'One of the truly prophetic figures of the space age'   *New Yorker*

'Quite masterly'   *The Times*

'Arthur C. Clarke is awesomely informed about physics and astronomy, and blessed with one of the most astounding imaginations ever encountered in print'   *New York Times*

'One of the best novels Clarke has written ... packed with suspense and mystery'   *Sunday Times* on *Rendezvous with Rama*

ALSO BY ARTHUR C. CLARKE FROM GOLLANCZ:

RAMA

THE OMNIBUS

THE COMPLETE RAMA STORY

ARTHUR C. CLARKE
AND GENTRY LEE

GOLLANCZ
London

This omnibus copyright © Arthur C. Clarke, Gentry Lee 2011
Rendezvous with Rama copyright © Arthur C. Clarke 1973
Rama II © Arthur C. Clarke, Gentry Lee 1989
The Garden of Rama copyright © Arthur C. Clarke, Gentry Lee 1991
Rama Revealed copyright © Arthur C. Clarke, Gentry Lee 1993
All rights reserved

The right of Arthur C. Clarke and Gentry Lee to be identified as the
authors of this work has been asserted by them in accordance
with the Copyright, Designs and Patents Act 1988.

First published in Great Britain in 2011 by Gollancz
An imprint of the Orion Publishing Group
Orion House, 5 Upper St Martin's Lane, London WC2H 9EA
An Hachette UK Company

A CIP catalogue record for this book
is available from the British Library

ISBN 978 0 575 09686 8

1 3 5 7 9 10 8 6 4 2

Typeset by Deltatype Ltd, Birkenhead, Merseyside

Printed and bound by CPI Group (UK) Ltd, Croydon, CR0 4YY

The Orion Publishing Group's policy is to use papers that
Are natural, renewable and recyclable products and made
from wood grown in sustainable forests. The logging and
manufacturing processes are expected to conform to the
environmental regulations of the country of origin.

To discover more about how the legacy of Sir Arthur is being honoured today, please visit
www.clarkefoundation.org

www.orionbooks.co.uk

CONTENTS

RENDEZVOUS
WITH RAMA

To Sri Lanka
where I climbed
the Stairway of the Gods

1 SPACEGUARD

Sooner or later, it was bound to happen. On 30 June 1908, Moscow escaped destruction by three hours and four thousand kilometres – a margin invisibly small by the standards of the universe. Again, on 12 February 1947, yet another Russian city had a still narrower escape, when the second great meteorite of the twentieth century detonated less than four hundred kilometres from Vladivostok, with an explosion rivalling that of the newly invented uranium bomb.

In those days, there was nothing that men could do to protect themselves against the last random shots in the cosmic bombardment that had once scarred the face of the Moon. The meteorites of 1908 and 1947 had struck uninhabited wilderness; but by the end of the twenty-first century, there was no region left on Earth that could be safely used for celestial target practice. The human race had spread from pole to pole. And so, inevitably ...

At 09.46 GMT on the morning of 11 September, in the exceptionally beautiful summer of the year 2077, most of the inhabitants of Europe saw a dazzling fireball appear in the eastern sky. Within seconds it was brighter than the sun, and as it moved across the heavens – at first in utter silence – it left behind it a churning column of dust and smoke.

Somewhere above Austria it began to disintegrate, producing a series of concussions so violent that more than a million people had their hearing permanently damaged. They were the lucky ones.

Moving at fifty kilometres a second, a thousand tons of rock and metal impacted on the plains of northern Italy, destroying in a few flaming moments the labour of centuries. The cities of Padua and Verona were wiped from the face of the earth; and the last glories of Venice sank forever beneath the sea as the waters of the Adriatic came thundering landwards after the hammer-blow from space.

Six hundred thousand people died, and the total damage was more than a trillion dollars. But the loss to art, to history, to science – to the whole human race, for the rest of time – was beyond all computation. It was as if a great war had been fought and lost in a single morning; and few could draw much pleasure from the fact that, as the dust of destruction slowly settled, for months the whole world witnessed the most splendid dawns and sunsets since Krakatoa.

After the initial shock, mankind reacted with a determination and a unity that no earlier age could have shown. Such a disaster, it was realised, might not occur again for a thousand years – but it might occur tomorrow. And the next time, the consequences could be even worse.

Very well; *there would be no next time.*

A hundred years earlier a much poorer world, with far feebler resources, had squandered its wealth attempting to destroy weapons launched, suicidally, by mankind against itself. The effort had never been successful, but the skills acquired then had not been forgotten. Now they could be used for a far nobler purpose, and on an infinitely vaster stage. No meteorite large enough to cause catastrophe would ever again be allowed to breach the defences of Earth.

So began Project spaceguard. Fifty years later – and in a way that none of its designers could ever have anticipated – it justified its existence.

2 INTRUDER

By the year 2130, the Mars-based radars were discovering new asteroids at the rate of a dozen a day. The SPACEGUARD computers automatically calculated their orbits, and stored away the information in their enormous memories, so that every few months any interested astronomer could have a look at the accumulated statistics. These were now quite impressive.

It had taken more than a hundred and twenty years to collect the first thousand asteroids, since the discovery of Ceres, largest of these tiny worlds, on the very first day of the nineteenth century. Hundreds had been found and lost and found again; they existed in such swarms that one exasperated astronomer had christened them 'vermin of the skies'. He would have been appalled to know that SPACEGUARD was now keeping track of half a million.

Only the five giants – Ceres, Pallas, Juno, Eunomia and Vesta – were more than two hundred kilometres in diameter; the vast majority were merely oversized boulders that would fit into a small park. Almost all moved in orbits that lay beyond Mars; only the few that came far enough sunwards to be a possible danger to Earth were the concern of SPACEGUARD. And not one in a thousand of these, during the entire future history of the solar system, would pass within a million kilometres of Earth.

The object first catalogued as 31/439, according to the year and the order of its discovery, was detected while still outside the orbit of Jupiter. There was nothing unusual about its location; many asteroids went beyond Saturn before turning once more towards their distant master, the sun. And Thule II, most far-ranging of all, travelled so close to Uranus that it might well have been a lost moon of that planet.

But a first radar contact at such a distance was unprecedented; clearly, 31/439 must be of exceptional size. From the strength of the echo, the computers deduced a diameter of at least forty kilometres; such a giant had not been discovered for a hundred years. That it had been overlooked for so long seemed incredible.

Then the orbit was calculated, and the mystery was resolved – to be replaced by a greater one. 31/439 was not travelling on a normal asteroidal path, along an ellipse which it retraced with clockwork precision every few years. It was a lonely wanderer between the stars, making its first and last visit to the solar system – for it was moving so swiftly that the gravitational field of the sun could never capture it. It would flash inwards past the orbits of Jupiter, Mars, Earth, Venus and Mercury, gaining speed as it did so, until it rounded the sun and headed out once again into the unkown.

It was at this point that the computers started flashing their 'Hi there! We have something interesting' sign, and for the first time 31/439 came to the attention of human beings. There was a brief flurry of excitement at SPACE-GUARD Headquarters, and the interstellar vagabond was quickly dignified by a name instead of a mere number. Long ago, the astronomers had exhausted Greek and Roman mythology; now they were working through the Hindu pantheon. And so 31/439 was christened Rama.

For a few days, the news media made a fuss of the visitor, but they were badly handicapped by the sparsity of information. Only two facts were known about Rama – its unusual orbit, and its approximate size. Even this was merely an educated guess, based upon the strength of the radar echo. Through the telescope, Rama still appeared as a faint, fifteenth magnitude star – much too small to show a visible disc. But as it plunged in towards the heart of the solar system, it would grow brighter and larger, month by month; before it vanished forever, the orbiting observatories would be able to gather more precise information about its shape and size. There was plenty of time, and perhaps during the next few years some spaceship on its ordinary business might be routed close enough to get good photographs. An actual rendezvous was most unlikely; the energy cost would be far too great to permit physical contact with an object cutting across the orbits of the planets at more than a hundred thousand kilometres an hour.

So the world soon forgot about Rama; but the astronomers did not. Their excitement grew with the passing months, as the new asteroid presented them with more and more puzzles.

First of all, there was the problem of Rama's light curve. It didn't have one.

All known asteroids, without exception, showed a slow variation in their brilliance, waxing and waning within a period of a few hours. It had been recognised for more than two centuries that this was an inevitable result of their spin, and their irregular shape. As they toppled end over end along their orbits the reflecting surfaces they presented to the sun were continually changing, and their brightness varied accordingly.

Rama showed no such changes. Either it was not spinning at all or it was perfectly symmetrical. Both explanations seemed equally unlikely.

There the matter rested for several months, because none of the big orbiting telescopes could be spared from their regular job of peering into the remote depths of the universe. Space astronomy was an expensive hobby, and time on a large instrument could easily cost a thousand dollars a minute. Dr William Stenton would never have been able to grab the Farside two-hundred-metre reflector for a full quarter of an hour, if a more important programme had not been temporarily derailed by the failure of a fifty cent capacitor. One astronomer's bad luck was his good fortune.

Bill Stenton did not know what he had caught until the next day, when he was able to get computer time to process his results. Even when they were finally flashed on his display screen, it took him several minutes to understand what they meant.

The sunlight reflected from Rama was not, after all, absolutely constant in its intensity. There was a very small variation – hard to detect, but quite unmistakable, and extremely regular. Like all the other asteroids, Rama was undeed spinning. But whereas the normal 'day' for an asteroid was several hours, Rama's was only four *minutes*.

Dr Stenton did some quick calculations, and found it hard to believe the results. At its equator, this tiny world must be spinning at more than a thousand kilometres an hour; it would be rather unhealthy to attempt a landing anywhere except at the poles. The centrifugal force at Rama's equator must be powerful enough to flick any loose objects away from it at an acceleration of almost one gravity. Rama was a rolling stone that could never have gathered any cosmic moss; it was surprising that such a body had managed to hold itself together, and had not long ago shattered into a million fragments.

An object forty kilometres across, with a rotation period of only four minutes – where did that fit into the astronomical scheme of things? Dr Stenton was a somewhat imaginative man, a little too prone to jump to conclusions. He now jumped to one which gave him a very uncomfortable few minutes indeed.

The only specimen of the celestial zoo that fitted this description was a collapsed star. Perhaps Rama was a dead sun – a madly spinning sphere of neutronium, every cubic centimetre weighing billions of tons ...

At this point, there flashed briefly through Dr Stenton's horrified mind the memory of that timeless classic, H. G. Wells' *The Star*. He had first read it as a very small boy, and it had helped to spark his interest in astronomy. Across more than two centuries of time, it had lost none of its magic and terror. He would never forget the images of hurricanes and tidal waves, of cities sliding into the sea, as the other visitor from the stars smashed into Jupiter and then fell sunwards past the Earth. True, the star that old Wells described was not cold, but incandescent, and wrought much of its destruction by heat. That scarcely mattered; even if Rama was a cold body, reflecting only the light of the sun, it could kill by gravity as easily as by fire.

Any stellar mass intruding into the solar system would completely distort the orbits of the planets. The Earth had only to move a few million kilometres sunwards – or starwards – for the delicate balance of climate to be destroyed. The Antarctic icecap could melt and flood all low-lying land; or the oceans could freeze and the whole world be locked in an eternal winter. Just a nudge in either direction would be enough ...

Then Dr Stenton relaxed and breathed a sigh of relief. This was all nonsense; he should be ashamed of himself.

Rama could not possibly be made of condensed matter. No star-sized mass could penetrate so deeply into the solar system without producing disturbances which would have betrayed it long ago. The orbits of all the planets would have been affected; that, after all, was how Neptune, Pluto and Persephone had been discovered. No, it was utterly impossible for an object as massive as a dead sun to sneak up unobserved.

In a way, it was a pity. An encounter with a dark star would have been quite exciting.

While it lasted ...

3 RAMA AND SITA

The extraordinary meeting of the Space Advisory Council was brief and stormy. Even in the twenty-second century, no way had yet been discovered of keeping elderly and conservative scientists from occupying crucial administrative positions. Indeed, it was doubted if the problem ever would be solved.

To make matters worse, the current Chairman of the SAC was Professor (Emeritus) Olaf Davidson, the distinguished astrophysicist. Professor Davidson was not very much interested in objects smaller than galaxies, and never bothered to conceal his prejudices. And though he had to admit that ninety per cent of his science was now based upon observations from space-borne instruments, he was not at all happy about it. No less than three times during his distinguished career, satellites specially launched to prove one of his pet theories had done precisely the opposite.

The question before the Council was straightforward enough. There was no doubt that Rama was an unusual object – but was it an important one? In a few months it would be gone forever, so there was little time in which to act. Opportunities missed now would never recur.

At rather a horrifying cost, a space-probe soon to be launched from Mars to beyond Neptune could be modified and sent on a high-speed trajectory to meet Rama. There was no hope of a rendezvous; it would be the fastest fly-by on record, for the two bodies would pass each other at two hundred thousand kilometres an hour. Rama would be observed intensively for only a few minutes – and in real closeup for less than a second. But with the right instrumentation, that would be long enough to settle many questions.

Although Professor Davidson took a very jaundiced view of the Neptune probe, it had already been approved and he saw no point in sending more good money after bad. He spoke eloquently on the follies of asteroid-chasing, and the urgent need for a new high-resolution interferometer on the Moon to prove the newly-revived Big Bang theory of creation, once and for all.

That was a grave tactical error, because the three most ardent supporters of the Modified Steady State Theory were also members of the Council. They secretly agreed with Professor Davidson that asteroid-chasing was a waste of money; nevertheless ...

He lost by one vote.

Three months later the space-probe, rechristened Sita, was launched from Phobos, the inner moon of Mars. The flight time was seven weeks, and the instrument was switched to full power only five minutes before interception. Simultaneously, a cluster of camera pods was released, to sail past Rama so that it could be photographed from all sides.

The first images, from ten thousand kilometres away, brought to a halt the activities of all mankind. On a billion television screens, there appeared a tiny, featureless cylinder, growing rapidly second by second. By the time it had doubled its size, no one could pretend any longer that Rama was a natural object.

Its body was a cylinder so geometrically perfect that it might have been turned on a lathe – one with centres fifty kilometres apart. The two ends were quite flat, apart from some small structures at the centre of one face, and were twenty kilometres across; from a distance, when there was no sense of scale, Rama looked almost comically like an ordinary domestic boiler.

Rama grew until it filled the screen. Its surface was a dull, drab grey, as colourless as the Moon, and completely devoid of markings except at one point. Halfway along the cylinder there was a kilometre-wide stain or smear, as if something had once hit and splattered, ages ago.

There was no sign that the impact had done the slightest damage to Rama's spinning walls; but this mark had produced the slight fluctuation in brightness that had led to Stenton's discovery.

The images from the other cameras added nothing new. However, the trajectories their pods traced through Rama's minute gravitational field gave one other vital piece of information – the mass of the cylinder.

It was far too light to be a solid body. To nobody's great surprise, it was clear that Rama must be hollow.

The long-hoped-for, long-feared encounter had come at last. Mankind was about to receive its first visitor from the stars.

4 RENDEZVOUS

Commander Norton remembered those first TV transmissions, which he had replayed so many times, during the final minutes of the rendezvous. But there was one thing no electronic image could possibly convey – and that was Rama's overwhelming size.

He had never received such an impression when landing on a natural body like the Moon or Mars. Those were worlds, and one expected them to be big. Yet he had also landed on Jupiter VIII, which was slightly larger than Rama – and that had seemed quite a small object.

It was very easy to resolve the paradox. His judgement was wholly altered by the fact that this was an artifact, millions of times heavier than anything that Man had ever put into space. The mass of Rama was at least ten million million tons; to any spaceman, that was not only an awe-inspiring, but a terrifying thought. No wonder that he sometimes felt a sense of insignificance, and even depression, as that cylinder of sculptured, ageless metal filled more and more of the sky.

There was also a sense of danger here, that was wholly novel to his experience. In every earlier landing he had known what to expect; there was always the possibility of accident, but never of surprise. With Rama, surprise was the only certainty.

Now *Endeavour* was hovering less than a thousand metres above the North Pole of the cylinder, at the very centre of the slowly turning disc. This end has been chosen because it was the one in sunlight; as Rama rotated, the shadows of the short enigmatic structures near the axis swept steadily across the metal plain. The northern face of Rama was a gigantic sundial, measuring out the swift passage of its four-minute day.

Landing a five-thousand-ton spaceship at the centre of a spinning disc was the least of Commander Norton's worries. It was no different from docking at the axis of a large space-station; *Endeavour*'s lateral jets had already given her a matching spin, and he could trust Lieutenant Joe Calvert to put her down as gently as a snowflake, with or without the aid of the nav computer.

'In three minutes,' said Joe, without taking his eyes from the display, 'we'll know if it's made of anti-matter.'

Norton grinned, as he recalled some of the more hair-raising theories about Rama's origin. If that unlikely speculation was true, in a few seconds there would be the biggest bang since the solar system was formed. The total annihilation of ten thousand tons would, briefly, provide the planets with a second sun.

Yet the mission profile had allowed even for this remote contingency; *Endeavour* had squirted Rama with one of her jets from a safe thousand kilometres away. Nothing whatsoever had happened when the expanding cloud of vapour arrived on target – and a matter-anti-matter reaction involving even a few milligrams would have produced an awesome firework display.

Norton, like all space commanders, was a cautious man. He had looked long and hard at the northern face of Rama, choosing the point of touchdown. After much thought, he had decided to avoid the obvious spot – the exact centre, on the axis itself. A clearly marked circular disc, a hundred metres in diameter, was centred on the Pole, and Norton had a strong suspicion that this must be the outer seal of an enormous airlock. The creatures who had built this hollow world must have had some way of taking their ships inside. This was the logical place for the main entrance, and Norton thought it might be unwise to block the front door with his own vessel.

But this decision generated other problems. If *Endeavour* touched down even a few metres from the axis, Rama's rapid spin would start her sliding away from the pole. At first, the centrifugal force would be very weak, but it would be continuous and inexorable. Commander Norton did not relish the thought of his ship slithering across the polar plain, gaining speed minute by minute until it was slung off into space at a thousand kilometres an hour when it reached the edge of the disc.

It was possible that Rama's minute gravitational field – about one thousandth of Earth's – might prevent this from happening. It would hold *Endeavour* against the plain with a force of several tons, and if the surface was sufficiently rough the ship might stay near the Pole. But Commander Norton had no intention of balancing an unknown frictional force against a quite certain centrifugal one.

Fortunately, Rama's designers had provided an answer. Equally spaced around the polar axis were three low, pill-box shaped structures, about ten metres in diameter. If *Endeavour* touched down between any two of these, the centrifugal drift would fetch her up against them and she would be held firmly in place, like a ship glued against a quayside by the incoming waves.

'Contact in fifteen seconds,' said Joe. As he tensed himself above the duplicate controls, which he hoped he would not have to touch, Commander Norton became acutely aware of all that had come to focus on this instant of time. This, surely, was the most momentous landing since the first touchdown on the Moon, a century and a half ago.

The grey pill-boxes drifted slowly upwards outside the control port. There was the last hiss of a reaction jet, and a barely perceptible jar.

In the weeks that had passed, Commander Norton had often wondered what he would say at this moment. But now that it was upon him, History chose his words, and he spoke almost automatically, barely aware of the echo from the past:

'Rama Base. *Endeavour* has landed.'

As recently as a month ago, he would never have believed it possible. The ship had been on a routine mission, checking and emplacing asteroid warning beacons, when the order had come. *Endeavour* was the only spacecraft in the solar system which could possibly make a rendezvous with the intruder before it whipped round the sun and hurled itself back towards the stars. Even so, it had been necessary to rob three other ships of the Solar Survey, which were now drifting helplessly until tankers could refuel them. Norton feared that it would be a long time before the skippers of *Calypso*, *Beagle* and *Challenger* would speak to him again.

Even with all this extra propellant, it had been a long hard chase; Rama was already inside the orbit of Venus when *Endeavour* caught up with her. No other ship could ever do so; this privilege was unique, and not a moment of the weeks ahead was to be wasted. A thousand scientists on Earth would have cheerfully mortgaged their souls for this opportunity; now they could only watch over the TV circuits, biting their lips and thinking how much better *they* could do the job. They were probably right, but there was no alternative. The inexorable laws of celestial mechanics had decreed that *Endeavour* was the first, and the last, of all Man's ships that would ever make contact with Rama.

The advice he was continually receiving from Earth did little to alleviate Norton's responsibility. If split-second decisions had to be made, no one could help him; the radio time-lag to Mission Control was already ten minutes, and increasing. He often envied the great navigators of the past, before the days of electronic communications, who could interpret their sealed orders without continual monitoring from headquarters. Why *they* made mistakes, no one ever knew.

Yet at the same time, he was glad that some decisions could be delegated to Earth. Now that *Endeavour*'s orbit had coalesced with Rama's they were heading sunwards like a single body; in forty days they would reach perihelion, and pass within twenty million kilometres of the sun. That was far too close for comfort; long before then, *Endeavour* would have to use her remaining fuel to nudge herself into a safer orbit. They would have perhaps three weeks of exploring time, before they parted from Rama forever.

After that, the problem would be Earth's. *Endeavour* would be virtually helpless, speeding on an orbit which could make her the first ship to reach the stars – in approximately fifty thousand years. There was no need to worry, Mission Control had promised. Somehow, regardless of cost, *Endeavour* would be refuelled – even if it proved necessary to send tankers after her, and abandon them in space once they had transferred every gramme of propellant. Rama was a prize worth any risk, short of a suicide mission.

And, of course, it might even come to that. Commander Norton had no illusions on this score. For the first time in a hundred years an element of total uncertainty had entered human affairs. Uncertainty was one thing that neither scientists nor politicians could tolerate. If that was the price of resolving it, *Endeavour* and her crew would be expendable.

5 FIRST EVA

Rama was as silent as a tomb – which, perhaps, it was. No radio signals, on any frequency; no vibrations that the seismographs could pick up, apart from the micro-tremors undoubtedly caused by the sun's increasing heat; no electrical currents; no radioactivity. It was almost ominously quiet; one might have expected that even an asteroid would be noisier.

What did we expect? Norton asked himself. A committee of welcome? He was not sure whether to be disappointed or relieved. The initiative, at any rate, appeared up to him.

His orders were to wait for twenty-four hours, then to go out and explore. Nobody slept much that first day; even the crew members not on duty spent their time monitoring the ineffectually probing instruments, or simply looking out of the observation ports at the starkly geometrical landscape. Is this world alive? they asked themselves, over and over again. Is it dead? Or is it merely sleeping?

On the first EVA, Norton took only one companion – Lieut-Commander Karl Mercer, his tough and resourceful life-support officer. He had no intention of getting out of sight of the ship, and if there was any trouble it was unlikely that a larger party would be safe. As a precaution, however, he had two more crew members, already suited up, standing by in the airlock.

The few grammes of weight that Rama's combined gravitational and centrifugal fields gave them were neither help nor hindrance; they had to rely entirely on their jets. As soon as possible, Norton told himself, he would string a cat's-cradle of guide ropes between the ship and the pill-boxes, so that they could move around without wasting propellants.

The nearest pill-box was only ten metres from the airlock, and Norton's first concern was to check that the contact had caused no damage to the ship. *Endeavour*'s hull was resting against the curving wall with a thrust of several tons, but the pressure was evenly distributed. Reassured, he began to drift around the circular structure, trying to determine its purpose.

Norton had travelled only a few metres when he came across an interruption in the smooth, apparently metallic wall. At first, he thought it was some peculiar decoration, for it seemed to serve no useful function. Six radial grooves, or slots, were deeply recessed in the metal, and lying in them were six crossed bars like the spokes of a rimless wheel, with a small hub at the centre. But there was no way in which the wheel could be turned, as it was embedded in the wall.

Then he noticed, with growing excitement, that there were deeper recesses at the ends of the spokes, nicely shaped to accept a clutching hand (claw? tentacle?). If one stood *so*, bracing against the wall, and pulled on the spoke so ...

Smooth as silk, the wheel slid out of the wall. To his utter astonishment – for he had been virtually certain that any moving parts would have become vacuum-welded ages ago – Norton found himself holding a spoked wheel. He might have been the captain of some old wind-jammer standing at the helm of his ship.

He was glad that his helmet sunshade did not allow Mercer to read his expression.

He was startled, but also angry with himself; perhaps he had already make his first mistake. Were alarms now sounding inside Rama, and had his thoughtless action already triggered some implacable mechanism?

But *Endeavour* reported no change; its sensors still detected nothing but faint thermal crepitations and his own movements.

'Well, Skipper – are you going to turn it?'

Norton thought once more of his instructions. 'Use your own discretion, but proceed with caution.' If he checked every single move with Mission Control, he would never get anywhere.

'What's your diagnosis, Karl?' he asked Mercer.

'It's obviously a manual control for an airlock – probably an emergency back-up system in case of power failure. I can't imagine *any* technology, however advanced, that wouldn't take such precautions.'

'And it would be fail-safe,' Norton told himself. 'It could only be operated if there was no possible danger to the system ...'

He grasped two opposing spokes of the windlass, braced his feet against the ground, and tested the wheel. It did not budge.

'Give me a hand,' he asked Mercer. Each took a spoke; exerting their utmost strength, they were unable to produce the slightest movement.

Of course, there was no reason to suppose that clocks and corkscrews on Rama turned in the same direction as they did on Earth ...

'Let's try the other way,' suggested Mercer.

This time, there was no resistance. The wheel rotated almost effortlessly through a full circle. Then, very smoothly, it took up the load.

Half a metre away, the curving wall of the pill-box started to move, like a slowly opening clamshell. A few particles of dust, driven by wisps of escaping air, streamed outwards like dazzling diamonds as the brilliant sunlight caught them.

The road to Rama lay open.

6 COMMITTEE

It had been a serious mistake, Dr Bose often thought, to put the United Planets Headquarters on the Moon. Inevitably, Earth tended to dominate the proceedings – as it dominated the landscape beyond the dome. If they *had* to build here, perhaps they should have gone to the Farside, where that hypnotic disc never shed its rays ...

But, of course, it was much too late to change, and in any case there was no real alternative. Whether the colonies liked it or not, Earth would be the cultural and economic overlord of the solar system for centuries to come.

Dr Bose had been born on Earth, and had not emigrated to Mars until he was thirty, so he felt that he could view the political situation fairly dispassionately. He knew now that he would never return to his home planet, even though it was only five hours away by shuttle. At 115, he was in perfect health, but he could not face the reconditioning needed to accustom him to three times the gravity he had enjoyed for most of his life. He was exiled forever from the world of his birth; not being a sentimental man, this had never depressed him unduly.

What did depress him sometimes was the need for dealing, year after year, with the same familiar faces. The marvels of medicine were all very well, and certainly he had no desire to put back the clock – but there were men around this conference table with whom he had worked for more than half a century. He knew exactly what they would say and how they would vote on any given subject. He wished that, some day, one of them would do something totally unexpected – even something quite crazy.

And probably they felt exactly the same way about him ...

The Rama Committee was still manageably small, though doubtless that would soon be rectified. His six colleagues – the UP representatives for Mercury, Earth, Luna, Ganymede, Titan and Triton – were all present in the flesh. They had to be; electronic diplomacy was not possible over solar system distances. Some elder statesmen, accustomed to the instantaneous communications which Earth had long taken for granted, had never reconciled themselves to the fact that radio waves took minutes, or even hours, to journey across the gulfs between the planets. 'Can't you scientists do something about it?' they had been heard to complain bitterly, when told

17

that face-to-face conversation was impossible between Earth and any of its remoter children. Only the Moon had that barely acceptable one-and-a-half-second delay – with all the political and psychological consequences which it implied. Because of this fact of astronomical life, the Moon – and *only* the Moon – would always be a suburb of Earth.

Also present in person were three of the specialists who had been co-opted to the Committee. Professor Davidson, the astronomer, was an old acquaintance; today, he did not seem his usual irascible self. Dr Bose knew nothing of the infighting that had preceded the launch of the first probe to Rama, but the Professor's colleagues had not let him forget it.

Dr Thelma Price was familiar through her numerous television appearances, though she had first made her reputation fifty years ago during the archaeological explosion that had followed the draining of that vast marine museum, the Mediterranean.

Dr Bose could still recall the excitement of that time, when the lost treasures of the Greeks, Romans and a dozen other civilizations were restored to the light of day. That was one of the few occasions when he was sorry to be living on Mars.

The exobiologist, Carlisle Perera, was another obvious choice; so was Dennis Solomons, the science historian. Dr Bose was slightly less happy about the presence of Conrad Taylor, the celebrated anthropologist, who had made his reputation by uniquely combining scholarship and eroticism in his study of puberty rites in late twentieth-century Beverley Hills.

No one, however, could possibly have disputed the right of Sir Lewis Sands to be on the Committee. A man whose knowledge was matched only by his urbanity, Sir Lewis was reputed to lose his composure only when called the Arnold Toynbee of his age.

The great historian was not present in person; he stubbornly refused to leave Earth, even for so momentous a meeting as this. His stereo image, indistinguishable from reality, apparently occupied the chair to Dr Bose's right; as if to complete the illusion, someone had placed a glass of water in front of him. Dr Bose considered that this sort of technological *tour de force* was an unnecessary gimmick, but it was surprising how many undeniably great men were childishly delighted to be in two places at once. Sometimes this electronic miracle produced comic disasters; he had been at one diplomatic reception where somebody had tried to walk through a stereogram – and discovered, too late, that it was the real person. And it was even funnier to watch projections trying to shake hands ...

His Excellency the Ambassador for Mars to the United Planets called his wandering thoughts to order, cleared his throat, and said: 'Gentlemen, the Committee is now in session. I think I am correct in saying that this is a gathering of unique talents, assembled to deal with a unique situation. The directive that the Secretary-General has given us is to evaluate that situation, and to advise Commander Norton when necessary.'

This was a miracle of over-simplification, and everyone knew it. Unless there was a real emergency, the Committee might never be in direct contact with Commander Norton – if, indeed, he ever heard of its existence. For the Committee was a temporary creation of the United Planets' Science Organisation, reporting through its Director to the Secretary-General. It was true that the Space Survey was part of the UP – but on the *Operations*, not the Science side. In theory, this should not make much difference; there was no reason why the Rama Committee – or anyone else for that matter – should not call up Commander Norton and offer helpful advice.

But Deep Space Communications are expensive. *Endeavour* could be contacted only through planetcom, which was an autonomous corporation, famous for the strictness and efficiency of its accounting. It took a long time to establish a line of credit with planetcom; somewhere, someone was working on this; but at the moment, planetcom's hard-hearted computers did not recognize the existence of the Rama Committee.

'This Commander Norton,' said Sir Robert Mackay, the Ambassador for Earth. 'He has a tremendous responsibility. What sort of person is he?'

'I can answer that,' said Professor Davidson, his fingers flying over the keyboard of his memory pad. He frowned at the screenful of information, and started to make an instant synopsis.

'William Tsien Norton, Born 2077, Brisbane, Oceana. Educated Sydney, Bombay, Houston. Then five years at Astrograd, specialising in propulsion. Commissioned 2102. Rose through usual ranks – Lieutenant on the Third Persephone expedition, distinguished himself during fifteenth attempt to establish base on Venus ... um ... um ... exemplary record ... dual citizenship, Earth and Mars ... wife and one child in Brisbane, wife and *two* in Port Lowell, with option on third ...'

'Wife?' asked Taylor innocently.

'No, child of course,' snapped the Professor, before he caught the grin on the other's face. Mild laughter rippled round the table, though the overcrowded terrestrials looked more envious than amused. After a century of determined effort, Earth had still failed to get its population below the target of one billion ...

'... appointed commanding officer Solar Survey Research Vessel *Endeavour*. First voyage to retrograde satellites of Jupiter ... um, that was a tricky one ... on asteroid mission when ordered to prepare for this operation ... managed to beat deadline ...'

The Professor cleared the display and looked up at his colleagues.

'I think we were extremely lucky, considering that he was the only man available at such short notice. We might have had the usual run-of-the-mill captain.' He sounded as if he was referring to the typical peg-legged scourge of the spaceways, pistol in one hand and cutlass in the other.

'The record only proves that he's competent,' objected the Ambassador from Mercury (population: 112,500 but growing). 'How will he react in a wholly novel situation like this?'

On Earth, Sir Lewis Sands cleared his throat. A second and a half later, he did so on the Moon.

'Not exactly a novel situation,' he reminded the Hermian, 'even though it's three centuries since it last occurred. If Rama is dead, or unoccupied – and so far all the evidence suggests that it is – Norton is in the position of an archaeologist discovering the ruins of an extinct culture.' He bowed politely to Dr Price, who nodded in agreement. 'Obvious examples are Schliemann at Troy or Mouhot at Angkor Vat. The danger is minimal, though of course accident can never be completely ruled out.'

'But what about the booby-traps and trigger mechanisms these Pandora people have been talking about?' asked Dr Price.

'Pandora?' asked the Hermian Ambassador quickly. 'What's that?'

'It's a crackpot movement,' explained Sir Robert, with as much embarrassment as a diplomat was ever likely to show, 'which is convinced that Rama is a grave potential danger. A box that shouldn't be opened, you know.' He doubted if the Hermian *did* know: classical studies were not encouraged on Mercury.

'Pandora – paranoia,' snorted Conrad Taylor. 'Oh, of course, such things are *conceivable*, but why should any intelligent race went to play childish tricks?'

'Well, even ruling out such unpleasantness,' Sir Robert continued, 'we still have the much more ominous possibility of an active, inhabited Rama. Then the situation is one of an encounter between two cultures – at very different technological levels. Pizzaro and the Incas. Peary and the Japanese. Europe and Africa. Almost invariably, the consequences have been disastrous – for one or both parties. I'm not making any recommendations: I'm merely pointing out precedents.'

'Thank you, Sir Robert,' replied Dr Bose. It was a mild nuisance, he thought, having two 'Sirs' on one small committee; in these latter days knighthood was an honour which few Englishmen escaped. 'I'm sure we've all thought of these alarming possibilities. But if the creatures inside Rama are – er – malevolent – will it really make the slightest difference what we do?'

'They might ignore us if we go away.'

'What – after they've travelled billions of miles and thousands of years?'

The argument had reached the take-off point, and was now self-sustaining. Dr Bose sat back in his chair, said very little, and waited for the consensus to emerge.

It was just as he had predicted. Everyone agreed that, once he had opened the first door, it was inconceivable that Commander Norton should not open the second.

7 TWO WIVES

If his wives ever compared his videograms, Commander Norton thought with more amusement than concern, it would involve him in a lot of extra work. Now, he could make one long 'gram and dupe it, adding only brief personal messages and endearments before shooting the almost identical copies off to Mars and Earth.

Of course, it was highly unlikely that his wives ever would do such a thing; even at the concessionary rates allowed to spacemen's families, it would be expensive. And there would be no point in it; his families were on excellent terms with each other, and exchanged the usual greetings on birthdays and anniversaries. Yet, on the whole, perhaps it was just as well that the girls had never met, and probably never would. Myrna had been born on Mars and so could not tolerate the high gravity of Earth. And Caroline hated even the twenty-five minutes of the longest possible terrestrial journey.

'Sorry I'm a day late with this transmission,' said the Commander after he had finished the general-purpose preliminaries, 'but I've been away from the ship for the last thirty hours, believe it or not …

'Don't be alarmed – everything is under control, going perfectly. It's taken us two days, but we're almost through the airlock complex. We could have done it in a couple of hours, if we'd known what we do now. But we took no chances, sent remote cameras ahead, and cycled all the locks a dozen times to make sure they wouldn't seize up behind us – *after* we'd gone through …

'Each lock is a simple revolving cylinder with a slot on one side. You go in through this opening, crank the cylinder round a hundred and eighty degrees – and the slot then matches up with another door so that you can step out of it. Or float, in this case.

'The Ramans really made sure of things. There are three of these cylinder-locks, one after the other just inside the outer hull and below the entry pill-box. I can't imagine how even one would fail, unless someone blew it up with explosives, but if it did, there would be a second back-up, and then a third …

'And *that's* only the beginning. The final lock opens into a straight corridor, almost half a kilometre long. It looks clean and tidy, like everything else we've seen; every few metres there are small ports that probably held lights,

21

but now everything is completely black and, I don't mind telling you, scary. There are also two parallel slots, about a centimetre wide, cut in the walls and running the whole length of the tunnel. We suspect that some kind of shuttle runs inside these, to tow equipment – or people – back and forth. It would save us a lot of trouble if we could get it working ...

'I mentioned that the tunnel was half a kilometre long. Well, from our seismic soundings we knew that's about the thickness of the shell, so obviously we were almost through it. And at the end of the tunnel we weren't surprised to find another of those cylindrical airlocks.

'Yes, *and* another. *And* another. These people seem to have done everything in threes. We're in the final lock chamber now, awaiting the OK from Earth before we go through. The interior of Rama is only a few metres away. I'll be a lot happier when the suspense is over.

'You know Jerry Kirchoff, my Exec, who's got such a library of *real* books that he can't afford to emigrate from Earth? Well, Jerry told me about a situation just like this, back at the beginning of the twenty-first – no, twentieth century. An archaeologist found the tomb of an Egyptian king, the first one that hadn't been looted by robbers. His workmen took months to dig their way in, chamber by chamber, until they came to the final wall. Then they broke through the masonry, and he held out a lantern and pushed his head inside. He found himself looking into a whole roomful of treasure – incredible stuff, gold and jewels ...

'Perhaps this place is also a tomb; it seems more and more likely. Even now, there's still not the slightest sound, or hint of any activity. Well, tomorrow we should know.'

Commander Norton switched the record to HOLD. What else, he wondered, should he say about the work before he began the separate personal messages to his families? Normally, he never went into so much detail, but these circumstances were scarcely normal. This might be the last 'gram he would ever send to those he loved; he owed it to them to explain what he was doing.

By the time they saw these images, and heard these words, he would be inside Rama – for better or for worse.

8 THROUGH THE HUB

Never before had Norton felt so strongly his kinship with that long dead Egyptologist. Not since Howard Carter had first peered into the tomb of Tutankhamen could any man have known a moment such as this – yet the comparison was almost laughably ludicrous.

Tutankhamen had been buried only yesterday – not even four thousand years ago; Rama might be older than mankind. That little tomb in the Valley of the Kings could have been lost in the corridors through which they had already passed, yet the space that lay beyond this final seal was at least a million times greater. And as for the treasure it might hold – that was beyond imagination.

No one had spoken over the radio circuits for at least five minutes; the well-trained team had not even reported verbally when all the checks were complete. Mercer had simply given him the OK sign and waved him towards the open tunnel. It was as if everyone realised that this was a moment for History, not to be spoiled by unnecessary small-talk. That suited Commander Norton, for at the moment he too had nothing to say. He flicked on the beam of his flashlight, triggered his jets, and drifted slowly down the short corridor, trailing his safety line behind him. Only seconds later, he was inside.

Inside *what*? All before him was total darkness; not a glimmer of light was reflected back from the beam. He had expected this, but he had not really believed it. All the calculations had shown that the far wall was tens of kilometres away; now his eyes told him that this was indeed the truth. As he drifted slowly into that darkness, he felt a sudden need for the reassurance of his safety line, stronger than any he had ever experienced before, even on his very first EVA. And that was ridiculous; he had looked out across the light-years and the megaparsecs without vertigo; why should he be disturbed by a few cubic kilometres of emptiness?

He was still queasily brooding over this problem when the momentum damper at the end of the line braked him gently to a halt, with a barely perceptible rebound. He swept the vainly-probing beam of the flashlight down from the nothingness ahead, to examine the surface from which he had emerged.

He might have been hovering over the centre of a small crater, which was itself a dimple in the base of a much larger one. On either side rose a complex of terraces and ramps – all geometrically precise and obviously artificial – which extended for as far as the beam could reach. About a hundred metres away he could see the exit of the other two airlock systems, identical with this one.

And that was all. There was nothing particularly exotic or alien about the scene: in fact, it bore a considerable resemblance to an abandoned mine. Norton felt a vague sense of disappointment; after all this effort, there should have been some dramatic, even transcendental revelation. Then he reminded himself that he could see only a couple of hundred metres. The darkness beyond his field of view might yet contain more wonders than he cared to face.

He reported briefly to his anxiously-waiting companions, then added: 'I'm sending out the flare – two minutes delay. Here goes.'

With all his strength, he threw the little cylinder straight upwards – or outwards – and started to count seconds as it dwindled along the beam. Before he had reached the quarter minute it was out of sight; when he had got to a hundred he shielded his eyes and aimed the camera. He had always been good at estimating time; he was only two seconds off when the world exploded with light. And this time there was no cause for disappointment.

Even the millions of candlepower of the flare could not light up the whole of this enormous cavity, but now he could see enough to grasp its plan and appreciate its titanic scale. He was at one end of a hollow cylinder at least ten kilometres wide, and of indefinite length. From his viewpoint at the central axis he could see such a mass of detail on the curving walls surrounding him that his mind could not absorb more than a minute fraction of it; he was looking at the landscape of an entire world by a single flash of lightning, and he tried by a deliberate effort of will to freeze the image in his mind.

All round him, the terraced slopes of the 'crater' rose up until they merged into the solid wall that rimmed the sky. No – that impression was false; he must discard the instincts both of earth and of space, and reorientate himself to a new system of coordinates.

He was not at the lowest point of this strange, inside-out world, but the highest. From here, all directions were *down*, not up. If he moved away from this central axis, towards the curving wall which he must no longer think of as a wall, gravity would steadily increase. When he reached the inside surface of the cylinder, he could stand upright on it at any point, feet towards the stars and head towards the centre of the spinning drum. The concept was familiar enough; since the earliest dawn of spaceflight, centrifugal force had been used to simulate gravity. It was only the scale of this application which was so overwhelming, so shocking. The largest of all spacestations, Syncsat Five, was less than two hundred metres in diameter. It would take some little while to grow accustomed to one a hundred times that size.

The tube of landscape which enclosed him was mottled with areas of light and shade that could have been forests, fields, frozen lakes or towns; the distance, and the fading illumination of the flare, made identification impossible. Narrow lines that could be highways, canals, or well-trained rivers formed a faintly visible geometrical network; and far along the cylinder, at the very limit of vision, was a band of deeper darkness. It formed a complete circle, ringing the interior of this world, and Norton suddenly recalled the myth of Oceanus, the sea which, the ancients believed, surrounded the Earth.

Here, perhaps, was an even stranger sea – not circular, but *cylindrical*. Before it became frozen in the inter-stellar night, did it have waves and tides and currents – and fish?

The flare guttered and died; the moment of revelation was over. But Norton knew that as long as he lived these images would be burned on his mind. Whatever discoveries the future might bring, they could never erase this first impression. And History could never take from him the privilege of being the first of all mankind to gaze upon the works of an alien civilization.

9 RECONNAISSANCE

'We have now launched five long-delay flares down the axis of the cylinder, and so have a good photo-coverage of its full length. All the main features are mapped; though there are very few than we can identify, we've given them provisional names.

'The interior cavity is fifty kilometres long and sixteen wide. The two ends are bowl-shaped, with rather complicated geometries. We've called ours the Northern Hemisphere and are establishing our first base here at the axis.

'Radiating away from the central hub, a hundred and twenty degrees apart, are three ladders that are almost a kilometre long. They all end at a terrace or ring-shaped plateau, that runs right round the bowl. And leading on from *that*, continuing the direction of the ladders, are three enormous stairways, which go all the way down to the plain. If you imagine an umbrella with only three ribs, equally spaced, you'll have a good idea of this end of Rama.

'Each of those ribs is a stairway, very steep near the axis and then slowly flattening out as it approaches the plain below. The stairways – we've called them Alpha, Beta, Gamma – aren't continuous, but break at five more circular terraces. We estimate there must be between twenty and thirty thousand steps ... presumably they were only used for emergencies, since it's inconceivable that the Ramans – or whatever we're going to call them – had no better way of reaching the axis of their world.

'The Southern Hemisphere looks quite different; for one thing, it has no stairways, and no flat central hub. Instead, there's a huge spike – kilometres long – jutting along the axis, with six smaller ones around it. The whole arrangement is very odd, and we can't imagine what it means.

'The fifty-kilometre-long, cylindrical section between the two bowls we've called the Central Plain. It may seem crazy to use the word "plain" to describe something so obviously curved, but we feel it's justified. It will appear flat to us when we get down there – just as the interior of a bottle must seem flat to an ant crawling round inside it.

'The most striking feature of the Central Plain is the ten-kilometre-wide dark band running completely round it at the half-way mark. It looks like ice, so we've christened it the Cylindrical Sea. Right out in the middle there's a large oval island, about ten kilometres long and three wide, and covered with

26

tall structures. Because it reminds us of Old Manhattan, we've called it New York. Yet I don't think it's a city; it seems more like an enormous factory or chemical processing plant.

'But there are some cities – or at any rate, towns. At least six of them; if they were built for human beings, they could each hold about fifty thousand people. We've called them Rome, Peking, Paris, Moscow, London, Tokyo ... They are linked with highways and something that seems to be a rail system.

'There must be enough material for centuries of research in this frozen carcass of a world. We've four thousand square kilometres to explore, and only a few weeks to do it in. I wonder if we'll ever learn the answer to the two mysteries that have been haunting me ever since we got inside; who were they – *and what went wrong*?'

The recording ended. On Earth and Moon, the members of the Rama Committee relaxed, then started to examine the maps and photographs spread in front of them. Though they had already studied these for many hours, Commander Norton's voice added a dimension which no pictures could convey. He had actually been there – had looked with his own eyes across this extraordinary inside-out world, during the brief moments while its age-long night had been illuminated by the flares. And he was the man who would lead any expedition to explore it.

'Dr Perera, I believe you have some comments to make?'

Ambassador Bose wondered briefly if he should have first given the floor to Professor Davidson, as senior scientist and the only astronomer. But the old cosmologist still seemed to be in a mild state of shock, and was clearly out of his element. All his professional career he had looked upon the universe as an arena for the titanic impersonal forces of gravitation, magnetism, radiation; he had never believed that life played an important role in the scheme of things, and regarded its appearance on Earth, Mars and Jupiter as an accidental aberration.

But now there was proof that life not only existed outside the solar system, but had scaled heights far beyond anything that man had achieved, or could hope to reach for centuries to come. Moreover, the discovery of Rama challenged another dogma that Professor Olaf had preached for years. When pressed, he would reluctantly admit that life probably did exist in other star systems – but it was absurd, he had always maintained, to imagine that it could ever cross the interstellar gulfs ...

Perhaps the Ramans had indeed failed, if Commander Norton was correct in believing that their world was now a tomb. But at least they had attempted the feat, on a scale which indicated a high confidence in the outcome. If such a thing had happened once, it must surely have happened many times in this Galaxy of a hundred thousand million suns ... and someone, somewhere, would eventually succeed.

This was the thesis which, without proof but with considerable arm-waving, Dr Carlisle Perera had been preaching for years. He was now a very happy man, though also a most frustrated one. Rama had spectacularly confirmed his views – but he could never set foot inside it, or even see it with his own eyes. If the devil had suddenly appeared and offered him the gift of instantaneous teleportation, he would have signed the contract without bothering to look at the small print.

'Yes, Mr Ambassador, I think I have some information of interest. What we have here is undoubtedly a "Space Ark". It's an old idea in the astronautical literature; I've been able to trace it back to the British physicist J. D. Bernal, who proposed this method of interstellar colonization in a book published in 1929 – yes, two hundred years ago. And the great Russian pioneer Tsiolkovski put forward somewhat similar proposals even earlier.

'If you want to go from one star system to another you have a number of choices. Assuming that the speed of light is an absolute limit – and that's *still* not completely settled, despite anything you may have heard to the contrary' – there was an indignant sniff, but no formal protest from Professor Davidson – 'you can make a fast trip in a small vessel, or a slow journey in a giant one.

'There seems no technical reason why spacecraft cannot reach ninety per cent, or more, of the speed of light. That would mean a travel time of five to ten years between neighbouring stars – tedious, perhaps, but not impracticable, especially for creatures whose life spans might be measured in centuries. One can imagine voyages of this duration, carried out in ships not much larger than ours.

'But perhaps such speeds are impossible, with reasonable payloads; remember, you have to carry the fuel to slow down at the end of the voyage, even if you're on a one-way trip. So it may make more sense to take your time – ten thousand, a hundred thousand years ...

'Bernal and others thought this could be done with mobile worldlets a few kilometres across, carrying thousands of passengers on journeys that would last for generations. Naturally, the system would have to be rigidly closed, recycling all food, air and other expendables. But, of course, that's just how the Earth operates – on a slightly larger scale.

'Some writers suggested that these Space Arks should be built in the form of concentric spheres; others proposed hollow, spinning cylinders so that centrifugal force could provide artificial gravity – exactly what we've found in Rama—'

Professor Davidson could not tolerate this sloppy talk.

'No such thing as centrifugal *force*. It's an engineer's phantom. There's only inertia.'

'You're quite right, of course,' admitted Perera, 'though it might be hard to convince a man who'd just been slung off a carousel. But mathematical rigour seems unnecessary—'

'Hear, hear,' interjected Dr Bose, with some exasperation. 'We all know what you mean, or think we do. Please don't destroy our illusions.'

'Well, I was merely pointing out that there's nothing conceptually novel about Rama, though its size is startling. Men have imagined such things for two hundred years.

'Now I'd like to address myself to another question. Exactly how long has Rama been travelling through space?

'We now have a very precise determination of its orbit and its velocity. Assuming that it's made no navigational changes, we can trace its position back for millions of years. We expected that it would be coming from the direction of a nearby star – but that isn't the case at all.

'It's more than *two hundred thousand years* since Rama passed near any star, and that particular one turns out to be an irregular variable – about the most unsuitable sun you could imagine for an inhabited solar system. It has a brightness range of over fifty to one; any planets would be alternately baked and frozen every few years.'

'A suggestion,' put in Dr Price. 'Perhaps that explains everything. Maybe this was once a normal sun and became unstable. That's why the Ramans had to find a new one.'

Dr Perera admired the old archaeologist, so he let her down lightly. But what would *she* say, he wondered, if he started pointing out the instantly obvious in her own speciality ...

'We did consider that,' he said gently. 'But if our present theories of stellar evolution are correct, this star could *never* have been stable – could never have had life-bearing planets. So Rama has been cruising through space for at least two hundred thousand years, and perhaps for more than a million.

'Now it's cold and dark and apparently dead, and I think I know why. The Ramans may have had no choice – perhaps they were indeed fleeing from some disaster – but they miscalculated.

'No closed ecology can be one hundred per cent efficient; there is always waste, loss – some degradation of the environment, and build-up of pollutants. It may take billions of years to poison and wear out a planet – but it will happen in the end. The oceans will dry up, the atmosphere will leak away ...

'By our standards, Rama is enormous – yet it is still a very tiny planet. My calculations, based on the leakage through its hull, and some reasonable guesses about the rate of biological turnover, indicate that its ecology could only survive for about a thousand years. At the most, I'll grant ten thousand ...

'That would be long enough, at the speed Rama is travelling, for a transit between the closely-packed suns in the heart of the Galaxy. But not out here, in the scattered population of the spiral arms. Rama is a ship which exhausted its provisions before it reached its goal. It's a derelict, drifting among the stars.

'There's just one serious objection to this theory, and I'll raise it before anybody else does. Rama's orbit is aimed so accurately at the solar system that coincidence seems ruled out. In fact, I'd say it's now heading much too close to the sun for comfort: *Endeavour* will have to break away long before perihelion, to avoid overheating.

'I don't pretend to understand this. Perhaps, there may be some form of automatic terminal guidance still operating, steering Rama to the nearest suitable star ages after its builders are dead.

'And they *are* dead; I'll stake my reputation on that. All the samples we've taken from the interior are absolutely sterile – we've not found a single micro-organism. As for the talk you may have heard about suspended animation, you can ignore it. There are fundamental reasons why hibernation techniques will only work for a very few centuries – and we're dealing with time spans a thousand-fold longer.

'So the Pandorans and their sympathizers have nothing to worry about. For my part, I'm sorry. It would have been wonderful to have met another intelligent species.

'But at least we have answered one ancient question. We are not alone. The stars will never again be the same to us.'

10 DESCENT INTO DARKNESS

Commander Norton was sorely tempted – but as captain his first duty was to his ship. If anything went badly wrong on this initial probe, he might have to run for it.

So that left his second officer, Lieut-Commander Mercer, as the obvious choice. Norton willingly admitted that Karl was better suited for the mission. *The* authority on life-support systems, Mercer had written some of the standard textbooks on the subject. He had personally checked out unnumerable types of equipment, often under hazardous conditions, and his biofeedback control was famous. At a moment's notice he could cut his pulse-rate by fifty per cent, and reduce respiration to almost zero for up to ten minutes. These useful little tricks had saved his life on more than one occasion.

Yet despite his great ability and intelligence, he was almost wholly lacking in imagination. To him the most dangerous experiments or missions were simply jobs that had to be done. He never took unnecessary risks, and had no use at all for what was commonly regarded as courage.

The two mottoes on his desk summed up his philosophy of life. One asked WHAT HAVE YOU FORGOTTEN? The other said HELP STAMP OUT BRAVERY. The fact that he was widely regarded as the bravest man in the Fleet was the only thing that ever made him angry.

Given Mercer, that automatically selected the next man – his inseparable companion Lt Joe Calvert. It was hard to see what the two had in common; the lightly-built, rather highly strung navigating officer was ten years younger than his stolid and imperturbable friend, who certainly did not share his passionate interest in the art of the primitive cinema.

But no one can predict where lightning will strike, and years ago Mercer and Calvert had established an apparently stable liaison. That was common enough; much more unusual was the fact that they also shared a wife back on Earth, who had borne each of them a child. Commander Norton hoped that he could meet her one day; she must be a very remarkable woman. The triangle had lasted for at least five years, and still seemed to be an equilateral one.

Two men were not enough for an exploring team; long ago it had been found that three was the optimum – for if one man was lost, two might

31

still escape where a single survivor would be doomed. After a good deal of thought, Norton had chosen Technical Sergeant Willard Myron. A mechanical genius who could make anything work – or design something better if it wouldn't – Myron was the ideal man to identify alien pieces of equipment. On a long sabbatical from his regular job as Associate Professor at Astrotech, the Sergeant had refused to accept a commission on the grounds that he did not wish to block the promotion of more deserving career officers. No one took this explanation very seriously and it was generally agreed that Will rated zero for ambition. He might make it to Space Sergeant, but would never be a full professor. Myron, like countless NCOs before him, had discovered the ideal compromise between power and responsibility.

As they drifted through the last airlock and floated out along the weightless axis of Rama, Lt Calvert found himself, as he so often did, in the middle of a movie flashback. He sometimes wondered if he should attempt to cure himself of this habit, but he could not see that it had any disadvantages. It could make even the dullest situations interesting and – who could tell? – one day it might save his life. He would remember what Fairbanks or Connery or Hiroshi had done in similar circumstances ...

This time, he was about to go over the top, in one of the early-twentieth-century wars; Mercer was the sergeant leading a three-man patrol on a night raid into no-man's land. It was not too difficult to imagine that they were at the bottom of an immense shell-crater, though one that had somehow become neatly tailored into a series of ascending terraces. The crater was flooded with light from three widely-spaced plasma-arcs, which gave an almost shadowless illumination over the whole interior. But beyond that – over the rim of the most distant terrace – was darkness and mystery.

In his mind's eye, Calvert knew perfectly well what lay there. First there was the flat circular plain over a kilometre across. Trisecting it into three equal parts, and looking very much like broad railroad tracks, were three wide ladders, their rungs recessed into the surface so that they would provide no obstruction to anything sliding over it. Since the arrangement was completely symmetrical, there was no reason to choose one ladder rather than another; that nearest to Airlock Alpha had been selected purely as a matter of convenience.

Though the rungs of the ladders were uncomfortably far apart, that presented no problem. Even at the rim of the Hub, half a kilometre from the axis, gravity was still barely one thirtieth of Earth's. Although they were carrying almost a hundred kilos of equipment and life-support gear, they would still be able to move easily hand-over-hand.

Commander Norton and the back-up team accompanied them along the guide ropes that had been stretched from Airlock Alpha to the rim of the crater; then, beyond the range of the floodlights, the darkness of Rama lay before them. All that could be seen in the dancing beams of the helmet lights was the first few hundred metres of the ladder, dwindling away across a flat and otherwise featureless plain.

And now, Karl Mercer told himself, I have to make my first decision. Am I going *up* that ladder, or *down* it?

The question was not a trivial one. They were still essentially in zero gravity, and the brain could select any reference system it pleased. By a simple effort of will, Mercer could convince himself that he was looking out across a horizontal plain, or up the face of a vertical wall, or over the edge of a sheer cliff. Not a few astronauts had experienced grave psychological problems by choosing the wrong coordinates when they started on a complicated job.

Mercer was determined to go head-first, for any other mode of locomotion would be awkward; moreover, this way he could more easily see what was in front of him. For the first few hundred metres, therefore, he would imagine he was climbing upwards; only when the increasing pull of gravity made it impossible to maintain the illusion would be switch his mental directions one hundred and eighty degrees.

He grasped the first rung and gently propelled himself along the ladder. Movement was as effortless as swimming along the seabed – more so, in fact, for there was no backward drag of water. It was so easy that there was a temptation to go too fast, but Mercer was much too experienced to hurry in a situation as novel as this.

In his earphones, he could hear the regular breathing of his two companions. He needed no other proof that they were in good shape, and wasted no time in conversation. Though he was tempted to look back, he decided not to risk it until they had reached the platform at the end of the ladder.

The rungs were spaced a uniform half metre apart, and for the first portion of the climb Mercer missed the alternate ones. But he counted them carefully, and at around two hundred noticed the first distinct sensations of weight. The spin of Rama was starting to make itself felt.

At rung four hundred, he estimated that his apparent weight was about five kilos. This was no problem, but it was now getting hard to pretend that he was climbing, when he was being firmly dragged *upwards*.

The five hundredth rung seemed a good place to pause. He could feel the muscles in his arms responding to the unaccustomed exercise, even though Rama was now doing all the work and he had merely to guide himself.

'Everything OK, Skipper,' he reported. 'We're just passing the halfway mark. Joe, Will – any problems?'

'I'm fine – what are you stopping for?' Joe Calvert answered.

'Same here,' added Sergeant Myron. 'But watch out for the Coriolis force. It's starting to build up.'

So Mercer had already noticed. When he let go of the rungs he had a distinct tendency to drift off to the right. He knew perfectly well that this was merely the effect of Rama's spin, but it seemed as if some mysterious force was gently pushing him away from the ladder.

Perhaps it was time to start going feet-first, now that 'down' was beginning to have a physical meaning. He would run the risk of a momentary disorientation.

'Watch out – I'm going to swing round.'

Holding firmly on to the rung, he used his arms to twist himself round a hundred and eighty degrees, and found himself momentarily blinded by the lights of his companions. Far above them – and now it really *was* above – he could see a fainter glow along the rim of the sheer cliff. Silhouetted against it were the figures of Commander Norton and the back-up team, watching him intently. They seemed very small and far away, and he gave them a reassuring wave.

He released his grip, and let Rama's still feeble pseudo-gravity take over. The drop from one rung to the next required more than two seconds; on Earth, in the same time, a man would have fallen thirty metres.

The rate of fall was so painfully slow that he hurried things up a trifle by pushing with his hands, gliding over spans of a dozen rungs at a time, and checking himself with his feet whenever he felt he was travelling too fast.

At rung seven hundred, he came to another halt and swung the beam of his helmet-lamp downwards; as he had calculated, the beginning of the stairway was only fifty metres below.

A few minutes later, they were on the first step. It was a strange experience, after months in space, to stand upright on a solid surface, and to feel it pressing against one's feet. Their weight was still less than ten kilogrammes, but that was enough to give a feeling of stability. When he closed his eyes, Mercer could believe that he once more had a real world beneath him.

The ledge or platform from which the stairway descended was about ten metres wide, and curved upwards on each side until it disappeared into the darkness. Mercer knew that it formed a complete circle and that if he walked along it for five kilometres he would come right back to his starting-point, having circumnavigated Rama.

At the fractional gravity that existed here, however, real walking was impossible; one could only bound along in giant strides. And therein lay danger.

The stairway that swooped down into the darkness, far below the range of their lights, would be deceptively easy to descend. But it would be essential to hold on to the tall handrail that flanked it on either side; too bold a step might send an incautious traveller arching far out into space. He would hit the surface again perhaps a hundred metres lower down; the impact would be harmless, but its consequences might not be – for the spin of Rama would have moved the stairway off to the left. And so a falling body would hit against the smooth curve that swept in an unbroken arc to the plain almost seven kilometres below.

That, Mercer told himself, would be a hell of a toboggan ride; the terminal speed, even in this gravity, could be several hundred kilometres an hour. Perhaps it would be possible to apply enough friction to check such a headlong descent; if so, this might even be the most convenient way to reach the inner surface of Rama. But some very cautious experimenting would be necessary first.

'Skipper,' reported Mercer, 'there were no problems getting down the ladder. If you agree, I'd like to continue towards the next platform. I want to time our rate of descent on the stairway.'

Norton replied without hesitation.

'Go ahead.' He did not need to add, 'Proceed with caution.'

It did not take Mercer long to make a fundamental discovery. It was impossible, at least at this one-twentieth-of-a-gravity level, to walk down the stairway in the normal manner. Any attempt to do so resulted in a slow-motion dream-like movement that was intolerably tedious; the only practical way was to ignore the steps, and to use the handrail to pull oneself downwards.

Calvert had come to the same conclusion.

'This stairway was built to walk *up*, not down!' he exclaimed. 'You can use the steps when you're moving against gravity, but they're just a nuisance in this direction. It may not be dignified, but I think the best way down is to slide along the handrail.'

'That's ridiculous,' protested Sergeant Myron. 'I can't believe the Ramans did it this way.'

'I doubt if they ever used this stairway – it's obviously only for emergencies. They must have had some mechanical transport system to get up here. A funicular, perhaps. That would explain those long slots running down from the Hub.'

'I always assumed they were drains – but I suppose they could be both. I wonder if it ever rained here?'

'Probably,' said Mercer. 'But I think Joe is right, and to hell with dignity. Here we go.'

The handrail – presumably it *was* designed for something like hands – was a smooth, flat, metal bar supported on widely-spaced pillars a metre high. Commander Mercer straddled it, carefully gauged the braking power he could exert with his hands, and let himself slide.

Very sedately, slowly picking up speed, he descended into the darkness, moving in the pool of light from his helmet-lamp. He had gone about fifty metres when he called the others to join him.

None would admit it, but they all felt like boys again, sliding down the banisters. In less than two minutes, they had made a kilometre descent in safety and comfort. Whenever they felt they were going too fast, a tightened grip on the handrail provided all the braking that was necessary.

'I hope you enjoyed yourselves,' Commander Norton called when they stepped off at the second platform. 'Climbing back won't be quite so easy.'

'That's what I want to check,' replied Mercer, who was walking experimentally back and forth, getting the feel of the increased gravity. 'It's already a tenth of a gee here – you really notice the difference.'

He walked – or, more accurately, glided – to the edge of the platform, and shone his helmet-light down the next section of the stairway. As far as his beam could reach, it appeared identical with the one above – though careful examination of photos had shown that the height of the steps steadily decreased with the rising gravity. The stair had apparently been designed so that the effort required to climb it was more or less constant at every point in its long curving sweep.

Mercer glanced up towards the Hub of Rama, now almost two kilometres above him. The little glow of light, and the tiny figures silhouetted against it, seemed horribly far away. For the first time, he was suddenly glad that he could not see the whole length of this enormous stairway. Despite his steady nerves and lack of imagination, he was not sure how he would react if he could see himself like an insect crawling up the face of a vertical saucer more than sixteen kilometres high – and with the upper half overhanging above him. Until this moment, he had regarded the darkness as a nuisance; now he almost welcomed it.

'There's no change of temperature,' he reported to Commander Norton. 'Still just below freezing. But the air-pressure is up, as we expected – around three hundred millibars. Even with this low oxygen content, it's almost breathable; further down there will be no problems at all. That will simplify exploration enormously. What a find – the first world on which we can walk without breathing gear! In fact, I'm going to take a sniff.'

Up on the Hub, Commander Norton stirred a little uneasily. But Mercer, of all men, knew exactly what he was doing. He would already have made enough tests to satisfy himself.

Mercer equalized pressure, unlatched the securing clip of his helmet, and opened it a crack. He took a cautious breath; then a deeper one.

The air of Rama was dead and musty, as if from a tomb so ancient that the last trace of physical corruption had disappeared ages ago. Even Mercer's ultra-sensitive nose, trained through years of testing life-support systems to and beyond the point of disaster, could detect no recognisable odours. There was a faint metallic tang, and he suddenly recalled that the first men on the Moon had reported a hint of burnt gunpowder when they repressurised the lunar module. Mercer imagined that the moon-dust-contaminated cabin on *Eagle* must have smelled rather like Rama.

He sealed the helmet again, and emptied his lungs of the alien air. He had extracted no sustenance from it; even a mountaineer acclimatised to the summit of Everest would die quickly here. But a few kilometres further down, it would be a different matter.

What else was there to do here? He could think of nothing, except the enjoyment of the gentle, unaccustomed gravity. But there was no point in growing used to that, since they would be returning immediately to the weightlessness of the Hub.

'We're coming back, Skipper,' he reported. 'There's no reason to go further – until we're ready to go *all* the way.'

'I agree. We'll be timing you, but take it easy.'

As he bounded up the steps, three or four at a stride, Mercer agreed that Calvert had been perfectly correct; these stairs were built to be walked *up*, not down. As long as one did not look back, and ignored the vertiginous steepness of the ascending curve, the climb was a delightful experience. After about two hundred steps, however, he began to feel some twinges in his calf muscles, and decided to slow down. The others had done the same; when he ventured a quick glance over his shoulder, they were considerably further down the slope.

The climb was wholly uneventful – merely an apparently endless succession of steps. When they stood once more on the highest platform, immediately beneath the ladder, they were barely winded, and it had taken them only ten minutes. They paused for another ten, then started on the last vertical kilometre.

Jump – catch hold of a rung – jump – catch – jump – catch … it was easy, but so boringly repetitious that there was danger of becoming careless. Halfway up the ladder they rested for five minutes: by this time their arms as well as their legs had begun to ache. Once again, Mercer was glad that they could see so little of the vertical face to which they were clinging; it was not too difficult to pretend that the ladder only extended just a few metres beyond their circle of light, and would soon come to an end.

Jump – catch a rung – jump – then, quite suddenly, the ladder *really* ended. They were back at the weightless world of the axis, among their anxious friends. The whole trip had taken under an hour, and they felt a sense of modest achievement.

But it was much too soon to feel pleased with themselves. For all their efforts, they had traversed less than an eighth of that cyclopean stairway.

11 MEN, WOMEN AND MONKEYS

S ome women, Commander Norton had decided long ago, should not be allowed aboard ship; weightlessness did things to their breasts that were too damn distracting. It was bad enough when they were motionless; but when they started to move, and sympathetic vibrations set in, it was more than any warm-blooded male should be asked to take. He was quite sure that at least one serious space accident had been caused by acute crew distraction, after the transit of a well-upholstered lady officer through the control cabin.

He had once mentioned this theory to Surgeon-Commander Laura Ernst, without revealing who had inspired his particular train of thought. There was no need; they knew each other much too well. On Earth, years ago, in a moment of mutual loneliness and depression, they had once made love. Probably they would never repeat the experience (but could one ever be *quite* sure of that?) because so much had changed for both of them. Yet whenever the well-built Surgeon oscillated into the Commander's cabin, he felt a fleeting echo of an old passion, she knew that he felt it, and everyone was happy.

'Bill,' she began, 'I've checked our mountaineers, and here's my verdict. Karl and Joe are in good shape – all indications normal for the work they've done. But Will shows signs of exhaustion and body-loss – I won't bother about the details. I don't believe he's been getting all the exercise he should, and he's not the only one. There's been some cheating in the centrifuge; if there's any more, heads will roll. Please pass the word.'

'Yes, Ma'am. But there's some excuse. The men have been working very hard.'

'With their brains and fingers, certainly. But not with their bodies – not *real* work in kilogramme-metres. And that's what we'll be dealing with, if we're going to explore Rama.'

'Well, can we?'

'Yes, if we proceed with caution. Karl and I have worked out a very conservative profile – based on the assumption that we can dispense with breathing gear below Level Two. Of course, that's an incredible stroke of luck, and changes the whole logistics picture. I still can't get used to the idea of a world with oxygen ... So we only need to supply food and water and thermosuits, and we're in business. Going down will be easy; it looks as if we can slide most of the way, on that very convenient banister.'

'I've got Chips working on a sled with parachute braking. Even if we can't risk it for crew, we can use it for stores and equipment.'

'Fine; *that* should do the trip in ten minutes; otherwise it will take about an hour.

'Climbing up is harder to estimate; I'd like to allow six hours, including two one-hour periods. Later, as we get experience – *and* develop some muscles – we may be able to cut this back considerably.'

'What about psychological factors?'

'Hard to assess, in such a novel environment. Darkness may be the biggest problem.'

'I'll establish searchlights on the Hub. Besides its own lamps, any party down there will always have a beam playing on it.'

'Good – that should be a great help.'

'One other point: should we play safe and send a party only halfway down the stair – and back – or should we go the whole way on the first attempt?'

'If we had plenty of time, I'd be cautious. But time is short, and I can see no danger in going all the way – and looking around when we get there.'

'Thanks, Laura – that's all I want to know. I'll get the Exec working on the details. And I'll order all hands to the centrifuge – twenty minutes a day at half a gee. Will that satisfy you?'

'No. It's point six gee down there in Rama, and I want a safety margin. Make it three quarters—'

'Ouch!'

'– for ten minutes—'

'I'll settle for that—'

'– *twice* a day.'

'Laura, you're a cruel, hard woman. But so be it. I'll break the news just before dinner. That should spoil a few appetites.'

It was the first time that Commander Norton had ever seen Karl Mercer slightly ill at ease. He had spent the fifteen minutes discussing the logistics problem in his usual competent manner, but something was obviously worrying him. His captain, who had a shrewd idea of what it was, waited patiently until he brought it out.

'Skipper,' Karl said at length, 'are you *sure* you should lead this party? If anything goes wrong, I'm considerably more expendable. And I've been further inside Rama than anyone else – even if only by fifty metres.'

'Granted. But it's time the commander led his troops, and we've decided that there's no greater risk on this trip than on the last. At the first sign of trouble, I'll be back up that stairway fast enough to qualify for the Lunar Olympics.'

He waited for any further objections, but none came, though Karl still

39

looked unhappy. So he took pity on him and added gently: 'And I bet Joe will beat me to the top.'

The big man relaxed, and a slow grin spread across his face. 'All the same, Bill, I wish you'd taken someone else.'

'I wanted *one* man who'd been down before, and we can't both go. As for Herr Doktor Professor Sergeant Myron, Laura says he's still two kilos overweight. Even shaving off that moustache didn't help.'

'Who's your number three?'

'I still haven't decided. That depends on Laura.'

'She wants to go herself.'

'Who doesn't? But if she turns up at the top of her own fitness list, I'll be very suspicious.'

As Lieut-Commander Mercer gathered up his papers and launched himself out of the cabin, Norton felt a brief stab of envy. Almost all the crew – about eighty-five per cent, by his minimum estimate – had worked out some sort of emotional accommodation. He had known ships where the captain had done the same, but that was not his way. Though discipline aboard the *Endeavour* was based very largely on the mutual respect between highly trained and intelligent men and women, the commander needed something more to underline his position. His responsibility was unique, and demanded a certain degree of isolation, even from his closest friends. Any liaison could be damaging to morale, for it was almost impossible to avoid charges of favouritism. For this reason, affairs spanning more than two degrees of rank were firmly discouraged; but apart from this, the only rule regulating shipboard sex was 'So long as they don't do it in the corridors and frighten the simps'.

There were four superchimps aboard *Endeavour*, though strictly speaking the name was inaccurate, because the ship's non-human crew was not based on chimpanzee stock. In zero gravity, a prehensile tail is an enormous advantage, and all attempts to supply these to humans had turned into embarrassing failures. After equally unsatisfactory results with the great apes, the Superchimpanzee Corporation had turned to the monkey kingdom.

Blackie, Blondie, Goldie and Brownie had family trees whose branches included the most intelligent of the Old and New World monkeys, plus synthetic genes that had never existed in nature. Their rearing and education had probably cost as much as that of the average spaceman, and they were worth it. Each weighed less than thirty kilos and consumed only half the food and oxygen of a human being, but each could replace 2.75 men for housekeeping, elementary cooking, tool-carrying and dozens of other routine jobs.

That 2.75 was the Corporation's claim, based on innumerable time-and-motion studies. The figure, though surprising and frequently challenged, appeared to be accurate, for simps were quite happy to work fifteen hours a day and did not get bored by the most menial and repetitious tasks. So they freed human beings for human work; and on a spaceship, that was a matter of vital importance.

Unlike the monkeys who were their nearest relatives *Endeavour*'s simps were docile, obedient and uninquisitive. Being cloned, they were also sexless, which eliminated awkward behavioural problems. Carefully house-trained vegetarians, they were very clean and didn't smell; they would have made perfect pets, except that nobody could possibly have afforded them.

Despite these advantages, having simps on board involved certain problems. They had to have their own quarters – inevitably labelled 'The Monkey House'. Their little mess-room was always spotless, and was well-equipped with TV, games equipment and programmed teaching machines. To avoid accidents, they were absolutely forbidden to enter the ship's technical areas; the entrances to all these were colour-coded in red, and the simps were conditioned so that it was psychologically impossible for them to pass the visual barriers.

There was also a communications problem. Though they had an equivalent IQ of sixty, and could understand several hundred words of English, they were unable to talk. It had proved impossible to give useful vocal chords either to apes or monkeys, and they therefore had to express themselves in sign language.

The basic signs were obvious and easily learned, so that everyone on board ship could understand routine messages. But the only man who could speak fluent Simpish was their handler – Chief Steward McAndrews.

It was a standing joke that Sergeant Ravi McAndrews *looked* rather like a simp – which was hardly an insult, for with their short, tinted pelts and graceful movements they were very handsome animals. They were also affectionate, and everyone on board had his favourite; Commander Norton's was the aptly-named Goldie.

But the warm relationship which one could so easily establish with simps created another problem, often used as a powerful argument against their employment in space. Since they could only be trained for routine, low-grade tasks, they were worse than useless in an emergency; they could then be a danger to themselves and to their human companions. In particular, teaching them to use spacesuits had proved impossible, the concepts involved being quite beyond their understanding.

No one liked to talk about it, but everybody knew what had to be done if a hull was breached or the order came to abandon ship. It had happened only once; then the simp handler had carried out his instructions more than adequately. He was found with his charges, killed by the same poison. Thereafter the job of euthing was transferred to the chief medical officer, who it was felt would have less emotional involvement.

Norton was very thankful that this responsibility, at least, did not fall upon the captain's shoulders. He had known men he would have killed with far fewer qualms than he would Goldie.

12 THE STAIRWAY OF THE GODS

I n the clear, cold atmosphere of Rama, the beam of the searchlight was completely invisible. Three kilometres down from the central Hub, the hundred-metre wide oval of light lay across a section of that colossal stairway. A brilliant oasis in the surrounding darkness, it was sweeping slowly towards the curved plain still five kilometres below; and in its centre moved a trio of ant-like figures, casting long shadows before them.

It had been, just as they had hoped and expected, a completely uneventful descent. They had paused briefly at the first platform, and Norton had walked a few hundred metres along the narrow, curving ledge before starting the slide down to the second level. Here they had discarded their oxygen gear, and revelled in the strange luxury of being able to breathe without mechanical aids. Now they could explore in comfort, freed from the greatest danger that confronts a man in space, and forgetting all worries about suit integrity and oxygen reserve.

By the time they had reached the fifth level, and there was only one more section to go, gravity had reached almost half its terrestrial value. Rama's centrifugal spin was at last exerting its real strength; they were surrendering themselves to the implacable force which rules every planet, and which can exert a merciless price for the smallest slip. It was still very easy to go downwards; but the thought of the return, up those thousands upon thousands of steps, was already beginning to prey upon their minds.

The stairway had long ago ceased its vertiginous downward plunge and was now flattening out towards the horizontal. The gradient was now only about one in five; at the beginning, it had been five in one. Normal walking was now both physically, and psychologically, acceptable; only the lowered gravity reminded them that they were not descending some great stairway on Earth. Norton had once visited the ruins of an Aztec temple, and the feelings he had then experienced came echoing back to him – amplified a hundred times. Here was the same sense of awe and mystery, and the sadness of the irrevocably vanished past. Yet the scale here was so much greater, both in time and space, that the mind was unable to do it justice; after a while, it ceased to respond. Norton wondered if, sooner or later, he would take even Rama for granted.

42

And there was another respect in which the parallel with terrestrial ruins failed completely. Rama was hundreds of times older than any structure that had survived on Earth – even the Great Pyramid. *But everything looked absolutely new; there was no sign of wear and tear.*

Norton had puzzled over this a good deal, and had arrived at a tentative explanation. Everything that they had so far examined was part of an emergency back-up system, very seldom put to actual use. He could not imagine that the Ramans – unless they were physical fitness fanatics of the kind not uncommon on Earth – ever walked up and down this incredible stairway, or its two identical companions completing the invisible Y far above his head. Perhaps they had only been required during the actual construction of Rama, and had served no purpose since that distant day. That theory would do for the moment, yet it did not feel right. There was something wrong, somewhere ...

They did not slide for the last kilometre but went down the steps two at a time in long, gentle strides; this way, Norton decided, they would give more exercise to muscles that would soon have to be used. And so the end of the stairway came upon them almost unawares; suddenly, there were no more steps – only a flat plain, dull grey in the now weakening beam of the Hub searchlight, fading away into the darkness a few hundred metres ahead.

Norton looked back along the beam, towards its source up on the axis more than eight kilometres away. He knew that Mercer would be watching through the telescope, so he waved to him cheerfully.

'Captain here,' he reported over the radio. 'Everyone in fine shape – no problems. Proceeding as planned.'

'Good,' replied Mercer. 'We'll be watching.'

There was a brief silence; then a new voice cut in. 'This is the Exec, on board ship. Really, Skipper, this isn't good enough. You know the news services have been screaming at us for the last week. I don't expect deathless prose, but can't you do better than that?'

'I'll try,' Norton chuckled. 'But remember there's nothing to see yet. It's like – well, being on a huge, darkened stage, with a single spotlight. The first few hundred steps of the stairway rise out of it until they disappear into the darkness overhead. What we can see of the plain looks perfectly flat – the curvature's too small to be visible over this limited area. And that's about it.'

'Like to give any impressions?'

'Well, it's still very cold – below freezing – and we're glad of our thermosuits. And *quiet* of course, quieter than anything I've ever known on Earth, or in space, where there's always some background noise. Here, every sound is swallowed up; the space around us is so enormous that there aren't any echoes. It's weird, but I hope we'll get used to it.'

'Thanks, Skipper. Anyone else – Joe, Boris?'

Lt Joe Calvert, never at a loss for words, was happy to oblige.

'I can't help thinking that this is the first time – *ever* – that we've been able to walk on another world, breathing its natural atmosphere – though I suppose "natural" is hardly the word you can apply to a place like this. Still, Rama must resemble the world of its builders; our own spaceships are all miniature earths. Two examples are damned poor statistics, but does this mean that all intelligent life-forms are oxygen eaters? What we've seen of their work suggests that the Ramans were humanoid, though perhaps about fifty per cent taller than we are. Wouldn't you agree, Boris?'

Is Joe teasing Boris? Norton asked himself. I wonder how he's going to react? ...

To all his shipmates, Boris Rodrigo was something of an enigma. The quiet, dignified communications officer was popular with the rest of the crew, but he never entered fully into their activities and always seemed a little apart – marching to the music of a different drummer.

As indeed he was, being a devout member of the Fifth Church of Christ, Cosmonaut. Norton had never been able to discover what had happened to the earlier four, and he was equally in the dark about the Church's rituals and ceremonies. But the main tenet of its faith was well known: it believed that Jesus Christ was a visitor from space, and had constructed an entire theology on that assumption.

It was perhaps not surprising that an unusually high proportion of the Church's devotees worked in space in some capacity or other. Invariably, they were efficient, conscientious and absolutely reliable. They were universally respected and even liked, especially as they made no attempt to convert others. Yet there was also something slightly spooky about them; Norton could never understand how men with advanced scientific and technical training could possibly believe some of the things he had heard Christers state as incontrovertible facts.

As he waited for Lt Rodrigo to answer Joe's possibly loaded question, the commander had a sudden insight into his own hidden motives. He had chosen Brois because he was physically fit, technically qualified, and completely dependable. At the same time, he wondered if some part of his mind had not selected the lieutenant out of an almost mischievous curiosity. How could a man with such religious beliefs react to the awesome reality of Rama? Suppose he encountered something that confounded his theology ... or, for that matter, confirmed it?

But Boris Rodrigo, with his usual caution, refused to be drawn.

'They were certainly oxygen breathers, and they *could* be humanoid. But let's wait and see. With any luck, we should discover what they were like. There may be pictures, statues – perhaps even bodies, over in those towns. If they are towns.'

'And the nearest is only eight kilometres away,' said Joe Calvert hopefully.

Yes, thought the commander, but it's also eight kilometres back – and then there's that overwhelming stairway to climb again. Can we take the risk?

A quick sortie to the 'town' which they had named Paris had been among the first of his contingency plans, and now he had to make his decision. They had ample food and water for a stay of twenty-four hours; they would always be in full view of the back-up team on the Hub, and any kind of accident seemed virtually impossible on this smooth, gently curving, metal plain. The only foreseeable danger was exhaustion; when they got to Paris, which they could do easily enough, could they do more than take a few photographs and perhaps collect some small artefacts, before they had to return?

But even such a brief foray would be worth it; there was so little time, as Rama hurtled sunwards towards a perihelion too dangerous for *Endeavour* to match.

In any case, part of the decision was not his to make. Up in the ship, Dr Ernst would be watching the outputs of the bio-telemetering sensors attached to his body. If she turned thumbs-down, that would be that.

'Laura, what do you think?'

'Take thirty minutes' rest, and a five hundred calorie energy module. Then you can start.'

'Thanks, Doc,' interjected Joe Calvert. 'Now I can die happy. I always wanted to see Paris. Montmartre, here we come.'

45

13 THE PLAIN OF RAMA

After those interminable stairs, it was a strange luxury to walk once more on a horizontal surface. Directly ahead, the ground was indeed completely flat; to right and left, at the limits of the floodlit area, the rising curve could just be detected. They might have been walking along a very wide, shallow valley; it was quite impossible to believe that they were really crawling along the inside of a huge cylinder, and that beyond this little oasis of light the land rose up to meet – no, to *become* – the sky.

Though they all felt a sense of confidence and subdued excitement, after a while the almost palpable silence of Rama began to weigh heavily upon them. Every footstep, every word, vanished instantly into the unreverberant void; after they had gone little more than half a kilometre, Lt Calvert could stand it no longer.

Among his minor accomplishments was a talent now rare, though many thought not rare enough – the art of whistling. With or without encouragement he could reproduce the themes from most of the movies of the last two hundred years. He started appropriately with Heigh-ho, heigh-ho, 'tis off to work we go, found that he couldn't stay down comfortably in the bass with Disney's marching dwarfs, and switched quickly to River Kwai. Then he progressed, more or less chronologically, through half a dozen epics, culminating with the theme from Sid Krassman's famous late-twentieth-century *Napoleon*.

It was a good try, but it didn't work, even as a morale-builder. Rama needed the grandeur of Bach or Beethoven or Sibelius or Tuan Sun, not the trivia of popular entertainment. Norton was on the point of suggesting that Joe save his breath for later exertions, when the young officer realised the inappropriateness of his efforts. Thereafter, apart from an occasional consultation with the ship, they marched on in silence. Rama had won this round.

On his initial traverse, Norton had allowed for one detour. Paris lay straight ahead, halfway between the foot of the stairway and the shore of the Cylindrical Sea, but only a kilometre to the right of their track was a very prominent, and rather mysterious, feature which had been christened the Straight Valley. It was a long groove or trench, forty metres deep and a hundred wide, with gently sloping sides; it had been provisionally identified as an irrigation ditch or canal. Like the stairway itself, it had two similar counterparts, equally spaced around the curve of Rama.

The three valleys were almost ten kilometres long, and stopped abruptly just before they reached the Sea – which was strange, if they were intended to carry water. And on the other side of the Sea the pattern was repeated: three more ten-kilometre-trenches continued on to the South Polar region.

They reached the end of the Straight Valley after only fifteen minutes' comfortable walking, and stood for a while staring thoughtfully into its depths. The perfectly smooth walls sloped down at an angle of sixty degrees; there were no steps or footholds. Filling the bottom was a sheet of flat, white material that looked very much like ice. A specimen could settle a good many arguments; Norton decided to get one.

With Calvert and Rodrigo acting as anchors and paying out a safety rope, he rapelled slowly down the steep incline. When he reached the bottom, he fully expected to find the familiar slippery feel of ice underfoot, but he was mistaken. The friction was too great; his footing was secure. This material was some kind of glass or transparent crystal; when he touched it with his fingertips, it was cold, hard and unyielding.

Turning his back to the searchlight and shielding his eyes from its glare, Norton tried to peer into the crystalline depths, as one may attempt to gaze through the ice of a frozen lake. But he could see nothing; even when he tried the concentrated beam of his own helmet-lamp, he was no more successful. This stuff was translucent, but not transparent. If it was a frozen liquid, it had a melting-point very much higher than water.

He tapped it gently with the hammer from his geology kit; the tool rebounded with a dull, unmusical 'clunk'. He tapped harder, with no more result, and was about to exert his full strength when some impulse made him desist.

It seemed most unlikely that he could crack this material; but what if he did? He would be like a vandal, smashing some enormous plate-glass window. There would be a better opportunity later, and at least he had discovered valuable information. It now seemed more unlikely than ever that this was a canal; it was simply a peculiar trench that stopped and started abruptly, but led nowhere. And if at any time it had carried liquid, where were the stains, the encrustations of dried-up sediment, that one would expect? Everything was bright and clean, as if the builders had left only yesterday ...

Once again he was face to face with the fundamental mystery of Rama, and this time it was impossible to evade it. Commander Norton was a reasonably imaginative man, but he would never have reached his present position if he had been liable to the wilder flights of fancy. Yet now, for the first time, he had a sense – not exactly of foreboding, but of anticipation. Things were not what they seemed; there was something very, very odd about a place that was simultaneously brand new – and a million years old.

Very thoughtfully, he began to walk slowly along the length of the little valley, while his companions, still holding the rope that was attached to his waist, followed him along the rim. He did not expect to make any further discoveries, but he wanted to let his curious emotional state run its course. For something else was worrying him; and it had nothing to do with the inexplicable newness of Rama.

He had walked no more than a dozen metres when it hit him like a thunderbolt.

He knew this place. *He had been here before.* Even on Earth, or some familiar planet, that experience is disquieting, though it is not particularly rare. Most men have known it at some time or other, and usually they dismiss it as the memory of a forgotten photograph, a pure coincidence – or, if they are mystically inclined, some form of telepathy from another mind, or even a flashback from their own future.

But to recognise a spot which *no* other human being can possibly have seen – that is quite shocking. For several seconds, Commander Norton stood rooted to the smooth crystalline surface on which he had been walking, trying to straighten out his emotions. His well-ordered universe had been turned upside down, and he had a dizzying glimpse of those mysteries at the edge of existence which he had successfully ignored for most of his life.

Then, to his immense relief, common sense came to the rescue. The disturbing sensation of *déjà-vu* faded out, to be replaced by a real and identifiable memory from his youth.

It was true – he had once stood between such steeply sloping walls, watching them drive into the distance until they seemed to converge at a point indefinitely far ahead. But they had been covered with neatly trimmed grass; and underfoot had been broken stone, not smooth crystal.

It had happened thirty years ago, during a summer vacation in England. Largely because of another student (he could remember her face – but he had forgotten her name) he had taken a course of industrial archaeology, then very popular among science and engineering graduates. They had explored abandoned coal-mines and cotton mills, climbed over ruined blast-furnaces and steam-engines, goggled unbelievingly at primitive (and still dangerous) nuclear reactors, and driven priceless turbine-powered antiques along restored motor roads.

Not everything that they saw was genuine; much had been lost during the centuries, for men seldom bother to preserve the commonplace articles of everyday life. But where it was necessary to make copies, they had been reconstructed with loving care.

And so young Bill Norton had found himself bowling along, at an exhilarating hundred kilometres an hour, while he furiously shoveled precious coal into the firebox of a locomotive that looked two hundred years old, but was actually younger than he was. The thirty-kilometre stretch of the Great Western Railway, however, was quite genuine, though it had required a good deal of excavating to get it back into commission.

Whistle screaming, they had plunged into a hillside and raced through a smoky, flame-lit darkness. An astonishingly long time later, they had burst out of the tunnel into a deep, perfectly straight cutting between steep grassy banks. The long-forgotten vista was almost identical with the one before him now.

'What is it, Skipper?' called Lt Rodrigo. 'Have you found something?'

As Norton dragged himself back to present reality, some of the oppression lifted from his mind. There was mystery here – yes; but it might not be beyond human understanding. He had learned a lesson, though it was not one that he could readily impart to others. At all costs, he must not let Rama overwhelm him. That way lay failure – perhaps even madness.

'No,' he answered, 'there's nothing down here. Haul me up – we'll head straight to Paris.'

14 STORM WARNING

'I 've called this meeting of the Committee,' said His Excellency the Ambassador of Mars to the United Planets, 'because Dr Perera has something important to tell us. He insists that we get in touch with Commander Norton right away, using the priority channel we've been able to establish after, I might say, a good deal of difficulty. Dr Perera's statement is rather technical, and before we come to it I think a summary of the present position might be in order; Dr Price has prepared one. Oh yes – some apologies for absence. Sir Lewis Sands is unable to be with us because he's chairing a conference, and Dr Taylor asks to be excused.'

He was rather pleased about that last abstention. The anthropologist had rapidly lost interest in Rama, when it became obvious that it would present little scope for him. Like many others, he had been bitterly disappointed to find that the mobile worldlet was dead; now there would be no opportunity for sensational books and viddies about Raman rituals and behavioural patterns. Others might dig up skeletons and classify artifacts; *that* sort of thing did not appeal to Conrad Taylor. Perhaps the only discovery that would bring him back in a hurry would be some highly explicit works of art, like the notorious frescoes of Thera and Pompeii.

Thelma Price, the archaelogist, took exactly the opposite point of view. She preferred excavations and ruins uncluttered by inhabitants who might interfere with dispassionate, scientific studies. The bed of the Mediterranean had been ideal – at least until the city planners and landscape artists had started getting in the way. And Rama would have been perfect, except for the maddening detail that it was a hundred million kilometres away and she would never be able to visit it in person.

'As you all know,' she began, 'Commander Norton has completed one traverse of almost thirty kilometres, without encountering any problems. He explored the curious trench shown on your maps as the Straight Valley; its purpose is still quite unknown, but it's clearly important as it runs the full length of Rama – except for the break at the Cylindrical Sea – and there are two other identical structures a hundred and twenty degrees apart round the circumference of the world.

'Then the party turned left – or East, if we adopt the North Pole convention

50

– until they reached Paris. As you'll see from this photograph, taken by a telescope camera at the Hub, it's a group of several hundred buildings, with wide streets between them.

'Now *these* photographs were taken by Commander Norton's group when they reached the site. If Paris is a city, it's a very peculiar one. Note that none of the buildings have windows, or even doors! They are all plain rectangular structures, an identical thirty-five metres high. And they appear to have been extruded out of the ground – there are no seams or joints – look at this close-up of the base of a wall – there's a smooth transition into the ground.

'My own feeling is that this place is not a residential area, but a storage or supply depot. In support of that theory, look at this photo ...

'These narrow slots or grooves, about five centimetres wide, run along all the streets, and there's one leading to every building – going straight into the wall. There's a striking resemblance to the street-car tracks of the early twentieth century; they are obviously part of some transport system.

'We've never considered it necessary to have public transport direct to every house. It would be economically absurd – people can always walk a few hundred metres. But if these buildings are used for the storage of heavy materials, it would make sense.'

'May I ask a question?' said the Ambassador for Earth.

'Of course, Sir Robert.'

'Commander Norton couldn't get into a single building?'

'No; when you listen to his report, you can tell he was quite frustrated. At one time he decided that the buildings could only be entered from underground; then he discovered the grooves of the transport system, and changed his mind.'

'Did he try to break in?'

'There was no way he could, without explosives or heavy tools. And he doesn't want to do that until all other approaches have failed.'

'I have it!' Dennis Solomons suddenly interjected. 'Cocooning!'

'I beg your pardon?'

'It's a technique developed a couple of hundred years ago,' continued the science historian. 'Another name for it is moth-balling. When you have something you want to preserve, you seal it inside a plastic envelope, and then pump in an inert gas. The original use was to protect military equipment between wars; it was once applied to whole ships. It's still widely used in museums that are short of storage space; no one knows what's inside some of the hundred-year-old cocoons in the Smithsonian basement.'

Patience was not one of Carlisle Perera's virtues; he was aching to drop his bombshell, and could restrain himself no longer.

'*Please*, Mr Ambassador! This is all very interesting, but I feel my information is rather more urgent.'

'If there are no other points – very well, Dr Perera.'

The exobiologist, unlike Conrad Taylor, had not found Rama a disappointment. It was true that he no longer expected to find life – but sooner or later, he had been quite sure, some remains would be discovered of the creatures who had built this fantastic world. The exploration had barely begun, although the time available was horribly brief before *Endeavour* would be forced to escape from her present sun-grazing orbit.

But now, if his calculations were correct, Man's contact with Rama would be even shorter than he had feared. For one detail had been overlooked – because it was so large that no one had noticed it before.

'According to our latest information,' Perera began, 'one party is now on its way to the Cylindrical Sea, while Commander Norton has another group setting up a supply base at the foot of Stairway Alpha. When that's established, he intends to have at least two exploratory missions operating at all times. In this way he hopes to use his limited manpower at maximum efficiency.

'It's a good plan, but there may be no time to carry it out. In fact, I would advise an immediate alert, and a preparation for total withdrawal at twelve hours' notice. Let me explain ...

'It's surprising how few people have commented on a rather obvious anomaly about Rama. It's now well inside the orbit of Venus – yet the interior is still frozen. But the temperature of an object in direct sunlight at this point is about five hundred degrees!

'The reason of course, is that Rama hasn't had time to warm up. It must have cooled down to near absolute zero – two hundred and seventy below – while it was in interstellar space. Now, as it approaches the sun, the outer hull is already almost as hot as molten lead. But the inside will stay cold, until the heat works its way through that kilometre of rock.

'There's some kind of fancy dessert with a hot exterior and ice-cream in the middle – I don't remember what it's called—'

'Baked Alaska. It's a favourite at UP banquets, unfortunately.'

'Thank you, Sir Robert. That's the situation in Rama at the moment, but it won't last. All these weeks, the solar heat has been working its way through, and we expect a sharp temperature rise to begin in a few hours. *That's* not the problem; by the time we'll have to leave anyway, it will be no more than comfortably tropical.'

'Then what's the difficulty?'

'I can answer in one word, Mr Ambassador. *Hurricanes.*'

15 THE EDGE OF THE SEA

There were now more than twenty men and women inside Rama – six of them down on the plain, the rest ferrying equipment and expendables through the airlock system and down the stairway. The ship itself was almost deserted, with the minimum possible staff on duty; the joke went around that *Endeavour* was really being run by the four simps and that Goldie had been given the rank of Acting-Commander.

For these first explorations, Norton had established a number of ground-rules; the most important dated back to the earliest days of man's space-faring. Every group, he had decided, must contain one person with prior experience. But not *more* than one. In that way, everybody would have an opportunity of learning as quickly as possible.

And so the first party to head for the Cylindrical Sea, though it was led by Surgeon-Commander Laura Ernst, had as its one-time veteran Lt Boris Rodrigo, just back from Paris. The third member, Sergeant Pieter Rousseau, had been with the back-up teams at the Hub; he was an expert on space reconnaissance instrumentation, but on this trip he would have to depend on his own eyes and a small portable telescope.

From the foot of Stairway Alpha to the edge of the Sea was just under fifteen kilometres – or an Earth-equivalent of eight under the low gravity of Rama. Laura Ernst, who had to prove that she lived up to her own standards, set a brisk pace. They stopped for thirty minutes at the mid-way mark, and made the whole trip in a completely uneventful three hours.

It was also quite monotonous, walking forward in the beam of the search-light through the anechoic darkness of Rama. As the pool of light advanced with them, it slowly elongated into a long, narrow ellipse; this foreshortening of the beam was the only visible sign of progress. If the observers up on the Hub had not given them continual distance checks, they could not have guessed whether they had travelled one kilometre, or five, or ten. They just plodded onwards through the million-year-old night, over an apparently seamless metal surface.

But at last, far ahead at the limits of the now weakening beam, there was something new. On a normal world, it would have been a horizon; as they approached, they could see that the plain on which they were walking came to an abrupt stop. They were nearing the edge of the Sea.

'Only a hundred metres,' said Hub Control. 'Better slow down.'

That was hardly necessary, yet they had already done so. It was a sheer straight drop of fifty metres from the level of the plain to that of the Sea – if it was a sea, and not another sheet of that mysterious crystalline material. Although Norton had impressed upon everyone the danger of taking anything for granted in Rama, few doubted that the Sea was really made of ice. But for what conceivable reason was the cliff on the southern shore five hundred metres high, instead of the fifty here?

It was as if they were approaching the edge of the world; their oval of light, cut off abruptly ahead of them, became shorter and shorter. But far out on the curved screen of the Sea their monstrous foreshortened shadows had appeared, magnifying and exaggerating every movement. Those shadows had been their companions every step of the way, as they marched down the beam, but now that they were broken at the edge of the cliff they no longer seemed part of them. They might have been creatures of the Cylindrical Sea, waiting to deal with any intruders into their domain.

Because they were now standing on the edge of a fifty-metre cliff, it was possible for the first time to appreciate the curvature of Rama. But no one had ever seen a frozen lake bent upwards into a cylindrical surface; that was distinctly unsettling, and the eye did its best to find some other interpretation. It seemed to Dr Ernst, who had once made a study of visual illusions, that half the time she was really looking at a *horizontally* curving bay, not a surface that soared up into the sky. It required a deliberate effort of will to accept the fantastic truth.

Only in the line directly ahead, parallel to the axis of Rama, was normalcy preserved. In this direction alone was there agreement between vision and logic. Here – for the next few kilometres at least – Rama looked flat, and *was* flat ... And out there, beyond their distorted shadows and the outer limit of the beam, lay the island that dominated the Cylindrical Sea.

'Hub Control,' Dr Ernst radioed, 'please aim your beam at New York.'

The night of Rama fell suddenly upon them, as the oval of light went sliding out to sea. Conscious of the now invisible cliff at their feet, they all stepped back a few metres. Then, as if by some magical stage transformation, the towers of New York sprang into view.

The resemblance to old-time Manhattan was only superficial; this star-born echo of Earth's past possessed its own unique identity. The more Dr Ernst stared at it, the more certain she became that it was not a city at all.

The real New York, like all of Man's habitations, had never been finished; still less had it been designed. *This* place, however, had an overall symmetry and pattern, though one so complex that it eluded the mind. It had been conceived and planned by some controlling intelligence – and then it had been completed, like a machine devised for some specific purpose. After that, there was no possibility of growth or change.

The beam of the searthlight slowly tracked along those distant towers and domes and interlocked spheres and criss-crossed tubes. Sometimes there would be a brilliant reflection as some flat surface shot the light back towards them; the first time this happened, they were all taken by surprise. It was exactly as if, over there on that strange island, someone was signaling to them ...

But there was nothing that they could see here that was not already shown in greater detail on photographs taken from the Hub. After a few minutes, they called for the light to return to them, and began to walk eastwards along the edge of the cliff. It had been plausibly theorized that, somewhere, there must surely be a flight of steps, or a ramp, leading down to the Sea. And one crewman, who was a keen sailor, had raised an interesting conjecture.

'Where there's a sea,' Sergeant Ruby Barnes had predicted, 'there must be docks and harbours – and ships. You can learn everything about a culture by studying the way it builds boats.' Her colleagues thought this a rather restricted point of view, but at least it was a stimulating one.

Dr Ernst had almost given up the search, and was preparing to make a descent by rope, when Lt Rodrigo spotted the narrow stairway. It could easily have been over-looked in the shadowed darkness below the edge of the cliff, for there was no guard-rail or other indication of its presence. And it seemed to lead nowhere; it ran down the fifty-metre vertical wall at a steep angle, and disappeared below the surface of the Sea.

They scanned the flight of steps with their helmet-lights, could see no conceivable hazard, and Dr Ernst got Commander Norton's permission to descend. A minute later, she was cautiously testing the surface of the Sea.

Her foot slithered almost frictionlessly back and forth. The material felt exactly like ice. It *was* ice.

When she struck it with her hammer, a familiar pattern of cracks radiated from the impact point, and she had no difficulty in collecting as many pieces as she wished. Some had already melted when she held up the sample holder to the light; the liquid appeared to be slightly turbid water, and she took a cautious sniff.

'Is that safe?' Rodrigo called down, with a trace of anxiety.

'Believe me, Boris,' she answered, 'if there are any pathogens around here that have slipped through my detectors, our insurance policies lapsed a week ago.'

But Boris had a point. Despite all the tests that had been carried out, there was a very slight risk that this substance might be poisonous, or might carry some unknown disease. In normal circumstances, Dr Ernst would not have taken even this minuscule chance. Now, however, time was short and the stakes were enormous. If it became necessary to quarantine *Endeavour*, that would be a very small price to pay for her cargo of knowledge.

'It's water, but I wouldn't care to drink it – it smells like an algae culture that's gone bad. I can hardly wait to get it to the lab.'

'Is the ice safe to walk on?'

'Yes, solid as a rock.'

'Then we can get to New York.'

'Can we, Pieter? Have you ever tried to walk across four kilometers of ice?'

'Oh – I see what you mean. Just imagine what Stores would say, if we asked for a set of skates! Not that many of us would know how to use them, even if we had any aboard.'

'And there's another problem,' put in Boris Rodrigo. 'Do you realise that the temperature is already above freezing? Before long, that ice is going to melt. How many spacemen can swim four kilometres? Certainly not this one ...'

Dr Ernst rejoined them at the edge of the cliff, and held up the small sample bottle in triumph.

'It's a long walk for a few cc's of dirty water, but it may teach us more about Rama than anything we've found so far. Let's head for home.'

They turned towards the distant lights of the Hub, moving with the gentle, loping strides which had proved the most comfortable means of walking under this reduced gravity. Often they looked back, drawn by the hidden enigma of the island out there in the centre of the frozen sea.

And just once, Dr Ernst thought she felt the faint suspicion of a breeze against her cheek.

It did not come again, and she quickly forgot all about it.

16 KEALAKEKUA

'**A**s you know perfectly well, Dr Perera,' said Ambassador Bose in a tone of patient resignation, 'few of us share your knowledge of mathematical meteorology. So please take pity on our ignorance.'

'With pleasure,' answered the exobiologist, quite unabashed. 'I can explain it best by telling you what is going to happen inside Rama – very soon.

'The temperature is now about to rise, as the solar heat pulse reaches the interior. According to the latest information I've received, it's already above freezing point. The Cylindrical Sea will soon start to thaw; and unlike bodies of water on Earth, it will melt from the bottom upwards. That may produce some odd effects; but I'm much more concerned with the atmosphere.

'As it's heated, the air inside Rama will expand – and will attempt to rise towards the central axis. And this is the problem. At ground level, although it's apparently stationary, it's actually sharing the spin of Rama – over eight hundred kilometres an hour. As it rises towards the axis it will try to retain that speed – and it won't be able to do so, of course. The result will be violent winds and turbulence; I estimate velocities of between two and three hundred kilometres an hour.

'Incidentally, very much the same thing occurs on Earth. The heated air at the Equator – which shares the Earth's sixteen-hundred-kilometres-an-hour spin – runs into the same problem when it rises and flows north and south.'

'Ah, the Trade Winds! I remember that from my geography lessons.'

'Exactly, Sir Robert. Rama will have Trade Winds, with a vengeance. I believe they'll last only a few hours, and then some kind of equilibrium will be restored. Meanwhile, I should advise Commander Norton to evacuate – as soon as possible. Here is the message I propose sending.'

With a little imagination, Commander Norton told himself, he could pretend that this was an improvised night camp at the foot of some mountain in a remote region of Asia or America. The clutter of sleeping pads, collapsible chairs and tables, portable power plant, lighting equipment, electrosan toilets, and miscellaneous scientific apparatus would not have looked out of place on Earth – especially as there were men and women working here without life support systems.

Establishing Camp Alpha had been very hard work, for everything had had to be man-handled through the chain of airlocks, sledded down the slope from the Hub, and then retrieved and unpacked. Sometimes, when the braking parachutes had failed, a consignment had ended up a good kilometre away out on the plain. Despite this, several crew members had asked permission to make the ride; Norton had firmly forbidden it. In an emergency, however, he might be prepared to reconsider the ban.

Almost all this equipment would stay here, for the labour of carrying it back was unthinkable – in fact, impossible. There were times when Commander Norton felt an irrational shame at leaving so much human litter in this strangely immaculate place. When they finally departed, he was prepared to sacrifice some of their precious time to leave everything in good order. Improbable though it was, perhaps millions of years hence, when Rama shot through some other star system, it might have visitors again. He would like to give them a good impression of Earth.

Meanwhile, he had a rather more immediate problem. During the last twenty-four hours he had received almost identical messages from both Mars and Earth. It seemed an odd coincidence; perhaps they had been commiserating with each other, as wives who lived safely on different planets were liable to do under sufficient provocation. Rather pointedly, they had reminded him that even though he was now a great hero, he still had family responsibilities.

The Commander picked up a collapsible chair, and walked out of the pool of light into the darkness surrounding the camp. It was the only way he could get any privacy, and he could also think better away from the turmoil. Deliberately turning his back on the organised confusion behind him, he began to speak into the recorder slung around his neck.

'Original for personal file, dupes to Mars and Earth. Hello, darling – yes, I know I've been a lousy correspondent, but I haven't been aboard ship for a week. Apart from a skeleton crew, we're all camping inside Rama, at the foot of the stairway we've christened Alpha.

'I have three parties out now, scouting the plain, but we've made disappointingly slow progress, because everything has to be done on foot. If only we had some means of transport! I'd be very happy to settle for a few electric bicycles ... they'd be perfect for the job.

'You've met my medical officer, Surgeon-Commander Ernst—' He paused uncertainly; Laura had met *one* of his wives, but which? Better cut that out—

Erasing the sentence, he began again.

'My MO, Surgeon-Commander Ernst, led the first group to reach the Cylindrical Sea, fifteen kilometres from here. She found that it was frozen water, as we'd expected – but you wouldn't want to drink it. Dr Ernst says it's a dilute organic soup, containing traces of almost any carbon compound you care to name, as well as phosphates and nitrates and dozens of metallic salts. There's not the slightest sign of life – not even any dead micro-organisms. So

58

we still know nothing about the biochemistry of the Ramans ... though it was probably not wildly different from ours.'

Something brushed lightly against his hair; he had been too busy to get it cut, and would have to do something about that before he next put on a space-helmet ...

'You've seen the viddies of Paris and the other towns we've explored on this side of the Sea ... London, Rome, Moscow. It's impossible to believe that they were ever built for anything to *live* in. Paris looks like a giant storage depot. London is a collection of cylinders linked together by pipes connected to what are obviously pumping stations. Everything is sealed up, and there's no way of finding what's inside without explosives or lasers. We won't try these until there are no alternatives.

'As for Rome and Moscow—'

'Excuse me, Skipper. Priority from Earth.'

What now? Norton asked himself. Can't a man get a few minutes to talk to his families?

He took the message from the Sergeant, and scanned it quickly, just to satisfy himself that it was not immediate. Then he read it again, more slowly.

What the devil was the Rama Committee? And why had he never heard of it? He knew that all sorts of associations, societies, and professional groups – some serious, some completely crackpot – had been trying to get in touch with him; Mission Control had done a good job of protection, and would not have forwarded this message unless it was considered important.

'Two-hundred-kilometre winds – probably sudden onset.' – well, that was something to think about. But it was hard to take it too seriously, on this utterly calm night; and it would be ridiculous to run away like frightened mice, when they were just starting effective exploration.

Commander Norton lifted a hand to brush aside his hair, which had some-how fallen into his eyes again. Then he froze, the gesture uncompleted.

He *had* felt a trace of wind, several times in the last hour. It was so slight that he had completely ignored it; after all, he was the commander of a *space*-ship, not a sailing ship. Until now the movement of air had not been of the slightest professional concern. What would the long-dead captain of that earlier *Endeavour* have done in a situation such as this?

Norton had asked himself that question at every moment of crisis in the last few years. It was his secret, which he had never revealed to anyone. And like most of the important things in life, it had come about quite by accident.

He had been captain of *Endeavour* for several months before he realised that it was named after one of the most famous ships in history. True, during the last four hundred years there had been a dozen *Endeavours* of sea and two of space, but the ancestor of them all was the 370-ton Whitby collier that Captain James Cook, RN, had sailed round the world between 1768 and 1771.

With a mild interest that had quickly turned to an absorbing curiosity

– almost an obsession – Norton had begun to read everything he could find about Cook. He was now probably the world's leading authority on the greatest explorer of all time, and knew whole sections of the *Journals* by heart.

It still seemed incredible that one man could have done so much, with such primitive equipment. But Cook had been not only a supreme navigator, but a scientist and – in an age of brutal discipline – a humanitarian. He treated his own men with kindness, which was unusual; what was quite unheard of was that he behaved in exactly the same way to the often hostile savages in the new lands he discovered.

It was Norton's private dream, which he knew he would never achieve, to retrace at least one of Cook's voyages around the world. He had made a limited but spectacular start, which would certainly have astonished the Captain, when he once flew a polar orbit directly above the Great Barrier Reef. It had been early morning on a clear day, and from four hundred kilometres up he had had a superb view of that deadly wall of coral, marked by its line of white foam along the Queensland coast.

He had taken just under five minutes to travel the whole two thousand kilometres of the Reef. In a single glance he could span weeks of perilous voyaging for that first *Endeavour*. And through the telescope, he had caught a glimpse of Cooktown and the estuary where the ship had been dragged ashore for repairs, after her near-fatal encounter with the Reef.

A year later, a visit to the Hawaii Deep-Space Tracking Station had given him an even more unforgettable experience. He had taken the hydrofoil to Kealakekua Bay, and as he moved swiftly past the bleak volcanic cliffs, he felt a depth of emotion that had surprised and even disconcerted him. The guide had led his group of scientists, engineers and astronauts past the glittering metal pylon that had replaced the earlier monument, destroyed by the Great Tsunami of '68. They had walked on for a few more yards across black, slippery lava to the small plaque at the water's edge. Little waves were breaking over it, but Norton scarcely noticed them as he bent down to read the words:

NEAR THIS SPOT
CAPTAIN JAMES COOK
WAS KILLED
14 FEBRUARY, 1779
ORIGINAL TABLET DEDICATED 28 AUGUST, 1928
BY COOK SESQUICENTENNIAL COMMISSION
REPLACED BY TRICENTENNIAL COMMISSION
14 FEBRUARY, 2079

That was years ago, and a hundred million kilometres away. But at moments like this, Cook's reassuring presence seemed very close. In the secret depths of his mind, he would ask: 'Well, Captain – what is *your* advice?' It was a little game he played, on occasions when there were not enough facts for sound judgement, and one had to rely on intuition. That had been part of Cook's genius; he always made the right choice – until the very end, at Kealakekua Bay.

The Sergeant waited patiently, while his Commander stared silently out into the night of Rama. It was no longer unbroken, for at two spots about four kilometres away, the faint patches of light of exploring parties could be clearly seen.

In an emergency, I can recall them within the hour, Norton told himself. And that, surely, should be good enough.

He turned to the Sergeant, 'Take this message. Rama Committee, care of Spacecom. Appreciate your advice and will take precautions. Please specify meaning of phrase "sudden onset". Respectfully, Norton, Commander, *Endeavour.'*

He waited until the Sergeant had disappeared towards the blazing lights of the camp, then switched on his recorder again. But the train of thought was broken, and he could not get back into the mood. The letter would have to wait for some other time.

It was not often that Captain Cook came to his aid when he was neglecting his duty. But he suddenly remembered how rarely and briefly poor Elizabeth Cook had seen her husband in sixteen years of married life. Yet she had borne him six children – and outlived them all.

His wives, never more than ten minutes away at the speed of light, had nothing to complain about ...

17 SPRING

During the first 'nights' on Rama, it had not been easy to sleep. The darkness and the mysteries it concealed were oppressive, but even more unsettling was the silence. Absence of noise is not a natural condition; all human senses require some input. If they are deprived of it, the mind manufactures its own substitutes.

And so many sleepers had complained of strange noises – even of voices – which were obviously illusions, because those awake had heard nothing. Surgeon-Commander Ernst had prescribed a very simple and effective cure; during the sleeping period, the camp was now lulled by gentle, unobtrusive background music.

This night, Commander Norton found the cure inadequate. He kept straining his ears into the darkness, and he knew what he was listening for. But though a very faint breeze did caress his face from time to time, there was no sound that could possibly be taken for that of a distant, rising wind. Nor did either of the exploring parties report anything unusual.

At least, around Ship's midnight, he went to sleep. There was always a man on watch at the communications console, in case of any urgent messages. No other precautions seemed necessary.

Not even a hurricane could have created the sound that did wake him, and the whole camp, in a single instant. It seemed that the sky was falling, or that Rama had split open and was tearing itself apart. First there was a rending crack, then a long-drawn-out series of crystalline crashes like a million glass-houses being demolished. It lasted for minutes, though it seemed like hours; it was still continuing, apparently moving away into the distance, when Norton got to the message centre.

'Hub Control! What's happened?'

'Just a moment, Skipper. It's over by the Sea. We're getting the light on it.'

Eight kilometres overhead, on the axis of Rama, the searchlight began to swing its beam out across the plain. It reached the edge of the Sea, then started to track along it, scanning around the interior of the world. A quarter of the way round the cylindrical surface, it stopped.

Up there in the sky – or what the mind still persisted in calling the sky – something extraordinary was happening. At first, it seemed to Norton that the

Sea was boiling. It was no longer static and frozen in the grip of an eternal winter; a huge area, kilometers across, was in turbulent movement. And it was changing colour; a broad band of white was marching across the ice.

Suddenly a slab perhaps a quarter of a kilometre on a side began to tilt upwards like an opening door. Slowly and majestically, it reared into the sky, glittering and sparkling in the beam of the searchlight. Then it slid back and vanished underneath the surface, while a tidal wave of foaming water raced outwards in all directions from its point of submergence.

Not until then did Commander Norton fully realise what was happening. *The ice was breaking up.* All these days and weeks, the Sea had been thawing, far down in the depths. It was hard to concentrate because of the crashing roar that still filled the world and echoed round the sky, but he tried to think of a reason for so dramatic a convulsion. When a frozen lake or river thawed on Earth, it was nothing like this ...

But of course! It was obvious enough, now that it had happened. The Sea was thawing from *beneath* as the solar heat seeped through the hull of Rama. And when ice turns into water, it occupies less volume ...

So the Sea had been sinking below the upper layer of ice, leaving it unsupported. Day by day the strain had been building up; now the band of ice that encircled the equator of Rama was collapsing, like a bridge that had lost its central pier. It was splintering into hundreds of floating islands, that would crash and jostle into each other until they too melted. Norton's blood ran suddenly cold, when he remembered the plans that were being made to reach New York by sledge ...

The tumult was swiftly subsiding; a temporary stalemate had been reached in the war between ice and water. In a few hours, as the temperature continued to rise, the water would win and the last vestiges of ice would disappear. But in the long run, ice would be the victor, as Rama rounded the sun and set forth once more into the interstellar night.

Norton remembered to start breathing again; then he called the party nearest the Sea. To his relief, Lieutenant Rodrigo answered at once. No, the water hadn't reached them. No tidal wave had come sloshing over the edge of the cliff. 'So now we know,' he added very calmly, 'why there *is* a cliff.' Norton agreed silently; but that hardly explains, he thought to himself, why the cliff on the southern shore is ten times higher ...

The Hub searchlight continued to scan round the world. The awakened Sea was steadily calming, and the boiling white foam no longer raced outwards from capsizing ice-floes. In fifteen minutes, the main disturbance was over.

But Rama was no longer silent; it had awakened from its sleep, and ever and again there came the sound of grinding ice as one berg collided with another.

Spring had been a little late, Norton told himself, but winter had ended.

And there was that breeze again, stronger than ever. Rama had given him enough warnings; it was time to go.

*

As he neared the halfway mark, Commander Norton once again felt gratitude to the darkness that concealed the view above – and below. Though he knew that more than ten thousand steps still lay ahead of him, and could picture the steeply ascending curve in his mind's eye, the fact that he could see only a small portion of it made the prospect more bearable.

This was his second ascent, and he had learned from his mistakes on the first. The great temptation was to climb too quickly in this low gravity; every step was so easy that it was very hard to adopt a slow, plodding rhythm. But unless one did this, after the first few thousand steps strange aches developed in the thighs and calves. Muscles that one never knew existed started to protest, and it was necessary to take longer and longer periods of rest. Towards the end he had spent more time resting than climbing, and even then it was not enough. He had suffered painful leg-cramps for the next two days, and would have been almost incapacitated had he not been back in the zero-gravity environment of the ship.

So this time he had started with almost painful slowness, moving like an old man. He had been the last to leave the plain, and the others were strung out along the half-kilometre of stairway above him; he could see their lights moving up the invisble slope ahead.

He felt sick at heart at the failure of his mission, and even now hoped that this was only a temporary retreat. When they reached the Hub, they could wait until any atmospheric disturbances had ceased. Presumably, it would be a dead calm there, as at the centre of a cyclone, and they could wait out the expected storm in safety.

Once again, he was jumping to conclusions, drawing dangerous analogies from Earth. The meteorology of a whole world, even under steady-state conditions, was a matter of enormous complexity. After several centuries of study, terrestrial weather-forecasting was still not absolutely reliable. And Rama was not merely a completely novel system; it was also undergoing rapid changes, for the temperature had risen several degrees in the last few hours. Yet still there was no sign of the promised hurricane, though there had been a few feeble gusts from apparently random directions.

They had now climbed five kilometres, which in this low and steadily diminishing gravity was equivalent to less than two on Earth. At the third level, three kilometres from the axis, they rested for an hour, taking light refreshments and massaging leg muscles. This was the last point at which they could breathe in comfort; like old-time Himalayan mountaineers, they had left their oxygen supplies here, and now put them on for the final ascent.

An hour later, they had reached the top of the stairway – and the beginning of the ladder. Ahead lay the last, vertical kilometre, fortunately in a gravity field only a few per cent of Earth's. Another thirty-minute rest, a careful check of oxygen, and they were ready for the final lap.

Once again, Norton made sure that all his men were safely ahead of him, spaced out at twenty-metre intervals along the ladder. From now on, it would be a slow, steady haul, extremely boring. The best technique was to empty the mind of all thoughts and to count the rungs as they drifted by – one hundred, two hundred, three hundred, four hundred …

He had just reached twelve hundred and fifty when he suddenly realised that something was wrong. The light shining on the vertical surface immediately in front of his eyes was the wrong colour – and it was much too bright.

Commander Norton did not even have time to check his ascent, or to call a warning to his men. Everything happened in less than a second.

In a soundless concussion of light, dawn burst upon Rama.

18 DAWN

The light was so brilliant that for a full minute Norton had to keep his eyes clenched tightly shut. Then he risked opening them, and stared through barely-parted lids at the wall a few centimetres in front of his face. He blinked several times, waited for the involuntary tears to drain away, and then turned slowly to behold the dawn.

He could endure the sight for only a few seconds; then he was forced to close his eyes again. It was not the glare that was intolerable – he could grow accustomed to that – but the awesome spectacle of Rama, now seen for the first time in its entirety.

Norton had known exactly what to expect; nevertheless the sight had stunned him. He was seized by a spasm of uncontrollable trembling; his hands tightened round the rungs of the ladder with the violence of a drowning man clutching at a lifebelt. The muscles of his forearms began to knot, yet at the same time his legs – already fatigued by hours of steady climbing – seemed about to give way. If it had not been for the low gravity, he might have fallen.

Then his training took over, and he began to apply the first remedy for panic. Still keeping his eyes closed and trying to forget the monstrous spectacle around him, he started to take deep, long breaths, filling his lungs with oxygen and washing the poisons of fatigue out of his system.

Presently he felt much better, but he did not open his eyes until he had performed one more action. It took a major effort of will to force his right hand to open – he had to talk to it like a disobedient child – but presently he manoeuvred it down to his waist, unclipped the safety belt from his harness, and hooked the buckle to the nearest rung. Now, whatever happened, he could not fall.

Norton took several more deep breaths; then – still keeping his eyes closed – he switched on his radio. He hoped his voice sounded calm and authoritative as he called: 'Captain here. Is everyone OK?'

As he checked off the names one by one, and received answers – even if somewhat tremulous ones – from everybody, his own confidence and self-control came swiftly back to him. All his men were safe, and were looking to him for leadership. He was the commander once more.

'Keep your eyes closed until you're quite sure you can take it,' he called.

'The view is – overwhelming. If anyone finds that it's too much, keep on climbing without looking back. Remember, you'll soon be at zero gravity, so you can't possibly fall.'

It was hardly necessary to point out such an elementary fact to trained spacemen, but Norton had to remind himself of it every few seconds. The thought of zero-gravity was a kind of talisman, protecting him from harm. Whatever his eyes told him, Rama could not drag him down to destruction on the plain eight kilometres below.

It became an urgent matter of pride and self-esteem that he should open his eyes once more and look at the world around him. But first, he had to get his body under control.

He let go of the ladder with *both* hands, and hooked his left arm under a rung. Clenching and unclenching his fists, he waited until the muscle cramps had faded away; then, when he felt quite comfortable, he opened his eyes and slowly turned to face Rama.

His first impression was one of blueness. The glare that filled the sky could not have been mistaken for sunlight; it might have been that of an electric arc. So Rama's sun, Norton told himself, must be hotter than ours. That should interest the astronomers ...

And now he understood the purpose of those mysterious trenches, the Straight Valley and its five companions; they were nothing less than gigantic strip-lights. Rama had six linear suns, symmetrically ranged around its interior. From each, a broad fan of light was aimed across the central axis, to shine upon the far side of the world. Norton wondered if they could be switched alternately to produce a cycle of light and darkness, or whether this was a planet of perpetual day.

Too much staring at those blinding bars of light had made his eyes hurt again; he was not sorry to have a good excuse to close them for a while. It was not until then, when he had almost recovered from this initial visual shock, that he was able to devote himself to a much more serious problem.

Who, or what, had switched on the lights of Rama?

This world was sterile, by the most sensitive tests that man could apply to it. But now something was happening that could not be explained by the action of natural forces. There might not be life here, but there could be consciousness, awareness; robots might be waking after a sleep of aeons. Perhaps this outburst of light was an unprogrammed, random spasm – a last dying gasp of machines that were responding wildly to the warmth of a new sun, and would soon lapse again into quiescence, this time for ever.

Yet Norton could not believe such a simple explanation. Bits of the jigsaw puzzle were beginning to fall into place, though many were still missing. The absence of all signs of wear, for example – the feeling of *newness*, as if Rama had just been created ...

These thoughts might have inspired fear, even terror. Somehow, they did nothing of the sort. On the contrary, Norton felt a sense of exhilaration

– almost of delight. There was far more here to discover than they had ever dared to hope. 'Wait,' he said to himself, 'until the Rama Committee hears about *this*!'

Then, with a calm determination, he opened his eyes again and began a careful inventory of everything he saw.

First, he had to establish some kind of reference system. He was looking at the largest enclosed space ever seen by man, and needed a mental map to find his way around it.

The feeble gravity was very little help, for with an effort of will he could switch Up and Down in any direction he pleased. But some directions were psychologically dangerous; whenever his mind skirted these, he had to vector it hastily away.

Safest of all was to imagine that he was at the bowl-shaped bottom of a gigantic well, sixteen kilometres wide and fifty deep. The advantage of this image was that there could be no danger of falling further; nevertheless, it had some serious defects.

He could pretend that the scattered towns and cities, and the differently coloured and textured areas, were all securely fixed to the towering walls. The various complex structures that could be seen hanging from the dome overhead were perhaps no more disconcerting than the pendent candelabra in some great concert-hall on Earth. What was quite unacceptable was the Cylindrical Sea ...

There it was, halfway up the well-shaft – a band of water, wrapped completely round it, with no visible means of support. There could be no doubt that it *was* water; it was a vivid blue, flecked with brilliant sparkles from the few remaining ice-floes. But a vertical sea forming a complete circle twenty kilometres up in the sky was such an unsettling phenomenon that after a while he began to seek an alternative.

That was when his mind switched the scene through ninety degrees. Instantly, the deep well became a long tunnel, capped at either end. 'Down' was obviously in the direction of the ladder and the stairway he had just ascended; and now with this perspective, Norton was at last able to appreciate the true vision of the architects who had built this place.

He was clinging to the face of a curving sixteen-kilometre-high cliff, the upper half of which overhung completely until it merged into the arched roof of what was now the sky. Beneath him, the ladder descended more than five hundred metres, until it ended at the first ledge or terrace. There the stairway began, continuing almost vertically at first in this low-gravity regime, then slowly becoming less and less steep until, after breaking at five more platforms, it reached the distant plain. For the first two or three kilometres he could see the individual steps, but thereafter they had merged into a continuous band.

The downward swoop of that immense stairway was so overwhelming that it was impossible to appreciate its true scale. Norton had once flown round

Mount Everest, and had been awed by its size. He reminded himself that this stairway was as high as the Himalayas, but the comparison was meaningless.

And no comparison at all was possible with the other two stairways, Beta and Gamma, which slanted up into the sky and then curved far out over his head. Norton had now acquired enough confidence to lean back and glance up at them – briefly. Then he tried to forget that they were there ...

For too much thinking along those lines evoked yet a third image of Rama, which he was anxious to avoid at all costs. This was the viewpoint that regarded it once again at a vertical cylinder or well – but now he was at the *top*, not the bottom, like a fly crawling upside down on a domed ceiling, with a fifty-kilometre drop immediately below. Every time Norton found this image creeping up on him, it needed all his willpower not to cling to the ladder again in mindless panic.

In time, he was sure, all these fears would ebb. The wonder and strangeness of Rama would banish its terrors, at least for men who were trained to face the realities of space. Perhaps no one who had never left Earth, and had never seen the stars all around him, could endure these vistas. But if any men could accept them, Norton told himself with grim determination, it would be the captain and crew of *Endeavour*.

He looked at his chronometer. This pause had lasted only two minutes, but it had seemed a lifetime. Exerting barely enough effort to overcome his inertia and the fading gravitational field, he started to pull himself slowly up the last hundred metres of the ladder. Just before he entered the airlock and turned his back upon Rama, he made one final swift survey of the interior.

It had changed, even in the last few minutes; a mist was rising from the Sea. For the first few hundred metres the ghostly white columns were tilted sharply forward in the direction of Rama's spin; then they started to dissolve in a swirl of turbulence, as the uprushing air tried to jettison its excess velocity. The Trade Winds of this cylindrical world were beginning to etch their patterns in its sky; the first tropical storm in unknown ages was about to break.

19 A WARNING FROM MERCURY

It was the first time in weeks that every member of the Rama Committee had made himself available. Professor Solomons had emerged from the depths of the Pacific, where he had been studying mining operations along the mid-ocean trenches. And to nobody's surprise, Dr Taylor had reappeared, now that there was at least a possibility that Rama held something more newsworthy than lifeless artifacts.

The Chairman had fully expected Dr Carlisle Perera to be even more dogmatically assertive than usual, now that his prediction of a Raman hurricane had been confirmed. To His Excellency's great surprise, Perera was remarkably subdued, and accepted the congratulations of his colleagues in a manner as near to embarrassment as he was ever likely to achieve.

The exobiologist, in fact, was deeply mortified. The spectacular break-up of the Cylindrical Sea was a much more obvious phenomenon than the hurricane winds – yet he had completely overlooked it. To have remembered that hot air rises, but to have forgotten that hot ice contracts, was not an achievement of which he could be very proud. However, he would soon get over it, and revert to his normal Olympian self-confidence.

When the Chairman offered him the floor, and asked what further climatic changes he expected, he was very careful to hedge his bets.

'You must realise,' he explained, 'that the meteorology of a world as strange as Rama may have many other surprises. But if my calculations are correct, there will be no further storms, and conditions will soon be stable. There will be a slow temperature rise until perihelion – and beyond – but that won't concern us, as *Endeavour* will have had to leave long before then.'

'So it should soon be safe to go back inside?'

'Er – probably. We should certainly know in forty-eight hours.'

'A return is imperative,' said the Ambassador for Mercury. 'We have to learn everything we possibly can about Rama. The situation has now changed completely.'

'I think we know what you mean, but would you care to elaborate?'

'Of course. Until now, we have assumed that Rama is lifeless – or at any rate uncontrolled. But we can no longer pretend that it is a derelict. Even if there are no life-forms aboard, it may be directed by robot mechanisms, programmed to carry out some mission – perhaps one highly disadvantageous to us. Unpalatable though it may be, we must consider the question of self-defence.'

There was a babble of protesting voices, and the Chairman had to hold up his hand to restore order.

'Let His Excellency finish!' he pleaded. 'Whether we like the idea or not, it should be considered seriously.'

'With all due respect to the Ambassador,' said Dr Conrad Taylor in his most disrespectful voice, 'I think we can rule out as naïve the fear of malevolent intervention. Creatures as advanced as the Ramans must have correspondingly developed morals. Otherwise, they would have destroyed themselves – as we nearly did in the twentieth century. I've made that quite clear in my new book *Ethos and Cosmos*. I hope you received your copy.'

'Yes, thank you, though I'm afraid the pressure of other matters has not allowed me to read beyond the introduction. However, I'm familiar with the general thesis. We may have no malevolent intentions towards an ant-heap. But if we want to build a house on the same site ...'

'This is as bad as the Pandora Party! It's nothing less than interstellar xenophobia!'

'Please, *gentlemen*! This is getting us nowhere. Mr Ambassador, you still have the floor.'

The Chairman glared across three hundred and eighty thousand kilometres of space at Conrad Taylor, who reluctantly subsided, like a volcano biding its time.

'Thank you,' said the Ambassador for Mercury. 'The danger may be unlikely, but where the future of the human race is involved, we can take no chances. And, if I may say so, we Hermians may be particularly concerned. We may have more cause for alarm than anyone else.'

Dr Taylor snorted audibly, but was quelled by another glare from the Moon.

'Why Mercury, more than any other planet?' asked the Chairman.

'Look at the dynamics of the situation. Rama is already inside our orbit. It is only an assumption that it will go round the sun and head on out again into space. Suppose it carries out a braking manoeuvre? If it does so, this will be at perihelion, about thirty days from now. My scientists tell me that if the entire velocity change is carried out there, Rama will end up in a circular orbit only twenty-five million kilometres from the sun. From there, it could dominate the solar system.'

For a long time nobody – not even Conrad Taylor – spoke a word. All the members of the Committee were marshalling their thoughts about those difficult people the Hermians, so ably represented here by their Ambassador.

To most people, Mercury was a fairly good approximation of Hell; at least, it would do until something worse came along. But the Hermians were proud of their bizarre planet, with its days longer than its years, its double sunrises and sunsets, its rivers of molten metal ... By comparison, the Moon and Mars had been almost trivial challenges. Not until men landed on Venus (if they ever did) would they encounter an environment more hostile than that of Mercury.

And yet this world had turned out to be, in many ways, the key to the solar system. This seemed obvious in retrospect, but the Space Age had been almost a century old before the fact was realised. Now the Hermians never let anyone forget it.

Long before men reached the planet, Mercury's abnormal density hinted at the heavy elements it contained; even so, its wealth was still a source of astonishment, and had postponed for a thousand years any fears that the key metals of human civilisation would be exhausted. And these treasures were in the best possible place, where the power of the Sun was ten times greater than on frigid Earth.

Unlimited energy – unlimited metal; *that* was Mercury. Its great magnetic launchers could catapult manufactured products to any point in the solar system. It could also export energy, in synthetic transuranium isotopes or pure radiation. It had even been proposed that Hermian lasers would one day thaw out gigantic Jupiter, but this idea had not been well received on the other worlds. A technology that could cook Jupiter had too many tempting possibilities for interplanetary blackmail.

That such a concern had ever been expressed said a good deal about the general attitude towards the Hermians. They were respected for their toughness and engineering skills, and admired for the way in which they had conquered so fearsome a world. But they were not liked, and still less were they completely trusted.

At the same time, it was possible to appreciate their point of view. The Hermians, it was often joked, some times behaved as if the Sun was their personal property. They were bound to it in an intimate love-hate relationship – as the Vikings had once been linked to the sea, the Nepalese to the Himalayas, the Eskimos to the Tundra. They would be most unhappy if something came between them and the natural force that dominated and controlled their lives.

At last, the Chairman broke the long silence. He still remembered the sun of India, and shuddered to contemplate the sun of Mercury. So he took the Hermians very seriously indeed, even though he considered them uncouth technological barbarians.

'I think there is some merit in your argument, Mr Ambassador,' he said slowly. 'Have you any proposals?'

'Yes, sir. Before we know what action to take, we must have the facts. We know the geography of Rama – if one can use that term – but we have no idea of its capabilities. And the key to the whole problem is this: does Rama have a propulsion system? *Can it change orbit?* I'd be very interested in Dr Perera's views.'

'I've given the subject a good deal of thought,' answered the exobiologist.

'Of course, Rama must have been given its original impetus by some launching device, but that could have been an external booster. If it does have onboard propulsion, we've found no trace of it. Certainly there are no rocket exhausts, or anything similar, anywhere on the outer shell.'

'They could be hidden.'

'True, but there would seem little point in it. And where are the propellant tanks, the energy sources? The main hull is solid – we've checked that with seismic surveys. The cavities in the northern cap are all accounted for by the airlock systems.

'That leaves the southern end of Rama, which Commander Norton has been unable to reach, owing to that ten-kilometre-wide band of water. There are all sorts of curious mechanisms and structures up on the South Pole – you've seen the photographs. What they are is anybody's guess.

'But I'm reasonably sure of this. If Rama does have a propulsion system, it's something completely outside our present knowledge. In fact, it would have to be the fabulous "Space Drive" people have been talking about for two hundred years.'

'You wouldn't rule that out?'

'Certainly not. If we can prove that Rama has a Space Drive – even if we learn nothing about its mode of operation – that would be a major discovery. At least we'd know that such a thing is possible.'

'What *is* a Space Drive?' asked the Ambassador for Earth, rather plaintively.

'Any kind of propulsion system, Sir Robert, that doesn't work on the rocket principle. Anti-gravity – if it is possible – would do very nicely. At present, we don't know where to look for such a drive, and most scientists doubt if it exists.'

'It doesn't,' Professor Davidson interjected. 'Newton settled *that*. You can't have action without reaction. Space Drives are nonsense. Take it from me.'

'You may be right,' Perera replied with unusual blandness. 'But if Rama doesn't have a Space Drive, it has no drive at all. There's simply no room for a conventional propulsion system, with its enormous fuel tanks.'

'It's hard to imagine a whole world being pushed around,' said Dennis Solomons. 'What would happen to the objects inside it? Everything would have to be bolted down. Most inconvenient.'

'Well, the acceleration would probably be very low. The biggest problem would be the water in the Cylindrical Sea. How would you stop that from ...'

Perera's voice suddenly faded away, and his eyes glazed over. He seemed to be in the throes of an incipient epileptic fit, or even a heart attack. His colleagues looked at him in alarm; then he made a sudden recovery, banged his fist on the table and shouted: 'Of course! That explains everything! The southern cliff – *now* it makes sense!'

'Not to me,' grumbled the Lunar Ambassador, speaking for all the diplomats present.

'Look at this longitudinal cross-section of Rama,' Perera continued excitedly, unfolding his map. 'Have you got your copies? The Cylindrical Sea is enclosed between two cliffs, which completely circle the interior of Rama. The one on the north is only fifty metres high. The southern one, on the other hand, is almost half a kilometre high. Why the big difference? No one's been able to think of a sensible reason.

'But suppose Rama *is* able to propel itself – accelerating so that the northern end is forward. The water in the Sea would tend to move back; the level at the south would rise – perhaps hundreds of metres. Hence the cliff. Let's see—'

Perera started scribbling furiously. After an astonishingly short time – it could not have been more than twenty seconds – he looked up in triumph.

'Knowing the height of those cliffs, we can calculate the maximum acceleration Rama can take. If it was more than two per cent of a gravity, the Sea would slosh over into the southern continent.'

'A fiftieth of a gee? That's not very much.'

'It is – for a mass of ten million megatons. And it's all you need for astronomical manoeuvring.'

'Thank you very much, Dr Perera,' said the Hermian Ambassador. 'You've given us a lot to think about. Mr Chairman – can we impress on Commander Norton the importance of looking at the South Polar region?'

'He's doing his best. The Sea is the obstacle, of course. They're trying to build some kind of raft – so that they can at least reach New York.'

'The South Pole may be even more important. Meanwhile, I am going to bring these matters to the attention of the General Assembly. Do I have your approval?'

There were no objections, not even from Dr Taylor. But just as the Committee members were about to switch out of circuit, Sir Lewis raised his hand.

The old historian very seldom spoke; when he did, everyone listened.

'Suppose we do find that Rama is – *active* – and has these capabilities. There is an old saying in military affairs that capability does not imply intention.'

'How long should we wait to find what its intentions are?' asked the Hermian. 'When we discover them, it may be far too late.'

'It is already too late. There is nothing we can do to affect Rama. Indeed, I doubt if there ever was.'

'I do not admit that, Sir Lewis. There are many things we can do – if it proves necessary. But the time is desperately short. Rama is a cosmic egg, being warmed by the fires of the sun. It may hatch at any moment.'

The Chairman of the Committee looked at the Ambassador for Mercury in frank astonishment. He had seldom been so surprised in his diplomatic career.

He would never have dreamed that a Hermian was capable of such a poetic flight of imagination.

20 BOOK OF REVELATION

When one of his crew called him 'Commander', or, worse still 'Mister Norton', there was always something serious afoot. He could not recall that Boris Rodrigo had ever before addressed him in such a fashion, so this must be doubly serious. Even in normal times, Lieut-Commander Rodrigo was a very grave and sober person.

'What's the problem, Boris?' he asked when the cabin door closed behind them.

'I'd like permission, commander, to use Ship Priority for a direct message to Earth.'

This *was* unusual, though not unprecedented. Routine signals went to the nearest planetary relay – at the moment, they were working through Mercury – and even though the transit time was only a matter of minutes, it was often five or six hours before a message arrived at the desk of the person for whom it was intended. Ninety-nine per cent of the time, that was quite good enough; but in an emergency more direct, and much more expensive, channels could be employed, at the captain's discretion.

'You know, of course, that you have to give me a good reason. All our available bandwidth is already clogged with data transmissions. Is this a personal emergency?'

'No, Commander. It is much more important than *that*. I want to send a message to the Mother Church.'

Uh-uh, said Norton to himself. How do I handle this?

'I'd be glad if you'll explain.'

It was not mere curiosity that prompted Norton's request – though that was certainly present. If he gave Boris the priority he asked, he would have to justify his action.

The calm, blue eyes stared into his. He had never known Boris to lose control, to be other than completely self-assured. All the Cosmo-Christers were like this; it was one of the benefits of their faith, and it helped to make them good spacemen. Sometimes, however, their unquestioning certainty was just a little annoying to those unfortunates who had not been vouchsafed the Revelation.

'It concerns the purpose of Rama, Commander. I believe I have discovered it.'

75

'Go on.'

'Look at the situation. Here is a completely empty, lifeless world – yet it is suitable for human beings. It has water, and an atmosphere we can breathe. It comes from the remote depths of space, aimed precisely at the solar system – something quite incredible, if it was a matter of pure chance. And it appears not only new; *it looks as if it has never been used.*'

We've all been through this dozens of times, Norton told himself. What could Boris add to it?

'Our faith has told us to expect such a visitation though we do not know exactly what form it will take. The Bible gives hints. If this is not the Second Coming, it may be the Second Judgement; the story of Noah describes the first. I believe that Rama is a cosmic Ark, sent here to save – those who are worthy of salvation.'

There was silence for quite a while in the Captain's cabin. It was not that Norton was at a loss for words; rather, he could think of too many questions, but he was not sure which ones it would be tactful to ask.

Finally he remarked, in as mild and non-committal a voice as he could manage: 'That's a very interesting concept, and though I don't go along with your faith, it's a tantalisingly plausible one.' He was not being hypocritical or flattering; stripped of its religious overtones, Rodrigo's theory was at least as convincing as half a dozen others he had heard. Suppose some catastrophe was about to befall the human race, and a benevolent higher intelligence knew all about it? That would explain everything, very neatly. However, there were still a few problems ...

'A couple of questions, Boris. Rama will be at perihelion in three weeks; then it will round the sun and leave the solar system just as fast as it came in. There's not much time for a Day of Judgement, or for shipping across those who are, er, selected – however *that's* going to be done.'

'Very true. So when it reaches perihelion, Rama will have to decelerate and go into a parking orbit – probably one with aphelion at Earth's orbit. There it might make another velocity change, and rendezvous with Earth.'

This was disturbingly persuasive. If Rama wished to remain in the solar system, it was going the right way about it. The most efficient way to slow down was to get as close to the sun as possible, and carry out the braking manoeuvre there. If there was any truth in Rodrigo's theory – or some variant of it – it would soon be put to the test.

'One other point, Boris. What's controlling Rama now?'

'There is no doctrine to advise on that. It could be a pure robot. Or it could be – a spirit. That would explain why there are no signs of biological life-forms.'

The Haunted Asteroid; why had that phrase popped up from the depths of memory? Then he recalled a silly story he had read years ago; he thought it best not to ask Boris if he had ever run into it. He doubted if the other's tastes ran to that sort of reading.

'I'll tell you what we'll do, Boris,' said Norton, abruptly making up his mind. He wanted to terminate this interview before it got too difficult, and thought he had found a good compromise.

'Can you sum up your ideas in less than – oh, a thousand bits?'

'Yes, I think so.'

'Well, if you can make it sound like a straightforward scientific theory, I'll send it, top priority, to the Rama Committee. Then a copy can go to your Church at the same time, and everyone will be happy.'

'Thank you, Commander, I really appreciate it.'

'Oh, I'm not doing this to save my conscience. I'd just like to see what the Committee makes of it. Even if I don't agree with you all along the line, you may have hit on something important.'

'Well, we'll know at perihelion, won't we?'

'Yes. We'll know at perihelion.'

When Boris Rodrigo had left, Norton called the bridge and gave necessary authorisation. He thought he had solved the problem rather neatly; besides, just suppose that Boris *was* right.

He might have increased his chances of being among the saved.

21 AFTER THE STORM

As they drifted along the now familiar corridor of the Alpha Airlock complex, Norton wondered if they had let impatience overcome caution. They had waited aboard *Endeavour* for forty-eight hours – two precious days – ready for instant departure if events should justify it. But nothing had happened; the instruments left in Rama had detected no unusual activity. Frustratingly, the television camera on the Hub had been blinded by a fog which had reduced visibility to a few metres and had only now started to retreat.

When they operated the final airlock door, and floated out into the cat's-cradle of guide-ropes around the Hub, Norton was struck first by the change in the light. It was no longer harshly blue, but was much more mellow and gentle, reminding him of a bright, hazy day on Earth.

He looked outwards along the axis of the world – and could see nothing except a glowing, featureless tunnel of white, reaching all the way to those strange mountains at the South Pole. The interior of Rama was completely blanketed with clouds, and nowhere was a break visible in the overcast. The top of the layer was quite sharply defined; it formed a smaller cylinder inside the larger one of this spinning world, leaving a central core, five or six kilometers wide, quite clear except for a few stray wisps of cirrus.

The immense tube of cloud was lit from underneath by the six artificial suns of Rama. The locations of the three on this Northern continent were clearly defined by diffuse strips of light, but those on the far side of the Cylindrical Sea merged together into a continuous, glowing band.

What is happening down beneath those clouds? Norton asked himself. But at least the storm, which had centrifuged them into such perfect symmetry about the axis of Rama, had now died away. Unless there were some other surprises, it would be safe to descend.

It seemed appropriate, on this return visit, to use the team that had made the first deep penetration into Rama. Sergeant Myron – like every other member of *Endeavour*'s crew – now fully met Surgeon-Commander Ernst's physical requirements; he even maintained, with convincing sincerity, that he was never going to wear his old uniforms again.

As Norton watched Mercer, Calvert and Myron 'swimming' quickly and confidently down the ladder, he reminded himself how much had changed. That first time they had descended in cold and darkness; now they were going towards light and warmth. And on all earlier visits, they had been confident that Rama was dead. That might yet be true, in a biological sense. But something was stirring; and Boris Rodrigo's phrase would do as well as any other. The spirit of Rama was awake.

When they had reached the platform at the foot of the ladder and were preparing to start down the stairway, Mercer carried out his usual routine test of the atmosphere. There were some things that he never took for granted; even when the people around him were breathing perfectly comfortably, without aids, he had been known to stop for an air check before opening his helmet. When asked to justify such excessive caution, he had answered: 'Because human senses aren't good enough, that's why. You may think you're fine, but you could fall flat on your face with the next deep breath.'

He looked at his meter, and said 'Damn!'

'What's the trouble?' asked Calvert.

'It's broken – reading too high. Odd; I've never known that to happen before. I'll check it on my breathing circuit.'

He plugged the compact little analyser into the test point of his oxygen supply, then stood in thoughtful silence for a while. His companions looked at him with anxious concern; anything that upset Karl was to be taken very seriously indeed.

He unplugged the meter, used it to sample the Rama atmosphere again, then called Hub Control.

'Skipper! Will you take an O_2 reading?'

There was a much longer pause than the request justified. Then Norton radioed back: 'I think there's something wrong with my meter.'

A slow smile spread across Mercer's face.

'It's up fifty per cent, isn't it?'

'Yes, what does that mean?'

'It means that we can all take off our masks. Isn't that convenient?'

'I'm not sure,' replied Norton, echoing the sarcasm in Mercer's voice. 'It seems too good to be true.' There was no need to say any more. Like all spacemen, Commander Norton had a profound suspicion of things that were too good to be true.

Mercer cracked his mask open a trifle, and took a cautious sniff. For the first time at this altitude, the air was perfectly breathable. The musty, dead smell had gone; so had the excessive dryness, which in the past had caused several respiratory complaints. Humidity was now an astonishing eighty per cent; doubtless the thawing of the Sea was responsible for this. There was a muggy feeling in the air, though not an unpleasant one. It was like a summer evening. Mercer told himself, on some tropical coast. The climate inside Rama had improved dramatically during the last few days ...

And why? The increased humidity was no problem; the startling rise in oxygen was much more difficult to explain.

As he recommended the descent, Mercer began a whole series of mental calculations. He had not arrived at any satisfactory result by the time they entered the cloud layer.

It was a dramatic experience, for the transition was very abrupt. At one moment they were sliding downwards in clear air, gripping the smooth metal of the handrail so that they would not gain speed too swiftly in this quarter-of-a-gravity region. Then, suddenly, they shot into a blinding white fog, and visibility dropped to a few metres. Mercer put on the brakes so quickly that Calvert almost bumped into him – and Myron *did* bump into Calvert, nearly knocking him off the rail.

'Take it easy,' said Mercer. 'Spread out so we can just see each other. And don't let yourself build up speed, in case I have to stop suddenly.'

In eerie silence, they continued to glide downwards through the fog. Calvert could just see Mercer as a vague shadow ten metres ahead, and when he looked back, Myron was at the same distance behind him. In some ways, this was even spookier than descending in the complete darkness of the Raman night; then, at least, the searchlight beams had shown them what lay ahead. But *this* was like diving in poor visibility in the open sea.

It was impossible to tell how far they had travelled, and Calvert guessed they had almost reached the fourth level when Mercer suddenly braked again. When they had bunched together, he whispered: 'Listen! Don't you hear something?'

'Yes,' said Myron, after a minute. 'It sounds like the wind.'

Calvert was not so sure. He turned his head back and forth, trying to locate the direction of the very faint murmur that had come to them through the fog, then abandoned the attempt as hopeless.

They continued the slide, reached the fourth level, and started on towards the fifth. All the while the sound grew louder – and more hauntingly familiar. They were half-way down the fourth stairway before Myron called out: 'Now do you recognise it?'

They would have identified it long ago, but it was not a sound they would ever have associated with any world except Earth. Coming out of the fog, from a source whose distance could not be guessed, was the steady thunder of falling water.

A few minutes later, the cloud ceiling ended as abruptly as it had begun. They shot out into the blinding glare of the Raman day, made more brilliant by the light reflected from the low-hanging clouds. There was the familiar curving plain – now made more acceptable to mind and senses, because its full circle could no longer be seen. It was not too difficult to pretend that they were looking along a broad valley, and that the upward sweep of the Sea was really an *outward* one.

They halted at the fifth and penultimate platform, to report that they were through the cloud cover and to make a careful survey. As far as they could tell, nothing had changed down there on the plain; but up here on the Northern dome, Rama had brought forth another wonder.

So there was the origin of the sound they had heard. Descending from some hidden source in the clouds three or four kilometres away was a waterfall, and for long minutes they stared at it silently, almost unable to believe their eyes. Logic told them that on this spinning world no falling object could move in a straight line, but there was something horribly unnatural about a curving waterfall that curved sideways, to end many kilometres away from the point directly below its source ...

'If Galileo had been born in this world,' said Mercer at length, 'he'd have gone crazy working out the laws of dynamics.'

'I thought I knew them,' Calvert replied, 'and I'm going crazy anyway. Doesn't it upset you, Prof?'

'Why should it?' said Sergeant Myron. 'It's a perfectly straightforward demonstration of the Coriolis Effect. I wish I could show it to some of my students.'

Mercer was staring thoughtfully at the globe-circling band of the Cylindrical Sea.

'Have you noticed what's happened to the water?' he said at last.

'Why – it's no longer so blue. I'd call it pea-green. What does that signify?'

'Perhaps the same thing that it does on Earth. Laura called the Sea an organic soup waiting to be shaken into life. Maybe that's exactly what's happened.'

'In a couple of days! It took millions of years on Earth.'

'Three hundred and seventy-five million, according to the latest estimate. So *that's* where the oxygen's come from. Rama's shot through the anerobic stage and has got to photosynthetic plants – in about forty-eight hours. I wonder what it will produce tomorrow?'

22 TO SAIL THE CYLINDRICAL SEA

When they reached the foot of the stairway, they had another shock. At first, it appeared that something had gone through the camp, overturning equipment, even collecting smaller objects and carrying them away. But after a brief examination, their alarm was replaced by a rather shame-faced annoyance.

The culprit was only the wind; though they had tied down all loose objects before they left, some ropes must have parted during exceptionally strong gusts. It was several days before they were able to retrieve all their scattered property.

Otherwise, there seemed no major changes. Even the silence of Rama had returned, now that the ephemeral storms of spring were over. And out there at the edge of the plain was a calm sea, waiting for the first ship in a million years.

'Shouldn't one christen a new boat with a bottle of champagne?'

'Even if we had any on board, I wouldn't allow such a criminal waste. Anyway, it's too late. We've already launched the thing.'

'At least it does float. You've won your bet, Jimmy. I'll settle when we get back to Earth.'

'It's got to have a name. Any ideas?'

The subject of these unflattering comments was now bobbing beside the steps leading down into the Cylindrical Sea. It was a small raft, constructed from six empty storage drums held together by a light metal framework. Building it, assembling it at Camp Alpha and hauling it on demountable wheels across more than ten kilometres of plain had absorbed the crew's entire energies for several days. It was a gamble that had better pay off.

The prize was worth the risk. The enigmatic towers of New York, gleaming there in the shadowless light five kilometres away, had taunted them ever since they had entered Rama. No one doubted that the city – or whatever it might be – was the real heart of this world. If they did nothing else, they must reach New York.

'We still don't have a name. Skipper – what about it?'

Norton laughed, then became suddenly serious.

'I've got one for you. Call it *Resolution*.'

'Why?'

'That was one of Cook's ships. It's a good name – may she live up to it.'

There was a thoughtful silence; then Sergeant Barnes, who had been principally responsible for the design, asked for three volunteers. Everyone present held up a hand.

'Sorry – we only have four life-jackets. Boris, Jimmy, Pieter – you've all done some sailing. Let's try her out.'

No one thought it in the least peculiar that an Executive Sergeant was now taking charge of the proceedings. Ruby Barnes had the only Master's Certificate aboard, so that settled the matter. She had navigated racing tri-marans across the Pacific, and it did not seem likely that a few kilometres of dead-calm water could present much of a challenge to her skills.

Ever since she had set eyes upon the Sea, she had been determined to make this voyage. In all the thousands of years that man had had dealings with the waters of his own world, no sailor had ever faced anything remotely like this. In the last few days a silly little jingle had been running through her mind, and she could not get rid of it. 'To sail the Cylindrical Sea ...' Well, that was precisely what she was going to do.

Her passengers took their places on the improvised bucket seats, and Ruby opened the throttle. The twenty-kilowatt motor started to whirr, the chain-drives of the reduction gear blurred, and *Resolution* surged away to the cheers of the spectators.

Ruby had hoped to get fifteen kph with this load, but would settle for anything over ten. A half-kilometre course had been measured along the cliff, and she made the round trip in five and a half minutes. Allowing for turning time, this worked out at twelve kph; she was quite happy with that.

With no power, but with three energetic paddlers helping her own more skilful blade, Ruby was able to get a quarter of this speed. So even if the motor broke down, they could get back to shore in a couple of hours. The heavy-duty power cells could provide enough energy to circumnavigate the world; she was carrying two spares, to be on the safe side. And now that the fog had completely burned away, even such a cautious mariner as Ruby was prepared to put to sea without a compass.

She saluted smartly as she stepped ashore.

'Maiden voyage of *Resolution* successfully completed, Sir. Now awaiting your instructions.'

'Very good ... Admiral. When will you be ready to sail?'

'As soon as stores can be loaded aboard, and the Harbour Master gives us clearance.'

'Then we leave at dawn.'

'Aye, aye, Sir.'

*

Five kilometres of water does not seem very much on a map; it is very different when one is in the middle of it. They had been cruising for only ten minutes, and the fifty-metre cliff facing the Northern Continent already seemed a surprising distance away. Yet, mysteriously, New York hardly appeared much closer than before ...

But most of the time they paid little attention to the land; they were still too engrossed in the wonder of the Sea. They no longer made the nervous jokes that had punctuated the start of the voyage; this new experience was too overwhelming.

Every time, Norton told himself, he felt that he had grown accustomed to Rama, it produced some new wonder. As *Resolution* hummed steadily forward, it seemed that they were caught in the trough of a gigantic wave – a wave which curved up on either side until it became vertical – then overhung until the two flanks met in a liquid arch sixteen kilometres above their heads. Despite everything that reason and logic told them, none of the voyagers could for long throw off the impression that at any minute those millions of tons of water would come crashing down from the sky.

Yet despite this, their main feeling was one of exhilaration; there was a sense of danger, without any *real* danger. Unless, of course, the Sea itself produced any more surprises.

That was a different possibility, for as Mercer had guessed, the water was now alive. Every spoonful contained thousands of spherical, single-celled micro-organisms, similar to the earliest forms of plankton that had existed in the oceans of Earth.

Yet they showed puzzling differences; they lacked a nucleus, as well as many of the other minimum requirements of even the most primitive terrestrial life-forms. And although Laura Ernst – now doubling as research scientist as well as ship's doctor – had proved that they definitely generated oxygen, there were far too few of them to account for the augmentation of Rama's atmosphere. They should have existed in billions, not mere thousands.

Then she discovered that their numbers were dwindling rapidly, and must have been far higher during the first hours of the Raman dawn. It was as if there had been a brief explosion of life, recapitulating on a trillion-fold swifter time-scale the early history of Earth. Now, perhaps, it had exhausted itself; the drifting micro-organisms were disintegrating, releasing their stores of chemicals back into the Sea.

'If you have to swim for it,' Dr Ernst had warned the mariners, 'keep your mouths closed. A few drops won't matter – if you spit them out right away. But all those weird organo-metallic salts add up to a fairly poisonous package, and I'd hate to have to work out an antidote.'

This danger, fortunately, seemed very unlikely. *Resolution* could stay afloat if any two of her buoyancy tanks were punctured. (When told of this, Joe Calvert had muttered darkly: 'Remember the *Titanic*!') And even if she sank, the crude but efficient life-jackets would keep their heads above water.

Although Laura had been reluctant to give a firm ruling on this, she did not think that a few hours' immersion in the Sea would be fatal; but she did not recommend it.

After twenty minutes of steady progress, New York was no longer a distant island. It was becoming a real place, and details which they had seen only through telescopes and photo-enlargements were now revealing themselves as massive, solid structures. It was now strikingly apparent that the 'city', like so much of Rama, was triplicated; it consisted of three identical, circular complexes or super-structures, rising from a long, oval foundation. Photographs taken from the Hub also indicated that each complex was *itself* divided into three equal components, like a pie sliced into 120-degree portions. This would greatly simplify the task of exploration; presumably they had to examine only one ninth of New York to have seen the whole of it. Even this would be a formidable undertaking; it would mean investigating at least a square kilometre of buildings and machinery, some of which towered hundreds of metres into the air.

The Ramans, it seemed, had brought the art of triple-redundancy to a high degree of perfection. This was demonstrated in the airlock system, the stairways at the Hub, the artificial suns. And where it really mattered, they had even taken the next step. New York appeared to be an example of triple-triple redundancy.

Ruby was steering *Resolution* towards the central complex, where a flight of steps led up from the water to the very top of the wall or levee which surrounded the island. There was even a conveniently-placed mooring post to which boats could be tied; when she saw this, Ruby became quite excited. Now she would never be content until she found one of the craft in which the Ramans sailed their extraordinary sea.

Norton was the first to step ashore; he looked back at his three companions and said: 'Wait here on the boat until I get to the top of the wall. When I wave, Pieter and Boris will join me. You stay at the helm, Ruby, so that we can cast off at a moment's notice. If anything happens to me, report to Karl and follow his instructions. Use your best judgement – but no heroics. Understood?'

'Yes, Skipper. Good luck!'

Commander Norton did not really believe in luck; he never got into a situation until he had analysed all the factors involved and had secured his line of retreat. But once again Rama was forcing him to break some of his cherished rules. Almost every factor here was unknown – as unknown as the Pacific and the Great Barrier Reef had been to his hero, three and a half centuries ago ... Yes, he could do with all the luck that happened to be lying around.

The stairway was a virtual duplicate of the one down which they had descended on the other side of the Sea; doubtless his friends over there were looking straight across at him through their telescopes. And 'straight' was now the correct word; in this one direction, parallel to the axis of Rama, the

Sea was indeed completely flat. It might well be the only body of water in the universe of which this was true, for on all other worlds, every sea or lake must follow the surface of a sphere, with equal curvature in all directions.

'Nearly at the top,' he reported, speaking for the record and for his intently listening second-in-command, five kilometres away, 'still completely quiet – radiation normal. I'm holding the metre above my head, just in case this wall is acting as a shield for anything. And if there are any hostiles on the other side, they'll shoot that first.'

He was joking, of course. And yet – why take any chances, when it was just as easy to avoid them?

When he took the last step, he found that the flat-topped embankment was about ten metres thick; on the inner side, an alternating series of ramps and stairways led down to the main level of the city, twenty metres below. In effect, he was standing on a high wall which completely surrounded New York, and so was able to get a grandstand view of it.

It was a view almost stunning in its complexity, and his first act was to make a slow panoramic scan with his camera. Then he waved to his companions and radioed back across the Sea: 'No sign of any activity – everything quiet. Come on up – we'll start exploring.'

23 NY, RAMA

It was not a city; it was a machine. Norton had come to that conclusion in ten minutes, and saw no reason to change it after they had made a complete traverse of the island. A city – whatever the nature of its occupants – surely had to provide some form of accommodation: there was nothing here of that nature, unless it was underground. And if that was the case, where were the entrances, the stairways, the elevators? He had not found anything that even qualified as a simple door ...

The closest analogy he had ever seen to this place on Earth was a giant chemical processing plant. However, there were no stockpiles of raw materials, or any indications of a transport system to move them around. Nor could he imagine where the finished product would emerge – still less what that product could possibly be. It was all very baffling, and more than a little frustrating.

'Anybody care to make a guess?' he said at last, to all who might be listening. 'If this is a factory, what does it make? And where does it get its raw materials?'

'I've a suggestion, Skipper,' said Karl Mercer, over on the far shore. 'Suppose it uses the Sea. According to Doc, that contains just about anything you can think of.'

It was a plausible answer, and Norton had already considered it. There could well be buried pipes leading to the Sea – in fact, there *must* be, for any conceivable chemical plant would require large quantities of water. But he had a suspicion of plausible answers; they were so often wrong.

'That's a good idea, Karl; but what does New York *do* with its seawater?'

For a long time, nobody answered from ship, Hub or Northern plain. Then an unexpected voice spoke.

'That's easy, Skipper. But you're all going to laugh at me.'

'No, we're not, Ravi. Go ahead.'

Sergeant Ravi McAndrews, Chief Steward and Simp Master, was the last person on this ship who would normally get involved in a technical discussion. His IQ was modest and his scientific knowledge was minimal, but he was no fool and had a natural shrewdness which everyone respected.

'Well, it's a factory all right, Skipper, and maybe the Sea provides the raw material ... after all, that's how it all happened on Earth, though in a different way ... I believe New York is a factory for making – Ramans.'

Somebody, somewhere, snickered, but became quickly silent and did not identify himself.

'You know, Ravi,' said his commander at last, 'that theory is crazy enough to be true. And I'm not sure if I want to see it tested ... at least, until I get back to the mainland.'

This celestial New York was just about as wide as the island of Manhattan, but its geometry was totally different. There were few straight thoroughfares; it was a maze of short, concentric arcs, with radial spokes linking them. Luckily, it was impossible to lose one's bearings inside Rama; a single glance at the sky was enough to establish the north-south axis of the world.

They paused at almost every intersection to make a panoramic scan. When all these hundreds of pictures were sorted out, it would be a tedious but fairly straightforward job to construct an accurate scale model of the city. Norton suspected that the resulting jigsaw puzzle would keep scientists busy for generations.

It was even harder to get used to the silence here than it had been out on the plain of Rama. A city-machine should make some sound; yet there was not even the faintest of electric hums, or the slightest whisper of mechanical motion. Several times Norton put his ear to the ground, or to the side of a building, and listened intently. He could hear nothing except the pounding of his own blood.

The machines were sleeping: they were not even ticking over. Would they ever wake again, and for what purpose? Everything was in perfect condition, as usual. It was easy to believe that the closing of a single circuit, in some patient, hidden computer, would bring all this maze back to life.

When at last they had reached the far side of the city, they climbed to the top of the surrounding levee and looked across the southern branch of the Sea. For a long time Norton stared at the five-hundred-metre cliff that barred them from almost half of Rama – and, judging from their telescopic surveys, the most complex and varied half. From this angle, it appeared an ominous, forbidding black, and it was easy to think of it as a prison wall surrounding a whole continent. Nowhere along its entire circle was there a flight of stairways or any other means of access.

He wondered how the Ramans reached their southern land from New York. Probably there was an underground transport system running beneath the Sea, but they must also have aircraft as well; there were many open areas here in the city that could be used for landing. To discover a Raman vehicle would be a major accomplishment – especially if they could learn to operate it. (Though could any conceivable power-source still be functioning, after several hundred thousand years?) There were numerous structures that had the functional look of hangars or garages, but they were all smooth and windowless, as if they had been sprayed with sealant. Sooner or later, Norton had told himself grimly, we'll be forced to use explosives, and laser beams. He was determined to put off this decision to the last possible moment.

His reluctance to use brute force was based partly on pride, partly on fear. He did not wish to behave like a technological barbarian, smashing what he could not understand. After all, he was an uninvited visitor in this world, and should act accordingly.

As for his fear – perhaps that was too strong a word; apprehension might be better. The Ramans seemed to have planned for everything; he was not anxious to discover the precautions they had taken to guard their property. When he sailed back to the mainland, it would be with empty hands.

24 DRAGONFLY

Lieutenant James Pak was the most junior officer on board *Endeavour*, and this was only his fourth mission into deep space. He was ambitious, and due for promotion; he had also committed a serious breach of regulations. No wonder, therefore, that he took a long time to make up his mind.

It would be a gamble; if he lost, he could be in deep trouble. He could not only be risking his career; he might even be risking his neck. But if he succeeded, he would be a hero. What finally convinced him was neither of these arguments; it was the certainty that, if he did nothing at all, he would spend the rest of his life brooding over his lost opportunity. Nevertheless, he was still hesitant when he asked the Captain for a private meeting.

What is it *this* time? Norton asked himself, as he analysed the uncertain expression of the young officer's face. He remembered his delicate interview with Boris Rodrigo; no, it wouldn't be anything like that. Jimmy was certainly not the religious type; the only interests he had ever shown outside his work were sport and sex, preferably combined.

It could hardly be the former, and Norton hoped it was not the latter. He had encountered most of the problems that a commanding officer could encounter in this department – except the classical one of an unscheduled birth during a mission. Though this situation was the subject of innumerable jokes, it had never happened yet; but such gross incompetence was probably only a matter of time.

'Well, Jimmy, what is it?'

'I have an idea, Commander. I know how to reach the southern continent – even to the South Pole.'

'I'm listening. How do you propose to do it?'

'Er – by flying there.'

'Jimmy, I've had at least five proposals to do that – more if you count crazy suggestions from Earth. We've looked into the possibility of adapting our spacesuit propulsors, but air drag would make them hopelessly inefficient. They'd run out of fuel before they could go ten kilometres.'

'I know that. But I have the answer.'

Lt Pak's attitude was a curious mixture of complete confidence and barely suppressed nervousness. Norton was quite baffled; what was the kid worried about? Surely he knew his commanding officer well enough to be certain that no reasonable proposal would be laughed out of court.

'Well, go on. If it works, I'll see your promotion is retro-active.'

That little half-promise, half-joke didn't go down as well as he had hoped. Jimmy gave a rather sickly smile, made several false starts, then decided on an oblique approach to the subject.

'You know, Commander, that I was in the Lunar Olympics last year.'

'Of course. Sorry you didn't win.'

'It was bad equipment; I know what went wrong. I have friends on Mars who've been working on it, in secret. We want to give everyone a surprise.'

'Mars? But I didn't know ...'

'Not many people do – the sport's still new there; it's only been tried in the Xante Sportsdome. But the best aerodynamicists in the solar system are on Mars; if you can fly in *that* atmosphere, you can fly anywhere.

'Now, my idea was that if the Martians could build a good machine, with all their know-how, it would *really* perform on the Moon – where gravity is only half as strong.'

'That seems plausible, but how does it help us?'

Norton was beginning to guess, but he wanted to give Jimmy plenty of rope.

'Well, I formed a syndicate with some friends in Lowell City. They've built a fully aerobatic flyer with some refinements that no one has ever seen before. In lunar gravity, under the Olympic dome, it should create a sensation.'

'And win you the gold medal.'

'I hope so.'

'Let me see if I follow your train of thought correctly. A sky-bike that could enter the Lunar Olympics, at a sixth of a gravity, would be even more sensational inside Rama, with no gravity at all. You could fly it right along the axis, from the North Pole to the South – and back again.'

'Yes – easily. The one-way trip would take three hours, non-stop. But of course you could rest whenever you wanted to, as long as you kept near the axis.'

'It's a brilliant idea, and I congratulate you. What a pity sky-bikes aren't part of regular Space Survey equipment.'

Jimmy seemed to have some difficulty in finding words. He opened his mouth several times, but nothing happened.

'All right, Jimmy. As a matter of morbid interest, and purely off the record, how did you smuggle the thing aboard?'

'Er – "Recreational Stores".'

'Well, you weren't lying. And what about the weight?'

'It's only twenty kilogrammes.'

'*Only!* Still, that's not as bad as I thought. In fact, I'm astonished you can build a bike for that weight.'

'Some have been only fifteen, but they were too fragile and usually folded up when they made a turn. There's no danger of *Dragonfly* doing that. As I said, she's fully aerobatic.'

'*Dragonfly* – nice name. So tell me just how you plan to use her; then I can decide whether a promotion or a court martial is in order. Or both.'

25 MAIDEN FLIGHT

*D*ragonfly was certainly a good name. The long, tapering wings were almost invisible, except when the light struck them from certain angles and was refracted into rainbow hues. It was as if a soap-bubble had been wrapped round a delicate tracery of aerofoil sections; the envelope enclosing the little flyer was an organic film only a few molecules thick, yet strong enough to control and direct the movements of a fifty-kph air flow.

The pilot – who was also the powerplant and the guidance system – sat on a tiny seat at the centre of gravity, in a semi-reclining position to reduce air resistance. Control was by a single stick which could be moved backwards and forwards, right and left; the only 'instrument' was a piece of weighted ribbon attached to the leading edge, to show the direction of the relative wind.

Once the flyer had been assembled at the Hub, Jimmy Pak would allow no one to touch it. Clumsy handling could snap one of the single-fibre structural members, and those glittering wings were an almost irresistible attraction to prying fingers. It was hard to believe that there was *really* something there ...

As he watched Jimmy climb into the contraption, Commander Norton began to have second thoughts. If one of those wire-sized struts snapped when *Dragonfly* was on the other side of the Cylindrical Sea, Jimmy would have no way of getting back – even if he was able to make a safe landing. They were also breaking one of the most sacrosanct rules of space exploration; a man was going *alone* into unknown territory, beyond all possibility of help. The only consolation was that he would be in full view and communication all the time; they would know exactly what had happened to him, if he did meet with disaster.

Yet this opportunity was far too good to miss; if one believed in fate or destiny, it would be challenging the gods themselves to neglect the only chance they might ever have of reaching the far side of Rama, and seeing at close quarters the mysteries of the South Pole. Jimmy knew what he was attempting, far better than anyone in the crew could tell him. This was precisely the sort of risk that had to be taken; if it failed, that was the luck of the game. You couldn't win them all ...

'Now listen to me carefully, Jimmy,' said Surgeon-Commander Ernst. 'It's very important not to over-exert yourself. Remember, the oxygen level here at the axis is still very low. If you feel breathless at any time, stop and hyper-ventilate for thirty seconds – but no longer.'

Jimmy nodded absentmindedly as he tested the controls. The whole rudder-elevator assembly, which formed a single unit on an outrigger five metres behind the rudimentary cockpit, began to twist around; then the flap-shaped ailerons, halfway along the wing, moved alternately up and down.

'Do you want me to swing the prop?' asked Joe Calvert, unable to suppress memories of two-hundred-year-old war movies. 'Ignition! Contact!' Probably no one except Jimmy knew what he was talking about, but it helped to relieve the tension.

Very slowly, Jimmy started to move the foot-pedals. The flimsy, broad fan of the airscrew – like the wing, a delicate skeleton covered with shimmering film – began to turn. By the time it had made a few revolutions, it had disap-peared completely; and *Dragonfly* was on her way.

She moved straight outwards from the Hub, moving slowly along the axis of Rama. When she had travelled a hundred metres, Jimmy stopped pedal-ling; it was strange to see an obviously aerodynamic vehicle hanging motion-less in mid-air. This must be the first time such a thing had ever happened, except possibly on a very limited scale inside one of the larger space-stations.

'How does she handle?' Norton called.

'Response good, stability poor. But I know what the trouble is – no gravity. We'll be better off a kilometre lower down.'

'Now wait a minute – is that safe?'

By losing altitude, Jimmy would be sacrificing his main advantage. As long as he stayed precisely on the axis, he – and *Dragonfly* – would be completely weightless. He could hover effortlessly, or even go to sleep if he wished. But as soon as he moved away from the central line around which Rama spun, the pseudo-weight of centrifugal force would reappear.

And so, unless he could maintain himself at this altitude, he would con-tinue to lose height – and at the same time, *to gain weight*. It would be an accelerating process, which could end in catastrophe. The gravity down on the plain of Rama was twice that in which *Dragonfly* had been designed to operate. Jimmy might be able to make a safe landing; he could certainly never take off again.

But he had already considered all this, and he answered confidently enough: 'I can manage a tenth of a gee without any trouble. And she'll handle more easily in denser air.'

In a slow, leisurely spiral, *Dragonfly* drifted across the sky, roughly follow-ing the line of Stairway Alpha down towards the plain. From some angles, the little sky-bike was almost invisible; Jimmy seemed to be sitting in mid-air pedalling furiously. Sometimes he moved into spurts of up to thirty kilometres an hour; then he would coast to a halt, getting the feel of the controls, before accelerating again. And he was always very careful to keep a safe distance from the curving end of Rama.

It was soon obvious that *Dragonfly* handled much better at lower altitudes; she no longer rolled around at any angle, but stabilized so that her wings were parallel to the plain seven kilometres below. Jimmy completed several wide orbits, then started to climb upwards again. He finally halted a few metres above his waiting colleagues and realised, a little belatedly, that he was not quite sure how to land this gossamer craft.

'Shall we throw you a rope?' Norton asked half-seriously.

'No, Skipper – I've got to work this out myself. I won't have anyone to help me at the other end.'

He sat thinking for a while, then started to ease *Dragonfly* towards the Hub with short bursts of power. She quickly lost momentum between each, as air drag brought her to rest again. When he was only five metres away, and the sky-bike was still barely moving, Jimmy abandoned ship. He let himself float towards the nearest safety line in the Hub webwork, grasped it, then swung around in time to catch the approaching bike with his hands. The manoeuvre was so neatly executed that it drew a round of applause.

'For my *next* act—' Joe Calvert began.

Jimmy was quick to disclaim any credit.

'That was messy,' he said. 'But now I know how to do it. I'll take a sticky-bomb on a twenty-metre line; then I'll be able to pull myself in wherever I want to.'

'Give me your wrist, Jimmy,' ordered the Doctor, 'and blow into this bag. I'll want a blood sample, too. Did you have any difficulty in breathing?'

'Only at this altitude. Hey, what do you want the blood for?'

'Sugar level; then I can tell how much energy you've used. We've got to make sure you carry enough fuel for the mission. By the way, what's the endurance record for sky-biking?'

'Two hours twenty-five minutes three point six seconds. On the Moon, of course – a two kilometre circuit in the Olympic Dome.'

'And you think you can keep it up for six hours?'

'Easily, since I can stop for a rest at any time. Sky-biking on the Moon is at least twice as hard as it is here.'

'OK Jimmy – back to the lab. I'll give you a Go-No-Go as soon as I've analysed these samples. I don't want to raise false hopes – but I think you can make it.'

A large smile of satisfaction spread across Jimmy Pak's ivory-hued countenance. As he followed Surgeon-Commander Ernst to the airlock, he called back to his companions: 'Hands off, *please*! I don't want anyone putting his fist through the wings.'

'I'll see to that, Jimmy,' promised the Commander. '*Dragonfly* is off limits to *everybody* – including myself.'

26 THE VOICE OF RAMA

The real magnitude of his adventure did not hit Jimmy Pak until he reached the coast of the Cylindrical Sea. Until now, he had been over known territory; barring a catastrophic structural failure, he could always land and walk back to base in a few hours.

That option no longer existed. If he came down in the Sea, he would probably drown, quite unpleasantly, in its poisonous waters. And even if he made a safe landing in the southern continent, it might be impossible to rescue him before *Endeavour* had to break away from Rama's sunward orbit.

He was also acutely aware that the foreseeable disasters were the ones most unlikely to happen. The totally unknown region over which he was flying might produce any number of surprises; suppose there were flying creatures here, who objected to his intrusion? He would hate to engage in a dog-fight with anything larger than a pigeon. A few well-placed pecks could destroy *Dragonfly*'s aerodynamics.

Yet, if there were no hazards, there would be no achievement – no sense of adventure. Millions of men would gladly have traded places with him now. He was going not only where no one had ever been before – but where no one would ever go again. In all of history, he would be the only human being to visit the southern regions of Rama. Whenever he felt fear brushing against his mind, he could remember that.

He had now grown accustomed to sitting in mid-air, with the world wrapped around him. Because he had dropped two kilometres below the central axis, he had acquired a definite sense of 'up' and 'down'. The ground was only six kilometres below, but the arch of the sky was ten kilometres overhead. The 'city' of London was hanging up there near the zenith; New York, on the other hand, was the right way up, directly ahead.

'*Dragonfly*,' said Hub Control, 'you're getting a little low. Twenty-two hundred metres from the axis.'

'Thanks,' he replied. 'I'll gain altitude. Let me know when I'm back at twenty.'

This was something he'd have to watch. There was a natural tendency to lose height – and he had no instruments to tell him exactly where he was. If he got too far away from the zero-gravity of the axis, he might never be able to climb back to it. Fortunately, there was a wide margin for error, and there was always someone watching his progress through a telescope at the Hub.

He was now well out over the Sea, pedalling along at a steady twenty kilometres an hour. In five minutes, he would be over New York; already the island looked rather like a ship, sailing for ever round and round the Cylindrical Sea.

When he reached New York, he flew a circle over it, stopping several times so that his little TV camera could send back steady, vibration-free images. The panorama of buildings, towers, industrial plants, power stations – or whatever they were – was fascinating but essentially meaningless. No matter how long he stared at its complexity, he was unlikely to learn anything. The camera would record far more details than he could possibly assimilate; and one day – perhaps years hence – some student might find in them the key to Rama's secrets.

After leaving New York, he crossed the other half of the Sea in only fifteen minutes. Though he was not aware of it, he had been flying fast over water, but as soon as he reached the south coast he unconsciously relaxed and his speed dropped by several kilometres an hour. He might be in wholly alien territory – but at least he was over land.

As soon as he had crossed the great cliff that formed the Sea's southern limit, he panned the TV camera completely round the circle of the world.

'Beautiful!' said Hub Control. 'This will keep the map-makers happy. How are you feeling?'

'I'm fine – just a little fatigue, but no more than I expected. How far do you make me from the Pole?'

'Fifteen point six kilometres.'

'Tell me when I'm at ten; I'll take a rest then. And make sure I don't get low again. I'll start climbing when I've five to go.'

Twenty minutes later the world was closing in upon him; he had come to the end of the cylindrical section, and was entering the southern dome.

He had studied it for hours through the telescopes at the other end of Rama, and had learned its geography by heart. Even so, that had not fully prepared him for the spectacle all around him.

In almost every way the southern and northern ends of Rama differed completely. Here was no triad of stairways, no series of narrow, concentric plateaux, no sweeping curve from hub to plain. Instead, there was an immense central spike, more than five kilometres long, extending along the axis. Six smaller ones, half this size, were equally spaced around it; the whole assembly looked like a group of remarkable symmetrical stalactites, hanging from the roof of a cave. Or, inverting the point of view, the spires of some Cambodian temple, set at the bottom of a crater ...

Linking these slender, tapering towers, and curving down from them to merge eventually in the cylindrical plain, were flying buttresses that looked massive enough to bear the weight of a world. And this, perhaps, was their function, if they were indeed the elements of some exotic drive units, as some had suggested.

Lieutenant Pak approached the central spike cautiously, stopped pedalling while he was still a hundred metres away, and let *Dragonfly* drift to rest. He checked the radiation level, and found only Rama's very low background. There might be forces at work here which no human instruments could detect, but that was another unavoidable risk.

'What can you see?' Hub Control asked anxiously.

'Just Big Horn – it's absolutely smooth – no markings – and the point's so sharp you could use it as a needle. I'm almost scared to go near it.'

He was only half joking. It seemed incredible that so massive an object should taper to such a geometrically perfect point. Jimmy had seen collections of insects impaled upon pins, and he had no desire for his own *Dragonfly* to meet a similar fate.

He pedalled slowly forward until the spike had flared out to several metres in diameter, then stopped again. Opening a small container, he rather gingerly extracted a sphere about as big as a baseball, and tossed it towards the spike. As it drifted away, it played out a barely visible thread.

The sticky-bomb hit the smoothly curving surface – and did not rebound. Jimmy gave the thread an experimental twitch, then a harder tug. Like a fisherman hauling in his catch, he slowly wound *Dragonfly* across to the tip of the appropriately christened 'Big Horn', until he was able to put out his hand and make contact with it.

'I suppose you could call this some kind of touchdown,' he reported to Hub Control. 'It feels like glass – almost frictionless, and slightly warm. The sticky-bomb worked fine. Now I'm trying the mike ... let's see if the suction pad holds as well ... plugging in the leads ... anything coming through?'

There was a long pause from the Hub; then Control said disgustedly: 'Not a damn thing, except the usual thermal noises. Will you tap it with a piece of metal? Then at least we'll find if it's hollow.'

'OK. Now what?'

'We'd like you to fly along the spike, making a complete scan every half-kilometre, and looking out for anything unusual. Then, if you're sure it's safe, you might go across to one of the Little Horns. But only if you're certain you can get back to zero gee without any problems.'

'Three kilometres from the axis – that's slightly above lunar gravity. *Dragonfly* was designed for that. I'll just have to work harder.'

'Jimmy, this is the Captain. I've got second thoughts on that. Judging by your pictures, the smaller spikes are just the same as the big one. Get the best coverage of them you can with the zoom lens. I don't want you leaving the low-gravity region ... unless you see something that looks very important. Then we'll talk it over.'

'OK, Skipper,' said Jimmy, and perhaps there was just a trace of relief in his voice. 'I'll stay close to Big Horn. Here we go again.'

He felt he was dropping straight downwards into a narrow valley between a group of incredibly tall and slender mountains. Big Horn now towered a kilometre above him, and the six spikes of the Little Horns were looming up all around. The complex of buttresses and flying arches which surrounded the lower slopes was approaching rapidly; he wondered if he could make a safe landing somewhere down there in that Cyclopean architecture. He could no longer land on Big Horn itself, for the gravity on its widening slopes was now too powerful to be counteracted by the feeble force of the sticky-bomb.

As he came even closer to the South Pole, he began to feel more and more like a sparrow flying beneath the vaulted roof of some great cathedral – though no cathedral ever built had been even one hundredth the size of this place. He wondered if it was indeed a religious shrine, or something remotely analogous, but quickly dismissed the idea. Nowhere in Rama had there been any trace of artistic expression; everything was purely functional. Perhaps the Ramans felt that they already knew the ultimate secrets of the universe, and were no longer haunted by the yearnings and aspirations that drove mankind.

That was a chilling thought, quite alien to Jimmy's usual not-very-profound philosophy; he felt an urgent need to resume contact, and reported his situation back to his distant friends.

'Say again, *Dragonfly*,' replied Hub Control. 'We can't understand you – your transmission is garbled.'

'I repeat – I'm near the base of Little Horn number Six, and am using the sticky-bomb to haul myself in.'

'Understand only partially. Can you hear me?'

'Yes, perfectly. Repeat, perfectly.'

'Please start counting numbers.'

'One, two, three, four ...'

'Got part of that. Give us beacon for fifteen seconds, then go back to voice.'

'Here it is.'

Jimmy switched on the low-powered beacon which would locate him anywhere inside Rama, and counted off the seconds. When he went over to voice again he asked plaintively: 'What's happening? Can you hear me now?'

Presumably Hub didn't, because the controller then asked for fifteen seconds of TV. Not until Jimmy had repeated the question twice did the message get through.

'Glad you can hear us OK, Jimmy. But there's something very peculiar happening at your end. Listen.'

Over the radio, he heard the familiar whistle of his own beacon, played back to him. For a moment it was perfectly normal; then a weird distortion crept into it. The thousand-cycle whistle became modulated by a deep, throbbing pulse so low that it was almost beneath the threshold of hearing; it was a kind of *basso-profundo* flutter in which each individual vibration could be heard. And the modulation was itself modulated; it rose and fell, rose and fell with a period of about five seconds.

Never for a moment did it occur to Jimmy that there was something wrong with his radio transmitter. This was from outside; though what it was, and what it meant, was beyond his imagination.

Hub Control was not much wiser, but at least it had a theory.

'We think you must be in some kind of very intense field – probably magnetic – with a frequency of about ten cycles. It may be strong enough to be dangerous. Suggest you get out right away – it may only be local. Switch on your beacon again, and we'll play it back to you. Then you can tell when you're getting clear of the interference.'

Jimmy hastily jerked the sticky-bomb loose and abandoned his attempt to land. He swung *Dragonfly* round in a wide circle, listening as he did so to the sound that wavered in his earphones. After flying only a few metres, he could tell that its intensity was falling rapidly; as Hub Control had guessed, it was extremely localized.

He paused for a moment at the last spot where he could hear it, like a faint throbbing deep in his brain. So might a primitive savage have listened in awestruck ignorance to the low humming of a giant power transformer. And even the savage might have guessed that the sound he heard was merely the stray leakage from colossal energies, fully controlled, but biding their time ...

Whatever this sound meant, Jimmy was glad to be clear of it. This was no place, among the overwhelming architecture of the South Pole, for a lone man to listen to the voice of Rama.

27 ELECTRIC WIND

As Jimmy turned homewards, the northern end of Rama seemed incredibly far away. Even the three giant stairways were barely visible, as a faint Y etched on the dome that closed the world. The band of the Cylindrical Sea was a wide and menacing barrier, waiting to swallow him up if, like Icarus, his fragile wings should fail.

But he had come all this way with no problems, and though he was feeling slightly tired he now felt that he had nothing to worry about. He had not even touched his food or water, and had been too excited to rest. On the return journey, he would relax and take it easy. He was also cheered by the thought that the homeward trip could be twenty kilometres shorter than the outward one, for as long as he cleared the Sea, he could make an emergency landing anywhere in the northern continent. That would be a nuisance, because he would have a long walk – and much worse, would have to abandon *Dragonfly* – but it gave him a very comforting safety margin.

He was now gaining altitude, climbing back towards the central spike; Big Horn's tapering needle still stretched for a kilometre ahead of him, and sometimes he felt it was the axis on which this whole world turned.

He had almost reached the tip of Big Horn when he became aware of a curious sensation; a feeling of foreboding, and indeed of physical as well as psychological discomfort, had come over him. He suddenly recalled – and this did nothing at all to help – a phrase he had once come across: '*Someone is walking over your grave.*'

At first he shrugged it off, and continued his steady pedalling. He certainly had no intention of reporting anything as tenuous as a vague malaise to Hub Control, but as it grew steadily worse he was tempted to do so. It could not possibly be psychological; if it was, his mind was much more powerful than he realised. For he could, quite literally, feel his skin beginning to crawl ...

Now seriously alarmed, he stopped in mid-air and began to consider the situation. What made it all the more peculiar was the fact that this depressed heavy feeling was not completely novel; he had known it before, but could not remember where.

He looked around him. Nothing had changed. The great spike of Big Horn was a few hundred metres above, with the other side of Rama spanning the sky beyond that. Eight kilometres below lay the complicated patchwork of the Southern continent, full of wonders that no other man would ever see. In all the utterly alien yet now familiar landscape, he could find no cause for his discomfort.

Something was tickling the back of his hand; for a moment, he thought an insect had landed there, and brushed it away without looking. He had only half-completed the swift motion when he realised what he was doing and checked himself, feeling slightly foolish. Of course, no one had ever seen an insect in Rama ...

He lifted his hand, and stared at it, mildly puzzled because the tickling sensation was still there. It was then that he noticed that every individual hair was standing straight upright. All the way up his forearm it was the same – and so it was with his head, when he checked with an exploring hand.

So *that* was the trouble. He was in a tremendously powerful electric field; the oppressed, heavy sensation he had felt was that which sometimes precedes a thunderstorm on Earth.

The sudden realisation of his predicament brought Jimmy very near to panic. Never before in his life had he been in real physical danger. Like all spacemen, he had known moments of frustration with bulky equipment, and times when, owing to mistakes or inexperience, he had wrongly believed he was in a perilous situation. But none of these episodes had lasted more than a few minutes, and usually he was able to laugh at them almost at once.

This time there was no quick way out. He felt naked and alone in a suddenly hostile sky, surrounded by titanic forces which might discharge their furies at any moment. *Dragonfly* – already fragile enough – now seemed more insubstantial than the finest gossamer. The first detonation of the gathering storm would blast her to fragments.

'Hub Control,' he said urgently. 'There's a static charge building up around me. I think there's going to be a thunderstorm at any moment.'

He had barely finished speaking when there was a flicker of light behind him; by the time he had counted ten, the first crackling rumble arrived. Three kilometres – that put it back around the Little Horns. He looked towards them and saw that every one of the six needles seemed to be on fire. Brush discharges, hundreds of metres long, were dancing from their points, as if they were giant lightning conductors.

What was happening back there could take place on an even larger scale near the tapering spike of Big Horn. His best move would be to get as far as possible from this dangerous structure, and to seek clear air. He started to pedal again, accelerating as swiftly as he could without putting too great a strain on *Dragonfly*. At the same time he began to lose altitude; even though this would mean entering the region of higher gravity, he was now prepared to take such a risk. Eight kilometres was much too far from the ground for his peace of mind.

The ominous black spike of Big Horn was still free of visible discharges, but he did not doubt that tremendous potentials were building up there. From time to time the thunder still reverberated behind him, rolling round and round the circumference of the world. It suddenly occurred to Jimmy how strange it was to have such a storm in a perfectly clear sky; then he realised that this was not a meteorological phenomenon at all. In fact, it might be only a trivial leakage of energy from some hidden source, deep in the southern cap of Rama. But why *now*? And, even more important – *what next*?

He was now well past the tip of Big Horn, and hoped that he would soon be beyond the range of any lightning discharges. But now he had another problem; the air was becoming turbulent, and he had difficulty in controlling *Dragonfly*. A wind seemed to have sprung up from nowhere, and if conditions became much worse the bike's fragile skeleton would be endangered. He pedalled grimly on, trying to smooth out the buffeting by variations in power and movements of his body. Because *Dragonfly* was almost an extension of himself, he was partly successful; but he did not like the faint creaks of protest that came from the main spar, nor the way in which the wings twisted with every gust.

And there was something else that worried him – a faint rushing sound, steadily growing in strength, that seemed to come from the direction of Big Horn. It sounded like gas escaping from a valve under pressure, and he wondered if it had anything to do with the turbulence which he was battling. Whatever its cause, it gave him yet further grounds for disquiet.

From time to time he reported these phenomena, rather briefly and breathlessly, to Hub Control. No one there could give him any advice, or even suggest what might be happening; but it was reassuring to hear the voices of his friends, even though he was now beginning to fear that he would never see them again.

The turbulence was still increasing. It almost felt as if he was entering a jet stream – which he had once done, in search of a record, while flying a high-altitude glider on Earth. But what could possibly create a jet stream inside Rama?

He had asked himself the right question; as soon as he had formulated it, he knew the answer.

The sound he had heard was the electric wind carrying away the tremendous ionisation that must be building up around Big Horn. Charged air was spraying out along the axis of Rama, and more air was flowing into the low-pressure region behind. He looked back at that gigantic and now doubly threatening needle, trying to visualise the boundaries of the gale that was blowing from it. Perhaps the best tactic would be to fly by ear, getting as far as possible away from the ominous hissing.

Rama spared him the necessity of choice. A sheet of flame burst out behind him, filling the sky. He had time to see it split into six ribbons of fire, stretching from the tip of Big Horn to each of the Little Horns. Then the concussion reached him.

28 ICARUS

Jimmy Pak had barely time to radio: 'The wing's buckling – I'm going to crash – I'm going to crash!' when *Dragonfly* started to fold up gracefully around him. The left wing snapped cleanly in the middle, and the outer section drifted away like a gently falling leaf. The right wing put up a more complicated performance. It twisted round at the root, and angled back so sharply that its tip became entangled in the tail. Jimmy felt that he was sitting in a broken kite, slowly falling down the sky.

Yet he was not quite helpless; the airscrew still worked, and while he had power there was still some measure of control. He had perhaps five minutes in which to use it.

Was there any hope of reaching the Sea? No – it was much too far away. Then he remembered that he was still thinking in terrestrial terms; though he was a good swimmer, it would be hours before he could possibly be rescued, and in that time the poisonous waters would undoubtedly have killed him. His only hope was to come down on land; the problem of the sheer southern cliff he would think about later – if there was any 'later'.

He was falling very slowly, here in this tenth-of-a-gravity zone, but would soon start to accelerate as he got further away from the axis. However, air-drag would complicate the situation, and would prevent him from building up too swift a rate of descent. *Dragonfly*, even without power, would act as a crude parachute. The few kilogrammes of thrust he could still provide might make all the difference between life and death; that was his only hope.

Hub had stopped talking; his friends could see exactly what was happening to him and knew that there was no way their words could help. Jimmy was now doing the most skilful flying of his life; it was too bad, he thought with grim humour, that his audience was so small, and could not appreciate the finer details of his performance.

He was going down in a wide spiral, and as long as its pitch remained fairly flat his chances of survival were good. His pedalling was helping to keep *Dragonfly* airborne, though he was afraid to exert maximum power in case the broken wings came completely adrift. And every time he swung southwards, he could appreciate the fantastic display that Rama had kindly arranged for his benefit.

The streamers of lightning still played from the tip of Big Horn down to the lesser peaks beneath, but now the whole pattern was rotating. The six-pronged crown of fire was turning against the spin of Rama, making one revolution every few seconds. Jimmy felt that he was watching a giant electric motor in operation, and perhaps that was not hopelessly far from the truth.

He was halfway down to the plain, still orbiting in a flat spiral, when the firework display suddenly ceased. He could feel the tension drain from the sky and knew, without looking, that the hairs on his arms were no longer straining upright. There was nothing to distract or hinder him now, during the last few minutes of his fight for life.

Now that he could be certain of the general area in which he must land, he started to study it intently. Much of this region was a checkerboard of totally conflicting environments, as if a mad landscape gardener had been given a free hand and told to exercise his imagination to the utmost. The squares of the checkerboard were almost a kilometre on a side, and though most of them were flat he could not be sure if they were solid, their colours and textures varied so greatly. He decided to wait until the last possible minute before making a decision – if indeed he had any choice.

When there were a few hundred metres to go, he made a last call to the Hub.

'I've still got some control – will be down in half a minute – will call you then.'

That was optimistic, and everyone knew it. But he refused to say goodbye; he wanted his comrades to know that he had gone down fighting, and without fear.

Indeed, he felt very little fear, and this surprised him, for he had never thought of himself as a particularly brave man. It was almost as if he was watching the struggles of a complete stranger, and was not himself personally involved. Rather, he was studying an interesting problem in aerodynamics, and changing various parameters to see what would happen. Almost the only emotion he felt was a certain remote regret for lost opportunities – of which the most important was the forthcoming Lunar Olympics. One future at least was decided; *Dragonfly* would never show her paces on the Moon.

A hundred metres to go; his ground speed seemed acceptable, but how fast was he falling? And here was one piece of luck – the terrain was completely flat. He would put forth all his strength in a final burst of power, starting – now!

The right wing, having done its duty, finally tore off at the roots. *Dragonfly* started to roll over, and he tried to correct by throwing the weight of his body against the spin. He was looking directly at the curving arch of landscape sixteen kilometres away when he hit.

It seemed altogether unfair and unreasonable that the sky should be so hard.

29 FIRST CONTACT

When Jimmy Pak returned to consciousness, the first thing he became aware of was a splitting headache. He almost welcomed it; at least it proved that he was still alive.

Then he tried to move, and at once a wide selection of aches and pains brought themselves to his attention. But as far as he could tell, nothing seemed to be broken.

After that, he risked opening his eyes, but closed them at once when he found himself staring straight into the band of light along the ceiling of the world. As a cure for headache, that view was not recommended.

He was still lying there, regaining his strength and wondering how soon it would be safe to open his eyes, when there was a sudden crunching noise from close at hand. Turning his head very slowly towards the source of the sound, he risked a look – and almost lost consciousness again.

Not more than five metres away, a large crab-like creature was apparently dining on the wreckage of poor *Dragonfly*. When Jimmy recovered his wits he rolled slowly and quietly away from the monster, expecting at every moment to be seized by its claws, when it discovered that more appetizing fare was available. However, it took not the slightest notice of him; when he had increased their mutual separation to ten metres, he cautiously propped himself up in a sitting position.

From this greater distance, the thing did not appear quite so formidable. It had a low, flat body about two metres long and one wide, supported on six triple-jointed legs. Jimmy saw that he was mistaken in assuming that it had been eating *Dragonfly*; in fact, he could not see any sign of a mouth. The creature was actually doing a neat job of demolition, using scissor-like claws to chop the sky-bike into small pieces. A whole row of manipulators, which looked uncannily like tiny human hands, then transferred the fragments to a steadily growing pile on the animal's back.

But *was* it an animal? Though that had been Jimmy's first reaction, now he had second thoughts. There was a purposefulness about its behaviour which suggested fairly high intelligence; he could see no reason why any creature of pure instincts should carefully collect the scattered pieces of his sky-bike – unless, perhaps, it was gathering material for a nest.

Keeping a wary eye on the crab, which still ignored him completely, Jimmy struggled to his feet. A few wavering steps demonstrated that he could still walk, though he was not sure if he would outdistance those six legs. Then he switched on his radio, never doubting that it would be operating. A crash that *he* could survive would not even have been noticed by its solid-state electronics.

'Hub Control,' he said softly. 'Can you receive me?'

'Thank God! Are you OK?'

'Just a bit shaken. Take a look at this.'

He turned his camera towards the crab, just in time to record the final demolition of *Dragonfly*'s wing.

'What the devil is it – and why is it chewing up your bike?'

'Wish I knew. It's finished with *Dragonfly*. I'm going to back away, in case it wants to start on me.'

Jimmy slowly retreated, never taking his eyes off the crab. It was now moving round and round in a steadily widening spiral, apparently searching for fragments it might have overlooked, and so Jimmy was able to get an overall view of it for the first time.

Now that the initial shock had worn off, he could appreciate that it was quite a handsome beast. The name 'crab' which he had automatically given it was perhaps a little misleading; if it had not been so impossibly large, he might have called it a beetle. Its carapace had a beautiful metallic sheen; in fact, he would almost have been prepared to swear that it *was* metal.

That was an interesting idea. Could it be a robot, and not an animal? He stared at the crab intently with this thought in mind, analysing all the details of its anatomy. Where it should have had a mouth was a collection of manipulators that reminded Jimmy strongly of the multi-purpose knives that are the delight of all red-blooded boys; there were pinchers, probes, rasps and even something that looked like a drill. But none of this was decisive. On Earth, the insect world had matched all these tools, and many more. The animal-or-robot question remained in perfect balance in his mind.

The eyes, which might have settled the matter, left it even more ambiguous. They were so deeply recessed in protective hoods that it was impossible to tell whether their lenses were made of crystal or jelly. They were quite expressionless, and of a startlingly vivid blue. Though they had been directed towards Jimmy several times, they had never shown the slightest flicker of interest. In his perhaps biased opinion, that decided the level of the creature's intelligence. An entity – robot or animal – which could ignore a human being could not be very bright.

It had now stopped its circling, and stood still for a few seconds, as if listening to some inaudible message. Then it set off, with a curious rolling gait, in the general direction of the Sea. It moved in a perfectly straight line at a steady four or five kilometres an hour, and had already travelled a couple of hundred metres before Jimmy's still slightly-shocked mind registered the fact that the last sad relics of his beloved *Dragonfly* were being carried away from him. He set off in a hot and indignant pursuit.

His action was not wholly illogical. The crab was heading towards the Sea – and if any rescue was possible, it could only be from this direction. Moreover, he wanted to discover what the creature would do with its trophy; that should reveal something about its motivation and intelligence.

Because he was still bruised and stiff, it took Jimmy several minutes to catch up with the purposefully-moving crab. When he had done so, he followed it at a respectful distance, until he felt sure that it did not resent his presence. It was then that he noticed his water-flask and emergency ration pack among the debris of *Dragonfly*, and instantly felt both hungry and thirsty.

There, scuttling away from him at a remorseless five kilometres an hour, was the only food and drink in all this half of the world. Whatever the risk, he had to get hold of it.

He cautiously closed in on the crab, approaching from right rear. While he kept station with it, he studied the complicated rhythm of its legs, until he could anticipate where they would be at any moment. When he was ready, he muttered a quick 'Excuse *me*,' and shot swiftly in to grab his property. Jimmy had never dreamed that he would one day have to exercise the skills of a pickpocket, and was delighted with his success. He was out again in less than a second, and the crab never slackened its steady pace.

He dropped back a dozen metres, moistened his lips from the flask, and started to chew a bar of meat concentrate. The little victory made him feel much happier; now he could even risk thinking about his sombre future.

While there was life, there was hope; yet he could imagine no way in which he could possibly be rescued. Even if his colleagues crossed the Sea, how could he reach them, half a kilometre below? 'We'll find a way down *somehow*,' Hub Control had promised. 'That cliff can't go right round the world, without a break anywhere.' He had been tempted to answer 'Why not?', but had thought better of it.

One of the strangest things about walking inside Rama was that you could always see your destination. Here, the curve of the world did not hide – it *revealed*. For some time Jimmy had been aware of the crab's objective; up there in the land which seemed to rise before him was a half-kilometre-wide pit. It was one of three in the southern continent; from the Hub, it had been impossible to see how deep they were. All had been named after prominent lunar craters, and he was approaching Copernicus. The name was hardly appropriate, for there were no surrounding hills and no central peaks. This Copernicus was merely a deep shaft or well, with perfectly vertical sides.

When he came close enough to look into it, Jimmy was able to see a pool of ominous, leaden-green water at least half a kilometre below. This would put it just about level with the Sea, and he wondered if they were connected.

Winding down the interior of the well was a spiral ramp, completely re-cessed into the sheer wall, so that the effect was rather like that of rifling in an immense gun-barrel. There seemed to be a remarkable number of turns; not until Jimmy had traced them for several revolutions, getting more and more confused in the process, did he realise that there was not one ramp but *three*, totally independent and 120 degrees apart. In any other background than Rama, the whole concept would have been an impressive architectural *tour de force*.

The three ramps led straight down into the pool and disappeared beneath its opaque surface. Near the waterline Jimmy could see a group of black tunnels or caves; they looked rather sinister, and he wondered if they were inhabited. Perhaps the Ramans were amphibious ...

As the crab approached the edge of the well, Jimmy assumed that it was going to descend one of the ramps – perhaps taking the wreckage of *Dragonfly* to some entity who would be able to evaluate it. Instead, the creature walked straight to the brink, extended almost half its body over the gulf without any sign of hesitation, though an error of a few centimetres would have been disastrous – and gave a brisk shrug. The fragments of *Dragonfly* went fluttering down into the depths; there were tears in Jimmy's eyes as he watched them go. So much, he thought bitterly, for *this* creature's intelligence.

Having disposed of the garbage, the crab swung around and started to walk towards Jimmy, standing only about ten metres away. Am I going to get the same treatment? He wondered. He hoped the camera was not too unsteady as he showed Hub Control the rapidly approaching monster. 'What do you advise?' he whispered anxiously, without much hope that he would get a useful answer. It was some small consolation to realise that he was making history, and his mind raced through the approved patterns for such a meeting. Until now, all of these had been purely theoretical. He would be the first man to check them in practice.

'Don't run until you're sure it's hostile,' Hub Control whispered back at him. Run where? Jimmy asked himself. He thought he could out-distance the thing in a hundred metre sprint, but had a sick certainty that it could wear him down over the long haul.

Slowly, Jimmy held up his outstretched hands. Men had been arguing for two hundred years about this gesture; would every creature, everywhere in the universe, interpret this as 'See – no weapons?' But no one could think of anything better.

The crab showed no reaction whatsoever, nor did it slacken its pace. Ignoring Jimmy completely, it walked straight past him and headed purposefully into the south. Feeling extremely foolish, the acting representative of *Homo sapiens* watched his First Contact stride away across the Raman plain, totally indifferent to his presence.

He had seldom been so humiliated in his life. Then Jimmy's sense of humour came to his rescue. After all, it was no great matter to have been ignored by an animated garbage truck. It would have been worse if it had greeted him as a long-lost brother ...

He walked back to the rim of Copernicus, and stared down into its opaque waters. For the first time, he noticed that vague shapes – some of them quite large – were moving slowly back and forth beneath the surface. Presently one of them headed towards the nearest spiral ramp, and something that looked like a multi-legged tank started on the long ascent. At the rate it was going, Jimmy decided, it would take almost an hour to get here; if it was a threat, it was a very slow-moving one.

Then he noticed a flicker of much more rapid movement, near those cave-like openings down by the waterline. Something was travelling very swiftly along the ramp, but he could not focus clearly upon it, or discern any definite shape. It was as if he was looking at a small whirlwind or 'dust-devil', about the size of a man ...

He blinked and shook his head, keeping his eyes closed for several seconds. When he opened them again, the apparition was gone.

Perhaps the impact had shaken him up more than he had realised; this was the first time he had ever suffered from visual hallucinations. He would not mention it to Hub Control.

Nor would he bother to explore those ramps, as he had half-thought of doing. It would obviously be a waste of energy.

The spinning phantom he had merely imagined seeing had nothing to do with his decision.

Nothing at all; for, of course, Jimmy did not believe in ghosts.

30 THE FLOWER

Jimmy's exertions had made him thirsty, and he was acutely conscious of the fact that in all this land there was no water that a man could drink. With the contents of his flask, he could probably survive a week – but for what purpose? The best brains of Earth would soon be focused on his problem; doubtless Commander Norton would be bombarded with suggestions. But he could imagine no way in which he could lower himself down the face of that half-kilometre cliff. Even it he had a long rough rope, there was nothing to which he could attach it.

Nevertheless, it was foolish – and unmanly – to give up without a struggle. Any help would have to come from the Sea, and while he was marching towards it he could carry on with his job as if nothing had happened. No one else would ever observe and photograph the varied terrain through which he must pass, and that would guarantee a posthumous immortality. Though he would have preferred many other honours, that was better than nothing.

He was only three kilometres from the Sea as poor *Dragonfly* could have flown, but it seemed unlikely that he could reach it in a straight line; some of the terrain ahead of him might prove too great an obstacle. That was no problem, however, as there were plenty of alternative routes. Jimmy could see them all, spread out on the great curving map that swept up and away from him on either side.

He had plenty of time; he would start with the most interesting scenery, even if it took him off his direct route. About a kilometre away towards the right was a square that glittered like cut glass – or a gigantic display of jewellery. It was probably this thought that triggered Jimmy's footsteps. Even a doomed man might reasonably be expected to take some slight interest in a few thousand square metres of gems.

He was not particularly disappointed when they turned out to be quartz crystals, millions of them, set in a bed of sand. The adjacent square of the checkerboard was rather more interesting, being covered with an apparently random pattern of hollow metal columns, set very close together and ranging in height from less than one to more than five metres. It was completely impassable; only a tank could have crashed through that forest of tubes.

111

Jimmy walked between the crystals and the columns until he came to the first crossroads. The square on the right was a huge rug or tapestry made of woven wire; he tried to prise a strand loose, but was unable to break it.

On the left was a tessellation of hexagonal tiles, so smoothly inlaid that there were no visible joints between them. It would have appeared a continuous surface, had the tiles not been coloured all the hues of the rainbow. Jimmy spent many minutes trying to find two adjacent tiles of the same colour, to see if he could then distinguish their boundaries, but he could not find a single example of such coincidence.

As he did a slow pan right around the crossroads, he said plaintively to Hub Control: 'What do *you* think this is? I feel I'm trapped in a giant jigsaw puzzle. Or is this the Raman Art Gallery?'

'We're as baffled as you, Jimmy. But there's never been any sign that the Ramans go in for art. Let's wait until we have some more examples before we jump to any conclusions.'

The two examples he found at the next crossroads were not much help. One was completely blank – a smooth, neutral grey, hard but slippery to the touch. The other was a soft sponge, perforated with billions upon billions of tiny holes. He tested it with his foot, and the whole surface undulated sickeningly beneath him like a barely stabilised quicksand.

As the next cross-roads he encountered something strikingly like a ploughed field – except that the furrows were a uniform metre in depth, and the material of which they were made had the texture of a file or rasp. But he paid little attention to this, because the square adjacent to it was the most thought-provoking of all that he had so far met. At last there was something that he could understand; and it was more than a little disturbing.

The entire square was surrounded by a fence, so conventional that he would not have looked at it twice had he seen it on Earth. There were posts – apparently of metal – five metres apart, with six strands of wire strung taut between them.

Beyond this fence was a second, identical one – and beyond that, a third. It was another typical example of Raman redundancy; whatever was penned inside this enclosure would have no chance of breaking out. There was no entrance – no gates that could be swung open to drive in the beast, or beasts, that were presumably kept here. Instead, there was a single hole, like a smaller version of Copernicus, in the centre of the square.

Even in different circumstances, Jimmy would probably not have hesitated, but now he had nothing to lose. He quickly scaled all three fences, walked over to the hole, and peered into it.

Unlike Copernicus, this well was only fifty metres deep. There were three tunnel exits at the bottom, each of which looked large enough to accommodate an elephant. And that was all.

After staring for some time, Jimmy decided that the only thing that made sense about the arrangement was for the floor down there to be an elevator. But *what* it elevated he was never likely to know; he could only guess that it was quite large, and possibly quite dangerous.

During the next few hours, he walked more than ten kilometres along the edge of the Sea, and the checkerboard squares had begun to blur together in his memory. He had seen some that were totally enclosed in tent-like structures of wire mesh, as if they were giant bird-cages. There were others which seemed to be pools of congealed liquid, full of swirl-patterns; however, when he tested them gingerly, they were quite solid. And there was one so utterly black that he could not even see it clearly; only the sense of touch told him that anything was there.

Yet now there was a subtle modulation into something he could understand. Ranging one after the other towards the south was a series of – no other word would do – *fields*. He might have been walking past an experimental farm on Earth; each square was a smooth expanse of carefully levelled earth, the first he had ever seen in the metallic landscapes of Rama.

The great fields were virgin, lifeless – waiting for crops that had never been planted. Jimmy wondered what their purpose could be, since it was incredible that creatures as advanced as the Ramans would engage in any form of agriculture; even on Earth, farming was no more than a popular hobby and a source of exotic luxury foods. But he could swear that these were potential farms, immaculately prepared. He had never seen earth that looked so clean; each square was covered with a great sheet of tough, transparent plastic. He tried to cut through it to obtain a sample, but his knife would barely scratch the surface.

Further inland were other fields, and on many of them were complicated constructions of rods and wires, presumably intended for the support of climbing plants. They looked very bleak and desolate, like leafless trees in the depths of winter. The winter they had known must have been long and terrible indeed, and these few weeks of light and warmth might be only a brief interlude before it came again.

Jimmy never knew what made him stop and look more closely into the metal maze to the south. Unconsciously, his mind must have been checking every detail around him; it had noticed, in this fantastically alien landscape, something even more anomalous.

About a quarter of a kilometre away, in the middle of a trellis of wires and rods, glowed a single speck of colour. It was so small and inconspicuous that it was almost at the limit of visibility; on Earth, no one would have looked at it twice. Yet undoubtedly one of the reasons he had noticed it now was because it reminded him of Earth ...

He did not report to Hub Control until he was sure that there was no mistake, and that wishful thinking had not deluded him. Not until he was only a few metres away could he be completely sure that life as he knew it had intruded into the sterile, aseptic world of Rama. For blooming here in lonely splendour at the edge of the southern continent was a flower.

As he came closer, it was obvious to Jimmy that something had gone wrong. There was a hole in the sheathing that, presumably, protected this layer of earth from contamination by unwanted life-forms. Through this break extended a green stem, about as thick as a man's little finger, which twined its way up through the trellis-work. A metre from the ground it burst into an efflorescence of bluish leaves, shaped more like feathers than the foliage of any plant known to Jimmy. The stem ended, at eye-level, in what he had first taken to be a single flower. Now he saw, with no surprise at all, that it was actually three flowers tightly packed together.

The petals were brightly coloured tubes about five centimetres long; there were at least fifty in each bloom, and they glittered with such metallic blues, violets and greens, that they seemed more like the wings of a butterfly than anything in the vegetable kingdom. Jimmy knew practically nothing about botany, but he was puzzled to see no trace of any structures resembling petals or stamens. He wondered if the likeness to terrestrial flowers might be a pure coincidence; perhaps this was something more akin to a coral polyp. In either case, it would seem to imply the existence of small, airborne creatures to serve either as fertilizing agents – or as food.

It did not really matter. Whatever the scientific definition, to Jimmy this was a flower. The strange miracle, the un-Raman-like accident of its existence here reminded him of all that he would never see again; and he was determined to possess it.

That would not be easy. It was more than ten metres away, separated from him by a lattice-work made of thin rods. They formed a cubic pattern, repeated over and over again, less than forty centimetres on either side. Jimmy would not have been flying sky-bikes unless he had been slim and wiry, so he knew he could crawl through the interstices of the grid. But getting out again might be quite a different matter; it would certainly be impossible for him to turn around, so he would have to retreat backwards.

Hub Control was delighted with his discovery, when he had described the flower and scanned it from every available angle. There was no objection when he said: 'I'm going after it.' Nor did he expect there to be; his life was now his own, to do with as he pleased.

He stripped off all his clothes, grasped the smooth metal rods, and started to wriggle into the framework. It was a tight fit; he felt like a prisoner escaping through the bars of his cell. When he had inserted himself completely into the lattice he tried backing out again, just to see if there were any problems. It was considerably more difficult, since he now had to use his outstretched arms for pushing instead of pulling, but he saw no reason why he should get helplessly trapped.

Jimmy was a man of action and impulse, not of introspection. As he squirmed uncomfortably along the narrow corridor of rods, he wasted no time asking himself just why he was performing so quixotic a feat. He had never been interested in flowers in his whole life, yet now he was gambling his last energies to collect one.

It was true that this specimen was unique, and of enormous scientific value. But he really wanted it because it was his last link with the world of life and the planet of his birth.

Yet when the flower was in his grasp, he had sudden qualms. Perhaps it was the only flower that grew in the whole of Rama; was he justified in picking it?

If he needed any excuse, he could console himself with the thought that the Ramans themselves had not included it in their plans. It was obviously a freak, growing ages too late – or too soon. But he did not really require an excuse, and his hesitation was only momentary. He reached out, grasped the stem, and gave a sharp jerk.

The flower came away easily enough; he also collected two of the leaves, then started to back slowly through the lattice. Now that he had only one free hand, progress was extremely difficult, even painful, and he soon had to pause to regain his breath. It was then that he noticed that the feathery leaves were closing, and the headless stem was slowly unwinding itself from its supports. As he watched with a mixture of fascination and dismay, he saw that the whole plant was steadily retreating into the ground, like a mortally injured snake crawling back into its hole.

I've murdered something beautiful, Jimmy told himself. But then Rama had killed him. He was only collecting what was his rightful due.

31 TERMINAL VELOCITY

Commander Norton had never yet lost a man, and he had no intention of starting now. Even before Jimmy had set off for the South Pole, he had been considering ways of rescuing him in the event of accident; the problem, however, had turned out to be so difficult that he had found no answer. All that he had managed to do was to eliminate every obvious solution.

How does one climb a half-kilometre vertical cliff; even in reduced gravity? With the right equipment – and training – it would be easy enough. But there were no piton-guns aboard *Endeavour*, and no one could think of any other practical way of driving the necessary hundreds of spikes into that hard, mirror surface.

He had glanced briefly at more exotic solutions, some frankly crazy. Perhaps a simp, fitted with suction pads, could make the ascent. But even if this scheme was practical, how long would it take to manufacture and test such equipment – and to train a simp to use it? He doubted if a man would have the necessary strength to perform the feat.

Then there was more advanced technology. The EVA propulsion units were tempting, but their thrust was too small, since they were designed for zero-gee operation. They could not possibly lift the weight of a man, even against Rama's modest gravity.

Could an EVA thrust be sent up on automatic control, carrying only a rescue line? He had tried out this idea on Sergeant Myron, who had promptly shot it down in flames. There were, the engineer pointed out, severe stability problems; they might be solved, but it would take a long time – much longer than they could afford.

What about balloons? There seemed a faint possibility here, if they could devise an envelope and a sufficiently compact source of heat. This was the only approach that Norton had not dismissed, when the problem suddenly ceased to be one of theory, and became a matter of life and death, dominating the news in all the inhabited worlds.

While Jimmy was making his trek along the edge of the Sea, half the crackpots in the solar system were trying to save him. At Fleet Headquarters, all the suggestions were considered, and about one in a thousand was forwarded

116

to *Endeavour*. Dr Carlisle Perera's arrived twice – once via the Survey's own network, and once by PLANETCOM, RAMA PRIORITY. It had taken the scientist approximately five minutes of thought and one millisecond of computer time.

At first, Commander Norton thought it was a joke in very poor taste. Then he saw the sender's name and the attached calculations, and did a quick double-take.

He handed the message to Karl Mercer.

'What do you think of this?' he asked, in as non-committal a tone of voice as he could manage.

Karl read it swiftly, then said, 'Well I'm damned! He's right, of course.'

'Are you *sure*?'

'He was right about the storm, wasn't he? We should have thought of this; it makes me feel a fool.'

'You have company. The next problem is – how do we break it to Jimmy?'

'I don't think we should ... until the last possible minute. That's how I'd prefer it, if I was in his place. Just tell him we're on the way.'

Though he could look across the full width of the Cylindrical Sea, and knew the general direction from which *Resolution* was coming, Jimmy did not spot the tiny craft until it had already passed New York. It seemed incredible that it could carry six men – and whatever equipment they had brought to rescue him.

When it was only a kilometre away, he recognised Commander Norton, and started waving. A little later the skipper spotted him, and waved back.

'Glad to see you're in good shape, Jimmy,' he radioed. 'I promised we wouldn't leave you behind. Now do you believe me?'

Not quite, Jimmy thought; until this moment he had still wondered if this was all a kindly plot to keep up his morale. But the Commander would not have crossed the Sea just to say goodbye; he must have worked out *something*.

'I'll believe you, Skipper,' he said, 'when I'm down there on the deck. *Now* will you tell me how I'm going to make it?'

Resolution was now slowing down, a hundred metres from the base of the cliff; as far as Jimmy could tell, she carried no unusual equipment – though he was not sure what he had expected to see.

'Sorry about that, Jimmy – but we didn't want you to have too many things to worry about.'

Now *that* sounded ominous; what the devil did he mean?

Resolution came to a halt, fifty metres out and five hundred below; Jimmy had almost a bird's-eye view of the Commander as he spoke into his microphone.

'This is it, Jimmy. You'll be perfectly safe, but it will require nerve. We know you've got plenty of that. *You're going to jump*.'

'Five hundred metres!'

'Yes, but at only half a gee.'

'So – have you ever fallen two hundred and fifty on Earth?'

'Shut up, or I'll cancel your next leave. You should have worked this out for yourself ... it's just a question of terminal velocity. In this atmosphere, you can't reach more than ninety kilometres an hour – whether you fall two hundred or two thousand metres. Ninety's a little high for comfort, but we can trim it some more. This is what you'll have to do, so listen carefully ...'

'I will,' said Jimmy. 'It had better be good.'

He did not interrupt the Commander again, and made no comment when Norton had finished. Yes, it made sense, and was so absurdly simple that it would take a genius to think of it. And, perhaps, someone who did not expect to do it himself ...

Jimmy had never tried high-diving, or made a delayed parachute drop, which would have given him some psychological preparation for this feat. One could tell a man that it was perfectly safe to walk a plank across an abyss – yet even if the structural calculations were impeccable, he might still be unable to do it. Now Jimmy understood why the Commander had been so evasive about the details of the rescue. He had been given no time to brood, or to think of objections.

'I don't want to hurry you,' said Norton's persuasive voice from half a kilometre below. 'But the sooner the better.'

Jimmy looked at his precious souvenir, the only flower in Rama. He wrapped it very carefully in his grimy handkerchief, knotted the fabric, and tossed it over the edge of the cliff.

It fluttered down with reassuring slowness, but it also took a very long time getting smaller, and smaller, and smaller, until he could no longer see it. But then *Resolution* surged forward, and he knew that it had been spotted.

'Beautiful!' exclaimed the Commander enthusiastically. 'I'm sure they'll name it after you. OK – we're waiting ...

Jimmy stripped off his shirt – the only upper garment anyone ever wore in this now tropical climate – and stretched it thoughtfully. Several times on his trek he had almost discarded it; now it might help to save his life.

For the last time, he looked back at the hollow world he alone had explored, and the distant, ominous pinnacles of the Big and Little Horns. Then, grasping the shirt firmly with his right hand, he took a running jump as far out over the cliff as he could.

Now there was no particular hurry; he had a full twenty seconds in which to enjoy the experience. But he did not waste any time, as the wind strengthened around him and *Resolution* slowly expanded in his field of view. Holding his shirt with both hands, he stretched his arms above his head, so that the rushing air filled the garment and blew it into a hollow tube.

As a parachute, it was hardly a success; the few kilometres an hour it subtracted from his speed was useful, but not vital. It was doing a much more important job – keeping his body vertical, so that he would arrow straight into the sea.

He still had the impression that he was not moving at all, but that the water below was rushing up towards him. Once he had committed himself, he had no sense of fear; indeed, he felt a certain indignation against the skipper for keeping him in the dark. Did he *really* think that he would be scared to jump, if he had to brood over it too long?

At the very last moment, he let go of his shirt, took a deep breath, and grabbed his mouth and nose with his hands. As he had been instructed, he stiffened his body into a rigid bar, and locked his feet together. He would enter the water as cleanly as a falling spear ...

'It will be just the same,' the Commander had promised, 'as stepping off a diving board on Earth. Nothing to it – *if* you make a good entry.'

'And if I don't?' he had asked.

'Then you'll have to go back and try again.'

Something slapped him across the feet – hard, but not viciously. A million slimy hands were tearing at his body; there was a roaring in his ears, a mounting pressure – and even though his eyes were tightly closed, he could tell that darkness was falling as he arrowed down into the depths of the Cylindrical Sea.

With all his strength, he started to swim upwards towards the fading light. He could not open his eyes for more than a single blink; the poisonous water felt like acid when he did so. He seemed to have been struggling for ages, and more than once he had a nightmare fear that he had lost his orientation and was really swimming downwards. Then he would risk another quick glimpse, and every time the light was stronger.

His eyes were still clenched tightly shut when he broke water. He gulped a precious mouthful of air, rolled over on his back, and looked around.

Resolution was heading towards him at top speed; within seconds, eager hands had grabbed him and dragged him aboard.

'Did you swallow any water?' was the Commander's anxious question.

'I don't think so.'

'Rinse out with this, anyway. That's fine. How do you feel?'

'I'm not really sure. I'll let you know in a minute. Oh ... thanks, everybody.' The minute was barely up when Jimmy was only too sure how he felt.

'I'm going to be sick,' he confessed miserably. His rescuers were incredulous.

'In a dead calm – on a flat sea?' protested Sergeant Barnes, who seemed to regard Jimmy's plight as a direct reflection on her skill.

'I'd hardly call it *flat*,' said the Commander, waving his arm around the band of water that circled the sky. 'But don't be ashamed – you may have swallowed some of that stuff. Get rid of it as quickly as you can.'

Jimmy was still straining, unheroically and unsuccessfully, when there was a sudden flicker of light in the sky behind them. All eyes turned towards the South Pole, and Jimmy instantly forgot his sickness. The Horns had started their firework display again.

There were the kilometre-long streamers of fire, dancing from the central spike to its smaller companions. Once again they began their stately rotation, as if invisible dancers were winding their ribbons around an electric maypole. But now they began to accelerate, moving faster and faster until they blurred into a flickering cone of light.

It was a spectacle more awe-inspiring than any they had yet seen here, and it brought with it a distant crackling roar which added to the impression of overwhelming power. The display lasted for about five minutes; then it stopped as abruptly as if someone had turned a switch.

'I'd like to know what the Rama Committee make of *that*.' Norton muttered to no one in particular. 'Has anyone here got any theories?'

There was no time for an answer, because at that moment Hub Control called in great excitement.

'*Resolution!* Are you OK? Did you feel that?'

'Feel *what*?'

'We think it was an earthquake – it must have happened the minute those fireworks stopped.'

'Any damage?'

'I don't think so. It wasn't really violent – but it shook us up a bit.'

'We felt nothing at all. But we wouldn't, out here in the Sea,'

'Of course, silly of me. Anyway, everything seems quiet now ... until next time.'

'Yes, until the next time,' Norton echoed. The mystery of Rama was steadily growing; the more they discovered about it, the less they understood.

There was a sudden shout from the helm.

'Skipper – look – up there in the sky!'

Norton lifted his eyes, swiftly scanning the circuit of the Sea. He saw nothing, until his gaze had almost reached the zenith, and he was staring at the other side of the world.

'My God,' he whispered slowly, as he realised that the 'next time' was already almost here.

A tidal wave was racing towards them, down the eternal curve of the Cylindrical Sea.

32 THE WAVE

Yet even in that moment of shock, Norton's first concern was for his ship.

'*Endeavour!*' he called. 'Situation report!'

'All OK, Skipper,' was the reassuring answer from the Exec. 'We felt a slight tremor, but nothing that could cause any damage. There's been a small change of attitude – the bridge says about point two degrees. They also think the spin rate has altered slightly – we'll have an accurate reading on that in a couple of minutes.'

So it's beginning to happen, Norton told himself, and a lot earlier than we expected; we're still a long way from perihelion, and the logical time for an orbit change. But some kind of trim was undoubtedly taking place – and there might be more shocks to come.

Meanwhile, the effects of this first one were all too obvious, up there on the curving sheet of water which seemed perpetually falling from the sky. The wave was still about ten kilometres away, and stretched the full width of the Sea from northern to southern shore. Near the land, it was a foaming wall of white, but in deeper water it was a barely visible blue line, moving much faster than the breakers on either flank. The drag of the shoreward shallows was already bending it into a bow, with the central portion getting further and further ahead.

'Sergeant,' said Norton urgently. 'This is *your* job. What can we do?'

Sergeant Barnes had brought the raft completely to rest and was studying the situation intently. Her expression, Norton was relieved to see, showed no trace of alarm – rather a certain zestful excitement, like a skilled athlete about to accept a challenge.

'I wish we had some soundings,' she said. 'If we're in deep water, there's nothing to worry about.'

'Then we're all right. We're still four kilometres from shore.'

'I hope so, but I want to study the situation.'

She applied power again, and swung *Resolution* around until it was just under way, heading directly towards the approaching wave. Norton judged that the swiftly moving central portion would reach them in less than five minutes, but he could also see that it presented no serious danger. It was only a racing ripple a fraction of a metre high, and would scarcely rock the boat. The walls of foam lagging far behind it were the real menace.

Suddenly, in the very centre of the Sea, a line of breakers appeared. The wave had clearly hit a submerged wall, several kilometres in length, not far below the surface. At the same time, the breakers on the two flanks collapsed, as they ran into deeper water.

Anti-slosh plates, Norton told himself. Exactly the same as in *Endeavour*'s own propellant tanks – but on a thousand-fold greater scale. There must be a complex pattern of them all around the Sea, to damp out any waves as quickly as possible. The only thing that matters now is: are we right on top of one?

Sergeant Barnes was one jump ahead of him. She brought *Resolution* to a full stop and threw out the anchor. It hit bottom at only five metres.

'Haul it up!' she called to her crewmates. 'We've got to get away from here!'

Norton agreed heartily; but in which direction? The Sergeant was headed full speed *towards* the wave, which was now only five kilometres away. For the first time, he could hear the sound of its approach – a distant, unmistakable roar which he had never expected to hear inside Rama. Then it changed in intensity; the central portion was collapsing once more – and the flanks were building up again.

He tried to estimate the distance between the submerged baffles, assuming that they were spaced at equal intervals. If he was right, there should be one more to come; if they could station the raft in the deep water between them, they would be perfectly safe.

Sergeant Barnes cut the motor, and threw out the anchor again. It went down thirty metres without hitting bottom.

'We're OK,' she said, with a sigh of relief. 'But I'll keep the motor running.'

Now there were only the lagging walls of foam along the coast; out here in the central Sea it was calm again, apart from the inconspicuous blue ripple still speeding towards them. The Sergeant was just holding *Resolution* on course towards the disturbance, ready to pour on full power at a moment's notice.

Then, only two kilometres ahead of them, the Sea started to foam once more. It humped up in white-maned fury, and now its roaring seemed to fill the world. Upon the sixteen-kilometre-high wave of the Cylindrical Sea, a smaller ripple was superimposed, like an avalanche thundering down a mountain slope. And that ripple was quite large enough to kill them.

Sergeant Barnes must have seen the expressions on the faces of her crewmates. She shouted above the roar: 'What are you scared about? I've ridden bigger ones than this.' That was not quite true; nor did she add that her earlier experience had been in a well-built surf-boat, not an improvised raft. 'But if we *have* to jump, wait until I tell you. Check your life-jackets.'

She's magnificent, thought the Commander – obviously enjoying every minute, like a Viking warrior going into battle. And she's probably right – unless we've miscalculated badly.

The wave continued to rise, curving upwards and over. The slope above them probably exaggerated its height, but it looked enormous – an irresistible force of nature that would overwhelm everything in its path.

Then, within seconds, it collapsed, as if its foundations had been pulled out from underneath it. It was over the submerged barrier, in deep water again. When it reached them a minute later *Resolution* merely bounced up and down a few times before Sergeant Barnes swung the raft around and set off at top speed towards the north.

'Thanks, Ruby – that was splendid. But will we get home before it comes round for the second time?'

'Probably not; it will be back in about twenty minutes. But it will have lost all its strength then; we'll scarcely notice it.'

Now that the wave had passed, they could relax and enjoy the voyage – though no one would be completely at ease until they were back on land. The disturbance had left the water swirling round in random eddies, and had also stirred up a most peculiar acidic smell – 'like crushed ants', as Jimmy aptly put it. Though unpleasant, the odour caused none of the attacks of sea-sickness that might have been expected; it was something so alien that human physiology could not respond to it.

A minute later, the wave front hit the next underwater barrier, as it climbed away from them and up the sky. This time, seen from the rear, the spectacle was unimpressive and the voyagers felt ashamed of their previous fears. They began to feel themselves masters of the Cylindrical Sea.

The shock was therefore all the greater when, not more than a hundred metres away, something like a slowly rotating wheel began to rear up out of the water. Glittering metallic spokes, five metres long, emerged dripping from the sea, spun for a moment in the fierce Raman glare, and splashed back into the water. It was as if a giant starfish with tubular arms had broken the surface.

At first sight, it was impossible to tell whether it was an animal or a machine. Then it flopped over and lay half-awash, bobbing up and down in the gentle aftermath of the wave.

Now they could see that there were nine arms, apparently jointed, radiating from a central disc. Two of the arms were broken, snapped off at the outer joint. The others ended at a complicated collection of manipulators that reminded Jimmy very strongly of the crab he had encountered. The two creatures came from the same line of evolution – or the same drawing-board.

At the middle of the disc was a small turret, bearing three large eyes. Two were closed, one open – and even that appeared to be blank and unseeing. No one doubted that they were watching the death-throes of some strange monster, tossed up to the surface by the submarine disturbance that had just passed.

Then they saw that it was not alone. Swimming round it, and snapping at its feebly moving limbs, were two small beasts like overgrown lobsters. They were efficiently chopping up the monster, and it did nothing to resist, though its own claws seemed quite capable of dealing with the attackers.

Once again, Jimmy was reminded of the crab that had demolished *Dragonfly*. He watched intently as the one-sided conflict continued, and quickly confirmed his impression.

'Look, Skipper,' he whispered. 'Do you see – they're not eating it. They don't even have any mouths. *They're simply chopping it to pieces.* That's exactly what happened to *Dragonfly*.'

'You're right. They're dismantling it – like – like a broken machine.' Norton wrinkled his nose. 'But no dead machine ever smelled like that!'

Then another thought struck him.

'My God – suppose they start on us! Ruby, get us back to shore as quickly as you can!'

Resolution surged forward with reckless disregard for the life of her power cells. Behind them, the nine spokes of the great starfish – they could think of no better name for it – were clipped steadily shorter, and presently the weird tableau sank back into the depths of the Sea.

There was no pursuit, but they did not breathe comfortably again until *Resolution* had drawn up to the landing stage and they had stepped thankfully ashore. As he looked back across that mysterious and now suddenly sinister band of water, Commander Norton grimly determined that no one would ever sail it again. There were too many unknowns, too many dangers ...

He looked back upon the towers and ramparts of New York, and the dark cliff of the continent beyond. They were safe now from inquisitive man.

He would not tempt the gods of Rama again.

33 SPIDER

From now on, Norton had decreed, there would always be at least three people at Camp Alpha, and one of them would always be awake. In addition, all exploring parties would follow the same routine. Potentially dangerous creatures were on the move inside Rama, and though none had shown active hostility, a prudent commander would take no chances.

As an extra safeguard, there was always an observer up on the Hub, keeping watch through a powerful telescope. From this vantage point, the whole interior of Rama could be surveyed, and even the South Pole appeared only a few hundred metres away. The territory round any group of explorers was to be kept under regular observation; in this way, it was hoped to eliminate any possibility of surprise. It was a good plan – and it failed completely.

After the last meal of the day, and just before the 22.00 hour sleep period, Norton, Rodrigo, Calvert and Laura Ernst were watching the regular evening news telecast specially beamed to them from the transmitter at Inferno, Mercury. They had been particularly interested in seeing Jimmy's film of the Southern continent, and the return across the Cylindrical Sea – an episode which had excited all viewers. Scientists, news commentators, and members of the Rama Committee had given their opinions, most of them contradictory. No one could agree whether the crab-like creature Jimmy had encountered was an animal, a machine, a genuine Raman – or something that fitted none of these categories.

They had just watched, with a distinctly queasy feeling, the giant starfish being demolished by its predators when they discovered that they were no longer alone. There was an intruder in the camp.

Laura Ernst noticed it first. She froze in sudden shock, then said: 'Don't move, Bill. Now look slowly to the right.'

Norton turned his head. Ten metres away was a slender-legged tripod surmounted by a spherical body no larger than a football. Set around the body were three large, expressionless eyes, apparently giving 360 degrees of vision, and trailing beneath it were three whiplike tendrils. The creature was not quite as tall as a man, and looked far too fragile to be dangerous, but that did not excuse their carelessness in letting it sneak up on them unawares. It reminded Norton of nothing so much as a three-legged spider, or daddy-long-legs, and he wondered how it had solved the problem – never challenged by any creature on Earth – of tripedal locomotion.

'What do you make of it, Doc?' he whispered, turning off the voice of the TV newscaster.

'Usual Raman three-fold symmetry. I don't see how it could hurt us, though those whips might be unpleasant – and they could be poisonous, like a coelenterate's. Sit tight and see what it does.'

After regarding them impassively for several minutes, the creature suddenly moved – and now they could understand why they had failed to observe its arrival. It was *fast*, and it covered the ground with such an extraordinary spinning motion that the human eye and mind had real difficulty in following it.

As far as Norton could judge – and only a high-speed camera could settle the matter – each leg in turn acted as a pivot around which the creature whirled its body. And he was not sure, but it also seemed to him that every few 'steps' it reversed its direction of spin, while the three whips flickered over the ground like lightning as it moved. Its top speed – though this also was very hard to estimate – was at least thirty kilometres an hour.

It swept swiftly round the camp, examining every item of equipment, delicately touching the improvised beds and chairs and tables, communication gear, food containers, Electrosans, cameras, water tanks, tools – there seemed to be nothing that it ignored, except the four watchers. Clearly, it was intelligent enough to draw a distinction between humans and their inanimate property; its actions gave the unmistakable impression of an extremely methodical curiosity or inquisitiveness.

'I wish I could examine it!' Laura exclaimed in frustration, as the creature continued its swift pirouette. 'Shall we try to catch it?'

'How?' Calvert asked, reasonably enough.

'You know – the way primitive hunters bring down fast-moving animals with a couple of weights whirling around at the end of a rope. It doesn't even hurt them.'

'That I doubt,' said Norton. 'But even if it worked, we can't risk it. We don't know how intelligent this creature is – and a trick like that could easily break its legs. Then we would be in real trouble – from Rama, Earth and everyone else.'

'But I've got to have a specimen!'

'You may have to be content with Jimmy's flower – unless one of these creatures cooperates with you. Force is out. How would you like it if something landed on Earth and decided that *you* would make a nice specimen for dissection?'

'I don't want to dissect it,' said Laura, not at all convincingly. 'I only want to examine it.'

'Well, alien visitors might have the same attitude towards you, but you could have a very uncomfortable time before you believed them. We must make no move that could possibly be regarded as threatening.'

He was quoting from Ship's Orders, of course, and Laura knew it. The claims of science had a lower priority than those of space-diplomacy.

In fact, there was no need to bring in such elevated considerations; it was merely a matter of good manners. They were all visitors here, and had never even asked permission to come inside ...

The creature seemed to have finished its inspection. It made one more high-speed circuit of the camp, then shot off at a tangent – towards the stairway.

'I wonder how it's going to manage the steps?' Laura mused. Her question was quickly answered; the spider ignored them completely, and headed up the gently sloping curve of the ramp without slackening its speed.

'Hub Control,' said Norton. 'You may have a visitor shortly; take a look at the Alpha Stairway Section Six. And incidentally, thanks a lot for keeping such a good watch on us.'

It took a minute for the sarcasm to sink in; then the Hub observer started to make apologetic noises.

'Er – I can just see *something*, Skipper, now you tell me it's there. But what is it?'

'Your guess is as good as mine,' Norton answered, as he pressed the *General Alert* button. 'Camp Alpha calling all stations. We've just been visited by a creature like a three-legged spider, with very thin legs, about two metres high, small spherical body, travels very fast with a spinning motion. Appears harmless but inquisitive. It may sneak up on you before you notice it. Please acknowledge.'

The first reply came from London, fifteen kilometres to the east.

'Nothing unusual here, Skipper.'

The same distance to the west, Rome answered, sounding suspiciously sleepy.

'Same here, Skipper. Uh, just a moment ...'

'What is it?'

'I put my pen down a minute ago – it's gone! What – oh!'

'Talk sense!'

'You won't believe this, Skipper. I was making some notes – you know I like writing, and it doesn't disturb anybody – I was using my favourite ball-point, it's nearly two hundred years old – well, now it's lying on the ground, about five metres away! I've got it – thank goodness – it isn't damaged.'

'And how do you suppose it got there?'

'Er – I may have dozed off for a minute. It's been a hard day.'

Norton sighed, but refrained from comment; there were so few of them, and they had so little time in which to explore a world. Enthusiasm could not always overcome exhaustion, and he wondered if they were taking unnecessary risks. Perhaps he should not split his men up into such small groups, and try to cover so much territory. But he was always conscious of the swiftly passing days, and the unsolved mysteries around them. He was becoming more and more certain that something was about to happen, and that they would have to abandon Rama even before it reached perihelion – the moment of truth when any orbit change must surely take place.

'Now listen, Hub, Rome, London – everyone,' he said. 'I want a report at every half-hour through the night. We must assume that from now on we may expect visitors at any time. Some of them may be dangerous, but at all costs we have to avoid incidents. You all know the directives on this subject.'

That was true enough; it was part of their training – yet perhaps none of them had ever really believed that the long-theorised 'physical contact with intelligent aliens' would occur in their lifetimes – still less that they would experience it themselves.

Training was one thing, reality another; and no one could be sure that the ancient, human instincts of self-preservation would not take over in an emergency. Yet it was essential to give every entity they encountered in Rama the benefit of the doubt, up to the last possible minute – and even beyond.

Commander Norton did not want to be remembered by history as the man who started the first interplanetary war.

Within a few hours there were hundreds of the spiders, and they were all over the plain. Through the telescope, it could be seen that the southern continent was also infested with them – but not, it seemed, the island of New York.

They took no further notice of the explorers, and after a while the explorers took little notice of them – though from time to time Norton still detected a predatory gleam in his Surgeon-Commander's eye. Nothing would please her better, he was sure, than for one of the spiders to have an unfortunate accident, and he would not put it past her to arrange such a thing in the interests of science.

It seemed virtually certain that the spiders could not be intelligent; their bodies were far too small to contain much in the way of brains, and indeed it was hard to see where they stored all the energy to move. Yet their behaviour was curiously purposeful and coordinated; they seemed to be everywhere, but they never visited the same place twice. Norton frequently had the impression that they were *searching* for something. Whatever it was, they did not seem to have discovered it.

They went all the way up to the central Hub, still scorning the three great stair ways. How they managed to ascend the vertical sections, even under almost zero gravity, was not clear; Laura theorised that they were equipped with suction pads.

And then, to her obvious delight, she got her eagerly desired specimen. Hub Control reported that a spider had fallen down the vertical face and was lying, dead or incapacitated, on the first platform. Laura's time up from the plain was a record that would never be beaten.

When she arrived at the platform, she found that, despite the low velocity of impact, the creature had broken all its legs. Its eyes were still open, but it showed no reactions to any external tests. Even a fresh human corpse would have been livelier, Laura decided; as soon as she got her prize back to *Endeavour*, she started to work with her dissecting kit.

The spider was so fragile that it almost came to pieces without her assistance. She disarticulated the legs, then started on the delicate carapace, which split along three great circles and opened up like a peeled orange.

After some moments of blank incredulity – for there was nothing that she could recognise or identify – she took a series of careful photographs. Then she picked up her scalpel.

Where to start cutting? She felt like closing her eyes, and stabbing at random, but that would not have been very scientific.

The blade went in with practically no resistance. A second later, Surgeon-Commander Ernst's most unlady-like yell echoed the length and breadth of *Endeavour*.

It took an annoyed Sergeant McAndrews a good twenty minutes to calm down the startled simps.

34 HIS EXCELLENCY REGRETS

'As you are all aware, gentlemen,' said the Martian Ambassador, 'a great deal has happened since our last meeting. We have much to discuss – and to decide. I'm therefore particularly sorry that our distinguished colleague from Mercury is not here.'

That last statement was not altogether accurate. Dr Bose was not particularly sorry that HE the Hermian Ambassador was absent. It would have been much more truthful to say that he was worried. All his diplomatic instincts told him that something was happening, and though his sources of information were excellent, he could gather no hints as to what it might be.

The Ambassador's letter of apology had been courteous and entirely uncommunicative. His Excellency had regretted that urgent and unavoidable business had kept him from attending the meeting, either in person or by video. Dr Bose found it very hard to think of anything more urgent – or more important – than Rama.

'Two of our members have statements to make. I would first like to call on Professor Davidson.'

There was a rustle of excitement among the other scientists on the Committee. Most of them had felt that the astronomer, with his well-known cosmic viewpoint, was not the right man to be Chairman of the Space Advisory Council. He sometimes gave the impression that the activities of intelligent life were an unfortunate irrelevance in the majestic universe of stars and galaxies, and that it was bad manners to pay too much attention to it. This had not endeared him to exobiologists such as Dr Perera, who took exactly the opposite view. To them, the only purpose of the Universe was the production of intelligence, and they were apt to talk sneeringly about purely astronomical phenomena. 'Mere dead matter' was one of their favourite phrases.

'Mr Ambassador,' the scientist began, 'I have been analysing the curious behaviour of Rama during the last few days, and would like to present my conclusions. Some of them are rather startling.'

Dr Perera looked surprised, then rather smug. He strongly approved of anything that startled Professor Davidson.

'First of all, there was the remarkable series of events when that young lieutenant flew over to the Southern hemisphere. The electrical discharges themselves, though spectacular, are not important; it is easy to show that they contained relatively little energy. But they coincided with a change in Rama's rate of spin, and its attitude – that is, its orientation in space. *This* must have involved an enormous amount of energy; the discharges which nearly cost Mr – er Pak his life were merely a minor by-product – perhaps a nuisance that had to be minimised by those giant lightning conductors at the South Pole.

'I draw two conclusions from this. When a spacecraft – and we must call Rama a spacecraft, despite its fantastic size – makes a change of attitude, that usually means it is about to make a change of orbit. We must therefore take seriously the views of those who believe that Rama may be preparing to become another planet of our sun, instead of going back to the stars.

'If this is the case. *Endeavour* must obviously be prepared to cast off – is that what spaceships do? – at a moment's notice. She may be in very serious danger while she is still physically attached to Rama. I imagine that Commander Norton is already well aware of this possibility, but I think we should send him an additional warning.'

'Thank you very much, Professor Davidson. Yes – Dr Solomons?'

'I'd like to comment on that,' said the science historian. 'Rama seems to have made a change of spin *without* using any jets or reaction devices. This leaves only two possibilities, it seems to me.

'The first one is that it has internal gyroscopes, or their equivalent. They must be enormous; where are they?

'The second possibility – which would turn all our physics upside down – is that it has a reactionless propulsion system. The so-called Space Drive, which Professor Davidson doesn't believe in. If this is the case, Rama may be able to do almost anything. We will be quite unable to anticipate its behaviour, even on the gross physical level.'

The diplomats were obviously somewhat baffled by this exchange, and the astronomer refused to be drawn. He had gone out on enough limbs for one day.

'I'll stick to the laws of physics, if you don't mind, until I'm forced to give them up. If we've not found any gyroscopes in Rama, we may not have looked hard enough, or in the right place.'

Ambassador Bose could see that Dr Perera was getting impatient. Normally, the exobiologist was as happy as anyone else to engage in speculation; but now, for the first time, he had some solid facts. His long-impoverished science had become wealthy overnight.

'Very well – if there are no other comments – I know that Dr Perera has some important information.'

'Thank you, Mr Ambassador. As you've all seen, we have at last obtained a specimen of a Raman life-form, and have observed several others at close quarters. Surgeon-Commander Ernst, *Endeavour*'s medical officer, has sent a full report on the spider-like creature she dissected.

'I must say at once that some of her results are baffling, and in any other circumstances I would have refused to believe them.

'The spider is definitely organic, though its chemistry differs from ours in many respects – it contains considerable quantities of light metals. Yet I hesitate to call it an animal, for several fundamental reasons.

'In the first place, it seems to have no mouth, no stomach, no gut – no method of ingesting food! Also no air intakes, no lungs, no blood, no reproductive system …

'You may wonder what it *has* got. Well, there's a simple musculature, controlling its three legs and the three whip-like tendrils or feelers. There's a brain – fairly complex, mostly concerned with the creature's remarkably developed triocular vision. But eighty per cent of the body consists of a honeycomb of large cells, and this is what gave Dr Ernst such an unpleasant surprise when she started her dissection. If she'd been luckier she might have recognised it in time, because it's the one Raman structure that *does* exist on Earth – though only in a handful of marine animals.

'Most of the spider is simply a battery, very much like that found in electric cells and rays. But in this case, it's apparently not used for defence. *It's the creature's source of energy.* And that is why it has no provisions for eating and breathing; it doesn't need such primitive arrangements. And incidentally, this means that it would be perfectly at home in a vacuum …

'So we have a creature which, to all intents and purposes, is nothing more than a mobile eye. It has no organs of manipulation; those tendrils are much too feeble. If I had been given its specifications, I would have said it was merely a reconnaissance device.

'Its behaviour certainly fits that description. All the spiders ever do is to run around and look at things. That's all they *can* do …

'But the other animals are different. The crab, the starfish, the sharks – for want of better words – can obviously manipulate their environment and appear to be specialised for various functions. I assume that they are also electrically powered since, like the spider, they appear to have no mouths.

'I'm sure you'll appreciate the biological problems raised by all this. Could such creatures evolve naturally? I really don't think so. They appear to be *designed* like machines, for specific jobs. If I had to describe them, I would say that they are robots – biological robots – something that has no analogy on Earth.

'If Rama is a spaceship, perhaps they are part of its crew. As to how they are born – or created – that's something I can't tell you. But I can guess that the answer's over there in New York. If Commander Norton and his men can wait long enough, they may encounter increasingly more complex creatures, with unpredictable behaviour. Somewhere along the line they may meet the Ramans themselves – the real makers of this world.

'And when *that* happens, gentlemen, there will be no doubt about it all …'

35 SPECIAL DELIVERY

Commander Norton was sleeping soundly when his personal communicator dragged him away from happy dreams. He had been holidaying with his family on Mars, flying past the awesome, snow-capped peak of Nix Olympica – mightiest volcano in the solar system. Little Billie had started to say something to him; now he would never know what it was.

The dream faded; the reality was his executive officer, up on the ship.

'Sorry to wake you, Skipper,' said Lieutenant-Commander Kirchoff. 'Triple A priority from Headquarters.'

'Let me have it,' Norton answered sleepily.

'I can't. It's in code – Commander's Eyes Only.'

Norton was instantly awake. He had received such a message only three times in his whole career, and on each occasion it had meant trouble.

'Damn!' he said. 'What do we do now?'

His Exec did not bother to answer. Each understood the problem perfectly; it was one that Ship's Orders had never anticipated. Normally, a commander was never more than a few minutes away from his office and the code book in his personal safe. If he started now, Norton might get back to the ship – exhausted – in four or five hours. That was not the way to handle a Class AAA Priority.

'Jerry,' he said at length. 'Who's on the switchboard?'

'No one; I'm making the call myself.'

'Recorder off?'

'By an odd breach of regulations, yes.'

Norton smiled. Jerry was the best Exec he had ever worked with. He thought of everything.

'OK. You know where my key is. Call me back.'

He waited as patiently as he could for the next ten minutes, trying – without much success – to think of other problems. He hated wasting mental effort; it was very unlikely that he could out-guess the message that was coming, and he would know its contents soon enough. *Then* he would start worrying effectively.

When the Exec called back, he was obviously speaking under considerable strain.

'It's not really *urgent* Skipper – an hour won't make any difference. But I prefer to avoid radio. I'll send it down by messenger.'

'But *why*— Oh, very well – I trust your judgement. Who will carry it through the airlocks?'

'I'm going myself; I'll call you when I reach the Hub.'

'Which leaves Laura in charge.'

'For one hour, at the most. I'll get right back to the ship.'

A medical officer did not have the specialised training to be acting commander, any more than a commander could be expected to do an operation. In emergencies, both jobs had sometimes been successfully switched; but it was not recommended. Well, one order had already been broken tonight ...

'For the record, you never leave the ship. Have you woken Laura?'

'Yes. She's delighted with the opportunity.'

'Lucky that doctors are used to keeping secrets. Oh – have you sent the acknowledgement?'

'Of course, in your name.'

'Then I'll be waiting.'

Now it was quite impossible to avoid anxious anticipations. 'Not *really* urgent – but I prefer to avoid radio ...'

One thing was certain. The Commander was not going to get much more sleep this night.

36 BIOT WATCHER

Sergeant Pieter Rousseau knew why he had volunteered for this job; in many ways, it was a realisation of a childhood dream. He had become fascinated by telescopes when he was only six or seven years old, and much of his youth had been spent collecting lenses of all shapes and sizes. These he had mounted in cardboard tubes, making instruments of ever-increasing power until he was familiar with the moon and planets, the nearer space-stations, and the entire landscape within thirty-kilometres of his home.

He had been lucky in his place of birth, among the mountains of Colorado; in almost every direction, the view was spectacular and inexhaustible. He had spent hours exploring, in perfect safety, the peaks which every year took their toll of careless climbers. Though he had seen much, he had imagined even more; he had liked to pretend that over each crest of rock, beyond the reach of his telescope, were magic kingdoms full of wonderful creatures. And so for years he had avoided visiting the places his lenses brought to him, because he knew that the reality could not live up to the dream.

Now, on the central axis of Rama, he could survey marvels beyond the wildest fantasies of his youth. A whole world lay spread out before him – a small one, it was true, yet a man could spend an entire lifetime exploring four thousand square kilometres, even when it was dead and changeless.

But now life, with all its infinite possibilities, had come to Rama. If the biological robots were not living creatures, they were certainly very good imitations.

No one knew who invented the word 'biot'; it seemed to come into instant use, by a kind of spontaneous generation. From his vantage point on the Hub, Pieter was Biot-Watcher-in-Chief, and he was beginning – so he believed – to understand some of their behaviour patterns.

The Spiders were mobile sensors, using vision – and probably touch – to examine the whole interior of Rama. At one time there had been hundreds of them rushing around at high speed, but after less than two days they had disappeared; now it was quite unusual to see even one.

They had been replaced by a whole menagerie of much more impressive creatures; it had been no minor task, thinking of suitable names for them. There were the Window Cleaners, with large padded feet, who were apparently polishing their way the whole length of Rama's six artificial suns. Their enormous shadows, cast right across the diameter of the world, sometimes caused temporary eclipses on the far side.

The crab that had demolished *Dragonfly* seemed to be a Scavenger. A relay chain of identical creatures had approached Camp Alpha and carried off all the debris that had been neatly stacked on the outskirts; they would have carried off everything else if Norton and Mercer had not stood firm and defied them. The confrontation had been anxious but brief; thereafter, the Scavengers seemed to understand what they were allowed to touch, and arrived at regular intervals to see if their services were required. It was a most convenient arrangement, and indicated a high degree of intelligence – either on the part of the Scavengers themselves, or some controlling entity elsewhere.

Garbage disposal on Rama was very simple; everything was thrown into the Sea, where it was, presumably, broken down into forms that could be used again. The process was rapid; *Resolution* had disappeared overnight, to the great annoyance of Ruby Barnes. Norton had consoled her by pointing out that it had done its job magnificently – and he would never have allowed anyone to use it again. The Sharks might not be as discriminating as the Scavengers.

No astronomer discovering an unknown planet could have been happier than Pieter when he spotted a new type of biot and secured a good photo of it through his telescope. Unfortunately, it seemed that all the interesting species were over at the South Pole, where they were performing mysterious tasks round the Horns. Something that looked like a centipede with suction pads could be seen from time to time exploring Big Horn itself, while round the lower peaks Pieter had caught a glimpse of a burly creature that could have been a cross between a hippopotamus and a bulldozer. And there was even a double-necked giraffe, which apparently acted as a mobile crane.

Presumably, Rama, like any ship, required testing, checking and repairing after its immense voyage. The crew was already hard at work; when would the passengers appear?

Biot classifying was not Pieter's main job; his orders were to keep watch on the two or three exploring parties that were always out, to see that they did not get into trouble, and to warn them if anything approached. He alternated every six hours with anyone else who could be spared, though more than once he had been on duty for twelve hours at a stretch. As a result, he now knew the geography of Rama better than any man who would ever live. It was as familiar to him as the Colorado mountains of his youth.

When Jerry Kirchoff emerged from Airlock Alpha, Pieter knew at once that something unusual was happening. Personnel transfers never occurred during the sleeping period, and it was now past midnight by Mission Time. Then Pieter remembered how short-handed they were, and was shocked by a much more startling irregularity.

'Jerry – who's in charge of the ship?'

'*I* am,' said the Exec coldly, as he flipped open his helmet. 'You don't think I'd leave the bridge while I'm on watch, do you?'

He reached into his suit carry-all, and pulled out a small can still bearing the label: CONCENTRATED ORANGE JUICE: TO MAKE FIVE LITRES.

'You're good at this Pieter. The skipper is waiting for it.'

Pieter hefted the can, then said, 'I hope you've put enough mass inside it – sometimes they get stuck on the first terrace.'

'Well, you're the expert.'

That was true enough. The Hub observers had had plenty of practice, sending down small items that had been forgotten or were needed in a hurry. The trick was to get them safely past the low-gravity region, and then to see that the Coriolis effect did not carry them too far away from the Camp during the eight-kilometre roll downhill.

Pieter anchored himself firmly, grasped the can, and hurled it down the face of the cliff. He did not aim directly towards Camp Alpha, but almost thirty degrees away from it.

Almost immediately, air resistance robbed the can of its initial speed, but then the pseudo-gravity of Rama took over and it started to move downwards at a constant velocity. It hit once near the base of the ladder, and did a slow-motion bounce which took it clear of the first terrace.

'It's OK now,' said Pieter. 'Like to make a bet?'

'No,' was the prompt reply. 'You know the odds.'

'You're no sportsman. But I'll tell you now – it will stop within three hundred metres of the Camp.'

'That doesn't sound very close.'

'You might try it some time. I once saw Joe miss by a couple of kilometres.'

The can was no longer bouncing; gravity had become strong enough to glue it to the curving face of the North Dome. By the time it had reached the second terrace it was rolling along at twenty or thirty kilometres an hour, and had reached very nearly the maximum speed that friction would allow.

'Now we'll have to wait,' said Pieter, seating himself at the telescope, so that he could keep track of the messenger. 'It will be there in ten minutes. Ah, here comes the skipper – I've got used to recognising people from this angle – now he's looking up at us.'

'I believe that telescope gives you a sense of power.'

'Oh, it does. I'm the only person who knows everything that's happening in Rama. At least, I *thought* I did,' he added plaintively, giving Kirchoff a reproachful look.

'If it will keep you happy, the skipper found he'd run out of toothpaste.'

After that, conversation languished; but at last Pieter said: 'Wish you'd taken that bet ... he's only got to walk fifty metres ... now he sees it ... mission complete.'

'Thanks, Pieter – a very good job. Now you can go back to sleep.'

'Sleep! I'm on watch until 0400.'

'Sorry – you *must* have been sleeping. Or how else could you have dreamed all this?'

SPACE SURVEY HQ TO COMMANDER SSV ENDEAVOUR.
PRIORITY AAA. CLASSIFICATION YOUR EYES ONLY.
NO PERMANENT RECORD.
SPACE GUARD REPORTS ULTRA HIGH SPEED VEHICLE
APPARENTLY LAUNCHED MERCURY TEN TO TWELVE DAYS
AGO ON RAMA INTERCEPT. IF NO ORBIT CHANGE ARRIVAL
PREDICTED DATE 322 DAYS 15 HOURS. MAY BE NECESSARY
YOU EVACUATE BEFORE THEN. WILL ADVISE FURTHER.

C IN C

Norton read the message half a dozen times to memorise the date. It was hard to keep track of time inside Rama; he had to look at his calendar watch to see that it was now Day 315. That might leave them only one week ...

The message was chilling, not only for what it said, but for what it implied. The Hermians had made a clandestine launch – that in itself a breach of Space Law. The conclusion was obvious; their 'vehicle' could only be a missile.

But *why*? It was inconceivable – well, almost inconceivable – that they would risk endangering *Endeavour*, so presumably he would receive ample warning from the Hermians themselves. In an emergency, he could leave at a few hours' notice, though he would do so only under extreme protest, at the direct orders of the Commander-in-Chief.

Slowly, and very thoughtfully, he walked across to the improvised life-support complex and dropped the message into an electrosan. The brilliant flare of laser light bursting out through the crack beneath the seat-cover told him that the demands of security were satisfied. It was too bad, he told himself, that all problems could not be disposed of so swiftly and hygienically.

37 MISSILE

The missile was still five million kilometres away when the glare of its plasma braking jets became clearly visible in *Endeavour*'s main telescope. By that time the secret was already out, and Norton had reluctantly ordered the second and perhaps final evacuation of Rama; but he had no intention of leaving until events gave him no alternative.

When it had completed its braking manoeuvre, the unwelcome guest from Mercury was only fifty kilometres from Rama, and apparently carrying out a survey through its TV cameras. These were clearly visible – one fore and one aft – as were several small omni-antennas and one large directional dish, aimed steadily at the distant star of Mercury. Norton wondered what instructions were coming down that beam, and what information was going back.

Yet the Hermians could learn nothing that they did not already know; all that *Endeavour* had discovered had been broadcast throughout the solar system. This spacecraft – which had broken all speed records to get here – could only be an extension of its makers' will, an instrument of their purpose. That purpose would soon be known, for in three hours the Hermian Ambassador to the United Planets would be addressing the General Assembly.

Officially, the missile did not yet exist. It bore no identification marks, and was not radiating on any standard beacon frequency. This was a serious breach of law, but even spaceguard had not yet issued a formal protest. Everyone was waiting, with nervous impatience, to see what Mercury would do next.

It had been three days since the missile's existence – and origin – had been announced; all that time, the Hermians had remained stubbornly silent. They could be very good at that, when it suited them.

Some psychologists had claimed that it was almost impossible to understand fully the mentality of anyone born and bred on Mercury. Forever exiled from Earth by its three-times-more-powerful gravity, Hermians could stand on the Moon and look across the narrow gap to the planet of their ancestors – even of their own parents – but they could never visit it. And so, inevitably, they claimed that they did not want to.

They pretended to despise the soft rains, the rolling fields, the lakes and seas, the blue skies – all the things that they could know only through recordings.

Because their planet was drenched with such solar energy that the daytime temperature often reached six hundred degrees, they affected a rather swaggering roughness that did not bear a moment's serious examination. In fact, they tended to be physically weak, since they could only survive if they were totally insulated from their environment. Even if he could have tolerated the gravity, a Hermian would have been quickly incapacitated by a hot day in any equatorial country on Earth.

Yet in matters that really counted, they *were* tough. The psychological pressures of that ravening star so close at hand, the engineering problems of tearing into a stubborn planet and wrenching from it all the necessities of life – these had produced a Spartan and in many ways highly admirable culture. You could rely on the Hermians; if they promised something, they would do it – though the bill might be considerable. It was their own joke that, if the sun ever showed signs of going nova, they would contract to get it under control – once the fee had been settled. It was a non-Hermian joke that any child who showed signs of interest in art, philosophy or abstact mathematics was ploughed straight back into the hydroponic farms. As far as criminals and psychopaths were concerned, this was not a joke at all. Crime was one of the luxuries that Mercury could not afford.

Commander Norton had been to Mercury once, had been enormously impressed – like most visitors – and had acquired many Hermian friends. He had fallen in love with a girl in Port Lucifer, and had even contemplated signing a three-year contract, but parental disapproval of anyone from outside the orbit of Venus had been too strong. It was just as well.

'Triple A message from Earth, Skipper,' said the bridge. 'Voice and back-up text from Commander-in-Chief. Ready to accept?'

'Check and file text; let me have the voice.'

'Here it comes.'

Admiral Hendrix sounded calm and matter-of-fact, as if he was issuing a routine fleet order, instead of handling a situation unique in the history of space. But then, he was not ten kilometres from the bomb.

'C-in-C to Commander, *Endeavour*. This is a quick summary of the situation as we see it now. You know that the General Assembly meets at fourteen hundred hours and you'll be listening to the proceedings. It is possible that you may then have to take action immediately, without consultation; hence this briefing.

'We've analysed the photos you have sent us; the vehicle is a standard space-probe, modified for high-impulse and probably laser-riding for initial boost. Size and mass are consistent with fusion bomb in the five hundred to one thousand megaton range; the Hermians use up to one hundred megatons routinely in their mining operations, so they would have had no difficulty in assembling such a warhead.

'Our experts also estimate that this would be the minimum size necessary to assure destruction of Rama. If it was detonated against the thinnest part of the shell – underneath the Cylindrical Sea – the hull would be ruptured and the spin of the body would complete its disintegration.

'We assume that the Hermians, if they are planning such an act, will give you ample time to get clear. For your information, the gamma-ray flash from such a bomb could be dangerous to you up to a range of a thousand kilometres.

'But that is not the most serious danger. The fragments of Rama, weighing tons and spinning off at almost a thousand kilometres an hour, could destroy you at an *unlimited* distance. We therefore recommend that you proceed along the spin axis, since no fragments will be thrown off in that direction. Ten thousand kilometres should give an adequate safety margin.

'This message cannot be intercepted; it is going by multiple-pseudo-random routing, so I can talk in clear English. Your reply may not be secure, so speak with discretion and use code when necessary. I will call you immediately after the General Assembly discussion. Message concluded. C-in-C, out.'

38 GENERAL ASSEMBLY

According to the history books – though no one could really believe it – there had been a time when the old United Nations had 172 members. The United planets had only seven; and that was sometimes bad enough. In order of distance from the Sun, they were Mercury, Earth, Luna, Mars, Ganymede, Titan and Triton.

The list contained numerous omissions and ambiguities which presumably the future would rectify. Critics never tired of pointing out that most of the United Planets were not planets at all, but satellites. And how ridiculous that the four giants, Jupiter, Saturn, Uranus and Neptune were not included ...

But no one lived on the Gas Giants, and quite possibly no one ever would. The same might be true of the other major absentee, Venus. Even the most enthusiastic of planetary engineers agreed that it would take centuries to tame Venus; meanwhile the Hermians kept their eyes on her, and doubtless brooded over long-range plans.

Separate representation for Earth and Luna had also been a bone of contention; the other members argued that it put too much power in one corner of the solar system. But there were more people on the Moon than all the other worlds except Earth itself – and it *was* the meeting place of the UP. Moreover, Earth and Moon hardly every agreed on anything, so they were not likely to constitute a dangerous bloc.

Mars held the asteroids in trust – except for the Icarian group (supervised by Mercury) and a handful with perihelions beyond Saturn – and thus claimed by Titan. One day the larger asteroids, such as Pallas, Vesta, Juno and Ceres, would be important enough to have their own ambassadors, and membership of the UP would then reach two figures.

Ganymede represented not only Jupiter – and therefore more mass than all the rest of the solar system put together – but also the remaining fifty or so Jovian satellites, if one included temporary captures from the asteroid belt (the lawyers were still arguing over this). In the same way, Titan took care of Saturn, its rings and the other thirty-plus satellites.

The situation for Triton was even more complicated. The large moon of Neptune was the outermost body in the solar system under permanent habitation; as a result, its ambassador wore a considerable number of hats.

He represented Uranus and its eight moons (none yet occupied); Neptune and its other three satellites; Pluto and its solitary moon; and lonely, moonless Persephone. If there were planets beyond Persephone, they too would be Triton's responsibility. And as if that was not enough, the Ambassador for the Outer Darkness, as he was sometimes called, had been heard to ask plaintively: 'What about comets?' It was generally felt that this problem could be left for the future to solve.

And yet, in a very real sense, that future was already here. By some definitions, Rama *was* a comet; they were the only other visitors from the interstellar deeps, and many had travelled on hyperbolic orbits even closer to the Sun than Rama's. Any space-lawyer could make a very good case out of that – and the Hermian Ambassador was one of the best.

'We recognise His Excellency the Ambassador for Mercury.'

As the delegates were arranged counter-clockwise in order of distance from the sun, the Hermian was on the President's extreme right. Up to the very last minute, he had been interfacing with his computer; now he removed the synchronizing spectacles which allowed no one else to read the message on the display screen. He picked up his sheaf of notes, and rose briskly to his feet.

'Mr President, distinguished fellow delegates, I would like to begin with a brief summary of the situation which now confronts us.'

From some delegates, that phrase 'a brief summary' would have evoked silent groans among all listeners; but everyone knew that Hermians meant exactly what they said.

'The giant spaceship, or artificial asteroid, which has been christened Rama was detected over a year ago, in the region beyond Jupiter. At first it was believed to be a natural body, moving on a hyperbolic orbit which would take it round the sun and on to the stars.

'When its true nature was discovered, the Solar Survey Vessel *Endeavour* was ordered to rendezvous with it. I am sure we will all congratulate Commander Norton and his crew for the efficient way in which they have carried out their unique assignment.

'At first, it was believed that Rama was dead – frozen for so many hundreds of thousands of years that there was no possibility of revival. This may still be true, in a strictly biological sense. There seems general agreement, among those who have studied the matter, that no living organism of any complexity can survive more than a very few centuries of suspended animation. Even at absolute zero, residual quantum effects eventually erase too much cellular information to make revival possible. It therefore appeared that, although Rama was of enormous archaeological importance, it did not present any major astropolitical problems.

'It is now obvious that this was a very naïve attitude, though even from the first there were some who pointed out that Rama was too precisely aimed at the Sun for pure chance to be involved.

'Even so, it might have been argued – indeed, it was argued – that here was an experiment that had failed. Rama had reached the intended target, but the controlling intelligence had not survived. This view also seems very simple-minded; it surely underestimates the entities we are dealing with.

'What we failed to take into account was the possibility of *non*-biological survival. If we accept Dr Perera's very plausible theory, which certainly fits all the facts, the creatures who have been observed inside Rama did not exist until a short time ago. Their patterns, or templates, were stored in some central information bank, and when the time was ripe they were manufactured from available raw materials – presumably the metallo-organic soup of the Cylindrical Sea. Such a feat is still somewhat beyond our own ability, but does not present any theoretical problems. We know that solid state circuits, unlike living matter, can store information without loss, for indefinite periods of time.

'So Rama is now in full operating condition, serving the purpose of its builders – whoever they may be. From our point of view, it does not matter if the Ramans themselves have all been dead for a million years, or whether they too will be re-created, to join their servants, at any moment. With or without them, their will is being done – and will continue to be done.

'Rama has now given proof that its propulsion system is still operating. In a few days, it will be at perihelion, where it would logically make any major orbit change. We may therefore soon have a new planet – moving through the solar space over which my government has jurisdiction. Or it may, of course, make additional changes and occupy a final orbit at any distance from the sun. It could even become a satellite of a major planet – such as Earth ...

'We are therefore, fellow delegates, faced with a whole spectrum of possibilities, some of them very serious indeed. It is foolish to pretend that these creatures *must* be benevolent and will not interfere with us in any way. If they come to our solar system, they need something from it. Even if it is only scientific knowledge – consider how that knowledge may be used ...

'What confronts us now is a technology hundreds – perhaps thousands – of years in advance of ours, and a *culture* which may have no points of contact whatsoever. We have been studying the behaviour of the biological robots – the biots – inside Rama, as shown on the films that Commander Norton has relayed, and we have arrived at certain conclusions which we wish to pass on to you.

'On Mercury we are perhaps unlucky in having no indigenous life-forms to observe. But, of course, we have a complete record of terrestrial zoology, and we find in it one striking parallel with Rama.

'This is the termite colony. Like Rama, it is an artificial world with a controlled environment. Like Rama, its functioning depends upon a whole series of specialised biological machines – workers, builders, farmers – *warriors*. And although we do not know if Rama has a queen, I suggest that the island known as New York serves a similar function.

144

'Now, it would obviously be absurd to press this analogy too far; it breaks down at many points. But I put it to you for this reason.

'What degree of cooperation or understanding would ever be possible between human beings and termites? When there is no conflict of interest, we tolerate each other. But when either needs the other's territory or resources, no quarter is given.

'Thanks to our technology and our intelligence, we can always win, if we are sufficiently determined. But sometimes it is not easy, and there are those who believe that, in the long run, final victory may yet go to the termites ...

'With this in mind, consider now the appalling threat that Rama may – I do not say *must* – present to human civilisation. What steps have we taken to counter it, if the worst eventuality should occur? None whatsoever; we have merely talked and speculated and written learned papers.

'Well, my fellow delegates, Mercury has done more than this. Acting under the provisions of Clause 34 of the Space Treaty of 2057, which entitled us to take any steps necessary to protect the integrity of our solar space, we have dispatched a high-energy nuclear device to Rama. We will indeed be happy if we never have to utilise it. But now, at least, we are not helpless – as we were before.

'It may be argued that we have acted unilaterally, without prior consultation. We admit that. But does anyone here imagine – with all respect, Mister President – that we could have secured any such agreement in the time available? We consider that we are acting not only for ourselves, but for the whole human race. All future generations may one day thank us for our foresight.

'We recognised that it would be a tragedy – even a crime – to destroy an artifact as wonderful as Rama. If there is any way in which this can be avoided, *without risk to humanity*, we will be very happy to hear of it. We have not found one, and time is running out.

'Within the next few days, before Rama reaches perihelion, the choice will have to be made. We will, of course, give ample warning to *Endeavour* – but we would advise Commander Norton always to be ready to leave at an hour's notice. It is conceivable that Rama may undergo further dramatic transformations at any moment.

'That is all, Mister President, fellow delegates. I thank you for your attention. I look forward to your cooperation.'

39 COMMAND DECISION

'Well, Rod, how do the Hermians fit into your theology?'

'Only too well, Commander,' replied Rodrigo with a humourless smile. 'It's the age-old conflict between the forces of good and the forces of evil. And there are times when men have to take sides in such a conflict.'

I thought it would be something like that, Norton told himself. This situation must have been a shock to Boris, but he would not have resigned himself to passive acquiescence. The Cosmo-Christers were very energetic, competent people. Indeed, in some ways they were remarkably like the Hermians.

'I take it you have a plan, Rod.'

'Yes, Commander. It's really quite simple. We merely have to disable the bomb.'

'Oh, And how do you propose to do that?'

'With a small pair of wire-cutters.'

If this had been anyone else, Norton would have assumed that they were joking. But not Boris Rodrigo.

'Now just a minute! It's bristling with cameras. Do you suppose the Hermians will just sit and watch you?'

'Of course; that's all they *can* do. When the signal reaches them, it will be far too late. I can easily finish the job in ten minutes.'

'I see. They certainly *will* be mad. But suppose the bomb is booby-trapped so that interference sets it off?'

'That seems very unlikely; what would be the purpose? This bomb was built for a specific deep-space mission, and it will be fitted with all sorts of safety devices to prevent detonation *except* on a positive command. But that's a risk I'm prepared to take – and it can be done without endangering the ship. I've worked everything out.'

'I'm sure you have,' said Norton. The idea was fascinating – almost seductive in its appeal; he particularly liked the idea of the frustrated Hermians, and would give a good deal to see their reactions when they realised – too late – what was happening to their deadly toy.

But there were other complications, and they seemed to multiply as Norton surveyed the problem. He was facing by far the most difficult, and the most crucial, decision in his entire career.

And that was a ridiculous understatement. He was faced with the most difficult decision *any* commander had ever had to make; the future of the entire human race might well depend upon it. For just suppose the Hermians were right?

When Rodrigo had left, he switched on the DO NOT DISTURB sign; he could not remember when he had last used it, and was mildly surprised that it was working. Now, in the heart of his crowded, busy ship, he was completely alone – except for the portrait of Captain James Cook, gazing at him down the corridors of time.

It was impossible to consult with Earth; he had already been warned that any messages might be tapped – perhaps by relay devices on the bomb itself. That left the whole responsibility in his hands.

There was a story he had heard somewhere about a President of the United States – was it Roosevelt or Perez? – who had a sign on his desk saying 'The buck stops here'. Norton was not quite certain what a buck was, but he knew when one had stopped at his desk.

He could do nothing, and wait until the Hermians advised him to leave. How would that look in the histories of the future? Norton was not greatly concerned with posthumous fame or infamy, yet he would not care to be remembered for ever as the accessory to a cosmic crime – which it had been in his power to prevent.

And the plan was flawless. As he had expected, Rodrigo had worked out every detail, anticipated every possibility even the remote danger that the bomb might be triggered when tampered with. If that happened, *Endeavour* could still be safe, behind the shield of Rama. As for Lieutenant Rodrigo himself, he seemed to regard the possibility of instant apotheosis with complete equanimity.

Yet, even if the bomb was successfully disabled, that would be far from the end of the matter. The Hermians might try again – unless some way could be found of stopping them. But at least weeks of time would have been bought; Rama would be far past perihelion before another missile could possibly reach it. By then, hopefully, the worst fears of the alarmists might have been disproved. Or the reverse ...

To act, or not to act – that was the question. Never before had Commander Norton felt such a close kinship with the Prince of Denmark. Whatever he did, the possibilities for good and evil seemed in perfect balance. He was faced with the most morally difficult of all decisions. If his choice was wrong, he would know very quickly. But if he was correct – he might never be able to prove it ...

It was no use relying any further on logical arguments and the endless mapping of alternative futures. That way, one could go round and round in circles for ever. The time had come to listen to his inner voices.

He returned the calm, steady gaze across the centuries.

'I agree with you, Captain,' he whispered. 'The human race has to live with its conscience. Whatever the Hermians argue, survival is not everything.'

He pressed the call button for the bridge circuit and said slowly, 'Lieutenant Rodrigo – I'd like to see you.'

Then he closed his eyes, hooked his thumbs in the restraining straps of his chair, and prepared to enjoy a few moments of total relaxation.

It might be some time before he would experience it again.

40 SABOTEUR

The scooter had been stripped of all unnecessary equipment; it was now merely an open framework holding together propulsion, guidance and life-support systems. Even the seat for the second pilot had been removed, for every kilogramme of extra mass had to be paid for in mission time.

That was one of the reasons, though not the most important, why Rodrigo had insisted on going alone. It was such a simple job that there was no need for any extra hands, and the mass of a passenger would cost several minutes of flight time. Now the stripped-down scooter could accelerate at over a third of a gravity; it could make the trip from *Endeavour* to the bomb in four minutes. That left six to spare; it would be sufficient.

Rodrigo looked back only once when he had left the ship; he saw that, as planned, it had lifted from the central axis and was thrusting gently away across the spinning disc of the North Face. By the time he reached the bomb, it would have placed the thickness of Rama between them.

He took his time, flying over the polar plain. There was no hurry here, because the bomb's cameras could not yet see him, and he could therefore conserve fuel. Then he drifted over the curving rim of the world – and there was the missile, glittering in sunlight fiercer even than that shining on the planet of its birth.

Rodrigo had already punched in the guidance instructions. He initiated the sequence; the scooter spun on its gyros, and came up to full thrust in a matter of seconds. At first the sensation of weight seemed crushing; then Rodrigo adjusted to it. He had, after all, comfortably endured twice as much inside Rama – and had been born under three times as much on Earth.

The huge, curving exterior wall of the fifty-kilometre cylinder was slowly falling away beneath him as the scooter aimed itself directly at the bomb. Yet it was impossible to judge Rama's size, since it was completely smooth and featureless – so featureless, indeed, that it was difficult to tell that it was spinning.

One hundred seconds into the mission; he was approaching the halfway point. The bomb was still too far away to show any details, but it was much brighter against the jet-black sky. It was strange to see no stars – not even brilliant Earth or dazzling Venus; the dark filters which protected his eyes against the deadly glare made that impossible. Rodrigo guessed that he was breaking a record; probably no other man had ever engaged in extra-vehicular work so close to the sun. It was lucky for him that solar activity was low.

At two minutes ten seconds the flip-over light started flashing, thrust dropped to zero, and the scooter spun through a hundred and eighty degrees. Full thrust was back in an instant, but now he was decelerating at the same mad rate of three metres per second squared – rather better than that, in fact, since he had lost almost half his propellent mass. The bomb was twenty-five kilometres away; he would be there in another two minutes. He had hit a top speed of fifteen hundred kilometres an hour – which, for a space-scooter, was utter insanity, and probably another record. But this was hardly a routine EVA, and he knew precisely what he was doing.

The bomb was growing; and now he could see the main antenna, holding steady on the invisible star of Mercury. Along that beam, the image of his approaching scooter had been flashing at the speed of light for the last three minutes. There were still two to go, before it reached Mercury.

What would the Hermians do, when they saw him? There would be consternation, of course; they would realise instantly that he had made a rendezvous with the bomb several minutes before they even knew he was on the way. Probably some stand-by observer would call higher authority – that would take more time. But even in the worst possible case – even if the officer on duty had authority to detonate the bomb, and pressed the button immediately – it would take another five minutes for the signal to arrive.

Though Rodrigo was not gambling on it – Cosmo-Christers *never* gambled – he was quite sure that there would be no such instantaneous reaction. The Hermians would hesitate to destroy a reconnaissance vehicle from *Endeavour*, even if they suspected its motives. They would certainly attempt some form of communication first – and that would mean *more* delay.

And there was an even better reason; they would not waste a gigaton bomb on a mere scooter. Wasted it would be, if it was detonated twenty kilometres from its target. They would have to move it first. Oh, he had plenty of time ... but he would still assume the very worst.

He would act as if the triggering impulse would arrive in the shortest possible time – just five minutes.

As the scooter closed in across the last few hundred metres, Rodrigo quickly matched the details he could now see with those he had studied in the photographs taken at long range. What had been only a collection of pictures became hard metal and smooth plastic – no longer abstract, but a deadly reality.

The bomb was a cylinder about ten metres long and three in diameter – by a strange coincidence, almost the same proportions as Rama itself. It was attached to the framework of the carrier vehicle by an open lattice-work of short I-beams. For some reason, probably to do with the location of the centre of mass, it was supported at *right angles* to the axis of the carrier, so that it conveyed an appropriately sinister hammer-head impression. It was indeed a hammer, one powerful enough to smash a world.

From each end of the bomb, a bundle of braided cables ran along the cylindrical side and disappeared through the lattice-work into the interior of the vehicle. All communication and control was here; there was no antenna of any kind on the bomb itself. Rodrigo had only to cut those two sets of cables and there would be nothing here but harmless, inert metal.

Although this was exactly what he had expected, it still seemed a little too easy. He glanced at his watch; it would be another thirty seconds before the Hermians, even if they had been watching when he rounded the edge of Rama, could know of his existence. He had an absolutely certain five minutes for uninterrupted work – and a ninety-nine per cent probability of much longer than that.

As soon as the scooter had drifted to a complete halt, Rodrigo grappled it to the missile framework so that the two formed a rigid structure. That took only seconds; he had already chosen his tools, and was out of the pilot's seat at once, only slightly hampered by the stiffness of his heavy-insulation suit.

The first thing he found himself inspecting was a small metal plate bearing the inscription:

DEPARTMENT OF POWER ENGINEERING
Section D,
47, Sunset Boulevard,
Vulcanopolis, 17464
For information apply to Mr Henry K. Jones

Rodrigo suspected that, in a very few minutes, Mr Jones might be rather busy.

The heavy wire-cutters made short work of the cable. As the first strands parted, Rodrigo gave scarcely a thought to the fires of hell that were pent up only centimetres away; if his actions triggered them, he would never know.

He glanced again at his watch; this had taken less than a minute, which meant that he was on schedule. Now for the back-up cable – and then he could head for home, in full view of the furious and frustrated Hermians.

He was just beginning to work on the second cable assembly when he felt a faint vibration in the metal he was touching. Startled, he looked back along the body of the missile.

The characteristic blue-violet glow of a plasma thruster in action was hovering round one of the attitude control jets. The bomb was preparing to move.

The message from Mercury was brief, and devastating. It arrived two minutes after Rodrigo had disappeared around the edge of Rama.

COMMANDER ENDEAVOUR FROM MERCURY SPACE CON-
TROL, INFERNO WEST. YOU HAVE ONE HOUR FROM RECEIPT
OF THIS MESSAGE TO LEAVE VICINITY OF RAMA. SUGGEST
YOU PROCEED MAXIMUM ACCELERATION ALONG SPIN AXIS.
REQUEST ACKNOWLEDGEMENT. MESSAGE ENDS.

Norton read it with sheer disbelief, then anger. He felt a childish impulse to
radio back that all his crew were inside Rama, and it would take hours to get
everyone out. But that would achieve nothing – except perhaps to test the
will and nerve of the Hermians.

And why, several days before perihelion, had they decided to act? He
wondered if the mounting pressure of public opinion was becoming too
great, and they decided to present the rest of the human race with a *fait
accompli*. It seemed an unlikely explanation; such sensitivity would have been
uncharacteristic.

There was no way in which he could recall Rodrigo, for the scooter was
now in the radio shadow of Rama and would be out of contact until they
were in line of sight again. That would not be until the mission was completed – or had failed.

He would have to wait it out; there was still plenty of time – a full fifty minutes. Meanwhile, he had decided on the most effective answer to Mercury.

He would ignore the message completely, and see what the Hermians did
next.

Rodrigo's first sensation, when the bomb started to move, was not one of
physical fear; it was something much more devastating. He believed that the
universe operated according to strict laws, which not even God Himself could
disobey – much less the Hermians. No message could travel faster than light;
he was five minutes ahead of anything that Mercury could do.

This could only be a coincidence – fantastic, and perhaps deadly, but no
more than that. By chance, a control signal must have been sent to the bomb
at about the time he was leaving *Endeavour*; while he was travelling fifty
kilometres, it had covered eighty million.

Or perhaps this was only an automatic change of attitude, to counter
over-heating somewhere in the vehicle. There were places where the skin
temperature approached fifteen hundred degrees, and Rodrigo had been very
careful to keep in the shadows as far as possible.

A second thrusters started to fire, checking the spin given by the first. No,
this was *not* a mere thermal adjustment. The bomb was re-orientating itself,
to point towards Rama ...

Useless to wonder *why* this was happening at this precise moment in time.
There was one thing in his favour; the missile was a low acceleration device.
A tenth of a gee was the most that it could manage. He could hang on.

He checked the grapples attaching the scooter to the bomb framework, and re-checked the safety line on his own suit. A cold anger was growing in his mind, adding to his determination. Did this manoeuvre mean that the Hermians were going to explode the bomb without warning, giving *Endeavour* no chance to escape? That seemed incredible – an act not only of brutality but of folly, calculated to turn the rest of the solar system against them. And what would have made them ignore the solemn promise of their own Ambassador?

Whatever their plan, they would not get away with it.

The second message from Mercury was identical with the first, and arrived ten minutes later. So they had extended the deadline – Norton still had one hour. And they had obviously waited until a reply from *Endeavour* could have reached them before calling him again.

Now there was another factor; by this time they must have seen Rodrigo, and would have had several minutes in which to take action. Their instructions could already be on the way. They could arrive at any second.

He should be preparing to leave. At any moment, the sky-filling bulk of Rama might become incandescent along the edges, blazing with a transient glory that would far outshine the sun.

When the main thrust came on, Rodrigo was securely anchored. Only twenty seconds later, it cut off again. He did a quick mental calculation; the delta vee could not have been more than fifteen kilometres an hour. The bomb would take over an hour to reach Rama; perhaps it was only moving in close to get a quicker reaction. If so, that was a wise precaution; but the Hermians had left it too late.

Rodrigo glanced at his watch, though by now he was almost aware of the time without having to check. On Mercury, they would now be seeing him heading purposefully towards the bomb, and less than two kilometres away from it. They could have no doubt of his intentions, and would be wondering if he had already carried them out.

The second set of cables went as easily as the first; like any good workman, Rodrigo had chosen his tools well. The bomb was disarmed; or, to be more accurate, it could no longer be detonated by remote command.

Yet there was one other possibility, and he could not afford to ignore it. There were no external contact fuses, but there might be internal ones, armed by the shock of impact. The Hermians still had control over their vehicle's movements, and could crash it into Rama whenever they wished. Rodrigo's work was not yet completely finished.

Five minutes from now, in that control room somewhere on Mercury, they would see him crawling back along the exterior of the missile, carrying the modestly-sized wire-cutters that had neutralized the mightiest weapon ever built by man. He was almost tempted to wave at the camera, but decided that it would seem undignified; after all, he was making history, and millions would watch this scene in the years to come. Unless, of course, the Hermians destroyed the recording in a fit of pique; he would hardly blame them.

He reached the mounting of the long-range antenna, and drifted hand-over-hand along it to the big dish. His faithful cutters made short work of the multiplex feed system, chewing up cables and laser wave guides alike. When he made the last snip, the antenna started to swing slowly around; the unexpected movement took him by surprise, until he realised that he had destroyed its automatic lock on Mercury. Just five minutes from now, the Hermians would lose all contact with their servant. Not only was it impotent; now it was blind and deaf.

Rodrigo climbed slowly back to the scooter, released the shackles, and swung it round until the forward bumpers were pressing against the missile, as close as possible to its centre of mass. He brought thrust up to full power, and held it there for twenty seconds.

Pushing against many times its own mass, the scooter responded very sluggishly. When Rodrigo cut the thrust back to zero, he took a careful reading of the bomb's new velocity vector.

It would miss Rama by a wide margin – and it could be located again with precision at any future time. It was, after all, a very valuable piece of equipment.

Lieutenant Rodrigo was a man of almost pathological honesty. He would not like the Hermians to accuse him of losing their property.

41 HERO

'Darling,' began Norton, 'this nonsense has cost us more than a day, but at least it's given me a chance to talk to you.

'I'm still in the ship, and she's heading back to station at the polar axis. We picked Rod up an hour ago, looking as if he'd just come off duty after a quiet watch. I suppose neither of us will ever be able to visit Mercury again, and I'm wondering if we're going to be treated as heroes or villains when we get back to Earth. But *my* conscience is clear; I'm sure we did the right thing. I wonder if the Ramans will ever say "thank you".

'We can stay here only two more days; unlike Rama, we don't have a kilometre-thick skin to protect us from the sun. The hull's already developing dangerous hotspots and we've had to put out some local screening. I'm sorry – I didn't want to bore you with my problems ...

'So there's time for just one more trip into Rama, and I intend to make the most of it. But don't worry – I'm not taking any chances.'

He stopped the recording. That, to say the least, was stretching the truth. There was danger and uncertainty about every moment inside Rama; no man could ever feel really at home there, in the presence of forces beyond his understanding. And on this final trip, now that he knew they would never return and that no future operations would be jeopardized, he intended to press his luck just a little further.

'In forty-eight hours, then, we'll have completed this mission. What happens then is still uncertain; as you know, we've used virtually all our fuel getting into this orbit. I'm still waiting to hear if a tanker can rendezvous with us in time to get back to Earth, or whether we'll have to make planet-fall at Mars. Anyway, I should be home by Christmas. Tell Junior I'm sorry I can't bring a baby biot; there's no such animal ...

'We're all fine, but we're very tired. I've earned a long leave after all this, and we'll make up for lost time. Whatever they say about me, you can claim you're married to a hero. How many wives have a husband who saved a world?'

As always, he listened carefully to the tape before duping it, to make sure that it was applicable to both his families. It was strange to think that he did not know which of them he would see first; usually, his schedule was determined at least a year in advance, by the inexorable movements of the planets themselves.

But that was in the days before Rama; now nothing would ever be the same again.

42 TEMPLE OF GLASS

'If we try it,' said Karl Mercer, 'do you think the biots will stop us?'

'They may; that's one of the things I want to find out. Why are you looking at me like that?'

Mercer gave his slow, secret grin, which was liable to be set off at any moment by a private joke he might or might not share with his shipmates.

'I was wondering, Skipper, if you think you own Rama. Until now, you've vetoed any attempt to cut into buildings. Why the switch? Have the Hermians given you ideas?'

Norton laughed, then suddenly checked himself. It was a shrewd question, and he was not sure if the obvious answers were the right ones.

'Perhaps I have been ultra-cautious – I've tried to avoid trouble. But this is our last chance; if we're forced to retreat we won't have lost much.'

'Assuming that we retreat in good order.'

'Of course. But the biots have never shown hostility; and except for the Spiders, I don't believe there's anything here that can catch us – if we do have to run for it.'

'*You* may run, Skipper, but I intend to leave with dignity. And incidentally, I've decided why the biots are so polite to us.'

'It's a little late for a new theory.'

'Here it is, anyway. They think we're Ramans. They can't tell the difference between one oxy-eater and another.'

'I don't believe they're *that* stupid.'

'It's not a matter of stupidity. They've been programmed for their particular jobs, and we simply don't come into their frame of reference.'

'Perhaps you're right. We may find out – as soon as we start to work on London.'

Joe Calvert had always enjoyed those old bank-robbery movies, but he had never expected to be involved in one. Yet this was, essentially, what he was doing now.

The deserted streets of 'London' seemed full of menace, though he knew that was only his guilty conscience. He did not *really* believe that the sealed and windowless structures ranged all around them were full of watchful inhabitants, waiting to emerge in angry hordes as soon as the invaders laid a hand on their property. In fact, he was quite certain that this whole complex – like all the other towns – was merely some kind of storage area.

Yet a second fear, also based on innumerable ancient crime dramas, could be better grounded. There might be no clanging alarm bells and screaming sirens, but it was reasonable to assume that Rama would have some kind of warning system. How otherwise did the biots know when and where their services were needed?

'Those without goggles, turn your backs,' ordered Sergeant Myron. There was a smell of nitric oxides as the air itself started to burn in the beam of the laser torch, and a steady sizzling as the fiery knife sliced towards secrets that had been hidden since the birth of man.

Nothing material could resist this concentration of power, and the cut proceeded smoothly at a rate of several metres a minute. In a remarkable short time, a section large enough to admit a man had been sliced out.

As the cut-away section showed no signs of moving, Myron tapped it gently – then harder – then banged on it with all his strength. It fell inwards with a hollow, reverberating crash.

Once again, as he had done during that very first entrance into Rama, Norton remembered the archaeologist who had opened the old Egyptian tomb. He did not expect to see the glitter of gold; in fact, he had no preconceived ideas at all, as he crawled through the opening, his flashlight held in front of him.

A Greek temple made of glass – that was his first impression. The building was filled with row upon row of vertical crystalline columns, about a metre wide and stretching from floor to ceiling. There were hundreds of them, marching away into the darkness beyond the reach of his light.

Norton walked towards the nearest column and directed his beam into its interior. Refracted as through a cylindrical lens, the light fanned out on the far side to be focused and refocused, getting fainter with each repetition, in the array of pillars beyond. He felt that he was in the middle of some complicated demonstration in optics.

'Very pretty,' said the practical Mercer, 'but what does it mean? Who needs a forest of glass pillars?'

Norton rapped gently on one column. It sounded solid, though more metallic than crystalline. He was completely baffled, and so followed a piece of useful advice he had heard long ago: 'When in doubt, say nothing and move on.'

As he reached the next column, which looked exactly like the first, he heard an exclamation of surprise from Mercer.

'I could have sworn this pillar was empty – now there's something inside it.'

Norton glanced quickly back.

'Where?' he said. 'I don't see anything.'

He followed the direction of Mercer's pointing finger. It was aimed at nothing; the column was still completely transparent.

'You can't see it?' said Mercer incredulously. 'Come around this side. Damn – now I've lost it!'

'What's going on here?' demanded Calvert. It was several minutes before he got even the first approximation to an answer.

The columns were not transparent from every angle or under all illuminations. As one walked around them, objects would suddenly flash into view, apparently embedded in their depths like flies in amber – and would then disappear again. There were dozens of them, all different. They looked absolutely real and solid, yet many seemed to occupy the identical volume of space.

'Holograms,' said Calvert. 'Just like a museum on Earth.'

That was the obvious explanation, and therefore Norton viewed it with suspicion. His doubts grew as he examined the other columns, and conjured up the images stored in their interiors.

Hand-tools (though for huge and peculiar hands), containers, small machines with keyboards that appeared to have been made for more than five fingers, scientific instruments, startlingly conventional domestic utensils, including knives and plates which apart from their size would not have attracted a second glance on any terrestrial table ... they were all there, with hundreds of less identifiable objects, often jumbled up together in the same pillar. A museum, surely, would have some logical arrangement, some segregation of related items. This seemed to be a completely random collection of hardware.

They had photographed the elusive images inside a score of the crystal pillars when the sheer variety of items gave Norton a clue. Perhaps this was not a collection, but a *catalogue*, indexed according to some arbitrary but perfectly logical system. He thought of the wild juxtapositions that any dictionary or alphabetized list will give, and tried the idea on his companions.

'I see what you mean,' said Mercer. 'The Ramans might be equally surprised to find us putting – ah– camshafts next to cameras.'

'Or books beside boots', added Calvert, after several seconds' hard thinking. One could play this game for hours, he decided, with increasing degrees of impropriety.

'That's the idea,' replied Norton. 'This may be an indexed catalogue for 3-D images – templates – solid blue-prints, if you like to call them that.'

'For what purpose?'

'Well, you know the theory about the biots ... the idea that they don't exist until they're needed and then they're created – synthesised – from patterns stored somewhere?'

'I see,' said Mercer slowly and thoughtfully. 'So when a Raman needs a left-handed blivet, he punches out the correct code number, and a copy is manufactured from the pattern in here.'

'Something like that. But please don't ask me about the practical details.'

The pillars through which they had been moving had been steadily growing in size, and were now more than two metres in diameter. The images were correspondingly larger; it was obvious that, for doubtless excellent reasons, the Ramans believed in sticking to a one-to-one scale. Norton wondered how they stored anything *really* big, if this was the case.

To increase their rate of coverage, the four explorers had now spread out through the crystal columns and were taking photographs as quickly as they could get their cameras focused on the fleeting images. This was an astonishing piece of luck, Norton told himself, though he felt that he had earned it; they could not possibly have made a better choice than this Illustrated Catalogue of Raman Artifacts. And yet, in another way, it could hardly have been more frustrating. There was nothing actually *here*, except impalpable patterns of light and darkness; these apparently solid objects did not really exist.

Even knowing this, more than once Norton felt an almost irresistible urge to laser his way into one of the pillars, so that he could have something material to take back to Earth. It was the same impulse, he told himself wryly, that would prompt a monkey to grab the reflection of a banana in a mirror.

He was photographing what seemed to be some kind of optical device when Calvert's shout started him running through the pillars.

'Skipper – Karl – Will – look at *this*!'

Joe was prone to sudden enthusiasms, but what he had found was enough to justify any amount of excitement.

Inside one of the two-metre columns was an elaborate harness, or uniform, obviously made for a vertically-standing creature, much taller than a man. A very narrow central metal band apparently surrounded the waist, thorax or some division unknown to terrestrial zoology. From this rose three slim columns, tapering outwards and ending in a perfectly circular belt, an impressive metre in diameter. Loops equally spaced along it could only be intended to go round upper limbs or arms. *Three* of them ...

There were numerous pouches, buckles, bandoliers from which tools (or weapons?) protruded, pipes and electrical conductors, even small black boxes that would have looked perfectly at home in an electronics lab on Earth. The whole arrangement was almost as complex as a spacesuit, though it obviously provided only partial covering for the creature wearing it.

And was that creature a Raman? Norton asked himself. We'll probably never know; but it must have been intelligent – no mere animal could cope with all that sophisticated equipment.

'About two and a half metres high,' said Mercer thoughtfully, 'not counting the head – whatever *that* was like.'

'With three arms – and presumably three legs. The same plan as the Spiders, on a much more massive scale. Do you suppose that's a coincidence?'

'Probably not. We design robots in our own image; we might expect the Ramans to do the same.'

Joe Calvert, unusually subdued, was looking at the display with something like awe.

'Do you suppose they know we're here?' he half-whispered

'I doubt it,' said Mercer. 'We've not even reached their threshold of consciousness – though the Hermians certainly had a good try.'

They were still standing there, unable to drag themselves away, when Pieter called from the Hub, his voice full of urgent concern.

'Skipper – you'd better get outside.'

'What is it – biots heading this way?'

'No – something much more serious. *The lights are going out.*'

43 RETREAT

When he hastily emerged from the hole they had lasered, it seemed to Norton that the six suns of Rama were as brilliant as ever. Surely, he thought, Pieter must have made a mistake … that's not like him at all …

But Pieter had anticipated just this reaction.

'It happened so slowly,' he explained apologetically, 'that it was a long time before I noticed any difference. But there's no doubt about it – I've taken a metre reading. The light level's down forty per cent.'

Now, as his eyes readjusted themselves after the gloom of the glass temple, Norton could believe him. The long day of Rama was drawing to it close.

It was still as warm as ever, yet Norton felt himself shivering. He had known this sensation once before, during a beautiful summer day on Earth. There had been an inexplicable weakening of light as if darkness was falling from the air, or the sun had lost its strength – though there was not a cloud in the sky. Then he remembered; a partial eclipse was in progress.

'This is it,' he said grimly. 'We're going home. Leave all the equipment behind – we won't need it again.'

Now, he hoped, one piece of planning was about to prove its worth. He had selected London for this raid because no other town was so close to a stairway; the foot of Beta was only four kilometers away.

They set off at the steady, loping trot which was the most comfortable mode of travelling at half a gravity. Norton set a pace which, he estimated, would get them to the edge of the plain without exhaustion, and in the minimum of time. He was acutely aware of the eight kilometers they would still have to climb when they had reached Beta, but he would feel much safer when they had actually started the ascent.

The first tremor came when they had almost reached the stairway. It was very slight, and instinctively Norton turned towards the south, expecting to see another display of fireworks around the Horns. But Rama never seemed to repeat itself exactly; if there were any electrical discharges above those needle-sharp mountains, they were too faint to be seen.

'Bridge,' he called, 'did you notice that?'

'Yes, Skipper – very small shock. Could be another attitude change. We're watching the rate gyro – nothing yet. Just a minute! Positive reading! Can just detect it – less than a microradian per second, but holding.'

So Rama was beginning to turn, though with almost imperceptible slowness. Those earlier shocks might have been a false alarm – but this, surely, was the real thing.

'Rate increasing – five microrad. Hello, did you feel *that* shock?'

'We certainly did. Get all the ship's systems operational. We may have to leave in a hurry.'

'Do you expect an orbit change already? We're still a long way from perihelion.'

'I don't think Rama works by our textbooks. Nearly at Beta. We'll rest there for five minutes.'

Five minutes was utterly inadequate, yet it seemed an age. For there was now no doubt that the light was failing, and failing fast.

Though they were all equipped with flashlights, the thought of darkness here was now intolerable; they had grown so psychologically accustomed to the endless day that it was hard to remember the conditions under which they had first explored this world. They felt an overwhelming urge to escape – to get out into the light of the Sun, a kilometre away on the other side of these cylindrical walls.

'Hub Control!' called Norton. 'Is the searchlight operating? We may need it in a hurry.'

'Yes, Skipper. Here it comes.'

A reassuring spark of light started to shine eight kilometers above their heads. Even against the now fading day of Rama, it looked surprisingly feeble; but it had served them before, and would guide them once again if they needed it.

This, Norton was grimly aware, would be the longest and most nerve-wracking climb they had ever done. Whatever happened, it would be impossible to hurry; if they over-exerted themselves, they would simply collapse somewhere on that vertiginous slope, and would have to wait until their protesting muscles permitted them to continue. By this time, they must be one of the fittest crews that had ever carried out a space mission; but there were limits to what flesh and blood could do.

After an hour's steady plodding they had reached the fourth section of the stairway, about three kilometres from the plain. From now on, it would be much easier; gravity was already down to a third of Earth value. Although there had been minor shocks from time to time, no other unusual phenomena had occurred, and there was still plenty of light. They began to feel more optimistic, and even to wonder if they had left too soon. One thing was certain, however; there was no going back. They had all walked for the last time on the plain of Rama.

It was while they were taking a ten-minute rest on the fourth platform that Joe Calvert suddenly exclaimed:

'What's that noise, Skipper?'

'Noise! – I don't hear anything.'

'High-pitched whistle – dropping in frequency, you *must* hear it.'

'Your ears are younger than mine – oh, now I do.'

The whistle seemed to come from everywhere. Soon it was loud, even piercing, and falling swiftly in pitch. Then it suddenly stopped.

A few seconds later it came again, repeating the same sequence. It had all the mournful, compelling quality of a lighthouse siren sending out its warnings into the fog-shrouded night. There was a message here, and an urgent one. It was not designed for their ears, but they understood it. Then, as if to make doubly sure, it was reinforced by the lights themselves.

They dimmed almost to extinction, then started to flash. Brilliant beads, like ball lightning, raced along the six narrow valleys that had once illuminated this world. They moved from both Poles towards the Sea in a synchronized, hypnotic rhythm which could have only one meaning. 'To the Sea!' the lights were calling. 'To the Sea!' And the summons was hard to resist; there was not a man who did not feel a compulsion to turn back, and to seek oblivion in the water of Rama.

'Hub Control!' Norton called urgently. 'Can you see what's happening?'

The voice of Pieter came back to him; he sounded awed, and more than a little frightened.

'Yes, Skipper. I'm looking across at the Southern continent. There are still scores of biots over there – including some big ones. Cranes, Bulldozers – lots of Scavengers. And they're all rushing back to the Sea faster than I've ever seen them move before. There goes a Crane – right over the edge! Just like Jimmy, but going down a lot quicker ... it smashed to pieces when it hit ... and here come the Sharks – they're tearing into it ... ugh; it's not a pleasant sight ...

'Now I'm looking at the plain. Here's a Bulldozer that seems to have broken down ... it's going round and round in circles. Now a couple of Crabs are tearing into it, pulling it to pieces ... Skipper, I think you'd better get back right away.'

'Believe me,' Norton said with deep feeling, 'we're coming just as quickly as we can.'

Rama was battening down the hatches, like a ship preparing for a storm. That was Norton's overwhelming impression, though he could not have put it on a logical basis. He no longer felt completely rational; two compulsions were warring in his mind – the need to escape, and the desire to obey those bolts of lightning that still flashed across the sky, ordering him to join the biots in their march to the sea.

One more section of stairway – another ten-minute pause, to let the fatigue poisons drain from his muscles. Then on again – another two kilometres to go, but let's try not to think about that—

The maddening sequence of descending whistles abruptly ceased. At the same moment, the fireballs racing along the slots of the Straight Valleys stopped their seaward strobing; Rama's six linear suns were once more continuous bands of light.

But they were fading fast, and sometimes they flickered, as if tremendous jolts of energy were being drained from waning power sources. From time to time, there were slight tremors underfoot; the bridge reported that Rama was still swinging with imperceptible slowness, like a compass needle responding to a weak magnetic field. This was perhaps reassuring; it was when Rama *stopped* its swing that Norton would really begin to worry.

All the biots had gone, so Pieter reported. In the whole interior of Rama, the only movement was that of human beings, crawling with painful slowness up the curving face of the north dome.

Norton had long since overcome the vertigo he had felt on that first ascent, but now a new fear was beginning to creep into his mind. They were so vulnerable here, on this endless climb from plain to Hub. Suppose that, when it had completed its attitude change, Rama started to accelerate?

Presumably its thrust would be along the axis. If it was in the northward direction, that would be no problem; they would be held a little more firmly against the slope which they were ascending. But if it was towards the south, they might be swept off into space, to fall back eventually on the plain far below.

He tried to reassure himself with the thought that any possible acceleration would be very feeble. Dr Perera's calculations had been most convincing; Rama could not possibly accelerate at more than a fiftieth of a gravity, or the Cylindrical Sea would climb the southern cliff and flood an entire continent. But Perera had been in a comfortable study back on Earth, not with kilometres of overhanging metal apparently about to crash down upon his head. And perhaps Rama was designed for periodic flooding—

No, that was ridiculous. It was absurd to imagine that all these trillions of tons could suddenly start moving with sufficient acceleration to shake him loose. Nevertheless, for all the remainder of the ascent, Norton never let himself get far from the security of the handrail.

Lifetimes later, the stairway ended; only a few hundred metres of vertical, recessed ladder were left. It was no longer necessary to climb this section since one man at the Hub, hauling on a cable, could easily hoist another against the rapidly diminishing gravity. Even at the bottom of the ladder a man weighed less than five kilos; at the top, practically zero.

So Norton relaxed in the sling, grasping a rung from time to time to counter the feeble Coriolis force still trying to push him off the ladder. He almost forgot his knotted muscles, as he had his last view of Rama.

It was about as bright now as a full moon on Earth; the overall scene was perfectly clear, but he could no longer make out the finer details. The South Pole was now partially obscured by a glowing mist; only the peak of Big Horn protruded through it – a small, black dot, seen exactly head-on.

The carefully-mapped but still unknown continent beyond the Sea was the same apparently random patchwork that it had always been. It was too foreshortened, and too full of complex detail, to reward visual examination, and Norton scanned it only briefly.

He swept his eyes round the encircling band of the Sea, and noticed for the first time a regular pattern of disturbed water, as if waves were breaking over reefs set at geometrically precise intervals. Rama's manoeuvring was having some effect, but a very slight one. He was sure that Sergeant Barnes would have sailed forth happily under these conditions, had he asked her to cross the Sea in her lost *Resolution*.

New York, London, Paris, Moscow, Rome ... he said farewell to all the cities of the northern continent, and hoped the Ramans would forgive him for any damage he had done. Perhaps they would understand that it was all in the cause of science.

Then, suddenly, he was at the Hub, and eager hands reached out to grab him, and to hurry him through the airlocks. His overstrained legs and arms were trembling so uncontrollably that he was almost unable to help himself, and he was content to be handled like a half-paralysed invalid.

The sky of Rama contracted above him, as he descended into the central crater of the Hub. As the door of the inner airlock shut off the view for ever, he found himself thinking: 'How strange that night should be falling, now that Rama is closest to the sun!'

44 SPACE DRIVE

A hundred kilometres was an adequate safety margin, Norton had decided. Rama was now a huge black rectangle, exactly broadside-on, eclipsing the sun. He had used this opportunity to fly *Endeavour* completely into shadow, so that load could be taken off the ship's cooling systems and some overdue maintenance could be carried out. Rama's protective cone of darkness might disappear at any moment, and he intended to make as much use of it as he could.

Rama was still turning; it had now swung through almost fifteen degrees, and it was impossible to believe that some major orbit change was not imminent. On the United Planets, excitement had now reached a pitch of hysteria, but only a faint echo of this came to *Endeavour*. Physically and emotionally, her crew was exhausted; apart from a skeleton watch, everyone had slept for twelve hours after take-off from the North Polar Base. On doctor's orders, Norton himself had used electro-sedation; even so, he had dreamed that he was climbing an infinite stairway.

The second day back on ship, everything had almost returned to normal; the exploration of Rama already seemed part of another life. Norton started to deal with the accumulated office work and to make plans for the future; but he refused the requests for interviews that had somehow managed to insinuate themselves into the Survey and even spaceguard radio circuits. There were no messages from Mercury, and the UP General Assembly had adjourned its session, though it was ready to met again at an hour's notice.

Norton was having his first good night's sleep, thirty hours after leaving Rama, when he was rudely shaken back to consciousness. He cursed groggily, opened a bleary eye at Karl Mercer – and then, like any good commander, was instantly wide awake.

'It's stopped turning?'

'Yes. Steady as a rock.'

'Let's go to the bridge.'

The whole ship was awake; even the simps knew that something was afoot, and made anxious, meeping noises until Sergeant McAndrews reassured them with swift hand-signals. Yet as Norton slipped into his chair and fastened the restraints round his waist, he wondered if this might be yet another false alarm.

Rama was now foreshortened into a stubby cylinder, and the searing rim of the sun had peeked over one edge. Norton jockeyed *Endeavour* gently back into the umbra of the artificial eclipse, and saw the pearly splendour of the corona reappear across a background of the brighter stars. There was one huge prominence, at least half a million kilometres high, that had climbed so far from the sun that its upper branches looked like a tree of crimson fire.

So now we have to wait, Norton told himself. The important thing is not to get bored, to be ready to react at a moment's notice, to keep all the instruments aligned and recording, no matter how long it takes ...

That was strange. The star field was shifting, almost as if he had actuated the Roll thrusters. But he had touched no controls, and if there had been any real movement, he would have sensed it at once.

'Skipper!' said Calvert urgently from the Nav position, 'we're rolling – look at the stars! *But I'm getting no instrument readings!*'

'Rate gyros operating?'

'Perfectly normal – I can see the zero jitter. But we're rolling several degrees a second!'

'That's impossible!'

'Of course it is – but look for yourself ...'

When all else failed, a man had to rely on eyeball instrumentation. Norton could not doubt that the star field was indeed slowly rotating – there went Sirius, across the rim of the port. Either the universe, in a reversion of pre-Copernican cosmology, had suddenly decided to revolve around *Endeavour*; or the stars were standing still, and the ship was turning.

The second explanation seemed rather more likely, yet it involved apparently insoluble paradoxes. If the ship was really turning at this rate, he would have *felt* it – literally by the seat of his pants, as the old saying went. And the gyros could not all have failed, simultaneously and independently.

Only one answer remained. Every atom of *Endeavour* must be in the grip of some force – and only a powerful gravitational field could produce this effect. At least, no other *known* field ...

Suddenly, the stars vanished. The blazing disc of the sun had emerged from behind the shield of Rama, and its glare had driven them from the sky.

'Can you get a radar reading? What's the Doppler?'

Norton was fully prepared to find that this too was inoperative, but he was wrong.

Rama was under way at last, accelerating at the modest rate of 0.015 gravities. Dr Perera, Norton told himself, would be pleased; he had predicted a maximum of 0.02. And *Endeavour* was somehow caught in its wake like a piece of flotsam, whirling round and round behind a speeding ship ...

Hour after hour, that acceleration held constant; Rama was falling away from *Endeavour* at steadily increasing speed. As its distance grew, the anomalous behaviour of the ship slowly ceased; the normal laws of inertia started to operate again. They could only guess at the energies in whose backlash they had been briefly caught, and Norton was thankful that he had stationed *Endeavour* at a safe distance before Rama had switched on its drive.

As to the nature of that drive, one thing was now certain, even though all else was mystery. There were no jets of gas, no beams of ions or plasma thrusting Rama into its new orbit. No one put it better than Sergeant-Professor Myron when he said, in shocked disbelief: 'There goes Newton's Third Law.'

It was Newton's Third law, however, upon which *Endeavour* had to depend the next day, when she used her very last reserves of propellent to bend her own orbit outwards from the sun. The change was slight, but it would increase her perihelion distance by ten million kilometres. That was the difference between running the ship's cooling system at ninety-five per cent capacity – and a certain fiery death.

When they had completed their own manoeuvre, Rama was two hundred thousand kilometres away, and difficult to see against the glare of the sun. But they could still obtain accurate radar measurements of its orbit; and the more they observed, the more puzzled they became.

They checked the figures over and over again, until there was no escaping from the unbelievable conclusion. It looked as if all the fears of the Hermians, the heroics of Rodrigo, and the rhetoric of the General Assembly, had been utterly in vain.

What a cosmic irony, said Norton as he looked at his final figures, if after a million years of safe guidance Rama's computers had made one trifling error – perhaps changing the sign of an equation from plus to minus.

Everyone had been so certain that Rama would lose speed, so that it could be captured by the sun's gravity and thus become a new planet of the solar system. It was doing just the opposite.

It was gaining speed – and in the worst possible direction.

Rama was falling ever more swiftly into the sun.

45 PHOENIX

As the details of its new orbit became more and more clearly defined, it was hard to see how Rama could possibly escape disaster. Only a handful of comets had ever passed as close to the sun; at perihelion, it would be less than half a million kilometres above that inferno of fusing hydrogen. No solid material could withstand the temperature of such an approach; the tough alloy that comprised Rama's hull would start to melt at ten times that distance.

Endeavour had now passed its own perihelion, to everyone's relief, and was slowly increasing its distance from the sun. Rama was far ahead on its closer, swifter orbit, and already appeared well inside the outermost fringes of the corona. The ship would have a grandstand view of the drama's final stage.

Then, five million kilometres from the sun, and still accelerating, Rama started to spin its cocoon. Until now, it had been visible under the maximum power of *Endeavour's* telescopes as a tiny bright bar; suddenly it began to scintillate, like a star seen through horizon mists. It almost seemed as if it was disintegrating; when he saw the image breaking up, Norton felt a poignant sense of grief at the loss of so much wonder. Then he realised that Rama was still there, but that it was surrounded by a shimmering haze.

And then it was gone. In its place was a brilliant, star-like object, showing no visible disc – as if Rama had suddenly contracted into a tiny ball.

It was some time before they realised what had happened. Rama had indeed disappeared: it was now surrounded by a perfectly reflecting sphere, about a hundred kilometres in diameter. All that they could now see was the reflection of the sun itself, on the curved portion that was closest to them. Behind this protective bubble, Rama was presumably safe from the solar inferno.

As the hours passed, the bubble changed its shape. The image of the sun became elongated, distorted. The sphere was turning into an ellipsoid, its long axis pointed in the direction of Rama's flight. It was then that the first anomalous reports started coming in from the robot observatories, which, for almost two hundred years, had been keeping a permanent watch on the sun.

Something was happening to the solar magnetic field, in the region around Rama. The million-kilometre-long lines of force that threaded the corona, and drove its wisps of fiercely ionized gas at speeds which sometimes defied even the crushing gravity of the sun, were shaping themselves around that glittering ellipsoid. Nothing was yet visible to the eye, but the orbiting instruments reported every change in magnetic flux and ultra-violet radiation.

And presently, even the eye could see the changes in the corona. A faintly-glowing tube or tunnel, a hundred thousand kilometres long, had appeared high in the outer atmosphere of the sun. It was slightly curved, bending along the orbit which Rama was tracing, and Rama itself – or the protective cocoon around it – was visible as a glittering head racing faster and faster down that ghostly tube through the corona.

For it was still gaining speed; now it was moving at more than two thousand kilometres a second, and there was no question of it ever remaining a captive of the sun. Now, at last, the Raman strategy was obvious; they had come so close to the sun merely to tap its energy at the source, and to speed themselves even faster on the way to their ultimate unknown goal ...

And presently it seemed that they were tapping more than energy. No one could ever be certain of this, because the nearest observing instruments were thirty million kilometres away, but there were definite indications that matter was flowing from the sun *into Rama itself*, as if it was replacing the leakages and losses of ten thousand centuries in space.

Faster and faster Rama swept around the sun moving now more swiftly than any object that had ever travelled through the solar system. In less than two hours, its direction of motion had swung through more than ninety degrees, and it had given a final, almost contemptuous proof of its total lack of interest in all the worlds whose peace of mind it had so rudely disturbed.

It was dropping out of the Ecliptic, down into the southern sky, far below the plane in which all the planets move. Though that, surely, could not be its ultimate goal, it was aimed squarely at the Greater Magellanic Cloud, and the lonely gulfs beyond the Milky Way.

46 INTERLUDE

'Come in,' said Commander Norton absentmindedly at the quiet knock on his door.

'Some news for you, Bill. I wanted to give it first, before the crew gets into the act. And anyway, it's my department.'

Norton still seemed far away. He was lying with his hands clasped under his head, eyes half shut, cabin light low – not really drowsing, but lost in some reverie or private dream.

He blinked once or twice, and was suddenly back in his body.

'Sorry Laura – I don't understand. What's it all about?'

'Don't say you've forgotten!'

'Stop teasing, you wretched woman. I've had a few things on my mind recently.'

Surgeon-Commander Ernst slid a captive chair across in its slots and sat down beside him.

'Though interplanetary crises come and go, the wheels of Martian bureaucracy grind steadily away. But I suppose Rama helped. Good thing you didn't have to get permission from the Hermians as well.'

Light was dawning.

'Oh – Port Lowell has issued the permit!'

'Better than that – it's already being acted on.' Laura glanced at the slip of paper in her hand. 'Immediate,' she read. 'Probably right now, your new son is being conceived. Congratulations.'

'Thank you. I hope he hasn't minded the wait.'

Like every astronaut, Norton had been sterilized when he entered the service; for a man who would spend years in space, radiation-induced mutation was not a risk – it was a certainty. The spermatozoon that had just delivered its cargo of genes on Mars, two hundred million kilometres away, had been frozen for thirty years, awaiting its moment of destiny.

Norton wondered if he would be home in time for the birth. He had earned rest, relaxation – such normal family life as an astronaut could ever know. Now that the mission was essentially over, he was beginning to unwind, and to think once more about his own future, and that of both his families. Yes, it would be good to be home for a while, and to make up for lost time – in many ways ...

'This visit,' protested Laura rather feebly, 'was purely in a professional capacity.'

'After all these years,' replied Norton, 'we know each other better than that. Anyway, you're off duty now.'

'*Now* what are you thinking?' demanded Surgeon-Commander Ernst, very much later. 'You're not becoming sentimental, I hope.'

'Not about us. About Rama. I'm beginning to miss it.'

'Thanks very much for the compliment.'

Norton tightened his arms around her. One of the nicest things about weightlessness, he often thought, was that you could really hold someone all night, without cutting off the circulation. There were those who claimed that love at one gee was so ponderous that they could no longer enjoy it.

'It's a well-known fact, Laura, than men, unlike women, have *two*-track minds. But seriously – well, *more* seriously – I do feel a sense of loss.'

'I can understand that.'

'Don't be so clinical; that's not the only reason. Oh, never mind.' He gave up. It was not easy to explain, even to himself.

He had succeeded beyond all reasonable expectation; what his men had discovered in Rama would keep scientists busy for decades. And, above all, he had done it without a single casualty.

But he had also failed. One might speculate endlessly, but the nature and the purpose of the Ramans was still utterly unkown. They had used the solar system as a refueling stop – as a booster station – call it what you will, and had then spurned it completely, on their way to more important business. They would probably never even know that the human race existed; such monumental indifference was worse than any deliberate insult.

When Norton had glimpsed Rama for the last time, a tiny star hurtling outwards beyond Venus, he knew that part of his life was over. He was only fifty-five, but he felt he had left his youth down there on the curving plain, among mysteries and wonders now receding inexorably beyond the reach of man. Whatever honours and achievements the future brought him, for the rest of his life he would be haunted by a sense of anticlimax, and the knowledge of opportunities missed.

So he told himself; but even then, he should have known better.

And on far-off Earth, Dr Carlisle Perera had as yet told no one how he had woken from a restless sleep with the message from his subconscious still echoing in his brain:

The Ramans do everything in threes.

RAMA II

1 RAMA RETURNS

The great radar pulse generator Excalibur, powered by nuclear explosions, had been out of service for almost half a century. It had been designed and developed in a frantic effort during the months following the transit of Rama through the solar system. When it was first declared operational in 2132, Excalibur's announced purpose was to give Earth ample warning of any future alien visitors: one as gigantic as Rama could be detected at interstellar distances – years, it was hoped, before it could have any effect on human affairs.

The decision to build Excalibur had been made even before Rama had passed perihelion. As the first extraterrestrial visitor rounded the sun and headed out toward the stars, armies of scientists studied the data from the only mission that had been able to rendezvous with the intruder.

Rama, they announced, was an intelligent robot with absolutely no interest in our solar system or its inhabitants. The official report offered no explanations for the many mysteries encountered by the investigators; however, the experts did convince themselves that they understood one basic principle of Raman engineering. Since most of the major systems and subsystems encountered inside Rama by the human explorers had two functional backups, it appeared that the aliens engineered everything in threes. Therefore, since the entire giant vehicle was assumed to be a machine, it was considered highly likely that two more Rama spacecraft would be following the first visitor.

But no new spaceships entered the solar neighbourhood from the empty reaches of interstellar space. As the years passed the people on Earth confronted more pressing problems. Concern about the Ramans, or whoever it was that had created that drab cylinder fifty kilometres long, abated as the lone alien incursion passed into history. The visit of Rama continued to intrigue many scholars, but most members of the human species were forced to pay attention to other issues. By the early 2140s the world was in the grip of a severe economic crisis. There was no money left to maintain Excalibur. Its few scientific discoveries could not justify the enormous expense of assuring the safety of its operation. The great nuclear pulse generator was abandoned.

Forty-five years later it took thirty-three months to return Excalibur to operational status. The primary justification for the refurbishment of Excalibur was scientific. During the intervening years radar science had flourished and produced new methods of data interpretation that had greatly enhanced the value of the Excalibur observations. As the generator again took images of the distant heavens, almost nobody on Earth was expecting the arrival of another Rama spacecraft.

The operations manager at Excalibur Station did not even inform his supervisor the first time the strange blip appeared on his data processing display. He thought it was an artifact, a bogey created by an anomalous processing algorithm. When the signature repeated several times, however, he paid closer attention. The manager called in the chief Excalibur scientist, who analysed the data and decided the new object was a long period comet. It was another two months before a graduate student proved that the signature belonged to a smooth body at least forty kilometres in its longest dimension.

By 2179 the world knew that the object hurtling through the solar system toward the inner planets was a second extraterrestrial spacecraft. The International Space Agency (ISA) concentrated its resources to prepare a mission that would intercept the intruder just inside the orbit of Venus in late February of 2200. Again the eyes of humanity looked outward, toward the stars, and the deep philosophical questions raised by the first Rama were again debated by the populace on Earth. As the new visitor drew nearer and its physical characteristics were more carefully resolved by the host of sensors aimed in its direction, it was confirmed that this alien spacecraft, at least from the outside, was identical to its predecessor. Rama had returned. Mankind had a second appointment with destiny.

2 TEST AND TRAINING

The bizarre metallic creature inched along the wall, crawling up toward the overhang. It resembled a skinny armadillo, its jointed snail body covered by a thin shell that curled over and around a compact grouping of electronic gadgetry astride the middle of its three sections. A helicopter hovered about two metres away from the wall. A long flexible arm with a pincer on the end extended from the nose of the helicopter and just missed closing its jaws around the odd creature.

'Dammit,' muttered Janos Tabori, 'this is almost impossible with the 'copter bouncing around. Even in perfect conditions it's hard to do precision work with these claws at full extension.' He glanced over at the pilot. 'And why can't this fantastic flying machine keep its altitude and attitude constant?'

'Move the helicopter closer to the wall,' ordered Dr David Brown.

Hiro Yamanaka looked at Brown without expression and entered a command into the control console. The screen in front of him flashed red and printed out the message, COMMAND UNACCEPTABLE. INSUFFICIENT TOLERANCES. Yamanaka said nothing. The helicopter continued to hover in the same spot.

'We have fifty centimetres, maybe seventy-five, between the blades and the wall,' Brown thought out loud. 'In another two or three minutes the biot will be safe under the overhang. Let's go to manual and grab it. Now. No mistakes this time, Tabori.'

For an instant a dubious Hire Yamanaka stared at the balding, bespectacled scientist sitting in the seat behind him. Then the pilot turned, entered another command into the console, and switched the large black lever to the left position. The monitor flashed, IN MANUAL MODE. NO AUTOMATIC PROTECTION. Yamanaka gingerly eased the helicopter closer to the wall.

Engineer Tabori was ready. He inserted his hands in the instrumented gloves and practised opening and closing the jaws at the end of the flexible arm. Again the arm extended and the two mechanical mandibles deftly closed around the jointed snail and its shell. The feedback loops from the sensors on the claws told Tabori, through his gloves, that he had successfully captured his prey. 'I've got it,' he shouted exultantly. He began the slow process of bringing the quarry back into the helicopter.

A sudden draught of wind rolled the helicopter to the left and the arm with the biot banged against the wall. Tabori felt his grip loosening. 'Straighten it up,' he cried, continuing to retract the arm. While Yamanaka was struggling to null the rolling motion of the helicopter, he inadvertently tipped the nose down just slightly. The three crew members heard the sickening sound of the metal rotor blades crashing against the wall.

The Japanese pilot immediately pushed the emergency button and the craft returned to automatic control. In less than a second, a whining alarm sounded and the cockpit monitor flashed red. EXCESSIVE DAMAGE. HIGH PROBABILITY OF FAILURE. EJECT CREW. Yamanaka did not hesitate. Within moments he blasted out of the cockpit and had his parachute deployed. Tabori and Brown followed. As soon as the Hungarian engineer removed his hands from the special gloves, the claws at the end of the mechanical arm relaxed and the armadillo creature fell the hundred metres to the flat plain below, smashing into thousands of tiny pieces.

The pilotless helicopter descended erratically toward the plain. Even with its onboard automatic landing algorithm active and in complete control, the damaged flying machine bounced hard on its struts when it hit the ground and tipped over on its side. Not far from the helicopter's landing site, a portly man, wearing a brown military suit covered with ribbons, jumped down from an open elevator. He had just descended from the mission control centre and was clearly agitated as he walked briskly to a waiting rover. He was followed by a scrambling lithe blonde woman in an ISA flight suit with camera equipment hanging over both her shoulders. The military man was General Valeriy Borzov, commander-in-chief of Project Newton. 'Anyone hurt?' he asked the occupant of the rover, electrical engineer Richard Wakefield.

'Janos apparently banged his shoulder pretty hard during the ejection. But Nicole just radioed that he had no broken bones or separations, only a lot of bruises.'

General Borzov climbed into the front seat of the rover beside Wakefield, who was sitting behind the vehicle control panel. The blonde woman, video journalist Francesca Sabatini, stopped recording the scene and started to open the back door of the rover. Borzov abruptly waved her away. 'Go check on des Jardins and Tabori,' he said, pointing across the level plain. 'Wilson's probably there already.'

Borzov and Wakefield headed in the opposite direction in the rover. They travelled about four hundred metres before they pulled alongside a slight man, about fifty, in a new flight suit. David Brown was busy folding up his parachute and replacing it in a stuff bag. General Borzov stepped down from the rover and approached the American scientist.

'Are you all right, Dr Brown?' the general asked, obviously impatient to dispense with the preliminaries.

Brown nodded but did not reply. 'In that case,' General Borzov continued in a measured tone, 'perhaps you could tell me what you were thinking about when you ordered Yamanaka to go to manual. It might be better if we discussed it here, away from the rest of the crew.'

'Did you even see the warning lights?' Borzov added after a lengthy silence. 'Did you consider, even for a moment, that the safety of the other cosmonauts might be jeopardized by the manoeuvre?'

Dr David Brown eventually looked over at Borzov with a sullen, baleful stare. When he finally spoke, his speech was clipped and strained, belying the emotion he was suppressing. 'It seemed reasonable to move the helicopter just a little closer to the target. We had some clearance left and it was the only way that we could have captured the biot. Our mission, after all, is to bring home—'

'You don't need to tell me what our mission is,' Borzov interrupted with passion. 'Remember, I helped write the policies myself. And I will remind you again that the number one priority, *at all times,* is the safety of the crew. Especially during these simulations ... I must tell you that I am absolutely flabbergasted by this crazy stunt of yours. The helicopter is damaged, Tabori is injured, you're lucky that nobody was killed.'

David Brown was no longer paying attention to General Borzov. He had turned around to finish stuffing his parachute into its transparent package. From the set of his shoulders and the energy he was expending on this routine task, it was obvious that he was very angry.

Borzov returned to the rover. After waiting for several seconds he offered Dr Brown a ride back to the base. The American shook his head without saying anything, hoisted his pack onto his back, and walked off in the direction of the helicopter and the elevator.

3 CREW CONFERENCE

Outside the meeting room in the training facility, Janos Tabori was sitting on an auditorium chair underneath an array of small but powerful portable lights. 'The distance to the simulated biot was at the limit of the reach of the mechanical arm,' he explained to the tiny camera that Francesca Sabatini was holding. 'Twice 1 tried to grab it and failed. Dr Brown then decided to put the helicopter on manual and take it a little closer to the wall. We caught some wind ...'

The door from the conference room opened and a smiling, ruddy face appeared. 'We're all here waiting for you,' said General O'Toole pleasantly. 'I think Borzov's becoming a little impatient.'

Francesca switched off the lights and put her video camera back in the pocket of her flight suit. 'All right, my Hungarian hero,' she said with a laugh, 'we'd better stop for now. You know how our leader dislikes waiting.' She walked over and put her arms gently around the small man. She patted him on his bandaged shoulder. 'But we're really glad you're all right.'

A handsome black man in his early forties had been sitting just out of the camera frame during the interview, taking notes on a flat, rectangular keyboard about a foot square. He followed Francesca and Janos into the conference room. 'I want to do a feature this week on the new design concepts in the teleoperation of the arm and the glove,' Reggie Wilson whispered to Tabori as they sat down. 'There are a bunch of my readers out there who find all this technical crap absolutely fascinating.'

'I'm glad that the three of you could join us,' Borzov's sarcastic voice boomed across the conference room. 'I was starting to think that perhaps a crew meeting was an imposition on all of you, an activity that interrupted the far more important tasks of reporting our misadventures or writing erudite scientific and engineering papers.' He pointed at Reggie Wilson, whose ubiquitous flat keyboard was on the table in front of him. 'Wilson, believe it or not, you're supposed to be a member of this crew first and a journalist second. Just one time do you think you can put that damn thing away and listen? I have a few things to say and I want them to be off the record.'

Wilson removed the keyboard and put it in his briefcase. Borzov stood up and walked around the room as he talked. The table in the crew conference room was a long oval about two metres across at its widest point. There were twelve places around the table (guests and observers, when they attended, sat in the extra chairs over against the walls), each one equipped with a computer keyboard and monitor slightly inset into the surface and covered, when not being used, by a polished grain top that matched the quality simulated wood on the rest of the table. As always, the other two military men on the expedition, European admiral Otto Heilmann (the hero of the Council of Governments intercession in the Caracas crisis) and American air force general Michael Ryan O'Toole, flanked Borzov at one end of the oval. The other nine Newton crew members did not always sit in the same seats, a fact that particularly frustrated the compulsively orderly Admiral Heilmann and, to a lesser extent, his commanding officer Borzov.

Sometimes the four 'nonprofessionals' in the crew would cluster together around the other end of the table, leaving the 'space cadets,' as the five cosmonaut graduates of the Space Academy were known, to create a buffer zone in the middle. After almost a year of constant media attention, the public had relegated each member of the Newton dozen to one of three subgroups – the nonpros, consisting of the two scientists and two journalists; the military troika; and the five cosmonauts who did most of the skilled work during the mission.

On this particular day, however, the two nonmilitary groups were thoroughly mixed. The famed Japanese interdisciplinary scientist Shigeru Takagishi, widely regarded as the foremost expert in the world on the first Raman expedition seventy years earlier (and also the author of the *Atlas of Rama* that was required reading for all of the crew), was sitting in the middle of the oval between Soviet pilot Irina Turgenyev and the brilliant but often zany British cosmonaut/electrical engineer Richard Wakefield. Opposite them were life science officer Nicole des Jardins, a statuesque copper brown woman with a fascinating French and African lineage, the quiet, almost mechanical Japanese pilot Yamanaka, and the stunning Signora Sabatini. The final three positions at the 'south' end of the oval, facing the large maps and diagrams of Rama on the opposite wall, were occupied by American journalist Wilson, the inimitable and garrulous Tabori (a Soviet cosmonaut from Budapest), and Dr David Brown. Brown looked very businesslike and serious; he had a set of papers spread out in front of him as the meeting began.

'It is inconceivable to me,' Borzov was saying while he strode purposefully around the room, 'that any of you could ever forget, even for a moment, that you have been selected to go on what could be the most important human mission of all time. But on the basis of this last set of simulations, I must admit that I am beginning to have my doubts about some of you.

'There are those who believe that this Rama craft will be a copy of its predecessor,' Borzov continued, 'and that it will be equally uninterested and uninvolved with whatever trifling creatures come to survey it. I admit it certainly appears to be at least the same size and same configuration, based on the radar data that we have been processing for the past three years. But even if it does turn out to be another dead ship built by aliens that vanished thousands of years ago, this mission is still the most important one of our lifetime. And I would think that it demands the very best effort from each of you.'

The Soviet general paused to collect his thoughts. Janos Tabori started to ask a question but Borzov interrupted him and launched again into his monologue. 'Our performance as a crew on this last set of training exercises has been absolutely abominable. Some of you have been outstanding – you know who you are – but just as many of you have acted as if you had no idea what this mission was about. I am convinced that two or three of you do not even read the relevant procedures or the protocol listings before the exercises begin. I grant you that they are dull and sometimes tedious, but all of you *agreed*, when you accepted your appointments ten months ago, to learn the procedures and to follow the protocols and project policies. Even those of you with no prior flight experience.'

Borzov had stopped in front of one of the large maps on the wall, this one an inset view of one corner of the city of 'New York' inside the first Raman spaceship. The area of tall thin buildings resembling Manhattan skyscrapers, all huddled together on an island in the middle of the Cylindrical Sea, had been partially mapped during the previous human encounter. 'In six weeks we will rendezvous with an unknown space vehicle, perhaps one containing a city like this, and all of mankind will depend on us to represent them. We have no way of knowing what we will find. Whatever preparation we will have completed before then may well be not enough. Our knowledge of our preplanned procedures must be perfect and automatic, so that our brains are free to deal with any new conditions we may encounter.'

The commander sat down at the head of the table. 'Today's exercise was nearly a complete disaster. We could easily have lost three valuable members of our team as well as one of the most expensive helicopters ever built. I want to remind you all, one more time, of the priorities of this mission as agreed to by the International Space Agency and the Council of Governments. The top priority is the safety of the crew. Second priority is the analysis and/ or determination of any threat, if it exists, to the human population of the planet Earth.' Borzov was now looking directly down the table at Brown, who returned the commander's challenging look with a stony stare of his own. 'Only after those two priorities are satisfied and the Raman craft is adjudged harmless does the capturing of one or more of the biots have any significance.'

'I would like to remind General Borzov,' David Brown said almost immediately in his sonorous voice, 'that some of us do not believe the priorities should be blindly applied in a serial fashion. The importance of the biots to the scientific community cannot be overstated. As I have said repeatedly, both in cosmonaut meetings and on my many television news appearances, if this second Rama craft is just like the first – which means that it will ignore our existence completely – and we proceed so slowly that we fail even to capture a single biot before we must abandon the alien ship and return to Earth, then an absolutely unique opportunity for science will have been sacrificed to assuage the collective anxiety of the world's politicians.'

Borzov started to reply but Brown stood up and gestured emphatically with his hands. 'No, no, hear me out. You have essentially accused me of incompetence in my conduct of today's exercise and I have a right to respond.' He held up some computer printout and waved it at Borzov. 'Here are the initial conditions for today's simulation, as posted and defined by *your* engineers. Let me refresh your memory with a few of the more salient points, in case you've forgotten. Background Condition #1: It is near the end of the mission and it has already been firmly established that Rama II is totally passive and represents no threat to the planet Earth. Background Condition #2: During the expedition biots have only been seen sporadically, and never in groups.'

Brown could tell from the body language of the rest of the crew that his presentation had had a successful beginning. He drew a breath and continued. 'I assumed, after reading those background conditions, that this particular exercise might represent the last chance to capture a biot. During the test I kept thinking what it would mean if we could bring one or several of them back to the Earth – in all the history of humanity, the only absolutely certain contact with an extraterrestrial culture took place in 2130 when our cosmonauts boarded that first Rama spaceship.

'Yet the long-term scientific benefit from that encounter was less than it might have been. Granted, we have reams of remote sensing data from that first investigation, including the information from the detailed dissection of the spider biot done by Dr Laura Ernst. But the cosmonauts brought home only one artifact, a tiny piece of some kind of biomechanical flower whose physical characteristics had already irreversibly changed before any of its mysteries could be understood, We have nothing else in the way of souvenirs from that first excursion. No ashtrays, no drinking glasses, not even a transistor from a piece of equipment that would teach us something about Raman engineering. Now we have a second chance.'

Brown looked up at the circular ceiling above him. His voice was full of power. 'If we could somehow find and return two or three different biots to the Earth, and if we could then analyse these creatures to unlock their secrets, then this mission would without doubt be the most significant historical event of all time. For in understanding in depth the engineering minds of the Ramans, we would, in a real sense, achieve a first contact.'

Even Borzov was impressed. As he often did, David Brown had used his eloquence to turn a defeat into a partial victory. The Soviet general decided to alter his tactics, 'Still,' Borzov said in a subdued tone during the pause in Brown's rhetoric, 'we must never forget that human lives are at stake on this mission and that we must do nothing to jeopardize their safety.' He looked around the table at the rest of the crew. 'I want to bring back biots and other samples from Rama as much as any of you,' he continued, 'but I must confess that this blithe assumption that the second craft will be exactly like the first disturbs me a great deal. What evidence do we have from the first encounter that the Ramans, or whoever they are, are benevolent? None at all. It could be dangerous to seize a biot too soon.'

'But there's no way of ever being certain, Commander, one way or the other.' Richard Wakefield spoke from the side of the table between Borzov and Brown. 'Even if we verify that this spaceship is exactly like the first one almost seventy years ago, we still have no information about what will happen once we make a concerted effort to capture a biot. I mean, suppose for a moment that the two ships are just supersophisticated robots engineered millions of years ago by a now vanished race from the opposite side of the galaxy. How can we predict what kinds of subroutines might be programmed into those biots to deal with hostile acts? What if the biots are integral parts, in some way that we have not been able to discern, of the fundamental operation of the ship? Then it would be natural, even though they are machines, that they would be programmed to defend themselves. And it is conceivable that what might look like an initial hostile act on our part could be the trigger that changes the way the entire ship functions. I remember reading about the robot lander that crashed into the ethane sea on Titan in 2012 – it had stored entirely different sequences depending on what it—'

'Halt,' Janos Tabori interrupted with a friendly smile. 'The arcana of the early robotic exploration of the solar system is not on the agenda for today's postmortem.' He looked down the table at Borzov. 'Skipper, my shoulder is hurting, my stomach is empty, and the excitement of today's exercise has left me exhausted. All this talk is wonderful, but if there's no more specific business would it be out of line to suggest an early end to this meeting so that we will have adequate time, for once, to pack our bags?'

Admiral Heilmann leaned forward on the table. 'Cosmonaut Tabori, General Borzov is in charge of the crew meetings. It is up to him to determine—'

The Soviet commander waved his arm at Heilmann. 'Enough, Otto, I think that Janos is right. It has been a long day at the end of an extremely busy seventeen days of activity. This conversation will be better when we are all fresh.'

Borzov stood up. 'All right, we will break for now. The shuttles will leave for the airport right after dinner.' The crew started preparing to leave. 'During your short rest period,' Borzov said as an afterthought, 'I want all of you to think about where we are in the schedule. We have left only two more weeks of simulations here at the training centre before the break for the end-of-the-year holiday. Immediately thereafter we begin the intensive prelaunch activities. This next set of exercises is our last chance to get it right. I expect each of you to return fully prepared for the remaining work – and recommitted to the importance of this mission.'

4 THE GREAT CHAOS

The intrusion of the first Raman spacecraft into the inner solar system in early 2130 had a powerful impact on human history. Although there were no immediate changes in everyday life after the crew headed by Commander Norton returned from encountering Rama I, the clear and unambiguous proof that a vastly superior intelligence existed (or, as a minimum, *had* existed) somewhere else in the universe forced a rethinking of the place of homo sapiens in the overall scheme of the cosmos. It was now apparent that other chemicals, doubtless also fabricated in the great stellar cataclysms of the heavens, had risen to consciousness in some other place, at some other time. Who were these Ramans? Why had they built a giant sophisticated spacecraft and sent it on an excursion into our neighbourhood? Both in public and private conversation, the Ramans were the number one topic of interest for many months.

For well over a year mankind waited more or less patiently for another sign of the Ramans' presence in the universe. Intense telescopic investigations were conducted at all wavelengths to see if any additional information associated with the retreating alien spaceship could be identified. Nothing was found. The heavens were quiet. The Ramans were departing as swiftly and inexplicably as they had arrived.

Once Excalibur was operational and its initial search of the heavens turned up nothing new, there was a noticeable change in the collective human attitude toward that first contact with Rama. Overnight the encounter became a historical event, something that *had* happened and was now completed. The tenor of newspaper and magazine articles that had earlier begun with phrases like 'when the Ramans return ...' changed to 'if there is ever another encounter with the creatures who built the huge spaceship discovered in 2130 ...' What had been a perceived threat, a lien in a sense on future human behaviour, was quickly reduced to a historical curiosity. There was no longer an urgency to deal with such fundamental issues as the return of the Ramans or the destiny of the human race in a universe peopled by intelligent creatures. Mankind relaxed, at least for a moment. Then it exploded in a paroxysm of narcissistic behaviour that made all previous historical periods of individual selfishness pale by comparison.

187

The surge of unabashed self-indulgence on a global scale was easy to understand. Something fundamental in the human psyche had changed as a result of the encounter with Rama I. Prior to that contact, humanity stood alone as the only known example of advanced intelligence in the universe. The idea that humans could, as a group, control their destiny far into the future had been a significant lynchpin in almost every working philosophy of life. That the Ramans existed (or had existed – whatever the tense, the philosophic logic came to the same conclusion) changed everything. Mankind was not unique, maybe not even special. It was just a question of time before the prevailing homocentric notion of the universe was to be irrevocably shattered by clearer awareness of the Others. Thus it was easy to comprehend why the life patterns of most human beings suddenly veered toward self-gratification, reminding literary scholars of a similar time almost exactly five centuries earlier, when Robert Herrick had exhorted the virgins to make the most of their fleeting time in a poem that began, 'Gather Ye Rosebuds While Ye May; Old Time is Still A-Flying ...'

An unrestrained burst of conspicuous consumption and global greed lasted for just under two years. Frantic acquisition of everything the human mind could create was superimposed on a weak economic infrastructure that had been already poised for a downturn in early 2130, when the first Raman spaceship flew through the inner solar system. The looming recession was first postponed throughout 2130 and 2131 by the combined manipulative efforts of governments and financial institutions, even though the fundamental economic weaknesses were never addressed. With the renewed burst of buying in early 2132, the world jumped directly into another period of rapid growth. Production capacities were expanded, stock markets exploded, and both consumer confidence and total employment hit all-time highs. There was unprecedented prosperity and the net result was a short-term but significant improvement in the standard of living for almost all humans.

By the end of the year in 2133, it had become obvious to some of the more experienced observers of human history that the 'Raman Boom' was leading mankind toward disaster. Dire warnings of impending economic doom started being heard above the euphoric shouts of the millions who had recently vaulted into the middle and upper classes. Suggestions to balance budgets and limit credit at all levels of the economy were ignored. Instead, creative effort was expended to come up with one way after another of putting more spending power in the hands of a populace that had forgotten how to say 'wait', much less 'no', to itself.

The global stock market began to sputter in January of 2134 and there were predictions of a coming crash. But to most humans spread around the Earth and throughout the scattered colonies in the solar system, the concept of such a crash was beyond comprehension. After all, the world economy had been expanding for over nine years, the last two years at a rate unparalleled in the previous two centuries. World leaders insisted that they had finally found the mechanisms that could truly inhibit the downturns of the capitalistic cycles. And the people believed them – until early May of 2134.

During the first three months of the year the global stock markets went inexorably down, slowly at first, then in significant drops. Many people, reflecting the superstitious attitude toward cometary visitors that had been prevalent for two thousand years, somehow associated the stock market's difficulties with the return of Halley's Comet. Its appearance starting in March turned out to be far brighter than anyone expected. For weeks scientists all over the world were competing with each other to explain why it was so much more brilliant than originally predicted. After it swooped past perihelion in late March and began to appear in the evening sky in mid-April, its enormous tail dominated the heavens.

In contrast, terrestrial affairs were dominated by the emerging world economic crisis. On May 1, 2134, three of the largest international banks announced that they were insolvent because of bad loans. Within two days a panic had spread around the world. The more than one billion home terminals with access to the global financial markets were used to dump individual portfolios of stocks and bonds. The communications load on the Global Network System was immense. GNS data transfer machines were stretched far beyond their capabilities and design specifications. Data gridlock delayed transactions for minutes, then hours, contributing additional momentum to the panic.

By the end of a week two things were apparent – that over half of the world's stock value had been obliterated and that many individuals, large and small investors alike, who had used their credit options to the maximum, were now virtually penniless. The supporting data bases that kept track of personal bank accounts and automatically transferred money to cover margin calls were flashing disaster messages in almost twenty percent of the houses in the world.

In truth, however, the situation was much much worse. Only a small percentage of the transactions were actually clearing through all the supporting computers because the data rates in all directions were far beyond anything that had ever been anticipated. In computer language, the entire global financial system went into the 'cycle slip' mode. Billions and billions of information transfers at lower priorities were 'postponed' by the network of computers while the higher priority tasks were being serviced first.

The net result of these data delays was that in most cases individual electronic bank accounts were not properly debited, for hours or even days, to account for the mounting stock market losses, Once the individual investors realised what was occurring, they rushed to spend whatever was still showing in their balances before the computers completed all the transactions. By the time governments and financial institutions understood fully what was going on and acted to stop all this frenetic activity, it was too late. The confused system had crashed completely. To reconstruct what had happened required carefully dumping and interleaving the backup checkpoint files stored at a hundred or so remote centres around the world.

For over three weeks the electronic financial management system that governed all money transactions was inaccessible to everybody. Nobody knew how much money he had – or how much anyone else had. Since cash had long ago become obsolete, only eccentrics and collectors had enough bank notes to buy even a week's groceries. People began to barter for necessities. Pledges based on friendship and personal acquaintance enabled many people to survive temporarily. But the pain had only begun. Every time the international management organisation that oversaw the global financial system would announce that they were going to try to come back 'on-line' and would plead with people to stay off their terminals 'except for emergencies', their pleas would be ignored, processing requests would flood the system, and the computers would crash again.

It was only two more weeks before the scientists of the world agreed on an explanation for the additional brightness in the apparition of Halley's Comet. But it was over four months before people could count again on reliable data base information from the GNS. The cost to human society of the enduring chaos was incalculable. By the time normal electronic economic activity had been restored, the world was in a violent financial down-spin that would not bottom out until twelve years later. It would be well over fifty years before the Gross World Product would return to the heights reached before the Crash of 2134.

5 AFTER THE CRASH

There is unanimous agreement that the Great Chaos profoundly altered human civilization in every way. No segment of society was immune. The catalyst for the relatively rapid collapse of the existing institutional infrastructure was the market crash and subsequent breakdown of the global financial system; however, these events would not have been sufficient, by themselves, to project the world into a period of unprecedented depression. What followed the initial crash would have been only a comedy of errors if so many lives had not been lost as a result of the poor planning. Inept world political leaders first denied or ignored the existing economic problems, then overreacted with a suite of individual measures that were baffling and/or inconsistent, and finally threw up their arms in despair as the global crisis deepened and spread. Attempts to coordinate international solutions were doomed to failure by the increasing need of each of the sovereign nations to respond to its own constituency.

In hindsight, it was obvious that the internationalisation of the world that had taken place during the twenty-first century had been flawed in at least one significant way. Although many activities – communications, trade, transportation (including space), currency regulation, peacekeeping, information exchange, and environmental protection, to name the most important – had indeed become international (even interplanetary, considering the space colonies), most of the agreements that established these international institutions contained codicils that allowed the individual nations to withdraw, upon relatively short notice, if the policies promulgated under the accords no longer served the interests of the country in question. In short, each of the nations participating in the creation of an international body had the right to abrogate its national involvement, unilaterally, when it was no longer satisfied with the actions of the group.

The years preceding the rendezvous with the first Raman spaceship in early 2130 had been an extraordinarily stable and prosperous time. After the world recovered from the devastating cometary impact near Padua, Italy, in 2077, there was an entire half century of moderate growth. Except for a few relatively short, and not too severe, economic recessions, living conditions improved in a wide range of countries throughout the time period. Isolated wars and civil disturbances did erupt from time to time, primarily in the undeveloped nations, but the concerted efforts of the global peacekeeping forces always contained these problems before they became too serious. There were no major crises that tested the stability of the new international mechanisms.

Immediately following the encounter with Rama I, however, there were rapid changes in the basic governing apparatus. First, emergency appropriations to handle Excalibur and other large Rama-related projects drained revenues from established programmes. Then, starting in 2132, a loud clamour for tax cuts, to put more money into the hands of the individuals, reduced even further the allocations for needed services. By late 2133, most of the newer international institutions had become understaffed and inefficient. Thus the global market crash took place in an environment where there was already growing doubt in the minds of the populace about the efficacy of the entire network of international organisations. As the financial chaos continued, it was an easy step for the individual nations to stop contributing funds to the very global organisations that might have been able to turn the tide of disaster if they had been used properly, that were vitiated by the near-sighted political leaders.

The horrors of the Great Chaos have been chronicled in thousands of history texts. In the first two years the major problems were skyrocketing unemployment and bankruptcies, both personal and corporate, but these financial difficulties seemed unimportant as the ranks of the homeless and starving continued to swell. Tent and box communities appeared in the public parks of all the big cities by the winter of 2136–37 and the municipal governments responded by striving valiantly to find ways to provide services to them. These services were intended to limit the difficulties created by the supposedly temporary presence of these hordes of idle and underfed individuals. But when the economy did not recover, the squalid tent cities did not disappear. Instead they became permanent fixtures of urban life, growing cancers that were worlds unto themselves with an entire set of activities and interests fundamentally different from the host cities that were supporting them. As more time passed and the tent communities turned into hopeless, restless cauldrons of despair, these new enclaves in the middle of the metropolitan areas threatened to boil over and destroy the very entities that were allowing them to exist. Despite the anxiety caused by this constant Damocles' sword of urban anarchy, the world squeaked through the brutally cold winter of 2137-38 with the basic fabric of modem civilization still more or less intact.

In early 2138 a remarkable series of events occurred in Italy. These events, focused around a single individual named Michael Balatresi, a young Franciscan novitiate who would later become known everywhere as St Michael of Siena, occupied much of the attention of the world and temporarily forestalled the disintegration of the society. Michael was a brilliant combination of genius and spirituality and political skills, a charismatic polyglot speaker with an unerring sense of purpose and timing. He suddenly appeared on the world stage in Tuscany, coming seemingly out of nowhere, with a passionate religious message that appealed to the hearts and minds of many of the world's frightened and/or disenfranchised citizens. His following grew rapidly and spontaneously and paid no heed to international boundaries. He became a potential threat to almost all the identified leadership coteries of the world with his unwavering call for a collective response to the problems besetting the species. When he was martyred under appalling circumstances in June of 2138, mankind's last spark of optimism seemed to perish. The civilized world that had been held together for many months by a flicker of hope and a slim thread of tradition abruptly crumbled into pieces.

The four years from 2138 to 2142 were not good years to be alive. The litany of human woes was almost endless. Famine, disease, and lawlessness were everywhere. Small wars and revolutions were too numerous to count. There was an almost total breakdown in the standard institutions of modern civilization, creating a phantasmagoric life for everyone in the world except the privileged few in their protected retreats. It was a world gone wrong, the ultimate in entropy. Attempts to solve the problems by well-meaning groups of citizens could not work because the solutions they conceived could only be local in scope and the problems were global.

The Great Chaos also extended to the human colonies in space and brought a sudden end to a glorious chapter in the history of exploration. As the economic disaster spread on the home planet, the scattered colonies around the solar system, which could not exist without regular infusions of money, supplies, and personnel, quickly became the forgotten stepchildren of the people on Earth. As a result almost half of the residents of the colonies had left to return home by 2140, the living conditions in their adopted homes having deteriorated to the point where even the twin difficulties of readjustment to Earth's gravity and the terrible poverty throughout the world were preferred over continuing to stay (most likely to die) in the colonies. The emigration process accelerated in 2141 and 2142, years characterized by mechanical breakdowns in the artificial ecosystems at the colonies and the beginning of a disastrous shortage of spare parts for the entire fleet of robot vehicles used to sustain the new settlements.

By 2143 only a very few hard core colonists remained on the Moon and Mars. Communications between Earth and the colonies had become intermittent and erratic. Monies to maintain even the radio links with the outlying settlements were no longer available. The United Planets had ceased to exist two years previously. There was no all-human forum addressing the problems of the species; the Council of Governments would not be formed for five more years. The two remaining colonies struggled vainly to avoid death.

In the following year, 2144, the last significant manned space mission of the time period took place. The mission was a rescue sortie piloted by an amazing Mexican woman named Benita Garcia. Using a jerryrigged spacecraft thrown together from old parts, Ms Garcia and her three-man crew somehow managed to reach the geosynchronous orbit of the lame cruiser *James Martin*, the last interplanetary transport vehicle in service, and save twenty-four members from the crew of a hundred women and children being repatriated from Mars. In every space historian's mind, the rescue of the passengers on the *James Martin* marked the end of an era. Within six more months the last remaining space stations were abandoned and no human lifted off the Earth, bound for orbit, until almost forty years later.

By 2145 the struggling world had managed to see the importance of some of the international organizations neglected and maligned at the beginning of the Great Chaos. The most talented members of mankind, after having eschewed personal political involvement during the benign early decades of the century, began to understand that it would only be through the collective skills of the brightest and most capable humans that any semblance of civilized life could ever be restored. At first the monumental cooperative efforts that resulted were only modestly successful; but they rekindled the fundamental optimism of the human spirit and started the renewal process. Slowly, ever so slowly, the elements of human civilization were put back into place.

It was still another two years before the general recovery finally showed up in economic statistics. By 2147 the Gross World Product had dwindled to 7% of its level six years earlier. Unemployment in the developed nations averaged 35%; in some of the undeveloped nations the combination of unemployed and underemployed amounted to 90% of the population. It is estimated that as many as one hundred million people starved to death during the awful summer of 2142 alone, when a great drought and concomitant famine girdled the world in the tropical regions. The combination of an astronomical death rate from many causes and a minuscule birthrate (for who wanted to bring a child into such a hopeless world?) caused the world's population to drop by almost a billion in the decade ending in 2150.

The experience of the Great Chaos left a permanent scar on an entire generation. As the years passed, and the children born after its conclusion reached adolescence, they were confronted by parents who were cautious to the point of phobia. Life as a teenager in the 2160s and even the 2170s was very strict. The memories of the terrible traumas of their youth during the Chaos haunted the adult generation and made them extremely rigid in their application of parental discipline. To them life was not a joyride at an amusement park. It was a deadly serious affair and only through a combination of solid values, self-control, and a steady commitment to a worthwhile goal was there a chance to achieve happiness.

The society that emerged in the 2170s was therefore dramatically different from the freewheeling laissez-faireism of fifty years earlier. Many very old, established institutions, among them the nation-state, the Roman Catholic church, and the English monarchy, had enjoyed a renaissance during the half century interim. These institutions had prospered because they had adapted quickly and taken leadership positions in the restructuring that followed the Chaos.

By the late 2170s, when a semblance of stability had returned to the planet, interest in space began to build again. A new generation of observation and communication satellites was launched by the reconstituted International Space Agency, one of the administrative arms of the Council of Governments. At first the space activity was cautious and the budgets were very small. Only the developed nations participated actively. When piloted flights recommenced and were successful, a modest schedule of missions was planned for the decade of the 2190s. A new Space Academy to train cosmonauts for those missions opened in 2188 and had its first graduates four years later.

On Earth growth was achingly slow but regular and predictable for most of the twenty years preceding the discovery of the second Raman spaceship in 2196. In a technological sense, mankind was at approximately the same overall level of development in 2196 as it had been, sixty-six years earlier, when the first extraterrestrial craft had appeared. Recent spaceflight experience was much less, to be certain, at the time of the second encounter; however, in certain critical technical areas like medicine and information management, the human society of the last decade of the twenty-second century was considerably more advanced than it had been in 2130. In one other component the civilizations encountered by the two Raman spacecraft were markedly different: Many of the human beings alive in 2196, especially those who were older and held the policy-making positions in the governing structure, had lived through some of the very painful years of the Great Chaos. They knew the meaning of the word 'fear.' And that powerful word shaped their deliberations as they debated the priorities that would guide a human mission to rendezvous with Rama II.

6 LA SIGNORA SABATINI

'S o you were working on your doctorate in physics at SMU when your husband made his famous prediction about supernova 2191a?'

Elaine Brown was sitting in a large soft chair in her living room. She was dressed in a stark brown suit, sexless, with a high-collar blouse. She looked stiff and anxious, as if she were ready for the interview to be completed.

'I was in my second year and David was my dissertation adviser,' she said carefully, her eyes glancing furtively at her husband. He was across the room, watching the proceedings from behind the cameras. 'David worked very closely with his graduate students. Everybody knew that. It was one of the reasons why I choose SMU for my graduate work.'

Francesca Sabatini looked beautiful. Her long blonde hair was flowing freely over her shoulders. She was wearing an expensive white silk blouse, trimmed by a royal blue scarf neatly folded around her neck. Her lounging pants were the same colour as the scarf. She was sitting in a second chair next to Elaine. Two coffee cups were on the small table between them.

'Dr Brown was married at the time, wasn't he? I mean during the period when he was your adviser.'

Elaine reddened perceptibly as Francesca finished her question. The Italian journalist continued to smile at her, a disarmingly ingenuous smile, as if the question she had just asked was as simple and straightforward as two plus two. Mrs Brown hesitated, drew a breath, and then stammered slightly in giving her response. 'In the beginning, yes, I believe that he still was,' she answered. 'But his divorce was final before I finished my degree.' She stopped again and then her face brightened. 'He gave me an engagement ring for a graduation present,'' she said awkwardly.

Francesca Sabatini studied her subject. *I could easily tear you apart on that reply,* she thought rapidly. *With just a couple more questions. But that would not serve my purpose.*

'Okay, cut' Francesca blurted out suddenly. 'That's a wrap. Let's take a look and then you can put all the equipment back in the truck.' The lead cameraman walked over to the side of robot camera #1, which had been programmed to in stay a close-up òn Francesca, and entered three commands into the miniature keyboard on the side of the camera housing. Meanwhile, because Elaine had risen from her seat, robot camera #2 was automatically backing away on its tripod legs and retracting its zoom lens. Another cameraman motioned to Elaine to stand still until he was able to disconnect the second camera.

Within seconds the director had programmed the automatic monitoring equipment to replay the last five minutes of the interview. The output of all three cameras was shown simultaneously, split screen, the composite picture of both Francesca and Elaine occupying the centre of the monitor with the tapes from the two close-up cameras on either side. Francesca was a consummate professional. She could tell quickly that she had the material she needed for this portion of the show. Dr David Brown's wife, Elaine, was young, intelligent, earnest, plain, and not comfortable with the attention being focused on her. And it was all clearly there on tape.

While Francesca was wrapping up the details with her crew and arranging to have the annotated interview composite delivered to her hotel at the Dallas Transportation Complex before her flight in the morning, Elaine Brown came back into the living room with a standard robot server, two different kinds of cheese, a bottle of wine, and plenty of glasses for everyone. Francesca glimpsed a frown on David Brown's face as Elaine announced that there would now be 'a small party' to celebrate the end of the interview.

The crew and Elaine gathered around the robot and the wine. David excused himself and walked out of the living room into the long hall that connected the back of the house, where all the bedrooms were, with the living quarters in the front. Francesca followed him.

'Excuse me, David,' she said. He turned around, his impatience clear. 'Don't forget that we still have some unfinished business. I promised an answer to Schmidt and Hagenest upon my return to Europe. They are anxious to proceed with the project.'

'I haven't forgotten,' he replied. 'I just want to make certain first that your friend Reggie is finished interviewing my children.' He heaved a sigh. 'There are times when I wish I was a total unknown in the world.'

Francesca walked up close to him. 'I don't believe that for a minute,' she said, her eyes fixed on his. 'You're just nervous today because you can't control what your wife and children are saying to Reggie and me. And nothing is more important to you than control.'

Dr Brown started to reply but was interrupted by a shriek of *'Mommeee'* reverberating down the hall from its origin in a distant bedroom. Within seconds a small boy, six or seven years old, swept past David and Francesca and raced pell-mell into the arms of his mother, who was now standing in the doorway connecting the hall and the living room. Some of Elaine's wine sloshed out of her glass from the force of the collision with her son; she unconsciously licked it off her hand as she sought to comfort the little boy.

'What is it, Justin?' she asked.

'That black man broke my dog,' Justin whined between sobs. 'He kicked it in the butt and now I can't make it work.'

The little boy pointed back down the hall. Reggie Wilson and a teenage girl, tall, thin, very serious, were walking toward the rest of the group. 'Dad,' said the girl, her eyes imploring David for help, 'Mr Wilson was talking to me about my pin collection when that damned robot dog came in and bit him on the leg. After peeing on him first. Justin had programmed him to make mischief—'

'She's lying,' the crying little boy interrupted her with a shout. 'She doesn't like Wally. She's never liked Wally.'

Elaine had one hand on the back of her nearly hysterical son and the other firmly around the stem of her wineglass. She would have been unsettled by the scene even if she hadn't noticed the disapproval she was receiving from her husband. She quaffed the wine and put the glass on a nearby bookshelf. 'There, there, Justin,' she said, looking embarrassed, 'calm down and tell Mom what happened.'

'That black man doesn't like me. And I don't like him. Wally knew it, so he bit him. Wally always protects me.'

The girl, Angela, became more agitated. 'I knew something like this would happen. When Mr Wilson was talking to me, Justin kept coming into my room and interrupting us, showing Mr Wilson his games, his pets, his trophies, and even his clothes, Eventually Mr Wilson had to speak sharply to him. Next thing we know Wally is running wild and Mr Wilson has to defend himself.'

'She's a liar, Mom. A big liar. Tell her to stop—'

Dr David Brown had had enough of this commotion. *'Elaine,'* he shouted angrily above the din, 'get ... *him* ... out of here.' He turned to his daughter as his wife pulled the weeping little boy through the door into the living room. 'Angela,' he said, his anger now raw and unconcealed, 'I thought I told you not to fight with Justin today under any circumstances.'

The girl recoiled from her father's attack. Tears welled up in her eyes. She started to say something but Reggie Wilson walked between her and her father. 'Excuse me, Dr Brown,' he interceded, 'Angela really didn't do anything. Her story is basically correct. She—'

'Look, Wilson,' David Brown said sharply, 'if you don't mind, I can handle my own family.' He paused a moment to calm his anger. 'I'm terribly sorry for all this confusion,' he continued in a subdued tone, 'but it will all be finished in another minute or so.' The look he gave his daughter was cold and unkind. 'Go back to your room, Angela. I'll talk to you later. Call your mother and tell her that I want her to pick you up before dinner.'

Francesca Sabatini watched with great interest as the entire scene unfolded. She saw David Brown's frustration, Elaine's lack of self-confidence. *This is perfect,* Francesca thought, *even better than I might have hoped. He will be very easy.*

*

The sleek silver train cruised the North Texas countryside at two hundred and fifty kilometres per hour. Within minutes the lights from the Dallas Transportation Complex appeared on the horizon. The DTC covered a mammoth area, almost twenty-five square kilometres. It was part airport, part train station, part small city. Originally constructed in 2185 both to handle the burgeoning long-distance air traffic and to provide an easy nexus for transferring passengers to the high-speed train system, it had grown, like other similar transportation centres around the world, into an entire community. More than a thousand people, most of whom worked at the DTC and found life easier when there was no commute, lived in the apartments that formed a semicircle around the shopping centre south of the main terminal. The terminal itself housed four major hotels, seventeen restaurants, and over a hundred different shops, including a branch of the chic Donatelli fashion chain.

'I was nineteen at the time,' the young man was saying to Francesca as the train approached the station, 'and had had a very sheltered upbringing. I learned more about love and sex in that ten weeks, watching your series on television, than I had learned in my whole life before. I just wanted to thank you for that programme.'

Francesca accepted the compliments gracefully. She was accustomed to being recognized when she was in public. Wlien the train stopped and she descended onto the platform, Francesca smiled again at the young man and his date. Reggie Wilson offered to carry her camera equipment as they walked toward the people mover that would take them to the hotel. 'Does it ever bother you?' he asked. She looked at him quizzically. 'All the attention, being a public figure?' he added in explanation.

'No,' she answered, 'of course not.' She smiled to herself. *Even after six months this man does not understand me. Maybe he's too engrossed with himself to figure out that some women are as ambitious as men.*

'I knew that your two television series had been popular,' Reggie was saying, 'before I met you during the personnel screening exercises. But I had no idea that it would be impossible to go out to a restaurant or to be seen in a public place without running into one of your fans.'

Reggie continued to chat as the people mover eased out of the train station and into the shopping centre. Near the track at one end of the enclosed mall a large group of people were milling around outside a theatre. The marquee proclaimed that the production inside was *In Any Weather*, by the American playwright Linzey Olsen.

'Did you ever see that play?' Reggie idly asked Francesca. 'I saw the movie when it first came out,' he continued without waiting for her to answer, 'about five years ago. Helen Caudill and Jeremy Temple. Before she was really big. It was a strange story, about two people who had to share a hotel room during a snowstorm in Chicago. They're both married. They fall in love while talking about their failed expectations. As I said, it was a weird play.'

Francesca was not listening. A boy who reminded her of her cousin Roberto had climbed into the car just in front of them at the first stop in the shopping centre. His skin and hair were dark, his facial features handsomely chiseled. *How long has it been since I have seen Roberto?* she wondered. *Must be three years now. It was down in Positano with his wife, Maria.* Francesca sighed and remembered earlier days, from long ago. She could see herself laughing and running on the streets of Orvieto. She was nine or ten, still innocent and unspoiled. Roberto was fourteen. They were playing with a soccer ball in the piazza in front of Il Duomo. She had loved to tease her cousin. He was so gentle, so unaffected. Roberto was the only good thing from her childhood.

The people mover stopped outside the hotel. Reggie was looking at her with a fixed stare. Francesca realised that he had just asked her a question. 'Well?' he said, as they descended from their car.

'I'm sorry, dear,' she answered. 'I was daydreaming again. What did you ask?'

'I didn't know I was that boring,' Reggie said without humour. He turned dramatically to ensure that she was paying attention. 'What choice did you make for dinner tonight? I had narrowed it down to Chinese or Cajun.'

At that particular moment the thought of having dinner with Reggie did not appeal to Francesca. 'I'm very tired tonight,' she said. 'I think I'll just eat by myself in the room and do a little work afterward.' She could have predicted the hurt look on his face. She reached up and kissed him lightly on the lips. 'You can come by my room for a nightcap about ten.'

Once inside her hotel suite, Francesca's first action was to activate her computer terminal and check for messages. She had four altogether. The printed menu told her the originator of each message, the time of its transmission, the duration of the message, and its urgency priority. The Urgency Priority System was a new innovation of International Communications, Inc., one of the three surviving communications companies that were finally flourishing again after massive consolidation during the middle years of the century. A UPS user entered his daily schedule early in the morning and identified what priority messages could interrupt which activities. Francesca had chosen to accept forwarding of only Priority One (Acute Emergency) messages to the terminal at David Brown's house; the taping of David and his family had to be accomplished in one day and she had wanted to minimize the chances of an interruption and delay, The rest of her messages had been retained at the hotel.

She had a single Priority Two message, three minutes long, from Carlo Bianchi. Francesca frowned, entered the proper codes into the terminal, and turned on the video monitor. A suave middle-aged Italian dressed in après-ski clothes, sitting on a couch with a burning fireplace behind him, came into view. 'Buon giomo, cara,' he greeted her. After allowing the video camera to pan around the living room at his new villa in Cortina d'Ampezzo, Signor

Bianchi came right to the point. Why was she refusing to appear in the advertisements for his summer line of sportswear? His company had offered her an incredible amount of money and had even tailored the advertising campaign to pick up on the space theme. The spots would not be shown until after the Newton mission would be over, so there was no conflict with her ISA agreements. Carlo acknowledged that they had had some differences in the past, but according to him they were many years ago. He needed an answer in a week.

Screw you, Carlo, Francesca thought, surprised at the intensity of her reactions. There were few people in the world who could upset Francesca, but Carlo Bianchi was one of them. She entered the necessary commands to record a message to her agent, Darrell Bowman, in London. 'Hi Darrell. It's Francesca in Dallas. Tell that weasel Bianchi I wouldn't do his ads even if he offered me ten million marks. And by the way, since I understand that his main competition these days is Donatelli, why don't you find their advertising director, Gabriela something or other, I met her once in Milano, and let her know that I would be happy to do something for them after Project Newton is over. April or May.' She paused for a moment. 'That's it. Back in Rome tomorrow night. My best to Heather.'

Francesca's longest message was from her husband, Alberto, a tall, greying, distinguished executive almost sixty years old. Alberto ran the Italian division of Schmidt and Hagenest, the multimedia German conglomerate that owned, among other things, over one third of the free newspapers and magazines in Europe as well as the leading commercial television networks in both Germany and Italy. In his transmission Alberto was sitting in the den in their home, wearing a rich charcoal suit and sipping a brandy. His tone was warm, familiar, but more like a father than a husband. He told Francesca that her long interview with Admiral Otto Heilmann had been on the news throughout Europe that day, that he had enjoyed her comments and insights as always, but that he had thought Otto came across as an egomaniac. *Not surprising,* Francesca had mused when she heard her husband's comment, *since he absolutely is. But he is often useful to me.*

Alberto shared some good news about one of his children (Francesca had three stepchildren, all of whom were older than she) before telling her that he missed her and was looking forward to seeing her the next night. *Me too,* Francesca thought before responding to his message. *It is comfortable living with you. I have both freedom and security.*

Four hours later Francesca was standing outside on her balcony, smoking a cigarette in the cold Texas December air. She was wrapped tightly in the thick robe supplied to the rooms by the hotel. *At least it's not like California,* she thought to herself as she pulled a deep drag into her lungs. *At least in Texas some of the hotels do have smoking balconies. Those zealots on the American West Coast would make smoking a felony if they could.*

201

She walked over to the side of the railing so that she would have a better view of a supersonic airliner approaching the airport from the west. In her mind's eye she was inside the plane, as she would be the next day on her flight home to Rome. She imagined that this particular flight had come from Tokyo, the undisputed economic capital of the world before the Great Chaos. After being devastated by their lack of raw materials during the lean years in the middle of the century, the Japanese were now prosperous again as the world returned to a free market. Francesca watched the plane land and then looked up at the sky full of stars above her. She took another pull on her cigarette and then followed the exhaled smoke as it drifted slowly away from her into the air.

And so, Francesca, she reflected, *now comes what may be your greatest assignment. A chance to become immortal? At least I should be remembered a long time as one of the Newton crew.* Her mind turned to the Newton mission itself and briefly conjured up images of fantastic creatures who might have created the pair of gargantuan spaceships and sent them to visit the solar system. But her thoughts jumped back quickly to the real world, to the contracts that David Brown had signed just before she had left his home that afternoon.

That makes us partners, my esteemed Dr Brown. And completes the first phase of my plan. And unless I miss my guess, that was a gleam of interest in your eyes today. Francesca had given David a perfunctory kiss when they had finished discussing and signing the contracts. They had been alone together in his study. For a moment she had thought he was going to return the kiss with a more meaningful one.

Francesca finished her cigarette, stubbed it out in the ashtray, and went back into her hotel room. As soon as she opened the door she could hear the sound of heavy breathing. The oversized bed was in disarray and a naked Reggie Wilson was lying across it on his back, his regular snores disturbing the silence of the suite. *You have great equipment, my friend,* she commented silently, *both for life and for lovemaking. But neither is an athletic contest. You would be more interesting if there was some subtlety, perhaps even a little finesse.*

7 PUBLIC RELATIONS

The solitary eagle soared high above the marshes in the early morning light. It banked on a gust of wind coming from the ocean and turned north along the coast. Far below the eagle, starting at the light brown and white sands beside the ocean and continuing through the collection of islands and rivers and bays that stretched for miles toward the western horizon, an intermittent complex of diverse buildings connected by paved roads broke up the grassland and swamp. Seventy-five years earlier, the Kennedy Spaceport had been one of a half dozen locations on the Earth where travellers could disembark from their high-speed trains and airplanes to catch a shuttle flight up to one of the LEO (Low Earth Orbit) space stations. But the Great Chaos had changed the spaceport into a ghostly reminder of a once flourishing culture. Its portals and fancy connecting passageways were abandoned for years to the grasses, water birds, alligators, and ubiquitous insects of Central Florida.

In the 2160s, after twenty years of complete atrophy, the reactivation of the spaceport had begun. It had been used first as an airport and then had evolved again into a general transportation centre serving the Florida Atlantic coast. When launches to space recommenced in the mid-2170s, it was natural that the old Kennedy launch pads would be recommissioned. By December of 2199 more than half of the old spaceport had been refurbished to handle the steadily growing traffic between Earth and space.

From one of the windows of his temporary office Valeriy Borzov watched the magnificent eagle glide gracefully back to its nest high in one of the few tall trees within the centre. He loved birds. He had been fascinated by them for years, beginning in his early boyhood in China. In his most vivid recurring dream General Borzov was always living on an amazing planet where the skies swarmed with flying creatures, He could still remember asking his father if there had been any flying biots inside the first Rama spacecraft and then being acutely disappointed with the reply.

General Borzov heard the sound of a large transport vehicle and looked out his west-facing window. Across the way, in front of the test facility, the propulsion module that would be used by both Newton vehicles was emerging from its test complex, on a huge platform moving on multiple tracks. The repaired module, sent back to the subsystem test area because of a problem with its ion controller, would be placed that afternoon inside a cargo shuttle and transferred to the spacecraft assembly facility at space station LEO-2, where it would be retrofitted prior to the final integrated vehicle tests just before Christmas. Both of the two Newton flight spacecraft were currently undergoing final checkout and test at LEO-2. All of the simulation exercises for the cosmonauts, however, were conducted over at LEO-3 with the backup equipment. The cosmonauts would only use the actual flight systems at LEO-2 during the last week before launch.

On the south side of the building, an electric bus pulled to a stop outside the office complex and discharged a small handful of people. One of the passengers was a blonde woman wearing a long-sleeved yellow blouse with vertical black stripes and a pair of black silk pants. She walked with an effortless grace over to the building entrance. General Borzov admired her from a distance, reminding himself that Francesca had been a successful model before becoming a television journalist. He wondered what it was that she wanted and why she had insisted on seeing him privately before the medical briefing this morning.

A minute later he greeted her at the door to his office. 'Good morning, Signora Sabatini,' he said.

'Still so formal, General?' she replied, laughing, 'even when there's only the two of us? You and the two Japanese men are the only members of the team who refuse to call me Francesca.' She noticed that he was staring strangely at her. She looked down at her clothing to see if something was wrong. 'What's the matter?' she asked him after a momentary hesitation.

'It must be your blouse,' General Borzov answered with a start. 'For just a moment I had the distinct impression that you were a tiger poised to pounce on a hapless antelope or gazelle. Maybe it's old age. Or my mind has started playing tricks on me,' He invited her to come into his office.

'I have had men tell me before that I resemble a cat. But never a tiger.' Francesca sat down in the chair beside the general's desk. She meowed with a mischievous smile. 'I'm just a harmless tabby housecat. '

'I don't believe that for a moment,' Borzov said with a chuckle. 'Many adjectives can be used to describe you, Francesca, but harmless would never be one of them.' He suddenly became very businesslike. 'Now, what can I do for you? You said that you had something very important to discuss with me that absolutely could not wait.'

Francesca pulled a large sheet of paper out of her soft briefcase and handed it to General Borzov. 'This is the press schedule for the project,' she said. 'I reviewed it in detail only yesterday with both the public information office and the world television networks. Notice that of the in-depth personal interviews with the cosmonauts, only five have already been completed. Four more were originally scheduled for this month. But notice also that when you added that extra three-day simulation to this coming set of exercises, you wiped out the time that had been allotted to interview Wakefield and Turgenyev.'

She paused for a moment to make sure he was following her. 'We can still catch Takagishi next Saturday and will tape the O'Tooles on Christmas Eve in Boston. But both Richard and Irina say that they now have no time for their interviews. In addition, we still have an old problem: Neither you nor Nicole is scheduled at all ...'

'You insisted on a meeting at seven-thirty this morning to discuss this *press* schedule,' Borzov interrupted, his voice clearly conveying the relative importance that he assigned to such activities.

'Among other things,' Francesca answered nonchalantly. She ignored the implied criticism in his comment. 'Of the people on this mission,' she continued, 'the polls show that the public has the greatest interest in you, me, Nicole des Jardins, and David Brown. So far, I have been unable to pin you down on a date for your personal interview and Madame des Jardins says that she does not intend to have one at all. The networks are unhappy. My prelaunch coverage is going to be incomplete. I need some help from you.'

Francesca looked directly at General Borzov. 'I am asking you to cancel the additional simulation, to set a definite time for your personal interview, and to talk to Nicole on my behalf.'

He frowned. The general was both angered and annoyed by Francesca's presumption. He was going to tell her that the scheduling of personal publicity interviews was not high on his priority list. But something held him back. Both his sixth sense and a lifetime of experience in dealing with people told him to hesitate, that there was more to this discussion than he had yet heard. He temporized by changing the subject.

'Incidentally, I must tell you that I am growing increasingly concerned about the lavish scope of this New Year's Eve party that your friends in the Italian government/business coalition are hosting. I know we agreed at the beginning of our training that we would participate, as a group, in that one social function. But I had no idea that it was going to be billed as "the party of the century", as it was called last week by one of those American personality magazines. You know all those people; can't you do something to downplay the party?'

'The gala was another item on my agenda,' Franceses replied, carefully avoiding the thrust of his comment. 'I need your assistance there as well. Four of the Newton cosmonauts now say that they do not plan to attend and two or three more have suggested that they may have other commitments – even though we all agreed to the party back in March. Takagishi and Yamanaka want to celebrate the holiday with their families in Japan and Richard Wakefield tells me that he has made reservations to go scuba diving in the Cayman Islands. And then there's that Frenchwoman again, who simply says that she's not coming and refuses to offer any kind of explanation.'

Borzov could not suppress a grin. 'Why are you having such a hard time with Nicole des Jardins? I would think that since both of you are women, you would be able to speak to her more easily than the others.'

'She is entirely unsympathetic with the role of the press in this mission. She has told me so several times. And she is very stubborn about her privacy.' Francesca shrugged her shoulders. 'But the public is absolutely fascinated with her. After all, not only is she a doctor and a linguist and a former Olympic champion, but also she is the daughter of a famous novelist and the mother of a fourteen-year-old daughter, despite never having been married ...'

Valeriy Borzov was looking at his watch. 'Just for my information,' he interrupted, 'how many more items are on your "agenda", as you call it? We are due in the auditorium in ten more minutes.' He smiled back at Francesca. 'And I feel compelled to remind you that Madame des Jardins went out of her way today to accommodate your request for press coverage of this briefing.'

Francesca studied General Borzov for several seconds. *I think he's ready now,* she thought to herself. *And unless I misjudged him he will understand immediately.* She pulled a small cubic object out of her briefcase and handed it across the desk. 'This is the only other item on my agenda,' she said.

The Newton commander-in-chief seemed puzzled. He turned the cube over in his hands. 'A freelance journalist sold it to us,' Francesca said in a very serious tone. 'We were assured it was the only copy in existence.'

She paused a moment while Borzov loaded the cube into the appropriate part of his desk computer. He blanched noticeably when the first video segment from the cube appeared on the monitor. He watched the wild rantings of his daughter, Natasha, for about fifteen seconds. 'I wanted to keep this out of the hands of the tabloid press,' Francesca added softly.

'How long is the tape?' General Borzov asked quietly.

'Almost half an hour,' she replied. 'I'm the only one who has seen the entire thing.'

General Borzov heaved a sigh. This was the moment his wife, Petra, had dreaded ever since it was first made official that he would be the commanding officer of the Newton. The institute director at Sverdlovsk had promised that no reporters would have access to his daughter. Now here was a videotape with a thirty-minute interview with her. Petra would be mortified.

He stared out the window. In his mind he was assessing what would happen to the mission if his daughter's acute schizophrenia were paraded before the public. It would be embarrassing, he conceded, but the mission would not be damaged in any serious way ... General Borzov looked across at Francesca. He hated making deals. And he wasn't certain that Francesca herself had not commissioned the interview with Natasha. Nevertheless ...

Borzov relaxed and forced a smile. 'I guess I could thank you,' he said, 'but somehow it doesn't seem appropriate.' He paused for a moment. 'I assume I'm expected to show some gratitude.'

So far, so good, Francesca thought. She knew better than to say anything just yet.

'All right,' the general continued after the lengthy silence, 'I will cancel the extra simulation. Others have already complained about it.' He turned the data cube over in his hands. 'And Petra and I will come to Rome early, as you once suggested, for the personal interview. I will remind all the cosmonauts tomorrow about the party on New Year's Eve and tell them that it is their duty to attend. But neither I nor anyone else can require Nicole des Jardins to talk to you about anything except her work.' He stood up abruptly. 'Now it's time for us to go to that biometry meeting.'

Francesca reached up and kissed him on the cheek. 'Thank you, Valeriy,' she said.

8 BIOMETRY

The medical briefing had already begun when Francesca and General Borzov arrived. All the rest of the cosmonauts were present, as well as twenty-five or thirty additional engineers and scientists associated with the mission. Four newspaper reporters and a television crew completed the audience. At the front of the small auditorium stood Nicole des Jardins, wearing her grey flight outfit as always, and holding a laser pointer in her hand. To the side of her was a tall Japanese man in a blue dress suit. He was listening carefully to a question from the audience. Nicole interrupted him to acknowledge the new arrivals.

'Sumimasen, Hakamatsu-san,' she said. 'Let me introduce our commander, General Valeriy Borzov of the Soviet Union, as well as the journalist-cosmonaut Francesca Sabatini.'

She turned toward the latecomers. 'Dobriy Utra,' Nicole said to the general, quickly nodding a greeting in Francesca's direction as well. 'This is the esteemed Dr Toshiro Hakamatsu,' Nicole said. 'He designed and developed the biometry system that we are going to use in flight, including the tiny probes that will be inserted into our bodies.'

General Borzov extended his hand. 'I am glad to meet you, Hakamatsu-san,' he said. 'Madame des Jardins has made us all very much aware of your outstanding work.'

'Thank you,' the man replied, bowing in the direction of Borzov after shaking his hand. 'It is an honour for me to be part of this project.'

Francesca and General Borzov took the two empty seats at the front of the auditorium and the meeting continued. Nicole aimed her pointer at a keyboard on the side of a small podium and a full-scale, multicoloured male model of the human cardiovascular system, with veins marked in blue and arteries in red, appeared, as a three-dimensional holographic image in the front of the room. Tiny white markers circulating inside the flowing blood vessels indicated the direction and rate of flow. 'The Life Sciences Board of the ISA just last week gave final approval to the new Hakamatsu probes as our key health monitoring system for the mission,' Nicole was saying. 'They withheld their approval until the last minute so that they could properly assess the results of the stress testing, in which the new probes were asked to perform in a wide variety of off-nominal situations. Even under those conditions there was no sign that any rejection mechanisms were triggered in any of the test subjects.

'We are fortunate that we will be able to use this system, for it will make life much easier both for me, as your life science officer, and for you. During the mission you will not be subjected to the routine injection/scanning techniques that have been used on previous projects. These new probes are injected one time, maybe twice at the most during our one-hundred-day mission, and they do not need to be replaced.'

'How did the long-term rejection problem get solved?' came a question from another doctor in the audience, interrupting Nicole's train of thought.

'I will discuss that in detail during our splinter session this afternoon,' she replied. 'For now, it should be sufficient for me to mention that since the key chemistry governing rejection focuses on four or five critical parameters, including acidity, the probes are coated with chemicals that adapt to the local chemistry at the implantation site. In other words, once the probe arrives at its destination, it noninvasively samples its ambient biochemical environment and then exudes a thin coating for itself that is designed to be consistent with the chemistry of the host and thereby avoid rejection.

'But I am getting ahead of myself,' Nicole said, turning to face the large model showing blood circulation in the human being. 'The family of probes will be inserted here, in the left arm, and the individual monitors will disperse according to their prescribed guidance programs to thirty-two distinct locales in the body. There they will embed themselves in the host tissue.' The inside of the holographic model became animated as she spoke and the audience watched as thirty-two blinking lights started from the left arm and scattered throughout the body. Four went to the brain, three more to the heart, four to the primary glands of the endocrine system, and the remaining twenty-one monitors spread out to assorted locations and organs ranging from the eyes to the fingers and toes.

'Each of the individual probes contains both an array of microscopic sensors to sample important health parameters and a fancy data system that first stores and then transmits the recorded information upon receipt of an enabling command from the scanner. In practice, I would expect to scan each of you and dump all your health telemetry once a day, but the recorders can handle data covering up to four days if necessary.' Nicole stopped and looked at the audience. 'Are there any questions so far?' she asked.

'Yes,' said Richard Wakefield in the front row. 'I see how this system gathers trillions of bits of data. But that's the easy part. There's no way you or any other human being could look at all that information. How does the data get synthesised or analysed so that you can tell if anything irregular is happening?'

'You'd make a great straight man, Richard,' Nicole said with a smile. 'That's my next subject.' She held up a small, flat, thin object with a keyboard on it. 'This is a standard programmable scanner that permits the monitored information to be sampled in many different ways. I can call for a full dump from any and/or all channels, or I can request transmission only of warning data ...'

Nicole saw many confused looks in her audience. 'I'd better back up and start this part of the explanation again,' she said. 'Each measurement made by each instrument has an "expected range" – one that will vary of course from individual to individual – and a much wider "tolerance range" used to identify a true emergency. If a particular measurement only exceeds the expected range, it is entered in the warning file and that specific channel is marked with an alarm identifier. One of my options using the scanner is to read out only these warning lists. If an individual cosmonaut is feeling fine, my normal procedure would be just to see if there are any entries in the warning buffer.'

'But if you have a measurement outside the tolerance range,' interjected Janos Tabori, who was the backup life science officer, 'then watch out. The monitor turns on its emergency transmitter and uses all its internal power to send out a "beep, beep" noise that is frightening. I know, it happened to me during a short test with what turned out to be improper tolerance values. I thought I was dying.' His comment caused general laughter. The image of little Janos walking around emitting a high-pitched beep was amusing.

'No system is foolproof,' Nicole continued, 'and this one is only as good as the set of values that are entered to trigger both the warnings and the emergencies. So you can see why calibration data is essential. We have examined each of your medical histories with extreme care and entered initial values in the monitors. But we must see actual results with the real probes inserted in your bodies. That's the reason for today's activity. We will insert your probe set today, monitor your performance during the four final simulation exercises that begin on Thursday, and then update the trigger values, if necessary, before we actually launch.'

There was some involuntary squirming as the cosmonauts thought about the prospect of tiny medical laboratories indefinitely embedded in their critical organs. They were accustomed to the regular investigative probes that were placed in the body to obtain some specific information, like the amount of plaque blocking the arteries, but those probes were temporary. The thought of permanent electronic invasion was to say the least disquieting. General Michael O'Toole asked two questions that were bothering most of the crew.

'Nicole,' he inquired in his usual earnest manner, 'can you tell us how you make sure that the probes actually go to the right places. Even more important, what happens if one malfunctions?'

'Of course, Michael,' she answered pleasantly. 'Remember these things will be inside me as well and I had to ask the same questions.' Nicole des Jardins was in her middle thirties. Her skin was a shiny copper brown, her eyes dark brown and almond-shaped, her hair a luxurious jet black. There was an unshakable self-confidence radiating from her that was sometimes mistaken for arrogance. 'You won't leave the clinic today until we have verified that all the probes are properly positioned,' she was saying. 'Based on recent past experience, one or two of you may have a monitor wander off course. It is an easy matter to track it with the lab equipment and then send overwrite commands as necessary to move it to the proper spot.

'As far as the malfunction issue is concerned, there are several levels of fault protection. First, each specific monitor tests its own battery of sensors more than twenty times a day. Any individual instrument failing a test is turned off immediately by the executive software in its own monitor. In addition, each of the probe packages undergoes a full and rigorous self-test twice a day. Failure of self-test is one of many fault conditions that causes the monitor to secrete chemicals causing self-destruction, with eventual harmless absorption by the body. Lest you become unduly concerned, we have rigorously verified all these fault paths with test subjects during the past year.'

Nicole wound up her presentation and stood quietly in front of her colleagues. 'Any more questions?' she asked. After a few seconds' hesitation she continued, 'Then I need a volunteer to walk up here beside the robot nurse and be inoculated. My personal probe set was injected and verified last week. Who wants to be next?'

Francesca stood up. 'All right, we'll start with la bella signora Sabatini,' Nicole said. She gestured to the television personnel. 'Focus those cameras on the tracer simulation. It's quite a show when these electronic bugs swarm through the bloodstream.'

9 DIASTOLIC IRREGULARITY

Through the window Nicole could barely discern the Siberian snow fields in the oblique December light. They were more than fifty thousand feet below her. The supersonic plane was slowing now as it moved south toward Vladivostok and the islands of Japan. Nicole yawned. After only three hours of sleep, it would be a fight all day to keep her body awake. It was almost ten in the morning in Japan but back home at Beauvois, in the Loire Valley not far from Tours, her daughter, Genevieve, still had four more hours of sleep until her alarm would awaken her at seven o'clock,

The video monitor in the back of the seat in front of Nicole automatically turned on and reminded her that in only fifteen minutes the plane would land at the Kansai Transportation Centre. The lovely Japanese girl on the screen suggested that now would be an excellent time to make or confirm ground transportation and housing arrangements. Nicole activated the communication system in her seat and a thin rectangular tray with a keyboard and small display area slid in front of her. In less than a minute Nicole arranged both her train ride to Kyoto and her electric trolley passage from there to her hotel. She used her Universal Credit Card to pay for all transactions, after first correctly identifying herself by indicating that her mother's maiden name was Anawi Tiasso. When she was finished a small printed schedule listing her train and trolley identifiers, along with the times of arrival and transit (she would reach her hotel at 11:14 am Japanese time), popped out of one end of the tray.

As the plane prepared for its landing, Nicole thought about the reason for her sudden trip one third of the way around the world. Just twenty-four hours ago she had been planning to spend this day around her home, alternating some office work in the morning with some language practice for Genevieve in the afternoon. It was the beginning of the holiday break for the cosmonauts and, except for that stupid party in Rome at the end of the year, Nicole was supposedly free until she had to report to LEO-3 on January 8. But while she had been sitting in her office at home the previous morning, routinely checking the biometry from the final set of simulations, Nicole had come across a curious phenomenon. She had been studying Richard Wakefield's heart and blood pressure during a variable gravity test and had

212

not understood a particularly rapid surge in his pulse rate. She had then decided to check Dr Takagishi's detailed heart biometry for comparison, since he had been engaged in a strenuous physical activity with Richard at the time of the pulse surge.

What she had found when she had examined a full dump of Takagishi's heart information had been an even bigger surprise. The Japanese professor's diastolic expansion was decidedly irregular, maybe even pathological. But no warnings had been issued by the probe and no data channels had been alarmed. What was going on? Had she detected a malfunction in the Haka-matsu system?

An hour's worth of detective work had resulted in the identification of more peculiarities. During the full set of simulations, there had been four separate intervals during which Takagishi's problem had occurred. The abnormal behaviour was sporadic and intermittent. Sometimes the extra long diastole, reminiscent of a valve problem during the filling of the heart with blood, would not appear for as long as thirty-eight hours. However, the fact that it did recur four different times suggested that there was definitely an abnormality of some kind.

What had mystified Nicole was not the raw data itself – it was the failure of the system to trigger the proper alarms in the presence of the wildly irregular observations. As part of her analysis she had traced laboriously through the Takagishi medical history, paying special attention to the cardiology report. She had found no hint of any kind of abnormality, so had convinced herself that she was seeing a sensor error and not a true medical problem.

So *if the system was working correctly,* she had reasoned, *the onset of the long diastole should have immediately sent the heart monitor outside the expected range and triggered an alarm. But it didn't. Neither the first time nor any other time. Is it possible that we have a double failure here? If so, how did the unit continue to pass self-test?*

At first Nicole had thought about phoning one of her assistants in the life science office at ISA to discuss the anomaly she had found, but she decided instead, since it was a holiday for ISA, to telephone Dr Hakamatsu in Japan. That phone call to him had completely bewildered her. He had told her flatly that the phenomenon she had observed must have been in the patient, that no combination of component failures in his probe could have produced such strange results. 'But then why were there no entries in the warning file?' she had asked the Japanese electronics designer.

'Because no expected range values were exceeded,' he answered confi-dently. 'For some reason an extremely wide expected range must have been entered for this particular cosmonaut. Have you looked at his medical history?'

Later on in the conversation, when Nicole told Dr Hakamatsu that the unexplained data had actually come from the probes inside one of his countrymen, namely cosmonaut-scientist Takagishi, the usually restrained engineer had actually shouted into the phone. 'Wonderful,' he had said, 'then I'll be able to clear up this mystery in a hurry. I'll contact Takagishi-san over at Kyoto University and let you know what I find.'

Three hours later Nicole's video monitor had revealed the sombre face of Dr Shigeru Takagishi. 'Madame des Jardins,' he had said very politely, 'I understand that you have been talking with my colleague Hakamatsu-san about my biometry output during the simulations. Would you be kind enough to explain to me what you have found?'

Nicole had then presented all the information to her fellow cosmonaut, concealing nothing and expressing her personal belief that the source of the erroneous data had indeed been a probe malfunction.

A long silence followed Nicole's explanation. At length the worried Japanese scientist had spoken again. 'Hakamatsu-san just visited me here at the university and checked out the probe set inside me. He will report that he found no problems with his electronics.' Takagishi had then paused, seemingly deep in thought. 'Madame des Jardins,' he had said a few seconds later, 'I would like to ask you a favour. It is a matter of the utmost importance to me. Could you possibly come to see me in Japan in the very near future? I would like to talk with you personally and explain something that may be related to my irregular biometry data.'

There had been an earnestness in Takagishi's face that Nicole could neither overlook nor misinterpret. He was clearly imploring her to help him. Without asking any more questions, she had agreed to visit him immediately. A few minutes later she had reserved a seat on the overnight supersonic flight from Paris to Osaka.

'It was never bombed during the great war with America,' Takagishi said, waving his arms at the city of Kyoto spread out below them, 'and it suffered almost no damage when the hoodlums took over for seven months in 2141. I admit that I am prejudiced,' he said, smiling, 'but to me Kyoto is the most beautiful city in the world.'

'Many of my countrymen feel that way about Paris,' Nicole answered. She pulled her coat rightly around her. The air was cold and damp. It felt as if it might snow at any moment. She was wondering when her associate was going to start talking about their business. She had not flown five thousand miles for a tour of the city, although she did admit that this Kyomizu Temple set among the trees on a hillside overlooking the city was certainly a magnificent spot.

'Let's have some tea,' Takagishi said. He led her to one of the several outside tearooms flanking the main part of the old Buddhist temple. *Now,* Nicole said to herself as she stifled a yawn, *he's going to tell me what this is all about.* Takagishi had met her at the hotel when she had arrived. He had suggested that she have some lunch and a short nap before he returned. After he had picked her up at three o'clock, they had come directly to this temple.

He poured the thick Japanese tea into the two cups and waited for Nicole to take a sip. The hot liquid warmed her mouth even though she didn't care for the bitter taste. 'Madame,' Takagishi began, 'you are doubtless wondering why I have asked you to come all the way to Japan on such short notice. You see,' he spoke slowly but with great intensity, 'all my life I have dreamed that perhaps another Rama spacecraft would return while I was still alive. During my studies at the university and during my many years of research I was preparing myself for one single event, the return of the Ramans. On that March morning in 2197 when Alastair Moore called me to say that the latest images from Excalibur indicated that we had another extraterrestrial visitor, I nearly wept with joy. I knew immediately that the ISA would mount a mission to visit the spaceship. I resolved to be part of that mission.'

The Japanese scientist took a drink from his tea and looked to his left, out across the manicured green trees and the slopes above the city. 'When I was a boy,' he continued, his careful English barely audible, 'I would climb these hills on a clear night and stare into the sky, searching for the home of the special intelligence that had created that incomparable giant machine. Once I came with my father and we huddled together in the cold night air, looking at the stars, while he told me what it had been like in his village during the days of the first Rama encounter twelve years before I was born. I believed on that night' – he turned to look at Nicole and she could again see the passion in his eyes – 'and I still believe today, that there was some reason for that visit, some purpose for the appearance of that awesome spaceship. I have studied all the data from that first encounter, hoping to find a clue that would explain why it came. Nothing has been conclusive. I have developed several theories on the subject, but I do not have enough evidence to support any of them.'

Again Takagishi stopped talking to drink some of his tea. Nicole had been both surprised and impressed by the depth of feeling he had exhibited. She sat patiently and said nothing while she waited for him to continue. 'I knew that I had a good chance to be selected as a cosmonaut,' he said, 'not only because of my publications, including the *Atlas*, but also because one of my closest associates, Hisanori Akita, was the Japanese representative on the selection board. When the number of scientists remaining in the competition had been reduced to eight and I was one of them, Akita-san suggested to me that it looked as if the two leading contenders were myself and David Brown. You'll recall that up until that time, no physical examinations of any kind had been conducted.'

That's right, Nicole remembered. *The potential crew was first reduced to forty-eight and then we were all taken to Heidelberg for the physicals. The German doctors in charge insisted that each of the candidates must pass every single medical criterion. The academy graduates were the first group tested and five out of twenty failed. Including Alain Blamont.*

'When your countryman Blamont, who had already flown half a dozen major missions for the ISA, was disqualified from consideration because of that trivial heart murmur – and the Cosmonaut Selection Board subsequently upheld the doctors by denying his appeal – I completely panicked.' The proud Japanese physicist was now staring directly into Nicole's eyes, entreating her to understand. 'I was afraid that I was going to lose the most important opportunity of my career because of a minor physical problem that had never before affected any part of my life.' He paused to choose his words carefully. 'I know that what I did was wrong and dishonourable, but I convinced myself at the time it was all right, that my chance to decipher the greatest puzzle in man's history should not be blocked by a group of small-minded doctors defining acceptable health only in terms of numerical values.

Dr Takagishi told the rest of his story without embellishment or obvious emotion. The passion he had fleetingly demonstrated during his discussion of the Ramans had vanished. His monotonic recital was crisp and clear. He explained how he had cajoled his family physician into falsifying his medical history and providing him with a new drug that would prevent the occurrence of his diastolic irregularity during the two days of his physical at Heidelberg. Although there had been some risk of deleterious side effects from the new drug, everything went according to plan. Takagishi passed the rigorous physical and was ultimately selected as one of the two mission scientists, along with Dr David Brown. He had never thought again about the medical issue until about three months ago, when Nicole had first explained to the cosmonauts that she was planning to recommend the usage of the Hakamatsu probe system during the mission instead of the standard temporary probe scans once every week.

'You see,' Takagishi explained, his brow now starting to furrow, 'under the old mission technique I could have used that same drug once a week and neither you nor any other life science officer would ever have seen my irregularity, But a permanent monitoring system cannot be fooled – the drug is much too dangerous for constant use.'

So you somehow worked out a deal with Hakamatsu, Nicole thought, jumping ahead of him in her own mind. *Either with or without his explicit knowledge. And you input expected value ranges that would not trigger in the presence of your abnormality. You hoped that nobody analyzing the tests would call for a full biometry dump.* Now she understood why he had summoned her urgently to Japan. *And you want me to keep your secret.*

'Watakuski no dõryõ wa, wakarimas,' Nicole said kindly, changing into Japanese to show her sympathy for her colleague's anguish. 'I can tell how much distress this is causing you. You need not explain in detail how you tampered with the Hakamatsu probes.' She paused and watched his face relax. 'But if I understand you correctly, what you want is for me to become an accomplice to your deception. You recognize of course that I cannot even consider preserving your secret unless I am absolutely convinced that your minor physical problem, as you call it, represents no possible threat to the mission. Otherwise I would be forced ...'

'Madame des Jardins,' Takagishi interrupted her, 'I have the utmost respect for your integrity. I would never, *never* ask you to keep my heart irregularity out of the record unless you agreed that it was really an insignificant problem.' He looked at her in silence for several seconds. 'When Hakamatsu first phoned me last evening,' he continued quietly, 'I thought originally that I would call a press conference and then resign from the project. But while I was thinking about what I would say in my resignation, I kept seeing this image of Professor Brown. He is a brilliant man, my American counterpart, but he is also, in my opinion, too certain of his own infallibility. The most likely replacement for me would be Professor Wolfgang Heinrich from Bonn. He has published many fine papers about Rama but he, like Brown, believes that these celestial visits represent random events, totally without connection in any way to us and our planet.' The intensity and passion had returned to his eyes. 'I cannot quit now. Unless I have no choice. Both Brown and Heinrich might miss the clue.'

Behind Takagishi, on the path that the led back to the main wooden building of the temple, three Buddhist monks walked briskly past. Despite the cold, they were dressed lightly in their usual charcoal grey smocks, their feet exposed to the cold in open sandals. The Japanese scientist was proposing to Nicole that they spend the rest of the day at the office of his personal physician, where they could study his complete and uncensored medical history dating back to his childhood. If she would be willing, he added, they would give her a data cube containing all the information to take back to France and study at her leisure.

Nicole, who had been listening intently to Takagishi for almost an hour, momentarily diverted her attention to the three monks now purposefully climbing the stairs in the distance. *Their eyes are so serene*, she thought. *Their lives so free of contradiction. Onemindedness can be a virtue. It makes all the answers easy.* For just a moment she was envious of the monks and their ordered existence. She wondered how well they would handle the dilemma that Dr Takagishi was presenting her. *He is not one of the space cadets,* she was now thinking, *so his role is not absolutely critical to mission success. And in a sense he is right. The doctors on the project have been too strict. They never should have disqualified Alain. It would be a shame if . . .*

'Daijobu,' she said before he had finished talking. 'I will go with you to see your doctor and if I don't find anything that bothers me, I will take the entire file home with me to study during the holidays.' Takagishi's face lit up. 'But let me warn you again,' she added, 'if there is anything in your history that I find questionable, or if I have the slightest shred of evidence that you have withheld any information from me, then I will ask you to resign immediately.'

'Thank you, thank you so much,' Dr Takagishi replied, standing and bowing to his female colleague. 'Thank you so much,' he repeated.

10 THE COSMONAUT AND THE POPE

General O'Toole could not have slept more than two hours altogether. The combination of excitement and jet lag had kept his mind active all night long. He had studied the lovely bucolic mural on the wall opposite the bed in his hotel room and counted all the animals twice. Unfortunately, he had remained wide awake after he had finished both counts.

He took a deep breath, hoping that it would help him relax. *So why all this nervousness?* he thought. *He is just a man like all the rest on Earth. Well, not exactly.* O'Toole sat up straight in his chair and smiled. It was ten o'clock in the morning and he was sitting in a small anteroom inside the Vatican. He was about to have a private audience with the Vicar of Christ himself, Pope John-Paul V.

During his childhood, Michael O'Toole had often dreamed of someday becoming the first North American pope. 'Pope Michael', he had called himself during the long Sunday afternoons when he had studied his catechism alone. As he had repeated the words of his lessons over and over and committed them to memory, he had imagined himself, maybe fifty years in the future, wearing the cassock and papal ring, celebrating mass for thousands in the great churches and stadia of the world. He would inspire the poor, the hopeless, the downtrodden. He would show them how God could lead them to a better life.

As a young man Michael O'Toole had loved all learning, but three subjects had especially intrigued him. He could not read enough about religion, history, and physics. Somehow his facile mind found it easy to jump between these different disciplines. It never bothered him that the epistemologies of religion and physics were one hundred and eighty degrees apart. Michael O'Toole had no difficulty recognizing which questions in life should be answered by physics and which ones by religion.

All three of his favourite scholastic subjects merged in the study of creation. It was, after all, the beginning of everything, including religion, history, and physics. How had it happened? Was God present, as the referee perhaps, for the kickoff of the universe eighteen billion years ago? Wasn't it He who had provided the impetus for the cataclysmic explosion known as the Big

Bang that produced all matter out of energy? Hadn't He foreseen that those original pristine hydrogen atoms would coalesce into giant clouds of gas and then collapse under gravitation to become the stars in which would be manufactured the basic chemical building blocks of life?

And I have never lost my fascination for creation, O'Toole said to himself as he waited for his papal audience. *How did it all happen? What is the significance of the particular sequence of events?* He remembered his questions of the priests when he was a teenager. *I probably decided not to become a priest because it would have limited my free access to scientific truth. The church has never been as comfortable as I am with the apparent incompatibilities between God and Einstein.*

An American priest from the Vatican state department had been waiting at his hotel in Rome the previous evening when O'Toole had returned from his day as a tourist. The priest had introduced himself and apologized profusely for not having responded to the letter that General O'Toole had written from Boston in November. It would have 'facilitated the process', the priest had remarked in passing, if the general had pointed out in his letter that he was *the* General O'Toole, the Newton cosmonaut. Nevertheless, the priest had continued, the papal schedule had been juggled and the Holy Father would be delighted to see O'Toole the next morning. As the door to the papal office swung open, the American general instinctively stood up. The priest from the night before walked into the room, looking very nervous, and quickly shook O'Toole's hand. They both glanced toward the doorway, where the pope, wearing his normal white cassock, was concluding a conversation with a member of his staff. John-Paul V came forward into the anteroom, a pleasant smile on his face, and extended his hand toward O'Toole. The cosmonaut automatically dropped to one knee and kissed the papal ring.

'Holy Father,' he murmured, astonished at the excited pounding of his heart, 'thank you for seeing me. This is indeed a great honour for me.'

'For me as well,' the pope replied in lightly accented English. 'I have been following the activities of you and your colleagues with great interest.'

He gestured toward O'Toole and the American general followed the church leader into a grand office with high ceilings. A very large, dark wood desk stood on one side of the room under a life-size portrait of John-Paul IV, the man who had become pope during the darkest days of the Great Chaos and had provided both the world and the church with twenty years of energetic and inspirational leadership. The gifted Venezuelan, a poet and historical scholar in his own right, had demonstrated to the world between 2139 and 2158 how positive a force the organized church could be at a time when virtually every other institution was collapsing and was, therefore, unable to give any succour to the bewildered masses.

The pope sat down on a couch and motioned for O'Toole to sit next to him. The American priest left the room. In front of O'Toole and the pope were great windows that opened onto a balcony overlooking the Vatican gardens some twenty feet below. In the distance O'Toole could see the Vatican museum where he had spent the previous afternoon.

'You wrote in your letter,' the Holy Father said, without referring to any notes, 'that there were some theological issues that you would like to discuss with me. I assume these are in some way related to your mission.'

O'Toole looked at the seventy-year-old Spaniard who was the spiritual leader of a billion Catholics. The pope's skin was olive, his features sharp, his thick black hair now mostly grey. His brown eyes were soft and clear. *He certainly doesn't waste any time,* O'Toole thought, recalling an article in a Catholic magazine in which one of the leading cardinals in the Vatican administration had praised John-Paul V for his management efficiency.

'Yes, Holy Father,' O'Toole said. 'As you know, I am about to embark on a journey of the utmost significance for humankind. As a Catholic, I have some questions that I thought it might be helpful for me to discuss with you.' He paused for a moment. 'I certainly don't expect you to have all the answers. But maybe you can guide me a little with your accumulated wisdom.'

The pope nodded and waited for O'Toole to continue. The cosmonaut took a deep breath, 'The issue of redemption is one that's bothering me, even though I guess it's just a part of a bigger concern that I have in reconciling the Ramans with our faith.'

The pope's brow furrowed and O'Toole could tell that he was not communicating very well. 'I have no trouble whatsoever,' the general added as an explanation, 'with the concept of God creating the Ramans – that's easy to comprehend. But did the Ramans follow a similar pattern of spiritual evolution and therefore need to be redeemed, at some point in their history, like human beings on Earth? And if so, did God send Jesus, or perhaps his Raman equivalent, to save them from their sins? Do we humans thus represent an evolutionary paradigm that has been repeated over and over throughout the universe?'

The pope's smile broadened almost into a grin. 'Goodness, General,' he said with humour, 'you have romped over a vast intellectual territory very quickly. You must know that I do not have fast answers to such profound questions. The church has had its scholars addressing the issues raised by Rama for almost seventy years and, as you would expect, our research has recently intensified because of the discovery of the second spacecraft.'

'But what do you personally believe, Your Holiness?' O'Toole persisted. 'Did the creatures who made these two incredible space vehicles commit some original sin and also need a saviour sometime in their history? Is the story of Jesus unique for us here on Earth, or is it just one small chapter in a book of nearly infinite length that covers all sentient beings and a general requirement for redemption to achieve salvation?'

'I'm not certain,' the Holy Father replied after several seconds. 'Sometimes it is nearly impossible for me to fathom the existence of other intelligence in any form out there in the rest of the universe. Then, as soon as I acknowledge that it certainly wouldn't look like us, I struggle with images and pictures that sidetrack my thinking from the kinds of theological questions that you have raised this morning.' He paused for a moment, reflecting. 'But most of the time I imagine that the Ramans too had lessons to learn in the beginning, that God did not create them perfect either, and that at some time in their development He must have sent them Jesus ...'

The pope interrupted himself and looked intently at General O'Toole. 'Yes,' he continued softly, 'I said Jesus. You asked me what I believed personally. To me Jesus is both the true saviour and the only son of God. It would be He who would be sent to the Ramans also, albeit in a different guise.'

O'Toole's face had brightened at the end of the pontiff's remarks. 'I agree with you, Holy Father,' he said excitedly. 'And therefore all intelligence is united, everywhere throughout the universe, by a similar spiritual experience. In a very very real sense, assuming that the Ramans have also been saved, we are all brothers. After all, we are made from the same basic chemicals. That means that Heaven will not be limited just to humans but will encompass all beings everywhere who have understood His message.'

'I can see where you might come to that conclusion,' John-Paul replied. 'But it is certainly not one that is universally accepted. Even within the church there are those who have an altogether different view of the Ramans.'

'You mean the homocentric group that uses quotations from St Michael of Siena for support?'

The pope nodded.

'For myself,' General O'Toole said, 'I find their narrow interpretation of St Michael's sermon on the Ramans much too confining. In saying that the extraterrestrial spacecraft might have been a herald, like Elijah or even Isaiah, foretelling the second coming of Christ, Michael was not restricting the Ramans to having only that particular role in our history and no other function or existence. He was simply explaining one possible view of the event from a human spiritual perspective.'

Again the pontiff was smiling, 'I can tell that you have spent considerable time and energy thinking about all this. My advance information about you was only partially correct. Your devotion to God, the church, and your family were all cited in your dossier. But there is little mention of your active intellectual interest in theology.'

'I consider this mission to be by far the most important assignment of my life. I want to make certain that I properly serve both God and mankind. So I am trying to prepare myself in every possible way, including discovering whether or not the Ramans may have a spiritual component. It could affect my actions on the mission.'

O'Toole paused a few seconds before continuing. 'By the way, your holiness, have your researchers found any evidence of possible Raman spirituality, based on their analysis of the first rendezvous?'

John-Paul V shook his head. 'Not really, However, one of my most devout archbishops, a man whose religious zeal sometimes overshadows his logic, insists that the structural order inside the first Raman craft – you know, the symmetries, geometric patterns, even the repetitive redundant designs based on the number three – is suggestive of a temple. He could be right. We just don't know. We don't see any evidence either way about the spiritual nature of the beings who created that first spaceship.'

'Amazing!' said General O'Toole. 'I had never thought of that before. Imagine if it really was created as some kind of a temple. That would stagger David Brown.' The general laughed. 'Dr Brown insists,' he said in explanation, 'that we poor ignorant human beings would not have any chance of ever determining the purpose of such a spaceship, for the technology of its builders is so far advanced beyond our comprehension that it would be impossible for us ever to understand any of it. And, according to him, of course there could be no Raman religion. In his opinion they would have left all the superstitious mumbo jumbo behind eons before they developed the capability to construct such a fabulous interstellar spacecraft.'

'Dr Brown is an atheist, isn't he?' the pope asked.

O'Toole nodded. 'An outspoken one. He believes that all religious thinking impairs the proper functioning of the brain. He regards anyone who doesn't agree with his point of view as an absolute idiot.'

'And the rest of the crew? Are they as strongly opinionated on the subject as Dr Brown?'

'He is the most vocal atheist, although I suspect Wakefield, Tabori, and Turgenyev all share his basic attitudes. Strangely enough, my intuitive sense tells me that Commander Borzov has a soft spot in his heart for religion. That's true of most of the survivors of The Chaos. Anyway, Valeriy seems to enjoy asking me questions about my faith.'

General O'Toole stopped for a moment as he mentally completed his survey of the religious beliefs of the Newton crew. 'The European women des Jardins and Sabatini are nominally Catholic, although they would not be considered devout by any stretch of the imagination. Admiral Heilmann is a Lutheran on Easter and Christmas, Takagishi meditates and studies Zen. I don't know about the other two,'

The pontiff stood up and walked to the window. 'Somewhere out there a strange and wonderful space vehicle, created by beings from another star, is headed toward us. We are sending a crew of a dozen to rendezvous with it.' He turned toward General O'Toole. 'This spaceship may be a messenger from God, but probably only you will be able to recognize it as such.'

O'Toole did not reply. The pope stared out the window again and was quiet for almost a minute. 'No, my son,' he finally said softly, as much to himself as to General O'Toole. 'I do not have the answers to your questions. Only God has them. You must pray that He will provide the answers when you need them.' He faced the general. 'I must tell you that I am delighted to find you so concerned with these issues. I am confident that God also has purposely selected you for this mission.'

General O'Toole could tell that the audience was coming to an end.

'Holy Father,' he said, 'thank you again for seeing me and sharing this time. I feel deeply honoured.'

John-Paul V smiled and walked over to his guest. He embraced him in the European manner and escorted General O'Toole out of his office.

11 ST MICHAEL OF SIENA

The exit from the subway station was opposite the entrance to the International Peace Park. As the escalator deposited General O'Toole on the upper level and he walked out into the afternoon light, he could see the domed shrine to his right, not more than two hundred yards away. To his left, at the other end of the park, the top of the ancient Roman Colosseum was visible behind a complex of administrative buildings.

The American general walked briskly into the park and turned right on the sidewalk leading to the shrine. He passed a lovely small fountain, part of a monument to the children of the world, and stopped to watch the animated, sculptured figures playing in the cold water. O'Toole was full of anticipation. *What an incredible day,* he was thinking. *First I have an audience with the pope. And now I finally visit the shrine of St Michael.*

When Michael of Siena was canonized in 2188, fifty years after his death (and, perhaps more significantly, three years after John-Paul V had been elected as the new pope), there had been an immediate consensus that the perfect place to locate a major shrine in his honour would be in the International Peace Park. The great park stretched from the Piazza Venezia to the Colosseum, wandering around and among those few ruins from the old Roman fora that had somehow survived the nuclear holocaust. Choosing the exact spot for the shrine had been a delicate process. The Memorial to the Five Martyrs, honouring those courageous men and women who had dedicated themselves to the restoration of order in Rome during the months immediately following the disaster, had been the feature attraction of the park for years. There was considerable feeling that the new shrine to St Michael of Siena must not be allowed to overshadow the dignified, open, marble penta-gon that had occupied the southeast corner of the park since 2155.

After much debate it was decided that St Michael's shrine should be located in the opposite, northwest corner of the park, its foundation symbolically centreed on the actual epicenter of the blast, only ten yards from the place where Trajan's Column had stood until it was instantaneously vaporized by the intense heat at the core of the fireball. The first floor of the round shrine was entirely for meditation and worship. There were twelve alcoves or chapels attached to the central nave, six with sculpture and artwork following classical Roman Catholic motifs and the other six each honouring one of the world's major religions. This eclectic partition of the ground floor was purposely designed to provide comfort for the many non-Catholics who made pilgrimages to the shrine to pay their respects to the memory of the beloved St Michael.

General O'Toole did not spend much time on the first level. He knelt and said a prayer in the chapel of St Peter, and looked briefly at the famous wood sculpture of Buddha in the nook beside the entrance, but like most tourists he could not wait to see the incomparable frescoes on the second floor. O'Toole was overwhelmed by both the size and the beauty of the famous paintings the moment he stepped out of the elevator. Directly in front of him was a life-size portrait of a lovely girl of eighteen with long blonde hair. She was bending down in an old church in Siena on Christmas Eve in 2115 and leaving behind a curly-haired baby, wrapped in a blanket and placed in a basket, on the cold church floor. This painting represented the night of St Michael's birth and was the first in a sequence of twelve panels of frescoes that completely circled the shrine and told the story of the saint's life.

General O'Toole walked over to the small kiosk beside the elevator and rented a forty-five-minute audio tour cassette that was ten centimetres square and easily fit in his coat pocket. He picked up one of the tiny disposable receivers and clipped it into his ear. After choosing English as his language, he pushed the button marked 'introduction' and listened as a lovely feminine British voice explained what he was about to see.

'Each of the twelve frescoes is six metres high,' the woman was saying as the general was studying the features of the baby Michael in the first panel. 'The lighting in the room is a combination of natural light from the outside, coming through filtered skylights, and artificial illumination from the electronic arrays in the dome. Automatic sensors determine the ambient conditions and mix the natural with the artificial light so that the viewing of the frescoes is always perfect.

'The twelve panels on this level correspond to the twelve alcoves on the floor below. The arrangement of the frescoes themselves, which follow the life of the saint in a chronological order, flows in a clockwise direction. Thus the final painting, commemorating Michael's canonization ceremony at Rome in 2188, is right next to the painting of his birth in the Siena cathedral seventy-two years earlier.

'The frescoes were designed and implemented by a team of four artists, including the master Feng Yi from China, who appeared suddenly in the spring of 2190 without any prior notification. Despite the fact that very little was known outside China of his skill, the other three artists, Rosa da Silva from Portugal, Fernando Lopez from Mexico, and Hans Reichwein from Switzerland, immediately welcomed Feng Yi to their team on the strength of the superb sketches that he had brought with him.'

O'Toole glanced around the circular room as he listened to the lyrical voice on the cassette. On this last day of 2199, there were more than two hundred people on the second floor of St Michael's shrine, including three tour groups. The American cosmonaut progressed slowly around the circle, stopping in front of each panel to study the artwork and listen to the discussion on the cassette.

The major events of St Michael's life were depicted in detail in the frescoes. The second through fifth panels featured his days as a Franciscan novitiate in Siena, his fact-finding tour around the world during the Great Chaos, the beginning of his religious activism when he returned to Italy, and Michael's use of the church resources to feed the hungry and house the homeless. The sixth painting showed the tireless saint inside the television studio donated by a wealthy American admirer. Here Michael, who spoke eight languages, repeatedly proclaimed his message of the fundamental unity of all humanity and the requirement for the wealthy to care for the less fortunate.

The seventh fresco was Feng Yi's portrait of the confrontation in Rome between Michael and the old and dying pope. It was a masterpiece of contrast. Using colour and light brilliantly, the painting conveyed the image of an energetic, vibrant, and vital young man being wrongly censured by a world-weary prelate anxious to live out his final days in peace and quiet. In Michael's facial expression could be seen two distinctly different reactions to what he was being told: obedience to the papacy and disgust that the church was more concerned with style and order than substance.

'Michael was sent to a monastery in Tuscany by the pope,' the audio guide continued, 'and it was there that the final transformations in his character took place. The eighth panel depicts God's appearances to Michael during this period of solitude. According to the saint, God spoke to him twice, the first time in the middle of a thunderstorm and the second time when a magnificent rainbow filled the sky. It was during the long and violent storm that God shouted out, on the claps of thunder, the new "Laws of Life" which Michael later proclaimed at his Easter sunrise service at Bolsena. On His second visitation God informed the saint that his message would be spread to the ends of the rainbow and that He would give the faithful a sign during the Easter mass.

'That most famous miracle of Michael's life, one that was watched on television by over a billion people, is shown in the ninth panel. The painting presents Michael preaching Easter mass to the multitudes gathered around the shores of Lake Bolsena. A vigorous spring shower is drenching the crowd, most of whom are dressed in the familiar blue robes that had become associated with his following. But while the rain falls all around St Michael, not a drop ever falls on the pulpit or on the sound equipment being used to amplify his voice. A perpetual radiant spotlight from the sun bathes the young saint's face as he announces God's new laws to the world. It was this crossover from being a purely religious leader ...'

General O'Toole switched off the cassette as he walked toward the tenth and eleventh paintings. He was familiar with the rest of the story. After the mass at Bolsena, Michael was beset by a flock of troubles. His life abruptly changed. Within two weeks most of his cable television licences were rescinded. Stories of corruption and immorality among his young devotees, whose numbers had grown into the hundreds of thousands in the Western world alone, were constantly in the press. There was an assassination attempt, which was foiled at the last minute by his staff. There were also baseless reports in the media that Michael had proclaimed himself the second Christ.

And so the leaders of the world became afraid of you. All of them. You were a threat to everyone with your Laws of Life. And they never understood what you meant by the final evolution. O'Toole stood in front of the tenth fresco. It was a scene he knew by heart. Almost every other educated person in the world would also recognize it instantly. The television replays of the last seconds before the terrorist bomb exploded were shown every year on June 28, the first day of the Feast of St Peter and St Paul and the anniversary of the day that Michael and almost a million others had perished in Rome on a fateful early summer morning in 2138.

You had called them to come to Rome to join you, To show the world that everyone was united. And so they came. The tenth painting showed Michael in his blue robes, standing high on the steps of the Vittorio Emmanuel Monument next to the Piazza Venezia. He was in the middle of a sermon. Around him in all directions, spilling over into the Roman fora along the jam-packed Via dei Fori Imperiali leading to the Colosseum, was a sea of blue. And faces. Eager, excited faces, mostly young, looking up and around the monuments of the ancient city to catch a glimpse of the boy-man who dared to suggest that he had a way, God's way, out of the despair and hopelessness that had engulfed the world.

Michael Ryan O'Toole, a fifty-seven-year-old American Catholic from Boston, fell on his knees and wept, like thousands before him, when he looked at the eleventh panel in the sequence. This painting depicted the same scene as the previous panel, but the time was more than an hour later, an hour *after* the seventy-five-kiloton nuclear bomb hidden in a sound truck near Trajan's Column had exploded and sent its hideous mushroom-shaped cloud into the skies above the city. Everything within two hundred metres of the epicenter had been instantly vaporized. There was no Michael, no Piazza Venezia, no huge Victor Emmanuel Monument. In the centre of the fresco was nothing but a hole. And around the perimeter of that hole, where the vaporization had not been quite as complete, were scenes of agony and horror that would shatter the complacency of even the most self-protected individuals.

Dear God, General O'Toole said to himself through his tears, *help me to comprehend the message in Saint Michael's life. Help me to understand how I can contribute, in whatever small way, to Your overall plan for us. Guide me as I prepare to be Your emissary to the Ramans.*

12 RAMANS AND ROMANS

'So, what do you think?' Nicole des Jardins stood up and turned around slowly in front of the camera beside the monitor. She was wearing a form-fitting white dress made from one of the new stretch fabrics. The hem of the dress was cut just below her knees and the long sleeves were marked by one black stripe that passed under her elbows as it ran from the shoulder to the wrist. The wide, jet-black belt matched both the colour of the stripe and the colour of her hair and high-heeled shoes. Her hair was pulled together by a comb at the back of her head and then left to tumble freely almost to her waist. Her only jewellery was a gold tennis bracelet containing three rows of small diamonds that she was wearing around her left wrist.

'You look beautiful, Maman,' her daughter, Genevieve, answered her from the screen. 'I've never seen you before both dressed up *and* with your hair down. What happened to your normal sweatsuit?' The fourteen-year-old grinned. 'And when does the party start?'

'At nine-thirty,' Nicole replied. 'Very fashionably late. We probably won't have dinner until an hour after that. I'm going to eat something in the hotel room before I leave so that I won't starve.'

'Maman, now don't forget your promise. Last week's *Aujourd'hui* said that my favourite singer, Julien LeClerc, would definitely be one of the guest entertainers. You have to tell him that your daughter thinks he's absolutely *divine!*'

Nicole smiled at her daughter. 'I will, darling, for you. Although it will probably be misinterpreted. From what I have heard your Monsieur LeClerc thinks that every woman in the world is in love with him.' She paused for a moment. 'Where's your grandfather? I thought you said he would be joining you in a few minutes.'

'Here I am,' Nicole's father said as his weathered, friendly face appeared on the screen next to his granddaughter. 'I was just finishing up a section of my new novel on Peter Abelard. I didn't expect you to call this early.' Pierre des Jardins was now sixty-six years old. A successful historical novelist for many years, his life since the early death of his wife had been blessed by fortune and accomplishment. 'You look stunning!' he exclaimed after seeing his daughter in her evening wear. 'Did you buy that dress in Rome?'

'Actually, Papa,' Nicole said, again turning around so that her father could see the entire outfit, 'I bought this for Francoise's wedding three years ago. But of course I never had a chance to wear it. Do you think it's too simple?'

'Not at all,' Pierre replied. 'In fact, I think it's just perfect for this kind of extravaganza. If it's like the big fêtes that I used to attend, every woman there will be wearing her fanciest and most expensive clothing and jewellery. You will stand out in your simple black and white. Particularly with your hair down like that. You took perfect.'

'Thanks,' Nicole said. 'Even though I know you're prejudiced, I still like to hear your compliments.' She looked at her father and daughter, her only two close companions for the last seven years. 'I'm really surprisingly anxious. I don't think I'll be this nervous on the day we encounter Rama. I often feel out of my element at big parties like this and tonight I have a peculiar sense of foreboding that I can't explain. You remember, Dad, like I felt the day before our dog died when I was a child.'

Her father's face became serious. 'Maybe you'd better consider staying in the hotel. Too many of your premonitions have been accurate in the past. I remember your telling me that something was wrong with your mother two days before we received that message ...'

'It's not that strong a feeling,' Nicole interrupted. 'And besides, what would I give as an excuse? Everyone's expecting me, especially the press, according to Francesca Sabatini. She's still annoyed with me for refusing to have a personal interview with her.'

'Then I guess you should go. But try to have some fun. Don't take things so seriously for this one night.'

'And remember to say hello to Julien LeClerc for me,' Genevieve added.

'I'll miss you both when midnight comes,' Nicole said. 'It will be the first time I've been away from you on New Year's Eve since 2194.' Nicole paused for a moment, remembering their family celebrations together. 'Take care, both of you. You know I love you very much.'

'I love you, too, Maman,' Genevieve shouted. Pierre waved goodbye.

Nicole switched off the videophone and checked her watch. It was eight o'clock. She still had an hour before she was supposed to meet her driver in the lobby. She walked over to the computer terminal to order something to eat. With a few commands she requested a bowl of minestrone and a small bottle of mineral water. The computer monitor told her to expect them both in between sixteen and nineteen minutes.

I really am high-strung tonight, Nicole thought as she leafed through the magazine *Italia* and waited for her food. The feature story in *Italia* was devoted to an interview with Francesca Sabatini. The article covered ten full pages and must have had twenty different photographs of 'la bella signora'. The interviewer discussed both of Francesca's highly successful documentary projects (the first on modern love and the second on drugs), stressing the point, in the middle of some questions about the drug series, that Francesca

229

repeatedly smoked cigarettes during the conversation.

Nicole perused the article in a hurry, noting as she read that there were facets to Francesca she had never considered. *But what motivates her?* Nicole wondered to herself. *What is it that she wants?* Near the end of the magazine story, the interviewer had asked Francesca her opinion of the other two women in the Newton crew. 'I feel that I'm actually the only woman on the mission,' Francesca had answered. Nicole slowed down to read the rest of the paragraph. 'The Russian pilot Turgenyev thinks and acts like a man and the French-African princess Nicole des Jardins has purposely suppressed her femininity, which is sad because she could be such a lovely woman.'

Nicole was only slightly angered by Francesca's glib comments. More than anything, she was amused. She felt a brief competitive surge but then chided herself for such a childish reaction. *I'll ask Francesca about this article at just the right time*, Nicole thought with a smile. *Who knows? Maybe I'll even ask her if seducing married men qualifies her as feminine.*

The forty-minute drive from the hotel to the party at Hadrian's Villa, which was located on the outskirts of the Roman suburbs not far from the resort town of Tivoli, was passed in total silence. The other passenger in Nicole's car was Hiro Yamanaka, the most taciturn of all the cosmonauts. In her television interview two months earlier with Yamanaka, a frustrated Francesca Sabatini, after ten minutes of two- and three-word, monosyllabic responses to all her questions, had asked Hiro if the rumor about his being an android were true.

'What?' Hiro Yamanaka had asked.

'Are you an android?' Francesca had repeated with a mischievous smile.

'No,' the Japanese pilot had responded, his features remaining absolutely expressionless while the camera zoomed in on his face.

When the car turned off the main road between Rome and Tivoli to drive the final mile to the Villa Adriana, the traffic became congested. Progress was very slow, not only because of the many cars carrying people to the gala, but also because of the hundreds of curious onlookers and paparazzi who were lining the narrow single carriageway road.

Nicole took a deep breath as the automobile finally pulled into a circular drive and stopped. Outside her tinted window she could see a bevy of photographers and reporters, poised to pounce on whoever climbed out of the car. Her door opened automatically and she stepped out slowly, pulling her black suede coat around her and trying to be careful not to catch her heels. 'Who's that?' she heard a voice say. 'Franco, over here, quick – it's cosmonaut des Jardins.' There was a smattering of applause and the flash of many cameras. A kindly looking Italian gentleman came forward and took Nicole by the hand. People moiled around her, several microphones were stuck in her face, and it seemed as if she were being given a hundred simultaneous questions and requests in four or five different languages,

'Why have you refused all personal interviews?'

'Please open your coat so we can see your dress.'

'Do the other cosmonauts respect you as a doctor?'

'Stop a moment. Please smile.'

'What is your opinion of Francesca Sabatini?'

Nicole said nothing as the security men held back the crowd and led her to a covered electric cart. The four-passenger cart moved slowly up a long hill, leaving the crowd behind, as a pleasant Italian woman in her mid-twenties explained in English to Nicole and Hiro Yamanaka what they were seeing around them. Hadrian, who had ruled the Roman empire between 117 and 138 AD, had built this immense villa, she told them, for his own enjoyment. The architectural masterpiece represented a blending of all the building styles Hadrian had seen on his many journeys to the distant provinces and was designed by the emperor himself on three hundred acres of plain at the foot of the Tiburtini Hills.

The initial cart ride past the ancient assortment of buildings was apparently an integral part of the evening's festivities. The lighted ruins themselves were only vaguely suggestive of their previous glory, for roofs were mostly missing, the decorative statuary had all been removed, and the rough stone walls were bare of adornment. But by the time the cart wound past the ruins of the Canopus, a monument built around a rectangular pool in the Egyptian style (it was the fifteenth or sixteenth building in the complex – Nicole had lost count), a general sense of the huge extent of the villa had definitely emerged.

This man died over two thousand years ago, Nicole thought to herself, remembering her history. *One of the smartest humans who ever lived. Soldier, administrator, linguist.* She smiled as she recalled the story of Antinous. *Lonely most of his life. Except for one brief, all consuming passion that ended in tragedy.*

The cart came to a stop at the end of a short walkway. The woman guide finished her monologue. 'To honour the great Pax Romana, an extended time of world peace two millennia ago, the Italian government, helped by generous donations from the corporations listed underneath the statue over there on your right, decided in 2189 to construct a perfect replica of Hadrian's Maritime Theatre. You may recall that we passed the ruins of the original at the beginning of the ride. The goal of the reconstruction project was to show what it would have been like to have visited a part of this villa during the emperor's lifetime. The building was finished in 2193 and has been used for state events ever since.'

The guests were met by formally clad young Italian men, uniformly tall and handsome, who escorted them along the walkway, up to and through Philosopher's Hall, and finally into the Maritime Theatre. There was a brief security check at the actual entrance and then the guests were free to roam as they pleased.

Nicole was enchanted by the building. It was basically round in shape,

231

about forty metres in diameter. An annulus of water separated an inner island – on which was located a large house with five rooms and a big yard – from the wide portico with its fluted columns. There was no roof above the water or the inner part of the portico, the open skies giving the entire theatre a wonderful feeling of freedom. Around the building the guests mixed and talked and drank; advanced robot waiters rolled around carrying large trays of champagne and wine and other alcoholic spirits. Across the two small bridges that connected the island with its house and yard to the portico and the rest of the building, Nicole could see a dozen people, all dressed in white, working to set up the dinner buffet.

A heavy blonde woman and her pint-size, jocular husband, a bald man wearing an old-fashioned pair of spectacles, were rapidly approaching Nicole from about thirty feet away. Nicole prepared for the coming onslaught by taking a small sip of the champagne and cassis cocktail that had been handed to her by a strangely insistent robot a few minutes before.

'Oh, Madame des Jardins,' the man said, waving at her and closing in with great speed. 'We just have to talk to you. My wife is one of your biggest fans.' He walked up beside Nicole and gestured to his wife. 'Come on, Cecelia,' he shouted, 'I've got her.'

Nicole took a deep breath and forced a wide smile. *It's going to be one of those evenings,* she said to herself.

Finally, Nicole was thinking, *maybe I'll have a few minutes of peace and quiet.* She was sitting by herself, her back purposely toward the door, at a small table in the comer of the room. The room was at the rear of the island house in the middle of the Maritime Theatre. Nicole finished the last few bites of her food and washed them down with some wine.

Whew, she thought, trying without success to remember even half the people she had met in the last hour. She had been like a prized photograph, passed from person to person and praised by everyone. She bad been embraced, kissed, hugged, pinched, flirted with (by both men and women), and even propositioned by a rich Swedish shipbuilder who had invited her to his 'castle' outside the city of Göteborg. Nicole had hardly said a word to any of them. Her face ached from polite smiling and she was a trifle tipsy from the wine and champagne cocktails.

'Well, as I live and breathe,' she heard a familiar voice behind her say, 'I believe the lady in the white dress is none other than my fellow cosmonaut, the ice princess herself, Madame Nicole des Jardins.' Nicole turned and saw Richard Wakefield staggering toward her. He bounced off a table, reached out to stabilize himself on a chair, and nearly fell in her lap.

'Sorry,' he said, grinning and managing to seat himself beside her. 'I'm afraid I've had too much gin and tonic.' He took a big gulp from the glass that had miraculously remained unspilled in his right hand. 'And now,' he said with a wink, 'if you don't mind, I'm going to take a nap before the dolphin show.'

Nicole laughed as Richard's head hit the wooden table with a splat and he feigned unconsciousness. After a moment she leaned over playfully and forced one of his eyelids open. 'If you don't mind, comrade, could you not pass out until after you explain to me the bit about the dolphin show.'

With great effort Richard sat up and began rolling his eyes. 'You mean you don't know? You, who always know *all* the schedules and *all* the procedures? That's impossible.'

Nicole finished her wine. 'Seriously, Wakefield. What are you talking about?'

Richard opened one of the small windows and stuck his arm through it, pointing at the pool of water that encircled the house. 'The great Dr Luigi Bardolini is here with his intelligent dolphins. Francesca is going to introduce him in about fifteen minutes.' He stared at Nicole with wild abandon. 'Dr, Bardolini is going to prove, here and tonight,' he shouted, 'that his dolphins can pass our university entrance exams.'

Nicole pulled back and looked carefully at her colleague. *He really is drunk,* she thought to herself. *Maybe he feels as out of place as I do.*

Richard was now gazing intently out the window. 'This party is really some zoo, isn't it?' Nicole said after a long silence. 'Where did they find ...'

'That's it,' Wakefield interrupted her suddenly, giving the table a triumphant pounding. 'That's why this place has seemed familiar to me since the moment we walked in.' He glanced at Nicole, who was eyeing him as if he had lost his mind. 'It's a miniature Rama, don't you see?' He jumped up, unable to contain his happiness at his discovery. 'The water surrounding this house is the Cylindrical Sea, the porticoes represent the Central Plain, and we, lovely lady, are sitting in the city of New York.'

Nicole was beginning to comprehend but could not keep up with the racing thoughts of Richard Wakefield. 'And what does similarity of design prove?' he thought out loud. 'What does it mean that human architects two thousand years ago constructed a theatre with some of the same guiding principles of design as those used in the Raman ship? Similarity of nature? Similarity of culture? Absolutely not.'

He stopped, now aware that Nicole was staring fixedly at him. 'Mathematics,' he said emphatically. A quizzical expression told him that she still didn't understand completely. 'Mathematics,' he said again, surprisingly lucid all of a sudden. 'That's the key. The Ramans almost certainly didn't look like us and clearly evolved on a world far different from the Earth. But they must have understood the same mathematics as the Romans.'

His face brightened. 'Hah,' he shouted again, causing Nicole to jump. He was pleased with himself. 'Ramans and Romans. That's what tonight is all about. And at some level of development in between is modern-day homo sapiens.'

Nicole shook her head as Richard exulted in the joy of his wit. 'You don't understand, lovely lady?' he said, extending his hand to help her up from her seat. 'Then perhaps you and I should go to watch a dolphin show and I will speak to you of Ramans there and Romans here, of cabbages and kings, of dum-de-dum and sealing wax, and whether pigs have wings.'

13 HAPPY NEW YEAR

After everyone had finished eating and all the plates had been cleared, Francesca Sabatini appeared in the centre of the yard with a microphone and spent ten minutes thanking all the gala sponsors. Then she introduced Dr Luigi Bardolini, suggesting that the techniques he had pioneered to communicate with the dolphins might prove extremely useful when humans try to talk to any extraterrestrials.

Richard Wakefield had disappeared just before Francesca had started speaking, ostensibly to find the rest room and obtain another drink. Nicole had caught sight of him briefly five minutes later, just after Francesca had finished with her introduction. He had been surrounded by a pair of buxom Italian actresses, both of whom were laughing heartily at his jokes. He had waved at Nicole and winked, pointing at the two women as if his actions were self-explanatory.

Good *for you, Richard,* Nicole had thought, smiling to herself. *At least one of us social misfits is having a good time.* She now watched Franceses walk gracefully across the bridge and start to move the crowd back from the water so that Bardolini and his dolphins would have plenty of room. Francesca was wearing a tight black dress, bare on one shoulder, with a starburst of gold sequins in the front. A gold scarf was tied around her waist. Her long blonde hair was braided and pinned against her head.

You really belong here, Nicole thought, truthfully admiring Francesca's ease in large crowds. Dr Bardolini began the first segment of his dolphin show and Nicole turned her attention to the circular pool of water. Luigi Bardolini was one of those controversial scientists whose work is brilliant but never quite as exceptional as he himself wants others to believe. It was true that he had developed a unique way of communicating with the dolphins and had isolated and identified the sounds of thirty to forty action verbs in their portfolio of squeaks. But it was not true, as he so often claimed, that two of his dolphins could pass a university entrance exam. Unfortunately, the way the twenty-second century international scientific community operated, if your most outrageous or advanced theories could not be substantiated, or were held up to ridicule, then your other discoveries, no matter how solid, were often disparaged as well. This behaviour had induced an endemic conservatism in science that was not altogether healthy.

Unlike most scientists, Bardolini was a brilliant showman. In the final segment of his show he had his two most famous dolphins, Emilio and Emilia, take an intelligence test in a real-time competition against two of the villa guides, one male and one female, who had been selected at random that evening. The construct of the competitive test was enticingly simple. On two of the four large electronic screens (one pair of screens was in the water and another pair was in the yard), a three-by-three matrix was shown with a blank in the lower right-hand corner. The other eight elements were filled with different pictures and shapes. The dolphins and humans taking the test were supposed to discern the changing patterns moving from left to right and top to bottom in the matrix, and then correctly pick out, from a set of eight candidates displayed on the companion screen, the element that should be placed in the blank lower right corner. The competitors had one minute to make their choice on each problem. The dolphins in the water, like the humans on the land above them, had a control panel of eight buttons they could push (the dolphins used their snouts) to indicate their selection.

The first few problems were easy, both for the humans and for the dolphins. In the first matrix, a single white ball was in the upper left corner, two white balls in the second column of the first row, and three white balls in the matrix element corresponding to row one and column three. Since the first element of the second row was a single ball as well, half white and half black, and since the beginning element of the third row was another single ball, now fully black, it was easy to read the entire matrix quickly and determine that what belonged in the blank lower right corner was three black balls.

Later problems were not so easy. With each successive puzzle, more complications were added. The humans made their first error on the eighth matrix, the dolphins on the ninth. Altogether Dr Bardolini exhibited sixteen matrices, the last one so complicated that at least ten separate changing patterns had to be recognized to properly identify what should be entered as the last element. The final score was a tie, Humans 12, Dolphins 12. Both pairs took a bow and the audience applauded.

Nicole had found the exercise fascinating. She wasn't certain if she believed Dr Bardolini's assertion that the competition was fair and unrehearsed, but it didn't matter to her. What she thought was interesting was the nature of the competition itself, the idea that intelligence could be defined in terms of an ability to identify patterns and trends. *Is there a way that synthesis can be measured?* she thought. *In children. Or even adults, for that matter.*

Nicole had participated in the test along with the human and dolphin contestants and had correctly answered the first thirteen, missing the fourteenth because of a careless assumption, and just finishing the fifteenth accurately before the buzzer sounded the end of the allocated time. She had had no idea where to begin on the sixteenth. *And what about you Ramans?* she was wondering, as Francesca returned to the microphone to introduce Genevieve's heartthrob, Julien LeClerc. *Would you have been able to answer all sixteen correctly in one tenth the time? One hundredth?* She gulped, as she realised the full range of possibilities. *Or maybe even one millionth?*

'I never lived, 'til I met you ... I never loved, 'til I saw you ...' The soft melody of the old recorded song swam in Nicole's memory and brought back an image from fifteen years before, from another dance with another man when she had still believed that love could conquer everything. Julien LeClerc misread her body signals and pulled her closer to him. Nicole decided not to fight it. She was already very tired and, if the truth were known, it felt good being held tightly by a man for the first time in several years.

She had honoured her agreement with Genevieve. When Monsieur LeClerc had finished his short set of songs, Nicole had approached the French singer and given him the message from her daughter. As she had anticipated, he had interpreted her approach to mean something entirely different. They had continued talking while Francesca had announced to the partygoers that there would be no more formal entertainment until after midnight and that all the guests were free to drink or snack or dance to the recorded music until then. Julien had offered his arm to Nicole and the two of them had walked back over to the portico, where they had been dancing ever since.

Julien was a handsome man, in his early thirties, but he was not really Nicole's type. First of all, he was too conceited for her. He talked about himself all the time and did not pay any attention when the conversation switched to other topics. Although he was a gifted singer, he had no other particularly outstanding characteristics. *But*, Nicole reasoned as their continued dancing brought stares from the other guests, *he's all right as a dancer and it beats standing around twiddling my thumbs.*

At a break in the music Francesca came over to talk to them. 'Good for you, Nicole,' she said, her open smile appearing genuine. 'I'm glad to see that you're enjoying yourself.' She extended a small tray with half a dozen dark chocolate balls lightly sprayed with white, possibly a sugar confection. 'These are fantastic,' Francesca said. 'I made them especially for the Newton crew.'

Nicole took one of the chocolates and popped it into her mouth. It was delicious. 'Now I have a favour to ask,' Francesca continued after several seconds. 'Since I was never able to schedule a personal interview with you and our mail indicates that there are millions of people out there who would like to find out more about you, do you think that you could come over to our studio here and give me ten or fifteen minutes before midnight?'

Nicole stared intently at Francesca. A voice inside her was sending out a warning, but her mind was somehow garbling the message.

'I agree,' Julien LeClerc said while the two women looked at each other. 'The press always talks about the "mysterious lady cosmonaut" or refers to you as "the ice princess". Show them what you've shown me tonight, that you're a normal, healthy woman like everybody else.'

Why not? Nicole finally decided, suppressing her interior voice. *At least by doing it here I don't have to involve Dad and Genevieve.*

They had started to walk toward the makeshift studio on the other side of the portico when Nicole saw Shigeru Takagishi across the room. He was leaning against a column and talking to a trio of Japanese businessmen dressed in formal attire. 'Just a minute,' Nicole said to her companions, 'I'll be right back.'

'Tanoshii shinnen, Takagishi-san,' Nicole greeted him. The Japanese scientist turned, startled at first, and smiled as he saw her approach. After he formally introduced Nicole to his associates, and they all bowed to acknowledge her presence and accomplishments, Takagishi started a polite conversation.

'O genki desu ka?' he asked.

'O kage same de,' she replied. Nicole leaned across to her Japanese colleague and whispered in his ear. 'I only have a minute. I wanted to tell you that I have carefully examined all your records and I am in complete agreement with your personal physician. There is no reason to say anything about your heart anomaly to the medical committee.'

Dr Takagishi looked as if he had just been told that his wife had given birth to a healthy son. He started to say something personal to Nicole but remembered he was in the midst of a group of his countrymen. 'Dōmō arigatō gozaimasu,' he said to the retreating Nicole, his warm eyes conveying the depth of his thanks.

Nicole felt great as she waltzed into the studio between Francesca and Julien LeClerc. She posed willingly for the still photographers while Signora Sabatini ensured that all the television equipment was in working order for the interview. She sipped some more champagne and cassis, making intermittent small talk with Julien. Finally she took a seat beside Francesca underneath the klieg lights. *How wonderful*, Nicole kept thinking about the earlier interaction with Takagishi, *to be able to help that brilliant little man.*

Francesca's first question was innocent enough. She asked Nicole if she was excited about the coming launch. 'Of course,' Nicole answered. She then gave a lively summary of the training exercises that the cosmonaut crew had been undergoing while waiting for the opportunity to rendezvous with Rama II. The entire interview was conducted in English. The questions flowed in an orderly pattern. Nicole was asked to describe her role in the mission, what she expected to discover ('I don't really know, but whatever we find will be extremely interesting'), and how she happened to go to the Space Academy in the first place. After about five minutes, Nicole was feeling at ease and very comfortable; it seemed to her that she and Francesca had fallen into a complementary rhythm.

Francesca then asked three personal questions, one about her father, a second about Nicole's mother and the Senoufo tribe in the Ivory Coast, and the third about her life with Genevieve. None of them were difficult. So Nicole was totally unprepared for Francesca's last question.

'It is obvious from your daughter's photographs that her skin is considerably lighter than yours,' Francesca said in the same tone and manner that she had used for all the other questions. 'Genevieve's skin colour suggests that her father was probably white. Who was the father of your daughter?'

Nicole felt her heart rate surge as she listened to the question. Then time seemed to stand still. A surprising flood of powerful emotions engulfed Nicole and she was afraid she was going to cry. A brilliant hot image of two entwined bodies reflected in a large mirror burst into her mind and made her gasp. She momentarily looked down at her feet, trying to regain her composure.

You stupid woman, she said to herself as she struggled to calm the combination of anger and pain and remembered love that had crashed upon her like a tidal wave. *You should have known better.* Again the tears threatened and she fought them. She looked up at the lights and Francesca. The gold sequins on the front of the Italian journalist's dress had grouped into a pattern, or so it seemed to Nicole. She saw a head in the sequins, the head of a large cat, its eyes gleaming and its mouth with sharp teeth just beginning to open.

At last, after what seemed to be forever, Nicole felt that she again had her emotions under control. She stared angrily at Francesca. 'Non voglio parlare di quello,' Nicole said quietly in Italian. 'Abbiamo terminate questa intervista.' She stood up, noticed that she was trembling, and sat down again. The cameras were still rolling. She breathed deeply for several seconds. At length Nicole rose from her chair and walked out of the temporary studio.

She wanted to flee, to run away from everything, to go somewhere where she could be alone with her private feelings. But it was impossible. Julien grabbed her as she exited from the interview. 'What a bitch!' he said, waving an accusing finger in Francesca's direction. There were people all around Nicole. All of them were talking at the same time. She was having trouble focusing her eyes and ears in all the confusion.

In the distance Nicole heard some music that she vaguely recognized but the song was more than half over before she realised it was 'Auld Lang Syne.' Julien had his arm around her back and was singing lustily. He was also leading the group of twenty or so people clustered around them in singing the final words. Nicole mouthed the last bar mechanically and tried to maintain her equilibrium. Suddenly a moist pair of lips was pressed against hers and an active tongue was trying to pry open her mouth and force its way inside. Julien was kissing her feverishly, photographers were snapping pictures all around, there was an incredible amount of noise. Nicole's head began to spin and she felt as if she were going to faint. She struggled hard, finally succeeding in freeing herself from Julien's grasp.

Nicole staggered backward and bumped into an angry Reggie Wilson. He pushed her aside in his haste to grab a couple sharing a deep New Year's kiss in the flashing lights. Nicole watched him disinterestedly, as if she were in a movie theatre, or even in one of her own dreams. Reggie pulled the pair apart and raised his right arm as if he were going to slug the other man.

Francesca Sabatini restrained Reggie as a confused David Brown retreated from her embrace.

'Keep your hands off her, you bastard,' Reggie shouted, still threatening the American scientist. 'And don't think for one minute that I don't know what you're doing.' Nicole could not believe what she was seeing. Nothing made any sense. Within seconds the room was full of security guards.

Nicole was one of many people ushered summarily away from the fracas while order was being restored. As she left the studio area she happened to pass Elaine Brown, sitting by herself in the portico with her back against a column. Nicole had met and enjoyed Elaine when she had gone to Dallas to talk to David Brown's family physician about his allergies. At the moment Elaine was obviously drunk and in no mood to talk to anybody. 'You shit,' Nicole heard her mutter, 'I never should have showed you the results until after I had published them myself. Then everything would have been different.'

Nicole left the gala as soon as she was able to arrange her transportation back to Rome. Francesca unbelievably tried to escort her out to the limousine as if nothing had happened. Nicole curtly rejected her fellow cosmonaut's offer and walked out alone.

It started to snow during the ride back to the hotel. Nicole concentrated on the falling snowflakes and was eventually able to clear her mind enough to assess the evening. Of one thing she was absolutely certain. There had been something unusual and very powerful in that chocolate ball she had eaten. Nicole had never before come so close to losing complete control of her emotions. *Maybe she gave one to Wilson too,* Nicole thought. *And that partially explains his eruption. But why?* she asked herself again. *What is she trying to accomplish?*

Back at the hotel she prepared quickly for bed. But just as she was ready to turn out the lights, Nicole thought she heard a light knock on the door. She stopped and listened, but there was no sound for several seconds. She had almost decided that her ears were playing tricks on her when she heard the knock again. Nicole pulled the hotel robe around her and approached the locked door very cautiously. 'Who's there?' she said forcefully but not convincingly. 'Identify yourself.'

She heard a sound of scraping and a piece of folded paper was thrust under the door. Nicole, still wary and frightened, picked up the paper and opened it. On it was written, in the original Senoufo script of her mother's tribe, three simple words – *Ronata. Omeh. Here.* Ronata was Nicole's name in Senoufo.

A mixture of panic and excitement caused Nicole to open the door without first checking on the monitor to see who was outside. Standing ten feet away from the door, his amazing old eyes already locked on hers, was an ancient, wizened man with his face painted in green and white horizontal streaks. He was wearing a full-length, bright green tribal costume, similar to a robe, on which were gold swashes and a collection of line drawings of no apparent meaning.

'Omeh!' Nicole said, her heart threatening to jump out of her chest. 'What are you doing here?' she added in Senoufo.

The old black man said nothing. He was holding out a stone and a small vial of some kind, both in his right hand. After several seconds he stepped deliberately forward into the room. Nicole backpedaled with each of his steps. His gaze never wavered from her. When they were in the centre of her hotel room and only three or four feet apart, the old man looked up at the ceiling and began to chant. It was a ritual Senoufo song, a general blessing and spell invocation used by the tribal shaman for hundreds of years to ward off evil spirits.

When he had finished the chant the old man Omeh stared again at his great-granddaughter and began to speak very slowly. 'Ronata,' he said, 'Omeh has sensed strong danger in this life. It is written in the tribal chronicles that the man of three centuries will chase the evil demons away from the woman with no companion. But Omeh cannot protect Ronata after Ronata leaves the kingdom of Minowe. Here,' he said, taking her hand and placing the stone and vial in it, 'these stay with Ronata always.'

Nicole looked down at the stone, a smooth, polished oval about eight inches long and four inches in each of the other two dimensions. The stone was mostly creamy white with a few strange brown lines wriggling across its surface. The small green vial that he had given her was no bigger than a travelling bottle of perfume.

'The water from the Lake of Wisdom can help Ronata,' Omeh said. 'Ronata will know the time to drink.' He tilted his head back and earnestly repeated the earlier chant, this time with his eyes closed. Nicole stood beside him in puzzled silence, the stone and the vial in her right hand. When he was finished singing, Omeh shouted three words that Nicole did not understand. Then he abruptly turned around and walked quickly toward the open door. Startled, Nicole ran out into the hall just in time to see his green gown disappear into the elevator.

14 GOODBYE HENRY

Nicole and Genevieve walked arm in arm up the hill through the light snow. 'Did you see the look on that American's face when I told him who you were?' Genevieve said with a laugh. She was very proud of her mother.

Nicole shifted her skis and poles over to the other shoulder as they approached the hotel. 'Guten Abend', an old man who would have made a perfect Santa Claus mumbled as he ambled by. 'I wish you wouldn't be so quick to tell people,' Nicole said, not really chastizing her daughter. 'Sometimes it's nice not to be recognized.'

There was a small shed for the skis beside the entrance to the hotel. Nicole and Genevieve stopped and placed their equipment in a locker. They exchanged their ski boots for soft snow slippers and walked back out into the fading light Mother and daughter stood together for a moment and looked back down the hill toward the village of Davos. 'You know,' said Nicole, 'there was a time today, during our race down that back piste toward Klosters, when I found it impossible to believe that I will actually be way out there' – she gestured at the sky – 'in less than two weeks, headed for a rendezvous with a mysterious alien spacecraft. Sometimes the human mind balks at the truth.'

'Maybe it's only a dream,' her daughter said lightly. Nicole smiled. She loved Genevieve's sense of play. Whenever the day-today drudgery of the hard work and tedious preparation would begin to overwhelm Nicole, she could always count on her daughter's easy nature to lighten her mood. They were quite a trio, the three of them that lived at Beauvois. Each of them was sorely dependent on the other two. Nicole did not like to think how the hundred-day separation might affect their harmonious accord.

'Does it bother you that I will be gone so long?' Nicole asked Genevieve as they entered the hotel lobby. A dozen people were sitting around a roaring fire in the middle of the room. An inconspicuous but efficient Swiss waiter was serving hot drinks to the apres-ski crew. There would be no robots in a Morosani hotel, not even for room service.

'I don't think of it that way,' her cheerful daughter responded. 'After all, I'll be able to talk with you almost every night on the videophone. The delay time will even make it fun. And challenging.' They walked past the old-fashioned registration desk. 'Besides,' Genevieve added, 'I'll be the centre of attention at school for the whole mission. My class project is already set; I'm going to draw a psychological portrait of the Ramans based on my conversations with you.'

Nicole smiled again and shook her head. Genevieve's optimism was always infectious. It was a shame—

'Oh, Madame des Jardins.' The voice interrupted her thought. The hotel manager was beckoning to her from the desk. Nicole turned around. 'There's a message for you,' the manager continued. 'I was told to deliver it to you personally.'

He handed her a small plain envelope. Nicole opened it and saw just the tiniest portion of a crest on the note card. Her heart raced into overdrive as she closed the envelope again. 'What is it, Mother?' Genevieve inquired. 'It must be special to be hand delivered. Nobody does things like that these days.'

Nicole tried to hide her feelings from her daughter. 'It's a secret memo about my work,' she lied. 'The deliveryman made a terrible mistake. He should never have given it even to Herr Graf. He should have put it in my hands only.'

'More confidential medical data about the crew?' Genevieve asked. She and her mother had often discussed the delicate role of the life science officer on a major space mission.

Nicole nodded. 'Darling,' she said to her daughter, 'why don't you run upstairs and tell your grandfather that I'll be along in a few minutes. We'll still plan dinner for seven-thirty. I'll read this message now and see if any urgent response is required.'

Nicole kissed Genevieve and waited until her daughter was on the elevator before walking back outside into the light snow. It was dark now. She stood under the streetlight and opened the envelope with her cold hands. She had difficulty controlling her trembling fingers. *You fool*, she thought, *you careless fool. After all this time. What if the girl had seen. . . .*

The crest was the same as it had been on that afternoon, fifteen and a half years ago, when Darren Higgins had handed her the dinner invitation outside the Olympic press area. Nicole was surprised by the strength of her emotions, She steeled herself and finally looked at the rest of the note below the crest.

'Sorry for the last-minute notice. Must see you tomorrow. Noon exactly. Warming hut #8 on the Weissfluhjoch. Come alone. Henry.'

The next morning Nicole was one of the first in line for the cable car that carried skiers to the top of the Weissfluhjoch. She climbed into the polished glass car with about twenty others and leaned against the window while the door automatically shut. *I have seen him only once in these fifteen years*, she thought to herself, *and yet . . .*

As the cable car ascended, Nicole pulled her snow glasses down over her eyes. It was a dazzling morning, not unlike the January morning seven years earlier when her father had called for her from the villa. They had had a rare snowfall at Beauvois the night before and, after much pleading, she had let Genevieve stay home from school to play in the snow. Nicole was working at the hospital in Tours at the time and was waiting to hear about her application to the Space Academy.

She had been showing her seven-year-old daughter how to make a snow angel when Pierre had called a second time from the house. 'Nicole, Genevieve, there's something special in our mail,' he had said. 'It must have come during the night.' Nicole and Genevieve had run to the villa in their snowsuits while Pierre posted the full text of the message on the wall video-screen.

'Most extraordinary,' Pierre had said. 'It seems we've all been invited to the English coronation, including the private reception afterward. This is extremely unusual.'

'Oh, Grandpapa,' Genevieve said excitedly, 'I want to go. Can we go? Do I get to meet a real king and queen?'

'There is no queen, darling,' her grandfather replied, 'unless you mean the queen mother. This king has not yet married.'

Nicole read the invitation several times without saying anything. After Genevieve had calmed down and left the room, her father had put his arms around Nicole.

'I want to go,' she had said quietly.

'Are you certain?' he had asked, pulling away and regarding her with an inquisitive stare.

'Yes,' she had answered firmly.

Henry had never seen her until that evening, Nicole was thinking as she checked first her watch and then her equipment in preparation for her ski run down from the summit. *Father had been wonderful. He had let me disappear at Beauvois and almost nobody knew I had a baby until Genevieve was almost a year old. Henry never even suspected. Not until that night at Buckingham Palace.*

Nicole could still see herself waiting in the reception line. The king had been late. Genevieve had been fidgety. At last Henry had been standing opposite her. 'The honourable Pierre des Jardins of Beauvois, France, with his daughter, Nicole, and granddaughter, Genevieve.' Nicole had bowed very properly and Genevieve had curtsied.

'So this is Genevieve,' the king had said. He had bent down for only a moment and put a hand under the child's chin. When the girl had lifted up her face he had seen something that he recognized. He had turned to look at Nicole, a trace of questioning in his glance. Nicole had revealed nothing with her smile. The crier was calling out the names of the next guests in the line. The king had moved on.

So *you sent Darren to the hotel,* Nicole thought as she schussed a short slope, aimed for a small jump, and was airborne for a second or two. *And he hummed and ha'ed and finally asked me if I would come have tea.* Nicole dug her edges into the snow and came to an abrupt stop. 'Tell Henry I can't,' she remembered saying to Darren in London seven years earlier.

She looked again at her watch. It was only eleven o'clock, too early to ski to the hut. She eased over to one of the lifts and took another ride to the summit.

It was two minutes past noon when Nicole arrived at the small chalet on the edge of the woods. She took off her skis, stuck them in the snow, and walked toward the front door. She ignored the conspicuous signs all around her that said EINTRITT VERBOTEN. From out of nowhere came two burly men, one of whom actually jumped between Nicole and the door to the hut. 'It's all right,' she heard a familiar voice say, 'we're expecting her.' The two guards vanished as quickly as they had appeared and Nicole saw Darren, smiling as always, occupying the doorway to the chalet.

'Hi there, Nicole,' he said in his normal friendly fashion. Darren had aged. There were a few flecks of grey around his temples and some salt with the pepper in his short beard. 'How are you?' he asked.

'I'm fine, Darren,' she answered, aware that despite all her lectures to herself, she was already starting to feel nervous. She reminded herself that she was now a professional, as accomplished in her own way as this king she was about to see. Nicole then strode forcefully into the chalet.

It was warm inside. Henry was standing with his back to a small fireplace. Darren closed the door behind her and left the two of them alone. Nicole self-consciously removed her scarf and opened her parka. She took off her snow glasses. They stared at each other for twenty, maybe thirty seconds, neither saying a word, neither wanting to interrupt the powerful flow of emotions that was carrying each of them back to two magnificent days fifteen years before.

'Hello, Nicole,' the king said finally. His voice was soft and tender.

'Hello, Henry,' she replied. He started to walk around the couch, to come close to her, perhaps to touch her, but there was something in her body language that stopped him. He leaned on the side of the couch.

'Won't you sit down?' he invited.

Nicole shook her head. 'I'd prefer to stand, if it's all right with you.' She waited a few more seconds. Their eyes again locked in a deep communication. She felt herself being drawn to him despite her strong internal warnings. 'Henry,' she blurted out suddenly, 'why did you summon me here? It must be important. It's not normal for the king of England to spend his days sitting in a chalet on the side of a Swiss ski mountain.'

Henry walked toward the corner of the room. 'I brought you a present,' he said as he bent down with his back to Nicole, 'in honour of your thirty-sixth birthday.'

Nicole laughed. Some of the tension was easing. 'That's tomorrow,' she said. 'You're a day early. But why ...'

He extended a data cube toward her. 'This is the most valuable gift I could find for you,' he said seriously, 'and it has taken many marks from the royal treasury to compile it.'

She looked at him quizzically,

'I have been worried for some time about this mission of yours,' Henry said, 'and in the beginning I could not understand why. But about four months ago, one night when I was playing with Prince Charles and Princess Eleanor, I realised what was bothering me. My intuitive sense tells me that this crew of yours will have problems. I know it sounds crazy, particularly coming from me, but I'm not worried about the Ramans. That megalomaniac Brown is probably right, the Ramans couldn't care less about us Earthlings. But you're about to spend a hundred days in confined quarters with eleven other ...'

He could tell that Nicole was not following him. 'Here,' he said, 'take this cube. 1 had my intelligence agents put together full and complete dossiers on every member of the Newton dozen, including you.' Nicole's brow furrowed. 'The information, most of which is not available in the official ISA files, confirmed my personal view that the Newton team contains quite a few unstable elements. I didn't know what to do with—'

'This is none of your business,' Nicole interrupted angrily. She was affronted by Henry's involvement in her professional life. 'Why are you meddling ...'

'Hey, hey, calm down, will you,' the king replied. '1 assure you my motives were all good. Look,' he added, 'you probably won't even need all this information, but I thought that maybe it could be useful. Take it. Throw it away if you like. You're the life science officer. You can treat it however you want.'

Henry could tell that he had botched the meeting. He walked away and sat down in a chair facing the fire. His back was toward Nicole.

'Take care of yourself, Nicole,' he mumbled.

She thought for a long moment, put the data cube inside her parka, and walked over behind the king. 'Thank you, Henry,' she said. Nicole let her hand fall on his shoulder. He didn't turn around. He reached up with his hand and very slowly wrapped his fingers around hers. They remained in that position for almost a minute.

'There was some data that eluded even my investigators,' he said in a low voice. 'One fact in particular in which I was extremely interested.'

Nicole could hear her heart amid the crackle of the logs in the fireplace. A voice inside her shouted *Tell him, tell him*. But another voice, full of wisdom, counseled silence.

She slowly withdrew her fingers from his. He turned around to look at her. She smiled. Nicole walked over to the door. She put her scarf back on her head and zipped her parka before going outside. 'Goodbye, Henry,' she said.

15 ENCOUNTER

The combined Newton spacecraft had manoeuvered so that Rama filled the expanded viewpoint in the control centre. The alien spaceship was immense. Its surface was a dull, drab grey, and its long body was a geometrically perfect cylinder. Nicole stood beside Valeriy Borzov in silence. For each of them, this first sight of the entire Rama vehicle in the sunlight was a moment to savour.

'Have you detected any differences?' Nicole said at length.

'Not yet,' Commander Borzov replied. 'It looks as if the two of them came off the same assembly line.' They were quiet again.

'Wouldn't you love to see that assembly line?' Nicole asked.

Valeriy Borzov nodded. A small flying craft, like a bat or a hummingbird zoomed past the viewport in the near field and headed off in the direction of Rama. 'The exterior drones will confirm the similarities. Each of them has a stored set of images from Rama I. Any variations will be logged and reported within three hours.'

'And if there are no unexplained variations?'

'Then we proceed as planned,' General Borzov answered with a smile. 'We dock, open up Rama, and release the interior drones.' He glanced at his watch. 'All of which should take place about twenty-two hours from now, provided the life science officer asserts that the crew is ready.'

'The crew is in fine shape,' Nicole reported. 'I've just finished looking at a synopsis of the cruise health data again. It's been surprisingly regular. Except for hormonal abnormalities in all three women, which were not totally unexpected, we have seen no significant anomalies in forty days.'

'So physically we're all ready to go,' the commander said thoughtfully, 'but what about our psychological readiness? Are you troubled about this recent spate of arguments? Or can we chalk it up to tension and excitement?'

Nicole was silent for a moment. 'I agree these four days since the docking have been a little rough. Of course, we knew about the Wilson-Brown problem even before launch. We partially solved it by having Reggie on your ship during most of the cruise, but now that we've joined the two spacecraft and the team is all together again, those two seem to be at each other at every opportunity. Particularly if Francesca is around.'

'I tried to talk to Wilson twice while the two ships were separated,' Borzov said in a frustrated tone. 'He wouldn't discuss it. But it's clear that he is very angry about something.'

General Borzov walked over to the control panel and started fiddling with the keyboards. Sequencing information appeared on one of the monitors. 'It must involve Sabatini,' he continued. 'Wilson didn't do much work during cruise, but his log indicates that he spent an inordinate amount of time on the videophone with her. And he was always in a foul mood. He even offended O'Toole.' General Borzov turned and looked intently at Nicole. 'As my life science officer, I want to know if you have any official recommendations about the crew, especially with respect to psychological interactions among the team members.'

Nicole had not expected this. When General Borzov had scheduled this final 'crew health assessment' with her, she had not thought that the meeting would extend to the mental health of the Newton dozen as well. 'You're asking for a professional psychological evaluation also?' she asked.

'Certainly,' General Borzov replied. 'I want an A5401 from you that attests to both the physical and psychological readiness of every one of the crew members. The procedure clearly states that the commanding officer, before each sortie, should request crew certification from the life science officer.'

'But during the simulations you asked only for physical health data.'

Borzov smiled. 'I can wait, Madame des Jardins,' he said, 'if you'd like time to prepare your report.'

'No, no,' Nicole said after some reflection. 'I can give my opinions now and then officially document them later tonight.' She hesitated several more seconds before continuing. 'I wouldn't put Wilson and Brown together as crew members on any subteam, at least not in the first sortie. And I'd even have some qualms, although this opinion is certainly not as strong, about combining Francesca in a group with either of the two men. I would place no other limitations of any kind on this crew.'

'Good. Good.' The commander grinned broadly, 'I appreciate your report, and not just because it confirms my own opinions. As you can understand, these matters can sometimes be fairly delicate.' General Borzov abruptly changed the subject. 'Now I have another question of an altogether different nature to ask you.'

'What's that?'

'Francesca came to me this morning and suggested that we have a party tomorrow night. She contends that the crew is tense and in need of some kind of release before the first sortie inside Rama. Do you agree with her?'

Nicole reflected for a moment. 'It's not a bad idea,' she replied. 'The strain has been definitely showing ... But what kind of party did you have in mind?'

'A dinner all together, here in the control room, some wine and vodka, maybe even a little entertainment.' Borzov smiled and put his arm on Nicole's shoulder. 'I'm asking your professional opinion, you understand, as my life science officer.'

'Of course,' Nicole said with a laugh. 'General,' she added, 'if you think it's time for the crew to have a party, then I'd be delighted to lend a hand ...'

Nicole finished her report and transferred the file by data line over to Borzov's's computer in the military ship. She had been very careful in her language to identify the problem as a 'personality conflict' rather than any kind of behavioural pathology. To Nicole, the problem between Wilson and Brown was straightforward: jealousy, pure and simple, the ancient green-eyed monster itself.

She was certain that it was wise to prevent Wilson and Brown from working closely together during sorties inside Rama. Nicole chastised herself for not having raised the issue with Borzov on her own. She realised that her mission portfolio included mental health as well, but somehow she had difficulty thinking of herself as the crew psychiatrist. *I avoid it because it's not an objective process*, she thought. *We have no sensors yet to measure good or bad mental health.*

Nicole walked down the hall of the living area. She was careful to keep one foot on the flóor at all times; she was so accustomed to the weightless environment that it was almost second nature. Nicole was glad that the Newton design engineers had worked so hard to minimize the differences between being in space and on the Earth. It made the job of being a cosmonaut much simpler by allowing the crew to concentrate on the more important elements of their work.

Nicole's room was at the end of the corridor. Although each of the cosmonauts had private quarters (the result of heated arguments between the crew and the system engineers, the latter having insisted that sleeping in pairs was a more efficient use of the space), the rooms were very small and confining. There were eight bedrooms on this larger vehicle, called the scientific ship by the crew members. The military ship had four more small bedrooms. Both spacecraft also had exercise rooms and 'lobbies,' common rooms where there was more comfortable furniture as well as some entertainment options not available in the bedrooms.

As Nicole passed Janos Tabori's room on her way to the exercise area, she heard his unmistakable laugh. His door was open as usual. 'Did you really expect me,' Janos was saying, 'to trade bishops and leave your knights in command of the centre of the board? Come on, Shig, 1 may not be a master, but I do learn from my mistakes. I fell for that one in an earlier game.'

Tabori and Takagishi were involved in their usual postprandial chess match. Almost every 'night' (the crew had stayed on a twenty-four-hour day that coincided with Greenwich Mean Time) the two men played for an hour or so before sleeping. Takagishi was a ranked chess master but he was also softhearted and wanted to encourage Tabori. So in virtually every game, after establishing a solid position, Takagishi would allow his edge to be eroded.

Nicole stuck her head in the door. 'Come in, beautiful,' Janos said with a grin. 'Watch me destroy our Asiatic friend in this pseudocerebral endeavor.' Nicole had started to explain that she was going to the exercise room when a strange creature, about the size of a big mouse, scurried through her legs and into Tabori's room. She jumped back involuntarily as the toy, or whatever it was, headed for the two men.

> The ousel cock, so black of hue
> with orange-tawny bill,
> the throstle, with his note so true
> the wren with little quill ...

The robot was singing as it skipped toward Janos. Nicole dropped down on her knees and examined the curious newcomer. It had the lower body of a human and the head of a donkey. It continued to sing. Tabori and Takagishi stopped their game and both laughed at the bewildered expression on Nicole's face.

'Go on,' said Janos, 'tell him that you love him. That's what the fairy queen Titania would do.'

Nicole shrugged her shoulders. The little robot was temporarily quiet. As Janos urged again, Nicole mumbled 'I love you' to the twenty-centimetre Athenian with a mule's head.

The miniature Bottom turned to Nicole. 'Methinks, mistress, you should have little reason for that. And yet, to say the truth, reason and love keep little company together nowadays.'

Nicole was amazed. She reached out to pick up the tiny figure but stopped herself when she heard another voice.

'Lord, what fools these mortals be. Now where is that player I changed into an ass. Bottom, where art thou?'

A second small robot, this one dressed as an elf, leapt into the room. When he saw Nicole, he jumped up from the floor and hovered at eye level for several seconds, his tiny back wings beating at a frantic pace. 'I be Puck, fair lass,' he said. 'I've not seen thee before.' The robot dropped to the ground and was silent. Nicole was now dumbfounded.

'What in the world ...' she started to say.

'Shh ...' Janos said, motioning for her to be quiet. He pointed at Puck. Bottom was sleeping in the corner near the edge of Janos' bed. Puck had now found Bottom and was spraying him with a fine light dust from a small pouch. As the three human beings watched, Bottom's head began to change. Nicole could tell that the small plastic and metal pieces making up the ass' head were simply rearranging themselves, but even she was impressed by the scope of the metamorphosis. Puck scampered off just as Bottom awakened with his new human head and started talking.

'1 have had a most rare vision,' Bottom said. 'I have had a dream, past the wit of man to say what dream it was. Man is but an ass if he go about to expound this dream.'

'Bravo, Bravo,' Janos shouted as the creature fell silent.

'O medetō,' Takagishi added.

Nicole sat down in the single unoccupied chair and looked at her companions. 'And to think,' she said, shaking her head, 'that I actually told the commander you two were psychologically sound.' She paused two or three seconds. 'Would one of you please tell me what is going on here?'

'It's Wakefield,' Janos said. 'The man is absolutely brilliant and, unlike some geniuses, also very clever. In addition he's a Shakespeare fanatic. He has a whole family of these little guys, although I think Puck is the only one that flies and Bottom's the only one that changes shape.'

'Puck doesn't fly,' Richard Wakefield said, coming into the room. 'He is barely capable of hovering, and only for a short period.' Wakefield seemed embarrassed. 'I didn't know you were going to be here,' he said to Nicole. 'Sometimes I entertain these two in the middle of their chess game.'

'One night,' Janos added as Nicole remained speechless, 'I had just conceded defeat to Shig when we heard what we thought was a fracas in the hall. Moments later, Tybalt and Mercutio entered the room, swearing and slashing their swords at each other.'

'This is a hobby of yours?' Nicole asked after several seconds, indicating the robots with a wave of her hand.

'My lady,' Janos interrupted before Wakefield could answer, 'never, *never* mistake a passion for a hobby. Our esteemed Japanese scientist does not play chess as a hobby. And this young man from The Bard's home town of Stratford-on-Avon does not create these robots as a hobby.'

Nicole glanced at Richard. She was trying to imagine the amount of energy and work that was necessary for the creation of sophisticated robots like the ones she had just seen. Not to mention talent and, of course, passion. 'Very impressive,' she said to Wakefield.

His smile acknowledged her compliment. Nicole excused herself and started to leave the room. Puck zoomed around her and stood in the doorway.

> If we shadows have offended,
> Think but this, and all is mended,
> That you have but slumbered here,
> While these visions did appear.

Nicole was laughing as she stepped over the sprite and waved good night to her friends.

Nicole stayed in the exercise room longer than she expected, Ordinarily thirty minutes of hard bicycling or running in place was enough to release her tensions and relax her body for sleep. On this evening, however, with the goal of their mission now so close at hand, it was necessary for her to work out for a longer time to calm her hyperactive system. Part of her difficulty was her residual concern about the report she had filed recommending that Wilson and Brown be separated on all important mission activities.

Was I too hasty? she asked herself. *Did I let General Borzov sway my opinion?* Nicole was very proud of her professional reputation and often constructively second-guessed her major decisions. Toward the end of her exercise she convinced herself again that she had filed the proper report. Her tired body told her that it was ready to sleep.

When she returned to the living area in the spacecraft, it was dark everywhere except in the hallway. As she started to turn left into the corridor that led to her room, she happened to glance beyond the lobby, in the direction of the small room where she kept all the medical supplies. *That's strange,* she thought, straining her eyes in the dim light. *It looks as if I left the supply room door open.*

Nicole walked across the lobby. The supply door was indeed ajar. She had already activated the automatic lock and had started to close the door when she heard a noise inside the dark room. Nicole reached in and turned on the light. She surprised Francesca Sabatini, who was sitting in the corner at a computer terminal. There was information displayed on the monitor in front of her and Francesca was holding a thin bottle in one of her hands.

'Oh, hello Nicole,' Francesca said nonchalantly, as if it were normal for her to be sitting in the dark at the computer in the medical supply room.

Nicole walked slowly over to the computer. 'What's going on?' she said casually, her eyes scanning the information on the screen. From the coded headings, Nicole could tell that Francesca had requested the inventory subroutine to list the birth control devices available onboard the spacecraft.

'What is this?' Nicole now asked, pointing at the monitor. There was a trace of irritation in her voice. All the cosmonauts knew that the medical supply room was off limits to everyone but the life science officer.

When Francesca still did not reply, Nicole became angry. 'How did you get in here?' she demanded. The two women were only a few centimetres apart in the small alcove next to the desk. Nicole suddenly reached over and grabbed the bottle out of Francesca's hand. While Nicole was reading the label, Francesca pushed her way through the narrow space and headed for the door. Nicole discovered that the liquid in her hand was for inducing abortions and quickly followed Francesca into the lobby.

'Are you going to explain this?' Nicole asked.

'Just give me the bottle, please,' Francesca said finally.

'I can't do that,' answered Nicole, shaking her head. 'This is a very strong medicine with serious side effects. What did you think you were going to do? Steal it and have it pass unnoticed? As soon as I completed an inventory comparison I would have known that it was gone.'

The two women stared at each other for several seconds. 'Look, Nicole,' Francesca said at length, managing a smile, 'this is really a very simple matter. I have discovered recently, much to my chagrin, that I am in the very early stages of pregnancy. I wish to abort the embryo. It's a private matter and I did not want to involve you or any of the rest of the crew.'

'You can't be pregnant,' Nicole replied quickly. 'I would have seen it in your biometry data.'

'I'm only four or five days. But I'm certain. I can already feel the changes in my body. And it's the right time of the month.'

'You know the proper procedures for medical problems,' Nicole said after some hesitation. 'This might have been very simple, to use your phrase, if you had first come to me. Most likely I would have respected your request for confidentiality. But now you've given me a dilemma ...'

'Will you stop with the bureaucratic lecture,' Francesca interrupted sharply. 'I'm really not interested in the goddamn rules. A man has made me pregnant and I intend to remove the foetus. Now, are you going to give me the bottle, or must I find another way?'

Nicole was outraged. 'You are amazing,' she responded to Francesca. 'Do you really expect me to hand you this bottle and walk away? Without asking any questions? You may be that cavalier about your life and health, but I certainly am not. I have to examine you first, check your medical history, determine the age of the embryo – only then would I even *consider* prescribing this medicine for you. Besides, I would feel compelled as well to point out to you that there are moral and psychological ramifications—'

Francesca laughed out loud. 'Spare me your ramifications, Nicole. I don't need your upper class Beauvois morality passing judgment on my life. Congratulations to you for raising a child as a single parent. My situation is much different. The father of this baby purposely stopped taking his pills, thinking my being pregnant would rekindle my love for him. He was wrong. This baby is unwanted. Now, should I be more graphic ...'

'That's enough,' Nicole interrupted, pursing her lips in disgust. 'The details of your personal life are really none of my business. I must decide what is best for you and for the mission.' She paused. 'In any event, I must insist on a proper examination, including the normal pelvic internal image set. If you refuse, then I won't authorize the abortion. And of course I'd be forced to make a complete report ...'

Francesca laughed. 'You don't need to threaten me. I am not *that* stupid. If it will make you feel better to stick your fancy equipment between my legs, then be my guest. But let's do it. I want this baby out of me before the sortie.'

Nicole and Francesca hardly exchanged a dozen words during the next hour. They went together to the small infirmary, where Nicole used her sensitive instruments to verify the existence and size of the embryo. She also tested Francesca for her acceptability to receive the abortion liquid. The foetus had been growing inside Francesca for five days. *Who might you be?*

Nicole thought as she looked on the monitor at the microscopic image of the tiny sac embedded in the walls of the uterus. Even in the microscope on the probe there was no way to tell that the collection of cells was a living thing. *But you are already alive. And much of your future is already programmed by your genes.*

Nicole made the printer list for Francesca what she could expect physically once she had ingested the medicine. The foetus would be swept away, rejected by her body, within twenty-four hours. There could possibly be some slight cramping with the normal menstruation that would follow immediately.

Francesca drank the liquid without hesitation. As her patient was dressing, Nicole thought back to the time when she had first suspected her own pregnancy. *Never once did I consider . . . And not just because her father was a prince. No. It was a question of responsibility. And love.*

'I can tell what you're thinking,' Francesca said when she was ready to leave. She was standing by the infirmary door. 'But don't waste your time. You have enough problems of your own.'

Nicole did not reply. 'So tomorrow the little bastard will be gone,' Francesca said coldly, her eyes tired and angry. 'It's a damn good thing. The world doesn't need another half-black baby.' Francesca didn't wait for Nicole's response.

16 RAMA RAMA BURNING BRIGHT

The touchdown near the entry port to Rama was smooth and without incident. Following the precedent of Commander Norton seventy years earlier, General Borzov instructed Yamanaka and Turgenyev to guide the Newton to a contact point just outside the hundred-metre circular disc centred on the spin axis of the giant cylinder. A set of low, pillbox-shaped structures temporarily held the spacecraft from Earth in place against the slight centrifugal force created by the spinning Rama. Within ten minutes strong attachments anchored the Newton firmly to its target.

The large disc was, as anticipated, the outer seal of the Raman air lock. Wakefield and Tabori departed from the Newton in their EVA gear and started searching for an embedded wheel. The wheel, which was the manual control for the air lock, was in exactly the predicted place. It turned as expected and exposed an opening in the outer shell of Rama. Since nothing about Rama II had yet varied from its predecessor in any way, the two cosmonauts continued with the entry procedure.

Four hours later, after considerable shuttling back and forth in the half kilometre of corridors and tunnels that connected the great hollow interior of the alien spaceship to the external air lock, the two men had finished opening the three redundant cylindrical doors. They had also deployed the transportation system that would ferry people and equipment from the Newton to the inside of Rama. This ferry had been designed by the engineers on Earth to slide along the parallel grooves the Ramans had cut into the walls of the outer tunnels unknown ages ago.

After a short break for lunch, Yamanaka joined Wakefield and Tabori and the three of them constructed the planned Alpha communications relay station at the inside end of the tunnel. The patterns of the arrayed antennae had been carefully engineered so that, if the second Raman vehicle was identical to the first, two-way communication would be possible between cosmonauts located anywhere on the stairways or in the northern half of the Central Plain. The master communication plan called for the establishment of another major relay station, to be called Beta, near the Cylindrical Sea; the pair of stations would provide strong links everywhere in the Northern Hemicylinder and would even extend to the island of New York.

Brown and Takagishi took their positions in the control centre once the operation of the Alpha relay station was verified. The countdown to interior drone deployment proceeded. Takagishi was obviously both nervous and excited as he finished his preflight tests with his drone. Brown seemed relaxed, even casual, as he completed his final preparations. Francesca Sabatini was sitting in front of the multiple monitors, ready to select the best images for real-time transmission to the Earth.

General Borzov himself announced the major events in the sequence. He paused for a dramatic breath before issuing the command to activate the two drones. The drones then flew away into the dark emptiness of Rama. Seconds later the main screen in the control centre, whose picture came directly from the drone being commanded by David Brown, was flooded with light as the first flare ignited. When the light became more manageable, the outline of the first wide-angle shot could be seen. It had always been planned that this initial picture would be a composite of the Northern Hemisphere, covering all the territory from the bowl-shaped end where they had entered down to the Cylindrical Sea at the midpoint of the artificial world. The sharp image that was eventually frozen on the screen was overwhelming. It was one thing to read about Rama and to conduct simulations inside its replica; it was quite another to be anchored to the gigantic spaceship near the orbit of Venus, and to be taking a first look inside... .

That the vista was familiar barely lessened the wonder of the image. In the end of the crater-shaped bowl, starting from the tunnels, a complex of terraces and ramps fanned out until they reached the main body of the spinning cylinder. Trisecting this bowl were three wide ladders, resembling broad railroad tracks, each of which later expanded into enormous stairways with more than thirty thousand steps each. The ladder/stairway combinations resembled three equally spaced ribs of an umbrella and provided a way to ascend (or descend) from the flat bottom of the crater to the vast Central Plain wrapped around the wall of the spinning cylinder.

The northern half of the Central Plain spread out to fill most of the picture on the screen. The huge expanse was broken into rectangular fields that had irregular dimensions except immediately around the 'cities.' The three cities in the wide-angle image – clusters of tall slim objects, resembling manmade buildings, that were connected by what looked like highways running along the edges of the fields – were immediately recognized by the crew as the Paris, Rome, and London named by the first Raman explorers. Equally striking in the image were the long straight grooves or valleys of the Central Plain. These three linear trenches, ten kilometres long and a hundred metres wide, were equally spaced around the curve of Rama. During the first Raman encounter these valleys had been the sources of the light that had filled the 'worldlet' shortly after the melting of the Cylindrical Sea.

The strange sea, a body of water running completely around the huge cylinder, was at the far edge of the image. It was still frozen, as expected, and in its centre was the mysterious island of towering skyscrapers that had been called New York since its original discovery. The skyscrapers stretched off the end of the picture, the looming towers beckoning to be visited.

The entire crew stared silently at the image for almost a minute. Then Dr David Brown started hooting. 'All right, Rama,' he said in a proud voice. 'You see, all you disbelievers,' he shouted loud enough for everyone to hear, 'it is *exactly* like the first one.' Francesca's video camera turned to record Brown's exultation. Most of the rest of the crew were still speechless, transfixed by the details on the monitor.

Meanwhile, Takagishi's drone was transmitting narrow-angle photos of the area just under the tunnel. These images were featured on the smaller screens around the control centre. The pictures would be used to reverify the designs of the communication and transportation infrastructure to be established inside Rama. This was the real 'job' of this phase of the mission – comparing the thousands of pictures that would be taken by these drones to the existing camera mosaics from Rama I. Although most of the comparisons could be done digitally (and therefore automatically), there would always be differences that would require human explanation. Even if the two space-ships were identical, the differing light levels at the times the images were taken would create some artificial miscompares.

Two hours later the last of the drones returned to the relay station and an initial summary of the photographic survey was complete. There were no major structural differences between Rama II and the earlier space vehicle down to a scale of a hundred metres. The only significant region of miscompares at that resolution was the Cylindrical Sea itself, and ice reflectivity was a notoriously difficult phenomenon to handle with a straightforward digital comparison algorithm. It had been a long and exciting day. Borzov announced that crew assignments for the first sortie would be posted in an hour and that a 'special dinner' would be served in the control centre two hours later.

'You cannot do this,' an angry David Brown shouted, bursting into the commander's office without knocking, and brandishing a hard-copy printout of the first sortie assignments.

'What are you talking about?' General Borzov responded. He was annoyed by Dr Brown's rude entrance.

'There must be some kind of mistake,' Brown continued in a loud voice. 'You can't really expect me to stay here on the Newton during the first sortie.' When there was no response from General Borzov, the American scientist changed tactics. 'I want you to know that I don't accept this. And the ISA management won't like it either.'

Borzov stood up behind his desk. 'Close the door, Dr Brown,' he said calmly. David Brown slammed the sliding door. 'Now *you* listen to me for a minute,' the general continued. 'I don't give a damn who you know. I am the commanding officer of this mission. If you continue to act like a prima donna, I'll see to it that you *never* set foot inside Rama.'

Brown lowered his voice. 'But I demand an explanation,' he said with undisguised hostility. 'I am the senior scientist on this mission. I am also the leading spokesman for the Newton project among the media. How can you possibly justify leaving me on board the Newton while nine other cosmonauts go inside Rama?'

'I don't have to justify my actions,' Borzov replied, for the moment enjoying his power over the arrogant American. He leaned forward. 'But for the record, and because I anticipated this childish outburst of yours, I will tell you why you're not going on the first sortie. There are two major purposes for our first visit: to establish the communications/transportation infrastructure and to complete a detailed survey of the interior, ensuring that this spaceship is exactly like the first one ...'

'That's already been confirmed by the drones,' Brown interrupted.

'Not according to Dr Takagishi,' Borzov rebutted. 'He says that—'

'Shit, General, Takagishi won't be satisfied until every square centimetre of Rama has been shown to be exactly the same as the first ship. You saw the results of the drone survey. Do you have any doubt in your mind ...'

David Brown stopped himself in midsentence. General Borzov was drumming on his desk with his fingers and regarding Dr Brown with a cold stare. 'Are you going to let me finish now?' Borzov said at length. He waited a few more seconds. 'Whatever you may think,' the commander continued, 'Dr Takagishi is considered to be the world expert on the interior of Rama. You cannot argue even for a minute that your knowledge of the details approaches his. I need all five of the space cadets for the infrastructure work. The two journalists must go inside, not only because there are two separate tasks, but also because world attention is focused on us at this time. Finally, I believe it is important for my subsequent management of this mission that I myself go inside at least once, and I choose to do it *now*. Since the procedures clearly state that at least three members of the crew must remain outside Rama during the early sorties, it is not difficult to figure out—'

'You don't fool me for a minute,' David Brown now interrupted nastily. 'I know what this is all about. You've concocted an apparently logical excuse to hide the real reason for my exclusion from the first sortie team. You're jealous, Borzov. You can't stand the fact that I am regarded by most people as the real leader of this mission.'

The commander stared at the scientist for over fifteen seconds without saying anything. 'You know, Brown,' he said finally, 'I feel sorry for you. You are remarkably talented, but your talent is exceeded by your own opinion of it. If you weren't such a ...' This time it was Borzov's turn to stop himself in midsentence. He looked away. 'Incidentally, since I know that you will go back to your room and immediately whine to the ISA, I should probably tell you that the life science officer's fitness report explicitly recommends against your sharing any mission duties with Wilson – because of the personal animosity that both of you have demonstrated.'

Brown's eyes narrowed. 'Are you telling me that Nicole des Jardins actually filed an official memorandum citing Wilson and me by name?'

Borzov nodded.

'The bitch,' Brown muttered.

'It's always someone else who is at fault, isn't it Dr Brown?' General Borzov said, smiling at his adversary.

David Brown turned around and stalked out of the office.

For the banquet, General Borzov ordered a few precious bottles of wine to be opened. The commanding officer was in an excellent mood. Francesca's suggestion had been a good one. There was a definite feeling of camaraderie among the cosmonauts as they brought the small tables together in the control centre and anchored them to the floor.

Dr David Brown did not come to the banquet. He remained in his room while the other eleven crew members feasted on game hens and wild rice. Francesca awkwardly reported that Brown was 'feeling under the weather', but when Janos Tabori playfully volunteered to go check the American scientist's health, Francesca hurriedly added that Dr Brown wanted to be left alone. Janos and Richard Wakefield, both of whom had several glasses of wine, bantered with Francesca at one end of the table while Reggie Wilson and General O'Toole engaged in an animated discussion about the coming baseball season at the opposite end. Nicole sat between General Borzov and Admiral Heilmann and listened to their reminiscences of peacekeeping activities in the early post-Chaos days.

When the meal was over, Francesca excused herself. She and Dr Takagishi disappeared for several minutes. When they returned Francesca asked the cosmonauts to turn their chairs to face the large screen. Then, with the lights out, she and Takagishi projected a full exterior view of Rama on the monitor. Except that this was not the dull grey cylinder everyone had seen before. No, this Rama had been cleverly coloured, using image processing subroutines, and was now a black cylinder with yellow-gold stripes. The end of the cylinder looked almost like a face. There was a momentary quiet in the room before Francesca began to recite.

> Tyger, tyger, burning bright,
> In the forests of the night,
> What immortal hand or eye,
> Could frame thy fearful symmetry?

Nicole des Jardins felt a cold chill run up her spine as she listened to Francesca begin the next verse.

In what distant deeps or skies,
Burnt the fire of thine eyes . . .

That is the real question after all, Nicole was thinking. *Who made this gargantuan spacecraft? That's much more important for our ultimate destiny than why.*

What the hammer? What the chain?
In what furnace was thy brain?
What the anvil? What dread grasp
Dare its deadly terrors clasp? . . .

Across the table General O'Toole was also mesmerized by Francesca's recitation. His mind was again struggling with the same fundamental questions that had been bothering him since he originally applied for the mission. *Dear God,* he was wondering, *how do these Ramans fit into your universe? Did You create them first, before us? Are they our cousins in some sense? Why have You sent them here at this time?*

When the stars threw down their spears
And water'd heaven with their tears,
Did He smile His work to see,
Did He who made the Lamb make thee?

When Francesca finished the short poem there was a brief silence and then spontaneous applause. She graciously mentioned that Dr Takagishi had provided all the image processing intelligence and the likable Japanese cosmonaut took an embarrassed bow. Then Janos Tabori stood at his chair. 'I think I speak for all of us, Shig and Francesca, in congratulating you on that original and thought-provoking performance,' he said with a grin. 'It almost, but not quite, made me feel serious about what we are doing tomorrow.'

'Speaking of which,' General Borzov said, rising at the head of the table with his recently opened bottle of Ukrainian vodka, from which he had already taken two strong swigs, 'it is now time for an ancient Russian tradition – the toasts. I brought along only two bottles of this national treasure and I propose to share them both with you, my comrades and colleagues, on this very special evening.'

He placed both bottles in General O'Toole's hands and the American adroitly used the liquid dispenser to channel the vodka into small covered cups that were passed around the table. 'As Irina Turgenyev knows,' the commander continued, 'there is always a small worm in the bottom of a bottle of Ukrainian vodka. Legend has it that he who eats the worm will be endowed with special powers for twenty-four hours. Admiral Heilmann has marked two of the cup bottoms with an infrared cross. The two people who drink from the marked cups will each be allowed to eat one of the vodka-saturated worms.'

'Yeuch,' said Janos a moment later, as he passed the infrared scanner to Nicole. He had first verified that he had no cross on the bottom of his cup. 'This is one contest I am glad to lose.'

Nicole's cup did have a marking on the bottom. She was one of the two lucky cosmonauts who would be able to eat a Ukrainian worm for dessert. She found herself wondering, *Must I do this?* and then answering her own question affirmatively as she saw the earnest look on her commanding officer's face. *Oh well,* she thought, *it probably won't kill me. Any parasites have probably been rendered harmless by the alcohol.*

General Borzov himself had the second cup with a cross on the bottom. The general smiled, placed one of the two tiny worms in his own cup and the other in Nicole's, and raised his vodka toward the ceiling of the spacecraft.

'Let us all drink to a successful mission,' he said. 'For each of us, these next few days and weeks will be the greatest adventure of our lives. In a real sense, we dozen are human ambassadors to an alien culture. Let us each resolve to do our best to properly represent our species.'

He took the cover off his cup, being careful not to jiggle it, and then drank it all in one gulp. He swallowed the worm whole. Nicole also swallowed the worm quickly, commenting to herself that the only thing she had ever eaten that tasted worse than the worm was that awful tuber during her Poro ceremony in the Ivory Coast.

After several more short toasts the lights in the room began to dim. 'And now,' General Borzov announced with a grand gesture, 'direct from Stratford, the Newton proudly presents Richard Wakefield and his talented robots.' The room became dark except for a square metre to the left of the table that was spotlit from above. In the middle of the light was a cutaway of an old castle. A female robot, twenty centimetres high and dressed in a robe, was walking around in one of the rooms. She was reading a letter at the beginning of the scene. After a few steps, however, she dropped her hands to her sides and began to speak.

> Glamis thou art, and Cawdor; and shalt be
> What thou art promised. Yet do I fear thy nature:
> It is too full o'th'milk of human kindness
> To catch the nearest way. Thou wouldst be great . . .

'I know that woman,' Janos said with a grin to Nicole. 'I have met her somewhere before.'

'Shh,' replied Nicole. She was fascinated by the precision in the movements of Lady Macbeth. *That Wakefield really is a genius,* she was thinking. *How is he able to design such extraordinary detail into those little things?* Nicole was astonished by the range of expressions on the robot's face.

As she concentrated, the tiny stage began to swim in Nicole's mind. She momentarily forgot she was watching robots in a miniature performance. A messenger came in and told Lady Macbeth both that her husband was drawing near and that King Duncan would be spending the night in their castle. Nicole watched Lady Macbeth's face explode with ambitious antici-pation as soon as the messenger had departed.

> ... Come you Spirits
> That tend on mortal thoughts. Unsex me here
> And fill me, from the crown to the toe, top-full
> Of direst cruelty! Make thick my blood ...

My God, Nicole thought, blinking her eyes to make certain they were not playing tricks on her, *she's changing!* Indeed she was. As the words 'Unsex me here' came from the robot, her (or its) shape began to change. The impres-sion of the breasts against the metal gown, the roundness of the hips, even the softness of the face all disappeared. An androgynous robot played on as Lady Macbeth.

Nicole was spellbound and floating in a fantasy induced both by her wild imagination and the sudden intake of alcohol. The new face on the robot was vaguely reminiscent of someone she knew. She heard a disturbance to her right and turned to see Reggie Wilson talking avidly with Francesca. Nicole glanced back and forth quickly from Francesca to Lady Macbeth. *That's it,* she said to herself. *This new Lady Macbeth resembles Francesca.*

A burst of fear, a premonition of tragedy, suddenly overwhelmed Nicole and plunged her into terror. *Something terrible is going to happen,* her mind was saying. She took several deep breaths and tried to calm herself but the eerie feeling would not go away. On the little stage King Duncan had just been greeted by his gracious hostess for the evening. To her left Nicole saw Francesca offer General Borzov the last sips of the wine. Nicole could not quell her panic.

'Nicole, what's the matter?' Janos asked. He could tell she was distressed.

'Nothing,' she said. She gathered all her strength and rose to her feet. 'Something I ate must have disagreed with me. I think I'll go to my room.'

'But you'll miss the movie after dinner,' Janos said humorously. Nicole forced a painted smile. He helped her stand up. Nicole heard Lady Macbeth berating her husband for his lack of courage and one more wave of premoni-tory fear surged through her. She waited until the adrenaline burst had subsided and then excused herself quietly from the group. She walked slowly back to her room.

17 DEATH OF A SOLDIER

In her dream Nicole was ten years old again and playing in the woods behind her home in the Paris suburb of Chilly-Mazarin. She had a sudden feeling that her mother was dying. The little girl panicked. She ran toward the house to tell her father. A small snarling cat blocked her path. Nicole stopped, She heard a scream. She left the path and went through the trees. The branches scraped her skin. The cat followed her. Nicole heard another scream. When she awakened a frightened Janos Tabori was standing over her. 'It's General Borzov,' Janos said. 'He's in excruciating pain.'

Nicole jumped swiftly out of bed, threw her robe around her, grabbed her portable medical kit, and followed Janos into the corridor, 'It looks like an appendicitis,' he mentioned as they hurried into the lobby, 'But I'm not certain.'

Irina Turgenyev was kneeling beside the commander and holding his hand. The general himself was stretched out on a couch. His face was white and there was sweat on his brow. 'Ah, Dr des Jardins has arrived.' He managed a smile. Borzov then tried to sit up, winced from the pain, and let himself lie back down. 'Nicole,' he said quietly, 'I am in agony. I've never felt anything like this in my life, not even when I was wounded in the army.'

'How long ago did it start?' she asked. Nicole had pulled out her scanner and biometry monitor to check all his vital statistics. Meanwhile Francesca and her video camera had moved over right behind Nicole's shoulder to film the doctor performing the diagnosis. Nicole impatiently motioned for her to back away.

'Maybe two or three minutes ago,' General Borzov said with effort. 'I was sitting here in a chair watching the movie, laughing heartily as I recall, when there was an intense, sharp pain, here on my lower right side. It felt as if something were burning me from the inside.'

Nicole programmed the scanner to search through the last three minutes of detailed data recorded by the Hakamatsu probes inside Borzov. She located the onset of the pain, easily identifiable in terms of both heart rate and endocrine secretions. She next requested a full dump over the time period of interest from all channels. 'Janos,' she then said to her colleague, 'go over to the supply room and bring me the portable diagnostician.' She handed Tabori the code card for the door.

'You have a slight fever, suggesting your body is fighting some infection,' Nicole told General Borzov. 'All the internal data confirms that you are feeling severe pain.' Cosmonaut Tabori returned with a small electronic array shaped like a box. Nicole extracted a small data cube from the scanner and inserted it into the diagnostician. In about thirty seconds the little monitor blinked and the words 94% LIKELY APPENDICITIS appeared. Nicole pressed a key and the screen displayed the other possible diagnoses, including hernia, internal muscle tear, and drug reaction. None were, according to the diagnostician, more than two percent probable.

I have two choices at this juncture, Nicole was thinking rapidly as General Borzov winced again from the pain. *I can send all the data down to Earth for a complete diagnostic, per the procedure* ... She glanced at her watch and quickly computed twice the round-trip light time plus the minimum duration of a physician's conference after the electronic diagnosis was complete. *By which time it might be too late.*

'What does it say, Doctor?' the general was asking. His eyes were entreating her to end the pain as quickly as possible.

'Most likely diagnosis is appendicitis,' Nicole answered.

'Dammit,' General Borzov responded. He looked around at all the others. Everyone was there except Wilson and Takagishi, both of whom had skipped the movie. 'But I won't make the project wait. We'll go ahead with the first and second sorties while I'm recuperating.' Another sharp pain jolted him and his face contorted,

'Whoa,' said Nicole. 'It's not certain yet. We need a little more data first.' She repeated the earlier data dump, now using the extra two minutes of information that had been recorded since she arrived in the lobby. This time the diagnosis read 92% LIKELY APPENDICITIS. Nicole was about to routinely check the alternative diagnoses when she felt the commander's strong hand on her arm.

'If we do this quickly, before too much poison builds up in my system, then this is a straightforward operation for the robot surgeon, isn't it?'

Nicole nodded.

'And if we spend the time to obtain a diagnostic concurrence from the Earth – *ouch!* – then my body may be in deeper trauma?'

He is reading my mind, Nicole thought at first. Then she realised that the general was only displaying his thorough knowledge of the Newton procedures.

'Is the patient trying to give the doctor a suggestion?' Nicole asked, smiling despite Borzov's obvious pain.

'I wouldn't be that presumptuous,' the commander answered with just a trace of a twinkle in his eye.

Nicole glanced back at the monitor. It was still blinking 92% LIKELY APPENDICITIS. 'Do you have anything to add?' she said to Janos Tabori.

'Only that I have seen an appendicitis before,' the little Hungarian answered, 'once, when I was a student, in Budapest. The symptoms were exactly like this.'

'All right,' Nicole said. 'Go prepare RoSur for the operation. Admiral Heilmann, will you and cosmonaut Yamanaka help General Borzov to the infirmary please?' She turned around to Francesca. 'I recognize that this is big news. I will allow you in the operating room on three conditions. You will scrub like all the surgical staff. You will stand quietly over against the wall with your camera, And you will absolutely obey any order that I give you.'

'Good enough,' Francesca nodded. 'Thank you.'

Irina Turgenyev and General O'Toole were still waiting in the lobby after Borzov left with Heilmann and Yamanaka. 'I'm certain that I speak for both of us,' the American said in his usual sincere manner. 'Can we help in any way?'

'Janos will assist me while RoSur performs the operation. But I could use one more pair of hands, as an emergency backup.'

'I would like to do that,' O'Toole said. 'I have some hospital experience from my charity work.'

'Fine,' replied Nicole. 'Now come with me to clean up.'

RoSur, the portable robot surgeon that had been brought along on the Newton mission for just this kind of situation, was not in the same class, in terms of medical sophistication, as the fully autonomous operating rooms at the advanced hospitals on Earth. But RoSur was a technological marvel in its own right. It could be packed in a small suitcase and weighed only four kilograms. Its power requirements were low. And there were more than a hundred configurations in which it could be used.

Janos Tabori unpacked RoSur. The electronic surgeon didn't look like much in its stowed configuration. All of its spindly joints and appendages were neatly arranged for easy storage. After Janos rechecked his RoSur User's Guide, he picked up the central control box of the robot surgeon and affixed it, as suggested, to the side of the infirmary bed where General Borzov was already lying. His pain had only subsided a little. The impatient commander was urging everyone to hurry.

Janos entered the code word identifying the operation. RoSur automatically deployed all its limbs, including its extraordinary scalpel/hand with four fingers, in the configuration needed to remove an appendix. Nicole then entered the room, her hands in gloves and her body covered with the white gown of the surgeon.

'Have you finished the software check?' she said.

Janos nodded his head.

'I'll complete all the pre-operation tests while you scrub,' she said to him. She motioned for Francesca and General O'Toole, both of whom were standing right outside the door, to enter the small room. 'Any better?' she said to Borzov.

'Not much,' he grumbled.

'That was a light sedative I administered. RoSur will give you the full anaesthetic as the first step in the operation.' Nicole had done all her memory refreshing in her room while she was dressing. She knew this operation inside out; it had been one of the surgical procedures they had performed during the test simulations. She entered Borzov's personal data file into RoSur, hooked up the electronic lines that would bring patient monitor information to RoSur during the appendectomy, and verified that all the software had passed self-test. As her last check, Nicole carefully tuned the pair of tiny stereo cameras that worked in concert with the surgical hand.

Janos came back into the room. Nicole pressed a button on the robot surgeon's control box and two hard copies of the operations sequence were quickly printed. Nicole took one and handed the other to Janos. 'Is everyone ready?' she asked, her eyes on General Borzov. The commanding officer of the Newton moved his head up and down. Nicole activated RoSur.

One of the robot surgeon's four hands gunned an anaesthetic into the patient and in one minute Borzov was unconscious. As Francesca's camera recorded every move of this historic operation (she was whispering occasional comments into her ultrasensitive microphone), the scalpel hand of RoSur, aided by its twin eyes, made the incisions necessary to isolate the suspect organ. No human surgeon had ever been so swift or deft. Armed with a battery of sensors checking hundreds of parameters every microsecond, RoSur had folded back all the requisite tissue and laid the appendix bare within two minutes. Programmed into the automatic sequence was a thirty-second inspection time before the robot surgeon would continue with the removal of the organ.

Nicole bent over the patient to check the exposed appendix. It was neither swollen nor inflamed. 'Look at this, quick, Janos,' she said, her eye on the digital clock counting down the inspection period. 'It looks perfectly healthy.' Janos leaned over from the opposite side of the operating table. *My God,* Nicole thought, *we're going to remove* ... The digital clock read 00:08. 'Stop it,' she shouted. 'Stop the operation.' Nicole and Janos both reached for the robot surgeon control box at the same time.

At that instant the entire Newton spacecraft lurched sideways. Nicole was thrown backward, against the wall. Janos fell forward, smacking his head against the operating table. His outstretched fingers landed on the control box and then slowly released as he slumped to the floor. General O'Toole and Francesca were both thrown against the far wall. A *beep, beep* from one of the inserted Hakamatsu probes indicated that someone in the room was in serious trouble physically. Nicole checked briefly to see that O'Toole and Sabatini were all right and then struggled against the continuing torque to regain her position next to the operating table. With great effort she pulled herself across the room on the floor, using the anchored legs of the table. When she was beside the table she steadied herself, still holding on to the legs, and stood up.

Blood spattered Nicole as her head crossed the plane of the operating table. She stared with disbelief at Borzov's body. The entire incision was full of blood and RoSur's scalpel/hand was buried inside, apparently still cutting away. It was Borzov's probe set that was going *beep, beep,* despite the fact that Nicole had inserted, by command, significantly wider emergency values just before the operation.

A wave of fear and nausea swept through Nicole as she realised that the robot had not aborted its surgical activities. Holding on tight against the powerful force trying to push her against the wall again, she somehow managed to reach over to the control box and switch off the power. The scalpel withdrew from the pool of blood and restowed itself against a stanchion, Nicole then tried to stop the massive haemorrhaging.

Thirty seconds later the unexplained force vanished as suddenly as it had appeared. General O'Toole clambered to his feet and came over beside the now desperate Nicole. The scalpel had done too much damage. The commander was bleeding to death before her eyes. 'Oh, no. Oh, God,' O'Toole said as he surveyed the wreckage of his friend's body. The insistent *beep, beep* continued. Now the life system alarms around the table sounded as well. Francesca recovered in time to record the final ten seconds of Valeriy Borzov's life.

It was a very long night for the entire Newton crew. In the two hours immediately after the operation, Rama went through a sequence of three more manoeuvres, each, like the first one, lasting one or two minutes. The Earth eventually confirmed that the combined manoeuvres had changed the attitude, spin rate, and orbit of the alien spaceship. Nobody could ascertain the exact purpose of the set of manoeuvres; they were just 'orientation changes,' according to the Earth scientists, that had altered the inclination and line of apsides of the Rama orbit. However, the energy of the trajectory had not been changed significantly – Rama was still on a hyperbolic escape path with respect to the Sun.

Everyone onboard the Newton and on Earth was stunned by the sudden death of General Borzov. He was eulogized by the press of all nations and his many accomplishments were lauded by his peers and associates. His death was reported as an accident, attributed to the untimely motion of the Rama spacecraft that had taken place during the middle of a routine appendectomy. But within eight hours after his death, knowledgeable people everywhere were asking tough questions. Why had the Rama spacecraft moved at exactly that time? Why had RoSur's fault protection system failed to stop the operation? Why were the human medical officers presiding over the procedure not able to switch off the power before it was too late?

Nicole des Jardins was asking herself the same questions. She had already completed the documents required when a death occurs in space and had sealed Borzov's body in the vacuum coffin at the back of the military ship's huge supply depot. She had quickly prepared and filed her report on the incident; O'Toole, Sabatini, and Tabori had all done the same. There was only one significant omission in the reports. Janos failed to mention that he had reached for the control box during the Raman manoeuvre. At the time Nicole did not think his omission was important.

The required teleconferences with ISA officials were extremely painful. Nicole was the person who bore the brunt of all the inane and repetitious questioning. She had to reach deep inside herself for extra reserves to keep from losing her temper several times. Nicole had expected that Francesca might hint at incompetence on the part of the Newton medical staff in her teleconference, but the Italian journalist was even-handed and fair in her reportage.

After a short interview with Francesca, in which Nicole discussed how horrified she had been at the moment she had first seen Borzov's incision filled with blood, the life science officer retired to her room, ostensibly to rest and/or sleep. But Nicole did not allow herself the luxury of resting. Over and over she reviewed the critical seconds of the operation. Could she have done anything to change the outcome? What could possibly explain RoSur's failure to stop itself automatically?

In Nicole's mind there was little or no probability that RoSur's fault protection algorithms had a design flaw; they wouldn't have passed all the rigorous prelaunch testing if they contained errors. So somewhere there must have been a human error, either negligence (had she and Janos, in their haste, forgotten to initialize some key fault protection parameter?) or an accident during those chaotic seconds following the unexpected torque. Her fruitless searching for an explanation and her almost total fatigue made her extremely depressed when she finally fell asleep. To her, one part of the equation was very clear. A man had died and she had been responsible.

18 POST MORTEM

As expected, the day after General Borzov's death was full of turmoil. The ISA investigation into the incident expanded and most of the cosmonauts were subjected to another long cross-examination. Nicole was interrogated about her sobriety at the time of the operation. Some of the questions were ugly and Nicole, who was trying to husband her energy for her own investigation of the events surrounding the tragedy, lost her patience twice with the interrogators.

'Look,' she exclaimed at one point, 'I have now explained four times that I had two glasses of wine and one glass of vodka three hours before the operation. I have admitted that I would not have drunk any alcohol prior to surgery, *if* I had known that I was going to operate. I have even acknowledged, in retrospect, that perhaps one of the two life science officers should have remained completely sober. But that's all hindsight. I repeat what I said earlier. Neither my judgment nor my physical abilities was in any way impaired by alcohol at the time of the operation.'

Back in her room, Nicole focused her attention on the issue of why the robot surgeon proceeded with the operation when its own internal fault protection should have aborted all activities. Based on the User's Guide to RoSur, it was evident that at least two separate sensor systems should have sent error messages to the central processor in the robot surgeon. The accelerometer package should have informed the processor that the environmental conditions were outside acceptable limits because of the untoward lateral force. And the stereo cameras should have transmitted a message indicating that the observed images were at variance with the predicted images. But for some reason neither sensor set was successful in interrupting the ongoing operation. What had happened?

It took Nicole almost five hours to rule out the possibility of a major error, either software or hardware, in the RoSur system itself. She verified that the loaded software and data base had been correct by doing a code comparison with the benchmark standard version of the software tested extensively during prelaunch. She also isolated the stereo imaging and accelerometer telemetry from the few seconds right after the spacecraft lurched. These data were properly transmitted to the central processor and should have resulted

269

in an aborted sequence. But they didn't. Why not? The only possible explanation was that the software had been changed by manual command between the time of loading and the performance of the appendectomy.

Nicole was now out of her league. Her software and system engineering knowledge had been stretched to the limit in satisfying herself that there had been no error in the loaded software. To determine whether and when commands might have changed the code or parameters after they were installed in RoSur required someone who could read machine language and carefully interrogate tbe billions of bits of data that had been stored during the entire procedure. Nicole's investigation was stalled until she could find someone to help her. *Maybe I should give this up?* a voice inside her said. *How could you,* another voice replied, *until you know for certain the cause of General Borzov's death?* At the root of Nicole's desire to know the answer was a desperate yearning to prove for certain that his death had not been her fault.

She turned away from her terminal and collapsed on her bed. As she was lying there, she remembered her surprise during the thirty-second inspection period when Borzov's appendix had been in plain view. *He definitely didn't have appendicitis,* she thought. Without having any particular motive, Nicole returned to her terminal and accessed the second set of data that she had had evaluated by the electronic diagnostician, just prior to her decision to operate. She glanced only briefly at the 92% LIKELY APPENDICITIS on the first screen, moving instead to the backup diagnoses. This time DRUG REACTION was listed as the second most likely cause, with a four percent probability. Nicole now called for the data to be displayed in another way. She asked a statistical routine to compute the likely cause of the symptoms, *given* the fact that it could not be an appendicitis.

The results flashed up on the monitor in seconds. Nicole was astonished. According to the data, if the biometry information input from Borzov's probe set was analysed under the assumption that the cause for the abnormalities could *not* be an appendicitis, then there was a 62 percent chance that it was due to a drug reaction. Before Nicole was able to complete any more analysis, there was a knock on her door.

'Come in,' she said, continuing to work at her terminal. Nicole turned and saw Irina Turgenyev standing in the doorway. The Soviet pilot said nothing for a moment.

'They asked me to come for you,' Irina said haltingly. She was very shy around everyone except her countrymen Tabori and Borzov. 'We're having a meeting of the crew down in the lobby.'

Nicole saved her temporary data files and joined Irina in the corridor. 'What sort of meeting is it?' she asked.

'An organizational meeting,' Irina answered. She said nothing more.

There was a heated exchange in process between Reggie Wilson and David Brown when the two women reached the lobby. 'Am I to understand, then,' Dr Brown was saying sarcastically, 'that you believe the Rama spacecraft *purposely* decided to manoeuvre at precisely that moment? Would you like to explain to all of us *how* this asteroid of dumb metal happened to know that General Borzov was having an appendectomy at that very minute? And while you're at it, will you explain why this supposedly malevolent spaceship has allowed us to attach ourselves and has done nothing to dissuade us from continuing our mission?'

Reggie Wilson glanced around the room for support. 'You're logic-chopping again, Brown,' he said, his frustration obvious. 'What you say always sounds logical on the surface. But I'm not the only member of this crew that found the coincidence unnerving. Look, here's Irina Turgenyev. She's the one who suggested the connection to me in the first place.'

Dr Brown acknowledged the arrival of the two women. There was an authority in the way he was asking the questions that suggested he was in control of the gathering. 'Is that right, Irina?' David Brown asked. 'Do you feel, like Wilson, that Rama was trying to send us some specific message by performing its manoeuvre during the general's operation?'

Irina and Hiro Yamanaka were the two cosmonauts who spoke the least during crew meetings. With all eyes turned toward her, Irina mumbled 'no' very meekly.

'But when we were discussing it last night—' Wilson insisted to the Soviet pilot.

'That's enough on that subject,' David Brown interrupted imperiously. 'I think we have a consensus, shared by our mission control officers on Earth, that the Raman manoeuvre was coincidence and not conspiracy.' He looked at the fuming Reggie Wilson. 'Now we have other more important issues to discuss. I would like to ask Admiral Heilmann to tell us what he has learned about the leadership problem.'

Otto Heilmann stood up on cue and read from his notes. 'According to the Newton procedures, in the event of the death or the incapacity of the commanding officer, the crew is expected to complete all sequences then under way in accordance with previous directions. However, once those "in process" activities are finished, the cosmonauts are supposed to wait for the Earth to name a new commanding officer.'

David Brown jumped back into the conversation. 'Admiral Heilmann and I started discussing our situation about an hour ago and we quickly realised that we had valid reasons for being concerned. The ISA is wrapped up in their investigation of General Borzov's death. They have not even begun to think about his replacement. Once they do start, it may take them weeks to decide. Remember, this is the same bureaucracy that was never able to select a deputy for Borzov, so they eventually decided that he didn't need one.' He paused several seconds to allow the rest of the crew members to consider what he was saying.

'Otto suggested that maybe we should not wait for the Earth to decide,' Dr Brown continued. 'It was his idea that we should develop our own management structure, one that is acceptable to all of us here, and then send it to the ISA as a recommendation. Admiral Heilmann thinks they will accept it because it will avoid what could be a protracted debate.'

'Admiral Heilmann and Dr Brown came to see me with this idea,' Janos Tabori now chimed in, 'and emphasized how important it is for us to get started with our mission inside Rama. They even laid out a strawman organisation that made sense to me. Since none of us has the broad experience of General Borzov, they suggested that maybe we should now have two leaders, possibly Admiral Heilmann and Dr Brown themselves. Otto would cover the military and spacecraft engineering issues; Dr Brown would lead the Rama exploration effort.'

'And what happens when they disagree or their areas of responsibility overlap?' asked Richard Wakefield.

'In that case,' Admiral Heilmann responded, 'we would submit the item in question to a vote of all the cosmonauts.'

'Isn't this cute?' said Reggie Wilson. He was still angry. He had been taking notes on his keyboard but now he stood up to address the rest of the cosmonauts. 'Brown and Heilmann just happened to be worrying about this critical problem and they just happened to have developed a new leadership structure in which all the power and responsibility are divided between them. Am I the only one here who smells something fishy?'

'Now come on, Reggie,' Francesca Sabatini said forcefully. She dropped her video camera to her side. 'There is sound logic in the strawman proposal. Dr Brown is our senior scientist. Admiral Heilmann has been a close colleague of Valeriy Borzov's for many years. None of us has a solid overall command of all aspects of the mission. To split the duties would be—'

It was difficult for Reggie Wilson to argue with Francesca. Nevertheless, he did interrupt her before she was finished. 'I disagree with this plan,' he said in a subdued tone. 'I think we should have a single leader. And based on what I have observed during my time with this crew, there's only one cosmonaut that we could all easily follow. That's General O'Toole.' He waved in the direction of his fellow American. 'If this is a democracy, I nominate him as our new commanding officer.'

There was a general uproar as soon as Reggie sat down. David Brown tried to restore order. 'Please, please,' he shouted, 'let's work one issue at a time. Do we want to decide our own leadership and then hand it to the ISA as a fait accompli? Once we handle that question, then we can settle who those leaders should be.'

'I had not thought about any of this before the meeting,' Richard Wakefield said. 'But I agree with the idea of cutting the Earth out of the loop. They have not lived with us on this mission. More importantly, they are not on board a spaceship affixed to an alien creation somewhere just inside the orbit of Venus. We are the ones who will suffer if a bad decision is made; we should decide our own organization.'

It was clear that everyone, with the possible exception of Wilson, preferred the idea of defining the leadership structure and then presenting it to the ISA. 'All right,' Otto Heilmann said a few minutes later, 'we must now choose our leaders. One strawman proposal has been advanced, suggesting a leadership split between myself and Dr Brown. Reggie Wilson has nominated General Michael O'Toole as the new commanding officer. Are there any other suggestions or discussion?'

The room was silent for about ten seconds. 'Excuse me,' General O'Toole then said, 'but I would like to make a few observations.' Everyone listened to the American general. Wilson was correct. Despite O'Toole's known preoccupation with religion (which he didn't force anyone else to share), he had the respect of the entire cosmonaut crew. 'I think we must be careful at this point not to lose the team spirit that we have worked so hard to develop during the past year. A contested election at this point could be divisive. Besides, it's not all that important or necessary. Regardless of who becomes our nominal leader, or leaders, each of us is trained to perform a specific set of functions. We will do them under any circumstances.'

Heads were nodding in agreement around the lobby. 'For myself,' General O'Toole continued, 'I must admit that I know little or nothing about the inside-Rama aspects of this mission. I have never trained to do anything except manage the two Newton spacecraft, assess any potential military threat, and act as a communications nexus on board. I'm not qualified to be the commanding officer.' Reggie Wilson started to interrupt but O'Toole continued without a pause. 'I'd like to recommend that we adopt the plan offered by Heilmann and Brown and move on with our primary task – namely the exploration of this alien leviathan that has come to us from the stars.'

At the conclusion of the meeting the two new leaders informed the rest of the cosmonauts that a rough draft of the first sortie scenario would be ready for review the following morning. Nicole headed for her room. On the way she stopped and knocked on the door of Janos Tabori. At first there was no response. When she knocked a second time, she heard Janos yell, 'Who is it?'

'It's me – Nicole,' she answered.

'Come in,' he said.

He was lying on his back on the small bed with an uncharacteristic frown on his face.

'What's the matter?' Nicole asked.

'Oh, nothing,' Janos answered. 'I just have a headache.'

'Did you take something?' Nicole inquired.

'No. It's not that serious.' He still didn't smile. 'What can I do for you?' he asked in an almost unfriendly tone.

Nicole was puzzled. She approached her subject cautiously. 'Well, I was rereading your report on Valeriy's death—'

'Why were you doing that?' Janos interrupted brusquely.

'To see if there was anything we might have done differently,' Nicole responded. It was obvious to her that Janos did not want to discuss the subject. After waiting a few seconds, Nicole spoke again. 'I'm sorry, Janos. I'm imposing on you. I'll come back another time.'

'No. No,' he said. 'Let's get this over with now.'

That's a curious way of putting it, Nicole was thinking as she formulated her question. 'Janos,' she said, 'nowhere in your report did you mention reaching for RoSur's control box right before the manoeuvre. And I could have sworn I saw your fingers on the keyboard panel as I was being swept over against the wall.'

Nicole stopped. There was no expression of any kind on Cosmonaut Tabori's face. It was almost as if he were thinking of something else. 'I don't remember,' he said at length, without emotion. 'You may be right. Perhaps my hitting my head erased part of my memory.'

Stop now, Nicole said to herself as she studied her colleague. *There's nothing more you can learn here.*

19 RITE OF PASSAGE

Genevieve suddenly broke into tears. 'Oh, Maman,' she said. 'I love you so much and this is absolutely awful.'

The teenager hurriedly moved out of the camera frame and was replaced by Nicole's father. Pierre looked off to his right for a few seconds, to make certain that his granddaughter was out of earshot, and then turned toward the monitor. 'These last twenty-four hours have been especially hard on her. You know how she idolises you. Some of the foreign press have been saying that you bungled the surgery. There was even a suggestion this evening from an American television reporter that you were drunk during the operation.'

He paused. The strain was showing on her father's face as well. 'Both Genevieve and I know that neither of these allegations is true. We love you completely and send all our support.'

The screen went dark. Nicole had initiated the videophone call and had, at first, been cheered by talking to her family. After her second transmission, however, when her father and daughter had reappeared on the screen twenty minutes later, it had been obvious that the events on board the Newton had unsettled life at Beauvois as well. Genevieve had been particularly distraught. She had cried intermittently while talking about General Borzov (she had met him several times and the avuncular Russian had always been especially nice to her) and had barely managed to compose herself before breaking into tears again right before the end of the call.

So I have embarrassed you as well, Nicole thought as she sat down on her bed. She rubbed her eyes. She was extremely tired. Slowly, without being aware of how depressed she had become, she undressed for bed. Her mind was plagued with pictures of her daughter at school in Luynes. Nicole winced as she imagined one of Genevieve's friends asking her about the operation and Borzov's death. *My darling daughter,* she thought, *you must know how much I love you. If only I could spare you from this pain.* Nicole wanted to reach out and comfort Genevieve, to hold her close, to share one of those mother-daughter caresses that chase away the demons. But it could not be. Genevieve was a hundred million kilometres away.

Nicole lay in bed on her back. She closed her eyes but did not sleep. She was aware of a deep and profound loneliness, a sense of isolation more acute than any she had felt before in her life. She knew that she was longing for some sympathy, for some human being who would tell her that her feelings of inadequacy were overblown and not consistent with reality. But there was nobody. Her father and daughter were back on Earth. Of the two Newton crew members she knew best, one was dead and the other was behaving suspiciously.

I have failed, Nicole was thinking as she was lying on her bed. *On my most important assignment I have failed.* She recalled another feeling of failure, when she was only sixteen. At that time Nicole had competed for the role of Joan of Arc in a huge national contest associated with the 750th anniversary of the death of the Maid. If she had won, Nicole would have portrayed Joan in a series of pageants over the next two years. She had thrown herself totally into the contest, reading every book she could find about Joan and watching scores of video presentations. Nicole had scored at the top in virtually every test category except 'suitability.' She should have won, but she didn't. Her father had consoled her by telling Nicole that France was not ready for its heroines to have dark skin.

But that was not exactly a failure, the Newton life science officer told herself. *And anyway I had my father to comfort me.* An image of her mother's funeral came to Nicole's mind. She had been ten years old at the time. Her mother had gone to the Ivory Coast by herself to visit their African relatives. Anawi had been in Nidougou when a virulent epidemic of Hogan fever had swept through the village. Nicole's mother had died quickly.

Five days later Anawi had been cremated as a Senoufo queen, Nicole had wept while Omeh chanted her mother's soul through the nether world and into the Land of Preparation, where beings rested while waiting to be selected for another life on Earth. As the flames had mounted the pyre and her mother's regal dress had begun to burn, Nicole had felt an overpowering sense of loss. And loneliness. *But that time also my father was there beside me,* she recalled. *He held my hand as we watched Mother disappear. Together it was easier to bear. I was much more lonely during the Poro. And more frightened.*

She could still remember the mixture of terror and helplessness that had filled her seven-year-old body at the Paris airport on that spring morning. Her father had caressed her very tenderly. 'Darling, darling Nicole,' he had said. 'I will miss you very much. Come back safely to me.'

'But why must I go, Papa?' she had replied. 'And why are you not coming with us?'

He had bent down beside her. 'You are going to become part of your mother's people. All Senoufo children go through the Poro at the age of seven.'

Nicole had started crying. 'But Papa, I don't want to go. I'm French, not African. I don't like all those strange people and the heat and the bugs ...'

Her father had placed his hands firmly on her cheeks. 'You must go, Nicole. Your mother and I have agreed.' Anawi and Pierre had indeed discussed it many times. Nicole had lived in France all her life. All she knew of her African heritage was what her mother had taught her and what she had learned from two month-long visits to the Ivory Coast with her family.

It had not been easy for Pierre to agree to send his beloved daughter off to the Poro. He knew that it was a primitive ceremony. He also knew that it was the cornerstone of the Senoufo traditional religion and that he had promised Omeh, at the time of his marriage to Anawi, that all their children would return to Nidougou for at least the first cycle of the Poro.

The hardest part for Pierre was staying behind. But Anawi was right. He was an outsider. He would not be able to participate in the Poro. He would not understand it. His presence would distract the little girl. There was an ache in his heart as Pierre kissed his wife and daughter and put them onto the plane to Abidjan.

Anawi was also apprehensive about the rite of passage ceremony for her only child, her little girl of barely seven years. She had prepared Nicole as well as she could. The child was a gifted linguist and had picked up the rudiments of the Senoufo language very easily. But there was no doubt that she was at a severe disadvantage with respect to the rest of the children. All of the others had lived their whole lives in and around the native villages. They were familiar with the area. To alleviate the orientation problem a little, Anawi and Nicole arrived in Nidougou a week ahead of time.

The fundamental idea of the Poro was that life was a succession of phases or cycles and that each transition should be carefully marked. Each cycle lasted seven years. There were three Poros in every normal Senoufo life, three metamorphoses that were necessary before the child could be transformed into an adult in the tribe. Despite the fact that many of the tribal customs faded away with the arrival of modern telecommunications devices in the Ivory Coast villages in the twenty-first century, the Poro remained an integral part of Senoufo society. In the twenty-second century, tribal practices enjoyed a renaissance of sorts, especially after the Great Chaos proved to most of the African leaders that it was dangerous to depend too much on the outside world.

Anawi kept a good acting smile upon her face during the afternoon that the tribal priests came to take Nicole away for the Poro. She didn't want her fear or anxiety to be transferred to her daughter. Nevertheless, Nicole could tell that her mother was troubled. 'Your hands are cold and sweaty, Mama,' she whispered in French as she hugged Anawi before departing. 'Don't worry. I'll be all right.' In fact, Nicole, the only brown face among the dozen dark black girls climbing into the carts, seemed almost cheery and expectant, as if she were going to an amusement park or a zoo.

There were four carts altogether, two carrying the little girls and two that were covered and unexplained. Nicole's friend from four years earlier,

Lutuwa, who was actually one of Nicole's cousins, explained to the rest of the girls that the other wagons contained the priests and the 'instruments of torture.' There was a long silence before one of the little girls had the courage to ask Lutuwa what she was talking about.

'I dreamed it all two nights ago,' Lutuwa said matter-of-factly. 'They are going to burn our nipples and stick sharp objects in all our holes. And as long as we don't cry, we won't feel any pain.' The other five girls in Nicole's cart, including Lutuwa, hardly said a word for the next hour.

By sunset they had travelled a long way east, past the abandoned microwave station, into the special area known only to the tribal religious leaders. The half dozen priests threw up temporary shelters and started building a fire. When it was dark, food and drink were served to the initiates, who sat cross-legged in a wide circle around the fire. After dinner the costumed dancing began. Omeh narrated the four dances, each of which featured one of the indigenous animals. Music for the dances came from tambourines and crude xylophones, the rhythm being maintained by the monotonic beat of the tom-tom. Occasionally an especially meaningful point in the story would be punctuated by a blast on the oliphant, the ivory hunting horn.

Just before bedtime Omeh, still wearing the great mask and headdress identifying him as the chieftain, handed each of the girls a large kit made of antelope hide and told them to study its contents very carefully. There was a flask of water, some dried fruit and nuts, two chunks of native bread, a cutting implement, some rope, two different kinds of unguents, and a tuber from an unknown plant.

'Tomorrow morning each child will be removed from this camp,' Omeh said, 'and placed in a specific location not too far away. The child will have only the gifts in the antelope hide. The child is expected to survive on her own and return to the same spot by the time the sun is full in the sky on the following day.

'The hide contains everything that is needed except for wisdom, courage, and curiosity. The tuber is something very special. Eating the fleshy root will terrify the child, but may also give abnormal powers of strength and vision.'

20 BLESSED SLUMBER

The little girl had been alone for almost two hours before she really understood what was happening to her. Omeh and one of the younger priests had placed Nicole right near a small, brackish pond, surrounded on all sides by the high grasses of the savanna. They had reminded her that they would return in the middle of the next day. Then they were gone.

At first Nicole had reacted as if the entire experience were a great game. She had taken out her kit made of antelope hide and carefully inventoried the contents. She had mentally divided the food into three parts, planning what she would eat for dinner, breakfast, and midmorning snack. There was not excessive food, but little Nicole judged that it would be enough. On the other hand, when she had visually measured the flask to determine the adequacy of her water supply, she had concluded that it was marginal. It would be good if she could find a spring or some pure running water that could be used in an emergency.

Nicole's next activity had been to create a mental map of her location, paying special attention to any landmarks that would help her identify the brackish pond from a distance. She was an extremely organized little girl and, back at Chilly-Mazarin, often played by herself in a wooded vacant lot very close to her house. In her room at home Nicole had maps of the wood that she had carefully drawn by hand, her secret hiding places marked with stars and circles.

It was when she came upon four striped antelope, grazing calmly under the steady afternoon sun, that Nicole first understood how utterly isolated she was. Her first instinct was to look for her mother, to show Anawi the beautiful animals she had found. *But mother is not here*, the little girl thought, her eyes scanning the horizon. *I am all alone.* The last word echoed through her mind and she felt an inchoate despair. She fought against the despair and looked off into the distance to see if she could find any indication of civilization. There were birds all around and some more grazing animals on the horizon at the limit of her vision, but no sign of any human beings. *I am all alone,* Nicole said to herself again, a slight shiver of fear running through her body.

She remembered that she wanted to find another source of water and walked off in the direction of a large grove of trees. The little girl had no idea about distances in the open savanna. Although she did carefully stop every thirty minutes or so to ensure that she could still find her way back to the pond, it amazed her that the distant grove did not appear to be coming any closer. She walked on and on. As the afternoon waned, she became tired and thirsty. She stopped to drink some of her water. The tsetse flies surrounded her, buzzing around her face as she tried to drink. Nicole took out the two unguents, smelled them both, and applied the worse smelling of the two to her face and arms. Her choice was apparently correct; the flies also found the unguent noisome and kept their distance.

She reached the trees about an hour before dark. She was delighted to find that she had fortuitously stumbled upon a small oasis in the middle of the great stretch of savanna. There was a strong spring in the grove where the water rushed out of the ground and formed a circular pool about ten metres in diameter. The excess water in turn trickled out of one edge of the pool and became a creek that ran from the oasis back into the savanna. Nicole was exhausted and sweaty from her long walk. The water in the pool was inviting. Without thinking she pulled off her clothes, except for her underpants, and jumped in for a swim.

The water invigorated and soothed her tired little body. With her head underwater and her eyes closed, she swam and swam and fantasized that she was in the community pool in her suburb near Paris. In her imagination she had gone to the piscine, as she generally did once a week, and was playing water sports with her friends. The memory comforted her. After a long time Nicole rolled over on her back and took a few strokes. She opened her eyes and looked at the trees above her. The rays from the late afternoon sun were making magic as they cut through the branches and the leaves.

Seven-year-old Nicole stopped swimming and trod water for several seconds, looking around the edge of the pool for her clothes. She didn't see them. Puzzled, she scanned the perimeter of the pool more carefully. Still she saw nothing. In her mind she reconstructed all the scenes of her arrival in the grove and conclusively remembered exactly where she had placed both her clothes and the kit made from antelope hide. She climbed out of the water and examined the spot more closely. *This is definitely the place,* she thought. *And my clothes and the kit are gone.*

There was no way to quell the panic. It overpowered her in an instant. Her eyes flooded with tears, a wail broke from her throat. She closed her eyes and wept, hoping that this was all a bad dream and that she would wake up in the next few seconds and see her mother and father. But when she opened her eyes again, the same scene was still there. A half-naked little girl was alone in the wilds of Africa with no food, no water, and no hope of rescue before the middle of the next day. And it was almost dark.

With great effort Nicole managed at last to control both her fright and her tears. She decided to look for her clothes. Where they had been before, she found fresh prints of some kind. Nicole had no way of knowing what kind of animal might have made the tracks, so she assumed that it was one of the gentle antelope that she had seen that afternoon in the savanna. *That would make sense,* the little girl thought logically. *This is probably the best water hole in the area. They stopped here and were curious about my things. My splashing must have scared them away.*

As the light faded she followed the tracks along a tiny pathway through the trees. After a short trek she found the antelope hide, or rather what was left of it, discarded on the side of the path. The kit was torn completely open. All the food was gone, the water flask was mostly drained, and everything else had fallen out except the unguents and the tuber. Nicole finished the water that was left in the flask and put it with the tuber in her right hand. She discarded the messy unguents. She was about to continue following the path when she heard a sound, halfway between a yelp and a cry. The sound was very close. The path opened into the savanna about fifty metres ahead. Nicole strained her eyes and thought she saw motion, but she couldn't make out anything specific. Then she heard the yelp again, louder this time. She dropped down on her stomach and crawled slowly along the path.

There was a small rise fifteen metres before the end of the grove. From that vantage point little Nicole saw the source of the yelp. Two lion cubs were playing with her green dress. Their watchful mother was on the opposite side, staring out into the savanna twilight. Nicole froze in terror as she comprehended that she was not visiting a zoo, that she was out in the wild and a real African lioness was only twenty metres away. Trembling with fear, she inched back along the path, very slowly, very quietly, lest she call attention to her presence.

Back near the pool she resisted the urge to jump up and run pell-mell into the savanna. *Then the lioness will see me for certain,* she thought. But where to spend the night? *I'll find a ditch among the trees,* she reasoned, *away from the path. And lie still. Then maybe I'll be safe.* Still clutching the flask and the tuber, Nicole walked softly over to the spring. She took a drink and filled her flask. Next she crawled into the grove and found a ditch. Then, convinced that she was as safe as she could possibly be under the circumstances, the exhausted little girl fell asleep.

She woke up suddenly with a sensation that bugs were crawling all over her. She reached down and rubbed her bare stomach. It was covered with ants. Nicole screamed, and then she realised what she had done. In a flash she heard the lioness crashing through the brush, searching for the creature that had made the noise. The little girl shuddered and scraped the ants off with a stick. Then she saw the lioness staring at her, the feral eyes piercing the dark. Nicole was near collapse. In her fright she somehow remembered what Omeh had said about the tuber. She put the dirt-covered root into her mouth and chewed vigorously. It tasted awful. She forced herself to swallow. A moment later Nicole was rushing through the trees with the lioness chasing her. Branches and leaves cut her face and chest. She slipped once and fell. When she reached the pool she did not stop. Nicole ran across the water, her feet barely touching the top. She flapped her arms. They had changed to wings, white wings. She was no longer touching the water. She was a great white heron soaring up, up into the night sky. She turned and looked at the puzzled lioness far below her. Laughing to herself, Nicole intensified her wing motion and rose above all the trees. The great savanna unfolded below her. She could see for over a hundred kilometres.

She flew across to the brackish pond, turned west, and spotted a campfire. She zoomed toward it, her bird shrieks piercing the calm of the night. Omeh awakened with a start, saw the solitary bird spread out against the sky, and made a loud bird cry of his own. 'Ronata?' his voice seemed to ask. But Nicole did not answer, She wanted to fly higher, even above the clouds.

On the other side of the clouds the Moon and stars were clear and bright. They beckoned to her. She thought she heard music in the distance, a tinkling like crystal bells, as she soared higher and higher. She tried to flap her wings. They would barely move. They had changed into control surfaces, which now extended to increase the lift in the ultrathin air. Her aft rockets began to fire. Nicole was now a silver shuttle, thin and sleek, leaving the Earth behind.

The music was louder out in orbit. There it was a magnificent symphony, enhancing the beauty of the majestic Earth below her. She heard her name being called. From where? Who could be calling way out here? The sound came from beyond the Moon. She changed her heading, pointed toward the void of deep space, and fired her rockets again. She swept past the Moon, heading away from the Sun. Her speed was still increasing exponentially. Behind her the Sun was growing smaller and smaller. It became a tiny light and then disappeared altogether. There was blackness all around. She held her breath and came to the surface of the water.

The lioness was prowling back and forth on the edge of the pool. Nicole could vividly see all the muscles in her powerful shoulders and read the expression on her face. *Please leave me alone,* Nicole said. *I won't hurt you or your babies.*

'I recognize your smell,' the lioness answered. 'My cubs were playing with that smell.'

I too am a cub, Nicole continued, *and I want to return to my mother. But I am afraid.*

'Come out of the water,' the lioness replied. 'Let me see you. I do not believe that you are what you say.'

Summoning all her courage, her eyes riveted on the lioness, the little girl walked slowly out of the water. The lioness didn't move. When the water was only waist deep, Nicole shaped her arms into a cradle and began to sing. It was a simple, peaceful melody, the one she remembered from the beginning of her life, when her mother or father would kiss her good night, put her down in the crib, and then turn out the light. The little animals in the mobile would go around and around while a woman's soft voice sang the Brahms lullaby.

'Lay thee down, now, and rest . . , May thy slumber be blessed.'

The lioness rocked back on her haunches and threatened to pounce. The girl, still softly singing, continued walking toward the animal. When Nicole was completely out of the water and only about five metres away, the lioness jumped aside and leapt back into the grove. Nicole kept walking, the soothing song giving her both comfort and strength. In a few minutes she was back out at the edge of the savanna. By sunrise she had reached the pond, where she lay down among the grasses and fell fast asleep. Omeh and the Senoufo priests found her lying there, half naked and still asleep, when the sun was high in the sky.

She could remember it all as if it were yesterday. *Almost thirty years ago now*, she recalled as she lay still awake in her small bed on the Newton, *and the lessons I learned have never stopped being valuable*, Nicole thought about the little seven-year-old girl who had been stranded in a completely alien world and had managed to survive. *So why am I feeling sorry for myself now?* she thought. *That was a much tougher situation.*

Immersing herself in her childhood experience had given her unexpected strength. Nicole was no longer depressed. Her mind was working overtime again, trying to formulate a plan that would give her the crucial answers to what had happened during the operation on Borzov. She had pushed her loneliness aside.

Nicole realised that she would have to stay on board the Newton during the first sortie if she wanted to do a thorough analysis of all aspects of the Borzov incident. She resolved to bring up the issue with Brown or Heilmann in the morning.

At length the exhausted woman fell asleep. As she was drifting into the twilight world that separates waking and sleeping, Nicole was humming a tune to herself. It was the Brahms lullaby.

21 PANDORA'S CUBE

Nicole could see David Brown sitting behind the desk. Francesca was leaning over him, pointing at something on a large chart that was spread out in front of the two of them. Nicole knocked on the door of the commander's office.

'Hello, Nicole,' Francesca said, as she opened the door. 'What can we do for you?'

'I came to see Dr Brown,' Nicole replied. 'About my assignment.'

'Come on in,' Francesca said.

Nicole shuffled in slowly and sat in one of the two chairs opposite the desk. Francesca sat in the other. Nicole looked at the walls of the office. They had definitely changed. General Borzov's photographs of his wife and children, along with his favourite painting, a picture of a solitary bird with outstretched wings soaring above the Neva River in Leningrad, had been replaced by huge sequencing charts. The charts, each one headed by a different name (First Sortie, Second Sortie, etc.), covered the side bulletin boards from one end of the wall to the other.

General Borzov's office had been warm and personal. This room was definitely sterile and intimidating. Dr Brown had hung laminated replicas of two of his most prestigious international scientific awards on the wall behind his desk. He had also raised the height of his chair so that he looked down on anyone else in the room who might be sitting.

'I have come to see you about a personal matter,' Nicole said. She waited several seconds, expecting David Brown to ask Francesca to leave the room. He said nothing. Finally Nicole glanced in Francesca's direction to make her concern obvious.

'She has been helping me with my administrative duties,' Dr Brown explained. 'I find that her feminine insight often detects signals that I have missed altogether.'

Nicole sat silently for another fifteen seconds. She had been prepared to talk to David Brown. She had not expected that it would be necessary also for her to explain everything to Francesca. *Maybe I should just leave*, Nicole thought fleetingly, somewhat surprised to find that she was irritated about Francesca's being there.

'I have read the assignments for the first sortie,' Nicole said eventually in a formal tone, 'and I would like to make a request. My duties, as outlined in the sequence, are minimal. Irina Turgenyev, it seems to me, is also underworked for the three-day sortie. I recommend that you give my non-medical tasks to Irina and I will stay on board the Newton with Admiral Heilmann and General O'Toole. I will follow the progress of the mission carefully and can be available immediately if there is any significant medical problem. Otherwise Janos can handle the life science responsibilities.'

Again there was silence in the room. Dr Brown stared at Nicole and then at Francesca. 'Why do you want to stay on board the Newton?' Francesca responded at length. 'I would have thought that you couldn't wait to see the inside of Rama.'

'As I said, it's mostly personal,' Nicole answered vaguely. 'I'm still extremely tired from the Borzov ordeal and I have a lot of paperwork to finish. The first sortie should be straightforward. I would like to be fully rested and prepared for the second.'

'It's a highly irregular request,' David Brown said, 'but under the circumstances, I think we can do it.' He glanced again at Francesca. 'But we'd like to ask a favour of you. If you're not going into Rama, then perhaps you'd be willing to spell O'Toole as communications officer from time to time? Then Admiral Heilmann could go inside ...'

'Certainly,' Nicole answered before Brown had finished.

'Good. Then I guess we're all agreed. We'll change the manifests for the first sortie. You will remain on board the Newton.' After Dr Brown was through talking, Nicole still made no move to leave her chair. 'Was there something else?' he asked impatiently.

'According to our procedures, the life science officer prepares certification memoranda on the cosmonauts prior to each sortie. Should I give a copy to Admiral—'

'Give all those memos to me,' Dr Brown interrupted her. 'Admiral Heilmann is not concerned with personnel matters.' The American scientist looked directly at Nicole. 'But you don't need to prepare new reports for the first sortie. I've read all the documents you wrote for General Borzov. They are quite adequate.'

Nicole did not let herself be cowed by the man's penetrating gaze. *So you know what I wrote about you and Wilson,* she thought, *and you think I should feel guilty or embarrassed. Well, I don't. My opinions have not changed just because you are now nominally in charge.*

That night Nicole continued with her investigation. Her detailed analysis of the biometry data from General Borzov showed that he had had extraordinary levels of two strange chemicals in his system just before his death. Nicole could not figure out where they had come from. Had he been taking medication without her knowledge? Could these chemicals, which were known to trigger pain (they were used, according to her medical encyclopedia, to test pain sensitivity in neurologically distressed patients), somehow have been manufactured internally in some kind of allergic reaction?

And what about Janos? Why couldn't he remember reaching for the control box? Why had he been reticent and withdrawn since Borzov's death? Just after midnight she stared at the ceiling of her small bedroom. *Today the crew enters Rama and I will be here alone. I should wait until then to continue my analysis.* But she couldn't wait. She was unable to push aside all the questions that were flooding her mind. *Could there be a connection between Janos and the drugs in Borzov? Is it possible that his death was not completely accidental?*

Nicole took her personal briefcase out of the tiny closet. She opened it hastily and the contents spilled into the air. She grabbed a group of family photographs that were floating above her bed. Then she gathered up most of the rest of the items and returned them to her briefcase. Nicole retained in her hand the data cube that King Henry had given her in Davos.

She hesitated before inserting the cube. At last she took a deep breath and placed it into the reader. Eighteen menu items were immediately displayed on the monitor. She could choose any of the twelve individual dossiers on the cosmonauts or six different compilations of crew statistics. Nicole called for the dossier on Janos Tabori. There were three submenus for his biography: Personal Data, Chronological Summary, and Psychological Assessment. She could tell from the listed file sizes that the Chronological Summary contained most of the details. Nicole accessed Personal Data first to gain familiarity with the format of the dossiers.

The brief chart did not tell her much that she didn't already know. Janos was forty-one and single. When he was not on duty for the ISA, he lived alone in an apartment in Budapest, only four blocks away from where his twice-divorced mother lived by herself. He had received an honours engineering degree from the University of Hungary in 2183. In addition to mundane items like height, weight, and number of siblings, the chart listed two other numbers: IE (for Intelligence Evaluation) and SC (for Socialization Coefficient). Tabori's numbers were +3.37 for IE and 64 for SC.

Nicole returned to the main menu and called up the Glossary to refresh her memory about the definitions of IE and SC. The IE numbers supposedly represented a composite measure of overall intelligence, based on a comparison with a similar worldwide student population. All students took a set of standardized tests at specified times between the ages of twelve and twenty. The index was actually an exponent in a decimal measuring system. An IE number of zero was average. An IE index of +1.00 meant the individual was above 90% of the population; +2.00 was above 99% of the population; +3.00 above 99.9%, etc. Negative IE indices indicated below-average intelligence. Janos' score of +3.37 placed him in the middle of the upper one tenth of one percent of the population in intelligence.

The SC numbers had a more straightforward explanation. They too were based on a battery of standardized tests administered to all students between the ages of twelve and twenty, but the interpretation here was easier to understand. The highest SC score was 100. A person scoring close to 100 was liked and respected by virtually everybody, would fit into most any group, was almost never quarrelsome or moody, and was very dependable. A footnote to the explanation of the SC scores acknowledged that written tests could not accurately measure personality traits in all cases, so the numbers should be used with discretion.

Nicole reminded herself to do a comparison sometime of all the cosmonaut IE and SC scores. Then she accessed the Chronological Summary file for Janos Tabori. The next sixty minutes was an eye-opening experience for Nicole. As the life science officer, she had of course studied the official ISA personnel files for the entire crew. But if the information about Janos Tabori on the cube given to her by King Henry was correct (and she had no way of knowing one way or the other), then the ISA files were woefully incomplete. Nicole had known previously that Janos had twice been selected as the outstanding engineering student at the University of Hungary; she had not known that he had been president for two years of the Gay Students Association of Budapest. She was aware that he had entered the Space Academy in 2192 and had graduated in only three years (because of his previous experience with major Soviet engineering projects); she had never been told that he had applied to the Academy twice previously and had been rejected both times. Despite sensational entrance scores, he had twice failed his personal interview – both times the interview committee had been headed by General Valeriy Borzov. Janos had been active in various gay organizations until 2190. Subsequently he had resigned from them all and never rejoined or participated in any organized gay activities. None of this information had been in his ISA file.

Nicole was stunned by what she had learned. It wasn't that Janos had been (or was) gay that disturbed her; she was free of prejudices where sexual orientation was concerned. What bothered her most was the likelihood that his official file had been deliberately censored to remove all references both to his homosexuality and to his earlier interactions with General Borzov.

The last entries in the Tabori Chronological Summary were also surprising for Nicole. According to the dossier, Janos had purportedly signed a contract with Schmidt and Hagenest, the German publishing conglomerate, in the last week of December, just before launch. His task was to perform unspecified 'consulting' for a wide variety of post-Newton media endeavors in support of what was referred to as the Brown-Sabatini project. Cosmonaut Tabori was paid an initial fee of three hundred thousand marks for signing. Three days later his mother, who had been waiting almost a year for one of the new artificial brain implants that reversed the damage from Alzheimer's disease, entered the Bavarian Hospital in Munich for neurological surgery.

*

287

Her eyes weary and burning, Nicole finished reading the extensive dossier on Dr David Brown. During the hours that she had been studying his Chronological Summary, she had created a special subfile for herself of those items in the summary that were of particular interest to her. Before trying again to sleep, Nicole scrolled through this special subfile one more time.

Summer 2161: Brown, eleven, enrolled in Camp Longhom by father over strenuous objections of mother. Typical outdoor summer camp in hill country of Texas for upper class boys, featuring athletics of all kinds, riflery, crafts, and hiking. Boys lived ten to a barracks, Brown was extremely unpopular immediately. On fifth day bunkmates seized him coming out of shower and painted his genitals black. Brown refused to move from bed until mother had travelled almost two hundred miles to pick him up and take him home. Father apparently ignored son altogether after this incident.

September 2166: After being valedictorian from private high school, Brown enrolled as freshman in physics at Princeton. Remained in New Jersey only eight weeks. Completed undergraduate work at SMU while living at home.

June 2173: Awarded Ph.D. in physics and astronomy by Harvard. Dissertation advisor Wilson Brownwell called Brown 'an ambitious, diligent student.'

June 2175: Brown completed post-doctorate research on the evolution of stars with Brian Murchison at Cambridge.

April 2180: Married Jeannette Hudson of Pasadena, California. Ms Hudson had been graduate student in astronomy at Stanford. Only child, daughter Angela, born in December 2184.

November 2181: Was refused tenure in astronomy department at Stanford because two members of evaluation committee believed Brown had falsified scientific data in several of his many scholarly publications. Issue was never resolved.

January 2184: Appointed to first ISA Advisory Committee. Prepared comprehensive plans for series of major new astronomical telescopes on far side of the moon.

May 2187: Brown named chairman of Department of Physics and Astronomy at SMU in Dallas, Texas.

February 2188: Fistfight with Wendell Thomas, Princeton professor, in atrium outside AAAS meeting in Chicago. Thomas insisted that Brown had stolen and published ideas they had discussed together.

April 2190: Electrified scientific world by not only publishing breakthrough models of supernova process, but also predicting nearby supernova to occur in mid-March 2191. Research done in collaboration with SMU doctoral student, Elaine Bernstein of New York. Strong suggestion from graduate associates of Ms Bernstein that she was actually one with the new insights. Brown catapulted to fame as a result of his bold and correct prediction.

June 2190: Brown divorced wife, from whom he had been separated for eighteen months. Separation had started three months after Elaine Bernstein had begun graduate work.

December 2190: Married Ms Bernstein in Dallas.

March 2191: Supernova 2191a filled night sky with light, as predicted by Brown et al.

June 2191: Brown signed two-year science reporting contract with CBS. Jumped to UBC in 2194 and then, at recommendation of agent, to INN in 2197.

December 2193: Brown awarded top ISA medal for Distinguished Scientific Achievement.

November 2199: Signed exclusive multimillion mark, multiyear contract with Schmidt and Hagenest to 'exploit' all possible commercial applications of Newton mission, including books, videos, and educational material. Teamed with Francesca Sabatini as other principal, cosmonauts Heilmann and Tabori as consultants. Signing bonus of two million marks deposited in secret account in Italy.

Her alarm awakened her after she had been asleep for only two hours. Nicole dragged herself out of bed and freshened up in the retractable wash-basin. She moved slowly into the corridor and turned toward the lobby. The other four space cadets were gathered around David Brown in the control centre, excitedly reviewing the details of the initial sortie.

'All right,' Richard Wakefield was saying, 'first priorities are the lightweight individual chairlifts by the right and left stairways and one heavy load elevator from the hub to the Central Plain. Then we set up a temporary control centre at the edge of the plain and assemble and test the three rovers. Crude campsite tonight, base camp at the Beta site near the edge of the Cylindrical Sea tomorrow. We will leave the assembly and deployment of the two helicopters for tomorrow, the icemobiles and motorboats for Day Three.'

'That's an excellent summary,' Dr Brown replied. 'Francesca will go with the four of you while you're setting up the infrastructure this morning. When the lightweight lifts are installed and operational, Admiral Heilmann and I will join you along with Dr Takagishi and Mr Wilson. We'll all sleep inside Rama tonight.'

'How many long duration flares do you have?' Janos Tabori asked Irina Turgenyev.

'Twelve,' she answered. 'That should be plenty for today.'

'And tonight, when we go to sleep in there, it will be the darkest night that any of us have ever seen,' Dr, Takagishi said. 'There will be no moon and no stars, no reflection off the ground, nothing but blackness all around.'

'What will the temperature be?' Wakefield asked.

'We don't know for certain,' the Japanese scientist answered. 'The initial drones carried only cameras. But the temperature in the region around the end of the tunnel was the same as in Rama I. If that's any indication, then it should be about ten degrees below freezing at the campsites.' Takagishi paused for a moment. 'And getting warmer,' he continued. 'We're now inside the orbit of Venus. We expect the lights to come on in another eight or nine days, and the Cylindrical Sea to melt from the bottom soon thereafter.'

'Hey,' kidded Brown. 'It sounds as if you're becoming converted. You no longer qualify *all* your statements, just some of them.'

'With each datum that indicates this spaceship is like its predecessor seventy years ago,' Takagishi replied, 'the probability that they are identical increases. Thus far, if we ignore the exact timing of the correction manoeuvre, everything about the two vehicles has been the same.'

Nicole approached the group. 'Well look who's here,' Janos said with his usual grin. 'Our fifth and final space cadet.' He noticed her swollen eyes. 'And our new commander was right. You do look as if you might benefit from some rest.'

'I, for one,' Richard Wakefield interjected, 'am disappointed that my rover assembly assistant will now be Yamanaka instead of Madame des Jardins. At least our life science officer talks. I may have to recite Shakespeare to myself to stay awake.' He elbowed Yamanaka in the ribs. The Japanese pilot almost smiled.

'I wanted to wish you all good luck,' Nicole said. 'As I'm sure Dr Brown has told you, I felt I was still too tired to be very helpful. I should be fresh and ready by the second sortie.'

'Well,' Francesca Sabatini remarked impatiently after her camera had panned around the room and captured one final close-up of each face. 'Are we finally ready?'

'Let's go,' said Wakefield. They headed toward the airlock at the front of the Newton spacecraft.

22 DAWN

Richard Wakefield worked quickly in the near darkness. He was halfway down the Alpha stairway, where the gravity due to the centrifugal force created by the spin of Rama had grown to one-fourth of a gee. The light from his headgear illuminated the near field. He was almost finished with another pylon.

He checked his air supply. It was already below the midpoint. By now they should have been deeper into Rama, closer to where they could breathe the ambient air. But they had underestimated how long it would take them to install the lightweight chairlifts. The concept was extremely simple and they had practised it several times in the simulations. The upper part of the job, when they had been in the vicinity of the ladders and virtually weightless, had been relatively straightforward. But at this level the installation of each pylon was a different process because of the increasing and changing gravity.

Exactly a thousand steps above Wakefield, Janos Tabori finished wrapping anchor lines around the metal banisters that lined the stairway. After almost four hours of tedious, repetitive work, he was becoming fatigued. He remembered the argument the engineering director had advanced when he and Richard had recommended a specialized machine for the installation of the lifts. 'It's not cost-effective to create a robot for non-recurring uses,' the man had said. 'Robots are only good for recurring tasks.'

Janos glanced below him but could not see as far as the next pylon, two hundred and fifty steps down the stairway. 'Is it time for lunch yet?' he said to Wakefield on his commpak.

'Could be,' was the response. 'But we're way behind. We didn't send Yamanaka and Turgenyev over to Gamma stairway until 10:30. At the rate we're going, we'll be lucky to finish these lightweight lifts and the crude campsite today. We'll have to postpone the heavy load elevator and the rovers until tomorrow.'

'Hiro and I are already eating,' they both heard Turgenyev say from the other side of the bowl. 'We were hungry. We finished the chair rack and the upper motor in half an hour. We're down to pylon #12.'

'Good work,' Wakefield said. 'But I'll warn you that you're in the easy part, around the ladders and the top of the stairway. Working weightless is a snap. Wait until the gravity is measurably different at each location.'

'According to the laser range finder, Cosmonaut Wakefield is exactly 8.13 kilometres away from me,' everyone heard Dr Takagishi interject.

'That doesn't tell me anything, Professor, unless I know where the hell you are.'

'I'm standing on the ledge just outside our relay station, near the bottom of the Alpha stairway.'

'Come on, Shig, won't you Orientals ever go along with the rest of the world? The Newton is parked on the *top* of Rama and you are at the *top* of the stairway. If we can't agree on up and down, how can we ever hope to communicate our innermost feelings? Much less play chess together.'

'Thank you, Janos. I am at the *top* of the Alpha stairway. By the way, what are you doing? Your range is increasing rapidly.'

'I'm sliding down the banister to meet Richard for lunch. I don't like eating fish and chips by myself.'

'I'm also coming down for lunch,' Francesca said. 'I just finished filming an excellent demonstration of the Coriolis force using Hiro and Irina. It will be great for elementary physics classes. I should be there in five minutes.'

'Say, signora' – it was Wakefield again – 'do you think we could talk you into some honest-to-goodness work? We stop what we're doing to accommodate your filming – maybe we can make a trade with you.'

'I'm willing,' answered Francesca. 'I'll help after lunch. But what I would like now is some light. Could you use one of your flares and let me capture you and Janos having a picnic on the Stairway of the Gods?'

Wakefield programmed a flare for a delayed ignition and climbed eighty steps to the nearest ledge. Cosmonaut Tabori arrived at the same spot half a minute before the light flooded them. From two kilometres above, Francesca panned across the three stairways and then zoomed in on the two figures sitting cross-legged on the ledge. From that perspective, Janos and Richard looked like two eagles nesting in a high mountain eyrie.

By late afternoon the Alpha chairlift was finished and ready for testing. 'We'll let you be the first customer,' Richard Wakefield said to Francesca, 'since you were good enough to help.' They were standing in full gravity at the foot of the incredible stairway. Thirty thousand steps stretched into the darkness of the artificial heavens above them. Beside them on the Central Plain the ultralight motor and the self-contained portable power station for the chairlift were already in operation. The cosmonauts had transported the electrical and mechanical subsystems in unassembled pieces on their backs and assembly had required less than an hour.

'The little chairs are not permanently connected to the cables,' Wakefield explained to Francesca. 'At each end there is a mechanism that attaches or detaches the chairs. That way it's not necessary to have an almost infinite number of seats.'

Francesca hesitantly sat down in the plastic structure that had been pulled away from a group of similar baskets hanging from a side cable. 'You're certain this is safe?' she said, staring at the darkness above her.

'Of course,' Richard said with a laugh. 'It's exactly like the simulation. And I'll be in the next chair behind you, only one minute or four hundred metres below. Altogether the ride takes forty minutes from bottom to top. Average speed is twenty-four kilometres per hour.'

'And I don't do anything,' Francesca remembered, 'except sit tight, hold on, and activate my breathing system about twenty minutes from the summit.'

'Don't forget to fasten your seat belt,' Wakefield reminded her with a smile. 'If the cable were to slow down or stop near the top, where you are weightless, your momentum could cause you to sail out into the Raman void.' He grinned. 'But since the entire chairlift runs beside the stairway, in the event of any emergency, you could always climb out of your basket and walk back up to the hub along the stairs.'

Richard nodded and Janos Tabori switched on the motor. Francesca was lifted off the ground and soon disappeared above them. 'I'll go right over to Gamma after I'm certain you're on your way,' Richard said to Janos. 'The second system should be easier. With all of us working together, we should be finished by 19:00 at the latest.'

'I'll have the campsite ready by the time you reach the summit,' Janos remarked, 'Do you think we're still going to stay down here tonight?'

'That doesn't make much sense,' David Brown said from above. He or Takagishi had monitored all cosmonaut communications throughout the day. 'The rovers aren't ready yet. We had hoped to do some exploring tomorrow.'

'If we each bring down a few subsystems,' Wakefield replied, 'Janos and I could assemble one rover tonight before we go to sleep. The second rover will probably be operational before noon tomorrow if we don't encounter any difficulties.'

'That's a possible scenario,' Dr Brown responded. 'Let's see how much progress we have made and how tired everyone is three hours from now.'

Richard climbed into his tiny chair and waited for the automatic loading algorithm in the processor to attach his seat to the cable. 'By the way,' he said to his companion as he started his ascent, 'thanks a lot for your good humour today. I might not have made it without the jokes.'

Janos smiled and waved at his friend. Looking upward from his moving chair, Richard Wakefield could barely make out the light from Francesca's headgear. *She's more than a hundred floors above me*, he thought. *But only two and a half percent of the distance from here to the hub. This place is immense.*

He reached in his pocket and pulled out the portable meteorological station that Takagishi had asked him to carry. The professor wanted a careful profile of all the atmospheric parameters in the north polar bowl of Rama. Of particular importance for his circulation models were the density and temperature of the air versus the distance below the airlock.

Wakefield watched the pressure readings, which started at 1.05 bars, fall below Earth levels, and continue their steady, monotonic decline. The temperature held fixed at a cold −8 degrees Celsius. He leaned back and closed his eyes. It was a strange feeling, riding a basket upward, ever upward in the dark. Richard turned down the volume of one channel on his commpak; the only ongoing conversation was between Yamanaka and Turgenyev and neither of them ever had very much to say. He increased the volume on Beethoven's Sixth Symphony, which was playing in the background on another channel.

As he listened to the music, Richard was surprised at how his internal visions of brooks and flowers and green fields on Earth evoked a powerful feeling of homesickness. It was almost impossible for him to fathom the miraculous concatenation of events that had carried him from his boyhood home in Stratford to Cambridge to the Space Academy in Colorado and finally to here, to Rama, where he was riding a chairlift in the dark along the Stairway to the Gods.

No, Prospero, he said to himself, *no magician could ever have conceived of such a place.* He remembered seeing *The Tempest* for the first time as a boy and being frightened by the portrayal of a world whose mysteries might be beyond our comprehension. *There is no magic,* he had said at the time. *There are only natural concepts that we cannot yet explain.* Richard smiled. *Prospero was not a mage; he was only a frustrated scientist*

A moment later Richard Wakefield was stupefied by the most amazing sight he had ever seen. As his chair was sailing soundlessly upward, parallel to the stairway, dawn burst upon Rama. Three kilometres below him, cut into the Central Plain, the long straight valleys that ran from the edge of the bowl to the Cylindrical Sea suddenly exploded with light. The six linear suns of Rama, three in each hemicylinder, were carefully designed to produce a balanced illumination throughout the alien world. Wakefield's first feelings were of vertigo and nausea. He was suspended in air by a thin cable, thousands of metres above the ground. He closed his eyes and tried to maintain his bearings. *You will not fall,* he said to himself.

'*Aieee,*' he heard Hiro Yamanaka yell.

From the ensuing conversation he could tell that Hiro, startled by the burst of light, had lost his footing near the middle of the Gamma stairway. He had apparently fallen twenty or thirty metres before he had adroitly (and luckily) managed to grab part of the banister.

'Are you all right?' David Brown asked.

'I think so,' Yamanaka answered breathlessly.

With the short crisis over, everyone started talking at once. 'This is fantastic!' Dr Takagishi was shouting. 'The light levels are phenomenal. And this is all happening *before* the thawing of the sea. It's different. It's altogether different.'

'Have another module ready for me as soon as I reach the top,' Francesca said. 'I'm almost out of film.'

'Such beauty. Such indescribable beauty,' General O'Toole added. He and Nicole des Jardins were watching the monitor on board the Newton. The real-time picture from Francesca's camera was being transmitted to them through the relay station at the hub.

Richard Wakefield said nothing. He simply stared, entranced by the world below him. He could barely discern Janos Tabori, the chairlift apparatus, and the half-completed campsite down at the bottom of the stairway. Nevertheless, the distance to them gave him some measure of this alien world. As he looked out across the hundreds of square kilometres of the Central Plain, he saw fascinating shapes in every direction. There were two features, however, that overwhelmed his imagination and vision: the Cylindrical Sea and the massive, pointed structures in the southern bowl opposite him, fifty kilometres away.

As his eyes grew more accustomed to the light, the gigantic central spire in the southern bowl seemed to grow larger and larger, It had been called Big Horn by the first explorers. *Can it really be eight kilometres tall?* Wakefield asked himself. The six smaller spires, surrounding the Big Horn in a hexagonal pattern and connected both to it and the walls of Rama by enormous flying buttresses, were each larger than anything made by man on Earth. Yet they were dwarfed by this neighbouring prominence originating from the very centre of the bowl and growing straight along the spin axis of the cylinder.

In the foreground, halfway between Wakefield's position near the north pole and that mammoth construction in the south, a band of bluish white ringed the cylindrical world. The frozen sea seemed illogical and out of place. It could never melt, the mind wanted to say, or all the water would fall toward the central axis. But the Cylindrical Sea was held in its banks by the centrifugal force of Rama. None knew better than the Newton crew that on its shore a human being would have the same weight as he would standing beside a terrestrial ocean.

The island city in the middle of the Cylindrical Sea was Rama's New York. To Richard its skyscrapers had not been too imposing in the views that had been offered by the light from the flares. But under the light of the Raman suns, it was clear that this city held centre stage. The eyes were drawn to New York from any point inside Rama – the dense oval island of buildings was the only break in the orderly annulus that formed the Cylindrical Sea.

'Just look at New York!' Dr Takagishi was gushing excitedly into his commpak. 'There must be almost a thousand buildings over two hundred metres tall.' He paused only a second. 'That's where *they* live. I know it. New York must be our target.'

After the initial outbursts there was a protracted silence while each of the cosmonauts privately integrated the sunlit world of Rama into his own consciousness. Richard could now clearly see Francesca, four hundred metres above him, as his chair crossed the transition between the stairways and the ladders and closed in on the hub.

'Admiral Heilmann and I have just had a quick conversation,' David Brown said, breaking the silence, 'with some advice from Dr Takagishi. There seems to be no obvious reason to change our plans for this sortie, at least not the early part. Unless something else unexpected occurs, we will go forward with Wakefield's suggestion. We will finish the two chairlifts, carry the rover down for assembly later this evening, and all sleep in the campsite at the foot of the stairway as planned.'

'Don't forget me,' Janos hollered into his commpak. 'I'm the only one who doesn't have much of a view!'

Richard Wakefield unfastened his seat belt and stepped out onto the ledge. He looked down to where the stairway disappeared from view. 'Roger, Cosmonaut Tabori. We have arrived back at Station Alpha. Whenever you give the signal, we will hoist you up to join us.'

23 NIGHTFALL

'... Considering the regular abuse that he received from his neurotic father and the emotional scars that must remain from his youthful marriage to British actress Sarah Tydings, Cosmonaut Wakefield is remarkably well adjusted. He underwent two years of professional therapy after his celebrated divorce, concluding a year before he entered the Space Academy in 2192. His scholastic record at the academy is still unequaled to this day; his professors in electrical engineering and computer sciences all insist that by the time of his graduation, Wakefield knew more than any member of the faculty ...

'... Except for a wariness where intimacy is concerned (particularly with women – he has apparently had no sustained emotional involvements since the breakup of his marriage), Wakefield exhibits none of the antisocial behaviour usually found in abused children. Although his SC was low as a youth, he has grown less arrogant as he has matured and is now less likely to force his brilliance upon others. His honesty and character are unassailable. Knowledge, not power or money, seems to be his goal ...'

Nicole finished reading the Psychological Assessment for Richard Wakefield and rubbed her eyes. It was very late. She had been studying the dossiers ever since the crew inside Rama had settled down to sleep. They would be awakening for their second day in that strange world in less than two hours. Her six-hour shift as communications officer would start in another thirty minutes. *So out of this entire bunch,* Nicole was thinking, *there are only three that are beyond question. Those four with their illegal media contract have already compromised themselves. Yamanaka and Turgenyev are unknowns. Wilson is marginally stable and has his own agenda anyway. That leaves O'Toole, Takagishi, and Wakefield.*

Nicole washed her face and hands and sat down again at the terminal. She exited from the Wakefield dossier and returned to the main menu of the data cube. She scanned the comparative statistics available and keyed a pair of displays to appear side by side on the screen. On the left-hand side was the ordered set of IE scores for each member of the crew; opposite, for comparison, Nicole had displayed the SC indices for the Newton dozen.

IE		SC	
Wakefield	+ 5.58	O'Toole	86
Sabatini	+ 4.22	Borzov	84
Brown	+ 4.17	Takagishi	82
Takagishi	+ 4.02	Wilson	78
Tabori	+ 3.37	des Jardins	71
Borzov	+ 3.28	Heilmann	68
des Jardins	+ 3.04	Tabori	64
O'Toole	+ 2.92	Yamanaka	62
Turgenyev	+ 2.87	Turgenyev	60
Yamanaka	+ 2.66	Wakefield	58
Wilson	+ 2.48	Sabatini	56
Heilmann	+ 2.24	Brown	49

Although Nicole had very quickly glanced through most of the information in the dossiers earlier, she had not read all the charts on all the crew members. Some of the indices she now saw for the first time. She was particularly surprised by the very high intelligence rating for Francesca Sabatini. *What a waste,* Nicole thought immediately. *All that potential being used for such ordinary pursuits.*

The overall intelligence level of the crew was quite impressive. Every cosmonaut was in the top one percent of the population. Nicole was 'one in a thousand' and she was only in the middle of the dozen. Wakefield's intelligence rating was truly exceptional and placed him in the supergenius category; Nicole had never before personally known someone with such high scores on the standardized tests.

Although her training in psychiatry had taught her to distrust attempts to quantify personality traits, Nicole was intrigued by the SC indices as well. She herself would have intuitively placed O'Toole, Borzov, and Takagishi at the top of the list. All three men seemed confident, balanced, and sensitive to others. But she was astonished by Wilson's high socialization coefficient. *He must have been an altogether different person before he became involved with Francesca.* Nicole wondered for a brief moment why her own SC index was no higher than a seventy-one; then she remembered that as a young woman she had been more withdrawn and self-centered.

So what about Wakefield? she asked herself, realizing that he was the only viable candidate to help her understand what had happened inside the RoSur software during Borzov's operation. Could she trust him? And could she enlist Richard's help without revealing some of her farfetched suspicions? Again the thought of abandoning her investigation altogether seemed very appealing. *Nicole,* she said to herself, *if this conspiracy idea of yours turns out to be a waste of time ...*

But Nicole was convinced that there were enough unanswered questions to warrant continuing her investigation. She resolved to talk to Wakefield.

After determining that she could add her own files to the king's data cube, she created a new file, a nineteenth file, simply called NICOLE. She called in her word processing subroutine and wrote a brief memorandum:

3-3-00 – Have determined for certain that RoSur malfunction during Borzov procedure due to external manual command after initial load and verification. Enlisting Wakefield for support.

Nicole pulled a blank data cube from the supply drawer adjacent to her computer. She copied onto it both her memorandum and all the information stored on the cube that she had been given by King Henry. When she dressed for her work shift in her flight suit, she put the duplicate cube in her pocket.

General O'Toole was dozing in the Command and Control Complex of the military spacecraft when Nicole arrived to give him a break. Although the visual displays in this smaller vehicle were not quite as breathtaking as those in the scientific ship, the layout of the military CCC as a communications centre was far superior, especially from a human engineering point of view. All the controls could easily be handled by a single cosmonaut.

O'Toole apologized for not being awake. He pointed to the three monitors that showed three different views of the same scene – the rest of the crew fast asleep inside the crude campsite at the foot of Alpha stairway. 'This last five hours has not been what you would call exciting,' he said.

Nicole smiled. 'General, you don't need to apologize to me. I know you've been on duty for almost twenty-four hours.'

General O'Toole stood up. 'After you left,' he summarized, checking his electronic log on one of the six monitors in front of him, 'they finished dinner and then they started the assembly of the first rover. The automatic navigation program failed its self-test, but Wakefield found the problem – a software bug in one of the subroutines that was changed in the last delivery – and fixed it. Tabori took the rover for a test drive before the crew prepared for sleep. At the end of the day Francesca did a stirring short piece for transmission to the Earth.' He paused for a moment. 'Would you like to see it?'

Nicole nodded. O'Toole activated the far right television monitor and Francesca appeared in a close-up outside the enclosed campsite. The frame showed a portion of the bottom of the stairway and the equipment for the chairlift as well. 'It is time to sleep in Rama,' she intoned. She looked up and around her. 'The lights in this amazing world came on unexpectedly about nine hours ago, showing us in more detail the elaborate handiwork of our intelligent cousins from across the stars.' A montage of still photographs and short videos, some taken by the drones and some taken by Francesca herself on that day, punctuated her tour of the artificial 'worldlet' that the crew was 'about to explore.' At the end of the brief segment the camera was again fixed on Francesca.

'Nobody knows why this second spacecraft in less than a century has invaded our little domain at the edge of the galaxy. Perhaps this magnificent creation has no explanation that would be even remotely comprehensible to us human beings. But perhaps somewhere in this vast and precise world of metal we will find some keys that will unlock the mysteries enshrouding the creatures who constructed this vehicle.' She smiled and her nostrils flared dramatically. 'And if we do, then perhaps we will have moved one step closer to an understanding of ourselves ... and maybe our gods as well.'

Nicole could tell that General O'Toole was moved by Francesca's oratory. Despite her personal antipathy for the woman, Nicole begrudgingly acknowledged again that Francesca was talented. 'She captures my feelings about this venture so well,' O'Toole said enthusiastically. 'I just wish I could be that articulate.'

Nicole sat down at the console and entered the handover code. She followed the listed procedure on the monitor and checked out all the equipment. 'All right, General,' she said as she turned around in her chair, 'I believe I can handle it from here.'

O'Toole lingered behind her. It was obvious that he wanted to talk. 'I had a long discussion with Signora Sabatini three nights ago,' he said. 'About religion. She told me that she had become an agnostic before finally coming back to the church. She told me that thinking about Rama had made her a Catholic again.'

There was a long silence. For some reason, the fifteenth century church in the old village of Sainte Etienne de Chigny, eight hundred metres down the road from Beauvois, came into Nicole's mind. She remembered standing inside the church with her father on a beautiful spring day and being fascinated by the light scattering through the stained glass windows.

'Did God make the colours?' Nicole had asked her father.

'Some say so,' he had answered laconically.

'And what do you think, Papa?' she had then asked.

'I must admit,' General O'Toole was saying as Nicole forced herself to return to the present, 'that this entire voyage has been spiritually uplifting for me. I feel closer to God now than I have ever felt before. There's something about contemplating the vastness of the universe that humbles you and makes you ...' He stopped himself. 'I'm sorry,' he started to apologise, 'I have imposed ...'

'No,' Nicole answered. 'No, you haven't. I find your religious certitude very refreshing.'

'Nevertheless, I hope I haven't offended you in any way. Religion is a very private matter.' He smiled. 'But sometimes it's hard not to share your feelings, particularly since both you and Signora Sabatini are Catholics as well.'

As O'Toole left the control complex, Nicole wished him a sound sleep during his nap. When he had gone, she removed the duplicate data cube from her pocket and placed it in the CCC cube reader. *At least this way,* she said to herself, *I have backed up my information sources.* Into her mind came a

300

picture of Francesca Sabatini listening intently while General O'Toole waxed philosophical about the religious significance of Rama. *You're an amazing woman,* Nicole thought. *You do whatever it takes. Even immorality and hypocrisy are acceptable.*

Dr Shigeru Takagishi stared in rapt silence at the towers and spheres of New York four kilometres away. From time to time he would walk over to the telescope that he had temporarily set up on the cliff overlooking the Cylindrical Sea and study a particular feature in that alien landscape.

'You know,' he said at length to Cosmonauts Wakefield and Sabatini, 'I don't believe the reports the first crew gave on New York are entirely accurate. Or else this is a different spaceship.' Neither Richard nor Francesca responded. Wakefield was engrossed in the last stages of assembly of the icemobile and Francesca, as usual, was busy video recording Wakefield's efforts.

'It looks as if there are certainly three identical parts to the city,' Dr Takagishi continued, primarily to himself, 'and three subdivisions within each of those parts. But all nine sections are not *absolutely* the same. There appear to be subtle differences.'

'There,' said Richard Wakefield, standing up with a satisfied smile. 'That ought to do it. A full day ahead of schedule. I'll just quickly test all the important engineering functions.'

Francesca glanced at her watch. 'We're almost half an hour behind the revised timeline. Are we still going to take a fast look at New York before dinner?'

Wakefield shrugged his shoulders and looked at Takagishi. Francesca walked over to the Japanese scientist. 'What do you say, Shigeru? Shall we take a quick run across the ice and give the people on Earth a close-up view of the Rama version of New York?'

'By all means,' Takagishi answered. 'I can't wait ...'

'Only if you will be back at camp by 19:30 at the latest,' David Brown interrupted. He was in the helicopter with Admiral Heilmann and Reggie Wilson. 'We need to do some serious planning tonight. We may want to revise the deployments for tomorrow.'

'Roger,' said Wakefield. 'If we forget about the pulley system for now and have no problem carrying the icemobile down the stairs, we should be able to cross the sea in ten minutes each way. That would get us back to camp in plenty of time.'

'We've overflown many of the features of the Northern Hemicylinder this afternoon,' Brown said. 'No biots anywhere. The cities look like duplicates of each other. There were no surprises anywhere in the Central Plain. I personally think that maybe we should attack the mysterious south tomorrow.'

'New York,' Takagishi shouted. 'A detailed reconnaissance of New York should be our goal for tomorrow.' Brown didn't answer. Takagishi walked out to the edge of the cliff and stared down at the ice fifty metres below. To his left the unimposing narrow stairway cut in the cliff descended in short steps. 'How heavy is the icemobile?' Takagishi asked.

'Not very,' Wakefield answered. 'But it's bulky. Are you certain you don't want to wait for me to install the pulleys? We can always go across tomorrow.'

'I can help carry it,' Francesca interjected. 'If we don't at least see New York, we will not be able to make educated inputs at the planning meeting tonight.'

'All right,' Richard replied, shaking his head in amusement at Francesca. 'Anything for journalism. I'll go first, so that most of the lifting is on my back. Francesca, get in the middle. Dr Takagishi at the top. Watch out for the runners. They are sharp on the edges.'

The climb down to the surface of the Cylindrical Sea was uneventful. 'Goodness,' Francesca Sabatini said as they prepared to cross the ice, 'that was easy. Why is a pulley system needed at all?'

'Because sometimes we may be carrying something else or, perish the thought, we may need to defend ourselves during ascent or descent.'

Wakefield and Takagishi sat in the front of the icemobile. Francesca was in the back with her video camera. Takagishi became more and more animated as they drew closer to New York. 'Just look at that place,' he said when the icemobile was about five hundred metres from the opposite shore. 'Can there be any doubt that this is the capital of Rama?'

As the trio approached the shore, the breathtaking sight of the strange city silenced all conversation. Everything about New York's complicated structure spoke of order and purposeful creation by intelligent beings; yet the first set of cosmonauts, seventy years earlier, had found it as empty of life as the rest of Rama. Was this vast complex, broken into nine sections, indeed an enormously complicated machine, as the first visitors had suggested, or was the long thin island (ten kilometres by three) actually a city whose denizens had long ago disappeared?

They parked the icemobile on the edge of the frozen sea and walked along a path until they found a stairway leading to the ramparts of the wall surrounding the city. The excited Takagishi loped along about twenty metres in front of Wakefield and Sabatini. As they ascended, more and more of the details of the city became apparent.

Richard was immediately intrigued by the geometrical shapes of the buildings. In addition to the normal tall, thin skyscrapers, there were scattered spheres, rectangular solids, even an occasional polyhedron. And they were definitely arranged in some kind of a pattern. *Yes,* he thought to himself as his eyes scanned the fascinating complex of structures, *over there is a dodecahedron, there a pentahedron ...*

His mathematical ruminations were interrupted when all the lights were suddenly extinguished and the entire interior of Rama was plunged into darkness.

24 SOUNDS IN THE DARKNESS

A t first Takagishi could see absolutely nothing. It was as if he had suddenly been struck blind. He blinked twice and stood motionless in the total darkness. The momentary silence on the commlinks erupted into hopeless noise as all the cosmonauts began to talk at the same time. Calmly, fighting against his growing fear, Takagishi tried to remember the scene that had been in front of his eyes at the moment the lights were extinguished.

He had been standing on the wall overlooking New York, about a metre from the dangerous edge. In the final second he had been looking off to the left and had just glimpsed a staircase descending into the city about two hundred metres away. Then the scene had vanished ...

'Takagishi,' he heard Wakefield calling, 'are you all right?'

He turned around to acknowledge the question and noticed that his knees had become weak. In the complete darkness he had lost his orientation. How many degrees had he turned? Had he been facing the city directly? Again he recalled the last image. The elevated wall was twenty or thirty metres above the floor of the city. A fall would be fatal.

'I'm here,' he said tentatively, 'But I'm too close to the edge.' He dropped down on all fours. The metal was cold against his hands.

'We're coming,' Francesca said. 'I'm trying to find the light on my video camera.'

Takagishi turned down the volume on his commpak and listened for the sound of his companions. A few seconds later he saw a light in the distance. He could barely make out the forms of his two associates.

'Where are you, Shigeru?' Francesca asked. The light from her camera illuminated only the area immediately around her.

'Up here. Up here.' He waved before he realised that they could not see him.

'I want complete quiet,' David Brown shouted over the communications system, 'until everyone is accounted for.' The conversations ceased after a few seconds. 'Now,' he continued, 'Francesca, what's going on down there?'

'We're climbing the stairway up the wall, on the New York side, David, about a hundred metres from where we parked the icemobile. Dr Takagishi was ahead of us, already at the top. We have the light from my camera. We're going to meet him.'

'Janos,' Dr Brown said next, 'where are you in rover #2?'

'About three kilometres from camp. The headlights are working fine. We could return in ten minutes or so.'

'Go back there and man the navigation console. We'll stay airborne until you verify that the homing system is operational from your side ... Francesca, be careful, but come back to camp as fast as you can. And give us a report every two minutes or so.'

'Roger, David,' she said. Francesca switched off her commpak and called for Takagishi again. Despite the fact that he was only thirty metres away, it took Francesca and Richard over a minute to find him in the dark.

Takagishi was relieved to touch his colleagues. They sat down beside him on the wall and listened to the renewed chatter on the commpak. O'Toole and des Jardins verified that there had been no other observed changes inside Rama at the time the lights had gone out. The half dozen portable scientific stations that had already been deployed in the alien spaceship had exhibited no meaningful perturbations. Temperatures, wind velocities and directions, seismic readings, and near field spectroscopic measurements were all unchanged.

'So the lights went out,' Wakefield said. 'I admit that it was scary, but it was no big deal. Probably—'.

'Shh' said Takagishi abruptly. He reached down and turned off both his and Walcefield's commpak. 'Do you hear that noise?'

To Wakefield the sudden silence was nearly as unnerving as the total darkness had been a few minutes before. 'No,' he said in a whisper, after listening for several seconds, 'but my ears are not very—'

'Shh.' Now it was Francesca's turn. 'Are you talking about that distant, high-pitched scraping sound?' she whispered.

'Yes,' said Takagishi, quietly but excitedly. 'Like something is brushing against a metallic surface. It suggests movement.'

Wakefield listened again. Maybe he could hear something. Maybe he was imagining it. 'Come on,' he said to the others out loud, 'let's go back to the icemobile.'

'Wait,' said Takagishi as Richard stood up. 'It seemed to stop just as you spoke.' He leaned over to Francesca. 'Turn off the light,' he said softly. 'Let's sit here in the darkness and see if we can hear it again.'

Wakefield sat back down beside his companions. With the camera light off it was absolutely black around them. The only sound was their breathing. They waited a full minute. They heard nothing. Just as Wakefield was about to insist that they leave, he heard a sound from the direction of New York. It was like hard brushes dragging across metal, but there was also an embedded high-frequency noise, as if a tiny voice were singing very fast, that punctuated the nearly constant scraping. The sound was definitely louder. And eerie. Wakefield felt his spine tingle.

'Do you have a tape recorder?' Takagishi whispered to Francesca. The scraping stopped at the sound of Takagishi's voice. The trio waited another fifteen seconds.

'Hey there, hey there,' they heard David Brown's loud voice on the emergency interrupt channel. 'Is everybody all right? You're way overdue for a report.'

'Yes, David,' Francesca replied. 'We're still here. We heard an unusual sound coming from New York.'

'Now's not the time for dilly-dallying. We have a major crisis on our hands. All our new plans have assumed that Rama would be constantly lit. We need to regroup.'

'All right,' Wakefield responded. 'We're leaving the wall now. If all goes well we should be back to the campsite in less than an hour.'

Dr Shigeru Takagishi was reluctant to leave New York with the mystery of the strange sound unresolved. But he understood completely that now was not the appropriate time for a scientific foray into the city. As the icemobile raced across the frozen Cylindrical Sea, the Japanese scientist smiled to himself. He was happy. He knew that he had heard a new sound, something decidedly different from any of the sounds catalogued by the first Rama team. This was a good beginning.

Cosmonauts Tabori and Wakefield were the last two to ride up the chair-lift beside the Alpha stairway. 'Takagishi was really quite irritated with Dr Brown, wasn't he?' Richard was saying to Janos as he helped the little Hungarian disembark from the chair. They glided along the ramp toward the ferry.

'I've never seen him so angry,' Janos replied. 'Shig is a consummate professional and he has great pride in his knowledge of Rama. For Brown to discount the noise you guys heard in such an offhand manner suggests an absence of respect for Takagishi. I don't blame Shig for being irritated.'

They climbed onboard the ferry and activated the transportation module. The vast darkness of Rama retreated behind them as they eased through the lighted corridor toward the Newton.

'It was a very strange sound,' Richard said. 'It really gave me the chills. I have no idea if it was a new sound, or if maybe Norton and his team heard the same thing seventy years ago. But I do know that I had a bad case of the willies while I was standing there on the wall.'

'Even Francesca was pissed off at Brown at first. She wanted to do a feature interview with Shig for her nightly report. Brown talked her out of it, but I'm not certain he completely convinced her that strange noises are not news. Luckily she had enough of a story with just the lights going out.'

The two men descended from the ferry and approached the air lock. 'Whew,' said Janos. 'I'm bushed. It has been a couple of long and hectic days.'

'Yeah,' Richard agreed. 'We thought we would be spending the next two nights at the campsite. Instead we're back up here. I wonder what surprises are in store for us tomorrow.'

Janos smiled at his friend. 'You know what's funny about all this?' he said. He did not wait for Wakefield to answer. 'Brown really believes he's in charge of this mission. Did you see how he reacted when Takagishi suggested that we could explore New York in the dark? Brown probably thinks it was *his* decision for us to return to the Newton and abort the first sortie.'

Richard looked at Janos with a quizzical smile. 'It wasn't, of course,' Janos continued. 'Rama made the decision for us to leave. And Rama will decide what we do next.'

25 A FRIEND IN NEED

In his dream he was lying on a futon in a seventeenth century ryokan. The room was very large, nine tatami mats in all. To his left, in the yard on the other side of the open screen, was a perfect miniaturized garden with tiny trees and a manicured stream. He was waiting for a young woman.

'Takagishi-san, are you awake?'

He stirred and reached out for the communicator. 'Hello,' he said, his voice betraying his grogginess. 'Who is it?'

'Nicole des Jardins,' the voice said. 'I'm sorry to call you so early, but I need to see you. It's urgent.'

'Give me three minutes,' Takagishi said,

There was a knock on his door exactly three minutes later. Nicole greeted him and entered the room. She was carrying a data cube. 'Do you mind?' she said, pointing to the computer console. Takagishi shook his head.

'Yesterday there were half a dozen separate incidents,' Nicole said gravely, pointing at some blips on the monitor, 'including the two largest aberrations I have ever seen in your heart data.' She looked at him. 'Are you certain that you and your doctor provided me with complete historical records?'

Takagishi nodded.

'Then I have reason for concern,' she continued. 'The irregularities yester-day suggest that your chronic diastolic abnormality has worsened. Perhaps the valve has sprung a new leak. Perhaps the long periods of weightlessness—'

'Or perhaps,' Takagishi interrupted with a soft smile, 'I became overly excited and my extra adrenaline aggravated the problem.'

Nicole stared at the Japanese scientist. 'That's possible, Dr Takagishi. One of the major incidents occurred just after the lights went out. I guess it was when you were listening to your strange sound.'

'And the other, by chance, could it have been during my argument with Dr Brown in the campsite? If so, that would support my hypothesis.'

Cosmonaut des Jardins touched several keys on the console and her software entered a new subroutine. She studied the data displayed on two sides of a split screen. 'Yes,' she said, 'it looks right. The second incident took place twenty minutes before we started leaving Rama. That would have been toward the end of the meeting.' She moved away from the monitor. 'But I can't dismiss

307

the bizarre behaviour of your heart just because you were excited.'

They stared at each other for several long seconds. 'What are you trying to tell me, Doctor?' Takagishi said softly. 'Are you going to confine me to my quarters on the Newton? Now, at the most significant moment in my professional career?'

'I'm considering it,' Nicole answered directly. 'Your health is more important to me than your career. I've already lost one member of the crew. I'm not certain that I could forgive myself if I lost another.'

She saw the entreaty in her colleague's face. 'I know how critical these sorties into Rama are to you. I'm trying to find some kind of rationalization that will allow me to overlook yesterday's data.' Nicole sat down at the far end of the bed and looked away. 'But as a doctor, not a Newton cosmonaut, it's very very tough.'

She heard Takagishi approach and felt his hand gently on her shoulder. 'I know how difficult it has been for you these last few days,' he said. 'But it was not your fault. All of us are aware that General Borzov's death was unavoidable.'

Nicole recognized the respect and friendship in Takagishi's gaze. She thanked him with her eyes, 'I very much appreciate what you did for me before launch,' he continued. 'If you feel compelled to limit my activities now, I will not object.'

'Dammit,' said Nicole, standing up quickly, 'it's not that simple. I've been studying your overnight data for almost an hour. Look at this. Your chart for the last ten hours is perfectly normal. There's not a trace of any anomaly. And you had had no incidents for weeks. Until yesterday. What is it with you, Shig? Do you have a bad heart? Or just a weird one?'

Takagishi smiled. 'My wife told me once that I had a strange heart. But I think she was referring to something altogether different.'

Nicole activated her scanner and displayed the data on the monitor in realtime. 'There we are again' – she shook her head— 'the signature of a perfectly healthy heart. No cardiologist in the world would argue with my conclusion.' She moved toward the door.

'So what's the verdict, Doc?' Takagishi asked.

'I haven't decided,' she answered. 'You could help. Have another one of your incidents in the next few hours and make it easy for me.' She waved goodbye. 'See you at breakfast.'

Richard Wakefield was coming out of his room as Nicole headed down the hall after leaving Takagishi. She made a spontaneous decision to talk to him about the RoSur software.

'Good morning, princess,' he said as he approached. 'What are you doing awake at this hour? Something exciting, I hope.'

'As a matter of fact,' Nicole replied in the same playful tone, 'I was coming to talk to you.' He stopped to listen. 'Do you have a minute?'

'For you, Madame Doctor,' he answered with an exaggerated smile, 'I have *two* minutes. But no more. Mind you, I'm hungry. And if I am not fed quickly when I'm hungry, I turn into an awful ogre.' Nicole laughed. 'What's on your mind?' he added lightly.

'Could we go into your room?' she asked.

'I knew it. I knew it,' he said, spinning around and sliding quickly toward his door. 'It's finally happened, just like in my dreams. An intelligent, beautiful woman is going to declare her undying affection ...'

Nicole could not suppress a chortle. 'Wakefield,' she interrupted, still grinning, 'you are hopeless. Are you never serious? I have some business to discuss with you.'

'Oh, darn,' Richard said dramatically. 'Business. In that case I'm going to limit you to the two minutes I allocated you earlier. Business also makes me hungry ... and grumpy.'

Richard Wakefield opened the door to his room and waited for Nicole to enter. He offered her the chair in front of his computer monitor and sat down behind her on the bed. She turned around to face him. On the shelf above his bed were a dozen tiny figurines similar to the ones she had seen before in Tabori's room and at the Borzov banquet.

'Allow me to introduce you to some of my menagerie,' Richard said, noticing her curiosity. 'You've met Lord and Lady Macbeth, Puck, and Bottom. This matched pair is Tybalt and Mercutio from *Romeo and Juliet*. Next to them are Iago and Othello, followed by Prince Hal, Falstaff, and the wonderful Mistress Quickly. The last one on the right is my closest friend, The Bard, or TB for short.'

As Nicole watched, Richard activated a switch near the head of his bed and TB climbed down a ladder from the shelf to the bed. The twenty-centimetre-high robot carefully navigated the folds in the bed coverings and came over to greet Nicole.

'And what be your name, fair lady?' TB said.

'I am Nicole des Jardins,' she replied.

'Sounds French,' the robot said immediately. 'But you don't look French. At least not Valois.' The robot appeared to be staring at her. 'You look more like a child of Othello and Desdemona.'

Nicole was astonished. 'How did you do that?' she asked.

'I'll explain later,' Richard said with a wave of his hand. 'Do you have a favourite Shakespearean sonnet?' he now inquired. 'If you do, recite a line, or give TB a number.'

'Full many a glorious morning ...' recalled Nicole.

'... have I seen,' the robot added,

> Flatter the mountain tops with sovereign eye,
> Kissing with golden face the meadows green.
> Gilding pale streams with heavenly alchemy ...

The little robot recited the sonnet with fluid head and arm movements as well as a wide range of facial expressions. Again Nicole was impressed by Richard Wakefield's creativity. She remembered the key four lines of the sonnet from her university days and mumbled them along with TB,

> Even so my sun one early morn did shine,
> With all-triumphant splendor on my brow;
> But, out alack, he was but one hour mine,
> The region cloud hath masked him from me now ...

After the robot finished the final couplet, Nicole, who was moved by the almost forgotten words, found herself applauding. 'And he can do all the sonnets?' she asked.

Richard nodded. 'Plus many, many of the more poetic dramatic speeches. But that's not his most outstanding capability. Remembering passages from Shakespeare only requires plenty of storage. TB is also a very intelligent robot. He can carry on a conversation better than ...'

Richard stopped himself in midsentence. 'I'm sorry, Nicole. I'm monopolizing the time. You said you had some business to discuss.'

'But you've already used my two minutes,' she said with a twinkle in her eye. 'Are you certain that you won't die of starvation if I take five more minutes of your time?'

Nicole quickly summarized her investigation into the RoSur software malfunction, including her conclusion that the fault protection algorithms must have been disabled by manual commands. She indicated that she could go no further with her own analysis and that she would like some help from Richard. She did not discuss her suspicions.

'Should be a snap,' he said with a smile. 'All I have to do is find the place in memory where the commands are buffered and stored. That could take a little time, given the size of the storage, but these memories are generally designed with logical architectures. However, I don't understand why you're doing all this detective work. Why don't you simply ask Janos and the others if they input any commands?'

'That's the problem,' Nicole replied. 'Nobody recalls commanding RoSur at any time after the final load and verify. When Janos hit his head during the manoeuvre, I thought his fingers were on the control box. He doesn't remember and I can't be certain.'

Richard's brow furrowed. 'It would be very unlikely that Janos just happened to toggle the fault protection enable switch with a random command. That would mean the overall design was stupid.' He thought for a moment. 'Oh well,' he continued, 'there's no need to speculate. Now you've aroused my curiosity. I'll look at the problem as soon as I have—'

'Break break. Break break.' They both heard Otto Heilmann's voice on the communicator. 'Will everyone come immediately to the science control centre for a meeting. We have a new development. The lights inside Rama just came on again.'

Richard opened the door and followed Nicole into the corridor. 'Thanks for your help,' Nicole said. 'I appreciate it very much.'

'Thank me after I do something,' Richard said with a grin. 'I'm notorious for promises. Now, what do you think is the meaning of all these games with the lights?'

26 SECOND SORTIE

David Brown had placed a single large sheet of paper on the table in the middle of the control centre. Francesca had divided it into partitions, representing hours, and was now busy writing down whatever he told her. 'The damn mission planning software is too inflexible to be useful in a situation like this,' Dr Brown was saying to Janos Tabori and Richard Wakefield. 'It's only good when the sequence of activities being planned is consistent with one of the preflight strategies.'

Janos walked over to one of the monitors. 'Maybe you can use it better than I can,' Dr Brown continued, 'but I have found it much easier this morning to rely on pencil and paper.' Janos called up a software program for mission sequencing and began to key in some data.

'Wait a minute,' Richard Wakefield interjected. Janos stopped typing on the keyboard and turned to listen to his colleague. 'We're getting all worked up over nothing. We don't need to plan the entire next sortie at this moment. In any case, we know the first major activity segment must be the completion of the infrastructure. That will take another ten or twelve hours. The rest of the sortie design can be done in parallel.'

'Richard's right,' Francesca added. 'We're trying to do everything too fast. Let's send the space cadets into Rama to finish setting up. While they're gone we can work out the details of the sortie.'

'That's impractical,' Dr Brown replied. 'The academy graduates are the only ones who know how long each of the various engineering activities should take. We can't make meaningful timelines without them.'

'Then one of us will stay here with you,' Janos Tabori said. He grinned. 'And we can use Heilmann or O'Toole inside, as an extra worker. That shouldn't slow us down too much.'

A consensus decision was reached in half an hour. Nicole would stay on board the Newton again, at least until the infrastructure was completed, and represent the cadets in the mission planning process. Admiral Heilmann would go into Rama with the four other professional cosmonauts. They would finish the remaining three infrastructure tasks: the assembly of the rest of the vehicles, the deployment of another dozen portable monitoring stations in the Northern Hemicylinder, and the construction of the Beta campsite/

communications complex on the north side of the Cylindrical Sea.

Richard Wakefield was in the process of reviewing all the detailed subtasks with his small team when Reggie Wilson, who had been virtually silent during the entire morning, suddenly jumped up from his chair. 'This is all bullshit,' he shouted. 'I can't believe all the nonsense I'm hearing.'

Richard stopped his review. Brown and Takagishi, who had already started discussing the sortie design, were suddenly silent. All eyes were focused on Reggie Wilson.

'A man died here four days ago,' he said. 'Killed, most likely, by whoever or whatever is operating that gigantic spacecraft. But we went inside exploring anyway. Next the lights go on and off unexpectedly.' Wilson looked around the room at the rest of the crew. His eyes were wild. His forehead was sweating. 'And what do we all do? Huh? How do we respond to this warning from alien creatures far superior to us? We sit down calmly and plan the rest of our exploration of their vehicle. Don't any of you get it? They don't want us in there. They want us to *leave*, to go home to Earth.'

Wilson's outburst was greeted by an uncomfortable silence. At length General O'Toole walked over beside Reggie Wilson. 'Reggie,' he said quietly, 'we were all upset by General Borzov's death. But none of the rest of us see any connection—'

'Then you're blind, man, you're blind. I was up in that goddamn helicopter when the lights went out. One minute it was bright as a summer day and the next, poof, it was pitch black. It was fucking weird, man. Somebody turned out *all* the lights. In this discussion never once have I heard anybody ask *why* the lights went out. What's the matter with you people? Are you too smart to be afraid?'

Wilson ranted for several minutes. His recurring theme was always the same. The Ramans had planned Borzov's death, they were sending a warning with the lights going on and off, there would be more disasters if the crew insisted on continuing with the exploration.

General O'Toole stood beside Reggie during the entire episode. Dr Brown, Francesca, and Nicole had a hurried discussion on the side and then Nicole approached Wilson. 'Reggie,' she said informally, interrupting his diatribe, 'why don't you and General O'Toole come with me? We can continue this conversation without delaying the rest of the crew.'

He looked at her suspiciously. 'You, Doctor? Why should I come with you? You weren't even in there. You haven't seen enough to know anything.' Wilson moved over in front of Wakefield. 'You were there, Richard,' he said. 'You saw that place. You know what kind of intelligence and power it would take to make a space vehicle that large and then launch it on a trip between the stars. Hey, man, we're *nothing* to them. We're less than ants. We haven't got a chance.'

'I agree with you, Reggie,' Richard Wakefield said calmly after a moment's hesitation. 'At least where our comparative capabilities are concerned. But we have no evidence they're hostile. Or even care about whether or not we explore their craft. On the contrary, the very fact that we are alive—'

'*Look,*' shouted Irina Turgenyev suddenly. 'Look at the monitor.' A solitary image was frozen on the giant screen in the control centre. A crablike creature filled the entire frame. It had a low, flat body, about twice as long as it was wide. Its weight was supported on six triple-jointed legs. Two scissorlike claws extended in front of the body and a whole row of manipulators, which looked uncannily like tiny human hands at first glance, nestled close to some kind of opening in the carapace. On closer inspection the manipulators were a veritable hardware store of capabilities – there were pincers, probes, rasps, and even something that resembled a drill.

Its eyes, if that's indeed what they were, were deeply recessed in protective hoods and raised like periscopes above the top of the shell. The eyeballs themselves were crystal or jelly, vivid blue in colour, and utterly expressionless.

From the legend on the side of the image it was clear that the photograph had been taken just moments before, by one of the long-range drones, at a spot roughly five kilometres south of the Cylindrical Sea. The frame, filmed with a telescopic lens, covered an area roughly six metres square.

'So we have company in Rama,' said Janos Tabori. The rest of the cosmonauts stared at the monitor in amazement.

All the crew later agreed that the image of the crab biot on the giant screen would not have been so frightening if it had not occurred at that precise moment. Although Reggie's behaviour was definitely aberrant, there was enough sense in what he was saying to remind each of them of the dangers in their expedition. None of the crew was completely free from fear. All of them had, in some private moment, confronted the disquieting fact that the super-advanced Ramans might not be friendly.

But most of the time they pushed aside their fears. It was part of their job. Like the early space shuttle astronauts in America, who knew that every so often the vehicle would crash or explode, the Newton cosmonauts accepted that there were uncontrollable risks associated with their mission. Healthy denial caused the group to avoid discussion of the unsettling issues most of the time and to focus on the more bounded (and therefore more controllable) items, such as the sequence of events for the following day.

Reggie's outburst and the simultaneous appearance of the crab biot on the monitor triggered one of the few philosophical group discussions that ever occurred on the project. O'Toole staked out his position early. Although he was fascinated by the Ramans, he did not fear them. God had seen fit to place him on this mission and, if He so chose, could decide that this extraordinary adventure would be O'Toole's last. In any case, whatever happened would be God's will.

Richard Wakefield articulated a point of view that was apparently shared by several of the other crew members. To him, the entire project was both a challenging voyage of discovery and a test of personal mettle. The uncertainties were there, to be sure, but they produced excitement as well as danger. The intense thrill of new learning, together with the possible monumental significance of this extraterrestrial encounter, more than compensated for the risks. Richard had no qualms about the mission. He was certain that this was the apotheosis of his life; if he didn't live beyond the end of the project, it would still have been worth it. He would have done something important during his brief existence on Earth.

Nicole listened attentively to the discussion. She didn't say much herself, but she found her own opinions crystallizing as she followed the flow of the conversation. She enjoyed watching the responses, both verbal and nonverbal, from the other cosmonauts. Shigeru Takagishi was clearly in the Wakefield camp. He was vigorously nodding his head the entire time Richard was talking about the excitement of participating in such a significant effort. Reggie Wilson, now subdued and probably embarrassed by his earlier tirade, did not say much. He commented only when asked a direct question. Admiral Heilmann looked uncomfortable from the beginning to the end. His entire contribution was to remind everyone of the passage of time.

Surprisingly, Dr David Brown did not add much to the philosophical discussion. He made several short comments and once or twice seemed on the verge of launching into a long, amplifying explanation. But he never did. His true beliefs about the nature of Rama were not revealed.

Francesca Sabatini initially acted as a kind of moderator or interlocuter, asking questions of clarification and keeping the conversation on an even keel. Toward the end of the discussion, however, she offered several personal, candid comments of her own. Her philosophical view of the Newton mission was altogether different from that expressed by O'Toole and Wakefield.

'I think you're making this entire thing much too complex and intellectual,' she said after Richard had delivered a long panegyric on the joys of knowledge. 'There was no need for me to do any deep soul-searching before I applied to be a Newton cosmonaut. I approached the issue the same way I do all my major decisions. I did a risk/reward trade-off. I judged that the rewards – considering all the factors, including fame, prestige, money, even adventure – more than warranted the risks. And I absolutely disagree with Richard in one respect. If I die on this mission I will not be at all happy. For me, most of the rewards from this project are delayed; I cannot benefit from them if I do not return to Earth.'

Francesca's comments aroused Nicole's curiosity. She wanted to ask the Italian journalist some more questions, but Nicole didn't think it was the proper time or place. After the meeting was over, she was still intrigued by what Francesca had said. *Can life really be that simple to her?* Nicole thought to herself. *Can everything be evaluated in terms of risks and rewards?* She remembered Francesca's lack of emotion when she drank the abortion liquid. *But what about principles or values? Or even feelings?* As the meeting broke up Nicole admitted to herself that Francesca was still very much a puzzle.

Nicole watched Dr Takagishi carefully. He was handling himself much better today. 'I have brought a printout of the Sortie Strategy, Dr Brown,' he was saying, waving a four-inch-thick set of papers in his hand, 'to remind us of the fundamental tenets of sortie design that resulted from over a year of unhurried mission planning. May I read from the summary?'

'I don't think you need to do that,' David Brown responded. 'We're all familiar with—'

'I'm not,' interrupted General O'Toole. 'I would like to hear it. Admiral Heilmann asked me to pay close attention and brief him on the issues.'

Dr Brown waved for Takagishi to continue. The diminutive Japanese scientist was borrowing a page from Brown's own portfolio. Even though he knew that David Brown personally favoured going after the crab biots on the second sortie, Takagishi still was attempting to convince the other cosmonauts that the top priority activity should be a scientific foray into the city of New York.

Reggie Wilson had excused himself an hour earlier and had gone to his room for a nap. The remaining five crew members on board the Newton had spent most of the afternoon struggling, without success, to reach an agreement on the activities for the second sortie. Since the two scientists Brown and Takagishi had radically different opinions on what should be done, no consensus was possible. Meanwhile, behind them on the large monitor, there had been intermittent views of the space cadets and Admiral Heilmann working inside Rama. The current picture showed Tabori and Turgenyev at the campsite adjoining the Cylindrical Sea. They had just finished assembling the second motorboat and were checking its electrical subsystems.

'... The sequence of sorties has been carefully designed,' Takagishi was reading, 'to be consistent with the Mission Policies and Priorities Document, ISA-NT-0014. The primary goals of the first sortie are to establish the engineering infrastructure and to examine the interior on at least a superficial level. Of particular importance will be the identification of any characteristics of this second Rama spacecraft that are in any way different from the first.

'Sortie #2 is designed to complete the mapping of the inside of Rama, focusing particularly on regions unexplored seventy years ago, as well as the collections of buildings called cities and any interior differences identified on the first sortie. Encounters with biots will be *avoided* on the second sortie, although the presence and location of the various kinds of biots will be part of the mapping process.

'Interaction with the biots will be delayed until the third sortie. Only after careful and *prolonged* observation will any attempt be made—'

'That's enough, Dr Takagishi,' David Brown interrupted. 'We all have the gist of it. Unfortunately that sterile document was prepared months before launch. The situation we face now was never contemplated. We have the lights going on and off. And we have located and are tracking a herd of six crab biots just beyond the southern edge of the Cylindrical Sea.'

'I disagree,' said the Japanese scientist respectfully. 'You said yourself that the unpredicted lighting profile did not represent a fundamental difference between the two spacecraft. We are not facing an unknown Rama. I submit that we should implement the sorties in accordance with the original mission plan.'

'So you favour dedicating this entire second sortie to mapping, including or perhaps even featuring a detailed exploration of New York?' asked O'Toole.

'Exactly, General O'Toole. Even if one takes the position that the strange sound heard by cosmonauts Wakefield, Sabatini, and myself does not constitute an official difference, the careful mapping of New York is clearly one of the highest priority activities. And it is vital that we accomplish it on this sortie. The temperature in the Central Plain has already risen to −5 degrees. Rama is carrying us closer and closer to the Sun. The spacecraft is heating from the outside in. I predict the Cylindrical Sea will begin to melt from the bottom in three or four more days—'

'I have never said that New York was not a legitimate target for exploration,' David Brown interrupted again, 'but I have maintained from the very beginning that the biots are the true scientific treasure of this voyage. Look at these amazing creatures,' he said, filling the centre screen with a film of the six crab biots moving slowly across a bland region in the Southern Hemisphere. 'We may never have another opportunity to capture one. The drones have almost finished reconnoitering the entire interior and no other biots have been spotted.'

The rest of the crew members, including Takagishi, looked at the monitor with rapt attention. The bizarre assemblage of aliens, arranged in a triangular formation with a slightly larger specimen in the lead, approached a jumbled mound of loose metal. The lead crab moved directly into the obstacle, paused a few seconds, and then used its claws to chop the elements of the mound into still smaller pieces. The two crabs in the second row transferred the metal fragments onto the backs of the remaining three members of the troop. This new material increased the size of the small piles already on the tops of the shells of the three crab biots in the back row.

'They must be the Raman garbage crew,' Francesca said. Everyone laughed.

'But you can see why I want to move quickly,' David Brown continued. 'Right now the short film we just saw is on its way to all the television networks on Earth. Over a billion of our fellow men and women will watch it today with the same mixture of fear and fascination that all of you just felt. Imagine what kind of laboratories we will be able to build to study such a creature. Imagine what we will learn—'

'What makes you think you can capture one?' General O'Toole asked. 'They look as if they could be quite formidable.'

317

'We are certain that these creatures, although they appear to be biological, are actually robots. Hence the name "biots," which became popular during and after the first Rama expedition. Based on all the reports from Norton and the other Rama I cosmonauts, each of these biots is designed to perform a singular function. They have no intelligence as we know it. We should be able to outsmart them ... and capture them.'

A camera close-up of the scissorlike claws appeared on the giant screen. They were obviously very sharp. 'I don't know,' said General O'Toole. 'I'd be inclined to follow Dr Takagishi's suggestion and observe them for quite a while before trying to catch one.'

'I disagree,' said Francesca. 'Speaking as a journalist, no story could be bigger than the attempted capture of one of those things. Everyone on Earth will watch. We may never have another chance like this.' She paused for a moment. 'The ISA has been pushing us for some upbeat news. The Borzov incident didn't exactly convince the taxpayers of the world that their space money is being wisely spent.'

'Why can't we do both tasks on the same sortie?' General O'Toole asked. 'One subteam could explore New York and the other would go after a crab.'

'No way,' replied Nicole. 'If the goal of this sortie is to seize a biot, then all of our resources should be applied in that direction. Remember, we are limited in both manpower and time.'

'Unfortunately,' David Brown now said with a wan smile, 'we can't make this decision by committee. Since we don't have complete agreement, I must make the choice ... Therefore, the purpose of the next sortie will be to capture a crab biot. I presume that Admiral Heilmann will agree with me. If he doesn't, we will submit the issue to a vote of the crew.'

The meeting broke up slowly. Dr Takagishi wanted to offer one more argument, to point out that the majority of the biot species seen by the first Rama explorers did not materialize until *after* the thawing of the Cylindrical Sea. But nobody wanted to listen anymore. Everyone was tired.

Nicole approached Takagishi and clandestinely activated her biometry scanner. The warning file was empty. 'Clean as a whistle,' she said with a smile.

Takagishi looked at her very seriously. 'Our decision is a mistake,' he said sombrely. 'We should be going into New York.'

27 TO CATCH A BIOT

'Be very careful,' Admiral Heilmann said to Francesca. 'It makes me nervous to see you leaning out like that.'

Signora Sabatini had hooked her ankles underneath the seats of the helicopter and was now stretching out beyond the plane of the door. She was holding a small video camera in her right hand. Three or four metres below her, apparently oblivious to the whirring machine overhead, the six crab biots plodded methodically along. They were still in their phalanx formation, arranged like the first three rows of a set of bowling pins.

'Move out over the sea,' Francesca shouted to Hiro Yamanaka. 'They're coming to the edge and will be turning again.'

The helicopter veered sharply to the left and flew over the side of the five-hundred-metre cliff that separated the southern half of Rama from the Cylindrical Sea. The bank here was ten times higher above the water than its northern counterpart. David Brown gasped as he looked down at the frozen sea half a kilometre below him,

'This is ridiculous, Francesca,' he said. 'What do you hope to accomplish? The automatic camera in the nose of the copter will take adequate pictures.'

'This camera was specifically designed for zoom action,' she said. 'Besides, a little jitter gives the images more verisimilitude.' Yamanaka steered back toward the bank. The biots were now about thirty metres directly ahead. The lead biot came up to within half a body length of the edge, paused for a fraction of a second, and then turned abruptly to its right. Another quick ninety-degree right turn completed the manoeuvre and left the biot heading in the exact opposite direction. The other five crabs followed their leader, executing their turns row by row with military precision.

'I got it that time,' Francesca said happily, pulling herself back into the helicopter. 'Head on and full frame. And I think I caught a glimmer of movement in the leader's blue eye just before it turned.'

The biots were now ambling away from the cliff at their normal speed of ten kilometres per hour. Their movement caused a slight indentation in the loamy soil. Their heading was along a path parallel to their last previous sweep toward the sea. From above, the whole region looked like a suburban yard in which part of the grass had been mowed – on one side the ground

319

was neat and packed, while in the territory not yet covered by the biots there was no orderly pattern in the soil markings.

'This could get boring,' Francesca said, playfully reaching up and putting her arms around David Brown's neck. 'We may have to amuse ourselves with something else.'

'We'll only watch them one more strip. Their pattern is fairly simple.' He ignored Francesca's light tickling on his neck. It seemed as if he were going through some kind of checklist in his mind. At length Brown spoke into the communicator. 'What do you think, Dr Takagishi? Is there anything else we should do at this time?'

Back in the scientific control centre on the Newton, Dr Takagishi was following the progression of the biots on the monitor. 'It would be extremely valuable,' he said, 'if we could find out more about their sensory capabilities before we try to capture one of them. So far they have not responded to noises or to distant visual stimuli. In fact, they have apparently not even noticed our presence. As I'm sure you would agree, we don't have enough data yet to come to any definitive conclusions. If we could expose them to an entire range of electromagnetic frequencies and calibrate their responses, then we might have a better idea ...'

'But that would take *days*,' Dr Brown interrupted. 'And in the final analysis we would still have to take our chances. I can't imagine what we might learn that would materially alter our plans.'

'If we found out more about them first,' Takagishi argued, 'then we could design a better, safer capture procedure. It might even occur that we would learn something that would dissuade us altogether ...'

'Unlikely,' was David Brown's abrupt response. As far as he was concerned, this particular discussion was over. 'Hey there, Tabori,' he now shouted. 'How are you guys coming with the huts?'

'We're almost finished,' the Hungarian answered. 'Another thirty minutes at the most. Then I'll be ready for a nap.'

'Lunch comes first,' Francesca interjected. 'You can't go to sleep on an empty stomach.'

'What are you cooking, beautiful?' Tabori bantered.

'Osso buco alla Rama.'

'That's enough,' Dr Brown said. He paused for a couple of seconds. 'O'Toole,' he then continued, 'can you handle the Newton all by yourself? At least for the next twelve hours?'

'Affirmative,' was the response.

'Then send down the rest of the crew. By the time we all meet at the new campsite, it should be ready for occupancy. We'll have some lunch and a brief nap. Then we'll plan our biot hunt.'

Below the helicopter the six crablike creatures continued their relentless march across the barren soil. The four human beings watched them encounter a distinct boundary, where the floor changed from dirt and small rocks into a fine wire mesh. As soon as they touched the narrow lane dividing the two sections, the biots executed a U-turn. They then headed back toward the sea along a parallel line adjacent to their last track. Yamanaka banked the helicopter, increased his altitude, and headed for the Beta campsite ten kilometres across the Cylindrical Sea,

They were all correct, Nicole was thinking. *Seeing it on the monitor is nothing by comparison.* She was descending on the chairlift into Rama. Now that she was beyond the halfway point, she had a breathtaking view in every direction. She remembered a similar feeling once, when she had been standing on the Tonto Plateau in the Grand Canyon National Park. *But that was made by nature and took over a billion years,* she said to herself. *Rama was actually built by somebody. Or something.*

The chair momentarily slowed. Shigeru Takagishi climbed off a kilometre below her. Nicole couldn't see him, but she could hear him talking to Richard Wakefield on the communicator. 'Hurry up,' she heard Reggie Wilson shout. 'I don't like sitting here in the middle of nowhere.' Nicole enjoyed being suspended on the chairlift. The amazing scene around her was temporarily almost static and she could study at her leisure any feature that was particularly interesting.

After one more stop for Wilson to disembark, Nicole was at last approaching the bottom of the Alpha chairlift herself. She watched, fascinated, as the resolution of her eyes improved quickly during the last three hundred metres of her descent. What had been a jumble of indistinct images resolved itself into a rover, three people, some equipment, and a small surrounding camp. After a few more seconds she could identify each of the three men. She had a quick flashback to another chairlift ride, this one in Switzerland some two months before. An image of King Henry flitted momentarily through her mind. It was replaced by the smiling face of Richard Wakefield just below her. He was giving her instructions on how best to ease herself out of the chair.

'It will never come to a complete stop,' he was saying, 'but it will slow down a lot. Unfasten your belt and then hit the ground walking, as if you were coming off a moving walkway.'

He grabbed her by the waist and lifted her off the platform. Takagishi and Wilson were already in the back seat of the rover. 'Welcome to Rama,' Wakefield said.

'All right, Tabori,' he then spoke into the communicator. 'We're all here and ready to go. We're switching now to the listen-only mode for our drive.'

'Hurry,' Janos urged him. 'We're having a hard time not eating your lunch ... By the way, Richard, will you bring tool box C when you come? We've been talking about nets and cages and I may need a wider variety of gadgets.'

'Roger,' Wakefield replied. He jogged over to the campsite and entered the only large hut. He emerged with a long rectangular metal box that was obviously very heavy. 'Shit, Tabori,' he said into the radio, 'what in the world is in here?'

They all heard a laugh. 'Everything you could possibly need to catch a crab biot. And then some.'

Wakefield switched off the transmitter and climbed in the rover. He started driving away from the stairway in the direction of the Cylindrical Sea. 'This biot hunt is the stupidest goddamn idea I've ever heard,' Reggie Wilson groused. 'Somebody is going to get hurt.'

There was quiet in the rover for almost a minute. To the right, at the limit of their vision, the cosmonauts could barely see the Raman city of London. 'Well, how does it feel to be part of the second team?' Wilson said to nobody in particular.

After an awkward silence, Dr Takagishi turned to address him. 'Excuse me, Mr Wilson,' he said politely, 'are you talking to me?'

'Sure I am,' Wilson replied, nodding his head up and down. 'Didn't anyone ever tell you that you were the number *two* scientist on this mission? I guess not,' Wilson continued after a short pause. 'But that's not surprising. Down on Earth I never knew that I was the number two journalist.'

'Reggie, I don't think—' Nicole said before she was interrupted.

'As for you, Doctor' – Wilson leaned forward in the rover – 'you may be the only member of the *third* team. I overheard our glorious leaders Heilmann and Brown talking about you. They'd like to leave you on the Newton permanently. But since we may need your skills—'

'That's enough,' Richard Wakefield broke in. There was a threatening edge in his voice. 'You can stop being so unpleasant.' Several tense seconds passed before Wakefield spoke again. 'By the way, Wilson,' he said in a friendlier tone, 'if I remember correctly, you're a racing fanatic. Would you like to drive this buggy?'

It was the perfect suggestion. A few minutes later Reggie Wilson was in the driver's seat beside Wakefield, laughing wildly as he accelerated the rover around a tight circle. Cosmonauts des Jardins and Takagishi were bumping around in the back seat.

Nicole was observing Wilson very carefully. *He's erratic again,* she was thinking. *That's at least three times in the last two days.* Nicole tried to recall when she had last done a full scan on Wilson. *Not since the day after Borzov died. I've checked the cadets twice in the interim ... Dammit,* she said to herself, *I let my preoccupation with the Borzov incident make me careless.* She made a mental note to scan everyone as soon as possible after she arrived at the Beta campsite.

'Say, my good professor,' Richard Wakefield said once Wilson had finally straightened out and was heading for camp, 'I have a question for you.' He turned around and faced the Japanese scientist. 'Have you figured out our strange sound from the other day? Or has Dr Brown convinced you that it was just a figment of our collective imagination?'

Dr Takagishi shook his head. 'I told you at the time that it was a new noise.' He stared off in the distance, across the unexplained mechanical fields of the Central Plain. 'This is a different Rama. I know it. The checkerboard squares in the south are laid out in an entirely new pattern and no longer extend to the shore of the Cylindrical Sea. The lights now go on before the sea melts. And they go off abruptly, without dimming for several hours as the first Rama explorers reported, The crab biots now appear in herds instead of individually.' He paused, still looking out across the fields. 'Dr Brown says that all these differences are trivial, but I think they mean something. It's just possible,' Takagishi said softly, 'that Dr Brown is wrong.'

'It's also possible that he's a complete son of a bitch,' said Wilson bitterly. He accelerated the rover to its maximum speed. 'Beta campsite, here we come!'

28 EXTRAPOLATION

Nicole completed her lunch of pressed duck, reconstituted broccoli, and mashed potatoes. The rest of the cosmonauts were still eating and it was temporarily quiet at the long table. In the corner, by the entrance, a monitor tracked the location of the crab biots. Their pattern had not changed. The blip representing the crabs would move in one direction for slightly more than ten minutes and then reverse itself.

'What happens after they finish this parcel?' Richard Wakefield asked. He was looking at a computer map of the area that was posted on a temporary bulletin board.

'Last time they followed one of those lanes between the chequerboard partitions until they came to a hole,' Francesca responded from the other end of the table. 'Then they dumped their garbage in it. They haven't picked up anything in this new territory, so what they will do when they finish is anybody's guess.'

'Everyone is convinced that our biots are in fact garbage men?' Richard asked.

'The evidence is fairly strong,' David Brown said. 'A similar solitary crab biot encountered by Jimmy Park inside the first Rama was also believed to be a garbage collector.'

'We flatter ourselves,' Shigeru Takagishi said softly after a long silence. He finished chewing his last bite and swallowed. 'Dr Brown himself was the one who first said that it was unlikely we human beings could comprehend what Rama was about. Our conversation reminds me of that old Hindu proverb about the blind men who felt the elephant. They all described it differently, for each of them touched only a small part of the animal. None of them was correct.'

'You don't think our crabs work for the Rama Sanitation Department?' Janos inquired.

'I didn't say that,' Takagishi replied. 'I merely suggested that it's hubris on our part to conclude so quickly that those six creatures have no purpose except cleaning up the garbage. Our observational data is woefully inadequate.'

'Sometimes it is necessary to extrapolate,' Dr Brown rejoined testily, 'and even speculate, based on minimal amounts of data. You know yourself that new science is based on maximum likelihood rather than certainty.'

'Before we become involved in an esoteric discussion about science and its methodology,' Janos now interrupted with a grin, 'I have a sporting proposition for you all.' He stood up at his place. 'Actually it was Richard's idea originally, but I've figured out how to make it into a game. It has to do with the lights.'

Janos took a quick drink of water from his cup. 'Since we first arrived here in Ramaland,' he intoned formally, 'there have been three transitions in the illumination state.'

'Boo. Hiss,' shouted Wakefield. Janos laughed.

'Okay, you guys,' the little Hungarian then continued in his normal offhand way, 'what's the deal with the lights? They've come on, gone off, and now come on again. What's going to happen in the future? I propose that we have a pool and contribute, say, twenty marks apiece. Each of us will make a prediction about the behaviour of the lights for the rest of the mission and whoever is closest will win the pot.'

'Who will judge the winner?' Reggie Wilson inquired sleepily. He had yawned several times during the preceding hour. 'Despite the impressive set of brains around this table, I don't think anyone has figured out Rama yet. My personal belief is that the lights will not follow any pattern. They will go on and off at random times to keep us guessing.'

'Write it down and send it on the modem to General O'Toole. Richard and I agreed that he would make a perfect judge. When the mission is over, he'll compare the predictions with actuality and someone will win a lucky dinner for two.'

Dr David Brown pushed his chair back from the table. 'Are you finished with your game, Tabori?' he asked. 'If so,' he added, without waiting for an answer, 'perhaps we can clean up this lunch mess and get on with our schedule.'

'Hey skipper,' Janos replied, 'I'm just trying to loosen things up. Everybody's getting tense ...'

Brown walked out of the hut before Cosmonaut Tabori had finished his sentence.

'What's bothering him?' Richard asked Francesca.

'I guess he's anxious about the hunt,' Francesca answered. 'He has been in a bad mood since this morning. Maybe he's feeling all the responsibility.'

'Maybe he's just a jerk,' said Wilson. He too rose from his seat. 'I'm going to take a nap.'

As Wilson was leaving the large hut Nicole remembered that she wanted to check everyone's biometry before the hunt. It was a simple enough task. All she needed was to stand close to each cosmonaut for about forty-five seconds with her activated scanner and then read the critical data off the monitor. If there were no entries in the warning files, the entire procedure was quite straightforward. On this particular check everyone was clean, including Takagishi. 'Nice going,' Nicole said to her Japanese colleague very quietly.

She walked outside to look for David Brown and Reggie Wilson. Dr Brown's hut was at the far end of the campsite. Like the rest of the individual dwellings, his hut resembled a tall skinny hat sitting on the ground. All the huts were off-white in colour, about two and a half metres tall, with a circular base just under two metres in diameter. They were manufactured with super-lightweight, flexible materials that combined easy packing and storage with formidable strength. Nicole remarked to herself that the huts looked something like native American Indian teepees.

David Brown was in his hut, sitting cross-legged on the ground in front of a portable computer monitor. On the screen was text from the chapter on biots in Takagishi's *Atlas of Rama*. 'Excuse me, Dr Brown,' Nicole said as she stuck her head in his door.

'Yes,' he said, 'what is it?' He made no attempt to hide his annoyance at the interruption.

'I need to check your biometry data,' Nicole said. 'You haven't been dumped since right before the first sortie.'

Brown gave her an irritated glance. Nicole held her ground. The American shrugged his shoulders, half grunted, and turned back to the monitor. Nicole knelt beside him and activated her scanner.

'There are some folding chairs over in the supply hut,' Nicole offered as Dr Brown shifted his weight uncomfortably on the ground. He ignored her comment. *Why is he so rude to me?* Nicole found herself wondering. *Is it because of that report on Wilson and him? No,* she thought, answering her own question, *it's because I have never been properly deferential,*

Data began to appear on Nicole's screen. She carefully keyed in several inputs that permitted a synopsis of the warning data to be shown. 'Your blood pressure has been too high for intermittent intervals during the last seventy-two hours, including almost all of today,' she said without emotion. 'This particular kind of pattern is usually associated with stress.'

Dr Brown stopped reading about biots and turned to face his life science officer. He looked at the displayed data without understanding it. 'This graph shows the amplitudes and durations of your out-of-tolerance excursions,' Nicole said, pointing at the screen. 'None of the individual occurrences would be serious by itself. But the overall pattern is cause for concern.'

'I have been under some pressure,' he mumbled. David Brown watched while Nicole called up other displays showing data that corroborated her original statements. Many of Brown's warning files were overflowing.

The lights continued to flash on the monitor. 'What's the worst-case scenario?' he inquired.

Nicole eyed her patient. 'A stroke with paralysis or death,' she replied. 'If the condition persists or worsens.'

He whistled. 'What should I do?'

'In the first place,' Nicole answered, 'you must start by getting more sleep. Your metabolic profile shows that since the death of General Borzov you have only had a total of eleven hours of solid rest. Why didn't you tell me you were having trouble sleeping?'

'I thought it was just excitement. I even took a sleeping pill one night and it had no effect.'

Nicole's brow furrowed. 'I don't remember giving you any sleeping pills.'

Dr Brown smiled. 'Shit,' he said, 'I forgot to tell you. I was talking to Francesca Sabatini about my insomnia one night and she offered me a pill. I took it without thinking.'

'Which night was that?' Nicole asked. She changed displays again on her monitor and called for more data from the storage buffers.

'I'm not certain,' Dr Brown said after some hesitation. 'I think it was—'

'Oh, here it is,' Nicole said. 'I can see it in the chemical analysis. That was March third, the second night after Borzov's death. The day you and Heilmann were selected as joint commanders. From the breakout in this spectrometry data, I would guess that you took a single medvil.'

'You can tell *that* from my biometry data?'

'Not exactly,' Nicole said with a smile. 'The interpretation is not unique. What was it you said at lunch? Sometimes it's necessary to extrapolate . . , and speculate.'

Their eyes met for a moment. *Could that be fear?* Nicole wondered as she tried to interpret what she was seeing in his gaze. Dr Brown looked away. 'Thank you, Dr des Jardins,' he said stiffly, 'for your report on my blood pressure. I will try to relax and get plenty of sleep. And I apologize for not informing you about the sleeping pill.' He dismissed her with a wave of his hand.

Nicole started to protest her dismissal but decided against it. *He wouldn't follow my advice anyway,* she said to herself as she walked toward Wilson's hut. *And his blood pressure was certainly not dangerously high.* She thought about the strained final two minutes of their conversation, after she had astonished Dr Brown by correctly identifying the type of sleeping pill. *There's something not quite right here. What is it that I am missing?*

She could hear Reggie Wilson snoring before she arrived at the door of his tent. After a brief debate with herself, Nicole decided that she would scan him after his nap. She then returned to her own hut and quickly fell asleep. 'Nicole. Nicole des Jardins.' The voice intruded in her dream and awakened her. 'It's me. Francesca. I need to tell you something.'

Nicole sat up slowly on her cot. Francesca had already entered the hut. The Italian was wearing her friendliest smile, the one that Nicole had thought was always saved for the camera.

'I was talking to David just a few minutes ago,' Francesca said as she approached the cot, 'and he told me about your conversation after lunch.' Francesca kept talking as Nicole yawned and swung her legs around to the floor. 'I was, of course, very concerned to learn about his blood pressure – don't worry, he and I have already agreed that I won't use it – but what really bothered me was he reminded me that we never told you about the sleeping pill. I'm so embarrassed. We should have told you immediately.'

Francesca was talking too fast for Nicole. Just moments before she had been in a deep sleep, dreaming of Beauvois, and now all of a sudden she was expected to listen to a staccato confession from the Italian cosmonaut.

'Could you wait a minute until I wake up?' Nicole asked crossly. She leaned around Francesca to a makeshift table and took a cup of water. She drank slowly.

'Now am I to understand,' Nicole said, 'that you have awakened me to tell me that you gave Dr Brown a sleeping pill? Something I already know?'

'Yes,' Francesca said with a smile. 'I mean, that's part of it. But I realised that I had forgotten to tell you about Reggie also.'

Nicole shook her head. 'I'm not following you, Francesca. Are you talking about Reggie Wilson now?'

Francesca hesitated for a second. 'Yes,' she said. 'Didn't you check him with your scanner right after lunch?'

Nicole shook her head again. 'No, he was already asleep.' She looked at her watch. 'I had planned to scan him before the meeting started. Maybe an hour from now.'

Francesca was flustered. 'Well,' she said, 'when David told me that the medvil showed up in his biometry data, I thought ...' She stopped herself in mid-sentence. She seemed to be collecting her thoughts. Nicole waited patiently.

'Reggie started complaining of headaches over a week ago,' Francesca eventually continued, 'after the two Newton ships joined for the rendezvous with Rama. Since he and I have been close friends and he knew about my knowledge of drugs – you know, from all that work on my documentary series – he asked me if I would give him something for headaches. I refused at first, but finally, after he kept badgering me, I gave him some nubitrol.'

Nicole frowned. 'That's a very strong medicine for a simple headache. There are still doctors who believe it should never be prescribed unless everything else has failed ...'

'I told him all that,' Francesca said. 'He was adamant. You don't know Reggie. Sometimes you can't reason with him.'

'How much did you give him?'

'Eight pills altogether, a total of two hundred milligrams.'

'No wonder he's been acting so strangely.' Nicole leaned over and picked up her pocket computer sitting on the end table. She accessed her medical data base and read the short entry about nubitrol. 'Not much here,' she said. 'I'll have to ask O'Toole to transmit the full entry from the medical encyclopedia. But if I remember correctly, wasn't there a controversy about nubitrol remaining in the system for weeks?'

'I don't recall,' Francesca replied. She looked at the monitor in Nicole's hand and quickly read the text. Nicole was irritated. She started to lambast Francesca verbally but at the last moment changed her mind. *So you gave drugs to both David and Reggie,* she was thinking. Out of her memory came a vague recollection of Francesca handing Valeriy Borzov a glass of wine several hours before he died. A strange chill ran through Nicole's body. Could her intuition be correct?

Nicole turned around and fixed Francesca with a cold stare. 'Now that you have confessed to playing doctor and pharmacist for both David and Reggie, is there anything else you want to tell me?'

'What do you mean?' Francesca asked.

'Have you given drugs to any other member of the crew?'

Nicole felt her heart race as Francesca blanched, ever so slightly, and hesitated before replying.

'No. No, of course not,' was her answer.

29 THE HUNT

The helicopter very slowly dropped the rover to the ground. 'How much farther?' Janos Tabori asked over the communicator.

'About ten metres,' Richard Wakefield replied from below. He was standing in a spot about a hundred metres south of the edge of the Cylindrical Sea. Above him the rover dangled at the end of two long cables. 'Be careful to let it down gently. There are some delicate electronics in the chassis.'

Hiro Yamanaka commanded the helicopter into its tightest possible altitude control loop while Janos electronically extended the cables a few centimetres at a time. 'Contact,' shouted Wakefield. 'On the rear wheels. The front needs to come down another metre.'

Francesca Sabatini raced around to the side of the rover to record its historic touchdown in the Southern Hemicylinder of Rama. Fifty metres farther from the cliff, in the neighbourhood of a hut that was serving as a temporary head-quarters, the rest of the cosmonauts were preparing for the hunt to begin. Irina Turgenyev was checking the installation of the cable snare in the second helicopter. David Brown was by himself a few metres away from the hut, talking on the radio with Admiral Heilmann back at the Beta campsite. The two men were reviewing the details of the capture plan. Wilson, Takagishi, and des Jardins were watching the conclusion of the rover landing operation.

'Now we know who's really the boss of this outfit,' Reggie Wilson was saying to his two companions. He pointed at Dr Brown. 'This damn hunt is more like a military operation than anything we've done, yet our senior scientist is in charge and our ranking officer is manning the phones.' He spat on the ground. 'Christ, do we have enough equipment here? Two helicopters, a rover, three different kinds of cages – not to mention several large boxes of electrical and mechanical shit. Those poor bastard crabs don't have a chance.'

Dr Takagishi put the laser binoculars to his eyes. He found the target quickly. Half a kilometre to the east the crab biots were nearing the edge of the cliff again. Nothing about their motion had changed. 'We need all the equipment because of the uncertainty,' Takagishi said quietly. 'Nobody really knows what is going to happen.'

'I hope the lights go out,' Wilson said with a laugh.

'We're prepared for that,' David Brown interjected tersely as he walked up to join the other three cosmonauts. 'The shells of the crabs have been sprayed with a light fluorescent material and we have plenty of flares. While you were complaining about the length of our last meeting, we were finishing the contingency plans.' He stared truculently at his countryman. 'You know, Wilson, you could try—'

'Break break,' the voice of Otto Heilmann interrupted him. 'News. Hot news. I just received word from O'Toole that INN will be carrying our feed *live*, beginning twenty minutes from now.'

'Good work,' replied Brown. 'We should be ready by then. I see Wakefield heading this way in the rover.' He glanced at his watch. 'And the crabs should be turning again in another few seconds. Incidentally, Otto, do you still disagree with my suggestion to snare the lead biot?'

'Yes, David, I do. I think it's an unnecessary risk. What little we do know suggests that the lead crab has the most capability. Why take a chance? Any biot would be an incredible treasure to carry back to Earth, particularly if it's still functional. We can worry about the leader after we already have one in the bag.'

'Then I guess I'm outvoted on this one. Dr Takagishi and Tabori both agree with you. So does General O'Toole. We'll proceed with Plan B. The target biot will be number four, the back right biot as we approach from the rear.'

The rover carrying Wakefield and Sabatini arrived at the hut area at almost the same time as the helicopter. 'Good job, men,' Dr Brown said as Tabori and Yamanaka jumped down from the copter. 'Take a short breather, Janos. Then go over and make sure Turgenyev and the cable snare are both ready to go. I want you airborne in five minutes.

'All right,' Brown said, turning to the others, 'this is it. Wilson, Takagishi, and des Jardins in the rover with Wakefield. Francesca, you come with me in the second helicopter with Hiro.'

Nicole started walking toward the rover but Francesca intercepted her. 'Have you ever used one of these?' The Italian journalist extended a video camera the size of a small book.

'Once,' Nicole answered, studying the camera in Francesca's hand, 'eleven or twelve years ago. I recorded one of Dr Delon's brain operations. I guess—'

'Look,' interrupted Francesca, 'I could use some help. I'm sorry I didn't discuss it with you earlier, but I didn't know ... Anyway, I need another camera, one on the ground, especially now that we're live on INN. I'm not asking for miracles. You're the only one who—'

'What about Reggie?' Nicole replied. 'He's the other journalist.'

'Reggie won't help,' Francesca said quickly. Dr Brown called for her to come to the helicopter. 'Will you do it, Nicole? Please? Or should I ask someone else?'

Why not? ran through Nicole's mind. *I have nothing else to do unless an emergency comes up.* 'Sure,' she replied.

'Thanks a million,' Francesca shouted as she handed Nicole the camera and dashed off to the waiting helicopter.

'Well, well,' said Reggie Wilson as Nicole approached the rover with the camera cradled in her hands. 'I see that our crew doctor has been recruited by the number one journalist. I hope you asked for the minimum wage.'

'Lighten up, Reggie,' Nicole replied. 'It doesn't bother me to help others when I have nothing specific to do myself.'

Wakefield switched on the rover and began to drive east toward the biots. The headquarters had been intentionally established in the area already 'cleaned' by the crabs. The packed soil made progress very easy for the rover. They were within a hundred metres of the biots in less than three minutes. Overhead the two helicopters circled around the crabs.

'What exactly do you want me to do?' Nicole called to Francesca on the rover transmitter.

'Try to move parallel to the biots,' Francesca answered. 'You can probably run alongside, at least for some of the time. The most important moment is when Janos tries to close the snare.'

'We're all ready here,' Tabori announced a few seconds later, 'Just give the word.'

'Are we on the air?' Brown asked Francesca. She nodded her head. 'All right,' he said to Janos. 'Go ahead.'

From out of one of the helicopters came a long, thick cable with what looked like an inverted basket on the end. 'Janos will try to centre the snare on the target biot,' Wakefield explained to Nicole, 'and let the sides drape naturally over the corner of the shell. Then he will increase the tension and pull the biot off the ground. We will cage the crab after we return it to the Beta campsite.'

'Let's see what they look like from down there,' Nicole heard Francesca say. The rover was now right next to the biots. Nicole climbed out and jogged beside them. She was frightened at first. For some reason she had not expected them to be so large or so strange looking. Their metallic sheen reminded her of the cold exterior of many of the new buildings in Paris. As she ran along on the soil, the biots were only about two metres away from her. With the automatic focusing and framing of the camera, it was not difficult for Nicole to take the proper pictures.

'Don't get in front of them,' Dr Takagishi warned her. He didn't need to worry. Nicole had not forgotten what they had done to that mound of metal.

'Your pictures are really very good,' Francesca's voice boomed on the rover receiver. 'Nicole, try to speed up to the lead biot and then fall back little by little, letting the camera pan across each of the ranks.' She waited while Nicole moved to the front of the biots. 'Wow. That's superb. Now 1 know why we brought an Olympic champion with us.'

On his first two attempts Janos missed with the snare. However, on the third try it landed perfectly on the number four crab's back. The edges of the net or basket spread out to the limit of the shell. Nicole was starting to sweat. She had been running already for four minutes. 'From now on,' Francesca said to her from the helicopter, 'focus on the single target crab. Move up as close as you dare.'

Nicole reduced her distance from the closest biot to about a metre. She nearly slipped once and a cold chill swept over her. *If I were to fall across their path,* she thought, *they'd make mincemeat out of me.* Her camera was fixed on the right rear crab as Janos tightened the cables.

'Now!' he shouted. The snare, with the biot entrapped, began to rise off the ground. Everything happened very fast. The target biot used its scissor-like claws to snap through one of the metal threads of the snare. The other five biots came to a brief halt, for maybe one full second, and then immediately all attacked the snare with their claws. The metal net was completely shredded and the biot was freed in five seconds,

Nicole was amazed by what she was seeing. Despite her pounding heart she continued to film. The lead biot now sat down on the ground. The other five surrounded it in an extremely tight circle. Each of the biots attached one claw to the crab in the centre and the other to its neighbour on the right. The formation was finished in less than five more seconds. The biots were locked and motionless.

Francesca was the first to speak. 'Absolutely incredible,' she screamed in elation. 'We just made the hair stand up on every human being on Earth.'

Nicole felt Richard Wakefield beside her. 'Are you all right?' he asked.

'I think so,' she said. She was still shaking. The two of them glanced over at the biots. There was no movement.

'They're in a huddle,' Reggie Wilson said from the rover. 'The score is now Biots 7, Humans 0.'

'Since you are so convinced that there is no danger, I'll agree to go ahead. But I must confess that I myself am nervous about another attempt. Those things clearly communicate with each other. And I don't think they want to be captured.'

'Otto, Otto,' Dr Brown replied. 'This procedure is only a straightforward refinement of what we tried the first time. The line nexus will adhere to the shell of the crab and will wrap its thin cables tightly around the entire carapace. The other biots will not be able to use their claws. There will be no room between the line and the shell.'

'Admiral Heilmann, this is Dr Takagishi.' There was definite concern in his voice as he spoke into the communicator. 'I must register my strongest objection to proceeding with this hunt. We have seen already how little we understand about these creatures. As Wakefield said, our attempt to snare one of them has obviously triggered their main fault protection responses. We have no idea at all how they will react next.'

'We all understand that, Dr Takagishi,' David Brown interjected before

Heilmann could respond. 'But there are extenuating factors that override the uncertainties. First, as Francesca pointed out, the entire Earth will again be watching if we go after the biots right away. You heard what Jean-Claude Revoir said twenty minutes ago – we have already done more for space exploration than anyone since the original Soviet and American cosmonauts back in the twentieth century. Second, we are prepared to complete the hunt now. If we abandon the attempt and return all our equipment to Beta, then we will have wasted a huge amount of time and effort. Finally, there is no obvious danger. Why do you insist on making such dire predictions? All we saw the biots do was engage in some kind of self-defense activity.'

'Professor Brown,' the eminent Japanese scholar tried one last rational appeal, 'please look around you. Try to imagine the capabilities of the creatures who made this amazing vehicle. Try to appreciate the possibility that perhaps, just perhaps, what we are trying to do might be viewed as a hostile act and has somehow been communicated to whatever intelligence is managing this spacecraft. Suppose as a result that we, as representatives of the human species, are condemning not only ourselves, but also, in some larger sense, all of our fellow—'

'Poppycock,' David Brown scoffed. 'How can anyone ever accuse *me* of wild speculation ...?' He laughed heartily. 'This is absurd. The evidence overwhelmingly indicates that this Rama has the same purpose and function as its predecessor and is completely oblivious to our existence. Just because one single subfamily of robots bands together when threatened does not have overwhelming significance.' He looked around at the others. 'I say that's enough talk, Otto. Unless you object, we're going out to capture a biot.'

There was a short hesitation from across the Cylindrical Sea. Then the cosmonauts heard Admiral Heilmann's affirmative reply. 'Go ahead, David. But don't take any unnecessary chances.'

'Do you think we're really in danger?' Hiro Yamanaka asked Dr Takagishi while the new capture tactics were being reviewed by Brown, Tabori, and Wakefield. The Japanese pilot was staring off in the distance at the massive structures in the southern bowl, thinking, perhaps for the first time, of the vulnerability of their position.

'Probably not,' his countryman replied, 'but it's insane to take such—'

'Insane is a perfect word for it,' Reggie Wilson interrupted. 'You and I were the only two vocal opponents of continuing this stupidity. But our objections were made to sound foolish and even cowardly. Personally, 1 wish one of those goddamn things would challenge the esteemed Dr Brown to a duel. Or better still, a bolt of lightning would come shooting out of those spires over there.'

He pointed at the great horns that Yamanaka had been regarding earlier. Wilson's voice changed and there was a fearful edge to it. 'We are over our heads here. I can feel it in the air. We are being warned of danger by powers that none of us can begin to understand. But we are ignoring the warnings.'

Nicole turned away from her colleagues and glanced at the lively planning meeting taking place fifteen metres away from her. Engineers Wakefield and Tabori were definitely enjoying the challenge of outwitting the biots. Nicole wondered if perhaps Rama really was sending them some kind of a warning. *Poppycock,* she said to herself, repeating David Brown's expression. She shuddered involuntarily as she recalled the several seconds when the crab biots had devastated the metal snare. *I'm overreacting. And so is Wilson. There's no reason to be afraid.*

Yet, as she turned again and looked through the binoculars to study the biot formation half a kilometre away, there was a palpable fear in her that would not be assuaged. The six crabs had not moved in almost two hours. They were still locked in their original arrangement. *What are you really all about, Rama?* Nicole asked herself for the umpteenth time. Her next question startled her. She had never verbalised it before. *And how many of us will make it back to Earth to tell your tale?*

For the second capture attempt Francesca wanted to be on the ground beside the biots. As before, Turgenyev and Tabori were up in the prime helicopter along with the most important equipment. Brown, Yamanaka, and Wakefield were in the other helicopter. Dr Brown had invited Wakefield to provide him with realtime advice; Francesca had of course persuaded Richard to take some aerial pictures for her to complement the automatic images from the helicopter system.

Reggie Wilson drove the ground-based cosmonauts to the biot site in the rover. 'Now here's a good job for me,' he said as they approached the location of the alien crabs. 'Chauffeur.' He gazed up at the distant ceiling of Rama. 'You hear that, you guys? I'm versatile. I can do many things.' He looked over at Francesca beside him in the front seat. 'By the way, Mrs Sabatini, were you planning to thank Nicole for her spectacular work? It was her action shots on the ground that captured the audience in your last transmission.'

Francesca was busy checking all her video equipment and at first ignored Reggie's comment. When he repeated his jibe, she responded, without looking up, 'May I remind Mr Wilson that I do not need his unsolicited advice on how to conduct my business?'

'There was a time,' Reggie mused out loud, shaking his head, 'when things were very different.' He glanced at Francesca. There was no indication that she was even listening. 'Back when I still believed in love,' he said in a louder voice. 'Before I knew about betrayal. Or ambition and its selfishness.'

He jerked the rover wheel vigorously to the left and brought it to a stop about forty metres west of the biots. Francesca jumped out without a word.

Within three seconds she was chattering to David Brown and Richard Wakefield on the radio about the video coverage of the capture. The ever polite Dr Takagishi thanked Reggie Wilson for driving the rover.

'We're coming in,' Tabori shouted from above. He managed to position the dangling nexus properly on his second attempt. The nexus was a round, heavy sphere about twenty centimetres in diameter, with a dozen small holes or indentations on its surface. It was slowly dropped onto the centre of the shell of one of the outside biots. Next Janos, transmitting a barrage of commands from the hovering helicopter to the processor in the nexus, ordered the extension of the massed threads of metal rolled up inside the sphere. The crabs did not stir as the threads wrapped themselves around the target biot.

'What do you think, inspector?' Janos hollered at Richard Wakefield in the other helicopter.

Richard surveyed the strange apparatus. The thick cable was attached to a ring stanchion at the rear of the helicopter. Fifteen metres below, the metal ball sat on the back of the target biot, thin filaments extending from inside the ball around the top and bottom of the carapace. 'Looks fine,' Richard replied. 'Now there's only the single question remaining. Is the helicopter stronger than their collective grip?'

David Brown commanded Irina Turgenyev to lift the prey. She slowly increased the speed of the blades and tried to ascend. The tiny slack in the cable disappeared but the biots barely moved. 'They're either very heavy or they're holding onto the ground somehow,' Richard said. 'Hit them with a sharp burst.'

The sudden jolt in the cable lifted the entire biot formation momentarily skyward. The helicopter strained as the biot mass dangled two or three metres off the ground. The two crabs not attached to the target biot dropped first, falling into a motionless heap seconds after takeoff. The other three crabs lasted longer, ten seconds altogether before they finally disengaged their claws from their companion and fell to the ground below. There were universal cries of joy and congratulations as the helicopter climbed higher into the sky.

Francesca was filming the capture sequence from a distance of about ten metres. After the last three biots, including the leader, had released their grips on the target crab and fallen onto the Raman soil, she leaned back to record the helicopter as it headed for the banks of the Cylindrical Sea with its prey. It took her two or three seconds to realise that everyone was shouting at her.

The lead biot and its final two companion crabs had not crumpled into a heap when they had hit the ground. Although slightly damaged, they were active and on the move within moments after landing. While Francesca was filming the departure of the helicopter, the lead biot sensed her presence and headed toward her. The other two followed a step behind.

They were only four metres away when Francesca, still filming, finally understood that she was now the prey. She turned around and started to run. 'Run to the side,' Richard Wakefield screamed into the communicator, 'they can only go in straight lines.'

Francesca zigged and zagged but the biots continued to follow her. Her original burst of adrenaline enabled her to extend the distance separating her from the crabs to ten metres. Later, however, as she began to tire, the relentless biots were closing in on her. She slipped and almost fell. By the time Francesca regained her stride the lead biot was no more than three metres away.

Reggie Wilson had raced toward the rover as soon as it was clear that the biots were chasing Francesca. Once he was at the controls of the vehicle, he headed for her rescue at top speed. He had originally intended to pick her up and move her out of the way of the biot onslaught. They were too close to her, however, so Reggie decided to smash into the three crabs from the side. There was a crash of metal on metal as the lightweight vehicle rammed the biots. Reggie's plan worked. The momentum of the crash carried Reggie and the crabs several metres to the side. The threat to Francesca was over.

But the biots were not incapacitated. Far from it. Despite the fact that one of the follower crabs had lost a leg and the lead biot had a slightly damaged claw, within seconds all three of them were at work in the wreckage. They started slicing the rover into chunks with their claws, and then they used their fearful collection of probes and rasps to tear the chunks into still smaller pieces.

Reggie was momentarily stunned by the impact of the rover against the biots. The alien crabs had been heavier than he had anticipated and the damage to his vehicle was severe. As soon as he realised that the biots were still active, he started to jump out of the rover. But he couldn't. His legs were wedged underneath the collapsed dashboard.

His unmitigated terror lasted no longer than ten seconds. There was nothing anyone could do. Reggie Wilson's horrified shrieks echoed through the vastness of Rama as the biots chopped him apart exactly as if he were part of the rover. It was accomplished swiftly and systematically. Both Francesca and the automatic camera in the helicopter filmed the final seconds of his life. The pictures were transmitted live back to the Earth.

30 POSTMORTEM II

Nicole sat quietly in her hut at the Beta campsite. She could not erase from her mind the horrible image of Reggie Wilson's face, contorted in terror as he was being hacked to pieces. She tried to force herself to think of something else. *So what now,* she wondered. *What will happen to the mission now?*

Outside it was dark again in Rama. The lights had vanished abruptly three hours before, after a period of illumination thirty-four seconds less than during the previous Raman day. The disappearance of the lights should have prompted much discussion and speculation. But it didn't. None of the cosmonauts wanted to talk about anything. The awful memory of Wilson's death weighed too heavily on everyone.

The normal crew meeting after dinner had been postponed until morning because David Brown and Admiral Heilmann were in an extended conference with ISA officials back on Earth. Nicole had not participated in any of the conversations, but it was not difficult for her to imagine their content. She realised that there was a very real possibility the mission would now be aborted. The hue and cry from the public might demand it. After all, they had witnessed one of the most gruesome scenes....

Nicole thought of Genevieve sitting in front of the television at Beauvois, watching while Cosmonaut Wilson was being methodically subdivided by the biots. She shuddered. Then she chastised herself for being self-centered. *The real horror,* she said to herself, *must have been in Los Angeles.*

She had met the Wilson family twice during the early parties right after the crew selections were announced. Nicole remembered the boy particularly. Randy was his name. He was seven or eight, wide-eyed and beautiful. He loved sports. He had brought Nicole one of his prized possessions, a program from the 2184 Olympics in nearly perfect condition, and had asked her to sign the page featuring the women's triple jump. She had tousled his hair as he had thanked her with a huge smile.

The image of Randy Wilson watching his father die on television was too much for her. Several tears wedged themselves into the corners of her eyes. *What a nightmare this year has been for you, little boy,* she thought. *The roller-coaster of life. First the joy of having your father selected as a cosmonaut. Then all the Francesca nonsense and the divorce. Now this terrible tragedy.*

Nicole was becoming depressed and her mind was still too active for sleep. She decided that she wanted some company. She walked over to the next hut and knocked softly on the door.

'Is someone out there?' she heard from inside.

'Hai, Takagishi-san,' she replied. 'It's Nicole. May I come in?'

He walked over to the door and opened it. 'This is an unexpected surprise,' he said. 'Is the visit professional?'

'No,' she answered as she entered. 'Strictly informal. I was not ready to sleep. I thought ...'

'You are welcome to visit me any time,' he said with a friendly smile. 'You do not need a reason.' He looked at her for several seconds. 'I am deeply disturbed by what happened this afternoon. I feel responsible. I don't think I did enough to stop—'

'Come on, Shigeru,' Nicole replied. 'Don't be ridiculous. You're not to blame. At least you spoke up. I'm the doctor and I didn't even say anything.'

Her eyes wandered aimlessly around Takagishi's hut. Beside his cot, sitting on a small piece of cloth on the floor, Nicole saw a curious white figurine with black markings. She walked over to it and bent down on her knees, 'What's this?' she asked.

Dr Takagishi was slightly embarrassed. He came over beside Nicole and picked up the tiny fat oriental man. He held it between his index finger and his thumb. 'It's a netsuke heirloom from my wife's family,' he said. 'It's made from ivory.'

He handed the little man to Nicole. 'He is the king of the gods. His companion, a similarly plump queen, rests on the table beside my wife's bed in Kyoto. Back before elephants became endangered, many people collected figures like this. My wife's family has a superb collection.'

Nicole studied the little man in her hand. He had a benign, serene smile on his face. She imagined the beautiful Machiko Takagishi back in Japan and for a few seconds she envied their marital bond. *It would make events like Wilson's death much easier to deal with,* she thought.

'Would you like to sit down?' Dr Takagishi was saying. Nicole positioned herself on a box next to the cot and they talked for twenty minutes. Mostly they shared memories of their families. They referred obliquely to the afternoon disaster several times, but they avoided detailed discussion of Rama and the Newton mission altogether. What they both needed were the comforting images of their daily lives on Earth.

'And now,' Takagishi said, finishing his cup of tea and putting it on the end table beside Nicole's, 'I have a strange request for Dr des Jardins. Would you please go over to your hut and bring back your biometry equipment? I would like to be scanned.'

Nicole started to laugh but noticed the seriousness in her colleague's face.

339

When she returned with her scanner several minutes later, Dr Takagishi told her the reason for his request. 'This afternoon,' he said, 'I felt two very sharp pains in my chest. It was during the excitement, after Wilson crashed into the biots, and I realised ...' He did not complete his sentence. Nicole nodded and activated the scanning instrument.

Neither of them said anything for the next three minutes. Nicole checked all the warning data, displayed graphs and charts of his cardiac performance, and shook her head regularly. When she was finished she faced her friend with a grim smile. 'You've had a slight heart attack,' she said to Dr Takagishi. 'Maybe two very close together. And your heart has been irregular ever since.' She could tell that he had expected the news. 'I'm sorry,' she said. 'I have some medicine with me that I can give you, but it's only a stopgap measure. We must go back to the Newton immediately so we can treat this problem properly.'

'Well' – he smiled wanly – 'If our predictions are correct, then it will be light again in Rama in about twelve hours. I assume we'll go then.'

'Probably,' she answered. 'I'll talk to Brown and Heilmann about it right away. My guess is that you and I will leave first thing in the morning.'

He reached out and took her hand. 'Thank you, Nicole,' he said.

She turned away. For the second time in an hour there were tears in the corners of her eyes. Nicole left Takagishi's hut and headed for the edge of camp to talk to David Brown.

'Ah, it *is* you.' She heard Richard Wakefield's voice in the dark. 'I thought for certain you were asleep. I have some news for you.'

'Hello, Richard,' Nicole said as the figure holding the flashlight emerged from the darkness.

'I couldn't sleep,' he said. 'Too many grisly pictures in my head. So I decided to work on your problem.' He smiled. 'It was even easier than I thought. Would you like to come to my hut for an explanation?'

Nicole was confused. She had been preoccupied with what she was going to say to Brown and Heilmann about Takagishi. 'You do remember, don't you?' Richard inquired. 'The problem with the RoSur software and the manual commands.'

'You've been working on *that?*' she asked. 'Down here?'

'Certainly. All I had to do was have O'Toole transmit the data that I needed. Come on, let me show you.'

Nicole decided seeing Dr Brown could wait for a few more minutes. She walked beside Richard. He knocked on another hut as they went by. 'Hey Tabori, guess what?' he shouted. 'I found our lovely lady doctor wandering around in the dark. Do you want to join us?'

'I explained some of it to him first,' Richard said to Nicole. 'Your hut was dark and I figured you were asleep.'

Janos stumbled out of his door less than a minute later and acknowledged

Nicole with a smile. 'All right, Wakefield,' he said, 'but let's not prolong it. I was finally drifting off.'

Back in Wakefield's hut, the British engineer thoroughly enjoyed recounting what had happened to the robot surgeon when the Newton had experienced the unexpected torque. 'You were right, Nicole,' he said, 'that there were manual commands input to RoSur. And these commands did indeed shut down the normal fault protection algorithms. But none of them was input until *during* the Raman manoeuvre.'

Wakefield smiled and continued, watching Nicole carefully to ensure that she was following his explanation. 'Apparently, when Janos fell and his fingers hit the control box, he generated three commands. At least that's what RoSur thought; it was told that there were three manual commands in it's queue. Of course they were all garbage. But RoSur had no way of knowing this.

'Maybe now you can appreciate some of the nightmares that plague system software designers. There's just no way anybody could ever anticipate all possible contingencies. The designers had protected against *one* inadvertent garbage command – someone brushing the control box during an operation, for example – but not *several* bad commands. Manual commands were essentially considered to be emergencies by the overall system design. Hence they had the highest priority in the interrupt structure of the RoSur software and were always processed immediately, The design acknowledged, however, that there could be a single "bad" manual command and had the capability of rejecting it and moving on to the next priority interrupts, which included fault protection.'

'Sorry,' said Nicole. 'You've lost me. How could a design be structured to disregard a single bad command, but not several? I thought this simple processor operated in series.'

Richard turned to his portable computer and, working from notes, called up on the monitor a mass of numbers arrayed in rows and columns. 'Here are the operations, instruction by instruction, that the RoSur software implemented after there were manual commands in its queue.'

'They repeat,' Janos observed, 'every seven operations.'

'Exactly,' Richard replied. 'RoSur tried three times to process the first manual command, was unsuccessful in each attempt, and then went on to the next command. The software operated exactly as it was designed—'

'But why,' Tabori asked, 'did it go back to the first command afterward?'

'Because the software designers never considered the possibility of *multiple* bad manual commands. Or at least never designed for the condition. The internal question the software asks after finishing with the processing of each command is whether or not there is another manual command in the buffer. If there is *not*, then the software rejects the first command and is free to handle another interrupt. If there *is*, however, the software is told to store the rejected command and process the next command. Now, if two commands in a row are rejected, the software *assumes* that the command processor *hardware* is broken, swaps to the redundant hardware set, and tries again to process the same manual commands. You can understand the reasoning. Suppose one ...'

Nicole listened for several seconds as Richard and Janos talked about redundant subsystems, buffered commands, and queue structures. She had very little training in either fault protection or redundancy management and could not follow the exchange. 'Just a moment,' she interjected at length, 'you've lost me again. Remember, I'm not an engineer. Can't somebody give me a summary in normal English?'

Wakefield was apologetic. 'Sorry, Nicole,' he said. 'You know what an interrupt driven software system is?' She nodded. 'And you are familiar with the way priorities operate in such a system? Good. Then the explanation is simple. The fault protection interrupts based on the accelerometer and imaging data were lower priority than the manual commands inadvertently entered by Janos when he was falling. The system became locked in a software loop trying to process the bad commands and never had a chance to heed the fault signals from the sensor subsystems. That's why the scalpel kept cutting.'

For some reason Nicole was disappointed. The explanation was clear enough, and she had certainly not wanted the analysis to implicate Janos or any other member of the crew. But it was too simple. It had not been worth all her time and energy.

Nicole sat down on the cot in Richard Wakefield's hut. 'So much for my mystery,' she said.

Janos sat beside her. 'Cheer up, Nicole,' he said. 'This is good news. At least now we know for certain that we didn't foul up the initialisation process. There's a logical explanation for what happened.'

'Great,' she replied sarcastically. 'But General Borzov is still dead. And now Reggie Wilson is too.' Nicole thought about the American journalist's erratic behaviour over the last several days and remembered her earlier conversation with Francesca. 'Say,' she said spontaneously, 'did either of you ever hear General Borzov complain of headaches or any other discomfort? Especially on the day of the banquet?'

Wakefield shook his head. 'No,' said Janos. 'Why do you ask?'

'Well, I asked the portable diagnostician, based on Borzov's biometry data, to give me the possible causes of his symptoms, given that the general was *not* having an appendicitis. The most likely cause was listed as drug reaction. Sixty-two percent probable. I thought that maybe he might have had an adverse reaction to some medication.'

'Really?' Janos said, his curiosity piqued. 'Why have you never said anything about this to me before?'

'I was going to ... several times,' Nicole answered. 'But I didn't think you were interested. Remember when I stopped by your room on the Newton the day after General Borzov died? It was right after the crew meeting. From the way you responded I concluded that you didn't want to rehash—'

'Goodness.' Janos shook his head. 'How we humans fail to communicate. It was just a headache. Nothing more or less. I certainly didn't mean to give you the impression that I was unwilling to talk about Valeriy's death.'

'Speaking of communicating,' Nicole said as she rose wearily from the cot, 'I must go to see Dr Brown and Admiral Heilmann before I go to bed.' She looked at Wakefield. 'Thanks a lot for your help, Richard. I wish I could say that I felt better now.'

Nicole walked over beside Janos. 'I'm sorry, friend,' she said. 'I should have shared my whole investigation with you. It probably would have been over much faster ...'

'It's fine,' Janos replied. 'Don't worry about it.' He smiled. 'Come on, I'll walk with you as far as my suite.'

Nicole could hear the loud conversation inside before she knocked on the door to the hut. David Brown, Otto Heilmann, and Francesca Sabatini were arguing about how to reply to the latest directions from Earth.

'They're overreacting,' Francesca was saying. 'And they'll realise it as soon as they have some time to reflect. This is not the first mission to suffer a loss of human life. They didn't cancel the American space shuttle when that schoolteacher and her crew were killed.'

'But they have *ordered* us to return to the Newton as soon as possible,' Admiral Heilmann protested.

'So tomorrow we'll talk to them again and explain why we want to survey New York first. Takagishi says the sea will start to melt in another day or two and we'll have to leave anyway. Besides, Wakefield and Takagishi and I did hear something that night, even if David doesn't believe us.'

'I don't know, Francesca,' Dr Brown was starting to respond when he finally heard Nicole's knock. 'Who's there?' he asked crossly.

'Cosmonaut des Jardins, I have some important medical information—'

'Look, des Jardins,' Brown interrupted quickly, 'we're very busy. Can't it wait until morning?'

All right, Nicole said to herself. *I can wait until morning*. She wasn't anxious to answer Dr Brown's questions about Takagishi's heart condition anyway. 'Roger,' she said out loud, laughing at herself for using the expression.

Within seconds Nicole could hear the discussion start again behind her. She walked slowly back to her hut. *Tomorrow has to be a better day,* she said as she crawled on to her cot.

31 ORVIETO PRODIGY

'**G**ood night, Otto,' David Brown said as the German admiral left his hut.

'See you in the morning.' Dr Brown yawned and stretched. He looked at his watch. It was a little more than eight hours until the lights should come on again.

He pulled off his flight suit and had a drink of water. He had just laid down on his cot when Francesca entered his hut. 'David,' she said, 'we have more problems.' She walked over and gave him a short kiss. 'I've been talking to Janos. Nicole suspects that Valeriy was drugged.'

'Whaaat?' he replied. He sat up on his cot. 'How could she? There was no way ...'

'Apparently there was some evidence in his biometry data and she cleverly found it. She mentioned it to Janos tonight.'

'You didn't react when he told you, did you? I mean, we must be absolutely—'

'Of course not,' Francesca answered. 'Anyway, Janos would never suspect anything in a thousand years. He is a total innocent. At least where things like this are concerned.'

'Damn that woman,' David Brown said. 'And damn her biometry.' He rubbed his face with his hands. 'What a day. First that stupid Wilson tries to be a hero. Now this ... I told you we should have destroyed all the data from the operation. It would have been an easy matter to wipe out the central files. Then things would never—'

'She would still have his biometry records,' Francesca countered. 'That's where the prime evidence is. You would have to be an absolute genius to take the data from the operation itself and deduce anything.' She sat down and cradled Dr Brown's head against her chest. 'Our big mistake was not when we failed to destroy the files. That would have aroused suspicion at the ISA. Our error was in underestimating Nicole des Jardins.'

Dr Brown shook free from the embrace and stood up. 'Dammit, Francesca, it's your fault. I never should have let you talk me into it. I knew at the time—'

'You knew at the time' – Francesca sharply interrupted – 'that you, Dr David

Brown, were not going on the first sortie into Rama. You knew at the time that your future millions as the hero and perceived leader of this expedition would be seriously compromised if you stayed on board the Newton.' Brown stopped pacing and faced Francesca. 'You knew at the time,' she continued more softly, 'that I too had a vested interest in your going on the sortie. And that I could be counted on to provide you with support.'

She took his hands and pulled him back toward the cot. 'Sit down, David,' Francesca said. 'We've been over and over this. We did not kill General Borzov. We simply gave him a drug that created the symptoms of an appendicitis. We made the decision together. If Rama had not manoeuvered and the robot surgeon had not malfunctioned, then our plan would have worked perfectly. Borzov would be on the Newton today, recovering from his appendectomy, and you and I would be here leading the exploration of Rama.'

David Brown removed his hands from hers and started to wring them. 'I feel so ... so unclean,' he said. 'I've never done anything like this before. I mean, whether we like it or not, we are partially responsible for Borzov's death. Maybe even for Wilson's as well. We could be indicted.' He was shaking his head again. There was a forlorn expression on his face. 'I'm supposed to be a scientist,' he said. 'What has happened to me? How did I get mixed up in these things?'

'Spare me your righteousness,' Francesca said harshly. 'And don't try to kid yourself. Aren't you the man who stole the decade's most important astronomical discovery from a woman graduate student? And then married her to keep her quiet forever? Your integrity was compromised a long long time ago.'

'That's unfair,' Dr Brown said petulantly. 'I have mostly been honest. Except—'

'Except when it was important and worth a lot to you, What a pile of shit!' Francesca now stood up and paced around the hut herself. 'You men are so damn hypocritical. You preserve your lofty self-images with amazing rationalisations. You never admit to yourselves who you really are and what you really want. Most women are more honest. We acknowledge our ambitions, our desires, even our basest wants. We admit our weaknesses. We face ourselves as we are, not as we would like to be.'

She returned to the cot and took David's hands in hers again. 'Don't you see, darling?' she said earnestly. 'You and I are soulmates. Our alliance is based on the strongest bond of all – mutual self-interest. We are both motivated by the same goals of power and fame.'

'That sounds awful,' he said.

'But it's true. Even if you don't want to admit it to yourself. David, darling, can't you see that your indecisiveness comes from your failure to acknowledge your true nature? Look at me. I know exactly what I want and am never confused about what to do. My behaviour is automatic.'

The American physicist sat quietly beside Francesca for a long time. At length he turned and put his head on her shoulder. 'First Borzov, now Wilson,' he said with a sigh. 'I feel whipped. I wish none of this had happened.'

'You can't give up, David,' she said, stroking his head. 'We've come too far. And the big prize is now within our reach.'

Francesca reached across him and started to remove his shirt. 'It's been a long and trying day,' she said soothingly. 'Let's try to forget it.' David Brown closed his eyes as she caressed his face and chest.

Francesca bent over and kissed him slowly on the lips. A few moments later she abruptly stopped. 'You see,' she said, slowly removing her own clothes, 'as long as we are in this together, we can derive strength from each other.' She stood up in front of David, forcing him to open his eyes.

'Hurry,' he said impatiently, 'I was already ...'

'Don't worry so much about it,' Francesca replied, lazily pulling down her pants, 'you've never had a problem with me.' Francesca smiled again as she pushed his knees apart and pressed his face against her breasts. 'Remember,' she said, tugging easily at his shorts with her free hand, 'I'm not Elaine.'

She studied David Brown as he slept beside her. The strain and anxiety that had dominated his face just minutes before had been replaced by the carefree smile of a boy. *Men are so simple,* Francesca was thinking. *Orgasm is the perfect pain reliever. I wish it were that easy for us.*

She slipped off the small cot and put her clothes on again. Francesca was very careful not to disturb her sleeping friend. *But you and I still have a real problem,* she said to herself as she finished dressing, *which we need to address quickly. And it will be more difficult because we are dealing with a woman.*

Francesca walked outside her hut, into the black of Rama. There were a few lights near the supplies at the other end of the camp, but otherwise the Beta campsite was dark. Everyone else was asleep. She switched on her small flashlight and walked away in a southerly direction, toward the Cylindrical Sea.

What is it that you want, Madame Nicole des Jardins? she thought as she walked along. *And where's your weakness, your Achilles' heel?* For several minutes Francesca flipped through her entire memory bank on Nicole, attempting to find any personality or character flaw that could be exploited. *Money's not the answer. Sex. isn't either, at least not with me.* She laughed involuntarily. *And certainly not with David. Your dislike for him is obvious.*

What about blackmail? Francesca asked herself as she drew near to the banks of the Cylindrical Sea. She remembered Nicole's strong reaction to her question about Genevieve's father. *Maybe,* she thought, *if I knew the answer to that question ... But I don't.*

Francesca was temporarily stumped. She could not figure out any way to compromise Nicole des Jardins. By this time the lights from the campsite behind her were barely visible. Francesca extinguished her flashlight and very cautiously sat down to dangle her feet over the edge of the cliff.

Having her legs suspended above the frozen ice of the Cylindrical Sea brought back a suite of poignant memories from her childhood in Orvieto. At the age of eleven, despite the barrage of health warnings that assaulted her from every direction, the precocious Francesca had decided to start smoking cigarettes. Every day after school she would wind her way down the hill to the plain below the town and sit on the bank of her favourite creek. There she would smoke in silence, an act of solitary rebellion. On those lazy afternoons she would inhabit a fantasy world of castles and princes, millions of kilometres away from her mother and stepfather.

The memory of those adolescent moments produced an irresistible desire to smoke in Francesca. She had been taking her nicotine pills throughout the mission, but they satisfied only the physical addiction. She laughed at herself and reached into one of the special pockets of her flight suit. Francesca had hidden away three cigarettes in a special container that would preserve them in fresh condition. She had told herself before leaving the Earth that the cigarettes were there 'in case of an emergency' ...

Smoking a cigarette inside an extraterrestrial space vehicle was even more outrageous than smoking at the age of eleven. Francesca wanted to hoot with delight when she threw back her head and expelled the smoke into the Raman air. The act made her feel free, liberated. Somehow the threat represented by Nicole des Jardins did not seem so serious.

While she was smoking, Francesca recalled the acute loneliness of that young girl stealing down the slopes of old Orvieto. She also remembered the terrible secret that she had kept locked forever in her heart. Francesca had never told anyone about her stepfather, certainly not her mother, and she rarely thought about it anymore. But as she sat on the banks of the Cylindrical Sea, the anguish of her childhood appeared to her in sharp relief.

It began right after my eleventh birthday, she thought, plunging back into the details of her life eighteen years before. *I had no idea what the bastard wanted at first.* She took another deep drag from her cigarette. *Even after he started bringing me gifts for no reason.*

He had been the principal of her new school. When she had taken her first full set of aptitude tests, Francesca had made the highest scores in the history of Orvieto. She was off the scale, a prodigy. Until then he had never noticed her. He had married her mother eighteen months before and fathered the twins almost immediately. Francesca had been a nuisance, another mouth to feed, nothing more than a part of her mother's furniture.

For several months he was especially nice to me. Then Mother went to visit Aunt Carlo for a few days. The painful memories came fast, rushing like a torrent through her mind. She remembered the smell of wine on her stepfather's breath, his sweat against her body, her tears after he had left her room.

The nightmare had lasted for over a year. He had forced himself upon her whenever her mother was not in the house. Then one evening, while he was putting on his clothes and looking in the other direction, Francesca had smacked him in the back of the head with an aluminium baseball bat. Her stepfather had fallen to the floor, bloody and unconscious. She had dragged him into the living room and left him there.

He never touched me again, Francesca remembered, putting out her cigarette in the Raman dirt. *We were strangers in the same house. From then on I spent most of my time with Roberto and his friends. I was just waiting for my chance. I was ready when Carlo came.*

Francesca was fourteen during the summer of 2184. She spent most of her time that summer loitering around the main square of Orvieto. Her older cousin Roberto had just completed his certificate to be a tour guide for the cathedral in the square. The old Duomo, the chief tourist attraction of the town, had been built in phases, starting in the fourteenth century. The church was an artistic and architectural masterpiece. The frescoes by Luca Signorelli inside its San Brizio chapel were widely hailed as the finest examples of imaginative fifteenth century painting outside of the Vatican museum.

To have become an official Duomo guide was considered quite an accomplishment, especially at the age of nineteen. Francesca was very proud of Roberto. She sometimes accompanied him on his tours, but only if she agreed beforehand not to embarrass him with her wisecracks.

One August afternoon, right after lunch, a sleek limousine pulled into the piazza around Il Duomo and the chauffeur requested a guide from the tourist bureau. The gentleman in the limousine had not made a reservation and Roberto was the only guide available. Francesca watched with great curiosity as a short, handsome man in his late thirties or early forties climbed out of the back of the car and introduced himself to Roberto. Automobiles had been banned from upper Orvieto, except by special permit, for almost a hundred years, so Francesca knew the man must be an unusual individual.

As he always did, Roberto began his tour with the reliefs sculptured by Lorenzo Maitani on the outside portals of the church. Still curious, Francesca stood just off to the side, smoking quietly, while her cousin explained the significance of the weird demonic figures at the bottom of one of the columns. 'This is one of the earliest representations of Hell,' Roberto said, pointing at a group of Dantesque figures. 'The fourteenth century concept of Hell involved an extremely literal interpretation of the Bible.'

'Hah!' Francesca had suddenly interjected, dropping her cigarette on the cobblestones and walking toward Roberto and the handsome stranger. 'It was also a very masculine concept of Hell. Notice that many of the demons have breasts and most of the sins depicted are sexual. Men have always believed that they were created perfect; it is women who have taught them to sin.'

The stranger was astonished by the appearance of this gangly teenager expelling smoke from her mouth. His trained eye immediately recognized her natural beauty and it was clear that she was very bright. Who was she?

'This is my cousin, Francesca,' Roberto said, obviously flustered by her interruption.

'Carlo Bianchi,' the man said, extending his hand. His hand was moist Francesca looked up at his face and could see that he was interested. She could feel her heart pounding in her chest. 'If you listen to Roberto,' she said coyly, 'then all you'll get is the official tour. He leaves out the juicy bits.'

'And you, young lady—'

'Francesca,' she said.

'Yes, Francesca. Do you have a tour of your own?'

Francesca gave him her prettiest smile. 'I read a lot,' she said. 'I know all about the artists who worked on the cathedral, particularly the painter Luca Signorelli.' She paused for a moment. 'Did you know,' she continued, 'that Michelangelo came here to study Signorelli's nudes before he painted the ceiling at the Sistine Chapel?'

'No, I didn't,' Carlo said, laughing heartily. He was already fascinated. 'But I do now. Come. Join us. You can add to what your cousin Roberto says.'

She loved the way he kept staring at her. It was as if he were appraising her, as if she were a fine painting or a jeweled necklace, his eyes missing nothing as they roamed unabashedly over her figure. And his easy laughter spurred her on. Francesca's comments became increasingly outrageous and bawdy.

'You see that poor girl on the demon's back?' she said while they were gazing at the bewildering range of genius exhibited by Signorelli's frescoes inside the San Brizio chapel. 'She looks like she's humping the demon in the butt, right? You know who she is? Her face and naked body are portraits of Signorelli's girlfriend. While he was slaving in here day after day, she became bored and decided to diddle a duke or two on the side. Luca was really pissed, So he fixed her. He condemned her to ride a demon in perpetuity.'

When he stopped laughing, Carlo asked Francesca if she thought the woman's punishment was fair. 'Of course not,' the fourteen-year-old replied, 'it's just another example of the male chauvinism of the fifteenth century. The men could screw anybody they wanted and were called virile; but let a woman try to satisfy herself—'

'*Francesca!*' Roberto interrupted. 'Really. This is too much. Your mother would kill you if she heard what you are saying ...'

'My mother is irrelevant at this moment. I'm talking about a double standard that still exists today. Look at ...'

Carlo Bianchi could hardly believe his good fortune. A rich clothes designer from Milano, one who had established an international reputation by the time he was thirty, he had just happened to decide, on a whim, to hire a car to take him to Rome instead of going on the usual high-speed train. His sister, Monica, had always told him about the beauty of Il Duomo in Orvieto. It had been another last-minute decision to stop. And now. My, my. The girl was such a splendid morsel.

He invited Francesca to dinner when the tour was over. But when they reached the entrance to the fanciest restaurant in Orvieto, the young woman balked. Carlo understood. He took her to a store and bought her an expensive new dress with matching shoes and accessories. He was astonished by how beautiful she was. And only fourteen!

Francesca had never before drunk really fine wine. She drank it as if it were water. Each dish was so delicious that she positively squealed. Carlo was enchanted with his woman-child. He loved the way she let her cigarette dangle from the corner of her lips. It was so unspoiled, so perfectly gauche.

When the meal was over it was dark. Francesca walked with him back to the limousine parked in front of Il Duomo. As they went down a narrow alley, she leaned over and playfully bit his ear. He spontaneously pulled her to him and was rewarded with an explosive kiss. The surge in his loins overwhelmed him.

Francesca had felt it too. She did not hesitate a second when Carlo suggested they go for a ride in the car. By the time the limousine had reached the outskirts of Orvieto, she was sitting astride him in the back seat. Thirty minutes later, when they finished making love the second time, Carlo could not bear the thought of parting with this incredible girl. He asked Francesca if she would like to accompany him to Rome.

'Andiamo,' she replied with a smile.

So we went to Rome and then Capri, Francesca remembered. *Paris for a week. In Milano you had me live with Monica and Luigi. For appearances. Men are always so worried about appearances.*

Francesca's long reverie was broken when she thought she heard footsteps in the distance. She cautiously stood up in the dark and listened. It was hard for her to hear anything over her own breathing. Then she heard the sound again, off to the left. Her ears told her the sound was out on the ice. A burst of fear flooded her with an image of bizarre creatures attacking their camp from across the ice. She listened again very carefully, but heard nothing.

Francesca turned back toward the camp. *I loved you, Carlo,* she said to herself, *if I ever loved any man. Even after you began to share me with your friends.* More long-buried pain came to the surface and Francesca fought it with hard anger. *Until you started hitting me. That ruined everything. You proved that you were a real bastard.*

Francesca very deliberately pushed aside the memories. *Now, where were we?* she thought as she approached her hut. *Ah yes. The issue was Nicole des Jardins. How much does she really know? And what are we going to do about it?*

32 NEW YORK EXPLORER

The tiny bell on his wristwatch awakened Dr Takagishi from a deep sleep. For a few moments he was disoriented, unable to remember where he was. He sat up on his cot and rubbed his eyes. At length he recalled that he was inside Rama and that the alarm had been set to wake him up after five hours of sleep.

He dressed in the dark. When he was finished he picked up a large bag and fumbled around inside for several seconds. Satisfied with its contents, he threw the strap over his shoulder and walked to the door of his hut. Dr Takagishi peered out cautiously. He could not see lights in any of the other huts. He took a deep breath and tiptoed out the door.

The world's leading authority on Rama walked out of the camp in the direction of the Cylindrical Sea. When he reached the shore, he climbed slowly down to the icy surface on the stairs cut into the fifty-metre cliff. Takagishi sat on the bottom rung, hidden against the base of the cliff. He removed some special cleats from his bag and attached them to the bottom of his shoes. Before walking out on the ice, the scientist calibrated his personal navigator so that he would be able to keep a constant heading once he left the shoreline.

When he was about two hundred metres away from the shore, Dr Takagishi reached in his pocket to pull out his portable weather monitor. It dropped on the ice, making a short clacking sound in the quiet night. Takagishi picked it up a few seconds later. The monitor told him that the temperature was minus two degrees Centigrade and that a soft wind was blowing across the ice at eight kilometres per hour.

Takagishi inhaled deeply and was astonished by a peculiar but familiar odour. Puzzled, he inhaled again, this time concentrating on the smell, There was no doubt about it – it was cigarette smoke! He hurriedly extinguished his flashlight and stood motionless on the ice. His mind raced into overdrive, searching for an explanation. Francesca Sabatini was the only cosmonaut who smoked. Had she somehow followed him when he left the camp? Had she seen his light when he checked his weather monitor?

He listened for noises but heard nothing in the Raman night. Still he waited. When the cigarette smell had been gone for several minutes, Dr

Takagishi continued his trek across the ice, stopping every four or five steps to ensure that he was not being followed. Eventually he convinced himself that Francesca was not behind him. However, the cautious Takagishi did not turn on his flashlight again until he had walked more than a kilometre and had become worried that he might have drifted off course.

Altogether it took him forty-five minutes to reach the opposite edge of the sea and the island city of New York. When he was a hundred metres from the shore, the Japanese scientist took a larger flashlight from his bag and switched on its powerful beam. The ghostly silhouettes of the skyscrapers sent an exhilarating chill down his spine. At last he was here! At last he could seek the answers to his lifetime of questions unencumbered by someone else's arbitrary schedule.

Dr Takagishi knew exactly where he wanted to go in New York. Each of the three circular sections of the Raman city was further subdivided into three angular portions, like a pie divided into slices. At the centre of each of the three main sections was a central core, or plaza, around which the rest of the buildings and streets were arranged. As a boy in Kyoto, after reading everything he could find about the first Raman expedition, Takagishi had wondered what it would be like to stand in the centre of one of those alien plazas and stare upward at buildings created by beings from another star.

Takagishi felt certain not only that the secrets of Rama could be understood by studying New York, but also that its three plazas were the most likely locations for clues to the mysterious purpose of the interstellar vehicle.

The map of New York drawn by the earlier Raman explorers was as firmly etched in Takagishi's mind as the map of Kyoto, where he was born and raised. But that first Raman expedition had had only a limited time to survey New York. Of the nine functional units, only one had been mapped in detail; the prior cosmonauts had simply assumed, on the basis of limited observations, that all the other units were identical.

As Takagishi's brisk pace carried him deeper and deeper into the foreboding quiet of one part of the central section, some subtle differences between this particular segment of Rama and the one studied by Norton's crew (they had surveyed an adjacent slice) began to emerge. The layout of the major streets in the two units was the same; however, as Dr Takagishi drew closer to the plaza, the smaller streets broke into a slightly different pattern from the one that had been reported by the first explorers. The scientist in Takagishi forced him to stop often and note all the variations on his pocket computer.

He entered the region immediately surrounding the plaza, where the streets ran in concentric circles. He crossed three avenues and found himself standing opposite a huge octahedron, about a hundred metres tall, with a mirrored exterior. His powerful flashlight beam reflected off its surface and then bounced from building to building around him. Dr Takagishi walked slowly around the octahedron, searching for an entrance, but he did not find one.

On the other side of the eight-sided structure, in the centre of the plaza, was a broad circular space without tall buildings. Shigeru Takagishi moved deliberately around the entire perimeter of the circle, studying the surrounding buildings as he walked. He gained no new insights about the purpose of the structures. When he turned inward at regular intervals to survey the plaza area itself, he saw nothing unusual or particularly noteworthy. Nevertheless, he did enter into his computer the location of the many short, nondescript metallic boxes that divided the plaza into partitions.

When he was again in front of the octahedron, Dr Takagishi reached into his bag and pulled out a thin hexagonal plate densely covered with electronics. He deployed the scientific apparatus in the plaza, three or four metres away from the octahedron, and then spent ten minutes verifying with his transceiver that all the scientific instruments were properly working. When the Japanese scientist had completed checking the payload, he quickly left the plaza area and headed for the Cylindrical Sea.

Takagishi was in the middle of the second concentric avenue when he heard a short but loud popping noise behind him in the plaza. He turned around but didn't move. A few seconds later he heard a different sound. This one Takagishi recognized from his first sortie, both the dragging of the metal brushes and the embedded high-frequency singing. He shone his flashlight in the direction of the plaza. The sound stopped. He switched off his flashlight and stood quietly in the middle of the avenue.

Several minutes later the brush dragging began again. Takagishi moved stealthily across the two avenues and started around the octahedron in the direction of the noise. When he was almost to the plaza, a *beep, beep* from his bag broke his concentration. By the time he turned off the alarm, which was indicating that the scientific package he had just deployed in the plaza had already malfunctioned, there was total quiet in New York. Again Dr Takagishi waited, but this time the sound did not recur.

He took a deep breath to calm himself and summoned all his courage. Somehow his curiosity won out over his fear and Dr Takagishi returned to the plaza opposite the octahedron to find out what had happened to the scientific payload. His first surprise was that the hexagonal package had vanished from the spot where he had left it. Where could it have gone? Who or what could have taken it?

Takagishi knew that he was on the verge of a scientific discovery of overwhelming importance. He was also terrified. Fighting a powerful desire to flee, he shone his large flashlight around the plaza, hoping to find an explanation for the disappearance of the science station. The beam reflected off a small piece of metal some thirty to forty metres closer to the centre of the plaza. Takagishi realised immediately that the reflection was coming from the instrument package. He hurried over to it.

He bent down on his knees and examined the electronics. There was no damage that was obvious. He had just pulled out his transceiver to begin a methodical check of all the science instruments when he noticed a rope-like object about fifteen centimetres in diameter at the edge of the flashlight beam illuminating the science package. Dr Takagishi picked up his light and walked over to the object. It was striped, black and gold, and stretched off into the distance for twelve metres or so, disappearing behind an odd metal shed about three metres tall. He felt the thick rope. It was soft and fuzzy on the top. When he tried to turn it over to feel the bottom, the object began to move. Takagishi dropped it immediately and watched it slither slowly away from him toward the shed. The motion was accompanied by the sound of brushes dragging against metal.

Dr Takagishi could hear the sound of his own heartbeat. Again he fought the urge to run away. He remembered his dawn meditations as a college student in the garden of his Zen master. He would not be afraid. He ordered his feet to march in the direction of the shed.

The black and gold rope disappeared. There was silence in the plaza. Takagishi approached the shed with his light beam on the ground at the spot where the thick rope had last been visible. He came around the corner and thrust the beam into the shed. He could not believe what he saw. A mass of black and gold tentacles writhed underneath the light.

A high-frequency whine suddenly exploded in his ears. Dr Takagishi looked over his left shoulder and was thunderstruck. His eyes bugged out of his head. His scream was lost as the noise intensified and three of the tentacles reached out to touch him. The walls of his heart gave way and he slumped, already dead, into the grasp of the amazing creature.

33 MISSING PERSON

'Admiral Heilmann?'

'Yes, General O'Toole.'

'Are you by yourself?'

'Certainly. I just woke up a few minutes ago. My meeting with Dr Brown is not for another hour. Why are you calling so early?'

'While you were sleeping I received a coded top secret message from COG military headquarters. It's about Trinity. They wanted to know the status.'

'What do you mean, General?'

'Is this line secure, Admiral? Have you turned off the automatic recorder?'

'Now I have.'

'They asked two questions. Did Borzov die without telling anyone his RQ? Does anyone else on the crew know about Trinity?'

'You know the answers to both questions.'

'I wanted to be certain that you hadn't talked to Dr Brown. They insisted that I check with you before encoding my answer. What do you think this is all about?'

'I don't know, Michael. Maybe somebody down on Earth is getting nervous. Wilson's death probably scared them.'

'It certainly scared me. But not to the point that I would think about Trinity. I wonder if they know something that we don't.'

'Well, I guess we'll find out soon enough. All the ISA officials have been insisting that we should evacuate Rama at the first available opportunity. They didn't even like our decision to rest the crew for several hours first. This time I don't think they will change their minds.'

'Admiral, do you remember that hypothetical discussion we had with General Borzov during the cruise, about the conditions under which we would activate Trinity?'

'Vaguely. Why?'

'Do you still disagree with his insistence that we must know *why* the Trinity contingency is being called for? You said at the time that if the Earth thought great danger was imminent, you didn't personally need to understand the rationale.'

'I'm afraid I'm not following you, General. Why are you asking me these questions?'

'I would like your permission, Otto, when I encode the response to COG military headquarters, to find out why they are asking about the status of Trinity at this particular time. If we are in danger, we have a right to know.'

'You may request additional information, Michael, but I would bet that their inquiry is strictly routine.'

Janos Tabori awakened while it was still dark inside Rama. As he pulled on his flight suit, he made a mental list of the activities that would be required to transport the crab biot to the Newton. If the order to leave Rama was confirmed, they would be departing soon after dawn. Janos consulted the formal evacuation procedure stored on his pocket computer and updated it by adding the new tasks associated with the biot.

He checked his watch. Dawn was only fifteen minutes away, assuming of course that the Rama diurnal cycle was regular. Janos laughed to himself. Rama had produced so many surprises already that there was no certainty the lights would return on schedule. If they did, however, Janos wanted to watch the Raman 'sunrise.' He could eat his breakfast after dawn.

A hundred metres from his hut the caged crab biot was immobile, as it had been since it was hoisted away from its companions the previous day. Janos shone his flashlight through the tough, transparent cage wall and checked to see if there were any signs that the biot might have moved during the night. Having established that the biot had not changed position, Janos walked away from the Beta campsite in the direction of the sea.

As he waited for the burst of light, he found himself thinking about the very end of his conversation with Nicole the night before. There was something not quite right about her offhand revelation of the possible cause of General Borzov's pain on the night he died. Janos remembered vividly the healthy appendix; there was no doubt that the primary diagnosis had been incorrect. But why had Nicole not talked to him about the backup drug diagnosis? Especially if she was conducting an investigation into the issue ...

Janos reached the inescapable conclusion that Dr des Jardins had either lost faith in his ability or somehow suspected that he might have himself administered the drugs to General Borzov without consulting her. Either way he should find out what she was thinking. A strange idea, born from his own feelings of guilt, next crossed his mind. *Could it be*, he mused, *that Nicole somehow knows about the Schmidt and Hagenest project and suspects all four of us?*

For the first time, Janos himself wondered if perhaps Valeriy Borzov's pain had not been natural. He recalled the chaotic meeting the four of them had had two hours after David Brown had learned that he would be left onboard the Newton during the first sortie. 'You must talk to him, Otto,' a frustrated Dr Brown had said to Admiral Heilmann. 'You must convince him to change his mind.'

Otto Heilmann had then admitted it was unlikely General Borzov would change the personnel assignments based on his request. 'In that case,' Dr Brown had replied angrily, 'we can say goodbye to all the incentive awards in our contract.'

Throughout the meeting Francesca Sabatini had remained quiet and seemingly unworried. As he was leaving, Janos had overheard Dr Brown berating her. 'And why are you so calm?' he had said. 'You stand to lose as much as anyone else. Or do you have a plan I don't know about?'

Janos had glimpsed Francesca's smile for only a fraction of a second. But he had remarked to himself at the time that she had seemed oddly confident. Now, as Cosmonaut Tabori awaited dawn on Rama, that smile returned to haunt him. With Francesca's knowledge of drugs it would have been well within her capability to give General Borzov something that would induce appendicitis symptoms. But would she have done something so ... so blatantly dishonest, just to enhance the value of their postmission media project?

Again Rama was instantaneously flooded with light. As always, it was a feast for the eyes. Janos turned around slowly, looking in all directions and studying both bowls of the immense structure. With the light now brightly shining, he resolved to talk to Francesca at the first opportunity.

It was Irina Turgenyev, strangely enough, who asked the question. The cosmonauts were almost finished with their breakfast. Dr Brown and Admiral Heilmann, in fact, had already left the table to conduct another of their interminable conference calls with ISA management. 'Where's Dr Takagishi?' she said innocently. 'He's the last member of the crew that I would expect to be late for anything.'

'He must have slept through his alarm,' Janos Tabori answered, pushing his folding chair away from the table. 'I'll go check on him.'

When Janos returned a minute later he was perplexed. 'He wasn't there,' he said with a shrug of his shoulders. 'I guess he went out for a walk.'

Nicole des Jardins had an immediate sinking feeling in her stomach. She rose abruptly without finishing her breakfast. 'We should go look for him,' she said, her concern undisguised, 'or he won't be ready when we leave.'

The other cosmonauts all noticed Nicole's agitation. 'What's going on here?' Richard Wakefield said good-naturedly. 'One of our scientists takes a little morning walk on his own and the company doctor goes into panic?' He switched on his radio. 'Hello, Dr Takagishi, wherever you are. This is Wakefield. Will you please let us know that you're all right so that we can finish our breakfast.'

There was a long silence. Every member of the crew knew that it was an absolutely mandatory requirement to carry a communicator at all times. You could choose to turn off the transmission capability, but you had to listen under any and all circumstances.

'Takagishi-san,' Nicole said next with an urgent edge in her voice. 'Are you all right? Please respond.' During the extended silence, Nicole's sinking feeling in her stomach turned into a large knot. Something terrible had happened to her friend.

'I've explained that to you twice, Dr Maxwell,' David Brown said in exasperation. 'It makes no sense to evacuate part of the crew. The most efficient way to search for Dr Takagishi is to use the entire staff. Once we find him we will clear out of Rama with great haste. And to answer your last question, no, this is not a ploy on the part of the crew to avoid compliance with the evacuation order.'

He turned to Admiral Heilmann and handed him the microphone. 'Dammit, Otto,' he muttered, 'you talk to that bureaucratic nincompoop. He thinks he can command this mission better than we can, even though he's a hundred million kilometres away.'

'Dr Maxwell, this is Admiral Heilmann. I am in complete agreement with Dr Brown. Anyway, we really can't afford to argue with such long delay times. We are going to proceed with our plan. Cosmonaut Tabori will stay here with me at Beta and pack all the heavy equipment, including the biot. I will coordinate the search. Brown, Sabatini, and des Jardins will cross the ice to New York, the most likely destination if the professor went under his own power. Wakefield, Turgenyev, and Yamanaka will look for him in the helicopters.'

He paused for a moment. 'There's no need for you to respond to this transmission in a hurry. The search will already have begun before your next message will arrive.'

Back in her hut, Nicole very carefully packed her medical supplies. She criticized herself for not foreseeing that Takagishi might try one last time to visit New York. *You made another mistake*, Nicole said to herself. *The least you can do is make certain you're prepared when you find him.*

She knew the personal packing procedure by heart. Nevertheless, she skimped on her own supplies of food and water to ensure that she had whatever an injured or sick Takagishi might need. Nicole had mixed emotions about her two companions on the quest to find the Japanese scientist, but it never occurred to her that the grouping might have been purposely planned. Everyone knew Takagishi's fascination with New York. Given the circumstances, it was not surprising that Brown and Sabatini were accompanying her to the primary search area.

Just before Nicole left the hut, she saw Richard Wakefield at her door. 'May I come in?' he asked.

'Certainly,' she replied.

He walked in with an uncharacteristic uncertainty, as if he were confused or embarrassed. 'What is it?' Nicole asked after an awkward silence.

He smiled. 'Well,' he said sheepishly, 'it seemed like a good idea a few minutes ago. Now it strikes me as a little stupid – maybe even childish.'

Nicole noticed he was holding something in his right hand. 'I brought you something,' he continued. 'A good luck charm, I guess. I thought you might take it with you to New York.'

Cosmonaut Wakefield opened his hand. Nicole recognized the figurine of Prince Hal. 'You can say what you will about valour and discretion and all that, but sometimes a little luck is more important.'

Nicole was surprisingly touched. She took the little figurine from Wakefield and studied its intricate detail with admiration. 'Does the prince have any special qualities I need to know about?' she asked with a smile.

'Oh yes.' Richard brightened. 'He loves to spend witty evenings in pubs with fat knights and other unsavory characters. Or battle renegade dukes and earls. Or court beautiful French princesses.'

Nicole blushed slightly. 'If I'm lonely and want the prince to amuse me, what do I do?' she asked.

Richard came over beside Nicole and showed her a tiny keyboard just above Prince Hal's buttocks. 'He'll respond to many commands,' Richard said, handing her a very small baton the size of a pin. 'This will fit perfectly into any of the key slots. Try "T" for talk or "A" for action if you want him to show you his stuff.'

Nicole put the little prince and the baton in the pocket of her flight suit. 'Thank you, Richard,' she said. 'This is very sweet.'

Wakefield was flustered. 'Well, you know, it's no big deal. It's just that we've had a spate of bad luck and I thought, I mean, maybe—'

'Thanks again, Richard,' Nicole interrupted him. 'I appreciate your concern.' They walked out of her hut together.

34 STRANGE COMPANIONS

D r David Brown was the kind of abstract scientist who neither liked nor trusted machines. Most of his published papers were written about theoretical subjects because he abhorred the formality and detail of empirical science. Empiricists had to contend with instrumentation and, even worse, engineers. Dr Brown considered all engineers to be nothing more than glorified carpenters and plumbers. He tolerated their existence only because some of them were necessary if his theories were ever to be proved by actual data.

When Nicole innocently asked Dr Brown some simple questions about the workings of the icemobile, Francesca could not restrain a cackle. 'He has absolutely no idea,' the Italian journalist responded, 'and he couldn't care less. Would you believe that the man doesn't even know how to drive an electric cart? I've seen him stare at a simple food processing robot for over thirty minutes, trying without success to figure out how to use it. He would starve to death if nobody helped him.'

'Come on, Francesca,' Nicole replied as the two women climbed into the front seat of the icemobile, 'he can't be that bad. After all, he has to use all the crew computers and communication devices, as well as the image processing system on board the Newton. So you must be exaggerating.'

The tenor of the conversation was light and harmless. Dr David Brown slumped in the back seat and heaved a sigh. 'Surely you two exceptional women have something more important to discuss. If not, perhaps you could explain to me why a lunatic Japanese scientist takes off from our camp in the middle of the night.'

'According to Maxwell's assistant, that obsequious cipher named Mills, many people on Earth think our good Japanese doctor was kidnapped by the Ramans.'

'Come on, Francesca. Be serious. Why would Dr Takagishi decide to strike out on his own?'

'I have an idea,' Nicole said slowly, 'that he was impatient with the scheduled exploration process. You know how fervently he believes in the importance of New York. After the Wilson incident ... well, he was fairly certain that an evacuation would be ordered. By the time we come back inside, *if* we come back, the Cylindrical Sea may have melted and it will be more difficult to reach New York.'

Nicole's natural honesty was urging her to tell Brown and Sabatini about Takagishi's heart problems. But her intuitive sense told her not to trust her two companions. 'He just doesn't seem like the type to go off half-cocked,' Dr, Brown was saying. 'I wonder if he heard or saw something.'

'Maybe he had a headache or couldn't sleep for some other reason,' Francesca offered. 'Reggie Wilson used to prowl around at night when his head was bothering him.'

David Brown leaned forward, 'By the way,' he said to Nicole, 'Francesca tells me that you think Wilson's instability might have been exacerbated by the headache pills he was using. You certainly seem to know your drugs. I was extremely impressed by how quickly you identified the particular sleeping pill I had taken.'

'Speaking of drugs,' Francesca added after a short pause, 'Janos Tabori mentioned something about a discussion he had with you concerning Borzov's death. I may not have understood him correctly, but I thought he said that you believe a drug reaction may have been involved.'

They were driving steadily across the ice. The conversation had been even in tone, apparently casual. There was no obvious reason to be suspicious. *Nevertheless*, Nicole said to herself as she framed a response to Francesca's remarks, *those last two comments seemed too smooth. Almost practised.* She turned to look at David Brown. She suspected that Francesca could dissemble without effort, but Nicole was certain she would be able to tell from Dr Brown's facial expression whether or not their questions were rehearsed. He squirmed slightly under her unblinking gaze.

'Cosmonaut Tabori and I were having a conversation about General Borzov and we started speculating about what might have caused his pain,' Nicole said blandly. 'After all, his appendix was perfectly healthy, so something else must have been responsible for his acute discomfort. In the course of our conversation, I mentioned to Janos that an adverse drug reaction should be considered as one possible cause. It was not a very strong statement.'

Dr Brown seemed relieved and immediately changed the subject. However, Nicole's statement had not satisfied Francesca. *Unless I am mistaken, our lady journalist has more questions,* Nicole mused. *But she isn't going to ask them right now.* She watched Francesca and could tell that the Italian woman was not paying attention to Dr Brown's monologue in the back seat. While he was discussing the reaction on Earth to Wilson's death, Francesca was deep in thought. There was a momentary quiet after Brown finished his commentary. Nicole glanced around her at the miles of ice, the imposing cliffs on the sides of the Cylindrical Sea, and the skyscrapers of New York in front of her. Rama was a glorious world. She had a momentary pang of guilt about her distrust of Francesca and Dr Brown. *It's a shame that we humans are never able to pull in the same direction*, Nicole said to herself. *Not even when confronted by infinity.*

'I can't imagine how you have managed it,' Francesca said, suddenly breaking the silence. She had turned to address Nicole. 'Even after all this time, not even the tabloid videos have a legitimate lead. And it doesn't take a genius to figure out when it must have occurred.'

Dr Brown was completely lost. 'What in the world are you talking about?' he asked.

'Our famous life science officer,' Francesca replied. 'Don't you find it fascinating that after all this time, the identity of her daughter's father is still unknown to the public?'

'Signora Sabatini,' Nicole said immediately, switching to Italian, 'as I told you once before, this subject is none of your business. I will not tolerate this kind of intrusion into my private affairs—'

'I just wanted to remind you, Nicole,' Francesca interrupted quickly, also in Italian, 'that you have secrets you might not want exposed.'

David Brown stared blankly at the two women. He had not understood a word in the last exchange and was confused by the obvious tension. 'So, David,' Francesca said in a patronizing tone, 'you were telling us about the mood on Earth. Do you think we're going to be ordered home? Or are we merely going to abort this particular sortie?'

'The COG Executive Council has been called into special session for later this week,' he answered after a puzzled hesitation. 'Dr Maxwell's current guess is that we will be told to abandon the project.'

'That would be a typical overreaction from a group of government officials whose primary objective has always been to minimize the downside risk. For the first time in history, adequately prepared human beings are exploring the interior of a vehicle built by another intelligence. Yet on Earth, the politicians continue to act as if nothing unusual has happened. They are incapable of vision. It's amazing.'

Nicole des Jardins did not listen to the rest of Francesca's conversation with Dr Brown. Her mind was still focused on their earlier exchange. *She must think I have proof about the drugs in Borzov,* Nicole said to herself. *There's no other possible explanation for the threat.*

When they reached the edge of the ice, Francesca spent ten minutes setting up the robot camera and sound equipment for a sequence showing the three of them preparing to search the alien city for their missing colleague. Nicole's complaints to Dr Brown about the waste of time went unheeded. She did, however, make the fact that she was annoyed obvious by refusing to participate in the video sequence. While Francesca was completing her preparations, Nicole climbed the nearby stairway and studied the amazing city of skyscrapers. Behind and below her, Nicole could hear Francesca invoking the drama of the moment for the millions of viewers back on Earth.

'Here I stand on the outskirts of the mysterious island city of New York. It was near this very spot that Dr Takagishi, Cosmonaut Wakefield, and I heard some strange sounds earlier this week. We have reason to suspect that New

York may have been the professor's destination when he took off from Beta campsite last night to do some solitary and unauthorized exploration ...

'What has happened to the professor? Why does he not respond when called on the commpak? Yesterday we witnessed a terrible tragedy when journalist Reggie Wilson, risking his own life to save this reporter, was trapped inside the rover and was unable to escape the powerful claws of the crab biots. Has a similar fate befallen our Rama expert? Did the extraterrestrials who built this amazing vehicle eons ago perhaps create a sophisticated trap designed to subdue and ultimately destroy any unsuspecting visitors? We don't know for certain. But we ...'

From her vantage point on top of the wall, Nicole tried to ignore Francesca and imagine in what direction Dr Takagishi might have gone. She consulted the maps stored in her pocket computer. *He would have gone toward the exact geometrical centre of the city,* she concluded. *He was certain there was meaning in the geometry.*

35 INTO THE PIT

They had walked the bewildering maze of streets for only twenty minutes, but they would have already been hopelessly lost without their personal navigators. They had no thorough plan for the search. They simply wandered up and down streets in a quasi-random pattern. Every three or four minutes there would be another transmission from Admiral Heilmann to Dr Brown and the search party would have to look for a location where the signal strength was satisfactory.

'At this rate,' Nicole remarked as once again they faintly heard Otto Heilmann's voice on the communicator, 'our search is going to take forever Dr Brown, why don't you just stay in one spot? Then Francesca and I—'

'Break break,' they heard Otto more clearly as David Brown moved into a space between two tall buildings. 'Did you copy that last transmission?'

'Afraid not, Otto,' Dr Brown replied. 'Would you please repeat it.'

'Yamanaka, Wakefield, and Turgenyev have covered the bottom third of the Northern Hemicylinder. No sign of Takagishi. It's unlikely that he could have gone farther north, unless he went to one of the cities. In that case we should have seen his footprints somewhere, So you're probably on the right track.

'Meanwhile we have big news here. Our captured crab biot started to move about two minutes ago. It is trying to escape, but so far its tools have barely dented the cage. Tabori is working feverishly to build a larger, stronger cage that will go around the entire apparatus. I'm bringing Yamanaka's copter back to Beta so he can give Tabori a hand. He should be here in a minute – Wait.... There's an urgent coming through from Wakefield.... I'll put him on.'

Richard Wakefield's British accent was unmistakable, though he could barely be heard by the trio in New York. 'Spiders,' he shouted in response to a question from Admiral Heilmann. 'You remember the spider biot dissected by Laura Ernst? Well, we can see six of them just beyond the southern cliff. They're all over that temporary hut we built. And something has apparently repaired those two dead crab biots, for our prisoner's brothers are trundling toward the south pole ...'

'Pictures!' Francesca Sabatini screamed into the radio. 'Are you taking pictures?'

'What's that? Sorry, I did not copy.'

'Francesca wants to know if you're taking pictures,' Admiral Heilmann clarified.

'Of course, love,' Richard Wakefield said. 'Both the automatic imaging system in the helicopter and the hand camera you gave me this morning have been running without interruption. The spider biots are amazing. I've never seen anything move so fast ... By the way, any sign of our Japanese professor?'

'Not yet,' David Brown hollered from New York. 'It's slow going in this maze. I feel as if I'm looking for a needle in a haystack.'

Admiral Heilmann repeated the status of the missing person search for Wakefield and Turgenyev in the helicopter. Richard then said that they were coming back to Beta to refuel. 'What about you, David?' Heilmann asked. 'In view of everything, including the need to keep those bastards on Earth informed, don't you think you should return to Beta yourself? Cosmonauts Sabatini and des Jardins can continue the search for Dr Takagishi. If necessary we can send someone to replace you when the helicopter picks you up.'

'I don't know, Otto, I haven't—' Francesca turned off the transmit switch on David Brown's radio in the middle of his reply. He shot her an angry glance that quickly softened.

'We need to talk about this,' she said firmly. 'Tell him you'll call him back in a couple of minutes.'

Nicole was flabbergasted by the conversation that ensued between Francesca Sabatini and David Brown. Neither one of them seemed to be even slightly concerned about the fate of Dr Takagishi. Francesca insisted that she had to return to Beta immediately to cover *all* the breaking stories. Dr Brown was anxious because he was away from the 'primary' action of the expedition.

Each argued that his reasons for returning were more important. What if they both left New York? No, that would leave cosmonaut des Jardins alone. Maybe she should come with them and they could reinitiate the search for Takagishi when things calmed down in several hours ...

Nicole finally exploded. *'Never,'* she shouted suddenly at them, 'never in my life have I seen such egotistical ...' She could not think of a good noun. 'One of our colleagues is missing and almost certainly needs our help. He may be injured or dying, yet all you two can do is argue about your own petty prerogatives. It's really disgusting.'

She paused a second to catch her breath. 'Let me tell you one thing,' Nicole continued, still fuming. 'I am not going back to Beta right now. I don't give a damn if you order me. I am staying here and finishing the search. At least I have my priorities straight. I know a man's life is more important than image or status or even a stupid media project,'

David Brown blinked twice, as if he had been slapped in the face. Francesca smiled. 'Well, well,' she said, 'so our reclusive life science officer knows more than we have given her credit for.' She looked over at David and then back at Nicole. 'Will you excuse us for a moment, dear? We have a few matters to discuss in private.'

Francesca and Dr Brown moved over beside the base of a skyscraper about twenty metres away and began an animated conversation. Nicole turned the other way. She was angry with herself for losing her temper. She was especially irritated that she had revealed her knowledge of their contract with Schmidt and Hagenest. *They will assume Janos told me,* she thought. *After all, we have been close friends.*

Francesca walked back to join Nicole while Dr Brown radioed Admiral Heilmann. 'David is calling for the helicopter to meet him next to the icemobile. He assures me that he can find his way out. I will stay here with you and search for Takagishi. At least that way I can photograph New York.'

There was no emotion in Francesca's pronouncement. Nicole was unable to read her mood. 'One other thing,' Francesca added. 'I promised David we would conclude our search and be ready to return to camp in four hours or less.'

The two women hardly talked during the first hour of their search. Francesca was content to let Nicole choose the path. Every fifteen minutes they stopped to radio the Beta camp and obtain an updated fix on their position. 'You're now about two kilometres south and four kilometres east of the icemobile,' Richard Wakefield told them when they stopped for lunch. He had been delegated the job of keeping track of their progress. 'You're just east of the central plaza.'

They had gone to the central section first, for Nicole had thought that Takagishi would have headed there. They had found the open circular plaza with many low structures, but no sign of their colleague. Since then, Francesca and Nicole had visited the two other plazas and carefully combed the length of two of the central pie portions. They had found nothing. Nicole admitted she was running out of ideas.

'This is quite an astonishing place,' Francesca responded as she began to eat her lunch. They were sitting on a square metal box about a metre high. 'My photographs can barely begin to capture it. Everything is so quiet, so tall, so ... alien.'

'Some of these buildings could not be described without your pictures. The polyhedrons, for example. There's at least one in each slice, with the biggest one always right around the plaza. I wonder what they signify, if anything? And why are they located where they are?'

The emotional tension just below the surface in the two women remained suppressed. They chatted a little about what they had seen in their trek across New York. Francesca had been especially fascinated by a large trellis arrangement that they had found connecting two tall skyscrapers in the central unit. 'What do you suppose that lattice or net thing was all about?' she asked idly.

'It must have had twenty thousand loops and must have been fifty metres tall.'

'I guess it's ridiculous for us to try to understand any of this,' Nicole said with a wave of her hand. She finished her lunch and glanced at her companion. 'Ready to continue?'

'Not quite,' Francesca said purposefully. She cleaned up the remains of her lunch and put them in the garbage pouch of her flight suit. 'You and I still have some unfinished business.'

Nicole looked at her quizzically. 'I think it's time we took off the masks and faced each other honestly,' Francesca said in what was a deceptively friendly manner. 'If you suspect that I gave Valeriy Borzov some medication on the day that he died, why don't you ask me directly?'

Nicole stared at her adversary for several seconds. 'Did you?' she asked at length.

'Do you think I did?' Franceses replied coyly. 'And if so, why did 1 do it?'

'You're just playing the same game at another level,' Nicole said after a pause. 'You're not willing to admit anything. You just want to find out how much I know. But I don't need a confession from you. Science and technology are supporting me. Eventually the truth will be obvious.'

'I doubt it,' Francesca said casually. She jumped down from the box. 'The truth always eludes those who search for it.' She smiled. 'Now let's go find the professor.'

On the western side of the central plaza the two women encountered another unique structure. From a distance it resembled a huge barn. The peak of its black roof was easily forty metres above the ground and it was more than a hundred metres long. There were two especially fascinating features about the barn. First, the two ends of the building were open. Second, although one could not see into it from the outside, all the walls and the roof were transparent from the *inside*. Francesca and Nicole took turns proving that it was not an optical illusion, Someone inside the barn could indeed see in all directions except down. In fact, the adjacent reflective skyscrapers had been precisely aligned so that all the nearby streets were visible from inside the barn.

'Fantastic,' said Francesca as she photographed Nicole standing on the other side of the wall.

'Dr Takagishi told me,' Nicole said as she came around the comer, 'that it was impossible to believe that New York was purposeless. The rest of Rama? Maybe. But nobody could have spent this much time and effort without some reason.'

'You almost sound religious,' Francesca said.

Nicole stared quietly at her Italian colleague. *She's needling me now,* Nicole said to herself. *She doesn't really care what I think. Maybe what anybody thinks.*

'Hey. Look at this,' Francesca said after a short silence. She had walked a short way into the interior of the barn and was pointing at the ground. Nicole came up beside her. In front of Francesca a narrow rectangular pit was cut in the floor. The pit was about five metres long, a metre and a half wide, and quite deep, maybe as much as eight metres. Most of the bottom was in shadow. The walls of the pit were straight up and down, without any sign of indentation.

'There's another one over here. And another there ...' Altogether there were nine pits, each constructed in exactly the same manner, that were scattered over the south half of the barn. In the north half, nine small spheres rested on the surface in a carefully measured array. Nicole found herself wishing for a legend of some kind, an instructional guide that would explain the meaning or purpose of all these objects. She was starting to feel bewildered.

They had crossed almost the entire length of the barn when they heard a faint emergency signal on their communicators. 'They must have found Dr Takagishi,' Nicole said out loud as she rushed out one of the open ends of the barn. As soon as she was no longer underneath the roof, the volume of the emergency signal nearly shattered her eardrums. 'Okay. Okay,' she radioed. 'We can hear you. What's up?'

'We've been trying to call you for over two minutes,' she heard Richard Wakefield say. 'Where in the hell have you been? I only used the emergency signal because of its higher gain.'

'We were inside this amazing barn,' Francesca replied from behind Nicole. 'It's like a surrealistic world, with one-way mirrors and weird reflections—'

'That's great,' Richard interrupted, 'but we don't have time to chat. You ladies are to march forthwith to the closest spot on the Cylindrical Sea. A helicopter will pick you up in ten minutes. We'd come into New York itself if there was a place for us to land.'

'Why?' Nicole asked. 'What's the hurry all of a sudden?'

'Can you see the South Pole from where you are?'

'No. We have too many tall buildings in the way.'

'Something weird is happening around the little horns. Huge arcs of lightning are bouncing from spire to spire. It's an impressive display. We all feel something unusual is about to happen.' Richard hesitated a second. 'You should leave New York immediately.'

'Okay,' Nicole answered. 'We're on our way.'

She switched off the transmitter and turned to Francesca. 'Did you hear how loud the emergency signal was the moment we came out of the barn?' Nicole thought for several seconds. 'The material in the walls and roof of that building must block radio signals.' Her face now brightened. 'That explains what happened to Takagishi – he must be inside a barn, or something similar.'

Francesca was not following Nicole's line of thought. 'So what?' she said, taking one last panoramic image of the barn with her video camera. 'It's really not important now. We must hurry out to meet the helicopter.'

'Maybe he's even in one of those very pits,' Nicole continued excitedly. 'Sure. It could have happened. He was exploring in the dark. He could have fallen ... Wait here,' she said to Francesca. 'I'll only be a minute.'

Nicole dashed back inside the barn and bent down beside one of the holes. Holding the side of the pit with her hand, she shone the beam from her flashlight down into the bottom. Something was there! She waited a few seconds for her eyes to focus. It was a pile of material of some kind. She moved quickly to the next pit. 'Doctor Takagishi,' she yelled. 'Are you here, Shig?' she shouted in Japanese.

'Come on!' Francesca hollered at Nicole from the end of the barn. 'Let's go. Richard sounded very serious.'

At the fourth pit the shadows made it very difficult for Nicole to see the bottom even with the beam from her flashlight. She could make out some objects, but what were they? She laid down on her stomach and eased slightly into the pit at an angle to try to confirm that the shapeless mass below her was not the body of her friend.

The lights in Rama began flashing on and off. Inside the barn, the optical effect was startling. And disorienting. Nicole glanced up to see what was happening and lost her balance. Most of her body slid into the pit. 'Francesca,' she yelled, pressing her hands against the opposite wall of the pit for support. 'Francesca, I need some help,' Nicole shouted again.

Nicole waited almost a minute before she concluded that Cosmonaut Sabatini must have already left the barn area. Her arms were tiring rapidly. Only her feet and the very bottoms of her legs were safely resting on the barn floor. Her head was next to one of the pit walls about eighty centimetres below floor level. The remainder of her body was suspended in midair, prevented from falling only by her intense arm pressure against the wall.

The lights continued to flash off and on at short intervals. Nicole lifted her head to see if she could possibly reach the top of the pit with one of her arms, while holding her position secure with the other. It was hopeless. Her head was too deep in the hole. She waited several more seconds, her desperation growing as the fatigue in her arms increased. Finally Nicole made an attempt both to throw her body upward and to grab onto the lip of the pit in one connected motion. She was almost successful. Her arms could not stop her downward momentum when she fell. Her feet followed her body into the hole and she smacked her head against the wall. She tumbled unconscious to the bottom of the pit.

36 IMPACT COURSE

rancesca had also been startled when the lights of Rama had suddenly begun to flash. Her initial impulse had been to run inside, just under the roof of the barn. Once there, she felt slightly more protected. *What's going on now?* she thought as the reflected lights from the adjacent buildings forced her to close her eyes to keep from becoming dizzy.

When she heard Nicole's cry for help, Francesca started to rush over to help her fellow cosmonaut. However, she tripped on one of the spheres and banged her knee as she fell. When she rose, Francesca could see in the strobing light that Nicole's position was very precarious. Only the backs of Nicole's shoes were visible. Francesca stood quite still and waited. Her mind had already raced ahead. She had a nearly perfect image of the pits in her memory, including a fairly accurate assessment of the depth. *If she falls she'll be injured,* she thought, *maybe even killed.* Francesca remembered the smooth walls. *She won't be able to climb out.*

The flashing lights gave an eerie overtone to the scene. As Francesca watched, she saw Nicole's body rise barely out of the pit and her hands scramble for a hold on the lip. In the next flashes of light the shoes changed angle with respect to the pit and then abruptly disappeared. Francesca heard no scream.

If she had not controlled herself, Francesca would have hurried over to the pit and looked into it. *No,* she said to herself, still standing amid the small spheres, *I must not look. If by chance she is still conscious, she might see me. Then I will have no options.*

Already Francesca was thinking about the possibilities offered by Nicole's fall. She was certain, based on their earlier exchange, that Nicole intended to do her utmost to prove that Borzov had ingested a pain-inducing drug on the last day of his life. It might be possible for Nicole even to identify the particular compound and then eventually, since it was not common, to trace its purchase back to Francesca. The scenario was unlikely, even implausible. But it could happen.

Francesca remembered using her special permits to buy the dimethyldexil, along with a batch of other items, at a hospital pharmacy in Copenhagen two years earlier. At the time there had been a suggestion that the drug, in very small doses, could produce mild feelings of euphoria in highly stressed individuals. A single journal article in an obscure Swedish mental health publication the following year had contained the information that sizable doses of dimethyldexil would produce acute pain that simulated an appendicitis.

As Francesca walked rapidly away from the barn in a northerly direction, her agile mind worked through all the possibilities. She was performing her usual risk/reward trade-off. The primary issue she was facing, now that she had left Nicole in the pit, was whether or not to tell the truth about Nicole's fall. But why did you leave her there? somebody would ask. Why didn't you radio us that she had fallen and stand by until help could arrive?

Because I was confused and frightened and the lights were flashing. And Richard had sounded so very concerned about our leaving. I thought it would be easier for us to all talk together at the helicopter. Was that believable? Barely. But it was easy to keep straight. *So I still have the partial truth option,* Francesca thought as she passed the octahedron near the central plaza. She realised she had walked too far to the east, checked her personal navigator, and then changed her direction. The lights of Rama continued to flash.

And what are my other choices? Wakefield talked with us just outside the barn. He knows where we were. A search party would definitely find her.

Unless ... Francesca thought again about the possibility that Nicole might eventually implicate her in the drugging of General Borzov. The resulting scandal would certainly result in a messy investigation and probably a criminal indictment. In any case, Francesca's reputation would be sullied and her future career as a journalist would be seriously compromised.

With Nicole out of the picture, on the other hand, there was virtually zero probability that anyone would ever learn that Francesca had drugged Borzov. The only person who knew the facts was David Brown, and he had been a co-conspirator. Besides, he had even more to lose than she did.

So the issue, Francesca thought, *is whether or not I can make up a believable story that both reduces the chance Nicole will be found and does not implicate me if she is. That's a very difficult task.*

She was nearing the Cylindrical Sea. Her personal navigator told her that she was only six hundred metres away. *Dammit,* Francesca answered herself after thinking very carefully about her situation, *I don't really have a completely safe option. I will have to choose one or the other. Either way there's a significant risk.*

Francesca stopped moving north and paced back and forth between two skyscrapers. As she was walking, the ground underneath her feet began to tremble. Everything was shaking. She dropped to her knees to steady herself. She heard Janos Tabori's voice very faintly on the radio. 'It's all right, everybody, don't be alarmed. It looks as if our vehicle is undergoing a manoeuvre. That must have been what the warnings were all about ... By the way, Nicole, where are you and Francesca? Hiro and Richard are about to take off in the helicopter.'

'I'm close to the sea, maybe two minutes away,' Francesca answered. 'Nicole went back to check on something.'

'Roger,' Janos replied. 'Are you there, Nicole? Do you copy, cosmonaut des Jardins?'

There was silence on the radio.

'As you know, Janos,' Francesca interjected, 'communications are very spotty from here. Nicole knows where to meet the helicopter. She'll be along quickly, I'm certain.' She paused a moment. 'Say, where are the others? Is everyone all right?'

'Brown and Heilmann are on the radio with Earth. ISA management will be completely freaked out now. They were already demanding that we leave Rama before this manoeuvre began.'

'We're just boarding the helicopter,' Richard Wakefield said. 'We'll be there in a few minutes.'

It's done. I've made my choice, Francesca said to herself when Richard was finished. She was surprisingly elated. Immediately she began to rehearse her story. 'We were near the large octahedron in the central plaza when Nicole spotted an alley off to our right that we had not noticed before. The street leading to the alley was extremely narrow and she remarked that it was probably a region where communications could not penetrate. I was already tired – we had been walking so fast. She told me to go ahead to the helicopter ...'

'And you never saw her again?' Richard Wakefield interrupted. Francesca shook her head. Richard was standing on the ice next to her. Beneath them the ice was vibrating as the long manoeuvre continued. The lights were now on. They had stopped their flashing when the manoeuvre began.

Pilot Yamanaka was sitting in the cockpit of his helicopter. Richard checked his watch. 'It's almost five minutes since we landed here. Something must have happened to her.' He glanced around. 'Maybe she's coming out somewhere else.'

Richard and Francesca climbed into the helicopter and Yamanaka took off. They cruised up and down the island coast, twice circling over the solitary icemobile. 'Edge into New York,' Wakefield commanded. 'Maybe we'll be able to spot her.'

From the helicopter it was virtually impossible to see the ground in the city. The copter had to fly above the tallest buildings. The streets were very narrow and the shadows played games with the eyes. Once Richard thought he saw something moving between the buildings, but it turned out to be an optical illusion.

'All right, Nicole, all right. Where in the hell are you?'

'Wakefield,' Dr David Brown's sonorous voice sounded in the helicopter, 'I want you three to come back to Beta immediately. We need to have a meeting.' Richard was surprised to hear that it was Dr Brown. Janos had been the one monitoring their communication link since they had left Beta.

'What's the hurry, boss?' Wakefield replied. 'We still haven't made our scheduled rendezvous with Nicole des Jardins. She should be coming out of New York any minute.'

'I'll give you the details when you get here. We have some difficult decisions to make. I'm certain that des Jardins will radio when she reaches the shore.'

It did not take them long to cross the frozen sea. Near the Beta campsite, Yamanaka landed the helicopter on the shaking ground and the three cosmonauts descended. The remaining four members of the crew were waiting for them.

'This is one incredibly long manoeuvre,' Richard said with a smile as he approached the others. 'I hope the Ramans know what they're doing.'

'They probably do,' Dr Brown said sombrely. 'At least the Earth thinks that they do.' He looked carefully at his watch. 'According to the navigation section in mission control, we should expect this manoeuvre to last another nineteen minutes, give or take a few seconds.'

'How do they know?' inquired Wakefield. 'Have the Ramans landed on Earth and handed out a flight plan while we've been up here exploring?'

Nobody laughed. 'If the vehicle stays at this attitude and acceleration rate,' Janos said with uncharacteristic seriousness, 'then in nineteen more minutes it will be on an impact course.'

'Impact with what?' Francesca asked.

Richard Wakefield did some quick mental computations. 'With the Earth?' he guessed. Janos nodded.

'Jesus!' Francesca exclaimed.

'Exactly,' David Brown said. 'This mission has become an Earth security concern. The COG Executive Council is meeting at this very moment to consider all contingencies. We have been told in the strongest possible language that we must leave Rama as soon as the manoeuvre is completed. We are to take nothing except the crab biot and our personal belongings. We are—'

'What about Takagishi? And des Jardins?' Wakefield asked.

'We will leave the icemobile where it is, along with a rover here at Beta. They are both easy to operate. We will still be in radio contact from the Newton.' Dr Brown stared directly at Richard. 'If this spacecraft is really on an Earth impact course,' he said dramatically, 'our individual lives are no longer very important. The entire course of history is about to be changed.'

'But what if the navigation engineers are wrong? What if Rama has just happened to make a manoeuvre that momentarily intersects an Earth impact trajectory? It could be—'

'Extremely unlikely. You remember that group of short-burst manoeuvres at the time of Borzov's death? They changed the orientation of Rama's orbit so that an Earth impact could be achieved with one long manoeuvre at exactly the right time. The engineers on Earth figured it out thirty-six hours ago. They radioed O'Toole before dawn this morning to expect the manoeuvre. I didn't want to say anything while everyone was out looking for Takagishi.'

'That explains why everyone is so anxious for us to clear out of here,' Janos noted.

'Only partially,' Dr Brown continued. 'There is clearly a different feeling about Rama and the Ramans down on Earth. ISA management and the world leaders on the COG Executive Council are apparently convinced that Rama is implacably hostile.'

He stopped for several seconds, as if he were reassessing his own attitude.

'I think they are reacting emotionally myself, but I cannot persuade them differently. I personally see no evidence of hostility, only a disinterest in and disregard for a wildly inferior being. But the televised account of Wilson's death has done its damage. The world's populace cannot be here beside us, cannot grasp the majesty of this place. They can only react viscerally to the horror—'

'If you don't think the Ramans have hostile intentions,' Francesca interrupted, 'then how do you explain this manoeuvre? It can't be coincidence. They or it has decided for some reason to head for the Earth. No wonder the people down there are traumatized. Remember, the first Rama never acknowledged its visitors in any way. This is a dramatically different response. The Ramans are telling us they know—'

'Hold it. Hold it,' Richard said. 'I think we're jumping to conclusions a little too fast. We have twelve more minutes before we should start pushing the panic buttons.'

'All right, Cosmonaut Wakefield,' Francesca said, now remembering that she was a reporter and activating her video camera, 'for the record, what do you think it will mean if this manoeuvre does culminate in a trajectory that impacts the Earth?'

When Richard finally spoke he was very serious. 'People of the Earth,' he said dramatically, 'if Rama has indeed changed its course to visit our planet, it is not necessarily a hostile act. There is nothing, I repeat nothing, that any of us have seen or heard that indicates the species that created this space vehicle wishes us any harm. Certainly Cosmonaut Wilson's death was disturbing, but it was probably an isolated response from a specific set of robots rather than a part of a sinister plan.

'I see this magnificent spacecraft as a single machine, almost organic in its complexity. It is extraordinarily intelligent and programmed for long-term survival. It is neither hostile nor friendly. It could easily have been designed to track any incoming satellites and compute where the visiting spacecraft must have originated. Rama's orbit change to fly in the vicinity of the Earth might therefore be nothing more than its standard response to an encounter initiated by another spacefaring species. It may simply be coming to find out more about us.'

'Very good,' Janos Tabori said with a grin. 'That was borderline philosophical.'

Wakefield laughed nervously.

'Cosmonaut Turgenyev,' Francesca said as she changed the direction of the camera, 'do you agree with your colleague? Right after General Borzov died, you openly expressed some concern that perhaps some "higher force," meaning the Ramans, might have had a hand in his death. What are your feelings now?'

The normally taciturn Soviet pilot stared directly into the camera with her sad eyes. 'Da,' she said, 'I think Cosmonaut Wakefield is a very brilliant engineer. But he has not answered the difficult questions. Why did Rama manoeuvre during General Borzov's operation? Why did the biots cut Wilson to pieces? Where is Professor Takagishi?'

Irina Turgenyev paused a moment to control her emotions. 'We will not find Nicole des Jardins. Rama may be only a machine, but we cosmonauts have already seen how dangerous it can be. If it is heading for the Earth, I fear for my family, my friends, for all humanity. There is no way to predict what it might do. And we would be powerless to stop it.'

Several minutes later Francesca Sabatini carried her automatic video equipment out beside the frozen sea for one final sequence. She carefully checked the time before switching on the camera at precisely fifteen seconds before the manoeuvre was expected to end. 'The picture you are seeing is jumping up and down,' she said in her best journalistic voice, 'because the ground underneath us here on Rama has been shaking continuously since this manoeuvre started forty-seven minutes ago. According to the navigation engineers, the manoeuvre will stop in the next few seconds if Rama has changed course to impact the Earth. Their calculations are, of course, based on assumptions about Rama's intentions—'

Francesca stopped in midsentence and took a deep breath. 'The ground is no longer shaking. The manoeuvre is over. Rama is now on an Earth impact trajectory.'

37 MAROONED

When Nicole awakened the first time she was groggy and had great difficulty holding any idea fixed in her mind. Her head hurt and she could feel sharp pains in her back and legs. She did not know what had happened to her. She was barely able to find her water flask and take a drink. *I must have a concussion,* she thought as she fell back asleep.

It was dark when Nicole woke up again. But her mind was no longer in a fog. She knew where she was. She remembered looking for Takagishi and sliding into the pit. Nicole also remembered calling for Francesca and the painful, terrible fall. She immediately took her communicator from the belt of her flight suit.

'Hello there, Newton team,' she said as she stood up slowly. 'This is cosmonaut des Jardins checking in. I've been, well, indisposed might be a good word. I fell down into a hole and knocked myself out. Sabatini knows where I am ...'

Nicole broke off her monologue and waited. There was no response from her receiver. She turned up the gain but only succeeded in picking up some strange static. *It's dark already,* she thought, *and it had only been light for two hours at most ...* Nicole knew that the periods of light inside Rama had been lasting about thirty hours. Had she been unconscious that long? Or had Rama thrown them another curveball? She looked at her wristwatch, which showed time elapsed since the start of the second sortie, and did a quick calculation. *I have been down here for thirty-two hours. Why has nobody come?*

Nicole thought back to the last minutes before she fell. They had talked to Wakefield, and then she had dashed in to check the pits. Richard always did a navigation fix when they were in two-way lock and Francesca knew exactly ...

Could something have happened to the entire crew? But if not, why had nobody discovered her? Nicole smiled to herself as she fought the onset of panic. *Of course,* she reasoned, *they found me, but I was unconscious, so they decided,* ... Another voice in her head told her that her thought pattern didn't make sense. Under any circumstances, she would have been retrieved from the pit if they had found her.

She shuddered involuntarily as she feared, for a brief moment, that perhaps she would *never* be found. Nicole forced her mind to change subjects and began an assessment of the physical damage she had suffered during the fall. She ran her fingers carefully across all portions of her skull. There were several bumps, including a large one on the very back of her head. *That must have been responsible for the concussion,* she surmised. But there were no skull fractures and what little bleeding there had been had stopped hours ago.

She checked her arms and legs, then her back. There were bruises everywhere, but miraculously no bones were broken. The occasional sharp pain just below her neck suggested that she had either crushed part of a vertebra or pinched some nerves. Other than that, she would heal. The discovery that her body had survived more or less intact temporarily buoyed her spirits.

Nicole next surveyed her new domain. She had fallen in the middle of a deep but narrow rectangular pit. It was six paces from end to end and one and a half paces across. Using her flashlight and outstretched arm, she estimated the depth of the hole at eight and a half metres.

The pit was empty except for a jumbled collection of small metallic pieces, ranging in length from five to fifteen centimetres, that were stacked over at one end of the hole. Nicole examined them carefully under the beam from her flashlight. There were over a hundred altogether and maybe a dozen different individual types. Some were long and straight, others curved, a few jointed – they reminded Nicole of industrial trash from a modern steel mill.

The walls of the pit were absolutely straight. The wall material felt like a metal/rock hybrid to Nicole. It was cold, very cold. There were no anomalies, no wrinkles that might have been used as footholds, nothing that would encourage her to believe she could climb out. She tried to chip or scrape the wall surface using her portable medical tools. She was unable to make any mark.

Discouraged by the perfect construction of the pit walls, Nicole walked back to the metal pile to see if there was any way she could put together a ladder or scaffold, some kind of support that would elevate her to the point where she could climb out using her own strength. It was not encouraging. The metal pieces were small and thin. A quick mental calculation told her there was not enough mass to support her weight.

Nicole became even more discouraged when she ate a small snack. She remembered that she had brought very little food and water with her because she had wanted to carry extra medical supplies for Takagishi. Even if she rationed it carefully, her water would only last a day and her food no more than thirty-six hours.

She shone her flashlight directly upward. The beam bounced off the roof of the barn. Thinking about the barn reminded her again of the events preceding her fall. Nicole remembered the increased amplitude of the emergency signal once she exited the building. *Great,* she thought despondently. *The interior of this fantastic barn is probably a radio blackout zone. No wonder nobody heard me.*

*

She slept because there was nothing else to do. Eight hours later Nicole woke up with a start from a frightening dream. She had been sitting with her father and daughter in a lovely provincial restaurant in France. It was a magnificent spring day; Nicole could see flowers in the garden adjoining the restaurant. When the waiter had come, he had placed a plate of escargots smothered in herbs and butter in front of Genevieve. Pierre received a mountainous serving of chicken cooked in a mushroom and wine sauce. The waiter had smiled and left. Slowly it had dawned on Nicole that there was nothing for *her* ...

She had never dealt with real hunger before. Even during the Poro, after the lion cubs took her food, Nicole had not been seriously hungry. She had told herself before she slept that she would carefully ration her remaining food, but that was before the hunger pangs had become overpowering. Now Nicole tore into her food packets with trembling hands and just barely stopped herself from eating all the food that was left. She wrapped the paltry remainder, put it back into one of her pockets, and buried her face in her hands. Nicole allowed herself to cry for the first time since she had fallen.

She also allowed herself to acknowledge that starving to death would be a terrible way to die. Nicole tried to imagine what it would feel like to weaken from hunger and then ultimately to perish. Would it be a gradual process, each successive stage more horrible than the one before? *Then let it come soon*, Nicole said out loud, momentarily abandoning all hope. Her digital watch was glowing in the dark, counting off the last precious minutes of her life.

Several hours passed. Nicole grew weaker and more despondent. She sat with her head bowed in the cold corner of the pit. Just as she was about to give up completely and accept her death, however, from inside her there came a different voice, an assertive, optimistic voice that refused to let her quit. It told her that *any* time of being alive was precious and wonderful, that simply being conscious at all, *ever*, was an overwhelming miracle of nature. Nicole took a slow, deep breath and opened her eyes. *If I'm to die here*, she said to herself, *then at least let me do it with élan.* She resolved that she would spend whatever time remained concentrating on the outstanding moments of her thirty-six years.

Nicole still retained a tiny hope of being rescued. But she had always been a practical woman, and logic told her that what was left of her life was probably measured in hours. During her unhurried trip into her treasured memories, Nicole wept several times, without inhibition, tears of joy at the past recaptured, bittersweet tears because she knew, as she relived each episode, that it was probably her last visit to that particular portion of her memory.

There was no pattern to her wanderings through the life that she had lived. She did not categorize, measure, or compare her experiences. Nicole simply lived them again as they came to her, each old event transformed and enriched by her heightened awareness.

Her mother occupied a special place in her memory. Because she had died when Nicole was only ten, her mother had retained all the attributes of a queen or goddess. Anawi Tiasso had indeed been beautiful and regal, a jet-black African woman of uncommon stature. All Nicole's images of her were bathed in soft, glowing light.

She remembered her mother in the living room of their home in Chilly-Mazarin, gesturing to Nicole to come sit upon her lap. Anawi read a book to her daughter every night before bedtime. Most of the stories were fairy tales about princes and castles and beautiful, happy people who overcame every obstacle. Her mother's voice was soft and mellow. She would sing lullabies to Nicole as the little girl's eyes grew heavier and heavier.

The Sundays of her childhood were special days. In the spring they would go to the park and play on the wide fields of grass. Her mother would teach Nicole how to run. The little girl had never seen anything as beautiful as her mother, who had been an international class sprinter as a young woman, racing gracefully across the meadow.

Of course Nicole remembered vividly all the details of her trip with Anawi to the Ivory Coast for the Poro. It was her mother who had held her during the nights in Nidougou before the ceremony. During those long, frightening nights, the little girl Nicole had struggled with all her fears. And each day, calmly and patiently, her mother had answered all her questions and had reminded her that many many other girls had passed through the transitional rite without undue difficulty.

Nicole's fondest memory from that trip was set in the hotel room in Abidjan, the night before she and Anawi returned to Paris. She and her mother had discussed the Poro only slightly during the thirty hours since Nicole and the other girls had finished the ceremonies. Anawi had not yet offered any praise. Omeh and the village elders had told Nicole that she had been exceptional, but to a seven-year-old girl no appraisal is as important as the one from her mother. Nicole had summoned her courage just before dinner.

'Did I do all right, Maman?' the little girl had said tentatively. 'At the Poro, I mean.'

Anawi had burst into tears. 'Did you do all right? Did you do all right?' She had wrapped her long sinuous arms around her daughter and picked her up off the floor. 'Oh, darling,' her mother had said as she had held Nicole high above her head. 'I'm so proud of you that I could split.' Nicole had jumped into her mother's arms and they had hugged and laughed and cried for fifteen minutes.

Nicole lay on her back in the bottom of the pit, the tears from her memories rolling sideways across her face and down into her ears. For almost an hour she had been thinking about her daughter, starting with her birth and then going through each of the major events of Genevieve's life. Nicole was recalling the vacation trip to America that they had taken together, three years earlier when Genevieve had been eleven. How very close they had been on that trip, especially on the day they had hiked down the South Kaibab trail into the Grand Canyon.

Nicole and Genevieve had stopped at each of the markers along the trail, studying the imprint of two billion years of time on the surface of the planet Earth. They had lunched on a promontory overlooking the desert desiccation of the Tonto plateau. That night, mother and daughter had spread their sleeping mats, side by side, right next to the mighty Colorado River. They had talked and shared dreams and held hands throughout the night.

I would not have taken that trip, Nicole mused, beginning to think about her father, *if it hadn't been for you. You were the one who knew it was the right time to go*. Nicole's father was the cornerstone of her life. Pierre des Jardins was her friend, confessor, intellectual companion, and most ardent supporter. He had been there when she was born and at every significant moment of her life. It was he whom she missed the most as she lay in the bottom of the pit inside Rama. It was he with whom she would have chosen to have had her final conversation.

There was no single memory of her father that jumped out at her, that demanded renewal above all the rest. Nicole's mental montage of Pierre framed all the events of her own life. Not all of them were happy. She remembered clearly, for example, the two of them in the savanna not far from Nidougou, silently holding hands as they both wept quietly while the funeral pyre for Anawi burned into the African night. She could also still feel his arms around her as she sobbed without cease following her failure, at the age of fifteen, to win the nationwide Joan of Arc competition.

They had lived together at Beauvois, an unlikely pair, from a year after the death of her mother until Nicole had finished her third year of studies at the University of Tours. It had been an idyllic existence. Nicole roamed through the woods around their villa after she bicycled home from school. Pierre wrote his novels in the study. In the evening Marguerite rang the bell and called them both to dinner before the lady climbed on her own bicycle, her day's work complete, and returned to her husband and children in Luynes.

During the summers Nicole travelled with her father throughout Europe, visiting the medieval towns and castles that were the primary venues of his historical novels. Nicole knew more about Eleanor of Aquitaine and her husband Henry Plantagenet than she knew about the active political leaders of France and Western Europe. When Pierre won the Mary Renault Prize for historical fiction in 2181, she went with him to Paris to receive the award. Nicole sat on the first row in the large auditorium, dressed in the tailored white skirt and blouse that Pierre had helped her choose, and listened to the speaker extol her father's virtues.

Nicole could still recite parts of her father's acceptance speech from memory. 'I have often been asked,' her father had said near the end of his delivery, 'if I have accumulated any wisdom that I would like to share with future generations.' He had then looked directly at her in the audience. 'To my precious daughter Nicole, and all the young people of the world, I offer one simple insight. In my life I have found two things of priceless worth – learning and loving. Nothing else – not fame, not power, not achievement for its own sake – can possibly have the same lasting value. For when your life is over, if you can say "I have learned" and "I have loved", you will also be able to say "I have been happy".'

I have been happy, Nicole said as another group of tears ran down the side of her face, *and mostly because of you. You never disappointed me. Not even in my most difficult moment.* Her memory turned, as she knew it would, to the summer of 2184, when her life had accelerated at such a fantastic pace that she had lost control of its direction. In one six-week period Nicole won an Olympic gold medal, conducted a short but torrid affair with the Prince of Wales, and returned to France to tell her father that she was pregnant.

Nicole could remember the key events from that period as if they had happened only yesterday. No emotion in her life had ever quite matched the joy and exhilaration that she had felt when she was standing on the victory stand in Los Angeles, the gold medal around her neck and the cheers of a hundred thousand people echoing in her ears. It was her moment. For almost a week she was the darling of the world media. She was on the front page of every newspaper, highlighted in every major broadcast on sports.

After her final interview in the television studio adjoining the Olympic stadium, a young Englishman with an engaging smile had introduced himself as Darren Higgins and handed her a card. Inside was a handwritten invitation to dinner from none other than the Prince of Wales, the man who would become Henry XI of Great Britain.

The dinner was magical, Nicole recalled, her desperate situation in Rama temporarily forgotten. *He was charming. The next two days were absolutely wonderful.* But thirty-nine hours later, when she awakened in Henry's bedroom suite in Westwood, her fairy tale was suddenly over. Her prince who had been so attentive and affectionate was now frowning and fretful. As the inexperienced Nicole tried unsuccessfully to understand what had gone wrong, it slowly dawned on her that her flight of fantasy was over. *I was just a conquest,* she remembered, *the celebrity of the moment. I was unsuitable for any permanent relationship.*

Nicole would never forget the last words the prince had said to her in Los Angeles. He had been circling her while she was hurriedly packing. He could not understand why she was so distraught. Nicole had not replied to any of his questions and had resisted his attempts to embrace her. 'What did you expect?' he had asked finally, his frustration obvious. 'That we would ride off into the sunset and live happily ever after? Come on, Nicole, this is the real world. You must know that the English people would never accept a half-black woman as their queen.'

Nicole had escaped before Henry saw her tears. *And so, my darling Genevieve,* Nicole said to herself in the bottom of the pit in Rama, *I left Los Angeles with two new treasures. I had a gold medal and a wonderful baby girl within my body.* Her thoughts quickly skipped across the following weeks of anxiety to the desperate, lonely moment when she finally summoned her courage to talk to her father.

'I ... I don't know what to do,' Nicole had said tentatively to Pierre on that September morning in the living room of their villa at Beauvois. 'I know that I have disappointed you terribly – I have disappointed myself – but I want to ask you if it's all right. I mean, if I want to, Papa, can I stay here and try—'

'Of course, Nicole,' her father had interrupted her. He was softly crying. It was the only time Nicole had seen him cry since the death of her mother. 'We'll do whatever's right,' he had said as he pulled her into his embrace.

I was so lucky, Nicole thought. *He was so accepting. He never faulted me. He never asked anything. When I told him that Henry was the father and that I never wanted anyone else to know, least of all Henry or the child, he promised he would keep my secret. And he has.*

The lights came on suddenly and Nicole stood up to survey her prison under the new conditions. Only the centre of the pit was fully lighted; both the ends were in shadow. Considering her situation, she was feeling amazingly cheerful and upbeat.

She looked up to the roof of the barn and through it to the nondescript sky of Rama. Nicole thought about her last few hours and had a sudden impulse. She had not said a prayer in over twenty years but she dropped down on her knees in the full light in the middle of the pit. *Dear God,* she said, *I know it's a little late, but thank you for my father, my mother, and my daughter. And all the wonders of life.* Nicole glanced up at the ceiling. She was smiling and had a twinkle in her eye. *And right now, dear God, I could use a little help.*

38 VISITORS

The tiny robot strode out into the light and unsheathed his sword. The English army had arrived at Harfleur.

> Once more unto the breach, dear friends, once more,
> Or close the wall up with our English dead.
> In peace there's nothing so becomes a man
> As modest stillness and humility:
> But when the blast of war blows in our ears,
> Then imitate the action of the tiger ...

Henry V, new king of England, continued to exhort his imaginary soldiers. Nicole smiled as she listened. She had spent the better part of an hour following Wakefield's Prince Hal from the debauchery of his youth, on to the battlefields fighting against Hotspur and the other rebels, and thence to the throne of England. Nicole had only once read the three Henry plays, and that had been years before, but she was well aware of the historical period because of her lifelong fascination with Joan of Arc.

'Shakespeare made you into something you never were,' she said out loud to the little robot as she bent beside it to insert Richard's baton in the 'Off' slot. 'You were a warrior, to be sure, nobody would argue with that. But you were also a cold and heartless conqueror. You made Normandy bleed under your powerful yoke. You almost crushed the life out of France.'

Nicole laughed nervously at herself. *Here I am*, she thought, *talking to a senseless ceramic prince twenty centimetres high*. She remembered her feelings of hopelessness an hour earlier after she had tried one more time to figure out a way to escape. The fact that her time was running out had been reinforced when she had drunk the next to last swig of water. *Oh well*, she mused, turning back to Prince Hal, *at least this is better than feeling sorry for myself*.

'And what else can you do, my little prince?' Nicole said. 'What happens if I insert this pin in the slot marked C?'

The robot activated, walked a few steps, and finally approached her left foot. After a long silence Prince Hal spoke, not in the rich actor's voice he had used during his earlier recitals, but instead in Wakefield's British twang.

'C stands for converse, my friend, and I have a considerable repertoire. But I don't speak until you say something first.'

Nicole laughed. 'All right, Prince Hal,' she said after a moment's thought, 'tell me about Joan of Arc,'

The robot hesitated and then frowned. 'She was a witch, dear lady, burned at the stake in Rouen a decade after my death. During my reign the north of France had been subjugated by my armies. The French witch, claiming she was sent by God—'

Nicole stopped listening and jerked her head up as a shadow crossed over them. She thought she saw something flying above the roof of the barn. Her heart pounded furiously. 'Here. I'm here,' she shouted at the top of her voice. Prince Hal droned on in the background about how Joan of Arc's success had sadly resulted in the return of his conquests to the realm of France. 'So English. So typically English,' Nicole said as she once again inserted the baton in Prince Hal's off button.

Moments later the shadow was large and completely darkened the bottom of the pit. Nicole looked up and her heart caught in her throat. Hovering over the pit, its wings spread and flapping, was a gigantic birdlike creature. Nicole shrank back and screamed involuntarily. The creature stuck its neck into the pit and uttered a set of noises. The sounds were harsh yet slightly musical. Nicole was paralysed. The thing repeated almost the same set of noises and then tried, without success because its wings were too large, to lower itself slowly into the narrow pit.

During this brief period Nicole, her traumatic terror giving way to normal fear, studied the great flying alien. Its face, except for two soft eyes that were a deep blue surrounded by a brown ring, reminded her of the pterodactyls that she had seen in the French museum of natural history. The beak was quite long and hooked. The mouth was toothless and the two talons, bilaterally symmetrical about the main body, each had four sharp digits.

Nicole would have guessed the avian's mass at about a hundred kilograms. Its body, except for the face and beak, the ends of the wings, and the talons, was covered by a thick black material that resembled velvet. When it was clear to the avian that it would not be able to fly down to the bottom of the pit, it sounded two sharp notes, pulled itself up, and disappeared.

Nicole did not move at all during the first minute after the creature departed. Then she sat down and tried to collect her thoughts. The adrenaline from her fright was still coursing through her body. She tried to think rationally about what she had seen. Her first idea was that the thing was a biot, like all the rest of the mobile creatures that had been seen previously in Rama. *If that's a biot,* she said to herself, *then it's extremely advanced.* She pictured the other biots she had seen, both the crabs from the Southern Hemicylinder and the wide variety of weird creations filmed by the first Raman expedition. Nicole could not convince herself that the avian was a biot. There was something about the eyes ...

She heard wings flapping in the distance and her body tensed. Nicole cowered in the shadowy corner just as the light in the pit was again obscured by a huge hovering body. Actually it was two bodies. The first avian had returned with a companion, the second one considerably the larger. The new bird stuck its neck down and stared at Nicole with its blue eyes while it hovered over the pit. It made a sound, louder and less musical than the other, and then craned its neck around to look at its companion. While the two avians jabbered back and forth, Nicole noticed that this one was covered with a polished surface, like linoleum, but in all other respects except size was identical to her first visitor. At length the new bird ascended and the strange pair landed on the side of the pit, still jabbering. They observed Nicole quietly for a minute or two. Then, after a brief conversation, they were gone.

Nicole was exhausted after her bout with fear. Within minutes after her flying visitors departed, she was curled up and asleep in the corner of the pit. She slept soundly for several hours. She was awakened by a loud noise, a crack that resounded through the barn like the report of a gun. She woke up quickly, but heard no more unexplained sounds. Her body reminded her that she was hungry and thirsty. She pulled out what was left of her food. *Should I make two tiny meals out of this?* she asked herself wearily, *or should I eat it all now and accept whatever comes?*

With a deep sigh, Nicole decided to finish off her food and water with one last meal. She was thinking that the two combined might give her enough sustenance that she could temporarily forget about food. She was wrong. While Nicole was drinking the last sip of water from her water flask, her mind was bombarded with images of the bottled spring water that she and her family always had on the table at Beauvois.

There was another loud crack in the distance after Nicole had finished her meal. She stopped to listen, but again there was silence. Her thoughts were dominated by escape ideas, all of them using the avians in some way to help her out of the pit. She was angry with herself for not having tried to communicate with them while she had the chance. Nicole laughed to herself. *Of course, they might have decided to eat me. But who's to say starving to death is preferable to being eaten?*

Nicole was certain that the avians would come back. Perhaps her certainty was reinforced by the hopelessness of her situation, but nevertheless she started making plans for what she would do when they did return. *Hello,* she imagined herself saying. She would stand up with an outstretched palm and walk forcefully to the centre of the pit, right under the hovering creature. Nicole would then use a special set of gestures to communicate her plight: pointing repeatedly first at herself and then the pit would indicate that she couldn't escape; waving at both the avians and the barn roof would ask them for their help.

Two loud sharp noises brought Nicole back to reality. After a brief pause she heard still another crack. Nicole searched through the 'Environments' chapter in her computerized *Atlas of Rama* and then laughed at herself for not having recognized immediately what was occurring. The loud reports were the sound of the ice breaking up as the Cylindrical Sea melted from the bottom. Rama was still inside the orbit of Venus (although the last midcourse manoeuvre had placed it onto a trajectory whose distance from the sun was now increasing again), and the solar input had finally brought the temperature inside Rama to above the freezing point of water.

The *Atlas* warned of fierce windstorms, hurricanes that would be created by the atmospheric thermal instabilities following the melting of the sea. Nicole walked to the centre of the pit. 'Come on, you birds, or whatever you are,' she yelled. 'Come get me now and let me have a chance to escape.'

But the avians did not come back. Nicole sat awake in the corner for ten hours, slowly growing weaker as the frequency of the loud reports reached a peak and then gradually diminished. The wind began to blow. At first it was just a breeze, but it became a gale by the time the cracks from the ice breaking up had stopped. Nicole was completely discouraged. When she fell asleep again she told herself that she would probably not be awake more than once or twice more.

The winds pummeled New York as the hurricane raged for hours. Nicole huddled lifelessly in a corner. She listened to the howling wind and remembered sitting in a ski chalet during a blizzard in Colorado. She tried to remember the pleasures of skiing but she could not. Her hunger and fatigue had weakened her imagination as well. Nicole sat very still, her mind devoid of thoughts except for wondering occasionally what it would feel like to die.

She couldn't remember falling asleep, but then she couldn't remember waking up either. She was very weak. Her mind was telling her that something had blown into her hole. It was dark again. Nicole crawled from her end of the pit toward the end with the jumbled metal. She did not switch on her flashlight. She bumped into something and started, then she felt it with her hands. The object was big, as large as a basketball. It had a smooth exterior and was oval in shape.

Nicole became more alert. She found her flashlight in her flight suit and illuminated the object. It was off-white and shaped like an egg. She examined it thoroughly. When she pressed on it hard, it gave slightly under the pressure. *Can I eat it?* her mind asked, her hunger so severe that she had no worries about what it might do to her.

Nicole pulled out her knife and was able to cut it with difficulty. She feverishly chopped off a chunk and forced it into her mouth. It was tasteless. Nicole spat it out and started to cry. She kicked the object angrily and it rolled over. She thought she heard something. Nicole reached out and pushed it hard, rolling it over again. *Yes,* she said to herself, *yes. That was a sloshing sound.*

It was slow cutting through the outside with her knife. After several minutes Nicole retrieved her medical equipment and started working on the object with her power scalpel. Whatever it was, the object was made of three separate and distinct layers. The covering was tough, like the skin of a football, and relatively difficult to manipulate. The second layer was a soft, moist, royal blue compound the consistency of a melon. Inside, in the centre, were several quarts of a greenish liquid. Trembling with anticipation, Nicole stuck a cupped hand into the incision and pulled the liquid to her lips. It had an odd, medicinal taste, but it was refreshing. She drank two hurried swallows and then her years of medical training interceded.

Fighting against her desire to drink more, Nicole inserted the probe from her mass spectrometer into the liquid to analyze its chemical constituents. She was in such a hurry that she made a mistake with the first specimen and had to repeat the process. When the results of the analysis were displayed on the tiny modular monitor that could be affixed to any of her instruments, Nicole began to weep with joy. The liquid would not poison her. On the contrary, it was rich in proteins and minerals in the kinds of chemical combinations that the body could process.

'All right, all right!' Nicole shouted out loud. She stood up quickly and nearly fainted. More cautious now, she sat back down on her knees and began the feast of her life. She drank the liquid and ate the moist meat until she was absolutely stuffed. Then she fell into a deep, satisfied sleep.

Nicole's primary concern when she awakened was to determine the quantity of 'manna melon,' as she called it, that was available to her. She had been a glutton, and knew it, but that was in the past. What she needed to do now was to husband the manna melon until she could somehow enlist the aid of the avians.

Nicole measured the melon carefully. Its gross weight had originally been almost ten kilograms, but only a little over eight remained. Her approximate assessment indicated that the inedible outer portion comprised roughly two kilograms, leaving her six kilograms of nourishment split roughly evenly between the liquid and the royal blue meat. *Let's see*, she was thinking, *three liquid kilograms makes—*

Nicole's thought processes were interrupted as the lights came on again. *Yessirree*, she said to herself, checking her wristwatch, *right on time, with the same secular drift.* She looked up from her watch and saw the egg-shaped object for the first time in the full light. Her recognition was immediate. *Oh my God*, Nicole thought as she walked over and traced with her fingers the brown lines wriggling on the creamy-white surface. *I had almost forgotten*. She reached into her flight suit and pulled out the polished stone that Omeh had given her on New Year's Eve in Rome. She stared at it and then glanced over at the oval object in the pit. *Oh my God*, Nicole repeated.

She replaced the stone in her pocket and removed the small green vial, 'Ronata will know the time to drink,' she heard her great-grandfather say again. Nicole sat down in the corner and emptied the vial in one gulp.

39 WATERS OF WISDOM

Immediately Nicole's vision began to blur. She closed her eyes for a second. When she opened them again she was blinded by a riot of bright colours, streaming by her in geometrical patterns as if she were moving very fast. In the centre of her sight, way off in the distance, a black dot emerged from the background amid a brilliant set of alternating red and yellow forms. Nicole concentrated on the dot as it continued to grow. It rushed toward her and expanded to fill her vision. She saw a man, an old black man, running across the African savanna on a perfect starry night. Nicole clearly saw his face as he turned to climb a mountain of rocks. The man looked like Omeh but also, somewhat strangely, like her mother.

He raced up the rock mountain with amazing agility. At the top he stood in silhouette, his arms outspread, and stared into the sky at the crescent moon on the horizon. Nicole heard the sound of a firing rocket engine and turned to her left. She watched a small spacecraft descend to the surface of the moon. Two men in space suits started down a ladder. She heard Neil Armstrong say 'That's one small step for a man, one giant leap for mankind.'

Buzz Aldrin joined Armstrong on the lunar surface and they both pointed off to their right. They were staring at an old black man standing on a nearby lunar scarp. He smiled. His teeth were very white.

His face loomed ever larger in Nicole's vision as the lunar landscape behind him began to fade. He started to chant slowly, in Senoufo, but at first Nicole could not comprehend what he was saying. All of a sudden she realised that he was talking to *her* and that she could understand every word. 'I am one of your ancestors from long ago,' he said. 'As a boy I went out to meditate the night that people landed on the moon. Because I was thirsty, I drank deeply the waters from the Lake of Wisdom. I flew first to the moon, where I talked with the astronauts, and then to other worlds. I met The Great Ones. They told me you would come to bring the story of Minowe to the stars.'

As Nicole watched, the old man's head began to grow. His teeth became vicious, long, his eyes yellow. He transformed into a tiger and leapt for her throat. Nicole screamed as she felt the teeth upon her neck. She prepared to die. But the tiger became limp, an arrow was buried deep in its side. Nicole heard a noise and looked up. Her mother, wearing a magnificent flowing red robe and carrying a golden bow, was running gracefully toward a gilded chariot parked in the middle of the air. 'Mother wait,' Nicole shouted.

The figure turned. 'You were seduced,' her mother said. 'You must be more careful. Only three times can I save you. Beware of what you cannot see but know is there.' Anawi climbed into the chariot and took the reins. 'You must not die. I love you, Nicole.' The winged red horses arched higher and higher until Nicole could no longer see them.

The colour pattern returned to her vision. Nicole heard music now, first far off in the distance, then much closer. It was synthetic, like the sound of crystal bells. Beautiful, haunting, ethereal. There was loud applause. Nicole was sitting in the front row at a concert with her father. On the stage an Oriental man with hair down to the floor, his eyes fixed in a gaze of rapture, stood next to three odd-shaped instruments. The sound was all around her. It made her want to cry.

'Come on,' her father said. 'We must go,' As Nicole was watching her father turned into a sparrow. He smiled at her. She flapped her own sparrow wings and they were airborne together, leaving the concert behind. The music faded. The air rushed by them. Nicole could see the lovely Loire Valley and a glimpse of their villa at Beauvois. She was content to be going home. But her sparrow father descended instead at Chinon, farther down the Loire. The two sparrows landed in a tree on the castle grounds.

Beneath them, standing in the crisp December air, Henry Plantagenet and Eleanor of Aquitaine were arguing about the succession to the throne of England. Eleanor walked over under the tree and noticed the sparrows. 'Why hello, Nicole,' she said, 'I didn't know you were there,' Queen Eleanor reached up and stroked the sparrow's underbelly. Nicole thrilled to the softness of her touch. 'Remember, Nicole,' she said, 'destiny is more important than love of any kind. You can endure anything if you are certain of your destiny.'

Nicole smelled fire and sensed they were needed somewhere else. She and her father ascended, turning north toward Normandy. The fire smell grew stronger. They heard a cry for help and urgently flapped their wings.

In Rouen a plain girl with lights in her eyes looked up at them as they approached. The fire below had reached her feet, the first smell of burning flesh was in the air. The girl lowered her eyes in prayer as a makeshift cross was held above her head by a priest. 'Blessed Jesus,' she said, tears running down her cheeks.

'We'll save you, Joan,' Nicole shouted as she and her father dropped into the crowded square. Joan embraced them as they untied her from the stake. The fire exploded around them and everything went black. In the next instant Nicole was flying again, but this time as a great white heron. She was alone, inside Rama, flying high over the city of New York. She banked to avoid one of the avians, who regarded her with shock.

Nicole could see everything in New York in incredible detail. It was as if she had multispectral eyes with a wide-range of lenses. She could spot movement in four different places. Close to the barn, a centipede biot was trudging slowly toward the south end of the building. From the vicinity of each of the three central plazas, heat was emanating from underground sources, causing coloured patterns in her infrared vision. Nicole circled down toward the barn and landed safely in her pit.

40 ALIEN INVITATION

I must be prepared for rescue, Nicole said to herself. She had finished filling her flask with the greenish liquid from the centre of the manna melon. After carefully sectioning the moist melon flesh and putting the pieces in her old food container packets, Nicole sat back down in her usual corner.

Whew! she thought, returning to the wild mental excursion she had taken after drinking the contents of the vial. *What in the world was that all about?* Nicole recalled her vision during the Poro, when she was still a child, and the brief conversation about it that she had had with Orneh three years later when Nicole had returned to Nidougou for the funeral of her mother.

'Where did Ronata go?' Omeh had asked one evening when the old man and the girl had been alone together.

She had known immediately what he was asking. 'I became a big white bird,' she bad answered. '1 flew beyond the Moon and Sun to the great void.'

'Ah,' he had said, 'Omeh thought so.'

And why didn't you ask him then what had happened to you? the scientist in the adult Nicole asked her former ten-year-old self. *Then maybe some of this would make sense.* But somehow Nicole knew that the vision was beyond analysis, that it existed in a realm as yet unfathomed by the deductive processes that made science so powerful. She thought instead about her mother, about how beautiful she had been in her long flowing red robes. Anawi had saved her from the tiger. *Thank you, Mother,* Nicole thought. She wished that she had talked longer with her.

It was a weird sound, like dozens of unshod baby feet on a linoleum floor, and it was definitely coming in her direction. Nicole didn't have much time to wonder. Seconds later the head and antennae of a centipede biot appeared at the edge of her pit and, without slowing down in any way, proceeded directly down the wall at the opposite end.

Altogether the biot was four metres long. It clambered down the wall without difficulty, placing each of its sixty legs directly against the smooth surface and holding on by some kind of suction. Nicole put on her backpack and watched for her opportunity. She was not *that* surprised by the appearance of the biot. After what she had seen in her vision, she was certain that she was going to be rescued by some means.

The centipede biot consisted of fifteen attached, jointed segments, each with four legs, and an insectlike head with a bizarre array of sensors, two of which were long and thin and resembled antennae. The jumbled pile of metal at the other end of the pit was apparently its spare parts. While Nicole was watching, the biot replaced three of its legs, the carapace for one of its segments, and two knobby protruberances on the side of its head. The entire process took no more than five minutes. When it was finished, the biot started again up the wall.

Nicole jumped on the centipede biot's back when three-fourths of its body was heading upward. The sudden extra weight was too much. The biot lost its grasp and fell, along with Nicole, back into the pit. Moments later it tried again to scale the wall. This time Nicole waited until the entire length of the centipede was heading up the wall, hoping that the strength of the extra segments would make the difference. It was to no avail. The biot and Nicole collapsed into a heap.

One of its front legs had been severely injured during the second fall, so the biot made the necessary repairs before trying to ascend the wall a third time. Nicole, meanwhile, pulled all her strongest suture material out of her medical pack and tied one end of a long octuple thickness around the three back sections of the biot. In the other end of the suture thread she made a loop. After she first put on gloves to protect her hands and then fashioned a waistband to keep the thread from cutting, Nicole tied the loop around her waist.

This could be a disaster, Nicole realised as she imagined all the possible outcomes of her scheme. *If the thread does not hold, I could fall. The second time I might not be so lucky.*

The centipede inched its way up the wall as before. Several small steps after it was completely elongated, the biot felt Nicole's weight from below. This time, however, it did not fall. The struggling biot managed to continue slowly on its upward path. Nicole kept her body perpendicular to the surface, as if she were rock climbing, and held onto the suture thread with both her hands.

Nicole was about forty centimetres behind the last segment of the biot as they scaled the wall. When the head of the centipede reached the top of the pit, Nicole was almost halfway out. Her slow and steady climb continued as, segment after segment, a portion of the biot left the pit above her. A few minutes later, however, her progress slowed markedly, stopping altogether when the number of centipede segments remaining on the wall dropped to four. Nicole could almost touch the rear segment of the centipede if she stretched her arms above her. Only about one metre's length of the biot was still on the wall, but nevertheless it was apparently stuck. Nicole was putting too much strain on the joints attaching the rear segments.

Grim scenarios ran through Nicole's mind as she dangled more than six metres above the floor of the pit. *This is great,* she thought sarcastically, as she pulled tightly on the suture line and placed her feet firmly against the wall.

There are three possible outcomes, none of them good. The thread could break. The biot could collapse. Or I might remain suspended here forever.

Nicole considered her alternatives. The only plan she could conceive with even a reasonable probability of success, and it was still very risky, was for her to climb up the suture thread to the last segment and then, somehow using the body or legs of the centipede as handholds, to muscle her way to the top of the pit.

Nicole glanced down and remembered her first fall. *I think I'll wait awhile first and see if this machine gets moving again.* A minute passed. Then another. Nicole took a deep breath. She reached up high on the suture line and pulled herself up the wall. She repeated the process with the other hand. She was now right behind the last segment. Nicole reached out and grabbed one of the legs, but as soon as she tried to put any weight on it, it pulled free from the wall.

So much for that plan, she thought after a moment's fright. She had restabilized herself just behind the biot. Nicole studied the centipede again very carefully. The carapace of each segment was made of overlapping pieces. *It might be possible to grab one of those flaps ...* Nicole reconstructed her first two attempts to ride on the back of the biot. *It was the suction force of the feet that gave out,* she thought. *Now most of the biot is on the level ground above. It should be able to hold me.*

Nicole realised that once she was on the back of the biot, she no longer had any protection against falling. To test the concept, she pulled herself to the top of the suture line and grabbed the carapace flap. She was able to get a firm grip. The only question was whether the flap could support her weight. Nicole tried to assess its strength while holding onto the suture with her other hand for safety. So far, so good.

Nicole grasped the flap on the rear biot segment and cautiously pulled herself up. She released her grip on the suture thread. Then she wrapped her legs around the side of the centipede's body and scooted along until she could reach the next flap. The legs of the rear segment popped off the wall, but the centipede did not move otherwise.

She repeated the process twice more, moving from segment to segment. Nicole was almost at the top. While she was on her final climb, she had a brief scare when the biot slipped a few centimetres back into the pit. Holding on breathlessly, she waited until the biot was stable and then crawled forward to the first segment that was on level ground. As she was crawling, the biot began walking again, but Nicole just rolled off sideways and landed on her back on the ground. 'Hallelujah!' she shouted.

As she stood on the wall around New York and stared out at the rolling waters of the Cylindrical Sea, Nicole wondered why there had been no answer to her call for help. The self-test status flag on her radio indicated that it was working properly, yet she had tried three separate times without success to establish contact with the rest of the crew. Nicole was well aware of the commlinks available to the cosmonauts. Failure to receive a reply meant both that no crew members were within six to eight kilometres of her at present *and* that the Beta relay station was not operational. *If Beta were working*, Nicole thought, *then they would be able to talk to me from anywhere, even the Newton.*

Nicole told herself that the crew was doubtless on board their own space-craft, preparing for another sortie, and that the Beta communications station had probably been disabled by the hurricane. What bothered her, though, was that it had already been forty-five hours since the onset of the melting and more than ninety hours since she had fallen into the pit. Why was nobody looking for her?

Nicole's eyes scanned the sky for some sign of a helicopter. The atmosphere now contained clouds, as predicted. The melting of the Cylindrical Sea had substantially altered the weather patterns on Rama. The temperature had warmed up considerably. Nicole glanced at her thermometer and confirmed her estimate, that it was now four degrees above freezing.

The most likely situation, Nicole reasoned, returning to the question of the whereabouts of her colleagues, *is that they will return soon. I need to stay close to this wall so that I can be easily seen.* Nicole did not waste much time thinking about other, less likely scenarios. She considered only briefly the possibility that the crew had had a major disaster and nobody had yet been available to look for her. *But even in that case*, she said to herself, *I should follow the same approach. They would come sooner or later.*

To pass the time, Nicole took a sample of the sea and tested it. It had very few of the organic poisons found by the first Raman expedition. *Maybe they flourished and died while I was still in the pit*, she thought. *Anyway they're virtually all gone now.* Nicole noted to herself that in an emergency a strong swimmer might be able to make it across without a boat. However, she recalled the pictures of the shark biots and other denizens of the sea reported by Norton and his crew and slightly modified her assessment.

Nicole walked along the ramparts for several hours. While she was sitting down quietly eating her manna melon lunch (and thinking about methods she could employ to retrieve the rest of the melon, in the event that she still wasn't rescued in another seventy-two hours), she heard what she thought was a cry coming from New York. She thought immediately of Dr Takagishi.

She tried her radio one more time. Nothing. Again Nicole checked the sky for some sign of a helicopter. She was still debating whether or not to forsake her lookout on the wall when she heard another cry. This time she had a better fix on its location. She located the nearest stairway and walked south into the centre of New York.

Nicole had not yet updated the map of New York stored in her computer. After she crossed the annular streets near the central plaza, she stopped near the octahedron and entered all her new discoveries, including the barn with the pits and anything else she could remember. A moment later, while Nicole was admiring the beauty of the bizarre, eight-sided building, she heard a third cry. Only this time it was more like a shriek. If it was Takagishi, he was certainly making a peculiar noise.

She jogged across the open plaza, trying to close in on the sound while it was still fresh in her mind. As Nicole approached the buildings on the opposite side, the shriek sounded again. This time she also heard an answer. She recognized the voices. They sounded like the avian pair that had visited her while she was in the pit. Nicole became more cautious. She walked in the direction of the sound. It seemed to be coming from the area around the lattice nets that Francesca Sabatini had found so fascinating.

In less than two minutes, Nicole was standing between two tall skyscrapers that were connected at the ground by a thick mesh lattice that rose fifty metres into the air. About twenty metres above the ground, the velvet-bodied avian struggled against its trap. The avian's talons and wings were ensnared in the cords of the stringy lattice. It screamed again when it saw Nicole. Its larger companion, presently circling near the top of the buildings, dove down in her direction.

Nicole cowered against the facade of one of the buildings as the avian drew near. It jabbered at Nicole, as if it were scolding her, but it did not touch her. The velvet avian then said something and, after a short exchange, the huge linoleum bird withdrew to a nearby ledge about twenty metres away.

After she had calmed herself (and keeping one eye on the linoleum avian on its perch), Nicole walked over to the lattice and inspected it. She and Francesca had not had any time to spare when they had been searching for Takagishi, so this was Nicole's first chance for a detailed examination. The lattice was made of a ropelike material, about four centimetres thick, that had some elasticity. There were thousands of intersections in the lattice, and at each one of them there was a small knot, or node. The nodes were a little sticky, but not enough to make Nicole think that the whole lattice was some kind of spider web for catching flying creatures.

While she was studying the bottom of the lattice, the free avian flew over Nicole's head and landed close to its trapped friend. Being very careful to avoid becoming snared itself, it played with the individual strands with its talons. It also stretched and twisted the cords, with some difficulty. Next the linoleum bird gingerly stepped over to where its companion was trapped and made an awkward attempt either to break or untie the lattice links holding the other avian. When it was finished, the huge bird stepped back and stared at Nicole.

What is it doing? Nicole said to herself. *I'm certain that it's trying to tell me something... .* When Nicole did not move, the avian laboriously repeated the entire demonstration. This time Nicole thought she understood that the alien creature was trying to tell her that it couldn't free its friend. Nicole smiled and waved. Then, still staying at the bottom of the lattice, she tied a few of the adjacent cords together. When she subsequently untied them, the two avians shrieked their approval. She repeated the process twice and then pointed, first at herself and then at the velvet creature trapped above her.

There was a flurry of talk in their loud, sometimes musical tongue and the larger of the pair returned to his ledge. Nicole stared up at the velvet creature. It was caught in three different places; in each case its struggle had resulted in its being wedged more tightly in the elastic cord. Nicole surmised that the avian must have been caught in the violent hurricane winds and had been blown into the lattice during the preceding night. The cords had probably deformed under the momentum of the contact, and when they had snapped back to their normal size, the great bird was trapped in the mesh. It was not a difficult climb. The lattice was carefully anchored to the two buildings and the rope itself was heavy enough that Nicole did not sway very much. But twenty metres off the ground is a considerable height, taller than a normal six-story building, so Nicole was having some second thoughts when she finally reached the altitude where the avian was trapped.

Nicole was panting from the effort of her climb. She eased gingerly over to the avian to ensure that she had not misunderstood anything in their strange communication. The alien bird followed her fixedly with its huge blue eyes. One of the wings was snared very close to the avian's head. Nicole began trying to free the wing, first wrapping strands of the lattice around her own ankles to make certain that she would not fall. It was slow work. At one point Nicole caught a whiff of the creature's powerful breath. *I know that smell,* Nicole said to herself. It only took an instant for Nicole to connect the smell with the manna melon that she had been eating earlier. *So you eat the same thing?* Nicole thought. *But where does it come from?* Nicole wished that she could talk to these strange and wonderful creatures.

She struggled with the first knot. It was very tight. She was afraid she might injure the creature's wing if she pulled with more force. Nicole reached into her pack and retrieved her power scalpel.

Instantly the other avian was upon her, jabbering and shrieking and scaring Nicole half to death. It would not go away and permit her to proceed until Nicole moved away from the trapped bird and showed its companion how the scalpel could cut through the lattice cord.

Using the scalpel the freeing operation was completed quickly. The velvet avian soared into the air, its musical cries of happiness resounding throughout the area. Its companion joined in the celebration with shrieks of its own as the two played, almost like lovebirds, in the air above the lattice. They disappeared a moment later and Nicole climbed slowly down to the ground. Nicole was pleased with herself. She was ready now to return to the wall and wait for the rescue that she was certain was imminent. She walked toward the north, singing a folk song of the Loire that she remembered from her adolescence.

After several minutes Nicole had company again. More accurately, she had a guide. Whenever she would make a wrong turn, the velvet avian, flying overhead, would make an incredible racket. The noise would only cease when Nicole would go in the proper direction. *I wonder where we're going?* Nicole asked herself.

In the plaza area, not more than forty metres from the octahedron, the avian swooped down on an utterly unobtrusive portion of the metallic ground. It tapped its talons several times and then hovered over the spot. A covering of some kind slid away and the creature disappeared under the plaza. Twice it flew out, said something in Nicole's direction, and then descended,

Nicole understood the message. *I think I'm being invited home to meet the family,* she said to herself. *Let's just hope that I'm not the dinner.*

41 A FRIEND INDEED

Nicole had no idea what to expect. She was not fearful as she walked over and gazed at the hole in the ground. Curiosity was her dominant feeling. She worried momentarily that her rescue team might arrive while she was under the ground, but Nicole convinced herself that they would return later.

The rectangular cover was large, about ten metres long and six metres wide. When the avian saw that Nicole was following, it flew into the hole and waited on the third ledge. Nicole squatted beside the opening and stared into the depths. She could see some lights close by and more were flickering in the distance below her. She could not estimate accurately to what depth the corridor descended, but it was obviously more than twenty or thirty metres.

The downward climb was not easy for a non-flying species. The vertical corridor was essentially a large hole with a series of broad ledges along its sides. Each of the ledges was exactly the same size, about five metres long and one metre wide, and they were separated one from another by about two metres in depth. Nicole had to be very careful.

What light there was in the vertical corridor came from the opening to the plaza and some lanterns hanging on the walls every four ledges along the descent. The lanterns were enclosed in transparent wrappings that were very flimsy and paperlike. Each lantern contained a small, burning fire, together with some liquid substance that Nicole assumed was the fuel.

Nicole's velvet-bodied friend watched her patiently throughout the descent, always staying three ledges below her. Nicole had the feeling that if she were to slip, the avian would catch her in midair, but she didn't want to test her hypothesis. Her mind was running at a rapid pace. Nicole had already decided that the creatures were definitely not biots. That meant they were an alien species of some kind. *But they couldn't possibly be the Ramans,* Nicole reasoned. *Their level of technological development is totally inconsistent with this incredible spacecraft.*

Nicole remembered from her history courses the poor and backward Mayans found in Mexico by the conquistadors. The Spanish had deemed it impossible that the ancestors of those ignorant and impoverished people could possibly have built such impressive ceremonial centres. *Could that have happened here?* Nicole wondered. *Might these strange avians be all that is left of the master species that constructed this vehicle?'*

About twenty metres below the surface Nicole heard what sounded like running water. The noise increased as she dropped onto a ledge that was actually an extension of a horizontal tunnel heading off behind her. Across the vertical corridor Nicole could see a similar dark hallway going in the opposite direction, also parallel to the surface.

Her avian guide was, as usual, three ledges below. Nicole pointed down the tunnel at her rear. The creature flew up close to her and systematically hovered over each of the two ledges immediately below Nicole, making it perfectly clear that Nicole was expected to descend.

Nicole was not willing to give up so easily. She took out her flask and made a drinking motion. Then Nicole pointed behind her at the dark tunnel. The avian fluttered about, apparently weighing the decision, and then flew over Nicole's head into the blackness. Forty seconds later Nicole saw a light in the distance that continued to grow as it approached her. The avian returned carrying a large torch in one of its talons.

Nicole followed the avian for about fifteen metres. They came to a room, off to the left of the tunnel, that contained a large cistern full of water. Fresh water fell into the cistern from a pipe embedded in the wall. Nicole pulled out her mass spectrometer and tested the liquid. It was virtually pure H_2O; no other chemicals were present above one part in a million. Careful to remember her manners, Nicole cupped her hands and drank from the waterfall. It was unbelievably delicious.

After she had finished drinking, Nicole continued to walk down the tunnel in the same direction. The avian went into a frenzy, flying up and down and jabbering incessantly, until Nicole reversed her direction and returned to the main vertical corridor. When she renewed her descent, she noticed that the ambient light level had dropped considerably. Nicole glanced above her. The opening to the plaza in New York was now closed. *I hope that doesn't mean I'm here for good,* she thought.

Twenty metres more below the surface, another pair of dark horizontal tunnels ran perpendicular to the main corridor. At this second level the velvet avian, still carrying the torch, led Nicole down one of the horizontal tunnels for about two hundred metres. She followed the bird into a large, circular room with a high ceiling. The avian used its torch to light several wall lanterns around the room. Then it disappeared. It was gone for almost an hour. Nicole sat as patiently as she could, at first staring around the black room that reminded her of a cave or grotto. There were no decorations. At length Nicole began to concentrate on how she would inform the avians that she was ready to leave.

When her velvet friend eventually returned, it brought four associates. Nicole heard them flapping their wings in the hallway and jabbering intermittently. Her avian's companion (who Nicole assumed was a mate of some kind) and two additional linoleum-surfaced creatures flew in first. They landed and then awkwardly walked up very close to Nicole to conduct a visual examination. After they had sat down on the opposite side of the room, another velvet-bodied creature, this one brown instead of black, flew in last. It was carrying a small manna melon in its talons.

The melon was placed in front of Nicole. All of the avians watched expectantly. Nicole neatly cut a one-eighth section out of the melon with her scalpel, picked it up to drink a small draught from the greenish liquid in the middle, and then carried the remaining melon over to her hosts. They shrieked appreciatively, admiring the precision of the cut as they passed the melon among themselves.

Nicole watched the avians eat. They shared the melon, one with another, and at no time were any portions meted out. The two velvet avians were surprisingly deft and dainty with their talons, making as little mess as possible and leaving no waste whatsoever. The larger avians were much clumsier; their eating reminded Nicole of animals on Earth. Like Nicole, none of the avians ate the tough outer covering of the manna melon.

When the meal was over the avians, who had not talked at all while they were eating, huddled in a circle for several seconds. The huddle broke up after the brown velvet one jabbered something that sounded to Nicole like a song. One at a time, they then flew over for another close-up look at her and disappeared out the door.

Nicole sat quietly and wondered what would happen next. The avians had left the lights on in the dining room (or banquet hall, or whatever it was), but it was pitch black in the corridor outside. They clearly intended for her to stay where she was, at least for the time being. It had been a long time since Nicole had had any sleep and she was pleasantly full from the meal. *Oh well,* she thought to herself, curling up on the floor after a short internal debate, *maybe a short nap will refresh me.*

In her dream she heard someone calling her name, but it was very far away. She had to strain to hear the voice. Nicole woke with a start and tried to remember where she was. She listened carefully but didn't hear anything. When she checked her watch, she learned that she had been asleep for four hours. *I'd better get out of here,* Nicole thought. *It will be dark soon and I don't want to miss my chance to be rescued.*

She moved out into the hallway and switched on her small flashlight. Nicole reached the vertical corridor in less than a minute. Immediately she began scrambling up the ledges. Just below where she had stopped during her descent for a drink of water, Nicole heard a strange noise above her. She stopped to catch her breath. She leaned slightly into the gaping hole and shone her light above, in the direction of the sound. Something large was moving back and forth on the portion of the first level that jutted out into the vertical corridor,

Nicole cautiously climbed up to the ledge directly underneath the new phenomenon and crouched beneath it. Whatever it was, it was covering each square centimetre of the ledge in front of the tunnel entrance once every five seconds. There was no way Nicole could avoid it. She couldn't possibly pull herself up and then climb to the next ledge above in less than five seconds.

She moved down to one end of her ledge and listened intently to the sound above her. When the thing turned and went in the opposite direction, Nicole pulled her head over the edge of the next level. The object was moving rapidly on treads and looked altogether like an armored tank from the rear. She had only a brief glimpse, for the top half of the tank spun around quickly at the other end as it prepared to reverse its field.

One thing is certain, Nicole said to herself as she stood on the ledge below. *That tank is some kind of sentinel.* Nicole wondered whether or not it had any sensors – certainly it had given no indication that it had heard her – but decided that she couldn't afford to find out. *It wouldn't be much of a guard if it couldn't at least see an intruder.*

Nicole climbed slowly down the ledges to the dining room level. She was sorely disappointed and now angry with herself for having come into the avian lair in the first place. It still did not make sense to her that the avians might be holding her as a captive. After all, hadn't the creature invited her to visit after Nicole had saved its life?

Nicole was also puzzled by the tank sentinel. Its existence was baffling, and completely inconsistent with the level of technological development of everything else in the lair. What was its purpose? Where did it come from? *Curiouser and curiouser,* Nicole thought.

When she was back on the second underground level, Nicole looked around to see if there was any other way she could get out of the lair. There was an identical set of ledges on the opposite side of the vertical corridor. If she could jump across, then maybe ...

Before considering seriously such a plan, Nicole had to determine whether or not a tank, or equivalent sentinel, was guarding the opposite horizontal tunnel on the first level. She couldn't tell from where she was standing, so Nicole, muttering to herself about her stupidity, climbed back up the ledges on her side to obtain a good view across the corridor. She was in luck. The ledge in front of the opposite tunnel was empty.

By the time she returned to the second underground level again, Nicole was fatigued from all the climbing. She stared across the corridor and at the lights in the abyss below her. She would almost certainly die if she fell. Nicole was a very good judge of distance and correctly reckoned that it was about four metres from the edge of the ledge extension in front of her tunnel to the edge on the opposite side. *Four metres,* she mused, *four and a half at the most. Allowing for some room at both ends, I need a five-metre jump to clear it. In flight suit with backpack.*

Nicole remembered a Sunday afternoon at Beauvois four years earlier, when Genevieve was ten and both mother and daughter were watching the 2196 Olympics on television. 'Can you still jump a long way, Maman?' the little girl had asked, having a hard time picturing her mother as an Olympic champion.

Pierre had cajoled her into taking Genevieve to the athletics field adjacent to the secondary school at Luynes. Her timing had been way off in the triple jump, but after thirty minutes of warmup and practice Nicole had managed to long jump six and a half metres. Genevieve had not been that impressed. 'Mama,' her daughter had said while they were bicycling home through the green countryside, 'Danielle's big sister can jump almost that far, and she's only a university student.'

The memory of Genevieve stirred a profound sadness in Nicole. She longed to hear her daughter's voice, help her with her hair, or go boating with her on their small private pond beside the Bresme. *We never value enough the time we have,* she thought, *until they're no longer around.*

Nicole started back down the tunnel to where the avians had left her. She wouldn't try the jump. It was too dangerous. If she slipped ...

'Nicole des Jardins, where the hell are you?' Nicole froze the moment she heard the call, very faint, off in the distance. Had she imagined it? 'Nicole,' she heard again. It was definitely Richard Wakefield's voice. She ran back to the vertical corridor and started to shout. *No,* she thought rapidly, *that will wake them. It will not take me more than five minutes. I can jump ...*

Nicole's adrenaline was pumping at an incredible rate. She marked off her steps and soared across the chasm with plenty of room to spare. She climbed up the ledges at breakneck speed. Toward the top she heard Wakefield calling her again.

'I'm here, Richard. Below you,' she shouted. 'Underneath the plaza.'

Nicole reached the top ledge and started pushing on the covering. It wouldn't budge. 'Shit,' she shouted as the puzzled Richard paced around in the vicinity. 'Richard, come over here. Where you hear my voice. Beat on the ground.'

Richard began to knock hard on the covering. They were shouting at each other. The noise was deafening. From far below Nicole heard the flapping of wings. As the avians rose in the corridor, they began to shriek and jabber.

'Help me,' Nicole hollered at them as they drew close. She pointed up at the cover. 'My friend is out there.'

Richard continued to pound. Only the two avians who had originally found Nicole in the pit came up to where she was. They hovered around her, flapping their wings and jabbering back at the five others who were one level below. The creatures were apparently having an argument, for the black velvet avian twice extended its neck down toward its associates and uttered a fearsome screech.

The covering suddenly opened. Richard had to scramble to keep from falling in. When he looked down into the hole he saw Nicole and two gigantic bird creatures, one of which flew right by him as Nicole crawled out of the opening. *'Bloody hell!'* he exclaimed, his eyes following the flight of the avian.

Nicole was overcome with joy. She ran into Wakefield's arms. 'Richard, oh Richard,' she said, 'I'm so glad to see you.'

He grinned at her and returned the hug. 'If I had known you felt like this,' he said, 'I would have come earlier.'

42 TWO EXPLORERS

'Let me get this straight.. You're telling me that you're *alone?* And we have no way to cross the Cylindrical Sea?'

Richard nodded. It was too much for Nicole. Five minutes earlier she had been exultant. Her ordeal had finally been over. She had imagined returning to the Earth and seeing her father and daughter again. Now he was telling her ...

She walked away quickly and leaned her head against one of the buildings surrounding the plaza. Tears rolled down her cheeks as she gave vent to her disappointment. Richard followed her at a distance.

'I'm sorry,' he said.

'It's not your fault,' Nicole replied after she had regained her composure. 'It just never occurred to me that I might see one of the crew again and *still* not be rescued ...' She stopped herself. It was not fair for her to make Richard suffer. She walked over to him and forced a smile.

'I'm not usually this emotional,' Nicole said. 'And I interrupted your story right in the middle.' She paused a second to wipe her eyes. 'You were telling me about the shark biots chasing the motorboat. You saw them first when you were about halfway across the sea?'

'More or less,' Richard replied. Her disappointment had subdued him. He tried a nervous laugh. 'Do you remember, after one of the simulations, when the review board criticized us for not having sent a pilotless version of our motorboat into the water first, just to make sure that there wasn't something peculiar to the new design that would disturb the "ecological equilibrium" in some way? Well, I thought their suggestion at the time was ridiculous. Now I'm not so certain. Those shark biots hardly bothered the Newton vessels, but they were definitely angry about my high-speed motorboat.'

Richard and Nicole had sat down together on one of the grey metal boxes that dotted the plaza area. 'I managed to dodge them once,' Richard continued, 'but I was extremely lucky. When I had no other choice I simply jumped out and swam. Fortunately for me, they were mostly after the boat. I didn't see one again while I was swimming until I was only a hundred metres from shore.'

'How long have you been inside Rama altogether now?' Nicole asked.

'About seventeen hours. I left the Newton two hours after dawn. I spent

404

too much damn time trying to repair the communications station at Beta. But it was impossible.'

Nicole felt his flight suit. 'Except for your hair, I can't even tell you've been wet.'

Richard laughed. 'Ob, the miracles of fabric engineering. Would you believe that this suit was almost dry by the time I changed my thermals? By then I was having a hard time convincing even myself that I had spent that twenty minutes swimming in the cold water.' He looked at his companion. She was loosening up very slowly. 'But I'm surprised at you, Cosmonaut des Jardins. You haven't even asked me the most important question. How did I know where you were?'

Nicole had pulled out her scanner and was reading Richard's biometry. Everything was within tolerances, despite his recent harrowing swim. She was a little slow to understand his question. 'You *knew* where I was?' she said finally, knitting her brow. 'I figured you were just wandering around—'

'Come on, lady. New York is small, but not *that* small. There's twenty-five square kilometres of territory inside these walls. And radio around here is completely unreliable.' He grinned. 'Let's see, if I stood and called your name in each square metre, I would have to call you twenty-five million times. At one call every ten seconds – allowing myself time to listen for a response and move to the next square metre – that would be six calls a minute. So it would take four million minutes, which is slightly more than sixty thousand hours, or twenty-five hundred Earth days—'

'Okay. Okay,' Nicole interrupted. She was finally laughing. 'Tell me how you knew where I was.'

Richard stood up. 'May I?' he said dramatically, extending his fingers toward the breast pocket of Nicole's flight suit.

'I suppose so,' she answered. 'Although I can't imagine what ...'

Richard reached into her pocket and pulled out Prince Hal. 'He led me to you,' Wakefield said. 'You're a good man, my prince, but for a while I thought you'd failed me.'

Nicole had no idea what Richard was talking about. 'Prince Hal and Falstaff have matching navigation beacons,' he explained. 'They put out fifteen strong pulses a second. With Falstaff fixed in my hut at Beta and with an equivalent transceiver over at Alpha campsite, I could follow you by triangulation. So I knew exactly where you were – at least in terms of x-y coordinates. My simple tracking algorithm wasn't designed for excursions in z.'

'That's what an engineer would call my visit to the avian lair?' Nicole said with another smile. 'An excursion in z?'

'That's one way of describing it.'

Nicole shook her head. 'I don't know about you, Wakefield. If you really knew where I was all this time, why the hell did you wait so long—'

'Because we lost you, or thought we had, before we found you ... after I came back to retrieve Falstaff.'

'Have I become a dullard in the last week, or is this roundabout explanation incredibly confusing?'

It was Richard's turn to laugh. 'Maybe I should try to make my presentation more orderly.' He paused to arrange his mental notes. 'I was really irritated,' he began, 'back in June when the Engineering Steering Group decided not to use navigation beacons as backup personnel locators. I had argued, unsuccessfully, that there might be emergency situations, or unforeseen circumstances, in which the signal-to-noise ratio on the regular voice link would be below threshold. So I equipped three of my own robots just in case ...'

Nicole studied Richard Wakefield while he talked. She had forgotten that he was both amazing and amusing. She was certain that if she asked the right questions, he could talk on this subject alone for a full hour.

'... Then Falstaff lost the signal,' he was saying. 'I wasn't present myself at the time, for I was preparing to come with Hiro Yamanaka to pick you and Francesca up in the helicopter, But Falstaff has a small recorder and timetags all the data. After you didn't show up, I replayed the data from the recorder and found that the signal had abruptly disappeared.

'It came back on only briefly, while we were talking on the radio a few minutes later, but several seconds after our last conversation the signal was gone for good. The signature suggested a hardware failure to me. I thought Prince Hal had malfunctioned. When Francesca said that you had been with her up until the plaza, then I was virtually certain that Prince Hal—'

Nicole had only been listening with one ear but she bolted to attention when Richard mentioned Francesca. 'Stop,' Nicole interrupted, holding up her hand. 'What did you say she told you?'

'That you and she had left the barn together and that you had walked away from her several minutes later to look for Takagishi ...'

'That's complete bullshit,' Nicole said.

'What do you mean?' Richard asked.

'It's a lie. An absolute and total untruth. I fell into that pit I told you about while Francesca was there, or at least no more than a minute after she left. She never saw me again.'

Richard thought for a moment. 'That explains why Falstaff lost you. You were in the barn all that time and the signal was blocked.' Now it was his turn to be puzzled. 'But why would Francesca make up such a story?'

That's what I would like to know, Nicole thought to herself. *She must have poisoned Borzov on purpose. Otherwise why would she deliberately ...*

'Was there something between the two of you?' Richard was saying. 'I always thought I detected—'

'Probably some jealousy,' Nicole interrupted, 'going both ways. Francesca and I are light years apart.'

'You can say that again,' Richard said with a chuckle. 'I've spent the better part of a year giving off signals that I find you intelligent and interesting and attractive. Yet I've never received anything but a restrained and courteous professional response. Francesca, on the other hand, notices if you happen to look at her with your head tilted sideways.'

'There are other, more substantive differences,' Nicole replied, not altogether displeased that Richard had finally verbalised his interest in her as a woman.

There was a momentary pause in the conversation. Nicole glanced at her watch. 'But I don't want to spend any more time talking about Francesca Sabatini,' she said, 'it's going to be dark again in an hour and we have an escape from this island to plan. We also have certain, uh, logistical issues to address, such as food, water, and other unmentionable items that made confinement in a small pit reasonably disgusting.'

'I brought a portable hut – if we need one.'

'That's great,' Nicole replied. 'I'll remember that when it rains.' She reached automatically into her backpack for some manna melon but did not pull it out. 'By the way,' she said to Richard, 'did you bring any *human* food?'

The hut came in handy when they were ready for sleep. They decided to pitch it just to the side of the central plaza. Nicole felt safer being close to the avians. In some sense they were her friends and they might help if an emergency arose. They were also the only known source of food. Between them, Richard and Nicole had barely enough food and water to last for another two Raman days.

Nicole had not objected to Richard's suggestion that they share the hut. He had gallantly offered to sleep outside, 'if that would make you more comfortable,' but the huts were plenty large enough for two sleeping mats as long as there were no other furnishings. Lying about half a metre apart made their conversation very easy. Nicole gave a detailed rendition of her hours alone, omitting only the part about the vial and the vision. That was too personal for her to share. Richard was fascinated by her entire story and absolutely intrigued by the avians.

'I mean, look,' he said, propping his head up on his elbow, 'try to figure out how the hell they got here. From what you've said, except for that tank sentinel – and I completely agree with you that it's an anomaly – they're no more advanced than prehistoric man. What a boggle it would be to learn their secret.

'You can't rule out completely that they're biots,' he continued, barely able to contain his enthusiasm. 'They might not be impressive as biology, but Jesus, as artificial intelligence they would be state of the art.' He sat up on his mat. 'Just think about what it would mean either way. We must find out all these answers. You're a linguist – maybe you could learn to talk to them.'

Nicole was amused. 'Has it occurred to you, Richard,' she asked, 'that all of this discussion will be academic if nobody ever rescues us?'

'A couple of times,' Richard said with a laugh. He was lying down again. 'That damn Heilmann took me aside, right before I came back inside Rama, and told me that I was acting "in violation of all procedures" by returning here. He promised me that they would not come after me under *any* circumstances.'

'So why did you come back?'

'I'm not completely certain,' he said slowly. 'I know I wanted to pick up Falstaff and see if, by some wild happenstance, he had ever received any more signals from your beacon. But I think there were other reasons. The mission was becoming more politics than science. It was obvious to me that the bureaucrats on Earth were going to abort the mission, "for security reasons", and the crew was not going to return to Rama. I knew the political discussions would continue for another day or two.' He paused a second. 'And I wanted one last look at the most incredible sight of my life.'

Nicole was quiet for a moment. 'You obviously weren't afraid,' she said softly, 'because you show no sign of fear even now. Doesn't the thought of being left to die on board Rama bother you at all?'

'A little,' Richard answered. 'But dying in an exciting situation is much better than living in a boring one.' Again he propped himself up on his elbow. 'I have been looking forward to this mission for three years. I thought from the beginning that I had a good chance of being selected. Except for my robots and Shakespeare, there is nothing in my life but my work. I have no family or friends to think of ...'

His voice trailed off. 'And I'm as much afraid of going back as I am of dying. At least Richard Wakefield, Newton cosmonaut, has a clearly defined purpose.' He started to say something else but stopped himself. Richard lay back down and closed his eyes.

43 EXOBIOLOGICAL PSYCHOLOGY

/'There's another reason not to give up hope,' Richard said cheerfully as soon as he saw Nicole open her eyes, 'and I forgot to mention it last night.'

Nicole had always awakened very slowly. Even as a child. She liked to savour the last part of her dream state before confronting harsh reality. At home Genevieve and Pierre both knew not to talk to her about anything important until after she had had her morning coffee. She blinked at Richard, who was shining his small flashlight in the gap between them.

'This space vehicle is now headed for the Earth,' he said. 'Even if the Newton leaves, there might be another human spacecraft here sooner or later.'

'What's that?' Nicole said, sitting up and rubbing her eyes.

'In all the excitement last night,' Richard replied, 'I left out one of the most important points. The manoeuvre – I guess you missed it because you were unconscious at the bottom of that pit – put Rama on an Earth impact course. That made our evacuation imperative.'

Richard noticed that Nicole was staring at him as if he had lost his mind. 'The spaceship is still on a hyperbola with respect to the Sun,' he clarified, 'but it's blasting full speed toward the Earth. We will impact in twenty-three days.'

'Richard,' Nicole said, longing intensely for that fresh cup of coffee, 'I do not like jokes early in the morning. If you have spent your energy making up—'

'No, no,' he interrupted. 'I'm serious. It's true. Believe me.'

Nicole pulled out her pocket thermometer and checked it. 'Then tell me, my engineering genius, why is the temperature in here still increasing? If we are now going away from the Sun, shouldn't it be dropping?'

'You're smarter than that, Nicole.' Richard shook his head. 'The thermal input from the Sun on the exterior of Rama diffuses very slowly through the outer shell and then into the interior. The thermal conductivity is obviously very low. I wouldn't expect the temperatures to reach a peak for another two weeks at least.'

Nicole remembered enough of her basic thermodynamics to realise he was making sense. It was too early in the morning for thermal diffusion. Nicole struggled with the idea that Rama was now bound for the Earth, She asked Richard for a drink of water. *What is going on here?* she thought. *Why is Rama now headed for our planet?*

Richard must have been reading her mind. 'You should have heard the silly discussions about why Rama had changed its trajectory and what it was likely to do. There was a seven-hour conference call on the subject.'

He laughed out loud. 'The ISA has an employee – a Canadian, I think – whose specialty is exobiological psychology. Can you believe it? This jerk actually participated in the conference call and offered insights into the motives behind the Raman manoeuvre.' Richard shook his head vigorously. 'All bureaucracies are the same. They drain the life out of the truly creative people and develop mindless paper-pushers as their critical mass.'

'What was the final result of the call?' Nicole asked after a short silence.

'Most of the sane people guessed that Rama would go into orbit around the Earth and conduct passive remote observations. But they were in the minority. Sanity and logic took a holiday, in my opinion. Even David Brown – who acted very strangely, it seemed to me, after we returned to the Newton – acknowledged that there was a high probability that Rama would do something hostile. He clarified his position by stating that it would *not*, in reality, be a hostile act; however, its attempt to learn more about the Earth might result in actions that would be *perceived* by us as hostile.'

The agitated Richard was now standing up. 'Have you ever heard such gobbledygook in your life? And Dr Brown was one of the more coherent speakers. The entire ISA Advisory Board was polled as to which of the projected scenarios each of them favoured. Do you think that bunch of plenipotentiaries could respond simply with "I believe in Option A, direct impact with resultant destruction and climate alteration", or "I favour Option C, Earth orbit with bellicose intentions"? Hell no! Each one of them had to deliver a lecture of some kind. That weird Dr Alexander, the one who asked you all the questions after your open biometry meeting in November, even spent fifteen minutes explaining how Rama's existence had exposed a flaw in the ISA charter. As if anybody gave a shit!' Richard sat down again and put his hands on his cheeks. 'The whole thing was unbelievable.'

Nicole was now fully awake. 'I assume,' she said, sitting up on her mat, 'judging from your obvious irritation, that you disagreed with the consensus.'

Richard nodded. 'Almost three-fourths of the large group participating in the call – which included all the Newton cosmonauts as well as most of the senior scientists and executives in the ISA – were convinced that the Raman manoeuvre was likely to be harmful to the Earth in some significant way. Almost all of them focused on the same issue. Since the first Rama apparently ignored our existence altogether, they argued, the fact that Rama II altered its trajectory to achieve a rendezvous with the Earth shows that this spacecraft is operating under different principles. I certainly agree with that conclusion.

But what I cannot understand is why everyone necessarily assumes that the Raman action is hostile. It seems just as likely to me that the aliens could be motivated by curiosity, or even a desire to be our benefactors in some way.'

The British engineer paused for a moment to reflect, 'Francesca says that the polls on Earth are indicating that a huge majority of the average people as well, almost ten to one according to her, is terrified by Rama's approach. They are clamouring for the politicians to do something.'

Richard opened the hut and walked out into the dark plaza. He idly shone his flashlight on the octahedron. 'At a second meeting eighteen hours later it was decreed that the Newton team would not go inside Rama again. Technically, I am not in violation of that order, because I left the Newton before the official proclamation. But it was obvious that the order was coming.'

'While the leaders of the planet Earth are discussing what to do with a spacecraft the size of an asteroid that is aimed directly at them,' Nicole said as she walked out into the plaza behind him, 'you and I have a more tractable problem. We must cross the Cylindrical Sea.' She managed a wan smile. 'Shall we do a little exploring while we talk?'

Richard directed his flashlight beam into the bottom of the pit. The manna melon was clearly identifiable but the individual pieces in the pile of jumbled metal were very hard to resolve. 'So those are spare parts from a centipede biot?'

Nicole nodded. They were kneeling side by side on the lip. 'Even in the daylight the ends of the pit are in shadows. I needed to be certain that I wasn't looking at Takagishi's body.'

'I would love to see a centipede biot repair itself.' Richard stood up and walked over to the wall of the barn. He knocked. 'And the material scientists would love this stuff. Normal radio waves are blocked both ways and you can't see in from the outside. Yet the wall is somehow transparent if you're inside the barn looking out.' He turned to Nicole. 'Bring your scalpel over here. Let's see if we can cut off a piece.'

Nicole was trying to decide if one of them should drop down into the pit and retrieve the melon. It wouldn't be too difficult, assuming the suture line would hold. At length she pulled out her scalpel and walked over beside Richard.

'I'm not certain we should do this,' she said. She hesitated before applying the scalpel to the barn wall. 'In the first place, the scalpel could be damaged. We might need it later. Second, uh, it might be considered vandalism.'

'Vandalism?' he said rhetorically. Richard regarded Nicole with a peculiar look. 'What a curiously homocentric concept.' He shrugged his shoulders and headed toward one end of the barn. 'Never mind,' he said, 'you're probably right about the scalpel.'

Richard had entered some data into his pocket computer and was studying the small monitor when Nicole came over beside him. 'You and Francesca were standing right about here, correct?' Nicole gave him an affirmative reply. 'Then you went back into the barn to look into one of the pits?'

'We've been over this before,' Nicole replied. 'Why are you asking again?'

'I think Francesca saw you fall into one of the pits and purposely misled us with that story about you wandering off to search for our Japanese professor. She didn't want anybody to find you.'

Nicole stared at Richard in the dark. 'I agree,' she responded slowly. 'But why do *you* think so?'

'It's the only explanation that makes any sense. I had a bizarre encounter with her right before I came back inside. She came into my room under the pretence of wanting an interview, supposedly to find out why I was returning to Rama. When I mentioned Falstaff and your navigation beacon, she switched off her camera. Then she became quite animated and asked me many detailed technical questions. Before she left, she told me she was convinced that none of us should ever have entered Rama in the first place. I thought she was going to beg me not to go back.'

'I can understand her not wanting me to find out that she had tried to maroon you in the pit,' Richard continued after a brief pause. 'What I can't fathom is why she left you there in the first place.'

'You remember the night you explained to me why RoSur's fault protection had failed?' Nicole said after a moment's reflection. 'That same night I also asked you and Janos if either of you had seen General Borzov ...'

As they walked back in the direction of the central plaza and their hut, Nicole spent fifteen minutes explaining to Richard her entire hypothesis about the conspiracy. She told him about the media contract, the drugs Francesca had given to both David Brown and Reggie Wilson, and Nicole's personal interactions with all the principals. She did not tell him about the data cube. Richard agreed that the evidence was very compelling.

'So you think she left you there in the pit to avoid being unmasked as a conspirator?'

Nicole nodded.

Richard whistled. 'Then everything fits. It was apparent to me that Francesca was running the show when we returned to the Newton. Both Brown and Heilmann were taking orders from her.' He put his arm around Nicole. 'I wouldn't want that woman as my enemy. She clearly has no scruples whatsoever.'

412

44 ANOTHER LAIR

Richard and Nicole had bigger concerns than Francesca. When they returned to the central plaza, they found their hut had disappeared. Repeated knocks on the avian cover produced no response. The precariousness of their situation became clearer to both of them.

Richard grew moody and uncommunicative. He apologized to Nicole, saying that it was a characteristic of his personality for him to withdraw from people when he felt insecure. He played with his computer for several hours, only stopping occasionally to ask Nicole questions about the geography of New York.

Nicole lay down on her sleeping mat and thought about swimming across the Cylindrical Sea. She was not an exceptionally good swimmer. During training it had taken her about fifteen minutes to swim one kilometre. That had been in a placid swimming pool. To cross the sea she would be forced to swim five kilometres through cold, choppy water. And she might be accompanied by lovely creatures like the shark biots.

A jolly fat man twenty centimetres high interrupted her contemplation. 'Would you like a drink, fair lass?' Falstaff asked her. Nicole rolled over and studied the robot from up close. He hoisted a large mug of fluid and drank it, spilling some on his beard. He wiped it off with his sleeve and then he burped. 'And if you want nothing to drink,' he said in a heavy British accent, thrusting his hand down into his codpiece, 'then perhaps Sir John could teach you a thing or two between the sheets.' The tiny face was definitely leering. It was crude, but very funny.

Nicole laughed. So did Falstaff. 'I am not only witty in myself,' the robot said, 'but the cause that wit is in other men.'

'You know,' Nicole said to Richard, who was watching from several metres away, 'if you ever became tired of being a cosmonaut, you could make millions in children's toys.'

Richard came over and picked up Falstaff. He thanked Nicole for her compliment. 'As I see it, we have three options,' he then said very seriously. 'We can swim the sea, we can explore New York to see if we can forage enough material to construct some kind of boat, or we can wait here until someone comes. I'm not optimistic about our chances in any of the cases.'

'So what do you suggest?'

'I propose a compromise. When it's light, let's carefully search the key areas of the city, particularly around the three plazas, and see if we can find anything that could be used to build a boat. We'll allot one Raman day, maybe two, to the exploration. If nothing turns up, we'll swim for it. I have no faith we'll ever see a rescue team.'

'Sounds all right to me. But I would like to do one other thing first. We don't have a lot of food, to make a rather obvious understatement, I'd feel better if we pulled up the manna melon first, before we did any more exploring. That way we could be protected against any surprises.'

Richard agreed that establishing the food supply would probably be a prudent initial action. But he didn't like the idea of using the suture thread again. 'You were lucky in many ways,' he told Nicole. 'Not only did the line not break, it didn't even slip off that waistband you made. However, it did cut completely through your gloves in two places and almost through the waistband.'

'You have another idea?' Nicole asked.

'The lattice material is the obvious choice,' Richard replied. 'It should be perfect, provided that we don't have any trouble obtaining it. Then I can go down in the pit and spare you the trouble—'

'Wrong,' Nicole interrupted. She smiled. 'With all due respect, Richard, now is not the time for any macho derring-do. Using the lattice is a great idea. But you're too heavy. If something happened, I would never be able to pull you out.' She patted him on the shoulder. 'And I hope it doesn't hurt your feelings, but I'm probably the more athletic of the two of us.'

Richard feigned hurt pride. 'But whatever happened to tradition? The man always performs the feats of physical strength and agility. Don't you remember your childhood cartoons?'

Nicole laughed heartily. 'Yes, my dear,' she said lightly. 'But you aren't Popeye. And I'm not Olive Oyl.'

'I'm not certain I can deal with this,' he said, shaking his head vigorously. 'To discover at the age of thirty-four that I'm not Popeye.... What a blow to my self-image.' He cuddled Nicole gently. 'What do you say?' he continued. 'Should we try to sleep some more before it's light?'

Neither of them was able to sleep. They lay side by side on their mats in the open plaza, each occupied with their own thoughts. Nicole heard Richard's body move. 'You're awake too?' she said in a whisper.

'Yeah,' he answered. 'I've even counted Shakespearean characters with no success. I was up to more than a hundred.'

Nicole propped herself up on an elbow and faced her companion. 'Tell me, Richard,' she said, 'where did this preoccupation of yours with Shakespeare come from? I know you grew up in Stratford, but it's hard for me to imagine how an engineer like you, in love with computers and calculations and gadgets, could become so fascinated with a playwright.'

'My therapist told me it was an "escapist compulsion",' Richard replied a few seconds later. 'Since I didn't like the real world or the people in it, he said, I made up another one. Except that I didn't create it from scratch. I just extended a wonderful universe already fabricated by a genius.

'Shakespeare was my God,' Richard continued after a moment. 'When I was nine or ten, I would stop in that park along the Avon – the one beside all the theatres, with the statues of Hamlet, Falstaff, Lady Macbeth, and Prince Hal – and spend the afternoon hours making up additional stories about my favourite characters. That way I put off going home until the last possible moment. I dreaded being around my father ... I never knew what he would do—

'But you don't want to hear this' – Richard interrupted himself suddenly – 'everyone has memories of childhood pain. We should talk about something else.'

'We should talk about whatever we're feeling,' Nicole responded, surprising even herself. 'Which is something I hardly ever do,' she added softly.

Richard turned and looked in her direction. He extended his hand slowly. She gently wrapped her fingers around his. 'My father worked for British Rail,' he said. 'He was a very smart man, but socially clumsy, and he had difficulty finding a job that fitted him after he finished the university at Sussex. Times were still tough. The economy had just started to recover from the Great Chaos... .

'When my mother told him that she was pregnant, he was overwhelmed by the responsibility of it all. He looked for a safe, secure position. He had always scored well on tests and the government had forced all the national transportation monopolies, including the rail system, to staff positions based on objective test results. So my father became the manager of operations at Stratford.

'He hated the job. It was boring and repetitive, no challenge at all for a man who had an honours degree. Mother told me that when I was very small he applied for other positions, but he always seemed to botch the interviews. Later on, when I was older, he never even tried. He sat at home and complained. And drank. And then made everyone around him miserable.'

There was a long silence. Richard was having a difficult time struggling with the demons of his childhood. Nicole squeezed his hand. 'I'm sorry,' she said.

'So was I,' Richard replied with a slight break in his voice. 'I was just a small child with an incredible sense of wonder and love of life. I would come home enthusiastic about something new I had learned or something that had happened at school, and my Dad would just growl.

'Once, when I was only eight, I came home from school in the early afternoon and I got into an argument with him. It was his day off and he had been drinking, as usual. Mother was out at the store. I don't remember what it was about now, but I do recall telling him that he was wrong about some trivial fact. When I continued to argue with him, he suddenly hit me in the nose with all his might. I fell against the wall with my broken nose gushing blood. From that time on, until I was fourteen and felt I could protect myself, I never walked in that house when he was there unless I was certain that my mother was home.'

Nicole tried to imagine an adult man slugging an eight-year-old child. *What kind of human being could break his own son's nose?* she wondered.

'I had always been very shy,' Richard was saying, 'and had convinced myself that I had inherited my father's social clumsiness, so I didn't have many friends my own age. But I still yearned for human interaction.' He looked over at Nicole and paused, remembering. 'I made Shakespeare's characters my friends. I read his plays every afternoon in the park and immersed myself in his imaginative world. I even memorized entire scenes. Then I talked to Romeo or Ariel or Jaques while I was walking home.'

It was not difficult for Nicole to visualize the rest of Richard's story. *I can picture you as an adolescent,* she thought. *Solitary, awkward, emotionally repressed. Your obsession with Shakespeare gave you an escape from your pain. All the theatres were near your home. You saw your friends become alive on the stage.*

On impulse Nicole leaned over and kissed Richard lightly on the cheek. 'Thanks for telling me,' she said.

As soon as it was daylight they walked over to the lattice. Nicole was surprised to find that the incisions she had made when she had freed the avian had all been repaired. The lattice was like new. 'Obviously a repair biot has already been here,' Richard commented, no longer extremely impressed after all the wonders he had already witnessed-

They cut off several long strands of the lattice and headed for the barn. On the way Richard tested the elasticity of the material. He found that it stretched about fifteen percent and always restored itself, albeit very slowly at times, to its original length. The restoration time varied significantly, depending on how long the piece had been fully stretched. Richard had already begun his examination of the inside structure of the cord when they arrived at the barn.

Nicole did not waste any time. She tied one end of the lattice material around a stumpy object just outside the barn and lowered herself down the wall. Richard's function was to make certain that nothing untoward occurred and to be available if there was some kind of an emergency. Down in the bottom of the pit Nicole shuddered once as she remembered how helpless she had felt there just a few days earlier. But she quickly turned her attention to her task, inserting a makeshift handle made from her medical probes deep into the manna melon and then securing the other end of the handle to her backpack. Her ascent was vigorous and uneventful.

'Well.' She smiled at Richard as she handed him the melon to carry. 'Should we now continue with Plan A?'

'Roger,' he replied. 'Now we know where our next ten meals are coming from.'

'Nine,' Nicole corrected with a laugh. 'I've made a slight adjustment in the estimate now that I've watched you eat a couple of times.'

Richard and Nicole marched quickly from the barn to the western plaza. They crisscrossed the open area and combed the narrow alleys nearby, but they did not find anything that would help them build a boat. Richard did have an encounter with a centipede biot, however; in the middle of their search one had entered the plaza and then moved diagonally across it. Richard had done everything possible, including lying in front of it and beating it over the head with his backpack, to try to induce the biot to stop. He had not been successful. Nicole was laughing at him when Richard returned, a little frustrated, to her side.

'That centipede is absolutely useless,' he complained. 'What the hell is it for? It's not carrying anything. It has no sensors that I can see. It just travels merrily along.'

'The technology of an advanced extraterrestrial species,' she reminded Richard of one of his favourite quotes, 'will be indistinguishable from magic.'

'But that damn centipede's not magic,' he replied, a little annoyed at Nicole's laughter, 'it's goddamn stupid!'

'And what would you have done if it had stopped?' Nicole inquired.

'Why, I would have examined it, of course. What did you think?'

'I think we'd be better off concentrating our energy in other areas,' she replied. 'I don't imagine a centipede biot is going to help us get off this island.'

'Well,' Richard said a little brusquely, 'it's obvious to me already we're going about this process all wrong. We're not going to find anything on the surface. The biots probably clean it up regularly. We should be looking for another hole in the ground, like the avian's lair. We can use the multispectral radar to identify any places where the ground is not solid.'

It took them a long time to find the second hole, even though it was not more than two hundred metres from the centre of the western plaza. At first Richard and Nicole were much too restrictive in their search. After an hour, though, they finally convinced themselves that the ground underneath the plaza area was solid everywhere. They expanded their search to include the small streets and lanes nearby, off the concentric avenues. On a dead-end alley with tall buildings on three sides, they found another covering in the centre of the road. It was not camouflaged in any way. This second cover was the same size as the one at the avian lair, a rectangle ten metres long and six metres wide.

45 NIKKI

'**D**o you think the avian cover opens in the same way?' Nicole asked, after Richard had very carefully searched the environs and found a flat plate on one of the buildings that looked decidedly out of place. Pressing hard against the plate had caused the cover to open.

'Probably,' he answered. 'We'll have to go back and check.'

'Then these places are not very secure,' Nicole said. The two of them walked back onto the street and knelt down to look in the hole. A broad, steep ramp descended from beside them and disappeared into the darkness below. They could only see about ten metres into the hole.

'It looks like one of those ancient parking lots,' Richard remarked. 'Back when everybody had automobiles.' He stepped on the ramp. 'It even feels like concrete.'

Nicole watched as her companion moved slowly down the ramp. When Richard's head was below the ground level, he turned and spoke to her. 'Aren't you coming?' he asked. He had switched on his flashlight beam and had illuminated a small landing another few metres below.

'Richard,' Nicole said from above. 'I think we should discuss this. I don't want to be stuck—'

'Ah-ha!' Richard exclaimed. As soon as his foot hit the first landing, some lights around him automatically lit the next phase of the descent. 'The ramp doubles back,' he shouted, 'and continues down. Looks just the same.' He turned and disappeared from Nicole's field of view.

'Richard,' Nicole now yelled, a little exasperated, 'will you please stop for a minute? We must talk about what we're doing.'

A few seconds later Richard's smiling face reappeared. The two cosmonauts discussed their options. Nicole insisted that she was going to stay outside, in New York, even if Richard was going to continue with his exploration. At least that way, she argued, she could guarantee that they would not be stranded in the hole.

While she was talking, Richard was standing on the first landing and surveying the area around him. The walls were made of the same material Nicole had found in the avian lair. Small strip lights, looking not unlike normal fluorescent lights on Earth, ran along the wall to illuminate the path.

'Move away just a second, will you?' Richard shouted in the middle of their conversation.

At first puzzled, Nicole backed away from the entrance to the rectangular hole. 'Farther,' she heard Richard yell. Nicole walked over and stood against one of the surrounding buildings.

'Is this far enough?' she had just finished shouting when the covering on the hole began to close. Nicole ran forward and tried to stop the motion of the cover, but it was much too heavy. 'Richard,' she cried as the hole disappeared beneath her.

Nicole pounded on the cover and remembered her own feelings of frustration when she had been locked in the avian lair. She quickly ran back over to the building and pressed the embedded flat panel. Nothing happened. Almost a minute passed. Nicole became anxious. She ran back into the street and called for her colleague.

'I'm right here, under the cover,' he answered, bringing Nicole considerable relief. 'I found another plate near the first landing and pressed it. I think it toggles the cover closed or open, but it may have a timing delay constraint. Give me a few minutes. Don't you try to open the cover. And don't stand too near it.'

Nicole backed away and waited. Richard had been correct. Several minutes later the cover opened and he emerged from the hole with a big grin on his face. 'See,' he said, 'I told you not to worry ... Now what's for lunch?'

As they descended the ramp, Nicole heard the familiar sound of running water. In a little room about twenty metres behind the landing, they found the identical piping and cistern that had been in the avian lair. Richard and Nicole both filled their flasks with the fresh, delicious water.

Outside the room there were no horizontal tunnels leading off in both directions, only another descending ramp dropping five more metres beneath the floor. Richard's flashlight beam crawled slowly across the dark walls near the water room. 'Look here, Nicole,' he said, pointing at what was a very subtle variation in building material. 'See, it arches around to the other side.'

She followed his beam as it inscribed a long circular arc on the wall. 'It looks as if there were at least two phases of construction.'

'Exactly,' he replied. 'Maybe there were horizontal tunnels here as well, at least in the beginning, and they were sealed off later.' Neither of them said anything else as they continued their descent. Back and forth went the identical ramps. Whenever Richard and Nicole touched a new landing, the next descending ramp was illuminated.

They were fifty metres underneath the surface when the ceilings above them opened up and the ramps terminated in a large cavern. The circular floor of the cave was about twenty-five metres in diameter. There were four dark tunnels, five metres in height and equally spaced at ninety degrees around the circle, that exited from the cavern.

'Eenie, Meenie, Mynie, Moe,' Richard said.

'I'll take Moe,' Nicole said. She headed toward one of the tunnels. When she was within a few metres of the entrance, the lights in the near portion of the tunnel switched on.

This time it was Richard's turn to be hesitant. He stared cautiously into the tunnel and made some quick entries into his computer. 'Does it look to you as if this tunnel curves slightly to the right? See, there at the end of the lights?'

Nicole nodded. She looked over Richard's shoulder to see what he was doing. 'I'm making a map,' he said in response to her curiosity. 'Theseus had string and Hansel and Gretel had bread. We have them both beat. Aren't computers wonderful?'

She smiled. 'So what's your guess?' Nicole said while they were walking along in the near part of the tunnel. 'Will it be a Minotaur or a gingerbread house with a wicked witch?'

We should be so lucky, Nicole thought. Her fear was increasing as they penetrated deeper and deeper into the tunnel. She recalled that awful moment of terror in the pit when she had first seen the avian hovering over her with its beak and talons extending in her direction. An icy chill ran down her spine. *There it is again,* she said to herself, *that feeling that something terrible is going to happen.*

She stopped. 'Richard,' she said, 'I don't like this. We should turn back ...'

They both heard the noise at the same time. It was definitely *behind* them, back in the vicinity of the circular cavern they had just left. It sounded like hard brushes dragging against metal.

Richard and Nicole huddled together. 'That's the same sound,' he whispered, 'that I heard the first night in Rama, when we were at the walls of New York.'

The tunnel behind them curved slightly to the left. When they looked back in that direction, the lights were off at the limit of their vision. The second time they heard the sound, however, some lights came on in the far distance almost simultaneously, indicating something was near the entrance to their tunnel.

Nicole bolted. She must have covered the next two hundred metres in thirty seconds, despite her flight suit and backpack. She stopped and waited for Richard. Neither of them heard the sound again and no new lights were illuminated in the distant reaches of the tunnel.

'I'm sorry,' Nicole said when Richard finally arrived. 'I panicked. I think I've been in this alien wonderland too long.'

'Jesus,' Richard responded with a disapproving frown. 'I've never seen anybody run that fast.' His frown changed into a smile. 'Don't feel bad, Nikki,' he said. 'I was scared shitless too. But I was frozen in place.'

Nicole continued taking deep breaths and stared at Richard. 'What did you call me?' she asked, somewhat belligerently.

'Nikki,' he replied. 'I thought it was time for me to have my own special name for you. Don't you like it?'

Nicole was speechless for ten full seconds. Her mind was millions of kilometres and fifteen years away, in a hotel suite in Los Angeles, her body experiencing wave after wave of pleasure. 'That was remarkable, Nikki, truly wonderful,' the prince had said several minutes later. She had told Henry on that night fifteen years before not to call her Nikki, that it sounded like a name for a buxom showgirl or a tart.

Richard was snapping his fingers in front of her face. 'Hello, hello. Anybody home?'

Nicole smiled. 'Sure, Richard,' she replied. 'Nikki's just fine – as long as you don't use it all the time.'

They continued to walk slowly along the tunnel. 'So where did you go back there?' Richard asked.

Somewhere I can never tell you about, Nicole mused. *Because each of us is the sum of all we have ever experienced. Only the very young have a clean slate. The rest of us must live forever with everything we have ever been.* She slid her arm through Richard's. *And have the good sense to know when to keep it private.*

The tunnel seemed endless. Richard and Nicole had almost decided to turn around when they came to a dark entryway off to their right. With no hesitation they both walked inside. The lights came on immediately. Inside the room, on the big wall to the left of them, were twenty-five flat rectangular objects, arranged in five orderly rows with five columns each. The opposite wall was empty. Within seconds after their entrance, the two cosmonauts heard a high-frequency squeaky sound coming from the ceiling. They tensed briefly, but relaxed as the squeaking continued and there were no new surprises.

They held hands and walked to one end of the long narrow room. The objects on the wall were photographs, most of them recognizable as having been taken somewhere inside Rama. The great octahedron near the central plaza was featured in several of the photos. The remaining pictures were a balance between scenes of the buildings of New York and wide-angle shots of panoramas around the interior of Rama.

Three of the photographs were particularly fascinating to Richard. They depicted sleek, aerodynamically curved boats plying the Cylindrical Sea; in one of the photographs a great wave was about to crash over the top of a large boat. 'Now there's what we need,' Richard said to Nicole excitedly. 'If we could find one of them, our troubles would be over.'

The squeaking above them continued with very little modulation. A spotlight moved from picture to picture at moments when there was a pause in the squeak. Nicole and Richard easily concluded that they were in a museum on some kind of tour, but there was nothing else they could know for certain. Nicole sat down against a side wall. 'I'm having a lot of trouble with all this,' she said. 'I feel totally out of control.'

Richard sat down beside her. 'Me too,' he said, nodding. 'And I just arrived in New York. So I can imagine what all this is doing to you.'

They were silent for a moment. 'You know what bothers me the most?' Nicole said, trying to give some expression to the helplessness she was feeling. 'It's how very little I understood and appreciated my own ignorance. Before I came on this voyage, I thought I knew the general dimensions of the relationship between my own knowledge and the knowledge of mankind. But what is staggering about this mission is how very small the *entire range* of human knowledge might be compared to what *could* be known. Just think, the sum of everything all human beings know or have ever known might be nothing more than an infinitesimal fraction of the *Encyclopedia Galactica*—'

'It is really frightening,' Richard interrupted enthusiastically. 'And thrilling at the same time ... Sometimes when I'm in a bookstore or a library, I am overwhelmed by all the things that I do not know. Then I am seized by a powerful desire to read all the books, one by one. Imagine what it would be like to be in the *true* library, one that combined the knowledge of all the species in the universe ... The very thought makes me woozy.'

Nicole turned to him and slapped his leg. 'All right, Richard,' she said jokingly, changing the mood, 'now that we have reaffirmed how incredibly stupid we are, what's our plan? I figure we have already covered about a kilometre in this tunnel. Where do we go from here?'

'I propose we walk another fifteen minutes in the same direction. In my experience tunnels always lead somewhere. If we don't find anything, we'll turn around.'

He helped Nicole up and gave her a small hug. 'All right, Nikki,' he said with a wink. 'Half a league onward.'

Nicole frowned and shook her head. 'Twice is enough for one day,' she said, extending her hand toward Richard.

46 THE BETTER PART OF VALOUR

The huge circular hole below them extended into the darkness. Only the top five metres of the shaft were lit. Metal spikes, about a metre long, protruded from the wall, each separated from its neighbours by the same distance.

'This is definitely the destination of the tunnels,' Richard muttered to himself. He was having some difficulty integrating this huge, cylindrical hole with its walls of spikes into his overall conception of Rama. He and Nicole had walked around the perimeter twice. They had even backtracked several hundred metres down the other, adjacent tunnel, concluding from its slight curvature to the right that it had probably originated at the same cavern as the tunnel they had followed earlier.

'Well,' Richard said at length, shrugging his shoulders, 'here we go,' He put his right foot on one of the spikes to test its ability to hold his weight. It was firm. He moved his left leg down to another of the spikes and descended one more level with his right leg. 'The spacing is nearly perfect,' he said, glancing back at Nicole. 'It shouldn't be a difficult climb.'

'Richard Wakefield,' Nicole said from the rim of the hole, 'are you trying to tell me that you intend to climb down into that chasm? And that you expect me to follow?'

'I don't expect anything of you,' he replied. 'But I can't see the point of turning back now. What's our alternative? Should we go back down the tunnel to the ramps and exit? For what? To see if anyone has found us yet? You saw the photographs of the boats. Maybe they're right here at the bottom. Maybe there's even a secret river that runs underground into the Cylindrical Sea.'

'Maybe,' Nicole said, starting to descend slowly now that Richard's progress had triggered another bank of lights below them, 'one of those things that made the bizarre noise is waiting for us down at the bottom.'

'I'll find out,' Richard said. 'Hallooo, down there. We two human-type beings are coming down.' He waved and momentarily lost his balance.

'Don't be a show-off,' Nicole said, coming down beside him. She paused to catch her breath and look around. Her two feet were resting on spikes and she was holding tightly to two others with her hands. *I must be insane,* she said to herself, *just look at this place. It's easy to imagine a hundred gruesome deaths.* Richard had dropped down to another pair of spikes. *And look at him. Is he totally immune to fear? Or just reckless? He actually seems to be enjoying all this.*

The third bank of lights illuminated a lattice on the opposite wall below them. It was hanging among all the spikes and, from a distance in the dim light, looked startlingly like a smaller version of the object that had been attached to the two skyscrapers in New York. Richard hurried around the cylinder to examine the lattice. 'Come over here,' he shouted at Nicole. 'I think it's the same damn material.'

The lattice was anchored to the wall by small bolts. At Richard's insistence, Nicole cut off a piece and handed it to him. He stretched it and watched it regain its shape. He studied its internal structure. 'It *is* the same stuff,' he said. His brow knitted into furrows. 'But what the hell does it mean?'

Nicole stood beside him and idly shone her flashlight into the depths below them. She was about to suggest that they climb out and head for more familiar terrain when she thought she saw a reflection from a floor about twenty metres below. 'I'm going to make you a proposition,' Nicole said to Richard. 'While you're studying that lattice cord, I'll drop down another several metres. We may be near the bottom of this bizarre well of spikes, or whatever it is. If not, then we'll abandon this place.'

'All right,' Richard said absentmindedly. He was already involved in his examination of the lattice cord, using the microscope he had taken from his backpack.

Nicole nimbly descended to the floor. 'I guess you'd better come down,' she called to Richard. 'There are two more tunnels, one large and one small. Plus another hole in the centre ...' He was beside her immediately. He had climbed down as soon as he had seen the lower platform illuminated by lights.

Richard and Nicole were now standing on a ledge three metres wide at the bottom of the spiked cylinder. The ledge formed a ring around another smaller descending hole that also had spikes growing out of its walls. To their left and right, dark arched tunnels were cut into the rock or metal that was the base construction material for the extensive underground world. The tunnel on their left was five to six metres high; the tiny tunnel on the opposite side, one hundred and eighty degrees around the ring, was only half a metre tall.

Running out of each of the two tunnels, and penetrating half a ledge-width into the ring, were two small parallel strips of unknown material that were fastened to the floor. The strips were very close together in the smaller tunnel and more widely spaced in the other. Richard was sitting on his knees examining the strips in front of the large tunnel when he heard a distant rumble. 'Listen,' he said to Nicole, as the two of them instinctively backed away.

The rumbling increased and changed into a whining sound, as if something were moving swiftly through the air. Far off in the tunnel, which ran straight as an arrow, Richard and Nicole could see some lights switch on. They tensed.

They didn't need to wait long for an explanation. A vehicle that resembled a hovering subway car burst into view and sped toward them, stopping suddenly with its front edge just over the farthest extension of the strips on the floor.

Richard and Nicole had recoiled as the vehicle had hurtled toward them. Both were dangerously close to the edge of the ring. For several seconds they stood in silence, each staring at the aerodynamic shape hovering in front of them. Then they looked at each other and laughed simultaneously. 'Okay,' Nicole said nervously, 'I get it. We've crossed into some new dimension. In this one it's just a little difficult to find the subway station.... This is so totally absurd. We climb down a spiked barrel and end up in a Metro station ... I don't know about you, Richard, but I've had enough. I'll take a few *normal* avians and manna melon any day of the week....'

Richard had walked over beside the vehicle. A door in the side had opened and they could both see the lit interior. There were no seats, only thin cylindrical poles, spaced in no obvious pattern, that ran the three metres from the ceiling to the floor. 'It can't go far,' Richard said, sticking his head inside the door but leaving his feet on the ledge outside. 'There's no place to sit down.'

Nicole came over to inspect for herself. 'Maybe they have no old or crippled people – and the grocery stores are all close to home.' She laughed again as Richard leaned farther into the car so he could see the ceiling and walls more clearly. 'Don't get any crazy ideas,' she said. 'It would be certifiably insane for us to climb aboard that car. Unless we were out of food and it was our last hope.'

'I guess you're right,' Richard replied. He was definitely disappointed as he withdrew from the subway car. 'But what an amazing—' He stopped himself in midsentence. He was staring across the platform at the opposite side of the ledge. There, in the middle of the now illuminated entrance to the tiny tunnel, an identical vehicle, one-tenth the size of the one next to them, was hovering off the floor. Nicole followed Richard's gaze.

'That must be the road to Lilliput over there,' Nicole said. 'Giants descend another floor and normal-size creatures take this subway. It's all very simple.'

Richard walked swiftly around the ring. 'That's perfect,' he said out loud, taking off his backpack and setting it on the ledge beside him. He began to rummage in one of the large pockets.

'What are you doing?' Nicole asked.

Richard pulled two tiny figures out of the pack and showed them to her. 'It's perfect,' he repeated, his excitement unmistakable. 'We can send Prince Hal and Falstaff. I'll only need a few minutes to adjust their software.'

Already Richard had spread his pocket computer out on the ledge beside the robots and was busily working away. Nicole sat down with her back against the wall between two spikes. She glanced over at Richard. *He is truly a rare species,* she said with admiration, thinking back over their hours together. *A genius, that's obvious. Almost without guile or meanness. And somehow he has retained the curiosity of the child.*

Nicole suddenly felt very tired. She smiled to herself as she was watching Richard. He was absorbed in his work. Nicole closed her eyes for a moment.

'I'm sorry that I took so long,' Richard was saying. 'I kept thinking of new things to add and I needed to rearrange the linkage ...'

Nicole woke up from her nap very slowly. 'How long have we been here?' she said as she yawned.

'A little over an hour,' Richard answered sheepishly. 'But everything is all set. I'm ready to put the boys in the subway.' Nicole glanced around her. 'Both the cars are still here,' she commented.

'I think they work like all the lights. I bet they will stay in the station as long as we're on the platform.'

Nicole stood up and stretched. 'So here's the plan,' Richard said. 'I have the controlling transceiver in my hand. Hal and Sir John each have audio, video, and infrared sensors that will acquire data continuously. We can choose which channel to monitor on our computers and send new commands as necessary.'

'But will the signals penetrate the walls?' Nicole asked, remembering her experience inside the barn.

'As long as they don't have to travel through too much material. The system is way overdesigned in terms of signal to noise to accommodate some attenuation ... Besides, the large subway came at us along a straight line. I'm hoping this one will be similar.'

Richard gingerly set the two robots down on the ledge and commanded them to walk toward the subway. Doors opened on both sides as they drew near. 'Remember me to Mistress Quickly,' Falstaff said as he climbed aboard. 'She was a stupid lass, but with a good heart.'

Nicole gave Richard a puzzled glance. 'I didn't overwrite all their earlier programming,' he said with a laugh. 'From time to time they will probably make some absurd random comments.'

The two robots stood on the subway for a minute or two. Richard hastily checked their sensors and made one more set of calibrations on the monitor. At length the doors of the subway closed, the vehicle waited for another ten seconds, and then it rushed away into the tunnel.

Richard commanded Falstaff to face the front, but there was not much to be seen out the window. It was a surprisingly long ride at a very high speed. Richard estimated that the little subway had travelled more than a kilometre before it finally slowed to a stop.

Richard waited before commanding the two robots to leave the subway. He wanted to make certain that they did not get off at an intermediate stop. However, there was no need to worry: the first full set of imaging data from Prince Hal and Falstaff showed that the subway had indeed reached the end of the line.

The two robots walked around the flat platform beside the vehicle and photographed more of their surroundings. The subway station had arches and columns, but it was basically one long, connected room. Richard estimated from the images that the ceiling height was about two metres. He commanded Hal and Falstaff to follow a long hallway that moved off to the left, perpendicular to the subway track.

The hallway terminated in front of another tunnel, this one barely five centimetres high. As the robots examined the floor, finding two tiny strips extending almost to their feet, a subway of minuscule proportions arrived in the station. With its doors open and its interior lit, Richard and Nicole could see that the new subway car was identical, except for its size, to the two they had seen before.

The cosmonauts were sitting together with their knees on the ledge, both avidly watching the small computer monitor. Richard commanded Falstaff to take a picture of Prince Hal standing next to the tiny subway. 'The car itself,' Richard said to Nicole after studying the image, 'is less than two centimetres tall. What's going to ride in it? Ants?'

Nicole shook her head and said nothing. She was feeling bewildered again. At that moment she was also thinking about her initial reactions to Rama. *Never in my wildest imagination,* she thought, recalling her awe at that first panoramic sight, *did I foresee that there would be so many new mysteries. The first explorers hardly scratched the surface* ...

'Richard,' Nicole said, interrupting her own thoughts.

He commanded the robots to walk back down the hallway and then glanced up from the monitor. 'Yes?' he said.

'How thick is the outer shell of Rama?'

'About four hundred metres altogether, I think,' he said with a slightly puzzled expression. 'But that's at one of the ends. We have no definite way of knowing how thick the shell is anywhere else. Norton and crew reported that the depth of the Cylindrical Sea was highly variable – as little as forty metres in some places and as much as a hundred and fifty elsewhere. That would suggest to me a shell thickness of several hundred metres at least.'

Richard checked the monitor quickly. Prince Hal and Falstaff were almost back at the station where they had climbed off the subway. He transmitted a stop command and turned to Nicole. 'Why are you asking? It's not like you to ask idle questions.'

'There's obviously an entire unexplored world down here,' Nicole replied. 'It would take a lifetime—'

'We don't have that long,' Richard broke in with a laugh. 'At least not a normal lifetime ... But back to your thickness question, remember the entire Southern Hemicylinder has a floor level four hundred and fifty metres above the north. So unless there are some major structural irregularities – and we certainly haven't seen any from the outside – the thickness should be substantially greater in the south.'

Richard waited for Nicole to say something additional. When she remained silent for several seconds, he turned back to the monitor and continued his surrogate exploration with the robots.

There had been a good reason for Nicole's question about the thickness of the shell. She had a picture in her mind that she could not shake. Nicole was imagining coming to the end of one of these long underground tunnels, opening a door, and then being blinded by the light of the Sun. *Wouldn't it be incredible,* she was thinking, *to be an intelligent creature living in this maze of dim light and tunnels and then, by chance, to stumble onto something that would irrevocably change your entire concept of the Universe? How could you return ...*

'Now what in the world is that?' Richard was asking. Nicole stopped her mental drifting and focused on the monitor. Prince Hal and Falstaff had entered a large room at the opposite end of the subway station and were standing in front of a conglomeration of loose, spongelike webbing. The infrared image of the scene showed a nested sphere, inside the web, that was radiating heat. At Nicole's suggestion, Richard commanded the robots to walk around the object and survey the rest of this new domain.

The room was immense. It extended into the distance farther than the resolution of the video devices carried by the robots. The ceiling was about twenty metres high and the two side walls were separated by more than fifty metres. Several other similar spherical objects encased in spongy masses could be seen scattered about the room in the distance. A lattice, stretching almost all the way across the room but stopping five metres above the floor, dangled from the high ceiling in the foreground. Another lattice could barely be discerned a hundred metres or so behind the first one.

Richard and Nicole discussed what the robots should do next. There were no other exits from either the subway station or the large room. A panoramic image around the room revealed nothing nearby of interest except the sphere embedded in its spongy exterior, Nicole wanted to bring the robots back and leave the lair altogether. Richard's curiosity demanded at least a cursory investigation of one of the spherical objects.

The two robots were able, with some difficulty, to climb around and through the webbed material to reach the sphere in the centre. The ambient temperature increased as they neared the sphere. One of the purposes of the external material was clearly to absorb heat. When the robots reached the nested sphere, their internal monitors flashed a warning that the outside temperatures exceeded their safe operating limits.

Richard moved quickly. Directing the robots on a nearly continuous basis, he determined that the sphere was virtually impenetrable and was probably made of a thick metal alloy with a very hard surface. Falstaff banged on the sphere several times with his arm; the resulting sound damped quickly, indicating the sphere was full, possibly with a liquid. The two robots were weaving their way out of the sponge webbing when their audio systems picked up the sound of brushes dragging against metal.

Richard tried to speed up their escape. Hal was able to increase his pace but Falstaff, whose subsystem temperatures had risen too high during his proximity to the sphere, was prevented by his own internal processor logic from accelerating his actions. The brush sound continued to grow louder.

The computer monitor on the ledge between the two cosmonauts was changed to split screen. Prince Hal reached the edge of the sponge, hit the floor, and headed for the subway without waiting for his companion. Falstaff continued to climb slowly through the webbing. 'Tis too much work for a drinking man,' he mumbled, as he crawled over another barrier.

The dragging metal sound abruptly stopped and Falstaff's camera recorded an image of a long, skinny object with black and gold stripes. Moments later the camera frame went to all black and the little robot's 'Terminal Fault Imminent' alarm began to sound. Richard and Nicole had one more fleeting glimpse of a picture from Falstaff; it showed what might have been a giant eye, from up close, a black gelatinous mixture tinged with blue. Then all transmissions from the robot, including emergency telemetry, abruptly ceased.

Meanwhile Hal had entered the waiting subway. During the several seconds before the subway left the station, the ominous dragging sound was heard again. But the subway departed anyway, with the robot inside, and started speeding through the tunnel toward the two cosmonauts. Richard and Nicole breathed a sigh of relief.

Not more than a second later a loud sound like breaking glass was picked up by Prince Hal's audio system. Richard commanded the robot to turn in the direction of the sound and Hal's camera photographed a solitary black and gold tentacle in midair. The tentacle had broken the window and was moving inexorably toward the robot. Both Richard and Nicole realised what was happening at the same moment. The thing was on top of the subway! And it was coming toward them!

Nicole was climbing the spikes in a flash. Richard wasted several valuable seconds picking up his computer monitor and putting all his equipment in the backpack. He heard Prince Hal's 'Terminal Fault Imminent' alarm when he was halfway up the spikes. Richard turned around to look just as the subway pulled into the tunnel below him.

What he saw made his blood run cold. On top of the subway was a large dark creature whose central body, if that was indeed what it was, was flattened against the roof. Striped tentacles extended in all directions. Four of them had pierced the windows of the train and grabbed the robot. The thing quickly climbed off the subway and wrapped one of its eight tentacles around the lowest spikes. Richard didn't watch anymore. He clambered up the rest of the cylinder and started racing through the tunnel at the top, following the steps of Nicole far ahead of him in the distance.

As he ran, Richard noticed that the tunnel was curving slightly to the right. He reminded himself that even though this was not the same tunnel they had used before, it should still lead them to the ramps. After several hundred metres Richard stopped to listen for the sound of his pursuer. He heard nothing. Richard had just taken two deep breaths and started to run again when his ears were assaulted by a terrible wail in front of him. It was Nicole. *Oh shit,* he thought, as he rushed forward to find her.

47 PROGRESSIVE MATRICES

'Never, never in my entire life,' Nicole said to Richard, 'have I ever seen anything that terrified me like that.' The two cosmonauts were sitting with their backs against the bottom of one of the skyscrapers surrounding the western plaza. They were both still breathing heavily, exhausted from their frantic escape. Nicole took a long drink of water.

'I had just started to relax,' she continued. 'I could hear you behind me – and nothing else. I decided I would stop in the museum and wait for you to catch up. It hadn't yet occurred to me that we were in the "other" tunnel.

'It should have been obvious, of course, because the opening was on the wrong side. But I wasn't thinking logically at that moment ... Anyway, I stepped inside the room, the lights came on, and there he was, not more than three metres in front of me. I thought my heart had stopped altogether ...'

Richard remembered Nicole running into his arms in the tunnel and sobbing for several seconds. 'It's Takagishi ... stuffed like a deer or a tiger ... in the opening to the right,' she had said in fits and starts. After Nicole had regained her composure, the two of them had walked back down the tunnel together. Inside the opening, standing upright just opposite the entrance, Richard had been shocked to see Newton cosmonaut Shigeru Takagishi. He was dressed in his flight suit and looked exactly as he had the last time they had seen him at the Beta campsite. His face was fixed in a pleasant smile and his arms were at his sides.

'What the hell?' Richard had said, blinking twice, his curiosity only slightly stronger than his terror. Nicole had averted her eyes. Even though she had seen the sight before, the stuffed Takagishi was much too lifelike for her.

They had only stayed in the large room for a minute. Alien taxidermy had also performed wonders on an avian with a broken wing that was hanging from the ceiling next to Takagishi. Against the wall behind the Japanese scientist was Richard and Nicole's hut that had disappeared the day before. The hexagonal electronics board from the Newton portable science station was on the floor next to Takagishi's feet, not far from a full-scale model of a bulldozer biot. Other biot replicas were scattered around the room.

Richard had started to study the varied collection of biots in the room when

431

they had faintly heard the familiar dragging noise coming from behind them in the tunnel. They had not wasted any more time. Their flight down the tunnel and up the ramps had been broken only by a brief stop at the cistern to replenish their supply of fresh water.

'Dr Takagishi was a gentle, sensitive man,' Nicole was saying to Richard, 'with passionate feelings about his work. Just before launch I visited him in Japan and he told me that his lifelong ambition had been to explore a second Rama spacecraft.'

'It's a shame he had to die such an unpleasant death,' Richard grimly replied. 'I guess that octospider, or one of its friends, must have dragged him down here for a visit to the taxidermist almost immediately. They certainly wasted no time putting him on display.'

'You know, I don't think they killed him,' Nicole said. 'Maybe I'm hopelessly naive, but I didn't see any evidence of foul play in his ... his statue.'

'You think they just scared him to death?' Richard retorted sarcastically.

'Yes,' said Nicole firmly. 'At least it's possible.' She spent the next five minutes explaining Takagishi's heart situation to Richard.

'I'm surprised at you, Nicole,' Richard replied after listening carefully to her disclosure. 'I had you figured all wrong. I thought you were Miss Prim and Proper, play it by the rules all the way. I never gave you credit for having a mind of your own. Not to mention a strong streak of compassion.'

'In this instance it's not clear that either was an asset. If I had faithfully enforced the rules, Takagishi would be alive and living with his family in Kyoto.'

'And he would have missed the singular experience of his life ... which brings me to an interesting question, my dear doctor. Surely you are aware, as we sit here, that the odds do not favour our escape. We are both likely to die without ever seeing another human face. How do you feel about that? Where does your death, or any death, for that matter, fit into your overall scheme of things?'

Nicole looked at Richard. She was surprised by the tenor of his question. She tried without success to read the expression on his face. 'I'm not afraid, if that's what you mean,' she answered carefully. 'As a doctor I've thought often about death. And of course since my mother died when I was very young, even as a child I was forced to have some perspective on the subject.'

She paused for a moment. 'For myself, I know that I would like to stay alive until Genevieve is grown – so that I can be a grandmother to her children. But just being alive is not the most important thing. Life must have quality to be worthwhile. And to have quality we must be willing to take a few risks ... I'm not being very focused, am I?'

Richard smiled. 'No,' he said, 'but I like your general drift. You have mentioned the key word. Quality.... Have you ever considered suicide?' he asked suddenly.

'No,' Nicole replied, shaking her head. 'Never. There's always been too much to live for.' *There must be some reason for his question,* she was thinking. 'What about you?' she said after a short silence. 'Did you think about suicide during any of that pain with your father?'

'No, strangely enough,' he answered. 'My father's beatings never made me lose my zest for life. There was too much to learn. And I knew that I would outgrow him and be on my own eventually.' There was a long pause before he continued. 'But there was one period in my life when I did seriously consider suicide,' Richard said. 'My pain and anger were so great that I did not think I could endure them.'

He became silent, locked in his thoughts. Nicole waited patiently. Eventually she slipped her arm through his. 'Well, my friend,' she said lightly, 'you can tell me about it someday. Neither of us is accustomed to sharing our deepest secrets. Maybe in time we can learn. I'm going to start by telling you why I believe we are not going to die and why I think we should go over to search the area around the eastern plaza next.'

Nicole had never told anyone, not even her father, about her 'trip' during the Poro. Before she finished telling her story to Richard, not only had Nicole covered what had happened to her as a seven-year-old at the Poro, but also she had recounted the story of Omeh's visit to Rome, the Senoufo prophecies about the 'woman without companion' who scatters her progeny 'among the stars,' and the details of her vision after drinking the vial at the bottom of the pit.

Richard was speechless. The entire set of stories was so foreign to his mathematical mind that he did not even know how to react. He stared at Nicole with awe and amazement. At length, embarrassed by his silence, he started to speak. 'I don't know what to say ...'

Nicole put her fingers to his lips. 'You don't need to say anything,' she said. 'I can read your reaction in your face. We can talk about it tomorrow, after you've had some time to think about what I told you.'

Nicole yawned and looked at her watch. She pulled her sleeping mat out of her backpack and unrolled it on the ground. 'I'm exhausted,' she said to Richard. 'Nothing like a little terror to produce instant fatigue. I'll see you in four hours.'

'We've been searching now for an hour and a half,' Richard said impatiently. 'Look at this map. There's no place within five hundred metres of the plaza centre that we haven't been to at least twice.'

'Then we're doing something wrong,' Nicole replied. 'There were *three* heat sources in my vision.' Richard frowned. 'Or be logical, if you prefer. Why would there be three plazas and only two underground lairs? You said yourself that the Ramans always followed a reasonable plan.'

They were standing in front of a dodecahedron that faced the eastern plaza. 'And another thing,' Richard growled to himself, 'what's the purpose of all these damn polyhedrons? There's one in every sector and the three biggest are in the plazas … Wait a minute,' he said, as his eyes went from one of the twelve faces of the dodecahedron to an opposite skyscraper. His head then turned quickly around the plaza. 'Could it be?' he said. 'No,' he answered, 'that would be impossible.'

Richard saw that Nicole was staring at him. 'I have an idea,' he said excitedly. 'It may be completely farfetched … Do you remember Dr Bardolini and his progressive matrices? With the dolphins? … What if the Ramans also left a pattern here in New York of subtle differences that change from plaza to plaza and section to section? … Look, it's no crazier than your visions.'

Already Richard was on his knees on the ground, working with his maps of New York. 'Can I use your computer too?' he said to Nicole a few minutes later. 'That will speed up the process.'

For hours Richard Wakefield sat beside the two computers, mumbling to himself and trying to solve the puzzle of New York. He explained to Nicole, when he took a break for dinner at her insistence, that the location of the third underground hole could only be determined if he thoroughly understood the geometric relationships between the polyhedrons, the three plazas, and all the skyscrapers immediately opposite the principal faces of the polyhedrons in each of the nine sectors. Two hours before dark Richard dashed off hurriedly to an adjacent section to obtain extra data that had not yet been recorded on their computer maps.

Even after dark he did not rest. Nicole slept the first part of the fifteen-hour night. When she awoke after five hours, Richard was still working feverishly on his project. He didn't even hear Nicole clear her throat. She arose quietly and put her hands on his shoulders. 'You must get some sleep, Richard,' she said quietly,

'I'm almost there,' he said. She saw the bags under his eyes when he turned around. 'No more than another hour.'

Nicole returned to her mat. When Richard awakened her later, he was full of enthusiasm. 'Wouldn't you know it?' he said with a grin. 'There are three possible solutions, each of which is consistent with all the patterns.' He paced for almost a minute. 'Could we go look now?' he then said pleadingly. 'I don't think I can sleep until I find out.'

None of Richard's three solutions for the location of the third lair was close to the plaza. The nearest one was over a kilometre away, at the edge of New York opposite the Northern Hemicylinder. He and Nicole found nothing there. They then marched another fifteen minutes in the dark to the second possible location, a spot very near the southeast corner of the city. Richard and Nicole walked down the indicated street and found the covering in the exact spot that Richard had predicted. 'Hallelujah,' he shouted, spreading out his sleeping mat beside the cover. 'Hooray for mathematics.'

Hooray for Omeh, Nicole thought. She was no longer sleepy but she wasn't anxious to explore any new territory in the dark. *What comes first,* she asked herself after they had returned to camp and she was lying awake on her mat, *intuition or mathematics? Do we use models to help us find the truth? Or do we know the truth first, and then develop the mathematics to explain it?*

They were both up at daylight. 'The days are still growing slightly shorter,' Richard mentioned to Nicole. 'But the sum of daytime and nighttime is remaining constant at forty-six hours, four minutes, and fourteen seconds.'

'How long before we reach the Earth?' Nicole inquired as she was stuffing her sleeping mat into its protective package.

'Twenty Earth days and three hours,' he replied after consulting his computer. 'Are you ready for another adventure?'

She nodded. 'I presume you also know where to find the panel that opens this cover?'

'No, but I bet it's not hard to find,' he said confidently. 'And after we find this one, the avian lair opening will be duck soup because we'll have the whole pattern.'

Ten minutes later Richard pushed on a metal plate and the third covering swung open. The descent into this third hole was down a wide staircase broken by occasional landings. Richard took Nicole's hand as they walked down the stairs. They used their flashlights to find their way, as no lights illuminated their descent.

The water room was in the same place as in the other underground lairs. There were no sounds in the horizontal tunnels that led off from the central stairway at either of the two main levels. 'I don't think anyone lives here,' Richard said.

'At least not yet,' Nicole answered.

48 WELCOME EARTHLINGS

Richard was puzzled. In the first room off one of the top horizontal tunnels he had found an array of strange gadgets that he had decoded in less than an hour. He now knew how to regulate the lights and temperature throughout each particular portion of the underground lair. But if it was that easy, and all the lairs were similarly constructed, why did the avians not use the lights that had been provided? While they were eating breakfast Richard quizzed Nicole about the details of the avian lair.

'You're overlooking more fundamental issues,' Nicole said, as she took a bite of manna melon. 'The avians aren't that important by themselves. The real question is, where are the Ramans? And why did they put these holes under New York in the first place?'

'Maybe they're all Ramans,' Richard replied. 'The biots, the avians, the octospiders – maybe they all came originally from the same planet. At the beginning they were all one happy family. But as the years and generations passed, different species evolved in separate ways. Individual lairs were constructed and the—'

'There are too many problems with that scenario,' Nicole interrupted. 'First, the biots are definitely machines. The avians may or may not be. The octospiders almost certainly aren't, although a technological level that could create this spaceship in the first place might have progressed further in artificial intelligence than we can possibly imagine. My intuitive sense, however, says that those things are organic.'

'We humans would never be able to distinguish between a living creature and a versatile machine created by a truly advanced species.'

'I agree with that. But we can't possibly resolve this argument by ourselves. Besides, there is another question that I want to discuss with you.'

'What's that?' Richard asked.

'Did the avians and the octospiders and these underground regions exist also on Rama I? If so, how did the Norton crew miss them altogether? If not, why are they on this spacecraft and not the first one?'

Richard was quiet for several seconds. 'I see where you're heading,' he said finally. 'The fundamental premise has always been that the Rama spacecraft were created millions of years ago, by unknown beings from another region of the galaxy, and that they were totally uninvolved with and disinterested in whatever they encountered during their trek. If they were created that long ago, why would two vehicles that were presumably built at virtually the same time have such striking differences?'

'I'm starting to believe that our colleague from Kyoto was right,' Nicole answered. 'Maybe there *is* a meaningful pattern to all this. I'm fairly confident that the Norton crew was thorough and accurate in its survey and that all the distinctions between Rama I and Rama II are indeed real. As soon as we acknowledge that the two spacecraft are different, we face a more difficult issue. *Why* are they different?'

Richard had finished eating and was now pacing in the dimly lit tunnel. 'There was a discussion just like this before it was decided to abort the mission. At the teleconference the main question was, why did the Ramans change course to encounter the Earth? Since the first spacecraft had not done so, it was considered hard evidence that Rama II was different. And the people participating in that meeting knew nothing of the avians or octospiders.'

'General Borzov would have loved the avians,' Nicole commented after a short silence. 'He thought that flying was the greatest pleasure in the world.' She laughed. 'He once told me that his secret hope in life was that reincarnation was on the level and that he would come back as a bird.'

'He was a fine man,' Richard said, stopping his pacing momentarily. 'I don't think we ever properly appreciated all his talents.'

As Nicole replaced part of the manna melon in her backpack and prepared to continue the exploration, she smiled at her peripatetic friend. 'One more question, Richard?'

He nodded.

'Do you think we've met any Ramans yet? By that I mean the creatures who made this vehicle. Or any of their descendants.'

Richard shook his head vigorously. 'Absolutely not,' he said. 'Maybe we've met some of their creations. Or even other species from the same planet. But we haven't seen the main characters yet.'

They found the White Room off to the left of a horizontal tunnel at the second level below the surface. Until then the exploration had been almost boring. Richard and Nicole had walked down many tunnels and had peered into one empty room after another. Four times they had found a set of gadgets for regulating the lights and temperature. Until they reached the White Room, they had seen nothing else of interest.

Both Richard and Nicole were astonished when they entered a room whose walls were painted a crisp white. In addition to the paint, the room was fascinating because one corner was cluttered with objects that turned out, on closer inspection, to be quite familiar. There was a comb and a brush, an empty lipstick container, several coins, a collection of keys, and even something that looked like an old walkie-talkie. In another pile there was a ring and a wristwatch, a tube of toothpaste, a nail file, and a small keyboard with Latin letters. Richard and Nicole were stunned. 'Okay, genius,' she said with a wave of her hand. 'Explain all this, if you can.'

He picked up the tube of toothpaste, opened the cap, and squeezed. A white material came out. Richard put his finger in it and then placed the finger in his mouth. 'Yuck,' he said, spitting out the paste. 'Bring your mass spectrometer over here.'

While Nicole was examining the toothpaste with her sophisticated medical instruments, Richard picked up each of the other objects. The watch in particular fascinated him. It was indeed keeping proper time, second by second, although its reference point was completely unknown. 'Did you ever go to the space museum in Florida?' he asked Nicole.

'No,' she answered distractedly.

'They had a display of the common objects taken by the crew on the first Rama mission. This watch looks exactly like the one in the display – I remember it well because I bought a similar one in the museum shop.'

Nicole walked over with a puzzled look on her face. 'This stuff isn't toothpaste, Richard. I don't know what it is. The spectra are astonishing, with an abundance of super-heavy molecules.'

For several minutes the two cosmonauts rummaged in the odd collection of items, trying to make some sense out of their latest discovery. 'One thing is certain,' Richard said as he was trying unsuccessfully to open up the walkie-talkie, 'these objects are definitely associated with human beings. There's simply too many of them for some kind of strange interspecies coincidence.'

'But how did they get here?' Nicole asked. She was trying to use the brush but its bristles were far too soft for her hair. She examined it in more detail. 'This is not really a brush,' she announced. 'It *looks* like a brush, and *feels* like a brush, but it's useless in the hair.'

She bent down and picked up the nail file. 'And this can't be used to file any human's fingernails.' Richard came over to see what she was talking about. He was still struggling with the walkie-talkie. He dropped it in disgust and took the nail file that Nicole had extended toward him.

'So these things look human, but aren't?' he said, pulling the file against the end of his longest fingernail. The nail was unchanged. Richard gave the file back to Nicole. 'What's going on here?' he shouted in a frustrated tone.

'I remember reading a science fiction novel while I was at the university,' Nicole said a few seconds later, 'in which an extraterrestrial species learned about human beings solely from our earliest television programs. When they finally met us, they offered cereal boxes and soaps and other objects the aliens had seen on our television commercials. The packages were all properly designed, but the contents were either nonexistent or absolutely wrong.'

Richard had not been listening carefully to Nicole. He had been fiddling with the keys and surveying the collection of objects in the room. 'Now what do all these things have in common?' he said, mostly to himself.

They both arrived at the same answer several seconds later. 'They were all carried by the Norton crew,' Richard and Nicole said in unison.

'So the two Rama space vehicles must have some kind of communication linkup,' Richard said.

'And these objects have been planted here on purpose, to show us that the visit to Rama I was observed and recorded.'

'The spider biots that inspected the Norton campsites and the equipment must have contained imaging sensors.'

'And all of these things were fabricated from pictures transmitted from Rama I to Rama II.'

After Nicole's last comment both of them were silent, each following their own thought pattern. 'But why do they want us to know all this? What is it we're supposed to do now?' Richard stood up and began to pace around the room. Suddenly he started laughing. 'Wouldn't it be amazing,' he said, 'if David Brown was right after all, if the Ramans really were completely disinterested in anything they found, but programmed their space vehicles to *act* interested in any visitors? They could flatter whatever species they encountered by making midcourse corrections and by fashioning simple objects. What an incredible irony. Since all immature species are probably hopelessly self-centered, the visitors to the Raman craft would be totally occupied trying to understand an assumed message—'

'I think you're getting carried away,' Nicole interrupted. 'All we know at this point is that this spacecraft apparently received pictures from Rama I, and that reproductions of small, everyday objects that were carried by the Norton crew have been placed here in this room for us to find.'

'I wonder if the keyboard is as useless as everything else,' Richard said as he picked it up. He spelled the word 'Rama' with the keys. Nothing happened. He tried 'Nicole.' Still nothing.

'Don't you remember how the old models worked?' Nicole said with a grin. She took the keyboard. 'They all had a separate power key.' She pressed the unmarked button in the upper right-hand corner of the keyboard. A portion of the opposite wall slid away, revealing a large black square area about one metre on a side.

The small keyboard was based on the ones that had been attached to the portable computers on the first Rama mission. It had four rows of twelve characters, with an extra power button in the upper right-hand corner. The twenty-six Latin letters, ten Arabic numerals, and four mathematical operands were marked on forty of the individual keys. The other eight keys contained either dots or geometrical figures on their surfaces and, in addition, could be set in either an 'up' or 'down' position. Richard and Nicole quickly learned that these special keys were the true controls of the Raman system. By trial and error they also discovered that the result from striking any individual action key was a function of the positioning of the *other* seven keys. Thus, pressing any specific command key could produce as many as 128 different results. Altogether, then, the system provided for 1,024 separate actions that could be initiated from the keyboard.

Making a command dictionary was a laborious process. Richard volunteered for the duty. Using their own computers to keep notes, he began the process of developing the rudiments of a language to translate the special keyboard commands. The initial goal was simple – to be able to use the Raman computer like one of their own. Once the translation was developed, any given input into the Newton portable computers would contain, as part of its output, what set of key impressions on the Raman board would produce a similar response on the square black screen.

Even with Richard's intelligence and computer expertise, the task was a formidable one. It was also not something that could easily be shared. At Richard's suggestion, Nicole climbed out of the lair twice during the first Raman day they were in the White Room. Both times she took long walks around New York, casting her eyes to the sky from time to time to look for a helicopter. On the second excursion Nicole went back to the barn where she had fallen in the pit. Already so much had happened that her frightening experience at the bottom seemed like ancient history.

She thought often about Borzov, Wilson, and Takagishi. All the cosmonauts had known when they left the Earth that there were uncertainties in the mission. They had trained often to handle vehicle emergencies, problems with their own spacecraft that might prove to be life threatening ... but none of them had actually believed that there would be any fatalities on the mission. *If Richard and I perish here in New York,* Nicole remarked to herself, *then almost half the crew will have died. That will be the worst disaster since we started flying piloted missions again.*

She was standing outside the barn, in almost the exact spot where she and Francesca had talked to Richard on the communicator the last time. *So why did you lie, Francesca?* Nicole wondered. *Did you think somehow my disappearance would silence all suspicion?*

On the final morning at the Beta campsite, before she and the others had set out to look for Takagishi, Nicole had transmitted all the notes in her own portable computer in Rama through the networking system to the desktop in her room on the Newton. At the time Nicole had made the data transfer to give herself extra memory, if she should need it, in her travelling computer. *But it's all there,* she recalled, *if some diligent detective ever looks for it. The drugs, David's blood pressure, even a cryptic reference to the abortion. And of course Richard's solution to the RoSur malfunction.*

On her two walks Nicole saw several centipede biots, and even a bulldozer once, at the far limit of her vision. She didn't see any avians and neither heard nor saw an octospider. *Maybe they only come out at night,* she mused as she returned to have dinner with Richard.

49 INTERACTION

'We're almost out of food,' Nicole said. They packed up what remained of the manna melon and stuffed it in Richard's backpack.

'I know,' he replied. 'I have a plan for you to obtain some more.'

'*Me?*' asked Nicole. 'Why is it my job?'

'Well, first of all, it only requires one person. Working with graphics on the Raman computer gave me the idea. Second, I can't spare the time. I think I'm on the verge of breaking into the operating system. There are about two hundred commands that I can't explain unless they allow entry into another level, some kind of higher-order space in the hierarchy.'

Richard had explained to Nicole during dinner that he had now figured out how to use the Raman computer like one on the Earth. He could store and retrieve data, perform mathematical computations, design graphics, even create new languages. 'But I haven't begun to tap its potential,' he had said. 'Tonight and tomorrow I must discover more of its secrets. We're running out of time.'

His plan for obtaining food was, indeed, deceptively simple. After the long Raman night (during which Richard could not have slept more than three hours), Nicole walked over to the central plaza to implement the plan. Based on his progressive matrix analysis, Richard gave her three possible locations for the panel to open the covering above the avian lair. He was so confident of his analysis that he wouldn't even discuss what she should do if she didn't find the plate. Richard was correct. Nicole found the panel easily. Then she opened the cover and shouted down the vertical corridor. There was no response.

She shone her flashlight into the darkness below her. The tank sentinel was on duty, going to and fro in front of the horizontal tunnel that led past the water room. Nicole shouted again. If she could avoid it, she did not want to descend even to the first ledge. Even though Richard had assured her he would come to her rescue if she was overdue, Nicole did not relish the prospect of being hemmed in with the avians again.

Was that a distant jabbering she heard? Nicole thought so. She took one of the coins that she had found in the White Room and dropped it into the vertical corridor. It sailed far down, hitting a ledge somewhere near the second main level. This time there was loud jabbering. One of the avians flew up into her flashlight beam and over the tank sentinel's head. Moments later the cover began to close and Nicole had to move away.

She had discussed this contingency with Richard. Nicole waited several minutes and then pushed the panel again. When she yelled into the depths of the avian lair the second time, there was an immediate response. This time her friend, the black velvet avian, flew up to within five metres of the surface and jabbered at her. It was clear to Nicole that she was being told to go away. Before the avian turned around, however, Nicole pulled out her computer monitor and activated a stored program. Two manna melons appeared on the screen in graphic depiction. As the avian watched, the melons became coloured and then a neat incision displayed the texture and colour inside one of them.

The black velvet avian had flown up closer to the opening for a better look. Now it turned and screeched back into the dark below. Within seconds a second familiar bird, the likely mate for the black velvet one, flew up and landed on the first ledge below the ground. Nicole repeated the display. The two birds talked and then flew deeper into the lair.

Minutes went by. Nicole could hear occasional jabbering from the depths of the corridor. At length her two friends returned, each carrying a small manna melon in its talons. They landed in the plaza near the opening. Nicole walked over toward the melons, but the avians continued to clutch them. What followed was (Nicole assumed) a long lecture. The two birds jabbered both individually and together, always looking at her and often tapping on the melons. Fifteen minutes later, apparently satisfied that they had communicated their message, the avians took flight, swooped around the plaza, and vanished into their lair.

I think they were telling me that melons are in short supply, Nicole thought as she walked back toward the eastern plaza. The melons were heavy. She had one in each of the two backpacks that she had emptied that morning before she left the White Room. Or *maybe that I should not disturb them in the future. Whatever it was, we will not be welcome any more.*

She thought that Richard would be ecstatic when she returned to the White Room. He was, but not because of Nicole and the manna melons. He had a grin on his face from one ear to the other and was holding one hand behind his back. 'Wait until I show you what I have,' he said as Nicole unloaded the backpacks. Richard brought his hand around in front of him and opened it. The hand contained a solitary black ball about ten centimetres in diameter.

'I'm nowhere near figuring out all the logic, or How much information can go in the request,' Richard said. 'But I have established a fundamental principle. We can ask for and receive "things" using the computer.'

'What do you mean?' Nicole asked, still not certain why Richard was so excited about a small black ball.

'They made this for me,' he said, handing her the ball again. 'Don't you understand? Somewhere here they have a factory and can make things for us.'

'Then maybe "they", whoever they are, can start making us some food,' said Nicole. She was a little annoyed that Richard had neither congratulated her nor thanked her for the melons. 'The avians are not likely to give us any more.'

'It will be no problem,' Richard said. 'Eventually, once we learn the full range of the request process, we may be able to order fish and chips, steak and potatoes, anything, as long as we can state what we want in unambiguous scientific terms.'

Nicole stared at her friend. With his unkempt hair, his unshaven face, the bags under his eyes, and his wild grin, he looked at the moment like a fugitive from an insane asylum. 'Richard,' she asked, 'will you slow down a little? If you've found the Holy Grail, can you at least spend a second explaining it to me?'

'Look at the screen,' he said, Using the keyboard he drew a circle, then scratched it out and made a square. In less than a minute Richard had carefully drawn a cube in three dimensions. When he was finished with the graphics, he put the eight action keys into a predetermined configuration and then pressed the key with the small rectangle designator. A set of strange symbols appeared on the black monitor. 'Don't worry,' Richard said, 'we don't need to understand the details. They are just asking for the dimensional specifications on the cube.'

Richard next made a string of entries from the normal alphanumeric keys. 'Now,' he said, turning back to face Nicole, 'if I have done it correctly, we will have a cube, made from the same material as that ball, in about ten minutes.'

They ate some of the new melon while they waited. It tasted the same as the others. *Steak and potatoes would be unbelievably good,* Nicole was thinking, when suddenly the end wall lifted up half a metre above the floor and a black cube appeared in the gap.

'Wait a minute, don't touch it yet,' Richard said as Nicole went over to investigate. 'Look here!' He shone his flashlight into the darkness behind the cube. 'There are vast tunnels beyond these walls,' he said, 'and they must lead to factories so advanced we couldn't even recognize them. Imagine! They can even make objects on request.'

Nicole was beginning to understand why Richard was so ecstatic. 'We now have the capability to control our own destiny in some small way,' he continued, 'If I can break the code fast enough, we should be able to request food, maybe even what we need to build a boat.'

'Without loud motors, I hope,' quipped Nicole.

'No motors,' agreed Richard. He finished his melon and turned back to the keyboard.

*

443

Nicole was becoming worried. Richard had succeeded in making only one new breakthrough in a full Raman day. All he had to show for thirty-eight hours of work (he had only slept eight hours during the entire period) was one new material. He could make 'light' black objects like the first ball, whose specific gravity was close to balsa wood, or he could make 'heavy' black objects of density similar to oak or pine. He was wearing himself out with his work. And he could not, or would not, share any of the load with Nicole.

What if his first discovery was just blind luck? Nicole said to herself as she climbed the stairs for her dawn walk. *Or what if the system cannot make anything but two kinds of black objects?* She could not help worrying about wasted time. It was only sixteen more days until Rama would encounter the Earth. There was no sign of a rescue team. At the back of her mind was the thought that perhaps she and Richard had been abandoned altogether.

She had tried to talk to Richard about their plans the previous evening, but he had been exhausted. Richard hadn't responded in any way when Nicole had mentioned to him that she was very concerned. Later, after she had carefully outlined all their options and asked his opinion about what they should do, she noticed that he had fallen asleep. When Nicole awakened after a brief nap herself, Richard was already working again at the keyboard and refused to be distracted by either breakfast or conversation. Nicole had stumbled over the growing array of black objects on the floor as she had exited the White Room for her early morning exercise.

Nicole was feeling very lonely. The last fifty hours, which she had spent mostly by herself, had passed very slowly. Her only escape had been the pleasure of reading. She had the text of five books stored in her computer. One was her medical encyclopedia, but the other four were all for recreation. *I bet all of Richard's discretionary memory is filled with Shakespeare,* she thought as she sat on the wall surrounding New York. She stared out at the Cylindrical Sea. In the far distance, barely visible in her binoculars through the mist and clouds, she could see the northern bowl where they had entered Rama the first time.

She had two of her father's novels stored in the computer. Nicole's personal favourite was *Queen for All Ages,* the story of Eleanor of Aquitaine's younger years, beginning with her adolescence at the ducal court in Poitiers. The story line followed Eleanor through her marriage to Louis Capet of France, their crusade to the Holy Land, and her extraordinary personal appeal for an annulment from Pope Eugenius. The novel culminated with Eleanor's divorce from Louis and betrothal to the young and exciting Henry Plantagenet.

The other Pierre des Jardins novel in her computer's memory was his universally acclaimed chef d'oeuvre, *I, Richard Coeur de Lion,* a mixture of first-person diary and interior monologue, set during two winter weeks at the end of the twelfth century. In the novel Richard and his soldiers, embarked on another crusade, are quartered near Messina under the protection of the

Norman king of Sicily, While there the famous warrior-king and homo-sexual son of Eleanor of Aquitaine and Henry Plantagenet, in a burst of self-examination, relives the major personal and historical events of his life.

Nicole remembered a long discussion with Genevieve after her daughter had read *I, Richard* the previous summer. The young teenager had been fascinated by the story, and had surprised her mother by asking extremely intelligent questions. Thoughts of Genevieve made Nicole wonder what her daughter might be doing at Beauvois at the very moment. *They have told you that I have disappeared,* Nicole surmised. *What does the military call it? Missing in action?*

In her mind's eye Nicole could see her daughter riding home from school each day on her bicycle. 'Any news?' Genevieve would probably say to her grandfather as she crossed the portal of the villa. Pierre would just shake his head sorrowfully.

It has been two weeks now since anyone has officially seen me. Do you still have hope, my darling daughter? The bereft Nicole was struck by an overwhelming desire to talk to Genevieve. For a moment, suspending reality, Nicole could not accept the fact that she was separated from her daughter by millions of kilometres and had no way to communicate with her. She rose to return to the White Room, thinking in her temporary confusion that she could phone Genevieve from there.

When her sanity returned several seconds later, Nicole was astonished at how easily her mind had tricked itself. She shook her head and sat down on the wall overlooking the Cylindrical Sea. She remained on the wall for almost two hours, her thoughts roaming freely over a variety of subjects. Toward the end of the time, when she was preparing to return to the White Room, her mind focused on Richard Wakefield. *I have tried, my British friend,* Nicole said to herself. *I have been more open with you than with anyone since Henry. But it would be just my luck to be here with someone even less trusting than myself.*

Nicole was feeling an undefined sadness as she trekked down the stairs to the second level and turned right at the horizontal tunnel. Her sadness changed to surprise when she entered the White Room. Richard jumped up from his small black chair and greeted her with a hug. He had shaved and brushed his hair. He had even cleaned his fingernails. Laid out on the black table in the middle of the room was a neatly sectioned manna melon. One piece sat on each of the two black plates in front of the chairs.

Richard pulled out her chair and indicated for Nicole to sit down. He went around the table and sat in his own seat. He reached across the table and took both of Nicole's hands. 'I want to apologize,' he said with great intensity, 'for being such a boor. I have behaved very badly these last few days.

'I have thought of thousands of things to tell you during these hours I've been waiting,' he continued hesitantly, a strained smile playing across his lips, 'but I can't remember most of them ... I know I wanted to explain to you how very important Prince Hal and Falstaff were to me. They were my closest friends … It has not been easy for me to deal with their deaths. My grief is still very intense …'

Richard took a drink of water and swallowed. 'But most of all,' he said, 'I'm sorry that I have not told you what a spectacular person you are. You are intelligent, attractive, witty, sensitive – everything I ever dreamed of finding in a woman. Despite our situation, I've been afraid to tell you how I felt. I guess my fear of rejection runs very deep.'

Tears welled out of the corner of Richard's eyes and ran down his cheeks. He was trembling slightly. Nicole could tell what an incredible effort it had been for him. She brought his hands up against her cheeks. 'I think you're very special too,' she said.

50 HOPE SPRINGS ETERNAL

Richard continued to work with the Rama computer, but he limited himself to short sessions and involved Nicole whenever he could. They took walks together and chatted like old friends. Richard entertained Nicole by acting out entire scenes from Shakespeare. The man had a prodigious memory. He tried to play both sides in the love scenes from *Romeo and Juliet*, but every time he broke into his falsetto, Nicole would erupt with laughter.

One night they talked for over an hour about Omeh, the Senoufo tribe, and Nicole's visions. 'You understand that it's difficult for me to accept the physical reality of some of these stories,' Richard said, attempting to qualify his curiosity. 'Nevertheless, I admit that I find them absolutely fascinating.' Later he showed keen interest in analyzing all the symbolism in her visions.

It was obvious that he acknowledged Nicole's mystical attributes as just another component in her rich personality.

They slept nuzzling together before they made love. When they did finally have intercourse, it was gentle and unhurried, surprising both of them with its ease and satisfaction. A few nights later, Nicole was lying with her head on Richard's chest, quietly drifting in and out of sleep. He was in deep thought. 'Several days ago,' he said, nudging her awake, 'back before we became so intimate, I told you that I considered committing suicide once. At the time I was afraid to tell you the story. Would you like to hear it now?'

Nicole opened her eyes. She rolled over and put her chin on his stomach. 'Uh-huh,' she said. She reached up and kissed him on the eyes before he began his tale.

'I guess you know I was married to Sarah Tydings when both of us were very young,' he began. 'It was also before she was famous. She was in her first year with the Royal Shakespeare Company and they were performing *Romeo and Juliet, As You Like It,* and *Cymbeline* in repertory at Stratford. Sarah was Rosalind and Juliet and fantastic at both.

'She was eighteen at the time, just out of school. I fell in love with her the first night I saw her as Juliet. I sent her roses in the dressing room every evening and used most of my savings to see all the performances. We had two long dinners together and then I proposed. She accepted more from astonishment than love.

'I went to graduate school at Cambridge after the summer was over. We lived in a modest flat and she commuted to the theatre in London. I would go with her whenever I could, but after several months my studies demanded more of my time.'

Richard stopped his narrative and glanced down at Nicole. She had not moved. She was lying partially across him, a smile of love on her face. 'Go on,' she said softly.

'Sarah was an adrenaline junkie. She craved excitement and variety. The mundane and tedious angered her. Grocery shopping, for example, was a colossal bore. It was just too much trouble for her to turn on the set and decide what to order. She also found any kind of schedule incredibly constraining.

'Lovemaking had to be performed in a different position or be accompanied by some different music every time; otherwise it was old hat. For a while I was creative enough to satisfy her. I also took care of all the routine tasks to free her from the drudgery of housework. But there were only so many hours in the day. Ultimately, despite my considerable abilities, my graduate studies began to suffer because I was spending all my energy making life interesting for her.

'After we had been married for a year, Sarah wanted to rent a flat in London, so that she didn't need to make the long commute every night after a performance. Actually she had already been spending a couple of nights a week in London, ostensibly with one of her actress friends. But her career was soaring and we had plenty of money, so why should I say no?

'It was not long before rumours about her behaviour became quite widespread. I chose to ignore them, fearing, I guess, that she wouldn't deny them if I asked her. Then one night, late, while I was studying for an examination, I received a phone call from a woman. She was very polite, although obviously distraught. She told me that she was the wife of the actor Hugh Sinclair, and that Mr Sinclair – who at that time was starring with Sarah in the American drama *In Any Weather* – was having an affair with my wife. "In fact," she told me, "he is over at your wife's flat at this very moment." Mrs Sinclair started crying and then hung up.'

Nicole reached up and softly caressed Richard's cheek with her hand. 'I felt as if my chest had exploded,' he said, remembering the pain. 'I was angry, terrified, frantic. I went to the station and took the late train to London. When the taxi dropped me at Sarah's place, I ran to the door.

'I did not knock. I bolted up the stairs and found the two of them sleeping naked in the bed. I picked Sarah up and flung her against the wall – I can still remember the sound of her head smashing into the mirror. Then I fell on him in a rage, punching his face over and over, until it was nothing but a mass of blood. It was awful... .'

Richard stopped himself and began to cry noiselessly. Nicole put her arms around his heaving chest and wept with him. 'Darling, darling,' she said.

'I was an animal,' he cried. 'I was worse than my father ever was. I would have killed them both if the people in the next flat hadn't restrained me.'

Neither of them said anything for several minutes. When Richard spoke again his voice was subdued, almost remote. 'The next day, after the police station and the tabloid reporters and all the recriminations with Sarah, I wanted to kill myself. I would have done it, too, if I had owned a gun. I was considering the gruesome alternatives – pills, slitting my wrists with a razor blade, jumping off a bridge – when another student called to ask me a detailed question on relativity. There was no way, after fifteen minutes of thinking about Mr Einstein, that suicide was still a viable option. Divorce, certainly. Celibacy, highly likely. But death was out of the question. I could never have prematurely terminated my love affair with physics.' His voice trailed off.

Nicole wiped her eyes and placed her hands in his. She leaned her naked body across Richard's and kissed him. 'I love you,' she said.

Nicole's sounding alarm indicated that it was daylight again in Rama. *Ten more days,* she noted after a quick mental calculation. *We'd better have a serious talk now.*

The alarm had awakened Richard as well. He turned and smiled at his sleeping partner. 'Darling,' Nicole said, 'the time has come—'

'The walrus said, to speak of many things.'

'Come on now, be serious. We have to decide what we're going to do. It's fairly obvious that we're not going to be rescued.'

'I agree,' said Richard. He sat up and reached across Nicole's mat for his shirt. 'I have been dreading this moment for days. But I guess we have finally reached the point where we should consider swimming across.'

'You don't think there's any chance of making a boat out of our black stuff?'

'No,' he answered. 'One material is too light and the other too heavy. We could probably build a hybrid that would be seaworthy, *if* we had some nails, but without any sails we would still have to row across.... Our best bet is to swim.'

Richard stood up and walked over to the black square on the wall. 'My fancy plans didn't pan out, did they?' He thumped lightly on the square. 'And I was going to produce steak and potatoes as well as a boat.'

'The best laid plans of mice and men gang aft agley.'

'What a weird poet old Robbie was. I never could understand what people saw in him.'

Nicole finished dressing and started doing some stretching exercises. 'Whew,' she said, 'I'm out of shape. I haven't had any heavy physical activity in days.' She smiled at Richard, who was looking at her coyly. '*That* doesn't count,' she added, shaking her head.

'It's almost the only exercise I've ever liked,' Richard replied with a grin. 'I used to hate it at the academy when we had those special physical training weekends.'

Richard had laid out small portions of manna melon on the black table, 'Three more meals after this one,' he said without emotion. 'I guess we swim before it's dark again.'

'You don't want to go this morning?' Nicole asked.

'No,' he replied. 'Why don't you go survey the coast and pick a spot. I found something last night on the computer that has me baffled. It won't give us food or sailboats, but it looks as if I may have finally broken through into another kind of structure.'

After breakfast, Nicole kissed Richard goodbye and wandered up to the surface. It did not take her long to reconnoitre the coast. There really were no reasons to pick one embarkation point over another. The grim reality of the coming swim oppressed Nicole. *The odds are good,* she told herself, *that neither Richard nor I will be alive when it is dark again in Rama.*

She tried to imagine what it would be like to be eaten by a shark biot. Would it be a quick death? Or would you drown aware that your legs had just been amputated? Nicole shuddered at the idea. *Maybe we should try to obtain another melon....* She knew that was useless. Sooner or later, they had to swim.

Nicole turned her back on the sea. *At least these last few days have been good,* she said to herself, not wanting to think anymore about their predicament. *He has been an excellent companion. In every way.* She allowed herself the momentary luxury of recalling their shared pleasure. Then Nicole smiled and started walking back toward the lair.

'But what am I looking at?' Nicole asked as another image flashed up on the black square.

'I'm not completely certain,' Richard replied. 'All I know is that I have tapped into a long list of some kind. You remember that one particular command configuration that produces the lines of symbols that look like Sanskrit? Well, I was scrolling through the gibberish and eventually I noticed a pattern. I stopped at the beginning of the pattern, changed the position of the last three keys, and then hit the double dot again. Suddenly an image was on the screen. And every time I hit an alphanumeric, the picture changed.'

'But how do you know you're looking at sensor output?'

Richard entered a command and there was a change in the image. 'Occasionally I see something I recognize,' he said. 'Look at that one, for example. Couldn't that be the Beta stairway viewed from a camera in the middle of the Central Plain?'

Nicole studied the picture. 'Possibly,' she said, 'but I don't see how you could ever tell for certain.'

Richard commanded the screen to change again. The next three pictures were unintelligible. The fourth one showed a feature tapering to a point at the top of the frame. 'And that one,' he said. 'Couldn't it be one of the little horns, as seen from a sensor near the top of the Big Horn?'

No matter how hard she tried, Nicole could not visualize what the view would be like from the top of the giant spire in the centre of the southern bowl. Richard continued to flip through the pictures. Only about one in five was even partially clear. 'Somewhere in this system there must be some enhancement algorithms,' he said to himself. 'Then I can sharpen up all the images.'

Nicole could tell that Richard was about to begin another long work session. She walked over to him and put her arms around his neck. 'Could I talk you into a little distraction first?' she said, reaching up and kissing him on the mouth.

'I guess so,' he replied, dropping the keyboard on the floor. 'It will probably be good for me to clear my mind.'

Nicole was in the middle of a beautiful dream. She was home again at her villa in Beauvois. Richard was sitting beside her on the couch in the living room and was holding her hand. Her father and daughter were opposite them in the soft chairs.

Her dream was broken by Richard's insistent voice. When Nicole opened her eyes her lover was standing over her, his voice crackling with excitement. 'Wait until you see this, darling,' he said, extending a hand to pull her up. 'It's fantastic! Somebody is still here.'

Nicole shook the dream from her mind and looked over at the black square where Richard was pointing. 'Can you believe it?' he said, jumping up and down. 'There's no doubt about it The military ship is still docked.'

Only then did Nicole realise that she was looking at a picture of the outside of Rama. She blinked her eyes and listened to Richard's rambling explanation. 'Once I figured out the code for the enhancement parameters, almost every frame became clear. That set of pictures I showed you earlier must be the realtime output from hundreds of Rama's imaging sensors. And I think I have figured out how to access the other sensor data bases as well.'

Richard was exultant. He threw his arms around Nicole and lifted her off the ground. He hugged and kissed her and bounced around the room like a lunatic.

When he finally calmed down a little, Nicole spent almost a full minute studying the image that was projected on the black square. It was definitely the Newton military ship; she could read the markings. 'So the science space-craft has gone home,' she commented to Richard.

'Yes,' he answered, 'as I expected. I was afraid they would *both* be gone and that after we swam across the sea, we would find ourselves still trapped, this time in a larger prison.'

The same concern had bothered Nicole. She smiled at Richard. 'It's relatively straightforward, then, isn't it? We swim across the Cylindrical Sea and walk over to the chairlift. Someone will be waiting for us at the top.'

Nicole started packing her belongings. Richard, meanwhile, continued to flash new images on the screen. 'What are you doing now, darling?' Nicole asked gently. 'I thought we were going to make our swim.'

'I haven't made a full pass through the sensor list since I located the enhancement parameters,' Richard replied. 'I just want to make certain we're not missing anything critical. It will only take another hour or so.'

Nicole stopped packing and sat down in front of the screen beside Richard. The pictures were indeed interesting. Some were exterior shots, but most were images of different regions inside Rama, including the underground lairs. One magnificent photo was taken from the top of the large room where the hot spheres in their sponge webbing rested on the floor beneath the hanging lattices. Richard and Nicole watched the picture for a moment, hoping to see a black and gold octospider, but they detected no movement.

They were near the end of the list when an image of the bottom third of the Alpha stairway stunned them both. There, climbing down the stairs, were four human figures in space suits. Richard and Nicole watched the figures descend for five seconds and then exploded with joy. 'They're coming!' Richard said, throwing his arms into the air. 'We're going to be rescued!'

51 ESCAPE HARNESS

Richard was becoming impatient. He and Nicole had been standing on the walls of New York for over an hour, scanning the skies for some sign of a helicopter. 'Where the hell are they?' he grumbled. 'It only takes fifteen minutes by rover from the bottom of Alpha stairway to the Beta campsite.'

'Maybe they're looking somewhere else,' Nicole said encouragingly.

'That's ridiculous!' Richard said. 'Surely they would go to Beta first – and even if they couldn't repair the comm system, at least they'd find my last message. I said I was taking one of the motorboats to New York.'

'They probably know that there's no place for a helicopter to land in the city. They may be coming across in a boat themselves.'

'Without first seeing if they could spot us from the helicopter? That's unlikely.' Richard turned his eyes to the sea and searched for a sail. 'A boat A boat. My kingdom for a boat.'

Nicole laughed but Richard barely managed a little smile. 'Two men could assemble the sailboat in the supply hut at Beta in less than thirty minutes,' he fretted. 'Dammit, what's holding them up?'

In his frustration Richard switched on the transmitter in his communicator. 'Now hear this, you guys. If you're anywhere near the Cylindrical Sea, identify yourselves. And then hurry your asses over here. We're standing on the wall and we're tired of waiting.'

There was no response. Nicole sat down on the wall. 'What are you doing?' Richard asked.

'I think you're worrying enough for both of us,' she responded. 'And I'm tired of standing up and waving my arms.' She stared across the Cylindrical Sea. 'It would be so much easier,' Nicole said wistfully, 'if we could just fly across ourselves.'

Richard cocked his head to one side and looked at her. 'What a great idea,' he said several seconds later. 'Why didn't we think of it before?' He immediately sat down and started doing some calculations on his computer. 'Cowards die many times before their deaths,' he mumbled to himself, 'the valiant never taste of death but once.'

Nicole watched her friend furiously pounding his keyboard. 'What are

453

you doing, dear?' she inquired, glancing over his shoulder at the computer monitor.

'Three!' he shouted, after finishing a computation. 'Three should be enough.' Richard looked up at the puzzled Nicole. 'Do you want to hear the most outrageous plan in interplanetary history?' he asked her.

'Why not?' she said with a doubtful smile.

'We are going to build ourselves harnesses out of the lattice material and the avians are going to fly us across the Cylindrical Sea.'

Nicole stared at Richard for several seconds. 'Assuming we can make the harnesses,' she said skeptically, 'how do we talk the avians into doing their part?'

'We convince them it's in their own best interest,' Richard replied. 'Or alternatively we threaten them in some way. ... I don't know, you can work on that issue.'

Nicole was incredulous. 'Anyway,' Richard continued, grabbing her hand and walking down the wall, 'it beats standing around here waiting for the helicopter or the boat.'

Five hours later there was still no sign of the rescue team. When they had finished making the harnesses, Richard had left Nicole at the wall and gone back to the White Room to check through the sensor set again. He returned with the news that he thought he had seen the human figures in the vicinity of the Beta campsite, but that the resolution on that particular frame had been very poor. As they had agreed, Nicole had been calling every half hour on the communicator. There had been no response.

'Richard,' she said, while he was programming some graphics on his computer, 'why do you think the rescue team was using the stairway?'

'Who knows?' he replied. 'Maybe the chairlift malfunctioned and there were no engineers left.'

'It seems strange to me,' Nicole mused. *Something about this is bothering me,* she thought, *but I don't dare share it with Richard until I can explain it. He doesn't believe in intuition.* Nicole glanced at her watch. *It's a good thing we rationed the melon. If the rescue team doesn't show up and this wild scheme doesn't work, we won't be swimming until next daylight.*

'Preliminary design complete,' Richard stated emphatically. He waved to Nicole to join him. 'If you approve the line drawing,' he said, pointing at the monitor in his hand, 'then I will proceed with the detailed graphics.'

In the picture three large avians, each with one line wrapped around its body, were flying in formation across a sea. Dangling underneath them, and attached by three lines, was a stick figure human being sitting in a flimsy harness. 'Looks good to me,' said Nicole, never thinking for a minute that such an event would actually happen.

*

'I can't believe we're doing this,' Nicole remarked, pushing the plate to open the avian lair for the second time.

Their first attempt to renew contact had resulted in the expected cold shoulder. This second time it was Richard who shouted into the avian lair. 'Listen to me, you avians,' he growled in his fiercest voice, 'I need to talk to you. Right *now*. Get up here on the double.' Nicole had to restrain a laugh.

Richard began dropping black objects into the lair. 'See,' he said with a grin, 'I knew these damn things would be good for something.' Eventually they could hear some activity at the bottom of the vertical corridor. The same pair of avians they had seen before flew up to the top of the lair and started screeching at Richard and Nicole. They did not even look at the monitor when Richard held it out for them. When they were finished screeching, the pair flew over the top of the tank sentinel and the cover closed again.

'It's no use, Richard,' Nicole said when he asked her to open the cover a third time. 'Even our friends are against us.' She paused before pressing the plate. 'What are we going to do if they attack us?'

'They won't attack,' Richard said, indicating for Nicole to open the cover. 'But just in case, I want you to stay over there. I will deal with our feathered friends.'

There was jabbering from the lair as soon as the cover opened the third time. Richard immediately started shouting back and pitching black objects down the corridor. One of them hit the tank sentinel and prompted a small explosion, like a gunshot.

The two familiar avians flew up to the opening and screamed at Richard. Three or four of their comrades were just behind. The noise was unbelievable. Richard did not back down. He kept yelling and pointing at the computer monitor. Finally he was able to get their attention.

The group of avians watched the graphic depiction of the flight across the sea. Richard then held up one of the harnesses in his left hand and started running the demonstration on his monitor again. Frantic conversation among the avians ensued. At the end, however, Richard sensed that he had lost. As a pair of the other avians flew over the top of the tank sentinel, Richard climbed down into the lair, onto the first ledge. 'Hold it,' he shouted at the top of his lungs.

The mate of the black velvet avian lunged forward, its threatening beak no more than a metre from Richard's face. The noise from all the screeching and jabbering was deafening. Richard was undaunted. Despite the avian protests, he descended to the second ledge. Now he would not be able to escape if the cover started to close.

Again he held up the harness and pointed at the monitor. A chorus of screeches told him the response. Then, above the avian howl, he heard another sound, like a Klaxon alarm announcing a fire drill at a school or hospital. All the avians immediately calmed down. They settled quietly on the ledges and stared down at the tank sentinel.

The lair was strangely silent. After a few seconds Richard heard the beating of wings and moments later a new avian flew into the vertical corridor. It rose slowly up to his level and hovered just opposite him. It had a grey velvet body and sharp grey eyes. Two thick rings of bright cherry red were wrapped around its neck.

The creature studied Richard and landed on the ledge opposite him, across the corridor. The avian that had been in that spot scurried out of the way. When the grey velvet bird spoke, it was soft and very clear. After the speech was finished, the black velvet avian flew up beside the new arrival and apparently explained the furore. Several times the two avians stared across at Richard. The last time, thinking that perhaps their nodding heads were a cue, Richard displayed the graphic flight one more time and held up the harnesses. The bird with the cherry rings flew over beside him for a closer look.

The creature made a sudden movement, frightening Richard, and he nearly fell off the ledge. What may have been avian laughter was silenced by a few words from the grey velvet leader, who then sat quite still, as if it were thinking, for over a minute. At length the avian leader gestured toward Richard with one talon, opened its huge wings, and soared out through the opening into daylight.

For several seconds Richard did not move. The great creature rose up, up into the sky above the lair and was soon followed by the two more familiar avians. Moments later Nicole's head appeared in the opening. 'Are you coming?' she asked. 'I don't know how you did it, but it looks as if our friends are ready.'

52 FLIGHT 302

Richard pulled the harness tight around Nicole's waist and buttocks. 'Your feet will dangle,' he said, 'and at first, when the lattice cord is stretching, you will have the feeling that you're falling.'

'What if I hit the water?' Nicole asked.

'You have to trust the avians to fly high enough that you won't,' Richard replied. 'I think they're quite intelligent, especially the one with the red rings.'

'Do you think it's the king?' Nicole asked, adjusting the harness for comfort.

'Probably their equivalent,' Richard answered. 'He has made it clear from the beginning that he intends to fly in the middle of the formation.'

Richard walked up the steep incline to the wall, carrying all three harness lines in his hands. The avians were sitting quietly together, staring out at the sea. They acquiesced as he tied the harness around their midsections, just behind the backs of the wings. Then they watched his computer monitor as he again showed them the graphics of the takeoff. The avians were to lift off together, slowly, pull the harness lines taut directly over Nicole's head, and then lift her straight up before flying north across the sea.

He checked that the knots were secure and then returned to Nicole's side at the bottom of the incline. She was only about five metres from the water. 'If, by some chance, the avians do not return for me,' Richard told her, 'don't wait forever. Once you find the rescue team, assemble the sailboat and come across. I will be down in the White Room.' He took a deep breath. 'Be safe, my darling,' he added. 'Remember that I love you.'

Nicole could tell from the pounding of her heart that the moment of takeoff had finally arrived. She kissed Richard slowly on the lips. 'And I love you,' she murmured.

When they broke their embrace, Richard waved at the avians on the wall. The grey velvet avian cautiously rose in the air, followed immediately by its two companions. They hovered in formation directly over Nicole. She felt the three lines pull tight and was momentarily lifted into the air.

Seconds later, as the elastic cord began to stretch, Nicole was falling toward the ground again. The avians flew higher, heading out over the water, and Nicole felt as if she were a yo-yo, bouncing up and down as the cord would stretch and then contract with a jerk when the avians rose swiftly to a higher altitude.

!t was an exciting flight. She touched the water once, just barely, while she was still close to shore. She was temporarily frightened, but the avians lifted her quickly before anything more than her feet were wet. Once the lattice cord was at its full extension, the ride was fairly smooth. Nicole sat in her harness, her hands holding on to two of the three lines, her feet dangling below her about eight metres from the tops of the waves.

The middle of the sea was quite calm. About halfway across Nicole saw two great, dark figures swimming along beneath her, parallel to her course. She was certain they were shark biots. She also detected two or three other species in the water, including one, long and skinny like an eel, that reared itself out of the sea and watched her fly by. *Whew,* Nicole thought as she surveyed the water, *I'm certainly glad that I didn't swim.*

The landing was easy. Nicole had been concerned that the avians might not realise there was a fifty-metre cliff on the opposite side of the sea. She needn't have worried. As they approached landfall in the Northern Hemicylinder, the avians gently increased their altitude. Nicole was set down gingerly about ten metres from the edge.

The huge birds landed close by. Nicole climbed out of her harness and walked over to the avians. She thanked them profusely and tried to pat them on the backs of their heads, but they jerked away from her touch. The creatures rested for several minutes and then, at a signal from their leader, they flew off across the sea toward New York.

Nicole was surprised at the intensity of her emotions. She knelt down and kissed the ground. It was only then that she realised she had never really expected to escape safely from New York. For a moment, before she started searching for the rescue team with her binoculars, she reviewed everything that had happened to her since that fateful crossing in the icemobile. *Before New York is a lifetime ago,* she said to herself. *Now everything has changed.*

Richard untied the harness from the avian leader and dropped it on the ground. All the birds were now free. The creature with the grey velvet body craned its neck around to see if Richard was finished. The rich cherry red of its rings was even clearer in the full daylight. Richard wondered about the rings and what they signified, knowing there was a high likelihood he would never see these magnificent aliens again.

Nicole came over beside Richard. When he had landed she had embraced him passionately. The avians had boldly stared, signaling their curiosity. *They too,* Nicole thought, *must be wondering about us.* The linguist in her imagined what it would be like actually to talk to an extraterrestrial species, to begin to understand how an altogether different intelligence might operate ...

'I wonder how we say goodbye and thank you,' Richard was saying.

'I don't know,' Nicole replied, 'but it would be nice ...'

She stopped to watch the avian leader. It had called the other two creatures to come beside it and the three birds were standing facing Richard and Nicole. On a signal they all spread their wings, to their full extent, and formed into a circle. They turned around one full revolution and then fell back into a straight line facing the humans.

'Come on,' Nicole said. 'We can do that.'

Nicole and Richard stood side by side, their arms outstretched, and faced their avian friends. Nicole then put her arms on Richard's shoulders and led him through a circular turn. Richard, who was sometimes not very graceful, stumbled once but managed to complete the movement. Nicole imagined that the avian leader was smiling when she and Richard straightened out after their revolution.

The three avians took off seconds later. Higher and higher in the sky they rose, until they were at the limit of Nicole's vision. Then they flew south, across the sea toward home.

'Good luck,' Nicole whispered as they departed.

The rescue team was not in the vicinity of the Beta campsite. In fact, Richard and Nicole had not seen any sign of them during a thirty-minute drive in the rover along the coast of the Cylindrical Sea. 'These guys must really be stupid,' Richard groused. 'My message was in plain view there at Beta. Could it be that they haven't even come down this far yet?'

'It's less than three hours until dark,' Nicole replied. 'They may have returned to the Newton already.'

'All right, then, to hell with them,' Richard said. 'Let's have a bite to eat and then head for the chairlift.'

'Do you think we should save any of the melon?' Nicole asked a few minutes later, while they were eating. Richard gave her a puzzled glance. 'Just in case,' she added.

'Just in case what?' Richard rejoined. 'Even if we don't find that idiotic rescue bunch and must climb all the stairs ourselves, we'll still be out of here right after dark. Remember, we become weightless again at the top of the stairway.'

Nicole smiled. 'I guess I'm naturally more cautious,' she said. She put several bites of melon back into her pack.

They had driven three-fourths of the way toward the chairlift and the Alpha stairway when they spotted the four human figures in space suits. It looked as if they were leaving the conglomeration of buildings that had been designated as the Raman Paris. The figures were walking in the opposite direction from the rover.

'I told you the guys were idiots,' Richard exclaimed. 'They don't even have the sense to take off their space suits. It must be a special team, sent up in the spare Newton vehicle just to find us and bring us back.'

He steered the rover across the Central Plain in the direction of the humans. Richard and Nicole both started shouting when they were within a hundred metres, but the men in the space suits continued their slow procession toward the west. 'They probably can't hear us,' Nicole offered. 'They still have on their helmets and communication gear.'

A frustrated Richard drove up to within five metres of the single-file line, stopped the rover, and jumped out in a hurry. He ran quickly around to the leader, shouting all the way. 'Hey, guys,' he yelled. 'We're here, behind you. All you have to do is turn around ...'

Richard stopped cold as he stared at the blank expression of the man in the lead. He recognized the face. Jesus, it was Norton! He shuddered involuntarily as a tingle ran down his spine. Richard barely jumped out of the way as the four-man procession walked slowly past him. Numb from the shock, he quietly studied the other three faces, none of which changed expression as they marched past. They were three other cosmonauts from the Rama I crew.

Nicole was at his side only seconds after the final figure passed him. 'What's the matter?' she said. 'Why didn't they stop?' The blood had all drained out of Richard's face. 'Darling, are you all right?'

'They're biots,' Richard mumbled. 'Goddamn human biots.'

'Whaaat?' Nicole replied, a streak of terror in her voice. She ran quickly to the head of the line and stared at the face behind the helmet glass. It was definitely Norton. Every feature of the face, even the colour of the eyes and the slight mustache, was absolutely perfect. But the eyes didn't say anything.

The motion of the body, too, now that she noticed it, seemed artificial. Each pair of steps was a repeated pattern. There were only slight variations from figure to figure. *Richard is right,* Nicole thought. *These are human biots. They must have been made from the images, just like the toothpaste and the brush.* A momentary panic swelled in her chest. *But we don't need a rescue team,* she told herself, calming her anxiety. *The military ship is still docked at the top of the bowl.*

Richard was stunned by the discovery of the human biots. He sat in the rover for several minutes, unwilling to drive, asking questions of Nicole and himself that he could not possibly have answered. 'So what's going on here?' he said over and over again. 'Are all these biots based on real species, found somewhere in the universe? And why are they being fabricated in the first place?'

Before they drove over to the chairlift, Richard insisted that they both shoot many minutes of video footage of the human biots. 'The avians and octospiders are fascinating,' he said as he took a special close-up of 'Norton's' leg motion, 'but this tape will blow everyone away.'

Nicole reminded him that it was less than two hours until dark and that it still might be necessary for them to climb the Stairway of the Gods. Satisfied that he had recorded the bizarre procession for posterity, Richard slid into the driver's seat of the rover and headed toward the Alpha stairway.

There was no need to perform any tests to see if the chairlift was working properly; it was running when they drove up beside it. Richard jumped out of the rover and ran into the control room.

'Someone's coming down,' he said, pointing up the lift.

'Or something,' Nicole said grimly.

The five-minute wait seemed like an eternity. At first neither Richard nor Nicole said anything. Later, however, Richard suggested that maybe they should sit in the rover in case they needed to make a quick escape.

Each of them trained binoculars on the long cable stretching upward to the heavens. 'It's a man!' cried Nicole.

'It's General O'Toole!' said Richard a few moments later.

Indeed it was. General Michael Ryan O'Toole, American air force officer, was descending in the chairlift. He was still several hundred metres above Richard and Nicole, but had not yet seen them. He was busy studying with his binoculars the beauty of the alien landscape around him.

General O'Toole had been preparing to leave Rama for the final time when, as he rode up in the chairlift, he had spotted what looked like three birds flying far to the south in the Rama sky. The general had decided to return to see if he could find those birds again. He was unprepared for the joyous greeting that awaited him when he reached the bottom of his ride.

53 TRINITY

When Richard Wakefield had left the Newton to go back inside Rama, General O'Toole had been the last crew member to say goodbye. The general had waited patiently while the other cosmonauts had finished their conversations with Richard. 'You're really certain you want to do this?' Janos Tabori had said to his British friend. 'You know the full committee is going to declare Rama off limits within hours.'

'By then,' Richard had grinned at Janos, 'I will be on my way to Beta. Technically I will not have violated their order.'

'That's bullshit,' Admiral Heilmann had interjected tersely. 'Dr Brown and I are in charge of this mission. We have both told you to stay on board the Newton.'

'And I've told you several times,' Richard said firmly, 'that I left some personal items inside Rama that are very important to me. Besides, you know as well as I do that there's nothing for any of us here to do over the next couple of days. Once the abort decision is definitely made, all the major scheduling activities will be on the ground. We will be told when to undock and head for Earth.'

'I will remind you, one more time,' Otto Heilmann had replied, 'that I consider what you are doing an act of insubordination. When we return to Earth I intend to prosecute to the fullest—'

'Save it, will you, Otto?' Richard interrupted. There was no rancour in his tone. He adjusted his spacesuit and started to put on his helmet. As always Francesca was recording the scene on her video camera. She had been strangely silent since her private conversation with Richard an hour earlier. She seemed detached, as if her mind were somewhere else.

General O'Toole walked up to Richard and extended his hand. 'We haven't spent much time together, Wakefield,' he said, 'but I've admired your work. Good luck in there. Don't take any unnecessary chances.'

Richard had been surprised by the general's warm smile. He had expected the American military officer to try to talk him out of leaving. 'It's magnificent in Rama, General,' Richard had said. 'Like a combination of the Grand Canyon, the Alps, and the Pyramids all at once.'

'We've lost four crew members already,' O'Toole replied. 'I want to see you back here safe and sound. God bless you.'

Richard finished shaking the general's hand, put on his helmet, and stepped across into the airlock. Moments later, when Wakefield was gone, Admiral Heilmann was critical of General O'Toole's behaviour. 'I'm disappointed in you, Michael,' he said. 'From that warm send-off the young man might have concluded that you actually approved of his action.'

O'Toole faced the German admiral. 'Wakefield has courage, Otto,' he said. 'And conviction as well, He is not afraid of either the Ramans or the ISA disciplinary process. I admire that kind of self-confidence.'

'Nonsense,' Heilmann rejoined. 'Wakefield is a brash, arrogant school-boy. You know what he left inside? A couple of those stupid Shakespearean robots. He just doesn't like taking orders. He wants to do what's uppermost on his own personal agenda.'

'That makes him a lot like the rest of us,' Francesca remarked. The room was quiet for a moment. 'Richard is very smart,' she said in a subdued tone. 'He probably has reasons for going back into Rama that none of us under-stand.'

'I just hope he comes back before dark, as he promised,' Janos said. 'I'm not certain I could stand to lose another friend.'

The cosmonauts filed out of the atrium into the hallway. 'Where's Dr Brown?' Janos asked Francesca as he walked along beside her.

'He's with Yamanaka and Turgenyev. They're reviewing possible crew assignments for the trip home. As shorthanded as we are, a lot of cross train-ing will be necessary before we leave.' Francesca laughed. 'He even asked me if I could be a backup navigation engineer. Can you imagine that?'

'Easily,' Janos replied. 'You probably could learn any of the engineering assignments at this point.'

Behind them Heilmann and O'Toole shuffled down the corridor. When they reached the hall leading to the private crew quarters, General O'Toole started to leave. 'Just a minute,' Otto Heilmann said. 'I need to talk to you about something else. This damn Wakefield thing almost made it slip my mind. Can you come to my office for an hour or so?'

'Essentially,' Otto Heilmann said, pointing at the unscrambled cryptogram on the monitor, 'this is a major change to the Trinity procedure. It's not surprising. Now that we know much more about Rama, you would expect the deployment to be somewhat different.'

'But we never anticipated using all five weapons,' O'Toole responded. 'The extra pair were only loaded on board in case of failures. That much mega-tonnage could vaporize Rama.'

'That's the intent,' Heilmann said. He sat back in his chair and smiled. 'Just between us chickens,' he said, 'I think there's a lot of pressure on the general staff down there. The feeling is that Rama's capabilities were vastly underrated initially.'

'But why do they want to put the two largest weapons in the ferry passageway? Surely one of the bombs would accomplish the desired result.'

'What if it didn't explode for some reason? There has to be a backup.' Heilmann leaned forward eagerly on his desk. 'I think this change to the procedure clearly defines the strategy. The two at the end will ensure that the structural integrity of the vehicle will be absolutely destroyed – that's essential to guarantee that it is impossible for Rama to manoeuvre again after the blast. The other three bombs are scattered around the interior to make certain that no part of Rama is safe. It's equally important that the explosions should result in enough velocity change that all the remaining pieces miss the Earth.'

General O'Toole constructed a mental image of the giant spacecraft being annihilated by five nuclear bombs. It was not a pleasant picture. Once, fifteen years before, he and twenty other members of the COG general staff had flown into the South Pacific to watch a hundred-kiloton weapon explode. The COG system engineering personnel had convinced the political leaders, and the world press, that one nuclear test was necessary 'every twenty years or so' to ensure that all the old weapons would indeed fire in an emergency. O'Toole and his team had observed the demonstration, ostensibly to learn as much as possible about the effects of nuclear weapons.

General O'Toole was deep in his memory, recalling the spine-tingling horror of that fireball rising in the peaceful South Pacific sky. He was not aware that Admiral Heilmann had asked him a question. 'I'm sorry, Otto,' he said. 'I was thinking about something else.'

'I had asked you how long you thought it might take to get approval for Trinity.'

'You mean in our case?' O'Toole said with disbelief.

'Of course,' Heilmann responded.

'I can't imagine it,' O'Toole said quickly. 'The weapons were included in the mission manifest solely to guard against openly hostile actions by the Ramans. I even remember the baseline scenario – an unprovoked attack against the Earth by the alien spacecraft, using high-technology weapons beyond the capabilities of our defences. The current situation is altogether different.'

The German admiral studied his American colleague. 'No one ever envisioned the Rama spacecraft on a collision course with the Earth,' Heilmann said. 'If it does not alter its trajectory, it will gouge an enormous hole in the surface and kick up such dust that the temperatures will drop all over the world for several years ... At least, that's what the scientists say,'

'But that's preposterous,' O'Toole argued. 'You heard all the discussion during the conference call. No rational person really believes that Rama will actually hit the Earth.'

'Impact is only one of several disaster scenarios. What would you do if you were chief of staff? Destroying Rama now is a safe solution. Nobody loses.'

Visibly shaken by the conversation, Michael O'Toole excused himself from the meeting with Admiral Heilmann and headed for his room. For the first time in his entire association with the Newton mission, O'Toole thought that he might actually be ordered to use his RQ code to activate the weapons. Never before, never for a moment, had he considered that the bombs in the metal containers at the back of the military ship were anything more than a palliative for the fears of the civilian politicians.

Sitting at the computer terminal in his room, the concerned O'Toole recalled the words of Armando Urbina, the Mexican peace activist who had advocated a total dismantling of the COG nuclear arsenal. 'As we have seen both at Rome and Damascus,' Senor Urbina had said, 'if the weapons exist, they can be used. Only if there are no weapons at all can we guarantee that human beings will never again suffer the horror of nuclear devastation.'

Richard Wakefield did not return before the Raman nightfall. Since the communication station at Beta had been knocked out of commission by the hurricane (the Newton had monitored the breakup of the Cylindrical Sea and the onset of the windstorm through telemetry relayed by Beta before it was silenced), Richard had moved out of communications range when he was halfway across the Central Plain. His last transmission to Janos Tabori, who had volunteered to man the commlink, had been typically Wakefield. As the signal from inside Rama was fading, Janos, in a lighthearted tone, had asked Richard how he wanted to be remembered 'to your fans' in case he was 'swallowed by the Great Galactic Ghoul.'

'Tell them that I loved Rama not wisely, but too well,' Richard had shouted into his communicator.

'What's that?' Otto Heilmann had puzzled. The admiral had come looking for Janos to discuss a Newton engineering problem.

'He killed her,' Janos had said, trying without success to lock up the signal again.

'Who killed – What are you talking about?'

'It's not important,' Janos had answered, spinning around in his chair and floating into the air. 'Now, what can I do for you, Herr Admiral?'

Richard's failure to return was not considered serious until several hours after the following Raman dawn. The cosmonauts remaining on the Newton had convinced themselves the night before that Wakefield had become absorbed in some task ('Probably fixing the Beta comm station,' Janos had offered), had lost track of the time, and had decided not to take a solitary ride out in the dark. But when he didn't return in the morning, a feeling of gloom began to pervade the conversation of the crew.

'I don't know why we won't admit it,' Irina Turgenyev said suddenly during a period of quiet at dinnertime. 'Wakefield is not coming back either. Whatever got Takagishi and des Jardins got him as well.'

'That's ridiculous, Irina,' Janos replied heatedly.

'Da,' she remarked. 'That's what you've always said. Ever since the beginning when General Borzov was cut to pieces. Then it was an accident that
the crab biot attacked Wilson. Cosmonaut des Jardins disappears down an
alley ...'

'Coincidence,' Janos shouted, 'all coincidence!'

'You're stupid, Janos,' Irina shouted back. 'You trust everybody and
everything. We should blow the damn thing to pieces before it does any
more—'

'Stop, stop, you two!' David Brown said loudly as the two Soviet colleagues
continued to argue.

'All right, now,' added General O'Toole. 'We're all a little tense. There's no
need for us to quarrel.'

'Will anyone be going in to look for Richard?' the emotional Janos asked
no one in particular.

'Who would be crazy enough—' Irina began to respond.

'No,' interrupted Admiral Heilmann firmly. 'I told him that his visit was
unauthorized and that we would not come after him under any circumstances. Besides, Dr Brown and the two pilots tell me that we can barely
fly the two Newton ships home with the manpower remaining – and their
analysis assumed Wakefield was with us. We cannot take any more risks.'

There was a long and sombre silence at the dinner table. 'I had planned
to tell everyone when the meal was over,' David Brown then said, standing
up beside his chair, 'but it looks to me as if this group could use some good
news now. An hour ago we received our orders. We're to depart for Earth
at 1-14 days, a little over a week from now. Between now and then we will
cross-train the personnel, rest for the voyage home, and make certain that all
the Newton engineering systems are working properly.'

Cosmonauts Turgenyev, Yamanaka, and Sabatini all shouted their approval.
'If we're going to leave without returning to Rama,' Janos inquired, 'why are
we waiting so long? Surely we can be well enough prepared in three or four
days.'

'As I understand it,' Dr Brown replied, 'our two military colleagues have a
special task that will occupy most of their time – and some of ours – for much
of the next three days.' He glanced over at Otto Heilmann. 'Do you want to
tell them?'

Admiral Heilmann stood up at his place. 'I need to discuss the details first
with General O'Toole,' he said in a ringing voice. 'We'll explain it to everyone
else in the morning.'

O'Toole didn't need Otto Heilmann to show him the message that had
been received only twenty minutes before. He knew what it said. In compliance with the procedure, there were only three words:

Proceed with Trinity.

54 ONCE A HERO

Michael O'Toole could not sleep. He tossed and turned, switched on his favourite music, and repeated both the 'Hail Mary' and 'Our Father' litanies over and over. Nothing worked. He longed for a distraction, something that would make him forget his responsibilities and allow his soul some repose.

PROCEED WITH TRINITY, he thought to himself at last, focusing on the true cause of his disquiet. What exactly did that mean? Use the teleoperator forklifts, open up the containers, pick up the weapons (they were about the size of refrigerators), check out the subsystems, put the bombs in a pod, carry them over to the Rama seal, ferry them to the heavy load elevator ...

And what else? he thought. One more thing. It wouldn't take much more than a minute at each weapon, but it was by far the most important. Each bomb had a redundant pair of tiny numerical keyboards on its side. He and Admiral Heilmann each had to use the keyboards to input a special sequence of digits, an RQ code it was called, before the weapons could be activated. Without those codes the bombs would remain absolutely dormant, forever. The original debates over whether or not to include nuclear weapons in the limited Newton supply manifest had echoed through the corridors of COG military headquarters in Amsterdam for several weeks. The ensuing vote had been close. It was decided that the Newton would carry the nuclear weapons, but to allay widespread concerns it was also decided to implement rigorous safety measures that would guard against their unwarranted use.

During these same meetings, the COG military leadership avoided public outcry by placing a top secret classification on the fact that the Newton was transporting nuclear bombs to its rendezvous with Rama. Not even the civilian members of the Newton crew had been told about the existence of the weapons.

The secret working group on Trinity safety procedures had met seven times at four different locations around the world prior to the Newton launch. To make the deployment process immune to untoward electronic inputs, manual action had been chosen as the method of activation for the nuclear weapons. Thus neither a lunatic on the Earth nor a frightened cosmonaut on the Newton could trigger the process with a simple electronic command. The

467

current COG chief of staff, a brilliant but passionless disciplinarian named Kazuo Norimoto, had expressed concern that without electronic command capability the military was unduly dependent upon the humans selected for the mission. He had been persuaded, however, that it was far better to depend on the Newton military officers than to worry about a terrorist or fanatic somehow gaining possession of the activation code.

But what if one of the Newton military officers were seized by panic? How could the system be protected against a unilateral act of nuclear warfare by a crew member? When all the discussions were completed, the resultant safety system was relatively simple. There would be three military officers in the crew. Each of them would have an RQ code known only to himself. Manual input of any two of the long numerical sequences would arm the nuclear devices. The system was thus protected against either a recalcitrant officer or a frightened one. It sounded like a foolproof system.

But our current situation was never considered in the contingency analyses, O'Toole thought as he lay in his bed. *In the event of any dangerous action, either military or civilian, each of us was supposed to designate an alternate to learn our code. But who would have thought that an appendectomy was dangerous? Valeriy's RQ died with him. Which means the system now requires two for two.*

O'Toole rolled over on his stomach and pressed his face against the pillow. He now clearly understood why he was still awake. *If I don't input my code those bombs cannot be used.* He remembered a luncheon on the military ship with Valeriy Borzov and Otto Heilmann during the leisurely cruise toward Rama. 'It's a perfect set of checks and balances,' the Soviet general had joked, 'and probably played a role in our individual selections. Otto would pull the trigger at the slightest provocation and you, Michael, would agonize over its morality even if your life were threatened. I'm the tiebreaker.'

But you are dead, General O'Toole said to himself, *and we have been ordered to activate the bombs.* He rose from the bed and walked over to his desk. As he had done all his life when facing a tough decision, O'Toole pulled a small electronic notebook from his pocket and made two short lists, one summarising the reasons for following his orders to destroy Rama and the other presenting arguments against it. He had no strictly logical reasons to oppose the destruction command – the giant vehicle was probably a lifeless machine, his three colleagues were almost certainly dead, and there was a non-trivial implied threat to the Earth. But still O'Toole hesitated. There was something about committing such a flagrantly hostile act that offended his sensibilities.

He returned to his bed and rolled over on his back. *Dear God,* he prayed, staring at the ceiling, *how can I possibly know what is right in this situation? Please show me the way.*

Only thirty seconds after his morning alarm, Otto Heilmann heard a soft knock on his door. General O'Toole walked in moments later. The American was already dressed for the day. 'You're up early, Michael,' Admiral Heilmann said, fumbling for his morning coffee that had been automatically heating for five minutes already.

'I wanted to talk to you,' O'Toole said pleasantly. He courteously waited for Heilmann to pick up his coffee packet.

'What is it?' the admiral asked.

'I want you to call off the meeting this morning.'

'Why?' Heilmann replied. 'We need some assistance from the rest of the crew, as you and I discussed last night. The longer we wait to get started, the more chance we will delay our departure.'

'I'm not ready just yet,' O'Toole said.

Admiral Hermann's brow furrowed. He took a long sip from his coffee and studied his companion. 'I see,' he said quietly. 'And what else is needed before you will be ready?'

'I want to talk to someone, General Norimoto perhaps, to understand why we are destroying Rama. I know you and I talked about it yesterday, but I want to hear the reasons from the person giving the order.'

'It is a military officer's duty to follow orders. Asking questions could be viewed as a disciplinary breach—'

'I understand all that, Otto,' O'Toole interrupted, 'but this is not a battlefield situation. I am not refusing to comply with the order. I just want to be certain ...' His voice trailed off and O'Toole stared off in the distance.

'Certain of what?' Heilmann asked.

O'Toole took a deep breath. 'Certain that I'm doing the right thing.'

A video conference with Norimoto was arranged and the Newton crew meeting was delayed. Since it was the middle of the night in Amsterdam, it was some time before the encoded transmission could be translated and presented to the COG chief of staff. In his typical manner, General Norimoto then requested several more hours to prepare his response, so that he could obtain 'staff consensus' on what he was going to say to O'Toole.

The general and Admiral Heilmann were sitting together in the Newton military control centre when the transmission from Norimoto began. General Norimoto was dressed in his full military uniform. He did not smile when he greeted the Newton officers. He put on his glasses and read from a prepared text.

'General O'Toole, we have carefully reviewed the questions contained in your last transmission. All your concerns were included on the issues list that was discussed here on Earth before we reached the decision to proceed with Trinity. Under the unique provisions contained in the ISA-COG operating protocols, you and the other Newton military personnel are temporarily part of my special staff; therefore, I am your commanding officer. The message that was transmitted to you should be treated as an order.'

General Norimoto managed just a glimmer of a smile. 'Nevertheless,' he continued reading, 'because of the significance of the action contained in your order and your obvious concern about its repercussions, we have prepared three summary statements that should help you to understand our decision:

'One: We do not know if Rama is hostile or friendly. We have no way of obtaining additional data to resolve the issue.

'Two: Rama is hurtling toward Earth. It might impact our home planet, take hostile action once it's in our neighbourhood, or perform benign activities that we can't define.

'Three: By implementing Trinity when Rama is still ten or more days away, we can guarantee the safety of the planet, regardless of Rama's intentions or future actions.'

The general paused for the briefest of moments. 'That is all,' he then concluded. 'Proceed with Trinity.'

The screen went blank. 'Are you satisfied?' Admiral Heilmann asked.

'I guess so,' O'Toole said with a sigh. 'I didn't hear anything new, but I shouldn't have expected anything else.'

Admiral Heilmann looked at his watch. 'We've wasted almost an entire day,' he said. 'Should we have the crew meeting after dinner?'

'I'd rather not,' O'Toole replied. 'This episode has exhausted me and I hardly slept at all last night. I'd prefer to wait until the morning.'

'All right,' Heilmann said after a pause. He stood up and put his arm on O'Toole's shoulder. 'We'll get started first thing after breakfast.'

In the morning General O'Toole did not attend the scheduled crew meeting. He phoned Heilmann and asked the admiral to proceed with the discussion without him. O'Toole's excuse was that he had a 'vicious stomach upset.' He doubted if Admiral Heilmann really believed his explanation, but it didn't really matter.

O'Toole watched and listened to the meeting on the video monitor in his room, never interrupting or adding to the proceedings. None of the other cosmonauts seemed particularly surprised that the Newton was carrying a nuclear arsenal. Heilmann did a thorough job of explaining what was to be done. He enlisted the help of Yamanaka and Tabori, as he and O'Toole had discussed, and outlined a sequence of events that would be complete with the weapons deployed inside Rama in seventy-two hours. That would leave the crew another three days to prepare for departure.

'When will the bombs detonate?' Janos Tabori asked nervously after Admiral Heilmann was finished.

'They will be set to explode sixty hours after our scheduled departure. According to the analytical models, we should be out of the debris field in twelve hours, but for safety we have specified, in our procedure, that the weapons will not be exploded unless we are at least twenty-four hours away ... If our departure is delayed because of some crisis, we can always overwrite the detonation time by electronic command.'

470

'That's reassuring,' Janos remarked.

'Any more questions?' Heilmann asked.

'Just one,' Janos said. 'As long as we're inside Rama putting these things in their proper locations, I assume that it's all right if we look around for our lost friends. In case they may be wandering—'

'The timeline is very tight, Cosmonaut Tabori,' the admiral replied, 'and the deployment itself, inside the structure, only takes a few hours. Unfortunately, due to our delays in starting the procedure, we will place the weapons in their designated positions during the time that Rama is dark.'

Great, O'Toole thought in his room, *that's something else that can be blamed on me.* All in all, though, he felt that Admiral Heilmann had handled the meeting very well. *It was nice of Otto not to say anything about the code*, O'Toole told himself. *He probably figures I'll come around. And he's probably right.*

When O'Toole woke up from a short nap it was past lunchtime and he had a ravenous appetite. There was nobody in the dining room except Francesca Sabatini; she was finishing her coffee and studying some kind of engineering data on a nearby computer monitor.

'Feeling better, Michael?' she said when she saw him.

He nodded. 'What are you reading?' O'Toole asked.

'I'm looking at the executive software manual,' Francesca replied. 'David is very concerned that without Wakefield we won't even know if the Newton software is working properly or not. I'm learning how to read the self-test diagnostic output.'

'Whew,' O'Toole whistled. 'That's pretty heavy for a journalist.'

'It's really not that complicated.' Francesca said with a laugh. 'And it's extremely logical. Maybe in my next career I'll be an engineer.'

O'Toole made himself a sandwich, picked up a package of milk, and joined Francesca at the table. She put a hand on his forearm. 'Speaking of next careers, Michael, have you given any thought to yours?'

He looked at her quizzically. 'What are you talking about?'

'I'm trapped in the usual professional dilemma, my dear friend. My duties as a journalist are in direct conflict with my feelings.'

O'Toole stopped chewing. 'Heilmann told you?'

She nodded. 'I'm not stupid, Michael. I would have found out sooner or later. And this is a big, big story. Maybe one of the biggest of the mission. Can't you see the trailer on the nightly news? "American general refuses to follow order to destroy Rama. Tune in at five."'

The general became defensive. 'I haven't refused. The Trinity procedure does not call for me to input my code until after the weapons are out of the containers ...'

'... and ready for placement in the pods,' Francesca finished. 'Which is about eighteen hours from now. Tomorrow morning, as near as I can figure ... I plan to be on hand to record the historic event.' She rose from the table,

'And Michael, in case you're wondering, I haven't mentioned your call to Norimoto in any of my reports. I may refer to your conversation with him in my memoirs, but I won't publish them for at least five years '

Francesca turned and looked directly in O'Toole's eyes. 'You're about to go from being an international hero to a bum overnight. I hope you've carefully considered all the ramifications of your decision.'

55 THE VOICE OF MICHAEL

General O'Toole spent the afternoon in his room, watching on the video monitor as Tabori and Yamanaka checked out the nuclear weapons. He was excused, on the basis of his presumed stomach upset, from his assigned task of checking out the weapon subsystems. The procedure was surprisingly straightforward; no one would have suspected that the cosmonauts were initiating an activity designed to destroy the most impressive work of engineering ever seen by humans.

Before dinner O'Toole placed a call to his wife. The Newton was rapidly approaching the Earth now and the delay time between transmission and reception was under three minutes. Old-fashioned two-way conversations were even possible. His talk with Kathleen was cordial and mundane. General O'Toole thought briefly about sharing his moral dilemma with his wife, but he realised that the videophone was not secure and decided against it, They both expressed excitement about being reunited again in the very near future.

The general ate dinner with the crew. Janos was in one of his boisterous moods, entertaining the others with stories about his afternoon with 'the bullets,' as he insisted on calling the nuclear bombs. 'At one point,' Janos said to Francesca, who had been laughing nonstop since his narrative began, 'we had all the bullets lightly anchored to the floor and lined up in a row, like dominoes. I scared the shit out of Yamanaka. I pushed the front one over and they all fell, clang, bang, in every direction. Hiro was certain they were going to explode.'

'Weren't you worried that you might injure some critical components?' David Brown asked.

'Nope,' Janos replied. 'The manuals that Otto gave me said that you couldn't hurt those things if you dropped them from the top of the Trump Tower. Besides,' he added, 'they aren't even armed yet. Right, Herr Admiral?'

Heilmann nodded and Janos launched into another story. General O'Toole drifted away, into his own mind, struggling impossibly with the relationship between those metal objects in the military ship and the mushroom-shaped cloud in the Pacific... .

Francesca interrupted his reverie. 'You have an urgent call on your private line, Michael,' she said. 'President Bothwell will be on in five minutes.'

The conversation at the table stopped. 'Well,' said Janos with a grin, 'you must be some special person. It's not just everybody that receives a call from Slugger Bothwell.'

General O'Toole excused himself politely from the table and went to his room. *He must know,* he was thinking as he waited impatiently for the call to connect. *But of course. He's the president of the United States.*

O'Toole had always been a baseball fan and his favourite team, naturally enough, was the Boston Red Sox. Baseball had gone into receivership at the height of the Great Chaos, in 2141, but a new group of owners had put the leagues back in business four years later. When Michael was six, in 2148, his father had taken him to Fenway Dome to watch a game between the Red Sox and the Havana Hurricanes. It was the beginning of a lifelong love affair for O'Toole.

Sherman Bothwell had been a left-handed, power-hitting first baseman for the Red Sox between 2172 and 2187. He had been immensely popular. A Missouri boy by birth, his genuine modesty and old-fashioned dedication to hard work were as exceptional as the 527 home runs he had hit during his sixteen years in the major leagues. During the last year of his baseball career, Bothwell's wife had died in a terrible boating accident. Sherman's uncomplaining courage in facing the responsibility of raising his children as a single parent was applauded in every American home.

Three years later, when he married Linda Black, the darling daughter of the governor of Texas, it was obvious to many people that old Sherman had a political career in mind. He advanced through the ranks with great speed. First lieutenant governor, then governor and presidential hopeful. He was elected to the White House by a landslide in 2196; it was anticipated that he would soundly defeat the Christian Conservative candidate in the forthcoming general election of 2200.

'Hello, General O'Toole,' the man in the blue suit with the friendly smile said when the screen was no longer blank. 'This is Sherman Bothwell, your president.'

The president was using no notes. He was leaning forward in a simple chair, his elbows resting on his thighs and his hands folded in front of him. He was talking as if he were sitting beside General O'Toole in someone's cozy living room.

'I have been following your Newton mission with great interest – as has everybody in my family, including Linda and the four kids – ever since you launched. But I have been *especially* attentive these last several weeks, as the tragedies have rained down upon you and your courageous colleagues. My, my. Who would have ever thought that such a thing as that Rama ship could exist? It is truly staggering ...

'Anyway, I understand from our COG representatives that the order has been given to destroy Rama. Now, I know that decisions like that are not made lightly, and that it places quite a large responsibility on folks like your-self. Nevertheless, I'm certain it's the right action.

'Yessirree, I know it's correct. Why, you know, my daughter Courtney – that's the eight-year-old – she wakes up with nightmares almost every night. We were watching when you all were trying to capture that *biot*, the one that looked like a crab, and my, it was positively awful. Now, Courtney knows – it's been all over the television – that Rama is heading *directly* for the Earth and she is really scared. Terrified. She thinks the whole country will be overrun by those crab things and that she and all her friends will be chopped up just like journalist Wilson.

'I'm telling you all this, General, because I know you're facing a big decision. And I've heard on the grapevine that you may be hesitant to destroy that humongous spacecraft and all its wonders. But General, I've told Courtney about you. I've told her that you and your crew are going to blow Rama to smithereens long before it reaches the Earth, 'That's why 1 called. To tell you that I'm counting on you. And so is Courtney.'

General O'Toole had thought, before listening to the president, that he might take advantage of the call and lay his dilemma in front of the leader of the American people. He had imagined that he might even question Slugger Bothwell about the nature of a species that destroys to protect against an unlikely downside risk. But after the practically perfect short speech from the ex-first baseman, O'Toole had nothing to say. After all, how could he refuse to respond to such a plea? All the Courtney Bothwells on the entire planet were counting on him.

After sleeping for five hours O'Toole awakened at three o'clock. He was aware that the most important action of his life was facing him. It seemed to him that everything he had done – his career, his religious studies, even his family activities – had been preparing him for this moment. God had trusted him with a monumental decision. But what did God want him to do? His forehead broke out in a sweat as O'Toole knelt before the image of Jesus on the cross that was behind his desk.

Dear Lord, he said, clasping his hands earnestly, *my hour approaches and I still do not see Thy will clearly. It would be so easy for me just to follow my orders and do what everyone wants. Is that Thy desire? How can I know for certain?*

Michael O'Toole closed his eyes and prayed for guidance with a fervor surpassing any he had ever felt previously. As he prayed, he recalled another time, years before, when he had been a young pilot working as part of a temporary peacekeeping force in Guatemala. O'Toole and his men had awakened one morning to find their small air base in the jungle completely surrounded by the right-wing terrorists that were trying to bring the fledgling democratic government to its knees. The subversives wanted the planes. In exchange they would guarantee safe passage to O'Toole and his men.

Major O'Toole had taken fifteen minutes to deliberate and pray before deciding to fight it out. In the ensuing battle the planes were destroyed and almost half his men were killed, but his symbolic stand against terrorism emboldened the young government and many others throughout Central America at a time when the poor countries were struggling desperately to overcome the ravages of two decades of depression. O'Toole had been awarded the Order of Merit, the highest COG military accolade, for his exploits in Guatemala.

On board the Newton years later, General O'Toole's decision process was much less straightforward. In Guatemala the young major had not had any questions about the morality of his actions. His order to destroy Rama, however, was altogether different. In O'Toole's opinion, the alien ship had not taken any overtly bellicose actions. In addition, he knew that the order was based primarily on two factors: fear of what Rama *might* do and the uproar of xenophobic public opinion. Historically, both fear and public opinion were notoriously unconcerned about morality. If somehow he could learn what Rama's true purpose was, then he could ...

Below the painting of Jesus on the desk in his room was a small statue of a young man with curly hair and wide eyes. This figure of St Michael of Siena had accompanied O'Toole on every journey he had made since his marriage to Kathleen. Seeing the statue gave him an idea. General O'Toole reached into one of the desk drawers and pulled out an electronic template. He switched on the power, checked the template menu, and accessed a concordance indexing the sermons of St Michael.

Under the word 'Rama,' the general found a host of different references in the concordance. The one that he was looking for was the only one marked in a bold font. That specific reference was the saint's famous 'Rama sermon,' delivered in camp to a group of five thousand of Michael's neophytes three weeks before the holocaust in Rome. O'Toole began to read.

'As the topic for my talk to you today, I am going to address an issue raised by Sister Judy in our council, namely what is the basis for my statement that the extraterrestrial spacecraft called Rama might well have been the first announcement of the second coming of Christ. Understand that at this point I have had no clear revelation one way or the other; God has, however, suggested to me that the heralds of Christ's next coming will have to be extraordinary or the people on Earth will not notice. A simple angel or two blowing trumpets in the heavens won't suffice. The heralds must do things that are truly spectacular to engage attention,

'There is a precedent, established in the old testament prophecies foretelling the coming of Jesus, of prophetic announcements originating in the heavens. Elijah's chariot was the Rama of its time. It was, technologically speaking, as much beyond the understanding of its observers as Rama is today. In that sense there is a certain conforming pattern, a symmetry that is not inconsistent with God's order.

'But what I think is most hopeful about the arrival of the first Rama spacecraft eight years ago – and I say first because I am certain there will be others – is that it forces humanity to think of itself in an extraterrestrial perspective. Too often we limit our concept of God and, by implication, our own spirituality. We belong to the universe. We are its children. It's just pure chance that our atoms have risen to consciousness here on this particular planet.

'Rama forces us to think of ourselves, and God, as beings of the universe. It is a tribute to His intelligence that He has sent such a herald at this moment. For as I have told you many times, we are overdue for our final evolution, our recognition that the entire human race is but a single organism. The appearance of Rama is another signal that it is time for us to change our ways and begin that final evolution.'

General O'Toole put down the template and rubbed his eyes. He had read the sermon before – right before his meeting with the pope in Rome, in fact – but somehow it had not seemed as significant then as it did now. *So which are you, Rama?* he thought. *A threat to Courtney Bothwell or a herald of Christ's second coming?*

During the hour before breakfast General O'Toole was still vacillating. He genuinely did not know what his decision would be. Weighing heavily upon him was the fact that he had been given an explicit order by his commanding officer. O'Toole was well aware that he had sworn, when he had received his commission, not only to follow orders, but also to protect the Courtney Bothwells of the planet. Did he have any evidence that this particular order was so immoral that he should abrogate his oath?

As long as he thought of Rama as only a machine, it was not too difficult for General O'Toole to countenance its destruction. His action would not, after all, kill any Ramans. But what was it that Wakefield had said? That the Raman spaceship was probably more intelligent than any living creatures on Earth, including human beings? And shouldn't superior machine intelligence have a special place among God's creations, perhaps even above lower life forms?

Eventually General O'Toole succumbed to fatigue. He simply had no energy left to deal with the unending stream of questions without answers. He reluctantly decided to cease his internal debate and prepared to implement his orders.

His first action was to rememorize his RQ code, the specific string of fifty integers between zero and nine that was known only by him and the processors inside the nuclear weapons. O'Toole had personally entered his code and checked that it had been properly stored in each of the weapons before the Newton mission had been launched from Earth. The string of digits was long to minimize the probability of its being duplicated by a repetitive, electronic search routine. Each of the Newton military officers had been counseled to derive a sequence that met two criteria: the code should be almost impossible to forget and should not be something straightforward, like all the phone numbers in the family, that an outside party might figure out easily from the personnel files.

For sentimental reasons, O'Toole had wanted nine of the numbers in his code to be his birthdate, 3-29-42, and the birthdate of his wife, 2-7-46. He knew that any decryption specialist would immediately look for such obvious selections, so the general resolved to hide the birthdates in the fifty digits. But what about the other forty-one digits? That particular number, forty-one, had intrigued O'Toole ever since a beer and pizza party during his sophomore year at MIT. One of his associates then, a brilliant young number theorist whose name he had long forgotten, had told O'Toole in the middle of a drunken discussion that forty-one was a 'very special number, the initial integer in the longest continuous string of quadratic primes.'

O'Toole never fully comprehended what exactly was meant by the expression 'quadratic prime.' However, he did understand, and was fascinated by, the fact that the string 41, 43, 47, 53, 61, 71, 83, 97, where each successive number was computed by increasing the difference from the previous number by two, resulted in exactly forty consecutive prime numbers. The sequence of primes ended only when the forty-first number in the string turned out to be a nonprime, namely 41 × 41 = 1681. This little known piece of information O'Toole had shared only one time in his life, with his wife Kathleen on her forty-first birthday, and he had received such a lacklustre response that he had never told anybody about it again.

But it was perfect for his secret code, particularly if he disguised it properly. To build his fifty-digit number, General O'Toole first constructed a sequence of forty-one digits, each coming from the sum of the first two digits in the corresponding term in the special quadratic prime sequence beginning with 41. Thus '5' was the initial digit, representing 41, followed by '7' for 43, '1' for 47 (4 + 7 = 11 and then truncate), '8' for 53, etc. O'Toole next scattered the numbers of the two birthdates using an inverse Fibonacci sequence (34, 21, 13, 8, 5, 3, 2, 1, 1) to define the locations of the nine new integers in the original forty-one-digit string.

It was not easy to commit the sequence to memory, but the general did not want to write it down and carry it with him to the activation process. If his code were written down, then anyone could use it, with or without his permission, and his option to change his mind again would be precluded. Once he had rememorized the sequence, O'Toole destroyed all his computations and went to the dining room to have breakfast with the rest of the cosmonauts.

'Here's a copy of my code for you, Francesca, and one for you, Irina, and the final one goes to Hiro Yamanaka. Sorry, Janos,' Admiral Heilmann said with a big smile, 'but I'm all out of bullets. Maybe General O'Toole will let you enter his code into one of the bombs.'

'It's all right, Herr Admiral,' Janos said wryly. 'Some privileges in life I can do without.'

Heilmann was making a big production out of activating the nuclear weapons, He had had his fifty-digit number printed out multiple times and had enjoyed explaining to the other cosmonauts how clever he had been in the conception of his code. Now, with uncharacteristic flair, he was allowing the rest of the crew to participate in the process.

Francesca loved it. It was definitely good television. It occurred to O'Toole that Francesca had probably suggested such a staging to Heilmann, but the general didn't spend much time thinking about it. O'Toole was too busy being astonished by how calm he himself had become. After his long and agonizing soul-searching, he was apparently going to perform his duty without qualms.

Admiral Heilmann became confused during the entering of his code (he admitted that he was nervous) and temporarily lost track of where he was in his sequence. The system designers had foreseen this possibility and had installed two lights, one green and one red, right above the numerical key-boards on the side of the bomb. After every tenth digit one of the two lights would illuminate, indicating whether or not the previous decade of code was a successful match. The safety committee had expressed concern that this 'extra' feature compromised the system (it would be easier to decrypt five ten-digit strings than one fifty-digit string), but repeated human engineering tests prior to launch had shown that the lights were necessary.

At the end of his second decade of digits, Heilmann was greeted by the flashing red light. 'I've done something wrong,' he said, his embarrassment obvious.

'Louder,' shouted Francesca from where she was filming. She had neatly framed the ceremony so that both the weapons and the pods appeared in the picture.

'I've made a mistake,' Admiral Heilmann proclaimed. 'All this noise has distracted me. I must wait thirty seconds before I can start again.'

After Heilmann had successfully completed his code, Dr Brown entered the activation code on the second weapon. He seemed almost bored; cer-tainly he didn't push the keyboard with anything approaching enthusiasm. Irina Turgenyev activated the third bomb. She made a short but passionate comment underscoring her belief that the destruction of Rama was abso-lutely essential

Neither Hiro Yamanaka nor Francesca said anything at all. Francesca, however, did impress the rest of the crew by doing her first thirty digits from memory. Considering that she had supposedly never seen Hermann's code until an hour earlier, and had not been alone for more than two minutes since then, her feat was quite remarkable.

Next it was General O'Toole's turn. Smiling comfortably, he walked easily up to the first weapon. The other cosmonauts applauded, both showing their respect for the general and acknowledging his struggle. He asked everyone please to be quiet, explaining that he had committed his whole sequence to memory. Then O'Toole entered the first decade of digits.

He stopped for a second as the green light flashed. In that instant an image flashed into his mind of one of the frescoes on the second floor of the shrine of St Michael in Rome. A young man in a blue robe, his eyes uplifted to the heavens, was standing on the steps of the Victor Emmanuel Monument, preaching to an appreciative multitude. General O'Toole heard a voice, loudly and distinctly. The voice said 'No.'

The general spun around quickly. 'Did anybody say anything?' he said, staring at the other cosmonauts. They shook their heads. Befuddled, O'Toole turned back to the bomb. He tried to remember the second decade of digits. But it was no good. His heart was racing at breakneck speed. His mind kept saying, over and over again, *What was that voice?* His resolve to perform his duty had vanished.

Michael O'Toole took a deep breath, turned around again, and walked across the huge bay. When he passed his stunned colleagues he heard Admiral Heilmann yell, 'What are you doing?'

'I'm going to my room,' O'Toole said without breaking stride.

'Aren't you going to activate the bombs?' Dr Brown said behind him.

'No,' replied General O'Toole. 'At least not yet.'

56 AN ANSWERED PRAYER

General O'Toole stayed in his room the rest of the day. Admiral Heilmann dropped by about an hour after O'Toole's failure to enter his code. After some meaningless small talk (Heilmann was terrible at that sort of thing), the admiral asked the all-important question.

'Are you ready to proceed with the activation?'

O'Toole shook his head. 'I thought I was this morning, Otto, but ...' There was no need for him to say anything more.

Heilmann rose from his chair. 'I've given orders for Yamanaka to take the first two bullets to the passageway inside Rama. They'll be there by dinner if you change your mind. The other three will be left in the bay for the time being.' He stared at his colleague for several seconds. 'I hope you come to your senses before too much longer, Michael. We're already in deep trouble at headquarters.'

When Francesca came in with her camera two hours later, it was clear from her choice of words that the attitude toward the general, at least among the remaining cosmonauts, was that O'Toole was suffering from acute nervous tension. He wasn't being defiant. He wasn't making a statement. None of the rest of the crew could have tolerated those alternatives, because they would all look bad by association. No, it was obvious that there was something wrong with his nerves.

'I've told everyone not to bother you with calls,' Francesca said compassionately as she glanced around the room, her television mind already framing the images of the coming interview. 'The phones have been ringing like crazy, especially since I sent down the tape from this morning.' She walked over to his desk, checking the objects on its top. 'Is this Michael of Siena?' Francesca asked, picking up the small statue.

O'Toole managed a wan smile. 'Yes,' he said. 'And I think you know the man on the cross in the picture.'

'Very well,' Francesca replied. 'Very well indeed.... Look, Michael, you know what's coming. I would like for this interview to paint you in the best possible light. Not that I'm going to treat you with kid gloves, you understand, but I want to make certain that those wolves down there hear your side of the story—'

'They're already screaming for my hide?' O'Toole interrupted.

'Oh, yes,' she answered. 'And it will get much worse. The longer you delay activating the bombs, the more wrath will be aimed at you.'

'But why?' O'Toole protested. 'I haven't committed a crime. I've simply delayed activating a weapon whose destructive power exceeds—'

'That's irrelevant,' Francesca retorted, 'In *their* eyes you haven't done your job, namely to protect the people on the planet Earth. They're frightened. They don't understand all this extraterrestrial crap. They've been told that Rama will be destroyed and now you've refused to remove their nightmares.'

'Nightmares,' mumbled O'Toole, 'that's what Bothwell ...'

'What about President Bothwell?' inquired Francesca.

'Oh, nothing,' he said. He looked away from her probing eyes. 'What else?' O'Toole asked impatiently.

'As I was saying, I want you to look as good as possible. Comb your hair again and put on a fresh uniform, not a flight suit. I'll daub a little makeup on your face so you don't look washed out.' She returned to the desk. 'We'll place your family photos in full view next to Jesus and Michael. Think carefully about what you're going to say. Of course I'll ask why you failed to activate the weapons this morning.'

Francesca walked over and put her hand on O'Toole's shoulder. 'In my introduction I will have suggested that you've been under a strain. I don't want to put words in your mouth, but admitting a little weakness will probably play well. Particularly in your country.'

General O'Toole squirmed while Francesca finished the preparations for the interview. 'Do I have to do this?' he asked, becoming more and more uncomfortable as the journalist essentially rearranged his room.

'Only if you want anybody to think you're not Benedict Arnold,' was her curt reply.

Janos came in to visit just before dinner. 'Your interview with Francesca was very good,' he lied. 'At least you raised some moral issues that all of us should consider.'

'It was dumb of me to bring up all that philosophical crap,' O'Toole fretted. 'I should have followed Francesca's advice and blamed everything on my fatigue.'

'Well, Michael,' said Janos, 'what's done is done. I didn't come in here to review the events of the day. I'm certain you've done that plenty of times already. I came in here to see if I could be any help.'

'I don't think so, Janos,' he replied. 'But I do appreciate the thought.'

There was a long hiatus in the conversation. At length Janos stood up and shuffled toward the door. 'What do you do now?' he asked quietly.

'I wish I knew,' O'Toole answered. 'I don't seem to be able to come up with a plan.'

*

The combined Rama-Newton spacecraft continued to hurtle toward the Earth. With each passing day the Rama threat loomed greater, a huge cylinder moving at hyperbolic speed toward what would be a calamitous impact if no new midcourse corrections were made. The estimated crash point was in the state of Tamil Nadu, in south India, not far from the city of Madurai. Physicists were on the network news every night, explaining what could be expected. 'Shock waves' and 'ejecta' became terms bandied about at dinner parties.

Michael O'Toole was vilified by the global press. Francesca had been right. The American general became the focus of a world's fury. There were even suggestions that he should be court-martialed and executed, on board the Newton, for his failure to follow orders. A lifetime of important accomplishments and selfless contributions was forgotten. Kathleen O'Toole was forced to leave the family apartment in Boston and take refuge with a friend in Maine.

The general was tortured by his indecision. He knew that he was doing irreparable damage to his family and his career by his failure to activate the weapons. But each time he convinced himself he was ready to execute the order, that loud and resounding 'No' echoed again in his ears.

O'Toole was only marginally coherent in his final interview with Francesca, the day before the scientific ship left to return to the Earth. She asked some very tough questions. When Francesca asked him why, if Rama were going to orbit the Earth, it had not yet made a deflection manoeuvre, the general perked up momentarily and reminded her that aerobraking – dissipating energy in the atmosphere as heat – was the most efficient method of achieving orbit around a planetary body with an atmosphere. But when she gave him a chance to amplify his statement, to discuss how Rama might reconfigure itself to have aerodynamic surfaces, O'Toole did not answer. He just stared at her distractedly.

O'Toole came out of his room for the final dinner the night before Brown, Sabatini, Tabori, and Turgenyev departed for home. His presence spoiled the last supper. Irina was extremely nasty to him, upbraiding the general venomously, and refusing to sit at the same table. David Brown ignored him altogether, choosing instead to discuss in excruciating detail the laboratory being designed in Texas to accommodate the captured crab biot. Only Francesca and Janos were friendly, so General O'Toole returned to his room right after dinner without formally saying goodbye to anyone.

The next morning, less than an hour after the scientific ship had left, O'Toole buzzed Admiral Heilmann and asked for a meeting. 'So you have finally changed your mind?' the German said excitedly when the general entered his office. 'Good. It's not too late yet. It's only 1-12 days. If we hurry we can still detonate the bombs at 1-9.'

'I'm getting closer, Otto,' O'Toole replied, 'but I'm not there yet. I've been thinking about all this very carefully. There are two things I would still like to do. I'd like to talk to Pope John-Paul and I want to go inside to see Rama for myself.'

O'Toole's response left Heilmann deflated. 'Shit,' he said. 'Here we go again. We'll probably ...'

'You don't understand, Otto,' the American said. He stared fixedly at his colleague. 'This is good news. Unless something totally unexpected occurs, either during my call to the pope or while I'm exploring Rama, I'll be ready to enter my code the minute I come out.'

'Are you certain?' Heilmann asked.

'I give you my word,' O'Toole replied.

General O'Toole held nothing back in his long, emotional transmission to the pope. He was aware that his call was being monitored, but it no longer mattered. A single thing was uppermost in his mind: making the decision to activate the nuclear weapons with a clear conscience.

He waited impatiently for the reply. When Pope John-Paul V finally appeared on the screen, he was sitting in the same room in the Vatican where O'Toole had had his audience just after Christmas. The pope was holding a small electronic pad in his right hand and occasionally glanced down as he spoke.

'I have prayed with you, my son,' the pontiff began in his precise English, 'particularly during this last week of your personal turmoil. I cannot tell you what to do. I do not have the answers any more than you do. We can only hope together that God, in His wisdom, will provide unambiguous answers to your prayers.

'In response to some of your religious inquiries, however, I can make a few comments. I offer them to you in the hope that they will be helpful ... I cannot say whether or not the voice you heard was that of St Michael, or if you had what is known as a religious experience. I can affirm that there is a category of human experience, usually called religious for lack of a better term, that exists and cannot be explained in purely rational or scientific terms. Saul of Tarsus was definitely blinded by a light from the heavens as part of his conversion to Christianity, before he became the apostle Paul. Your voice may have been St Michael. Only you can decide.

'As we discussed three months ago, God certainly created the Ramans, whoever they were. But he also created the viruses and bacteria that cause human death and suffering. We cannot glorify God, either individually or as a species, if we do not survive. It seems unlikely to me that God would expect us to take no action if our very survival were threatened.

'The possible role of Rama as a herald for the second coming of Christ is a difficult issue. There are some priests inside the church who agree with St Michael, although they are a distinct minority. Most of us feel that the Rama craft are too spiritually sterile to be heralds. They are incredible engineering marvels, to be sure, but there is nothing about them that suggests any warmth or compassion or any other redeeming characteristic that is associated with Christ. It therefore seems very unlikely that Rama has any strictly religious significance.

'In the end it is a decision you must make yourself. You must continue your prayers, as I'm certain you realise, but maybe expect a little less fanfare in God's response. He does not speak to everyone in the same way; nor will each of His messages to you come in the same form. Please remember one more thing. As you explore Rama in search of God's will, the prayers of many on Earth will go with you. You can be certain that God will give you an answer; your challenge is to identify and interpret it.'

John-Paul ended his transmission with a blessing and a recitation of the Lord's prayer. General O'Toole knelt automatically and spoke the words along with his spiritual leader. When the screen was blank, he reviewed what the pontiff had said and felt reassured. *I must be on the right track,* O'Toole said to himself. *But I should not expect a heavenly proclamation with accompanying trumpets.*

O'Toole was not prepared for his powerful emotional response to Rama. Perhaps it was the sheer scale of the spacecraft, so much larger than anything ever built by human beings. Perhaps also his long confinement on the Newton and heightened emotional state contributed to the intensity of his feelings. Whatever the reasons, Michael O'Toole was totally overwhelmed by the spectacle as he made his solitary way into the giant spacecraft.

There was no specific feature that dominated the rest in O'Toole's mind. His throat caught and his eyes brimmed with tears of wonder on several different occasions: riding down the chairlift on his initial descent and looking out across the Central Plain with its long illuminated strips that were Rama's light; standing beside the rover on the shores of the Cylindrical Sea and staring through his binoculars at the mysterious skyscrapers of New York; and gawking many times, like all the cosmonauts before him, at the gigantic horns and buttresses that adorned the southern bowl. O'Toole's dominant feelings were awe and reverence, much as he had felt the first time he had entered one of the old European cathedrals.

He spent the Raman night at Beta, using one of the extra huts left by the cosmonauts on the second sortie. He found Wakefield's message dated two weeks earlier, and had a momentary desire to assemble the sailboat and cross over to New York. But O'Toole restrained himself and focused on the true purpose of his visit.

He admitted to himself that although Rama was a spectacular achievement, its magnificence should not be a relevant factor in his evaluation process. Was there anything he had seen that would cause him to alter his tentative conclusion? No, he grudgingly answered. When the lights came on again inside the giant cylinder, O'Toole was confident that before the next Raman nightfall he would activate the weapons.

Still he procrastinated, He drove the entire length of the coastline, examining New York and the other vistas from different vantage points and observing the five-hundred-metre cliff on the opposite side of the sea. On one last pass through the Beta campsite, O'Toole decided to pick up some odds and ends, including a few personal mementos left behind by the other crew members in their hasty retreat from Rama. Not many items had escaped the hurricane, but he found some souvenirs that had been trapped in comers against the supply crates.

General O'Toole took a long nap before he guided the rover back to the bottom of the chairlift. Realizing what he was going to do when he reached the Newton, O'Toole knelt down and prayed one last time before ascending. Shortly into his ride, when he was still less than half a kilometre above the Central Plain, he turned in his chair and looked back across the Raman panorama. *Soon this will all be gone,* O'Toole thought, *enveloped in a solar furnace unleashed by man.* His eyes lifted from the plain and focused on New York. He thought he saw a moving black speck in the Raman sky.

With trembling hands he lifted his binoculars to his eyes. In a few seconds O'Toole located the enlarged speck. He quickly changed the binocular resolution and the speck split into three parts, each a bird soaring in formation far off in the distance. O'Toole blinked but the image did not change. There were indeed three birds flying in the Raman sky!

Joy filled General O'Toole. He yelled with delight as he followed the birds with his binoculars until he could no longer see them. The remaining thirty minutes of the ride to the top of the Alpha stairway seemed like a lifetime.

The American officer immediately climbed into another chair and descended again into Rama. He wanted desperately to see those birds one more time. *If I could somehow photograph them,* he thought, planning to drive back to the Cylindrical Sea if necessary, *then I could prove to everyone that there are also living creatures in this amazing world.*

Starting two kilometres above the floor O'Toole searched in vain for the birds as he descended. Only slightly disheartened by his failure to find them, he was subsequently dumbfounded by what he saw when he dropped his binoculars from his eyes and prepared to disembark from the chair. Richard Wakefield and Nicole des Jardins were standing side by side at the bottom of the lift.

General O'Toole embraced them each with a vigorous hug and then, with tears of happiness running down his cheeks, he knelt on the soil of Rama. 'Dear God,' he said as he offered his silent prayer of thanks. 'Dear God,' he repeated.

57 THREE'S COMPANY

The three cosmonauts talked avidly for over an hour. There was so much to tell. When Nicole told of her fright upon encountering the dead Takagishi in the octospider lair, O'Toole was momentarily silent and then shook his head. 'There are so many unanswered questions here,' he said, staring up at the high ceiling. 'Are you really malevolent after all?' he asked rhetorically.

Richard and Nicole both praised the general's courage in not entering his code to activate the weapons. They were also both horrified that the COG had ordered the destruction of Rama. 'It is absolutely unforgivable for us to use nuclear weapons against this spaceship,' Nicole said. 'I am convinced that it is not fundamentally hostile. And I believe that Rama manoeuvered to intercept the Earth because it has a specific message for us.'

Richard lightly chided Nicole for developing her opinion more on the basis of emotions than facts. 'Perhaps,' she rejoined, 'but there is a serious logical flaw as well in this decision to destroy. We now have hard evidence that this vehicle communicated with its predecessor. There is good reason to suspect that a Rama III is out there somewhere, probably coming in this direction. If the Rama fleet *is* potentially hostile, there is no way the Earth will be able to escape. We may succeed in destroying this second craft – but in so doing we will almost certainly alert their next ship. Since their technology is so much more advanced than ours, we would have no possibility of surviving their concerted attack.'

General O'Toole looked at Nicole with admiration. 'That's an excellent point,' he said. 'It's a shame you weren't available for the ISA discussions. We never considered—'

'Why don't we postpone the rest of this conversation until we're back on the Newton?' Richard said suddenly. 'According to my watch, it will be dark again in another thirty minutes, before any of us have reached the top of the lift. I don't want to ride in the dark any longer than is necessary.'

Each of the three cosmonauts believed that they were leaving Rama for the last time. As the remaining minutes of light dwindled, each cosmonaut gazed intently at the magnificent alien landscape that stretched out into the distance. For Nicole, the dominant feeling was one of elation. Cautious by nature with her expectations, until this moment in the chairlift she had not allowed herself the intense pleasure of believing that she would ever again hold her beloved Genevieve in her arms. Her mind was now flooded by the bucolic beauty of Beauvois and she imagined in detail the joy of her reunion scene with her father and daughter. *It could be as little as a week or ten days,* Nicole said to herself expectantly. By the time she reached the top she was having difficulty containing her jubilation.

During his ride Michael O'Toole reviewed, one more time, his activation decision. When dark came to Rama, suddenly and at the predicted moment, he had finished developing his plan for communicating his decision to the Earth. They would phone ISA management immediately. Nicole and Richard would summarize their stories and Nicole would present her reasons for thinking that the destruction of Rama would be 'unforgivable.' O'Toole was convinced that his order to activate the weapons would then be rescinded.

The general switched on his flashlight just before his chair reached the top of the stairway. He stepped off in the weightless environment and stood beside Nicole. They waited for Richard Wakefield before proceeding together around the ramp to the ferry passageway, only a hundred metres away. After the trio had boarded the ferry and were ready to move through the Rama shell toward the Newton, Richard's flashlight beam fell on a large metal object on the side of the passage. 'Is that one of the bombs?' he asked.

The nuclear weapon system did indeed resemble an oversized bullet. *How curious,* Nicole thought, recoiling as an instant shudder ran through her system. *It could be any shape, of course. I wonder what subconscious aberration made the designers choose that particular form ...*

'But what's that weird contraption at the top?' Richard was asking O'Toole.

The general's brow furrowed as he stared at a bizarre object illuminated by the centre of the beam of light. 'I don't know,' he confessed. 'I've never seen it before.' He disembarked from the ferry. Richard and Nicole followed him.

General O'Toole shuffled over to the weapon and studied the strange attachment fixed above the numerical keyboard. It was a flat plate, slightly larger than the keyboard itself, that was anchored by angular joints to the sides of the weapon. On the underside of the plate, momentarily retracted, were ten tiny punches – at least that's what they looked like to O'Toole. His observation was confirmed seconds later when one of the punches extended and hit the number '5' on the keyboard several centimetres below. The '5' was followed in rapid succession by a '7,' and then by eight more numbers before a green light flashed the successful completion of the first decade.

Within seconds the apparatus entered ten more digits and another green light flashed. O'Toole froze in terror. *My God*, he thought, *that's my code! Somehow they've broken –* His panic subsided an instant later when, after the third decade of digits, the red light announced that an error had been made.

'Apparently,' General O'Toole said a short time later in response to an inquiry from Richard, 'they have jerryrigged this scheme to try to enter the code in my absence, They only have the first two decades correct. For a moment I was afraid ...' O'Toole paused, aware of strong emotions stirring within him.

'They must have assumed you weren't coming back,' Nicole said in a matter-of-fact tone.

'If Heilmann and Yamanaka did it,' O'Toole replied. 'Of course we can't rule out completely the possibility that the contraption might have been placed there by the aliens ... or even the biots.'

'Extremely unlikely,' Richard commented. 'The engineering is much too crude.'

'At any rate,' O'Toole said, opening his backpack for some tools to disconnect the apparatus, 'I'm not taking any chances.'

At the Newton end of the passageway, O'Toole, Wakefield, and des Jardins found the second bomb fitted with the same apparatus. The trio watched it punch out one code attempt – with the same result, a failure somewhere in the third decade – and then they disabled it as well. Afterward they opened up the seal and exited from Rama.

Nobody greeted them when they stepped inside the Newton military ship. General O'Toole assumed that both Admiral Heilmann and Yamanaka were asleep and went immediately to the bedrooms. He wanted to talk to Heilmann in private anyway. But the two men were not in their rooms. It did not take long to confirm, in fact, that the other two cosmonauts were nowhere in the comparatively small living and working area of the military ship.

A search of the supply area in the back of the ship was also futile. However, the threesome did discover that one of the extravehicular activity (EVA) pods was missing. This discovery raised another perplexing set of questions. Where could Heilmann and Yamanaka have gone in the pod? And why had they violated the top-priority project policy that at least one crew member should always stay on board the Newton?

The three cosmonauts were puzzled as they returned to the control centre to discuss their possible courses of action. O'Toole was the first to raise the spectre of foul play. 'Do you think those octospiders, or even some of the biots, might have come on board? After all, it's not difficult to enter the Newton unless it's in Self-Protection Mode.'

Nobody wanted to say what all three of them were thinking. If someone or something had captured or killed their two colleagues on the ship, then it might still be around and *they* might be in danger themselves... .

'Why don't we call the Earth and announce that we're alive?' Richard said, breaking the silence.

'Great idea.' General O'Toole smiled. He moved over to the control centre console and activated the panel. A standard system status display appeared on the large screen. 'That's strange,' the general commented. 'According to this, we have no video link with the Earth presently. Only low-rate tele-metry. Now, why would the data system configuration have been changed?'

He keyed in a simple set of commands to establish the normal multichannel high-rate link with the Earth. A swarm of error messages appeared on the monitor. 'What the hell?' Richard exclaimed. 'It looks as if the video system has died.' He turned to O'Toole. 'This is your speciality, General, what do you make of all this?'

General O'Toole was very serious. 'I don't like it, Richard. I've only seen this many error messages one time before – during one of our early simula-tions when some nincompoop forgot to load the communications software. We must have a major software problem. The probability of that many hard-ware failures in such a short time span is essentially zero.'

Richard suggested that O'Toole subject the video communications software to its standard self-test. During the test, the diagnostic printout reported that the error buffers in the self-test algorithm had overflowed when the procedure was less than one percent complete. 'So the vidcomm software is definitely the culprit,' Richard said, analyzing the data in the diagnostic. He entered some commands. 'It's going to take a while to straighten it out—'

'Just a minute,' Nicole interrupted. 'Shouldn't we spend our time trying to make some sense out of all this new information before we start on any specific tasks?' The two men stopped their activity and waited for her to continue. 'Heilmann, Yamanaka, and one pod are missing from this ship,' Nicole said, walking slowly around the control centre, 'and someone was trying to automatically activate the two nuclear bombs in the passageway. Meanwhile the vidcomm software, after functioning properly for hundreds of days – counting all the preflight simulations – has suddenly gone haywire. Do either of you have a coherent explanation for all this?'

There was a long silence. 'General O'Toole's suggestion of a hostile invasion of the Newton might work,' Richard offered. 'Heilmann and Yamanaka might have fled to save themselves and the aliens could have purposely screwed up the software.'

Nicole was not convinced. 'Nothing I have seen suggests that any aliens – or even any biots, for that matter – have been inside the Newton. Unless we see some evidence ...'

'Maybe Heilmann and Yamanaka were trying to break the general's code,' Wakefield invented, 'and they were afraid—'

'Stop. Stop,' Nicole shouted suddenly. 'Something's happening to the screen.' The two men turned around just in time to see Admiral Otto Heilmann's face materialise on the monitor.

'Hello, General O'Toole,' Heilmann said with a smile from the huge screen. 'This videotape was triggered by your entering the Newton airlock. Cosmo-naut Yamanaka and I prepared it just before we departed in one of the pods three hours before 1-9 days. We were ordered to evacuate less than an hour after you went inside to explore Rama. We delayed as long as we could but eventually had to follow our instructions.

'Your personal orders are simple and straightforward. You are to enter your activation code into the two weapons in the ferry passageway and the three remaining in the bay. You should depart in the final pod no more than eight hours thereafter. Don't be concerned about the electronic devices in operation on the two bombs in the Raman shell. COG military headquarters ordered them put in place to test some new top secret decryption techniques. You will discover they can easily be disabled with pliers and/or wirecutters.

'An extra, emergency propulsion system has been added to the pod and its software has been programmed to guide you to a safe location, where you will rendezvous with an ISA tug. All you need to do is code in the exact time of your departure. However, I must stress that the new pod navigation algorithms are valid *only* if you leave the Newton *before* 1-6 days. After that time, I am told the guidance parameters become increasingly invalid and it will be almost impossible to rescue you.'

There was a short pause in Heilmann's delivery and his voice took on an increased sense of urgency. 'Don't waste any more time, Michael. Activate the weapons and go directly to the pod. We have already supplied it with the food and other essentials that you will need ... Good luck on your voyage home. We'll see you back on Earth.'

58 HOBSON'S CHOICE

'm certain that Heilmann and Yamanaka were being extremely cautious,' Richard Wakefield explained. 'They probably left early so they could take extra supplies. And with these lightweight pods, each extra kilogram can be critical.'

'*How* critical?' asked Nicole.

'Well – it could make all the difference between getting into a safe orbit around Earth – or shooting past it so quickly that we couldn't be rescued.'

'Does that mean,' O'Toole inquired sombrely, 'that only one of us might be able to use the pod?'

Richard paused before answering. 'I'm afraid that's possible; it's a function of the time of departure. We'll have to do some quick calculations to determine exactly. But personally I see no reason why we shouldn't consider flying this entire spacecraft. I was trained as a backup pilot, after all ... We have only limited control authority, since the ship is so large, but if we jettison everything we don't absolutely need, we may be able to do it Again, we'll need to do the computations.'

Nicole's assignments from General O'Toole and Richard were to check the supplies that had been placed in the pod, determine their adequacy, and then approximate both the mass and packaging volume required to support either two or three travellers. In addition Richard, still favouring flying back to Earth in the military ship, asked Nicole to go through the Newton supply manifest and estimate how much mass could be thrown overboard.

While O'Toole and Wakefield used the computers in the control centre, Nicole worked alone in the huge bay. First she examined the remaining pod very carefully. Although the pods were normally used by a single person for EVA, they had also been designed as emergency escape vehicles. Two people could sit behind the tough, transparent front window with a week's supplies on the shelves at the rear of the small cabin. *But three people?* Nicole wondered. *Impossible. Someone would have to squeeze into the shelf space. And then there would not be adequate room for the supplies.* Nicole thought momentarily about being confined to the tiny shelves for seven or eight days. *It would be even worse than the pit in New York.*

She looked through the supplies that had been hastily thrown into the pod

492

by Heilmann and Yamanaka. The food allocation was more or less correct, both in quantity and variety, for a one-week voyage; the medical kit, however, was woefully inadequate. Nicole made a few notes, constructed what she considered to be a proper supply list for either a two or three person crew, and estimated the mass and packaging requirements. She then started to cross the bay.

Her eyes were drawn to the bullet-shaped nuclear weapons lying placidly on their sides right beside the pod airlock. Nicole walked over and touched the bombs, her hands idly running across the polished metal surface. *So these are the first great weapons of destruction,* she thought, *the outcome of the brilliant physics of the twentieth century.*

What a sad commentary on our species, Nicole mused, as she was walking among the nuclear bombs. *A visitor comes to see us. It cannot speak our language, but it does discover where we live. When it turns the corner on to our street, while its purpose is still utterly unknown, we blast it into oblivion.*

She shuffled across the bay toward the living quarters, aware of a profound feeling of sadness deep within her. *Your problem,* Nicole said to herself, *is that you always expect too much. From yourself. From those you love. Even from the human race. We are yet too immature a species.*

A momentary wave of nausea forced Nicole to stop for a moment. *What's this?* she thought. *Are these bombs making me ill?* In the back of her mind Nicole recalled a similar feeling of nausea fifteen years before, two hours into her flight from Los Angeles to Paris. *It can't be,* she told herself. *But I'll check just to be certain....*

'That's the second reason why the three of us cannot all fit in a single pod. Don't feel bad, Nicole. Even if the physical space could accommodate our bodies and the needed supplies, the velocity change capability of the pod with all that mass is barely enough to close the orbit around the Sun. Our chances of being rescued would be virtually nil.'

'Well,' Nicole replied to Richard, trying to be cheerful, 'at least we still have the other option. We can go home in this big vehicle. According to my estimates, we can dump in excess of ten thousand kilograms—'

'I'm afraid it doesn't matter,' General O'Toole interrupted.

Nicole looked at Richard. 'What's he talking about?'

Richard Wakefield stood up and walked over to Nicole. He took her hands in his. 'They screwed up the navigation system too,' Richard said. 'Their automatic search algorithms, the big number-crunchers being used to try to decrypt O'Toole's code, were overlaid into the general purpose computers on top of the vidcomm and navigation subroutines. This ship is useless as a transportation module.'

General O'Toole's voice was distant and lacked its usual upbeat timbre. 'They must have started only minutes after I left. Richard read the command buffers and found out that the decryption software was uplinked less than two hours after my departure.'

'But why would they incapacitate the Newton?' Nicole asked.

'Don't you understand?' O'Toole said with passion. 'The priorities had changed. Nothing was as important as detonating the nuclear weapons. They didn't want to waste the time for the radio signals to go back and forth to Earth. So they moved the computations up here, where each successive candidate code could be commanded from the computer without delay.'

'In fairness to mission control,' Richard interjected, now pacing around the room, 'we should acknowledge that the fully loaded Newton military ship actually has less orbit change capability than a two-person pod with an auxiliary propulsion system. In the eyes of the ISA safety manager, there was no increased risk associated with making this craft inoperable.'

'But none of this should have happened in the first place,' the general argued. 'Dammit! Why couldn't they just have waited for my return?'

Nicole sat down abruptly in one of the available chairs. Her head was spinning and she felt momentarily dizzy. 'What's the matter?' Richard said, approaching her with alarm.

'I have been having occasional periods of nausea today,' Nicole replied. 'I think I'm pregnant. I'll know for certain in about twenty minutes.' She smiled at the dumbfounded Richard. 'It's extremely rare for a woman to become pregnant within ninety days of an injection of neutrabriolate. But it has happened before. I don't suppose—'

'Congratulations,' an enthusiastic General O'Toole suddenly interrupted. 'I had no idea that the two of you were planning to have a family.'

'Nor did I,' Richard replied, still looking shocked. He gave Nicole a vigorous hug and held her close. 'Nor did I,' he repeated.

'There will be no more discussion of this subject,' General O'Toole said emphatically to Richard. 'Even if Nicole weren't pregnant with your child, I would insist that the two of you go in the pod and leave me here. It's the only sensible decision. In the first place, we both know that mass is the most critical parameter and I am the heaviest of the three of us by far. In addition, I am old and you two are both quite young. You know how to fly the pod; I've never even trained inside it a single time. Besides,' he added dryly, 'I will be court-martialed on Earth for refusing to follow orders.'

'As for you, my good doctor,' O'Toole continued moments later, 'I don't need to tell you that you are carrying a very special baby. He or she will be the only human child that was ever conceived inside an extraterrestrial space vehicle.' He stood up and glanced around. 'Now,' he said, 'I propose we open a bottle of wine and celebrate our last evening together.'

Nicole watched General O'Toole glide over to the larder. He opened it and started rummaging around. 'I'm perfectly happy with fruit juice, Michael,' she said. 'I shouldn't drink more than a single glass of wine now anyway.'

'Of course,' he replied quickly. 'I temporarily forgot. I was hoping that we could do something special on this last night. I wanted to share one last time ...' General O'Toole stopped himself and brought the wine and juice back to the table. He handed cups to both Richard and Nicole. 'I want you both to know,' he said quietly, his mood now subdued, 'that I cannot imagine a finer pair of people than the two of you. I wish you every success, especially with the baby.'

The three cosmonauts drank in silence for several seconds. 'We all know it, don't we?' General O'Toole said in a barely audible tone. 'The missiles must be on their way. How long do you figure I have, Richard?'

'Judging from what Admiral Heilmann said on the tape, I would say that the first missile will reach Rama at 1-5 days. That would be consistent both with the pod being outside the debris field and the deflection velocities that must be imparted to the surviving pieces of the spacecraft.'

'You two have lost me,' Nicole said. 'What missiles are we talking about?'

Richard leaned over toward her. 'Both Michael and I are certain,' he said gravely, 'that the COG has ordered a missile strike against Rama. They had no assurance that the general would ever return to the Newton and enter his code. And the search algorithm with the automatic punch was a long shot at best. Only a missile strike could guarantee that Rama would not have the capability of harming our planet.'

'So I have a little more than forty-eight hours to make my final peace with God,' General O'Toole said after reflecting for several seconds. 'I have lived a fabulous life. I have much to be thankful for. I will go into His arms without regret.'

59 DREAM OF DESTINY

As Nicole stretched her arms over her head and to her sides, she brushed against Richard on her left and one of the water containers hanging slightly out of the shelf behind her. 'It's going to be crowded,' she observed, squirming in her seat.

'Yes, it is,' Richard replied distractedly. His attention was focused on the display in front of the pilot's seat in the pod. He entered some commands and waited for the response. When it finally came, Richard frowned.

'I guess I'll make one more attempt to repackage the supplies,' Nicole said with a sigh. She turned around in her seat and stared at the shelves. 'I could save us some room and fourteen kilograms if our rescue was guaranteed in seven days,' she said.

Richard did not respond. 'Dammit,' he muttered when a set of numbers appeared on the display.

'What's the matter?' Nicole asked.

'There's something not quite right here,' Richard said. 'The navigation code was developed for considerably less payload mass – it may not converge if we lose one of the accelerometers.' Nicole waited patiently for Richard to explain. 'So if we have any hiccoughs along the way, we will probably have to stop for several hours and reinitialise.'

'But I thought you said there was plenty of fuel for the two of us.'

'Plenty of fuel, yes. However, there are some subtleties in the reprogrammed navigation algorithms that assume the pod contains less than a hundred kilograms, basically only O'Toole and his supplies.'

Nicole could read the concern in Richard's brow. 'We're all right, I think, if there are no malfunctions,' he continued. 'But no pod has ever been operated under conditions like this.'

Through the front window they could see General O'Toole walking across the bay toward them. He was carrying a small object in his hand. It was TB, one of Richard's tiny Shakespearean robots.

'I almost forgot I had him,' O'Toole said a minute later after he had been thanked profusely by Richard. Cosmonaut Wakefield was soaring around the supply depot like a joyous child, a wide smile on his delighted face.

'I thought I'd never see any of them again,' Richard yelled from one of the side walls where his exuberant momentum had carried him.

'I was passing your room,' General O'Toole shouted back, 'right before the scientific ship departed. Cosmonaut Tabori was arranging your things. He asked me to keep that particular robot, just in case—'

'Thank you, thank you, Janos,' Richard said. He walked carefully down the wall and anchored himself to the floor. 'This is a very special one, Michael,' he said with a gleam in his eye. He switched on TB's power. 'Do you know any Shakespearean sonnets?'

'There's one that Kathleen especially likes, if I can recall it. I think the first line is, "That time of year thou mayst" ...'

> That time of year thou mayst in me behold
> When yellow leaves, or none, or few, do hang
> Upon those boughs which shake against the cold,
> Bare ruined choirs where late the sweet birds sang,
> In me thou seest the twilight of such day
> As after sunset fadeth in the west ...

The feminine voice coming from TB startled both Nicole and General O'Toole. The words struck a resonant chord in O'Toole; he was deeply moved and a few tears welled up in the corners of his eyes. Nicole took the general's hand and squeezed it compassionately after TB had finished the sonnet.

'You didn't say anything to Michael about the problems you found with the pod navigation,' Nicole said. She and Richard were lying side by side in one of the small bedrooms on the military ship.

'No,' replied Richard quietly. 'I didn't want to worry him. He believes that we are going to be safe and I don't want him to think differently.'

Nicole extended her arm and touched Richard. 'We could stay here, darling – then at least Michael would survive.'

He rolled over toward her. She could tell he was looking at her, even though she couldn't see him very clearly in the dark. 'I thought about that,' Richard said. 'But he would never accept it ... I even thought about sending you by yourself. Would you want to do that?'

'No,' Nicole answered after thinking for a moment. 'I don't think so. I'd rather go with you, unless ...'

'Unless what?'

'Unless there really is a big difference in the odds. If one of us can survive but two of us are almost certainly doomed, it doesn't make much sense—'

'I can't give you an accurate probabilistic assessment,' Richard interrupted. 'But I don't think there's a major difference if we go together. My knowledge of the pod and its system might almost be worth the extra mass. But either way, we're better off in the pod than if we stay here.'

'You're absolutely convinced that missiles are on the way, aren't you?'

'Yes, indeed. Nothing else makes sense. I would bet that such a contingency plan was under development as soon as Rama changed course and headed for the Earth.'

They were silent again. Nicole tried to sleep but was unsuccessful. They had both decided to rest for six hours before departing so that they could store some energy for what would doubtless be an exhausting voyage. Nicole's mind, however, would not turn off. She kept imagining General O'Toole perishing in a nuclear fireball.

'He really is a wonderful man,' Nicole said very quietly. She wasn't certain if Richard was still awake.

'Yes, he is,' Richard answered in the same tone. 'I envy his inner strength. I can't imagine giving up my own life for someone else so willingly,' He paused for a moment. 'I guess that comes from his deep religious beliefs. He doesn't see death as an end, only as a transition.'

I could do it, Nicole thought. *I could give up my life for Genevieve. Maybe even for Richard and this unborn baby. Perhaps in O'Toole's religion everyone is part of his family.*

Richard, meanwhile, was struggling with his own emotions. Was he being selfish in not insisting that Nicole go alone? Could he really justify the extra risk of his presence in terms of his extra skills? He dismissed the questions and tried to think of something else.

'You haven't said much about the baby,' Nicole said softly after another short silence.

'I haven't really had time to integrate him, or her, into what's going on,' Richard replied. 'I guess I've been insensitive ... You know I'm happy about it. I just want to wait until we're rescued before I seriously start thinking about what it will be like to be a father.' He leaned over and gave Nicole a kiss. 'Now, darling, I hope you won't think I'm being rude, but I'm going to try to sleep. It could be a long time before we have another opportunity ...'

'Of course,' she said. 'I'm sorry.' Nicole's mind drifted to another picture, this one of a small baby. *I wonder if he'll be intelligent,* she thought. *And will he have Richard's blue eyes and long fingers?*

Nicole was curled up in a ball in the corner of the dimly lit room. The taste of manna melon was still in her mouth. She was awakened by a strange tapping on her shoulder. Nicole glanced up and saw the grey velvet avian bending over her. The cherry rings around its neck glowed in the dark. 'Come,' it said pleadingly. 'You must come with us.'

She followed the avian into the hallway and turned to the right, away from the vertical corridor. The other avians were standing quietly against the wall. They were all watching her carefully. The whole procession followed the grey avian down the tunnel.

In a few moments the tunnel expanded into a large room. There was a solitary small light on the far wall, but otherwise the room was dark. Others were present, but Nicole could not see them clearly. Occasionally she glimpsed their silhouettes as they moved across the beam from the single light source. Nicole started to say something but the avian leader interrupted her. 'Shh,' it said, 'they will be here soon.'

Nicole heard a noise coming toward them from the opposite side of the room. It sounded like a cart with wooden wheels moving on a dirt path. As it approached, the avians around Nicole backed up and pressed against her. Moments later there was a fire in front of them.

A bier was resting on top of a burning cart. Nicole gasped. Her mother's body, dressed in regal green robes, lay on top of the bier. In the light from the fire Nicole could see some of the others in the room. Richard was smiling at her, holding the hand of a dark little girl about two years old. General O'Toole was very close to the fire, kneeling in prayer beside it. Behind him were a variety of biots and two or three odd forms that must have been octospiders.

The flames consumed the bier and began to burn her mother's body. Her mother rose slowly from her supine position, When Anawi turned in Nicole's direction, her face changed. It was Omeh's head on top of her mother's body.

'Ronata,' he said distinctly, 'the prophecies must be heeded. The Senoufo blood will be spread, even unto the stars. Minowe will be left behind. Ronata must travel with those who come from far away. Go now, and save the strange ones and Ronata's children.'

60 RETURN TO RAMA

I can't believe I'm doing this, Nicole said to herself as she carried her final ferryload of supplies to the heavy elevator at the top of the Beta stairway. It was dark inside Rama. The beam from her flashlight shone into the black void,

The dream had been so incredibly vivid that Nicole had been completely disorientated for more than five minutes after she woke up. Even now, almost two hours later, when she closed her eyes Nicole could see Omeh's face perfectly and hear his magical voice intoning the words. *I hope Richard doesn't wake up before I'm gone,* Nicole thought. *There's no way he would ever understand.*

She returned to the ferry and made one last trip through the shell toward the Newton. For thirty minutes she had been drafting her goodbye remarks in her mind, but now that the moment had come, Nicole was apprehensive.

'Dear Michael and dearest Richard,' she would begin, 'last night I had the most compelling dream of my life. The old Senoufo chieftain Omeh appeared to me and told me that my destiny was with Rama.'

Nicole passed through the airlock and entered the control centre. She sat down in front of the camera and cleared her voice. *This is ridiculous,* she thought, just before she turned on the lights. *I must be insane.* But the power of Omeh's image in her mind calmed all of her last-minute doubts. Moments later she continued with her final remarks to her friends.

'There is no way I can summarize in this short farewell the importance of Omeh and my African background in my life. Michael, Richard can tell you some of the Senoufo stories as the two of you fly home to Earth. Suffice it to say that I have never been misled by the old shaman. I know well that voices in a dream have no substance and are most likely creations of my own subconscious, but nevertheless I have decided to follow the directions Omeh gave me.

'I intend to do whatever I can to communicate to Rama that nuclear missiles may be on the way. I don't know exactly how I will accomplish this, but I will have some hours to plan while I am assembling the sailboat to cross the Cylindrical Sea. I do remember, Richard, our discussion about the keyboard commands that might lead into the higher hierarchy ...

'It is extremely difficult for me to say goodbye like this, and I am keenly aware that it is a poor substitute for a final embrace. But if you two were awake, you would never let me go back inside Rama ... I love you, Richard, never doubt it for a moment. I know it's unlikely, but maybe somehow, someday we will be united in another place. I promise you that if I survive to give birth to our child, I will never cease telling her about the intelligence, wit, and sensitivity of her father.

'I have one last request. If it turns out that either of you reaches home safely and I never return to the Earth, please explain to Genevieve what happened to me. Tell her the whole story, about the dream, the vial and the vision, and the Poro when I was a child. And tell her that I loved her with all my heart.'

Tears were flowing down Nicole's cheeks when she finished her message. She stood up and rewound the tape. She played it for a minute, to make certain that it had recorded properly, and then walked over to the airlock. *Goodness*, she thought as she put on her helmet, *I'm really going to do it.*

During Nicole's eerie descent on the chairlift in the dark she had strong misgivings about her decision to return. It was only her supreme self-discipline that allowed her to chase away the lingering fears. As she climbed into the rover and started to drive toward the Cylindrical Sea, Nicole thought about how she would communicate with the intelligence governing Rama. *I'll definitely use pictures,* she said to herself, *and wherever possible the precise language of science. That much I have learned from Richard.*

The thought of Richard rekindled her anxieties. *He'll think that I have abandoned him,* she worried. *And how can I really expect him to think otherwise?* Nicole recalled the depressing first days of her pregnancy with Genevieve and how very lonely she had been having nobody with whom she could share her feelings. Again she felt a strong call to turn around and leave Rama. Her introspection was broken by the spectacular arrival of light. Dawn had come again to Rama. As before, Nicole was mesmerized by the sights around her. *There's nothing like this anywhere in the universe.*

When she reached what had been the Beta campsite, she first found and started to unpack the large sailboat. It was in good shape. It had been packed at the bottom of a large storage container. Working to assemble the sailboat kept Nicole from brooding too much about her decision to leave the Newton. Mechanical assembly was not her forte. She almost despaired once when she had to disassemble a major fitting that had taken her ten minutes to put together in the first place. The entire exercise reminded her of several frustrating Christmas Eves at Beauvois when she and Pierre had worked almost all night to put Genevieve's new toys together. 'There ought to be a law that stores can only sell assembled toys,' Nicole laughingly muttered as she struggled with the directions for the sailboat.

Nicole carried the hull of the boat down the steps and placed it right next to the water. Each of the major substructures she assembled on the cliff above, where the light was brighter. She was so engrossed in her work that she did not hear the footsteps until they were only two or three metres away. When Nicole, who was working on her knees, turned to her right and saw something approaching her from very close, she was frightened almost out of her wits.

Moments later she and Richard were kissing and hugging joyously. 'O'Toole's coming too,' he said, sitting down next to Nicole and immediately beginning to work on the sailboat. 'At first, when I explained that I wasn't leaving without you, that whatever life I could have on Earth wouldn't mean anything if you weren't with me, he told me that you and I were both crazy. But after we talked, and I explained to him that I thought we had a decent probability of warning the Ramans, he decided that he'd rather spend his last hours with us than take a chance on a lonely and painful death in the pod.'

'But I thought you said that it would be a safe trip for a solitary passenger.'

'It's not completely clear. The software loaded in the pod is a nightmare. You can tell from the programming that it was done hastily. And how could it have been properly checked? O'Toole by himself might have had a better chance than the two of us together... But remember, he would face serious problems upon his arrival on Earth. That court-martial comment was not idle chatter.'

'I don't think that Michael was afraid of a court-martial. He might have wanted to spare his family, but—'

A shout from the distance interrupted their conversation. General O'Toole was waving at them from an approaching rover. 'But I don't understand,' Nicole said. 'How did he get here so quickly? You didn't walk, did you?'

Richard laughed. 'Of course not. I left a beacon at the bottom of the chair-lift. After I arrived at Beta and saw that you had removed the sailboat and its parts, I sent the rover back on automatic.'

'That was brave of you,' Nicole said. 'What if I had set sail during the extra time that it took you to find me on foot?'

Richard peered over the cliff at the boat's hull down next to the water. 'Actually you've done better than I expected,' he said with a tease in his voice. 'You might have finished in another hour or two.'

He grabbed Nicole's hands as she tried to hit him.

General O'Toole was the only practised sailor among the three of them. Soon after they reached the midpoint of their sail, he relegated Richard to holding an oar as a possible weapon in case the pair of shark biots that were shadowing them decided to attack. 'It's not Marblehead or the Cape,' O'Toole said as he stared across at New York, 'but it's definitely an interesting sail.'

During the voyage Richard tried, without success, to convince a nervous Nicole that the shark biots were unlikely to bother them. 'After all,' he told her, 'they didn't bother the boats at all during the first Rama expedition.

They must have capsized me because of something special in the design of our new motorboats.'

'How can you be so certain?' Nicole asked, staring uncomfortably at the grey shadows in the water beside them. 'And if they are not going to attack us, why have they been following us for so long?'

'We're a curiosity, that's all,' Richard replied. Nevertheless, he braced himself when one of the shadows suddenly veered toward the boat. It disappeared underneath them and joined its companion on the other side. 'See,' he said, releasing his grip on the oar, 'I told you there was nothing to worry about.'

They moored the sailboat on the New York side before climbing up the nearby stairway. Since General O'Toole had never been to New York before and was naturally very curious about what he was seeing, Richard went ahead to start working on the computer while Nicole gave the briefest of tours to O'Toole along the way.

By the time Nicole and the general reached the White Room, Richard already had some progress to report. 'My hypothesis was correct,' he said only seconds after the other two had joined him. 'I'm fairly certain that I now have accessed the entire sensor list, They must have radar or its equivalent onboard. While I'm trying to locate it, why don't you two develop a flow diagram for how we will communicate our warning. Remember, keep it simple. We probably don't have more than twenty-four hours until the first missile arrives.'

Twenty-four hours, Nicole said to herself. *One more day.* She glanced over at Richard, hard at work at the keyboard, and General O'Toole, who was looking at some of the black objects still scattered in one of the corners. Nicole's momentary feelings of fondness for the two men were quickly truncated by a sharp burst of fear. The reality of their predicament overpowered her. *Will we all die tomorrow?* she wondered.

61 ENDANGERED SPACECRAFT

'We really shouldn't be surprised,' Richard said without emotion. The three of them were sitting in front of the large black screen. 'All of us expected it.'

'But we hoped otherwise,' O'Toole interjected. 'Sometimes it's depressing to be proven correct.'

'Are you positive, Richard,' Nicole asked, 'that each of those blips represents an object in space?'

'I don't think there's any doubt,' Richard replied. 'We know for certain that we're looking at sensor output. And look, I'll show you how to change the fields.' Richard called to the screen a display that showed a cylinder, definitely Rama, at the centre of a set of concentric circles. Next he keyed in another pair of commands, resulting in motion on the screen. The cylinder became smaller and smaller, ultimately collapsing to a point. The size of the concentric circles around the cylinder also diminished during the motion and new circles appeared at the edge of the screen. Eventually a group of dots, sixteen in all, appeared on the right side of the display.

'But how do you know they are missiles?' Nicole queried, indicating the small points of light.

'I don't,' Richard said. 'But I do know they are flying objects nearly on a straight line between Rama and the Earth. I suppose they might be peace envoys, but I doubt it seriously.'

'How long?' O'Toole asked.

'It's hard to tell exactly,' Richard answered after a moment's pause. 'I'd estimate eighteen to twenty·hours until the first one. They're spread out more than I would have expected. If we track them for an hour or so, we'll have a more precise estimate of the impact time.'

General O'Toole whistled and then reflected for several seconds before speaking. 'Before we try to tell this spacecraft that it's about to undergo a nuclear attack, will you answer one simple question for me?'

'If I can,' Richard replied,

'What makes you think that Rama can protect itself from these incoming missiles, even if we are able to communicate the warning?'

There was a protracted silence. 'Do you remember one time, Michael, almost a year ago,' Richard said, 'when we were flying together from London to Tokyo and we started talking about religion?'

'You mean when I was reading Eusebius?'

'I think so. You were telling me about the early history of Christianity ... Anyway, right in the middle of the discussion I suddenly asked you why you believed in God. Do you remember your answer?'

'Of course,' O'Toole replied. 'It's the same response I gave my oldest son when he declared himself an atheist at the age of eighteen.'

'Your answer on the plane perfectly captures my attitude in this current situation. We know that Rama is extremely advanced technologically. Certainly when it was designed there must have been some consideration of a possible hostile attack.... Who knows, maybe it even has a powerful propulsion system that we haven't yet discovered and will be able to manoeuvre out of the way. I bet—'

'Can I interrupt for a second?' Nicole said. 'I wasn't with you two on the flight to Tokyo. I'd like to know how Michael answered your question.'

The two men stared at each other for several seconds. Finally General O'Toole responded. 'Faith informed by thought and observation,' he said.

'The first part of your plan is not too difficult, and I agree with the approach, but I have no mental picture of how we will communicate the yield, or how to tie the nuclear chain reaction to the incoming missiles unambiguously.'

'Michael and I will work on those items while you develop the graphics for the first segment. He says he remembers his nuclear physics reasonably well.'

'Remember not to make too many assumptions,' Richard reminded Nicole. 'We must make certain that each part of the message is self-contained.'

General O'Toole was not with Richard and Nicole at the moment. After two hours of intense work he had walked away, out into the tunnel, about five minutes earlier. His two colleagues suddenly worried about his absence. 'He's probably going to the bathroom,' Richard said.

'He might be lost,' Nicole replied.

Richard moved over to the entrance to the White Room and hollered into the corridor. 'Hullo, Michael O'Toole,' he said. 'Are you all right?'

'Yes,' came the answer from the direction of the central stairway. 'Can you and Nicole come around here for a minute?'

'What's up?' Richard inquired a few moments later when he and Nicole joined the general at the foot of the stairway.

'Who built this lair?' O'Toole asked, his eyes focused on the ceiling high above him. 'And why do you think it was created in the first place?'

'We don't know,' Richard answered impatiently, 'and I don't think we'll resolve the issue in the next few minutes, or even hours. Meanwhile, we have work—'

'Indulge me for a little while,' O'Toole interrupted firmly. 'I need to have this discussion before I can proceed.' Richard and Nicole waited for him to continue. 'We are rushing pell-mell toward sending a warning to whatever intelligence is in control of this vehicle. Presumably, we are doing this so that Rama will be able to take measures to protect itself. How do we know that's the right action for us? How do we know that we're not being traitors to our species?'

General O'Toole waved his arms at the large cavern around him. 'There must be some reason, some grand plan for all this. Why were all those fake human objects left in the White Room? Why did the Ramans invite us to communicate with them? Who and what are the avians and the octospiders?' He shook his head, frustrated by all the unanswered questions. 'I was uncertain about destroying Rama; but I'm equally uncertain about sending the warning. What if Rama escapes the nuclear attack because of us and then destroys the Earth anyway?'

'That's extremely unlikely, Michael. The first Rama sailed through the solar system—'

'Just a minute, Nicole, if you don't mind,' Richard interrupted softly. 'Let me try to answer the general.'

He walked over and put his arm on General O'Toole's shoulder. 'Michael,' Richard said, 'what has impressed me the most about you since the first time we met has been your ability to understand the difference between the answers we can know, as a result of deduction or the scientific method, and those questions for which there is not even a valid logical approach. There is no way whatsoever that we can understand what Rama is all about at this juncture. We don't yet have enough data. It's like trying to solve a system of simultaneous linear equations when there are many more variables than constraints. Multiple hypersurfaces of correct solutions exist.'

O'Toole smiled and nodded his head. 'What we do know,' Richard continued, 'is that a fleet of missiles is now approaching Rama. They are probably armed with nuclear warheads. We have a choice, to warn or not to warn, and we must make it based on the information available to us at this moment.'

Richard pulled out his small computer and walked over beside O'Toole. 'You can represent this entire problem as a 3×2 matrix,' he said. 'Assume there are three possible descriptions of the Raman threat; never hostile, always hostile, and hostile only if attacked. Let these three situations represent the rows of the matrix. Now consider the decision facing us. We can either warn them, or choose not to. Note that it is only a *successful* warning that matters. So there are two columns to the matrix, Rama warned and Rama not warned.'

O'Toole and Nicole both looked over Richard's shoulder as he constructed the matrix and displayed it on his small monitor. 'If we now look at the outcomes of the six events represented by the individual elements in this matrix, and try to assign some probabilities wherever we can, we will have all the information we need to make our decision. Do you agree?'

General O'Toole nodded, impressed by how quickly and concisely Richard had structured their dilemma. 'The outcome of the second row is always the same,' Nicole now offered, 'independent of whether or not we warn them. If Rama is truly hostile, with their more advanced technology it makes no difference whether we warn them or not. Sooner or later, with this vehicle or one that comes in the future, they will either subjugate or destroy the human race.'

Richard paused a moment to ensure that O'Toole was following the conversation, 'Similarly,' he then said slowly, 'if Rama is *never* hostile, it cannot be wrong to warn them. In neither case, warned or unwarned, is the Earth in danger. And if we are successful in telling them about the nuclear missiles, then something extraordinary will have been saved.'

The general smiled. 'So the only possible problem, O'Toole's Anxiety, if you want to call it that, comes if Rama was not originally intending to be hostile, but will change its mind and attack the Earth once it learns that nuclear missiles have been launched against it.'

'Precisely,' said Richard. 'And I would argue that our warning itself would probably be a mitigating factor in that potentially hostile case. After all—'

'All right. All right,' O'Toole replied. 'I see where you're headed. Unless a very high probability is assigned to the case I'm worried about, the overall analysis suggests a better result from warning the Ramans.' He suddenly laughed. 'It's a good thing you don't work for COG military headquarters, Richard. You might have convinced me with logic to activate the code—'

'I doubt it,' Nicole said. 'Nobody could have made a solid case for that kind of paranoia.'

'Thank you.' The general smiled. 'I'm satisfied. You were very persuasive. Let's go back to work.'

Driven by the relentless approach of the missiles, the threesome worked tirelessly for hours. Nicole and Michael O'Toole designed the warning message in two discrete segments. The first segment, much of which was background to establish the basic communication technique, presented all the trajectory mechanics, including the Rama orbit as the vehicle entered the solar system, the two Newton craft leaving the Earth and joining just before rendezvous with the alien ship, the two Raman manoeuvres changing its trajectory, and finally the sixteen missiles blasting off from the Earth toward a Rama intercept. Richard, his long hours of work at the keyboard and black screen now paying off, transformed all these orbital events into graphic line drawings while the other two cosmonauts struggled with the complexity of the remainder of the message.

The second segment was exceedingly difficult to design. In it the humans wanted to explain that the incoming missiles carried nuclear warheads, that the explosive power of the bombs was generated by a chain reaction, and that the heat, shock, and radiation resulting from the explosion were all enormously powerful. Presenting the fundamental picture was not the challenge;

quantifying the destructive power in any terms that could be understood by an extraterrestrial intelligence was a formidable obstacle.

'It's impossible,' an exasperated Richard exclaimed when both O'Toole and Nicole insisted that the warning was not complete without some indication of the explosion temperature and the magnitude of the shock and radiation fields. 'Why don't we just indicate the quantity of fissionable material in the process? They must be great at physics. They can compute the yield and other parameters.'

Time was running out and all three of them were becoming exhausted. In the final hours, General O'Toole succumbed to fatigue and, at Nicole's insistence, took a substantial nap. His biometry output had indicated that his heart was in stress. Richard even slept for ninety minutes. But Nicole never allowed herself the luxury of rest. She was determined to figure out some way to depict in pictures the destructive power of the weapons.

When the men awakened, Nicole convinced them to append to the second segment an additional short section demonstrating what would happen to a city or forest on Earth if a one-megaton nuclear bomb exploded in the vicinity. For these pictures to make any sense, of course, Richard had to expand his earlier glossary, in which he had defined the chemical elements and their symbols with mathematical precision, to include some more measures of size. 'If they understand this,' he grumbled as he laboriously included scale tick marks beside his line drawings of buildings and trees, 'then they're smarter than even I gave them credit for.'

Finally the message was completed and stored. They reviewed the entire warning one last time and made a few corrections. 'Of the commands that I have never been able to understand,' Richard said, 'there are five that I have reason to suspect may be links to a different level processor. Of course, I am only guessing, but I believe it's an educated guess. I will transmit our message five times, using each of these particular commands a single time, and hope that our warning somehow reaches the central computer.'

While Richard entered all the proper commands into the keyboard, Nicole and General O'Toole went for a walk. They climbed up the stairway and wandered around the skyscrapers of New York. 'You believe that we were meant to board Rama and find the White Room, don't you?'

'Yes,' Nicole answered.

'But for what purpose?' asked the general. 'If the Ramans just wanted to make contact with us, why did they go to such elaborate lengths? And why are they risking our misinterpretation of their intent?'

'I don't know,' Nicole said. 'Maybe they're testing us in some way. To find out what we're like.'

'Goodness,' O'Toole replied, 'what a terrible thought. We may be catalogued as the creatures who launch nuclear attacks against visitors.'

'Exactly,' said Nicole.

Nicole showed O'Toole the barn with the pits, the lattice where she had rescued the avian, the stunning polyhedrons, and the entrances to the other two lairs. She was becoming very tired, but she knew that she would not sleep until everything was resolved.

'Should we head back?' O'Toole said after he and Nicole had walked down to the Cylindrical Sea and verified that the sailboat was still intact where they had left it.

'All right,' Nicole answered wearily. She checked her watch. It was exactly three hours and eighteen minutes until the first nuclear missile would arrive at Rama.

62 THE FINAL HOUR

Nobody had spoken for five minutes. Each of the three cosmonauts sat enmeshed in his own private world, aware that the first missile was now less than an hour away. Richard raced through all the sensor outputs hurriedly, searching vainly for any indication that Rama was taking some protective action. 'Shit,' he muttered, looking again at the close-up radar picture that showed the lead missile drawing closer and closer.

Richard walked over to where Nicole was sitting in the corner. 'We must have failed,' he said quietly. 'Nothing has changed.'

Nicole rubbed her eyes. 'I wish I weren't so tired,' she said. 'Then maybe we could do something interesting for our last fifty minutes.' She smiled grimly. 'Now I know what it must.be like to be on Death Row.'

General O'Toole approached from the other side of the room. He was holding two of the small black balls in his left hand. 'You know,' be said, 'often I have wondered what I would do if I ever had a specified, finite time before I died. Now here I am, and my mind keeps focusing on a single thing.'

'What's that?' Nicole asked.

'Have either of you ever been baptized?' he replied tentatively.

'Whaaat?' exclaimed Richard with a laugh of surprise.

'I thought not,' said General O'Toole. 'What about you, Nicole?'

'No, Michael,' she answered. 'My father's Catholicism was more tradition than ceremony.'

'Well,' persisted the general. 'I'm offering to baptize you both.'

'Here? Now?' inquired the astounded Wakefield. 'Are my ears deceiving me, Nikki, or did I just hear this gentleman suggest that we spend the last hour of our life being baptized?'

'It won't take—' O'Toole started to say.

'Why not, Richard?' Nicole interrupted. She stood up with a bright smile on her face. 'What else do we have to do? And it's a hell of a lot better than morbidly sitting around here waiting for the great fireball.'

Richard almost cackled. 'This is wonderful!' he exclaimed. 'I, Richard Wakefield, lifelong atheist, am considering being baptized on an extraterrestrial spaceship as the final action of my life. I love it!'

'Remember what Pascal wrote,' Nicole teased.

'Ah, yes,' Richard replied. 'A simple matrix from one of the world's great thinkers. "There may or may not be a God; I may or may not believe in Him. The only way I can lose is if there is a God and I do not believe in Him. Therefore I shall believe in Him to minimize my downside risk."' Richard chuckled. 'But I did not agree to believe in God, only to being baptized.'

'So you'll do it,' Nicole said.

'Why not?' he replied, parroting her earlier comment. 'Maybe that way I don't have to stay in Limbo with the virtuous pagans and unbaptized children.' He grinned at O'Toole. 'All right, General, we're all yours. Do your thing.'

'Now you listen closely to this, TB,' Richard said. 'You're probably the only robot ever to be in a human's pocket during a baptism.'

Nicole nudged Richard in the ribs. The patient General O'Toole waited a few moments and then began the ceremony.

At Richard's insistence, they had left the lair and walked out into the open plaza. Richard had wanted the sky of Rama overhead and neither of the other two had objected. Nicole had gone over to the Cylindrical Sea to fill the baptismal flask with water while General O'Toole completed his preparations. The American general was taking the baptism seriously but was apparently not offended by Richard's lighthearted banter.

Nicole and Richard knelt down in front of O'Toole. He sprinkled water on Richard's head. 'Richard Colin Wakefield, I baptize thee in the name of the Father, and the Son, and the Holy Spirit.'

When O'Toole had finished baptizing Nicole in the same simple way, Richard stood up and grinned. 'I don't feel any different,' he said. 'I'm just like I was before – scared shitless about dying in the next thirty minutes,'

General O'Toole had not moved. 'Richard,' he said softly, 'could I ask you to kneel again? I would like to say a short prayer.'

'What's this?' Richard asked. 'First a baptism, now a prayer?' Nicole looked up at him. Her eyes asked him to accede. 'All right,' he said, 'I guess I might as well go all the way.'

'Almighty God, please hear our prayer,' the general said in a strong voice. He also was kneeling now. His eyes were closed and his hands were clasped in front of him. 'We three have gathered here in what may be our final hour to pay homage to Thee. We beseech Thee to consider how we may serve Thee if we continue to live and, if it be Thy will, we ask Thee to spare us a painful and horrible death. If we are to die, we pray that we may be accepted into Thy heavenly kingdom. Amen.'

General O'Toole stopped for just a moment and then began to recite the Lord's prayer. After he had said, 'Our Father, Who art in heaven, hallowed be Thy name—' the lights in the great spaceship were abruptly extinguished. Another Raman day was over. Richard and Nicole waited respectfully until their friend had finished the prayer before pulling out their flashlights.

Nicole thanked the general and gave him a small hug. 'Well, here we are,' Richard jabbered nervously. 'Twenty-seven minutes and counting. We've had a baptism and a prayer. What should we do now? Who has an idea for the last, and I mean the very last, amusement? Should we sing? Dance? Play some kind of game?'

'I would prefer to remain up here by myself,' General O'Toole said solemnly, 'and face my death in atonement and prayer. And I imagine the two of you would like to be alone together.'

'All right, Nikki,' Richard said. 'Where shall we share our final kiss? On the shore of the Cylindrical Sea or back in the White Room?'

Nicole had been awake for thirty-two consecutive hours and was absolutely exhausted. She fell into Richard's arms and closed her eyes. At that moment scattered flashes of light intruded upon the new blackness of the Raman night.

'What's that?' General O'Toole asked anxiously.

'It must be the horns,' Richard answered excitedly. 'Come on, let's go.'

They ran to the south edge of the island and stared at the massive, enigmatic structures in the southern bowl. Filaments of light were darting between different pairs of the six spires surrounding the great monolith in the centre. The yellow arcs seemed to sizzle in the air, undulating gently back and forth in the middle while remaining connected to one of the little horns at each end. A distant cracking sound accompanied the spectacular sight.

'Amazing,' said O'Toole, overcome with awe. 'Absolutely amazing.'

'So Rama is going to manoeuvre,' Richard said. He could hardly contain himself. He hugged Nicole, then O'Toole, and finally kissed Nicole on the lips. 'Whoopee!' he yelled as he danced along the wall.

'But Richard,' Nicole shouted after him, 'isn't it too late? How can Rama move out of the way in such a short time?'

Richard ran back to his colleagues. 'You're right,' he said breathlessly. 'And those damn missiles probably have terminal guidance anyway.' He started running again, this time heading back toward the plaza. 'I'm going to watch on the radar.'

Nicole glanced over at General O'Toole. 'I'm coming,' he said. 'But I've already run enough for one day. I want to watch this show for another few seconds. You can go on without me if you want.'

Nicole waited. As the two of them walked briskly toward the plaza, General O'Toole thanked Nicole for allowing him to baptize her. 'Don't be silly,' she replied. 'I'm the one who should thank you.' She put her hand on his shoulder. *The baptism itself wasn't that important,* she continued in her private thoughts. *It was obvious that you were concerned about our souls. We agreed primarily to show our affection for you.* Nicole smiled to herself. *At least I think that was the reason....*

The ground underneath them began to shake vigorously and General O'Toole stopped, momentarily frightened. 'That's apparently what happened during the last manoeuvre,' Nicole said, steadying both of them by taking the general's hand, 'although I was personally lying unconscious at the bottom of a pit and missed the entire event.'

'Then the light show was just an announcement of the manoeuvre?'

'Probably. That's why Richard was so elated.'

They had barely opened the lair covering when Richard bolted up the stairs. 'They've done it!' he exclaimed. 'They've done it!'

O'Toole and Nicole stared at him as he caught his breath. 'They've deployed some kind of mesh or net – I don't know exactly what it is – about six, maybe eight hundred metres thick – all around the spacecraft.' He turned around. 'Come on,' he said, dashing down the steps three at a time.

Despite her fatigue, Nicole responded to his excitement with a final burst of adrenaline. She bounded down the stairs after Richard and ran to the White Room. He was standing in front of the black screen, flipping back and forth from the exterior image that showed the new material around the vehicle to the radar view that depicted the incoming missiles.

'They must have understood our warning,' he said to Nicole. Richard jubilantly picked her up off the ground, gave her a kiss, and held her in the air. 'It worked, darling,' he shouted. 'Thank you, oh thank you.'

Nicole too was excited. But she was not yet convinced that Rama's action would prevent the destruction of the vehicle. After General O'Toole came in and Richard explained to him what they were seeing on the screen, there were only nine minutes left. Nicole had butterflies the size of basketballs in her stomach. The ground continued to shake as Rama extended its manoeuvre.

The nuclear missiles obviously had terminal guidance, for despite the fact that Rama was definitely changing its trajectory, the missiles continued to approach along a straight line. The close-up radar picture showed that the sixteen attackers were quite spread out. Their estimated impact times ranged over a period slightly less than an hour.

Richard's frenetic activity increased. He paced wildly around the room. At one point he pulled TB out of his pocket, put him down on the floor, and began talking rapidly to the little robot as if TB were his closest friend. What Richard said was barely coherent. One moment Richard was telling TB to prepare for the coming explosion; a second later he was explaining to him how Rama was going to miraculously evade the oncoming missiles.

General O'Toole was trying to remain calm, but it was impossible with Richard flying around the room like a Tasmanian devil. He started to say something to Richard, but decided instead to step outside into the tunnel for some quiet.

During one of the rare moments that Richard was not moving, Nicole walked over to him and grabbed his hands. 'Darling,' she said, 'relax. There's nothing we can do.'

Richard looked down for a second at his friend and lover and then threw his arms around her. He kissed her wildly and then sat down on the shaking floor, pulling her down beside him. 'I'm scared, Nicole,' he said, his body trembling. 'I'm really scared. I hate not being able to do anything.'

'I'm frightened too,' she replied gently, taking his hands again. 'And so is Michael.'

'But neither of you *act* scared,' Richard said. 'I feel like an idiot, bouncing around here like Tigger in *Winnie the Pooh.*'

'Every person confronts death in a different way,' Nicole said. 'All of us feel fear. We just deal with it in our own individual fashion.'

Richard was calming down. He glanced over at the big monitor and then at his watch. 'Three more minutes until the first impact,' he said.

Nicole put her hands on his cheeks and kissed him softly on the lips. 'I love you, Richard Wakefield,' she said.

'And I love you,' he answered.

Richard and Nicole were sitting quietly on the floor, holding hands and watching the black screen, when the first missile reached the edge of the dense mesh that surrounded Rama. General O'Toole was standing behind them in the doorway – he had returned to the room about thirty seconds earlier. At the moment the missile made contact, the impacted part of the mesh yielded, cushioning the blow but allowing the missile to penetrate deeper into the netting. Simultaneously, other pieces of the mesh wrapped themselves rapidly about the missile, spinning a thick cocoon with amazing speed. It was all over in a fraction of a second. The missile was about two hundred metres from the outer shell of Rama, already enclosed in a thick wrapping, when its nuclear warhead detonated. The mesh on the screen flew around a little, but there was only a barely perceptible nudge inside the White Room.

'Wow!' said Richard first. 'Did you see that?'

He jumped up and approached the screen. 'It happened so fast,' Nicole commented, coming up beside him.

General O'Toole mumbled a very short prayer of thanks and joined his colleagues in front of the screen. 'How do you think it did that?' he asked Richard.

'I have no idea,' Richard replied. 'But somehow that cocoon contained the explosion. It must be a fantastic material.' He flipped back to the radar image. 'Let's watch this next one more closely. It should be here in a few—'

There was a brilliant flash of light and the screen went blank. Less than a second later a sharp lateral force hit them hard, knocking them to the floor. The lights went out in the White Room and the ground stopped shaking. 'Is everyone all right?' Richard asked, groping for Nicole's hand in the dark.

'I think so,' O'Toole replied. 'I hit the wall, but only with my back and elbow.'

'I'm fine, darling,' Nicole answered. 'What happened?'

'Obviously that one exploded early, before it reached the net. We were hit by the shock wave.'

'I don't understand,' O'Toole said. 'The bomb exploded in a vacuum. How could there be a shock wave?'

'It wasn't technically just a shock wave,' Richard replied, standing up as the lights came back on and the ground began to shake again. 'Hey, how about that!' he interrupted himself. 'The famous Raman redundancy scores again. You okay?' he said to Nicole, who looked unsteady as she was standing up.

'I bruised my knee,' she answered, 'but it's not serious.'

'The bomb destroyed the rest of its own missile,' Richard said, now answering O'Toole's question as he searched through the sensor list for the redundant imaging and radar outputs, 'vaporizing most of the casing and reducing the rest to fragments. The gas and debris moved outward at enormous speeds, creating the wave that hit us. The mesh attenuated the size of the shock.'

Nicole moved over against the wall and sat down. 'I want to be ready for the next one,' she said.

'I wonder how many bumps like that Rama can survive,' Richard said.

General O'Toole came over and sat down beside Nicole. 'Two down and fourteen to go,' he said. They all smiled. At least they weren't dead yet.

Richard located the redundant sensors a few minutes later. 'Uh-oh,' he said as he surveyed the remaining blips on the screen. 'Unless I'm mistaken, the last bomb that exploded was many kilometres away. We were lucky. We'd better hope one doesn't detonate just outside the mesh.'

The trio watched while two more missiles were trapped and wrapped in the material surrounding Rama. Richard stood up. 'We have a brief respite now'' he said. 'It will be three minutes or so before our next impact – then we'll have four more missiles in a hurry.'

Nicole rose to her feet also. She saw that General O'Toole was holding his back. 'Are you sure you're all right, Michael?' she asked. He nodded, still watching the screen. Richard came over beside Nicole and took her hand. A minute later they sat down together against the wall to wait for the next impacts.

They didn't wait long. A second lateral force, much stronger than the first one, hit them within twenty seconds. Again the lights went out and the floor stopped shaking. Nicole could hear O'Toole's labored breathing in the dark. 'Michael,' she said, 'are you hurt?'

When there was no immediate reply, Nicole started crawling in his direction. That was a mistake. She was not braced against anything when the powerful third blast hit. Nicole was thrown savagely into the wall, hitting it with the side of her head.

General O'Toole stayed beside Nicole while Richard went up into New York to survey the city. The men spoke quietly when Richard returned. He reported only minor damage. Thirty minutes after the final missile had been trapped, the lights came back on and the ground started shaking again. 'You see,' Richard said with a grin, 'I told you we'd be all right. They always do everything important in threes.'

Nicole remained unconscious for almost another hour. During the last few minutes she was vaguely aware of both the vibration of the floor and the conversation on the opposite side of the room. Nicole opened her eyes very slowly,

'The net effect,' she heard Richard say, 'is to increase our velocity along the hyperbola. So we will cross the Earth's orbit much earlier than previously, long before the planet itself has arrived.'

'How close will we come to the Earth?'

'Not too close. It depends on when this manoeuvre ends. If it stopped now we would miss by a million kilometres or so, more than twice the distance to the Moon.'

Nicole sat up and smiled. 'Good morning,' she said cheerfully.

The two men came over beside her. 'Are you all right, darling?' Richard asked.

'I think so,' Nicole said, feeling the bump on the side of her head. 'I may have occasional headaches for a while.' She looked at the two men. 'What about you, Michael? I seem to remember being worried about you right before the big blast.'

'The second one knocked the wind out of me,' O'Toole replied. 'Luckily I was better prepared for the third bomb. And my back seems fine now.'

Richard started to explain what he had learned from the output of Rama's celestial sensors. 'I heard the last part of it,' Nicole said. 'I gather we're now going to miss the Earth altogether.' Richard helped her to stand up. 'But where are we headed?'

Richard shrugged his shoulders. 'No planetary or asteroidal targets are anywhere close to our present trajectory. Our hyperbolic energy is increasing. If nothing changes we will escape from the solar system altogether.'

'And become interstellar travellers,' Nicole said quietly.

'If we live that long,' added the general.

'For my part,' Richard said with a playful smile, 'I am not going to worry about what happens next. At least not yet. I plan to celebrate our escape from the nuclear phalanx. I vote we go upstairs and introduce Michael to some new friends. Should it be the avians or the octospiders?'

Nicole shook her head and smiled. 'You're hopeless, Wakefield. Let me not in any way inhibit ...'

> Let me not to the marriage of true minds
> Admit impediments ...

TB suddenly interrupted. All three of the cosmonauts were startled. They stared down at the tiny robot and then erupted with laughter.

... love is not love
Which alters when it alteration finds
Or bends with the remover to remove.
Oh no, it is an ever-fixed mark ...

Richard picked up TB and switched him off. Nicole and Michael were still laughing. Richard embraced each of them individually. 'I can't think of three better traveling companions,' he said, holding the little robot over his head, 'wherever it is we're going.'

AFTERWORD

BY ARTHUR C. CLARKE

Writing is a lonely profession, and after a few decades even the most devout egotist may occasionally yearn for company. But collaboration in any work of art is a risky business, and the more people involved, the smaller the chances of success. Can you imagine *Moby Dick* by Herman Melville & Nat Hawthorne? Or *War and Peace* by Leo Tolstoy and Freddie Dostoyevsky. With Additional Dialogue by Van Turgenev?

Certainly I never imagined, until a few years ago, that I would ever collaborate with another writer on a work of fiction. *Non-fiction* was different: I've been involved in no less than 14 multi-author projects (two with the Editors of *Life*, and you don't get more multiplex than that). But fiction – no way! I was quite sure I would never let any outsider tamper with my unique brand of creativity ...

Well, a funny thing happened on the way to the word-processor. Early in 1986 my agent Scott Meredith called me in his most persuasive 'Don't-say-no-until-I've-finished' mode. There was, it seemed, this young genius of a movie producer who was determined to film something – *anything* – of mine. Though I'd never heard of Peter Guber, as it happened I had seen two of his movies (*Midnight Express, The Deep*), and been quite impressed by them. I was even more impressed when Scott told me that Peter's latest, *The Color Purple*, had been nominated for half-a-dozen Oscars.

However, I groaned inwardly when Scott went on to say that Peter had a friend with a brilliant idea he'd like me to develop into a screenplay. I groaned, because there are no new ideas in sf, and if it really was brilliant I'd have thought of it already. And I *hate* screenplays; they are incredibly boring, almost unreadable, and, as far as I'm concerned, unwritable. Like a musical score, they're a necessary intermediate stage in a production. Writing them requires considerable specialised skills, but they have no literary or artistic value of their own. (A musical score is at least pretty to look at.)

Then Scott explained who the friend was, and I did a double-take. The project suddenly looked very exciting indeed, for reasons that had nothing to do with Peter Guber, but a lot to do with Stanley Kubrick.

Flashback. Twenty years earlier, in *2001: A Space Odyssey*, Stanley and I had visited the moons of Jupiter – never dreaming that these completely unknown worlds would, in fact, be reconnoitred by robots long before the date of our movie. In March and July 1979, the two Voyager probes revealed that Io, Europa, Ganymede and Callisto were stranger places than we'd dared to imagine. The stunning views of Jupiter's giant satellites made it possible – no, imperative – for me to write *2010: Odyssey Two*. This time around, the Jovian sequences could be based on reality, not imagination; and when Peter Hyams filmed the book in 1984, he was able to use actual images from the Voyager spacecraft as backgrounds for much of the action.

Spectacular though the results of 1979 missions were, it was confidently hoped that they would be quite surpassed within a decade. The Voyager spacecraft spent only a few hours in the vicinity of Jupiter, hurtling past the giant planet and its moons on the way to Saturn. But in May 1986, NASA planned to launch Galileo, an even more ambitious space probe. This would make not a brief fly-by, but a *rendezvous*; Galileo would spend two years, starting in December 1988, on a detailed survey of Jupiter and its major moons. By 1990, if all went well, there would be such a flood of new information about these exotic worlds that a third Space Odyssey would be inevitable. *That* was what I was planning to write; I'd hitched my wagon to Galileo, and could hardly care less about some amateur science-fiction author's ideas. How to turn him down politely? I was still pondering this when Scott continued:

'Peter Guber wants to fly out to Sri Lanka, just for thirty-six hours, to introduce this guy to you. His name is Gentry Lee, and let me explain who he is. He works at the Jet Propulsion Laboratory, and he's the Chief Engineer on Project Galileo. Have you heard of that?'

'Yes,' I said faintly.

'And before that, he was Director of Mission Planning for the Viking landers, that sent back those wonderful pictures from Mars. Because he felt the public didn't appreciate what was going on in space, he formed a company with your friend Carl Sagan to make *Cosmos* – he was manager of the whole TV series –'

'Enough!' I cried. 'This man I have to meet. Tell Mr Gabor to bring him here right away.'

'The name,' said Scott, 'is *Guber*. Peter Guber.'

Well, it was agreed that the two of them would fly out to Sri Lanka, and if I liked Gentry's idea (and, equally important, Gentry) I'd develop an outline – perhaps a dozen pages, which would give characters, locations, plot and all the basic elements from which any competent script-writer could generate a screenplay.

They arrived in Colombo on 12 February 1986 – just two weeks after the *Challenger* disaster. 1986 was going to be the Big Year for Space, but now the entire NASA programme was in total disarray. In particular, Galileo would be delayed for years. It would be 1995 before there could be any further news from the moons of Jupiter. I could forget about *Odyssey Three* – just as Gentry could forget about doing anything with Galileo except getting it back from the cape and putting it in mothballs.

Happily, the Guber-Lee-Clarke Summit went well, and for the next few weeks. I filled floppy discs with concepts, characters, backgrounds, plots – anything which seemed even remotely useful to the story we'd decided to call *Cradle*. Someone once said that writing a book of fiction consists of the elimination of alternatives. Very true: at one time I calculated that, if I used all the elements I'd created in every possible combination, there'd be enough material for half a billion different *Cradles*.

I sent the one I finally selected, in the form of a 4,000 word outline, to Gentry. He liked it, and flew out to Sri Lanka again so that we could fill in the details. During a three-day marathon up in the mountains above the ancient capital, Kandy, despite the distraction of the most gorgeous panorama I know, we completed an 8,000 word demi-hemi-semi-final version which eventually became the basis of the novel. From then onwards, we were able to collaborate by making frequent phone calls, and flying yards of printout across the Pacific.

The writing took the best part of a year, though of course we were both involved in other projects as well. When I discovered that Gentry had a considerably better background in English *and French* literature than I did (by now I was immune to such surprises) I heroically resisted all attempts to impose my own style on him. This upset some longtime ACC readers, who when *Cradle* appeared under our joint names were put out by passages where I might have done a little more sanitising. The earthier bits of dialogue, I explained, were the result of Gentry's years with the hairy-knuckled, hard-drinking engineers and mathematicians of JPL's Astrodynamics Division, where the Pasadena cops often have to be called in to settle barefisted fights over Bessel functions and non-linear partial differential equations.

Yet so far, to the best of my knowledge, no school board has demanded that *Cradle* be removed from its shelves. I mention this because I have just discovered, to my astonished indignation, that this actually happened to *Imperial Earth* a decade ago. What's more, the board concerned then went on to ban *any* collection containing *anything* I'd ever written.

I wish I'd known about this at the time. I would have enjoyed telling these apprentice Ayatollahs that the 'Books for the Blind' version of the novel that offended them was recorded by a lady very unlikely to promote porn. She happens to be married to England's First Law Lord.

Although *Cradle* was originally conceived as a movie project, and a treatment was prepared for Warner Films, the chances of it ever reaching the screen now seem remote. By bad luck, a whole string of underwater extraterrestrial movies appeared around the time of the book's publication, and most of them sank without trace.

But Peter Guber, I'm happy to say, has gone on from strength to strength. His latest productions, *The Witches of Eastwick, Gorillas in the Mist* and *Rain*

Man have been very well received; even this short list shows his interest in unusual and worthwhile projects. Maybe he'll make *Cradle* when the cycle comes round again, as it inevitably will. 'There is a tide in the affairs of men' – and of movies.

Though I'd greatly enjoyed working with Gentry, when we'd finished rocking *Cradle* I had no plans for further collaboration – because Halley's Comet was now dominating my life, as it had failed to dominate terrestrial skies. I realised that its next appearance, in 2061, would provide a splendid opportunity for a third Space Odyssey. (If the much-delayed Galileo does perform as hoped in 1995, and beams back megabytes of new information from the Jovian system, there may be a Final Odyssey. But I make no promises.)

By the summer of 1987, *2061: Odyssey Three* was doing very nicely in the bookshops, thank you, and I was once again beginning to feel those nagging guilt pains that assail an author when he's not Working On A Project. Suddenly, I realised that one was staring me right in the face.

Fifteen years earlier, the very last sentence of *Rendezvous With Rama* had read: 'The Ramans did everything in threes.' Now, those words were a last-minute afterthought when I was doing the final revision. I had not – cross my heart – any idea of a sequel in mind; it just seemed the correct, open-ended way of finishing the book. (In real life, of course, no story every ends.)

Many readers – and reviewers – jumped to the conclusion that I had planned a trilogy from the beginning. Well, I hadn't – but now I realised it was a splendid idea. And Gentry was just the man for the job: he had all the background in celestial mechanics and space hardware to deal with the next appearance of the Ramans.

I quickly outlined a spectrum of possibilities, very much as I had done with *Cradle*, and in a remarkably short time *Rama II* was born. *The Garden of Rama* and *Rama Revealed* will follow during the 1989–91 period.

So once again Gentry Lee is communicating across the Pacific for brain-storming sessions in the Sri Lankan hills, and the postman is complaining about the bulky printouts he has to balance on his bicycle. This time round, however, technology has speeded up our intercontinental operations. The fax machine now allows us to exchange ideas almost in real time; it's far more convenient than the Electronic Mail Link Peter Hyams and I used when scripting *2010* (see *The Odyssey File*).

There is much to be said for this kind of long-distance collaboration; if they are too close together, co-authors may waste a lot of time on trivia. Even a solitary writer can think of endless excuses for not working; with two, the possibilities are at least squared.

However, there is no way of demonstrating that a writer is neglecting his job; even if his snores are deafening, his sub-conscious may be hard at work. And Gentry and I knew that our wildest excursions into literature, science, art or history might yield useful story elements.

For example, during the writing of *Rama II* it became obvious that Gentry was in love with Eleanor of Aquitaine (don't worry, Stacey – she's been dead for 785 years) and I had tactfully to dissuade him from devoting pages to her amazing career. (If you wonder how E of A could have the remotest connexion with interstellar adventures, you have pleasures in store.)

I certainly learned a lot of French and English history from Gentry that they never taught me at school. The occasion when Queen Eleanor berated her son, the intrepid warrior-king Richard the Lionheart *in front of his troops* for failing to produce an heir to the throne must have been one of the more piquant moments in British military history. Alas, there was no way we could work in this gallant but gay Corleone, who was often a Godfather, never a Father ... very unlike Gentry, whose fifth son arrived towards the end of *Rama II*.

But you will meet Gentry's most cherished creation, the yet-to-be-born Saint Michael of Siena. One day, I am sure, you'll encounter him again, in books that Gentry will publish under his own name, with the minimum of help or hindrance from me.

As I write these words, we're just coming up to the midway point of our four-volume partnership. And though we think we know what's going to happen next – I'm sure the Ramans have quite a few surprises in store for us ...

THE GARDEN
OF RAMA

NICOLE'S JOURNAL

I

Two nights ago, at 10:44 Greenwich time on the Earth, Simone Tiasso Wakefield greeted the universe. It was an incredible experience. I thought I had felt powerful emotions before, but nothing in my life – not the death of my mother, not the Olympic gold medal in Los Angeles, not my thirty-six hours with Prince Henry, and not even the birth of Genevieve under the watchful eyes of my father at the hospital in Tours – was as intense as my joy and relief when I finally heard Simone's first cry.

Michael had predicted that the baby would arrive on Christmas Day. In his usual lovable way, he told us that he believed God was going to 'give us a sign' by having our spacechild born on Jesus' assumed birthday. Richard scoffed, as my husband always does when Michael's religious fervor gets carried away. But after I felt the first strong contractions on Christmas Eve, even Richard almost became a believer.

I slept fitfully the night before Christmas. Just before I awakened, I had a deep, vivid dream. I was walking beside our pond at Beauvois, playing with my pet duck Dunois and his wild mallard companions, when I heard a voice calling me. I could not identify the voice, but I definitely knew it was a woman speaking. She told me that the birth was going to be extremely difficult and that I would need every bit of my strength to bring my second child into the light.

On Christmas itself, after we exchanged the simple presents that each of us had clandestinely ordered from the Ramans, I began to train Michael and Richard for a range of possible emergencies. I think Simone would indeed have been born on Christmas Day if my conscious mind had not been so aware that neither of the two men was even remotely prepared to help me in case of a major problem. My will alone probably delayed the baby's birth those final two days.

One of the contingency procedures we discussed on Christmas was a breech baby. A couple of months ago, when my unborn baby girl still had some freedom of movement inside my womb, I was fairly certain that she was upside down. But I thought she had turned around during the last week before she dropped into the birth position. I was only partially correct. She did manage to come headfirst down the birth canal; however, her face was upward, toward my stomach, and after the first serious set of contractions, the top of her little head became awkwardly wedged against my pelvis.

In a hospital on Earth the physician would probably have performed a caesarean section. Certainly a doctor would have been on guard for fetal stress and at work early with all the robot instruments, striving to turn Simone's head around before she wedged into such an uncomfortable position.

Toward the end the pain was excruciating. In between the strong contractions driving her against my unyielding bones, I tried to yell out orders to Michael and Richard. Richard was almost useless. He could not deal with my pain (or 'the mess,' as he later called it), much less either assist with the episiotomy or use the makeshift forceps we had obtained from the Ramans. Michael, bless his heart, sweat pouring off his forehead despite the cool temperature in the room, struggled gallantly to follow my sometimes incoherent instructions. He used the scalpel from my kit to open me up wider and then, after only a moment's hesitation due to all the blood, he found Simone's head with the forceps. Somehow he managed, on his third attempt, both to force her backward in the birth canal and to turn her over so she could be born.

Both men screamed when she crowned. I kept concentrating on my breathing pattern, worried that I might not maintain consciousness. Despite the intense pain, I too bellowed when my next powerful contraction shot Simone forward into Michael's hands. As the father it was Richard's job to cut the umbilical cord. When Richard had finished, Michael lifted Simone up for me to see. 'It's a girl,' he said with tears in his eyes. He laid her softly on my stomach and I rose up slightly to look at her. My first impression was that she looked exactly like my mother.

I forced myself to stay alert until the placenta was removed and I had finished stitching, with Michael's assistance, the cuts he had made with the scalpel. Then I collapsed. I don't remember many details from the next twenty-four hours. I was so tired from the labour and delivery (my contractions were down to five minutes apart *eleven* hours before Simone was actually born) that I slept at every opportunity. My new daughter nursed readily, without any urging, and Michael insists that she even nursed once or twice while I was only partially awake. My milk now surges into my breasts immediately after Simone begins to suckle. She seems quite satisfied when she's finished. I'm delighted that my milk is adequate for her – I was worried that I might have the same problem that I had with Genevieve.

One of the two men is beside me every time I wake up. Richard's smiles always seem a little forced, but they are appreciated nevertheless. Michael is quick to place Simone in my arms or at my breasts when I am awake. He holds her comfortably, even when she is crying, and keeps mumbling, 'She's beautiful.'

At the moment Simone is sleeping beside me wrapped in the quasi-blanket manufactured by the Ramans (it is extremely difficult to define fabrics, particularly quality words like 'soft', in any of the quantitative terms that our hosts can understand). She does indeed look like my mother. Her skin is quite dark, maybe even darker than mine, and the thatch of hair on her head is jet black. Her eyes are a rich brown. With her head still coned and misshapen from the difficult birth, it is not easy to call Simone beautiful. But of course Michael is right. She is gorgeous. My eyes can readily see the beauty beyond the fragile, reddish creature breathing with such frantic rapidity. Welcome to the world, Simone Wakefield.

2

I have been depressed now for two days. And tired, oh, so tired. Even though I am well aware that I have a typical case of post-partum syndrome, I have been unable to relieve my feelings of depression.

This morning was the worst. I woke before Richard and lay quietly on my portion of the mat. I looked over at Simone, who was sleeping peacefully in the Raman cradle against the wall. Despite my feelings of love for her, I could not manage any positive thoughts about her future. The glow of ecstasy that had surrounded her birth and lasted for seventy-two hours had completely vanished. An endless stream of hopeless observations and unanswerable questions kept running through my mind. What kind of life will you have, my little Simone? How can we, your parents, possibly provide for your happiness?

My darling daughter, you live with your parents and their good friend Michael O'Toole in an underground lair on board a gargantuan spacecraft of extraterrestrial origin. The three adults in your life are all cosmonauts from the planet Earth, part of the crew of the Newton expedition sent to investigate a cylindrical worldlet called Rama almost a year ago. Your mother, father, and General O'Toole were the only human beings still on board this alien craft when Rama abruptly changed its trajectory to avoid being annihilated by a nuclear phalanx launched from a paranoid Earth.

Above our lair is an island city of mysterious skyscrapers, which we call New York. It is surrounded by a frozen sea that completely circles this huge spacecraft and cuts it in half. At this moment, according to your father's calculations, we are just inside the orbit of Jupiter (although the great gasball itself is way over on the other side of the Sun), following a hyperbolic trajectory that will eventually leave the solar system altogether. We do not know where we are going. We do not know who built this spaceship or why they built it. We know there are other occupants on board, but we have no idea where *they* came from and, in addition, have reason to suspect that at least some of them may be hostile.

Over and over my thoughts the last two days have continued in this same pattern. Each time I come to the same depressing conclusion: It is inexcusable that we, as supposedly mature adults, would bring such a helpless and innocent being into an environment about which we understand so little and over which we have absolutely no control.

Early this morning, as soon as I realised that today was my thirty-seventh birthday, I began to cry. At first the tears were soft and soundless, but as the memories of all my past birthdays flooded into my mind, deep sobs replaced the soft tears. I was feeling an acute, aching sorrow, not just for Simone, but also for myself. And as I remembered the magnificent blue planet of our origin and could not imagine it in Simone's future, I kept asking myself the same question. Why have I given birth to a child in the middle of this mess?

There's that word again. It's one of Richard's favourites. In his vocabulary, mess has virtually unlimited applications. Anything that is chaotic and/or out of control, whether it is a technical problem or a domestic crisis (like a wife sobbing in the grips of a fierce postpartum depression), is referred to as a mess.

The men were not much help earlier this morning. Their futile attempts to make me feel better only added to my gloom. A question: Why is it that almost every man, when confronted by an unhappy woman, immediately assumes that her unhappiness is somehow related to him? Actually I'm not being fair. Michael has had three children in his life and knows something about the feelings I'm experiencing. Mostly he just asked me what he could do to help. But Richard was absolutely devastated by my tears. He was frightened when he woke up and could hear my weeping. At first he thought that I was having some terrible physical pain. He was only minimally reassured when I explained to him that I was simply depressed.

After first establishing that he was not to blame for my mood, Richard listened silently while I expressed my concerns about Simone's future. I admit that I was slightly overwrought, but he didn't seem to grasp *anything* I was saying. He kept repeating the same phrase – that Simone's future was no more uncertain than our own – believing that since there was no logical reason for me to be so upset, my depression should immediately vanish. Eventually, after over an hour of miscommunication, Richard correctly concluded that he was not helping and decided to leave me alone.

(Six hours later.) I'm feeling better now. There are still three more hours before my birthday is over. We had a small party tonight. I just finished nursing Simone and she is again lying beside me. Michael left us about fifteen minutes ago to go to his room down the hall. Richard fell asleep within five minutes after his head was on the pillow. He had spent all day working on my request for some improved diapers.

Richard enjoys spending his time supervising and cataloging our interactions with the Ramans, or whoever it is that operates the computers we activate by using the keyboard in our room. We have never seen anyone or anything in the dark tunnel immediately behind the black screen. So we don't know for certain if there really are creatures back there responding to our requests and ordering their factories to manufacture our odd items, but it is convenient to refer to our hosts and benefactors as the Ramans.

Our communication process with them is both complicated and straightforward. It is complicated because we talk to them using pictures on the black screen and precise quantitative formulas in the language of mathematics, physics, and chemistry. It is straightforward because the actual sentences we input using the keyboard are amazingly simple in syntax. Our most often used sentence is 'We would like' or 'We want' (of course, we could not possibly know the exact translation of our requests and are just assuming that we are being polite – it could be the instructions we activate are in the form of rude commands beginning with 'Give me'), followed by a detailed description of what we would like provided to us.

The hardest part is the chemistry. Simple everyday objects like soap, paper, and glass are very complex chemically and extremely difficult to specify exactly in terms of their number and kind of chemical compounds. Sometimes, as Richard discovered early in his work with the keyboard and black screen, we must also outline a manufacturing process, including thermal regimes, or what we receive does not bear any resemblance to what we ordered. The request process involves a lot of trial and error. In the beginning it was a very inefficient and frustrating interaction. All three of us kept wishing that we remembered more of our college chemistry. In fact, our inability to make satisfactory progress in equipping ourselves with everyday essentials was one of the catalysts for the Great Excursion, as Richard likes to call it, that occurred four months ago.

By then the ambient temperature, topside in New York as well as in the rest of Rama, was already five degrees below freezing and Richard had confirmed that the Cylindrical Sea was again solid ice. I was growing quite concerned that we were not going to be properly prepared for the baby's birth. It was taking us too long to accomplish everything. Procuring and installing a working toilet, for example, had turned out to be a month-long endeavor, and the result was still only marginally adequate. Most of the time our primary problem was that we kept providing incomplete specifications to our hosts. However, sometimes the difficulty was the Ramans themselves. Several times they informed us, using our mutual language of mathematical and chemical symbols, that they could not complete the manufacture of a specific item within our allocated time period.

Anyway, Richard announced one morning that he was going to leave our lair and try to reach the still-docked military ship from our Newton expedition. His expressed purpose was to retrieve the key components of the scientific data base stored on the ship's computers (this would help us immensely in formulating our requests to the Ramans), but he also acknowledged that he was terribly hungry for some decent food. We had been managing to stay healthy and alive with the chemical concoctions provided by the Ramans. However, most of the food had been either tasteless or terrible.

In all fairness, our hosts had been responding correctly to our requests. Although we knew generally how to describe the essential chemical ingredients our bodies needed, none of us had ever studied in detail the complex biochemical process that takes place when we taste something. In those early days eating was a necessity, never a pleasure. Often the goo was difficult, if not impossible, to swallow. More than once nausea followed a meal.

The three of us spent most of a day debating the pros and cons of the Great Excursion. I was in the 'heartburn' stage of my pregnancy and was feeling quite uncomfortable. Even though I did not relish the idea of remaining alone in our lair while the two men trekked across the ice, located the rover, drove across the Central Plain, and then rode or climbed the many kilometres to the Alpha relay station, I recognised that there were many ways in which they could help each other. I also agreed with them that a solo trip would be foolhardy.

Richard was quite certain the rover would still be operational but was less optimistic about the chairlift. We discussed at length the damage that might have been done to the Newton military ship, exposed as it was on the outside of Rama to the nuclear blasts that had occurred beyond the protective mesh shield. Richard conjectured that since there was no visible structural damage (using our access to the output of the Raman sensors, we had looked at images of the Newton military ship on the black screen several times during the intervening months), it was possible that Rama itself might have inadvertently protected the ship from all of the nuclear explosions and, as a result, there might not be any radiation damage inside either.

I was more sanguine about the prospects. I had worked with the environmental engineers on the designs for the spacecraft shielding and was aware of the radiation susceptibility of each of the subsystems of the Newton. Although I did think there was a high probability the scientific data base would be intact (both its processor and all its memories were made from radiation-hardened parts), I was virtually certain the food supply would be contaminated. We had always known that our packaged food was in a relatively unprotected location. Prior to launch, in fact, there had even been some concern that an unexpected solar flare might produce enough radiation to make the food unsafe to eat.

I was not afraid of staying alone for the few days or week that it might take for the men to make the round trip to the military ship. I was more worried about the possibility that one or both of them might not return. It wasn't just a question of the octospiders, or any other aliens that might be cohabiting this immense spaceship with us. There were environmental uncertainties to be considered as well. What if Rama suddenly started to manoeuvre? What if some other equally untoward event occurred and they couldn't make it back to New York?

Richard and Michael assured me that they would take no chances, that they would not do anything except go to the military ship and return. They departed just after dawn on a twenty-eight-hour Raman day. It was the first time I had been alone since my long, solitary sojourn in New York that started when I fell into the pit. Of course, I wasn't truly alone. I could feel Simone kicking inside me. It's an amazing feeling, carrying a baby. There's something indescribably wonderful about knowing there's another living soul inside you. Especially since the child is formed in significant part from your own genes. It's a shame that men are not able to experience being pregnant. If they could, maybe they would understand why we women are so concerned about the future.

By the third Earth day after the men left, I had developed a bad case of cabin fever. I decided to climb out of our lair and take a hike around New York. It was dark in Rama, but I was so restless I started to walk anyway. The air was quite cold. I zipped my heavy flight jacket around my bulging stomach. I had only been walking for a few minutes when I heard a sound in the distance. A chill ran down my spine and I stopped immediately. The adrenaline apparently surged into Simone as well, for she kicked vigorously while I listened for the noise. In about a minute I heard it again, the sound of brushes dragging across a metallic surface and accompanied by a high-frequency whine. The sound was unmistakable; an octospider was definitely wandering around in New York. I quickly went back to the lair and waited for dawn to come to Rama.

When it was light I returned to New York and wandered around. While I was in the vicinity of that curious barn where I fell into the pit, I began having my doubts about our conclusion that the octos only come out at night. Richard has insisted from the beginning that they are nocturnal creatures. During the first two months after we passed the Earth, before we built our protective grill that prevents unwelcome visitors from descending into our lair, Richard deployed a series of crude receivers (he had not yet perfected his ability to specify electronic parts to the Ramans) around the octospider lair covering and confirmed, at least to his satisfaction, that they only come topside at night. Eventually the octos discovered all his monitors and destroyed them, but not before Richard had what he believed to be conclusive data supporting his hypothesis.

Nevertheless, Richard's conclusion was no comfort to me when I suddenly heard a loud and totally unfamiliar sound coming from the direction of our lair. At the time I was standing inside the barn, staring into the pit where I had almost died nine months ago. My pulse immediately jumped up and my skin tingled. What disturbed me the most was that the noise was between me and my Raman home. I crept up on the intermittent sound cautiously, peering around buildings each time before committing myself. At length I discovered the source of the noise. Richard was cutting pieces of a lattice using a miniature chain saw that he had brought back from the Newton.

Actually he and Michael were having an argument when I discovered them. A relatively small lattice, about five hundred nodes altogether with square dimensions maybe three metres on a side, was affixed to one of those low, nondescript sheds about a hundred metres to the east of our lair opening. Michael was questioning the wisdom of attacking the lattice with a chain saw. At the moment they saw me, Richard was justifying his action by extolling the virtues of the elastic lattice material.

The three of us hugged and kissed for several minutes and then they reported on the Great Excursion. It had been an easy trip. The rover and the chairlift had worked without difficulty. Their instruments had shown that there was still quite a bit of radiation throughout the military ship, so they didn't stay long and didn't bring back any of the food. The scientific data base, however, had been in fine shape. Richard had used his data compression subroutines to strip much of the data base onto cubes compatible with our portable computers. They had also brought back a large backpack full of tools, like the chain saw, that they thought would be useful in finishing our living accommodations.

Richard and Michael worked incessantly from then until the birth of Simone. Using the extra chemical information contained in the data base, it became easier to order what we needed from the Ramans. I even experimented with sprinkling harmless esters and other simple organics on the food, resulting in some improvement in the taste. Michael completed his room down the corridor, Simone's cradle was constructed, and our bathrooms immeasurably improved. Considering all the constraints, our living conditions are now quite acceptable. Maybe soon ... Hark. I hear a soft cry from beside me. It's time to feed my daughter.

Before the last thirty minutes of my birthday is history, I want to return to the vivid images of previous birthdays that catalyzed my depression this morning. For me, my birthday has always been the most significant event of the year. The Christmas–New Year time period is special, but in a different way, for it is a celebration shared by everyone. A birthday focuses more directly on the individual. I have always used my birthdays as a time for reflection and contemplation about the direction of my life.

If I tried, I could probably remember something about every single one of my birthdays since I was five years old. Some memories, of course, are more poignant than others. This morning many of the pictures from my past celebrations evoked powerful feelings of nostalgia and homesickness. In my depressed state I railed against my inability to provide order and security to Simone's life. But even at the bottom of my depression, confronted by the immense uncertainty surrounding our existence here, I would not have really wished that Simone were not here to experience life with me. No, we are voyagers tied together by the deepest bond, parent and child, sharing the miracle of consciousness that we call life.

I have shared a similar bond before, not only with my mother and father, but also with my first daughter Genevieve. Hmm. It's amazing that all the images of my mother still stand out so sharply in my mind. Even though she died twenty-seven years ago, when I was only ten years old, she left me with a cornucopia of wonderful memories. My last birthday with her was quite extraordinary. The three of us went into Paris on the train. Father was dressed in his new Italian suit and looked extremely handsome. Mother had chosen to wear one of her bright, multicoloured native dresses. With her hair stacked in layers on her head, she looked like the Senoufo princess that she had been before she married Father.

We had dinner at a fancy restaurant just off the Champs-Elysées. Then we walked to a theatre where we watched an all-black troupe perform a set of native dances from the western regions of Africa. After the show, we were allowed backstage, where Mother introduced me to one of the dancers, a tall, beautiful woman of exceptional blackness. She was one of Mother's distant cousins from the Ivory Coast.

I listened to their conversation in the Senoufo tribal language, remembering bits and pieces from my training before the Poro three years earlier, and marvelled again at the way my mother's face always became more expressive when she was with her people. But fascinated as I was by the evening, I was only ten years old and would have preferred a normal birthday party with all my friends from school. Mother could tell I was disappointed while we were riding on the train back to our home in the suburb of Chilly-Mazarin. 'Don't be sad, Nicole,' she said, 'next year you can have a party. Your father and I wanted to take this opportunity to remind you again of the other half of your heritage. You are a French citizen and have lived your whole life in France, but part of you is pure Senoufo with roots deep in the tribal customs of West Africa.'

Earlier today, as I recalled the *danses ivoiriennes* performed by Mother's cousin and her associates, I imagined briefly, in my mind's eye, walking into a beautiful theatre with my ten-year-old daughter Simone beside me – but then the fantasy vanished. There are no theatres beyond the orbit of Jupiter. In fact, the whole concept of a theatre will probably never have any real meaning for my daughter. It is all so bewildering.

Some of my tears this morning were because Simone will never know her grandparents, and vice versa. They will be mythological characters in the fabric of her life and she will know them only from their photographs and videos. She will never have the joy of hearing my mother's amazing voice. And she will never see the soft and tender love in my father's eyes.

After Mother died, my father was very careful to make each of my birthdays very special. On my twelfth birthday, after we had just moved into the villa at Beauvois, Father and I walked together in the falling snow among the manicured gardens at the Chateau de Villandry. That day he promised me that he would always be beside me when I needed him. I tightened my grip on his hand as we walked along the hedges. I wept that day also, admitting to him (and to myself) how frightened I was that he too would abandon me. He cradled me against his chest and kissed my forehead. He never broke his promise.

Only last year, in what seems now to have been another lifetime, my birthday began on a ski train just inside the French border. I was still awake at midnight, reliving my noon encounter with Henry at the chalet on the side of the Weissfluhjoch. I had not told him, when he indirectly inquired, that he was Genevieve's father. I would not give him that satisfaction.

But I remember thinking on the train, is it fair for me to keep from my daughter the fact that her father is the king of England? Are my self-respect and pride so important that I can justify preventing my daughter from knowing that she is a princess? I was mulling these questions over in my mind, staring blankly out at the night, when Genevieve, as if on cue, appeared in my sleeping berth. 'Happy Birthday, Mother,' she said with a grin. She gave me a hug. I almost told her then about her father. I would have, I am certain, if I had known what was going to happen to the Newton expedition. I miss you, Genevieve. I wish that I had been allowed a proper goodbye.

Memories are very peculiar. This morning, in my depression, the flood of images from previous birthdays heightened my feelings of isolation and loss. Now, when I'm in a stronger mood, I savour those same recollections. I'm no longer terribly sad at this moment that Simone will not be able to experience what I have known. Her birthdays will be completely different from mine and unique to *her* life. It is my privilege and duty to make them as memorable and loving as I can.

3

26 MAY 2201

Five hours ago a series of extraordinary events began to occur inside Rama. We were sitting together at that time, eating our evening meal of roast beef, potatoes, and salad (in an effort to persuade ourselves that what we are eating is delicious, we have a code name for each of the chemical combinations that we obtain from the Ramans. The code names are roughly derived from the kind of nutrition provided – thus our 'roast beef' is rich in protein, 'potatoes' are primarily carbohydrates, etc.), when we heard a pure and distant whistle. All of us stopped eating and the two men bundled up to go topside. When the whistle persisted, I grabbed Simone and my heavy clothes, wrapped the baby in numerous blankets, and followed Michael and Richard up into the cold.

The whistle was much louder on the surface. We were fairly certain that it was coming from the south, but since it was dark in Rama we were leery about wandering away from our lair. After a few minutes, however, we began to see splashes of light reflecting off the mirrored surfaces of the surrounding skyscrapers, and our curiosity could not be contained. We crept cautiously toward the southern shore of the island, where no buildings would be between us and the imposing horns of the Southern bowl of Rama.

When we arrived at the shore of the Cylindrical Sea, a fascinating light show was already in progress. The arcs of multicoloured light flying around and illuminating the gigantic spires of the southern bowl continued for over an hour. Even baby Simone was mesmerised by the long streamers of yellow, blue, and red bouncing between the spires and making rainbow patterns in the dark. When the show abruptly ceased, we switched on our flashlights and beaded back toward our lair.

After a few minutes of walking, our animated conversation was interrupted by a distant long shriek, unmistakably the sound of one of the avian creatures that had helped Richard and me to escape from New York last year. We stopped abruptly and listened. Since we have neither seen nor heard any avians since we returned to New York to warn the Ramans of the incoming nuclear missiles, both Richard and I were very excited. Richard has been over to their lair a few times, but has never had any response to his shouts down the great vertical corridor. Just a month ago Richard said that he thought the avians had left New York altogether – the shriek tonight clearly indicates that at least one of our friends is still around.

Within seconds, before we had a chance to discuss whether or not one of us would go in the direction of the shriek, we heard another sound, also familiar, that was too loud for any of us to feel comfortable. Fortunately the dragging brushes were not between us and our lair. I put both of my arms around Simone and sprinted toward home, nearly running into buildings at least twice in my hurry in the dark. Michael was the last to arrive. By then I had finished opening both the cover and the grill. 'There's several of them,' Richard said breathlessly, as the sounds of the octospiders, growing louder, surrounded us. He cast his flashlight beam down the long lane leading east from our lair and we all saw two large, dark objects moving in our direction.

Normally we go to sleep within two or three hours after dinner, but tonight was an exception. The light show, the avian shriek, and the close encounter with the octospiders had energised all three of us. We talked and talked. Richard was convinced that something really major was about to happen. He reminded us that the Earth impact manoeuvre by Rama had also been preceded by a small light show in the southern bowl. At that time, he recalled, the consensus of the Newton cosmonauts had been that the entire demonstration was intended as an announcement or possibly as some kind of an alert. What, Richard wondered, was the significance of tonight's dazzling display?

For Michael, who was not inside Rama for any extended period of time before its close passage by the Earth and had never before had any direct contact with either the avians or the octospiders, tonight's events were of major proportions. The fleeting glance that he caught of the tentacled creatures coming toward us down the lane gave him some appreciation for the terror that Richard and I had felt when we were racing up those bizarre spikes and escaping from the octospider lair last year.

'Are the octospiders the Ramans?' Michael asked tonight. 'If so,' he continued, 'then why should we run from them? Their technology has advanced so far beyond ours that they can basically do with us as they see fit.'

'The octospiders are passengers on this vehicle,' Richard responded quickly, 'just as we are. So are the avians. The octos think we may be the Ramans, but they are not certain. The avians are a puzzle. Surely they cannot be a spacefaring species. How did they get on board in the first place? Are they perhaps a part of the original Raman ecosystem?'

I instinctively clutched Simone against my body. So many questions. So few answers. A memory of poor Dr Takagishi, stuffed like a huge fish or tiger and standing in the octospider museum, shot through my mind and gave me the shivers. 'If we are passengers,' I said quietly, 'then where are we going?'

Richard sighed. 'I've been doing some computations,' he said. 'And the results are not very encouraging. Even though we are travelling very fast with respect to the Sun, our speed is puny when the reference system is our local group of stars. If our trajectory does not change, we will exit the solar system in the general direction of Barnard's star. We will arrive in the Barnard system in several thousand years.'

Simone began to cry. It was late and she was very tired. I excused myself and went down to Michael's room to feed her while the men surveyed all the sensor outputs on the black screen – to see if they could determine what might be happening. Simone nursed fretfully at my breasts, even hurting me once. Her disquiet was extremely unusual. Ordinarily she is such a mellow baby. 'You feel our fear, don't you?' I said to her. I've read that babies can sense the emotions of the adults around them. Maybe it's true.

I still could not rest, even after Simone was sleeping comfortably on her blanket on the floor. My premonitory senses were warning me that tonight's events signaled a transition into some new phase of our life aboard Rama. I had not been encouraged by Richard's calculation that Rama might sail through the interstellar void for several thousand years. I tried to imagine living in our current conditions for the rest of my life and my mind balked. It would certainly be a boring existence for Simone. I found myself formulating a prayer, to God, or the Ramans, or whoever had the power to alter the future. My prayer was very simple. I asked that the forthcoming changes would somehow enrich the future life of my baby daughter.

28 MAY 2201

Again tonight there was a long whistle followed by a spectacular light show in the southern bowl of Rama. I didn't go to see it. I stayed in the lair with Simone. Michael and Richard did not encounter any of the other occupants of New York. Richard said that the show was approximately the same length as the first one, but the individual displays were considerably different. Michael's impression was that the only major change in the show was in the colours. In his opinion the dominant colour tonight was blue, whereas two days ago it had been yellow.

Richard is certain that the Ramans are in love with the number three and that, therefore, there will be another light show when night falls again. Since the days and nights on Rama are now approximately equal at twenty-three hours – a time period Richard calls the Raman equinox, correctly predicted by my brilliant husband in the almanac he issued to Michael and me four months ago – the third display will begin in another two Earth days. We all expect something unusual will occur soon after this third demonstration. Unless Simone's safety is in doubt, I will definitely watch.

30 MAY 2201

Our massive cylindrical home is now undergoing a rapid acceleration that began over four hours ago. Richard is so excited that he can hardly contain himself. He is convinced that underneath the elevated Southern Hemicylinder is a propulsion system operating on physical principles beyond the wildest imaginings of human scientists and engineers. He stares at the external sensor data on the black screen, his beloved portable computer in his hand, and makes occasional entries based on what he sees on the monitor. From time to time he mumbles to himself or to us about what he thinks the manoeuvre is doing to our trajectory.

I was unconscious at the bottom of the pit at the time that Rama made the midcourse correction to achieve the Earth impact orbit, so I don't know how much the floor shook during that earlier manoeuvre. Richard says those vibrations were trivial compared to what we are experiencing now. Just walking around at present is difficult. The floor bounces up and down at a very high frequency, as if a jackhammer were operating only a few metres away. We have been holding Simone in our arms ever since the acceleration started. We cannot put her down on the floor or in her cradle, because the vibration frightens her. I am the only one who moves around with Simone, and I am exceptionally cautious. Losing my balance and falling is a real concern – Richard and Michael have each fallen twice already – and Simone could be seriously injured if I fell in the wrong position.

Our meagre furniture is hopping all over the room. One of the chairs actually bounced out into the corridor and headed for the stairs half an hour ago. At first we replaced the furniture in its proper position every ten minutes or so, but now we just ignore it – unless it heads out the entryway into the hall.

Altogether it has been an unbelievable time period, beginning with the third and final light show in the south. Richard went out first that night, by himself, just before dark. He rushed back excitedly a few minutes later and grabbed Michael. When the two of them returned, Michael looked as if he had seen a ghost. 'Octospiders,' Richard shouted. 'Dozens of them are massed along the shoreline two kilometres to the east.'

'Now, you don't really know how many there are,' Michael said. 'We only saw them for ten seconds at most before the lights went out.'

'I watched them for longer when I was by myself,' Richard continued. 'I could see them very clearly with the binoculars. At first there were only a handful, but they suddenly started arriving in droves. I was just starting to count them when they organised themselves into some kind of an array. A giant octo with a red-and-blue-striped head appeared to be by itself at the front of their formation.'

'I didn't see the red and blue giant, or any "formation",' Michael added as I stared at the two of them with disbelief. 'But I definitely saw many of the creatures with the dark heads and the black and gold tentacles. In my opinion they were looking to the south, waiting for the light show to begin.'

'We saw the avians too,' Richard said to me. He turned to Michael. 'How many would you say were airborne in that flock?'

'Twenty-five, maybe thirty,' Michael replied.

'They soared high into the air over New York, shrieking as they rose, and then flew north, across the Cylindrical Sea.' Richard paused for a moment. 'I think those birds have been through this before. I think they know what is going to happen.'

I started wrapping Simone in her blankets. 'What are you doing?' Richard asked. I explained that I wasn't about to miss the final light show. I also reminded Richard that he had sworn to me that the octospiders only ventured out at night. 'This is a special occasion,' he replied confidently just as the whistle began to sound.

Tonight's show seemed more spectacular to me. Maybe it was my sense of anticipation. Red was definitely the colour of the night. At one point a fiery red arc inscribed a full and continuous hexagon connecting the tips of the six smaller horns. But as spectacular as the Raman lights were, they were not the highlight of the evening. About thirty minutes into the display, Michael suddenly shouted, 'Look!' and pointed down the shoreline in the direction where he and Richard had seen the octospiders earlier.

Several balls of light had ignited simultaneously in the sky above the frozen Cylindrical Sea. The 'flares' were about fifty metres off the ground and illuminated an area of roughly one square kilometre on the ice below them. During the minute or so that we could see some detail, a large black mass moved south across the ice. Richard handed me his binoculars just as the light from the flares was fading away. I could see some individual creatures in the mass. A surprisingly large number of the octospiders had coloured patterns on their heads, but most were dark charcoal grey, like the one that chased us in the lair. Both the black and gold tentacles and the shapes of their bodies confirmed that these creatures were the same species as the one we had seen climbing the spikes last year. And Richard was right. There were dozens of them.

When the manoeuvre began, we returned quickly to our lair. It was dangerous being outside in Rama during the extreme vibrations. Occasionally small parts of the surrounding skyscrapers would break free and crash to the ground. Simone began to cry as soon as the shaking started.

After a difficult descent into our lair, Richard began checking the external sensors, mostly looking at star and planet positions (Saturn is definitely identifiable in some of the Raman frames) and then making computations based on his observational data. Michael and I alternated holding Simone – eventually we sat in a corner of the room, where the two merging walls gave us some sense of stability – and talked about the amazing day.

Almost an hour later Richard announced the results of his preliminary orbit determination. He gave first the orbital elements, with respect to the Sun, of our hyperbolic trajectory *before* the manoeuvre started. Then he dramatically presented the new, osculating elements (as he called them) of our instantaneous trajectory. Somewhere in the recesses of my mind I must have stored the information that defines the term osculating element, but I luckily didn't need to fetch it. I was able, from the context, to understand that Richard was using a shorthand way of telling us how much our hyperbola had changed during the first three hours of the manoeuvre. However, the full implication of a change in hyperbolic eccentricity escaped me.

Michael remembered more of his celestial mechanics. 'Are you certain?' he said almost immediately.

'The quantitative results have wide error bars,' Richard replied. 'But there can be no doubt about the qualitative nature of the trajectory change.'

'Then our rate of escape from the solar system is *increasing*?' Michael asked.

'That's right,' Richard nodded. 'Our acceleration is virtually all going into the direction that increases our speed with respect to the Sun. The manoeuvre has already added many kilometres per second to our Sun-based velocity.'

'Whew,' Michael replied. 'That's staggering.'

I understood the gist of what Richard was saying. If we had retained any hope that we might be on a circuitous voyage that would magically return us to the Earth, those hopes were now being shattered. Rama was going to leave the solar system much faster than any of us had expected. While Richard waxed lyrical about the kind of propulsion system that could impart such a velocity change to this 'behemoth of a spacecraft,' I nursed Simone and found myself again thinking about her future. So we are definitely leaving the solar system, I thought, and going somewhere else. Will I ever see another world? Will Simone? Is it possible, my daughter, that Rama will be your home world for your entire lifetime?

The floor continues to shake vigorously, but it comforts me. Richard says our escape velocity is still increasing rapidly. Good. As long as we are going somewhere new, I want to travel there as fast as possible.

4

5 JUNE 2201

I awakened in the middle of last night after hearing a persistent knocking sound coming from the direction of the vertical corridor in our lair. Even though the normal noise level from the constant shaking is substantial, Richard and I could both clearly hear the pounding without any difficulty. After checking Simone – she was still comfortably sleeping in her cradle now mounted on Richard's makeshift shock absorbers – we walked cautiously over to the vertical corridor.

The knocking grew louder as we climbed the stairs toward the grill that protects us from unwanted visitors. At one landing Richard leaned over and whispered to me that it 'must be MacDuff knocking at the gate' and that our 'evil deed' would soon be discovered. I was too tense to laugh. When we were still several metres below the grill, we saw a large moving shadow projected on the wall in front of us. We stopped to study it. Both Richard and I realised immediately that our outside lair cover was open – there was daylight topside in Rama at the time – and that the Raman creature or biot responsible for the knocking was creating the bizarre shadow on the wall.

I instinctively clutched Richard's hand. 'What in the world is it?' I wondered out loud.

'It must be something new,' Richard said very softly.

I told him that the shadow resembled an old-fashioned oil pump going up and down in the middle of a producing field. He grinned nervously and agreed.

After waiting for what must have been five minutes and neither seeing nor hearing any change in the rhythmic knocking pattern of the visitor, Richard told me that he was going to climb to the grill, where he would be able to see something more definitive than a shadow. Of course that meant that whatever was outside beating on our door would also be able to see him, assuming that it had eyes or an approximate equivalent. For some reason I remembered Dr Takagishi at that moment, and a wave of fear swept through me. I kissed Richard and told him not to take any chances.

When he reached the final landing, just above where I was waiting, his

544

body was partially in the light and blocked the moving shadow. The knocking suddenly stopped abruptly. 'It's a biot, all right,' Richard shouted. 'It looks like a praying mantis with an extra hand in the middle of its face.'

His eyes suddenly widened. 'And now it's *opening* the grill,' he added, immediately jumping off the landing.

A second later he was beside me. He grabbed my hand and we raced down several flights of stairs together. We didn't stop until we were back on our living level several landings below.

We could hear the sound of motion above us. 'There was another mantis and at least one bulldozer biot behind the first mantis,' Richard said breathlessly. 'As soon as they saw me they started removing the grill ... Apparently they were just knocking to alert us to their presence.'

'But what do they want?' I asked rhetorically. The noise above us continued to grow. 'It sounds like an army,' I remarked.

Within seconds we could hear them moving down the stairs. 'We must be prepared to run for it,' Richard said frantically. 'You get Simone and I'll wake Michael.'

We moved swiftly down the corridor toward our living area. Michael had been awakened already by all the noise, and Simone was stirring as well. We huddled together in our main room, sitting on the shaking floor opposite the black screen, and waited for the alien invaders. Richard had prepared a keyboard request for the Ramans that would, upon the input of two additional commands, cause the black screen to lift up just as it did when our unseen benefactors were about to supply us with some new product. 'If we are attacked,' Richard said, 'we'll take our chances in the tunnels behind the screen.'

Half an hour passed. From the hubbub in the direction of the stairs we could tell that the intruders were already on our level in the lair, but none of them had yet entered the passage toward our living area. After another fifteen minutes curiosity overpowered my husband. 'I'll go check out the situation,' Richard said, leaving Michael with me and Simone.

He returned in less than five minutes. 'There are fifteen, maybe twenty of them,' he told us with a puzzled frown. 'Three mantises altogether, plus two different types of bulldozer biots. They seem to be building something on the opposite side of the lair.'

Simone had fallen asleep again. I put her in the cradle and then followed the two men toward the noise. When we reached the circular area where the stairs climb toward the opening to New York, we encountered a maelstrom of activity. It was impossible to follow all the work being done on the opposite side of the room. The mantises appeared to be supervising the bulldozer biots as they were widening a horizontal corridor on the other side of the circular room.

'Does anybody have any idea what they are doing?' Michael asked in a whisper.

'Not a clue,' Richard replied at the time.

It is almost twenty-four hours later now and it is still not clear exactly what the biots are building. Richard thinks that the corridor expansion has been made to accommodate some kind of a new facility. He has also suggested that all this activity almost certainly has something to do with us, for it is, after all, being done in our lair.

The biots work without stopping for rest, food, or sleep. The floor vibrations do not bother them at all. They seem to be following some master plan or procedure that has been thoroughly communicated, for none of them ever confer about anything. It is an awesome spectacle to watch their relentless activity. For their part, the biots have never once acknowledged that we are there watching them.

An hour ago Richard, Michael, and I talked briefly about the frustration we are all feeling because we do not know what is happening around us. At one point Richard smiled. 'It's really not dramatically different from the situation on Earth,' he said vaguely. When Michael and I pressed him to explain what he meant, Richard waved his hand in a sweeping gesture. 'Even at home,' he replied abstractedly, 'our knowledge is severely limited. The search for truth is always a frustrating experience.'

8 JUNE 2201

It is inconceivable to me that the biots could have finished the facility so quickly. Two hours ago the last of them, the foreman mantis that had signaled to us (using the 'hand' in the middle of its 'face') to inspect the new room early this afternoon, finally trundled up the stairs and disappeared. Richard says that it had remained in our lair until it was satisfied that we understood everything.

The only object in the new room is a narrow rectangular tank that has obviously been designed for us. It has shiny metal sides and is about three metres high. At either end there is a ladder that goes from the floor to the lip of the tank. A sturdy walkway runs around the outside perimeter of the tank just centimeters below the lip.

Inside the rectangular structure are four webbed hammocks secured against the walls. Each of these fascinating creations has been individually crafted for a specific member of our family. The hammocks for Michael and Richard are at each end of the tank; Simone and I have webbed beds in the middle, with her tiny hammock being right beside mine.

Of course Richard has already examined the entire arrangement in detail. Because there is a cover to the tank and the hammocks are set down into the cavity between half a metre and a metre from the top, he has concluded that the tank closes and is then probably filled with a fluid. But why was it built? Are we going to undergo some set of experiments? Richard is certain

546

that we are about to be tested in some way, but Michael says that our being used as guinea pigs is 'inconsistent with the Raman personality' we have observed heretofore. I had to laugh at his comment. Michael has now spread his incurable religious optimism to encompass the Ramans as well. He always assumes, like Voltaire's Dr Pangloss, that we are living in the best of all possible universes.

The foreman mantis hung around, mostly watching from the walkway of the tank, until each of the four of us had actually lain upon his or her hammock. Richard pointed out that although the hammocks had been positioned at varying depths along the walls, we each will 'sink' to approximately the same level when occupying the webbed beds. The webbing is slightly elastic, reminiscent of the lattice material we have encountered before in Rama. While I was 'testing' my hammock this afternoon, its bounce reminded me of both the fear and the exhilaration during my fantastic lattice harness ride across the Cylindrical Sea. When I closed my eyes it was easy to see myself again just above the water, suspended beneath the three great avians who were carrying me to freedom.

Along the lair wall, behind the tank from the point of view of our living area, there is a set of thick pipes that are connected directly to the tank. We suspect that their purpose is to carry some kind of fluid that fills up the volume of the tank. I guess we will find out soon enough.

So what do we do now? All three of us agree that we should just wait. Doubtless we will eventually be expected to spend some time in this tank. But we have to assume that we will be told when it is the proper time.

10 JUNE 2201

Richard was right. He was certain that the intermittent, low-frequency whistle early yesterday was announcing another mission phase transition. He even suggested that maybe we should go over to the new tank and be prepared to take positions on our individual hammocks. Michael and I both argued with him, insisting that there was not 'nearly enough information' to jump to such a conclusion.

We should have followed Richard's advice. Essentially we ignored the whistle and went on with our normal (if that term can ever be used for our existence inside this spacecraft of extraterrestrial origin) routine. About three hours later, the foreman mantis appeared suddenly in the doorway of our main room and scared me out of my wits. It pointed down the corridor with its peculiar fingers and made it clear that we were to move with some dispatch.

Simone was still asleep and not at all happy when I woke her up. She was also hungry, but the mantis biot would not let me take the time to feed her. So Simone was crying fitfully as we were herded across our lair to the tank.

A second mantis was waiting on the walkway that rings the lip of the tank. It was holding our transparent helmets in its strange hands. It must also have been the inspector, for this second mantis would not let us descend to our hammocks until it checked to ensure that the helmets were properly placed over our heads. The plastic or glass compound that forms the helmet front is remarkable; we can see perfectly through it. The bottoms of the helmets are also extraordinary. They are made of a sticky, rubberlike compound that adheres to the skin very tightly and creates an impermeable seal.

We had only been lying on our hammocks for thirty seconds when a powerful surge pressed us down against the webbed elements with such force that we sank halfway into the empty tank. An instant later tiny threads (they seemed to grow out of the hammock material) wrapped themselves around the trunks of our bodies, leaving only our arms and necks free. I glanced over at Simone to see if she was crying; she had a big smile on her face.

The tank had already begun to fill with a light green liquid. In less man a minute we were surrounded by the fluid. Its density was very close to our own, for we half floated on the surface until the top of the tank closed and the liquid completely filled the volume. Although I considered it unlikely that we were in any actual danger, I was frightened when the lid closed over our heads. There is a little claustrophobia in each of us.

All this time the strong acceleration continued. Luckily it wasn't completely dark inside the tank. There were tiny lights scattered around the tank cover. I could see Simone next to me, her body bouncing like a buoy, and I could even see Richard in the distance.

We were inside the tank for slightly more than two hours. Richard was extremely excited when we were finished. He told Michael and me that he was certain we had just completed a 'test' to see how we could withstand 'excessive' forces.

'They are not satisfied with the paltry accelerations that we have been experiencing heretofore,' he exuberantly informed us. 'The Ramans want to *really* increase the velocity. To accomplish that, the spacecraft must be subjected to long duration, high G-forces. This tank has been designed to provide us with enough cushioning that our biological construction can accommodate the unusual environment.'

Richard spent all day doing calculations and a few hours ago showed us his preliminary reconstruction of yesterday's 'acceleration event.' 'Look at this,' he shouted, barely able to contain himself. 'We made an equivalent velocity change of *seventy* kilometres per second during that short two-hour period. That is absolutely monstrous for a spacecraft the size of Rama! We were accelerating at close to *ten* gees the entire time.' He then grinned at us. 'This ship has one hell of an overdrive mode.'

When we finished the test in the tank, I inserted a new set of biometry probes in all of us, including Simone. I have not seen any unusual responses, at least nothing that has triggered a warning, but I admit that I am still a little concerned about how our bodies will react to the stress. A few minutes ago Richard chided me. 'The Ramans are certainly watching too,' he said, indicating that he thought the biometry was unnecessary. 'I bet they are taking their own data through those threads.'

5

My vocabulary is inadequate to describe my experiences of the last several days. The word 'amazing', for example, falls far short of conveying the true sense of how extraordinary these long hours in the tank have been. The only remotely similar experiences in my life were both induced by the ingestion of catalytic chemicals, first during the Poro ceremony in the Ivory Coast when I was seven years old and then, more recently, after drinking Omeh's vial while I was at the bottom of the pit in Rama. But both those trips or visions or whatever were isolated incidents and comparatively short in duration. My recent episodes in the tank have lasted for hours.

Before throwing myself totally into a description of the world inside my mind, I should summarise first the 'real' events of the past week so that the hallucinatory episodes can be placed in context. Our daily life has now evolved into a repeating pattern. The spacecraft continues to manoeuvre, but in two separate modes: 'regular,' when the floor shakes and everything moves but a quasi-normal life can be lived, and 'overdrive,' when Rama accelerates at a ferocious rate that Richard now estimates is in excess of eleven gees.

When the spacecraft is in overdrive, the four of us must be inside the tank. The overdrive periods last for just under eight hours out of each twenty-seven-hour, six-minute cycle in the repetitive pattern. We are clearly intended to sleep during the overdrive segments. The tiny lights above our heads in the closed tank are extinguished after the first twenty minutes of each segment and we lie there in the total darkness until five minutes before the end of the eight-hour period.

All this rapid velocity change, according to Richard, is speeding our escape from the Sun. If the current manoeuvre remains consistent in both magnitude and direction, and continues for as long as a month, we will then be travelling at half the speed of light with respect to our solar system.

'Where are we going?' Michael asked yesterday.

'It's still too early to tell,' Richard responded. 'All we know is that we're blasting away at a fantastic rate.'

The temperature and density of the liquid inside the tank have been carefully adjusted each period until they are now exactly equal to ours. As a result, when I lie there in the dark, I can feel nothing at all except a barely perceptible downward force. My mind always tells me that I am inside an acceleration tank, surrounded by some kind of fluid cushioning my body against the powerful force, but the absence of sensation eventually causes me to lose my sense of body altogether. That's when the hallucinations begin. It's almost as if some normal sensory input to the brain is necessary to keep me properly functioning. If no sounds, no sights, no tastes, no smells, and no pain reach my brain, then its activity becomes unregulated.

I tried to discuss this phenomenon with Richard two days ago, but he just looked at me as if I were crazy. He has had no hallucinations. He spends his time in the 'twilight zone' (his name for the period of no sensory input prior to deep sleep) doing mathematical calculations, conjuring up a wide variety of maps of the Earth, or even reliving his most outstanding sexual moments. He definitely *manages* his brain, even in the absence of sensory input. That is why we are so different. My mind wants to find a direction of its own when it is not being used for chores such as processing the billions of pieces of data coming from all the other cells in my body.

The hallucinations usually begin with a coloured speck of red or green that appears in the total dark surrounding me. As the speck enlarges, it is joined by other colours, often yellow, blue, and purple. Each of the colours rapidly forms into its own irregular pattern and spreads across my vision screen. What I am seeing becomes a kaleidoscope of bright colours. The movement in the field accelerates until hundreds of strips and splotches fuse into one raging explosion.

In the middle of this riot of colour a coherent image always forms. At first I cannot tell exactly what it is, for the figure or figures are very small, as if they are far, far away. As the image moves closer, it changes colours several times, adding both to the surreal overtone of the vision and to my inner sense of dread. More than half the time the image that eventually resolves itself contains my mother, or some animal like a cheetah or a lioness that I intuitively recognise as my mother in disguise. As long as I just watch, and make no volitional attempt to interact with my mother, she remains a character in the changing image. However, if I try to contact Mother in any way, she, or the animal representing her, immediately disappears, leaving me with an overwhelming feeling of having been abandoned.

During one of my recent hallucinations the waves of colour broke into geometric patterns and these in turn changed to human silhouettes marching single file across my field of view. Omeh was leading the procession in a bright green robe. The two figures at the rear of the group were both women, the heroines of my adolescence, Joan of Arc and Eleanor of Aquitaine. When I first heard their voices the procession dissolved and the scene instantly shifted. Suddenly I was in a small rowboat in the early morning fog on the small duck pond near our villa at Beauvois. I shivered with fear and began to weep uncontrollably. Joan and Eleanor appeared in the fog and mist to assure me that my father was not going to marry Helena, the English duchess with whom he had gone to Turkey on a vacation.

Another night the overture of colour was followed by a bizarre theatrical performance somewhere in Japan. There were only two characters in the hallucinatory play, both of whom were wearing brilliant, expressive masks. The man who was dressed in the Western suit and tie recited poetry and had magnificently clear, open eyes that could be seen through his friendly mask. The other man looked like a seventeenth century samurai warrior. His mask was a perpetual scowl. He began to threaten both me and his more modern colleague. I screamed at the end of this hallucination because the two men met in the middle of the stage and merged into a single character.

Some of my most powerful hallucinatory images have only lasted for a few seconds. On the second or third night, a naked Prince Henry, engorged with desire, his body a vibrant purple in colour, appeared for two or three seconds in the middle of another vision in which I was riding on a giant green octospider.

During yesterday's sleep period there were no colours for hours. Then, as I became aware of being incredibly hungry, a giant pink manna melon appeared in the darkness. When I attempted to eat the melon in my vision, it grew legs and scampered away, disappearing into unresolved colours.

Does any of this mean anything at all? Can I learn something about myself or my life from these apparently random outpourings of my undirected mind?

The debate about the significance of dreams has raged now for almost three centuries and is still unresolved. These hallucinations of mine, it seems to me, are even more removed from reality than normal dreams. In a sense they are distant cousins of the two psychedelic trips that I took earlier in my life, and any attempt to interpret them logically would be absurd. However, for some reason I still believe some fundamental truths are contained in these wild and seemingly unconnected rampagings of my mind. Maybe that's because I cannot accept that the human brain ever operates in a purely random manner.

22 JULY 2201

Yesterday the floor finally stopped shaking. Richard had predicted it. When we didn't go back into the tank two days ago at the customary time, Richard correctly conjectured that the manoeuvre was almost over.

So we enter still another phase of our incredible odyssey. My husband informs us that we are now travelling at a velocity of more than half the speed of light. That means we are covering the Earth–Moon distance approximately every two *seconds*. We are headed, more or less, in the direction of the star Sirius, the brightest true star in the night sky of our home planet. If there are no more manoeuvres, we will arrive in the vicinity of Sirius in another twelve years.

I am relieved that our life may now return to some kind of local equilibrium. Simone seems to have weathered the long periods in the tank without any noticeable difficulties, but I can't believe that such an experience will leave an infant totally unscathed. It is important for her that we now re-establish a daily routine.

In my moments alone I still think often about those vivid hallucinations during the first ten days in the tank. I must admit that I was delighted when I finally endured several 'twilight zones' of total sensory deprivation without the wild, coloured patterns and disjointed images flooding my mind. By that time I was starting to worry about my sanity and, quite frankly, was already way past 'overwhelm'. Even though the hallucinations abruptly stopped, my recollection of the strength of those visions still made me wary each time the lights in the top of the tank were extinguished during the last several weeks.

I had only one additional vision after those first ten days – and it may actually just have been an extremely vivid dream during a normal period of sleep. Despite the fact that this particular image was not as sharp as the earlier ones, I have nevertheless retained all the details because of its similarity to one of the hallucinatory segments while I was at the bottom of the pit last year.

In my final dream or vision I was sitting with my father at an outdoor concert in an unknown place. An old Oriental gentleman with a long white beard was by himself on the stage, playing music on some kind of strange stringed instrument. Unlike my vision at the bottom of the pit, however, my father and I did not turn into little birds and fly away to Chinon in France. Instead, my father's body disappeared completely, leaving only his eyes. Within a few seconds there were five other pairs of eyes forming a hexagon in the air above me. I recognised Omeh's eyes immediately, and my mother's, but the other three were unknown. The eyes at the vertices of the hexagon all stared at me, unblinking, as if they were trying to communicate something. Just before the music stopped I heard a single distinct sound. Several voices simultaneously uttered the word '*Danger*'.

What was the origin of my hallucinations and why was I the only one of the three of us to experience them? Richard and Michael also endured sensory deprivation, and they have each admitted seeing 'bizarre coloured patterns,' but their images were never coherent. If, as we have conjectured, the Ramans initially injected us with a chemical or two, using the tiny threads that wound around our bodies, to help us sleep in the unfamiliar surroundings, why was I the only one to respond with such wild visions?

Richard and Michael both think the answer is simple, that I am a 'drug labile individual with a hyperactive imagination'. As far as they are concerned, that's the entire explanation. They don't pursue the subject any further and, although they are polite when I raise the many issues associated with my 'trips', they don't even seem interested anymore. I might have expected that kind of a response from Richard, but certainly not from Michael.

Actually even our predictable General O'Toole has not been completely himself since we began our sessions in the tank. He has clearly been preoccupied with other matters. Only this morning did I obtain a small glimpse of what has been going on in his mind.

'I have always,' Michael finally said slowly, after I had been pestering him with friendly questions for several minutes, 'without consciously acknowledging it, redefined and relimited God with each new breakthrough in science. I had managed to integrate a concept of the Ramans into my Catholicism, but in so doing I had merely expanded my limited definition of Him. Now, when I find myself on board a robot spacecraft travelling at relativistic speeds, I see that I must completely unfetter God. Only then can He be the supreme being of all the particles and processes in the universe.'

The challenge of *my* life in the near future is at the other extreme. Richard and Michael are focused on profound ideas – Richard in the realm of science and engineering, Michael in the world of the soul. Although I thoroughly enjoy the stimulating ideas produced by each of them in his separate search for the truth, someone must pay attention to the everyday tasks of living. The three of us have the responsibility, after all, of preparing our only member of the next generation for her adult life. It looks as if the task of being the primary parent will always fall to me.

It is a responsibility I gladly embrace. When Simone smiles radiantly at me during a break from her nursing, I don't muse about my hallucinations, it really doesn't matter that much whether or not there is a God, and it is not of overwhelming significance that the Ramans have developed a method for using water as nuclear fuel. At that instant the only thing that is important is that I am Simone's mother.

31 JULY 2201

Spring has definitely come to Rama. The thaw began as soon as the manoeuvre was completed. By that time the temperature topside had reached a frigid twenty-five below zero, and we had begun to worry about how much lower the outside temperature could become before the system regulating the thermal conditions in our lair would be stretched to the limit. The temperature has been rising steadily almost a degree per day since then and, at that rate, will cross the freezing level within two more weeks.

We are now outside the solar system in the near-perfect vacuum that fills the immense voids between neighbouring stars. Our sun is still the dominant object in the sky, but none of the planets is even visible. Two or three times a week Richard searches through the telescopic data for some sign of the comets in the Oort Cloud, but thus far he has seen nothing.

Where is the heat coming from that is warming the interior of our vehicle?

Our master engineer, the handsome cosmonaut Richard Wakefield, had a quick explanation when Michael asked him that question yesterday. 'The same nuclear system that was providing the huge velocity change is probably now generating the heat. Rama must have two different operating regimes. When it is in the neighborhood of a heat source, like a star, it turns off all its primary systems, including propulsion and thermal control.'

Both Michael and I congratulated Richard for an eminently plausible explanation. 'But,' I asked him two days ago, 'there are still many other questions. *Why*, for example, does it have the two separate engineering systems? And why does it turn off the primary one at all?'

'Here I can only speculate,' Richard answered with his usual grin. 'Maybe the primary systems need periodic repairs and these can only be accomplished when there is an external source of heat and power. You have seen how the various biots maintain the surface of Rama. Maybe there's another set of biots who perform all the maintenance on the primary systems.'

'I have another idea,' Michael said slowly. 'Do you believe we are meant to be on board this spacecraft?'

'What do you mean?' Richard asked, his brow furrowed.

'Do you think it is a random event that we are here? Or is it a likely event, given all the probabilities and the nature of our species, that some members of the human race would be inside Rama at this moment?'

I liked Michael's line of reasoning. He was hinting, although he didn't yet understand it completely himself, that perhaps the Ramans were not just geniuses in the hard sciences and engineering. Perhaps they knew something about universal psychology as well. Richard wasn't following.

'Are you suggesting,' I asked, 'that the Ramans *purposely* used their secondary systems in the neighborhood of the Earth, expecting thereby to lure us into a rendezvous?'

'That's preposterous,' Richard said immediately.

'But Richard,' Michael rejoined, 'think about it. What would have been the probability of any contact if the Ramans had streaked into our system at a significant fraction of the speed of light, rounded the Sun, and then gone on their merry way? Absolutely zero. And, as you have indicated yourself, there may be other "foreigners," if we can call ourselves that, on this ship as well. I doubt if many species have the ability ...'

During a break in the conversation I reminded the men that the Cylindrical Sea would soon melt from below, and that there would be hurricanes and tidal waves immediately afterward. We all later agreed that we should retrieve the backup sailing boat from the Beta site.

It took the men slightly more than twelve hours to trek both ways across the ice. Night had already fallen by the time they returned. When Richard and Michael reached our lair, Simone, who is already completely aware of her surroundings, reached out her arms to Michael.

'I see someone is glad that I'm back,' Michael said jokingly.

'As long as it's just Simone,' Richard said. He seemed strangely tense and distant.

Last night his peculiar mood continued. 'What's the matter, darling?' I asked him when we were alone together on our mat. He didn't reply immediately, so I kissed him on the cheek and waited.

'It's Michael,' Richard said at length. 'I just realised today, when we were carrying the boat across the ice, that he's in love with you. You should hear him. All he talks about is you. You're the perfect mother, the perfect wife, the perfect friend. He even admitted that he was envious of me.'

I caressed Richard for a few seconds, trying to figure out how to respond. 'I think you're making too much of some casual statements, darling,' I said finally. 'Michael was simply expressing his honest affection. I am very fond of him as well ...'

'I know – that's what bothers me,' Richard interrupted me abruptly. 'He takes care of Simone most of the time when you're busy, the two of you talk for hours while I'm working on my projects ...'

He stopped and stared at me with a strange, forlorn look in his eyes. His gaze was scary. This was not the same Richard Wakefield that I have known intimately for over a year. A chill rushed through my system before his eyes softened and he reached over to kiss me.

After we made love and he fell asleep, Simone stirred and I decided to feed her. While I was nursing I thought back over the entire period of time since Michael found us at the foot of the chairlift. There was nothing I could cite that should have caused Richard the slightest bit of jealousy. Even our lovemaking has remained regular and satisfying throughout, although I will admit it hasn't been too imaginative since Simone's birth.

The crazy look that I had seen in Richard's eyes continued to haunt me even after Simone was finished nursing. I promised myself I would find more time to be alone with Richard in the coming weeks.

6

20 JUNE 2202

I verified today that I am indeed pregnant again. Michael was delighted, Richard surprisingly unresponsive. When I talked to Richard privately, he acknowledged that he had mixed feelings because Simone had finally reached the stage where she didn't need 'constant attention' anymore. I reminded him that when we had talked two months ago about having another child, he had given his enthusiastic consent. Richard suggested to me that his eagerness to father a second child had been strongly influenced by my 'obvious excitement' at the time.

The new baby should arrive in mid-March. By then we will have finished with the nursery and will have enough living space for the entire family. I am sorry that Richard is not thrilled about being a father again, but I am glad that Simone will now have a playmate.

15 MARCH 2203

Catharine Colin Wakefield (we will call her Katie) was born on the thirteenth of March at 6:16 in the morning. It was an easy birth, only four hours from the first strong contraction to delivery. There was no significant pain at any time. I delivered squatting on my haunches and was in such good shape that I cut the umbilical myself.

Katie already cries a lot. Both Genevieve and Simone were sweet, mellow babies, but Katie is obviously going to be a noisemaker. Richard is pleased that I wanted to name her after his mother. I had hoped that he might be more interested in his role as father this time, but at present he is too busy working on his 'perfect data base' (it will index and provide easy access to all our information) to pay much attention to Katie.

My third daughter weighed just under four kilograms at birth and was fifty-four centimetres long. Simone was almost certainly not as heavy when she was born, but we did not have an accurate scale at the time. Katie's skin colour is quite fair, almost white in fact, and her hair is much lighter than the dark black tresses of her sister. Her eyes are surprisingly blue. I know that it's not unusual for babies to have blue eyes and that often they darken significantly in the first year. But I never expected a child of mine to have blue eyes for even a moment.

18 MAY 2203

It's hard for me to believe that Katie is already more than two months old. She is such a demanding baby! By now I should have been able to teach her not to pull on my nipples, but I cannot break her of the habit. She is especially difficult when anyone else is present while I am nursing. If I even turn my head to talk to Michael or Richard, or especially if I try to answer one of Simone's questions, then Katie jerks on my nipple with a vengeance.

Richard has been extremely moody lately. At times he is his usual brilliant, witty self, keeping Michael and me laughing with his erudite banter; however, his mood can shift in an instant. A single seemingly innocuous observation by either of us can plunge him into depression or even anger.

I suspect that Richard's real problem these days is boredom. He has finished his data base project and not yet started another major activity. The fabulous computer he built last year contains subroutines that make our interface with the black screen almost routine. Richard could add some variety to his days by playing a more active part in Simone's development and education, but I guess it's just not his style. He does not seem to be fascinated, as Michael and I are, with the complex patterns of growth that are emerging in Simone.

When I was first pregnant with Katie, I was quite concerned about Richard's apparent lack of interest in children. I decided to attack the problem directly by asking him to help me set up a mini-laboratory that would enable us to analyse part of Katie's genome from a sample of my amniotic fluid. The project involved complex chemistry, a level of interaction with the Ramans deeper than any we had ever tried before, and the creation and calibration of some sophisticated medical instruments.

Richard loved the task. I did too, for it reminded me of my days in medical school. We worked together for twelve, sometimes fourteen hours a day (leaving Michael to take care of Simone – those two are certainly fond of each other) until we were finished. Often we would talk about our work late into the night, even while we were making love.

When the day came, however, that we completed the analysis of our own future child's genome, I discovered, much to my amazement, that Richard was more excited about the fact that the equipment and analysis met all our specifications than he was about the characteristics of our second daughter. I was astonished. When I told him that the child was a girl, and didn't have Down's or Whittingham's syndrome, and none of her a priori cancer tendencies were outside the acceptable ranges, he reacted matter-of-factly. But when I praised the speed and accuracy with which the system had completed the test, Richard beamed with pride. What a different man my husband is! He is much more comfortable with the world of mathematics and engineering than he is with other people.

Michael has noticed Richard's recent restlessness as well. He has encouraged Richard to create more toys for Simone like the brilliant dolls he made when I was in the final months of my pregnancy with Katie. Those dolls are still Simone's favourite playthings. They walk around on their own and even respond to a dozen verbal commands. One night, when Richard was in one of his exuberant moods, he programmed TB to interact with the dolls. Simone was almost hysterical with laughter after The Bard (Michael insists on calling Richard's Shakespeare-spouting robot by its full name) chased all three of the dolls into a corner and then launched into a medley of love sonnets.

Not even TB has cheered Richard these last two weeks. He's not sleeping well, which is unusual for him, and he has shown no passion for anything. Our regular and varied sex life has even been suspended, so Richard must be really struggling with his internal demons. Three days ago he left early in the morning (it was also just after dawn in Rama – every now and then our Earth clock in the lair and the Raman clock outside are in synch) and stayed up in New York for over ten hours. When I asked him what he had been doing, he replied that he had sat on the wall and stared at the Cylindrical Sea. Then he changed the subject.

Michael and Richard are both convinced that we are now alone on our island. Richard has entered the avian lair twice recently, both times staying on the side of the vertical corridor away from the tank sentry. He even descended once to the second horizontal passageway, where I made my leap, but he saw no signs of life. The octospider lair now has a pair of complicated grills between the covering and the first landing. For the past four months, Richard has been electronically monitoring the region around the octo lair again; even though he admits there may be some ambiguities in his monitor data, Richard insists he can tell from visual inspection alone that the grills have not been opened for a long time.

The men assembled the sailing boat a couple of months ago, and then spent two hours checking it out on the Cylindrical Sea. Simone and I waved to them from the shore. Fearful that the crab biots would define the boat as 'garbage' (as they apparently did the other boat – we never did figure out what happened to it; a couple of days after we escaped from the phalanx of nuclear missiles we returned to where we had left it and it was gone), Richard and Michael disassembled it again and brought it into our lair for safekeeping.

Richard has said several times that he would like to sail across the sea, toward the south, and see if he can find any place where the five-hundred-metre cliff can be scaled. Our information about the Southern Hemicylinder of Rama is very limited. Except for the few days when we were on the biot hunt with the original Newton cosmonaut team, our knowledge of the region is limited to the crude mosaics assembled in realtime from the initial Newton drone images. It would certainly be fascinating and exciting to explore the south – maybe we could even find out where all those octospiders went: But we can't afford to take any risks at this juncture. Our family is critically dependent on each of the three adults – the loss of any one of us would be devastating.

I believe Michael O'Toole is content with the life we have made for ourselves on Rama, especially since the addition of Richard's large computer has made so much more information readily available to us. We now have access to all the encyclopedic data that was stored on board the Newton military ship. Michael's current 'study unit,' as he calls his organised recreation, is art history. Last month his conversation was full of the Medici and the Catholic popes of the Renaissance, along with Michelangelo, Raphael, and the other great painters of the period. He is now involved with the nineteenth century, a time in art history that I find more interesting. We have had many recent discussions about the impressionist 'revolution,' but Michael does not accept my argument that impressionism was simply a natural by-product of the advent of the camera.

Michael spends hours with Simone. He is patient, tender, and caring. He has carefully monitored her development and has recorded her major milestones in his electronic notebook. At present Simone knows twenty-one of her twenty-six letters by sight (she confuses the pairs C and S, as well as Y and V, and for some reason cannot learn the K), and can count to twenty on a good day. Simone can also correctly identify drawings of an avian, an octospider, and the four most prevalent types of biots. She knows the names of the twelve disciples as well, a fact that does not make Richard happy. We have already had one 'summit meeting' about the spiritual education of our daughters, and the result was polite disagreement.

That leaves me. I am happy most of the time, although I do have some days when Richard's restlessness or Katie's crying or just the absurdity of our strange life on this alien spaceship combine to overwhelm me. I am always busy. I plan most of the family activities, decide what we're eating and when, and organise the children's days, including their naps. I never stop asking the question, where are we going? But it no longer frustrates me that I do not know the answer.

My personal intellectual activity is more limited than I might choose if I were left to my own devices, but I tell myself that there are only so many hours in the day. Richard, Michael, and I engage often in lively conversation, so there is certainly no dearth of stimulation. But neither of them has much interest in some intellectual areas that have always been a part of my life. My skills in languages and linguistics, for example, have been a source of considerable pride for me since my earliest days in school. Several weeks ago I had a terrifying dream in which I had forgotten how to write or speak in anything but English. For two weeks thereafter I spent two hours by myself each day, not just reviewing my beloved French, but also studying Italian and Japanese as well.

One afternoon last month Richard projected on the black screen a Raman external telescope output that included our Sun and another thousand stars in the field of view. The Sun was the brightest of the objects, but just barely. Richard reminded Michael and me that we are already more than twelve trillion kilometres away from our oceanic home planet in close orbit around that insignificant distant star.

Later the same evening we watched 'Eleanor the Queen', one of the thirty or so movies originally carried on board the Newton to entertain the cosmonaut crew. The movie was loosely based on my father's successful novels about Eleanor of Aquitaine and was filmed in many of the locations that I had visited with my father when I was an adolescent. The final scenes of the movie, showing the years before Eleanor died, all took place in L'Abbaye de Fontevrault. I remember being fourteen years old and standing in the abbey beside my father opposite the carved effigy of Eleanor, my hands trembling with emotion as I clutched his. 'You were a great woman,' I once said to the spirit of the queen who had dominated twelfth century history in France and England, 'and you have set an example for me to follow. I will not disappoint you.'

That night, after Richard was asleep and while Katie was temporarily quiet, I thought about the day again and was filled with a deep sorrow, a sense of loss that I could not quite articulate. The juxtaposition of the retreating Sun and the image of myself as a teenager, making bold promises to a queen who had been dead for almost a thousand years, reminded me that everything I had ever known before Rama is now finished. My two new daughters will never see any of the places that meant so much to me and Genevieve. They will never know the smell of freshly mown grass in springtime, the radiant beauty of the flowers, the songs of the birds, or the glory of the full moon rising out of the ocean. They will not know the planet Earth at all, or any of its inhabitants, except for this small and motley crew they will call their family, a meagre representation of the overflowing life on a blessed planet.

That night I wept quietly for several minutes, knowing even as I was weeping that by morning I would again be wearing my optimistic face. After all, it could be much worse. We have the essentials: food, water, shelter, clothing, good health, companionship, and, of course, love. Love is the most important ingredient for the happiness of any human life, either on Earth or on Rama. If Simone and Katie learn only of love from the world we've left behind, it will be enough.

7

Today was unusual in every respect. First, I announced as soon as everyone was awake that we were going to dedicate the day to the memory of Eleanor of Aquitaine, who died, if the historians are correct and we have properly tracked the calendar, exactly one thousand years ago today. To my delight, the entire family supported the idea and both Richard and Michael immediately volunteered to help with the festivities. Michael, whose art history unit has now been replaced by one on cooking, suggested that he prepare a special medieval brunch in honour of the queen. Richard dashed off with TB, whispering to me that the little robot was going to return as Henry Plantagenet.

I had developed a short history lesson for Simone, introducing her to Eleanor and the twelfth century world. She was unusually attentive. Even Katie, who never sits still for longer than five minutes, was cooperative and didn't interrupt us. She played quietly with her baby toys most of the morning. Simone asked me at the end of the lesson why Queen Eleanor had died. When I responded that the queen had died of old age, my three-year-old daughter then asked if Queen Eleanor had 'gone to heaven'.

'Where did you get that idea?' I asked Simone.

'From Uncle Michael,' she replied. 'He told me that good people go to heaven when they die and bad people go to hell.'

'Some people believe there is a heaven,' I said after a reflective pause. 'Others believe in what's called reincarnation, where people come back and live again as a different person or even as a different kind of animal. Some other people believe that each special life is a unique miracle, awakening from conception to birth, and going to sleep forever at death.' I smiled and tousled her hair.

'What do you believe, Mama?' my daughter then asked.

I felt something very close to panic. I temporised with a few comments while I tried to figure out what to say. An expression from my favourite TS Eliot poem, 'to lead you to an overwhelming question,' whisked in and out of my mind. Luckily I was rescued.

'Fare thee well, young lady.' The little robot TB, dressed in what was supposed to pass for medieval riding garb, walked into the room and informed Simone that he was Henry Plantagenet, king of England, and husband of Queen Eleanor. Simone's smile brightened. Katie looked up and grinned.

'The queen and I built a grand empire,' the robot said, making an expansive gesture with his little arms, 'that eventually included all of England, Scotland, Ireland, Wales, and half of what is now France.' TB recited a prepared lecture with gusto, amusing Simone and Katie with his winks and hand gestures. He then reached in his pocket and pulled out a miniature knife and fork, claiming that he had introduced the concept of eating utensils to the 'barbaric English'.

'But why did you put Queen Eleanor in prison?' Simone asked after the robot was finished. I smiled. She had indeed paid attention to her history lesson. The robot's head pivoted and looked in Richard's direction. Richard held up a finger, indicating a brief wait, and rushed out into the corridor. In no more than a minute TB, aka Henry II, returned. The robot walked over to Simone. 'I fell in love with another woman,' he said, 'and Queen Eleanor was angry. To get even with me, she turned my sons against me ...'

Richard and I had just started a mild argument about the *real* reasons why Henry imprisoned Eleanor (we have discovered many times that we each learned a different version of Anglo-French history) when we heard a distant but unmistakable shriek. Within moments all five of us were topside. The shriek repeated.

We looked up in the sky above us. A solitary avian was flying a wide pattern a few hundred metres above the tops of the skyscrapers. We hurried over to the ramparts, beside the Cylindrical Sea, so we could have a better look. Once, twice, three times the great creature flew around the perimeter of the island. At the end of each loop the avian emitted a single long shriek. Richard waved his arms and shouted throughout the flight, but there was no indication that he was noticed.

The children became restless after about an hour. We agreed that Michael would take them back to the lair and Richard and I would stay as long as there was any possibility of contact. The bird continued flying in the same pattern. 'Do you think it's looking for something?' I asked Richard.

'I don't know,' he said, shouting again and waving at the avian as it reached the point in its loop where it was closest to us. This time it changed course, inscribing long graceful arcs in its helical descent. As it grew closer, Richard and I could see both its grey velvet underbelly and the two bright, cherry-red rings around its neck.

'It's our friend,' I whispered to Richard, remembering the avian leader who had agreed to transport us across the Cylindrical Sea four years earlier.

But this avian was not the healthy, robust creature that had flown in the centre of the formation when we had escaped from New York. This bird was skinny and emaciated, its velvet dirty and unkempt. 'It's sick,' Richard said as the bird landed about twenty metres away from us.

The avian jabbered something softly and jerked its head around nervously, as if it were expecting more company. Richard took one step toward it and the creature waved its wings, flapped them once, and backed up a few metres. 'What food do we have available,' Richard said in a low voice, 'that is chemically most like the manna melon?'

I shook my head. 'We don't have any food at all except last night's chicken – Wait,' I said, interrupting myself, 'we do have that green punch the children like. It looks like the liquid in the centre of the manna melon.'

Richard was gone before I had finished my sentence. During the ten minutes until he returned, the avian and I stared silently at one another. I tried to focus my mind on friendly thoughts, hoping that somehow my good intentions would be communicated through my eyes. Once I did see the avian change its expression, but of course I had no idea what either expression meant.

Richard returned carrying one of our black bowls filled with the green punch. He set the bowl in front of us and pointed at it as we backed away six or eight metres. The avian approached it in small, halting steps, stopping eventually right in front of the bowl. The bird dropped its beak into the liquid, took a small sip, and then threw its head back to swallow. Apparently the punch was all right, for the liquid was drained in less than a minute. When the avian was finished, it backed up two steps, spread its wings to their full extent, and made a full circular turn.

'Now we should say "you're welcome",' I said, extending my hand to Richard. We executed our circular turn, as we had done when we had said goodbye and thank you four years earlier, and bowed slightly in the avian's direction when we were finished.

Both Richard and I thought that the creature smiled, but we readily admitted later that we might have imagined it. The grey velvet avian spread its wings, lifted off the ground, and soared over our heads into the air.

'Where do you think it's going?' I asked Richard.

'It's dying,' he replied softly. 'It's taking one last look around the world it has known.'

6 JANUARY 2205

Today is my birthday. I am now forty-one years old. Last night I had another of my vivid dreams. I was very old. My hair was completely grey and my face was heavily wrinkled. I was living in a castle – somewhere near the Loire, not too far from Beauvois – with two grown daughters (neither of whom looked, in the dream, like Simone or Katie or Genevieve) and three grandsons. The boys were all teenagers, healthy physically, but there was something wrong with each of them. They were all dull, maybe even retarded. I remember in the dream trying to explain to them how the molecule of haemoglobin carries oxygen from the pulmonary system to the tissues. None of them could understand what I was saying.

I woke up from the dream in a depression. It was the middle of the night and everyone else in the family was asleep. As I often do, I walked down the corridor to the nursery to make certain that the girls were still covered by their light blankets. Simone hardly ever moves at night but Katie, as usual, had thrown her blanket off with her thrashing around. I put the cover back over Katie and then sat down in one of the chairs.

What is bothering me? I wondered. Why have I been having so many dreams about children and grandchildren? One day last week I made a joking reference to the possibility of having a third child and Richard, who is going through another of his extended gloomy periods, almost jumped out of his skin. I think he's still sorry I talked him into having Katie. I dropped the subject immediately, not wanting to provoke another of his nihilistic tirades.

Would I really want another baby at this juncture? Does it make any sense at all, given the situation in which we find ourselves? Putting aside for the moment any personal reasons I might have for giving birth to a third child, there is a powerful biological argument for continuing to reproduce. Our best guess at our destiny is that we will never have any future contact with other members of the human species. If we are the last in our line, it would be wise for us to pay heed to one of the fundamental tenets of evolution: maximum genetic variation produces the highest probability of survival in an uncertain environment.

After I had thoroughly awakened from my dream last night, my mind carried the scenario even further. Suppose, I told myself, that Rama is really not going anywhere, at least not soon, and that we will spend the rest of our lives in our current conditions. Then, in all likelihood, Simone and Katie will outlive the three of us adults. What will happen next? I asked. Unless we have somehow saved some semen from either Michael or Richard (and both the biological and sociological problems would be formidable), my daughters will not be able to reproduce. They themselves may arrive at paradise or nirvana or some other world, but they will eventually perish and the genes they carry will die with them.

But suppose, I continued, that I give birth to a son. Then the two girls will have a male companion their age and the problem of succeeding generations will be dramatically lessened.

It was at this point in my thought pattern that a truly crazy idea jumped into my brain. One of my major areas of specialty during my medical training was genetics, especially hereditary defects. I remembered my case studies of the royal families of Europe between the fifteenth and eighteenth centuries and the many 'inferior' individuals produced from the excessive inbreeding. A son produced by Richard and me would have the same genetic ingredients as Simone and Katie. That son's children with either of the girls, our grand-children, would have a very high risk of defects. A son produced by *Michael* and me, on the other hand, would share only half his genes with the girls and, if my memory of the data serves me correctly, his offspring with Simone or Katie would have a drastically lower defect risk.

I immediately rejected this outrageous thought. It did not, however, go away. Later in the night, when I should have been sleeping, my mind returned to the same topic. What if I become pregnant by Richard again, I asked myself, and I have a third girl? Then it will be necessary to repeat the entire process. I'm already forty-one. How many more years do I have before the onset of menopause, even if I delay it chemically? On the basis of the two data points thus far, there is no evidence that Richard can produce a boy at all. We could establish a laboratory to permit male sperm selection from his semen, but it would take a monumental effort on our part and months of detailed interaction with the Ramans. And there would still remain the issues of sperm preservation and delivery to the ovaries.

I thought through the various proven techniques of altering the natural sex selection process (the man's diet, type and frequency of intercourse, timing with respect to ovulation, etc.) and concluded that Richard and I would probably have a good chance of producing a boy naturally, if we were very careful. But at the back of my mind the thought persisted that the odds would be still more favourable if Michael were the father. After all, he had two sons (out of three children) as a result of random behaviour. However much I might be able to improve the probabilities with Richard, the same techniques with Michael would virtually guarantee a son.

Before I fell back asleep I considered briefly the impracticality of the entire idea. A foolproof method of artificial insemination (which I would be required to supervise, even though I was the subject) would have to be devised. Could we do that, in our current situation, and *guarantee* both the sex and the health of the embryo? Even hospitals on Earth, with all the resources at their command, are not always successful. The other alternative was to have sex with Michael. Although I did not find that thought unpleasant, the sociological ramifications seemed so great that I abandoned the idea altogether.

(Six hours later.) The men surprised me tonight with a special dinner. Michael is becoming quite a cook. The food tasted, as advertised, like beef Wellington, although it looked more like creamed spinach. Richard and Michael also served a red liquid that was labeled wine. It wasn't terrible, so I drank it, discovering much to my surprise that it contained some alcohol and I actually felt a buzz.

All of us adults were, in fact, slightly tipsy by the end of the dinner. The girls, Simone especially, were puzzled by our behaviour. During our dessert of coconut pie, Michael told me that forty-one was a 'very special number'. He then explained to me that it was the largest prime that started a long quadratic sequence of other primes. When I asked him what a quadratic sequence was, he laughed and said he didn't know. He did, however, write out the forty-element sequence he was talking about: 41, 43, 47, 53, 61, 71, 83, 97, 113 ... concluding with the number 1,601. He assured me that every one of the forty numbers in the sequence was a prime. 'Therefore,' he said with a twinkle, 'forty-one must be a magic number.'

While I was laughing, our resident genius Richard looked at the numbers and then, after no more than a minute of playing with his computer, explained to Michael and me why the sequence was called 'quadratic'. 'The second differences are constant,' he said, showing us what he meant with an example. 'Therefore the entire sequence can be generated by a simple quadratic expression. Take $f(N) = N^2 - N + 41$,' he continued, 'where N is any integer from 0 to 40. That function will generate your entire sequence.

'Better still,' he said with a laugh, 'consider $f(N) = N^2 - 81N + 1681$, where N is an integer running from 1 to 80. This quadratic formula starts at the tail end of your string of numbers, $f(1) = 1601$, and proceeds through the sequence in decreasing order first. It reverses itself at $f(40) = f(41) = 41$, and then generates your entire array of numbers again in increasing order.'

Richard smiled. Michael and I just stared at him in awe.

13 MARCH 2205

Katie had her second birthday today and everyone was in a good mood, Richard especially. He does like his little girl, even though she manipulates him outrageously. For her birthday he took her over to the octospider lair cover and they rattled the grills together. Both Michael and I expressed our disapproval, but Richard laughed and winked at Katie.

At dinner Simone played a short piano piece that Michael has been teaching her and Richard served a quite remarkable wine, a Raman Chardonnay, he called it, with our poached salmon. In Rama poached salmon looks like scrambled eggs on Earth, which is a bit confusing, but we continue to adhere to our convention of labelling foods according to their nutritional content.

I'm feeling buoyantly happy, even though I must admit that I am slightly nervous about my coming discussion with Richard. He is very upbeat at the present time, mostly because he's busily working on not one, but two major projects. Not only is he making liquid concoctions whose taste and alcohol content rival the fine wines of the planet Earth, but also he is creating a new set of twenty-centimetre robots based on the characters from the plays of the twentieth century Nobel laureate Samuel Beckett. Michael and I have been urging Richard to reincarnate his Shakespeare troupe for several years, but the memory of his lost friends has always stopped him. But a new playwright – that's a different question. He has already finished the four characters in *Endgame*. Tonight the children laughed gleefully when the old folks 'Nagg' and 'Nell' rose out of their tiny garbage cans shouting, 'My Pap. Bring me my Pap.'

I am definitely going to present to Richard my idea of having a son with Michael as the father. He will, I am certain, appreciate the logic and the science of the suggestion, although I can hardly expect him to be terribly enthusiastic about it. Of course I have not mentioned my idea at all to Michael yet. He does know I have something serious on my mind, however, because I have asked him if he would look after the girls this afternoon while Richard and I go topside for a picnic and a talk.

My nervousness about this issue is probably unwarranted. It is doubtless based on a definition of proper behaviour that simply has no application to our present situation. Richard is feeling good these days. His wit has been very sharp lately. He may throw a few sharp zingers at me during our discussion, but I bet he will be in favour of the idea at the end.

8

This has been the spring of our discontent. Oh, Lord, what fools we mortals be. Richard, Richard, please come back.

Where to start? And how to begin? Do I dare to eat a peach? In a minute there are visions and revisions that a minute ... In the next room Michael and Simone come and go, talking of Michelangelo.

My father always told me that everyone makes mistakes. Why did mine have to be so colossal? The idea made good sense. My left brain said it was logical. But deep down inside the human being, reason does not always carry the day. Emotions are not rational. Jealousy is not the output of a computer program.

There were plenty of warnings. That first afternoon, as we sat beside the Cylindrical Sea and had our 'picnic,' I could tell from Richard's eyes that there was a problem. Uh-oh, back off, Nicole, I said to myself.

But later he seemed so reasonable. 'Of course,' Richard said that same afternoon, 'what you are suggesting is the genetically correct thing to do. I will go with you to tell Michael. Let's get this over as fast as we can, hoping one encounter will be all that is necessary.'

I felt elated at the time. It never occurred to me that Michael might balk. 'It would be a sin,' he said in the evening, after the girls were asleep, within seconds after he understood what we were proposing.

Richard took the offensive, arguing that the entire concept of sin was an anachronism even on Earth and that Michael was just being silly. 'Do you really want me to do this?' Michael asked Richard directly at the end of the conversation.

'No,' Richard answered after a brief hesitation, 'but it's clearly in the best interests of our children.' I should have paid more attention to the 'no'.

It never occurred to me that my plan might not work. I tracked my ovulation cycle very carefully. When the designated night finally arrived, I informed Richard and he stalked out of the lair for one of his long hikes in Rama. Michael was nervous and fighting his feelings of guilt, but even in my worst doomsday scenario I had not imagined that he might be unable to have intercourse with me.

When we took off our clothes (in the dark, so Michael would not feel uncomfortable) and lay beside each other on the mats, I discovered that his body was rigid and tense. I kissed him on the forehead and cheeks. Then I tried to loosen him up by rubbing his back and neck. After about thirty minutes of touching (but nothing that would be considered sexual foreplay), I snuggled my body against his in a suggestive way. It was obvious we had a problem. His penis was still completely flaccid.

I did not know what to do. My initial thought, which of course was completely irrational, was that Michael did not find me attractive. I felt terrible, as if someone had slapped me in the face. All my repressed feelings of inadequacy burst to the surface and I was surprisingly angry. Luckily I didn't say anything (neither of us talked during this entire period) and Michael couldn't see my face in the dark. But my body language must have signaled my disappointment.

'I'm sorry,' he said softly.

'It's all right,' I answered, trying to be nonchalant.

I propped myself up on an elbow and caressed his forehead with my other hand. I expanded my light massage, letting my fingers ran gently around his face, neck, and shoulders. Michael was completely passive. He lay on his back without moving, his eyes closed most of the time. Although I am certain he was enjoying the rub, he neither said anything nor uttered any murmurs of pleasure. By this time I was becoming exceedingly anxious. I found myself wanting Michael to caress *me*, to tell *me* that I was all right.

At length I rolled over with part of my body across his. I let my breasts drop gently on his torso while my right hand played with the hair on his chest. I leaned up to kiss him on the lips, intending to arouse him elsewhere with my left hand, but he pulled away quickly and then sat up.

'I can't do this,' Michael said, shaking his head.

'Why not?' I asked quietly, my body now in an awkward position beside him.

'It's wrong,' he answered with great solemnity.

I tried several times in the next few minutes to start a conversation, but Michael did not want to talk. Eventually, because there was nothing else for me to do, I dressed silently in the dark. Michael barely managed a meagre 'Good night' when I left.

I did not return immediately to my room. Once I was out in the corridor I realised that I was not yet ready to confront Richard. I leaned against the wall and struggled with the powerful emotions engulfing me. Why had I assumed everything would be so simple? And what would I tell Richard now?

From the sound of Richard's breathing I knew that he was not asleep when I entered our room. If I had had more courage, I might have told him right then what had happened with Michael. But it was easier to ignore it for the moment. That was a serious mistake.

The next two days were strained. Nobody mentioned what Richard had once referred to as the 'fertilization event.' The men tried to act as if everything was normal. After dinner the second night I persuaded Richard to take a walk with me while Michael put the girls to bed.

Richard was explaining the chemistry of his new wine fermentation process as we stood on the ramparts overlooking the Cylindrical Sea. At one point I interrupted him and took his hand. 'Richard,' I said, my eyes searching for love and reassurance in his, 'this is very difficult ...' My voice trailed off.

'What is it, Nikki?' he asked, forcing a smile.

'Well,' I answered, 'it's Michael. You see,' I blurted out, 'nothing really happened ... He couldn't ...'

Richard stared at me for a long time. 'You mean he's impotent?' he asked.

I nodded first and then completely confused him by shaking my head. 'Probably not really,' I stammered, 'but he was the other night with me. I think he's just too tense or feels guilty or maybe it's been too long ...' I stopped myself, realizing I was saying too much.

Richard gazed across the sea for what seemed like an eternity. 'Do you want to try again?' he said eventually in a completely expressionless voice. He did not turn to look at me.

'I ... I don't know,' I answered. I squeezed his hand. I was going to say something else, to ask him if he could deal with the situation if I tried one more time, but Richard abruptly walked away from me. 'Let me know when you make up your mind,' he said tersely.

For a week or two I was certain that I was going to abandon the entire idea. Slowly, very slowly, a semblance of cheer returned to our little family. The night after my period was over Richard and I made love twice for the first time in a year. He seemed especially pleased and was very talkative as we cuddled after the second intercourse.

'I must say I was really worried there for a while,' he said. 'The thought of your having sex with Michael, even for supposedly logical reasons, was driving me crazy. I know it doesn't make rational sense, but I was terribly afraid that you might like it – do you understand? – and that somehow our relationship might be affected.'

Richard was obviously assuming that I wasn't going to try again to become pregnant with Michael's child. I didn't argue with him that night because I too was momentarily content. A few days later, however, when I began reading about impotence in my medical books, I realised myself that I was still determined to proceed with my plan.

During the week before I ovulated again, Richard was busy brewing his wine (and maybe tasting it a bit more often than necessary – more than once he was a little drunk before dinner) and creating little robots out of Samuel Beckett's characters. My attention was focused on impotence. My curriculum at medical school had virtually ignored the subject. And since my own sexual experience has been comparatively limited, I had never personally been exposed to it before. I was surprised to learn that impotence is an extremely common malady, primarily psychological but very often with an exacerbating physical component as well, and that there are many well-defined treatment patterns, all of which focus on lessening the 'performance anxiety' in the man.

Richard saw me preparing my urine for ovulation testing one morning. He didn't say anything, but I could tell from his face that he was hurt and disappointed. I wanted to reassure him, but the children were in the room and I was afraid there might be a scene.

I didn't tell Michael that we were going to make a second attempt. I thought that his anxiety would be reduced if he didn't have time to think about it. My plan almost worked. I went with Michael to his room, after we had put the children to bed, and explained to him what was happening while we undressed. He had the beginnings of an erection and, despite his mild protests, I moved quickly to sustain it. I am certain that we would have been successful if Katie had not started screaming 'Mommy, Mommy' just when we were ready to begin intercourse.

Of course I left Michael and ran down the corridor to the nursery. Richard was already there. He was holding Katie in his arms. Simone was sitting up on her mat, rubbing her eyes. The three of them all stared at my naked body in the doorway. 'I had a terrible dream,' Katie said, holding tightly to Richard. 'An octospider was eating me.'

I walked into the room. 'Are you feeling better now?' I asked, reaching out to take Katie. Richard continued to hold her and she made no effort to come to me. After an uncomfortable moment I went over to Simone and draped my arm across her shoulder.

'Where are your pajamas, Mother?' my four-year-old asked. Most of the time both Richard and I sleep in the Raman version of pajamas. The girls are quite accustomed to my naked body – the three of us shower together virtually every day – but at night, when I come into the nursery, I'm almost always wearing my pyjamas.

I was going to give Simone a flippant answer when I noticed that Richard too was staring at me. His eyes were definitely hostile. 'I can take care of things here,' he said harshly. 'Why don't you finish what you were doing?'

I returned to Michael to try one more time to achieve intercourse and conception. It was a bad decision. I made a futile attempt to arouse Michael for a couple of minutes and then he pushed my hand away. 'It's useless,' he said. 'I'm almost sixty-three years old and I haven't had intercourse for five years. I never masturbate and I consciously try not to think about sex. My erection earlier was just a temporary stroke of luck.' He was silent for almost a minute. 'I'm sorry, Nicole,' he then added, 'but it's not going to work.'

We lay silently side by side for several minutes. I was dressing and preparing

572

to leave when I noticed that Michael had fallen into the rhythmic breathing pattern that precedes sleep. I suddenly remembered from my reading that men with psychological impotence often have erections during their sleep, and my mind dreamed up another crazy idea. I laid awake beside Michael for quite a while, waiting until I was certain he was in a deep sleep.

I stroked him very softly at first. I was delighted that he responded very quickly. After a while I slightly increased the vigour of my massage, but I was extremely careful not to wake him up. When he was definitely ready I prepared myself and moved over on top of him. I was only moments away from achieving intercourse when I jostled him too roughly and he awakened. I tried to continue, but in my haste I must have hurt him, for he uttered a yelp and looked at me with wild, startled eyes. Within seconds his erection had vanished.

I rolled over on my back and heaved a deep sigh. I was terribly disappointed. Michael was asking me questions, but I was too distraught to answer. Tears suffused my eyes. I dressed in a hurry, kissed Michael lightly on the forehead, and stumbled out into the corridor. I stood there for another five minutes before I had the strength to return to Richard.

My husband was still working. He was down on his knees beside Pozzo, from *Waiting for Godot*. The little robot was in the middle of one of his long, rambling speeches about the uselessness of everything. Richard ignored me at first. Then, after silencing Pozzo, he turned around. 'Do you think you took long enough?' he asked sarcastically.

'It still didn't work,' I answered dejectedly. 'I guess ...'

'Don't give me that shit,' Richard suddenly shouted angrily. 'I'm not *that* stupid. Do you expect me to believe that you spent *two hours* naked with him and nothing happened? I know about you women. You think that ...'

I don't remember the rest of what he said. I do recall my terror as he advanced toward me, his eyes full of anger. I thought he was going to hit me and I braced myself. Tears burst from my eyes and rolled down my cheeks. Richard called me horrible names and even made a racist slur. He was insane. When he raised his arm in a fury I bolted from the room, rushing down the corridor toward the stairs to New York. I nearly ran over little Katie, who had been awakened by the shouting and was standing dumbfounded at the door of the nursery.

It was light in Rama. I walked around, crying intermittently, for most of an hour. I was furious with Richard, but I was also deeply unhappy with myself. In his rage Richard had said that I was 'obsessed' with this idea of mine and that it was just a 'clever excuse' to have intercourse with Michael so that I could be the 'queen bee of the hive'. I hadn't replied to any of his rantings. Was there even a smidgin of truth in his accusation? Was any part of my excitement about the project a desire on my part to have sex with Michael?

I convinced myself that my motivations had all been proper, whatever that means, but that I had been incredibly stupid about this entire affair from the very beginning. I, of all people, should have known that what I was suggesting was impossible. Certainly after I saw Richard's initial response (and Michael's too, for that matter), I should have immediately forsaken the idea. Maybe Richard was right in some ways. Maybe I am stubborn, even obsessed with the idea of providing maximum genetic variation to our offspring. But I know for certain that I did not concoct the entire thing just so I could have sex with Michael.

It was dark in our room when I returned. I changed into my pyjamas and plopped down, exhausted, on my mat. After a few seconds Richard rolled over, hugged me fiercely, and said, 'My darling, Nicole, I'm so, so sorry. Please forgive me.'

I have not heard his voice since then. He has been gone now for six days. I slept soundly that night, unaware that Richard was packing his things and leaving me a note. At seven o'clock in the morning, an alarm sounded. There was a message filling the black screen. It said, 'FOR NICOLE DES JARDINS ONLY – Push K when you want to read.' The children were not yet awake, so I pushed the K button on the keyboard.

'Dearest Nicole,' the note began, 'this is the most difficult letter I have ever written in my life. I am temporarily leaving you and the family. I know that this will create considerable hardship for you, Michael, and the girls, but believe me, it is the only way. After last night it is apparent to me that there is no other solution.

'My darling, I love you with all my heart and know, when my brain is in control of my emotions, that what you are trying to do is in the best interests of the family. I feel terrible about the accusations that I made last night. I feel even worse about all the names I called you, especially the racial epithets and my frequent use of the word "bitch". I hope that you can forgive me, even though I'm not certain I can forgive myself, and will remember my love for you instead of my insane, unbridled anger.

'Jealousy is a terrible thing. "It doth mock the meat it feeds upon" is an understatement. Jealousy is completely consuming, totally irrational, and absolutely debilitating. The most wonderful people in the world are nothing but raging animals when trapped in the throes of jealousy.

'Nicole, darling, I did not tell you the complete truth last year about the end of my marriage to Sarah. I suspected for months that she was seeing other men on those nights she was spending in London. There were plenty of tell-tale signs – her uneven interest in sex, new clothes that were never worn with me, sudden fascinations with new positions or different sexual practices, phone calls with nobody on the other end – but I loved her so madly, and was so certain that our marriage would be over if I confronted her, that I didn't do anything until I was enraged by my jealousy.

'Actually, as I would lie in my bed at Cambridge and picture Sarah having intercourse with another man, my jealousy would become so powerful that I could not fall asleep until I had imagined Sarah dead. When Mrs Sinclair called me that night and I knew I could no longer pretend that Sarah was faithful, I went to London with the express intention of killing both my wife and her lover.

'Luckily I had no gun and my rage upon seeing them together made me forget the knife I had placed in the pocket of my overcoat. But I definitely *would* have killed them if the mêlée had not aroused the neighbours and I had not been restrained.

'You may be wondering what all this has to do with you. You see, my love, each of us develops definitive patterns of behaviour in his life. My pattern of insane jealousy was already present before I met you. During the two times that you have gone to be intimate with Michael, I have been unable to stop the memories of Sarah from returning. I *know* you are not Sarah, and that you are not cheating on me, but nevertheless, my emotions return in that same lunatic pattern. In a very strange sense, because the idea of your betraying me is so impossible to conceive, I feel worse, *more* frightened, when you are with Michael than I did when Sarah was with Hugh Sinclair or any of her other actor friends.

'I hope some of this makes sense. I am leaving because I cannot control my jealousy, even though I acknowledge it to be irrational. I do not want to become like my father, drinking away my misery and ruining the lives of everyone around me. I sense that you will achieve this conception, one way or another, and I would prefer to spare you my bad behaviour during the process.

'I expect that I will be back soon, unless I encounter unforeseen dangers in my explorations, but I do not know exactly when. I need a period of healing, so that I can again be a solid contributor to our family. Tell the girls that I am off on a journey. Be kind especially to Katie – she will miss me the most.

'I love you, Nicole. I know that it will be difficult for you to understand why I am leaving, but please try,

Richard.'

13 MAY 2205

Today I spent five hours topside in New York searching for Richard. I went over to the pits, to both lattices, to all three plazas. I walked the perimeters of the island along the ramparts. I shook the grill on the octospider lair and descended briefly into the land of the avians. Everywhere I called his name. I remember that Richard found me five years ago because of the navigation beacon he had placed on his Shakespearean robot Prince Hal. I could have used a beacon today.

There were no signs of Richard anywhere. I believe that he has left the island. Richard is an excellent swimmer – he could easily have made it across to the Northern Hemicylinder – but what about the weird creatures inhabiting the Cylindrical Sea? Did they let him across?

Come back, Richard. I miss you. I love you.

He had obviously been thinking about leaving for several days. He had updated and arranged our catalogue of interactions with the Ramans to make it as easy as possible for Michael and me. He took the largest of our packs and his best friend TB, but he left the Beckett robots behind.

Our family meals have been dreadful affairs since Richard left. Katie is nearly always angry. She wants to know when her daddy will be back and why he has been gone so long. Michael and Simone endure their sorrow in quiet. Their bond continues to deepen – they seem to be able to comfort one another quite well. For my part, I have tried to pay more attention to Katie, but I am no substitute for her beloved Daddy.

The nights are terrible. I do not sleep. I go over and over all my interactions with Richard the last two months and relive all my mistakes. His letter before departing was very revealing. I never would have thought that his earlier difficulties with Sarah would have had the slightest impact on his marriage to me, but I recognise now what he was saying about patterns.

There are patterns in my emotional life as well. My mother's death when I was only ten taught me the terror of abandonment. Fear of losing a strong connection has made intimacy and trust difficult for me. Since my mother, I have lost Genevieve, my father, and now, at least temporarily, Richard. Each time the pattern recurs all the chimeras of the past are reactivated. When I cried myself to sleep two nights ago, I realised that I was missing not only Richard, but also Mother, Genevieve, and my marvellous father. I was feeling each of those losses all over again. So I can understand how my being with Michael could trigger Richard's painful memories of Sarah.

The process of learning never stops. Here I am, forty-one years old, and I am discovering another facet of the truth about human relationships. I have obviously wounded Richard deeply. It doesn't matter that there is no logical basis for Richard's concern that my sleeping with Michael might lead to an alienation of my affection for him. Logic has no application here. Perception and feeling are what count.

I had forgotten how devastating loneliness can be. Richard and I have been together for five years. He might not have had all the attributes of my Prince Charming, but he has been a wonderful companion and is, without a doubt, the smartest human being I have ever met. It would be an immeasurable tragedy if he were never to return. I grieve when I think, even for a moment, that I may have seen him for the last time.

At nights, when I am especially lonely, I often read poetry. Baudelaire and Eliot have been my favourites since my university days, but the last few evenings I have been finding comfort in the poems of Benita Garcia. During her days as a cadet at the Space Academy in Colorado, her wild passion for life caused her lots of pain. She threw herself into her cosmonaut studies and the arms of the men surrounding her with equal élan. When Benita was called before the cadet disciplinary committee for no transgression except her uninhibited sexuality, she realised how schizophrenic men were where sex was concerned.

Most of the literary critics prefer her first volume of poetry, *Dreams of a Mexican Girl*, which established her reputation when she was still a teenager, over the wiser, less lyrical book of poems she published during her final year at the academy. With Richard now gone and my mind still struggling to understand what has really occurred during these last months, it is Benita's poems of late adolescent angst and questioning that resonate with me. Her path to adulthood was extremely difficult. Although her work remained rich in images, Benita was no longer Pollyanna walking among the ruins at Uxmal. Tonight I read several times one of her university poems that I particularly like.

> My dresses brighten up my room,
> Like desert flowers after rain.
> You come tonight, my newest love,
> But which me do you want to see?
> The pale pastels are best for books,
> My blues and greens, an evening make,
> As friend, or even wife to be.
> But if it's sex that's in your mind,
> Then red or black and darkened eyes,
> Become the whore that I must be.
>
> My childhood dreams were not like this,
> My prince came only for a kiss,
> Then carried me away from pain,
> Can I not see him once again?
> The masks offend me, college boy,
> I wear my dress without much joy.
> The price I pay to hold your hand,
> Belittles me as you have planned.

9

14 DECEMBER 2205

I guess I should celebrate, but I feel that I have won a pyrrhic victory. I am finally pregnant with Michael's child. But what a cost. We still have heard nothing from Richard and I fear that I may have alienated Michael as well.

Michael and I each separately accepted the full responsibility for Richard's departure. I dealt with my culpability as well as I could, recognizing that I would have to put it behind me to be any kind of meaningful mother to the girls. Michael, on the other hand, responded to Richard's action and his own guilt by pouring himself into religious devotion. He is still reading his Bible at least twice every day. He prays before and after every meal, and often chooses not to take part in family activities so that he can 'communicate' with God. The word 'atonement' is currently very big in Michael's vocabulary.

He has swept Simone along in his reborn Christian zeal. My mild protests are essentially ignored. She loves the story of Jesus, even though she can't have more than the slightest notion of what it is really about. The miracles especially fascinate Simone. Like most children, she has no difficulty suspending her disbelief. Her mind never asks 'how' when Jesus walks on the water or turns the water into wine.

My comments are not completely fair. I'm probably jealous of the rapport that exists between Michael and Simone. As her mother I should be delighted that they are so compatible. At least they have each other. Try as we might, poor Katie and I remain unable to make that deep connection.

Part of the problem is that Katie and I are both extremely stubborn. Although she is only two and a half years old, she already wants to control her own life. Take something simple, for example, like the planned set of activities for the day. I have been creating the schedules for everybody in the family since our first days in Rama. Nobody else has ever argued seriously with me, not even Richard. Michael and Simone always accept whatever I recommend – as long as there is ample unstructured time.

But Katie is a different story. If I schedule a walk topside in New York before an alphabet lesson, she wants to change the order. If I plan chicken for dinner, she wants pork or beef. We start virtually every morning with a fight about the activities for the day. When she doesn't like my decisions, Katie sulks, or pouts, or cries for her 'Daddy.' It really hurts when she calls for Richard.

Michael says that I should acquiesce to her desires. He insists that it's just a phase of growing up. But when I point out to him that neither Genevieve nor Simone were ever like Katie, he smiles and shrugs.

Michael and I do not always agree on parenting techniques. We have had several interesting discussions about family life in our bizarre circumstances. Toward the end of one of the conversations, I was slightly miffed about Michael's assertion that I was 'too strict' with the girls, so I decided to bring up the religion issue. I asked Michael why it was so important to him that Simone learn about the minutiae in Jesus' life.

'Someone has to carry on the tradition,' he said vaguely.

'So you believe that there will be a tradition to carry on, that we are not going to drift forever in space and die one by one in terrifying loneliness.'

'I believe that God has a plan for all human beings,' he answered.

'But what is His plan for us?' I asked.

'We don't know,' Michael replied. 'Any more than those billions of people still back on Earth know what His plan is for them. The process of living is searching for His plan.'

I shook my head and Michael continued. 'You see, Nicole, it should be much easier for us. We have far fewer distractions. There is no excuse for our not remaining close to God. That's why my earlier preoccupations with food and art history are so difficult to forgive. In Rama, human beings have to make a major effort to fill up their time with something *other* than prayer and devotion.'

I admit that his certitude annoys me at times. In our present circumstances, the life of Jesus seems to have no more relevance than the life of Attila the Hun or any other human being who has ever been alive on that distant planet two light-years away. We are no longer part of the human race. We are either doomed, or the beginning of what will essentially be a new species. Did Jesus die for all our sins as well, those of us who will never see the Earth again?

If Michael had not been a Catholic and programmed from birth in favour of procreation, I never would have convinced him to conceive a child. He had a hundred reasons why it was not the right thing to do. But in the end, maybe because I was disturbing his nightly devotions with my persistent attempts to persuade him, he finally consented. He warned me that it was highly likely that 'it would never work' and that he 'would not take any responsibility' for my frustration.

It took us three months to produce an embryo. During the first two ovulation cycles I was unable to arouse him. I tried laughter, body massage, music, food – everything mentioned in any of the articles about impotence. His guilt and tension were always stronger than my ardour. Fantasy finally provided the solution. When I suggested to Michael one night that he should imagine I was his wife Kathleen throughout the entire affair, he was finally able to sustain an erection. The mind is indeed a wonderful creation.

Even with fantasy, making love with Michael was not an easy task. In the first place, and this is probably an unkind thing for me to say, his preparations alone were enough to put any ordinary woman out of the mood. Just before he took off his clothes, Michael always offered a prayer to God. What did he pray for? It would be fascinating to know the answer.

Eleanor of Aquitaine's first husband, Louis VII of France, had been raised as a monk and only became king because of a historical accident. In my father's novel about Eleanor there is a long interior monologue in which she complains about making love 'surrounded by solemnity and piety and the coarse cloth of the Cistercians'. She longed for gaiety and laughter in the bedroom, for bawdy talk and wanton passion. I can understand why she divorced Louis and married Henry Plantagenet.

So I am now pregnant with the boychild (I hope) who will bring genetic variation to our progeny. It has been quite a struggle and almost certainly not worth it. Because of my desire to have Michael's child, Richard is gone and Michael is, at least temporarily, no longer the close friend and companion that he was during our first years on Rama. I have paid the price for my success. Now I must hope that this spacecraft does indeed have a destination.

1 MARCH 2206

I repeated the partial genome test this morning to verify my initial results. There is no doubt about it. Our unborn baby boy definitely has Whittingham's syndrome. Fortunately there are no other identifiable defects, but Whittingham's is bad enough.

I showed the data to Michael when we had a few moments alone after breakfast. At first he didn't understand what I was telling him, but when I used the word retarded, he reacted immediately. I could tell that he was envisioning a child who would be completely unable to take care of himself. His concerns were only partially allayed when I explained that Whittingham's is nothing more than a learning disability, a simple failure of the electrochemical processes in the brain to operate properly.

When I performed the first partial genome test last week, I suspected Whittingham's, but since there was a possible ambiguity in the results, I didn't say anything to Michael. Before drawing a second amniotic sample, I wanted to review what was known about the condition. My abridged medical encyclopedia unfortunately did not contain enough information to satisfy me.

This afternoon, while Katie was napping, Michael and I asked Simone if she would read a book in the nursery for an hour or so. Our perfect angel readily complied. Michael was much calmer than he had been in the morning.

He acknowledged that he had been devastated at first by the news about Benjy (Michael wants to name the child Benjamin Ryan O'Toole, after his grandfather). Apparently reading the Book of Job had played a major role in helping him regain his perspective.

I explained to Michael that Benjy's mental development would be slow and tedious. He was comforted, however, when I informed him that many Whittingham's sufferers had eventually achieved twelve-year-old equivalency after twenty years of schooling. I assured Michael there would be no physical signs of the defect, as there are in Down's, and that since Whittingham's is a blocked recessive trait, there was little likelihood that any possible offspring would be affected before the third generation at the earliest.

'Is there any way of knowing which one of us has the syndrome in our genes?' Michael asked when we were near the end of our conversation.

'No,' I replied. 'It's a very difficult disorder to isolate because it apparently arises from several different defective genes. Only if the syndrome is active is the diagnosis straightforward. Even on Earth attempts to identify carriers have not been successful.'

I started to tell him that since the disease was first diagnosed in 2068, there have been almost no cases in either Africa or Asia. It has been basically a Caucasian disorder, with the highest frequency of occurrence in Ireland. I decided Michael would learn this information soon enough (it is all in the main article in the medical encyclopedia – which he is reading now), and I didn't want him to feel any worse than he already did.

'Is there any cure?' he asked next.

'None for us,' I said, shaking my head. 'There was some indication in the last decade that genetic counter-measures could be effective, if used during the second trimester of pregnancy. However, the procedure is complicated, even on Earth, and can result in losing the foetus altogether.'

That would have been a perfect time in the discussion for Michael to mention the word 'abortion'. He didn't. His set of beliefs is so steadfast and unwavering that I'm certain he never even considered it. For him, abortion is an absolute wrong, on Rama as well as Earth. I found myself wondering if there were any conditions under which Michael would have considered an abortion. What if the baby had Down's syndrome and also was blind? Or had multiple congenital problems that guaranteed an early death?

If Richard had been here, we would have had a logical discussion about the advantages and disadvantages of an abortion. He would have created one of his famous Ben Franklin sheets, with pros and cons listed separately on the two sides of the large screen. I would have added a long list of emotional reasons (which Richard would have omitted in his original list) for not having an abortion, and in the end we almost certainly would have all agreed to bring Benjy into Rama. It would have been a rational, community decision.

I want to have this baby. But I also want Michael to reaffirm his commitment as Benjy's father. A discussion of the possibility of abortion would have elicited that renewed commitment. Blind acceptance of the rules of God or the church or any structured dogma can sometimes make it too easy for an individual to withhold his own support for a specific decision. I hope that Michael is not that kind of person.

10

Benjy came early. Despite my repeated assurances that he would look perfectly healthy, Michael seemed relieved when the boy was born three days ago with no physical abnormalities. It was another easy birth. Simone was surprisingly helpful during both the labour and delivery. For a girl who is not yet six years old, she is extremely mature.

Benjy also has blue eyes, but they're not as light as Katie's and I don't think they will stay blue. His skin is light brown, just a little darker than Katie's, but lighter than mine or Simone's. He weighed three and a half kilograms at birth and was fifty-two centimetres long.

Our world remains unchanged. We don't talk about it very much, but all of us except Katie have given up hope that Richard will ever return. We are headed for Raman winter again, with the long nights and the shorter days. Periodically either Michael or I goes topside and searches for some sign of Richard, but it's a mechanical ritual. We don't really expect to find anything. He has been gone now for sixteen months.

Michael and I now take turns computing our trajectory with the orbit determination program that Richard designed. In the beginning it took us several weeks to figure out how to use it, despite the fact that Richard had left explicit instructions with us. We reverify once a week that we are still headed in the direction of Sirius, with no other star system along our path.

Despite Benjy's presence, it seems that I have more time to myself than I have ever had before. I have been reading voraciously and have rekindled my fascination for the two heroines who dominated my adolescent mind and imagination. Why have Joan of Arc and Eleanor of Aquitaine always appealed so much to me? Because not only did they both display inner strength and self-sufficiency, but also each woman succeeded in a male-dominated world by ultimately relying on her own abilities.

I was a very lonely teenager. My physical surroundings at Beauvois were magnificent and my father's love was overflowing, but I spent virtually my entire adolescence by myself. In the back of my mind I was always terrified that death or marriage would take my precious father away from me. I wanted to make myself more self-contained to avoid the pain that would occur if I were ever separated from Father. Joan and Eleanor were perfect role models. Even today, I find reassurance in reading about their lives. Neither woman allowed the world around her to define what was really important in life.

Everyone's health continues to be good. This past spring, as much to keep myself busy as anything, I inserted a set of the leftover biometry probes in each of us and monitored the data for a few weeks. The monitoring process reminded me of the days of the Newton mission – can it really be more than six years since the twelve of us left the Earth to rendezvous with Rama?

Anyway, Katie was fascinated by the biometry. She would sit beside me while I was scanning Simone or Michael and ask dozens of questions about the data on the displays. In no time at all she understood how the system worked and what the warning files were all about. Michael has commented that she is extraordinarily bright. Like her father. Katie still misses Richard terribly.

Although Michael talks about feeling ancient, he is in excellent shape for a sixty-four-year-old man. He is very concerned about being physically active enough for the children and has been jogging twice a week since the beginning of my pregnancy. Twice a week. What a funny concept. We have held faithfully to our Earth calendar, even though it has absolutely no meaning here on Rama. The other night Simone asked about days, months, and years. As Michael was explaining the rotation of the Earth, the seasons of the year, and the orbit of the Earth around the Sun, I suddenly had a vision of a magnificent Utah sunset that I had shared with Genevieve on our trip to the American west. I wanted to tell Simone about it. But how can you explain a sunset to someone who has not seen the Sun?

The calendar reminds us of what we were. If we ever arrive at a new planet, with a real day and night instead of this artificial one in Rama, then we will most certainly abandon the Earth calendar. But for now, holidays, the passage of months, and most especially birthdays, all remind us of our roots on that beautiful planet we can no longer even find with the best Raman telescope.

Benjy is now ready to nurse. His mental capabilities may not be the best, but he certainly has no problem letting me know when he is hungry. Michael and I, by mutual consent, have not yet told Simone and Katie about their brother's condition. That he will take attention away from them while he is an infant will be difficult enough for them to handle. That his need for attention will continue, and even grow, when he becomes a toddler and a little boy is more than they can be expected to grasp at this point in their young lives.

13 MARCH 2207

Katie is four years old today. When I asked her two weeks ago what she wanted for her birthday, she didn't hesitate a second. 'I want my Daddy back,' she said.

She is a solitary, isolated little girl. Extremely quick to learn, she is also the moodiest child I have ever had. Richard was also extremely volatile. He would sometimes be so elated and exuberant that he couldn't contain himself, usually when he had just experienced something exciting for the first time. But his depressions were formidable. There were times when he would go a week or more without laughing or even smiling.

Katie has inherited his gift for mathematics. She can already add, subtract, multiply, and divide – at least with small numbers. Simone, who is certainly no slouch, appears more evenly talented. And more generally interested in a wide range of subjects. But Katie is certainly pressing her in maths.

In the almost two years since Richard has been gone, I have tried without success to replace him in Katie's heart. The truth is that Katie and I clash. Our personalities are not compatible as mother and daughter. The individuality and wildness that I loved in Richard is threatening in Katie. Despite my best intentions, we always end up in a contest.

We could not, of course, produce Richard for Katie's birthday. But Michael and I did try very hard to have some interesting presents for her. Even though neither of us is particularly skilled at electronics, we did manage to create a small video game (it took many interactions with the Ramans to produce the right parts – and many nights working together to make something Richard probably could have finished in a day) called 'Lost in Rama'. We made it very simple, because Katie is only four years old. After playing with it for two hours she had exhausted all the options and had figured out how to get home to our lair from any starting point in Rama.

Our biggest surprise came tonight, when we asked her (this has become a tradition for us in Rama) what she would like to do on her birthday evening. 'I want to go inside the avian lair,' Katie said with a mischievous sparkle in her eyes.

We tried to talk her out of it by pointing put that the distance between the ledges was greater than her height. In response, Katie went over to the rope ladder of lattice material hanging at the side of the nursery and showed us that she could climb it. Michael smiled. 'Some things she has inherited from her mother,' he said.

'Please, Mom?' Katie then said in her precocious little voice. 'Everything else is so boring. I want to look at the tank sentry myself, from only a few metres away.'

Even though I had some misgivings, I walked over to the avian lair with Katie and told her to wait topside while I put the rope ladder in place. At the first landing, opposite the tank sentry, I stopped for a moment and looked across the chasm at that perpetual motion machine protecting the entry to the horizontal tunnel. Are you always there? I wondered. And have you ever been replaced or repaired during all this time?

'Are you ready, Mom?' I heard my daughter call from above. Before I could scramble up to meet her, Katie was already descending the ladder. I scolded her when I caught up with her at the second ledge, but she ignored me. She was terribly excited. 'Did you see, Mom?' she said. 'I did it by myself.'

I congratulated her even though my mind was still reeling from a mental picture of Katie slipping off the ladder, banging into one of the ledges, and then careening into the bottomless depths of the vertical corridor. We continued down the ladder with my helping her from below until we reached the first landing and pair of horizontal tunnels. Across the chasm the tank sentry continued its repetitive motion. Katie was ecstatic.

'What's behind that tank thing?' she asked. 'Who made it? What's it doing there? Did you really jump across this hole? ...'

In response to one of her questions, I turned and took several steps into the tunnel behind us, following my flashlight beam and assuming Katie was following me. Moments later, when I discovered that she was still standing back on the edge of the chasm, I froze with fear. I watched her pull a small object out of the pocket of her dress and throw it across the chasm at the tank sentry.

I yelled at Katie, but it was too late. The object hit the front of the tank. Immediately there was a loud pop like gunshots, and two metal projectiles smashed into the wall of the lair not more than a metre above her head.

'Yippee,' Katie shouted as I jerked her back from the abyss. I was furious. My daughter began to cry. The noise in the lair was deafening.

She stopped crying abruptly several seconds later. 'Did you hear it?' she asked.

'What?' I said, my heart still pounding wildly.

'Over there,' she said. She pointed across the vertical corridor into the blackness behind the sentry. I shone the flashlight into the void, but we could see nothing.

We both stood absolutely still, holding hands. There *was* a sound coming from the tunnel behind the sentry. But it was at the very limit of my hearing, and I could not identify it.

'It's an avian,' Katie said with conviction. 'I can hear its wings flapping. *Yippee*,' she shouted again in her loudest voice.

The sound ceased. Although we waited fifteen minutes before climbing out of the lair, we never heard anything else. Katie told Michael and Simone that we had heard an avian. I couldn't corroborate her story but chose not to argue with her. She was happy. It had been an eventful birthday.

8 MARCH 2208

Patrick Erin O'Toole, a perfectly healthy baby in every respect, was born yesterday at 2:15 in the afternoon. The proud father is holding him at this very moment, smiling as my fingers dart across the keyboard on my electronic notebook.

It is late at night now. Simone put Benjy to sleep, as she does every night at nine o'clock, and then went to bed herself. She was very tired. She took care of Benjy without any help from anyone during my surprisingly long labour. Every time I would shout, Benjy would cry out in response and Simone would try to soothe him.

Katie has already claimed Patrick as her baby brother. She is very logical. If Benjy is Simone's, then Patrick must belong to Katie. At least she is showing some interest in another member of the family.

Patrick was not planned, but both Michael and I are delighted that he showed up to join our family. His conception was sometime late last spring, probably in the first month after Michael and I started sharing his bedroom at night. It was my idea that we should sleep together, although I'm certain that Michael had thought about it as well.

On the night that Richard had been gone for exactly two years, I was completely unable to sleep. I was feeling lonely, as usual. I tried to imagine sleeping all the rest of my nights by myself and I became very despondent. Just after midnight I walked down the corridor to Michael's room.

Michael and I have been relaxed and easy with each other from the beginning this time. I guess we were both ready. After Benjy's birth Michael was very busy helping me with all the children. During that period he eased up a little on his religious activities and made himself more accessible to all of us, including me. Eventually our natural compatibility reasserted itself. All that was left was for us both to acknowledge that Richard was never going to return.

Comfortable. That's the best way to describe my relationship with Michael. With Henry, it was ecstasy. With Richard, it was passion and excitement, a wild roller-coaster ride in life and bed. Michael comforts me. We sleep holding hands, the perfect symbol for our relationship. We make love rarely, but it is enough.

I have made some concessions. I even pray some, now and then, because it makes Michael happy. For his part, he has become more tolerant about exposing the children to ideas and value systems outside of his Catholicism. We have agreed that what we are seeking is harmony and consistency in our mutual parenting.

There are six of us now, a single family of human beings closer to several other stars than we are to the planet and star of our birth. We still do not know if this giant cylinder hurtling through space is really going anywhere. At times it does not seem to matter. We have created our own world here in Rama and, although it is limited, I believe that we are happy.

11

I had forgotten what it felt like to have adrenaline coursing through my system. In the last thirty hours our calm and placid life on Rama has been utterly destroyed.

It all began with two dreams. Yesterday morning, just before I woke up, I had a dream about Richard that was extraordinarily vivid. Richard wasn't actually in my dream – I mean, he didn't appear alongside Michael, Simone, Katie, and me. But Richard's face was inset in the upper left-hand corner of my dream screen while the four of us were engaged in some normal, everyday activity. He kept calling my name over and over. His call was so loud that I could still hear it when I awakened.

I had just begun to tell Michael about the dream when Katie appeared at the doorway in her pyjamas. She was trembling and frightened. 'What is it, darling?' I asked, beckoning to her with my open arms.

She came over and hugged me tightly. 'It's Daddy,' she said. 'He was calling me last night in my dreams.'

A chill ran down my spine and Michael sat up on his mat. I comforted Katie with my words, but I was unnerved by the coincidence. Had she heard my conversation with Michael? Impossible. We had seen her the moment she arrived at our room.

After Katie returned to the nursery to change her clothes, I told Michael that I could not possibly ignore the two dreams. He and I have often discussed my occasional psychic powers. Although he generally discounts the whole idea of extrasensory perception, Michael has always admitted that it is impossible to state categorically that my dreams and visions do not foreshadow the future.

'I must go topside and look for Richard,' I told him after breakfast. Michael had expected me to make such an effort and was prepared to look after the children. But it was dark in Rama. We both agreed that it would be better if I waited until our evening, when it would again be light in the spacecraft world above our lair.

I took a long nap so that I would have plenty of energy for a thorough search. I slept fitfully, and kept dreaming that I was in danger. Before I left,

I made certain that there was a reasonably accurate graphics drawing of Richard stored in my portable computer. I wanted to be able to show the object of my quest to any avians that I might encounter.

After kissing the children good night, I headed straight for the avian lair. I was not that surprised when I found that the tank sentry was gone. Years ago, when I was first invited into the lair by one of the avian residents, the tank sentry had also not been present. Could it be that I was somehow being invited again? And what did all this have to do with my dream? My heart was pounding like crazy as I passed the room with the cistern of water and headed deeper into the tunnel that the absent sentry had usually guarded.

I never heard a sound. I walked for almost a kilometre before I came to a tall doorway on my right. I cautiously peered around the corner. The room was dark, like everywhere in the avian lair except the vertical corridor. I switched on my flashlight. The room was not very deep, maybe fifteen metres at the most, but it was extremely tall. Against the wall opposite the door were rows and rows of oval storage bins. The beam from my light showed that the rows extended all the way to the high ceiling, which must have been just under one of the plazas in New York.

It did not take me long to figure out the purpose of the room. Each of the storage bins was the size and shape of a manna melon. Of course, I thought to myself. This must have been where the food supply was kept. No wonder they didn't want anybody in here.

After verifying that all the bins were indeed empty, I started to walk back toward the vertical corridor. Then, on a hunch, I reversed my direction, passed the storage room, and continued on down the tunnel. It must go somewhere, I reasoned, or it would have ended at the melon room.

After another half a kilometre the tunnel widened gradually until it entered a large circular chamber. In the centre of the room, which had a high ceiling, was a broad domed structure. Around the walls were about twenty alcoves, cut into the walls at regular intervals. There was no light except my flashlight beam, so it took several minutes to integrate the room, with the domed building in the middle, into a composite picture.

I walked completely around the perimeter, examining the alcoves one after another. Most were empty. In one of them I found three identical tank sentries neatly arrayed against the back wall. My initial impulse was to be wary of the sentries, but it was not necessary. They were all dormant.

By far the most interesting of the alcoves, however, was the one at the centre of the room, exactly one hundred and eighty degrees around the circle from the entrance tunnel. This special alcove was carefully organised and had thick shelves cut into its walls. There were fifteen shelves in all, five each on the two sides and five more on the wall opposite the doorway to the alcove. The shelves on the sides had objects arranged on them (everything was very orderly); the shelves against the far wall each had five round pits hollowed out along their lengths.

The contents of these pits, which were each further subdivided into sections, like portions of a pie, were fascinating. One of the sections in each of the pits contained a very fine material, like ash. A second section contained one, two, or three rings, either cherry red or gold, that I immediately recognised because of their similarity to the rings we had seen around the neck of our grey velvet avian friend. There did not seem to be any particular pattern to the rest of the articles in the pits – in fact, some of the pits were empty except for the ash and the rings.

Eventually I turned around and approached the domed structure. Its front door faced the special alcove. I examined the door with my flashlight. An intricate design was carved on its rectangular surface. There were four separate panels, or quadrants, in the design. An avian was in the top left quadrant, with a manna melon in the adjacent panel, on the right. The lower two quadrants contained unfamiliar pictures. On the left side was a carving of a jointed, striped creature running on six legs. The final panel, on the bottom right, featured a large box filled with very thin mesh or webbing.

After some hesitation I pushed open the door. I nearly jumped out of my skin when a loud alarm, like a klaxon, pierced the silence. I stood inside the door without moving while the alarm sounded for almost a minute. When it was over, I still did not move. I was trying to hear if anyone (or anything) was responding to the alarm.

No sound disturbed the silence. After a few minutes I began examining the inside of the building. A transparent cube, roughly two and a half metres in each dimension, occupied the centre of the single room. The walls of the cube were stained in spots, partially obscuring my vision, but I could still see that the bottom ten centimetres were covered by a fine, dark material. The room around the cube was decorated with geometric patterns on the walls, floors, and ceiling. One of the cube faces had a narrow entryway that permitted access to the cube interior.

I went inside. The fluffy black material appeared to be ash, but it was a slightly different consistency than the similar stuff I had found in the alcove pits. My eyes followed the beam of my flashlight as it moved in an orderly pattern around the cube. Near the centre there was an object partially buried in the ash. I walked over, picked up the object, shook it off, and nearly fainted. It was Richard's robot TB.

TB was considerably altered. His exterior was blackened, his tiny control panel had melted off, and he no longer operated. But it was unmistakably him. I put the little robot to my lips and kissed him. In my mind's eye I could see him spouting one of Shakespeare's sonnets as Richard listened with rapt enjoyment.

It was obvious that TB had been in a fire. Had Richard also been trapped in an inferno inside the cube? I sifted through the ash carefully but found no bones. I did wonder, however, what it was that had burned and created all the ash. And what was TB doing inside the cube in the first place?

I was convinced that Richard was somewhere in the avian lair, so I spent another eight long hours scrambling up and down ledges and exploring tunnels. I visited all the places I had been before, during my short sojourn long ago, and even found some interesting new chambers of unknown purpose. But there were no signs of Richard. There were, in fact, no signs of life of any kind. Mindful that the short Raman day was almost over and that the four children would be waking up soon in our own lair, I finally returned, tired and dejected, to my Raman home.

Both the cover and the grill to our lair were open when I arrived. Although I was fairly certain that I had closed them both before leaving, I could not remember my exact actions at departure. Eventually I told myself that perhaps I had been too excited at the time and had forgotten to close everything. I had just started to descend when I heard Michael call 'Nicole' from behind me.

I turned around. Michael was approaching from the lane to the east. He was moving quickly, which was unusual for him, and was carrying baby Patrick in his arms. 'There you are,' he said, panting as I walked up to him. 'I was beginning to worry ...'

He stopped abruptly, stared at me for an instant, and then looked around quickly. 'But where's Katie?' he said anxiously.

'What do you mean, where's Katie?' I asked, the look on Michael's face causing me alarm.

'Isn't she with you?' he asked.

When I shook my head and said that I hadn't seen her, Michael suddenly erupted in tears. I rushed forward and comforted little Patrick, who was frightened by Michael's sobs and started crying himself.

'Oh, Nicole,' Michael said. 'I'm so, so sorry. Patrick was having a bad night, so I brought him into my room. Then Benjy had a stomach ache and Simone and I had to nurse him for a couple of hours. We all fell asleep while Katie was alone in the nursery. About two hours ago, when we all woke up, she was gone.'

I had never seen Michael so distraught before. I tried to comfort him, to tell him that Katie was probably just playing in the neighborhood somewhere (and when we find her, I was thinking, I will give her a scolding she'll never forget), but Michael argued with me.

'No, no,' he said, 'she's nowhere around. Patrick and I have been looking for over an hour.'

Michael, Patrick, and I went downstairs to check on Simone and Benjy. Simone informed us that Katie had been extremely disappointed when I had decided to look for Richard alone. 'She had hoped,' Simone said serenely, 'that you would take her with you.'

'Why didn't you tell me this last night?' I asked my eight-year-old daughter.

'It didn't seem that important,' Simone said. 'Besides, it never occurred to me that Katie would try to find Daddy by herself.'

Michael and I were both exhausted, but one of us had to look for Katie. I was the correct choice. I washed my face, ordered breakfast for everybody from the Ramans, and told a quick version of my descent into the avian lair. Simone and Michael turned the blackened TB over slowly in their hands. I could tell they too were wondering what had happened to Richard.

'Katie said that Daddy went to find the octospiders,' Simone commented just before I left. 'She said it was more exciting in their world.'

I was filled with dread as I trudged over to the plaza near the octospider lair. While I was walking, the lights went out and it was night again in Rama. 'Great,' I muttered to myself. 'Nothing like trying to find a missing child in the darkness.'

Both the octospider covering and the pair of protective grills were open. I had never seen the grills open before. My heart skipped a beat. I knew instinctively that Katie had gone down into their lair and that, despite my fear, I was about to follow her. First I bent down on my knees and shouted 'Katie' twice into the blackness beneath me. I heard her name echoing through the tunnels. I strained to listen for a response, but there were no sounds at all. At least, I told myself, I also don't hear any dragging brushes accompanied by a high-frequency whine.

I descended the ramp to the large cavern with the four tunnels that Richard and I had once labeled 'Eenie, Meenie, Mynie, and Moe.' It was difficult, but I forced myself to enter the tunnel that Richard and I had followed before. After a few steps, however, I stopped myself, backed up, and then went into the adjacent tunnel. This second corridor also led to the descending barrel corridor with the protruding spikes, but it passed the room that Richard and I called the octospider museum along the way. I remembered clearly the terror I had felt nine years earlier when I had found Dr Takagishi, stuffed like a hunting trophy, hanging in that museum.

There was a reason I wanted to visit the octospider museum that was not necessarily related to my search for Katie. If Richard had been killed by the octospiders (as Takagishi apparently was – although I am still not convinced that he did not die from a heart attack), or if they had found his body somewhere else in Rama, then perhaps it too would be in the room. To say that I wasn't anxious to see an alien taxidermist's version of my husband would be an understatement; however, above all I wanted to know what *had* happened to Richard. Especially after my dream.

I took a deep breath when I arrived at the entrance to the museum. I turned slowly left through the doorway. The lights came on as soon as I crossed the threshold, but fortunately Dr Takagishi was not staring directly in my face. He had been moved across the room. In fact, the whole museum had been rearranged in the intervening years. All the biot replicas, which had occupied most of the space in the room when Richard and I had visited it briefly before, had been removed. The two 'exhibits,' if one could call them that, were now the avians and the human beings.

The avian display was closer to the door. Three individuals were hanging from the ceiling, their wings outspread. One of them was the grey velvet avian with the two cherry red neck rings that Richard and I had seen just before its death. There were other fascinating objects and even photographs in the avian exhibit, but my eyes were drawn across the room, to the display surrounding Dr Takagishi.

I sighed with relief when I realised that Richard was not in the room. Our dinghy was there, however, the one that Richard, Michael, and I had used to cross the Cylindrical Sea. It was on the floor right next to Dr Takagishi. There was also an assortment of items that had been salvaged from our picnics and other activities in New York. But the centre of the exhibit was a set of framed pictures on the back and side walls.

From across the room I could not tell much about the content of the pictures. I gasped, however, as I approached them. The images were photographs, set in rectangular frames, many of which showed life *inside* our lair. There were photos of all of us, including the children. They showed us eating, sleeping, even going to the bathroom. I was feeling numb as I scanned the display. 'We are being watched,' I commented to myself, 'even in our own home.' I felt a terrible chill.

On the side wall was a special collection of pictures that dismayed and embarrassed me. On Earth they would have been candidates for an erotic museum. The images showed me making love with Richard in several different positions. There was one picture of Michael and me as well, but it wasn't as sharp because it had been dark in our bedroom that night.

The line of pictures below the sex scenes were all photographs of the children's births. Each birth was shown, including Patrick's, confirming that the eavesdropping was still continuing. The juxtaposition of the sex and birth images made it clear that the octospiders (or the Ramans?) had definitely figured out our reproductive process.

I was totally consumed with the photographs for probably fifteen minutes. My concentration was finally broken when I heard a very loud sound of brushes dragging against metal coming from the direction of the museum door. I was absolutely terrified. I stood still, frozen in my spot, and looked around wildly. There was no other escape from the room.

Within seconds Katie came bouncing through the door. '*Mom*!' she shouted when she saw me. She raced across the museum, nearly toppling Dr Takagishi, and jumped into my arms.

'Oh, Mom,' she said, hugging and kissing me fiercely, 'I knew you'd come.'

I closed my eyes and held my lost child with all my strength. Tears cascaded down my cheeks. I swung Katie from side to side, comforting her by saying, 'It's all right, darling, it's all right.'

When I wiped my eyes and opened them, an octospider was standing in the museum doorway. It was momentarily not moving, almost as if it were watching the reunion between mother and daughter. I stood transfixed, swept by a wave of emotions ranging from joy to sheer terror.

Katie felt my fear. 'Don't worry, Mother,' she said, looking over her shoulder at the octospider. 'He won't hurt you. He just wants to look. He's been close to me many times.'

My adrenaline level was at an all-time high. The octospider continued to stand (or sit, or whatever octos do when they're not moving) in the door. Its large black head was almost spherical and sat on a body that spread, near the floor, into the eight black-and-gold-striped tentacles. In the centre of its head were two parallel indentations, symmetric about an invisible axis, that ran from the top to the bottom. Precisely centred in between those two indentations, roughly a metre above the floor, was an amazing square lens structure, ten centimetres on a side, that was a gelatinous combination of grid lines plus flowing black and white material. While the octospider was staring at us, that lens was teeming with activity.

There were other organs embedded in the body between the two indentations, both above and below the lens, but I had no time to study them. The octospider moved toward us in the room and, despite Katie's assurances, my fear returned with full force. The brush sound was made by cilia-like attachments to the bottom of the tentacles as they moved across the floor. The high-frequency whine was emanating from a small orifice in the lower right side of the head.

For several seconds fear immobilised my thought processes. As the creature drew closer, my natural flight responses took over. Unfortunately, they were useless in this situation. There was nowhere to run.

The octospider didn't stop until it was a scant five metres away. I had backed Katie against the wall and was standing between her and the octo. I held up my hand. Again there was a flurry of activity in its mysterious lens. Suddenly I had an idea. I reached into my flight suit and pulled out my computer. With my fingers trembling (the octospider had raised a pair of tentacles in front of its lens – in retrospect I wonder if it thought I was going to produce a weapon), I called the image of Richard up on the monitor and thrust it out toward the octospider.

When I made no additional movement the creature slowly returned its two protective tentacles to the floor. It stared at the monitor for almost a full minute and then, much to my astonishment, a wave of bright purple colouring ran completely around its head, starting at the edge of its indentation. This purple was followed a few seconds later by a rainbow pattern of red, blue, and green, each band a different thickness, that also came out of the same indentation and, after circling the head, retreated into the parallel indentation almost three hundred and sixty degrees away.

Katie and I both stared in awe. The octospider picked up one of its tentacles, pointed at the monitor, and repeated the wide purple wave. Moments later, as before, came the identical rainbow pattern.

'It's talking to us, Mommy,' Katie said softly.

'I think you're right,' I replied. 'But I don't have any idea what it's saying.'

After waiting for what seemed like forever, the octospider began to move backward toward the doorway, its extended tentacle beckoning us to follow. There were no more bands of colour. Katie and I held hands and cautiously followed. She started looking around and noticed the photographs on the wall for the first time. 'Look, Mommy,' she said, 'they have pictures of our family.'

I shushed her and told her to please pay attention to the octospider. It backed into the tunnel and headed toward the spiked vertical corridor and the subways. That was the opening we needed. I picked Katie up, told her to hang on tight, and raced down the tunnel at top speed. My feet scarcely touched the floor until I was up on the ramp and back in New York.

Michael was ecstatic to see Katie safe, even though he was very concerned (as I still am) that there were cameras hidden in the walls and ceilings of our living quarters, I never did scold Katie properly for going off on her own – I was too relieved to find her at all. Katie told Simone that she had had a 'fabulous adventure' and that the octospider was 'nice.' Such is the world of the child.

4 FEBRUARY 2209

Oh, joy of joys! We have found Richard! He is still alive! Just barely, for he is in a deep coma and has a high fever, but he is nevertheless alive.

Katie and Simone found him this morning, lying on the ground not fifty metres from the opening to our lair. The three of us had been planning to play some soccer in the plaza and were ready to leave the lair when Michael called me back for something. I told the girls to wait for me in the area around the lair entrance. When they both started screaming a few minutes later, I thought something terrible had happened. I rushed up the stairs and immediately saw Richard's comatose body in the distance.

At first I was afraid that Richard was dead. The doctor in me immediately went to work, checking his vital signs.

The girls hung over me while I was examining him. Especially Katie. She kept saying, over and over, 'Is Daddy alive? Oh, Mommy, make Daddy be all right.'

Once I had confirmed that he was in a coma, Michael and Simone helped me carry Richard down the stairs. I injected a set of biometry probes into his system and have been monitoring the output ever since.

I took his clothes off and checked him from head to toe. He has some scratches and bruises that I have not seen before, but that's to be expected after all this time. His blood cell counts are peculiarly close to normal – I would have expected white cell abnormalities with his almost forty-degree temperature.

There was another big surprise when we examined Richard's clothing in detail. In his jacket pocket we found the Shakespearean robots Prince Hal and Falstaff, who had disappeared nine years ago in the strange world below the spiked corridor in what we thought was the octospider lair. Somehow Richard must have convinced the octos to return his playmates.

I have been sitting here beside Richard now for seven hours. Most of the time this morning other members of the family have also been here, but for the last hour Richard and I have been alone. My eyes have feasted on his face for minutes on end, my hands have roamed across his neck, his shoulders, and his back. My touching him has evoked a flood of memories and my eyes have often been filled with tears. I never thought I would see or touch him again. Oh, Richard, welcome home. Welcome home to your wife and family.

12

We have had an incredible day. Just after lunch, while I was sitting beside Richard and routinely checking all his biometry, Katie asked me if she could play with Prince Hal and Falstaff. 'Of course,' I told her without thinking. I was certain that the little robots were not functioning and, to tell the truth, I wanted her out of the room so that I could try another technique for bringing Richard out of his coma.

I have never seen a coma even remotely like Richard's. Most of the time his eyes are open, and occasionally they even seem to be following an object in his field of vision. But there are no other signs of life or consciousness. No muscles ever move. I have used a variety of stimuli, some mechanical, mostly chemical, to try to rouse him from his comatose state. None of them have worked. That's why I was so unprepared for what happened today.

After Katie had been gone for about ten minutes, I heard a very strange mix of sounds coming from the nursery. I left Richard's side and walked into the corridor. Before I reached the nursery the strange noise resolved itself into clipped speech with a very peculiar rhythm. 'Hello,' a voice that sounded as if it were in the bottom of a well said. 'We are peaceful. Here is your man.'

The voice was coming from Prince Hal, who was standing in the middle of the room when I entered the nursery. The children were on the floor surrounding the robot, somewhat tentatively except for Katie. She was clearly excited.

'I was just playing with the buttons,' Katie said to me in explanation when I gave her a questioning glance, 'and suddenly he started talking.'

No motions accompanied Prince Hal's speech. How peculiar, I thought, remembering that Richard took pride in the fact that his robots always moved and spoke in concert. Richard did not do this, a voice inside my head told me, but I initially dismissed the idea. I dropped down on the floor beside the children.

'Hello. We are peaceful. Here is your man,' Prince Hal said again several seconds later. This time an eerie feeling swept through me. The girls were still laughing, but they quickly stopped when they noticed the strange expression on my face. Benjy crawled over beside me and grabbed my hand.

We were sitting on the floor with our backs to the door. I suddenly had a feeling there was someone behind me. I turned around and saw Richard standing in the doorway. I gasped and jumped up just as he fell and lost consciousness.

The children all screamed and began to cry. I tried to comfort them after quickly examining Richard. Since Michael was topside in New York having his afternoon walk, I cared for Richard on the floor outside the nursery for over an hour. During that time I watched him very closely. He was exactly as he had been when I left him in the bedroom earlier. There was no obvious sign that he had been awake for thirty or forty seconds in the interim.

When Michael returned he helped me carry Richard to the bedroom. We talked for over an hour about why Richard had awakened so abruptly. Later I read and reread every article about coma in my medical books. I am convinced that Richard's coma is caused by a mixture of physical and psychological problems. In my opinion the sound of that strange voice induced a trauma in him that temporarily overwhelmed the factors creating the coma.

But why did he then relapse so quickly? That's a more difficult issue. Perhaps he had exhausted his small energy base by walking down the hall. There's no way we can really know. In fact, we cannot answer most of the questions about what happened today, including the one that Katie keeps asking – *who* is it that is peaceful?

1 MAY 2209

Let it be recorded that on this day Richard Colin Wakefield actually acknowledged his family and spoke his first words. For almost a week he has been working up to this moment, initially by giving signs of recognition with his face and eyes and then by moving his lips as if to make words. He smiled at me this morning and almost said my name, but his first actual word was 'Katie,' spoken this afternoon after his cherished daughter gave him one of her energetic hugs.

There is a feeling of euphoria in the family, especially among the girls. They are celebrating the return of their father. I have told Simone and Katie repeatedly that Richard's rehabilitation will almost certainly be long and painful, but I guess they are too young to comprehend what that means.

I am a very happy woman. It was impossible for me to restrain the tears when Richard distinctly whispered 'Nicole' in my ear just before dinner. Even though I realise that my husband is not yet anywhere near normal, I am now certain that he will eventually recover and that fills my heart with joy.

18 AUGUST 2209

Slowly but surely Richard continues to improve. He only sleeps twelve hours a day now, can walk almost a mile before becoming fatigued, and is able to concentrate occasionally on a problem if it's especially interesting. He has not yet begun to interact with the Ramans through the keyboard and screen. He has, however, taken Prince Hal apart and tried unsuccessfully to determine what caused the strange voice in the nursery.

Richard is the first to admit that he is not himself. When he can talk about it, he says that he is 'in a fog, like a dream but not quite as sharp'. It has been over three months since he regained consciousness, but he still can't remember very much about what happened to him after he left us. He believes he was in the coma for the last year or so. His estimate is based more on vague feelings than on any particular fact.

Richard insists that he lived in the avian lair for some months and that he was present at a spectacular cremation. He can't supply any other details. Richard has also twice contended that he explored the Southern Hemicylinder and found the main city of the octospiders near the Southern Bowl, but since what he *can* remember changes from day to day, it is difficult to place much credence in any specific recollection.

I have replaced Richard's biometry set twice already and have very lengthy records of all his critical parameters. His charts are normal except in two areas – his mental activity and his temperature. His daily brain waves defy description. There is nothing in my medical encyclopedia that will allow me to interpret any pair of these charts, much less the entire set. Sometimes the level of activity in his brain is astronomically high; sometimes it seems to stop altogether. The electrochemical measurements are equally peculiar. His hippocampus is virtually dormant – that could explain why Richard's having such difficulty with his memory.

His temperature is also weird. It has been stable now, for two months, at 37.8 degrees Celsius, eight tenths of a degree above normal for an average human. I have checked all his preflight records; Richard's 'normal' temperature on Earth was a very steady 36.9. I cannot explain why this elevated temperature persists. It's almost as if his body and some pathogen are in stable equilibrium, neither able to subdue the other. But what pathogen could it be that would elude all my attempts to identify it?

All the children have been especially disappointed in Richard's lackadaisical behaviour. During his absence we probably mythologised him somewhat, but there's no doubt he was a very energetic man before. This new Richard is only a shadow of his former self. Katie swears she remembers wrestling and playing vigorously with her Daddy when she was only two (her memory has undoubtedly been reinforced by the stories that Michael, Simone, and I told her while Richard was gone), and is often quite angry that he spends so little time with her now. I try to explain to her that 'Daddy is still sick,' but I don't think she is mollified by my explanation.

Michael moved all my things back to this room within twenty-four hours after Richard's return. He is such a sweet man. He went through another heavy religious phase for several weeks (I expect in his mind he needed forgiveness for some fairly grievous sins) but has since moderated because of the workload on me. He has been marvellous with the children.

Simone acts as a backup mother. Benjy worships her and she has incredible patience with him. Since she had commented several times that Benjy was 'a little slow,' Michael and I have told Simone about his Whittingham's syndrome. We still have not told Katie. Right now Katie is having a difficult time. Not even Patrick, who follows her around like a pet dog, can cheer her up.

We all know, even the children, that we are being watched. We searched the walls in the nursery very carefully, almost as if it were a game, and found several minute irregularities in the surface finish that we declared to be cameras. We chipped them away with our tools, but we could not positively say that we had indeed found monitoring devices. They may be so small that we couldn't see them without a microscope. At least Richard remembered his favourite saying, about advanced alien technology being indistinguishable from magic.

Katie was the most disturbed about the prying cameras of the octospiders. She spoke openly and resentfully of their intrusion into her 'private life.' She probably has more secrets than any of us. When Simone told her younger sister that it was really not important, because 'after all, God is also watching us all the time', we had our first sibling religious argument. Katie replied with 'Bullshit', a rather unpleasant word for a six-year-old girl to use. Her expression reminded me to be more careful with my own language.

One day last month I took Richard over to the avian lair to see if perhaps being there would refresh his memory. He became very frightened as soon as we were in the tunnel off the vertical corridor. 'Dark,' I heard him mumble. 'I cannot see in the dark. But *they* can see in the dark.' He wouldn't walk any more after we passed the water and the cistern, so I brought him back to our lair.

Richard knows that both Benjy and Patrick are Michael's sons and probably suspects that Michael and I lived as husband and wife for part of the time he was gone, but he has never commented about it. Both Michael and I are prepared to ask for Richard's forgiveness and to stress to him that we were not lovers (except for Benjy's conception) until he had been gone for two years. At the moment, however, Richard doesn't seem much interested in the subject.

Richard and I have shared our old conjugal mat since soon after he awakened from his coma. We have touched a lot and been very friendly, but until two weeks ago there had never been any sex. In fact, I was starting to think that sex was another of the things that had been erased from his memory, so unresponsive had he been to my occasional provocative kisses.

Then came a night, however, when the old Richard was suddenly in bed with me. This is a pattern that has been occurring in other areas as well – every now and then his old wit, energy, and intelligence are all present for a short period of time. Anyway, the old Richard was ardent, funny, and imaginative. It was like heaven for me. I remembered levels of pleasure that I had long since buried.

His sexual interest continued for three consecutive nights. Then it departed as abruptly as it had arrived. At first I was disappointed (Isn't that human nature? Most of the time we want it to be better. When it's as good as it can be, we want it to last forever), but now I have accepted that this facet of his personality must also undergo a healing process.

Last night Richard computed our trajectory for the first time since he has been back with us. Both Michael and I were delighted. 'We're still holding the same direction,' he pronounced proudly. 'We're now less than three light years from Sirius.'

6 JANUARY 2210

Forty-six years old. My hair is now mostly grey on the sides and in front. Back on Earth I would be debating whether or not to colour my hair. Here on Rama it does not matter.

I am too old to be pregnant. I should tell that to the little girl growing inside my womb. I was quite astonished when I realised that I was indeed pregnant again. The onset of menopause had already begun, with its strange hot flashes, moments of daffiness, and totally unpredictable menstruations. But Richard's sperm has made one more baby, another addition to this homeless family adrift in space.

If we never encounter another human being (and Eleanor Joan Wakefield turns out to be a healthy baby, which seems likely at this point), then there will be a total of six possible combinations of parents for our grandchildren. Almost certainly all of those permutations will not occur, but it's fascinating to imagine. I used to think that Simone would mate with Benjy, and Katie with Patrick, but where will Ellie fit into the equation?

This is my tenth birthday on board Rama. It seems utterly impossible that I have spent only twenty percent of my life in this giant cylinder. Did I have another life once, back on that oceanic planet trillions of kilometres away? Did I really know adult people other than Richard Wakefield and Michael O'Toole? Was my father actually Pierre des Jardins, the famous writer of historical fiction? Did I have a secret, dream affair with Henry, Prince of Wales, that produced my wonderful first daughter Genevieve?

None of it seems possible. At least not today, not on my forty-sixth birthday. It's funny. Richard and Michael have asked me, one time each, about Genevieve's father. I have still never told anyone. Isn't that ridiculous? What possible difference could it make here on Rama? None at all. But it has been my secret (shared only with my father) since the moment of Genevieve's conception. She was *my* daughter. I brought her into the world and I raised her. Her biological father, I always told myself, was of no importance.

That is, of course, poppycock. Hah. There's that word again. Dr David Brown used it often. Goodness. I haven't thought about the other Newton cosmonauts for years. I wonder if Francesca and her friends made their millions off the Newton mission. I hope Janos got his share. Dear Mr Tabori, an absolutely delightful man. Hmm. I also wonder how Rama's escape from the nuclear phalanx was explained to the citizens of Earth. Ah, yes, Nicole, this is a typical birthday. A long, unstructured voyage down memory lane.

Francesca was so beautiful. I was always jealous of how well she handled herself with people. Did she drug Borzov and Wilson? Probably. I don't think for a minute she meant to kill Valeriy. But she had a truly twisted morality. Most genuinely ambitious people do.

I am amused, now when I look back, at how obsessed I was as a young mother in my twenties. I had to succeed at everything. My ambition was quite different from Francesca's. I wanted to show the world that I could play by all the rules and still win, just as I had done with the triple jump in the Olympic games. What could be more impossible for an unmarried mother than to be selected as a cosmonaut? I was certainly full of myself during those years. Lucky for me, and for Genevieve, that Father was there.

I knew, of course, every time I looked at Genevieve that Henry's imprint was obvious. From the top of her lips to the bottom of her chin, Genevieve's face is exactly like his. And I did not really want to deny the genetics. It was just so important to me to make it on my own, to show at least myself that I was a superb mother and woman even if I was unsuitable to be the queen.

I was too black to be Queen Nicole of England, or even Joan of Arc in one of those French anniversary pageants. I wonder how many years it will be before skin colour is no longer an issue among human beings on Earth. Five hundred years? A thousand? What was it that the American William Faulkner said – something about Sambo will be free only when all of his neighbors wake up in the morning and say, both to themselves and to their friends, that Sambo is free. I think he is right. We have seen that racial prejudice cannot be eradicated by legislation. Or even by education. Each person's journey through life must have an epiphany, a moment of true awareness, when he (or she) realises, once and for all, that Sambo and every other individual in the world who is in any way different from him (or her) *must* be free if we are to survive.

When I was down at the bottom of that pit ten years ago and certain that I was going to die, I asked myself what particular moments of my life I would live over if I were offered the opportunity. Those hours with Henry leapt into my mind, despite the fact that he later broke my heart. Even today I would gladly soar again with my prince. To have experienced total happiness, even if it's just for a few minutes or hours, is to have been alive. It is not that important, when you are faced with death, that your companion in your great moment subsequently disappointed or betrayed you. What is important is that sense of momentary joy so great you feel you have transcended the Earth.

It embarrassed me a little, in the pit, that my memories of Henry were on a level equal to my memories of my father, mother, and daughter. But I have since realised that I am not unique in cherishing my recollections of those hours with Henry. Each person has very special moments or events that are uniquely hers and are zealously protected by the heart.

My only close friend at the university, Gabrielle Moreau, spent a night with Genevieve and me at Beauvois the year before the Newton expedition was launched. We had not seen each other for seven years and spent most of the night talking, primarily about the major emotional events of our lives. Gabrielle was extremely happy. She had a handsome, sensitive, successful husband, three healthy, gorgeous children, and a beautiful manor house near Chinon, But Gabrielle's 'most wonderful' moment, she confided to me after midnight with a girlish smile, had occurred before she met her husband. She had had a powerful schoolgirl crush on a famous movie star who one day happened to be on location in Tours. Gabrielle somehow managed to meet him in his hotel room and talk to him privately for almost an hour. She kissed him a single time on the lips before she left. That was her most precious memory.

Oh, my prince, it was ten years ago yesterday that I saw you for the last time. Are you happy? Are you a good king? Do you ever think of the black Olympic champion who gave herself to you, her first love, with such reckless abandon?

You asked me an indirect question, that day on the ski mountain, about the father of my daughter. I denied you the answer, not realizing that my denial meant I had still not forgiven you completely. If you were to ask me today, my prince, I would gladly tell you. Yes, Henry Rex, King of England, *you* are the father of Genevieve des Jardins. Go to her, know her, love her children. I cannot. I am more than fifty trillion kilometres away.

13

Everyone was too excited to sleep last night. Except for Benjy, bless his heart, who simply could not grasp what we were telling him. Simone has explained to him many times that our home is inside a giant cylindrical spacecraft – she has even shown him on the black screen the different views of Rama from the external sensors – but the concept continues to elude him.

When the whistle sounded yesterday Richard, Michael, and I stared at each other for several seconds. It had been so long since we last heard it. Then we all started talking at once. The children, including little Ellie, were full of questions and could feel our excitement. The eight of us went topside immediately. Richard and Katie ran over to the sea without waiting for the rest of the family. Simone walked with Benjy, Michael with Patrick. I carried Ellie because her little legs just wouldn't move fast enough.

Katie was bursting with enthusiasm when she ran back to greet us. 'Come on, come on,' she said, grabbing Simone by the hand. 'You've got to see it. It's amazing. The colours are fantastic.'

Indeed they were. The rainbow arcs of light crackled from horn to horn, filling the Raman night with an awesome display. Benjy stared southward with his mouth open. After many seconds he smiled and turned to Simone. 'It's beau-ti-ful,' he said slowly, proud of his use of the word.

'Yes, it is, Benjy,' Simone replied. 'Very beautiful.'

'Ve-ry beau-ti-ful,' Benjy repeated, turning back to look at the lights.

None of us said very much during the show itself. But after we returned to the lair the conversation was nonstop for hours. Of course, someone had to explain everything to the children. Simone was the only one born at the time of the last manoeuvre, and she was just an infant. Richard was the chief explainer. The whistle and light show really energised him – he seemed more like himself last night than he has at any time since he returned – and he was both entertaining and informative as he recounted everything we knew about whistles, light shows, and Raman manoeuvres.

'Do you think the octospiders are going to return to New York?' Katie asked expectantly.

'I don't know,' Richard said. 'But that's definitely a possibility.'

Katie spent the next fifteen minutes telling everyone, for the umpteenth time, about our encounter with the octospider four years ago. As usual, she embellished and exaggerated some of the details, especially from the solo part of the story before she saw me in the museum.

Patrick loves the tale. He wants Katie to tell it all the time. 'There I was,' Katie said last night, 'lying on my stomach, my head peering over the edge of a gigantic round cylinder that dropped into the black gloom. Silver spikes were sticking out of the sides of the cylinder, and I could see them flashing in the dim light. "Hey," I shouted, "anybody down there?"

'I heard a sound like dragging metal brushes together with a whine. Lights came on below me. At the bottom of the cylinder, beginning to climb the spikes, was a black *thing* with a round head and eight tentacles of black and gold. The tentacles wrapped around the spikes as it climbed swiftly in my direction ...'

'Oc-to-spi-der,' Benjy said.

When Katie was finished with her story, Richard told the children that in four more days the floor was probably going to start shaking. He stressed that everything should be carefully anchored to the ground and that each of us should be prepared for another set of sessions in the deceleration tank. Michael pointed out that we needed at least one new toy box for the children, and several sturdy boxes for our stuff as well. We have accumulated so much junk over the years that it will be quite a task to secure everything in the next few days.

When Richard and I were lying alone on our mat, we held hands and talked for over an hour. At one point I told him that I hoped this coming manoeuvre signaled the beginning of the end of our journey in Rama.

'Hope springs eternal in the human breast.
Man never is, but always to be blessed.'

he replied. He sat up for a moment and looked at me, his eyes twinkling in the near darkness. 'Alexander Pope,' he said. Then he laughed. 'I bet he never thought he would be quoted sixty trillion kilometres away from Earth.'

'You seem better, darling,' I said, stroking his arm.

His brow furrowed. 'Right now everything seems clear. But I don't know when the fog will descend again. It could be any minute. And I still cannot remember more than the barest outline of what happened during the three years that I was gone.'

He laid back down. 'What do you think will happen?' I asked.

'I'm guessing we'll have a manoeuvre,' he replied. 'And I hope it's a big one. We are approaching Sirius very quickly and will need to slow down considerably if our target is anywhere in the Sirius system.' He reached over and took my hand. 'For you,' he said, 'and especially for the children, I hope this is not a false alarm.'

8 JULY 2213

The manoeuvre began four days ago, right on schedule, as soon as the third and final light show was finished. We didn't see or hear any avians or octospiders, as we haven't for four years now. Katie was very disappointed. She wanted to see the octospiders all return to New York.

Yesterday a pair of the mantis biots came into our lair and went straight to the deceleration tank. They were carrying a large container, in which were the five new webbed beds (Simone, of course, needs a different size now) and all the helmets. We watched them from a distance while they installed the beds and checked out the tank system. The children were fascinated. The short visit from the mantises confirmed that we will soon be undergoing a major change in velocity.

Richard was apparently correct with his hypothesis about the connection between the main propulsion system and the overall thermal control of Rama. The temperature has already started to drop topside. In anticipation of a long manoeuvre, we have been busy using the keyboard to order cold-weather clothing for all the children.

The constant shaking is again disrupting our lives. At first it was amusing for the children, but they are already complaining about it. For myself, I am hoping that we are now near our ultimate destination. Although Michael has been praying 'God's will be done', my few prayers have definitely been more selfish and specific.

1 SEPTEMBER 2213

Something new is definitely happening. For the last ten days, ever since we finished in the tank and the manoeuvre ended, we have been approaching a solitary light source situated about thirty astronomical units away from the star Sirius. Richard has ingeniously manipulated the sensor list and the black screen so that this source is dead centre on our monitor at all times, regardless of which particular Raman telescope is observing it.

Two nights ago we began to see some definition in the object. We speculated that perhaps it was an inhabited planet and Richard rushed around computing the heat input from Sirius on a planet whose distance was roughly equal to Neptune's distance from our Sun. Even though Sirius is much larger, brighter, and hotter than the Sun, Richard concluded that our paradise, if this was indeed our destination, was still going to be very cold.

Last night we could see our target more clearly. It is an elongated construction (Richard says it therefore cannot be a planet – anything 'that size' that is decidedly non-spherical 'must be artificial'), shaped like a cigar, with two rows of lights along the top and bottom. Because we don't know exactly how far away it is, we don't know its size for certain. However, Richard has been making some 'guesstimates,' based on our closing velocity, and he thinks the cigar is roughly a hundred and fifty kilometres long and fifty kilometers tall.

The entire family sits in our main room and stares at the monitor. This morning we had another surprise. Katie showed us that there were two other vehicles in the vicinity of our target. Richard had taught her last week how to change the Raman sensors providing input to the black screen and, while the rest of us were talking, she accessed the distant radar sensor that we had first used thirteen years ago to identify the nuclear missiles coming from Earth. The cigar-shaped object appeared at the edge of the radar field of view. Standing right in front of the cigar, almost indistinguishable from it in the wide field, were the two other blips. If the giant cigar is indeed our destination, then perhaps we are about to have company.

8 SEPTEMBER 2213

There is no way I can adequately describe the astounding events of the last five days. The language does not have adjectives superlative enough to capture what we have seen and experienced. Michael has even commented that heaven may pale by comparison beside the wonders that we have witnessed.

At this moment our family is on board a driverless small shuttle craft, no larger than a city bus on Earth, that is whizzing us from the way station to an unknown destination. The cigar-shaped way station is still visible, but just barely, out the domed window at the rear of the craft. To our left, our home for thirteen years, the cylindrical spaceship we call Rama, is headed in a slightly different direction than we are. It departed from the way station a few hours after we did, lit like a Christmas tree on the outside, and we are presently separated from it by about two hundred kilometres.

Four days and eleven hours ago our Rama spacecraft came to a stop relative to the way station. We were the third vehicle in an amazing queue. In front of us was a spinning starfish about one tenth the size of Rama and a giant wheel, with a hub and spokes, that entered the way station within hours after we stopped.

The way station itself turned out to be hollow. When the giant wheel moved into the centre of the way station, gantries and other deployable elements rolled out to meet the wheel and fix it in place. A suite of special vehicles in three unusual shapes (one looked like a balloon, another like a blimp, and the third resembled a bathysphere on Earth) then entered the wheel from the way station. Although we couldn't see what was going on inside the wheel, we did see the special vehicles emerge, one by one, at odd intervals over the next two days. Each vehicle was met by a shuttle, like the one in which we are now flying but larger in size. These shuttles had all been parked in the dark in the right-hand side of the way station and had been moved into place thirty minutes or so before the rendezvous.

As soon as the shuttles were loaded, they always took off in a direction directly opposite our queue. About an hour after the final vehicle had emerged from the wheel and the last shuttle had departed, the many pieces of mechanical equipment attached to the wheel were retracted and the great circular spacecraft itself eased out of the way station.

The starfish in front of us had already entered the way station and was being handled by another set of gantries and attachments when a loud whistle summoned us topside in Rama. The whistle was followed by a light show in the southern bowl. However, this display was completely different from the ones that we had seen before. The Big Horn was the star of the new show. Circular rings of colour formed near its tip and then sailed slowly north, centred along the spin axis of Rama. The rings were huge. Richard estimated they were at least a kilometer in diameter, with a ring thickness of forty metres.

The dark Raman night was illuminated by as many as eight of these rings at a time. The order remained the same – red, orange, yellow, green, blue, brown, pink, and purple – for three repetitions. As a ring would break up and disappear near the Alpha relay station at the northern bowl of Rama, a new ring of the same colour would form back near the tip of the Big Horn.

We stood transfixed, our mouths agape, as this spectacle took place. As soon as the last ring disappeared from the third set, another astonishing event occurred. All the lights came on inside Rama! The Raman night had only begun three hours earlier – for thirteen years the sequence of night and day had been completely regular. Now, all of a sudden, it was changed. And it wasn't just the lights. There was music as well; at least I guess you could call it music. It sounded like millions of tiny bells and it seemed to be coming from everywhere.

None of us moved for many seconds. Then Richard, who had the best pair of binoculars, spied something flying toward us. 'It's the avians,' he shouted, jumping up and down and pointing at the sky. 'I just remembered something. I visited them in their new home in the north while I was on my odyssey.'

One at a time we each looked through his binoculars. At first it wasn't certain that Richard was correct in his identification, but as they came closer the fifty or sixty specks resolved themselves into the great birdlike creatures we know as the avians. They headed straight for New York. Half the avians hovered in the sky, maybe three hundred metres above their lair, as the other half dove down to the surface.

'Come on, Daddy,' Katie yelled. 'Let's go.'

Before I could raise any objection, father and daughter were off at a sprint. I watched Katie run. She is already very fast. In my mind's eye I could see my mother's graceful stride across the grass in the park at Chilly-Mazarin – Katie has definitely inherited some characteristics from her mother's side of the family, even though she is first and foremost her father's daughter.

Simone and Benjy had already started toward our lair. Patrick was concerned about the avians. 'Will they hurt Uncle Richard and Katie?' he asked.

I smiled at my handsome five-year-old son. 'No, darling,' I answered, 'not if they're careful.' Michael, Patrick, Ellie, and I returned to the lair to watch the starfish being processed in the way station.

We couldn't see much because all the ports of entry to the starfish were on the opposite side, away from the Raman cameras. But we assumed some kind of unloading activity was occurring, because eventually five shuttles departed for some new location. The starfish was finished with its processing very quickly. It had already left the way station before Richard and Katie returned.

'Start packing,' Richard said breathlessly as soon as he arrived. 'We're leaving. We're all leaving.'

'You should have seen them,' Katie said to Simone almost simultaneously. 'They were huge. And ugly. They went down in their lair ...'

'The avians returned to get some special things from their lair,' Richard interrupted her. 'Maybe they were mementos of some kind. Anyway, everything fits. We're getting out of here.'

As I raced around trying to put our essentials into a few of the sturdy boxes, I criticised myself for not having figured everything out sooner. We had watched both the wheel and the starfish 'unload' at the way station. But it had not occurred to us that we might be the cargo to be unloaded by Rama.

It was impossible to decide what to pack. We had been living in those six rooms (including the two we had fixed up for storage) for thirteen years. We had probably requested an average of five items a day using the keyboard. Granted, most of the objects had long since been thrown away, but still ... We didn't know where we were going. How could we know what to take?

'Do you have any idea what's going to happen to us?' I asked Richard.

My husband was beside himself trying to figure out how to take his large computer. 'Our history, our science – all that remains of our knowledge is there,' he said, pointing at the computer in agitation. 'What if it's irretrievably lost?'

It weighed only eighty kilograms altogether. I told him we could all help him carry the computer after we had packed clothing, personal items, and some food and water.

'Do you have any idea where we're going?' I repeated.

Richard shrugged his shoulders. 'Not the slightest,' he replied. 'But wherever it is, I bet it will be amazing.'

Katie came into our room. She was holding a small pouch and her eyes were alive with energy. 'I'm packed and ready,' she said. 'Can I go topside and wait?'

Her father's affirmative nod was barely in motion when Katie bolted out the door. I shook my head, giving Richard a disapproving look, and went down the hall to help Simone with the other children. The process of packing for the boys was an ordeal. Benjy was cranky and confused. Even Patrick was irritable, Simone and I had just finished (the job was impossible until we forced the boys to take a nap) when Richard and Katie returned from topside.

'Our vehicle is here,' Richard said calmly, suppressing his excitement.

'It's parked on the ice,' Katie added, taking off her heavy jacket and gloves.

'How do you know it's ours?' Michael asked. He had entered the room only moments after Richard and Katie.

'It has eight seats and room for our bags,' my ten-year-old daughter replied. 'Who else could it be for?'

'*Whom*,' I said mechanically, trying to integrate this latest new information. I felt as if I had been drinking from a fire hose for four consecutive days.

'Did you see any octospiders?' Patrick asked.

'Oc-to-spi-der,' Benjy repeated carefully.

'No,' answered Katie, 'but we did see four mammoth planes, real flat, with wide wings. They flew over our heads, coming from the south. We think the flat planes were carrying the octos, don't we, Dad?'

Richard nodded.

I took a deep breath. 'All right, then,' I said. 'Bundle up, everybody. Let's go. Carry the bags first. Richard, Michael, and I will make a second trip for the computer.'

An hour later we were all in the vehicle. We had climbed the stairs of our lair for the last time. Richard pressed a flashing red button and our Raman helicopter (I call it that because it went straight up, not because it had any rotary blades) lifted off the ground.

Our flight path was slow and vertical for the first five minutes. Once we were close to the spin axis of Rama, where there was no gravity and very little atmosphere, the vehicle hovered in place for two or three minutes while it changed its external configuration.

It was an awesome final view of Rama. Many kilometres below us our island home was but a small patch of greyish brown in the middle of the frozen sea that circled the giant cylinder. I could see the horns in the south clearer than ever before. Those amazing long structures, supported by massive flying buttresses larger than small towns on the Earth, all pointed directly north.

I felt strangely emotional as our craft began to move again. After all, Rama had been my home for thirteen years. I had given birth to five children there. I have also matured, I remember telling myself, and may finally be growing into the person I have always wanted to be.

There was very little time to dwell on what had been. Once the external configuration change was complete, our vehicle zipped along the spin axis to the northern hub in a matter of a few minutes. Less than an hour later we were all safely in this shuttle. We had left Rama. I knew we would never return. I wiped the tears from my eyes as our shuttle pulled out of the way-station.

AT THE NODE

1

Nicole was dancing. Her partner in the waltz was Henry. They were young and very much in love. The beautiful music filled the huge ballroom as the twenty or so couples moved in rhythm around the floor. Nicole looked stunning in her long white gown. Henry's eyes were fixed on hers. He held her firmly at the waist, but somehow she felt completely free.

Her father was one of the people standing around the edge of the dance floor. He was leaning against a massive column that rose almost twenty feet to the domed ceiling. He waved and smiled as Nicole danced by in the arms of her prince.

The waltz seemed to last forever. When it was finally over, Henry held her hands and told Nicole that he had something very important to ask her. At just that moment her father touched her on the back. 'Nicole,' he whispered, 'we must go. It's very late.'

Nicole curtsied to the prince. Henry was reluctant to let go of her hands. 'Tomorrow,' he said, 'We'll talk tomorrow.' He blew her a kiss as she left the dance floor.

When Nicole walked outside it was almost sunset. Her father's sedan was waiting. Moments later, as they raced down the highway beside the Loire, she was dressed in blouse and jeans. Nicole was younger now, maybe fourteen, and her father was driving much faster than usual. 'We don't want to be late,' he said. 'The pageant starts at eight o'clock.'

The Chateau d'Ussé loomed before them. With its many towers and spires, the castle had been the inspiration for the original story of Sleeping Beauty. It was only a few kilometres down the river from Beauvois and had always been one of her father's favourite places.

It was the evening of the annual pageant, when the story of Sleeping Beauty was replayed in front of a live audience. Pierre and Nicole attended every year. Each time Nicole longed desperately for Aurora to avoid the deadly spinning wheel that would throw her into a coma. And each year she wept adolescent tears when the kiss of the handsome prince awakened the beauty from her deathlike sleep.

The pageant was over, the audience gone. Nicole was climbing up the

circular steps that led to the tower where the real Sleeping Beauty had supposedly lapsed into her coma. The teenager was racing up the steps, laughing,
leaving her father far behind.

Aurora's room was on the other side of the long window. Nicole caught her
breath and stared at all the sumptuous furnishings. The bed was canopied,
the dressers richly decorated. Everything in the room was trimmed in white.
It was magnificent. Nicole glanced back at the sleeping, girl and gasped. It was
she, Nicole, lying in the bed in a white gown!

Her heart pounded furiously as she heard the door open and the footsteps coming toward her in the room. Her eyes remained closed as the first
aroma of his mint breath reached her nose. This is it, she thought excitedly to
herself. He kissed her, gently, on the lips. Nicole felt as if she were flying on
the softest of clouds. Music was all around her. She opened her eyes and saw
Henry's smiling face only centimetres away. She reached her arms out to him
and he kissed her again, this time with passion, as a man kisses a woman.

Nicole kissed him back, reserving nothing, allowing her kiss to tell him that
she was his. But he pulled away. Her special prince was wearing a frown. He
pointed at her face. Then he backed up slowly and left the room.

She had just started to cry when a distant sound intruded on her dream.
A door was opening, light was coming into the room. Nicole blinked, then
closed her eyes again to protect them against the light. The complicated set
of ultra-thin, plastic-like wires that were attached to her body automatically
rewound themselves into their containers on either side of the canvas mat on
which she was sleeping.

Nicole awakened very slowly. The dream had been extremely vivid. Her
feelings of unhappiness had not vanished as quickly as the dream. She tried
to chase her despair by reminding herself that none of what she had dreamed
was real.

'Are you going to just lie there forever?' Her daughter Katie, who had been
asleep beside her on the left, was already up and bending over her.

Nicole smiled. 'No,' she said, 'but I admit I am more than a little bit groggy.
I was in the middle of a dream ... How long did we sleep this time?'

'A day short of five weeks,' Simone answered from the other side. Her
older daughter was sitting up, casually arranging her long hair that had
become matted during the test.

Nicole glanced at her watch, verified that Simone was correct, and sat up
herself. She yawned. 'So how do you feel?' she said to the two girls.

'Full of energy,' eleven-year-old Katie answered with a grin. 'I want to
run, jump, wrestle with Patrick ... I hope this was our last long sleep.'

'The Eagle said it should be,' Nicole replied. 'They're hoping that they
will have enough data now.' She smiled. 'The Eagle says we women are
more difficult to understand – because of the wild monthly variations in our
hormones.'

Nicole stood up, stretched, and gave Katie a kiss. Then she eased over and hugged Simone. Although not quite fourteen, Simone was almost as tall as Nicole. She was a striking young woman with a dark brown face and soft, sensitive eyes. Simone always seemed calm and serene, in marked contrast to the restlessness and impatience of Katie.

'Why didn't Ellie come with us for this test?' Katie asked a little querulously. 'She's a girl too, but it seems like she never has to do anything.'

Nicole put her arm around Katie's shoulder as the three of them headed for the door and the light. 'She's only four years old, Katie, and according to The Eagle, Ellie's too small to give them any of the critical data they still need.'

In the small illuminated foyer, directly outside the room where they had been sleeping for five weeks, they put on their tight body suits, transparent helmets, and the slippers that anchored their feet on the floor. Nicole checked the two girls carefully before activating the outside door of the compartment. She needn't have worried. The door wouldn't have opened if any of them were unprepared for the environmental changes.

If Nicole and her daughters had not seen the large room outside their compartment several times before, they would have stopped in amazement and stared for several minutes. Stretching in front of them was a long chamber, a hundred or more metres in length and fifty metres wide. The ceiling above them, filled with banks of lights, was about five metres high. The room looked like a mixture of a hospital operating room and a semiconductor-manufacturing plant on the Earth. There were no walls or cubicles dividing the room into partitions, yet its rectangular dimensions were clearly sub-allocated into different tasks. The room was busy – the robots were all either analysing data from one set of tests or preparing for another set. Around the edges of the room were compartments, like the one in which Nicole, Simone, and Katie had slept for five weeks, in which the 'experiments' were carried out.

Katie walked over to the closest compartment on the left. It was set back in the corner and was suspended from the wall and ceiling along two perpendicular axes. A display screen built next to the metallic door showed a wide array of what was presumably data in some bizarre cuneiform-like script.

'Weren't we in this one last time?' Katie asked, pointing at the compartment. 'Wasn't this the place where we slept on that peculiar white foam and felt all the pressure?'

Her question was transmitted inside the helmets of her mother and sister. Nicole and Simone both nodded and then joined Katie in staring at the unintelligible screen.

'Your father thinks they are trying to find a way that we can sleep through an entire acceleration regime lasting for several months,' Nicole said. 'The Eagle will neither confirm nor deny this conjecture.'

Although the three women had undergone four separate tests together in this laboratory, none of them had ever seen any forms of life or intelligence except for the dozen or so mechanical aliens that apparently were in charge.

The humans called these beings 'block robots' because, except for their cylindrical 'feet' which allowed them to roll around the floor, the creatures were all made of rectangular solid chunks that looked like the blocks that human children played with on Earth.

'Why do you think we've never seen any of the Others?' Katie now asked. 'I mean, in here. We see them for a second or two in the tube and that's all. We know they're here – we aren't the only ones being tested.'

'This room is scheduled very carefully,' her mother replied. 'It's obvious that we weren't *meant* to see the Others, except in passing.'

'But *why*? The Eagle ought ...' Katie persisted.

'Excuse me,' Simone interrupted. 'But I think Big Block is coming over to see us.'

The largest of the block robots usually stayed in the square control area in the centre of the room and monitored all the experiments that were under way. At that moment he was moving toward them down one of the lanes that formed a grid in the room.

Katie walked over to another compartment about twenty metres away. From the active monitor on its exterior wall, she could tell that an experiment was under way inside.

Suddenly she pounded on the metal quite sharply with her gloved hand.

'*Katie,*' Nicole shouted.

'Stop that.' A sound came from Big Block almost simultaneously. He was about fifty metres away and approaching them very rapidly. 'You must not do that,' he said in perfect but clipped English.

'And what are you going to do about it?' Katie said defiantly as Big Block, all five square metres of him, ignored Nicole and Simone and headed for the young girl. Nicole ran over to protect her daughter.

'You must leave now,' Big Block said, hovering over Nicole and Katie from only a couple of metres away. 'Your test is over. The exit is over there where the lights are flashing.'

Nicole tugged firmly on Katie's arm and the girl reluctantly accompanied her mother toward the exit. 'But what *would* they do,' Katie said stubbornly, 'if we decided to stay here until another experiment was finished? Who knows? Maybe one of our octospiders is in there right now. Why are we never allowed to meet anyone else?'

'The Eagle has explained several times,' Nicole replied, a trace of anger in her voice, 'that during "this phase" we will be permitted "sightings" of other creatures but no additional contact. Your father has repeatedly asked why and The Eagle has always answered that we will find out in time ... And I wish you would try not to be so difficult, young lady.'

'It's not much different from being in prison,' Katie groused. 'We have only limited freedom here. And we're never told the answers to the really important questions.'

They had reached the long passageway that connected the transportation centre to the laboratory. A small vehicle, sitting at the edge of a moving sidewalk, was waiting for them. When they sat down, the top of the car closed over them and interior lights were illuminated. 'Before you ask,' Nicole said to Katie, pulling off her helmet as they started to move, 'we are not allowed to see out during this part of the transfer because we pass portions of the Engineering Module that are off limits to us. Your father and Uncle Michael asked this set of questions after their first sleep test.'

'Do you agree with Daddy,' Simone inquired after they had been riding in silence for several minutes, 'that we have been having all these sleep tests in preparation for some kind of space voyage?'

'It seems likely,' Nicole answered. 'But of course we don't know for certain.'

'And where are they going to send us?' asked Katie.

'I have no idea,' Nicole replied. 'The Eagle has been very evasive on all questions about our future.'

The car was moving about twenty kilometres per hour. After a fifteen-minute ride it stopped. The 'lid' of the vehicle rolled itself back as soon as all the helmets were properly in place again. The women exited into the main transportation centre of the Engineering Module. It was laid out in a circle and was twenty metres tall. In addition to half a dozen moving sidewalks leading to locations interior to the module, the centre contained two large, multilevel structures from which the sleek tubes departed. These tubes transported equipment, robots, and living creatures back and forth among the Habitation, Engineering, and Administration modules, the three huge spherical complexes that were the primary components of The Node.

As soon as they were inside the station, Nicole and her daughters heard a voice on their helmet receivers. 'Your tube will be on the second level. Take the escalator on the right. You will be departing in four minutes.'

Katie rolled her head from side to side, surveying the transportation centre. She could see racks of equipment, cars waiting to take travellers to destinations inside the Engineering Module, lights, escalators, and station platforms. But there was nothing moving. No robots and no living creatures.

'What would happen,' she said to her sister and mother, 'if we refused to go up there?' She stopped in the middle of the station. 'Then your schedule would be all fouled up,' she shouted at the tall ceiling.

'Come on, Katie,' Nicole said impatiently, 'we just went through this in the laboratory.'

Katie started walking again. 'But I *do* want to see something different,' she complained. 'I know that this place is not always this empty. Why are we kept isolated? It's as if we're unclean or something.'

'Your tube will depart in two minutes,' the disembodied voice said. 'Second level on the right.'

'Isn't it amazing that the robots and controllers can communicate with each and every species in its own language?' Simone commented as they reached the escalator.

'I think it's freaky,' Katie replied. 'Just for once, I'd like to see whoever or whatever controls this place make a mistake. Everything is too slick. I'd like to hear them speak avian to us. Or for that matter, speak avian to the avians.'

On the second level they shuffled along a platform for about forty metres until they reached a transparent vehicle, shaped like a bullet, the size of an extremely large automobile on Earth. It was parked, as always, on a track on the left side of the median. There were four parallel tracks on the platform altogether, two on either side of the median. All the others were currently empty.

Nicole turned and looked across the transportation centre. Sixty degrees around the circle was an identical tube station. The tubes on that side went to the Administration Module. Simone was watching her mother. 'Have you ever been over there?' she asked.

'No,' replied Nicole. 'But I bet it would be interesting. Your father says it looks wonderfully strange from up close.'

Richard just had to explore, Nicole thought, remembering the night almost a year ago when her husband set out to 'hitch' a ride to the Administration Module. Nicole shuddered. She had gone out into the atrium of their apartment with Richard and tried to dissuade him while he was putting on his space suit. He had figured out how to fool the door monitor (the next day a new, foolproof system was in place) and could hardly wait to take an 'unsupervised' look around.

Nicole had barely slept that night. In the wee hours of the morning their light panel had signaled that someone or something was in the atrium. When she had looked on the monitor, there was a strange birdman standing there, holding her unconscious husband in his arms. That had been their first contact with The Eagle ...

The thrust of the tube momentarily pinned them against the backs of their seats and returned Nicole to the present. They zoomed away from the Engineering Module. In less than a minute they were hurtling at full speed down the long, extremely narrow cylinder that connected the two modules.

The median and four tube tracks were at the centre of the long cylinder. Out to their right, in the far distance, the lights of the spherical Administration Module shone against a blue background of space. Katie had her tiny binoculars out. 'I want to be ready,' she said. 'They always go by so fast.'

Several minutes later she announced 'It's coming' and the three women pressed against the right side of the vehicle. In the far distance another tube approached on the opposite side of the track. Within instants it was upon them and the humans had no more than a second to stare across at the occupants of the vehicle heading for the Engineering Module.

'Wow!' said Katie as the tube rushed past.

'There were two different types,' said Simone.

'Eight or ten creatures altogether.'

'One set was pink, the other gold. Both mostly spherical.'

'And those long stringy tentacles, like gossamer. How big would you guess they were, Mother?'

'Five, maybe six metres in diameter,' Nicole said. 'Much bigger than we are.'

'Wow!' said Katie again. 'That was really something.' There was excitement in her eyes. The girl loved the feeling of adrenaline rushing through her system.

I too have never stopped being amazed, Nicole thought. *Not once during these thirteen months. But is this all there is? Were we brought all the way here from Earth just to be tested? And titillated by the existence of creatures from other worlds? Or is there some other, deeper purpose?*

There was a momentary silence in the speeding vehicle. Nicole, who was sitting in the middle, drew her daughters closer to her. 'You know I love you, don't you?' she said.

'Yes, Mother,' Simone replied. 'And we love you too.'

2

The reunion party was a success. Benjy embraced his beloved Simone the moment she walked into the apartment. Katie had Patrick pinned to the floor no more than a minute later.

'See,' she said, 'I can still beat you.'

'But not by much,' Patrick replied. 'I'm getting stronger. You'd better watch out.'

Nicole hugged both Richard and Michael before little Ellie ran over and leapt into her arms. It was evening, two hours after dinner on the twenty-four-hour clock used by the family, and Ellie had been almost ready for bed when her mother and sisters had arrived. The little girl walked down the hall to her room after proudly showing Nicole that she could now read 'cat', 'dog', and 'boy'.

The adults let Patrick stay awake until he was exhausted. Michael carried him to bed and Nicole tucked him in. 'I'm glad you're back, Mommy,' he said. 'I missed you very much.'

'And I missed you too,' Nicole answered. 'I don't think I'll be going away for so long again.'

'I hope not,' the six-year-old said. 'I like having you here.'

Everyone but Nicole was asleep by one o'clock in the morning. Nicole was not tired. After all, she had just finished sleeping for five weeks. After lying restlessly beside Richard in bed for thirty minutes, she decided to take a walk.

Although their apartment itself had no windows, the small atrium just off the entrance hall had an exterior window that offered a breathtaking view of the other two vertices of The Node. Nicole walked into the atrium, put on her space suit, and stood in front of the outer door. It did not open. She smiled to herself. *Maybe Katie's right. Maybe we are just prisoners here.* It had been clear very early in their stay that the outside door was locked intermittently; The Eagle had explained that it was 'necessary' to keep them from seeing things they 'couldn't understand.'

Nicole gazed out the window. At that moment a shuttle vehicle, similar in shape to the one that had brought them to The Node thirteen months before, was approaching the Habitation Module transportation centre. *What kind of wonderful creatures do you contain?* Nicole thought. *And are they as astounded as we were when we first arrived?*

Nicole would never forget those first views of The Node. All of the family had thought, after they had left The Waystation, that they would reach their next destination within several hours. They had been wrong. Their separation from the illuminated Rama craft had grown slowly until after six hours they could no longer see Rama at all on their left. The lights of The Waystation behind them were becoming faint. They were all tired. Eventually the entire family had fallen asleep.

It had been Katie who had awakened them. 'I see where we're going,' she had shouted triumphantly, her excitement unrestrained. She had pointed out the front shuttle window, a little to the right, where one strong and growing light was dividing itself into three. For the next four hours the image of The Node grew and grew. From that distance it had been an awesome sight, an equilateral triangle with three glowing, transparent spheres at its vertices. And what a scale! Even their experience with Rama had not prepared them for the majesty of this incredible engineering creation. Each of the three sides, actually long transportation corridors connecting the three spherical modules, was over a hundred and fifty kilometres in length. The spheres at each vertex were twenty-five kilometres in diameter. Even from a great distance the humans could discern activity on many of the separate levels inside the modules.

'What is going to happen now?' Patrick had anxiously asked Nicole as the shuttle had altered its path and started heading toward one of the vertices of the triangle.

Nicole had picked Patrick up and held him in her arms. 'I don't know, darling,' she had said softly to her son. 'We have to wait and see.'

Benjy had been completely awestruck. He had stared for hours at the great illuminated triangle in space. Simone had often stood beside him, holding his hand. While the shuttle was making its final approach to one of the spheres, she had felt his muscles tense. 'Don't worry, Benjy,' Simone had said reassuringly, 'everything will be all right.'

Their shuttle had entered a narrow corridor cut into the sphere and then docked in a berth at the edge of the transportation centre. The family had cautiously left the craft, carrying with them their bags and Richard's computer. Then the shuttle had immediately departed, unnerving even the adults by its swift disappearance. Less than a minute later they heard the first disembodied voice.

'Welcome,' it had said in an unmodulated tone. 'You have arrived at the Habitation Module. Proceed straight ahead and stand in front of the grey wall.'

'Where is that voice coming from?' Katie had asked. Her voice contained the fright they all were feeling.

'Everywhere,' Richard had answered. 'It's above us, around us, even below us.' They all scanned the walls and ceiling.

'But how does it know English?' Simone had inquired. 'Are there other people here?'

Richard laughed nervously. 'Unlikely,' he replied. 'Probably this place has been in contact with Rama in some way and has a master language algorithm. I wonder ...'

'Please move forward,' the voice had interrupted. 'You are in a transportation complex. The vehicle that will take you to your section of the module is waiting on a lower level.'

It had taken them several minutes to reach the grey wall. The children had never been in unconfined weightlessness before. Katie and Patrick jumped off the platform and did flips and rolls in the air. Benjy, watching their fun, tried to copy their antics. Unfortunately, he was not able to figure out how to use the ceiling and walls to return to the platform. He was completely disoriented by the time Simone rescued him.

When the entire family and its baggage were properly positioned in front of the wall, a wide door opened and they entered a small room. Special tight-fitting suits, helmets, and slippers were neatly arranged on a bench. 'The transportation centre and most of the common areas here at The Node,' the voice said in its absolute monotone, 'do not have an atmosphere that is suitable for your species. You will need to wear this clothing unless you are inside your apartment.'

When they were all dressed, a door on the opposite side of the room opened and they entered the main hall of the Habitation Module transportation centre. The station was identical to the one they would later encounter at the Engineering Module. Nicole and her family descended two levels, as directed by the voice, and then proceeded around the circular periphery to where their 'bus' was waiting. The closed vehicle was comfortable and well lit, but they were unable to see out during the hour and a half that it travelled through a maze of passageways. At length the bus halted and its top lifted off.

'Take the hall to your left,' another, similar voice had directed as soon as all eight of them were standing on the metallic floor. 'The hall splits into two pathways after four hundred metres. Take the path to your right and stop in front of the third square marker on the left. That is the door to your apartment.'

Patrick had sprinted off down one of the halls. 'That is the wrong hall,' the voice had announced without inflection. 'Return to the dock and take the next hall on your left.'

There was nothing for them to see on the walk from the dock to their apartment. In the succeeding months, they would make the walk many times, either going to the exercise room or, occasionally, for tests over in the Engineering Module, and they would still never see anything except walls and ceilings and the square markers they would come to recognise as doors.

The place was obviously carefully monitored. Nicole and Richard both felt certain, from the very beginning, that some, perhaps many, of the apartments in their area were occupied by someone or something, but they never ever saw any of the Others in the corridors.

After finding and entering the specified door to their apartment, Nicole and her family removed their special clothing in the atrium and stored it in the cabinets created for that purpose. The children took turns looking out the window at the other two spherical modules while they waited for the inner door to open. A few minutes later they saw the interior of their new home for the very first time.

They were all overwhelmed. Compared to the relatively primitive conditions in which they had been living in Rama, the family's apartment at the Node was paradise. Each of the children had his or her own room. Michael had a suite for himself at one end of the unit; Richard and Nicole's master bedroom, complete even with a king-sized bed, was at the opposite end of the apartment, just off the entrance hall. There were four bathrooms altogether, plus a kitchen, a dining room, and even a playroom for the children. The furniture in each room was surprisingly appropriate and tastefully designed. The apartment contained over four hundred square metres of living space.

Even the adults were stunned. 'How in the world could they have done this?' Nicole had asked Richard that first night, out of earshot of the overjoyed children.

Richard had cast a bewildered glance around them. 'I can only surmise,' he had replied, 'that somehow all our actions in Rama were monitored and telemetered here to The Node. They must also have had access to our data bases and extracted the way we live from that set of information.' Richard grinned. 'And of course, even way out here, if they have sensitive receivers, they could be picking up television signals from Earth. Isn't it embarrassing to think that we are represented by such ...'

'Welcome,' another identical voice had interrupted Richard's thought. Again the sound seemed to be coming from all directions. 'We hope everything in your apartment is satisfactory. If it is not, please tell us. We cannot possibly respond to everything that all of you say at all times. Therefore, a simple communication regimen has been established. On your kitchen counter is a white button. We will assume that everything said by an individual after pushing the white button is directed at us. When you are finished with your communication, push the white button again. In that way ...'

'I have one question first,' Katie had then interrupted. She had run into the kitchen to push the button. 'Just who are you, anyway?'

A tiny delay of maybe one second had preceded the answer. 'We are the collective intelligence that governs The Node. We are here to assist you, to make you more comfortable, and to supply you with the essentials for living. We will also, from time to time, ask you to perform certain tasks that will help us to understand you better ...'

*

Nicole could no longer see the shuttle she had been watching out the window. Actually, she had been so deeply immersed in her memory of their arrival at The Node that she had temporarily forgotten the newcomers. Now, as she returned to the present, in her mind's eye she imagined an assemblage of strange creatures disembarking on a platform and being startled upon hearing a voice address them in their native language. *The experience of wonder must be universal*, she thought. *belonging to all conscious chemicals.*

Her eyes lifted from the near field and focused on the Administration Module in the distance. *What goes on over there?* Nicole wondered. *We hapless creatures move back and forth between Habitation and Engineering. All our activities appear to be logically orchestrated. But by whom? And for what? Why has someone brought all these beings to this artificial world?*

Nicole had no answer to these infinite questions. As usual, they gave her a powerful sense of her own insignificance. Her immediate impulse was to go back inside and hug one of her children. She laughed at herself. *Both pictures are true indications of our position in the cosmos,* she thought. *We are both desperately important to our children and absolutely nothing in the grand scheme of things. It takes enormous wisdom to see that there is no inconsistency in those two points of view.*

3

Breakfast was a celebration. They ordered a feast from the exceptional cooks who prepared their food. The designers of their apartment had considerately provided them with a variety of ovens and a full refrigerator, in case they wanted to prepare their own meals from the raw materials. However, the alien (or robot) cooks were so good, and so quickly trained, that Nicole and her family almost never prepared the meals themselves – they just pushed the white button and ordered.

'I want pancakes this morning,' Katie announced in the kitchen.

'Me too, me too,' her sidekick Patrick added.

'What kind of pancakes?' the voice intoned. 'We have four different types in our memory. There is buckwheat, buttermilk ...'

'Buttermilk,' interrupted Katie. 'Three altogether.' She glanced at her little brother. 'Better make it four.'

'With butter and maple syrup,' Patrick shouted.

'Four pancakes with butter and maple syrup,' said the voice. 'Will that be all?'

'One apple juice and one orange juice as well,' Katie said after a brief consultation with Patrick.

'Six minutes and eighteen seconds,' the voice said.

When the food was ready, the family gathered at the round table in the kitchen. The youngest children explained to Nicole what they had been doing during her absence. Patrick was especially proud of his new personal record in the fifty-meter dash over in the exercise room. Benjy laboriously counted to ten and everyone applauded. They had just finished breakfast and were cleaning the dishes off the table when the doorbell rang.

The adults looked at each other and Richard walked over to the control console, where he turned on the video monitor. The Eagle was standing outside their door.

'I hope it's not another test,' said Patrick spontaneously.

'No ... no, I doubt it,' Nicole replied, moving toward the entryway. 'He's probably here to give us the results of the last experiments.'

Nicole took a deep breath before she opened the door. No matter how many times she encountered The Eagle, her adrenaline level always increased in his presence. Why was that? Was it his awesome knowledge that frightened her? Or his power over them? Or just the bewildering fact of his existence?

The Eagle greeted her with what she had come to recognise as a smile. 'May I come in?' he said pleasantly. 'I would like to talk to you, your husband, and Mr O'Toole.'

Nicole stared at him (or *it*, her mind instantly flashed), as she always did. He was tall, maybe two and a quarter metres, and shaped like a human being from the neck down. His arms and torso, however, were covered with small, tightly woven charcoal grey feathers – except for the four fingers on each hand, which were creamy white and featherless. Below his waist, the surface of The Eagle's body was flesh-coloured, but it was obvious from the sheen of his outer layer that no attempt had been made to duplicate real human skin. There was no hair below his waist and neither visible joints nor genitalia. His feet had no toes. When The Eagle walked, wrinkles developed around the knee area, but they disappeared when he was standing still.

The Eagle's face was mesmerizing. His head had two large, powder blue eyes on either side of a protruding greyish beak. When he talked the beak opened and his perfect English came from some kind of electronic voice box at the back of the throat. The feathers on the top of his head were white and contrasted sharply with the dark grey of his face, neck, and back. The feathering on his face was quite sparse and scattered.

'May I come in?' The Eagle repeated politely when Nicole did not move for several seconds.

'Of course ... of course,' she replied, moving away from the door. 'I'm sorry ... I just hadn't seen you for so long.'

'Good morning, Mr Wakefield, Mr O'Toole. Hello, children,' The Eagle said as he strode into the living room.

Patrick and Benjy both backed away from him. Of all the children, only Katie and little Ellie did not seem to be afraid.

'Good morning,' Richard replied. 'And what can we do for you today?' he inquired. The Eagle *never* made social calls. There was always some purpose for his visits.

'As I told your wife at the door,' The Eagle replied, 'I need to talk to all three of you adults. Can Simone take care of the other children while we chat for an hour or so?'

Nicole had already started herding the children back into the playroom when The Eagle stopped her. 'That won't be necessary,' he said. 'They can use the whole apartment. The four of us are going to the conference room across the hall.'

Uh-oh, Nicole thought immediately. *This is something big ... We've never left the children alone in the apartment before.*

She was suddenly very concerned about their safety. 'Excuse me, Mr Eagle,' she said. 'Will the children be all right here? I mean, they're not going to have any special visitors or anything like that ...?'

'No, Mrs Wakefield,' The Eagle responded matter-of-factly. 'I give you my word that nothing will interfere with your children.'

Out in the atrium, when the three humans started to put on their space suits, The Eagle stopped them. 'That won't be necessary,' he said. 'Last night we reconfigured this portion of the sector. We have sealed off the hall just before the junction and transformed this whole area into an Earthlike habitat. You'll be able to use the conference room without putting on any special clothing.'

The Eagle started talking as soon as they sat down in the large conference room across the hall. 'Since our first encounter you have repeatedly asked me questions about what you are doing here and I have not given you direct answers. Now that your final set of sleep tests is completed – successfully, I might add – I have been empowered to inform you about the next phase of your mission.

'I have also been given permission to tell you something about myself. As all of you have suspected, I am not a living creature – at least not by your definition.' The Eagle laughed. 'I was created by the intelligence that governs The Node to interface with you on sensitive issues. Our early observations of your behaviour indicated a reluctance on your part to interact with the disembodied voices. It had already been decided to create me, or something similar, as an emissary to your family when you, Mr Wakefield, nearly caused serious chaos in this sector by trying to make an unscheduled and unapproved visit to the Administration Module. My appearance at that time was designed to preclude further untoward behaviour.

'We have now entered,' The Eagle continued after only a momentary hesitation, 'the most important time period of your stay here. The spaceship you call Rama is over at the Hangar undergoing major refurbishment and engineering redesign. You human beings will now take part in that redesign process, for some of you will be returning with Rama to the solar system in which you originated.'

Richard and Nicole both started to interrupt. 'Let me finish first,' The Eagle said. 'We have very carefully prepared my remarks to cover your anticipated questions.'

The alien birdman glanced at each of the three humans around the table before continuing at a slower pace. 'Notice that I did not say that you will be going back to Earth. If the nominal plan succeeds, those of you who return will interact with other human beings in your solar system, but not on your home planet. Only if there is some required deviation from the baseline plan will you actually return to Earth.

'Notice also that only *some* of you will be returning. Mrs Wakefield,' The Eagle said directly to Nicole, 'you will definitely be travelling again in Rama. This is one of the constraints that we are placing on the mission. We will let you and the rest of your family decide who will accompany you on the journey. You can go alone if you choose, leaving everyone else here at The

Node, or you can take some of the others. However, you cannot *all* make the voyage on Rama. At least one reproductive pair must stay here at The Node – to ensure some data for our encyclopedia in the unlikely event that the mission is unsuccessful.

'The primary purpose of The Node is to catalogue life-forms in this part of the galaxy. Spacefaring life forms have the highest priority and our specifications call for us to collect vast amounts of data about each and every spacefarer we encounter. To accomplish this task, we have worked out, over hundreds of thousands of years of your time, a method of gathering this data that minimises the likelihood of a cataclysmic intrusion into the evolutionary pattern of those spacefarers while at the same time maximizing the probability of our obtaining the vital data.

'Our basic approach involves sending observing spacecraft on reconnaissance missions, hoping to lure spacefarers to us so they can be identified and phenotyped. Repeat spacecraft are later sent to the same target, first to expand the degree of interaction, and ultimately to capture a representative subset of the spacefaring species so that long-term and detailed observations can take place in an environment of our choice.'

The Eagle paused. Nicole's mind and heart were both racing at a frantic pace. She had so many questions. Why had she been especially selected to return? Would she be able to see Genevieve? And what exactly did The Eagle mean by the word 'capture' – did he understand that the word was usually interpreted in a hostile manner? Why did ...

'I think I understood most of what you said,' Richard spoke first, 'but you have omitted some crucial information. Why are you gathering all this data about spacefaring species?'

The Eagle smiled. 'In our information hierarchy there are three basic levels. Access to each level by an individual or a species is permitted or denied based on a set of established criteria. With my earlier statements we have given you, as representatives of your species, Level Two information for the first time. It is a tribute to your intelligence that your initial question seeks an answer which is classified as Level Three.'

'Does all that gobbledygook mean you're not going to tell us?' Richard asked, laughing nervously.

The Eagle nodded.

'*Will* you tell us why I alone am required to make the return voyage?' Nicole now asked.

'There are many reasons,' The Eagle answered. 'First, we believe you are the best suited physically for the return voyage. Our data also indicates that your superior communication skills will be invaluable after the capture phase of the mission is completed. There are additional considerations as well, but those two are the most important.'

'When will we be leaving?' Richard asked.

'That's not certain. Part of the schedule is dependent on you. We will let you know when a firm departure date is established. I will tell you, however, that it will almost certainly be in less than four of your months.'

We're going to leave very soon, Nicole thought. *And at least two of us must stay here. But who* ...

'*Any* reproductive pair can be left here at The Node?' Michael now inquired, following the same pattern of thought as Nicole.

'Almost, Mr O'Toole,' The Eagle replied. 'The youngest girl Ellie would not be acceptable with you as a partner – we might not be able to keep you alive and fertile until she reaches sexual maturity – but any other combination would be fine. We must have a high probability of successfully producing healthy offspring.'

'Why?' Nicole asked.

'There exists a very small probability that your mission will not be successful and that the pair left at The Node will be the only humans we are able to observe. As infant spacefarers, having reached that stage without the usual assistance, you are especially interesting to us.'

The conversation could have lasted indefinitely. However, after several more questions, The Eagle abruptly rose and announced that his participation in the conference was over. He encouraged the humans to deal quickly with the issue of 'allocation,' as he called it, for he intended to begin work almost immediately with those members of the family who would be returning in the direction of Earth. It would be their job to help him design the 'Earth module inside Rama'. Without any additional explanation, he left the room.

The three adults agreed not to tell the children the most important details of their meeting with The Eagle for at least a day, until after they had had a chance to reflect and converse among themselves. That night, after the children had gone to bed, Nicole, Richard, and Michael talked quietly in the living room of their apartment.

Nicole opened the conversation by admitting that she was feeling angry and powerless. Despite the fact that The Eagle had been very nice about it, she said, he had basically ordered them to participate in the return mission. And how could they refuse? The entire family was absolutely dependent upon The Eagle – or at least the intelligence that he represented – for its survival. No threats had been made, but no threats were needed. They had no choice but to comply with The Eagle's instructions.

But who among the family should stay at The Node? Nicole wondered aloud. Michael said it was absolutely essential that at least one adult remain at The Node. His argument was persuasive. Any two of the children, even Simone and Patrick, would need the benefit of an adult's experience and wisdom to have any chance for happiness under the circumstances. Michael then volunteered to stay at The Node, saying that it was unlikely he would survive a return trip anyway.

All three of them agreed that it was clearly the Nodal intelligence's intention to have the humans sleep most of the way back to the solar system. Otherwise, what was the purpose of all the sleep tests? Nicole did not like the idea of the children missing out on the critical development periods of their lives. She suggested that she should return alone, leaving everyone else in the family at The Node. After all, she reasoned, it's not as if the children would have a 'normal' life on Earth after they make the journey.

'If we are interpreting The Eagle correctly,' she said, 'anybody who returns will end up ultimately as a passenger on Rama heading to some other location in the Galaxy.'

'We don't know that for certain,' Richard argued. 'On the other hand, whoever stays here is almost certainly doomed to never seeing any humans other than the family.'

Richard added that he intended to make the return trip under any circumstances, not just to be a companion for Nicole, but also to experience the adventure.

The trio could not reach a final agreement about the deployment of the children during that first evening's discussion. But they did firmly resolve the issue of what the adults were going to do. Michael O'Toole would stay at the Node. Nicole and Richard would make the return journey to the solar system.

In bed after the meeting Nicole could not sleep. She kept running through all the options in her mind. She was certain that Simone would make a better mother than Katie. Besides, Simone and Uncle Michael were extremely compatible and Katie would not want to be separated from her father. But who should be left to mate with Simone? Should it be Benjy, who loved his sister madly, but would never be able to engage in an intelligent conversation?

Nicole tossed and turned for hours. In truth, she didn't like any of the choices. She understood well the source of her disquiet. However the issue was resolved, she would be forced once again to separate, probably permanently, from at least a few members of the family that she loved. As she lay in her bed in the middle of the night the ghosts and pain of past separations returned to haunt her. Nicole's heart ached as she imagined the parting that would come in a few months. Pictures of her mother, her father, and Genevieve tugged at her heartstrings. *Maybe that's all life is,* she thought in her temporary depression. *An endless sequence of painful partings.*

4

'Mother, Father, wake up. I want to talk to you.'

Nicole had been dreaming. She had been walking in the woods behind her family villa at Beauvois. It had been springtime and the flowers had been magnificent. It took her a few seconds to realise that Simone was sitting on their bed.

Richard reached over and kissed his daughter on the forehead. 'What is it, dear?' he asked.

'Uncle Michael and I were saying our matins together and I could tell that he was distressed.' Simone's serene eyes moved slowly back and forth from one parent to the other. 'He told me everything about your conversation yesterday with The Eagle.'

Nicole sat up quickly as Simone continued. 'I've had over an hour now to think carefully about everything. I know I'm only a thirteen-year-old girl, but I believe I have a solution to this, uh, allocation issue that will make everybody in the family happy.'

'My dear Simone,' Nicole replied, reaching out for her daughter, 'it's not your responsibility to solve ...'

'No, Mother,' Simone gently interrupted. 'Please hear me out. My solution involves something that none of you adults would ever even consider. It could only come from me. And it's obviously the best plan for everyone concerned.'

Richard's brow was now furrowed. 'What are you talking about?' he said.

Simone took a deep breath, 'I want to stay at The Node with Uncle Michael. I will become his wife and we will be The Eagle's "reproductive pair". Nobody else needs to stay, but Michael and I would be happy to keep Benjy with us as well.'

'*Whaat?*' Richard shouted. He was flabbergasted. 'Uncle Michael is seventy-two years old! You're not even fourteen yet. It's preposterous, ridiculous ...' He was suddenly silent.

The mature young woman who was his daughter smiled. 'More preposterous than The Eagle?' she replied. 'More ridiculous than the fact that we have travelled eight light-years from the Earth to rendezvous with a giant intelligent triangle that is now going to send some of us back in the opposite direction?'

Nicole regarded Simone with awe and admiration. She said nothing, but reached out and gave her daughter a strong hug. Tears swam in Nicole's eyes.

'It's all right, Mother,' Simone said after the embrace was ended. 'After you recover from the initial shock, you'll realise that what I'm suggesting is by far the best solution. If you and Father make the return trip together – as I think you should – then either Katie or Ellie or I must stay here at The Node and mate with Patrick or Benjy or Uncle Michael. The only combination that is genetically sound is either Katie or I with Uncle Michael. I've thought through all the possibilities. Michael and I are very close. We have the same religion. If we stay and marry, then each of the other children is free to choose. They can either remain here with us or return to the solar system with you and Daddy.'

Simone put her hand on her father's forearm. 'Daddy, I know that in many ways this will be harder on you than it is on Mother. I have not yet mentioned my idea to Uncle Michael. He certainly did not suggest it. If you and Mother don't give me your support, then it can't work. This marriage will be difficult enough for Michael to accept even if you don't object.'

Richard shook his head. 'You are amazing, Simone.' He embraced her. 'Please let us think about it for a while. Promise me you won't say another word about this until your mother and I have had a chance to talk.'

'I promise,' Simone said. 'Thank you both very much. I love you,' she added at the door to their bedroom.

She turned and walked down the illuminated hall. Her long black hair reached almost to her waist. *You have become a woman,* Nicole thought, watching Simone's graceful walk. *And not just physically. You are mature way beyond your years.* Nicole imagined Michael and Simone as husband and wife and was surprised that she didn't find it at all objectionable. Considering everything, Nicole said to herself, realizing that after his protests Michael O'Toole would be very happy, *your idea may be the least unsatisfactory choice in our difficult situation.*

Simone did not waver from her intention even when Michael objected strenuously to what he called her 'proposed martyrdom.' She explained to him, patiently, that her marriage to him was the only one possible since Katie and he were, by everyone's assessment, incompatible personalities, and anyway Katie was still only a girl, a year or eighteen months away from sexual maturity. Would he prefer that she marry one of her half-brothers and commit incest? No, no, he responded.

Michael assented when he saw that there were no other viable choices and that neither Richard nor Nicole raised any strong objections to the marriage. Richard, of course, tempered his approval with the phrase 'in these unusual circumstances,' but Michael could tell that Simone's father had at least partially accepted the idea of his thirteen-year-old daughter marrying a man old enough to be her grandfather.

Within a week it had been decided, with the children's involvement, that Katie, Patrick, and little Ellie would all make the return trip on Rama with Richard and Nicole. Patrick was reluctant to leave his father, but Michael O'Toole graciously agreed that his six-year-old son would probably have a 'more interesting and fulfilling' life if he stayed with the rest of the family. That left only Benjy. The adorable boy, chronologically eight but mentally equivalent to an average three-year-old, was told that he would be welcome either in Rama or at The Node. He could barely comprehend what was going to happen to the family, and was certainly not prepared to make such a momentous choice. The decision frightened and confused him; he became quite distraught and lapsed into a deep depression. As a result, the family postponed discussions of Benjy's fate until an undefined time in the future.

'We will be gone a day and a half, maybe two,' The Eagle said to Michael and the children. 'Rama is being reconditioned at a facility about ten thousand kilometres from here.'

'But I want to go too,' Katie said petulantly. 'I also have some good ideas for the Earth module.'

'We'll involve you in later phases of the process,' Richard assured Katie. 'We'll have a design centre right here beside us, in the conference room.'

Eventually Richard and Nicole finished their goodbyes and joined The Eagle in the hallway. They put on their special suits and crossed over into the common area of the sector. Nicole could tell that Richard was excited. 'You do love adventure, don't you, darling?' she said.

He nodded. 'I think it was Goethe who said that everything a human being wants can be divided into four components – love, adventure, power, and fame. Our personalities are shaped by how much of each component we seek. For me, adventure has always been numero uno.'

Nicole was contemplative as they entered a waiting car along with The Eagle. The lid closed over them and again they could not see anything during their ride to the transportation centre. *Adventure is very important to me also,* Nicole thought, *and as a young girl fame was my uppermost goal.* She smiled to herself. *But now it's definitely love ... We would be boring if we never changed.*

They travelled in a shuttle identical to the one that had brought them to The Node originally. The Eagle sat in front, Richard and Nicole in the rear. The view behind them of the spherical modules, the transportation corridors, and the entire lighted triangle was absolutely sensational.

The direction they were going was toward Sirius, the dominant feature in the space surrounding The Node. The large, young white star glowed in the distance, appearing roughly the same size as their native sun would look from the asteroid belt.

'How did you happen to pick this location for The Node?' Richard asked The Eagle after they had been cruising for about an hour.

633

'What do you mean?' he replied.

'Why here, why in the Sirius system, instead of some other place?'

The Eagle laughed. 'This location is only temporary,' he said. 'We'll be moving again as soon as Rama departs.'

Richard was puzzled. 'You mean the entire Node *moves?*' He turned around and glanced back at the triangle glowing faintly in the distance. 'Where is the propulsion system?'

'There are small propulsion capabilities in each of the modules, but they are only used in case of an emergency. Transport between temporary holding sites is accomplished by what you would call tugs – they affix themselves to ports on the sides of the spheres and provide virtually all the trajectory change velocity.'

Nicole thought about Michael and Simone and became worried. 'Where will The Node go?' she asked.

'It's probably not specified exactly yet' The Eagle answered vaguely. 'It's always a stochastic function anyway, depending on how the various activities are proceeding.' He continued after a short silence. 'When our work in a specific place is finished, the entire configuration – Node, Hangar, and Way-station – are moved to another region of interest.'

Richard and Nicole stared silently at each other in the backseat. They were having difficulty grasping the magnitude of what The Eagle was telling them. The *entire* Node *moved*! It was too much to believe. Richard decided to change the subject.

'What is your definition of a spacefaring species?' he asked The Eagle.

'One that has ventured, either on its own or through its robot surrogates, outside the sensible atmosphere of its home planet. If its own planet has no atmosphere, or if the species has no home planet at all, then the definition is more complicated.'

'You mean there are intelligent creatures that have evolved in a vacuum? How can that be possible?'

'You're an atmospheric chauvinist,' The Eagle replied. 'Like all creatures, you limit the ways that life might express itself to environments similar to your own.'

'How many spacefaring species are there in our galaxy?' Richard asked a little later.

'That's one of the objectives of our project – to answer that question exactly. Remember, there are more than a hundred billion stars in the Milky Way. Slightly more than a quarter of them have planetary systems surrounding them. If only one out of every million stars with planets was home to a spacefaring species, then there would still be twenty-five thousand spacefarers in our galaxy alone.'

The Eagle turned around and looked at Richard and Nicole. 'The estimated number of spacefarers in the galaxy, as well as the spacefarer density in any specified zone, is Level Three information. But I can tell you one thing. There are Life Dense Zones in the galaxy where the average number of spacefarers is greater than one per thousand stars.'

Richard whistled. 'This is staggering stuff,' he said to Nicole excitedly. 'It means that the local evolutionary miracle that produced us is a common paradigm in the universe. We are unique, to be sure, for nowhere else would the process that produced us have been duplicated exactly. But the characteristic that is truly special about our species – namely our ability to model our world and understand both it and where we fit into its overall scheme – that capability must belong to thousands of creatures! For without that ability they could not have become spacefarers.'

Nicole was overwhelmed. She recalled a similar moment, years before when she was with Richard in the photograph room of the octospider lair in Rama, when she had struggled to grasp the immensity of the universe in terms of total information content. Again now she realised that the entire set of knowledge in the human domain, everything that any member of the human species had ever learned or experienced, was no more than a single grain of sand on the great beach representing everything that had ever been known by all the sentient creatures of the universe.

5

Their shuttle stopped several hundred kilometers from The Hangar. The facility had a strange shape, completely flat on the bottom but with rounded sides and top. The three factories in The Hangar – one at each end and another in the middle – each looked from the outside like geodesic domes. They rose sixty or seventy kilometers above the bottom of the structure. Between these factories the roof was much lower, only eight or ten kilometers above the flat plane, so the overall appearance of the top of The Hangar was what might have been expected from the back of a three-humped camel, if such a creature had ever existed.

The Eagle, Nicole, and Richard had stopped to watch a starfish craft which, according to The Eagle, had been reconditioned and was now ready for its next voyage. The starfish had come out of the left hump. Although small compared to either The Hangar or Rama, the starfish was still almost ten kilometers from its centre to the end of a ray. It had begun to spin as soon as it was free of The Hangar. As the shuttle remained 'parked' some fifteen kilometers away, the starfish increased its spin rate to ten revolutions per minute. Once its spin rate was stabilised, the starfish zoomed away to the left.

'That leaves only Rama out of this set,' The Eagle said. 'The giant wheel, which was first in your queue at The Waystation, left four months ago. It required only minimal refurbishing.'

Richard wanted to ask a question, but he restrained himself. He had already learned during the flight from The Node that The Eagle voluntarily gave them virtually all the information he was allowed to share. 'Rama has been quite a challenge,' The Eagle continued. 'And we're still not certain exactly when we will finish.'

The shuttle approached the right dome of The Hangar and lights began to shine at the five o'clock position on the dome's face. Upon closer inspection Richard and Nicole could see that some small doors had opened. 'You'll need your suits,' The Eagle said. 'It would have been a major engineering feat to have designed this huge place with a variable environment.'

Nicole and Richard dressed while the shuttle docked in a berth very similar to the one at their transportation centre. 'Can you hear me all right?' The Eagle said, testing the communication system.

'Roger,' Richard replied from inside his helmet. He and Nicole glanced at each other and laughed as they remembered their days as Newton cosmonauts.

The Eagle led them down a long, wide corridor. At the end they turned right through a door and came out on a broad balcony ten kilometers above a factory floor larger than anyone could possibly imagine. Nicole felt her knees weaken as she stared into the giant abyss. Despite the weightlessness, waves of vertigo swept through both Richard and Nicole. They both turned away at the same moment. They focused their eyes on each other while they tried to comprehend what they had just seen.

'It's quite a sight,' The Eagle commented.

What a colossal understatement, Nicole thought. She very slowly lowered her eyes again to the awesome spectacle. This time she held on to the rail with both hands to help her equilibrium.

The factory below them contained the entire Northern Hemicylinder of Rama, from the port end where they had docked the Newton and entered, down to the end of the Central Plain at the banks of the Cylindrical Sea. There was no sea, and no Raman city of New York, but there was almost as much real estate in this one enclosed factory as in the entire American state of Rhode Island.

The crater and bowl of the north end of Rama were still completely intact, including the outer shell. These segments of Rama were positioned to the right of Richard, Nicole, and The Eagle, almost behind them as they stood on the platform. Mounted in front of them on the railings were a dozen telescopes, each with a different resolution, through which the three of them could see the familiar ladders and stairways, resembling three ribs of an umbrella, that took thirty thousand steps to descend (or ascend) to the Central Plain of Rama.

The rest of the Northern Hemicylinder was split open and lying beneath them in parts, not directly connected to the bowl or to each other, but nevertheless lying with adjacent sectors in the proper alignment. Each part was roughly six to eight square kilometers and its edges rose, due to the curvature, substantially off the floor.

'It's easier to do the early work in this configuration,' The Eagle explained. 'Once we've closed the cylinder it's harder to get in and out with all the equipment.'

Through the telescopes Richard and Nicole could see that two different areas of the Central Plain were teeming with activity. They could not begin to count the number of robots going to and fro on the floor of the factory below them. Nor could they determine exactly what was being done in many cases. It was engineering on a scale never dreamed of by humans.

'I brought you up here first to give you an overview,' The Eagle said. 'Later we will go down on the floor and you can see more of the details.'

Richard and Nicole stared at him dumbfounded. The Eagle laughed and continued. 'If you look carefully, and put the pieces together in your mind, you will see that two vast regions of the Central Plain, one near the Cylindrical Sea and another covering an area almost up to the end of the stairways, have been completely cleared. That's where all the new construction is going on. Between these two areas Rama looks exactly as it did when you left it. We have a general engineering guideline here – we only change those regions that are going to be used on the next mission.'

Richard brightened. 'Are you telling us that this spacecraft is used *over and over*? And that for each mission only *required* changes are made?'

The Eagle nodded.

'Then that conglomeration of skyscrapers we call New York might have been built for some much *earlier* mission, and simply *left* there because no changes were required?'

The Eagle did not say anything in response to Richard's rhetorical question. He was pointing at the northern area of the Central Plain. 'That will be your habitat, over there. We have just finished the infrastructure, what you would call the "utilities", including water, power, sewer, and top-level environmental control. There is room for design flexibility in the rest of the process. That's why we have brought you over here.'

'What is that tiny domed building south of the cleared area?' Richard asked. He was still staggered by the idea that New York might have been a leftover, a remnant from an earlier Raman voyage.

'That's the control centre,' The Eagle replied. 'The equipment that manages your habitat will be stored there. Usually the control centre is hidden beneath the living area, in the shell of Rama, but in your case the designers decided to put it on the Plain.'

'What's that large region over there?' Nicole said, pointing at the cleared area immediately north of where the Cylindrical Sea would have been located if Rama had been completely reassembled.

'I'm not allowed to tell you what it's for,' The Eagle replied. 'In fact, I'm surprised that I have even been allowed to show you that it exists. Ordinarily our return voyagers are totally ignorant of the contents of their vehicle outside their own habitat. The nominal plan is, of course, for each species to stay within its own module.'

'Look at that mound or tower in the centre,' Nicole said to Richard, directing his attention to the other region. 'It must be almost two kilometers high.'

'And it's shaped like a doughnut. I mean, the centre is hollowed out.'

They could see that the outside walls of what was possibly a second habitat were already quite advanced. None of its interior would be visible from the factory floor.

'Can you give us a hint as to who or what is going to live *there*?' Nicole asked.

'Come on,' The Eagle said firmly, shaking his head. 'It's time for us to descend.'

Richard and Nicole disengaged themselves from the telescopes, took a quick look at the general layout of their own habitat (which was not nearly as far along in construction as the other one), and followed The Eagle back into the corridor. After five minutes of walking they reached what The Eagle told them was an elevator.

'You must buckle yourselves into these seats very carefully,' their guide said. 'This is quite a wild ride.'

The acceleration in their bizarre oval capsule was powerful and swift. Less than two minutes later, the deceleration was equally abrupt. They had reached the factory floor. 'This thing travels three hundred kilometres an hour?' Richard asked after doing some quick mental calculations.

'Unless it's in a hurry,' The Eagle replied.

Richard and Nicole followed him out onto the factory floor. It was immense. In many ways it was more staggering than Rama itself, because almost half of the giant spacecraft was lying on the floor around them. They both remembered the overpowering feelings they had had riding in the chairlifts in Rama and looking out across the Cylindrical Sea at the mysterious horns in the southern bowl. Those feelings of reverence and awe returned, and were even amplified, as Richard and Nicole stared at the activity going on around and above them in the factory.

The elevator had deposited them at the floor level just outside one of the portions of their habitat. The shell of Rama was in front of them. They checked its thickness as they walked across from the elevator exit. 'About two hundred metres thick,' Richard noted to Nicole, answering a question they had had since their first days in Rama.

'What will be beneath our habitat, in the shell?' Nicole asked.

The Eagle held up three of his four fingers, indicating that they were asking for Level III information. Both the humans laughed.

'Will you be going with us?' Nicole asked The Eagle a few moments later.

'Back to your solar system? No, I can't,' he answered. 'But I will admit that it would be interesting.'

The Eagle led them over to an area of intense activity. Several dozen robots were working on a large, cylindrical structure about sixty metres tall. 'This is the main fluid recycling plant,' The Eagle said. 'All the liquids that find their way into the drains or sewers in your habitat are eventually sent here. Purified water is piped back into the colony and the rest of the chemicals are retained for other possible uses. This plant will be sealed and impregnable. It uses technology far beyond your level of development.'

The Eagle then led them up a ladder and into the habitat itself. He gave them an exhausting tour. In each sector The Eagle showed Richard and Nicole the main features of that particular area and then, without a break, commandeered a robot to transport them to the next adjacent sector.

'What exactly do you want us to do here?' Nicole inquired after several hours, as The Eagle prepared to take them to still another part of their future home.

'Nothing specific,' The Eagle replied. 'This will be your only visit to Rama itself. We wanted you to have a feel for the size of your habitat, in case you needed that to be more comfortable with the design process. We have a one-twentieth percent scale model back at the Habitation Module – all the rest of our work will be done there.' He looked at Richard and Nicole. 'We can leave whenever you want.'

Nicole sat down on a grey metal box and gazed around her. The number and variety of the robots were enough to make her dizzy all by themselves. She had been overwhelmed since the moment she walked out on the balcony of the factory, and was now absolutely numb. She reached her hand out to Richard.

'I know I should be studying what I'm seeing, darling, but none of it makes sense anymore. I'm completely saturated.'

'I am too,' Richard confessed. 'I never would have thought it possible that there was something more astonishing and awesome than Rama, but this factory certainly is.'

'Have you wondered, since we've been here,' Nicole said, 'what the factory must look like that made this place? Better still, imagine the assembly line for The Node.'

Richard laughed. 'We can continue that comment into an infinite regression. If The Node is indeed a machine, as it appears to be, it assuredly is a higher order machine than Rama. Rama was probably designed here. It is controlled, I would guess, by The Node. But what created and controls The Node? Was it a creature like us, the result of biological evolution? And does it even still exist, in any sense that we can understand, or has it become some other kind of entity, content to let its influence be felt by the existence of these amazing machines that it created?'

Richard sat down beside his wife. 'It's even too much for me. I guess I've had enough as well … Let's go back to the children.'

Nicole leaned over and kissed him. 'You're a very smart man, Richard Wakefield,' she said. 'You know that's one of the reasons I love you.'

A large robot resembling a forklift trundled close by them, carrying some rolled metal sheets. Richard again shook his head in wonder. 'Thank you, darling,' he said after a pause. 'You know that I love you too.'

They stood up together and signaled The Eagle that they were ready to leave.

The next night, back at their apartment in the Habitation Module, both Richard and Nicole were still alert thirty minutes after making love. 'What is it, dear?' Nicole asked. 'Is something wrong?'

'I had another foggy spell today,' Richard said. 'It lasted for almost three hours.'

'Goodness,' Nicole said. She sat up in bed. 'Are you all right now? Should I get the scanner and see if I can tell anything from your biometry?'

'No,' Richard answered, shaking his head. 'My fogs have never registered on your machine. But this one really disturbed me. I realised how incapacitated I am during them. I can barely function at all, much less help you or the children in any kind of crisis. They scare me.'

'Do you remember what started this one?'

'Absolutely. Like always. I was thinking of our trip to The Hangar, especially about that other habitat. I inadvertently started remembering a few disconnected scenes from my odyssey and then suddenly there was the fog. It was total. I'm not certain I would have even recognised you during the first five minutes of its duration.'

'I'm sorry, darling,' Nicole said.

'It's almost as if something is monitoring my thoughts. And when I reach into a certain portion of my memory, then *bam*, I'm given some kind of warning.'

Richard and Nicole were silent for almost a minute.

'When I close my eyes,' Nicole said, 'I still see all those robots scurrying around inside Rama.'

'Me too.'

'And yet, I still have great difficulty believing it was a real scene and not something I dreamed or saw in a movie.' Nicole smiled. 'We have lived an utterly unbelievable life these last fourteen years, haven't we?'

'Absolutely,' Richard said, turning over on his side in his normal sleeping posture. 'And who knows? The most interesting part may be still ahead of us.'

6

The holographic model of New Eden was projected into the centre of the large conference room at a 1/2000 scale. Inside Rama the actual Earth habitat would occupy an area of one hundred and sixty square kilometres in the Central Plain, starting just opposite the bottom of the long northern stairway. Its enclosed volume would be twenty kilometres long in the direction around the cylinder, eight kilometres wide in the direction parallel to the cylindrical spin axis, and eight kilometres high from the colony floor to the towering ceiling.

The New Eden model at the Habitation Module, however, which The Eagle, Richard, and Nicole used for their design work, was a more manageable size. It fitted easily into the single large room, and the holographic projections made it easy for the designers to walk through and among the various structures. Changes were made using the computer-aided design subroutines that acted upon the voice commands of The Eagle.

'We've changed our minds again,' Nicole said, beginning their third marathon design discussion with The Eagle by encircling, with her black 'flashlight,' a concentration of buildings in the centre of the colony. 'We now think it's a bad idea to have everything in one place, with the people all on top of each other. Richard and I think it would make more sense if the living areas and small trade shops were in four separate villages at the corners of the rectangle. Only the buildings used by everyone in the colony would be in the central complex.'

'Of course, our new concept will completely change the transportation flow you and I discussed yesterday,' Richard added, 'as well as the specific coordinate assignments for the parks, Sherwood Forest, Lake Shakespeare, and Mount Olympus. But all the original elements can still be accommodated in our current design for New Eden – here, take a look at this sketch and you can see where we have moved everything.'

The Eagle seemed to grimace as he stared at his human helpers. After a second he looked at the map in Richard's electronic notebook. 'I hope this will be the last major alteration,' he commented. 'We don't make much progress if every time we meet we essentially start the design all over.'

'We're sorry,' Nicole said. 'But it has taken us a little while to grasp the magnitude of our task. We now understand that we're designing the long-term living situation for as many as two thousand human beings; if it takes several iterations to get it right, then we must spend the time.'

'I see you've increased again the number of large structures in the central complex,' The Eagle said. 'What's the purpose of this building behind the library and auditorium?'

'It's a sports and recreation building,' Nicole replied. 'It will have a track, a baseball diamond, a soccer field, tennis courts, a gymnasium, and a swimming pool – plus enough seating in each area to handle almost all the citizens. Richard and I imagine that athletics will be very important in New Eden, especially since so many of the routine tasks will be handled by the biots.'

'You've also expanded the sizes of the hospital and the schools ...'

'We were too conservative in our original allocations of the space,' Richard interrupted. 'We didn't leave enough unassigned floor area for activities that we cannot yet define specifically.'

The first two design meetings had lasted ten hours each. Both Richard and Nicole had marvelled initially at how quickly The Eagle was able to integrate their comments into specific design recommendations. By the third meeting they were no longer amazed by the speed and accuracy of his synthesis. But the alien biot did surprise them regularly by showing a keen interest in some of the cultural details. For example, he queried them at length about the name the humans had given to their new colony. After Nicole had explained to him that it was essential that the habitat have some specific name, The Eagle asked about the meaning and significance of 'New Eden.'

'The whole family discussed the name of the habitat for most of one evening,' Richard explained, 'and there were many good suggestions, mostly derived from the history and literature of our species. Utopia was a leading candidate. Arcadia, Elysium, Paradise, Concordia, and Beauvois were all seriously considered. But in the end we thought New Eden was the best choice.'

'You see,' Nicole added, 'the mythological Eden was a beginning, the start of what we might call our modern Western culture. It was a lush, verdant paradise, supposedly designed especially for humans by an all-powerful God who had also created everything else in the universe. That first Eden was rich in life forms but devoid of technology.

'New Eden is also a beginning. But in almost every other way it is the opposite of the ancient garden. New Eden is a technological miracle without any life-forms, at least initially, except a few human beings.'

Once the general layout of the colony was complete, there were still hundreds of details that had to be decided. Katie and Patrick were given the task of designing the neighborhood parks for each of the four villages. Even though neither of them had ever seen an actual blade of grass, a real flower, or a tall tree, they had watched plenty of movies and seen many, many photographs. They ended up with four different, tasteful designs for the five acres of open area, communal gardens, and peaceful walkways in each village.

'But where will we get the grass? And the flowers?' Katie asked The Eagle.

'They will be brought by the people from Earth,' The Eagle replied.

'How will they know what to bring?'

'We will tell them.'

It was also Katie who pointed out that the design of New Eden had omitted a key element, one that had played a major role in the bedtime stories her mother had told her when she was a little girl. 'I've never seen a zoo,' she said. 'Can we have one in New Eden?'

The Eagle altered the master plan during the next design session to include a small zoo at the edge of Sherwood Forest.

Richard worked with The Eagle on most of the technological details for New Eden. Nicole's area of speciality was the living environment. The Eagle had originally suggested one kind of house with a standard set of furniture for all the homes in the colony. Nicole had laughed out loud. 'You certainly haven't learned very much about us as a species,' she said. 'Human beings must have variety. Otherwise we become bored. If we make all the houses the same, people will start changing them immediately.'

Because she had only limited time (The Eagle's requests for information were keeping Richard and Nicole working ten to twelve hours a day – luckily Michael and Simone were happy to look after the children), Nicole decided on eight basic house plans and four modular furniture arrangements. Altogether, then, there were thirty-two different living configurations. By varying the external design of the buildings in each of the four villages (details that Nicole worked out with Richard, after some useful input from art historian Michael O'Toole), Nicole finally achieved her goal of creating a design for everyday living that was neither uniform nor sterile.

Richard and The Eagle agreed on the New Eden transportation and communication systems, both external and internal, in just a few hours. They had more difficulty with the overall environmental control and biot designs. The Eagle's original concept, on which the infrastructure supporting New Eden was based, assumed twelve hours of light and twelve hours of darkness every day. Periods of sunlight, clouds, and rain were to be regular and predictable. There was to be virtually no variation in the temperature as a function of place and time.

When Richard requested seasonal changes in the length of the day and more variability in all the weather parameters, The Eagle stressed that allowing those 'significant variations' in the enormous volume of air in the habitat would result in the use of much more 'critical computational resource' than had originally been allocated during the infrastructure design. The Eagle also indicated that the major control algorithms would have to be restructured and retested, and that the departure date would be delayed as a result. Nicole supported Richard on the weather issue and the seasons, explaining to The Eagle that true human behaviour ('which you and the Nodal Intelligence apparently want to observe') was definitely dependent on both these factors.

In the end a compromise was reached. The length of day and night throughout a year would match a location at thirty degrees latitude on the Earth. The weather in New Eden would be allowed to evolve naturally within specified limits, the master controller only acting when conditions reached the edge of the 'design box.' Thus the temperature, wind, and rainfall could freely fluctuate inside tolerances. The Eagle was adamant about two items, however. There could be no lightning and no ice. If either of those conditions (both of which introduced 'new complexities' into his computational model) were imminent, even if the rest of the parameters were still within the design box, then the control system would take over automatically and regularise the weather.

It had been The Eagle's original intention to retain the same kind of biots that had been in the first two Rama craft. Richard and Nicole both, however, stressed to him that the Raman biots, especially the ones like the centipedes, mantises, crabs, and spiders, were not at all appropriate.

'The cosmonauts that have boarded the two Rama craft,' Nicole explained, 'would not be considered average humans. Far from it, in fact. We were especially trained to deal with sophisticated machines – and even some of us were frightened by a few of your biots. The more ordinary humans who will probably form the bulk of the New Eden inhabitants will not be at all comfortable with these bizarre mechanical contraptions scurrying all over their realm.'

After several hours of discussion The Eagle agreed to redesign the biot maintenance staff. For example, garbage would be collected by robots that looked like typical garbage trucks on Earth – there just wouldn't be any drivers. Construction work, when required, would be done by robots whose shapes were the same as vehicles performing similar functions on Earth. Thus the strange machines would be familiar in appearance to the colonists, and their xenophobic fears should be mitigated.

'What about the performance of routine, everyday activities?' The Eagle asked at the end of one long meeting. 'We had thought we would use human biots, voice responsive, deployed in large numbers, to free your colonists of all drudgery. We've spent considerable time since you arrived perfecting the design.'

Richard liked the idea of having robot assistants, but Nicole was leery. 'It is imperative,' she said, 'that these human biots be absolutely identifiable. There should be no chance that anyone, not even a small child, could mistake one for a real human being.'

Richard chuckled. 'You've read too much science fiction,' he said.

'But this is a real worry,' Nicole protested. 'I can well imagine the quality of the human biots that would be made here at The Node. We're not talking about those vacant imitations we saw inside Rama. People would be terrified if they couldn't tell the difference between a human and a machine.'

'So we'll limit the number of varieties,' Richard responded. 'And they'll be easily classified by primary function. Does that satisfy your concern ... ? It would be a shame not to take advantage of this incredible technology.'

'That might work,' Nicole said, 'providing that one short briefing could easily familiarise everyone with the different types. We must absolutely ensure that there are no problems of misidentification.'

After several weeks of intense effort, most of the critical design decisions had been made and the workload dropped for Richard and Nicole. They were able to resume a more or less normal life with the children and Michael. One evening The Eagle dropped by and informed the family that New Eden was in its final test period, primarily verifying the ability of the new algorithms to monitor and control the environment over the wide range of possible conditions.

'Incidentally,' The Eagle continued, 'we've inserted gas exchange devices, or GEDs, in all the places – Sherwood Forest, the parks, along the shores of the lake and the sides of the mountain – where plants coming from Earth will eventually be growing. The GEDs act like plants, absorbing carbon dioxide and producing oxygen, and are quantitatively equivalent as well. They prevent the buildup of atmospheric carbon dioxide, which over a long period of time would undermine the efficacy of the weather algorithms. Operating the GEDs requires some power, so we've slightly reduced the wattage available for human consumption during the early days of the colony. However, once the plants are flourishing the GEDs can be removed and there will be abundant power for any reasonable purpose.'

'OK, Mr Eagle,' Katie said when he was finished. 'What we all want to know is when we are going to depart.'

'I was going to tell you on Christmas Day,' The Eagle replied, the small wrinkle that passed for a smile forming at the corner of his mouth, 'and that's still two days away.'

'Tell us now, oh, please, Mr Eagle,' Patrick said.

'Well ... all right,' their alien companion replied. 'Our target date for finishing with Rama in The Hangar is January 11. We expect to load you in the shuttle and depart from The Node two days later, on the morning of January 13.'

That's only three weeks, Nicole thought, her heart skipping a beat as the reality of their departure sunk in. *There is still so much to do.* She glanced across the room, where Michael and Simone were sitting beside each other on the couch. *Among other things, my beautiful daughter, I must prepare you for your wedding.*

'So we'll be married on your birthday, Mama,' Simone said. 'We've always said the ceremony would be one week before the rest of the family left.'

Tears crept involuntarily into Nicole's eyes. She lowered her head so that the children would not see. *I am not ready to say goodbye,* Nicole thought. *I cannot bear to think that I will never see Simone again.*

*

Nicole had chosen to leave the family parlour game that was going on in the living room. She had given, as her excuse, that she had some final design data to develop for The Eagle, but in reality she desperately needed a few moments alone to organise the last three weeks of her life at The Node. All during dinner she had been thinking of all the things she needed to do. She had been close to panic. Nicole feared that there wasn't enough time, or that she would forget something critical altogether. Once she had made a thorough list of her remaining tasks, however, along with a timetable for accomplishing them, Nicole relaxed somewhat. It was not an impossible list.

One of the items that Nicole had entered in her electronic notebook, in all capital letters, was 'BENJY??' As she sat on the side of her bed, thinking about her retarded eldest son and chastising herself for not having addressed the issue earlier, Nicole heard a loud knock on her open door. It was an astonishing coincidence.

'Mom-my,' Benjy said very slowly with his wide, innocent smile, 'can I talk to you?' He thought for a moment. 'Now?' he added.

'Of course, darling,' Nicole answered. 'Come in and sit beside me on the bed.'

Benjy came over next to his mother and gave her a big hug. He looked down at his lap and spoke haltingly. His emotional struggle was obvious. 'You and Rich-ard and the other chil-dren are go-ing a-way soon for a ve-ry long time,' he said.

'That's right,' Nicole replied, trying to be cheerful.

'Dad-dy and Si-mone will stay here and be mar-ried?'

This was more of a question. Benjy had lifted his head and was waiting for Nicole to corroborate his statement. When she nodded, tears rushed instantly into his eyes and his face contorted. 'What about Ben-jy?' he said. 'What will hap-pen to Ben-jy?'

Nicole pulled his head to her shoulder and cried with her son. His entire body shook with his sobs. Nicole was now furious with herself for having procrastinated so long. *He's known all along,* she thought. *Ever since that first conversation. He's been waiting. He thinks nobody wants him.*

'You have a choice, darling,' Nicole managed to say when she had collected her own emotions. 'We would love to have you come with us. And your father and Simone would be delighted if you stayed here with them.'

Benjy stared at his mother as if he did not believe her. Nicole repeated her statements very slowly. 'You are tel-ling me the truth?' he asked.

Nicole nodded vigourously.

Benjy smiled for a second and then looked away. He was silent for a long time. 'There will be no-bo-dy to play with here,' he said at length, still staring at the wall. 'And Simone will need to be with Dad-dy.'

Nicole was astonished at how concisely Benjy had summarised his considerations. He seemed to be waiting. 'Then come with us,' Nicole said softly.

'Your Uncle Richard and Katie and Patrick and Ellie and I all love you very much and want to have you with us.'

Benjy turned to look at his mother. Fresh tears were running down his cheeks. 'I will come with you, Mom-my,' he said, and put his head on her shoulder.

He had already made up his mind, Nicole thought, holding Benjy against her body. *He's smarter than we think. He only came in here to make certain he was wanted.*

'... and Dear Lord, let me properly cherish this wonderful young girl that I am about to marry. Let us share Thy gift of love and let us grow together in our knowledge of Thee ... I ask these things in the name of Thy son, whom Thou sent to Earth to show Thy love and to redeem us for our sins. Amen.'

Michael Ryan O'Toole, seventy-two years of age, unclasped his hands and opened his eyes. He was sitting at the desk in his bedroom. He checked his watch. *Only two more hours*, he thought, *until I will marry Simone*. Michael glanced briefly at the picture of Jesus and the small bust of St Michael of Siena in front of him on his desk. *And then later tonight, after the meal that is both wedding feast for us and birthday dinner for Nicole, I will hold that angel in my arms*. He could not stop the next thought from coming. *Dear Lord, please do not let me disappoint her*.

Michael reached into his desk and pulled out a small Bible. It was the only real book he owned. All the rest of his reading material was in the form of small data cubes that he inserted into his electronic notebook. His Bible was very special, a memento of a life once lived on a planet far away.

During his childhood and adolescence that Bible had gone everywhere with him. As Michael turned the small black book over in his hands, he was flooded with memories. In his first recollection he was a small boy, six or seven years old. His father had come into his bedroom at home. Michael had been playing a baseball game on his personal computer and was somewhat embarrassed – he always felt ill at ease when his serious father found him engaging in play.

'Michael,' his father had said, 'I want to give you a present. Your very own Bible. It is a true book, one that you read by turning the pages. We've put your name on the cover.'

His father had extended the book and little Michael had accepted it with a soft 'thank you.' The cover was leather and felt good to his touch. 'Inside that volume,' his father had continued, 'is some of the best teaching that human beings will ever know. Read it carefully. Read it often. And govern your life by its wisdom.'

That night I put the Bible under my pillow, Michael recalled. *And it stayed there. All through my childhood. Even through high school.* He remembered his machinations when his high school baseball team had won the city championship and was going to Springfield for the state tournament. Michael had taken his Bible with him, but he didn't want his teammates to see it. A Bible wasn't 'cool' for a high school athlete, and the young Michael O'Toole did not yet have enough self-esteem to overcome his fear of the laughter of his peers. So he designed a special compartment for his Bible in the side of his toiletry bag and stored the book there, enclosed in protective wrap. In his hotel room in Springfield he waited until his roommate took a bath. Then Michael removed the Bible from its hiding place and put it under his pillow.

I even took it on our honeymoon. Kathleen was so understanding. As she always was with everything. A brief memory of the bright sun and the white sand outside their suite in the Cayman Islands was quickly followed by a powerful feeling of loss. *'How are you doing, Kathleen?'* Michael said out loud. *'Where has life taken you?'* He could see her in his mind's eye, puttering around their brownstone condominium on Commonwealth Avenue in Boston. *Our grandson Matt must be a teenager by now*, he thought. *Are there others? How many altogether?*

The heartache deepened as he imagined his family – Kathleen, his daughter Colleen, his son Stephen, plus all the grandchildren – gathered around the long table for a Christmas feast without him. In his mental image a light snow was falling outside on the avenue. *I guess Stephen would give the family prayer now*, he thought. *He was always the most religious of the children.*

Michael shook his head, returning to the present, and opened the Bible to the first page. A beautiful script writing of the word 'Milestones' appeared at the top of the sheet. The entries were sparse, a total of eight altogether, the chronicle of major events in his life.

7-13-67	Married Kathleen Murphy in Boston, Massachusetts
1-30-69	Birth of son, Thomas Murphy O'Toole, in Boston
4-13-70	Birth of daughter, Colleen Gavin O'Toole, in Boston
12-27-71	Birth of son, Stephen Molloy O'Toole, in Boston
2-14-92	Death of Thomas Murphy O'Toole in Pasadena, Calif.

Michael's eyes stopped there, at the death of his first-born son, and they quickly filled with tears. He recalled vividly that terrible St Valentine's Day many years before. He had taken Kathleen out to dinner at a lovely seafood restaurant on Boston Harbor. They had been almost finished with their meal when they first heard the news. 'I'm sorry I'm late showing you the desserts,' apologised the young man who was their waiter. 'I've been watching the news in the bar. There has just been a devastating earthquake in Southern California.'

Their fear had been immediate. Tommy, their pride and joy, had won a scholarship in physics at Cal Tech after graduating as the valedictorian at Holy Cross. The O'Tooles had abandoned what was left of their meal and rushed into the bar. There they had learned that the earthquake had struck at 5:45

in the evening, Pacific time. The giant San Andreas fault had ripped apart near Cajon Pass and the poor people, cars, and structures within a hundred miles of the epicenter had been tossed about on the surface of the Earth like hapless boats at sea during a hurricane.

Michael and Kathleen had listened to the news all night long, alternately hoping and fearing, as the full magnitude of the nation's worst disaster of the twenty-second century had become better understood. The quake had been a fearsome 8.2 on the Richter scale. Twenty million people had been left without water, electricity, transportation, and communications. Fifty-foot-deep cracks in the Earth had engulfed entire shopping centres. Virtually all the roads had become impassable. The damage was worse, and more wide-spread, than if the Los Angeles metropolitan area had been hit with several nuclear bombs.

Early in the morning, before dawn even, the Federal Emergency Administration had issued a telephone number to call for inquiries. Kathleen O'Toole gave the message machine all the information they knew – the address and phone number at Tommy's apartment, the name and address of the Mexican restaurant where he worked to earn spending money, and his girlfriend's address and phone number.

We waited all day and into the night, Michael remembered. Then Cheryl called. She had managed somehow to drive to her parents' home in Poway. 'The restaurant collapsed, Mr O'Toole,' Cheryl had said through her tears. 'Then it caught fire. I talked to one of the other waiters, one who survived because he was out on the patio when the quake hit. Tommy had been working the closest station to the kitchen ...'

Michael O'Toole took a deep breath. *This is wrong,* he said to himself, struggling to force the painful memories of his son's death out of his mind. *This is wrong,* he repeated. *This is a time for joy, not sorrow. For Simone's sake I must not think of Tommy now.*

He closed the Bible and wiped his eyes. He stood up at his desk and walked into the bathroom. First he shaved, slowly and deliberately, and then he stepped into the hot shower.

Fifteen minutes later, when he opened his Bible again, this time with pen in hand, Michael O'Toole had exorcised the demons of his son's death. With a flourish he wrote an additional entry on the Milestones page, pausing when he was finished to read the final four lines.

10-31-97	Birth of grandson, Matthew Arnold Rinaldi, in Toledo, Ohio
8-27-06	Birth of son, Benjamin Ryan O'Toole, in Rama
3-7-08	Birth of son, Patrick Erin O'Toole, in Rama
1-6-15	Marriage to Simone Tiasso Wakefield

You are an old man, O'Toole, he said to himself, looking at his thin grey hair in the mirror. He had closed his Bible several minutes earlier and returned to the bathroom to brush his hair one final time. *Too old to be getting married again*. He remembered his first wedding, forty-seven years earlier. *My hair was thick and blonde then*, he recalled. *Kathleen was beautiful. The service was magnificent. I cried the moment I saw her at the end of the aisle*.

His picture of Kathleen in her wedding dress, holding on to her father's arm at the other end of the aisle in the cathedral, faded into another memory of her, this one also shrouded in tears. In this second image the tears belonged to his wife. She had been sitting beside him in the family room at Cape Kennedy when the time had come for him to check in for the flight to LEO-3 to join the rest of the Newton crew. 'Be careful,' she had said, in a surprisingly emotional farewell. They had hugged. 'I'm so proud of you, darling,' she had whispered in his ear. 'And I love you very much.'

'Because I love you very much,' Simone had also said when Michael had asked her if she really, *really* wanted to marry him and, if so, why. A soft image of Simone came into his mind as his memory of his final goodbye with Kathleen gently faded away. *You are so innocent and trusting, Simone*, Michael mused, thinking of his young bride-to-be. *Back on Earth you wouldn't even be dating yet. You'd still be considered just a girl*.

The thirteen years in Rama flashed through his mind in an instant. Michael recalled first the struggle of Simone's birth, including the glorious moment when she had finally cried and he had laid her gently on her mother's stomach. His next image was of a very young Simone, a serious girl of six or so, earnestly studying her catechism under his tutelage. In another picture Simone was skipping rope with Katie and singing a joyous song. The final fleeting image was a scene of the family picnicking beside the Cylindrical Sea in Rama. There was Simone, standing proudly beside Benjy as if she were his guardian angel.

She was already a young woman when we arrived at The Node, General Michael O'Toole thought to himself, his mind moving to a more recent sequence of images. *Extremely devout. Patient and selfless with the younger children. And nobody has ever made Benjy smile like Simone*.

There was a common theme to all these pictures of Simone. In Michael's mind, they were bathed in the unusual love that he felt for his child bride. It was not the kind of love that a man normally feels for the woman he is going to marry – it was more like an adoration. But it was love, nevertheless, and that love had forged a powerful bond between the unlikely pair.

I am a very lucky man, Michael thought as he finished adjusting his clothing. God has seen fit to show me His wonders in many ways.

In the master suite at the other end of the apartment, Nicole was helping Simone with her dress. It was not a wedding dress in the classical sense, but it was white and full with small straps over the shoulders. It was certainly not the casual attire that all of the family were accustomed to wearing on an everyday basis.

Nicole carefully placed the combs in her daughter's long black hair and studied Simone in the mirror. 'You look beautiful,' Nicole said.

She glanced at her watch. They had ten more minutes. And Simone was completely ready except for the shoes. *Good. Now we can talk*, Nicole thought fleetingly. 'Darling,' she started, her voice surprisingly catching in her throat.

'What is it, Mother?' Simone said pleasantly. She was sitting on the bed beside her mother, carefully putting the black shoes on her feet.

'When we had that talk last week about sex,' Nicole began again, 'there were several topics that we didn't discuss.' Simone looked up at her mother. Her attention was so complete that Nicole momentarily forgot what she was going to say. 'Did you read those books I gave you ...?' she eventually stammered.

Simone's wrinkled brow revealed her puzzlement. 'Yes, of course,' she replied. 'We discussed that yesterday.'

Nicole took her daughter's hands. 'Michael is a wonderful man,' she said. 'Kind, considerate, loving – but he is older. And when men are older ...'

'I'm not sure I'm following you, Mother,' Simone gently interrupted. 'I thought there was something you wanted to tell me about sex.'

'What I'm trying to say,' Nicole said after taking a deep breath, 'is that you may need to be very patient and tender with Michael in bed. Everything might not work right away.'

Simone stared at her mother for a long time. 'I had suspected that,' she said quietly, 'both from your nervousness about the subject and some unspoken anxiety that I have read in Michael's face. Don't worry, Mother, I do not have unreasonable expectations. In the first place, we are not marrying because of a desire for sexual gratification. And since I have no experience of any kind, except for holding hands occasionally during this last week, whatever pleasure I feel will be new and therefore wonderful.'

Nicole smiled at her amazingly mature thirteen-year-old daughter. 'You are a jewel,' she said, her eyes brimming with tears.

'Thank you,' Simone replied, hugging her mother. 'Remember,' she added, 'my marriage to Michael is blessed by God. Whatever problems we encounter, we will ask God to help us with. We will be fine.'

A sudden heartache devastated Nicole. *One more week*, a voice inside her said, and *you will never see this beloved girl again*. She continued to embrace Simone until Richard knocked on the door and told them that everyone was ready for the ceremony.

8

'Good morning,' Simone said with a soft smile. The rest of the family were all seated at the table having breakfast when she and Michael walked in, hand in hand.

'Good mor-ning,' Benjy replied. His mouth was stuffed with buttered toast and jam. He rose from his seat, walked slowly around the table, and hugged his favourite sister.

Patrick was right behind him. 'Are you going to help me with my math today?' he asked Simone. 'Mother says that now that we're going back I have to be serious about my studies.'

Michael and Simone sat down at the table after the boys had returned to their seats. Simone reached for the coffee pot. She was like her mother in one respect. She didn't function well in the morning until she had had her coffee.

'Well, is the honeymoon finally over?' Katie asked in her usual irreverent manner. 'After all, it's been three nights and two days. You must have listened to every piece of classical music in the data base.'

Michael laughed easily. 'Yes, Katie,' he said, smiling warmly at Simone. 'We've taken the "Do Not Disturb" sign off the door. We want to do whatever we can to help everyone pack for the voyage.'

'We're actually in pretty good shape,' Nicole commented, delighted to see Michael and her daughter so comfortable together after their long seclusion. *I needn't have worried*, she thought quickly. *In some ways Simone is more adult than I am.*

'I wish The Eagle would give us more specifics about our return trip,' Richard complained. 'He won't tell us how long the journey will take or whether or not we'll sleep all the way or anything definite.'

'He says he doesn't know for certain,' Nicole reminded her husband. 'There are "uncontrollable" variables that could result in many different scenarios.'

'You always believe him,' Richard countered. 'You are the most trusting...'

The doorbell interrupted their conversation. Katie went to the door and returned a few moments later with The Eagle. 'I hope I'm not disturbing your breakfast,' the birdman apologised, 'but we have much to accomplish today. I will need for Mrs Wakefield to come with me.'

Nicole took the final sip of her coffee and looked quizzically at The Eagle.

654

'Alone?' she said. She was aware of a vague fear inside her. She had never left the apartment by herself with The Eagle during their sixteen-month stay at the Node.

'Yes,' The Eagle replied. 'You'll be coming with me alone. There is a special task that only you can perform.'

'Do I have ten minutes to get ready?'

'Certainly,' The Eagle replied.

While Nicole was out of the room, Richard peppered The Eagle with questions. 'Okay,' Richard said at one juncture, 'I understand that as a result of all these tests, you are confident now that we can safely remain asleep throughout the acceleration and deceleration periods. But what about during normal cruise? Will we be awake or asleep?'

'Mostly asleep,' The Eagle replied, 'because that way we can both retard the aging process and ensure your good health. But there are many uncertainties in the schedule. It may be necessary to awaken you several times en route.'

'Why have you not told us this before?'

'Because it wasn't yet decided. The scenario for your mission is quite complicated and the baseline plan has only recently been defined.'

'I don't want my aging process to "be retarded",' Katie said. 'I want to be a grown woman when we meet other people from the Earth.'

'As I told your mother and father yesterday,' The Eagle said to Katie, 'it is important that we have the ability to slow the aging process while you and your family are asleep. We do not know exactly when you will return to your solar system. If you were to sleep for fifty years, for example ...'

'Whaaat?' Richard interrupted in consternation. 'Who said anything about fifty years? We reached here in twelve or thirteen. Why wouldn't ...'

'I'll be older than Mama,' Katie said, a frightened look on her face.

Nicole entered from the next room. 'What's this I heard about fifty years? Why will it take so long? Are we going someplace else first?'

'Obviously,' Richard said. He was angry. 'Why were we not told all this before we made the "allocation" decision? We might have done something differently ... My God, if it take fifty years, Nicole and I will be a hundred years old!'

'No, you won't,' The Eagle replied without emotion. 'We estimate that you and Mrs Wakefield will only age one year in five or six while we have you "suspended". For the children, the ratio will be closer to one year in two, at least until their growth subsides. We are wary of tampering too much with the growth hormones. And besides, the fifty years is an upper bound, what a human engineer would call a three-sigma number.'

'Now I'm completely confused,' Katie said, walking over and directly confronting The Eagle. 'How old will I be when I meet up with a human being who is not part of my family?'

'I can't answer that question exactly, because there are statistical uncertainties involved,' their alien colleague replied. 'But your body should be at the equivalent development level of your early to mid-twenties. At least that's a *most likely* answer.' The Eagle motioned to Nicole. 'Now that's all I'm going to say. I have business with your mother. We should return before dinner tonight.'

'As usual,' Richard grumbled, 'we're told almost nothing. Sometimes I wish that we had not been so co-operative.'

'You could have been more difficult,' The Eagle remarked as he and Nicole were leaving the room, 'and in fact our predictions, based on our observational data, were for less co-operation than we have had. In the end, though, there would have been no substantive difference in the outcome. This way it has been more pleasant for you.'

'Goodbye,' Nicole said.

'Goodbye,' said Benjy, waving to his mother after the door was already closed.

It was a long document. Nicole calculated that it would take her at least ten, maybe fifteen minutes to read the entire text out loud.

'Are you almost finished with your study?' The Eagle inquired again. 'We'd like to begin the shooting, as you call it, as soon as possible.'

'Explain to me again what happens to this video after I make it,' Nicole requested.

'We broadcast it toward the Earth several years before you arrive in your solar system. That gives your fellow human beings ample time to respond.'

'How do you know if they have actually heard it?'

'We have requested a simple return signal acknowledging receipt.'

'And what if you don't ever receive this return signal?'

'That's what contingency plans are for.'

Nicole had serious misgivings about reading the message. She asked if she could have some time to discuss the document with Richard and Michael.

'What is it that you are worried about?' The Eagle asked.

'Everything,' Nicole replied. 'It just doesn't seem right. I feel as if I'm being used to further your purpose – and since I don't know exactly what your purpose is, I'm afraid that I'm being a traitor to the human species.'

The Eagle brought Nicole a glass of water and sat down beside her in the alien studio. 'Let's look at this logically,' The Eagle said. 'We have very clearly told you that our primary objective is to gather detailed information about spacefaring species in the galaxy. Right?'

Nicole nodded.

'We have also constructed a habitat inside Rama for two thousand Earthlings and are sending you and your family back to gather those humans for an observational voyage. All you're doing, with that video, is informing the Earth that we are on our way and that the two thousand members of your species, along with the supporting artifacts of your culture, should meet us in Mars orbit. What could be wrong with that?'

'The text of this document,' Nicole protested, pointing at the electronic notebook The Eagle had given her, 'is extremely vague. I never indicate, for example, what will be the eventual fate of all these humans – only that they will be "cared for" and "observed" during some kind of a journey. There is also no mention of why the humans are being studied, or anything at all about The Node and its controlling intelligence. In addition, the tone is definitely threatening. I am telling the people on Earth who receive this transmission that if a contingent of humans does not rendezvous with Rama in Mars orbit, then the spaceship will approach closer to the Earth and "acquire its specimens in a less organised way". That is clearly a hostile statement.'

'You may edit the remarks, if you would like, just as long as the intent is not changed,' The Eagle replied. 'But I should tell you that we have a great deal of experience with this type of communication. With species similar to yours, we have always been more successful when the message has not been too specific.'

'But why won't you let me take the document back to the apartment? I could discuss it with Richard and Michael and we could jointly edit it to soften the tone.'

'Because the video must be prepared by you today,' The Eagle said stubbornly. 'We are open to discussing modifications to the content and will work with you as long as necessary. But the sequence must be completed before you return to your family.'

The voice sounded friendly but the meaning was absolutely clear. *I have no choice*, Nicole thought. *I am being ordered to do the video.* She stared for several seconds at the strange creature sitting beside her. *This Eagle is just a machine*, Nicole said to herself, feeling her anger rise. *He is carrying out his programmed instructions ... My quarrel is not with him.*

'No,' she said abruptly, astonishing even herself. She shook her head. 'I won't do it.'

The Eagle was not prepared for Nicole's response. There was a long silence. Despite her emotional agitation, Nicole was fascinated by her companion. *What's going on with him now?* she wondered. *Are complicated new logic loops being exercised in his equivalent of a brain? Or is he perhaps receiving signals from somewhere else?*

At length The Eagle stood up. 'Well,' he said, 'this is quite a surprise ... We never expected you to refuse to do the video.'

'Then you haven't been paying attention to what I've been saying ... I feel as if you, or whoever is commanding you, are using me ... and purposely telling me as little as possible. If you want me to do something for you, then at least some of my questions should be answered.'

'What is it *precisely* that you want to know?'

'I've told you already,' Nicole replied, her frustration showing. 'What the hell is really going on in this place? Who or what are you? Why do you want to observe us? And while you're at it, how about a good explanation of why you need for us to leave a "reproductive pair" here? I've never liked the idea of breaking up my family – I should have protested more forcefully at the beginning. If your technology is so wonderful that it can create something like this incredible Node, why can't you simply take a human egg and some sperm ...'

'Calm down, Mrs Wakefield,' The Eagle said. 'I've never seen you so agitated before. I had you classified as the most stable individual in your group.'

And most malleable too, I'll bet, Nicole thought. She waited for her anger to subside. *Somewhere in that bizarre brain is doubtless a quantitative assessment of the probability that I would meekly follow orders ... Well, I fooled you this time ...*

'Look, Mr Eagle,' Nicole said a few seconds later, 'I'm not stupid. I know who is in control here. I just think we humans deserve to be treated with a little more respect. Our questions are quite legitimate.'

'And if we answer them to your satisfaction?'

'You've been watching me carefully for over a year,' Nicole said. She smiled. 'Have I ever been completely unreasonable?'

'Where are we going?' Nicole asked.

'On a short tour,' The Eagle replied. 'That may be the best way to deal with your uncertainties.'

The strange vehicle was small and spherical, just large enough for The Eagle and Nicole. The entire front hemisphere was transparent. Behind the window, on the side where the alien birdman was sitting, was a small control panel. During the flight The Eagle occasionally touched the panel, but most of the time the craft seemed to be operating on its own.

Within seconds after they were seated inside, the sphere zipped down a long corridor and through a large set of double doors into total blackness. Nicole gasped. She felt as if she were floating in space.

'Each of the three spherical modules of The Node,' The Eagle said, as Nicole struggled vainly to see anything at all, 'has a hollow centre. We have now entered a passageway that leads to the core of the Habitation Module.'

After almost a minute some distant lights appeared in front of their small craft. Soon thereafter the vehicle emerged from the black passageway and entered the immense hollow core. The sphere flipped and turned, disorienting Nicole as it headed toward the darkness, away from the many lights on what must have been the inside of the main body of the Habitation Module.

'We observe everything that occurs with all our guest species, both temporary and permanent,' The Eagle said. 'As you have suspected, we have hundreds of monitoring devices inside your apartment. But all your walls are also one-way mirrors – from this core region we can watch your activities from a wider perspective.'

Nicole had grown accustomed to the wonders of The Node, but the new sights around her were still staggering. Dozens, maybe hundreds of tiny blinking lights moved about in the vast darkness of the core. They looked like a group of scattered fireflies on a dark summer night. Some of the lights were hovering near the walls; others were moving slowly across the void. Some were so far away that they seemed to be standing still.

'We have a major maintenance centre here as well,' The Eagle said, pointing in front of them at a dense collection of lights in the distance. 'Every element of the module can be reached very quickly from this core, in case there are engineering or any other kind of problems.'

'What's going on over there?' Nicole asked, tapping on the window. About twenty kilometers to the right a group of vehicles were stationed just away from a large, illuminated portion of the Habitation Module.

'That's a special observation session,' The Eagle replied, 'using our most advanced remote sensing monitors. Those particular apartments house an unusual species, one that has characteristics never before recorded in this sector of the Galaxy. Many of its individuals are dying and we do not understand why. We are trying to figure out how to save them.'

' So everything doesn't always work the way you planned it?'

'No,' replied The Eagle. In the reflected light the creature seemed to be smiling. 'That's why we have so many contingency plans.'

'What would you have done if no humans had ever come to find out about Rama in the first place?' Nicole suddenly asked.

'We have alternate methods of accomplishing the same goals,' The Eagle answered vaguely.

The vehicle accelerated along its chordal path in the darkness. Soon a similar sphere, slightly larger than theirs, approached them from the left. 'Would you like to meet a member of a species whose development level is approximately equal to yours?' The Eagle said. He touched the control panel and the interior of their craft was illuminated by soft lights.

Before Nicole could respond, the second vehicle was beside them. It also had a transparent forward hemisphere. This second sphere was filled with a colourless liquid, and two creatures were swimming about. They looked like large eels wearing capes, and they moved in undulations through the liquid. Nicole estimated that the creatures were about three metres long and twenty centimeters thick. The black cape, which spread out like a wing during movement, was about a metre wide when fully extended.

'The one on your right, without the coloured markings,' The Eagle said, 'is an artificial intelligence system. It serves a role similar to mine, acting as a host for the aquatic species. The other being is a spacefarer from another world.'

Nicole stared at the alien. It had folded its cape tightly around its slightly greenish body and was sitting nearly motionless in the liquid. The creature had arranged itself in a horseshoe configuration with both ends of its body facing her. A burst of bubbles came from one of its two ends.

'It says, "Hello, and wow, are you intriguing",' The Eagle said.

'How do you know that?' Nicole replied, unable to take her eyes off the bizarre being. Its two ends, one bright red and the other grey, had now wrapped around each other. Both were pressed against the window of the craft.

'My colleague in the other vehicle is translating and then communicating to me ... Do you wish to respond?'

Nicole's mind was a blank. *What do I say?* she thought, her eyes focused on the unusual wrinkles and protuberances on the alien's extremities. There were half a dozen separate features on each end, including a pair of white slits on the red 'face'. None of the markings looked like anything that Nicole had ever seen on Earth. She stared silently, remembering the many conversations that she and Richard and Michael had had about the questions they would ask if, and when, they were ever able to communicate directly with an intelligent extraterrestrial. *But we never imagined a situation like this*, Nicole thought.

More bubbles flooded the window opposite her. '"Our home planet accreted five billion years ago," The Eagle said, translating. '"Our binary stars reached stability a billion years later. Our system has fourteen major planets, on two of which some kind of life evolved. Our oceanic planet has three intelligent species, but we are the only spacefarers. We began our space exploration slightly more man two thousand years ago."'

Nicole was now embarrassed by her silence. 'Hello ... hello,' she said haltingly. 'It is a pleasure to meet you ... Our species has only been spacefarers for three hundred years. We are the only highly intelligent organism on a planet that is two thirds covered by water. Our heat and light come from a solitary, stable, yellow star. Our evolution began in the water, three or four billion years ago, but now we live on the land ...'

Nicole stopped. The other creature, its two ends still entwined, had now brought the rest of its body over against the window so that the details of its physical structure could be seen more clearly. Nicole understood. She stood up next to the window and turned around slowly. Then she held her hands out, wiggling her fingers. More bubbles followed.

'Do you have an alternate manifestation?' The Eagle translated a few seconds later.

'I don't understand,' Nicole replied. The Nodal host in the other sphere communicated her message using both body motions and bubbles.

'We have two manifestations,' the alien explained. 'My offspring will have appendages, not unlike yours, and will dwell mostly on ocean bottoms, building our homes and factories and spaceships. They in turn will produce another generation that looks like me.'

'No, no,' Nicole replied eventually. 'We have only a single manifestation. Our children always resemble their parents.'

The conversation lasted for five more minutes. The two spacefarers talked mostly about biology. The alien was especially impressed by the wide thermal range in which humans could function successfully. It told Nicole that members of its species were unable to survive if the ambient temperature of the surrounding liquid was outside a narrow range.

Nicole was fascinated by the creature's description of a watery planet whose surface was almost totally covered by huge mats of photosynthetic organisms. The caped eels, or whatever they were, lived in the shallows just below these hundreds of different organisms and used the photo-synthesisers for practically everything – food, building materials, even as reproductive aids.

At length The Eagle told Nicole that it was time to depart. She waved at the alien, which was still pressed against the window. It responded with a final flurry of bubbles and unwrapped its two ends. Seconds later the distance between the two capsules was already hundreds of metres.

It was dark again inside the moving sphere. The Eagle was silent. Nicole was exhilarated. Her mind continued to race, still actively formulating questions for the alien creature with whom she had had the brief encounter. *Do you have families?* she thought. *And if so, how do dissimilar creatures live together? Can you communicate with the bottom-dwellers who are your children?*

Another genre of question intruded into Nicole's stream of consciousness and she suddenly felt slightly disappointed in herself. *I was much too clinical, too scientific,* she thought. *I should have asked about God, life after death, even ethics.*

'It would have been virtually impossible to have had what you would call a philosophical conversation,' The Eagle said a few moments later after Nicole had expressed a lack of satisfaction in the topics that had been discussed. 'There was absolutely no common ground for such an exchange. Until each of you knew a few basic facts about the other, there were no references for a discussion of values or other meaningful issues.'

Still, Nicole reflected, I could have tried. Who knows? That horseshoe-shaped alien might have had some answers ...

Nicole was jolted out of her contemplation by the sound of human voices. As she looked questioningly at The Eagle, the sphere turned completely around and Nicole saw that they were hovering only a few metres away from her living quarters.

A light went on in the bedroom that Michael and Simone were sharing. 'Is that Benjy?' Nicole heard her daughter whisper to her husband of a few days. 'I think so,' Michael replied.

Nicole watched quietly as Simone rose from the bed, pulled her robe about her, and crossed into the hallway. When she switched on the light in the living room, Simone saw her retarded younger brother curled up on the sofa.

'What are you doing here, Benjy?' Simone asked kindly. 'You should be in bed – it's very, very late.' She stroked her brother's anxious brow.

'I could not sleep,' Benjy replied with effort. 'I was worried a-bout Ma-ma.'

'She'll be home soon,' Simone said soothingly. 'She'll be home soon.'

Nicole felt a lump in her throat and a few tears eased into her eyes. She looked over at The Eagle, then at the illuminated apartment in front of her, and finally at the firefly vehicles in the distance above her head. She took a deep breath. 'All right,' Nicole said slowly, 'I'm ready to do the video.'

'I'm jealous,' Richard said. 'I really am. I would have been willing to trade both my arms for a conversation with that creature.'

'It was amazing,' Nicole said. 'Even now, I'm still having difficulty believing that it actually happened ... It's also amazing that The Eagle somehow knew how I would respond to everything.'

'He was just guessing. He really could not have expected to have solved his problem with you that easily. You didn't even make him answer your question about their need for a reproductive couple ...'

'Yes, I *did*,' Nicole replied somewhat defencively. 'He explained to me that human embryology was such an astonishingly complicated process that even *they* couldn't possibly know the exact role played by a human mother without ever having watched a foetus mature and develop.'

'I'm sorry, darling,' Richard said quickly. 'I wasn't implying that you really had any choice ...'

'I felt as if they were at least *trying* to satisfy my objections.' Nicole sighed. 'Maybe I'm kidding myself. After all, in the end I did make the video, exactly as they had planned.'

Richard put his arms around Nicole. 'As I said, you really had no choice, darling. Don't be too hard on yourself.'

Nicole kissed Richard and sat up in bed. 'But what if they are taking this data so that they can prepare an efficient invasion, or something like that?'

'We've discussed all this before,' Richard replied. 'Their technological capabilities are so advanced they could take over the Earth in minutes if that was their goal. The Eagle himself has pointed out that if invasion and subjugation was their objective, they could accomplish it with a far less elaborate procedure.'

'Now who's the trusting one?' Nicole said, managing a smile.

'Not trusting. Just realistic. I'm certain that the overall welfare of the human species is not a significant factor in the priority queue of the Nodal Intelligence. But I do think you should stop worrying about being an accomplice in crime with your video. The Eagle is right. Most likely you have made the "acquisition process" less difficult for the inhabitants of Earth as well.'

They were silent for a few minutes. 'Darling,' Nicole said at length. 'Why do you think we're not going directly to the Earth?'

'My guess is that we must stop somewhere else first. Presumably to pick up another species in the same phase of the project as we are.'

'And they will live in that other module inside Rama?'

'That's what I would assume,' Richard replied.

9

The day of departure was January 13, 2215, according to the calendar that had been fastidiously kept by Richard and/or Nicole ever since Rama had escaped from the nuclear phalanx. Of course this date didn't really mean anything – except to them. Their long trip to Sirius at slightly more than half the speed of light had slowed time inside Rama, at least relative to the Earth, so the date they were using was a complete artifice. Richard estimated that the actual date on the Earth, at the time of their departure from the Node, was three to four years later, in 2217 or 2218. It was impossible for him to compute the Earth date exactly, since he did not have an accurate velocity time history from the years that they had travelled inside Rama. Thus Richard could only approximate the relativistic corrections necessary to transform their own time basis into the one being experienced on the Earth.

'The date on Earth right now really has no significance to us anyway,' Richard explained to Nicole soon after they had awakened for their final day at the Node. 'Besides,' he continued, 'it's almost certain that we will be returning to our solar system at extremely high velocities, meaning there will be additional time dilation before we rendezvous in Mars orbit.'

Nicole had never really understood relativity – it was totally inconsistent with her intuition – and she certainly wasn't going to spend any energy worrying about it on her last day before separating from Simone and Michael. She knew that the final partings would be extremely difficult, for everybody, and she wanted to concentrate all her resources on those last emotional moments.

'The Eagle said that he would come for us at eleven,' Nicole said to Richard while they were dressing. 'I was hoping that after breakfast we could all sit together in the living room. I want to encourage the children to express their feelings.'

Breakfast was light, even cheerful, but when the eight members of the family gathered together in the living room, each mindful that there were less than two hours remaining before The Eagle arrived to take everyone but Michael and Simone away, the conversation was forced and strained.

The newlyweds sat together on the love seat, facing Richard, Nicole, and the other four children. Katie, as usual, was completely frenetic. She talked constantly. She jumped from subject to subject, steering safely away from any discussion of the imminent departure. Katie was in the middle of a long monologue about a wild dream she had had the night before when her story was interrupted by the sound of two voices coming from the entryway to the master suite.

'Dammit, Sir John,' said the first variation in Richard's voice, 'this is our last chance. I'm going out there to say goodbye whether you're coming or not.'

'These goodbyes, my prince, do wrench my very soul. I'm not yet in my cups enough to deaden the pain. You yourself said the lass was the very apparition of an angel. How can I possibly ...'

'Well, then, I'm going out there without you,' said Prince Hal. All the eyes in the family were on Richard's tiny robot prince as he came down the hall to the living room. Falstaff staggered after him, stopping every four or five steps to take a drink from his flask.

Hal walked over in front of Simone. 'Dearest lady,' he said, bending down on one knee, 'I cannot find the words to express properly how much I will miss seeing your smiling face. Throughout my entire realm, there is not one member of the fairer sex who is your equal in beauty ...'

'Zounds,' Falstaff interrupted, throwing himself on both knees beside his prince. 'Mayhap Sir John has made a mistake. Why am I going with this motley crew (he waved his arm at Richard, Nicole, and the other children – all of whom were smiling broadly) when I could remain here, in the presence of such magnificent grace, and only this one old man for competition? I remember Doll Tearsheet ...'

While the pair of twenty-centimetre robots were entertaining the family, Benjy rose from his chair and approached Michael and Simone. 'Si-mone,' he said, fighting back his tears, 'I am go-ing to miss you. I love you.' Benjy paused for a moment, looking first at Simone and then at his father. 'I hope that you and Dad-dy will be ve-ry hap-py.'

Simone rose from her seat and put her arms around her trembling little brother. 'Oh, Benjy, thank you,' she said. 'I will miss you too. And I will carry your spirit with me every day.'

Her embrace was too much for the boy. Benjy's body was racked by sobs and his soft, sorrowful moan brought tears to the eyes of everyone else. Within moments Patrick had crawled into his father's lap. He buried his swollen eyes in Michael's chest. 'Daddy ... Daddy,' he kept saying over and over.

A choreographer could not have designed a more beautiful dance of goodbye. The radiant Simone, looking somehow still serene despite her tears, waltzed around the room, saying a meaningful farewell to each and every member of the family. Michael O'Toole remained sitting on the love seat, with Patrick on his lap and Benjy beside him. His eyes brimmed repeatedly as one by one the departing family members came to him for a final embrace.

I want to remember this moment forever. There is so much love here, Nicole said to herself as she glanced around the room. Michael was holding little Ellie in his arms; Simone was telling Katie how much she would miss their talks together. For once even Katie was in emotional knots – she was surprisingly silent when Simone walked back across the room to rejoin her husband.

Michael gently lifted Patrick off his lap and took Simone's extended hand. The two of them turned toward the others and dropped to their knees, their hands clasped in prayer. 'Our heavenly Father,' Michael said in a strong voice. He paused for several seconds while the rest of the family, even Richard, knelt beside the couple on the floor.

'We thank Thee for having allowed us the joyful love of this wonderful family. We thank Thee also for having shown us Thy miraculous handiwork throughout the universe. At this moment we beseech thee, if it be Thy will, to look after each of us as we go our separate ways. We know not if it is in Thy plan for us once again to share the camaraderie and love that has uplifted all of us. Stay with us all, wherever our paths take us in Thy amazing creation, and let us, O Lord, someday be joined together again – in this world or the next. Amen.'

Seconds later the doorbell rang. The Eagle had arrived.

Nicole left the house, purposely designed as a smaller version of her family villa at Beauvois in France, and walked down the narrow lane in the direction of the station. She passed other houses, all dark and empty, and tried to imagine what it would be like when they were full of people. *My life has been like a dream*, she said to herself. *Surely no human has ever had a more varied experience.*

Some of the houses cast shadows on the lane as the simulated Sun completed its arc in the ceiling far above her head. *Another remarkable world*, Nicole mused, surveying the village in the southeast corner of New Eden. *The Eagle was correct when he said that the habitat would be indistinguishable from Earth.*

For a fleeting moment Nicole thought of that blue, oceanic world nine light-years away. In her mental picture she was standing beside Janos Tabori, thirteen years earlier, as the Newton spaceship had pulled away from LEO-3. 'That's Budapest,' Janos had said, circling with his fingers a specific feature on the lighted globe shimmering in the observation window.

Nicole had then located Beauvois, or at least the general region, by backtracking up the Loire River from where it emptied into the Atlantic. 'My home is just about here,' she had said to Janos. 'Maybe my father and daughter are looking in this direction right now.'

Genevieve, Nicole thought as the brief recollection faded, *My Genevieve. You would be a young woman now. Almost thirty.* She continued to walk slowly down the lane near her new house in the Earth habitat inside Rama. Thinking of her first daughter made Nicole remember a short conversation she had had with The Eagle during a break in the video recording at The Node.

'Will I be able to see my daughter Genevieve while we are close to the Earth?' Nicole had asked.

'We don't know,' The Eagle had replied after a short hesitation. 'It depends entirely on how your fellow humans respond to your message. You yourself will stay inside Rama, even if the contingency plans are invoked, but it is possible that your daughter will be one of the two thousand who come from Earth to live in New Eden. It has happened before, with other spacefarers.'

'And what about Simone?' Nicole had asked when The Eagle was finished. 'Will I ever see her again?'

'That is more difficult to answer,' The Eagle had replied. 'There are many, many factors involved.' The alien creature had stared at his despondent human friend. 'I'm sorry, Mrs Wakefield,' he had said.

One daughter left on Earth. Another in an alien space world almost a hundred trillion kilometres away. And I will be somewhere else. Who knows where? Nicole was feeling extremely lonely. She stopped her walk and focused her eyes on the scene around her. She was standing beside a circular area in the village park. Inside the rock circumference was a slide, a sandbox, a jungle gym, and a merry-go-round – a perfect playground for Earth children. Underneath her feet, the network of GEDs was interleaved throughout the portions of the park that would eventually contain the grasses brought from Earth.

Nicole bent down to examine the individual gas exchange devices. They were compact round objects, only two centimetres in diameter. There were several thousand of them arrayed in rows and columns that crisscrossed the park. *Electronic plants*, Nicole thought. *Converting carbon dioxide to oxygen. Making it possible for us animals to survive.*

In her mind's eye Nicole could see the park with grass, trees, and lilies in the small pond, just as it had appeared in the holographic image in the conference room at the Node. But even though she knew that Rama was returning to the solar system to 'acquire' human beings who would fill up this technological paradise, it was still difficult for her to imagine this park teeming with children. *I have not seen another human being, except for my family, in almost fifteen years.*

Nicole left the park and continued toward the station. The residential houses that had lined the narrow lanes were now replaced by row buildings containing what would eventually be small shops. Of course they were all empty, as was the large, rectangular structure, destined to be a supermarket, that was right opposite the station.

She walked through the gate and boarded the waiting train in the front, just behind the control cab that was manned by a Benita Garcia robot. 'Almost dark,' Nicole said out loud.

'Eighteen more minutes,' the robot replied.

'How long to the somnarium?' Nicole asked.

'The ride to Grand Central Station takes ten minutes,' Benita answered as the train left the southeast station. 'Then you have a two-minute walk.'

Nicole had known the answer to her question. She had just wanted to hear another voice. This was her second day alone, and a conversation with a Garcia robot was better than talking to herself.

The train ride took her from the southeast corner of the colony to its geographic centre. Along the way, Nicole could see Lake Shakespeare on the left-hand side of the train and the slopes of Mount Olympus (which were covered with more GEDs) on the right. Electronic message monitors inside the train displayed information about the sights that were being passed, the time of day, and the distance that had been travelled.

You and The Eagle did a good job on this train system, Nicole thought, thinking of her husband Richard, now asleep along with all the other members of her family. *Soon I will be joining you in the big round room.*

The somnarium was, in reality, just an extension of the main hospital that was located about two hundred metres from the central train station. After leaving the train and walking past the library, Nicole entered the hospital, walked through it, and then reached the somnarium through a long tunnel. The rest of her family were all asleep in a large, circular room on the second floor. Each was in a 'berth' along the wall, a long, coffin-like contraption hermetically sealed against the outside environment. Only their faces were visible through the small windows near their heads. As she had been trained to do by The Eagle, Nicole examined the monitors containing the data about the physical condition of her husband, two daughters, and two sons. Everybody was fine. There were not even any hints of irregularities.

Nicole stopped and gazed longingly at each of her loved ones. This was to be her last inspection. According to the procedure, since everyone's critical parameters were well within tolerances, it was now time for Nicole to go to sleep herself. It could be many years before she saw any of her family again.

Dear, dear Benjy. Nicole sighed as she studied her retarded son in repose. *Of all of us, this break in life will be the hardest on you. Katie, Patrick, and Ellie will catch up quickly. Their minds are quick and agile. But you will miss the years that might have made you independent.*

The berths were held out from the circular wall by what looked like wrought-iron metalwork. The distance from the head of one berth to the foot of the next was only about a metre and a half. Nicole's empty berth was in the middle; Richard and then Katie were behind her head; Patrick, Benjy, and Ellie were at her feet.

She lingered for several minutes beside Richard's berth. He had been the last to go to sleep, two days before. As he had requested, Prince Hal and Falstaff were lying on his chest inside the sealed container. *Those final three days were wonderful, my love*, Nicole said to herself as she stared at her husband's expressionless face through the window. *I could not have asked for more.*

They had swum and even water-skied in Lake Shakespeare, climbed Mount Olympus, and made love whenever either one of them had had the slightest inclination. They had clung to each other all through one night in the big bed in their new home. Richard and Nicole had checked on the sleeping children, once each day, but had mostly used the time for a thorough exploration of their new realm.

It had been an exciting, emotional time. Richard's last words, before Nicole activated the system that put him to sleep, were 'You are a magnificent woman and I love you very much.'

Now it was Nicole's turn. She could procrastinate no longer. She climbed into her berth, as she had practised many times during their first week inside New Eden, and flipped all the switches except one. The foam around her was unbelievably comfortable. The top of the berth closed over her head. She had only to trip the final switch to bring the sleeping gas into her compartment.

She sighed deeply. As Nicole was lying on her back, she remembered the dream she had had about Sleeping Beauty during one of her final tests at the Node. Her mind then plunged backward to her childhood, to those wonderful weekends she had spent with her father watching the Sleeping Beauty pageants at the Chateau d'Ussé.

That's a nice way to go, she said to herself, feeling her drowsiness as the gas crept into her berth. *Thinking that it will be some Prince Charming who will awaken me.*

RENDEZVOUS AT MARS

1

'**M**rs Wakefield.'

The voice seemed far, far away. It intruded gently into her consciousness but did not quite awaken her from sleep.

'Mrs Wakefield.'

This time it was louder. Nicole tried to recall where she was before opening her eyes. She shifted her body and the foam reoriented itself to provide maximum comfort. Slowly her memory began to send signals to the remainder of her brain. *New Eden. Inside Rama. Back to the solar system,* she recalled. *Is this all just a dream?*

She finally opened her eyes. Nicole had difficulty focusing for several seconds. At length the figure bending over her resolved itself. It was her mother, dressed in a nurse's uniform!

'Mrs Wakefield,' the voice said. 'It is now time to wake up and prepare for the rendezvous.'

For a moment Nicole was in a state of shock. Where was she? What was her mother doing here? Then she remembered. *The robots,* she thought. *Mother is one of the five kinds of human robots. An Anawi Tiasso robot is a health and fitness specialist.*

The robot's helping arm steadied Nicole as she sat up in her berth. The room had not changed during the long time that she had been asleep. 'Where are we?' Nicole asked as she prepared to climb out of the berth.

'We have completed the major deceleration profile and entered your solar system,' the jet-black Anawi Tiasso replied. 'Mars orbit insertion will be in six months.'

Her muscles did not seem at all strange. Before Nicole had left The Node, The Eagle had informed her that each of the sleeping compartments included special electronic components that would not only regularly exercise the muscles and other biological systems to preclude any atrophy, but also monitor the health of all the vital organs. Nicole stepped down the ladder. When she reached the floor she stretched.

'How do you feel?' asked the robot. She was Anawi Tiasso Number 017. Her number was prominently displayed on the right shoulder of her uniform.

'Not bad,' answered Nicole. 'Not bad, 017,' she repeated while examining the robot. It did look remarkably like her mother. Richard and she had seen all the prototypes before they had left The Node, but only the Benita Garcias had been operational during the two weeks before they went to sleep. All the rest of the New Eden robots had been built and tested during the long flight. *It really does look just like Mother*, Nicole mused, admiring the handiwork of the unknown Raman artists. *They made all the changes to the prototype that I suggested.*

In the distance she heard footsteps coming toward them. Nicole turned around. Approaching them was a second Anawi Tiasso, also dressed in the white uniform of a nurse. 'Number 009 has been assigned to help with the initialization procedure as well,' the Tiasso robot beside her said.

'Assigned by whom?' Nicole asked, struggling to remember her discussions with The Eagle about the wake-up procedure.

'By the preprogrammed mission plan,' Number 017 replied. 'Once all you humans are alive and alert, we will take all our instructions from you.'

Richard woke up more rapidly but was quite clumsy descending the short ladder. It was necessary for the two Tiassos to support him to prevent his falling. Richard was clearly delighted to see his wife. After a long hug and a kiss, he stared at Nicole for several seconds. 'You look none the worse for wear,' he said jokingly. 'The grey in your hair has spread, but there are still healthy clutches of black in isolated spots.'

Nicole smiled. It was great to be talking to Richard again.

'By the way,' he asked a second later, 'how long did we spend in those crazy coffins?'

Nicole shrugged her shoulders. 'I don't know,' she answered. 'I haven't asked yet. The first thing I did was wake you up.'

Richard turned to the two Tiassos. 'Do you fine women know how long it has been since we left the Node?'

'You have slept for nineteen years of traveller's time,' Tiasso Number 009 replied.

'What does she mean, traveller's time?' Nicole asked.

Richard smiled. 'That's a relativistic expression, darling,' he said. 'Time doesn't mean anything unless you have a frame of reference. Inside Rama nineteen years have passed, but those years only pertain to ...'

'Don't bother,' Nicole interrupted. 'I didn't sleep all this time to wake up to a relativity lesson. You can explain it to me later, over dinner. Meanwhile, we have a more important issue. In what order should we awaken the children?'

'I have a different suggestion,' Richard replied after a moment's hesitation. 'I know you're eager to see the children. So am I. However, why don't we let them sleep for several more hours? It certainly won't hurt them ... And you and I have a lot to discuss. We can begin our preparations for the rendezvous, outline what we are going to do about the children's education, maybe even take a moment or two to become reacquainted ourselves ...'

Nicole *was* anxious to talk to the children, but the logical part of her mind could see the merit in Richard's suggestion. The family had developed only a rudimentary plan for what would happen after they woke up, primarily because The Eagle had insisted that there were too many uncertainties to specify the conditions exactly. It would be much easier to do some planning before the children were awake ...

'All right,' Nicole said at length, 'as long as I know for certain that everyone is all right.' She glanced over at the first Tiasso.

'All the monitor data indicates that each of your children survived the sleep period without any significant irregularities,' the biot said.

Nicole turned back to Richard and carefully studied his face. It had aged a little, but not as much as she had expected.

'Where's your beard?' she blurted out suddenly, realizing that his face was strangely clean-shaven.

'We shaved the men yesterday while they were sleeping,' Tiasso 009 replied. 'We also cut everybody's hair and gave everyone a bath – in accordance with the preprogrammed mission plan.'

The men? Nicole thought. She was momentarily puzzled. *Of course*, she said to herself. *Benjy and Patrick are now men*!

She took Richard's hand and they walked quickly over to Patrick's berth. The face she saw through the window was astonishing. Her little Patrick was no longer a boy. His features had lengthened considerably and the rounded contours of his face had disappeared. Nicole stared at her son silently for over a minute.

'His age equivalence is sixteen or seventeen,' Tiasso Number 017 said in response to Nicole's questioning glance. 'Mr Benjamin O'Toole remains a year and a half older. Of course, these ages are only approximations. As The Eagle explained before your departure from The Node, we have been able to retard somewhat the key aging enzymes in each of you – but not all at the same rate. When we say that Mr Patrick O'Toole is sixteen or seventeen now, we are referring only to his personal, internal biological clock. The age quoted is some kind of average across his growth, maturation, and subsystem aging processes.'

Nicole and Richard stopped at each of the other berths and stared for several minutes through the windows at their sleeping children. Nicole repeatedly shook her head in bewilderment. 'Where have my babies gone?' she said after seeing that even little Ellie had become a teenager during the long voyage.

'We knew this would happen,' Richard commented without emotion, not helping the mother in Nicole cope with the sense of loss that she was feeling.

'*Knowing* it is one thing,' said Nicole. 'But *seeing* it and experiencing it is another. This is not a case of a typical mother who suddenly realises her boys and girls have all grown up. What has happened to our children is truly staggering. Their mental and social development has been interrupted for the equivalent of ten to twelve years. We now have small children walking around in adult bodies. How can we prepare them to meet other humans in just six months?'

Nicole was overwhelmed. Had some part of her not believed The Eagle when he had described what was going to happen to her family? Perhaps. It was one more unbelievable event in a life that had long been beyond comprehension. *But as their mother,* Nicole thought to herself, *I have much to do and almost no time. Why didn't I plan for all this before we left The Node?*

While Nicole was struggling with her powerful emotional response to seeing her children suddenly grown, Richard chatted with the two Tiassos. They easily answered all his questions. He was extremely impressed with their capabilities, both physical and mental. 'Do all of you have such a wealth of information stored in your memories?' he asked the robots in the middle of their conversation.

'Only we Tiassos have the detailed historical health data on your family,' 009 replied. 'But all the human biots can access a wide range of basic facts. However, a portion of that knowledge will be removed at the moment of first contact with other humans. At that time the memory devices of all biot types will be partially purged. Any event or piece of data pertaining to The Eagle, The Node, or any situations that transpired before you awakened will not remain in our data bases after we rendezvous with the other humans. Only your personal health information will be available from that earlier time period – and this data will be localised in the Tiassos.'

Nicole had already been thinking about The Node before this last comment. 'Are you still in contact with The Eagle?' she suddenly asked.

'No.' It was Tiasso 017 who replied this time. 'It is safe to assume that The Eagle, or at least some representative of the Nodal Intelligence, is periodically monitoring our mission, but there is never any interaction with Rama once it leaves The Hangar. You, we, Rama – we are on our own until the mission objectives are fulfilled.'

Katie stood in front of the full-length mirror and studied her naked body. Even after a month it was still new to her. She loved to touch herself. She especially liked to run her fingers across her breasts and watch her nipples swell in response to the stimulation. Katie liked it even more at night when she was alone underneath the sheets. Then she could rub herself everywhere until waves of tingles rolled across her body and she wanted to cry out from pleasure.

Her mother had explained the phenomenon to her but had seemed a little uncomfortable when Katie had wanted to discuss it a second and a third time. 'Masturbation is a very private affair, darling,' Nicole had said in a low voice one night before dinner, 'and generally only discussed, if at all, with one's closest friends.'

Ellie was no help. Katie had never seen her sister examining herself, not even once. *She probably doesn't do it at all*, Katie thought. *And she certainly doesn't want to talk about it.*

'Are you through in the shower?' Katie heard Ellie call from the next room. Each of the girls had her own bedroom, but they shared the bath.

'Yes,' Katie shouted in response.

Ellie came into the bathroom, modestly wrapped in a towel, and glanced briefly at her sister standing completely naked in front of the mirror. The younger girl started to say something, but apparently changed her mind, for she dropped the towel and stepped gingerly into the shower.

Katie watched Ellie through the transparent door. She looked first at Ellie's body, and then glanced in the mirror, comparing every possible anatomical feature. Katie preferred her own face and skin colour – she was by far the lightest member of the family other than her father – but Ellie had a superior figure.

'Why do I have such a boyish shape?' Katie asked Nicole one evening two weeks later after Katie had finished reading through a data cube containing some very old fashion magazines.

'I can't explain exactly,' Nicole replied, looking up from her own reading. 'Genetics is a wonderfully complicated subject, far more complex than Gregor Mendel originally thought.'

Nicole laughed at herself, realizing immediately that Katie could not possibly have understood what she had just said. 'Katie,' she continued in a less pedantic tone, 'each child is a unique combination of the characteristics of her two parents. These identifying characteristics are stored in molecules called genes. There are literally billions of different ways the genes from one pair of parents can express themselves. That's why children from the same parents are not all identical.'

Katie's brow furrowed. She had been expecting a different kind of answer. Nicole quickly understood. 'Besides,' she added in a comforting tone, 'your figure is really not "boyish" at all. "Athletic" would be a more descriptive word.'

'At any rate,' Katie rejoined, pointing at her sister, who was studying hard over in the corner of the family room, 'I certainly don't look like Ellie. Her body is really attractive – her breasts are even larger and rounder than yours.'

Nicole laughed naturally. 'Ellie does have an imposing figure,' she said. 'But yours is just as good – it's simply different.' Nicole returned to her reading, thinking the conversation was over.

'They don't have many women with my kind of figure in these old magazines,' Katie persisted after a short silence. She was holding up her electronic notebook, but Nicole was no longer paying attention. 'You know, Mother,' her daughter then said, 'I think that The Eagle made some kind of mistake with the controls in my berth. I think I must have received some of the hormones that were meant for Patrick or Benjy.'

'Katie, darling,' Nicole replied, finally realizing that her daughter was obsessed with her figure, 'it is virtually certain that you have become the person your genes were programmed to be at conception. You are a lovely, intelligent young woman. You would be happier if you spent your time thinking about your many excellent attributes, instead of finding an imperfection in yourself and wishing to be somebody different.'

Since they had awakened, many of their mother-daughter conversations had had a similar pattern. To Katie, it seemed that her mother did not try to understand her and was too ready with a lecture and/or an epigram. 'There's far more to life than just feeling good' was a regular refrain that resounded in Katie's ears. On the other hand, her mother's praise for Ellie seemed effusive to Katie. 'Ellie is such a good student, even though she started so late,' 'Ellie is always helpful without our asking her,' or 'Why can't you be a little more patient with Benjy, like Ellie is?'

First Simone and now Ellie, Katie said to herself as she lay naked in bed late one night after she and her sister had quarreled and her mother had reprimanded only her. *I've never had a chance with Mother. We're just too different. I might as well stop trying.*

Her fingers roamed over her body, stimulating her desire, and Katie sighed in anticipation. *At least*, she thought, *there are some things that I don't need Mother for.*

'Richard,' Nicole said one evening in bed when they were only six weeks away from Mars.

'Mmmmmm,' he responded slowly. He had been almost asleep.

'I'm concerned about Katie,' she said. 'I'm happy with the progress the other children are making – especially Benjy, bless his heart. But I have real worries about Katie.'

'What exactly is it that's bothering you?' Richard said, propping himself up on one elbow.

'Her attitudes, mostly. Katie is incredibly self-centred. She also has a quick temper and is impatient with the other children, even Patrick, who absolutely adores her. She argues with me all the time, often when it's a nonsensical dispute. And I think she spends far too many hours alone in her room.'

'She's just bored,' Richard replied. 'Remember, Nicole, physically she's a young woman in her early twenties. She should be dating, asserting her independence. There's really nobody here who is a peer ... And you must admit that sometimes we treat her like a twelve-year-old.'

Nicole did not say anything. Richard leaned over and touched her arm. 'We've always known that Katie was the most high-strung of the children. Unfortunately, she's a lot like me.'

'But at least you channel your energy into worthwhile projects,' Nicole said. 'Katie is as likely to be destructive as constructive ... Really, Richard, I wish you would talk to her. Otherwise I'm afraid we're going to have big problems when we meet the other humans.'

'What do you want me to say to her?' Richard replied after a short silence. 'That life is not just one excitement after another? And why should I ask her not to retreat into her fantasy world in her own room? It's probably more interesting there. Unfortunately there's nothing very exciting for a young woman anywhere in New Eden at the present time.'

'I had hoped you would be a little more understanding,' Nicole replied, slightly miffed. 'I need your help, Richard ... and Katie responds better to you.'

Again Richard was silent. 'All right,' he said finally in a frustrated tone. He lay back down in the bed. 'I'll take Katie water-skiing tomorrow – she loves that – and at least ask her to be more considerate of the other members of the family.'

'Very good. Excellent,' Richard said, finishing his reading of the material in Patrick's notebook. He switched off the power and glanced over at his son, who was sitting somewhat nervously in the chair opposite Richard. 'You have learned algebra quickly,' Richard continued. 'You are definitely gifted in mathematics. By the time we have other people in New Eden, you will be almost ready for university courses – at least in mathematics and science.'

'But Mother says I'm still way behind in my English,' Patrick replied. 'She says that my compositions are those of a young child.'

Nicole overheard the conversation and walked in from the kitchen. 'Patrick, darling, Garcia 041 says that you do not take writing seriously. I know that you cannot learn everything overnight, but I don't want you to be embarrassed when we meet the other humans.'

'But I like maths and science better,' Patrick protested. 'Our Einstein robot says he could teach me calculus in three or four weeks – if I didn't have so many other subjects to study.'

The front door suddenly opened and Katie and Ellie breezed in. Katie's face was bright and alive. 'Sorry we're late,' she said, 'but we have had a *big* day.' She turned to Patrick. 'I drove the boat across Lake Shakespeare by *myself*. We left the Garcia on the shore.'

Ellie was not nearly as ecstatic as her sister. In fact, she looked a little piqued. 'Are you all right, dear?' Nicole said quietly to her younger daughter while Katie was regaling the rest of the family with her tales of their adventure on the lake.

Ellie nodded and didn't say anything.

'What was really exciting,' Katie enthused, 'was crossing over our own waves at high speeds. Bam-bam-bam, we bounced from wave to wave. Sometimes I felt as if we were flying.'

'Those boats are not toys,' Nicole commented a few moments later. She motioned for everyone to come to the dinner table. Benjy, who had been in the kitchen picking at the salad with his fingers, was the last to sit down.

'What would you have done if the boat had capsized?' Nicole asked Katie when everyone was seated.

'The Garcias would have rescued us,' Katie answered flippantly. 'There were three of them watching us from the shore ... After all, that's what they're for. Besides, we were wearing life vests and I can swim anyway.'

'But your sister can't,' Nicole replied quickly, a critical tone in her voice. 'And you know she would have been terrified if she had been thrown into the lake.'

Katie started to argue, but Richard interceded and changed the subject before the conflict escalated. In truth, the entire family was edgy. Rama had gone into orbit around Mars a month earlier and there was still no sign of the contingent from Earth that they were supposed to meet. Nicole had always assumed that their rendezvous with their fellow humans would take place immediately after Mars orbit insertion.

After dinner, the family went out into Richard's small backyard observatory to look at Mars. The observatory had access to all the external sensors on Rama (but none of the internal ones outside of New Eden – The Eagle had been very firm about this particular point during their design discussions) and could present a splendid telescopic view of the Red Planet for part of each Martian day.

Benjy especially liked the observing sessions with Richard. He proudly pointed out the volcanoes in the Tharsis region, the great canyon called Valles Marineris, and the Chryse area where the first Viking spacecraft had landed over two hundred years before. A dust storm was just forming south of Mutch Station, the hub of the large Martian colony that had been abandoned in the fitful days following the Great Chaos. Richard speculated that the dust might spread across the entire planet since it was the proper season for such global storms.

'What happens if the other Earthlings don't show up?' Katie asked during a quiet point in their Martian observations. 'And Mother, please give us a straight answer this time. After all, we're not children any more.'

Nicole ignored the challenging tone in Katie's comment. 'If I remember correctly, the baseline plan is for us to wait here in Mars orbit for six months,' she replied. 'If there is no rendezvous during that time, Rama will head for Earth.' She paused for several seconds. 'Neither your father nor I know what the procedure will be from that point forward. The Eagle told us that if any of the contingency plans are invoked, we will be told at the time as much as we are required to know.'

The room was quiet for almost a minute as images of Mars at different resolutions appeared on the giant screen on the wall. 'Where is Earth?' Benjy then asked.

'It's the planet just inside Mars, the next one closer to the Sun,' Richard answered. 'Remember, I showed you the planetary lineup in the subroutine in my computer.'

'That's not what I meant,' Benjy answered very slowly. 'I want to see Earth.'

It was a simple enough request. It had never occurred to Richard, although he had brought the family out to the observatory several times before, that the children might be interested in that barely blue light in the Martian night sky. 'Earth is not very impressive from this distance,' Richard said, interrogating his data base to obtain the right sensor output. 'In fact, it looks pretty much like any other bright object, such as Sirius, for example.'

Richard had missed the point. Once he had identified the Earth in a specific celestial frame and then centred the image around that apparently insignificant reflection, the children all stared with rapt attention.

That is their home planet. Nicole thought, fascinated by the sudden change of mood in the room. *Even though they have never been there.* Pictures of the Earth from her memory flooded Nicole as she too stared at the tiny light in the centre of the image. She became aware of a profound homesickness deep within her, a longing to return to that blessed, oceanic planet filled with so much beauty. Tears swelled into her eyes as she moved up closer to her children and put her arms around them.

'Wherever we go in this amazing universe,' she said softly, 'both now and in the future, that blue speck will always be our home.'

2

ai Buatong rose in the predawn dark. She slipped into a sleeveless cotton dress, stopped briefly to pay respects to her personal Buddha in the family's *hawng pra* adjacent to the living room, and then opened the front door without disturbing any of the other members of the family. The summer air was soft. In the breeze she could smell flowers mixed with Thai spices – someone was already cooking breakfast in the neighborhood.

Her sandals made no sound on the soft dirt lane. Nai walked slowly, her head turning from right to left, her eyes absorbing all the familiar shadows that would soon be only memories. *My last day*, she thought. *It has finally come.*

After a few minutes, she turned right onto the paved street that led to the small Lamphun business district. An occasional bicycle passed her, but the morning was mostly quiet. None of the shops were yet open.

As she approached a temple, Nai passed two Buddhist monks, one on either side of the road. Each of the monks was dressed in the customary saffron robe and was carrying a large metal urn. They were seeking their breakfasts, just as they did every morning throughout Thailand, and were counting on the generosity of the townspeople of Lamphun. A woman appeared in a shop doorway right in front of Nai and dropped some food in the monk's urn. No words were exchanged and the monk's expression did not visibly alter to acknowledge the donation.

They own nothing, Nai mused to herself, *not even the robes upon their backs. And yet they're happy.* She recited quickly the basic tenet, 'The cause of suffering is desire', and recalled the incredible wealth of her new husband's family in the Higashiyama district on the edge of Kyoto, Japan. *Kenji says his mother has everything but peace. It eludes her because she cannot buy it.*

For a moment the recent memory of the grand house of the Watanabes filled her mind, pushing aside the image of the simple Thai road along which she was walking. Nai had been overwhelmed by the opulence of the Kyoto mansion. But it had not been a friendly place for her. It had been immediately obvious that Kenji's parents viewed her as an interloper, an inferior foreigner who had married their son without their support. They had not been unkind, just cold. They had dissected her with questions about her family and educational background that had been delivered with emotionless and logical precision. Kenji had later comforted Nai by pointing out that his family would not be with them on Mars.

She stopped in the street in Lamphun and looked across at the temple of Queen Chamatevi. It was Nai's favourite place in town, probably her favourite place in all of Thailand. Parts of the temple were fifteen hundred years old; its silent stone sentinels had seen a history so different from the present that it might as well have occurred on another planet.

Nai crossed the street and stood in the courtyard, just inside the temple walls. It was an unusually clear morning. Just above the uppermost *chedi* of the old Thai temple a strong light shone in the dark morning sky. Nai realised that the light was Mars, her next destination. The juxtaposition was perfect. For all twenty-six years of her life (except for the four years she had spent at the University of Chiang Mai) this town of Lamphun had been her home. Within six weeks she would be on board a giant spaceship that would take her to her living quarters for the next five years, in a space colony on the red planet.

Nai sat down in the lotus position in a corner of the courtyard and stared fixedly at that light in the sky. *How fitting*, she thought, *that Mars is looking down on me this morning.* She began the rhythmic breathing that was the prelude for her morning meditation. But as she was preparing for the peace and calm that usually 'centred' her for the day ahead, Nai recognised that there were many powerful and unresolved emotions inside her.

First I must reflect, Nai thought, deciding to forgo her meditation temporarily. On this, my last day at home, I must make peace with the events that have changed my life completely.

Eleven months earlier Nai Buatong had been sitting in the identical spot, her French and English lesson cubes neatly packed beside her in a carrying case. Nai had been planning to organise her material for the coming school term, determined that she was going to be more interesting and energetic as a high school language teacher.

Before she had started working on her lesson outlines on that fateful day the previous year, Nai had read the daily Chiang Mai newspaper. Slipping the cube into her reader, she had flipped quickly through the pages, scarcely reading more than the headlines. On the back page there had been a notice, written in English, that had caught her eye.

DOCTOR, NURSE, TEACHER, FARMER

Are you adventurous, multilingual, healthy?

The International Space Agency (ISA) is mounting a major expedition to recolonise Mars. Outstanding individuals with the critical skills defined above are sought for a five-year assignment in the colony. Personal interviews will be held in Chiang Mai on Monday August

23, 2244. Pay and benefits are exceptional.. Applications may be requested from Thai Telemail # 462-62-4930.

When she had first submitted her application to the ISA, Nai had not thought that her chances were very high. She had been virtually certain that she would not pass the first screening and therefore would not even qualify for the personal interview. Nai was quite surprised, in fact, when six weeks later she received a notice in her electronic mailbox that she had been provisionally selected for the interviews. The notice also informed Nai that, according to the procedure, she should ask whatever personal questions she might have by mail first, before the interview. The ISA stressed that they only wanted to interview those candidates who intended to accept, if an assignment in the Martian colony were to be offered.

Nai responded by telemail with a single question. Could a significant portion of her earnings while she was living on Mars be directed to a bank on Earth? She added that this was an essential precondition for her acceptance.

Ten days later another electronic mail notice arrived. It was very succinct. Yes, the message said, a portion of her earnings could be regularly sent to a bank on Earth. However, it continued, Nai would have to be absolutely certain about her division of the monies – whatever split a colonist decided on could not be changed after he or she left the Earth.

Because the cost of living in Lamphun was low, the salary offered by the ISA for a language teacher in the Martian colony was almost double what Nai needed to handle all her family obligations. The young woman was heavily burdened with responsibility. She was the only wage earner in a family of five that included her invalid father, her mother, and her two younger sisters.

Her childhood had been difficult, but her family had managed to survive just above the poverty line. During Nai's final year at the university, however, disaster had struck. First her father had had a debilitating stroke. Then her mother, whose business sense was nonexistent, had ignored the recommendations of family and friends and had tried to manage the small family craft shop on her own. Within a year the family had lost everything and Nai was forced not only to use her personal savings to provide food and clothing for her family, but also to abandon her dream of doing literary translation work for one of the big publishing houses in Bangkok.

Nai taught school during the week and was a tourist guide on the weekend. On the Saturday before the ISA interview, Nai was conducting a tour in Chiang Mai, thirty kilometres from her home. In her group were several Japanese, one of whom was a handsome, articulate young man in his early thirties who spoke practically unaccented English. His name was Kenji Watanabe. He paid very close attention to everything Nai said, always asked intelligent questions, and was extremely polite.

Near the end of the tour of the Buddhist holy places in the Chiang Mai area, the group rode the cable car up the mountain Doi Suthep to visit the famous Buddhist temple on its summit. Most of the tourists were exhausted from the day's activities, but not Kenji Watanabe. First the man insisted on climbing the long dragon stairway, like a Buddhist pilgrim, rather than riding the funicular from the cable car exit to the top. Then he asked question after question while Nai was explaining the wonderful story of the founding of the temple. Finally, when they had descended and Nai was sitting by herself, having tea in the lovely restaurant at the foot of the mountain, Kenji left the other tourists in the souvenir shops and approached her table.

'*Kaw tode krap*,' he said in excellent Thai, astonishing Miss Buatong. 'May I sit down? I have a few more questions.'

'*Khun pode pasa thai dai mai ka*?' Nai asked, still shocked.

'*Pohm kao jai pasa thai dai nitnoy*,' he answered, indicating that he understood a little Thai. 'How about you? *Anata wa nihon go hanashimasu ka*?'

Nai shook her head. '*Nihon go hanashimasen.*' She smiled. 'Only English, French, and Thai. Although I can sometimes understand simple Japanese if it is spoken very slowly.'

'I was fascinated,' Kenji said in English, after sitting down opposite Nai, 'by the murals depicting the founding of the temple on Doi Suthep. It is a wonderful legend – a blend of history and mysticism – but as a historian, I'm curious about two things. First, couldn't this venerable monk from Sri Lanka have known, from some religious sources outside of the kingdom of Lan-na, that there was a relic of the Buddha in that nearby abandoned pagoda? It seems unlikely to me that he would have risked his reputation otherwise. Second, it seems too perfect, too much like life imitating art, for that white elephant carrying the relic to have climbed Doi Suthep by chance and then to have expired just when he reached the peak. Are there any non-Buddhist historical sources from the fifteenth century that corroborate the story?'

Nai stared at the eager Mr Watanabe for several seconds before replying. 'Sir,' she said with a wan smile, 'in my two years of conducting tours of the Buddhist sites of this region, I have never had anybody ask me either one of those questions. I certainly do not know the answers myself, but if you are interested, I can give you the name of a professor at Chiang Mai University who is extremely well versed in the Buddhist history of the kingdom of Lan-na. He is an expert on the entire time period, beginning with King Mengrai ...'

Their conversation was interrupted by an announcement that the cable car was now ready to accommodate passengers for the trip back to the city. Nai rose from her seat and excused herself. Kenji rejoined the rest of the group. As Nai watched him from afar, she kept recalling the intensity in his eyes. *They were incredible*, she was thinking. *I have never seen eyes so clear and so full of curiosity.*

She saw those eyes again the following Monday afternoon, when she went to the Dusit Thani Hotel in Chiang Mai for her ISA interview. She was astonished to see Kenji sitting behind a desk with the official ISA emblem on his shirt. Nai was initially flustered. 'I had not looked at your documents before Saturday,' Kenji said as an apology. 'I promise. If I had known you were one of the applicants, I would have taken a different tour.'

The interview eventually went smoothly. Kenji was extremely complimentary, both about Nai's outstanding academic record and her volunteer work with the orphanages in Lamphun and Chiang Mai. Nai was honest in admitting that she had not always had 'an overpowering desire' to travel in space, but since she was basically 'adventurous by nature' and this ISA position would also allow her to take care of her family obligations, she had applied for the assignment on Mars.

Toward the end of the interview there was a pause in the conversation. 'Is that all?' Nai asked pleasantly, rising from her chair.

'One more thing, perhaps,' Kenji Watanabe said, suddenly awkward. 'That is, if you're any good at interpreting dreams.'

Nai smiled and sat back down. 'Go on,' she said.

Kenji took a deep breath. 'Saturday night I dreamed I was in the jungle, somewhere near the foot of Doi Suthep – I knew where I was because I could see the golden *chedi* at the top of my dream screen. I was rushing through the trees, trying to find my way, when I encountered a huge python sitting on a broad branch beside my head.

'"Where are you going?" the python asked me.

'"I'm looking for my girlfriend," I answered.

'"She's at the top of the mountain," the python said.

'I broke free of the jungle, into the sunlight, and looked at the summit of Doi Suthep. My childhood sweetheart Keiko Murosawa was standing there waving down at me. I turned around and glanced back at the python.

'"Look again," it said.

'When I looked up the mountain the second time the woman's face had changed. It was no longer Keiko – it was you who was now waving to me from the top of Doi Suthep.'

Kenji was silent for several seconds. 'I have never had such an unusual or vivid dream. I thought perhaps ...'

Nai had had goose bumps on her arms while Kenji was telling the story. She had known the ending – that she, Nai Buatong, would be the woman waving from the top of the mountain – before he had finished. Nai leaned forward in her chair. 'Mr Watanabe,' she said slowly, 'I hope that what I am going to say does not offend you in any way ...'

Nai was quiet for several seconds. 'We have a famous Thai proverb,' she said at length, her eyes avoiding his, 'that says when a snake talks to you in a dream, you have found the man or woman that you will marry.'

Six weeks later I received the notice, Nai remembered. She was still sitting in the courtyard beside Queen Chamatevi's temple in Lamphun. *The package of ISA materials came three days afterward. Along with the flowers from Kenji.*

Kenji himself had appeared in Lamphun the following weekend. 'I'm sorry I didn't call or anything,' he had apologised, 'but it just didn't make sense to pursue the relationship unless you also were going to Mars.'

He had proposed on Sunday afternoon and Nai had quickly accepted. They had been married in Kyoto three months later. The Watanabes had graciously paid for Nai's two sisters and three of her other Thai friends to travel to Japan for the wedding. Her mother could not come, unfortunately, for there was nobody else to look after Nai's father.

Nai took a deep breath. Her review of the recent changes in her life was now over. She was ready to begin her meditation. Thirty minutes later she was quite serene, happy and expectant about the unknown life in front of her. The sun had risen and there were other people on the temple grounds. She walked slowly around the perimeter, trying to savour her last moments in her home village.

Inside the main *viharn*, after an offering and the burning of incense at the altar, Nai carefully studied every panel of the paintings on the walls she had seen so many times before. The pictures told the life story of Queen Chamatevi, her one and only heroine ever since childhood. In the seventh century the many tribes in the Lamphun area had had different cultures and had often been at war with each other. All they had in common at that particular epoch was a legend, a myth that said a young queen would arrive from the south, 'borne by huge elephants', and would unite all the diverse tribes into the Haripunchai kingdom.

Chamatevi had been only twenty-three when an old soothsayer identified her to some emissaries from the north as the future queen of the Haripunchai. She was a young and beautiful princess of the Mons, the Khmer people who would later construct Angkor Wat. Chamatevi was also extremely intelligent, a rare woman of the era, and very much favoured by everyone at the royal court.

The Mons were therefore stunned when she announced that she was giving up her life of leisure and plenty and heading north on a harrowing six-month journey across seven hundred kilometres of mountains, jungles, and swamps. When Chamatevi and her retinue, 'borne by huge elephants,' reached the verdant valley in which Lamphun lay, her future subjects immediately put aside their factional quarrels and placed the beautiful young queen on the throne. She ruled for fifty years in wisdom and justice, lifting her kingdom from obscurity into an age of social progress and artistic accomplishment.

When she was seventy years old, Chamatevi abdicated her throne and divided her kingdom in half, each ruled by one of her twin sons. The queen then announced that she was dedicating the remainder of her life to God. She entered a Buddhist monastery and gave away all of her possessions. She lived a simple, pious life in the monastery, dying at the age of ninety-nine. By then the golden age of the Haripunchai was over.

On the final wall panel inside the temple an ascetic and wizened woman is carried away to nirvana in a magnificent chariot. A younger Queen Chamatevi, radiantly beautiful beside her Buddha, sits above the chariot in the splendor of the heavens. Nai Buatong Watanabe, Martian colonist-designate, sat on her knees in the temple in Lamphun, Thailand, and offered a silent prayer to the spirit of her heroine from the distant past.

Dear Chamatevi, she said. *You have watched over me for these twenty-six years. Now I am about to leave for an unknown place, much as you did when you came north to find the Haripunchai. Guide me with your wisdom and insight as I go to this new and wonderful world.*

3

Yukiko was wearing a black silk shirt, white pants, and a black and white beret. She crossed the living room to talk to her brother. 'I wish you would come, Kenji,' she said. 'It's going to be the largest demonstration for peace that the world has ever seen.'

Kenji smiled at his younger sister. 'I would like to, Yuki,' he replied. 'But I only have two more days before I must leave and I want to spend the time with Mother and Father.'

Their mother entered the room from the opposite side. She looked harried, as usual, and was carrying a large suitcase. 'Everything is now packed properly,' she said. 'But I still wish you would change your mind. Hiroshima is going to be a madhouse. The Asahi Shimbun says they're expecting a *million* visitors, almost half of them from abroad.'

'Thank you, Mother,' Yukiko said, reaching for the suitcase. 'As you know, Satoko and I will be at the Hiroshima Prince Hotel. Now, don't worry. We will call every morning, before the activities begin. And I'll be home Monday afternoon.'

The young woman opened the suitcase and reached inside a special compartment, pulling out a diamond bracelet and a sapphire ring. She put them both on. 'Don't you think you should leave those things at home?' her mother fussed. 'Remember, there will be all those foreigners. Your jewellery may be too much temptation for them.'

Yukiko laughed in the uninhibited way that Kenji adored. 'Mother,' she said, 'you're such a worrywart. All your ever think about is what *bad* things might happen ... We're going to Hiroshima for the ceremonies commemorating the three hundredth anniversary of the dropping of the atomic bomb. Our prime minister will be there, as well as three of the members of the Central Council of the COG. Many of the world's most famous musicians will be performing in the evenings. This will be what Father calls an *enriching* experience – and all you can think about is who might steal my jewellery.'

'When I was young it was unheard of for two girls, not yet finished at the university, to travel around Japan unchaperoned ...'

'Mother, we've been through this before,' Yuki interrupted. 'I'm almost twenty-two years old. Next year, after I finish my degree, I'm going to live away from home, on my own, maybe even in another country. I'm no longer a child. And Satoko and I are perfectly capable of looking after one another.'

Yukiko checked her watch. 'I must go now,' she said. 'She is probably already waiting for me at the subway station.'

She strode gracefully over to her mother and gave her a perfunctory kiss. Yuki shared a longer embrace with her brother.

'Be well, *ani-san*,' she whispered in his ear. 'Take care of yourself and your lovely wife on Mars. We're all very proud of you.'

Kenji had never really known Yukiko very well. He was, after all, almost twelve years older than she. Yuki had been only four when Mr Watanabe had been assigned to the position of president of the American division of International Robotics. The family had moved across the Pacific to a suburb of San Francisco. Kenji had not paid much attention to his younger sister in those days. In California he had been much more interested in his new life, especially after he started at UCLA.

The elder Watanabes and Yukiko had returned to Japan in 2232, leaving Kenji as a sophomore in history at the university. He had had very little contact with Yuki since then. During his annual visits to his home in Kyoto, Kenji always meant to spend some private hours with Yukiko, but it never seemed to happen. Either she was too deeply involved in her own life, or his parents had scheduled too many social functions, or Kenji himself had just not left enough time.

Kenji was vaguely sad as he stood at the door and watched Yukiko disappear in the distance. *I'm leaving this planet,* he thought, *and yet I've never taken the time to know my own sister.*

Mrs Watanabe was talking in a monotone behind him, expressing her feeling that her life had been a failure because none of her children had any respect for her and they had all moved away. Now her only son, who had married a woman from Thailand just to embarrass them, was going off to live on Mars and she wouldn't see him for over five years. As for her middle daughter, she and her banker husband had at least given her two grandchildren, but they were as dull and boring as their parents ...

'How is Fumiko?' Kenji interrupted his mother. 'Will I have a chance to see her and my nieces before I leave?'

'They're coming over from Kobe for dinner tomorrow night,' his mother replied. 'Although I have no idea what I'm going to feed them ... Did you know that Tatsuo and Fumiko are not even teaching those girls how to use chopsticks? Can you imagine? A Japanese child who does not know how to use chopsticks? Is nothing sacred? We've given up our identity to become rich. I was telling your father ...'

Kenji excused himself from his mother's querulous monologue and sought refuge in his father's study. Framed photographs lined the walls of the room, the archives of a successful man's personal and professional life. Two of the pictures held special memories for Kenji as well. In one of the photos, he and his father were each holding on to a large trophy given by the country club to the winners in the annual father-son golf tournament. In the other, the beaming Mr Watanabe was presenting a large medal to his son after Kenji had won first prize in all Kyoto in the high school academic competition.

What Kenji had forgotten until seeing the photographs again was that Toshio Nakamura, the son of his father's closest friend and business associate, had been the runner-up in both contests. In both pictures the young Nakamura, almost a head taller than Kenji, was wearing an intense, angry frown on his face.

That was long before all his trouble, Kenji thought. He remembered the headline, 'Osaka Executive Arrested', which had proclaimed four years earlier the indictment of Toshio Nakamura. The article underneath the headline had explained that Mr Nakamura, who was at the time already a vice president in the Tomozawa Hotel Group, had been charged with very serious crimes, ranging from bribery to pandering to trafficking in human slavery. Within four months Nakamura had been convicted and sentenced to several years in detention. Kenji had been astonished. *What in the world happened to Nakamura?* he had wondered many times in the intervening four years.

While Kenji was remembering his boyhood rival, he felt very sorry for Keiko Murosawa, Nakamura's wife, for whom Kenji himself had had a special affection when he was a sixteen-year-old in Kyoto. Kenji and Nakamura had, in fact, vied for the love of Keiko for almost a year. When Keiko had finally made it clear that she preferred Kenji over Toshio, young Nakamura had been furious. He had even confronted Kenji one morning, near the Ryoanji Tempe, and threatened him physically.

I might have married Keiko myself, Kenji thought, *if I had stayed in Japan*. He gazed out the window at the moss garden. It was raining outside. He suddenly had an especially poignant memory of a rainy day during his adolescence.

Kenji had walked over to her house as soon as his father had told him the news. A Chopin concerto had greeted his ears the moment he turned into the lane leading to her house. Mrs Murosawa had answered the door and had addressed him sternly. 'Keiko is practising now,' she had said to Kenji. 'She won't be finished for over an hour.'

'Please, Mrs Murosawa,' the sixteen-year-old boy had said, 'it's very important.'

Her mother was about to close the door when Keiko herself caught sight of Kenji through the window. She stopped playing and rushed over, her radiant smile sending a rush of joy through the young man. 'Hi, Kenji,' she said. 'What's up?'

'Something *very* important,' he replied mysteriously. 'Can you come with me for a walk?'

Mrs Murosawa had grumbled about the coming recital, but Keiko convinced her mother that she could afford to miss practice for one day. The girl grabbed an umbrella and joined Kenji in front of the house. As soon as they were out of view of her home, she slipped her arm through his, as she always did when they walked together.

'So, my friend,' Keiko said as they followed their normal route toward the hills behind their section of Kyoto. 'What's so *very* important?'

'I don't want to tell you now,' Kenji answered. 'Not here, anyway. I want to wait until we're in the right place.'

Kenji and Keiko laughed and made small talk as they headed for Philosopher's Walk, a beautiful path that wound for several kilometers along the bottom of the eastern hills. The route had been made famous by the twentieth century philosopher Nishida Kitaro, who supposedly took the walk every morning. It led past some of Kyoto's most famous scenic spots, including Ginkaku-ji (the Silver Pavilion) and Kenji's personal favourite, the old Buddhist temple called the Honen-In.

Behind and to the side of the Honen-In was a small cemetery with about seventy or eighty graves and tombstones. Earlier that year Kenji and Keiko, while adventuring on their own, had discovered that the cemetery housed the remains of some of Kyoto's most prominent citizens of the twentieth century, including the celebrated novelist Junichiro Tanizaki and the doctor/poet Iwao Matsuo. After their discovery, Kenji and Keiko made the cemetery their regular meeting place. Once, after they had both read *The Makioka Sisters*, Tanizaki's masterpiece of Osaka life in the 1930s, they had laughingly argued for over an hour – while sitting beside the author's tombstone – about which of the Makioka sisters Keiko resembled the most.

On the day that Mr Watanabe informed Kenji that the family was moving to America, it had already started to rain by the time Kenji and Keiko reached the Honen-In. There Kenji turned right onto a small lane and headed toward an old gate with a woven straw roof. As Keiko expected, they did not enter the temple, but instead climbed the steps leading to the cemetery. But Kenji did not stop at Tanizaki's tomb. He climbed up higher, to another grave site.

'This is where Dr Iwao Matsuo is buried,' Kenji said, pulling out his electronic notebook. 'We are going to read a few of his poems.'

Keiko sat close beside her friend, the two of them nestled under her umbrella in the light rain, while Kenji read three poems. 'I have one final poem,' Kenji then said, 'a special haiku written by a friend of Dr Matsuo's.'

> One day in the month of June,
> After a cooling dish of ice cream,
> We bid each other farewell.

They were both silent for several seconds after Kenji recited the haiku from memory a second time. Keiko became alarmed and even a little frightened when Kenji's serious expression did not waver. 'The poem talks of a parting,' she said softly. 'Are you telling me that ...'

'Not by choice, Keiko,' Kenji interrupted her. He hesitated for several seconds. 'My father has been assigned to America,' he continued at length. 'We will move there next month.'

Kenji had never seen such a forlorn look on Keiko's beautiful face. When she looked up at him with those terribly sad eyes, he thought his heart would tear apart. He held her tightly in the afternoon rain, both of them crying, and swore he would love only her forever.

4

The younger waitress, the one in the light blue kimono with the old-fashioned obi, pulled back the sliding screen and entered the room. She was carrying a tray with beer and sake.

'*Osake onegai shimasu*,' Kenji's father said politely, holding up his sake cup as the lady poured.

Kenji took a drink of his cold beer. The older waitress now returned, soundlessly, with a small plate of hors d'oeuvres. In the centre was a shellfish of some kind, in a light sauce, but Kenji could not have identified either the mollusk or the sauce. He had not eaten more than a handful of these *kaiseki* meals in the seventeen years since he had left Kyoto.

'*Campai*,' Kenji said, clinking his beer glass against his father's sake cup. 'Thank you, Father. I am honoured to be having dinner here with you.'

Kicho was the most famous restaurant in the Kansai region, perhaps in all of Japan. It was also frighteningly expensive, for it preserved the full traditions of personal service, private eating rooms, and seasonal dishes with only the highest quality ingredients. Every course was a delight to the eye as well as to the palate. When Mr Watanabe had informed his son that they were going to dine alone, just the two of them, Kenji had never imagined that it would be at Kicho.

They had been talking about the expedition to Mars. 'How many of the other colonists are Japanese?' Mr Watanabe asked.

'Quite a few,' Kenji replied. 'Almost three hundred, if I remember correctly. There were many top-quality applications from Japan. Only America has a larger contingent.'

'Do you know any of the others from Japan personally?'

'Two or three. Yasuko Horikawa was briefly in my class in Kyoto in junior high school. You may remember her. Very, very smart. Buck teeth. Thick glasses. She is, or was, I should say, a chemist with Dai-Nippon.'

Mr Watanabe smiled. 'I think I do remember her,' he said. 'Did she come over to the house the night that Keiko played the piano?'

'Yes, I think so,' Kenji said easily. He laughed. 'But I have a hard time remembering anything other than Keiko from that night.'

Mr Watanabe emptied his sake cup. The younger attendant, who was sitting unobtrusively on her knees in a corner of the tatami mat room, came to the table to refill it. 'Kenji, I'm concerned about the criminals,' Mr Watanabe said as the young lady departed.

'What are you talking about, Father?' Kenji said.

'I read a long story in a magazine that said the ISA had recruited several hundred convicts to be part of your Lowell Colony. The article stressed that all of the criminals had perfect records during their times of detention, as well as outstanding skills. But why was it necessary to accept convicts at all?'

Kenji took a swallow from his beer. 'In truth, Father,' he replied, 'we have had some difficulty with the recruitment process. First, we had an unrealistic view of how many people would apply and we set up screening criteria that were far too tough. Second, the five-year minimum time requirement was a mistake. To young people in particular, a decision to do anything for that long a period is an overwhelming commitment. Most importantly, the press seriously undermined the entire staffing process. At the time we were soliciting applications, there were myriad articles in magazines and "specials" on television about the demise of the Martian colonies a hundred years ago. People were frightened that history might repeat itself and they too could be left permanently abandoned on Mars.'

Kenji paused briefly, but Mr Watanabe said nothing. 'In addition, as you are well aware, the project has had recurring financial crises. It was during a budget squeeze last year that we first began to consider skilled, model convicts as a way of solving some of our personnel and budgetary difficulties. Although they would be paid only modest salaries, there were still plenty of inducements to cause the convicts to apply. Selection meant granting of full pardons, and therefore freedom, when they returned to Earth after the five-year term. In addition, the ex-prisoners would be full citizens of Lowell Colony like everyone else, and would no longer have to tolerate the onerous monitoring of their every activity ...'

Kenji stopped as two small pieces of broiled fish, delicate and beautiful and sitting on a bed of variegated leaves, were placed upon the table. Mr Watanabe picked up a piece of fish with his chopsticks. '*Oishii desu*,' he commented, without glancing at his son.

Kenji reached for his piece of fish. The discussion of the convicts in Lowell Colony had apparently ended. Kenji looked behind his father, where he could see the lovely garden for which the restaurant was so famous. A tiny stream dropped down polished steps and ran beside a half dozen exquisite dwarf trees. The seat facing the garden was always the position of honour for a traditional Japanese meal. Mr Watanabe had insisted that Kenji should have the garden view during this last dinner.

'You were not able to attract any Chinese colonists?' his father asked after they had finished the fish.

Kenji shook his head. 'Only a few from Singapore and Malaysia. Both the Chinese and Brazilian governments forbade their citizens to apply. The

Brazilian decision was expected – their South American empire is virtually at war with the COG – but we had hoped that the Chinese might soften their stand. I guess a hundred years of isolation doesn't die that easily.'

'You can't really blame them,' Mr Watanabe commented. 'Their nation suffered terribly during the Great Chaos. All the foreign capital disappeared overnight and their economy immediately collapsed.'

'We did manage to recruit a few black Africans, maybe a hundred altogether, and a handful of Arabs. But most of the colonists are from the countries that contribute significantly to the ISA. That's probably to be expected.'

Kenji became suddenly embarrassed. The entire conversation since they had entered the restaurant had been about him and his activities. During the next few courses Kenji asked his father questions about his work at International Robotics. Mr Watanabe, who was now the chief operating officer of the corporation, always glowed with pride when he talked about 'his' company. It was the world's largest manufacturer of robots for the factory and the office. The annual sales of IR, as it was always called, placed it among the top fifty manufacturers in the world.

'I'll be sixty-two next year,' Mr Watanabe said, the many cups of sake making him unusually talkative, 'and I had thought that I might retire. But Nakamura says that would be a mistake. He says that the company still needs me ...'

Before the fruit arrived, Kenji and his father were again discussing the coming Martian expedition. Kenji explained that Nai and most of the other Asian colonists who were travelling on either the Pinta or the Nina were already at the Japanese training site in southern Kyushu. He would join his wife there as soon as he left Kyoto and, after ten more days of training, they and the rest of the passengers on the Pinta would be transported to a LEO (Low Earth Orbit) space station, where they would undergo a week of weightlessness training. The final leg of their near-Earth journey would be a ride aboard a space tug from LEO to the geosynchronous space station at GEO-4, where the Pinta was currently being assembled while undergoing its final checks and being outfitted for the long trip to Mars.

The younger waitress brought them two glasses of cognac. 'That wife of yours is really a magnificent creature,' Mr Watanabe said, taking a small sip of the liqueur. 'I have always thought that the Thai women were the most beautiful in the world.'

'She's also beautiful inside,' Kenji hastily added, suddenly missing his new bride, 'And she is quite intelligent as well.'

'Her English is excellent,' Mr Watanabe remarked. 'But your mother says her Japanese is awful.'

Kenji bristled. 'Nai tried to speak Japanese – which, incidentally, she has never studied – because Mother refused to speak English. It was deliberately done to make Nai feel ill at ease ...'

Kenji caught himself. His remarks defending Nai were not appropriate for the occasion.

'*Gomen nasai,*' he said to his father.

Mr Watanabe took a long drink from his cognac. 'Well, Kenji,' he said, 'this is the last time we will be alone together for at least five years. I have very much enjoyed our dinner and our conversation.' He paused. 'There is, however, one more item that I want to discuss with you.'

Kenji shifted his position (he was no longer used to sitting cross-legged on the floor for four hours at a time) and sat up straight, trying to clear his mind. He could tell from his father's tone that the 'one more item' was a serious one.

'My interest in the criminals in your Lowell Colony is not just idle curiosity,' Mr Watanabe began. He paused to gather his thoughts before continuing. 'Nakamura-san came into my office late last week, at the end of the business day, and told me that his son's second application for Lowell Colony had also been denied. He asked me if I would talk to you about looking into the matter.'

The comment hit Kenji like a thunderbolt. He had never even been told that his boyhood rival had applied for Lowell Colony. Now here was his father ...

'I have not been involved in the process of selecting the convict colonists,' Kenji replied slowly. 'That's an entirely different division in the project.'

Mr Watanabe did not say anything for several seconds. 'Our connections tell us,' he eventually continued, after finishing his cognac, 'that the only real opposition to the application is coming from a psychiatrist, a Dr Ridgemore from New Zealand, who has the opinion, despite Toshio's excellent record during his detention period, that Nakamura's son still does not recognise that he did anything wrong ... I believe that you were personally responsible for recruiting Dr Ridgemore for the Lowell Colony team.'

Kenji was staggered. This was no idle request his father was making. He had done extensive background research. *But why?* Kenji wondered. *Why is he so interested?*

'Nakamura-san is a brilliant engineer,' Mr Watanabe said. 'He has personally been responsible for many of the products that have established us as leaders in our field. But his laboratory has not been very innovative lately. In fact, its productivity began to drop around the time of his son's arrest and conviction.'

Mr Watanabe leaned toward Kenji, resting his elbows on the table. 'Nakamura-san has lost his self-confidence. He and his wife must visit Toshio in that detention apartment once a month. It is a constant reminder to Nakamura of how his family has been disgraced. If the son could go to Mars, then perhaps ...'

Kenji understood too well what his father was asking. Emotions that had long been suppressed threatened to erupt. Kenji was angry and confused. He was going to tell his father that his request was 'improper' when the elder Watanabe spoke again.

'It has been equally hard on Keiko and the little girl. Aiko is almost seven now. Every other weekend they dutifully ride the train to Ashiya ...'

Try as he might, Kenji could not prevent the tears from forming in the corners of his eyes. The picture of Keiko, broken and dejected, leading her daughter inside the restricted area for the biweekly visit with her father, was more than he could bear.

'I talked to Keiko myself last week,' his father added, 'at Nakamura-san's request. She was very despondent. But she seemed to perk up when I told her that I was going to ask you to intercede on her husband's behalf.'

Kenji took a deep breath and gazed at his father's emotionless face. He knew what he was going to do. He knew also that it was indeed 'improper' – not wrong, just improper. But it made no sense to agonise over a decision that was a foregone conclusion.

Kenji finished his cognac. 'Tell Nakamura-san that I will call Dr Ridgemore tomorrow,' he said.

What if his intuition was wrong? *Then I will have wasted an hour, ninety minutes at the most*, Kenji thought as he excused himself from the family gathering with his sister Fumiko and her daughters and ran out into the street. He turned immediately toward the hills. It was about an hour before sunset. *She'll be there*, he said to himself. *This will be my only chance to say goodbye.*

Kenji went first to the small Anraku-Ji temple. He walked inside the *hondo*, expecting to find Keiko in her favourite spot, in front of the side wooden altar commemorating two twelfth century Buddhist nuns, formerly members of the court harem, who had committed suicide when Emperor Go-Toba had ordered them to repudiate the teachings of St Honen. Keiko was not there. Nor was she outside where the two women were buried, just at the edge of the bamboo forest. Kenji began to think that he had been mistaken. *Keiko has not come*, he thought. *She feels that she has lost too much face.*

His only other hope was that Keiko was waiting for him in the cemetery beside the Honen-In, where seventeen years earlier he had informed her that he was moving away from Japan. Kenji's heart skipped a beat as he walked up the lane leading to the temple. Off in the distance to his right he could see a woman's figure. She was wearing a simple black dress and was standing beside the tomb of Junichiro Tanizaki.

Although her body was facing away from him and he could not see clearly in the fading twilight, Kenji was certain that the woman was Keiko. He raced up the steps and into the cemetery, finally stopping about five metres away from the woman in black.

'Keiko,' he said, catching his breath. 'I'm so glad ...'

'Watanabe-san,' the figure said formally, turning around with her head low and her eyes on the ground. She bowed very deeply, as if she were a servant. '*Domo arrigato gozaimasu*,' she repeated twice. Finally she rose, but she still did not look up at Kenji.

'Keiko, ' he said softly. 'It's only Kenji. I'm alone. Please look at me.'

'I cannot,' she answered in a voice that was scarcely audible. 'But I can thank you for what you have done for Aiko and me.' Again she bowed. '*Domo arrigato gozaimasu*,' she said.

Kenji bent down impulsively and put his hand under Keiko's chin. He gently raised her head until he could see her face. Keiko was still beautiful. But Kenji was shocked to see such sadness permanently carved into those delicate features.

'Keiko,' he murmured, her tears cutting into his heart like tiny knives.

'I must go,' she said. 'I wish you happiness.' She pulled away from his touch and bowed again. Then she rose, without looking at him, and walked slowly down the path in the twilight shadows.

Kenji's eyes followed her until she disappeared in the distance. It was only then that he realised he had been leaning on Tanizaki's tombstone. He stared for several seconds at the two Kanji characters, Ku and Jaku, on the grey markers. One of them said 'Emptiness'; the other 'Solitude'.

5

When the message from Rama was relayed to Earth from the tracking satellite system in 2241, it caused immediate consternation. Nicole's video was quickly classified top secret, of course, while the International Intelligence Agency (IIA), the security arm of the Council of Governments (COG), struggled to comprehend what it was all about. A dozen of the finest agents were soon assigned to the secure facility in Novosibirsk to analyse the signal that had been received from deep space and to develop a master plan for the COG response.

Once it was ascertained that neither the Chinese nor the Brazilians could have decoded the signal (their technological capabilities were not yet on a par with the COG), the requested acknowledgment was transmitted in the direction of Rama, thereby precluding any future replays of Nicole's video. Then the superagents focused on the detailed contents of the message itself.

They began by doing some historical research. It was widely accepted, despite some suggested (but discredited) evidence to the contrary, that the Rama II spacecraft had been destroyed by the barrage of nuclear missiles in April of 2200. Nicole des Jardins, the putative human being in the video, had been presumed dead before the Newton science ship had even left Rama. Certainly she, or what was left of her, must have been annihilated in the nuclear devastation. So the speaker could not actually be she.

But if the person or thing speaking in the television segment was a robot imitation or simulacrum of Madame des Jardins, it was vastly superior to any artificial intelligence designs on Earth. The preliminary conclusion, therefore, was that the Earth was again dealing with an advanced civilization of unbelievable capability, one that was consistent with the technological levels exhibited by the two Rama spacecraft.

There was no question about the implied threat in the message either, about that the superagents were unanimous. If there was indeed another Rama vehicle on its way to the solar system (although none had yet been detected by the pair of Excalibur stations), the Earth could certainly not ignore the message. Of course, there was some possibility that the entire thing was an elaborate hoax, concocted by the brilliant Chinese physicists (they were definitely the prime suspects), but until that was a confirmed fact, the COG needed to have a definitive plan.

Fortunately a multinational project had already been approved to establish a modest colony on Mars in the mid-2240s. During the two previous decades, a half dozen exploration missions to Mars had rekindled interest in the great idea of terra-forming the red planet and making it habitable for the human species. Already there were unmanned scientific laboratories on Mars that were conducting experiments that were either too dangerous or too controversial to be performed on Earth. The easiest way to meet the intent of the Nicole des Jardins video – and not alarm the populace of the planet Earth – would be to announce and fund a considerably larger colony on Mars. If the entire affair turned out subsequently to be a hoax, then the size of the colony could be scaled back to the original proposed size.

One of the agents, an Indian named Ravi Srinivasan, carefully researched the massive ISA data archives from the year 2200 and became convinced that Rama II had not been destroyed by the nuclear phalanx. 'It is possible,' Mr Srinivasan said, 'that this video is legitimate and that the speaker is really the esteemed Madame des Jardins.'

'But she would be seventy-seven years old today,' another of the agents countered.

'There is nothing in the video that indicates when it was made,' Mr Srinivasan argued. 'And if you compare the photographs of Madame des Jardins taken during the mission with the pictures of the woman in the transmission we received, they are decidedly different. Her face is older, maybe by as much as ten years. If the speaker in the video is a hoax or a simulacrum, then it is an amazingly clever one.'

Mr Srinivasan agreed, however, that the plan eventually developed by the IIA was the proper one even if the video was indeed presenting the truth. So it was not that important that he convince everyone that his point of view was correct. What was absolutely necessary, the superagents all agreed, was that a bare minimum of people know about the existence of the video.

The forty years since the beginning of the twenty-third century had seen some marked changes on the planet Earth. Following the Great Chaos, the Council of Governments (COG) had emerged as a monolithic organization controlling, or at least manipulating, the politics of the planet. Only China, which had retreated into isolation after its devastating experience during the Chaos, was outside the sphere of influence of the COG. But after 2200, there were signs that the unchallenged power of the COG was beginning to erode.

First came the Korean elections of 2209, when the people of that nation, disgusted with successive regimes of corrupt politicians who had grown rich at the expense of the populace, actually voted to federate with the Chinese. Of the major countries of the world, only China had a significantly different kind of government from the regulated capitalism practised by the wealthy nations of North America, Asia, and Europe. The Chinese government was a kind of socialist democracy based on the humanist principles espoused by the canonised twenty-second century Italian Catholic, St Michael of Siena.

The COG, and indeed the entire world, was dumbfounded by the stunning election results in Korea. By the time the IIA was able to foment a civil war (2211-2212), the new Korean government and their Chinese allies had already captured the hearts and minds of the people. The rebellion was easily quashed and Korea became a permanent part of the Chinese federation.

The Chinese openly acknowledged that they had no intention of exporting their form of government by military action, but the rest of the world did not accept their word. The COG military and intelligence budgets doubled between 2210 and 2220 as political tension returned to the world scene.

Meanwhile, in 2218, the three hundred and fifty million Brazilians elected a charismatic general, Joao Pereira, to head their nation. General Pereira believed that South America was mistreated and undervalued by the COG (he was not wrong) and he demanded changes in the COG character that would correct the problems. When the COG refused, Pereira galvanised South American regionalism by unilaterally abrogating the COG charter. Brazil seceded, in effect, from the Council of Governments, and over the next decade most of the rest of the South American nations, encouraged by the massive military strength in Brazil that successfully opposed the COG peacekeeping forces, followed suit. What emerged was a third player in the world geopolitical scene, a kind of Brazilian empire, energetically led by General Pereira.

At first the embargoes by the COG threatened to return Brazil and the rest of South America to the destitution that had ravaged the region in the wake of the Great Chaos. But Pereira fought back. Since the advanced nations of North America, Asia, and Europe would not buy his legal exports, he decided that he and his allies would export illegal products. Drugs became the primary trade of the Brazilian empire. It was an immensely successful policy. By 2240 there was a massive flow of all kinds and types of drugs from South America to the rest of the world.

It was in this political environment that Nicole's video was received on Earth. Although some cracks had appeared in the COG control of the planet, the organization still represented almost seventy percent of the population and ninety percent of the Earth's material wealth. It was natural that the COG and its implementing space agency, the ISA, should take the responsibility for managing the response. Carefully following the security criteria defined by the IIA, a fivefold increase in the number of people going to Mars as part of the Lowell Colony was announced in February 2242. Earth departure was scheduled for the late summer or early autumn of 2245.

The other four people in the room, all blonde and blue-eyed and members of the same family from Malmo, Sweden, filed out the door, leaving Kenji and Nai Watanabe alone. She continued to gaze down at the Earth thirty-five thousand kilometres below her. Kenji joined her in front of the huge observation window.

'I never fully realised,' Nai said to her husband, 'just what it meant to be in geosynchronous orbit. The Earth doesn't move from here. It looks suspended in space.'

Kenji laughed. 'Actually we're both moving – and very fast. But since our orbital period and the Earth's rotation period are the same, the Earth always presents us with the same picture.'

'It was different at that other space station,' Nai said, shuffling away from the window in her slippers. 'There the Earth was majestic, dynamic, much more impressive.'

'But we were only three hundred kilometres from the surface. Of course it was ...'

'*Shit*!' they heard a voice shout from the other side of the observation lounge. A husky young man in a plaid shirt and blue jeans was flailing in the air, slightly more than a metre off the floor, and his frantic motion was causing him to tumble sideways. Kenji crossed over and helped the newcomer to stand upright on his feet.

'Thanks,' the man said. 'I forgot to keep one foot on the floor at all times. This weightlessness is fucking weird for a farmer.'

He had a heavy southern accent. 'Oops, I'm sorry about the language, ma'am. I've lived among cows and pigs too long.' He extended his hand to Kenji. 'I'm Max Puckett from DeQueen, Arkansas.'

Kenji introduced himself and his wife. Max Puckett had an open face and a quick grin. 'You know,' Max said, 'when I signed up to go to Mars, I never realised we would be weightless for the whole goddamn trip ... What's going to happen to the poor hens? They'll probably never lay another egg.'

Max walked over to the window. 'It's almost noon at my home down there on that funny planet. My brother Clyde probably just opened a bottle of beer and his wife Winona is making him a sandwich.' He paused for several seconds and then turned to the Watanabes. 'What are you two going to do on Mars?'

'I'm the colony historian,' Kenji replied. 'Or at least one of them. My wife Nai is an English and French teacher.'

'Shit,' said Max Puckett. 'I was hoping you were one of the farming couples from Vietnam or Laos. I want to learn something about rice.'

'Did I hear you say something about hens?' Nai asked after a short silence. 'Are we going to have chickens on the Pinta?'

'Ma'am,' Max Puckett replied, 'there are fifteen thousand of Puckett's finest packed in cages in a cargo tug parked at the other end of this station. The ISA paid enough for those chickens that Clyde and Winona could rest for a whole damn year if they wanted ... If those hens are not going with us, I'd like to know what the hell they're going to do with them.'

'Passengers only occupy twenty percent of the space on the Pinta and the

Santa Maria,' Kenji reminded Nai. 'Supplies and other cargo elements take up the rest of the space. We will only have a total of three hundred passengers on the Pinta, most of them ISA officials and other key personnel necessary to initialise the colony ...'

'*E-nish-ul-eyes* the colony?' Max interrupted. 'Shit, man, you talk like one of them robots.' He grinned at Nai. 'After two years with one of those talking cultivators, I threw the son of a bitch away and replaced him with one of those earlier silent versions.'

Kenji laughed easily. 'I guess I do use a lot of ISA jargon. I was one of the first civilians selected for New Lowell, and I managed the recruiting in the Orient.'

Max had put a cigarette in his mouth. He glanced around in the observation lounge. 'I don't see a smoking sign anywhere,' he said. 'So I guess if I light up I'll set off all the alarms.' He put the cigarette behind his ear. 'Winona hates it when me and Clyde smoke. She says only farmers and whores smoke anymore.'

Max chuckled. Kenji and Nai laughed as well. He was a funny man. 'Speaking of whores,' Max said with a twinkle, 'where's all those convict women I saw on television? Whoo-eee, some of them were mighty fine. Damn sight better looking than my chickens and pigs.'

'All the colonists who had been held in detention on Earth are travelling on the Santa Maria,' Kenji said. 'We'll arrive about two months before them.'

'You know an awful lot about this mission,' Max said. 'And you don't speak garbled English like the Japs I've met in Little Rock and Texarkana. Are you somebody special?'

'No,' Kenji replied, unable to suppress another laugh. 'As I told you, I'm just the lead colony historian.'

Kenji was about to tell Max that he had lived in the United States for six years – which explained why his English was so good – when the door to the lounge opened and a dignified elderly gentleman in a grey suit and dark tie entered. 'Pardon me,' he said to Max, who had again placed the unlighted cigarette in his mouth, 'have I mistakenly ended up in the smoking room?'

'No, Pops,' Max answered. 'This room is the observation lounge. It's much too nice to be the smoking area. Smoking is probably confined to a small room, without windows, near the bathrooms. My ISA interviewer told me...'

The elderly gentleman was staring at Max as if the man were a biologist and Max was a rare but unpleasant species. 'My name, young man,' he interrupted, 'is not "Pop". It's Pyotr. Pyotr Mishkin, to be exact.'

'Glad to know you, Peter,' Max said, sticking out his hand. 'I'm Max. This couple here's the Wabanyabes. They're from Japan.'

'Kenji Watanabe,' Kenji said in correction. 'This is my wife Nai, who is a citizen of Thailand.'

'Mr Max,' Pyotr Mishkin said formally, 'my first name is Pyotr, not Peter. It is bad enough that I must speak English for five years. Surely I can ask that

702

my name at least retain its original Russian sound.'

'Okay, Pee-yot-ur,' Max said, again grinning. 'What do you do, anyway? No, let me guess ... you're the colony undertaker.'

For a fraction of a second Kenji was afraid that Mr Mishkin was going to explode in anger. Instead, however, the smallest of smiles began to form upon his face. 'It is apparent, Mr Max,' he said slowly, 'that you have a certain comic gift. I can see where that might be a virtue on a long and boring space trip.' He paused for a moment. 'For your information, I am not the undertaker. I was trained in the law. Until two years ago, when I retired of my own volition to seek a "new adventure", I was a member of the Soviet Supreme Court.'

'Holy shit,' Max Puckett exclaimed. 'Now I remember. I read about you in *Time* magazine ... Hey, Judge Mishkin, I'm sorry. I didn't recognise you ...'

'Not at all,' Judge Mishkin interrupted, an amused smile spreading across his face. 'It was fascinating to be unknown for a moment and to be taken for an undertaker. Probably the practised judge's mien is very close to the proper dour expression of the funeral attendant. By the way, Mr ...'

'Puckett, sir.'

'By the way, Mr Puckett,' Judge Mishkin continued, 'would you like to join me in the bar for a drink? A vodka would taste especially good right about now.'

'So would some tequila,' Max replied, walking toward the door with Judge Mishkin. 'Incidentally, I don't suppose you know what happens when you feed tequila to pigs, do you? ... I thought not ... Well, me and my brother Clyde ...'

They disappeared out the door, leaving Kenji and Nai Watanabe alone again. The couple glanced at each other and laughed. 'You don't think,' Kenji said, 'that those two are going to be friends, do you?'

'No chance,' Nai replied with a smile. 'What a pair of characters.'

'Mishkin is considered to be one of the finest jurists of our century. His opinions are required reading in all the Soviet law schools. Puckett was president of the Southwest Arkansas Farmers Cooperative. He has incredible knowledge of farming techniques, and farm animals as well.'

'Do you know the background of all the people in New Lowell?'

'No,' Kenji replied. 'But I have studied the files of everyone on the Pinta.'

Nai put her arms around her husband. 'Tell me about Nai Buatong Watanabe,' she said.

'Thai schoolteacher, fluent in English and French, IE equals 2.48, SC of 91...'

Nai interrupted Kenji with a kiss. 'You forgot the most important characteristic,' she said.

'What's that?'

She kissed him again. 'Adoring new bride of Kenji Watanabe, colony historian.'

6

Most of the world was watching on television when the Pinta was formally dedicated several hours before it was scheduled to depart for Mars with its passengers and cargo. The second vice president of the COG, a Swiss real estate executive named Heinrich Jenzer, was present at GEO-4 for the dedication ceremonies. He gave a short address to commemorate both the completion of the three large spacecraft and the opening of a 'new era of Martian colonization'. When he was finished, Mr Jenzer introduced Mr Ian Macmillan, the Scottish commander of the Pinta. Macmillan, a boring speaker who appeared to be the quintessential ISA bureaucrat, read a six-minute speech reminding the world of the fundamental objectives of the project.

'These three vehicles,' he said early in his speech, 'will carry almost two thousand people on a hundred-million-kilometre voyage to another planet, Mars, where this time a permanent human presence will be established. Most of our future Martian colonists will be transported in the second ship, the Nina, which will depart from here at GEO-4 three weeks from today. Our ship, the Pinta, and the final spacecraft, the Santa Maria, will each carry about three hundred passengers as well as the thousands of kilograms of supplies and equipment that will be necessary to sustain the colony.'

Carefully avoiding any mention of the demise of the first set of Martian outposts in the previous century, Commander Macmillan next tried to be poetic, comparing the forthcoming expedition to that of Christopher Columbus seven hundred and fifty years earlier. The language of the speech that had been written for him was excellent, but Macmillan's drab, monotonic delivery transformed words that would have been inspirational in the hands of an outstanding speaker into a dull and prosaic historical lecture.

He ended his speech by characterizing the colonists as a group, citing statistics about their ages, occupations, and countries of origin. 'These men and women, then,' Macmillan summarised, 'are a representative cross section of the human species in almost every way. I say *almost* because there are at least two attributes common to this group that would not be found in a random collection of human beings of this size. First, the future residents of Lowell Colony are extremely intelligent – their average IE is slightly above

1.86. Second, and this goes without saying, they must be courageous or they would not have applied for and then accepted a long and difficult assignment in a new and unknown environment.'

When he was finished, Commander Macmillan was handed a tiny bottle of champagne, which he broke across the 1/100 scale model of the Pinta that was displayed behind him and the other dignitaries on the dais. Moments later, as the colonists filed out of the auditorium and prepared to board the Pinta, Macmillan and Jenzer began the scheduled press conference.

'He's a jerk.'

'He's a marginally competent bureaucrat.'

'He's a fucking jerk.'

Max Puckett and Judge Mishkin were discussing Commander Macmillan in between bites of lunch. 'He has no goddamn sense of humour.'

'He is simply unable to appreciate things that are out of the ordinary.'

Max was chafing. He had been censured by the Pinta command staff during an informal hearing earlier that morning. His friend Judge Mishkin had represented Max in the hearing and had prevented the proceedings from getting out of control.

'Those assholes have no right to pass judgment on my behaviour.'

'You are most certainly correct, my friend,' Judge Mishkin replied, 'in the general sense. But we have a set of unique conditions on this spacecraft. *They* are the authority here, at least until we arrive at Lowell Colony and establish our own government ... At any rate, there's no real harm done. You are not inconvenienced in any way by their declaration that your actions were "untenable". It could have been much worse.'

Two nights earlier there had been a party celebrating the crossing of the halfway point in the Pinta's voyage from Earth to Mars. Max had flirted energetically for over an hour with lovely Angela Rendino, one of Macmillan's staff assistants. The bland Scotsman had then taken Max aside and strongly suggested that Max should leave Angela alone.

'Let her tell me that,' Max had said sensibly.

'She's an inexperienced young woman,' Macmillan had replied. 'And she's too gracious to tell you how repulsive your animal humour is.'

Max had been having a great time until then. 'What's your angle here, Commander?' he had asked, after first quaffing another margarita. 'Is she your private punch or something?'

Ian Macmillan had flushed crimson. 'Mr Puckett,' the spacecraft officer had replied a few seconds later, 'if your behaviour does not improve, I will be forced to confine you to your living quarters.'

The confrontation with Macmillan had ruined Max's evening. He had been incensed by the commander's use of his official authority in what was clearly a personal situation. Max had returned to his room, which he shared with another American, a pensive forester from the state of Oregon named Dave

Denison, and quickly finished an entire bottle of tequila. In his drunken state Max had been both homesick and depressed. He had then decided to go to the communications centre to phone his brother Clyde back in Arkansas.

By this time it was very late. To reach the communications complex, it was necessary for Max to cross the entire ship, passing first the common lounge where the party had just ended, and then the officers' quarters. In the central wing Max caught a fleeting glimpse of Ian Macmillan and Angela Rendino, arm in arm, going into the commander's private apartment.

'The son of a bitch,' Max said to himself.

The drunken Max paced outside Macmillan's door in the hall, growing angrier and angrier. After five minutes he finally had an idea that he liked. Remembering his award-winning pig call from his days at the University of Arkansas, Max split the evening quiet with a horrendous noise.

'Sooo-eee, *pig, pig,*' Max hollered.

He repeated the call another time and then disappeared in a flash, just before every door in the officers' wing (including Macmillan's) opened to see what the disturbance had been. Commander Macmillan was not at all happy that his entire crew saw him, along with Miss Rendino, in a state of undress.

The cruise to Mars was a second honeymoon for Kenji and Nai. Neither of them had much work to do. The journey was relatively uneventful, at least from the point of view of a historian, and Nai's duties were minimal since most of her high school students were on board the other two spaceships.

The Watanabes spent many evenings socializing with Judge Mishkin and Max Puckett. They played cards often (Max was as good at poker as he was terrible at bridge), talked about their hopes for Lowell Colony, and discussed the lives they had left behind on Earth.

When the Pinta was three weeks away from Mars, the staff announced a coming two-day communications outage and urged everyone to call home before the radio systems were temporarily out of commission. Since it was the year-end holiday period, it was the perfect time to phone.

Max hated the time delay and the long one-way conversations. After listening to a disjointed discussion of Christmas plans in Arkansas, Max informed Clyde and Winona that he wasn't going to call any more because he disliked 'waiting fifteen minutes to find out if anyone has laughed at my jokes.'

It had snowed early in Kyoto. Kenji's mother and father had prepared a video showing Ginkaku-ji and the Honen-In under a soft blanket of snow; if Nai had not been with him Kenji would have been unbearably homesick. In a brief call to Thailand, Nai congratulated one of her sisters on having won a scholarship to the university.

Pyotr Mishkin didn't telephone anyone. The old Russian's wife was dead and he had no children. 'I have wonderful memories,' he told Max, 'but there is nothing personal left for me on Earth.'

On the first day of the planned communications blackout, it was announced

706

that an important programme, required viewing for everybody, would be shown at two o'clock in the afternoon. Kenji and Nai invited Max and Judge Mishkin to their small apartment to watch.

'I wonder what stupid lecture this is going to be,' said Max, opposed, as always, to official pronouncements, which he considered a waste of his time.

When the video began, the president of the COG and the director of the ISA were shown sitting together at a large desk. The COG president underscored the importance of the message that they were about to receive from Werner Koch, the director of the ISA.

'Passengers on the Pinta,' Dr Koch began, 'four years ago our satellite tracking systems decoded a coherent signal that had apparently originated in deep space in the general direction of the star Epsilon Eridani. When properly processed, the signal contained an amazing video, one that you will see in its entirety in about five minutes.

'As you will hear, the video announces the return to our system of a Rama spacecraft. In 2130 and 2200, giant cylinders, fifty kilometres long and twenty kilometres wide, created by an unknown alien intelligence for a purpose we still have not fathomed, visited our family of planets in orbit around the Sun. The second intruder, usually referred to as Rama II, made a velocity correction while inside the orbit of Venus that put it on an impact course with the Earth. A fleet of nuclear missiles was dispatched to encounter the alien cylinder and destroy it before Rama came close enough to our planet to do any harm.

'The following video claims that another of these Rama spacecraft has now come to our neighbourhood with the sole purpose of "acquiring" a representative sample of two thousand human beings for "observation". As bizarre as this claim may be, it is important to note that our radar has indeed confirmed that a Rama class vehicle did enter orbit around Mars less than a month ago.

'Unfortunately, we must take this fantastic message from deep space seriously. Therefore, you colonists on the Pinta have been assigned to rendezvous with the new object in Mars orbit. We realise that this news will come as a severe shock to most of you, but we did not have many viable options. If, as we suspect, some misguided genius has planned and orchestrated an elaborate hoax, then, after the brief detour, you will continue on with your colonization of Mars as originally conceived. If, however, the video you are about to see is actually telling the truth, then you and your associates on board the Nina and the Santa Maria will become the contingent of human beings that the Raman intelligence will observe.

'You can well imagine that your mission now has uppermost priority among all COG activities. You can also understand the need for secrecy. From this moment forward, until this Rama issue is resolved one way or the other, all communication between your vehicle and the Earth will be strictly controlled. The IIA will monitor all the voice loops. Your friends and families will be told that you are safe, and eventually that you have landed on Mars, but that the Pinta communication systems have completely failed.

'You are being shown the following video now to give you three weeks to prepare for the encounter. A baseline plan and accompanying procedures for the rendezvous, worked out in great detail by the IIA in conjunction with ISA operations personnel, have already been transmitted to Commander Macmillan on the high-rate data stream. Each one of you will have a specific set of assignments. Each of you also has a personalised document packet that will provide you with the necessary background information for you to perform your duties.

'Of course we wish you well. Most likely this Rama affair will turn out to be nothing, in which case it will simply have delayed your initialization of Lowell Colony. If, however, this video is on the level, then you must move quickly to develop careful plans for accommodating the arrival of the Nina and the Santa Maria – none of the colonists on those other two spacecraft will have been told anything at all about Rama or the change in assignment.'

There was a momentary silence in the Watanabe apartment as the video abruptly concluded and was replaced on the screen by a text message, NEXT VIDEO IN TWO MINUTES. 'Well, I'll be goddamned,' was Max Puckett's only comment.

7

In the video Nicole was sitting on an ordinary brown chair with a featureless wall behind her. She was dressed in one of the ISA flight suits that
had been her regular apparel during the Newton mission. Nicole read the
message from an electronic notebook that she held in her hands.

'My fellow Earthlings,' she began, 'I am Newton cosmonaut Nicole des
Jardins, speaking to you from billions of kilometres away. I am on board a
Rama spacecraft similar to the two great cylindrical spaceships that visited
our solar system during the last two centuries. This third Rama vehicle is
also heading toward our tiny region of the Galaxy. Approximately four years
after your first receipt of this video, Rama Three will go into orbit around the
planet Mars.

'Since I left the Earth I have learned that the Rama class vehicles were
constructed by an advanced extraterrestrial intelligence as elements in a vast
information-gathering system whose ultimate objective is acquiring and cataloguing data about life in the universe. It is as part of this goal that this third
Rama craft is returning to the vicinity of our home planet.

'Inside Rama Three an Earthlike habitat has been designed to accommodate
two thousand human beings, plus significant numbers of other animals and
plants from our home planet. The exact biomass and other general specifications for these animals and plants are contained in the first appendix to this
video; however, it should be stressed that the plants, especially those that are
extremely efficient in the conversion of carbon dioxide to oxygen, are a key
feature in the basic design of the Earth habitat on board Rama. Without the
plants, life for the humans inside Rama will be seriously compromised.

'What is expected, as a result of this transmission, is that the Earth will
send a representative group of its inhabitants – together with the ancillary
supplies detailed in the second appendix – to make a rendezvous with Rama
Three in Mars orbit. The voyagers will be taken inside Rama and carefully
observed while they are living in a habitat that reproduces the environmental
conditions on the Earth.

'Because of the hostile response to Rama Two which, incidentally, resulted
in only minor damage to the alien spacecraft, the nominal mission plan for
this Rama vehicle involves no approach to Earth closer than Mars orbit. This

nominal plan *assumes*, of course, that the authorities on Earth will indeed comply with the requests contained in this transmission. If no human beings are sent to rendezvous with Rama Three in Mars orbit, I have no knowledge of how the spacecraft has been programmed to respond. I can say, however, based on my own observations, that it is easily within the capabilities of the extraterrestrial intelligence to acquire its desired observational data by other, less benign methods.

'With respect to the human beings to be transported to Mars, it goes without saying that the selected individuals should represent a broad cross section of humanity, including both sexes, all ages, and as many cultures as can be reasonably included. The large library of information about the Earth that is requested in the third video appendix will provide significant additional data that can be correlated with the observations taken inside Rama.

'I myself have no knowledge of how long the human beings will be inside Rama, or exactly where the spacecraft will take them, or even why the superior intelligence that created the Rama vehicles is gathering information about life in the universe. I can say, however, that the wonders I have witnessed since leaving our solar system have given me an entirely new sense of our place in the universe.'

The total time of the video, more than half of which was allocated to the detailed appendices, was just over ten minutes. Throughout the transmission the basic scene did not change. Nicole's delivery was measured and deliberate, punctuated by short pauses when her eyes moved from the camera to the notebook in her hands. Although there was some modulation in her tone, Nicole's earnest facial expression was virtually constant. Only when she implied that the Ramans might have 'other, less benign methods' of obtaining their data did any strong emotion flash in her dark eyes.

Kenji Watanabe watched the first half of the video with intense concentration. During the appendices, however, his mind began to stray and to start asking questions. *Who are these extraterrestrials?* he wondered. *Where did they come from? Why do they want to observe us? And why have they picked Nicole des Jardins as their spokesperson?*

Kenji laughed to himself, realizing that there was an endless stream of such infinite questions. He decided to focus on more tractable issues.

If Nicole were still alive today, Kenji thought next, *then she would be eighty-one years old.* The woman on the television screen had some grey hair, and many more wrinkles than cosmonaut des Jardins had had when the Newton was launched from the Earth, but her age in the video was certainly nowhere near eighty. *Maybe fifty-two or fifty-three at the very most,* Kenji said to himself.

So did she make this video thirty years ago? he wondered. *Or has her aging process been somehow retarded?* It did not occur to him to question whether or not the speaker was really Nicole. Kenji had spent enough time in the Newton archives to recognise immediately Nicole's facial expressions and mannerisms. *She should have made the video about four years ago*, Kenji was thinking, *but if so* ... He was still struggling with the entire situation when Nicole's transmission terminated and the director of the ISA appeared again on the monitor.

Dr Koch explained quickly that the video would be replayed twice in its entirety on all channels and then would be available to each of the passengers and crew at his leisure.

'What the hell is *really* going on here?' Max Puckett demanded to know as soon as Nicole's face appeared on the monitor again. He directed his question at Kenji.

'If I have understood correctly,' Kenji answered after watching for several seconds, 'we have been purposely misled by the ISA about one of the primary purposes of our endeavor. Apparently, this message was first received about four years ago, back when the funding for the Lowell Colony was still somewhat uncertain, and it was decided then – *after* all efforts to prove the video to be a hoax were unsuccessful – that the investigation of Rama III would be a secret objective of our project.'

'Shit,' said Max Puckett, shaking his head vigorously. 'Why the hell didn't they just tell us the truth?'

'My mind balks at the idea of supercreatures sending such awesome technology just to gather data about us,' Judge Mishkin commented after a short silence. 'On another level, however, at least now I understand some of the peculiarities in the personnel selection process. I was flabbergasted when that group of homeless American teenagers was added to the colony about eight months ago. Now I see that the selection criteria were based on satisfying the "broad cross section" requested by Madame des Jardins; whether or not our particular mix of individuals and skills would produce a sociologically viable colony on Mars must have always been a secondary consideration.'

'I *hate* lies and liars,' Max now said. He had stood up from his chair and was pacing around the room. 'All these politicians and government managers are the same – the bastards will lie without any conscience.'

'But what could they have done, Max?' Judge Mishkin replied. 'Almost certainly they didn't *really* take the video seriously. At least not until this new craft showed up in Mars orbit. And if they had told the truth from the beginning, there would have been worldwide panic.'

'Look, Judge,' Max said in a frustrated tone, 'I thought I was hired to be a fucking farmer on a colony on Mars. I don't know anything about ETs and, quite frankly, I don't want to know anything. It's hard enough for me to deal with chickens, pigs, and people.'

'Especially people,' Judge Mishkin said quickly, smiling at his friend. Despite himself, Max chuckled.

A few minutes later Judge Mishkin and Max said goodbye and left Kenji and Nai alone. Soon after their guests were gone, the videophone rang in Kenji and Nai's apartment. 'Watanabe?' they heard Ian Macmillan say.

'Yes, sir,' Kenji replied.

'Sorry to disturb you, Watanabe,' the commander said. 'But you have the first assignment given to anyone other than my immediate staff. Your orders are to brief the entire Pinta crew on the Newton expedition, the Ramas, and Cosmonaut des Jardins at 1900 tonight. I thought you might want to begin your preparations.'

'... All the media reported in 2200 that Rama Two was completely destroyed, vaporised by the multiple nuclear bombs that exploded in its vicinity. The missing cosmonauts des Jardins, O'Toole, Takagishi, and Wakefield were of course all considered to be dead. Actually, according to both the official documents of the Newton mission and the very successful books and television series distributed by Hagenest and Schmidt, Nicole des Jardins presumably died somewhere in New York, the island city in the middle of the Cylindrical Sea, weeks before the science ship of the Newton ever left Rama and returned to the Earth.'

Kenji paused to look at his audience. Even though Commander Macmillan had explained to the Pinta passengers and crew that a videotape of Kenji's presentation would be immediately available, many of the listeners were taking notes. Kenji was enjoying his moment in the limelight. He glanced at Nai and smiled before continuing.

'Cosmonaut Francesca Sabatini, the most famous survivor of the ill-fated Newton expedition, postulated in her memoirs that Dr des Jardins might have encountered a hostile biot, or had perhaps fallen, somewhere in one of the blackout regions of New York. Since the two women had been together for most of the day – they were searching for the Japanese scientist Shigeru Takagishi, who had mysteriously disappeared from the Beta campsite the night before – Signora Sabatini was well aware of the amount of food and water that Cosmonaut des Jardins was carrying. "Even with her consummate knowledge of the human body," Sabatini wrote, "Nicole could not possibly have survived more than a week. And if, in a delirious state, she had tried to obtain water from the ice of the poisonous Cylindrical Sea, she would have died even sooner."

'Of the half-dozen Newton cosmonauts who did not return from the encounter with Rama Two, it is Nicole des Jardins who has always attracted the most interest. Even before the brilliant statistician Roberto Lopez correctly conjectured seven years ago, on the basis of European genome information stored in The Hague, that the late King Henry XI of England was the father of Nicole's daughter Genevieve, Dr des Jardins's reputation had become legendary. Recently the attendance at her memorial near her family villa in Beauvois, France, has increased markedly, especially among young females. People flock there, not only to pay Cosmonaut des Jardins homage and to view the many photographs and videos commemorating her outstanding life, but also to see the two superb bronze statues created by the Greek sculptor Theo Pappas. In one the youthful Nicole is depicted in her track singlet and shorts with the Olympic gold medal around her neck; in the second she is shown as a mature woman, wearing an ISA flight suit similar to one you saw in the video.'

Kenji pointed to the back of the room in the small Pinta auditorium and the lights were extinguished. Moments later a slide show began on one of the two screens behind him. 'These are the few photographs of Nicole des Jardins that were stored in our Pinta files. The reference data base indicates that many more pictures, including historical film clips, are available in the reserve library stored out in the cargo bay, but those data are not accessible during cruise due to the limitations of the flight data network. The extra data are not needed, however, for it is clear from these photos that the individual who appeared in the transmission this afternoon is either Nicole des Jardins, *or an absolutely perfect copy of her.*'

A close-up still from the afternoon video was frozen on the left screen and juxtaposed to a head photo taken of Nicole the night of the New Year's Eve party at the Villa Adriani outside Rome. There was no question about it. The two pictures were definitely of the same woman. An appreciative murmur rose from the audience as Kenji paused in his presentation.

'Nicole des Jardins was born,' Kenji continued in a slightly subdued tone, 'on January 6, 2164. Therefore, if the video we watched this afternoon was actually filmed about four years ago, she should have been seventy-seven years old at the time. Now, we all know that Dr des Jardins was in superb physical condition, and that she exercised regularly, but if the woman we saw this afternoon was seventy-seven, then the ETs who built Rama must also have discovered the fountain of youth.'

Even though it was late at night and Kenji was very tired, he still could not sleep. The events of the day kept forcing themselves into his mind and exciting him again. Next to him in the small double bed Nai Buatong Watanabe was very much aware that her husband was awake.

'You're absolutely certain that we were seeing the real Nicole des Jardins, aren't you, dear?' Nai said softly after Kenji had turned over for the umpteenth time.

'Yes,' said Kenji. 'But Macmillan isn't. He demanded that I make that statement about the possibility of a perfect copy. He thinks everything in the video is a fake.'

'After our discussion this afternoon,' Nai said following a short pause, 'I was able to recall all the brouhaha about Nicole and King Henry from seven years ago. It was in most of the personality magazines. But I've forgotten something. How was it established for certain that Henry was Genevieve's father? Wasn't the king already dead? And doesn't the royal family in England keep its genome information private and secret?'

'Lopez used the genomes belonging to the parents and siblings of people who had married into the royal family. Then, employing a data correlation technique that he himself had invented, Dr Lopez showed that Henry, who was still the Prince of Wales during the 2184 Olympics, was more than three times as likely as any other person present in Los Angeles at the time to have been the father of Nicole's baby. After Darren Higgins admitted on his deathbed that Henry and Nicole had spent one night together during the Olympics, the royal family allowed a genetic specialist access to their genome data base. The expert concluded, beyond any reasonable doubt, that Henry was Genevieve's father.'

'What an amazing woman,' Nai said.

'She was indeed,' Kenji replied. 'But what prompted you to make that comment right now?'

'As a woman,' Nai said, 'I admire her protecting her secret and raising her princess herself as much or more than any of her other accomplishments.'

E ponine located Kimberly in the corner of the smoky room and sat down beside her. She accepted the cigarette her friend offered, lit it, and inhaled deeply.

'Ah, what pleasure,' Eponine said softly as she expelled the smoke in small circles and watched it rise slowly toward the ventilators.

'As much as you love tobacco and nicotine,' Kimberly said in a whisper from beside her, 'I know that you would absolutely adore kokomo.' The American girl took a drag from her cigarette. 'I know that you don't believe me, Eponine, but it's actually better than sex.'

'Not for me, mon amie,' Eponine replied in a warm, friendly tone. 'I have enough vices. And I could never, never control something that was truly better than sex.'

Kimberly Henderson laughed heartily, her long blonde locks bouncing on her shoulders. She was twenty-four, a year younger than her French colleague. The two of them were sitting in the smoking lounge attached to the women's shower. It was a tiny square room, no more than four metres on a side, in which a dozen women were currently standing or sitting, all smoking cigarettes.

'This room reminds me of the back room at Willie's in Evergreen, just outside Denver,' Kimberly said. 'While a hundred or more cowboys and rednecks would be dancing and drinking in the main bar, eight or ten of us would retreat into Willie's sacred "office", as he called it, and fuck ourselves completely up with kokomo.'

Eponine stared through the haze at Kimberly. 'At least in this lounge we aren't harassed by the men. They are absolutely impossible, even worse than the guys in the detention village at Bourges. These characters must think about nothing but sex all day long.'

'That's understandable,' Kimberly replied with another laugh. 'They're not being closely watched for the first time in years. When Toshio's men sabotaged all the hidden monitors, everybody was suddenly free.' She glanced over at Eponine. 'But there's a grim side as well. There were two more rapes today, one right in the co-ed recreation area.'

Kimberly finished one cigarette and immediately lit another. 'You need someone to protect you,' she continued, 'and I know Walter would love the job. Because of Toshio, the cons have mostly stopped trying to hit on me. My main concern now is the ISA guards – they think they're hot shit. Only that gorgeous Italian hunk, Marcello something or other, interests me at all. He told me yesterday that he would make me "moan with pleasure" if I would just join him in his room. I was sorely tempted until I saw one of Toshio's thugs watching the conversation.'

Eponine also lit another cigarette. She knew it was ridiculous to smoke them one after another, but the passengers on the Santa Maria were only allowed three half-hour 'breaks' each day and smoking was not permitted in the cramped living quarters. While Kimberly was momentarily sidetracked by a question from a burly woman in her early forties, Eponine thought about the first few days after they had left the Earth. *Our third day out*, she recalled, *Nakamura sent his go-between to see me. I must have been his first choice.*

The huge Japanese man, a sumo wrestler before he became a bill collector for a notorious gambling ring, had bowed formally when he had approached her in the co-ed lounge. 'Miss Eponine,' he had said in heavily accented English, 'my friend Nakamura-san has asked me to tell you that he finds you very beautiful. He offers you complete protection in exchange for your companionship and an occasional favour of pleasure.'

The offer was attractive in some ways, Eponine remembered, *and not unlike what most of the decent-looking women on the Santa Maria have eventually accepted. I knew at the time that Nakamura would be very powerful. But I didn't like his coldness. And I mistakenly thought that I could remain free.*

'Ready?' Kimberly repeated. Eponine snapped out of her reverie. She stubbed out her cigarette and walked with her friend into the dressing room. While they were taking off their clothes and preparing to shower, at least a dozen eyes feasted on their magnificent bodies.

'Doesn't it bother you,' Eponine asked when they were standing side by side in the shower, 'to have these dykes devouring you with their eyes?'

'Nope,' Kimberly replied. 'In a way I enjoy it. It's certainly flattering. There are not many women here who look like we do. It arouses me to have them stare so hungrily at me.'

Eponine rinsed the soapy lather off her full, firm breasts and leaned over to Kimberly. 'Then you have had sex with another woman?' she asked.

'Of course,' Kimberly replied with another deep laugh. 'Haven't you?'

Without waiting for a response, the American woman launched into one of her stories. 'My first dealer in Denver was a dyke. I was only eighteen and absolutely perfect from head to toe. When Loretta first saw me naked, she thought she'd died and gone to heaven. I had just entered nursing school and couldn't afford much dope. So I made a deal with Loretta. She could fuck me, but only if she kept me supplied with cocaine. Our affair lasted almost six months. By then I was dealing on my own and, besides, I had fallen in love with the Magician.

'Poor Loretta,' Kimberly continued as she and Eponine dried each other's backs in the lavatory that adjoined the shower. 'She was broken hearted. She offered me everything, including her client list. Eventually she became a nuisance, so I undercut her and had the Magician force her out of Denver.'

Kimberly saw a fleeting look of disapproval on Eponine's face. 'Jesus,' she said, 'there you go again, turning moral on me. You're the softest goddamn murderer I have ever met. Sometimes you remind me of all the goody two-shoes in my high school graduating class.'

As they were about to leave the shower area, a tiny black girl with her hair in braids came up behind them. 'You Kimberly Henderson?' she said.

'Yes.' Kimberly nodded, turning around. 'But why ...'

'Is your man the king Jap Nakamura?' the girl interrupted.

Kimberly did not reply. 'If so, I need your help,' the black girl continued.

'What do you want?' Kimberly asked in a noncommittal tone.

The girl suddenly broke into tears. 'My man Reuben didn't mean nothing. He was drunk on that shit the guards sell. He didn't know he was talking to the king Jap.'

Kimberly waited for the girl to dry her tears. 'What have you got?' she whispered.

'Three knives and two joints of dynamite kokomo,' the black girl replied in the same soft whisper.

'Bring them to me,' Kimberly said with a smile. 'And I'll arrange a time for your Reuben to apologise to Mr Nakamura.'

'You don't like Kimberly, do you?' Eponine said to Walter Brackeen. He was a huge American Negro with soft eyes and absolutely magical fingers on a keyboard. He was playing a light jazz medley and staring at his beautiful lady while his three roommates were out, by agreement, in the common areas.

'No, I don't,' Walter replied slowly. 'She's not like us. She can be very funny, but underneath I think she's truly bad.'

'What do you mean?'

Walter changed to a soft ballad, with an easier melody, and played for almost a full minute before speaking. 'I guess in the eyes of the law we're all equal, all murderers. But not in my eyes. I squashed the life out of a man who sodomised my baby brother. You killed a crazy bastard who was ruining your life.' Walter paused for a moment and rolled his eyes. 'But that friend of yours Kimberly, she and her boyfriend offed three people they didn't even know just for drugs and money.'

'She was stoned at the time.'

'No matter,' Walter said. 'Each of us is always responsible for his behaviour. If I put shit in me that makes me awful, that's my mistake. But I can't cop out of the responsibility for my actions.'

'She had a perfect record in the detention centre. Every one of the doctors who worked with her said she was an excellent nurse.'

Walter stopped playing his keyboard and stared at Eponine for several seconds. 'Let's not talk about Kimberly anymore,' he said. 'We have little enough time together ... Have you thought about my proposition?'

Eponine sighed. 'Yes, I have, Walter. And although I like you, and enjoy making love with you, the arrangement you suggested sounds too much like a commitment ... Besides, I think this is mostly for your ego. Unless I miss my guess, you prefer Malcolm ...'

'Malcolm has nothing to do with us,' Walter interrupted. 'He's been my close friend for years, since the very first days I entered the Georgia detention compound. We play music together. We share sex when we're both lonely. We're soul mates ...'

'I know, I know ... Malcolm's not really the central issue. It's more the principle of the thing that bothers me. I do like you, Walter, you know that. But ...' Her voice trailed off as Eponine struggled with her mixed feelings.

'We're three weeks away from Earth,' Walter said, 'and we have six more weeks before we reach Mars. I am the largest man on the Santa Maria. If I say that you're my girl, nobody will bother you for those six weeks.'

Eponine recalled an unpleasant scene just that morning where two German inmates had discussed how easy it would be to commit rape in the convict quarters. They had known that she was within earshot but had made no effort to lower their voices.

At length she put herself in Walter's huge arms. 'All right,' she said softly. 'But don't expect too much ... I'm sort of a difficult woman.'

'I think Walter may have a heart problem,' Eponine said in a whisper. It was the middle of the night and their other two roommates were asleep. Kimberly, in the bunk below Eponine, was still stoned on the kokomo she had smoked two hours earlier. Sleep would be impossible for her for several more hours.

'The rules on this ship are fucking stupid,' Kimberly said. 'Christ, even in the Pueblo Detention Complex there were fewer regulations. Why the hell can't we stay in the common areas after midnight? What harm are we doing?'

'He has occasional chest pains and, if we have vigorous sex, he often complains afterward of shortness of breath ... Do you think you could take a look at him?'

'And how about that Marcello? Huh! What a stupid ass! He tells me I can stay up all night if I want to come to his room. While I'm sitting there with Toshio. What does he think he's doing? I mean, not even the guards can mess with the king Jap ... What did you say, Eponine?'

Eponine raised herself on an elbow and leaned over the side of the bed. 'Walter Brackeen, Kim,' she said. 'I'm talking about Walter Brackeen. Can you slow yourself down enough to pay attention to what I'm saying?'

'All right. All right. What about your Walter? What does he want?

Everybody wants something from the king Jap. I guess that makes me the queen, at least in a way ...'

'I think Walter has a bad heart,' the exasperated Eponine repeated in a loud voice. 'I would like for you to look at him.'

'Shh,' Kimberly replied. 'They'll come bust us, like they did that crazy Swedish girl ... Shit, Ep, I'm no doctor. I can tell when a heartbeat is irregular, but that's all. You ought to take Walter to that con doctor who's really a cardiologist, what's his name, the super quiet one who stays to himself when he's not examining somebody ...'

'Dr Robert Turner,' Eponine interrupted.

'That's the one ... very professional, aloof, distant, never speaks except in doctorese, hard to believe he blew the heads off two men in a courtroom with a shotgun, it just doesn't figure ...'

'How do you know *that*?' Eponine said.

'Marcello told me. I was curious, we were laughing, he was teasing me, saying things like "Does that Jap make you moan?" and "How about that quiet heart doctor, can he make you moan?"'

'Christ, Kim,' Eponine said, now alarmed, 'have you been going to bed with Marcello too?'

Her roommate laughed. 'Only twice. He talks better than he fucks. And what an ego. At least the king Jap is appreciative.'

'Does Nakamura know?'

'Do you think I'm crazy?' Kimberly replied. 'I don't want to die. But he may be suspicious ... I won't do it again, but if that Dr Turner were to so much as whisper in my ear I would cream all over myself ...'

Kimberly continued her rambling chatter. Eponine thought briefly about Dr Robert Turner. He had examined Eponine soon after launch when she had been having some peculiar spotting. *He never even noticed my body*, she remembered. *It was a thoroughly professional examination.*

Eponine tuned Kimberly out of her mind and focused on an image of the handsome doctor. She was surprised to discover that she was feeling a spark of romantic interest. There was something definitely mysterious about the doctor, for there was nothing in his manner or personality that was the least bit consistent with a double murder. *There must be an interesting story*, she thought.

Eponine was dreaming. It was the same nightmare that she had had a hundred times since the murder. Professor Moreau was lying with his eyes closed on the floor of his studio, blood streaming out of his chest. Eponine walked over to the basin, cleaned the large carving knife, and placed it back on the counter. As she stepped over the body those hated eyes opened. She saw the wild insanity in his eyes. He reached out for her with his arms ...

'Nurse Henderson. Nurse Henderson.' The knocking on the door was louder. Eponine awakened from her dream and rubbed her eyes. Kimberly and another of their roommates reached the door almost simultaneously.

Walter's friend Malcolm Peabody, a diminutive, effete white man in his early forties, was standing at the door. He was frantic. 'Dr Turner sent me for a nurse. Come quickly. Walter's had a heart attack.'

As Kimberly began to dress, Eponine glided down from her bunk. 'How is he, Malcolm?' she asked, pulling on her robe. 'Is he dead?'

Malcolm was momentarily confused. 'Oh, hi, Eponine,' he said meekly. 'I had forgotten that you and Nurse Henderson ... When I left he was still breathing, but ...'

Being careful to keep one foot on the floor at all times, Eponine hurried out the door, down the corridor, into the central common area, and then into the men's living quarters. Alarms sounded as the main monitors followed her progress. When she reached the entrance to Walter's wing, Eponine paused for a moment to catch her breath.

A crowd of people was standing in the corridor outside of Walter's room. His door was open wide and the bottom third of his body was lying outside, in the hallway. Eponine pushed her way through the crowd and into the room.

Dr Robert Turner was kneeling beside his patient, holding electronic prods against Walter's naked chest. The big man's body recoiled with each jolt, and then rose slightly off the floor before the doctor pushed it down again against the surface.

Dr Turner glanced up when Eponine arrived. 'Are you the nurse?' he asked brusquely.

For a fleeting moment Eponine was speechless. And embarrassed. Here her friend was dying or dead and all she could think about was Dr Turner's practically perfect blue eyes. 'No,' she said at length, definitely flustered. 'I'm the girlfriend ... Nurse Henderson is my roommate ... She should be here any minute.'

Kimberly and two ISA guard escorts arrived at that moment. 'His heart stopped completely forty-five seconds ago,' Dr Turner said to Kimberly. 'It's too late to move him to the infirmary. I'm going to open him up and try to use the Komori stimulator. Did you bring your gloves?'

While Kimberly pulled on her gloves, Dr Turner ordered the crowd away from his patient. Eponine didn't move. When the guards grabbed her by the arms, the doctor mumbled something and the guards released her.

Dr Turner handed Kimberly his set of surgical tools and then, working with both incredible speed and skill, cut a deep incision into Walter's chest. He laid back the folds of the skin, exposing the heart and rib cage. 'Have you been through this procedure before, Nurse Henderson?' he asked.

'No,' Kimberly replied.

'The Komori stimulator is an electrochemical device that attaches to the heart, forcing it to beat and continue to pump blood. If the pathology is temporary, like a blood clot or a spastic valve, then sometimes the problem can be fixed and the patient's heart will start functioning again.'

Dr Turner inserted the stamp-sized Komori stimulator behind the left ventricle of the heart and applied the power from the portable control system on the floor beside him. Walter's heart began to beat slowly three or four seconds later. 'We have about eight minutes now to find the problem,' the doctor said to himself.

He finished his analysis of the organ's primary subsystems in less than a minute. 'No clots,' he mumbled, 'and no bad vessels or valves ... So why did it stop beating?'

Dr Turner gingerly lifted up the throbbing heart and inspected the muscles underneath. The muscular tissue around the right auricle was discoloured and soft. He touched it very lightly with the end of one of his pointed instruments and portions of the tissue flaked off.

'My God,' the doctor said, 'what in the world is this?' While Dr Turner was holding the heart up, Walter Brackeen's heart contracted again and one of the long fibre structures in the middle of the discoloured muscular tissue started to unravel. 'What the ...' Turner blinked twice and put his right hand on his cheek.

'Look at this, Nurse Henderson,' he said quietly. 'It's absolutely amazing. The muscles here have atrophied completely. I've never seen anything like it. We cannot help this man.'

Eponine's eyes filled with tears as Dr Turner withdrew the Komori stimulator and Walter's heart stopped beating again. Kimberly started to remove the clamps holding back the skin and tissue around the heart, but the doctor stopped her. 'Not yet,' he said. 'Let's take him over to the infirmary so I can perform a full autopsy. I want to learn whatever I can.'

The guards and two of Walter's roommates eased the large man onto a gurney and the body was removed from the living quarters. Malcolm Peabody sobbed quietly on Walter's bunk. Eponine walked over to him. They shared a silent hug and then sat together, holding hands, for most of the rest of the night.

9

'Y ou'll be in charge here while I'm inside,' Commander Macmillan said to his deputy, a handsome young Russian engineer named Dmitri Ulanov. 'Under all circumstances, your primary responsibility is the safety of the passengers and crew. If you hear or see anything threatening or even suspicious, blow the pyros and move the Pinta away from Rama.'

It was the morning of the first reconnaissance mission from the Pinta into the interior of Rama. The spacecraft from Earth had docked the previous day on one of the circular ends of the huge cylindrical spacecraft. The Pinta had been parked right beside the external seal, in the same general location as the earlier Raman expeditions in 2130 and 2200.

As part of the preparations for the initial sortie, Kenji Watanabe had briefed the scouting party the night before on the geography of the first two Ramas. When he had finished with his comments, he had been approached by his friend Max Puckett.

'Do you think our Rama will look like all those pictures you showed us?' Max had asked.

'Not exactly,' Kenji had replied. 'I expect some changes. Remember that the video said that an Earth habitat had been constructed somewhere inside Rama. Nevertheless, since the exterior of this spacecraft is identical to the other two, I don't think everything inside will be changed.'

Max had looked perplexed. 'This is all *way* beyond me,' he had said, shaking his head. 'By the way,' he had added a few seconds later, 'you're *sure* you're not responsible for me being in the scouting party?'

'As I told you this afternoon,' Kenji replied, 'none of us on board the Pinta had anything to do with the scouting selections. All sixteen members were chosen by the ISA and IIA back on Earth.'

'But why have I been equipped with this goddamn arsenal? I have a state-of-the-art laser machine gun, self-guiding grenades, even a set of mass-sensitive mines. I have more firepower now than I had during the peacekeeping invasion of Belize.'

Kenji had smiled. 'Commander Macmillan, as well as many members of the military staff at COG Headquarters, still believes this whole affair is a trap of some kind. Your designator in this scouting operation is "soldier". My personal belief is that none of your weapons will be necessary.'

Max was still grumbling the next morning when Macmillan left Dmitri Ulanov in charge of the Pinta and personally led the scouting party into Rama. Although he was weightless, the military equipment that Max was carrying on the outside of his space suit was unwieldy and severely restricted his freedom of movement. 'This is ridiculous,' he mumbled to himself. 'I'm a farmer, not a goddamn commando.'

The initial surprise came only minutes after the scouts from the Pinta had moved inside the external seal. Following a short walk down a broad corridor, the group came to a circular room from which three tunnels led deeper into the interior of the alien spaceship, Two of the tunnels were blocked with multiple metal gates. Commander Macmillan called Kenji in for consultation.

'This is a completely different design,' Kenji said in response to the commander's questions. 'We may as well throw out our maps.'

'Then I presume we should proceed down the unblocked tunnel?' Macmillan asked.

'That's your call,' Kenji replied, 'but I don't see any other option, except to return to the Pinta.'

The sixteen men trudged slowly down the open tunnel in their space suits. Every few minutes they would launch flares into the darkness ahead of them so that they could see where they were going. When they were about five hundred metres into Rama, two small figures suddenly appeared at the other end of the tunnel. Each of the four soldiers plus Commander Macmillan quickly pulled out his binoculars.

'They're coming toward us,' said one of the soldier scouts excitedly.

'Well, I'll be damned,' said Max Puckett, a shiver going down his spine, 'it's Abraham Lincoln!'

'And a woman,' said another, 'in some kind of uniform.'

'Prepare to fire,' ordered Ian Macmillan.

The four soldier scouts scurried to the head of the party and knelt down, their guns pointed down the tunnel. 'Halt,' shouted Macmillan as the two strange figures drew within two hundred metres of the scouting party.

Abraham Lincoln and Benita Garcia stopped. 'State your purpose,' they heard the commander shout.

'We are here to welcome you,' Abraham Lincoln said in a loud, deep voice.

'And to take you to New Eden,' Benita Garcia added.

Commander Macmillan was thoroughly confused. He did not know what to do next. While he hesitated, the others in the scouting party talked among themselves.

'It's Abraham Lincoln, come back as a ghost,' the American Terry Snyder said.

'The other one is Benita Garcia – I saw her statue in Mexico City once.'

'Let's get the hell out of here. This place gives me the creeps,' another scout said.

'What would ghosts be doing in orbit around Mars?'

'Excuse me, Commander,' Kenji said at length to the befuddled Macmillan. 'What do you intend to do now?'

The Scotsman turned to face his Japanese Rama expert. 'It's difficult to decide on exactly the proper action pattern, of course,' he said. 'I mean, those two certainly look harmless enough, but remember the Trojan horse. Hah! Well, Watanabe, what do you suggest?'

'Why don't I go forward, perhaps alone, or maybe even with one of the soldiers, to talk to them? Then we'll know ...'

'That's certainly brave of you, Watanabe, but unnecessary. No, I think we'll all go forward. Cautiously, of course. Leaving a couple of men at the rear to report in case we're zapped by a ray gun or something.'

The commander turned on his radio. 'Deputy Ulanov, Macmillan here. We've encountered two beings of some kind. They're either human or in human disguise. One looks like Abraham Lincoln and the other like that famous Mexican cosmonaut ... What's that, Dmitri? ... Yes, you copy correctly. Lincoln and Garcia. We've encountered Lincoln and Garcia in a tunnel inside Rama. You may report that to the others ... Now, I'm leaving Snyder and Finzi here while the rest of us advance toward the strangers.'

The two figures did not move as the fourteen explorers from the Pinta approached. The soldiers were spread out in front of the group, ready to fire at the first sign of trouble.

'Welcome to Rama,' Abraham Lincoln said when the first scout was only twenty metres away. 'We are here to escort you to your new homes.'

Commander Macmillan did not respond immediately. It was the irrepressible Max Puckett who broke the silence. 'Are you a ghost?' he shouted. 'I mean, are you *really* Abraham Lincoln?'

'Of course not,' the Lincoln replied matter-of-factly. 'Both Benita Garcia and I are human biots. You will find five categories of human biots in New Eden, each designed with specific capabilities to free humans from tedious, repetitive tasks. My areas of specialty arc clerical and legal work, accounting, bookkeeping and housekeeping, home and office management, and other organizational tasks.'

Max was dumbfounded. Ignoring his commander's order to 'stand back,' Max walked up to within several centimetres of the Lincoln. 'This is some fucking robot,' he muttered to himself. Oblivious to any possible danger, Max next reached out and put his fingers on the Lincoln's face, first touching the skin around the nose and then feeling the whiskers in the long black beard. 'Incredible,' he said out loud. 'Absolutely incredible.'

'We have been manufactured with very careful attention to detail,' the Lincoln now said. 'Our skin is chemically similar to yours and our eyes operate on the same basic optical principles as yours, but we are not dynamic, constantly renewing creatures like you. Our subsystems must be maintained and sometimes even replaced by technicians.'

Max's bold move had defused all the tension. By this time the entire scouting party, including Commander Macmillan, were poking and probing the two biots. Throughout the examination both the Lincoln and the Garcia answered questions about their design and implementation. At one point Kenji realised that Max Puckett had withdrawn from the rest of the scouting party and was sitting by himself against one of the walls of the tunnel.

Kenji walked over to his friend. 'What's the matter, Max?' he asked.

Max shook his head. 'What kind of genius could produce something like these two? It's positively scary.' He was silent for several seconds. 'Maybe I'm strange, but those two biots frighten me much more than this huge cylinder.'

The Lincoln and the Garcia walked with the scouting party to what appeared to be the end of the tunnel. Within seconds a door opened in the wall and the biots motioned for the humans to go inside. Under questioning from Macmillan, the biots explained that the humans were about to enter a 'transportation device' that would carry them to the outskirts of the Earth habitat.

Macmillan communicated what the biots had said to Dmitri Ulanov on the Pinta and told his Russian deputy to 'blast off' if he didn't hear anything from them within forty-eight hours.

The tube ride was astonishing. It reminded Max Puckett of the giant roller coaster at the state fair in Dallas, Texas. The bullet-shaped vehicle sped along an enclosed, helical track that dropped all the way from the bowl-shaped northern end of Rama to the Central Plain below. Outside the tube, which was encased in a heavy transparent plastic of some kind, Kenji and the others glimpsed the vast network of ladders and stairways that traversed the same territory as their ride. But they did not see the incomparable vistas reported by the previous Rama explorers – their view to the south was blocked by an extremely tall wall of metallic grey.

The ride took less than five minutes. It deposited them in an enclosed annulus that completely circumscribed the Earth habitat. When the Pinta scouts exited from the tube, the weightlessness in which they had been living since they had departed from Earth had vanished. The gravity was close to normal.

'The atmosphere in this corridor, like the atmosphere in New Eden, is just like your home planet,' the Lincoln biot said. 'But that is not the case in the region on our right, outside the walls protecting your habitat.'

The annulus surrounding New Eden was dimly lit, so the colonists were not prepared for the bright sunlight that greeted them when the huge door opened and they entered their new world. On the short walk to the nearby train station they carried their space helmets in their hands. The men passed empty buildings on both sides of the path – small structures that could be houses or shops, as well as a larger one ('That will be an elementary school,' the Benita Garcia informed them) right opposite the station itself.

A train was waiting for them when they arrived. The sleek subway car with soft, comfortable seats, and a constantly updating electronic status board, raced quickly toward the centre of New Eden, where they were to have a 'comprehensive briefing,' according to the Lincoln biot. The train ran first along the side of a beautiful, crystalline lake ('Lake Shakespeare,' the Benita Garcia said), and men turned to the left, heading away from the light grey walls that enclosed the colony. During the last part of the ride a large, barren mountain dominated the landscape on the right-hand side of the train.

Throughout the ride the entire contingent from the Pinta was very quiet. In truth they were all completely overwhelmed. Not even in the creative imagination of Kenji Watanabe had anything like what they were seeing ever been envisioned. It was all much too large, much more magnificent than they had pictured.

The central city, where all the major buildings had been located by the designers of New Eden, was the final stunner. The members of the party stood silently and gawked at the array of large and impressive structures that formed the heart of the colony. That the buildings were still empty only added to the mystical quality of the entire experience. Kenji Watanabe and Max Puckett were the last two men to enter the edifice where the briefing was to occur.

'What do you think?' Kenji asked Max as the two of them stood on the top of the stairs of the administration building and surveyed the astonishing complex around them.

'I cannot think,' answered Max, the awe in his tone quite obvious. 'This whole place defies thought. It is heaven, Alice's wonderland, and all the fairy tales of my boyhood wrapped up in one package. I keep pinching myself to make sure that I'm not dreaming.'

'On the screen in front of you,' the Lincoln biot said, 'is an overview map of New Eden. Each of you will be given a full packet of maps, including all the roads and structures in the colony. We are *here*, in Central City, which was designed to be the administrative centre of New Eden. Residences have been built, along with shops, small offices, and schools, in the four corners of the rectangle that is enclosed by the outside wall. Because the naming of these four towns will be left to the inhabitants, we will refer to them today as the northeast, northwest, southeast, and southwest villages. In doing this we are following the convention, adopted by earlier Raman explorers from the Earth, of referring to the end of Rama where your spacecraft docked as the north end.

'Each of the four sides of New Eden has an allocated geographic function. The freshwater lake along the south edge of the colony, as you have already been informed, is called Lake Shakespeare. Most of the fish and water life that you have brought with you will live there, although some of the specimens may be perfect for emplacement in the two rivers that empty into Lake Shakespeare from Mount Olympus, here on the east side of the colony, and Sherwood Forest on the west side.

'At present both the slopes of Mount Olympus and all the regions of Sherwood Forest, as well as the village parks and green belts throughout the colony, are covered with a fine lattice of gas exchange devices, or GEDs, as we call them. These tiny mechanisms serve but one function – they convert carbon dioxide into oxygen. In a very true sense they are mechanical plants. They are to be replaced by all the *real* plants that you have brought from the Earth,

'The north side of the colony, between the villages, is reserved for farming. Farm buildings have been constructed *here*, along the road that connects the two northern towns. You will grow most of your food in this area. Between the food supplies that you have brought with you and the synthetic food stored in the tall silos three hundred metres north of this building, you should be able to feed two thousand humans for at least a year, maybe eighteen months if waste is kept at a minimum. After that you are on your own. It goes without saying that farming, including the aquaculture that has been allocated to the eastern shores of Lake Shakespeare, will be an important component in your life in New Eden ...'

To Kenji, the briefing experience was like drinking out of a fire hose. The Lincoln biot kept the information rate exceedingly high for ninety minutes, dismissing all questions either by saying 'That's outside my knowledge base' or by referring to the page and paragraph numbers in the Basic Guidebook to New Eden that he had handed out. Finally there was a break in the briefing and everyone moved to an adjacent room, where a drink that tasted like Coca-Cola was served.

'Whew,' said Terry Snyder as he wiped his brow, 'am I the only one who is saturated?'

'Shit, Snyder,' replied Max Puckett with an impish grin. 'Are you saying you're inferior to that goddamn robot? He sure as hell ain't tired. I bet he could lecture all day.'

'Maybe even all week,' mused Kenji Watanabe. 'I wonder how often these biots need to be serviced. My father's company makes robots, some of them exceedingly complex, but nothing like this. The information content in that Lincoln must be astronomical.'

'The briefing will recommence in five minutes,' the Lincoln announced. 'Please be prompt.'

In the second half of the briefing the various kinds of biots in New Eden were introduced and explained. Based on their recent studies of the previous Raman expeditions, the colonists were prepared for the bulldozer and other construction biots. The five categories of human biots, however, elicited a more emotional response.

'Our designers decided,' the Lincoln told them, 'to limit the physical appearances of the human biots so that there could be no question of someone mistaking one of us for one of you. I have already listed my basic functions – all the other Lincolns, three of whom are now joining us, have been identically programmed. At least originally. We are, however, capable of some low level of learning that will allow our data bases to be different as our specific uses evolve.'

'How can we tell one Lincoln from another?' asked one bewildered member of the scouting party as the three new Lincolns circulated around the room.

'We each have an identification number, engraved both here, on the shoulder, and again here, on the left buttock. This same system is employed for the other categories of human biots. I, for example, am Lincoln 004. The three that just entered are 009, 024, and 071.'

When the Lincoln biots left the briefing room, they were replaced by five Benita Garcias. One of the Garcias outlined the specialties of her category – police and fire protection, farming, sanitation, transportation, mail handling – and then answered a few questions before they all departed.

The Einstein biots were next. The scouts erupted with laughter when four of the Einsteins, each a wild, unkempt, white-haired replica of the twentieth-century scientific genius, walked into the room together. The Einsteins explained that they were the engineers and scientists of the colony. Their primary function, a vital one encompassing many duties, was to 'ensure the satisfactory working of the colony infrastructure,' including of course the army of biots.

A group of tall, jet-black female biots introduced themselves as the Tiassos, specializing in health care. They would be the doctors, the nurses, the health officials, the ones who would provide child care when the parents were not available. Just as the Tiasso portion of the briefing was ending, a slight Oriental biot with intense eyes walked into the room. He was carrying a lyre and an electronic easel. He introduced himself as a Yasunari Kawabata before playing a beautiful, short piece on the lyre.

'We Kawabatas are creative artists,' he said simply. 'We are musicians, actors, painters, sculptors, writers, and sometimes photographers and cinematographers. We are few in number, but very important for the quality of life in New Eden.'

When the official briefing was finally over, the scouting party was served an excellent dinner in the large hall. About twenty of the biots joined the humans at the gathering, although of course they did not eat anything. The simulated roast duck was staggeringly authentic, and even the wines could have passed the inspection of all but the most learned oenologists on Earth.

Later in the evening, when the humans had grown more comfortable with their biot companions and were peppering them with questions, a solitary

female figure appeared in the open doorway. At first she was unnoticed But
the room quieted quickly after Kenji Watanabe jumped up from his seat and
approached the newcomer with an outstretched hand.

'Dr des Jardins, I presume,' he said with a smile.

10

Despite Nicole's assurances that everything in New Eden was completely consistent with her earlier remarks on the video, Commander Macmillan refused to allow the Pinta passengers and crew to enter Rama and occupy their new homes until he was certain there was no danger. After returning to the Pinta, he conferred at length with ISA personnel on Earth and then sent a small contingent headed by Dmitri Ulanov into Rama to obtain additional information. The chief medical officer of the Pinta, a dour Dutchman named Darl van Roos, was the most important member of Ulanov's team. Kenji Watanabe and two soldiers from the first scouting party also accompanied the Russian engineer.

The doctor's instructions were straightforward. He was to examine the Wakefields, all of them, and certify that they were indeed humans. His second assignment was to analyse the biots and categorise their non-biological features. Everything was accomplished without incident, although Katie Wakefield was uncooperative and sarcastic during the examination. At Richard's suggestion, an Einstein biot took apart one of the Lincolns and demonstrated, at a functional level, how the most sophisticated subsystems worked. Deputy Ulanov was duly impressed.

Two days later the voyagers from the Pinta began moving their possessions into Rama. A large cadre of biots helped with the unloading of the spacecraft and the movement of all the supplies into New Eden. The process took almost three days to complete. But where would everyone settle? In a decision that would later have significant consequences for the colony, almost all of the three hundred travellers on the Pinta elected to live in South-east Village, where the Wakefields had made their home. Only Max Puckett and a handful of farmers, who moved directly into the farming region along the northern perimeter of New Eden, decided to live elsewhere in the colony.

The Watanabes moved into a small house just down the lane from Richard and Nicole. From the very beginning Kenji and Nicole had had a natural rapport and their initial friendship had grown with each subsequent interaction. On the first evening that Kenji and Nai spent in their new home, they were invited to share a family dinner with the Wakefields.

'Why don't we go into the living room? It's more comfortable there,' Nicole said when the meal was completed. 'The Lincoln will clear the table and take care of the dishes.'

The Watanabes rose from their chairs and followed Richard through the entryway at the end of the dining room. The younger Wakefields politely waited for Kenji and Nai to go first, and then joined their parents and guests in the cosy living room at the front of the house.

It had been five days since the Pinta scouting party had entered Rama for the first time. *Five amazing days*, Kenji was thinking as he sat down in the Wakefield living room. His mind quickly scanned the kaleidoscope of jumbled impressions that were as yet unordered by his brain. *And in many ways this dinner was the most amazing of all. What this family has been through is incredible.*

'The stories you have told us,' Nai said to Richard and Nicole when everyone was seated, 'are absolutely astonishing. There are so many questions I want to ask, I don't know where to start ... I'm especially fascinated by this creature you call The Eagle. Was he one of the ETs who built The Node and Rama in the first place?'

'No,' said Nicole. 'The Eagle was a biot also. At least that's what he told us, and we have no reason not to believe him. He was created by the governing intelligence of The Node to give us a specific physical interface.'

'But then who *did* build The Node?'

'That's definitely a Level Three question,' Richard said with a smile.

Kenji and Nai laughed. Nicole and Richard had explained The Eagle's informational hierarchy to them during the long stories at dinner. 'I wonder if it is even possible,' Kenji mused, 'for us to conceive of beings so advanced that their machines can create other machines smarter than we are.'

'I wonder if it is even possible,' Katie now interrupted, 'for us to discuss some more trivial issues. For example, where are all the young people my age? So far I don't think I have seen more than two colonists between twelve and twenty-five.'

'Most of the younger set are on board the Nina,' Kenji responded. 'It should arrive here in about three weeks with the bulk of the colony population. The passengers on the Pinta were handpicked for the task of checking out the veracity of the video we received.'

'What's veracity!' Katie asked.

'Truth and accuracy,' Nicole said. 'More or less. It was one of your grandfather's favourite words ... And speaking of your grandfather, he was also a great believer that young people should always be permitted to *listen* to adult conversation, but not to interrupt it ... We have many things to discuss tonight with the Watanabes. The four of you don't have to stay.'

'I want to go out and see the lights,' Benjy said. 'Will you come with me, please, Ellie?'

Ellie Wakefield stood up and took Benjy by the hand. The two of them said goodnight politely and were followed out the door by Katie and Patrick.

'We're going to see if we can find anything exciting to do,' Katie said as they departed. 'Good night, Mr and Mrs Watanabe. Mother, we'll be back in a couple of hours or so.'

Nicole shook her head as the last of her children left the house. 'Katie has been so frenetic since the Pinta arrived,' she said in explanation, 'she is barely even sleeping at night. She wants to meet and talk to *everybody*.'

The Lincoln biot, who had now finished cleaning the kitchen, was standing unobtrusively by the door behind Benjy's chair. 'Would you like something to drink?' Nicole asked Kenji and Nai, motioning in the direction of the biot. 'We don't have anything as delicious as the fresh fruit drinks that you brought from Earth, but Linc can whip up some interesting synthetic concoctions.'

'I'm fine,' Kenji said, shaking his head. 'But I just realised we have spent the entire evening talking about your incredible odyssey. Certainly you must have questions for us. After all, forty-five years have passed on Earth since the Newton was launched.'

Forty-five years, Nicole suddenly thought. *Is that possible? Can Genevieve really be almost sixty years old?*

Nicole remembered clearly the last time she had seen her father and daughter on Earth. Pierre and Genevieve had accompanied her to the airport in Paris. Her daughter had hugged Nicole fiercely until the last call for boarding and then looked up at her mother with intense love and pride. The girl's eyes had been full of tears. Genevieve had been unable to say anything. *And during that forty-five years my father has died. Genevieve has become an older woman, a grandmother even, Kenji said. While I have been wandering in time and space. In a wonderland.*

The memories were too powerful for Nicole. She took a deep breath and steadied herself. There was still quiet in the Wakefield living room as she returned to the present.

'Is everything all right?' Kenji asked sensitively. Nicole nodded and stared at the soft, open eyes of her new friend. She imagined for a brief moment that she was talking to her fellow Newton cosmonaut Shigeru Takagishi. *This man is full of curiosity, as Shig was. I can trust him. And he has talked to Genevieve only a few years ago.*

'Most of the general Earth history has been explained to us, in bits and snippets, during our many conversations with other passengers from the Pinta,' Nicole said after a protracted silence. 'But we know absolutely nothing about our families except what you told us briefly that first night. Both Richard and I would like to know if you've remembered any additional details that might have been omitted in our first conversations.'

'As a matter of fact,' Kenji said, 'I went back through my journals this afternoon and read again the entries I made when I was doing the preliminary research for my book on the Newton. The most important thing that I neglected to mention in our earlier discussion was how much your Genevieve looks like her father, at least from the lips down. King Henry's face was striking, as I'm certain you remember. As an adult Genevieve's face lengthened and began to resemble his quite markedly ... Here, look at these, I managed to find a couple of photographs from my three days at Beauvois stored in my data base.'

Seeing the pictures of Genevieve overwhelmed Nicole. Tears rushed immediately into her eyes and overflowed onto her cheeks. Her hands trembled as she held the two photographs of Genevieve and her husband Louis Gaston. *Oh, Genevieve*, she cried to herself, *How I have missed you. How I would love to hold you in my arms for just a moment.*

Richard leaned over her shoulder to see the pictures. As he did so he caressed Nicole gently. 'She does look something like the prince,' he commented softly, 'but I think she looks much more like her mother.'

'Genevieve was also extremely courteous,' Kenji added, 'which surprised me considering how much she had suffered during all the media uproar in 2238. She answered my questions very patiently. I had intended to make her one of the centrepieces of the Newton book until my editor dissuaded me from the project altogether.'

'How many of the Newton cosmonauts are still alive?' Richard asked, keeping the conversation going while Nicole continued to gaze at the two photographs.

'Only Sabatini, Tabori, and Yamanaka,' Kenji replied. 'Dr David Brown had a massive stroke, and then died six months later under somewhat unusual circumstances. I believe that was in 2208. Admiral Heilmann died of cancer in 2214 or so. Irina Turgenyev suffered a complete mental breakdown, a victim of "Return to Earth" syndrome identified among some of the twenty-first century cosmonauts, and eventually committed suicide in 2211.'

Nicole was still struggling with her emotions. 'Until three nights ago,' she said to the Watanabes when the room was again silent, 'I had never even told Richard or the children that Henry was Genevieve's father. While I was living on Earth, only my father knew the truth. Henry may have suspected, but he didn't know for certain. Then, when you told me about Genevieve, I realised that I should be the one to tell my family. I ...'

Nicole's voice trailed off and more tears appeared in her eyes. She wiped her face with one of the tissues Nai handed her. 'I'm sorry,' Nicole said, 'I'm never like this. It's just such a shock to see a picture and to recall so many things ...'

'When we were living in Rama Two and then at The Node,' Richard said, 'Nicole was a model of stability. She was a rock. No matter what we encountered, no matter how bizarre, she was unflappable. The children and Michael O'Toole and I all depended on her. It's very rare to see her ...'

'Enough,' Nicole exclaimed after wiping her face. She put the photographs aside. 'Let's go on to other subjects. Let's talk about the Newton cosmonauts, Francesca Sabatini in particular. Did she get what she wanted? Fame and riches beyond compare?'

'Pretty much,' Kenji said. 'I wasn't alive during her heyday in the first decade of the century, but even now she is still very famous. She was one of the people interviewed on television recently about the significance of recolonizing Mars.'

Nicole leaned forward in her chair. 'I didn't tell you this during dinner, but I'm certain Francesca and Brown drugged Borzov, causing his appendicitis symptoms. And she purposely left me at the bottom of that pit in New York. The woman was totally without scruples.'

Kenji was silent for several seconds. 'Back in 2208, just before Dr Brown died, he had occasional lucid periods in his generally incoherent state. During one such period he gave a fantastic interview to a magazine reporter in which he confessed partial responsibility for Borzov's death and implicated Francesca in your disappearance. Signora Sabatini said the entire story was "poppycock – the crazy outpourings of a diseased brain", sued the magazine for a hundred million marks, and then settled comfortably out of court. The magazine fired the reporter and formally apologised to her.'

'Francesca always wins in the end,' Nicole remarked.

'I almost resurrected the whole story three years ago,' Kenji continued, 'when I was doing the research for my book. Since it had been more than twenty-five years, all the data from the Newton mission was in the public domain and therefore available to anyone who asked for it. I found the contents of your personal computer, including the data cube that must have come from Henry, scattered throughout the trickle telemetry. I became convinced that Dr Brown's interview had indeed contained some truth.'

'So what happened?'

'I went to interview Francesca at her palace in Sorrento. Soon thereafter I stopped working on the book ...'

Kenji hesitated for an instant. *Should I say more?* he wondered. He glanced over at his loving wife. *No*, he said to himself, *this is not the time or the place.*

'I'm sorry, Richard.'

He was almost asleep when he heard his wife's soft voice in the bedroom.

'Huh?' he said. 'Did you say something, dear?'

'I'm sorry,' Nicole repeated. She rolled over next to him and found his hand with hers underneath the covers. 'I should have told you about Henry years ago ... Are you still angry?'

'I was never angry,' Richard said. 'Surprised, yes, maybe even flabbergasted. But not angry. You had your reasons for keeping it secret.' He squeezed her hand. 'Besides, it was back on Earth, in another life. If you had told me when we first met, it might have mattered. I might have been jealous, and almost certainly would have felt inadequate. But not now.'

Nicole leaned over and gave him a kiss. 'I love you, Richard Wakefield,' she said.

'And I love you too,' he responded.

*

Kenji and Nai made love for the first time since they had left the Pinta and she fell asleep immediately. Kenji was still surprisingly alert. He lay awake in bed, thinking about the evening with the Wakefields. For some reason an image of Francesca Sabatini came into his mind. *The most beautiful seventy-year-old woman I have ever seen*, was his first thought. *And what a fantastic life.*

Kenji remembered clearly the summer afternoon when his train had pulled into the station at Sorrento. The driver of the electric cab had recognised the address immediately. 'Capisco,' he had said, waving his hands and then heading in the direction of 'il palazzo Sabatini'.

Francesca lived in a converted hotel overlooking the Bay of Naples. It was a twenty-room structure that had once belonged to a seventeenth century prince. From the office where Kenji waited for Signora Sabatini to appear, he could see a funicular carrying swimmers down a steep precipice to the dark blue bay below.

La signora was half an hour late and then quickly became impatient for the interview to be over. Twice Francesca informed Kenji that she had only agreed to talk to him at all because her publisher had told her he was an 'outstanding young writer.' 'Frankly,' she said in her excellent English, 'at this stage I find all discussion of the Newton extremely boring.'

Her interest in the conversation picked up considerably when Kenji told her about his 'new data,' the files from Nicole's personal computer that had been telemetered down to Earth in the 'trickle mode' during the final few weeks of the mission. Francesca became quiet, even pensive, as Kenji compared the internal notes that Nicole had made with the 'confession' given by Dr David Brown to the magazine reporter in 2208.

'I underestimated you,' Francesca said with a smile, when Kenji asked if she didn't think it was a 'remarkable coincidence' that Nicole's Newton diary and David Brown's confession had so many points of agreement. She never answered his questions directly. Instead she stood up in the office, insisted that he stay for the evening, and told Kenji that she would talk to him later.

Near dusk a note came to Kenji's room in Francesca's palace telling him that dinner would be at eight-thirty and that he should wear a coat and a tie. A robot arrived at the appointed time and led him to a magnificent dining room with walls covered in murals and tapestries, glittering chandeliers hanging from the high ceilings, and delicate carvings on all the mouldings. The table was set for ten. Francesca was already there, standing near a small robot server off to one side of the enormous room.

'*Kon ban wa*, Watanabe-san,' Francesca said in Japanese as she offered him a glass of champagne. 'I'm renovating the main sitting areas, so I'm afraid we're having our cocktails here. It's all very gauche, as the French would say, but it will have to do.'

Francesca looked magnificent. Her blonde hair was only slightly tinged by grey. It was stacked on top of her head, held by a large carved comb. A choker of diamonds was around her throat and an immense solitary sapphire dangled from an understated diamond necklace. Her strapless gown was white, with folds and pleats that accentuated the curves of her still youthful body. Kenji could not believe that she was seventy years old.

She took him by the hand, after explaining that she had quickly put together a dinner party in his honour, and led him over to the tapestries against the far wall. 'Do you know Aubusson at all?' she asked. When he shook his head, Francesca launched into a discussion of the history of European tapestries.

Half an hour later, Francesca took her seat at the head of the table. A music professor from Naples and his wife (supposedly an actress), two handsome, swarthy professional so ccer players, the curator of the Pompeii ruins (a man in his early fifties), a middle-aged Italian poetess, and two young women in their twenties, each stunningly attractive, occupied the other places. After some consultation with Francesca, one of the two young women sat opposite Kenji and the other beside him.

At first the armchair opposite Francesca, at the far end of the table, was empty. Francesca whispered something to her head waiter, however, and five minutes later a very old man, halt and almost blind, was led into the room. Kenji recognised him immediately. It was Janos Tabori.

The meal was wonderful, the conversation lively. The food was all served by waiters, not by the robots used in all but the most fashionable restaurants, and each course was enhanced by a different Italian wine. And what a remarkable group! Everyone, even the soccer players, spoke passable English. They were also both interested in and knowledgeable of space history. The young woman opposite Kenji had even read his most popular book on the early exploration of Mars. As the evening wore on, Kenji, who was a bachelor of thirty at the time, became less inhibited. He was aroused by everything – the women, the wine, the discussions of history and poetry and music.

Only once during the two hours at the table was there any mention of the afternoon interview. During a lull in the conversation after dessert and before the cognac, Francesca nearly shouted at Janos: 'This young Japanese man – he's very brilliant, you know – thinks he has found evidence from Nicole's personal computer that corroborates those awful lies David told before he died.'

Janos did not comment. His facial expression did not change. But after the meal he handed Kenji a note and then disappeared. '"You know nothing but the truth and have no tenderness",' the note said. '"Thus you judge unjustly." Aglaya Yepanchin to Prince Myshkin. *The Idiot*, by Fyodor Dostoyevsky.'

Kenji had only been in his room for five or ten minutes when there was a knock on his door. When he opened it he saw the young Italian woman who had been sitting opposite him at dinner. She was wearing a tiny bikini that revealed most of her exceptional body. She was also holding a man's bathing suit in her hand.

'Mr Watanabe,' she said with a sexy smile, 'please join us for a swim. This suit ought to fit you.'

Kenji felt an immediate and enormous surge of lust that did not quickly abate. Slightly embarrassed, he waited a minute or two after dressing before he joined the woman in the hall.

Three years later, even lying in his bed in New Eden next to the woman he loved, it was impossible for Kenji not to recall with sexual longing the night he spent in Francesca's palace. Six of them had taken the funicular down to the bay and swum in the moonlight. At the cabana next to the water, they had drunk and danced and laughed together. It had been a dream night.

Within an hour, Kenji remembered, *we were all happily naked. The game plan was clear. The two soccer players were for Francesca. The two Madonnas for me.*

Kenji squirmed in his bed recalling both the intensity of his pleasure and Francesca's free laughter when she found him entwined with the two young women at dawn in one of the oversized chaise lounges beside the bay.

When I reached New York four days later my editor told me that he thought I should abandon the Newton project. I didn't argue with him. I probably would have suggested it myself.

11

Ellie was fascinated by the porcelain figures. She picked one up, a little girl dressed in a light blue ballet gown, and turned it over in her hands. 'Look at this, Benjy,' she said to her brother. 'Someone made this – all by himself.'

'*That* one is actually a copy,' the Spanish shopkeeper said, 'but an artist did make the original from which the computer imprint was taken. The reproduction process is now so accurate that even the experts have a hard time telling which ones are the copies.'

'And you collected all these back on Earth?' Ellie waved her hand at the hundred or so figures on the table and in the small glass cases.

'Yes,' Mr Murillo said proudly. 'Although I was a civil servant in Seville – building permits and that sort of thing – my wife and I also owned a small shop. We fell in love with porcelain art about ten years ago and have been avid collectors ever since.'

Mrs Murillo, also in her late forties, came out of a back room where she was still unpacking merchandise.

'We decided,' she said, 'long before we learned that we had actually been selected as colonists by the ISA, that no matter how restrictive our baggage requirements were for the voyage on the Nina, we would bring our entire collection of porcelain with us.'

Benjy was holding the dancing girl only a few centimetres from his face. 'Beau-ti-ful,' he said with a broad smile.

'Thank you,' Mr Murillo said. 'We had hoped to start a collectors' society in Lowell Colony,' he added. 'Three or four of the other passengers on the Nina brought several pieces as well.'

'May we look at them?' Ellie asked. 'We'll be very careful.'

'Help yourself,' Mrs Murillo said. 'Eventually, once everything settles down, we will sell or barter some of the objects – certainly the duplicates. Right now they're just on display to be appreciated.'

While Ellie and Benjy were examining the porcelain creations, several other people entered the shop. The Murillos had opened for business only a few days before. They sold candles, fancy napkins, and other small household adornments.

'You certainly didn't waste any time, Carlos,' a burly American said to Mr Murillo several minutes later. From this initial greeting it was obvious that he had been a fellow passenger on the Nina.

'It was easier for us, Travis,' Mr Murillo said. 'We had no family and needed only a small place to live.'

'We haven't even settled into a house yet,' Travis complained. 'We're definitely going to live in this village, but Chelsea and the kids cannot find a house they all like. Chelsea is still spooked by the whole arrangement. She doesn't believe the ISA is telling us the truth even now.'

'I admit that it is extremely difficult to accept that this space station was built by aliens just so they can observe us ... and it would certainly be easier to believe the ISA story if there were pictures from that Node place. But why would they lie to us?'

'They have lied before. Nobody even mentioned this place until a day before the rendezvous ... Chelsea believes that we are part of an ISA space colony experiment. She says that we will stay here for a while, and then be transferred to the surface of Mars, so that the two types of colonies can be compared.'

Mr Murillo laughed. 'I see Chelsea hasn't changed since we left the Nina.' He became more serious. 'You know, Juanita and I had our doubts too, especially after the first week passed and nobody had seen any sign of the aliens. We spent two full days wandering around, talking to other people – we essentially conducted our own investigation. We finally concluded that the ISA story must be true. First of all, it's just too preposterous to be a lie. Second, that Wakefield woman was very convincing. In her open meeting she answered questions for almost two hours and neither Juanita nor I detected a single inconsistency.'

'It's hard for me to imagine anyone sleeping for twelve years,' Travis said, shaking his head.

'Of course. It was for us too. But we actually inspected that somnarium where the Wakefield family supposedly slept. Everything was exactly as Nicole had described it in the meeting. The overall building, incidentally, is immense. There are enough berths and rooms to house everyone in the colony, if necessary ... It certainly doesn't make sense that the ISA would have built such a huge facility to support a lie.'

'Maybe you're right.'

'Anyway, we've decided to make the best of it. At least for the time being. And we certainly can't complain about our living conditions. All the housing is first rate. Juanita and I even have our own Lincoln robot to give us a hand both at home and around the store.'

Ellie was following the discussion very closely. She remembered what her mother had told her the night before when she had asked if she and Benjy could go for a walk in the village. 'I guess so, darling,' Nicole had said, 'but if anyone recognises you as a Wakefield and starts to question you, don't talk to them. Be polite, and then come home as quickly as you can. Mr Macmillan does not want us talking to any non-ISA personnel about our experiences just yet.'

While Ellie was admiring the porcelain figures and listening intently to the conversation between Mr Murillo and the man named Travis, Benjy wandered off on his own. When Ellie realised he was not beside her, she started to panic.

'What are you staring at, buddy?' Ellie heard a harsh male voice say on the other side of the shop.

'Her hair is ve-ry pret-ty,' Benjy replied. He was blocking the aisle, preventing the man and his wife from moving forward. He smiled and reached out his hand toward the woman's magnificent long blonde hair. 'May I touch it?' he asked.

'Are you crazy? Of course not. Now get out of ...'

'Jason, I think he's retarded,' the woman said quietly, catching her husband's arm before he pushed Benjy.

At that moment Ellie walked up beside her brother. She realised that the man was angry, but she did not know what to do. She nudged Benjy gently on the shoulder. 'Look, Ellie,' he exclaimed, slurring his words in excitement, 'look at her pret-ty yel-low hair.'

'Is this goon a friend of yours?' the tall man asked Ellie.

'Benjy is my brother,' Ellie answered with difficulty.

'Well, get him out of here. He's bothering my wife.'

'Sir,' Ellie said after summoning her courage, 'my brother doesn't mean any harm. He's never seen long blonde hair up close before.'

The man's face wrinkled in anger and puzzlement. 'Whaaat?' he said. He glanced at his wife. 'What's with these two? One's a dummy and the other ...'

'Aren't you two of the Wakefield children?' a pleasant female voice behind Ellie interrupted.

The distraught Ellie turned around. Mrs Murillo stepped between the teenagers and the couple. She and her husband had crossed the shop as soon as they had heard the raised voices. 'Yes, ma'am,' Ellie said softly. 'Yes, we are.'

'You mean these are two of the children who came from outer space?' the man named Jason asked.

Ellie managed to pull Benjy quickly over to the door of the shop. 'We're very sorry,' Ellie said before she and Benjy departed. 'We didn't mean to cause any trouble.'

'Freaks!' Ellie heard somebody say as the door closed behind her.

It had been another exhausting day. Nicole was very tired. She stood in front of the mirror and finished washing her face. 'Ellie and Benjy had some kind of unpleasant experience down in the village,' Richard said from the bedroom. 'They wouldn't tell me much about it.'

Nicole had spent thirteen long hours that day helping to process the Nina passengers. No matter how hard she and Kenji Watanabe and the others had worked, it seemed as if nobody was ever satisfied and there were always more tasks that needed to be done. Many of the new colonists had been downright petulant when Nicole had tried to explain to them the procedures that the ISA had established for the allocation of food, living quarters, and working areas.

She had been too many days without enough sleep. Nicole looked at the bags under her eyes. *But we must finish with this group before the Santa Maria arrives*, she said to herself. *They will be far more difficult.*

Nicole wiped her face with a towel and crossed into the bedroom, where Richard was sitting up in his pajamas. 'How was your day?' she asked.

'Not bad ... Fairly interesting, in fact. Slowly but surely the human engineers are becoming more comfortable with the Einsteins.' He paused. 'Did you hear what I said about Ellie and Benjy?'

Nicole sighed. From the tone in Richard's voice she understood his real message. Despite her fatigue, she exited from the bedroom and headed down the hall.

Ellie was already asleep, but Benjy was still awake in the room he shared with Patrick. Nicole sat down beside Benjy and took his hand. 'Hel-lo, Ma-ma,' the boy said.

'Uncle Richard mentioned that you and Ellie went into the village this afternoon,' Nicole said to her eldest son.

An expression of pain creased the boy's face for a few seconds and then disappeared. 'Yes, Ma-ma,' he said.

'Ellie told me that they were recognised and that one of the new colonists called them some names,' Patrick said from the opposite side of the room.

'Is that right, darling?' Nicole asked Benjy, still holding and stroking his hands.

The boy made a barely perceptible affirmative motion with his head and then stared silently at his mother. 'What's a goon, Ma-ma?' he said suddenly, his eyes filling with tears.

Nicole put her arms around Benjy. 'Did someone call you a goon today?' she asked softly.

Benjy nodded. 'The word doesn't have a specific meaning,' Nicole answered. 'Anyone who is different, or perhaps objectionable, might be called a goon.' She caressed Benjy again. 'People use words like that when they aren't thinking. Whoever called you a goon was probably confused, or upset, by other events in his life, and he just lashed out at you because he didn't understand you ... Did you do anything to bother him?'

'No, Ma-ma. I just told him that I liked the wo-man's yellow hair.'

It took several minutes, but Nicole eventually learned the gist of what had occurred in the porcelain shop. When she thought that Benjy was all right, Nicole walked across the room to kiss Patrick good night. 'And how about you?' she said. 'Was your day all right?'

'Mostly,' Patrick said. 'I only had one disaster – down at the park.' He tried to smile. 'Some of the new boys were playing basketball and invited me to join them ... I was absolutely terrible. A couple of them laughed at me.'

Nicole gave Patrick a long and tender hug. *Patrick is strong*, Nicole said to herself when she was out in the hall, headed back to her bedroom. *But even he needs support.* She took a deep breath. *Am I doing the right thing?* she asked herself for the umpteenth time since she had become deeply involved in all aspects of the planning for the colony. *I feel so responsible for everything here. I want New Eden to begin properly ... But my children still need more of my time ... Will I ever achieve the right balance?*

Richard was still awake when Nicole snuggled in beside him. She shared Benjy's story with her husband. 'I'm sorry I wasn't able to help him,' Richard said. 'There are just some things that only a mother ...'

Nicole was so exhausted that she was falling asleep before Richard even finished his sentence. He touched her firmly on the arm. 'Nicole,' he said, 'there is something else we must talk about. Unfortunately it can't wait – we may not have any private time in the morning.'

She rolled over and looked at Richard quizzically. 'It's about Katie,' he said. 'I really need your help ... There's another of those youth get-acquainted dances tomorrow night – you remember we told Katie last week she could go, but only if Patrick went with her and she came home at a reasonable hour. Well, tonight I just happened to see her standing in front of her mirror in a new dress. It was short and very revealing. When I asked her about the dress, and then told her that it didn't seem like an appropriate outfit for a casual dance, she flew into a rage. She insisted that I was "spying on her" and then informed me that I was "hopelessly ignorant" about fashion.'

'What did you say?'

'I reprimanded her. She glared at me coldly and said nothing. Several minutes later she left the house without saying a word. The rest of the children and I ate dinner without her ... Katie came home only thirty minutes or so before you did. She smelled of tobacco and beer. When I tried to talk to her, she just said "Don't bother me", and then went to her room and slammed the door.'

I have been afraid of this, Nicole thought as she lay next to Richard in silence. *All the signs have been there since she was a little girl. Katie is brilliant, but she is also selfish and impetuous ...*

'I was going to tell Katie that she could not go to the dance tomorrow night,' Richard was saying, 'but then I realised that by any normal definition she is an adult. After all, her registry card at the administration office gives her age as twenty-four. We really can't treat her like a child.'

But she's maybe fourteen emotionally, Nicole thought, squirming as Richard began reciting all the difficulties they had had with Katie since the first other humans had entered Rama. *Nothing matters to her but adventure and excitement.*

Nicole remembered the day she had spent with Katie at the hospital. It had been a week before the colonists from the Nina had arrived. Katie had been fascinated by all the sophisticated medical equipment and genuinely interested in how it worked; however, when Nicole had suggested that Katie might want to work at the hospital until the university opened, the young woman had laughed. 'Are you kidding?' her daughter had said. 'I can't imagine anything more boring. Especially when there will be hundreds of new people to meet.'

There's not much either Richard or I can do, Nicole said to herself with a sigh. *We can ache for Katie, and offer her our love, but she has already decided that all our knowledge and experience is irrelevant.*

There was silence in the bedroom. Nicole reached over and kissed Richard. 'I will talk to Katie tomorrow about the dress,' she said, 'but I doubt if it will do much good.'

Patrick was sitting by himself in a folding chair against the wall of the school gymnasium. He took a sip from his soda and glanced at his watch as the slow music ended and a dozen couples dancing on the large floor slowed to a stop. Katie and Olaf Larsen, a tall Swede whose father was a member of Commander Macmillan's staff, shared a brief kiss before walking, arm in arm, in Patrick's direction.

'Olaf and I are going outside for a cigarette and another shot of whisky,' Katie said when the pair reached Patrick. 'Why don't you come with us?'

'We're already late, Katie,' Patrick replied. 'We said we would be home by twelve-thirty.'

The Swede gave Patrick a condescending pat on the back. 'Come on, boy,' he said. 'Loosen up. Your sister and I are having a good time.'

Olaf was already drunk. His fair face was flushed from the drinking and dancing. He pointed across the room. 'You see that girl with the red hair, white dress, and big boobs? Her name is Beth and she's a hot number. She's been waiting all night for you to ask her to dance. Would you like for me to introduce you?'

Patrick shook his head. 'Look, Katie,' he said. 'I want to go. I've been sitting here patiently ...'

'Half an hour more, baby brother,' Katie interrupted. 'I'll go outside for a little while, then come back for a couple of dances. After that we'll leave. OK?'

She kissed Patrick on the cheek and moved toward the door with Olaf. A fast dance began playing on the gymnasium sound system. Patrick watched in fascination as the young couples moved in tune with the heavy beat of the music.

'You don't dance?' a young man who was walking around the perimeter of the dance floor asked him.

'No,' said Patrick. 'I've never tried.'

The young man gave Patrick a strange look. Then he stopped and smiled.

'Of course,' he said, 'you're one of the Wakefields ... Hi, my name is Brian Walsh. I'm from Wisconsin, in the middle of the United States. My parents are the ones who are supposed to be organizing the university.'

Patrick had not exchanged more than a couple of words with anyone except Katie since they had arrived at the dance several hours earlier. He gladly shook hands with Brian Walsh and the two of them chatted amiably for a few minutes. Brian, who had been half finished with his undergraduate degree in computer engineering when his family had been selected for Lowell Colony, was twenty and an only child. He was also extremely curious about his companion's experiences.

'Tell me,' he said to Patrick when they had become more comfortable with each other, 'does this place called The Node really exist? Or is it part of sòme cockamamie story dreamed up by the ISA?'

'No,' said Patrick, forgetting that he was not supposed to discuss such things. 'The Node is definitely there. My father says it's an extraterrestrial processing station.'

Brian laughed easily. 'So somewhere out near Sirius is a gigantic triangle built by an unknown superspecies? And its purpose is to help *them* study other creatures who travel in space? Wow. That's the most fantastic tale I have ever heard. In fact, almost everything your mother told us at that open meeting was unbelievable. I will, however, admit that both the existence of this space station and the technological level of the robots do make her story more plausible.'

'Everything my mother said was true,' Patrick said. 'And some of the most incredible stories were purposely left out. For example, my mother had a conversation with a caped eel who talked in bubbles. Also ...' Patrick stopped himself, remembering Nicole's admonitions.

Brian was fascinated. 'A caped eel?' he said. 'How did she know what it was saying?'

Patrick looked at his watch. 'Excuse me, Brian,' he said abruptly, 'but I'm here with my sister and I'm supposed to meet her in a few minutes.'

'Is she the one with the little red dress cut *really* low?'

Patrick nodded. Brian put his arm around his new friend's shoulder. 'Let me give you some advice,' he said. 'Somebody needs to talk to your sister. The way she acts around all the guys makes people think she's an easy lay.'

'That's just Katie,' Patrick said defensively. 'She's never been around anyone except the family.'

'Sorry,' Brian said with a shrug. 'It's none of my business anyway ... Say, why don't you give me a call sometime? I've enjoyed our conversation very much.'

Patrick said goodbye to Brian and started walking toward the door. Where was Katie? Why had she not come back inside the gymnasium?

He heard her loud laugh within seconds after he was outside. Katie was standing on the playground with three men, one of whom was Olaf Larsen.

They were all smoking and laughing and drinking from a bottle that was being passed around.

'So what position do *you* like best?' a dark young man with a moustache asked.

'Oh, I prefer to be on top,' Katie said with a laugh. She took a gulp from the bottle. 'That way I'm in control.'

'Sounds good to me,' the man, whose name was Andrew, replied. He chuckled and placed his hand suggestively on her bottom. Katie pushed it away, still laughing. Seconds later she saw Patrick approaching.

'Come over here, baby brother,' Katie shouted. 'This shit we're drinking is dynamite.'

The three men, who had been drawn in close around Katie, moved slightly away from her as Patrick walked toward them. Although he was still quite skinny and undeveloped, his height made him an imposing figure in the dim light.

'I'm going home now, Katie,' Patrick said, refusing the bottle when he was beside her, 'and I think you should go with me.'

Andrew laughed. 'Some party girl you have here, Larsen,' he said sarcastically, 'with a teenage brother as a chaperon.'

Katie's eyes flared with anger. She took another swig from the bottle and handed it to Olaf. Then she grabbed Andrew and kissed him wildly on the lips, pressing her body tightly against his.

Patrick was embarrassed. Olaf and the third man cheered and whistled as Andrew returned Katie's kiss. After almost a minute Katie pulled away. 'Let's go now, Patrick,' she said with a smile, her eyes still fixed on the man she had kissed. 'I think that's enough for one night.'

12

Eponine stared out the second story window at the gently rolling slope. The GEDs covered the hillside, their fine gridwork pattern almost obscuring the brown soil underneath.

'So, Ep, what do you think?' Kimberly asked. 'It's certainly nice enough. And once the forest is planted, we'll have trees and grass and maybe even a squirrel or two outside our window. That's definitely a plus.'

'I don't know,' a distracted Eponine replied after a few seconds. 'It's a little smaller than the one I liked yesterday in Positano. And I have a few misgivings about living here, in Hakone. I haven't known that many Orientals ...'

'Look, roomie, we can't wait forever. I told you yesterday that we should have made backup choices. There were *seven* pairs that wanted the apartment in Positano – not surprising since there were only four units left in the whole village – and we just weren't lucky. All that's left now, except for those tiny flats over the shops on the main street in Beauvois – and I don't want to live there because there's absolutely no privacy – is either here or in San Miguel. And all the blacks and browns are living in San Miguel.'

Eponine sat down in one of the chairs. They were in the living room of the small two-bedroom apartment. It was furnished modestly, but adequately, with two chairs and a large sofa that were the same brown colour as the rectangular coffee table. Altogether the apartment, which had a single large bathroom and a small kitchen in addition to the living room and two bedrooms, was slightly more than one hundred square metres.

Kimberly Henderson paced around the room impatiently. 'Kim,' Eponine said slowly, 'I'm sorry, but I'm having a hard time concentrating on selecting an apartment when so much is happening to us. What is this place? Where are we? Why are we here?' Her mind flashed back quickly to the incredible briefing three days earlier, when Commander Macmillan had informed them that they were inside a spaceship built and equipped by extraterrestrials 'for the purpose of observing Earthlings'.

Kimberly Henderson lit a cigarette and expelled the smoke forcefully into the air. She shrugged. 'Shit, Eponine,' she said, 'I don't know the answers to any of those questions. But I do know that if we don't pick an apartment we'll be left with whatever nobody else has wanted.'

Eponine looked at her friend for several seconds and then sighed. 'I don't think this process has been very fair,' she complained. 'The passengers from the Pinta and the Nina were all able to pick their homes before we even arrived. We are being forced to choose among the rejects.'

'What did you expect?' Kimberly replied quickly. 'Our ship was carrying convicts – of course we got the dregs. But at least we're finally free.'

'So I guess you want to live in this apartment?' Eponine said at length.

'Yes,' replied Kimberly. 'And I also want to put in a bid on the other two apartments we saw this morning, near the Hakone market, in case we are aced out of this one. If we don't have a definite home after the drawing tonight, I'm afraid we'll really be in bad shape.'

This was a mistake, Eponine was thinking as she watched Kimberly walking around the room. *I never should have agreed to be her roommate ... But what choice did I have? The living accommodations that are left for single people are abysmal.*

Eponine was not accustomed to rapid changes in her life. Unlike Kimberly Henderson, who had had an enormous variety of experiences before she was convicted of murder at the age of nineteen, Eponine had lived a relatively sheltered childhood and adolescence. She had grown up in an orphanage outside Limoges, France, and until Professor Moreau took her to Paris to see the great museums when Eponine was seventeen, she had never even been outside her native province. It had been a very difficult decision for her to sign up for the Lowell Colony in the first place. But Eponine was facing a lifetime of detention in Bourges, and she was offered a chance for freedom on Mars. After a long deliberation she had courageously decided to submit her application to the ISA.

Eponine had been selected as a colonist because she had an outstanding academic record, especially in all the arts, was fluent in English, and had been a perfect prisoner. Her dossier in the ISA files had identified her most likely placement in the Lowell Colony as 'drama and/or art teacher in the secondary schools.' Despite the difficulties associated with the cruise phase of the mission after leaving the Earth, Eponine had felt a palpable rush of adrenaline and excitement when Mars had first appeared in the observation window of the Santa Maria. It would be a new life on a new world.

Two days before the scheduled encounter, however, the ISA guards had announced that the spacecraft was not going to deploy its landing shuttles as planned. Instead, they had told the convict passengers, the Santa Maria was going to take a 'temporary detour to rendezvous with a space station orbiting Mars.' Eponine had been both confused and concerned by the announcement. Unlike most of her associates, she bad read carefully all the ISA material for the colonists and she had never seen any mention of an orbiting space station around Mars.

It had not been until the Santa Maria was completely unloaded and all the people and supplies were inside New Eden that anyone had really told Eponine and the other convicts what was happening. And even after the

Macmillan briefing, very few of the convicts believed they were being told the truth. 'Come on, now,' Willis Meeker had said, 'does he really think we're that stupid? A bunch of ETs built this place and all those crazy robots? This whole thing is a setup. We're just testing some new kind of prison concept.'

'But Willis,' Malcolm Peabody had replied, 'what about all the others, the ones who came on the Pinta and the Nina? I've talked to some of them. They're normal people, I mean, they aren't convicts. If your theory is right, what are *they* doing here?'

'How the hell should I know, fag? I'm no genius. I just know that Macmillan dude is not giving us the straight shit.'

Eponine did not let her uncertainties about the Macmillan briefing deter her from going with Kimberly to Central City to submit requests for the three apartments in Hakone. They were fortunate in the drawing this time and were allocated their first choice. The two women spent a day moving into the apartment on the edge of Sherwood Forest and then reported to the employment office in the administrative complex for processing.

Because the other two spacecraft had arrived well before the Santa Maria, the procedures to integrate the convicts into the life in New Eden were quite carefully defined. It took virtually no time to assign Kimberly, who really did have an outstanding nursing record, to the central hospital.

Eponine interviewed with the school superintendent and four other teachers before accepting an assignment at Central High School. Her new job required a short commute by train, whereas she could have walked each day if she had decided to teach at Hakone Middle School. But Eponine thought it would be worth the trouble. She very much liked the principal and staff members who were teaching at the high school.

At first the other seven doctors working at the hospital were leery of the two convict physicians, especially Dr Robert Turner, whose dossier cryptically mentioned his brutal murders without detailing any of the extenuating circumstances. But after a week or so, during which time his extraordinary skill, knowledge, and professionalism became apparent to everyone, the staff unanimously selected him to be the director of the hospital. Dr Turner was quite astonished by his selection and pledged, in a brief acceptance speech, to dedicate himself completely to the welfare of the colony.

His first official act was to propose to the provisional government that a full physical examination be given to every citizen of New Eden so that all the personal medical files could be updated. When his proposal was accepted, Dr Turner deployed the Tiassos throughout the colony as paramedics. The biots performed all the routine examinations and gathered data for the doctors to analyse. Simultaneously, remembering the excellent data network that had existed among all the hospitals in the Dallas metropolitan area, the indefatigable Dr Turner began working with several of the Einsteins to design a fully computerised system for tracking the health of the colonists.

One evening during the third full week after the Santa Maria had docked with Rama, Eponine was home alone, as usual (Kimberly Henderson's daily pattern had already become established – she was almost never in the apartment. If she wasn't at work at the hospital, then she was out with Toshio Nakamura and his cronies), when her videophone sounded. It was Malcolm Peabody's face that appeared on the monitor. 'Eponine,' he said shyly, 'I have a favour to ask.'

'What is it, Malcolm?'

'I received a call from a Dr Turner at the hospital about five minutes ago. He says there were some "irregularities" in my health data taken by one of those robots last week. He wants me to come in for a more detailed examination.'

Eponine waited patiently for several seconds. 'I'm not following you,' she said at length. 'What's the favour?'

Malcolm took a deep breath. 'It must be serious, Eponine. He wants to see me now ... Will you come with me?'

'*Now?*' said Eponine, glancing at her watch. 'It's almost eleven o'clock at night.' In a flash she remembered Kimberly Henderson complaining that Dr Turner was a 'workaholic, as bad as those black robot nurses.' Eponine also recalled the amazing blue of his eyes.

'All right,' she said to Malcolm. 'I'll meet you at the station in ten minutes.'

Eponine had not been out much at night. Since her teaching appointment, she had spent most of her evenings working on her lesson plans. On one Saturday night she had gone out with Kimberly, Toshio Nakamura, and several other people to a Japanese restaurant that had just opened. But the food was strange, the company mostly Oriental, and several of the men, after drinking too much, made pathetic passes at her. Kimberly chided her for being 'picky and stand-offish,' but Eponine refused her roommate's later invitations to socialise.

Eponine reached the station before Malcolm. While she was waiting for him to arrive, she marvelled at how completely the village had been transformed by the presence of humans. *Let's see*, she was thinking, *the Pinta arrived here four months ago, the Nina five weeks after that. Already there are shops everywhere, both around the station and in the village itself. The accoutrements of human existence. If we stay here a year or two this colony will be indistinguishable from Earth.*

Malcolm was quite nervous and talkative during the short train ride. 'I know it's my heart, Eponine,' he said. 'I've been having sharp pains, here, ever since Walter died. At first I thought it was all in my mind.'

'Don't worry,' Eponine responded, comforting her friend. 'I bet it's nothing really serious.'

Eponine was having difficulty keeping her eyes open. It was after three o'clock in the morning. Malcolm was asleep on the bench beside her. *What's that doctor doing?* she wondered. *He said he wouldn't be long.*

Soon after their arrival, Dr Turner had examined Malcolm with a computerised stethoscope and then, telling him he needed 'more comprehensive tests,' bad taken him into a separate part of the hospital. Malcolm had returned to the waiting room an hour later. Eponine herself had seen the doctor only briefly, when he had admitted Malcolm to his office at the beginning of the examination.

'Are you Mr Peabody's friend?' a voice suddenly said. Eponine must have been dozing. When her vision was in focus, the beautiful blue eyes were staring at her from only a metre away. The doctor looked tired and upset.

'Yes,' Eponine said softly, trying not to disturb the man sleeping on her shoulder.

'He's going to die very soon,' Dr Turner said. 'Possibly in the next two weeks.'

Eponine felt her blood surge through her body. *Am I hearing correctly?* she thought. *Did he say Malcolm was going to die in the next two weeks?* Eponine was stunned.

'He will need a lot of support,' the doctor was saying. He paused for a moment, staring at Eponine. Was he trying to remember where he had seen her before? 'Will you be able to help him?' Dr Turner asked.

'I ... I hope so,' Eponine answered.

Malcolm began to stir. 'We must wake him up now,' the doctor said.

There was no emotion detectable in Dr Turner's eyes. He had delivered his diagnosis – no, his *assertion* – without a hint of feeling. *Kim is right*, Eponine thought. *He's as much an automaton as those Tiasso robots.*

At the doctor's suggestion, Eponine accompanied Malcolm down a corridor and into a room filled with medical instruments. 'Someone intelligent,' Dr Turner said to Malcolm, 'chose the equipment that was brought here from Earth. Although we are limited in staff, our diagnostic apparatus is first rate.'

The three of them walked over to a transparent cube about one metre on a side. 'This amazing device,' Dr Turner said, 'is called an organ projector. It can reconstruct, with detailed fidelity, almost all the major organs of the human body. What we are seeing now, when we look inside, is a computer graphic representation of your heart, Mr Peabody, just as it appeared ninety minutes ago when I injected the tracer material into your blood vessels.'

Dr Turner pointed at an adjacent room, where Malcolm had apparently undergone the tests. 'While you were sitting on that table,' he continued, 'you were scanned a million times a second by the machine with the big lens. From the location of the tracer material and those billions of instantaneous scans, an extremely accurate, three-dimensional image of your heart was constructed. That is what you are seeing inside the cube.'

Dr Turner stopped a moment, looked away quickly, and then fixed his eyes on Malcolm. 'I'm not trying to make it harder on you, Mr Peabody,' he said quietly, 'but I wanted to explain how I am able to know what's wrong with you. So that you will understand there has been no mistake.'

Malcolm's eyes were wild with fright. The doctor took him by the hand and led him to a specific position beside the cube. 'Look right there, on the back of the heart, near the top. Do you see the strange webbing and striation in the tissues? Those are your heart muscles and they have undergone irreparable decay.'

Malcolm stared inside the cube for what seemed like an eternity and then lowered his head. 'Am I going to die, Doctor?' he asked meekly.

Robert Turner took his patient's other hand. 'Yes, you are, Malcolm. On Earth, we could possibly wait for a heart transplant; here, however, it is out of the question since we have neither the right equipment nor a proper donor ... If you would like, I can open you up and take a first-hand look at your heart. But it's extremely unlikely that I would see anything that would change the prognosis.'

Malcolm shook his head. Tears began to run down his cheeks. Eponine put her arms around the little man and began to weep as well. 'I'm sorry it took me so long to complete my diagnosis,' Dr Turner said, 'but in a case this serious I needed to be absolutely certain.'

A few moments later Malcolm and Eponine walked toward the door. Malcolm turned around. 'What do I do now?' he asked the doctor.

'Whatever you enjoy,' Dr Turner replied.

When they were gone Dr Turner returned to his office, where hardcopy printouts of Malcolm Peabody's charts and files lay strewn across his desk. The doctor was deeply worried. He was virtually certain – he could not know definitely until he had completed the autopsy – that Peabody's heart was suffering from the same kind of malady that had killed Walter Brackeen on the Santa Maria. The two of them had been close friends for several years, going all the way back to the beginning of their detention terms in Georgia. It was unlikely that they had both *coincidentally* contracted the same heart disease. But if it was not a coincidence, then the pathogen must be communicable.

Robert Turner shook his head. Any disease that struck the heart was alarming. But one that could be passed from one person to another? The spectre was terrifying.

He was very tired. Before putting his head down on his desk Dr Turner made a list of the references on heart viruses that he wanted to obtain from the data base. Then he fell quickly asleep.

Fifteen minutes later the phone aroused him suddenly. A Tiasso was on the other end, calling from the Emergency Room. 'Two Garcias have found a human body out in Sherwood Forest,' it said, 'and are on the way here now. From the images they have transmitted, I can tell that this case will require your personal involvement.'

Dr Turner scrubbed his hands, put on his gown again, and reached the Emergency Room just before the two Garcias arrived with the body. As experienced as he was, Dr Turner had to turn away from the horribly mutilated corpse. The head had been almost completely severed from the body – it was hanging by only a thin strand of muscle – and the face had been hacked and disfigured beyond recognition. In addition, in the genital area of the trousers there was a bloody, gaping hole.

The pair of Tiassos immediately went to work, cleaning up the blood and preparing the body for autopsy. Dr Turner sat on a chair, away from the scene, and filled out the first death report in New Eden.

'What was his name?' he asked the biots.

One of the Tiassos rustled through what was left of the dead man's clothing and found his ISA identification card.

'Danni,' the biot replied. 'Marcello Danni.'

EPITHALAMION

1

The train from Positano was full. It stopped at the small station on the shores of Lake Shakespeare, halfway to Beauvois, and disgorged its mixture of humans and biots. Many were carrying baskets of food and blankets and folding chairs. Some of the smaller children raced from the station out onto the thick, freshly mown grass surrounding the lake. They laughed and tumbled down the gentle slope that covered the hundred and fifty metres between the station and the edge of the water.

For those who did not want to sit on the grass, wooden stands had been erected just opposite the narrow pier that extended fifty metres into the water before spreading out into a rectangular platform. A microphone, rostrum, and several chairs were set up on the platform; it was there that Governor Watanabe would deliver the Settlement Day address after the fireworks were finished.

Forty metres to the left of the stands the Wakefields and the Watanabes had placed a long table covered with a blue and white cloth. Finger foods were tastefully arranged on the table. Coolers underneath were filled with drinks. Their families and friends had gathered in the immediate area and were either eating, playing some kind of game, or engaged in animated conversation. Two Lincoln biots were moving around the group, offering drinks and canapés to those who were too far away from the table and the coolers.

It was a hot afternoon. Too hot, in fact, the third exceptionally warm day in a row. But as the artificial sun completed its mini-arc in the dome far above their heads and the light began to slowly dim, the expectant crowd on the banks of Lake Shakespeare forgot about the heat.

A final train arrived only minutes before the light disappeared completely. This one came from the Central City station to the north, bringing colonists who lived in Hakone or San Miguel. There were not many latecomers. Most of the people had arrived early to set up their picnics on the grass. Eponine was on the last train. She had originally planned not to attend the celebration at all, but had changed her mind at the last minute.

Eponine was confused when she stepped onto the grass from the station platform. There were so many people! *All of New Eden must be here*, she thought. For a moment she wished that she had not come. Everyone was with friends and family, and she was all alone.

Ellie Wakefield was playing horseshoes with Benjy when Eponine stepped off the train. She quickly recognised her teacher, even from the distance, because of her bright red armband. 'It's Eponine, Mother,' Ellie said, running over to Nicole. 'May I ask her to join us?'

'Of course,' Nicole replied.

A voice on the public address system interrupted the music being played by a small band to announce that the fireworks would begin in ten minutes. There was scattered applause.

'Eponine,' Ellie shouted. 'Over here.' Ellie waved her arms.

Eponine heard her name being called but could not see very clearly in the dim light. After several seconds she started in Ellie's direction. Along the way she inadvertently bumped into a toddler who was roaming by himself in the grass. 'Kevin,' a mother shrieked, 'stay away from her!'

In an instant a burly blonde man grabbed the little boy and held him away from Eponine. 'You shouldn't be here,' the man said. 'Not with decent people.'

A little shaken, Eponine continued toward Ellie, who was walking in her direction across the grass. 'Go home, Forty-one!' a woman who had watched the earlier incident shouted. A fat ten-year-old boy with a bulbous nose pointed his finger at Eponine and made an inaudible comment to his younger sister.

'I'm so glad to see you,' Ellie said when she reached her teacher. 'Will you come have something to eat?'

Eponine nodded. 'I'm sorry for all these people,' Ellie said in a voice loud enough for everyone around her to hear. 'It's a shame they are so ignorant.'

Ellie led Eponine back to the big table and made a general introduction. 'Hey, everybody, for those of you who don't know her, this is my teacher and friend Eponine. She has no last name, so don't ask her what it is.'

Eponine and Nicole had met several times before. They exchanged pleasantries now while a Lincoln offered Eponine some vegetable sticks and a soda. Nai Watanabe pointedly brought her twin sons, Kepler and Galileo, who had just had their second birthday the week before, over to meet the new arrival. A large nearby group of colonists from Positano was staring as Eponine lifted Kepler in her arms. 'Pretty,' the little boy said, pointing at Eponine's face.

'It must be very difficult,' Nicole said in French, her head nodding in the direction of the gawking bystanders.

'Oui,' Eponine replied. *Difficult?* she thought. *That's the understatement of the year. How about absolutely impossible? It's not bad enough that I have some horrible disease that will probably kill me. No. I must also wear an armband so that others can avoid me if they choose.*

Max Puckett glanced up from the chessboard and noticed Eponine. 'Hello,

hello,' he said. 'You must be the teacher I've heard so much about.'

'That's Max,' Ellie said, bringing Eponine over in his direction. 'He's a flirt, but he's harmless. And the older man who's ignoring us is Judge Pyotr Mishkin ... Did I say it correctly, Judge?'

'Yes, of course, young lady,' Judge Mishkin replied, his eyes not leaving the chessboard. 'Dammit, Puckett, what in the world are you trying to do with that knight? As usual, your play is either stupid or brilliant and I can't decide which.'

The judge eventually looked up, saw Eponine's red armband, and scrambled to his feet. 'I'm sorry, Miss, truly sorry,' he said. 'You are forced to endure enough without having to bear slights from this selfish old codger.'

A minute or two before the fireworks began, a large yacht could be seen approaching the picnic area from the western side of the lake. Brightly coloured lights and pretty girls decorated its long deck. The name *Nakamura* was emblazoned on the side of the boat. Above the main deck, Eponine recognised Kimberly Henderson standing beside Toshio Nakamura at the helm.

The party on the yacht waved at the people on the shore. Patrick Wakefield ran excitedly over to the table. 'Look, Mother,' he said, 'there's Katie on the boat.'

Nicole put on her glasses for a better look. It was indeed her daughter in a bikini bathing suit, waving from the deck of the yacht. 'That's just what we need,' Nicole mumbled to herself, as the first of the fireworks exploded above them, filling the dark sky with colour and light.

'Three years ago today,' Kenji Watanabe began his speech, 'a scouting party from the Pinta first set foot in this new world. None of us knew what to expect. All of us wondered, especially during the two long months that we spent eight hours each day in the somnarium, if anything resembling a normal life would ever be possible here in New Eden.

'Our early fears have not materialised. Our alien hosts, whoever they might be, have never once interfered with our lives. It may be true, as Nicole Wakefield and others have suggested, that they are continually observing us, but we do not feel their presence in any way. Outside our colony the Rama spacecraft is rushing toward the star we call Tau Ceti at an unbelievable speed. Inside, our daily activities are barely influenced by these remarkable external conditions of our existence.

'Before the days in the somnarium, while we were still voyagers inside the planetary system that revolves around our home star the Sun, many of us thought our "observation period" would be short. We believed that after a few months or so we would be returned to Earth, or maybe even our original destination Mars, and that this third Rama spacecraft would disappear in the distant reaches of space like its two predecessors. As I stand before you today, however, our navigators tell me that we are still moving away from our sun, as we have been for more than two and a half years, at approximately half the speed of light. If, indeed, it will be our good fortune someday to return to our own solar system, that day will be at least several years in the future.

'These factors dictate the primary theme of this, my last Settlement Day address. The theme is simple: fellow colonists, we must take full responsibility for our own destiny. We cannot expect the awesome powers that created our worldlet in the beginning to save us from our mistakes. We must manage New Eden as if we and our children will be here forever. It is up to us to ensure the quality of life here, both now and for our future generations.

'At present there are a number of challenges facing the colony. Notice that I call them challenges, not problems. If we work together we can meet these challenges. If we carefully weigh the long-term consequences of our actions, we will make the right decisions. But if we are unable to understand the concepts of "delayed gratification" and "for the good of all", then the future of New Eden will be bleak.

'Let me take an example to illustrate my point. Richard Wakefield has explained, both on television and in public fora, how the master scheme that controls our weather is based on certain assumptions about the atmospheric conditions inside our habitat. Specifically, our weather control algorithm assumes that both the carbon dioxide levels and the concentration of smoke particles are less than a given magnitude. Without understanding exactly how the mathematics works, you can appreciate that the computations governing the external inputs to our habitat will not be correct if the underlying assumptions are not accurate.

'It is not my intent today to give a scientific lecture about a very complex subject. What I really want to talk about is policy. Since most of our scientists believe that our unusual weather the last four months is a result of unduly high levels of carbon dioxide and smoke particles in the atmosphere, my government has made specific proposals to deal with these issues. All of our recommendations have been rejected by the Senate.

'And why? Our proposal to impose a gradual ban on fireplaces – which are totally unnecessary in New Eden in the first place – was called a "restriction on personal freedom". Our carefully detailed recommendation to reconstitute part of the GED network, so that the loss of plant cover resulting from the development of portions of Sherwood Forest and the northern grasslands could be offset, was voted down as well. The reason? The opposition argued that the colony cannot afford the task and, in addition, that the power consumed by the new segments of the GED network would result in painfully stringent electricity conservation measures.

'Ladies and gentlemen, it is ridiculous for us to bury our heads in the sand and hope that these environmental problems will go away. Each time that we postpone taking positive action means greater hardships for the colony in the future. I cannot believe that so many of you accept the opposition's wishful thinking, that somehow we will be able to figure out how the alien weather algorithms actually work and tune them to perform properly under conditions with higher levels of carbon dioxide and smoke particles. What colossal hubris!'

Nicole and Nai were both watching the reaction to Kenji's speech very carefully. Several of his supporters had urged Kenji to give a light, optimistic talk, without any discussion of me crucial issues. The governor, however, had been firm in his determination to make a meaningful speech.

'He's lost them,' Nai leaned over to whisper to Nicole. 'He's being too pedantic.'

There was definitely a restiveness in the stands, where approximately half the audience was now sitting. The Nakamura yacht, which had been anchored just offshore during the fireworks, had pointedly departed soon after Governor Watanabe began to speak.

Kenji switched topics from the environment to the retro-virus RV-41. Since this was an issue that aroused strong passions in the colony, the audience's attention increased markedly. The governor explained how the New Eden medical staff, under the leadership of Dr Robert Turner, had made heroic strides in understanding the disease but still needed to perform more extensive research to determine how to treat it. He then decried the hysteria that had forced the passage of a bill, even over his veto, requiring all those colonists with RV-41 antibodies in their system to wear red armbands at all times.

'Boo,' shouted a large group of mostly Oriental picnickers on the other side of the stands from Nicole and Nai.

'... These poor, unfortunate people face enough anguish ...' Kenji was saying.

'They're whores and fags,' a man cried from behind the Wakefield–Watanabe party. The people around him laughed and applauded.

'... Dr Turner has repeatedly affirmed that this disease, like most retro-viruses, cannot be transmitted except by blood and semen ...'

The crowd was becoming unruly. Nicole hoped that Kenji was paying attention and would cut his comments short. He had intended to discuss also the wisdom (or lack thereof) of expanding the exploration of Rama outside of New Eden, but he could tell that he had lost his audience.

Governor Watanabe paused a second and then issued an earsplitting whistle into the microphone. That temporarily quieted all the listeners. 'I have only a few more remarks,' he said, 'and they should not offend anyone ...

'As you know, my wife Nai and I have twin sons. We feel that we are richly blessed. On this Settlement Day I ask each of you to think about *your* children and envision another Settlement Day, a hundred or maybe even a thousand years into the future. Imagine that you are face-to-face with those whom you have begotten, your children's children's children. As you talk to them, and hold them in your arms, will you be able to say that you did everything reasonably possible to leave them a world in which they had a good chance of finding happiness?'

Patrick was excited again. Just as the picnic was ending, Max had invited him to spend the night and the next day at the Puckett farm. 'The new term at the university doesn't start until Wednesday,' the young man told his mother. 'May I go? Please?'

Nicole was still disturbed by the crowd's reaction to Kenji's speech and did not understand at first what her son was asking. After asking him to repeat his request she glanced at Max. 'You'll take good care of my son?'

Max Puckett grinned and nodded his head. Max and Patrick waited until the biots had finished cleaning up all the trash from the picnic and then headed for the train station together. Half an hour later they were in the Central City station waiting for the infrequent train that served the farming region directly. Across the platform from them, a group of Patrick's college classmates were entering the train to Hakone. 'You should come,' one of the young men yelled to Patrick. 'Free drinks for everybody all night long.'

Max watched Patrick's eyes follow his friends onto the train. 'Have you ever been to Vegas?' Max asked.

'No, sir,' he answered. 'My mother and father ...'

'Would you like to go?'

Patrick's hesitation was all Max needed. A few seconds later they boarded the train to Hakone with all the merrymakers. 'I'm not terribly fond of the place myself,' Max commented as they were riding. 'It seems too false, too superficial ... But it's certainly worth seeing and it's not a bad place to go for amusement when you're all alone.'

Slightly more than two and a half years earlier, very soon after the daily accelerations ended, Toshio Nakamura had correctly calculated that the colonists were likely to stay in New Eden and Rama for a long time. Before even the first meeting of the constitutional committee and its selection of Nicole des Jardins Wakefield as provisional governor, Nakamura had decided that he was going to be the richest and most powerful person in the colony. Building on the convict support base he had established during the cruise from Earth to Mars on the Santa Maria, he expanded his personal contacts and was able, as soon as banks and currency had been created in the colony, to begin building his empire.

Nakamura was convinced that the best products to sell in New Eden were those that provided pleasure and excitement. His first venture, a small gambling casino, was an immediate success. Next he bought some of the farmland on the east side of Hakone and built the colony's initial hotel, along with a second, larger casino just off the lobby. He added a small, intimate club, with female hostesses trained in the Japanese manner, and then a more raucous girlie club. Everything he did was successful. Parlaying his investments shrewdly, Nakamura was in a position, soon after Kenji Watanabe was elected governor, to offer to buy one fifth of Sherwood Forest from the government. His offer allowed the Senate to forestall higher taxes that would otherwise have been required to pay for the initial RV-41 research.

Part of the burgeoning forest was cleared and replaced with Nakamura's personal palace as well as a new, glittering hotel/casino, an entertainment arena, a restaurant complex, and several clubs. Consolidating his monopoly, Nakamura lobbied intensely (and successfully) for legislation that would limit gambling to the region around Hakone. His thugs then convinced all prospective entrepreneurs that nobody really wanted to enter the gambling business in competition with the 'king Jap.'

When his power was beyond attack, Nakamura permitted his associates to branch out into prostitution and drugs, neither of which were illegal in the New Eden society. Toward the end of the Watanabe term, when government policies began to conflict increasingly with his personal agenda, Nakamura decided he should control the government also. But he didn't want to be saddled with the boring job himself. He needed a dupe. So he recruited Ian Macmillan, the hapless ex-commander of the Pinta who had been an also-ran in the first gubernatorial election won by Kenji Watanabe. Nakamura offered Macmillan the governorship in exchange for the Scotsman's fealty.

There was nothing even remotely like Vegas anywhere else in the colony. The basic New Eden architecture designed by the Wakefields and The Eagle had all been spare, functional in the extreme, with simple geometries and plain facades. Vegas was overdone, garish, inconsistent – a mishmash of architectural styles. But it was interesting, and young Patrick O'Toole was visibly impressed when he and Max Puckett entered the outside gates of the compound.

'Wow,' he said, staring at the huge blinking sign above the portal.

'I don't want to diminish your appreciation any, my boy,' Max said, lighting a cigarette, 'but the power required to operate that one sign would drive almost a square kilometre of GEDs.'

'You sound like my mother and father,' Patrick replied.

Before entering the casino or any of the clubs, each person had to sign the master register. Nakamura missed no bets. He had a complete file on what every Vegas visitor had done every time he had come inside. That way Nakamura knew which portions of his business should be expanded *and*, more importantly, the special and favoured vice (or vices) of each of his customers.

Max and Patrick went into the casino. While they were standing by one of the two craps tables, Max tried to explain to the young man how the game worked. Patrick, however, could not keep his eyes off the cocktail waitresses in their scanty outfits.

'Ever been laid, boy?' Max asked.

'Excuse me, sir?' Patrick replied.

'Have you ever had sex – you know, intercourse with a woman?'

'No, sir,' the young man answered.

A voice inside Max's head told him that it was not his responsibility to usher the young man into the world of pleasure. The same voice also reminded Max that this was New Eden, and not Arkansas, or otherwise he would have taken Patrick over to the Xanadu and treated him to his first sex.

There were more than a hundred people in the casino, a huge crowd considering the size of the colony, and everyone seemed to be having fun. The waitresses were indeed dispensing free drinks just as fast as they could – Max grabbed a margarita and handed one to Patrick.

'I don't see any biots,' Patrick commented.

'There aren't any in the casino,' Max replied. 'Not even working the tables, where they would be more efficient than humans. The king Jap believes their presence inhibits the gambling instinct. But he uses them exclusively in all the restaurants.'

'Max Puckett. Well, I do declare.'

Max and Patrick turned around. A beautiful young woman in a soft, pink dress was approaching them. 'I haven't seen you in months,' she said.

'Hello, Samantha,' Max said after being uncharacteristically tongue-tied for several seconds.

'And who is this handsome young man?' Samantha said, batting her long eyelashes at Patrick.

'This is Patrick O'Toole,' Max answered. 'He is ...'

'Oh, my goodness,' Samantha exclaimed. 'I've never met one of the o-*rig*-inal colonists before.' She studied Patrick for a few seconds before continuing. 'Tell me, Mr O'Toole,' she said, 'is it really true that you went to sleep for *years*?'

Patrick nodded shyly.

'My friend Goldie says that the whole story is bullshit, that you and your family are really all agents for the IIA. She doesn't even believe we have ever left Mars orbit. Goldie says all that dreary time in the tanks was also part of the hoax.'

'I assure you, ma'am,' Patrick politely responded, 'that my family did indeed sleep for years. I was only six years old when my parents put me in a berth. I looked almost like I do now the next time I woke up.'

'Well, I find it *fas*-cinatin', even if I don't know what to make of it all ... So, Max, what are you up to? And by the way, are you going to officially introduce *me*?'

'I'm sorry. Patrick, this is Miss Samantha Porter from the great state of Mississippi. She works at the Xanadu ...'

'I'm a prostitute, Mr O'Toole. One of the very best ... Have you ever met a prostitute before?'

Patrick blushed. 'No, ma'am,' he said.

Samantha put a finger under his chin. 'He's cute,' she said to Max. 'Bring him over. If he's a virgin, I might do him for free.' She gave Patrick a small kiss on the lips and then turned around and departed.

Max couldn't think of anything appropriate to say after Samantha left. He thought about apologizing but decided it wasn't necessary. Max put his arm around Patrick and the two of them walked toward the back of the casino, where the higher stakes tables were cordoned off.

'All right, now, *yo*,' cried a young woman with her back toward them. 'Five and six makes a *yo*.'

Patrick glanced over at Max with surprise. 'That's Katie,' he said, hastening his step in her direction.

Katie was completely absorbed in the game. She took a quick drag from a cigarette, belted down the drink she was handed by the swarthy man on her right, and then held the dice high above her head. 'All the numbers,' she said, handing chips to the croupier. 'Here's twenty-six – plus five marks on the hard eight ... Now, be there, forty-four,' she said, flinging the dice against the opposite end of the table with a flick of her wrist. . '*Forty-four*,' the crowd around the table shouted in unison.

Katie jumped up and down in her place, gave her date a hug, quaffed another drink, and took a long, languorous pull from her cigarette.

'Katie,' Patrick said just as she was about to throw the dice again.

She stopped in mid-throw and turned around with a quizzical look on her face. 'Well, I'll be damned,' she said. 'It's my baby brother.'

Katie stumbled over to greet him as the croupiers and other players at the table yelled for her to continue the game.

'You're drunk, Katie,' Patrick said quietly while he was holding her in his arms.

'No, Patrick,' Katie replied, jerking herself backward toward the table. 'I am *flying*. I am on my own personal shuttle to the stars.'

She turned back to the craps table and raised her right arm high. 'All right, now, *yo*. Are you in there, *yo*?' she shouted.

2

Again the dreams came in the early morning hours. Nicole woke up and tried to remember what she had been dreaming, but all she could recall was an isolated image here and there. Omeh's disembodied face had been in one of her dreams. Her Senoufo great-grandfather had been warning her about something, but Nicole had not been able to understand what he was saying. In another dream Nicole had watched Richard walk into a quiet ocean just before a devastating wave came rushing toward the shore.

Nicole rubbed her eyes and glanced at the clock. It was just before four o'clock. *Almost the same time every morning this week*, she thought. *What do they mean?* She stood up and crossed into the bathroom.

Moments later she was in the kitchen dressed in her exercise clothes. She drank a glass of water. An Abraham Lincoln biot, who had been resting immobile against the wall at the end of the kitchen counter, activated and approached Nicole.

'Would you like some coffee, Mrs Wakefield?' he asked, taking the empty water glass from her.

'No, Linc,' she answered. 'I'm going out now. If anyone wakes up tell them I'll be back before six.'

Nicole walked down the hallway toward the door. Before leaving the house she passed the study on the right-hand side of the corridor. Papers were strewn all over Richard's desk, both beside and on top of the new computer he had designed and constructed himself. Richard was extremely proud of his new computer, which Nicole had urged him to build, even though it was unlikely that it would ever completely replace his favourite electronic toy, the standard ISA pocket computer. Richard had religiously carried the little portable since before the launch of the Newton.

Nicole recognised Richard's writing on some of the paper sheets but could not read any of his symbolic computer language. *He has spent many long hours in here recently*, Nicole thought, feeling a pang of guilt. *Even though he believes that what he's doing is wrong.*

At first Richard had refused to participate in the effort to decode the algorithm that governed the weather in New Eden. Nicole recalled their discussions clearly. 'We have agreed to participate in this democracy,' she had argued. 'If you and I choose to ignore its laws, then we set a dangerous example for the others ...'

'This is *not* a law,' Richard had interrupted her. 'It's only a resolution. And you know as well as I do that it's an incredibly dumb idea. You and Kenji both fought against it. And besides, aren't you the one who told me once that we have a *duty* to protest majority stupidity?'

'Please, Richard,' Nicole had replied. 'You may of course explain to everyone why you think the resolution is wrong. But this algorithm effort has now become a campaign issue. All the colonists know that we are close to the Watanabes. If you ignore the resolution it will look as if Kenji is purposely trying to undermine ...'

While Nicole was remembering her earlier conversation with her husband, her eyes roamed idly around the study. She was somewhat surprised, when her mind again focused on the present, to find that she was staring at three little figures on an open shelf above Richard's desk. *Prince Hal, Falstaff, TB,* she thought. *How long has it been since Richard entertained us with you?*

Nicole thought back to the long and monotonous weeks after her family had awakened from their years of sleep. While they were waiting for the arrival of the other colonists, Richard's robots had been their primary source of amusement. In her memory Nicole could still hear the children's mirthful laughter and see her husband smiling with delight. *Those were simpler, easier times,* she said to herself. She closed the door to the study and continued down the hall. *Before life became too complicated for play. Now your little friends just sit silently on the shelf.*

Out in the lane, underneath the streetlight, Nicole stopped for a moment beside the bicycle rack. She hesitated, looking at her bicycle, and then turned around and headed for the backyard. A minute later she had crossed the grassy area behind the house and was on the path that wound up Mount Olympus.

Nicole walked briskly. She was very deep in thought. For a long time she paid no attention to her surroundings. Her mind jumped around from subject to subject, from the problems besetting New Eden, to her strange dream patterns, to her anxieties about her children, especially Katie.

She arrived at a fork in the path. A small, tasteful sign explained that the path to the left led to the cable car station, eighty metres away, where one could ride to the top of Mount Olympus. Nicole's presence at the fork was electronically detected and prompted a Garcia biot to approach from the direction of the cable car.

'Don't bother,' Nicole shouted. 'I'm going to walk.'

The view became more and more spectacular as the switchbacks wound up the side of the mountain that faced the rest of the colony. Nicole paused at one of the viewpoints, five hundred metres in altitude and just under three kilometres walking distance from the Wakefield home, and looked out across New Eden. It had been a clear night, with little or no moisture in the air.

No rain today, Nicole thought, noting that the mornings were always damp with water vapor on the days that showers fell. Just below her was the village of Beauvois – the lights from the new furniture factory allowed her to identify most of the familiar buildings of her region, even from this distance. To the north the village of San Miguel was hidden behind the bulky mountain. But out across the colony, far on the other side of a darkened Central City, Nicole could discern the splashes of light that marked Nakamura's Vegas.

She was instantly plunged into a bad mood. *That damn place stays open all night long*, she grumbled silently, *using critical power resources and offering unsavoury amusements.*

It was impossible for Nicole not to think of Katie when she looked at Vegas. *Such natural talent*, Nicole remarked to herself, a dull heartache accompanying the image of her daughter. She could not help wondering if Katie was still awake in the glittering fantasy life on the other side of the colony. *And such a colossal waste*, Nicole thought, shaking her head.

Richard and she had discussed Katie often. There were only two subjects about which they fought – Katie and New Eden politics. And it wasn't entirely accurate to say they fought about politics. Richard basically felt that all politicians, except Nicole and *maybe* Kenji Watanabe, were essentially without principles. His method of discussion was to make sweeping pronouncements about the insipid goings-on in the Senate, or even in Nicole's own courtroom, and then to refuse to consider the subject anymore.

Katie was another issue. Richard always argued that Nicole was much too hard on Katie. *He also blames me*, Nicole thought as she gazed at the faraway lights, *for not spending enough time with her. He contends my jumping into colony politics left the children with only a part-time mother at the most critical period of their lives.*

Katie was almost never at home anymore. She still had a room in the Wakefield house, but she spent most of her nights in one of the fancy apartments that Nakamura had built inside the Vegas compound.

'How do you pay the rent?' Nicole had asked her daughter one night, just before the usual unpleasantness.

'How do you think, Mother?' Katie had answered belligerently. 'I work. I have plenty of time. I'm only taking three courses at the university.'

'What kind of work do you do?' Nicole had asked.

'I'm a hostess, an entertainer ... you know, whatever is needed,' Katie had answered vaguely.

Nicole turned away from the lights of Vegas. *Of course*, she said to, herself, *it is entirely understandable that Katie is confused. She never had any adolescence. But still, she doesn't seem to be getting any better* ... Nicole started walking briskly up the mountain again, trying to dispel her mounting gloom.

Between five hundred and a thousand metres in altitude, the mountain was covered with thick trees that were already five metres high. Here the path to the summit ran between the mountain and the outside wall of the colony in an extremely dark stretch that lasted for more than a kilometer. There was one break in the blackness, near the end, at a lookout point facing north.

Nicole had reached the highest point in her ascent. She stopped at the lookout and stared across at San Miguel. *There is the proof,* she thought, shaking her head, *that we have failed here in New Eden. Despite everything, there is poverty and despair in Paradise.*

She had seen the problem coming, had even accurately predicted it toward the end of her one-year term as provisional governor. Ironically, the process that had produced San Miguel, where the standard of living was only half what it was in the other three New Eden villages, had begun soon after the arrival of the Pinta. That first group of colonists had mostly settled in the south-east village, which would later become Beauvois, setting a precedent that was accentuated after the Nina reached Rama. As the free settlement plan was implemented, almost all the Orientals decided to live together in Hakone; the Europeans, white Americans, and middle Asians chose either Positano or what was left of Beauvois. The Mexicans, other Hispanics, black Americans, and Africans all gravitated toward San Miguel.

As governor, Nicole had tried to resolve the de facto segregation in the colony with a Utopian resettlement plan that would have allocated to each of the four villages racial percentages that mirrored the colony as a whole. Her proposal might have been accepted very early in the colony's history, especially right after the days in the somnarium, when most of the other citizens viewed Nicole as a goddess. But it was too late after more than a year. Free enterprise had already created gaps in both personal wealth and real estate values. Even Nicole's most loyal followers realised the impracticality of her resettlement concept at that point.

After Nicole's term as governor was completed, the Senate had resoundingly approved Kenji's appointment of Nicole as one of New Eden's five permanent judges. Nevertheless, her image in the colony suffered considerably when the remarks she had made in defence of the aborted resettlement plan became widely circulated. Nicole had argued that it was essential for the colonists to live in small, integrated neighborhoods to develop any real appreciation of racial and cultural differences. Her critics had thought that her views were 'hopelessly naive'.

Nicole stared at the twinkling lights of San Miguel for several more minutes as she warmed down from her strenuous climb up the mountain. Just before she turned around and headed back toward her home in Beauvois, she suddenly recalled another set of twinkling lights, from the town of Davos, in Switzerland, back on the planet Earth. During Nicole's last ski vacation, she and her daughter Genevieve had had dinner on the mountain above Davos and, after eating, had held hands in the bracing cold out on the restaurant balcony. The lights of Davos had shone like tiny jewels many kilometres below them. Tears came into Nicole's eyes as she thought of the grace and humour of her first daughter, whom she had not seen for so many years. *Thank you again, Kenji,* she mumbled as she began to walk, recalling the photographs her new friend had brought from Earth, *for sharing with me your visit with Genevieve.*

It was again black all around her as Nicole wound back down the side of the mountain. The outer wall of the colony was now on her left. She continued to think about life in New Eden. *We need special courage now,* she said to herself. *Courage, and values, and vision.* But in her heart she feared the worst was still ahead for the colonists. *Unfortunately,* she reflected gloomily, *Richard and I and even the children have remained outsiders, despite everything we have tried to do. It is unlikely that we will be able to change anything very much.*

Richard checked to ensure that the three Einstein biots had all properly copied the procedures and data that had been on the several monitors in his study. As the four of them were leaving the house, Nicole gave him a kiss.

'You are a wonderful man, Richard Wakefield,' she said.

'You're the only one who thinks so,' he replied, forcing a smile.

'I'm also the only one who knows,' Nicole said. She paused for a moment. 'Seriously, darling,' she continued, 'I appreciate what you're doing. I know ...'

'I won't be very late,' he interrupted. 'The three AIs and I have only two basic ideas left to try ... If we aren't successful today, we're giving up.'

With the three Einsteins following close behind him, Richard hurried down to the Beauvois station and caught the train for Positano. The train stopped momentarily by the big park on Lake Shakespeare where the Settlement Day picnic had been two months earlier. Richard and his supporting biot cast disembarked several minutes later at Positano and walked through the village to the southwest corner of the colony. There, after having their identification checked by one human and two Garcias, they were allowed to pass through the colony exit into the annulus that circumscribed New Eden. There was one more brief electronic inspection before they reached the only door that had been cut in the thick external wall surrounding the habitat. It swung open and Richard led the biots into Rama itself.

Richard had had misgivings when, eighteen months earlier, the Senate had voted to develop and deploy a penetrating probe to test the environmental conditions in Rama just outside their module. Richard had served on the committee that had reviewed the engineering design of the probe; he had been afraid that the external environment might be overwhelmingly hostile and that the design of the probe might not properly protect the integrity of their habitat. Much time and money had been spent guaranteeing that the boundaries of New Eden were hermetically sealed during the entire procedure, even while the probe was inching its way through the wall.

Richard had lost credibility in the colony when the environment in Rama had turned out to be not significantly different from that in New Eden. Outside there was permanent darkness, and some small, periodic variations in both atmospheric pressure and constituents, but the ambient Raman environment was so similar to the one in the colony that the human explorers did not even need their space suits. Two weeks after the first probe revealed the benign atmosphere in Rama, the colonists had completed the mapping of the area of the Central Plain that was now accessible to them.

New Eden and a second, almost identical rectangular construct to the south, which Richard and Nicole both believed to be a habitat for a second life-form, were enclosed together in a larger, also rectangular region whose extremely tall, metallic grey barriers separated it from the rest of Rama. The barriers on the north and south sides of this larger region were extensions of the walls of the habitats themselves. On both the east and west side of the two enclosed habitats, however, there were about two kilometres of open space.

At the four corners of this outer rectangle were massive cylindrical structures. Richard and the other technological personnel in the colony were convinced that the impenetrable corner cylinders contained the fluids and pumping mechanisms whereby the environmental conditions inside the habitats were maintained.

The new outer region, which had no ceiling except for the opposite side of Rama itself, covered most of the Northern Hemicylinder of the spacecraft. A large metal hut, shaped like an igloo, was the only building in the Central Plain between the two habitats. This hut was the control centre for New Eden and was located approximately two kilometers south of the colony wall.

When they exited from New Eden, Richard and the three Einsteins were headed for the control centre, where they had been working together for almost two weeks in an attempt to break into the master control logic governing the weather inside New Eden. Despite Kenji Watanabe's objection, the Senate had earlier appropriated funds for an 'all-out effort' by the colony's 'best engineers' to alter the alien weather algorithm. They had promulgated this legislation after hearing testimony from a group of Japanese scientists, who had suggested that stable weather conditions *could* indeed be maintained inside New Eden, even with the higher levels of carbon dioxide and smoke in the atmosphere.

It was an appealing conclusion for the politicians. If, perhaps, neither barring wood-burning nor deploying a reconstituted GED network were truly *required*, and it was only necessary to adjust a few parameters in the alien algorithm that had, after all, been initially designed with some assumptions that were no longer valid, well, then ...

Richard hated that kind of thinking. Avoid the issue as long as possible, he called it. Nevertheless, both because of Nicole's pleas and the total failure of the other colony engineers to understand any facet of the weather control process, Richard had agreed to tackle the task. He had insisted, however, that he work essentially alone, with only the Einsteins helping him.

On the day that Richard planned to make his last attempt to decode the New Eden weather algorithm, he and his biots stopped first near a site one kilometre away from the colony exit. Under the large lights Richard could see a group of architects and engineers working at a very long table.

'The canal will not be difficult to build – the soil is very soft.'

'But what about sewage? Should we dig cesspools, or haul the waste material back to New Eden for processing?'

'The power requirements for this settlement will be substantial. Not only the lighting, because of the ambient darkness, but also all the appliances. In addition, we're far enough away from New Eden that we must account for nontrivial losses on the lines ... Our best superconducting materials are too critical for this usage.'

Richard felt a mixture of disgust and anger as he listened to the conversations. The architects and engineers were conducting a feasibility study for an external village that could house the RV-41 carriers. The project, whose name was Avalon, was the result of a delicate political compromise between Governor Watanabe and his opposition. Kenji had permitted the study to be funded to show that he was 'open-minded' on the issue of how to deal with the RV-41 problem.

Richard and the three Einsteins continued down the path in a southerly direction. Just north of the control centre they caught up with a group of humans and biots headed toward the second habitat probe site with some impressive equipment.

'Hi, Richard,' said Marilyn Blackstone, the fellow Brit whom Richard had recommended to head the probe effort. Marilyn was from Taunton, in Somerset. She had received her engineering degree from Cambridge in 2232 and was extremely competent.

'How's the work coming?' Richard asked.

'If you have a minute, come take a look,' Marilyn suggested.

Richard left the three Einsteins at the control centre and accompanied Marilyn and her team across the Central Plain to the second habitat. As he was walking, he remembered his conversation with Kenji Watanabe and Dmitri Ulanov in the governor's office one afternoon before the probe project was officially approved.

'I want it understood,' Richard had said, 'that I am categorically against any and all efforts to intrude upon the sanctity of that other habitat. Nicole and I are virtually positive that it harbours another kind of life. There is no argument for penetration that is compelling.'

'Suppose it's empty,' Dmitri had replied. 'Suppose the habitat has been placed there for us, assuming we are clever enough to figure out how to use it.'

'Dmitri,' Richard had almost shouted, 'have you listened to anything that Nicole and I have been telling you all these months? You are still clinging to an absurd homocentric notion about our place in the universe. Because we are the dominant species on the planet Earth, you *assume* we are superior beings. We are *not*. There must be hundreds ...'

'Richard,' Kenji had interrupted him in a soft voice, 'we know your opinion on this subject. But the colonists of New Eden do not agree with you. They have never seen The Eagle, the octospiders, or any of the other wonderful creatures that you talk about. They want to know if we have room to expand...'

Kenji was already afraid then, Richard was thinking as he and the exploration team neared the second habitat. *He's still terrified that Macmillan will beat Ulanov in the election and turn the colony over to Nakamura.*

Two Einstein biots began working as soon as the team arrived at the probe site. They carefully installed the compact laser drill in the spot where a hole in the wall had already been created. Within five minutes the drill was slowly expanding the hole in the metal.

'How far have you penetrated?' Richard asked.

'Only about thirty-five centimeters so far,' Marilyn replied. 'We're taking it very slowly. If the wall has the same thickness as ours, it will be another three or four weeks before we are all the way through ... Incidentally, the spectrographic analysis of the wall parts indicates it's the same material as our wall.'

'And once you've penetrated into the interior?'

Marilyn laughed. 'Don't worry, Richard. We're following all the procedures you recommended. We will have a minimum of two weeks of passive observation before we continue to the next phase. We'll give *them* a chance to respond – if *they* are indeed inside.'

The scepticism in her voice was obvious. 'Not you too, Marilyn,' Richard said. 'What's the matter with everybody? Do you think Nicole and the children and I just made up all those stories?'

'Extraordinary claims require extraordinary evidence,' she replied.

Richard shook his head. He started to argue with Marilyn, but he realised he had more important things to do.

After a few minutes of polite engineering conversation, he walked back toward the control centre where his Einsteins were waiting.

The great thing about working with the Einstein biots was that Richard could try many ideas at once. Whenever he had a particular approach in mind, he could outline it to one of the biots and have complete confidence that it would be implemented properly. The Einsteins never suggested a new method themselves; however, they were perfect memory devices and often reminded Richard when one of his ideas was similar to an earlier technique that had failed.

All the other colony engineers attempting to modify the weather algorithm had tried first to understand the inner workings of the alien supercomputer that was located in the middle of the control centre. That had been their fundamental mistake. Richard, knowing a priori that the supercomputer's internal operation would be indistinguishable from magic to him, concentrated on isolating and identifying the output signals that emanated from the huge processor. After all, he reasoned, the basic structure of the process must be straightforward. Some set of measurements defines the conditions inside New Eden at any given time. The alien algorithms must use this measurement data to compute commands that are somehow passed to the huge cylindrical structures, where the actual physical activity takes place that leads to modifications in the atmosphere inside the habitat.

It did not take Richard long to draw a functional block diagram of the process. Because there were no direct electrical contacts between the control centre and the cylindrical structures, it was obvious that there was some kind of electromagnetic communication between the two entities. But what kind? When Richard scanned the spectrum to see at what wavelengths the communication was taking place, he found many potential signals.

Analyzing and interpreting those signals was a little like looking for a needle in a haystack. With the Einstein biots helping him, Richard eventually determined that the most frequent transmissions were in the microwave bandwidth. For a week he and the Einsteins catalogued the microwave exchanges, reviewing the weather conditions in New Eden both before and after, and trying to zero in on the specific parameter set modulating the strength of the response on the cylinder side of the interface. During that week Richard also tested and validated a portable microwave transmitter that he and the biots had constructed together. His goal was to create a command signal that would look as if it had come from the control centre.

His first serious attempt on the final day was a complete failure. Guessing that the accuracy of the timing of his transmission might be the problem, he and the Einsteins next developed a sequencing control routine that would enable them to issue a signal with femtosecond precision, so that the cylinders would receive the command within an extremely tiny time slice.

An instant after Richard had sent what he thought was a new set of parameters to the cylinders, a loud alarm sounded in the control centre. Within seconds a wraithlike image of The Eagle appeared in the air above Richard and the biots.

'Human beings,' the holographic Eagle said, 'be very careful. Great care and knowledge were used to design the delicate balance of your habitat. Do not change these critical algorithms unless there is a genuine emergency.'

Even though he was shocked, Richard acted immediately, ordering the Einsteins to record what they were seeing. The Eagle repeated his warning a second time and then vanished, but the entire scene was stored in the videorecording subsystems of the biots.

3

'Are you going to be depressed forever?' Nicole asked, looking across the breakfast table at her husband. 'Besides, thus far nothing terrible has happened. The weather has been fine.'

'I think it's better than before, Uncle Richard,' Patrick offered. 'You're a hero at the university – even if some of the kids do think you're part alien.'

Richard managed a smile. 'The government is not following my recommendations,' he said quietly, 'and is paying no heed whatsoever to The Eagle's warning. There are even some people in the engineering office who are saying I created the hologram of The Eagle myself. Can you imagine that?'

'Kenji believes what you told him, darling.'

'Then why is he letting those weather people continually increase the strength of the commanded response? They can't possibly predict the long-term effects.'

'What is it you're worried about, Father?' Ellie asked a moment later.

'Managing such a large volume of gas is a very complicated process, Ellie, and I have great respect for the ETs who designed the New Eden infrastructure in the first place. *They* were the ones who insisted the carbon dioxide and particulate concentrations must be maintained below specified levels. They must have known *some*thing.'

Patrick and Ellie finished their breakfasts and excused themselves. Several minutes later, after the children had left the house, Nicole walked around the table and put her hands on Richard's shoulders. 'Do you remember the night we discussed Albert Einstein with Patrick and Ellie?'

Richard looked at Nicole with a furrowed brow.

'Later on that night, when we were in bed, I commented that Einstein's discovery of the relationship between matter and energy was "horrible", because it led to the existence of nuclear weapons ... Do you remember your response?'

Richard shook his head.

'You told me that Einstein was a scientist, whose life work was searching for knowledge and truth. "There is no knowledge that is horrible," you said. "Only what other human beings *do* with that knowledge can be called horrible".'

Richard smiled. 'Are you trying to absolve me of responsibility on this weather issue?'

'Maybe,' Nicole replied. She reached down and kissed him on the lips. 'I know that you are one of the smartest, most creative human beings who ever lived and I don't like to see you carrying all the burdens of the colony on your shoulders.'

Richard kissed her back with considerable vigour. 'Do you think we can finish before Benjy wakes up?' he whispered. 'He doesn't have school today and he stayed up very late last night.'

'Maybe,' Nicole answered with a coquettish grin. 'We can at least try. My first case is not until ten o'clock.'

Eponine's senior class at Central High School, called simply 'Art and Literature,' encompassed many aspects of the culture that the colonists had at least temporarily left behind. In her basic curriculum, Eponine covered a multicultural, eclectic set of sources, encouraging the students to pursue independent study in any specific areas they found stimulating. Although she always used lesson plans and a syllabus in her teaching, Eponine was the kind of instructor who tailored each of her classes to the interests of the students.

Eponine herself thought *Les Misérables* by Victor Hugo was the greatest novel ever written, and the nineteenth century impressionist painter Pierre-Auguste Renoir, from her home city of Limoges, the finest painter who had ever lived. She included the works of both of her countrymen in the class, but carefully structured the rest of the source material to give fair representation to other nations and cultures.

Since the Kawabata biots helped her each year with the class play, it was natural to use the real Kawabata's novels *A Thousand Cranes* and *Snow Country* as examples of Japanese literature. The three weeks on poetry ranged from Frost to Rilke to Omar Khayyam. However, the principal poetic focus was Benita Garcia, not only because of the presence of the Garcia biots all over New Eden, but also because Benita's poetry and life were both fascinating to young people.

There were only eleven students in Eponine's senior class the year she was required to wear the red armband for having tested positive for RV-41 antibodies. The results of her test had presented the school administration with a difficult dilemma. Although the superintendent had courageously resisted the efforts of a strident group of parents, mostly from Hakone, who had demanded that Eponine be 'dismissed' from the high school, he and his staff had nevertheless bowed somewhat to the hysteria in the colony by making Eponine's senior course optional. As a result her class was much smaller than it had been in the previous two years.

Ellie Wakefield was Eponine's favourite student. Despite the great gaps in the young woman's knowledge due to her years asleep on the trip back to the solar system from the Node, her natural intelligence and hunger for learning made her a joy in the classroom. Eponine often asked Ellie to perform special tasks. On the morning that the class began its study of Benita Garcia, which was, incidentally, the same morning that Richard Wakefield had discussed with his daughter his worries about the weather control activities in the colony, Ellie had been asked to memorise one of the poems from Benita Garcia's first book, *Dreams of a Mexican Girl*, written when the Mexican woman was still a teenager. Before Ellie's recitation, however, Eponine tried to fire the imaginations of the young people with a short lecture on Benita's life.

'The *real* Benita Garcia was one of the most amazing women who ever lived,' Eponine said, nodding at the expressionless Garcia biot in the corner who helped her with all the routine chores of teaching. 'Poet, cosmonaut, political leader, mystic – her life was both a reflection of the history of her time and an inspiration for everyone.

'Her father was a large landowner in the Mexican state of Yucatan, far from the artistic and political heart of the nation. Benita was an only child, the daughter of a Mayan mother and a much older father. She spent most of her childhood alone on the family plantation that touched the marvellous Puuc Mayan ruins at Uxmal. As a small girl Benita often played among the pyramids and buildings of that thousand-year-old ceremonial centre.

'She was a gifted student from the beginning, but it was her imagination and élan that truly separated her from the others in her class. Benita wrote her first poem when she was nine, and by the age of fifteen, at which time she was in a Catholic boarding school in the Yucatecan capital of Merida, two of her poems had been published in the prestigious Diario de Mexico.

'After finishing secondary school, Benita surprised her teachers and her family by announcing that she wanted to be a cosmonaut. In 2129 she was the first Mexican woman ever admitted to the Space Academy in Colorado. When she graduated four years later, the deep cutbacks in space had already begun. Following the crash of 2134 the world plunged into the depression known as the Great Chaos and virtually all space exploration was stopped. Benita was laid off by the ISA in 2137 and thought that her space career was over.

'In 2144 one of the last interplanetary transport cruisers, the James Martin, limped home from Mars to Earth carrying mostly women and children from the Martian colonies. The spacecraft was barely able to make it into Earth orbit and it appeared as if all the passengers would die. Benita Garcia and three of her friends from the cosmonaut corps jerryrigged a rescue vehicle and managed to save twenty-four of the voyagers in the most spectacular space mission of all times ...'

Ellie's mind floated free from Eponine's narrative and imagined how exhilarating it must have been on Benita's rescue mission. Benita had flown her space vehicle manually, without a lifeline to mission operations on the Earth, and risked her life to save others. Could there be any greater commitment to one's fellow members of the species?

As she thought about Benita Garcia's selflessness, an image of her mother came into Ellie's mind. A montage of pictures of Nicole rapidly followed. First, Ellie saw her mother in her judge's robes speaking articulately before the Senate. Next Nicole was rubbing Ellie's father's neck in the study late at night, patiently teaching Benjy to read day after day, riding off beside Patrick on a bicycle for a game of tennis in the park, or telling Linc what to prepare for dinner. In the last image Nicole was sitting on Ellie's bed late at night, answering questions about life and love. *My mother is my hero*, Ellie suddenly realised. *She is as unselfish as Benita Garcia.*

'... Imagine, if you will, a young Mexican girl of sixteen, home from boarding school for vacation, climbing slowly up the steep steps of the Pyramid of the Magician in Uxmal. Below her, in the already warm spring morning, iguanas play among the rocks and the ruins.'

Eponine nodded at Ellie. It was time for her poem. She stood at her seat and recited.

> You have seen it all, old lizard
> Seen our joys, our tears,
> Our hearts full of dreams
> And terrible desires.
> And does it never change?
> Did my Indian mother's mother
> Sit here on these steps
> One thousand years ago
> And tell to you the passions
> She would not, could not share?
>
> At night I look unto the stars
> And dare to see myself among them.
> My heart soars above these pyramids,
> Flying free into the everything-can-be.
> Yes, Benita, the iguanas tell me,
> Yes to you and your mother's mother,
> Whose yearning dreams years ago
> Will now become fulfilled in you.

When Ellie had finished her cheeks were glistening from the silent tears that had fallen. Her teacher and the other students probably thought that she had been deeply moved by the poem and by the lecture on Benita Garcia. They couldn't have understood that Ellie had just experienced an emotional epiphany, that she had just discovered the true depth of her love and respect for her mother.

*

THE GARDEN OF RAMA

It was the last week of rehearsals for the school play. Eponine had picked an old work, *Waiting for Godot,* by the twentieth century Nobel laureate Samuel Beckett, because its theme was so germane to life in New Eden. The two main characters, both dressed in rags throughout, were played by Ellie Wakefield and Pedro Martinez, a handsome nineteen-year-old who had been one of the 'troubled' teenagers added to the colony contingent during the last months before launch.

Eponine could not have produced the play without the Kawabatas. The biots designed and created the sets and the costumes, controlled the lights, and even conducted rehearsals when she could not be present. The school had four Kawabatas altogether, and three of them were under Eponine's jurisdiction during the six weeks immediately preceding me play.

'Good work,' Eponine called out, approaching her students on the stage. 'Let's call it quits for today.'

'Miss Wakefield,' Kawabata Number 052 said, 'there were three places where your words were not exactly correct. In your speech beginning ...'

'Tell her tomorrow,' Eponine interrupted, gently waving the biot away. 'It will mean more to her then.' She turned to face the small cast. 'Are there any questions?'

'I know we've been through this before, Miss Eponine,' Pedro Martinez said hesitantly, 'but it would help me if we could discuss it again ... You told us that Godot was not a person, that he or it was actually a concept, or a fantasy ... that we were all waiting for something ... I'm sorry, but it's difficult for me to understand exactly what ...'

'The whole play is basically a commentary on the absurdity of life,' Eponine replied after a few seconds. 'We laugh because we see ourselves in those bums on the stage, we hear our words when they speak. What Beckett has captured is the essential longing of the human spirit. Whoever he is, Godot will make everything all right. He will somehow transform our lives and make us happy.'

'Couldn't Godot be God?' Pedro asked.

'Absolutely,' Eponine said. 'Or even the super advanced extraterrestrials who built the Rama spacecraft and oversaw The Node where Ellie and her family stayed. Any power or force or being that is a panacea for the woes of the world could be Godot. That's why the play is universal.'

'Pedro,' a demanding voice shouted from the back of the small auditorium, 'are you almost finished?'

'Just a minute, Mariko,' the young man answered. 'We're having an interesting discussion. Why don't you come join us?'

The Japanese girl remained in the doorway. 'No,' she said rudely. 'I don't want to – let's go now.'

Eponine dismissed the cast and Pedro jumped down from the stage. Ellie came over beside her teacher as the young man hurried toward the door.

'Why does he let her act that way?' Ellie mused out loud.

'Don't ask me,' Eponine replied with a shrug. 'I'm certainly no expert when it comes to relationships.'

That Kobayashi girl is trouble, Eponine thought, remembering how Mariko had treated both Ellie and her as if they were insects one night after rehearsal. *Men are so stupid sometimes.*

'Eponine,' Ellie asked, 'do you have any objections if my parents come to the dress rehearsal? Beckett is one of my father's favourite playwrights and...'

'That would be fine,' Eponine replied. 'Your parents are welcome anytime. Besides, I want to thank them ...'

'*Miss Eponine*,' a young male voice shouted from across the room. It was Derek Brewer, one of Eponine's students who had a schoolboy crush on her. Derek ran a few steps toward her and then shouted again. 'Have you heard the news?'

Eponine shook her head. Derek was obviously very excited. 'Judge Mishkin has ruled the armbands unconstitutional!'

It took a few seconds for Eponine to absorb the information. By then Derek was at her side, delighted to be the one giving her the news. 'Are ... are you certain?' Eponine asked.

'We just heard it on the radio in the office.'

Eponine reached for her arm and the hated red band. She glanced at Derek and Ellie and with one swift movement pulled the band off her arm and tossed it into the air. As she watched it arc toward the floor her eyes filled with tears.

'Thank you, Derek,' she said.

Within moments Eponine felt four young arms embracing her. 'Congratulations,' Ellie said softly.

4

The hamburger stand in Central City was completely run by biots. Two Lincolns managed the busy restaurant and four Garcias filled the customer orders. The food preparation was done by a pair of Einsteins and the entire eating area was kept spotless by a single Tiasso. The stand generated an enormous profit for its owner, because there were no costs except the initial building conversion and the raw materials.

Ellie always ate there on Thursday nights, when she worked at the hospital as a volunteer. On the day of what became known as the Mishkin Proclamation, Ellie was joined at the hamburger stand by her now bandless teacher Eponine.

'I wonder why I've never seen you at the hospital,' Eponine said as she took a bite of a French fried potato. 'What do you do there anyway?'

'Mostly I talk to the sick children,' Ellie replied. 'There are four or five with serious illnesses, one little boy even with RV-41, and they appreciate visits from humans. The Tiasso biots are very efficient at operating the hospital and performing all the procedures, but they are not that sympathetic.'

'If you don't mind my asking,' Eponine said after chewing and swallowing a bite of her hamburger, 'why do you do it? You are young, beautiful, healthy. There must be a thousand things you'd rather do.'

'Not really,' Ellie answered. 'My mother has a very strong sense of community, as you know, and I feel worthwhile after I talk to the kids.' She hesitated a moment. 'Besides, I'm socially awkward ... I'm physically nineteen or twenty, which is old for high school, but I have almost no social experience.' Ellie blushed. 'One of my girlfriends in school told me that the boys are convinced I'm an extraterrestrial.'

Eponine smiled at her protégée. *Even being an alien would be better than having RV-41*, she thought. *But the young men are really missing something if they're passing you by.*

The two women finished their dinner and left the small restaurant. They walked out into the Central City square. In the middle of the square was a monument, appropriately cylindrical in shape, that had been dedicated in the ceremonies associated with the first Settlement Day celebration. The monument was two and a half metres tall altogether. Suspended in the cylinder at eye level was a transparent sphere with a diameter of fifty centimetres. The small light at the centre of the sphere represented the Sun, the plane parallel to the ground was the ecliptic plane that contained the Earth and the other planets of the solar system, and the lights scattered throughout the sphere showed the correct relative positions of all the stars within a twenty-light-year radius of the Sun.

A line of illumination connected the Sun and Sirius, indicating the path that the Wakefields had taken on their odyssey to and from The Node. Another tiny line of light extended from the solar system along the trajectory that had been followed by Rama III since it had acquired the human colonists in Mars orbit. The host spacecraft, which was represented by a large, blinking red light, was currently in a position about one third of the way between the Sun and the star Tau Ceti.

'I understand the idea for this monument originally came from your father,' Eponine said as the two women stood beside the celestial sphere.

'Yes,' said Ellie, 'Father is really extremely creative where science and electronics are concerned.'

Eponine stared at the blinking red light. 'Does it bother him at all that we are going in a different direction, not toward Sirius or The Node at all?'

Ellie shrugged. 'I don't think so,' she said. 'We don't talk about it very much ... He told me one time that none of us was capable of understanding what the extraterrestrials were doing anyway.'

Eponine glanced around her in the square. 'Look at all the people, hurrying here and there. Most of them never even stop to see where we are ... I check our location at least once a week.' She was suddenly very serious. 'Ever since I was diagnosed with RV-41 I have had a compulsive need to know exactly where I am in the universe ... I wonder if that's part of my fear of dying.'

After a long silence Eponine put her arm on Ellie's shoulder. 'Did you ever ask The Eagle about death?' she said.

'No,' Ellie replied softly. 'But I was only four years old when I left The Node. I certainly had no concept of death.'

'When I was a child, I thought like a child,' Eponine said to herself. She laughed. 'What *did* you talk to The Eagle about?'

'I don't recall exactly,' Ellie said. 'Patrick told me that The Eagle especially liked to watch us play with our toys.'

'Really?' Eponine said. 'That's a surprise. From your mother's description I would have imagined The Eagle was much too serious to be interested in play.'

'I can still see him clearly in my mind's eye,' Ellie said, 'even though I was so young. But I can't remember what he sounded like.'

'Have you ever dreamed about him?' Eponine asked a few seconds later.

'Oh, yes. Many times. Once he was standing on top of a huge tree, looking down at me from the clouds.'

Eponine laughed again. Then she quickly checked her watch. 'Oh, my,' she said. 'I'm late for my appointment. What time are you due at the hospital?'

'Seven o'clock,' Ellie said.

'Then we'd better be on our way.'

When Eponine reported to Dr Turner's office for her biweekly checkup, the Tiasso in charge took her to the laboratory, obtained blood and urine specimens, and then asked her to take a seat. The biot informed Eponine that the doctor was 'running behind.'

A dark black man with sharp eyes and a friendly smile was also sitting in the waiting room. 'Hello,' he said when their eyes met, 'my name is Amadou Diaba. I'm a pharmacist.'

Eponine introduced herself, thinking that she had seen the man before.

'Great day, huh?' the man asked after a brief silence. 'What a relief to take off that cursed armband.'

Eponine now remembered Amadou. She had seen him once or twice in group meetings for the RV-41 sufferers. Someone had told Eponine that Amadou had contracted the retrovirus through a blood transfusion in the early days of the colony. *How many of us are there altogether?* Eponine thought. *Ninety-three. Or is it ninety-four? Five of whom caught the disease through a transfusion ...*

'It seems that big news always happens in pairs,' Amadou was saying. 'The Mishkin Proclamation was announced only hours before the leggie things were seen for the first time.'

Eponine looked at him quizzically. 'What are you talking about?' she asked.

'You haven't heard about the leggies yet?' Amadou said, laughing slightly. 'Where in the world have you been?'

Amadou waited a few seconds before launching into an explanation. 'The exploration team over at the other habitat has been in the process of widening their penetration site for the last few days. Today they were suddenly confronted by six strange creatures who crawled out of the hole that had been made in the wall. These leggies, as the television reporter called them, apparently live in the other habitat. They look like hairy golf balls attached to six giant, jointed legs, and they move very, very quickly ... They crawled all over the men, the biots, and the equipment for about an hour. Then they disappeared back into the penetration site.'

Eponine was about to ask some questions about the leggies when Dr Turner came out of his office. 'Mr Diaba and Miss Eponine,' he said. 'I have a detailed report for each of you. Who wants to be first?'

The doctor still had the most magnificent blue eyes. 'Mr Diaba was here before me,' Eponine replied. 'So ...'

'Ladies always go first,' Amadou interrupted. 'Even in New Eden.'

Eponine went into Dr Turner's inner office. 'So far, so good,' the doctor told her when they were alone. 'You definitely have the virus in your system, but there's no sign of any heart muscle deterioration. I don't know why for certain, but the disease definitely progresses more rapidly in some than others.'

How can it be, my handsome doctor, Eponine thought, that you follow all my health data so closely but never once have noticed the looks I've been giving you all this time?

'We'll keep you on the regular immune system medication. It has no serious side effects, and it may be partially responsible for our not seeing any evidence of the virus's destructive activities ... Are you feeling all right otherwise?'

They walked back out to the waiting room together. Dr Turner reviewed for Eponine the symptoms that would indicate the virus had moved to another stage in its development. While they were talking, the door opened and Ellie Wakefield came into the room. At first Dr Turner ignored her presence, but moments later he did an obvious double take.

'May I help you, young lady?' he said to Ellie.

'I've come to ask Eponine a question,' Ellie replied deferentially. 'If I'm disturbing you, I can wait outside.'

Dr Turner shook his head and then was surprisingly disorganised in his final comments to Eponine. At first she did not understand what had happened. But when Eponine started to leave with Ellie, she saw the doctor staring at her student. *For three years, Eponine thought, I have yearned to see a look like that in his eyes. I didn't think he was capable of it. And Ellie, bless her heart, missed it altogether.*

It had been a long day. Eponine was extremely tired by the time she walked from the station to her apartment in Hakone. The emotional release she had felt after removing her armband had passed. She was now a little depressed. Eponine was also fighting feelings of jealousy toward Ellie Wakefield.

She stopped in front of her apartment. The broad red stripe on her door reminded everyone that an RV-41 carrier lived inside. Thanking Judge Mishkin again, Eponine carefully pulled off the stripe. It left an outline on the door. *I'll paint it tomorrow*, Eponine thought.

Once in her apartment, she plopped down in her soft chair and reached for a cigarette. Eponine felt the surge of anticipatory pleasure as she put the cigarette in her mouth. *I never smoke at school in front of my students*, she rationalised. *I do not set a bad example for them. I smoke only here. At home. When I'm lonely.*

Eponine hardly ever went out at night. The villagers in Hakone had made it very clear to her that they didn't want her in their midst – two separate delegations had asked her to leave the village and there had been several nasty notes on her apartment door. But Eponine had stubbornly refused to move. Since Kimberly Henderson was never there, Eponine had much more living space than she would have been able to afford under normal circumstances. She also knew that an RV-41 carrier would not be welcomed in any neighbourhood in the colony.

Eponine had fallen asleep in her chair and was dreaming of fields of yellow flowers. She almost didn't hear the knock, even though it was very loud. She glanced at her watch – it was eleven o'clock. When Eponine opened the door, Kimberly Henderson entered the apartment.

'Oh, Ep,' she said, 'I'm so glad you're here. I need to talk to someone desperately. Someone I can trust.'

Kimberly lit a cigarette with a jerky motion and immediately burst into a rambling monologue. 'Yes, yes, I know,' Kimberly said, seeing the disapproval in Eponine's eyes. 'You're right, I'm stoned ... But I needed it ... Good old kokomo ... Artificial feelings of self-confidence are at least better than thinking of yourself as a piece of shit.'

She took a frantic drag and exhaled the smoke in short, choppy bursts. 'The asshole has really done it this time, Ep ... he's pushed me over the brink ... Cocky son of a bitch – thinks he can do whatever he wants ... I tolerated his affairs and even let some of the younger girls join me sometimes – the threesomes relieved the boredom ... but I was always ichiban, numero uno, or at least I thought I was ...'

Kimberly stubbed out her cigarette and began to wring her hands. She was close to tears. 'So tonight he tells me I'm moving ... "What," I say, "What do you mean?" ... "You're moving," he says ... No smile, no discussion ... "Pack your things," he says, "there's an apartment for you over behind Xanadu."

'"That's where the whores live," I answer ... He smiles a little and says nothing ... "That's it, I'm dismissed," I say ... I flew into a rage ... "You can't do this," I said ... I tried to hit him but he grabbed my hand and smacked me hard on the face ... "You'll do as I order," he says ... "I will *not*, you mother-fucker" ... I picked up a vase and threw it. It smashed into a table and shattered. In seconds two men had pinned my arms behind me ... "Take her away," the king Jap said.

'They took me to my new apartment. It was very nice. In the dressing room was a large box of rolled kokomo ... I smoked an entire number and was flying ... Hey, I said to myself, this is not so bad. At least I don't have to cater to Toshio's bizarre sexual desires ... I went over to the casino and was having fun, higher than a kite, until I saw them ... out in public in front of everybody else ... I went wild – hollering, screaming, cursing – I even attacked her ... Somebody hit me in the head ... I was down on the casino floor with Toshio bending over me ... "If you ever do anything like that again," he hissed, "you'll be buried beside Marcello Danni".'

Kimberly put her face in her hands and started to sob. 'Oh, Ep,' she said seconds later, 'I feel so helpless. I have nowhere to turn. What can I do?'

Before Eponine could say anything, Kimberly was talking again. 'I know, I know,' she said. 'I could go back to work at the hospital. They still need nurses, real ones – by the way, where is your Lincoln?'

Eponine smiled and pointed to the closet. 'Good for you.' Kimberly laughed. 'Keep the robot in the dark. Bring him out to clean the bathroom, wash the dishes, cook the meals. Then, whoosh, back in the closet ...' She chuckled. 'Their dicks don't work, you know. I mean, they have one, or sort of, anatomically perfect after all, but they don't get hard. One night when I was stoned and alone I had one mount me but he didn't know what I meant when I said "thrust". ... As bad as some men I've known.'

Kimberly jumped up and paced around the room. 'I'm not really sure why I came,' she said, lighting another cigarette. 'I thought maybe you and I ... I mean, we were friends for a while ...' Her voice trailed off. 'I'm coming down now, starting to feel depressed. It's awful, terrible. I can't stand it. I don't know what I expected, but you have your own life ... I'd better be going.'

Kimberly crossed the room and gave Eponine a perfunctory hug. 'Take care, now, OK?' Kimberly said. 'Don't worry about me, I'll be all right.'

It was only after the door closed and Kimberly left that Eponine realised she had not uttered one word while her ex-friend was in the room. Eponine was certain that she would never see Kimberly again.

5

t was an open meeting of the Senate and anyone in the colony could attend. The gallery had only three hundred seats and they were all filled. Another hundred people were standing along the walls and sitting in the aisles. On the main floor the twenty-four members of the New Eden legislative body were called to attention by their presiding officer, Governor Kenji Watanabe.

'Our budget hearings continue today,' Kenji said after striking the gavel several times to quiet the onlookers, 'with a presentation by the director of the New Eden Hospital, Dr Robert Turner. He will summarise what was accomplished with the health budget last year and present his requests for the coming year.'

Dr Turner walked to the rostrum and motioned to the two Tiassos who had been sitting beside him. The biots quickly set up a projector and a suspended cube screen for the visual material that would support Dr Turner's talk.

'We have made great strides in the last year,' Dr Turner began, 'both in building a solid medical environment for the colony and in understanding our nemesis, the RV-41 retrovirus that continues to plague our populace. During the last twelve months not only have we completely determined the life cycle of this complex organism, but also we have developed screening tests that allow us to identify accurately any and all persons who carry the disease ...

'Everyone in New Eden was tested during a three-week period that ended seven months ago. Ninety-six individuals in the colony were identified as being infected with the retrovirus at that time. Since the completion of the testing, only one new carrier has been found. There have been three deaths from RV-41 during the interim, so our current infected population is ninety-four ...

'RV-41 is a deadly retrovirus that attacks the muscles of the heart, causing them to atrophy irreversibly. Ultimately the human carrier dies. There is no known cure. We are experimenting with a variety of techniques for remitting the progression of the disease and have recently had some sporadic but inconclusive success. At this moment, until we score a significant breakthrough in our work, we must reluctantly assume that all individuals afflicted by the retrovirus will eventually succumb to its virulence.

'The chart I'm placing on the projection cube shows the various stages of the disease. The retrovirus is passed between individuals during a sharing of bodily fluids involving any combination of semen and blood. There is no indication that there is any other method of transfer. I repeat,' Dr Turner said, now shouting to be heard above the hubbub of the gallery, 'we have verified passage only where semen or blood is involved. We cannot categorically declare that other bodily fluids, such as sweat, mucus, tears, saliva, and urine, cannot be agents in the transfer, but our data thus far strongly suggests that RV-41 cannot be passed in these fluids.'

The talking in the gallery was now widespread. Governor Watanabe struck his gavel several times to quiet the room. Robert Turner cleared his throat and then continued. 'This particular retrovirus is very clever, if I can use that word, and especially well adapted to its human host. As you can see from the diagram on the cube, it is relatively benign in its first two stages, when it essentially just resides, without harm, inside the blood and semen cells. It may be that during this time it has already begun its attack on the immune system. We cannot say for certain, because during this stage all diagnostic data shows that the immune system is healthy.

'We do not know what triggers the decline of the immune system. Some inexplicable process in our complex bodies – and here is an area where we need to do more intensive research – suddenly signals to the RV-41 virus that the immune system is vulnerable and a mighty attack begins. The virus density in the blood and semen suddenly rises by several orders of magnitude: This is when the disease is the most contagious, and also when the immune system is overwhelmed.'

Dr Turner paused. He shuffled the papers from which he was reading before continuing. 'It is curious that the immune system *never* survives this attack. Somehow RV-41 knows when it can win, and never multiplies until that particular condition of vulnerability has been reached. Once the immune system is destroyed, the atrophy of the heart muscles begins and a predictable death follows.

'In the later stages of the disease, the RV-41 retrovirus disappears completely from the semen and the blood. As you can well imagine, this vanishing wreaks havoc with the diagnostic process. Where does it go? Does it "hide" in some way, become something else we have not yet identified? Is it supervising the gradual destruction of the heart muscles, or is the atrophy simply a side effect of the earlier attack on the immune system? All these questions we cannot answer at the present time.'

The doctor stopped momentarily for a drink of water. 'Part of our charter last year,' he then said, 'was to investigate the origin of this disease. There have been rumors that RV-41 was somehow indigenous to New Eden, perhaps placed here as some kind of diabolical extraterrestrial experiment. That kind of talk is complete nonsense. We definitely brought this retrovirus here from the Earth. Two passengers on the Santa Maria died from RV-41 within three months of each other, the first during the cruise from Earth to Mars. We can be certain, although this is hardly encouraging, that our friends and colleagues back on Earth are struggling with this devil as well.

'As for the origin of RV-41, here I can only speculate. If the medical data base that we had brought along from Earth had been an order of magnitude larger, then perhaps I would be able to identify its origin without any guessing ... Nevertheless, I will point out that the genome of this RV-41 retrovirus is astonishingly similar to a pathogen genetically engineered, by humans, as part of the vaccine envelope testing performed in the early years of the twenty-second century.

'Let me explain in more detail. After the successful development of preventive vaccines for the AIDS retrovirus, which was a horrible scourge during the last two decades of the twentieth century, medical technology took advantage of biological engineering to expand the range of all the available vaccines. Specifically, the biologists and the doctors purposely *engineered* new and more deadly retroviruses and bacteria to prove that a given vaccine class had a broad range of successful application. All this work was done, of course, under careful controls and at no risk to the populace.

'When the Great Chaos occurred, however, research monies were severely cut and many of the medical laboratories had to be abandoned. The dangerous pathogens stored in isolated spots around the world were presumably all destroyed. Unless ... and here is where my speculation enters into the explanation.

'The retrovirus that is afflicting us here in New Eden is amazingly similar to the AQT19 retrovirus engineered in 2107 at the Laffont Medical Laboratory in Senegal. It is possible, I will admit, that a naturally occurring agent could have a genome similar to AQT19, and therefore my speculation could be wrong. However, it is my belief that all the AQT19 in that abandoned lab in Senegal was *not* destroyed. I am convinced that this particular retrovirus somehow survived and mutated slightly in the subsequent century – perhaps by living in simian hosts – and eventually found its way into human beings. In that case, *we* are the ultimate creators of the disease that is killing us.'

There was an uproar in the gallery. Governor Watanabe again gaveled the audience to quiet, privately wishing that Dr Turner had kept his conjectures to himself. At this point the hospital director began his discussion of all the projects for which funding was needed in the coming year. Dr Turner was requesting an appropriation *double* what his department had had in the past year. There was an audible groan on the Senate floor.

The several speakers who immediately followed Robert Turner were really just window dressing. Everyone knew that the only other important speech of the day would be given by Ian Macmillan, the opposition candidate for governor in the elections three months hence. It was understood that both the current governor, Kenji Watanabe, and the choice of his political party,

Dmitri Ulanov, favoured a significant increase in the medical budget even if new taxes were required to finance it. Macmillan was reportedly opposed to any increase in Dr Turner's funds.

Ian Macmillan had been soundly defeated by Kenji Watanabe in the first general election held in the colony. Since that time, Mr Macmillan had moved his residence from Beauvois to Hakone, had been elected to the Senate from the Vegas district, and had taken a lucrative position in Toshio Nakamura's expanding business empire. It was the perfect marriage. Nakamura needed someone 'acceptable' to run the colony for him, and Macmillan, who was an ambitious man without any clearly defined values or principles, wanted to be governor.

'It is too easy,' Ian Macmillan began reading his speech, 'to listen to Dr Turner and then to open our hearts and purses, allocating funds for all his requests. That's what is wrong with these budget hearings. Each department head can make a strong case for his proposals. But by listening to each item separately, we lose sight of the larger picture. I do not mean to suggest that Dr Turner's programme is anything but worthy. However, I do think that a discussion of priorities is warranted at this time.'

Macmillan's speaking style had improved considerably since he had moved to Hakone. He had obviously been carefully coached. However, he was not a natural orator, so at times his practised gestures seemed almost comical. His primary point was that the RV-41 carriers made up less than five percent of the population of New Eden and the cost of helping them was incredibly expensive.

'Why should the rest of the citizens of the colony be forced to suffer deprivation for the benefit of such a small group?' he said. 'Besides,' he added, 'there are other, more compelling issues that require added monies, issues that touch each and every colonist and will likely impact our very survival.'

When Ian Macmillan presented his version of the story about the leggies that had 'rushed out' of the adjoining module in Rama and 'frightened' the colony exploration team, he made it sound as if their 'attack' had been the first foray in a planned interspecies war. Macmillan raised the spectre of the leggies being followed by 'more fearsome creatures' that would terrify the colonists, especially the women and children. 'Money for defence,' he said, 'is money spent for all of us.'

Candidate Macmillan also suggested that environmental research was another activity 'far more important for the general welfare of the colony' than the medical programme outlined by Dr Turner. He praised the work being done to control the environment, and envisioned a future where the colonists would have complete knowledge of the coming weather.

His speech was interrupted by applause from the gallery many times. When he did finally discuss the individuals suffering from RV-41, Mr Macmillan outlined a 'more cost-effective' plan to deal with 'their terrible tragedy'. 'We will create a new village for them,' he intoned, 'outside of New Eden, where they can live out their final days in peace.

'In my opinion,' he said, 'the RV-41 medical effort in the future should be restricted to isolating and identifying all the mechanisms by which this scourge is passed from individual to individual. Until this research is completed, it is in the best interests of everyone in the colony, including the unfortunate people who carry the disease, to quarantine the carriers so that there can be no more accidental contamination.'

Nicole and her family were all in the gallery. They had badgered Richard into coming, even though he disliked political gatherings. Richard was disgusted by Macmillan's speech. For her part, Nicole was frightened. What the man was saying had a certain appeal. *I wonder who is writing his material*, she thought at the conclusion of his speech. She chastised herself for having underestimated Nakamura.

Toward the end of Macmillan's oration, Ellie Wakefield quietly left her place in the gallery. Her parents were astonished, a few moments later, to see her down on the Senate floor approaching the rostrum. So were the other members of the gallery, who had thought that Ian Macmillan was the last speaker of the day. Everyone was preparing to depart. Most of them sat down again when Kenji Watanabe introduced Ellie.

'In our civics class in high school,' she started, her nervousness apparent in her voice, 'we have been studying the colony constitution and the Senate procedures. It's a little-known fact that *any* citizen of New Eden may address one of these open hearings ...'

Ellie took a deep breath before continuing. In the gallery, both her mother and her teacher Eponine leaned forward and grabbed the rail in front of them. 'I wanted to speak today,' Ellie said more forcefully, 'because I believe I have a unique point of view on this issue of the RV-41 sufferers. First, I am young, and second, until a little over three years ago I had never had the privilege of interacting with a human being other than my family.

'For both those reasons I treasure human life. My word was picked carefully. A treasure is something you value greatly. This man, this incredible doctor who works all day and sometimes all night to keep us healthy, obviously treasures human life as well.

'When he spoke earlier, Dr Turner didn't tell you why we should fund his programme, only *what* the disease was and *how* he would try to combat it. He assumed you all understood *why*. After listening to Mr Macmillan,' Ellie said, glancing at the previous speaker, 'I have some doubts.

'We must continue to study this horrible disease, until we can contain and control it, because a human life is a precious commodity. Each individual person is a unique miracle, an amazing combination of complex chemicals with special talents, dreams, and experiences. Nothing can be more important to the overall colony than an activity aimed at the preservation of human life.

'I understand from the discussion today that Dr Turner's programme is expensive. If taxes must be raised to pay for it, then perhaps each of us will have to do without some special item that we wanted. It is a small enough price to pay for the treasure of another human's company.

'My family and friends tell me sometimes that I am hopelessly naive. That may be true. But perhaps my innocence allows me to see things more clearly than other people can. In this case I believe there is only one question that needs to be asked. If you, or some member of your family, had been diagnosed with RV-41, would you support Dr Turner's programme? ... Thank you very much.'

There was an eerie silence as Ellie stepped away from the rostrum. Then thunderous applause erupted. Tears flowed in both Nicole's and Eponine's eyes. On the Senate floor Dr Robert Turner reached both his hands out to Ellie.

6

When Nicole opened her eyes Richard was sitting beside her on the bed. He was holding a cup of coffee. 'You told us to wake you at seven,' he said.

She sat up and took the coffee from him. 'Thank you, darling,' Nicole said. 'But why didn't you let Linc ...'

'I decided to bring your coffee myself ... There is news from the Central Plain again. I wanted to discuss it with you, even though I know how you dislike being jabbered at first thing in the morning.'

Nicole took a long, slow sip from her cup. She smiled at her husband. 'What's the news?' she said.

'There were two more leggie incidents last night. That makes almost a dozen this week. Our defence forces reportedly destroyed three leggies who were "harassing" the engineering crew.'

'Did the leggies make any attempts to fight back?'

'No, they didn't. At the first sound of gunfire they raced for the hole in the other habitat ... Most of them escaped, as they did the day before yesterday.'

'And you still think they're remote observers, like the spider biots in Rama One and Two?'

Richard nodded. 'And you can just imagine what kind of a picture the Others are developing of us. We fire on unarmed creatures without provocation ... we react in a hostile manner to what is certainly an attempt at contact...'

'I don't like it either,' Nicole said softly. 'But what can we do? The Senate explicitly authorised the exploration teams to defend themselves.'

Richard was about to reply when he noticed Benjy standing in the doorway. The young man was smiling broadly. 'May I come in, Mother?' he asked.

'Of course, dear,' Nicole replied. She opened her arms wide. 'Come give me a big birthday hug.'

'Happy birthday, Benjy,' Richard said as the boy, who was larger than most men, crawled onto the bed and embraced his mother.

'Thank you, Uncle Richard.'

'Are we still having a picnic in Sherwood Forest today?' Benjy asked slowly.

'Yes, indeed,' his mother answered. 'And then tonight we're having a big party.'

'Hooray,' Benjy said.

It was a Saturday. Patrick and Ellie were both sleeping late because they did not have classes. Linc served breakfast to Richard, Nicole, and Benjy while the adults watched the morning news on television. There was a short film of the most recent 'leggie confrontation' near the second habitat as well as comments from both of the gubernatorial candidates.

'As I have been saying for weeks now,' Ian Macmillan remarked to the television reporter, 'we must dramatically expand our defence preparations. We have finally started to upgrade the weapons available to our forces, but we need to move more boldly in this arena.'

An interview with the weather director concluded the morning news. The woman explained that the unusually dry and windy recent weather had been caused by a 'modelling error' in their computer simulation. 'All week long,' she said, 'we have been trying unsuccessfully to create rain. Now, of course, since it's the weekend, we have programmed sunshine ... But we promise it will rain next week.'

'They don't have the slightest idea what they're doing,' Richard grumbled, switching off the television. 'They're overcommanding the system and generating chaos.'

'What's k-oss, Uncle Richard?' Benjy asked.

Richard hesitated for a moment. 'I guess the simplest definition is the absence of order. But in mathematics, the word has a more precise meaning. It is used to describe unbounded responses to small perturbations.' Richard laughed. 'I'm sorry, Benjy. Sometimes I talk in scientific gobbledygook.'

Benjy smiled. 'I like it when you talk to me as if I'm nor-mal,' he said carefully. 'And some-times I do un-der-stand a lit-tle.'

Nicole seemed preoccupied while Linc was clearing the breakfast dishes off the table. When Benjy left the room to brush his teeth, she leaned toward her husband. 'Have you talked to Katie?' she asked. 'She didn't answer her phone yesterday afternoon or last night.'

Richard shook his head.

'Benjy will be crushed if she doesn't show up for his party. I'm going to send Patrick off to find her this morning.'

Richard stood up from his chair and walked around the table. He reached down and took Nicole's hand. 'And what about you, Mrs Wakefield? Have you scheduled some rest and relaxation anywhere in your busy programme? After all, it is the weekend.'

'I'm going by the hospital this morning to help train the two new paramedics. Then Ellie and I will leave here with Benjy at ten. On the way back I'll stop by the courtroom – I haven't even read the submitted briefs for the cases on Monday. I have a quick meeting with Kenji at two-thirty and my pathology lecture at three ... I should be home by four-thirty.'

'Which will give you just enough time to organise Benjy's party. Really, darling, you need to slow down. After all, you're not a biot.'

Nicole kissed her husband. 'You should talk. Aren't you the one who works twenty or thirty straight hours when you're involved in an exciting project?' She stopped a moment and became serious. 'All this is very important, darling ... I feel we're at a cusp in the affairs of the colony and that I really am making a difference here.'

'No question, Nicole. You are definitely having an impact. But you never have any time for yourself.'

'That's a luxury item,' Nicole said, opening the door to Patrick's room. 'To be savoured in my later years.'

As they emerged from the trees into the wide meadow, rabbits and squirrels scurried out of their way. On the opposite side of the meadow, quietly eating in the middle of a patch of tall purple flowers, was a young stag. He turned his head of new antlers toward Nicole, Ellie, and Benjy as they approached him, and then bounded away into the forest.

Nicole consulted her map. 'There should be some picnic tables here somewhere, right beside the meadow.'

Benjy was kneeling down over a group of yellow flowers that were full of bees. 'Ho-ney,' he said with a smile. 'Bees make ho-ney in their hives.'

After several minutes they located the tables and spread out a cloth on top of one of them. Linc had packed sandwiches – Benjy liked peanut butter and jelly best – plus fresh oranges and grapefruit from the orchards near San Miguel. While they were eating lunch, another family traipsed through the other side of the meadow. Benjy waved.

'Those peo-ple don't know it's my birth-day,' he said.

'But we do,' Ellie said, raising her cupful of lemonade to make a toast. 'Congratulations, brother.'

Just before they were finished eating, a small cloud passed overhead and the bright colours of the meadow momentarily dimmed. 'That's an unusually dark cloud,' Nicole commented to Ellie. Moments later it was gone and the grasses and flowers were again bathed in sunlight.

'Do you want your pudding now?' Nicole asked Benjy. 'Or do you want to wait?'

'Let's play catch first,' Benjy replied. He took the baseball equipment out of the picnic bag and handed a glove to Ellie. 'Let's go,' he said, running out into the meadow.

While her two children were throwing the baseball back and forth, Nicole cleaned up the remains of their lunch. She was about to join Ellie and Benjy when she heard the alarm on her wrist radio. She pressed the receive button and the digital time display was replaced with a television picture. Nicole turned up the volume so that she could hear what Kenji Watanabe had to say.

'I'm sorry to bother you, Nicole,' Kenji said, 'but we have an emergency. A rape complaint has been filed and the family wants an indictment immediately. It's a sensitive case, in your jurisdiction, and I think it should be handled now ... I don't want to say anything else on the line.'

'I'll be there in half an hour,' Nicole responded.

At first Benjy was crestfallen that his picnic was going to be cut short. However, Ellie convinced her mother that it was all right for her to stay in the forest with Benjy for another couple of hours. Just as she departed from the meadow, Nicole handed the map of Sherwood Forest to Ellie. At that moment another, larger cloud moved in front of the artificial New Eden sun.

There was no sign of any life at Katie's apartment. Patrick was temporarily stymied. Where should he look for her? None of his university friends lived in Vegas, so he really didn't know where to start.

He called Max Puckett from a public phone. Max gave Patrick the names, addresses, and phone numbers of three individuals he knew in Vegas. 'None of these people is the kind you would want to invite home to dinner with your parents, if you know what I mean,' Max said with a laugh, 'but they are all good-hearted and will probably help you find your sister.'

The only name Patrick recognised was Samantha Porter, whose apartment was just a few hundred metres from the phone booth. Even though it was the early afternoon, Samantha was still in her robe when she finally answered the door. 'I thought that was you, when I looked on the monitor,' she said with a sexy smile. 'You're Patrick O'Toole, aren't you?'

Patrick nodded and then shifted his feet uncomfortably during a long silence. 'Miss Porter,' he said at length, 'I have a problem ...'

'You're much too *young* to have a problem,' Samantha interrupted. She laughed heartily. 'Why don't you come inside and we'll talk about it?'

Patrick blushed. 'No, ma'am,' he said, 'it's not that kind of a problem ... I just can't find my sister Katie and I thought maybe you could help me.'

Samantha, who had half turned to lead Patrick into her apartment, turned back to stare at the young man. '*That's* why you've come to see me?' she said. She shook her head and laughed again. 'What a disappointment! I thought that you had come to fool around. Then I could tell everybody, once and for all, whether or not you really are an alien.'

Patrick continued to fidget in the entryway. After several seconds Samantha shrugged. 'I believe that Katie spends most of her time in the palace,' she said. 'Go to the casino and ask for Sherry. She'll know how to find your sister.'

'Yes, yes, Mr Kobayashi, I understand. *Wakarimasu*,' Nicole was saying to the Japanese gentleman in her office. 'I can appreciate what you must be feeling. You can be sure that justice will be done.'

She escorted the man into the waiting room, where he joined his wife. Mrs Kobayashi's eyes were still swollen from her tears. Their sixteen-year-old daughter Mariko was in the New Eden Hospital, undergoing a full medical examination. She had been badly beaten, but was not in critical condition.

Nicole called Dr Turner after she finished talking to the Kobayashis. 'There's fresh semen in the girl's vagina,' the doctor said, 'and bruises on almost every square centimetre of her body. She's an emotional wreck as well – rape is definitely a possibility.'

Nicole sighed. Mariko Kobayashi had named Pedro Martinez, the young man who had starred with Ellie in the school play, as the rapist. Could it be possible? Nicole rolled her chair across the floor of her office and accessed the colony data base through her computer.

MARTINEZ, PEDRO ESCOBAR ... born 26 May 2228, Managua, Nicaragua ... mother unwed, Maria Escobar, maid, domestic, often unemployed ... father probably Ramon Martinez, black dockworker from Haiti ... six half brothers and sisters, all younger ... convicted for selling kokomo, 2241, 2242 ... rape, 2243 ... eight months Managua Correction Home ... model prisoner ... transfer to Covenant House in Mexico City, 2244 ... IE 1.86, SC 52.

Nicole read the short computer entry twice before calling Pedro into her office. He sat down, as Nicole suggested, and then stared at the floor. A Lincoln biot stood in the corner throughout the interview and carefully recorded the conversation.

'Pedro,' Nicole said softly. There was no response. He did not even look up. 'Pedro Martinez,' she repeated more forcefully, 'do you understand that you have been accused of raping Mariko Kobayashi last night? I'm sure I don't need to explain to you that this is a very serious accusation ... You are being given a chance now to respond to her charges.'

Pedro still did not say anything. 'In New Eden,' Nicole continued at length, 'we have a judicial system that may be different from the one you experienced in Nicaragua. Here criminal cases cannot proceed to indictment unless a judge, after examining the facts, believes that there is sufficient reason for indictment. That is why I am talking to you.'

After a long silence the young man, without looking up at all, mumbled something that was inaudible.

'What?' Nicole asked.

'She's lying,' Pedro said, much louder. 'I don't know why, but Mariko's lying.'

'Would you like to tell me your version of what happened?'

'What difference would it make? Nobody is going to believe me anyway.'

'Pedro, listen to me. If, on the basis of an initial investigation, my court concludes that there is insufficient reason to proceed with the prosecution, your case can be dismissed. Of course, the seriousness of this charge demands a very thorough investigation, which means you will have to make a complete statement and answer some very tough questions.'

Pedro Martinez lifted his head and stared at Nicole with sorrowful eyes.

'Judge Wakefield,' he said quietly, 'Mariko and I *did* have sex last night ... but it was her idea. She thought it would be fun to go into the forest ...' The young man stopped talking and looked back down at the floor.

'Had you had intercourse with Mariko before?' Nicole asked after several seconds.

'Only once – about ten days ago,' Pedro answered.

'Pedro, was your lovemaking last night ... was it extremely physical?'

Tears eased out of Pedro's eyes and rolled onto his cheeks. 'I did not beat her,' he said passionately. 'I would never have hurt her.'

As he spoke there was a strange sound in the distance, like the cracking of a long whip, except much deeper in tone.

'What was that?' Nicole wondered out loud.

'Sounded like thunder,' Pedro remarked.

The thunder could also be heard in the village of Hakone, where Patrick was sitting in a luxurious suite in Nakamura's palace, talking to his sister Katie. She was dressed in an expensive blue silk lounging outfit.

Patrick ignored the unexplained noise. He was angry. 'Are you telling me that you won't even *try* to make it to Benjy's party tonight? What am I supposed to tell Mother?'

'Tell her anything you want,' Katie said. She took a cigarette from her case and placed it in her mouth. 'Tell her you couldn't find me.' She lit the cigarette with a gold lighter and blew the smoke in her brother's direction. He tried to wave it away with his hand.

'Come on, baby brother,' Katie said with a laugh. 'It won't kill you.'

'Not immediately, anyway,' he answered.

'Look, Patrick,' Katie said, standing up and starting to pace around the suite, 'Benjy's an idiot, a moron. We've never been very close. He won't even realise that I'm not there unless someone mentions it to him.'

'You're wrong, Katie. He's more intelligent than you think. He asks about you all the time.'

'That's crap, baby brother,' Katie replied. 'You're just saying it to make me feel guilty ... Look, I'm not coming. I mean, I might consider it if it were just you and Benjy and Ellie – although she's been a pain in the ass ever since her "wonderful" speech. But you know what it's like for me around Mother. She's on my case all the time.'

'She's worried about you, Katie.'

Katie laughed nervously and took a deep drag to finish her cigarette. 'Sure she is, Patrick. All she's really worried about is whether I'll embarrass the family.'

Patrick stood up to leave. 'You don't have to go now,' Katie said. 'Why don't you stay for a while? I'll put on some clothes and we'll go down to the casino. Remember how much fun we used to have together?'

Katie started toward the bedroom. 'Are you using drugs?' Patrick asked suddenly.

She stopped and stared at her brother. 'Who wants to know?' Katie said defiantly. 'You or Madame Cosmonaut Doctor Governor Judge Nicole des Jardins Wakefield?'

'I want to know,' Patrick said quietly.

Katie walked across the room and put her hands on Patrick's cheeks. 'I'm your sister and I love you,' she said. 'Nothing else is important.'

The dark clouds had all gathered over the small rolling hills of Sherwood Forest. Wind was sweeping through the trees, blowing Ellie's hair behind her. There was a bolt of lightning and an almost simultaneous crack of thunder.

Benjy recoiled and Ellie pulled him close beside her. 'According to the map,' she said, 'we're only about one kilometer from the edge of the forest.'

'How far is that?' Benjy asked.

'If we walk quickly,' Ellie shouted above the wind, 'then we can make it out in about ten minutes.' She grabbed Benjy's hand and pulled him alongside her on the path.

An instant later lightning split one of the trees beside them and a thick branch fell across the path. The branch struck Benjy on the back and knocked him down. He fell mostly on the path, but his head landed in the green plants and ivy at the base of the trees in the forest. The noise from the thunder nearly deafened him.

He lay on the forest floor for several seconds, trying to understand what had happened to him. At length he struggled to his feet. 'Ellie,' he said, looking at the prostrate form of his sister on the other side of the path. Her eyes were closed.

'*Ellie!*' Benjy now screamed, half walking, half crawling over to her side. He grabbed her by the shoulders and shook her lightly. Her eyes did not open. The swelling on her forehead, above and to the side of her right eye, was already the size of a large orange.

'What am I go-ing to do?' Benjy said out loud. He smelled smoke and glanced up into the trees at almost the same moment. He saw fire leaping from branch to branch, driven by the wind. There was another bolt of lightning, more thunder. In front of him, down the trail in the direction that Ellie and he had been going, Benjy could see that a larger fire was sweeping through the trees on both sides of the path. He started to panic.

He held his sister in his arms and slapped her lightly on the face. 'Ellie,' he said, 'please, please wake up.' She did not stir. The fire around him was spreading rapidly. Soon this entire portion of the forest would be an inferno.

Benjy was terrified. He tried to lift Ellie up, but stumbled and fell in the process. 'No, no, no,' he shouted, standing again and bending to lift Ellie to his shoulders.

The smoke was getting heavy. Benjy moved slowly down the path, away from the fire, with Ellie on his back.

He was exhausted when he reached the meadow. He gently placed Ellie on one of the concrete tables and sat on a bench himself. The fire was raging out of control on the north side of the meadow. *What do I do now?* he thought. His eye fell on the map sticking out of Ellie's shirt pocket. *That can help me.* He grabbed the map and looked at it. At first he could not understand any of it and he began to panic again.

Relax, Benjy, he heard his mother say in a soothing tone. *It's a little hard, but you can do it. Maps are very important. They tell us where to go ... Now, the first thing always is to orient the map so that you can read the writing. See. That's right. Most of the time the up direction is called north. Good. This is a map of Sherwood Forest ...*

Benjy turned the map over in his hands until the letters were all right side up. The lightning and thunder continued. A sudden change in the wind pushed smoke into his lungs and he coughed. He tried to read the words on the map.

Again he heard his mother's voice. *If you don't recognise the word at first, then take each letter and sound it out very slowly. Next let all the sounds fall together until it makes a word you understand.*

Benjy glanced at Ellie on the table. 'Wake up, oh, please wake up, Ellie,' he said. 'I need your help.' Still she did not move.

He bent down over the map and struggled to concentrate. With painstaking deliberation Benjy sounded out all the letters, over and over, until he had convinced himself that the green patch on the map was the meadow where he was sitting. *The white lines are the paths,* he said to himself. *There are three white lines running into the green patch.*

Benjy looked up from the map, counted the three paths leading out of the meadow, and felt a surge of self-confidence. Moments later, however, a gust of wind carried cinders across the meadow and ignited the trees on the southern side. Benjy moved quickly. *I must go,* he said, again lifting Ellie onto his back.

He now knew that the main fire was in the northern portion of the map, toward the village of Hakone. Benjy stared again at the paper in his hands. *So I must stay on white lines in the bottom part,* he thought.

The young man trundled down the path as another tree exploded in fire far above his head. His sister was over his shoulder, and the lifesaving map was in his right hand. Benjy stopped to look at the map every ten steps, each time verifying that he was still headed in the correct direction. When he finally came to a major trail junction, Benjy placed Ellie gingerly on the ground and traced the white lines on the map with his finger. After a minute he smiled broadly, picked up his sister again, and headed down the trail leading to the village of Positano. Lightning flashed one more time, the thunder boomed, and a drenching shower began to fall on Sherwood Forest.

7

Several hours later, Benjy was sleeping peacefully in his room. Meanwhile, across the colony, the New Eden hospital was a madhouse. Humans and biots were dashing about, gurneys with bodies were standing in the halls, patients were shouting in agony. Nicole was talking on the phone with Kenji Watanabe. 'We need every Tiasso in the colony sent here as quickly as possible. Try to replace those that are doing geriatric or infant care with a Garcia, or even an Einstein. Have humans staff the village clinics. The situation is very serious.'

She could barely hear what Kenji was saying above the noise in the hospital. 'Bad, really bad,' she said in response to his question. 'Twenty-seven admitted so far, four dead that we know of. The whole Nara area – that enclave of Japanese-style wood houses that is out behind Vegas, surrounded by the forest – is a disaster. The fire happened too fast. The people panicked.'

'Dr Wakefield, Dr Wakefield. Please come to Number 204 immediately.' Nicole hung up the phone and raced down the hall. She bounded up the stairs to the second floor. The man dying in room 204 was an old friend, a Korean, Kim Lee, who had been Nicole's liaison with the Hakone community during the time that she was provisional governor.

Mr Kim had been one of the first to build a new home in Nara. During the fire he had rushed into his burning house to save his seven-year-old son. The son would live, for Mr Kim had protected him carefully while he had walked through the flames. But Kim Lee himself had suffered third-degree burns over most of his body.

Nicole passed Dr Turner in the corridor. 'I don't think we can do anything for that friend of yours in 204,' he said. 'I'd like your opinion. Call me down in the emergency room. They just brought in another critical who was trapped in her house.'

Nicole took a deep breath and slowly opened the door to the room. Mr Kim's wife, a pretty Korean woman in her mid-thirties, was sitting quietly in the corner. Nicole walked over and embraced her. While Nicole was comforting Mrs Kim, the Tiasso who was monitoring all of Mr Kim's data brought over a set of charts. The man's condition was indeed hopeless. When Nicole glanced up from her reading, she was surprised to see her daughter Ellie, a large bandage on the right side of her head, standing beside Mr Kim's bed. Ellie was holding the dying man's hand.

'Nicole,' Mr Kim said in an agonised whisper as soon as he recognised her. His face was nothing but blackened skin. Even speaking one word was painful. 'I want to die,' the man said, nodding at his wife in the corner.

Mrs Kim stood up and approached Nicole. 'My husband wants me to sign the euthanasia papers,' she said. 'But I am unwilling unless you can tell me that there is absolutely no chance he can ever be happy again.' She started to cry but stopped herself.

Nicole hesitated for a moment. 'I cannot tell you that, Mrs Kim,' Nicole said grimly. She glanced back and forth between the burned man and his wife. 'What I can tell you is that he will probably die sometime in the next twenty-four hours and will suffer ceaselessly until his death. If a medical miracle occurs and he survives, he'll be seriously disfigured and debilitated for the rest of his life.'

'I want to die now,' Mr Kim repeated with effort.

Nicole sent the Tiasso for the euthanasia documents. The papers required signatures from the attending physician, the spouse, and the individual himself if, in the opinion of the doctor, he was competent to make his own decisions. While the Tiasso was gone, Nicole motioned to Ellie to meet her out in the hall.

'What are you doing here?' Nicole said quietly to Ellie when they were out of earshot. 'I told you to stay at home and rest. You had a bad concussion.'

'I'm all right, Mother,' Ellie said. 'Besides, when I heard that Mr Kim was badly burned, I wanted to do something to help. He was such a good friend back in the early days.'

'He's in terrible shape,' Nicole said, shaking her head. 'I can't believe he's still alive.'

Ellie reached out and touched her mother on the forearm. 'He wants his death to be useful,' she said. 'Mrs Kim talked to me about it. I've already sent for Amadou, but I need for you to talk to Dr Turner.'

Nicole stared at her daughter. 'What in the world are you talking about?'

'Don't you remember Amadou Diaba ...? Eponine's friend, the Nigerian pharmacist with the Senoufo grandmother. He's the one who caught RV-41 from a blood transfusion. . , . Anyway, Eponine told me that his heart is rapidly deteriorating.'

Nicole was silent for several seconds. She could not believe what she was hearing. 'You want me,' she said finally, 'to ask Dr Turner to perform a *manual* heart transplant, right now, in the middle of this crisis?'

'If he decides now, it can be done later tonight, can't it? Mr Kim's heart can be kept healthy at least that long.'

'Look, Ellie,' Nicole said, 'we don't even know ...'

'I already checked,' Ellie interrupted. 'One of the Tiassos verified that Mr Kim would be an acceptable donor.'

Nicole shook her head again. 'All right, all right,' she said. 'I'll think about it. Meanwhile, I want you to lie down and rest. A concussion is not a trivial injury.'

'You're asking me to do what?' an incredulous Dr Robert Turner said to Nicole.

'Now, Dr Turner,' Amadou said in his British accent, 'it is not Dr Wakefield who is really making the request. It is I. I beseech you to perform this operation. And please do not consider it risky. You have yourself told me that I will not live more than three months longer. I know full well that I may die on the operating table. But if I survive, according to the statistics you showed me, I have a fifty-fifty chance of living eight more years. I could even marry and have a child.'

Dr Turner spun around and glanced at the clock on his office wall. 'Forget for a moment, Mr Diaba, that it is past midnight and I have been working nine hours straight with burn victims. Consider what you are asking. I have not performed a heart transplant for *five* years. And I have never *ever* done one without being supported by the finest cardiological staff and equipment on the planet Earth. All the surgical work, for example, was always done by robots.'

'I understand all that, Dr Turner. But it is not really germane. I will certainly die without the operation. There will almost certainly not be another donor in the near future. Besides, Ellie told me that you have recently been reviewing all the heart transplant procedures, as part of your work in preparing your budget request for new equipment ...'

Dr Turner flashed a quizzical look at Ellie. 'My mother told me about your thorough preparation, Dr Turner. I hope you're not upset that I said something to Amadou.'

'I will be pleased to assist you in any way I can,' Nicole added. 'Although I have never done any heart surgery myself, I did complete my residency at a cardiological institute.'

Dr Turner looked around the room, first at Ellie, then at Amadou and Nicole. 'Then that settles it, I guess. I don't see where you've given me much choice.'

'You'll do it?' Ellie exclaimed with youthful excitement.

'I will try,' the doctor answered. He walked over to Amadou Diaba and extended both his hands. 'You do know, don't you, that there is very little chance you will ever wake up?'

'Yes, sir, Dr Turner. But very little chance is better than none ... I thank you.'

Dr Turner turned to Nicole. 'I'll meet you in my office for a procedure review in fifteen minutes. And by the way, Dr Wakefield, will you please have a Tiasso bring us a fresh pot of coffee?'

*

Preparing for the transplant operation brought back memories that Dr Robert Turner had buried in the recesses of his mind. Once or twice he even imagined for several seconds that he had actually returned to the Dallas Medical Centre. He remembered mostly how happy he had been in those distant days on another world. He had loved his work; he had loved his family. His life had been almost perfect.

Drs. Turner and Wakefield carefully wrote down the exact sequence of events that they would follow before they began the procedure. Then, during the operation itself, they stopped to check with each other after each major segment was completed. No untoward events occurred at any time during the procedure. When Dr Turner removed Amadou's old heart, he turned it over so that Nicole and Ellie (she had insisted on staying in case there was anything she could do to help) could see the badly atrophied muscles. The man's heart was a disaster. Amadou would probably have died in less than a month.

An automatic pump kept the patient's blood circulating while the new heart was 'hooked up' to all the principal arteries and veins. This was the most difficult and dangerous phase of the operation. In Dr Turner's experience, this segment had never ever been performed by human hands.

Dr Turner's surgical skills had been finely tuned by the many manual operations he had conducted during his three years in New Eden. He surprised even himself with the ease with which he connected the new heart to Amadou's critical blood vessels.

Toward the end of the procedure, when all of the dangerous phases had been completed, Nicole offered to perform the few remaining tasks. But Dr Turner shook his head. Despite the fact that it was almost dawn in the colony, he was determined to finish the operation himself.

Was it the extreme fatigue that caused Dr Turner's eyes to play tricks on him during the final minutes of the operation? Or could it perhaps have been the surge of adrenaline that accompanied his realization that the procedure was going to be successful? Whatever the cause, during the terminal stages of the operation, Robert Turner periodically witnessed remarkable changes in the face of Amadou Diaba. Several times his patient's face slowly altered before his eyes, the features of Amadou becoming those of Carl Tyson, the young black man that Dr Turner had murdered in Dallas. Once, after finishing a stitch, Dr Turner glanced up at Amadou and was frightened by Carl Tyson's cocky grin. The doctor blinked, and looked again, but it was only Amadou Diaba on the operating table.

After this phenomenon had occurred several times, Dr Turner asked Nicole if she had noticed anything unusual about Amadou's face. 'Nothing but his smile,' she replied. 'I've never seen anyone smile like that under anesthesia.'

When the operation was over and the Tiassos reported that all of the patient's vital signs were excellent, Dr Turner, Nicole, and Ellie were exultant despite their exhaustion. The doctor invited the two women to join him in his office, for one final celebratory cup of coffee. At that moment, he didn't yet realise that he was going to propose to Ellie.

Ellie was stunned. She just stared at the doctor. He glanced at Nicole and then returned his gaze to Ellie. 'I know it's sudden,' Dr Turner said. 'But there's no doubt in my mind. I have seen enough. I love you. I want to marry you. The sooner the better.'

The room was absolutely quiet for almost a minute. During the silence, the doctor walked over to his office door and locked it. He even disconnected his phone. Ellie started to speak. 'No,' he said to her with passion, 'don't say anything yet. There's something else I must do first.'

He sat down in his chair and took a deep breath. 'Something that I should have done long ago,' he said quietly. 'Besides, you both deserve to know the whole truth about me.'

Tears welled up in Dr Turner's eyes even before he began to tell the story. His voice broke the first time he spoke, but he then collected himself and eased into the narrative.

'I was thirty-three years old and blindly, outrageously happy. I was already one of the leading cardiac surgeons in America and I had a beautiful, loving wife with two daughters, aged three and two. We lived in a mansion with a swimming pool inside a country club community about forty kilometres north of Dallas, Texas.

'One night when I came home from the hospital – it was very late, for I had supervised an unusually delicate open heart procedure – I was stopped at the gate of our community by the security guards. They acted rattled, as if they didn't know what to do, but after a phone call and some peculiar glances in my direction, they waved me through.

'Two police cars and an ambulance were parked in front of my house. Three mobile television vans were scattered in the cul-de-sac just beyond my home. When I started to turn in to my driveway, a policeman stopped me. With flashbulbs popping all around and klieg lights from the television cameras blinding my eyes, the policeman led me into my house.

'My wife was lying under a sheet on a cot in the main hall beside the stairway to the second floor. Her throat had been slit. I heard some people talking upstairs and raced up to see my daughters. The girls were still lying where they had been killed – Christie on the floor in the bathroom and Amanda in her bed. The bastard had cut their throats as well.'

Huge, desolate sobs wrenched out of Dr Turner. 'I will never forget that horrible sight. Amanda must have been killed in her sleep, for there was no mark on her except for the cut ... What kind of human being could kill such innocent creatures?'

Dr Turner's tears were cascading down his cheeks. His chest was heaving uncontrollably. For several seconds he did not speak. Ellie quietly came over beside his chair and sat on the floor, holding his hand.

'The next five months I was totally numb. I could not work, I could not eat. People tried to help me – friends, psychiatrists, other doctors – but I could not function. I simply could not accept that my wife and children had been murdered.

'The police had a suspect in less than a week. His name was Carl Tyson. He was a young black man, twenty-three years old, who delivered groceries for a nearby supermarket. My wife always used the television for her shopping. Carl Tyson had been to our home several times before – I even remembered having seen him once or twice myself – and certainly knew his way around the house.

'Despite my daze during that period, I was aware of what was happening in the investigation of Linda's murder. At first, everything seemed so simple. Carl Tyson's fresh fingerprints were found all over the house. He had been inside our community that very afternoon on a delivery. Most of Linda's jewellery was missing, so robbery was the obvious motive. I figured the suspect would be summarily convicted and executed.

'The issue quickly became clouded. None of the jewellery was ever found. The security guards had marked Carl Tyson's entry and departure from the community on the master log, but he was only inside Greenbriar for twenty-two minutes, hardly enough time for him to deliver groceries and commit a robbery plus three murders. In addition, after a famous attorney decided to defend Tyson and helped him prepare his sworn statements, Tyson insisted that Linda had asked him to move some furniture that afternoon. This was a perfect explanation for the presence of his fingerprints all over the house ...'

Dr Turner paused, reflecting, the pain obvious in his face. Ellie squeezed his hand gently and he continued.

'By the time of the trial, the prosecution's argument was that Tyson had brought the groceries to the house in the afternoon and had discovered, after talking with Linda, that I would be in surgery until much later that night. Since my wife was a friendly and trusting woman, it was not unlikely that she might have chatted with the delivery boy and mentioned that I would not be home until late ... Anyway, according to the prosecutor, Tyson returned after he finished his shift at the supermarket. He climbed the rock wall that surrounded the country club development and walked across the golf course. Then he entered the house, intending to steal Linda's jewellery and expecting everyone in the family to be asleep. Apparently my wife confronted him and Tyson panicked, killing first Linda and then the children to ensure that there were no witnesses.

'Despite the fact that nobody saw Tyson return to our neighborhood, I thought the prosecution's case was extremely persuasive and that the man would be easily convicted. After all, he had no alibi whatsoever for the time period during which the crime was committed. The mud that was found on Tyson's shoes exactly matched the mud in the creek he would have crossed to reach the back side of the house. He did not show up for work for two days after the murders. In addition, when Tyson was arrested, he was carrying a large amount of cash that he said he won in a poker game.

'During the defence portion of the trial, I really began to have my doubts about the American judicial system. His attorney made the case a racial issue, depicting Carl Tyson as a poor, unfortunate black man who was being railroaded on circumstantial evidence. His lawyer argued emphatically that all Tyson had done on that October day was deliver groceries to my house. Someone else, his attorney said, some unknown maniac, had climbed the Greenbriar fence, stolen the jewellery, and then murdered Linda and the children.

'The last two days of the trial I became convinced, more from watching the body language of the jury than anything else, that Tyson was going to be acquitted. I went insane with righteous indignation. There was no doubt in my mind that the young man had committed the crime. The thought that he might be set free was intolerable.

'Every day during the trial – which lasted about six weeks – I showed up at the courthouse with my small medical bag. At first the security guards checked the bag each time I entered, but after a while, especially since most of them were sympathetic with my anguish, they just let me pass.

'The weekend before the trial concluded I flew to California, ostensibly to attend a medical seminar but actually to buy a black market shotgun that would fit in my medical bag. As I expected, on the day the verdict was being announced, the guards did not make me open my bag.

'When the acquittal was announced, there was an uproar in the courtroom. All the black people in the gallery shouted hooray. Carl Tyson and his attorney, a Jewish guy named Irving Bernstein, threw their arms around each other. I was ready to act. I opened my briefcase, quickly assembled the shotgun, jumped over the barrier, and killed them both, one with each barrel.'

Dr Turner took a deep breath and paused. 'I have never admitted before, not even to myself, that what I did was wrong. However, sometime during this operation on your friend Mr Diaba I understood clearly how much my emotional outrage has poisoned my soul for all these years ... My violent act of revenge did not return my wife and children to me. Nor did it make me happy, except for that sick animal pleasure I felt at the instant I knew that both Tyson and his attorney were going to die.'

There were now tears of contrition in Dr Turner's eyes. He glanced over at Ellie. 'Although I may not be worthy, I do love you, Ellie Wakefield, and very much want to marry you. I hope that you can forgive me for what I did years ago.'

Elite looked up at Dr Turner and squeezed his hand again. 'I know very little of romance,' she said slowly, 'for I have had no experience with it. But I do know that what I feel when I think about you is wonderful. I admire you,

I respect you, I may even love you. I would like to talk to my parents about this, of course … but yes, Dr Robert Turner, if they do not object I would be very happy to marry you.'

8

Nicole leaned over the basin and stared at her face in the mirror. She ran her fingers across the wrinkles under her eyes and smoothed her grey bangs. *You're almost an old woman,* she said to herself. Then she smiled. 'I grow old, I grow old, I shall wear the bottoms of my trousers rolled,' she said out loud.

Nicole laughed and backed up from the mirror, turning herself around so that she could see what she looked like from the back. The kelly green dress that she planned to wear in Ellie's wedding fitted snugly against her body, which was still trim and athletic after all the years. *Not too bad,* Nicole thought approvingly. *At least Ellie won't be embarrassed.*

On the end table beside her bed were the two photographs of Genevieve and her French husband that Kenji Watanabe had given her. After Nicole returned to the bedroom, she picked up the photos and stared at them. *I couldn't be at your wedding, Genevieve,* she thought suddenly with a burst of sadness. *I never even met your husband.*

Struggling with her emotions, Nicole crossed quickly over to the other side of the bedroom. She stared for almost a minute at a photograph of Simone and Michael O'Toole, taken the day of their wedding at The Node. *And I left you only a week after your wedding ... You were so very young, Simone,* Nicole thought to herself, *but in many ways you were far more mature than Ellie ...*

She did not let herself finish the thought. There was too much heartache in remembering either Simone or Genevieve. It was healthier to focus on the present. Nicole purposely reached up and grabbed the individual picture of Ellie that was hanging on the wall beside her brothers and sisters. *So you will be my third daughter to marry,* Nicole thought. *It seems impossible. Sometimes life moves much too fast.*

A montage of images of Ellie flashed through Nicole's mind. She saw again the shy little baby lying beside her in Rama II, Ellie's awestruck little girl face as they approached the Node in the shuttle, her new adolescent features at the moment of awakening from the long sleep, and finally Ellie's mature determination and courage as she spoke in front of the citizens of New Eden in defence of Dr Turner's programme. It was a powerful emotional journey into the past.

Nicole replaced Ellie's picture on the wall and started to undress. She had just hung her dress in the closet when she heard a strange sound, like someone crying, at the very limit of her hearing. *What was that?* she wondered. Nicole sat still for several minutes, but didn't hear any other noises. When she stood up, however, she suddenly had the eerie feeling that both Genevieve and Simone were in the room with her. Nicole glanced around her quickly, but she was still alone.

What is going on with me? she asked herself. *Have I been working too hard? Has the combination of the Martinez case and the wedding pushed me over the brink? Or is this another of my psychic episodes?*

Nicole tried to calm herself by breathing slowly and deeply. She was not, however, able to shake the feeling that Genevieve and Simone were indeed there in the room with her. Their presence beside her was so strong that Nicole had to restrain herself to keep from talking to them.

She remembered clearly the discussions that she had had with Simone prior to her marriage to Michael O'Toole. *Maybe that's why they are here*, Nicole thought. *They've come to remind me that I've been so busy with my work, I haven't had my wedding talk with Ellie.* Nicole laughed out loud nervously, but the goose bumps remained on her arm.

Forgive me, my darlings, Nicole said to both Ellie's photograph and the spirits of Genevieve and Simone in the room. *I promise that tomorrow ...*

This time the shriek was unmistakable. Nicole froze in her bedroom, the adrenaline coursing through her system. Within seconds she was running across the house to the study where Richard was working.

'Richard,' she said, just before reaching the door to the study, 'did you hear ...?'

Nicole stopped herself in midsentence. The study was a mess. Richard was on the floor, surrounded by a pair of monitors and a jumbled pile of electronic equipment. The little robot Prince Hal was in one hand and Richard's precious portable computer from the Newton mission was in the other. Three biots – two Garcias and a partially disassembled Einstein – were bending over him.

'Why, hello, darling,' Richard said nonchalantly. 'What are you doing here? I thought you'd be asleep by now.'

'Richard, I am certain that I heard an avian shriek. Only about a minute ago. It was close by.' Nicole hesitated, trying to decide whether or not to tell him about the visit from Genevieve and Simone.

Richard's brow furrowed. 'I didn't hear anything,' he replied. 'Did any of you?' he asked the biots. They all shook their heads, including the Einstein, whose chest was wide open and connected by four cables to the monitors on the floor.

'I *know* I heard something,' Nicole reiterated. She was silent for a moment. *Is this another sign of terminal stress?* she asked herself. Nicole now surveyed the chaos on the floor in front of her. 'By the way, darling, what are you doing?'

'This?' Richard said with a vague sweep of his hand. 'Oh, it's nothing special. Just another project of mine.'

'Richard Wakefield,' she said quickly, 'you are not telling me the truth. This mess all over the floor could not possibly be "nothing special" – I know you better than that. Now, what's so secret ...'

Richard had changed the displays on all three of his active monitors and was now shaking his head vigorously. 'I don't like this,' he mumbled. 'Not at all.' He glanced up at Nicole. 'Have you by any chance accessed my recent data files that are stored in the central supercomputer? Even inadvertently?'

'No, of course not. I don't even know your entry code ... But that's not what I want to talk about ...'

'Somebody has.' Richard quickly keyed in a diagnostic security subroutine and studied one of the monitors. 'At least five times in the last three weeks. You're certain that it wasn't you?'

'Yes, Richard,' Nicole said emphatically. 'But you're still trying to change the subject. I want you to tell me what *this* is all about.'

Richard set Prince Hal down on the floor in front of him and looked up at Nicole. 'I'm not quite ready to tell you, darling,' he said after a moment's hesitation. 'Please give me a couple of days.'

Nicole was puzzled. At length, however, her face brightened. 'All right, darling. If it's a wedding present for Ellie, then I'll gladly wait.'

Richard returned to his work. Nicole plopped down in the only chair in the room that was not cluttered. As she watched her husband, she realised how tired she was. She convinced herself that her fatigue must have caused her to imagine the shriek.

'Darling,' Nicole said softly a minute or two later.

'Yes,' he answered, glancing up at her from the floor.

'Do you ever wonder what's *really* going on here in New Eden? I mean, why have we been left so utterly alone by the creators of Rama? Most of the colonists go about their lives with hardly a thought about the fact that they're travelling in an interstellar spaceship constructed by extraterrestrials. How can this be possible? Why doesn't The Eagle or some other equally marvellous manifestation of their superior alien technology suddenly appear? Then maybe our petty problems ...'

Nicole stopped when Richard started laughing. 'What is it?' she said.

'This reminds me of a conversation that I had once with Michael O'Toole. He was frustrated because I would not accept on faith the eyewitness reports of the apostles. He then told me that God should have known that we were a species of doubting Thomases and should have scheduled frequent return visits from the resurrected Christ.'

'But that situation was entirely different,' Nicole argued.

'Was it?' Richard replied. 'What the early Christians reported about Jesus could not have been any harder to accept than our description of The Node and our long, time-dilating journey at relativistic velocities ... It's far more comforting for the other colonists to believe that this spaceship was created as an experiment by the ISA. Very few of them understand science well enough to know that Rama is way beyond our technological capability.'

Nicole was silent for a moment. 'Then is there *nothing* we can do to convince them ...'

She was interrupted by the triple buzz that indicated an incoming phone call was urgent. Nicole stumbled across the floor to answer it. Max Puckett's concerned face appeared on the monitor.

'We have a dangerous situation here outside the detention compound,' he said. 'There's an angry mob, maybe seventy or eighty people, mostly from Hakone. They want access to Martinez. They've already terminated two Garcia biots and attacked three others. Judge Mishkin is trying to reason with them, but they're in a nasty mood. Apparently Mariko Kobayashi committed suicide about two hours ago. Her whole family is here, including her father.'

Nicole was dressed in a sweat suit in less than a minute. Richard tried vainly to argue with her. 'It was *my* decision,' she said as she climbed on her bicycle. 'I should be the one to deal with the consequences.'

She eased down the lane to the main bicycle path and then began to pedal furiously. At top speed she would be at the administrative centre in four or five minutes, less than half the time it would take her by train at this time of night. *Kenji was wrong*, Nicole thought. *We should have had a press conference this morning. Then I could have explained the decision.*

Almost a hundred colonists were gathered in the main square of Central City. They were milling around in front of the New Eden detention complex where Pedro Martinez had been held since he was first indicted for the rape of Mariko Kobayashi. Judge Mishkin was standing at the top of the steps in front of the detention centre. He was speaking to the angry crowd through a megaphone. Twenty biots, mostly Garcias but with a couple of Lincolns and Tiassos in the group, had locked arms in front of Judge Mishkin and were preventing the mob from climbing the stairs to reach the judge.

'Now, folks,' the grey-haired Russian was saying, 'if Pedro Martinez is indeed guilty, then he will be convicted. But our constitution guarantees him a fair trial ...'

'Shut up, old man,' someone shouted from the audience.

'We want Martinez,' another voice said.

Off to the left, in front of the theatre, six young Orientals were finishing a makeshift scaffold. There was a cheer from the crowd as one of them tied a thick rope with a noose over the crossbar. A burly Japanese man in his early twenties pushed to the front of the crowd. 'Move out of the way, old man,' he said. 'And take these mechanical dolts with you. Our quarrel is not with you. We are here to secure justice for the Kobayashi family.'

'Remember Mariko,' a young woman shouted. There was a crashing sound as a red-haired boy struck one of the Garcias in the face with an aluminium baseball bat. The Garcia, its eyes destroyed and its face disfigured beyond recognition, made no response but did not give up its place in the cordon.

'The biots will not fight back,' Judge Mishkin said into the megaphone. 'They are programmed to be pacifists. But destroying them serves no purpose. It is senseless, inane violence.'

Two runners coming from Hakone arrived in the square and there was a momentary change in the focus of the crowd. Less than a minute later, the unruly mob cheered the appearance of two huge logs, carried by a dozen youths each. 'Now we will remove the biots that are protecting that murderer Martinez,' the young Japanese spokesman said. 'This is your last chance, old man. Move out of the way before you are hurt.'

Many individuals in the crowd ran over to take positions on the logs they intended to use as battering rams. At that moment Nicole Wakefield arrived in the square on her bicycle.

She jumped down quickly, walked through the cordon, and raced up the steps to stand beside Judge Mishkin. 'Hiro Kobayashi,' she shouted into the megaphone before the crowd had recognised her. 'I have come to explain to you why there will be no jury trial for Pedro Martinez. Will you come forward so that I can see you?'

The elder Kobayashi, who had been standing off to the side of the square, walked slowly over to the bottom of the steps in front of Nicole.

'Kobayashi-san,' Nicole said in Japanese, 'I was very sorry to hear about the death of your daughter ...'

'Hypocrite,' someone shouted in English, and the crowd began to buzz.

'... As a parent myself,' Nicole continued in Japanese, 'I can imagine how terrible it must be to experience the death of a child.

'Now,' she said, switching to English and addressing the crowd, 'Let me explain my decision today to all of you. Our New Eden constitution says that each citizen shall have a "fair trial". In all other cases since this colony was originally settled, criminal indictments have led to a trial by jury. In the case of Mr Martinez, however, because of all the publicity, I am convinced that no unbiased jury can be found.'

A chorus of whistles and boos briefly interrupted Nicole. 'Our constitution does not define,' she continued, 'what should be done to ensure a "fair trial" if no jury of peers is to be involved. However, our judges, have supposedly been selected to implement the law and are trained to decide cases on the basis of the evidence. That is why I have assigned the Martinez indictment to the jurisdiction of the New Eden Special Court. There all the evidence – some of which has never heretofore been made public – will be carefully weighed.'

'But we all know the boy Martinez is guilty,' a distraught Mr Kobayashi cried in response. 'He has even admitted he had sex with my daughter. And we also know he raped a girl in Nicaragua, back on Earth ... Why are you protecting him? What about justice for my family?'

'Because the law ...' Nicole started to answer, but was drowned out by the crowd.

'We want Martinez. We want Martinez.' The chant swelled as the huge logs, which had been laid on the pavement soon after Nicole's appearance, were again hoisted by the people in the square. As the mob struggled to set up a battering ram, one of the logs inadvertently crashed into the monument marking the celestial location of Rama. The sphere shattered and electronic parts that had indicated the nearby stars tumbled out onto the pavement. The small blinking light that had been Rama itself broke into hundreds of pieces.

'Citizens of New Eden,' Nicole shouted into the megaphone, 'hear me out. There is something about this case that none of you know. If you will just listen ...'

'*Kill the nigger bitch,*' shouted the red-haired boy who had struck the Garcia biot with the baseball bat.

Nicole glared at the young man with fire in her eyes. 'What did you say?' she thundered.

The chanting suddenly ceased. The boy was isolated. He glanced around nervously and grinned. 'Kill the nigger bitch,' he repeated.

Nicole was down the steps in an instant. The crowd moved aside as she headed straight for the red-haired boy. 'Say it one more time,' she said, her nostrils flaring, when she was less than a metre away from her antagonist.

'Kill ...' he started.

She slapped his cheek hard with her open hand. The smack resounded through the square. Nicole turned around abruptly and started toward the steps, but hands grabbed her from all sides. The shocked boy doubled up his fist ...

At that moment two loud booms shook the square. As everyone tried to ascertain what was happening, two more blasts were detonated in the sky over the heads of the crowd. 'That's just me and my shotgun,' Max Puckett said into the megaphone. 'Now, if you folks will just let the lady judge pass ... there, that's better ... and then head on home, we'll all be better off.'

Nicole broke free from the hands that were holding her, but the crowd did not disperse. Max raised the gun, aimed it at the thick knot of rope above the noose on the makeshift scaffold, and fired again. The rope exploded into pieces, parts of it falling into the crowd.

'Now, folks,' Max said. 'I'm a lot more ornery than these two judges. And I already know I'm going to spend some time in this here detention centre for violating the colony's gun laws. I'd sure as hell hate to have to shoot some of you as well.'

Max pointed his gun at the crowd. Everyone instinctively ducked. Max fired blanks over their heads and laughed heartily as the people began to scurry out of the square.

*

Nicole could not sleep. Over and over again she replayed the same scene. She kept seeing herself walking into the crowd and slapping the red-haired boy. *Which makes me no better than he is,* she thought.

'You're still awake, aren't you?' Richard said.

'Umm-hm.'

'Are you all right?'

There was a short silence. 'No, Richard,' Nicole answered. 'I'm not ... I'm extremely upset with myself for striking that boy.'

'Hey, come on,' he said. 'Stop beating yourself up. He deserved it. He insulted you in the worst way. People like that don't understand anything but force.'

Richard reached over and began rubbing Nicole's back. 'My God,' he said, 'I've never seen you so tense. You're in knots from one end to the other.'

'I'm worried,' Nicole said. 'I have a terrible feeling that the whole fabric of our life here in New Eden is about to come unravelled ... And that everything I have done or am doing is absolutely useless.'

'You have done your best, darling. I must confess that I am amazed by how hard you have tried.' Richard continued to rub Nicole's back very gently. 'But you must remember you're dealing with human beings. You can transport them to another world and give them a paradise, but they still come equipped with their fears and insecurities and cultural predilections. A new world could only *really* be new if all the humans involved began with totally empty minds, like new computers with no software and no operating systems, just loads of untapped potential.'

Nicole managed a smile. 'You're not very optimistic, darling.'

'Why should I be? Nothing I have seen here in New Eden or on Earth suggests to me that humanity is capable of achieving harmony in its relationship with itself, much less with any other living creatures. Occasionally there is an individual, or even a group, that is able to transcend the basic genetic and environmental drawbacks of the species ... But these people are miracles, certainly not the norm.'

'I don't agree with you,' Nicole said softly. 'Your view is too hopeless. I believe that most people desperately want to achieve that harmony. We just don't know how to do it. That's why we need more education. And more good examples.'

'Even that red-haired boy? Do you believe he could be educated out of his intolerance?'

'I have to think so, darling,' Nicole said. 'Otherwise ... I fear I would simply give up.'

Richard made a sound somewhere between a cough and a laugh.

'What is it?' Nicole asked.

'I was just wondering,' Richard said, 'if Sisyphus ever deluded himself into believing that maybe the next time the boulder would not roll down the hill again.'

Nicole smiled. 'He had to believe there was some chance the boulder would stay at the summit, or he could not have laboured so hard ... At least that's what I think.'

9

As Kenji Watanabe descended from the train at Hakone, it was impossible for him not to recall another meeting with Toshio Nakamura, years before, on a planet billions of kilometres away. *He had telephoned me that time too*, Kenji thought. *He had insisted that we talk about Keiko.*

Kenji stopped in front of a shop window and straightened his tie. In the distorted reflection he could easily imagine himself as an idealistic Kyoto teenager on his way to a meeting with a rival. *But that was long ago, Kenji thought to himself, with nothing at stake except our egos. Now the entire fate of our little world ...*

His wife Nai had not wanted him to meet with Nakamura at all. She had encouraged Kenji to call Nicole for another opinion. Nicole also had been opposed to any meeting between the governor and Toshio Nakamura. 'He's a dishonest, power-crazy megalomaniac,' Nicole had said. 'Nothing good can come from the meeting. He just wants to find your weaknesses.'

'But he has said that he can reduce tension in the colony.'

'At what price, Kenji? Watch out for the terms. That man never offers to do something for nothing.'

So why did you come? a voice inside Kenji's head asked him as he stared at the huge palace his boyhood associate had built for himself. *I'm not certain exactly*, another voice answered. *Maybe honour. Or self-respect. Something deep in my heritage.*

Nakamura's palace and the surrounding homes were built of wood in the classic Kyoto style. Blue tile roofs, carefully manicured gardens, sheltering trees, immaculately clean walkways – even the smell of the flowers reminded Kenji of his home city on a faraway planet.

He was met at the door by a lovely young girl in sandals and kimono, who bowed and said, '*Ohairi kudasai*,' in the very formal Japanese way. Kenji left his shoes on the rack and put on sandals himself. The girl's eyes were always on the floor as she guided him through the few Western rooms of the palace into the tatami mat area where, it was said, Nakamura spent most of his free time gamboling with his concubines.

After a short walk the girl stopped and pulled aside a paper screen decorated with cranes in flight. '*Dozo*,' she said, gesturing inside. Kenji walked into the six-mat room and sat cross-legged on one of the two cushions in front of a shiny black lacquer table. *He will be late*, Kenji thought. *That's all part of the strategy.*

A different young girl, also pretty, self-effacing, and dressed in a lovely pastel kimono, came noiselessly into the room carrying water and Japanese tea. Kenji sipped the tea slowly while his eyes roamed around the room. In one corner was a wooden screen with four panels. Kenji could tell from his distance of a few metres that it was exquisitely carved. He rose from his cushion to take a closer look.

The side facing toward him featured the beauty of Japan, one panel for each of the four seasons. The winter picture showed a ski resort in the Japanese Alps smothered in metres of snow; the spring panel depicted the cherry trees in blossom along the Kama River in Kyoto. Summer was a pristine clear day with Mount Fuji's snowcapped summit rising above the verdant countryside. The autumn panel presented a riot of colour in the trees surrounding the Tokugawa family shrine and mausoleum at Nikko.

All this amazing beauty, Kenji thought, suddenly feeling deeply homesick. *He has tried to recreate the world we have left behind. But why? Why does he spend his sordid money on such magnificent art? He is a strange, inconsistent man.*

The four panels on the backside of the screen told of another Japan. The rich colours displayed the battle of Osaka Castle, in the early seventeenth century, after which Ieyasu Tokugawa was virtually unopposed as shogun of Japan. The screen was covered with human figures – samurai warriors in battle, male and female members of the court scattered throughout the castle grounds, even the Lord Tokugawa himself, larger than the rest and looking supremely content with his victory. Kenji noticed with amusement that the carved shogun bore more than a passing resemblance to Nakamura.

Kenji was about to sit back down on the cushion when the screen opened and his adversary entered. '*Omachido sama deshita*,' Nakamura said, bowing slightly in his direction.

Kenji bowed back, somewhat awkwardly because he could not take his eyes off his countryman. Toshio Nakamura was dressed in a complete samurai outfit, including the sword and dagger! *This is all part of some psychological ploy*, Kenji told himself. *It is designed to confuse or scare me.*

'*Ano, hajememashoka*,' Nakamura said, sitting down on the cushion opposite Kenji. '*Kocha ga, oishii desu, ne?*'

'*Totemo oishii desu*,' Kenji replied, taking another sip. The tea was indeed excellent. *But he is not my shogun*, Kenji thought. *I must change this atmosphere before any serious discussion starts.*

'Nakamura-san, we are both busy men,' Governor Watanabe said in English. 'It is important to me that we dispense with the formalities and cut straight to the heart of the matter. Your representative told me on the phone this morning that you are "disturbed" about the events of the last twenty-four hours and have some "positive suggestions" for reducing the current tension in New Eden. This is why I have come to talk to you.'

Nakamura's face showed nothing; however, the slight hiss as he was speaking indicated his displeasure with Kenji's directness. 'You have forgotten your Japanese manners, Watanabe-san. It is grievously impolite to start a business discussion before you have complimented your host on the surroundings and inquired about his well-being. Such impropriety almost always leads to unpleasant disagreement, which can be avoided ...'

'I'm sorry,' Kenji interrupted with a trace of impatience, 'but I don't need a lesson from you, of all people, on manners. Besides, we are not in Japan, we are not even on Earth, and our ancient Japanese customs are about as germane now as the outfit you are wearing ...'

Kenji had not intended to insult Nakamura, but he could not have had a better strategy for causing his adversary to reveal his true intentions. The tycoon rose to his feet abruptly. For a moment the governor thought Nakamura was going to draw his samurai sword.

'All right,' said Nakamura, his eyes implacably hostile, 'we will do this your way ... Watanabe, you have lost control of the colony. The citizens are very unhappy with your leadership and my people tell me there is widespread talk of impeachment and/or insurrection. You have botched the environmental and RV-41 issues, and now your black woman judge, after innumerable delays, has announced that a nigger rapist will not be subject to a trial by jury. Some of the more thoughtful of the colonists, knowing that you and I have a common background, have asked me to intercede, to try to convince you to step aside before there is widespread bloodshed and chaos.'

This is incredible, Kenji thought as he listened to Nakamura. *The man is absolutely out of his mind*. The governor resolved to say very little in the conversation.

'So you believe I should resign?' Kenji asked after a protracted silence.

'Yes,' answered Nakamura, his tone growing more imperious. 'But not immediately. Not until tomorrow. Today you should exercise your executive privilege to change the jurisdiction for the Martinez case away from Nicole des Jardins Wakefield. She is obviously prejudiced. Judges Iannella or Rodriguez, either one, would be more appropriate. Notice,' he said, forcing a smile, 'that I am not suggesting the case be transferred to Judge Nishimura's court.'

'Is there anything else?' Kenji asked.

'Only one more thing. Tell Ulanov to withdraw from the election. He doesn't have any chance to win and continuing this divisive campaign will only make it more difficult for us to pull together after the Macmillan victory. We need to be united. I foresee a serious threat to the colony from whatever enemy inhabits the other habitat. The leggies, that you seem to believe are "harmless observers", are just their advance scouts ...'

Kenji was astonished by what he was hearing. How had Nakamura become so warped? Or had he always been this way?

'... I must stress that time is of the essence,' Nakamura was saying, 'especially with respect to the Martinez issue and your resignation. I have asked Kobayashi-san and the other members of the Asian community not to act too hastily, but after last night I'm not certain I can restrain them. His daughter was a beautiful, talented young woman. Her suicide note makes it clear that she could not live with the shame implied by the continual delays in the trial of her rapist. There is genuine anger throughout ...'

Governor Watanabe temporarily forgot his resolution to remain quiet. 'Are you aware,' he said, also standing up, 'that semen from two different individuals was found in Mariko Kobayashi after the night during which she was allegedly raped? And that both Mariko and Pedro Martinez repeatedly insisted that they were alone together the entire evening? Even when Nicole hinted to Mariko last week that there was evidence of additional intercourse, the young woman stuck to her story.'

Nakamura momentarily lost his composure. He stared blankly at Kenji Watanabe.

'We have not been able to identify the other party,' Kenji continued. 'The semen samples mysteriously disappeared from the hospital laboratory before the full DNA analysis could be completed. All we have is the record of the original examination.'

'That record could be wrong,' asserted Nakamura, his self-confidence returning.

'Very, very unlikely. But at any rate, now you can understand Judge Wakefield's dilemma. Everyone in this colony has already decided Pedro is guilty. She did not want a jury to convict him wrongly.'

There was a long silence. The governor started to depart. 'I'm surprised at you, Watanabe,' Nakamura said at length. 'You've missed the point of this meeting entirely. Whether or not that jigaboo Martinez raped Mariko Kobayashi is really not that important. I have promised her father that the Nicaraguan boy will be punished. And that's what counts.'

Kenji Watanabe stared at his boyhood classmate with disgust. 'I'm going to leave now,' he said, 'before I become really angry.'

'You will not be given another chance,' Nakamura said, his eyes again full of hostility. 'This was my first and final offer.'

Kenji shook his head, pulled back the paper screen himself, and walked out into the corridor.

Nicole was walking along a beach in beautiful sunlight. Ahead of her about fifty metres, Ellie was standing beside Dr Turner. She was wearing her wedding dress, but the groom was dressed in a bathing suit. Nicole's great-grandfather Omeh was performing the ceremony in his long green tribal robe.

Omeh placed Ellie's hands in Dr Turner's and began a Senoufo chant. He raised his eyes to the sky. A solitary avian soared overhead, shrieking in rhythm with the wedding chant. As Nicole watched the avian flying above her, the sky darkened. Storm clouds rushed in, displacing the placid sky.

The ocean began to churn and the wind to blow. Nicole's hair, now completely grey, streamed out behind her. The wedding party was in disarray. Everyone ran inland to escape the coming storm. Nicole could not move. Her eyes were fixed on a large object being tossed upon the waves.

The object was a huge green bag, like the plastic bags used for lawn trash back in the twenty-first century. The bag was full and was coming toward the shore. Nicole would have tried to grab it, but she was afraid of the moiling sea. She pointed at the bag. She yelled for help.

In the upper left-hand corner of her dream screen she saw a long canoe. As it drew closer, Nicole realised that the eight occupants of the canoe were extraterrestrials, orange in colour, smaller than humans. They looked as if they were made from bread dough. They had eyes and faces but no bodily hair. The aliens steered the canoe over to the large green bag and picked it up.

The orange extraterrestrials deposited the green bag on the beach. Nicole did not approach until they climbed back into their canoe and returned to the ocean. She waved goodbye to them and walked over to the bag. It had a zipper, which she carefully opened. Nicole pulled back the top half and stared at the dead face of Kenji Watanabe.

Nicole shuddered, screamed, and sat up in bed. She reached over for Richard, but the bed was empty. The digital clock on the table read 2:48 a.m. Nicole tried to slow her breathing and clear her mind of the horrible dream.

The vivid image of the dead Kenji Watanabe lingered in her mind. As she walked over to the bathroom, Nicole remembered her premonitory dreams about the death of her mother, back when she was only ten years old. What if Kenji is really going to die? she thought, feeling the first wave of panic. She forced herself to think about something else. Now where is Richard at this time of night? she wondered. Nicole pulled on her robe and left the bedroom area.

She walked quietly past the children's rooms toward the front of the house. Benjy was snoring, as usual. The light was on in the study, but Richard was not there. Two of the new biots plus Prince Hal were also gone. One of the monitors on Richard's work table still contained a display.

Nicole smiled to herself and remembered their agreement. She touched the keys NICOLE on the keyboard and the display changed. 'Dearest Nicole,' the message appeared, 'if you awaken before I return, do not worry. I plan to be back by dawn, eight o'clock tomorrow morning at the very latest. I have been doing some work with the 300 series biots – you remember, the ones that are not completely programmed in firmware and therefore can be designed for special tasks – and have reason to believe that someone has been spying on my work. Therefore, I have accelerated the completion of my current project and have gone outside New Eden for a final test. I love you. Richard.'

*

It was dark and cold out on the Central Plain. Richard tried to be patient. He had sent his upgraded Einstein (Richard referred to it as Super-Al) and Garcia 325 over to the second habitat probe site before him. They had explained to the night watchman, a standard Garcia biot, that the published experiment schedule had changed and that a special investigation was presently going to be conducted. With Richard still out of sight, Super-Al had then withdrawn all the equipment from the opening into the other habitat and placed it on the ground. The process had consumed over an hour of precious time. Now that Super-Al was finally finished, he signaled Richard to approach. Garcia 325 cleverly led the watchman biot off to another area around the probe site so it wouldn't be able to see Richard.

He wasted no time. Richard pulled Prince Hal out of his pocket and put him in the opening. 'Go quickly,' Richard said, setting his small monitor up on the floor of the passage. The opening into the other habitat had been gradually widened over the weeks so that it was now approximately a square, eighty centimetres on a side. There was more than enough room for the tiny robot.

Prince Hal hurried through to the other side. The drop from the passage to the inside floor was about a metre. The robot adroitly attached a small cable to a stanchion he glued to the floor of the passage and then let himself down. Richard watched Hal's every move on his screen and communicated instructions by radio.

Richard had expected that there would be an outer annulus protecting the second habitat. He was correct. *So the basic design of the two habitats is similar*, he thought. Richard had also anticipated that there would be an opening of some kind in the inner wall, some gate or door through which the leggies must come and go, and that Prince Hal would be small enough to enter the inside of the habitat by the same portal.

It did not take long for Hal to locate the entrance into the main part of the habitat. However, what was obviously a door was also more than twenty metres above the floor of the annulus. Having watched the video recordings of the leggies moving up vertical surfaces on the bulldozer biots at the Avalon survey site, Richard had prepared for this possibility as well.

'Climb,' he ordered Prince Hal after a nervous glance at his watch. It was almost six o'clock. Dawn would be coming soon in New Eden. Soon thereafter the regular scientists and engineers would be returning to this probe site.

The entrance to the inside of the habitat was one hundred times Prince Hal's height above the floor. The robot's ascent would be the equivalent of a human going straight up a sixty-storey building. At home Richard had had the little robot practise by scaling the house, but he had always been there beside him. Were there grooves for hand and footholds on the wall Hal was climbing? Richard could not tell from the monitor. Were all the correct equations in Prince Hal's mechanical engineering subprocessor? *I'll find out soon enough*, Richard thought as his star pupil began his climb.

Prince Hal slipped and dangled by his hands once, but eventually succeeded in making it to the top. However, the ascent took another thirty minutes. Richard knew he was running out of time. As Hal pulled himself onto the windowsill of a circular porthole, Richard saw that the robot's ingress into the habitat was blocked by a mesh screen. However, a small part of the interior was barely visible in the dim light. Richard carefully positioned Hal's tiny camera so that it could see through the gridwork.

'The watchman insists it must return to its main station,' Garcia 325 announced to Richard on the radio. 'It is required to make its daily report at 0630.'

Shit, thought Richard, *that's only six minutes*. He moved Hal slowly around on the lip of the porthole to see if he could identify any objects in the habitat interior. Richard could see nothing specific. 'Shriek,' Richard then ordered, switching the robot's audio volume to full. 'Shriek until I tell you to stop.'

Richard had not tested the new amplifier he had installed in Prince Hal at its maximum output. He was therefore astonished at the amplitude of Hal's avian mimicry. It resounded from the passage and Richard jumped back. *Pretty damn good*, Richard said after collecting himself, *at least if my memory is accurate*.

The watchman biot was soon upon Richard, following its preprogrammed instructions by demanding his personal papers and an explanation of what he was doing. Super-Al and Garcia 325 tried to confuse the watchman, but when it could not obtain Richard's cooperation, the biot insisted it must make an emergency report. On the monitor, Richard saw the entire mesh screen swing open and six leggies swarm onto Prince Hal. The robot continued to shriek.

The watchman Garcia began to broadcast its emergency. Richard was aware that he had only a few minutes before he would be forced to leave. *'Come, dammit, come,'* he said, watching the monitor in between furtive glances behind him in the Central Plain. There were no lights yet approaching from his home colony in the distance.

At first Richard thought he had imagined it. Then it repeated, the sound of large wings flapping. One of the leggies was partially obscuring his view, but moments later Richard definitely saw a familiar talon reaching out for Prince Hal. The avian shriek that followed confirmed the sighting. The image on the monitor became fuzzy.

'If you have a chance,' Richard screamed into the radio, 'try to return to the passage. I'll come back for you later.'

He turned around, quickly packing his monitor in his bag. 'Let's go,' Richard said to his two biot associates. They began to run toward New Eden.

Richard was triumphant as he hurried toward home. *My hunch was right*, he said exultantly to himself. *This changes everything ... now I have a daughter to give away.*

10

The wedding was scheduled to take place at seven o'clock in the evening in the theatre at Central High School. The reception, for a much larger group, was planned for the gymnasium, an adjacent building no more than twenty metres away. All day long Nicole struggled with last-minute items, rescuing the preparations from one potential disaster after another.

She did not have time to contemplate the significance of Richard's new discovery. He had come home full of excitement, wanting to discuss the avians, and even who might be spying on his research, but Nicole had simply not been able to focus on anything except the wedding. They had both agreed not to tell anyone else about the avians until after they had had a chance for a lengthy discussion.

Nicole had gone for a morning walk in the park with Ellie. They had talked about marriage, love, and sex for over an hour, but Ellie had been so excited about the wedding that she had not been able to concentrate fully on what her mother was saying. Toward the end of their walk, Nicole had stopped under a tree to summarise her message,

'Remember at least this one thing, Ellie,' Nicole had said, holding both her daughter's hands in hers. 'Sex is an important component of marriage, but it is not the most important. Because of your lack of experience, it is unlikely that sex will be wonderful for you at the beginning. However, if you and Robert love and trust each other, and both of you genuinely want to give and receive pleasure, you will find that your physical compatibility will increase year after year.'

Two hours before the ceremony Nicole, Nai, and Ellie arrived together at the school. Eponine was already there waiting for them. 'Are you nervous?' the teacher said with a smile. Ellie nodded. 'I'm scared to death,' Eponine added, 'and I'm only one of the bridesmaids.'

Ellie had asked her mother to be matron of honour. Nai Watanabe, Eponine, and her sister Katie were the bridesmaids. Dr Edward Stafford, a man who shared Robert Turner's passion for medical history, was the best man. Because he had no other close associates, except for the biots at the hospital, Robert picked the rest of his attendants from the Wakefield family and friends. Kenji Watanabe, Patrick, and Benjy were his three groomsmen.

'Mother, I feel nauseous,' Ellie said soon after they were all gathered in the dressing room. 'I'll be so embarrassed if I throw up on my wedding dress. Should I try to eat something?' Nicole had anticipated this situation. She handed Ellie a banana and some yogurt, assuring her daughter that it was completely normal to feel queasy before such a big event.

Nicole's uneasiness about the day increased as time passed and Katie did not show up. With everything in order in the bride's dressing room, she decided to cross the hall to talk to Patrick. The men had finished dressing before Nicole knocked on their door.

'How is the mother of the bride?' Judge Mishkin asked when she entered. The grand old judge was going to perform the wedding ceremony.

'A little spooked,' Nicole answered with a wan smile. She found Patrick in the back of the room, adjusting Benjy's clothes.

'How do I look?' Benjy asked his mother as she approached.

'Very, very handsome,' Nicole replied to her beaming son. 'Have you talked to Katie this morning?' she asked Patrick.

'No,' he said. 'But I reconfirmed the time with her, as you requested, just last night ... Is she not here yet?'

Nicole shook her head. It was already six-fifteen, only forty-five minutes before the ceremony was scheduled to start. She walked out in the hall to use the phone, but the smell of cigarette smoke told her that Katie had finally arrived.

'Just think, little sister,' Katie was saying in a loud voice as Nicole crossed back to the bride's dressing room, 'tonight you get to have your first sex. Oooeee! I bet the thought just drives that gorgeous body of yours absolutely wild.'

'Katie,' Eponine said, 'I don't think that's entirely appropriate ...'

Nicole walked into the room and Eponine fell silent. 'Why, Mother,' Katie said, 'how beautiful you look. I had forgotten that there was a woman lurking behind those judge's robes.'

Katie expelled smoke into the air and took a drink from the champagne bottle on the counter beside her. 'So here we are,' she said with a flourish, 'about to witness the marriage of my baby sister ...'

'Stop it, Katie, you've had too much to drink.' Nicole's voice was cold and hard. She picked up the champagne and Katie's pack of cigarettes. 'Just finish dressing and stop the clowning. You can have these back after the ceremony.'

'OK, Judge ... whatever you say,' Katie said, inhaling deeply and blowing out smoke rings. She grinned at the other ladies. Then, as Katie reached for the waste-basket to flick the ash off her cigarette, she lost her balance. Katie fell painfully against the counter, hitting several open bottles of cosmetics before landing on the floor in a mess. Eponine and Ellie both rushed over to help her.

'Are you all right?' Ellie asked.

'Watch out for your dress, Ellie,' Nicole said, looking disapprovingly at

Katie sprawled on the floor. Nicole grabbed some paper towels and began cleaning up what Katie had spilled.

'Yeah, Ellie,' Katie said sarcastically a few seconds later, when she was again standing up. 'Watch out for that dress. You want to be absolutely spotless when you marry your double murderer.'

Nobody breathed in the room. Nicole was livid. She approached Katie and then stood directly in front of her. 'Apologise to your sister,' she ordered.

'I will not,' Katie replied defiantly just moments before Nicole's open hand landed on her cheek. Tears burst into Katie's eyes. 'Ah-hah,' she said, wiping at her face, 'it's New Eden's most famous slapper. Only two days after resorting to physical violence in Central City Square, she strikes her own daughter in a replay of her most famous deed ...'

'Mother, don't ... please,' Ellie interrupted, fearing that Nicole would slap Katie again.

Nicole turned around and looked at the distraught bride. 'I'm sorry,' she mumbled.

'That's right,' said Katie angrily. 'Tell *her* you're sorry. *I'm* the one you hit, Judge. Remember me? Your older, unmarried daughter? The one you called "disgusting" only three weeks ago yesterday ... You told me that my friends were "sleazy and immoral" – are those the exact words? – yet your precious Ellie, that paragon of virtue, you hand over to a double murderer ... with another murderer as a bridesmaid to boot.'

All of the women realised at roughly the same moment that Katie was not just drunk and truculent. She was deeply disturbed. Her wild eyes condemned them all as she continued her rambling diatribe.

She is drowning, Nicole said to herself, *and crying desperately for help. Not only have I ignored her cries, I have pushed her deeper into the water.*

'Katie,' Nicole said quietly, 'I'm sorry. I acted foolishly and without thought.' She walked toward her daughter with her arms outstretched.

'No,' Katie replied, pushing her mother's arms away. 'No, no, no ... I don't want your pity.' She moved back toward the door. 'In fact, I don't want to be in this goddamn wedding ... I don't belong here. Good luck, little sister. Tell me someday how the handsome doctor is in bed.'

Katie turned around and stumbled through the door. Both Ellie and Nicole were silently weeping as she left.

Nicole tried to concentrate on the wedding, but her heart was heavy after the untoward scene with Katie. She helped Ellie put on her makeup again, repeatedly chastising herself for having responded angrily to Katie.

Just before the ceremony started, Nicole returned to the men's dressing room and informed them that Katie had decided not to be in the wedding. She then peeked briefly at the gathering crowd, noticing that there were about a dozen biots already seated. *My goodness*, Nicole thought, *we weren't specific enough in the invitations.* It was not abnormal for some of the colonists to bring their Lincolns or Tiassos with them to special functions, especially if they had children. Before she returned to the bride's dressing room, Nicole fretted momentarily about whether or not there would be enough seats for everybody.

Moments later, or so it seemed, the bridal party was gathered on the stage around Judge Mishkin and the music announced the arrival of the bride. Like everyone else, Nicole turned around and looked to the back of the theatre. There was her gorgeous youngest daughter, resplendent in her white dress with the red trim, coming down the aisle on Richard's arm. Nicole fought back the tears, but when she saw big drops glistening on the cheeks of the bride, she could control herself no longer. *I love you, my Ellie*, Nicole said to herself. *How I hope that you will be happy.*

Judge Mishkin had prepared an eclectic ceremony at the couple's request. It praised the love of a man and a woman, and talked about how important their bond was in the proper creation of a family. His words counseled tolerance, patience, and selflessness. He offered a nondenominational prayer, invoking God to 'call forth' from the bride and groom that 'compassion and understanding that ennobles the human species.'

The ceremony was short, but elegant. Dr Turner and Ellie exchanged rings and recited their vows with strong, positive voices. They turned to Judge Mishkin and he placed their hands together. 'With the authority granted me by the colony of New Eden, I pronounce Robert Turner and Eleanor Wakefield husband and wife.'

As Dr Turner was gently lifting Ellie's veil for the traditional kiss, a shot rang out, followed an instant later by another. Judge Mishkin pitched forward on the bridal couple, blood spurting from his forehead. Kenji Watanabe collapsed beside him. Eponine dove between the bridal couple and the guests as a third and fourth shots were heard. Everyone was screaming. There was chaos in the theatre.

Two more shots followed in rapid succession. In the third row Max Puckett finally disarmed the Lincoln biot that had been the gunman. Max had turned around almost instantly, as soon as he had heard the first shot, and had leapt over the chairs a second later. However, the Lincoln biot, who had risen from its seat at the word wife, fired its automatic gun a total of six times before Max subdued it completely.

Blood was all over the stage. Nicole crawled over and examined Governor Watanabe. He was already dead. Dr Turner cradled Judge Mishkin as the gracious old man closed his eyes for the final time. The third bullet had apparently been intended for Dr Turner, for Eponine had caught it in her side after her frantic dive to save the bride and groom.

Nicole picked up the microphone that had fallen with Judge Mishkin. 'Ladies and gentlemen. This is a terrible, terrible tragedy. Please do not panic. I believe there is no more danger. Please just hold your places until we can tend to the injured.'

The final four bullets had not done too much damage. Eponine was bleeding, but her condition was not critical. Max had struck the Lincoln just before it fired the fourth bullet, almost certainly saving Nicole's life, since that particular bullet had missed her by only centimetres. Two of the guests had been grazed by the final shots as the Lincoln was falling.

Richard joined Max and Patrick, who were restraining the killer biot. 'He won't answer a single goddamn question,' Max said.

Richard looked at the Lincoln's shoulder. The biot was number three hundred and thirty-three. 'Take him into the back,' Richard said. 'I want to look at him later.'

On the stage Nai Watanabe was sitting on her knees, holding the head of her beloved Kenji on her lap. Her body was trembling with deep, desperate sobs. Beside her the twins Galileo and Kepler were wailing with fright. Ellie, blood all over her wedding dress, was trying to comfort the little boys.

Dr Turner was attending to Eponine. 'An ambulance should be here in just a few minutes,' he said after dressing her wound. He kissed her on the forehead. 'There's no way that Ellie and I can ever thank you for what you did.'

Nicole was down with the guests, making certain that neither of the bystanders who had been struck by bullets was seriously injured. She was about to return to the microphone and tell everyone that they could begin to leave when a hysterical colonist burst into the theatre.

'An Einstein has gone mad,' he shouted before surveying the scene in front of him. 'Ulanov and Judge Iannella are both dead.'

'We should both leave. And now,' Richard said. 'But even if you won't, Nicole, I am going to go. I know too much about the three-hundred-series biots – and what Nakamura's people have done to change them. They'll be after me tonight or in the morning.'

'All right, darling,' Nicole replied. 'I understand. But I cannot go. Someone must stay to take care of the family. And to fight Nakamura. Even if it's hopeless. We must not submit to his tyranny.'

It was three hours after the aborted end of Ellie's wedding. Panic was sweeping the colony. The television had just reported that five or six biots had simultaneously gone mad and that as many as eleven of New Eden's most prominent citizens had been killed. Luckily the Kawabata biot performing the concert in Vegas had failed in its attack on gubernatorial candidate Ian Macmillan and noted industrialist Toshio Nakamura.

'Bullshit,' Richard had said as he had watched. 'That was just another part of their plan.'

He was certain that the entire assassination activity had been planned and orchestrated by the Nakamura camp. Moreover, Richard had no doubt that he and Nicole had also been intended targets. He was convinced that the day's events would result in a totally different New Eden under the control of Nakamura, with Ian Macmillan as his puppet governor.

'Won't you at least say goodbye to Patrick and Benjy?' Nicole asked.

'I'd better not,' Richard answered. 'Not because I don't love them, but because I'm afraid I might change my mind ...'

'Are you going to use the emergency exit?' Nicole said.

Richard nodded. 'They'd never let me out the normal way.'

While he was checking his diving apparatus Nicole came into the study. 'It was just reported on the news that people are smashing their biots all over the colony. One of the colonists interviewed said the entire mass murder was part of an alien plot.'

'Great,' Richard said grimly. 'The propaganda has already begun.'

He packed as much food and water as he thought he could comfortably carry. When he was ready, he held Nicole tightly against him for over a minute. There were tears in both their eyes as he departed.

'Do you know where you're going?' Nicole asked softly.

'More or less,' Richard answered as he stood in the back door. 'I'm not telling you, of course, so you can't be implicated ... '

'I understand,' she said. They both heard something at the front of the house and Richard dashed out into the backyard.

The train to Lake Shakespeare was not running. The Garcia operating an earlier train on the same track had been terminated by a group of angry colonists and the whole system had shut down. Richard began walking toward the eastern side of Lake Shakespeare.

As he trudged along carrying his heavy diving equipment and backpack, he had the feeling that he was being followed. Twice Richard thought he saw someone out of the corner of his eye, but when he stopped and looked around, he saw nothing. Finally he reached the lake. It was after midnight. He took one final look at the lights of the colony and began to put on his diving apparatus. Richard's blood ran cold as a Garcia came out of the bushes while he was undressing.

He expected to be killed. After several long seconds the Garcia spoke. 'Are you Richard Wakefield?' it asked.

Richard did not move or say anything. 'If you are,' the biot said at length, 'I am bringing a message from your wife. She says she loves you and Godspeed.'

Richard took a long slow breath. 'Tell her I love her also,' he said.

THE TRIAL

In the deepest part of Lake Shakespeare there was an open entrance to a long submarine channel that ran under both the village of Beauvois and the habitat wall. During the design of New Eden, Richard, who had had considerable practical experience with contingency engineering, had stressed the importance of an emergency exit from the colony.

'But what would you need it for?' The Eagle had asked.

'I don't know,' Richard had said. 'But unforeseen situations often arise in life. A robust engineering design always has contingency protection.'

Richard swam carefully through the tunnel, slowing down every several minutes to check his air supply. When he reached the end he moved through a series of locks that left him eventually in a dry subterranean passage. He walked for about a hundred metres before he removed his diving apparatus and stored it at the side of the tunnel. When he reached the exit, which was at the eastern edge of the enclosed area that included both the habitats in the Northern Hemicylinder of Rama, Richard pulled his thermal jacket out of his waterproof pack.

Even though he realised that nobody could possibly know where he was, Richard opened the round door in the passage ceiling very cautiously. Then he eased out into the Central Plain. *So far, so good*, he thought, breathing a sigh of relief. *Now for Plan B.*

For four days Richard remained on the eastern side of the plain. Using his excellent small binoculars, he could see the lights indicating activities around the control centre, the Avalon region, or the second habitat probe site. As Richard had anticipated, there were search parties out in the interhabitat region for a day or two, but only one group came in his direction and they were easy for him to avoid.

His eyes grew accustomed to what he had thought was total darkness in the Central Plain. Actually there was a small amount of background light, due to reflection off the surfaces of Rama. Richard conjectured that the source or sources of the light must be in the Southern Hemicylinder, on the other side of the far wall of the second habitat.

Richard wished that he could fly, so that he would be able to soar over the walls and move freely in the vastness of the cylindrical world. The existence of the very low levels of reflected light piqued his interest in the rest of Rama. Was there still a Cylindrical Sea to the south of the barrier wall? Did New York still exist as an island in that sea? And what, if anything, was in the Southern Hemicylinder, a region even larger than the one that contained the two northern habitats?

On the fifth day after his escape Richard awoke from an especially disturbing dream about his father and started to walk in the direction of what he now called the avian habitat. He had shifted his sleeping pattern to be directly opposite the diurnal cycle in New Eden, so the time inside the colony was about seven in the evening. He assumed that all the humans who were working at the probe site had already finished for the day.

When he was about half a kilometre away from the opening in the avian habitat wall, Richard stopped to verify, using his binoculars, that there were no longer any people in the region. He then sent Falstaff to decoy the site watchman biot.

Richard was not certain how uniform the passage was that led into the second habitat. He had drawn an eighty-centimetre square on the floor of his study, and had convinced himself that he should be able to crawl through it. But what if the size of the passage was irregular? *We'll find out soon enough,* Richard said to himself as he approached the site.

Only one set of cables and instruments had been reinserted into the passage, so it was not difficult for Richard to clear them out. Falstaff had also been successful – Richard neither heard nor saw the watchman biot. He threw his small pack into the opening and then tried to climb in himself. It was impossible. He took off his jacket first, then his shirt, pants, and shoes. Wearing only his underwear and socks, Richard could barely fit into the passage. He tied his clothes together in a bundle, affixed them to the side of his pack, and squeezed into the opening.

It was a very slow crawl. Richard inched forward on his stomach using his hands and elbows, pushing his pack in front of him. He brushed his body against the walls and the ceiling with every movement. He stopped, his muscles already beginning to tire, after he was fifteen metres into the tunnel. The other side was still almost forty metres away.

As he rested Richard realised that his elbows, knees, and even the top of his balding head were already scraped and bleeding. Retrieving bandages from his pack was out of the question – just rolling over on his back and looking behind him was a monumental effort in the cramped quarters.

He also realised that he was very cold. While he had been crawling, the energy required to make forward progress had kept him warm. Once he had stopped, however, his exposed body had chilled rapidly. Having so much of his body resting against cold, metallic surfaces did not help either. His teeth began to chatter.

Richard pressed on slowly, painfully, for another fifteen minutes. Then his right hip cramped and in his body's involuntary response he smashed his head against the top of the passage. A little woozy from the blow, he became alarmed when he felt blood running down the side of his head.

There was no light in front of him. The dim illumination that had allowed him to monitor Prince Hal's progress had vanished. He struggled to roll over and see behind him. It was dark everywhere and he was becoming cold again. Richard felt his head and tried to determine how severely he had been cut. His panic started when he realised that he was still haemorrhaging.

Until that moment he had not felt claustrophobic. Now, all of a sudden, wedged into a dark passage that Richard could feel pressing against him from all sides, he felt as if he could not breathe. The walls seemed to be crushing him. He could not control himself. He screamed.

In less than half a minute some kind of light was being shone into the passage from his rear. He heard the funny English accent of the Garcia biot but could not understand what it was saying. *Almost certainly*, he thought, *it is filing an emergency report. I'd better move quickly.*

He began to crawl again, ignoring his fatigue, his bleeding head, and his skinless knees and elbows. Richard estimated that he had only ten more metres to go, fifteen at the most, when the passage seemed to shrink. He couldn't get through! He strained every muscle, but it was useless. He was definitely stymied. While he was trying to find a different crawling position that might be more geometrically favourable, he heard a soft pitter-patter approaching him from the direction of the avian habitat.

Moments later they were all over him. Richard spent five seconds of absolute terror before his mind informed him that the tickling sensations he was feeling all over his skin were caused by the leggies. He remembered seeing them on television – little spherical creatures about two centimetres in diameter attached to six radially symmetrical, multijointed legs almost ten centimetres long if fully extended.

One had stopped and was directly on his face, its legs straddling his nose and mouth. He tried to brush it off but bumped his head again. Richard began squirming around to shake off the leggies and somehow managed to make forward progress. With the leggies still all over him, he crawled the final metres to the exit.

He reached the outer avian annulus just as he heard a human voice behind him. 'Hello, is there somebody in there?' it said. 'Whoever you are, please identify yourself. We're here to help you.' A strong searchlight illuminated the passage.

Richard now discovered he had another problem. His exit was one metre above the floor of the annulus. *I should have crawled backward*, he thought, *and dragged my pack and clothes. It would have been much easier.*

It was too late for hindsight. With his pack and clothes on the floor below him and a second human voice now asking questions from behind, Richard continued to crawl forward until his body was halfway out of the passage. When he felt himself falling, Richard put his hands behind his head, tucked his chin against his chest, and, tried to make himself into a ball. He then bounced and rolled into the avian annulus. As he was falling the leggies jumped off and disappeared in the darkness.

The lights the humans were shining into the passage reflected off the inner wall of the annulus. After first ascertaining that he was not injured, and that his head was no longer seriously bleeding, Richard picked up his belongings and hobbled two hundred metres to the left. He stopped just under the porthole where Prince Hal had been captured by the avian.

Despite his fatigue, Richard wasted no time scaling the wall. As soon as he had finished dressing and tending to his wounds, he started the ascent. He was certain that a deployable camera would soon be pushed into the annulus to look for him.

Fortunately, there was a small ledge in front of the porthole that was large enough to accommodate Richard. He sat there while he cut through the metal mesh screen and then pushed it aside. He expected the leggies to show up at any minute, but he remained alone. Richard didn't see or hear anything from the habitat interior. Although he twice tried to summon Prince Hal on his radio, there was no response to his call.

Richard stared into the complete darkness of the avian habitat. *What is in there?* he wondered. The atmosphere in the interior, he reasoned, must be the same as that in the annulus, because air was allowed to circulate freely back and forth. Richard had just decided to pull out his flashlight for a look into the habitat interior when he heard sounds below and behind him. Seconds later he saw a light beam coming in his direction down on the floor of the annulus.

He scrunched himself over toward the interior of the habitat as far as he dared, to avoid the light, and listened carefully to the sounds. *It's the deployable camera*, he thought. *But it has limited range. It cannot operate without the tether.*

Richard sat very still. *What do I do now?* he said to himself, when it became apparent that the light attached to the camera was continuing to sweep the same, area below the porthole. *They must have seen something. If I turn on my flashlight and there's any reflection, they'll know where I am.*

He dropped a small object from his pack into the habitat to ensure that its floor level was the same as the annulus. He heard nothing. Richard tried another, slightly larger object, but still there was no sound of it striking the floor.

His heart rate surged as his mind told him that the floor of the habitat interior was far below the floor of the annulus. He recalled the basic structure of Rama, with its thick external shell, and realised that the habitat bottom could be several hundred metres below where he was sitting. Richard leaned over and stared again into the void.

The deployable camera suddenly stopped moving and its light remained focused on a specific spot in the annulus. Richard guessed that something must have fallen out of his pack while he was hurriedly hobbling from the passage to the area underneath the porthole. He knew that other lights and cameras would be coming soon. In his mind's eye Richard envisioned being captured and taken back to New Eden. He did not know specifically which colony laws he had broken, but he knew that he had committed many violations. A deep resentment coursed through him as he contemplated spending months or even years in detention. *Under no circumstances*, he told himself, *will I let that happen.*

He reached down the inside wall of the habitat to ascertain if there were enough irregularities to find places to put his feet and hands. Satisfied that it was not an impossible descent, he fumbled in his pack for his climbing line and anchored one end of it to the hinges supporting the mesh door. *Just in case I should slip*, he told himself.

A second light was now in the annulus behind him. Richard eased himself into the habitat with the line wrapped securely around his waist. He did not rappel, but he did use the line for occasional support while he was groping for footholds in the dark. The climb was not technically difficult; there were many small ledges on which Richard could place his feet.

Down and down he went. When he estimated that he had descended sixty or seventy metres, Richard decided to stop and take his flashlight out of his pack. He was not comforted when he shone the light down the wall. He still could not see the bottom. What he could see, maybe fifty more metres below him, was very diffuse, like a cloud, or even fog. *Great*, thought Richard sarcastically, *that's just great.*

Another thirty metres and he had reached the end of his climbing line. Richard could already feel the moisture from the fog. By now he was extremely tired. Since he was not willing to give up the security of the line, he backtracked up the wall a few metres, wrapped the line around himself several times, and went to sleep with his body pressed against the wall.

2

His dreams were very strange. Often he was falling, head over heels, down, down, and never hitting a bottom. In the last dream before Richard awakened, Toshio Nakamura and two Oriental toughs were interrogating him in a small room with white walls.

When he woke up Richard did not know where he was for several seconds. His first movement was to pull his right cheek away from the metallic surface of the wall. A few moments later, after Richard recalled that he had gone to sleep in a vertical position on the wall in the interior of the avian habitat, he switched on his flashlight and looked down. His heart skipped a beat when he saw that the fog was no longer there. Instead he could see the wall extending far, far below, and what appeared to be water where the wall finally terminated.

He leaned his head back and gazed above him. Since he knew he was about ninety metres below the porthole (the climbing line was a hundred metres long), he estimated that the distance down to the water was about two hundred and fifty more metres. His knees became weak as his brain began to comprehend fully his predicament. When Richard started to untangle himself from the extra loops he had made in the line before going to sleep, he noticed that his arms and hands were trembling.

He had a tremendous desire to flee, to ascend again to the porthole, and then leave this alien world altogether. *No*, Richard told himself, fighting his instinctive reaction. *Not yet. Only if there are no other viable options.*

He decided he would first have something to eat. Very gingerly Richard freed himself from part of the line and pulled some food and water out of his pack. Then he turned partially around and pointed his light into the interior of the habitat. Richard thought he could see shapes and forms off in the distance, but he couldn't be certain. *It could be just my imagination*, he thought.

When he was finished eating, he checked his food and water supplies and then made a mental list of his options. *It's all very simple*, Richard said to himself with a nervous laugh. *I can return to New Eden and become a convict. Maybe even a corpse. Or I can give up the security of my line and continue on down the wall*. He paused a moment, glancing up and down. *Or I can stay here and hope for a miracle.*

Remembering that an avian had come quickly when Prince Hal had shrieked, Richard began to shout. After two or three minutes, he stopped shouting and started to sing. He sang intermittently for most of an hour. He began with tunes from his days at Cambridge University and then switched to songs that had been popular during his lonely teenage years. Richard was astonished by how well he remembered the lyrics. *The memory is an amazing device*, he mused to himself. *What accounts for its selective reliability? Why can I remember almost all the words of these dumb songs from my adolescence and virtually nothing from my odyssey in Rama?*

Richard was reaching into his pack for another drink of water when there was suddenly light in the habitat. He was so startled that his feet slipped off the wall and all his weight was on the climbing line for a few seconds. The light was not blinding, as it had been when dawn had arrived in Rama II while he was riding the chairlift, but it was light nevertheless. As soon as Richard was again secure, he surveyed the world that was now unveiled in front of him.

The source of the illumination was a great, hooded ball hanging from the ceiling of the habitat. Richard estimated that the ball was about four kilometres away from him and roughly one kilometre directly above the top of the most prominent structure in sight, a large brown cylinder in the geometrical centre of the habitat. An opaque hood covered the top three fourths of the glowing ball, so most of its light was directed downward.

The basic design principle of the habitat interior was radial symmetry. At its centre was the upright brown cylinder, looking as if it was made from soil, that probably measured fifteen hundred metres from top to bottom. Richard of course could only see one side of the structure, but from its curvature he estimated that its diameter was between two and three kilometres.

There were no windows or doors on the outside of the cylinder. No light escaped anywhere from its interior. The only pattern on the side of the structure was a set of widely spaced curved lines, each one of which started at the top and ran entirely around the cylinder before reaching the bottom directly underneath its point of origination. The bottom of the cylinder was sitting on an elevated plateau at approximately the same altitude as the porthole through which Richard had entered.

Circumscribing the cylinder was an array of small white structures that formed a ring about three hundred metres in diameter. The two northern quadrants (Richard had entered the avian habitat through the north porthole) of this ring were identical; each quadrant had fifty or sixty buildings that were laid out in the same pattern. Richard assumed from the symmetry that the other two quadrants would conform to the same design.

A thin circular canal, maybe seventy or eighty metres wide, surrounded the ring of structures. Both the canal and the white buildings were located on the plateau at the same altitude as the bottom of the brown cylinder. Outside the canal, however, a large region of what appeared to be growing things, primarily green in colour, occupied most of the rest of the habitat. The ground in this green region sloped monotonically down from the canal to the shores of the four-hundred-meter-wide moat that was just inside the interior wall. The four apparently identical quadrants in the green region were further subdivided into four sectors each, which Richard, basing his designations on Earth analogues, called jungle, forest, grassland, and desert.

For about ten minutes Richard stared quietly at the vast panorama. Because the level of illumination dropped in direct proportion to the distance from the cylinder, he could not see the closer regions any more clearly than those in the distance. Nevertheless, the details were still impressive. The more he looked, the more new things he noticed. There were small lakes and rivers in the green region, an occasional tiny island in the moat, and what looked like roads between the white buildings. *Of course*, he found himself thinking. *Why would I have expected otherwise? We have reproduced a small Earth in New Eden. This must represent, in some way, the home planet of the avians.*

His last thought reminded him that both Nicole and he had been convinced from the beginning that the avians were no longer (if they had ever been) a high-technology, spacefaring species. Richard pulled out his binoculars and studied the brown cylinder in the distance. *What secrets do you hold?* he wondered, thrilled momentarily by the possibilities for adventure and discovery.

Richard next searched the skies for some sign of the avians. He was disappointed. He thought he saw flying creatures once or twice at the top of the brown cylinder, but the flecks flitted in and out of his binocular vision so quickly that he couldn't be absolutely certain. Everywhere else he looked – in all parts of the green region, in the neighbourhood of the white buildings, even in the moat – he saw no evidence of movement. There was no positive indication that anything was alive in the avian habitat.

The light disappeared after four hours and Richard was again left in the dark in the middle of the vertical wall. He checked his thermometer, including its historical data base. The temperature had not varied more than half a degree from 26°C since he had entered the habitat. *Impressive thermal control*, Richard said to himself. *But why so stringent? Why use so much of the power resource to keep a fixed temperature?*

As the darkness stretched into hours, Richard became impatient. Even though he regularly rested each set of muscles by temporarily supporting himself in different ways with his line, his body was slowly wearing out. It was time for him to consider taking some action. Reluctantly he decided that it would be foolhardy for him to abandon the line and descend to the moat. *What would I do when I reached there anyway?* he thought. *Swim across? And then what? I'd still have to turn around if I didn't find food immediately.*

He began to climb slowly toward the porthole. While he was resting about halfway to the exit he thought he heard something very faint off to his right. Richard stopped and quietly reached into his pack for his receiver set. With a minimum of motion he turned the gain up to its highest level and put on the earphones. At first he heard nothing. But after several minutes he picked up a sound below him, coming from the moat. It was impossible to identify exactly what he was hearing – it could have been several boats moving through the water – but there was no doubt that some kind of activity was occurring down there.

Was that a faint flapping of wings as well, again somewhere off to his right? With no warning Richard suddenly screamed at the top of his lungs, and then truncated the scream abruptly. The flurry of wing sounds died out quickly, but for a second or two they were unmistakable.

Richard was exultant. 'I know you're there,' he shouted gleefully. 'I know you're watching me.'

He had a plan. It was certainly a long shot, but it was definitely better than nothing. Richard checked his food and water, assured himself that they were both marginally adequate, and took a deep breath. *It's now or never*, he thought.

He practised descending without relying on the line for support. It made progress more difficult, but he could do it. When he reached the end of the line, Richard unharnessed himself and shone his light down the wall. At least as far as the top of the fog, which by now had returned, there were plenty of ledges available. He continued down very carefully, admitting to himself that he was frightened. Several times he thought he could hear his own heart beating in his earphones.

Now, if I'm right, Richard thought when he descended into the fog, *I'm going to have company down here.* The moisture made the descent doubly difficult. Once he slipped and almost fell, but he managed to recover. Richard stopped at a spot where his hand and footholds were unusually solid. He estimated that he was about fifty metres above the moat. *I'll wait now until I hear something. They'll have to come closer in the fog.*

In a short while he heard the wings again. This time it sounded as if it was a pair of avians. Richard stood where he was for over an hour, until the fog began to thin. Several more times he heard the wings of his observers.

He had planned to wait until it was light again to descend all the way to the water. But when the fog lifted and the lights still did not return, Richard began to worry about the time. He started down the wall in the dark. About ten metres above the moat he heard his observers fly away. Two minutes later the interior of the avian habitat was again illuminated.

Richard wasted no time. His plan was simple. Based on the boat noises that he had heard in the dark, Richard assumed that there was something happening in the moat that was critical to the avians or whoever it was that lived in the brown cylinder. If not, he reasoned, why had they proceeded with the activity, knowing that he might hear it? If they had postponed it for even a few hours, he would almost certainly have been gone from the habitat.

Richard intended to enter the moat. *If the avians feel threatened in any way,* he reasoned, *they will take some action. If not, I will immediately begin my ascent and take my chances in New Eden.*

Just before he eased into the water, Richard took off his shoes and with some difficulty put them into his waterproof pack. At least they wouldn't be wet if he had to climb out. Seconds later, as soon as he was completely in the water, a pair of avians flew at him from where they had been hiding in the green region directly across the moat.

They were frantic. They jabbered and shrieked and acted as if they were going to tear Richard apart with their talons. He was so ecstatic that his plan had worked that he virtually ignored their displays. The avians hovered over him and tried to herd him back to the wall. He trod water and studied them closely.

These two were slightly different from the ones that he and Nicole had encountered in Rama II. These avians had the velvet body coverings, just like the others, but the velvet was purple. The single ring around each of their necks was black. They were also smaller (*Perhaps they're younger,* Richard thought) than the earlier avians, and much more frenetic. One of the creatures actually touched Richard's cheek with its talon when he didn't move swiftly enough to the wall.

At length Richard did climb up onto the wall, barely out of the water, but that did not seem to appease the avians. Almost immediately the two large birds began taking turns flying narrow patterns up the wall, showing Richard that they wanted him to ascend. When he didn't move they became more and more frantic.

'I want to go with you,' Richard said, pointing at the brown cylinder in the distance. Each time he repeated his hand signal the huge creatures shrieked and jabbered and flew up in the direction of the porthole.

The avians were becoming frustrated and Richard started to worry that perhaps they might attack him. Suddenly he had a brilliant idea. *But can I remember the entry code?* he asked himself excitedly. *It's been so many years.*

When he reached in his pack the avians flew away immediately. 'That proves,' Richard said out loud as he switched on his beloved portable computer, 'that the leggies are your electronic observers. How else could you have possibly known that human beings may keep weapons in packs like these?'

He punched five letters on the keyboard and then smiled broadly when the display activated. 'Come here,' Richard said, waving at the pair of avians who had retreated almost to the other side of the moat. 'Come here,' he repeated, 'I have something to show you.'

He held up the monitor and displayed the complex computer graphic that he had used many years before in Rama II to convince the creatures to carry Nicole and him across the Cylindrical Sea. It was an elegant graphic showing three avians carrying two human figures across a body of water in a harness. The two giant birds approached tentatively. *That's it,* Richard said to himself excitedly. *Come over here and take a good look.*

3

Richard did not know exactly how long he had been living in the dim room. He had lost track of time soon after they had taken his pack away from him. His routine had been the same, day after day. He slept in the corner of the room. Whenever he awakened, whether from a nap or a long sleep, two avians would enter his room from the corridor and hand him a manna melon to eat. He knew they came through the locked door at the end of the corridor, but if he tried to sleep near the door they simply denied him his food. It had been an easy lesson for Richard to learn.

Every other day or so a different pair of avians would enter his prison and clean up his wastes. His clothes were rank, and Richard knew that he was unbearably filthy, but he had not been able to communicate to his captors that he wanted a bath.

He had been exultant in the beginning. When the two juvenile avians had finally approached close enough to watch the graphic, and then had made their first attempt to take the computer from him several minutes later, Richard had decided to program the display to repeat indefinitely.

In less than an hour the largest avian he had ever seen, one with a grey velvet body and three brilliant cherry red rings around its neck, had returned with the two juveniles, and the three of them had picked Richard up in their talons. They had carried him across the moat, put him down temporarily in a desert area, and then, after a series of jabbers among the three of them that must have been a discussion about the optimal way of carrying him, they had lifted him high into the air.

It had been a breathtaking flight. The view that Richard had had of the landscape in the habitat had reminded him of a ride he had once taken in a hot air balloon in southern France. He had flown in the clutches of the avians all the way to the top of the brown cylinder, directly underneath the bright hooded ball. They had been met by a half dozen additional avians, one holding Richard's computer, which was still repeating its graphics. Later they had been escorted down a wide vertical corridor into the interior of the cylinder.

That first fifteen hours or so Richard had been taken from one large group of avians to another. He had thought that his hosts were just introducing him to all the citizens of avianland. Assuming that there were not too many avians who attended more than one of the short jabber and shriek sessions, Richard estimated that there were about seven hundred individual birds.

After his parade through the conference halls of the avian realm, Richard had been taken to a small room where the three-ringed avian and two of its associates, each large creatures as well with three red neck rings, watched him day and night for about a week. During that time Richard was allowed access to his computer and all the items in the pack. At the end of that observation period, however, they had taken away all his belongings and moved him to his prison.

That must have been three months ago, give or take a week, Richard said to himself one day as he began his twice-daily walk that was his primary regular exercise. The corridor outside his room was approximately two hundred metres long. He usually made eight complete laps, back and forth from the door at the end of the corridor to the rock wall just outside his room.

And during this entire period there has not been one single visit from the leaders. So the observation period must have been my trial – at least the avian equivalent ... And was I found guilty of something? Is that why I have been restricted to this dingy cell?

Richard's shoes were wearing out and his clothes were already tattered. Since the temperature was comfortable (he conjectured that it must be twenty-six degrees Celsius everywhere in the avian habitat), he wasn't worried about being cold. But for many reasons he wasn't looking forward to being naked all the time after his clothes eventually disintegrated. He smiled to himself, remembering his modesty during the observation period. *Taking a crap when three giant birds are watching your every move is certainty not an easy task.*

He had grown tired of eating manna melon for every meal, but at least it was nourishing. The liquid at the centre was refreshing and the moist meat had a pleasant taste. But Richard longed for something different to eat. *Even that synthetic stuff from the White Room would be a welcome change*, he had told himself several times.

In his solitude Richard's greatest challenge had been to retain his mental acumen. He had begun by doing mathematical problems in his head. More recently, worried that the sharpness of his memory had already decayed measurably because of his age, he had started to pass the time by reconstructing events and even entire major chronological segments of his life.

Of particular interest to him during these memory exercises were the huge gaps associated with his odyssey in Rama II during the voyage from the Earth to the Node. Although it was difficult for Richard to recall many specific events from the odyssey, eating the manna melon always evoked memory fragments from his long stay with the avians during that journey.

Once, after a meal, he had suddenly recalled a large ceremony with many avians. He had remembered a fire in a domelike structure and all the avians wailing in unison after the fire was over. Richard had been puzzled. He had not been able to remember anything about the context of the memory. *Where did that take place? Was that just before I was captured by the octospiders?* he had wondered. But as usual, when he had tried to remember something about what he had experienced with the octospiders, he had ended up with a whopping headache.

Richard was thinking about his earlier odyssey again when, on the last lap of his daily walk, he passed underneath the solitary light in the corridor. He looked in front of him and saw that the door to his prison was open. *That's it*, he said to himself, *I've finally gone crazy. Now I'm seeing things.*

But the door remained open as he approached it. Richard walked on through, stopping to touch the open door and to verify that he had not lost his sanity. He passed two more lights before he came to a small open storage room on the right. Eight or nine manna melons were neatly stacked on the shelves. *Ah, ha*, Richard thought. *I get it. They've expanded my prison. From now on I'm allowed to obtain my own food. Now, if there's just a bathroom somewhere ...*

Farther down the hallway there was indeed running water in another small room on the left. Richard drank heartily, washed his face, and was sorely tempted to bathe. However, his curiosity was too strong. He wanted to know the extent of his new domain.

The corridor that ran just outside his cell ended at a perpendicular intersection. Richard could go either way. Thinking perhaps that he was in some kind of maze to test his mental capabilities, he dropped his outer shirt at the intersection and proceeded to the right. There were definitely more lights in that direction.

After he had walked for twenty metres or so, he saw a pair of avians approaching in the distance. Actually he heard their jabber first, for they were involved in an animated discussion. When they were only five metres away Richard stopped. The two avians glanced at him, acknowledged him with a short shriek at a different pitch, and then continued on down the corridor.

He next encountered a trio of avians with roughly the same interaction. *What is going on here?* Richard wondered as he continued to walk. *Am I no longer in prison?*

In the first large room that he passed, four avians were sitting together in a circle, passing a set of polished sticks back and forth and jabbering constantly. Later, just before the hallway widened into a major meeting room, Richard stood in the doorway of another chamber and watched with fascination as a pair of leggies did what appeared to be push-ups on the top of a square table. Half a dozen quiet avians studied the leggies intently.

There were twenty of the birdlike creatures in the meeting room. They were all gathered around a table, staring at a paperlike document that had been spread out in front of them. One of the avians had a pointer in its talon and was using it to indicate specific items on the document. There were strange squiggles on the paper that were totally incomprehensible, but Richard convinced himself that the avians were looking at a map.

When Richard tried to move closer to the table so that he could see better, the avians in front of him graciously moved aside. Once in the ensuing conversation, Richard even thought from the body language around the table that one of the questions had been directed at him. *I really am losing my mind*, he told himself, shaking his head.

But I still don't know why I have been given all this freedom, Richard thought as he sat in his room and ate his manna melon. Six weeks had passed since he had found the door to his prison opened. Many changes had been made in his cell. Two of the lanternlike lights had been installed on his walls and Richard was now sleeping on a pile of material that reminded him of hay. There was even a constantly filled container of fresh water in the corner of his room.

Richard had felt certain, when his restrictions were initially lifted, that it was only a matter of hours or at most a day or two before something really significant happened. In a sense he had been correct, for the next morning two juvenile aliens had awakened him from his sleep and begun his avian language lessons. They had started with simple items, like the manna melon, water, and Richard himself, at which they would first point and then slowly repeat a sound, clearly the jabberword for that particular item. With some effort Richard had learned a great deal of vocabulary, although his ability to differentiate between closely related shrieks and jabbers was not too sharp. He was absolutely hopeless when it came to making the sounds on his own. He simply didn't have the physical equipment to speak in the avian language.

But Richard had expected that somehow his knowledge of the bigger picture would become clearer, and that had not happened. Certainly the avians were trying to educate him, and they had given him freedom to roam anywhere he wanted in their cylinder – he even ate with them occasionally when he was in their midst and the manna melons showed up – but what was it all for? The way they looked at him, especially the leaders, suggested to Richard that they were expecting some kind of response. *But what response?* Richard asked himself for the hundredth time as he finished his manna melon.

As far as Richard could tell, the avians did not have a written language. He had seen no books and none of the creatures ever wrote anything. There were those strange maplike documents that they occasionally studied, or at least that was Richard's interpretation of their activity, but they never created any of them ... or *marked* on any of them. It was a puzzle.

And what about the leggies? Richard encountered the creatures two or three times a week and once had a pair in his room for several hours, but they would never sit still and let him analyse one of them. One time, when he had tried to grasp a leggie in his hand, Richard had received a rude shock, an electric current almost certainly, that had caused him to release the leggie immediately.

Richard's mind jumped from image to image as he tried to ascertain some sensible pattern to his life in avianland. He was extremely frustrated. Yet he would not accept for a minute that there was *no* plan behind his capture and then subsequent increased freedom. He continued to search for an answer by reviewing all his experiences in their domain.

There was only one major area of the avian living quarters that was off limits to Richard, and he probably could not have reached it anyway since he was unable to fly. Occasionally he would see one or two avians descend in the great vertical corridor and go below the levels that he normally frequented. Once Richard even saw a pair of hatchlings, no larger than a human hand, being carried up from the dark regions below. On another occasion Richard had pointed down at the darkness and his accompanying avian had shaken its head. Most of the creatures had learned the simple head motions of yes and no in Richard's language.

But somewhere, Richard thought, *there must be additional information. I must be missing some clues.* He vowed to conduct an exhaustive survey of the entire avian living area, including not only the dense apartments on the opposite side of the vertical corridor, where he usually felt unwanted, but also the large manna melon storehouses on the bottom level. *I will make a thorough map,* he said to himself, *to make certain that I haven't neglected something critical.*

As soon as Richard had rendered the avian living area in his three-dimensional graphics, he knew what he had been overlooking. The often disorganised passageways in the cylinder, including horizontal and vertical corridors for both walking and flight, had never been synthesised by Richard into one coherent picture. *Of course*, he said to himself as he projected different views of his complex map onto his computer monitor. *How could I have been so stupid? More than seventy percent of the cylinder is still unaccounted for.*

Richard resolved to take his computer pictures to one of the avian leaders and request, somehow, to see the rest of the cylinder. It was not an easy task. Some kind of crisis was disturbing the avians that particular day, as the corridors were full of jabbers, shrieks, and avians rushing to and fro. Out in the great vertical corridor Richard watched thirty or forty of the largest creatures fly up and out of the cylinder in some kind of organised formation.

Finally Richard managed to obtain the attention of one of the three-ringed giants. It was fascinated by the detail it saw on the computer monitor and by all the different geometrical representations of its home. But Richard was unable to convey his primary message – that he wanted to see the rest of the cylinder.

The leader called in some colleagues to watch the demonstration and Richard was treated to appreciative avian jabber. He was dismissed, however, when another bird broke into their meeting with what must have been important news about their ongoing crisis.

Richard returned to his cell. He was dejected. He lay on his hay mat and thought of the family that he had left behind in New Eden. *Maybe it's time for me to leave*, he thought, wondering what the protocol was in avianland for obtaining permission to depart. While he was lying down a visitor came into his room.

Richard had never seen this particular avian before. It had four cobalt blue rings around its neck and the velvet covering of its body was a deep black with occasional white tufts. Its eyes were astonishingly clear and – or so Richard surmised – very sad. The avian waited for Richard to stand and then started speaking, very slowly. Richard understood some of the words, most importantly the oft-repeated combination 'follow me.'

Outside his cell three other avians were respectfully standing. They walked behind Richard and his important visitor. The group left Richard's cell area, crossed the single bridge that spanned the great vertical corridor, and entered the section of the cylinder where the manna melons were stored.

At the back of one of the manna melon storehouses were indentations in the wall that Richard had not noticed when he had conducted his survey. When Richard and the avians approached within a few metres of the indentations, the wall slid to the side and revealed what appeared to be an enormous elevator. The avian superleader gestured for him to enter.

Once he was inside, the four avians each jabbered 'goodbye' and formed into a circle to formalise their parting with a turn and a bow. Richard tried his best to imitate their jabber for goodbye before he also bowed and backed into the elevator. The wall closed seconds later.

4

The elevator ride was painfully slow. The immense car had a square floor approximately twenty metres on a side, with a ceiling that was another eight to ten metres above Richard's head. The floor of the car was flat everywhere except for two pairs of parallel grooves, one pair on either side of Richard, that ran from the door to the back of the elevator. *They can certainly transport huge loads in this*, Richard thought, staring at the ceiling far above him.

He tried to estimate the rate of descent of the elevator, but it was impossible. He had no frame of reference. According to Richard's map of the cylinder, the manna melon storehouses should have been about eleven hundred metres above the base. *So if we're going all the way to the bottom, at what would be a normal elevator speed on Earth, then this trip may take several minutes.*

It was the longest three minutes of his life. Richard had absolutely no idea what he would find when the elevator doors opened. *Maybe I'll be outside, he thought suddenly. Maybe I'll be on the edge of that region with the white structures ... Could they be sending me home?*

He had just begun to wonder how life might have changed in New Eden when the elevator came to a stop. The large doors opened and for several seconds Richard was certain that his heart had jumped out of his body. Standing directly in front of him, and obviously staring at him with all their eyes, were two creatures far stranger than any he had ever imagined.

Richard could not move. What he was seeing was so unbelievable that he was physically paralysed while his mind struggled with the bizarre inputs it was receiving from his senses. Each of the beings in front of him had four eyes on its 'head'. In addition to the two large, milky ovals on either side of an invisible line of symmetry that bisected the head, each creature had two additional eyes attached to stalks raised ten to twelve centimeters above the top of its forehead. Behind the large head, their bodies had three segments, with a pair of appendages for each segment, giving them six legs altogether. The aliens were standing upright on their two back legs, their front four appendages neatly tucked against their smooth, cream-coloured underbellies.

They moved toward him in the elevator and Richard backed away, frightened. The two creatures turned to each other and communicated in a high-frequency noise that originated from a small circular orifice below the oval eyes. Richard blinked, felt dizzy, and dropped down on one knee to steady himself. His heart was still pumping furiously.

The aliens also changed position, putting their middle legs on the floor. In that posture they resembled giant ants with their front two legs off the ground and their heads raised high. The entire time the black spheres at the end of the eye stalks continued to pivot, scanning the full three hundred and sixty degrees, and the milky material in the dark brown ovals moved from side to side.

For several minutes they sat more or less stationary, as if they were encouraging Richard to examine them. Fighting against his fear, he tried to study them in an objective, scientific fashion. The creatures were roughly the size of medium-sized dogs, but they certainly weighed much less. Their bodies were thin and quite trim. The front and back segments were larger than the middle one, and all three body divisions displayed a polished carapace on top that was made of some kind of hard material.

Richard would have classified them as very large insects except for their extraordinary appendages, which were thick, perhaps even muscled, and covered with a short, very dense, black-and-white-striped 'hair' that made it appear as if the creatures were wearing panty hose. Their hands, if that was the proper appellation, were free of the hairy covering and had four fingers each, including an opposing thumb on the front pair.

Richard had just summoned enough courage to look again at their incredible heads when there was a high-pitched, sirenlike noise behind the two aliens. They turned around. Richard stood up and saw a third creature approaching at a rapid clip. Its motion was marvellous to watch. It ran like a cat with six legs, stretching out parallel to the ground and pushing off with a different pair of legs at each point in its stride.

The three engaged in a quick conversation and the newcomer, lifting up its head and front legs, motioned unambiguously for Richard to leave the elevator. He walked out behind the trio and entered a very large chamber.

This room was a manna melon storehouse also, but that was its only similarity to the one in the avian portion of the cylinder. High technology and automated equipment were everywhere. In the ceiling ten metres above them, a mechanical cherry picker was moving on a rail system. It would grasp individual melons and load them in freight cars on grooves at one end of the room. While Richard and his hosts watched, a freight car moved down the groove and came to a stop in the elevator.

The creatures bounced off down one of the aisles in the room and Richard hastened to follow. They waited for him at the door, then raced to their left, looking backward to see if he was still in sight. Richard ran after them for most of the next two minutes, until they reached a wide open atrium, many metres high, with a transportation device in its centre.

The device was a remote cousin of the escalator. Actually there were two of them, one going up and another down, that spiraled around the two thick poles in the centre of the atrium. The escalators moved very quickly at quite a steep angle. Every five metres or so they reached the next level, or floor, and the passengers then walked a metre to the spiral escalator around the other pole. What passed for a railing on the side of the escalator was a barrier only thirty centimetres high. The alien creatures rode in the horizontal position, with all six legs on the moving ramp. Richard, who was standing originally, quickly dropped down to all fours to keep from falling out.

During the ride a dozen or so other aliens, riding on the down half of the escalator, passed Richard and gawked at him with their amazing faces. *But how do they eat?* Richard wondered, noting that the circular hole they used for communication was certainly not large enough for much food. There were no other orifices on their heads, although there were some small knobs and wrinkles whose purposes were unknown.

Where they were taking Richard was on the eighth or ninth level. All three of the creatures waited for him until he reached the appointed platform. Richard followed them into a hexagonal building with bright red markings on the front. *That's funny*, Richard thought, staring at the strange squiggles. *I've seen that writing before. , . . Of course, on the map or whatever document it was the avians were reading.*

Richard was placed in a room that was well lit and tastefully decorated in black and white with geometric patterns. There were objects around him of all shapes and sizes, but Richard had no idea what any of them were. The aliens used sign language to inform Richard that this was where he was going to stay. Then they departed. A weary Richard studied the furniture, trying to figure out which thing might be the bed, and then stretched out on the floor to sleep.

Myrmicats. That's what I'll call them. Richard had awakened after sleeping for four hours and could not stop thinking about the alien creatures. He wanted to give them a good name. After dismissing both cat-ant and catsect, he remembered that someone who studies ants is called a myrmecologist. He chose myrmicat because it looked better in his mind when spelled with an 'i' instead of an 'e'.

Richard's room was well lit. In fact, every place he had been in the myrmicat habitat had had good illumination, which was in marked contrast to the dark, catacomblike corridors of the upper portions of the brown cylinder. *I have not seen any of the avians since the elevator ride*, Richard was thinking. *So apparently these two species do not live together. At least not completely. But they both use manna melons ... What exactly is their connection?*

A pair of myrmicats bounded through the entry, placed a neatly sectioned melon and a cup of water in front of him, and then disappeared. Richard was both hungry and thirsty. Several seconds after he had finished with his breakfast, the pair of creatures returned. Using the hands on their front legs, the myrmicats gestured for him to stand up. Richard stared at them. *Are these the same creatures as yesterday?* he wondered. *And are they the same pair that brought the melon and the water?* He thought back over all the myrmicats he had seen, including those who had passed him going down the escalator. He could not recall a single distinguishing or identifying characteristic in any individual. *So they all look the same?* he thought. *Then how do they tell each other apart?*

The myrmicats led him out into the corridor and bolted away to the right. *This is great*, Richard said to himself, starting to jog after spending a few seconds admiring the beauty of their gait. *They must think humans are all athletes.* One of the myrmicats stopped about forty metres in front of him. It did not turn around, but Richard could tell it was watching him because both of its stalk eyes were bent back in his direction. 'I'm coming,' Richard shouted. 'But I can't run that fast.'

It wasn't long before Richard figured out that the pair of aliens was giving him a guided tour of the myrmicat domain. The tour was very logically planned. The first stop, a very brief one, was at a manna melon storehouse. Richard watched two freight cars filled with melons slide down grooves into an elevator similar to (or identical with) the one in which he had descended the day before.

After another five-minute jog, Richard entered an entirely different section of the myrmicat den. Whereas the walls in the other section had been mostly metallic grey or white, except in his room, here the rooms and corridors were all decorated profusely, either with colours or geometric patterns or both. One vast chamber was about the size of a theatre and had three liquid pools in its floor. About a hundred myrmicats were in this room, half apparently swimming in the pools (with only their stalk eyes and the top half of their carapaces above the water line), and the other half either sitting on the ridges dividing the three pools from each other, or milling around in a weird building on the far side of the room.

But were they actually swimming? On closer inspection Richard noticed that the creatures did not move around in the pool – they just submerged in a given spot and stayed under the water for several minutes. Two of the pools were quite thick, roughly the consistency of a rich, creamy soup on Earth, and the third, clear pool was almost certainly water. Richard followed a single myrmicat as it moved from one of the thick pools to the water, then over to the other thick pool. *What are they doing?* Richard wondered. *And why have they brought me here?*

As if on cue he was tapped on the back by one of the myrmicats. It pointed to Richard, then to the pools, and then to Richard's mouth. He had no idea what it was telling him. The guide myrmicat next walked down the slope toward the pools and submerged itself in one of the thicker pools. When it returned it stood on its back pair of legs and pointed to the grooves between the segments of its soft, cream-coloured underbelly.

It was clearly important to the myrmicats that Richard understand what was going on at the pools. At the next stop he watched a combination of myrmicats and some high-technology machines grinding up fibrous material and then mixing it with water and other liquids to create a thin slurry that looked like what was in one of the pools. At length one of the aliens put its ringer into the slurry and then touched the material to Richard's lips. *They must be telling me that the pools are for feeding,* Richard thought. *So they don't eat manna melon after all? Or at least they have a more varied diet? This is all fascinating.*

Soon they were off on another jog to another distant corner of the den. Here Richard saw thirty or forty smaller creatures, obviously juvenile myrmicats, engaged in activities with supervisory adults. In physical appearance the little ones resembled their elders except for one major difference – they had no carapace. Richard concluded that the hard top covering was probably not exuded by the creature until its growth was complete. Although Richard imagined that what he saw occurring with the juveniles was a rough approximation of school, or perhaps a nursery, he of course had no way of knowing for certain. But at one point he was sure that he heard the juveniles repeating in unison a sequence of sounds made by an adult myrmicat.

Richard next rode the escalator with his pair of tour guides. On about the twentieth level the creatures left the escalator and the open atrium, racing quickly down a corridor that ended in a vast factory filled with myrmicats and machines engaged in an impressive array of tasks. His guides always seemed to be in a hurry, so it was difficult for Richard to study any particular process. The factory was like a machine shop on Earth. There were noises of all kinds, smells of chemicals and metals, and the whine of myrmicat communication throughout the room. At one position Richard watched a pair of myrmicats repair a cherry picker similar to the machine that he had seen operating in the manna melon storehouse the day before.

In one corner of the factory was a special area that was sealed off from the rest of the work. Although his guides did not lead him in that direction, Richard's curiosity was piqued. Nobody stopped him when he crossed the threshold of the special area. Inside the large cubicle a myrmicat operator was presiding over an automated manufacturing process.

Long, skinny, jointed pieces of light metal or plastic came into the room on a conveyor belt from one direction. Small spheres about two centimetres in diameter entered from an adjacent cubicle on another conveyor. Where the two belts merged, a large, rectangular machine, mounted in housing that was hanging from the high ceiling, descended onto the parts with a peculiar sucking sound. Thirty seconds later the myrmicat operator caused the machine to withdraw and a pair of leggies scrambled off the belt, folded their long legs around them, and jumped into positions in a box that looked like a gigantic egg carton.

Richard watched the process repeat several times. He was fascinated. He was also slightly bewildered. *So the myrmicats make the leggies. And the maps.*

And probably the spacecraft too, wherever they and the avians come from. So what is this? Some advanced kind of symbiosis?

He shook his head as the leggie assembly process in front of him continued. Moments later Richard heard a myrmicat noise behind him. He turned around. One of his guides extended a slice of manna melon in his direction.

Richard was becoming exhausted. He had no idea how long he had been touring, but he felt as if it had been many, many hours.

There was no way he could possibly synthesise everything he had seen. After the ride in the small elevator to the upper reaches of the myrmicat region, where Richard not only had visited the avian hospital staffed and run by the myrmicats, but also had watched the avians hatching out of brown, leathery eggs under the watchful eyes of myrmicat doctors, Richard knew for certain that there was indeed a complex symbiotic relationship between the two species. *But why?* he wondered as his guides allowed him to rest temporarily near the top of the escalator. *The avians clearly benefit from the myrmicats. But what do these giant ant-cats get from the avians?*

His guides led him down a broad corridor toward a large door several hundred metres in the distance. For once they were not running. As they neared the door, three other myrmicats entered the hallway from smaller side corridors and the creatures began to talk in their high-frequency language. At one point all five of them stopped and Richard imagined that an argument was under way. He studied them carefully while they talked, especially their faces. Even the wrinkles and folds around the noise-making orifice and oval eyes were identical from creature to creature. There was absolutely no way of distinguishing one myrmicat from another.

At length the entire group began again to walk toward the door. From the distance Richard had underestimated its size. As he drew near, he could see that it was twelve to fifteen metres tall, and more than three metres wide. Its surface was intricately and magnificently carved, the central focus of the artwork being a square, four-panel decoration with a flying avian in the upper left quadrant, a manna melon in the upper right, a running myrmicat in the lower left partition, and something that looked like candyfloss with scattered thick, clustered lumps in the lower right.

Richard stopped to admire the artwork. At first he had a vague feeling that he had seen this door, or at least the design, before, but he told himself that it couldn't be possible. However, as he was running his fingers across the sculpted figure of the myrmicat, his memory suddenly awoke. *Yes*, Richard thought excitedly to himself, *of course. At the back of the avian lair in Rama II. That was where the fire was.*

Moments later the door swung open and Richard was ushered into what resembled a large underground cathedral. The room in which he found himself was over fifty metres tall. Its basic floor shape was a circle, about thirty metres in diameter, and there were six separate naves off to the side, around the circle. The walls were dazzling. Virtually every square inch contained sculptures or supporting frescoes meticulously created with great attention to detail. It was overwhelmingly beautiful.

At the centre of the cathedral was an elevated platform on which a myrmicat was standing and speaking. Below him were a dozen others, all sitting on their back four legs and watching the speaker with rapt attention.

As Richard wandered around in the room he realised that the decorations on the wall, in a metre-wide strip about eighty centimetres above the floor, were telling an orderly story. Richard quietly followed the artwork until he reached what he thought was the beginning of the story. The first decoration was a sculptured portrait of a manna melon. In the next three panels something could be seen growing inside the melon. Whatever was growing was tiny in the second panel, but by the fourth sculpture it occupied almost the entire interior of the melon.

In the fifth panel a tiny head with two milky, oval eyes, stalk nubs, and a small circular orifice below the eyes could be seen poking its way out of the melon. The sixth sculpture, which showed a juvenile myrmicat very much like the ones Richard had seen earlier in the day, confirmed what he had been surmising as he had been following the decorations. *Holy shit*, Richard said to himself, *so a manna melon is a myrmicat egg! His thoughts raced ahead. But that doesn't make sense. The avians eat the melons ... In fact, the myrmicats even feed them to me ... What's going on here?*

Richard was so astonished by what he had discovered (and so tired from all the running during the tour) that he sat down in front of the sculpture containing the juvenile myrmicats. He tried to figure out the relationship between the myrmicats and the avians. He could cite no parallel symbiosis on Earth, although he was well aware that species often worked together to improve each other's chances for survival. But how could one species remain friendly with another when its eggs were the sole food for the second species? Richard concluded that what he had thought were fundamental biological tenets did not apply to the avians and the myrmicats.

While Richard was pondering the strange new things he had learned, a group of myrmicats gathered around him. They all motioned for him to stand up. A minute later he was following them down a winding ramp on the other side of the room to a special crypt in the basement of their cathedral.

For the first time since Richard had entered the habitat the lighting was dim. The myrmicats beside him moved slowly, almost reverently, as they proceeded down a broad passage with an arched ceiling. At the other end of the passage was a pair of doors that opened into a large room filled with a soft white material. Although the material, which looked like cotton from a distance, was densely arrayed, its individual filaments were mostly very thin, except where they came together in clumps, or ganglia, that were scattered in no definable pattern throughout the large white volume.

Richard and the myrmicats stopped in the entryway, a metre or so away from where the material began. The cottony network extended in all directions for as far as Richard could see. While he was studying its intricate mesh construction, the elements of the material very slowly began to move, pulling apart to form a lane that would continue the path from the passage into the interior of its network. *It's alive*, Richard thought, his pulse racing as he watched in fascination and terror.

Five minutes later, an alley had opened up that was just large enough for Richard to walk ten metres into the material. The myrmicats around him were all pointing toward the cottony web. Richard started shaking his head. *I'm sorry, fellas*, Richard wanted to say, *but there's something about this situation that I don't like. So I'll just skip this part of the tour if it's all right with you.*

The myrmicats kept pointing. Richard had no choice, and he knew it. *What is it going to do to me?* he asked as he took his first step forward. *Eat me? Is that what this has been all about? That would make no sense at all.*

He turned around. The myrmicats had not moved. Richard took a deep breath and walked the full ten metres into the lane, to a spot where he could reach out and touch one of the odd ganglia in the living mesh. As he was examining the ganglion carefully, the material around him began to move again. Richard whirled around and saw that the lane behind him was closing. Momentarily frantic, he tried to run in that direction, back toward the passage, but it was a waste of energy. The net caught him and he resigned himself to accept whatever was going to happen next.

Richard stood perfectly still as the web enveloped him. The tiny elements, like threads, were about a millimetre wide. Slowly, steadily, they began to cover his body. *Wait*, Richard thought, *wait. You're going to suffocate me.*

But surprisingly, even though hundreds of filaments were already wrapping around his head and face, he was having no difficulty breathing.

Before his hands were immobilised, Richard tried to pull one of the tiny elements off his arm. It was almost impossible. As they had been wrapping around him, the threads had also been making insertions in his skin. After many tugs, he finally succeeded in freeing the white filaments from one small portion of his forearm, but he was bleeding in the areas that had been freed. Richard surveyed his body and estimated that he probably had a million or so pieces of the living mesh underneath the outer layer of his skin. He shuddered.

Richard was still amazed that he had not suffocated. As his mind began to wonder how air was getting to him through the web, he heard another voice inside his head. *Stop trying to analyse everything*, it said. *You'll never understand it anyway. For once in your life just experience the incredible adventure.*

5

Again Richard had lost track of time. Sometime during the days (or had it been weeks?) that he had been living inside the alien net, he had changed positions. During one of his early naps, the web had also removed his clothes. Richard was now lying on his back, supported by an extremely dense section of the fine mesh network enveloping his body.

His mind no longer actively wondered how he was managing to survive. Somehow, whenever he felt hunger or thirst, his needs were swiftly satisfied. His wastes always disappeared within minutes. Breathing was easy even though he was completely surrounded by the living web.

Richard passed many of his conscious hours studying the creature around him. If he looked carefully, he could see the tiny elements constantly in motion. The patterns in the net around him altered very slowly, but they definitely did change. Richard mentally plotted the trajectories of the ganglia that he could see. At one point three separate ganglia migrated into his vicinity and formed a triangle in front of his head.

The net developed a regular cycle of interacting with Richard. It would keep its millions of filaments attached to him for fifteen to twenty hours at a time, and then release him completely for several hours. Richard slept without dreaming whenever he was not attached to the web. If he happened to awaken still in the unattached mode, he was enervated and listless. But each time the threads began to wind around him again he felt a renewed surge of energy.

His dreams were active and vivid if he slept while attached to the alien net. Richard had never dreamed much before and had often laughed at Nicole's preoccupation with her dreams. But as his sleeping images became more complex, and in some cases quite bizarre, Richard began to appreciate why Nicole paid so much attention to them. One night he dreamed that he was again a teenager and was watching a theatrical performance of *As You Like It* in his hometown of Stratford-on-Avon. The lovely blonde girl who was playing Rosalind came down from the stage and whispered in his ear.

'Are you Richard Wakefield?' she asked in the dream.

'Yes,' he answered.

The actress began to kiss Richard, first slowly, then more passionately with a lively, tickling tongue darting around inside his mouth. He felt a surge of overpowering desire and then woke up abruptly, strangely embarrassed by both his nakedness and his erection. *Now, what was that all about?* Richard wondered, echoing the phrase he had often heard from Nicole.

At some stage in his captivity his recollections of Nicole became much sharper, more clearly delineated. Richard found to his surprise that in the absence of other stimuli he was able, if he concentrated, to recall entire conversations with Nicole, including such details as the kind of facial expressions she used to punctuate her sentences. In the protracted solitude of his long period inside the web, Richard often ached with loneliness, the vivid memories making him miss his beloved wife even more.

His memories of the children were equally sharp. He missed them all as well, especially Katie. He remembered his last conversation with his special daughter, several days before the wedding, when she had come by the house to pick up some of her clothes. Katie had been depressed, and needed support, but Richard had been unable to help her. *The connection just wasn't there*, Richard thought. The recent image of Katie as a sexy young woman was replaced by a picture of a reckless ten-year-old girl scampering across the plazas of New York. The juxtaposition of the two images provoked a profound feeling of loss in Richard. *I was never comfortable with Katie after she awakened*, he realised with a sigh. *I still wanted my little girl.*

The clarity of his recollections of Nicole and Katie convinced Richard that something extraordinary was happening to his memory. He discovered that he could also recall the exact scores of every World Cup quarter-final, semi-final, and final between 2174 and 2190. Richard had known all that useless information as a young man, for he had been an avid soccer fan. However, during the years before the launch of the Newton, when so many new things had crowded into his brain, he had often been unable, even during soccer discussions with his friends, to recall even the participants in a key World Cup match.

As the visual images from his memories continued to sharpen, Richard found that he was also recalling the emotions that had been associated with the pictures. It was almost as if he were completely reliving the experiences. In one long recollection he remembered not only the overpowering feelings of love and adoration that he had felt for Sarah Tydings when he had first seen her perform onstage, but also the thrill and excitement of their courtship, including the unbridled passion of their first night of love. It had left him breathless then; and now, many years later, enveloped by an alien creature resembling a neural net, Richard's response was equally powerful.

Soon it seemed as if Richard no longer had any control over which memories were activated in his brain. In the beginning, or so he believed, he had purposely thought about Nicole or his children or even his courtship with the young Sarah Tydings, just to make himself happy. *Now*, he said one day in an imaginary conversation with the sessile net, *after refreshing my memory – for*

God knows what purpose – it seems that you are reading it all out.

For many hours Richard enjoyed the forced memory readout, especially those portions covering his life at Cambridge and the Space Academy, when his days were enlivened by the constant joy of new knowledge. Quantum physics, the Cambrian explosion, probability and statistics, even the long-forgotten vocabulary words from his German lessons reminded him how much of his happiness in life had been due to the excitement of learning. In another particularly satisfying remembrance, his mind jumped swiftly from play to play, covering every live performance of Shakespeare that he had seen between the ages of ten and seventeen. *Everyone needs a hero*, Richard thought after the montage of scenes, *as impetus to bring out the best in himself. My hero was definitely William Shakespeare.*

Some of the memories were painful, especially those from his childhood. In one of them Richard was eight years old again, sitting on a bench at the small table in his family's dining room. The atmosphere at the table was tense. His father, drunk and angry at the world, was glowering at all of them as they ate their dinner in silence. Richard accidentally spilled some of his soup and seconds later the back of his father's hand hit him hard on the cheek, knocking him off his bench and into the corner of the room, where he trembled from fear and shock. He had not thought about that moment for years. Richard was unable to restrain his tears as he recalled how helpless and scared he had been around his neurotic, abusive father.

One day Richard suddenly began to remember details from his long odyssey in Rama II and a powerful headache almost blinded him. He saw himself in a strange room, lying on a floor surrounded by three or four octospiders. Dozens of probes and other instruments had been implanted in him and some kind of test was under way.

'Stop, stop,' Richard shouted, destroying the memory picture with his acute agitation. 'My head is killing me.'

Miraculously his headache began to fade and Richard was again among the octospiders in his memory. He recalled the days and days of testing that he had experienced and the tiny living creatures that had been inserted into his body. He recalled also a peculiar set of sexual experiments in which he had been subjected to all kinds of external stimulation and rewarded when he ejaculated.

Richard was startled by these new memories that he had never accessed before, never once since he had awakened from the coma in which his family had found him in New York. *Now I remember other things about the octospiders too*, he thought excitedly. *They talked to each other in colours that wrapped around their heads. They were basically friendly, but determined to learn everything they could about me. They ...*

The mental picture vanished and Richard's headache returned. The threads from the net had just disconnected. Richard was exhausted and quickly fell asleep.

*

After days and days of one memory after another, the readout abruptly ceased. Richard's mind was no longer driven by an external forcing function. The threads of the net remained unattached for long periods of time.

A week passed without incident. In the second week, however, an unusual spherical ganglion, far larger and more densely wrapped than the normal clumps in the living web, began to develop about twenty centimetres away from Richard's head. The ganglion grew until it was about the size of a basketball. Soon thereafter the immense clump issued hundreds of filaments that inserted themselves into the skin around the circumference of Richard's skull. *At last*, Richard thought, ignoring the pain caused by the invasion of the threads into his brain, *now we will see what this has all been about.*

He began immediately to see some kind of pictures, although they were so fuzzy that he could not identify anything specific. The quality of Richard's mental images improved very quickly, however, for he cleverly devised a rudimentary way of communicating with the web. As soon as the first image appeared in his mind, Richard concluded that the net, which had been reading his memory output for days, was now trying to write into his brain.

But the web obviously had no way of measuring the quality of the images that Richard was receiving. Remembering his trips to the eye doctor as a boy and the communication pattern that resulted in the final specifications for his eyeglass lenses, Richard pointed his thumb up or down to indicate whether each change the net made in its transmission process made the picture better or worse. In that manner Richard was soon able to 'see' what the alien was attempting to show him.

The first pictures were images of a planet taken from a spacecraft. The cloud-covered world with two smallish moons and a distant, solitary yellow star as its heat and light source was almost certainly the home planet of the sessile webs. The suite of pictures that followed showed Richard various landscapes from the planet.

Fog was ubiquitous on the home world of the sessiles. Below the fog in most of the images was a brown, rock-less, barren surface. Only in the littorals where the barren ground encountered the waves of the green liquid lakes and oceans was there any suggestion of life. In one of these oases Richard saw not only several avians, but also a fascinating mélange of other living things. Richard could have spent days examining just one or two of these pictures, but he was not in control of the image sequence. The net had some purpose for its communication, he was certain, and the first set of pictures was only an introduction.

All of the remaining images featured either an avian, a manna melon, a myrmicat, a sessile web, or some combination of the quartet. The scenes were all taken from what Richard assumed was 'normal life' on their home planet, and expanded on the general theme of symbiosis among the species. In several pictures the aliens were shown defending the subterranean colonies of the myrmicats and sessiles from invasions by what appeared to be small animals and plants. Other images depicted the myrmicats ministering to avian hatchlings or transporting large quantities of manna melons to an avian mound.

Richard was puzzled when he saw several pictures that showed tiny manna melons embedded inside the sessile creatures. *Why would the myrmicats lay their eggs in here?* he wondered. *For protection? Or are these weird webs a kind of thinking placenta?*

One definite impression left upon Richard by the sequence of images was that the sessiles were, in a hierarchical sense, the dominant species of the three. The pictures all suggested that both the myrmicats and the avians paid homage to the web creatures. *Do these nets, then, somehow do all the important thinking for the avians and myrmicats?* Richard asked himself. *What incredible symbiotic relationships ... How in the world could they possibly have evolved?*

There were several thousand frames altogether in the sequence. After it repeated twice, the filaments detached themselves from Richard and returned to the giant ganglion. In the days that followed Richard was essentially left alone, the attachments to his host being limited to those necessary for him to survive.

When a lane formed in the web and Richard could see the door through which he had entered many weeks before, he thought that he was going to be released. His momentary excitement, however, was quickly dampened. At his first attempt to move, the sessile net tightened its grip on all parts of his body.

So what is the purpose of the lane? As Richard watched, a trio of myrmicats entered from the hallway. The creature in the middle had two broken legs, and its back segment was crushed, as if it had been run over by a heavy car or truck. Its two companions carried the disabled myrmicat into the web and then departed. Within seconds the sessile began to wrap itself around the new arrival.

Richard was about two metres away from the crippled myrmicat. The region between him and the injured creature emptied of all filaments and clumps. Richard had never before seen such a gap inside the sessile. *So my education continues,* he mused. *What is it that I am supposed to learn now? That sessiles are doctors to the myrmicats, just as the myrmicats are doctors to the avians?*

The web did not limit its attention to the injured portions of the myrmicat. In fact, during one long waking period Richard watched the net completely enclose the creature in a tight cocoon. At the same time, the large ganglion in Richard's immediate vicinity migrated over to the cocoon.

Later, after a nap, Richard noticed that the ganglion had returned to his side. The cocoon across the gap had almost finished unravelling. Richard's pulse rate doubled as the cocoon completely disappeared and there was no trace of the myrmicat.

Richard didn't have much time to wonder what had happened to the myrmicat. Within minutes the filaments from the large ganglion were again attached to his skull and another picture show was playing inside his brain. In the very first image Richard saw five human soldiers camping on the shore of the moat inside the avian habitat. They were eating a meal. Beside them were an impressive array of weapons, including two machine guns.

The pictures that followed showed humans on the attack throughout the second habitat. Two of the early scenes were especially gruesome. In the first a juvenile avian had been decapitated in midair and was falling to the ground. A pair of satisfied humans congratulated each other in the lower left portion of the same frame. The second image depicted a large square hole in one of the grassland sectors of the green region. Inside the hole could be seen the remains of several dead avians. A human with a wheelbarrow containing another pair of avian corpses was approaching the mass grave from the left.

Richard was staggered by what he was seeing. *What are these pictures anyway?* he wondered. *And why am I seeing them now?* He quickly reviewed all the recent events in his sessile world and concluded, with considerable shock, that the disabled myrmicat must have actually seen everything Richard was being shown, and that the web creature had somehow removed the images from the mind of the myrmicat and transferred them into Richard's brain.

Once he understood what he was seeing, Richard paid more attention to the pictures themselves. He was completely outraged by the invasion and slaughter that he saw. In one of the later images three human soldiers were shown raiding an avian apartment complex inside the brown cylinder. There were no survivors.

These poor creatures are doomed, Richard said to himself, *and they must know it* ...

Tears suddenly formed in Richard's eyes and a profound sadness, deeper than any he had ever known, accompanied his realization that members of his own species were systematically exterminating the avians. *No, no!*, he shouted silently. *Stop, oh, please stop. Can't you see what you are doing? These avians, too, proclaim the miracle of chemicals raised to consciousness. They are like us. They are our brothers.*

In the next several seconds Richard's many interactions with the birdlike creatures flooded his memory and chased away the implanted images. *They saved my life*, he thought, his mind focusing on the flight long ago across the Cylindrical Sea. *With absolutely no benefit to themselves. What human*, he said to himself bitterly, *would have done such a good deed for an avian?*

Richard had rarely sobbed in his life. But his sorrow for the avians overpowered him. As he wept, all his experiences since entering the avian habitat filed through his mind. Richard recalled especially the sudden change in their treatment of him and his subsequent transfer to the realm of the myrmicats. *Then came the guided tour and my eventual placement here ... It's obvious they have been trying to communicate with me. But why?*

At that instant Richard had an epiphany of such power that tears rushed into his eyes again. *Because they are desperate,* he answered himself. *They are begging me to help.*

6

Again a large void was created in the interior of the sessile. Richard watched carefully as thirty small ganglia formed into a sphere with a diameter of about fifty centimetres on the other side of the gap. An unusually thick filament connected each of the ganglia with the centre of the sphere. At first, Richard could detect nothing inside the sphere. After the ganglia had moved to another location, however, he saw, where the sphere had been, a tiny green object with hundreds of infinitesimal threads anchoring it to the rest of the web.

It grew very slowly. The ganglia had already finished migrating to three new positions, repeating the same spherical configuration each time, before Richard recognised that what was growing in the sessile was a manna melon. He was thunderstruck. Richard could not imagine how the vanished myrmicat could possibly have left behind eggs that had taken so long to germinate. *And they must have been only a few cells then. Tiny, tiny embryos somehow nurtured here ...*

His own thoughts were interrupted by his realization that these new manna melons were developing in a region of the sessile that was almost twenty metres away from where the myrmicat had been cocooned. *So this web creature transported the eggs from one place to another? And then retained them for weeks?*

Richard's logical mind began to reject the hypothesis that the vanished myrmicat had laid any eggs at all. Slowly but surely, he developed an alternative explanation for what he had observed that suggested a biology more complex than any he had ever encountered on Earth. *What if,* he asked himself, *the manna melons, myrmicats, and this sessile web are all manifestations of what we would call the same species?*

Staggered by the ramifications of this simple thought, Richard spent two long waking periods reviewing everything he had seen inside the second habitat. As he stared at the four manna melons growing across the gap from him, Richard envisioned a cycle of metamorphosis in which the manna melons gave birth to the myrmicats, who in turn came to die and add new matter to the sessile net, which then laid the manna melon eggs that began the process again. There was nothing he had observed that was inconsistent with this explanation. But Richard's brain was exploding with thousands of questions, not only about *how* this intricate set of metamorphoses took place, but also about *why* this species had evolved into such a complex being in the first place.

Most of Richard's academic study had been in fields that he had always proudly called 'hard science.' Mathematics and physics had been the primary elements of his education. As he struggled to understand the possible life cycle of the creature in which he had been living for many weeks, Richard was bewildered by his ignorance. He wished that he had learned much more about biology. *For how can I help them?* he asked himself. *I have no idea even where to start.*

Much later, Richard would wonder if by this time in his stay inside the sessile, the creature had learned not only how to read his memory, but also how to interpret his thoughts. His visitors arrived a few days afterward. Again a lane formed in the sessile between Richard's position and the original entry way. Four identical myrmicats walked down the lane and gestured for Richard to join them. They were carrying his clothes. When Richard made an effort to move, his alien host did not try to restrain him. His legs were wobbly, but after dressing, Richard managed to follow the myrmicats back into the corridor deep within the brown cylinder.

The large chamber had obviously been recently modified. The vast mural on its walls was not yet completed. In fact, at the same time that Richard's myrmicat teacher was pointing to specific items in the painting that had already been finished, myrmicat artists were still at work on the remainder of the mural. During Richard's early lessons in the room, as many as a dozen of the creatures were engaged in sketching or painting the other sections.

Only one visit to the mural chamber was necessary for Richard to ascertain its purpose. The entire room was being created to give him information on how he could help the alien species survive. It was clear these extraterrestrials knew that they were about to be overrun and destroyed by the humans. The paintings in this room were their attempt to provide Richard with the data he might need to save them. But could he learn enough simply from the pictures?

The artwork was brilliant. From time to time Richard would suspend the activity in his left brain that was trying to interpret the messages in the paintings so that his right brain could appreciate the talent of the myrmicat artists. The creatures worked in the upright position, their back two legs on the floor and their four front legs operating together to implement the sketch or painting. They talked among themselves, apparently asking questions, but did not make so much noise that Richard was disturbed across the chamber.

The entire first half of the mural was a textbook in alien biology. It proved that Richard's fundamental understanding of the strange creature was correct. There were over a hundred individual paintings in the main sequence, of which two dozen showed different stages in the development of the myrmicat embryo, expanding considerably the knowledge that Richard had gleaned from the sculptures inside the myrmicat cathedral. The primary panels explaining the embryological progression followed a straight line around the walls of the chamber. Above and below these main sequence pictures were supporting or supplementary frames, most of which were beyond Richard's comprehension.

For example, a quartet of supporting paintings had been arranged around a picture of a manna melon that had recently been removed from a sessile web, but had not yet begun any myrmicat development activity in its interior. Richard was certain that these four additional pictures were trying to give him specific information about the ambient conditions required for the germination process to begin. However, the myrmicat artists had used scenes from their home planet, illustrating the desired conditions with landscapes of fogs and lakes and their native flora and fauna, to communicate the data. Richard just shook his head when the myrmicat teacher pointed at these paintings.

A diagram across the top of the main sequence used suns and moons to specify time scales. Richard understood from the arrangement that the lifetime of the myrmicat manifestation of the species was very short when compared with the lifetime of the sessiles. He was unable, however, to figure out anything else the diagram was trying to convey.

Richard was also somewhat confused about the numerical relationships among the different manifestations of the species. It was clear that each manna melon resulted in a single myrmicat (there were no examples of twins shown), and that a sessile could produce many manna melons. But what was the ratio of sessiles to myrmicats? In one frame a large sessile was presented with a dozen different myrmicats in its interior, each in a different phase of cocooning. What was that supposed to indicate?

Richard slept in a small room not far from the mural chamber. His lessons lasted three to four hours each, after which he would be fed or allowed to sleep. Sometimes, when he entered the chamber, Richard would glance over at the paintings, some still incomplete, in the second half of the mural. If that happened, the lights in the chamber would immediately be extinguished. The myrmicats wanted to be certain that Richard learned his biology first.

After about ten days the second half of the mural was finished. Richard was stunned when he was finally allowed to study it. The renderings of the many human beings and avians were exceptionally accurate. Richard himself appeared half a dozen times in the paintings. With his long hair and beard, both of them more than half white, he almost didn't recognise himself. *I could pass for Christ in these pictures*, he joked as he wandered around the chamber.

Part of the remaining mural was a historical summary of the invasion of the alien habitat by the humans. There was more detail than Richard had seen in his mental picture show while he was inside the sessile, but he did not learn anything substantively new. He was, however, again disturbed emotionally by the horrible details of the continuing massacre.

The pictures also triggered an interesting question in his mind. Why had the contents of this mural not been transferred *directly* to him by the sessile, thereby obviating the entire effort by the myrmicat artists? *Perhaps*, Richard mused, *the sessile is a recording device only, and is incapable of imagination. Maybe it can only show me what has already been seen by one of the myrmicats.*

What was left of the mural explicitly defined what the myrmicat/sessile creatures were asking Richard to do. In each of his portraits he was wearing a large blue pack over his shoulders. The pack had two large pockets in the front, and two more in the back, each containing a manna melon. There were two additional, smaller pockets on the sides of the pack. One was stuffed with a silver cylindrical tube about fifteen centimetres long and the other contained two small, leathery avian eggs.

The mural showed Richard's suggested activity in an orderly sequence. He would leave the brown cylinder through an exit below the ground level, and come out in the green region on the other side of both the ring of white buildings and the thin canal. There, guided by a pair of avians, he would descend to the shore of the moat, where he would be picked up by a small submarine. The submarine would dive under the module wall, enter a large body of water, and then surface on the shore of an island with many sky-scrapers.

Richard smiled as he studied the mural. *So both the Cylindrical Sea and New York are still here*, he thought. He remembered what The Eagle had said about not making unnecessary changes to Rama. *That means our lair may be there as well.*

There were many additional pictures surrounding Richard's escape sequence, some giving more details about the alien plants and animals in the green region, and others providing explicit instructions on how to operate the submarine. When Richard tried to copy what he thought was the most important of this information into his portable computer from the Newton, the myrmicat teacher suddenly seemed impatient. Richard wondered if the crisis situation had worsened.

The next day, after a long nap, Richard was outfitted with his pack and ushered into the sessile chamber by his hosts. There the four manna melons he had watched growing two weeks previously were removed from the web by the myrmicats and placed in his pack. They were quite heavy. Richard estimated that they weighed twenty kilograms altogether. Another myrmicat then used an instrument similar to a large scissors to remove from the sessile a cylindrical volume containing four ganglia and their associated filaments. This sessile material was placed in a silver tube and inserted in one of Richard's smaller side pockets. The avian eggs were the last elements to be loaded.

Richard took a deep breath. *This must be goodbye*, he thought as the myrmicats pointed down the corridor. For some reason he remembered Nai

Watanabe's insistence that the Thai greeting called the *wai*, a small bow with hands clasped together in front of the upper chest, was a universal sign of respect. Smiling to himself, Richard performed a *wai* to the half dozen myrmicats surrounding him. To his astonishment, each of them placed its four forward legs together in pairs in front of its underbelly and made a slight bow in his direction.

The deep basement of the brown cylinder was obviously uninhabited. After leaving the sessile chamber, Richard and his guide had first passed many other myrmicats, especially in the vicinity of the atrium. But once they had entered the ramp that descended to the basement, they had never encountered even a single myrmicat.

Richard's guide dispatched a leggie in front of them. It raced along the final narrow tunnel and through the vault-like emergency exit into the green region. When the leggie returned, it stood on the back of the myrmicat's head for several seconds and then scampered down to the floor. The guide motioned for Richard to proceed into the tunnel.

Outside, in the green region, Richard was met by two large avians who immediately became airborne. One of them had an ugly scar on its wing, as if it had been hit by a spray of bullets. Richard was in a moderately dense forest, with growth around him up to three or four metres off the ground. Even though the light was dim, it was not difficult for Richard to find a pathway or to follow the avians above him. Occasionally he heard sporadic gunfire off in the distance.

The first fifteen minutes passed without incident. The forest thickness lessened. Richard had just estimated that he should be at the moat for the rendezvous with the submarine in another ten minutes when, without any warning, a machine gun began to fire no more than a hundred metres away. One of the guide avians crashed to the ground. The other avian disappeared. Richard hid himself in a dark thicket when he heard the soldiers coming in his direction.

'Two rings for certain,' one of them said. 'Maybe even three. That would give me twenty rings this week alone.'

'Shit, man, that was no contest. It shouldn't even count. The damn bird didn't even know you were there.'

'That's his problem, not mine. I still get to count his rings. Ah, here he is ... Crap, he only has two.'

The men were only about fifteen metres away from Richard. He stood absolutely still, not daring to move, for more than five minutes. The soldiers, meanwhile, stayed in the vicinity of the avian corpse, smoking and talking about the war.

Richard began to feel pain in his right foot. He shifted his weight ever so slightly, thinking he would relieve whatever muscle was being strained, but the pain only increased. At length he glanced down and discovered to his horror that one of the rodentlike creatures he had seen in the mural chamber had eaten through what was left of his shoe and was now chomping on his foot. Richard tried to shake his leg vigorously but noiselessly. He was not completely successful. Although the rodent released his foot, the soldiers heard the sound and started moving toward him.

Richard could not run. Even if there had been an escape route, the extra weight he was carrying would have made him easy prey for the soldiers. Within a minute one of the men yelled, 'Over here, Bruce, I think there's something in this thicket.'

The man was pointing his gun in Richard's direction. 'Don't shoot,' Richard said. 'I'm a human.'

The second soldier had just joined his comrade. 'What the fuck are you doing out here alone?'

'I'm taking a hike,' Richard answered.

'Are you crazy?' the first soldier said. 'Come on out of there. Let us take a look at you.'

Richard slowly walked out of the underbrush. Even in the dim light he must have been an astonishing sight with his long hair and beard plus the bulging blue jacket.

'Jesus Christ. Who the hell are you? Where's your outfit positioned?'

'This ain't no goddamn soldier,' the other man said, still staring at Richard. 'This here's a loony tune. He must have escaped from the facility in Avalon and wandered over here by mistake ... Hey, asshole, don't you know this is dangerous territory? You could be killed ...'

'Look at his pockets,' the first soldier interrupted. 'He's carrying four *huge* goddamn melons ...'

Suddenly they struck from the sky. There must have been a dozen of the avians altogether, consumed by fury and shrieking as they attacked. The two human soldiers were knocked to the ground. Richard started to run. One of the avians landed on the face of the first soldier and began to tear it apart with its talons. Gunfire erupted as other soldiers in the vicinity, hearing the fracas, hurried into the area to help the patrol.

Richard did not know how he was going to find the submarine. He raced downhill as fast as his feet and his load would allow him. The gunfire behind him increased. He heard the screams of pain of the soldiers and the death shrieks of the avians.

He found the moat but there was no sign of the submarine. Richard could hear human voices coming down the slope behind him. Just when he was about to panic, he heard a short shriek from a large bush on his right. The leader avian with the four cobalt rings flew past his head, not far off the ground, and continued down the shore of the moat to the left.

They located the small submarine in three more minutes. The ship had already submerged before the pursuing humans broke into the clear in the green region. Inside, Richard took off his pack and placed it behind him in the small control compartment. He looked at his avian companion and tried a couple of simple jabber phrases. The avian leader replied, very slowly and very clearly, with the jabber equivalent of 'We all thank you very much.'

The journey took slightly more than an hour. Richard and the avian said very little to each other. During the early part of the voyage, Richard carefully watched the avian leader operating the submarine. He made notes in his computer and, during the second half of the trip, even took over the controls himself for a short period of time. When he was not too busy, Richard's mind was asking questions about everything he had experienced in the second habitat. Above all, he wanted to know why it was he in the submarine with the melons, the avian eggs, and the sessile slice, and not one of the myrmicats. *I must be missing something,* he mused to himself.

Soon thereafter the submarine surfaced and Richard was in familiar territory. The skyscrapers of New York loomed above him. 'Hallelujah,' Richard said out loud, carrying his full pack on to the island.

The avian leader anchored the submarine just offshore and quickly prepared to leave. He turned around in a circle, bowed slightly to Richard, and then took off toward the north. As he was watching the birdlike creature fly away, Richard realised that he was standing in the exact spot where he and Nicole had waited, many many years before in Rama II, for the three avians who would carry them across the Cylindrical Sea to freedom.

7

During the first second that Richard stood on the surface in New York, a hundred billion billion bits of data were acquired by the infinitesimal Raman sensors scattered throughout the giant cylindrical spacecraft. These data were transmitted in realtime to local data-handling centres, still microscopic in size, where they were stored until the allocated time for them to be relayed to the central telecommunications processor buried beneath the Southern Hemicylinder.

Every second of every hour of every day the Raman sensors acquire these hundred quintillion data bits. At the telecommunications processor, the data are labeled, sifted, analysed, compressed, and stored in recording devices whose individual components are smaller than an atom. After storage, the data are accessed by the dozens of distributed processors, each managing a separate function, that together control the Rama spacecraft. Thousands of algorithms spread among the processors then operate on the data, extracting trend and synthesis information in preparation for the regularly scheduled data bursts that transmit the mission status to the Nodal Intelligence.

The data bursts contain a mixture of raw, compressed, and synthesised data, depending on the exact formats selected by the different processors. The most important part of each burst is the narrative report, in which the unified but distributed intelligence of Rama presents its prioritised summary of the progress of the mission. The rest of the burst is essentially supporting information, images or measurements or sensor outputs that either provide additional background data or directly support the conclusions contained in the summary.

The language used for the narrative summary is mathematical in structure, precise in definition, and highly coded. It is also rich in footnotes, each equivalent phrase or sentence containing, as part of its transmission structure, the pointers to the actual data buttressing the particular statement being made. The report could not, in the truest sense, be translated into any language as primitive as the ones used by human beings. Nevertheless, what follows is a crude approximation of the summary report received by the Nodal Intelligence from Rama soon after Richard's arrival in New York.

REPORT Number 298
Time of Transmission: 156 307 872 491.5116
Time Since First-Stage Alert: 29.2873
References: Node 23-419
Spacecraft 947
Spacefarers 47 249 (A & B)
32 806
2 666

During the last interval the humans (Spacefarer Number 32 806) have continued to wage a successful war against the avian/sessile symbiotic pair (Number 47 249 – A & B). The humans now control almost all the interior of the avian/sessile habitat, including the upper portion of the brown cylinder where the avians formerly lived. The avians have fought courageously but vainly against the human invasion. They have been killed unmercifully, and less than a hundred of them now remain.

Thus far the humans have not breached the integrity of the sessile domain. They have, however, found the elevator shafts leading to the lower parts of the brown cylinder. The humans are currently developing plans for an attack on the sessile lair.

The sessiles are a defenceless species. There are no weapons of any kind in their domain. Even their mobile form, which has the physical dexterity to use weapons, is essentially nonviolent. To protect themselves from what they fear will be an inevitable invasion by the humans, the sessiles have directed the mobile myrmicats to build fortresses surrounding the four oldest and most developed of their species. Meanwhile, no more manna melons are being allowed to germinate and those myrmicats not involved in the construction process are cocooning early. If the humans delay their attack several more intervals, as seems likely, it is possible they will encounter only a few myrmicats during their invasion.

The human habitat continues to be dominated by individuals with characteristics decidedly different from the human contingent observed inside Rama II and at the Node. The focus of the current human leaders is the retention of personal power, without serious consideration of the welfare of the colony. Despite both the video message and the presence of messenger humans in their group, these leaders must not believe they are actually being watched, for their behaviour in no way reflects the possible existence of a set of values or ethical laws that supersedes their own dominion.

The humans have continued to prosecute the war against the avian/sessiles primarily because it distracts attention from the other problems in their colony, including the human-initiated environmental degradation and the recent precipitous decline in living standards. The human leaders, and indeed most of the colonists, have shown no remorse whatsoever over the destruction and possible extermination of the avians.

The human family that remained for over a year at The Node no longer has any significant impact on the affairs of the colony. The woman who was the primary messenger is still imprisoned, essentially because she opposes the actions of the existing leaders, and is in danger of being executed. Her husband has been living with the avians and sessiles and is now a critical component in their attempt to survive the human onslaught. The children are not yet mature enough to be a major factor in the human colony.

Very recently, the husband escaped from the sessile domain to the island in the middle of the spacecraft. He carried both avian and sessile embryos with him. He is currently located in a familiar environment, and therefore should be able both to survive and to nurture the young of the other species. His successful escape may have been at least partly due to the non-invasive intercession that began at the time of the first-stage alert. The intercession signals almost certainly played a role in the decision by the sessiles to trust their embryos to a human being.

There is no evidence, however, that the intercession transmissions have affected the behaviour of any of the humans. For the sessiles, information processing is a primary activity and, therefore, it is not surprising that they would be susceptible to intercessionary suggestions. The humans, however, especially the leaders, have their lives so filled with activity that there is very little, if any, time for cogitation.

There is an additional problem with humans and non-invasive intercession. As a species they are so varied, from individual to individual, that a transmission package cannot be designed with broad applicability. A set of signals that might result in a positive behaviour modification for one human will almost certainly have no impact on anyone else. Experiments with different types of intercession processes are currently being conducted, but it may well be that humans belong to that small group of spacefarers who are immune to noninvasive intercession.

In the south of the spacecraft, the octospiders (Number 2 666) continue to thrive in a colony almost indistinguishable from any of their other isolated colonies in space.

The full range of possible biological expression remains latent, primarily because of restricted territorial resources and no true competition. However, they are carrying with them the significant potential for expansion that has characterised their several successful transfers from one star system to another.

Until the humans probed through the wall of their own habitat and broke the seal on their enclosure, the octospiders paid very little attention to the other two species in the spacecraft. Since the humans began to explore, however, the octospiders have watched the events in the north with increasing interest. Their existence is still unknown to the humans, but the octospiders have already started formulating a contingency plan to cover a possible interaction with their aggressive neighbours.

The potential loss of the entire avian/sessile community greatly reduces the value of the mission. It is possible that the only sessile and avian survivors of the voyage will be those in the small octospider zoo and, perhaps, those raised by the human on the island. Even irrevocable loss of a single species does not call for a stage-two alert; nevertheless, the continued unpredictable and life-negative behaviour of the current human leaders provides an unmitigated worry that the mission may suffer additional serious losses. Intercessionary activity in the near future will be focused on those humans who both oppose the present leaders and have indicated, by their behaviour, growth beyond territorialism and aggression.

8

'My country was called Thailand. It had a king, whose name was also Rama, like our spaceship. Your grandmother and grandfather – my mother and father – probably still live there, in a town called Lamphun ... Here it is.'

Nai pointed at a spot on the faded map. The boys' attention had started to wander. *They're still too young*, she thought. *Even for bright children it's too much to expect at four.*

'All right, now,' she said, folding up the map, 'you can go outside and play.'

Galileo and Kepler put on their heavy jackets, picked up a ball, and raced out the door into the street. Within seconds they were engaged in a one-on-one soccer match. *Oh, Kenji*, Nai thought, watching the boys from the entryway. *How they have missed you. There's just no way one parent can be both mother and father.*

She had begun the geography lesson, as she always did, by reminding the boys that all of the colonists in New Eden had come originally from a planet called Earth. Nai had then shown the boys a world map for their home planet, first discussing the basic concept of continents and oceans, and then identifying Japan, their father's native country. The activity had made Nai both homesick and lonely.

Maybe these lessons aren't for you at all, she thought, still watching the soccer game under the dim streetlights of Avalon. Galileo dribbled around Kepler and fired at an imaginary goal. *Maybe they're really for me.*

Eponine was coming down the street in their direction. She picked up the ball and threw it back to the boys. Nai smiled at her friend. 'What a delight to see you,' she said. 'I can definitely use a happy face today,'

'What's the matter, Nai?' Eponine asked. 'Life in Avalon getting you down? ... At least it's a Sunday. You're not working in the gun factory and the boys aren't over at the centre.'

The two women walked inside. 'And certainly your living conditions cannot be the cause of your despair.' Eponine waved her arm at the room. 'After all, you have a large room for the three of you, half a toilet, and a bath you share with five other families. What more could you want?'

Nai laughed and hugged Eponine. 'You're a big help,' she said.

'Mommy, Mommy.' Kepler was standing in the doorway a moment later. 'Come quickly,' the little boy said. 'He's back ... and he's talking to Galileo.'

Nai and Eponine returned to the door. A man with a severely disfigured face was kneeling down in the dirt next to Galileo. The boy was obviously frightened. The man was holding a sheet of paper in his gloved hand. On it a large human face with long hair and a full beard had been carefully drawn.

'You know this face, don't you?' the man said insistently. 'It's Mr Richard Wakefield, isn't it?'

Nai and Eponine approached the man cautiously. 'We told you last time,' Nai said firmly, 'not to bother the boys any more. Now go back to the ward or we will call the police.'

The man's eyes were wild. 'I saw him again last night,' he said. 'He looked like Jesus, but he was Richard Wakefield all right. I started to shoot him and they attacked me. Five of them. They tore my face apart ...' The man started to weep.

An orderly came running down the street. He grabbed the man. 'I saw him,' the wild man shouted as he was led away. 'I know I did. Please believe me.'

Galileo was crying. Nai bent down to comfort her son. 'Mama,' the boy said, 'do you think that man really saw Mr Wakefield?'

'I don't know,' she answered. Nai glanced at Eponine. 'But some of us would like to believe it.'

The boys had finally fallen asleep in their beds in the corner. Nai and Eponine sat next to each other in the two chairs. 'The rumour is she's very ill,' Eponine said quietly. 'They hardly feed her at all. They make her suffer in every possible way.'

'Nicole will never give up,' Nai said proudly. 'I wish I had her strength and courage.'

'Neither Ellie nor Robert has been allowed to see her for over six months ... Nicole doesn't even know she has a granddaughter.'

'Ellie told me last week that she has filed another petition with Nakamura to visit her mother,' Nai said. 'I worry about Ellie. She continues to push very, very hard.'

Eponine smiled. 'Ellie is so wonderful, even if she is incredibly naive. She insists that if she obeys all the colony laws, Nakamura will leave her alone.'

'That's not surprising ... especially when you consider that Ellie still thinks her father is alive,' Nai said. 'She has talked with every one of the people who claim to have seen Richard since he disappeared.'

'All the stories about Richard give her hope,' Eponine said. 'We can still use a dosage of hope from time to time ...'

There was a momentary lull in the conversation. 'What about you, Eponine?' Nai asked. 'Do you allow yourself ...'.

'No,' Eponine interrupted. 'I am always honest with myself ... I am going to die soon; I just don't know when. Besides, why should I fight to keep living? Conditions here in Avalon are far worse than they were even in the detention camp at Bourges. If it weren't for the few children in the school ...'

They both heard the noise outside the door at the same time. Nai and Eponine sat completely still. If their conversation had been recorded by one of Nakamura's roving biots, then ...

The door suddenly swung open. The two women nearly jumped out of their skins. Max Puckett stumbled in, grinning. 'You're under arrest,' he said, 'for engaging in seditious conversation.'

Max was carrying a large wooden box. The two women helped him place it in the corner. Max took off his heavy jacket. 'Sorry to show up so late, ladies, but I couldn't help it.'

'Another food run to the troops?' Nai asked in a soft voice. She pointed at the sleeping twins.

Max nodded. 'The king Jap,' he said in a lower voice, 'always reminds me that an army travels on its stomach.'

'That was one of Napoleon's maxims.' Eponine looked at Max with a sarcastic smile. 'I don't suppose you ever heard of him out there in Arkansas.'

'Uh-oh,' Max replied. 'The lovely lady teacher is in a smartass mood tonight.' He pulled an unopened pack of cigarettes out of his shirt pocket. 'Maybe I should just keep her gift for myself.'

Eponine laughed and jumped up to grab the cigarettes. After a short mock struggle, Max surrendered them to her. 'Thanks, Max,' Eponine said in a genuine manner. 'There aren't many pleasures allowed to those of us ...'

'Now, look here,' Max said, still grinning. 'I didn't come all the way out here to listen to you feeling sorry for yourself. I stopped in Avalon to be inspired by your beautiful face. If you're going to be depressed, I'll just take my corn and tomatoes ...'

'Corn and tomatoes!' Nai and Eponine exclaimed in unison. The women ran over to the box. 'The children haven't had any fresh produce in weeks,' Nai said excitedly as Max opened the box with a steel bar.

'Be very, very careful with these,' Max said seriously. 'You know that what I am doing is absolutely illegal. There's barely enough fresh food for the army and the government leaders. But I decided you deserved something better than leftover rice.'

Eponine gave Max a hug. 'Thank you,' she said.

'The boys and I are very grateful, Max,' Nai said. 'I don't know how we'll ever repay you.'

'I'll find some way,' Max said.

The two women returned to their chairs and Max sat down on the floor between them. 'Incidentally,' he said, 'I ran into Patrick O'Toole over in the second habitat. He asked me to say hello to both of you.'

'How is he?' Eponine asked.

'Troubled, I would say,' Max replied. 'When he was drafted, he let Katie talk him into reporting to the army – which I'm certain he would never have done if either Nicole or Richard could have spoken to him even once – and I think he realises now what a mistake he made. He didn't say anything, but I could sense his distress. Nakamura keeps him in the front line because of Nicole.'

'Is this war almost over?' Eponine asked.

'I think so,' Max said. 'But it's not clear the king Jap wants it to be over. From what the soldiers told me, there's very little resistance left. They're mostly mopping up inside the brown cylinder.'

Nai leaned forward. 'We heard a rumour that another intelligent species was also living in the cylinder – something altogether different from the avians.'

Max laughed. 'Who knows what to believe? The television and newspaper say whatever Nakamura tells them, and everyone knows it. There are always hundreds of rumours. I myself have encountered some bizarre alien plants and animals inside that habitat, so nothing would surprise me.'

Nai stifled a yawn. 'I'd best be leaving,' Max said, standing up, 'and let our hostess go to bed.' He glanced at Eponine. 'Would you like someone to walk you home?'

'Depends on who the someone is,' Eponine said with a smile.

A few minutes later, Max and Eponine reached her tiny hut on one of the side streets of Avalon. Max dropped the cigarette they had been sharing and ground it into the dirt. 'Would you like someone ...' he started.

'Yes, Max, of course I would,' Eponine replied with a sigh. 'And if that someone were anyone, it would definitely be you.' She looked directly in his eyes. 'But if you shared my bed, even one time, then I would want more. And if, by some awful chance, no matter how careful we were, you were ever, *ever* to test positive for RV-41, I would never forgive myself.'

Eponine pressed herself against him to hide her tears. 'Thanks for everything,' she said. 'You're a good man, Max Puckett, maybe the only one left in this crazy universe.'

Eponine was in a museum in Paris surrounded by hundreds of masterpieces. A large group of tourists passed through the museum. They spent a total of forty-five seconds looking at five magnificent paintings by Renoir and Monet. 'Stop,' Eponine shouted in her dream. 'You can't possibly have *seen* them.'

The knocking on her door chased the dream away. 'It's us, Eponine,' she heard Ellie say. 'If it's too early, we can try to come back later, before you go to school. Robert was worried that we might get tied up in the psychiatric ward.'

Eponine leaned over and grabbed the robe hanging on the room's solitary chair. 'Just a minute,' she said, 'I'm coming.'

She opened the door for her friends. Ellie was in her nurse's uniform, with little Nicole in a makeshift carrier on her back. The sleeping baby was wrapped cleverly in cotton to protect her from the cold.

'May we come in?'

'Of course,' replied Eponine. 'I'm sorry,' she said, 'I must not have heard you ...'

'It's a ridiculous time for us to visit,' Ellie said. 'But with all our work at the hospital, if we didn't come out here early in the morning, we'd never make it.'

'How have you been feeling?' Dr Turner asked a few seconds later. He was holding a scanner in front of Eponine and data was already being displayed on the portable computer monitor.

'A little tired,' Eponine said. 'But it could be just psychological. Since you told me two months ago that my heart was beginning to show some signs of degradation, I have imagined myself having a heart attack at least once a day.'

During the examination Ellie operated the keyboard that was attached to the monitor. She made certain that the most important information from the checkup was recorded in the computer. Eponine craned around to see the screen. 'How's the new system working, Robert?'

'We've had several failures with the probes,' he replied. 'Ed Stafford says that's to be expected because of our inadequate testing. And we don't yet have a good data management scheme, but on the whole we're very pleased.'

'It's been a saviour, Eponine,' Ellie said without glancing up from the keyboard. 'With our limited funds, and all the wounded from the war, there would have been no way we could have kept the RV-41 files current without this kind of automation.'

'I only wish we had been able to use more of Nicole's expertise in the original design,' Robert Turner said. 'I hadn't realised she was such an expert on internal monitoring systems.' The doctor saw something unusual in a graph that appeared on the screen. 'Print a copy of that, will you, darling? I want to show it to Ed.'

'Have you heard anything new about your mother?' Eponine asked Ellie as the examination neared its completion.

'We saw Katie two nights ago,' Ellie replied very slowly. 'It was a difficult evening. She had another "deal" from Nakamura and Macmillan she wanted to discuss ...' Her voice trailed off. 'Anyway, Katie says that there will definitely be a trial before Settlement Day.'

'Has she seen Nicole?'

'No,' Ellie answered. 'As far as we know, nobody has. Her food is brought in by a Garcia and her monthly checkups are done by a Tiasso.'

Baby Nicole stirred and whimpered on her mother's back. Eponine reached down and touched the portion of the child's cheek that was exposed to the air. 'They are so unbelievably soft,' she said. At that moment the little girl's eyes opened and she began to cry.

'Do I have time to nurse her, Robert?' Ellie asked.

Dr Turner glanced at his watch. 'All right,' he said. 'We're basically finished here. Since both Wilma Margolin and Bill Tucker are in the next block, why don't I call on them by myself and then come back?'

'You can handle them without me?'

'With difficulty,' he said grimly. 'Especially poor Tucker.'

'Bill Tucker is dying very slowly,' Ellie said to Eponine in explanation. 'He's alone and in great pain. But since the government has now outlawed euthanasia, there's nothing we can do.'

'There's no indication of additional atrophy in your data,' Dr Turner said to Eponine a few moments later. 'I guess we should be thankful.'

She didn't hear him. In her mind's eye, Eponine was imagining her own slow and painful death. *I will not let it happen that way*, she told herself. *Never. As soon as I am no longer useful ... Max will bring me a gun.*

'I'm sorry, Robert,' she said. 'I must be sleepier than I thought. What did you say?'

'You're no worse.' Robert gave Eponine a kiss on the cheek and started for the door. 'I'll be back in about twenty minutes,' he said to Ellie.

'Robert looks very tired,' Eponine said when he departed.

'He is,' Ellie replied. 'He still works all the time ... and worries when he's not working.' Ellie was sitting on the dirt floor with her back against the wall of the hut. Nicole was cradled in her arms, suckling at a breast and cooing intermittently.

'That looks like fun,' Eponine said.

'Nothing I have ever experienced is even remotely similar. The pleasure is indescribable.'

It's not for me, Eponine's inner voice said. *Not now. Not ever.* In a fleeting moment Eponine recalled a night of passion when she almost hadn't said no to Max Puckett.

A deep feeling of bitterness welled up inside her. She struggled to fight it.

'I had a nice walk with Benjy yesterday,' she said, changing the subject.

'I'm sure he'll tell me all about it this morning,' Ellie said. 'He loves his Sunday walks with you. It's all he has left, except for my occasional visits ... You know that I am very grateful.'

'Forget it. I like Benjy. I also need to feel needed, if you know what I mean ... Benjy actually has adjusted surprisingly well. He doesn't complain as much as the 41s, and certainly not as much as the people assigned here to work at the gun factory.'

'He hides his pain,' Ellie replied. 'Benjy's much smarter than anyone thinks. He really dislikes the ward but knows that he can't take care of himself. And he doesn't want to be a burden to anybody ...'

Tears suddenly formed in Ellie's eyes and her body trembled slightly. Baby Nicole stopped nursing and stared at her mother. 'Are you all right?' Eponine asked.

Ellie shook her head affirmatively and wiped her eyes with the small cotton cloth that she was holding next to her breasts to catch any leakage.

Nicole resumed nursing. 'Suffering is difficult enough to watch,' Ellie said. 'Unnecessary suffering tears your heart out.'

The guard looked carefully at their identification papers and handed them to another uniformed man sitting behind him at a computer console. The second man made an entry into the computer and returned the documents to the guard.

'Why,' Ellie said, when they were out of earshot, 'does that man stare at our photographs every single day? He must have passed us through this checkpoint personally a dozen times in the last month.'

They were walking along the lane that led from the module exit to Positano. 'It's his job,' Robert replied, 'and he likes to feel important. If he doesn't make a ceremony out of it each time, then we might forget the power he has over us.'

'The process was much smoother when the biots were handling the entrance.'

'The ones that are still functioning are too critical to the war effort. Besides, Nakamura is afraid that the ghost of Richard Wakefield will appear and somehow confound the biots.'

They walked in silence for several seconds. 'You don't think my father is still alive, do you, darling?'

'No, dear,' Robert answered after a short hesitation. He was surprised by the directness of the question. 'But even though I don't *think* he's alive, I still *hope* that he is.'

Robert and Ellie finally reached the outskirts of Positano. A few new houses, European in style, lined the lane that sloped gently down into the heart of the village. 'By the way, Ellie,' Robert said, 'talking about your father reminded me of something I wanted to discuss with you ... Do you remember that project I was telling you about, the one that Ed Stafford is doing?'

Ellie shook her head.

'He's trying to classify and categorise the entire colony in terms of general genetic groupings. He thinks that such classifications, even though they are completely arbitrary, may offer clues about which individuals are likely to have which diseases. I don't completely agree with his approach – it seems too forced and numerical, rather than medical – but parallel studies have been done on Earth and they showed that people with similar genes do indeed have similar disease tendencies.'

Ellie stopped walking and looked at her husband quizzically. 'Why did you want to discuss this with me?'

Robert laughed. 'Yes, yes,' he said. 'I'm coming to that ... Anyway, Ed defined a difference metric – a numerical method of measuring how different any two individuals are, using the way in which the four basic amino acids are chained in the genome – and then, as a test, divided all the citizens of New Eden into groups. Now, the metric didn't really mean anything ...'

'Robert Turner,' Ellie interrupted. She was laughing. 'Will you please get to the point? What are you trying to tell me?'

'Well, it's weird,' he said. 'We don't quite know what to make of it. When Ed made his first classification structure, two of the people tested did not belong to any group. By fiddling with the definitions of the categories, he was eventually able to define a quantitative spread that covered one of them. But the amino acid chaining structure of the final person was so different from every other person in New Eden that she couldn't be placed into any of the groups ...'

Ellie was staring at Robert as if he had lost his mind.

'The two individuals were your brother Benjy and you,' Robert concluded awkwardly. 'You were the one outside all the groupings.'

'Should I be worried about this?' Ellie said after they had walked another thirty metres in silence.

'I don't think so,' Robert said casually. 'It's probably just an artifice of the particular metric that Ed chose. Or perhaps a mistake was made ... But it would be fascinating if somehow cosmic radiation might have altered your genetic structure during your embryological development.'

By this time they had arrived at the main square of Positano. Ellie leaned over and kissed her husband. 'That was very interesting, dear,' she said, teasing him a little, 'but I must admit that I'm still not sure what it was all about.'

A large bicycle rack occupied most of the square. Two dozen rows and as many columns of parking positions were spread out over the area in front of what had been the train station. All the colonists, with the exception of the government leaders, who had electric cars, now used bicycles for transportation.

The train service in New Eden had been discontinued soon after the war began. The trains had originally been constructed by the extraterrestrials from very light and exceptionally strong materials that the human factories in the colony had never been able to duplicate. These alloys were extremely valuable in many different military functions. By the middle stages of the war, therefore, the defence agency had requisitioned all the cars in the train system.

Ellie and Robert rode their bicycles, side by side along the banks of Lake Shakespeare. Little Nicole had awakened and was quietly watching the landscape around her.

They passed the park, where the Settlement Day picnic was always held, and turned toward the north.

'Robert,' Ellie said very seriously, 'have you thought any more about our long discussion last night?'

'About Nakamura and politics?'

'Yes,' she answered. 'I still think we should *both* oppose his edict suspending elections until after the war is over ... You have a lot of stature in the colony.

Most of the health professionals will follow your lead. Nai even thinks that the factory workers in Avalon might strike.'

'I can't do it,' Robert said after a long silence.

'Why not, darling?' Ellie asked.

'Because I don't think it will work. In your idealistic view of the world, Ellie, people act out of commitment to principles or values. In reality, they don't behave that way at all. If we were to oppose Nakamura, the most likely result is that we would both be imprisoned. What would happen then to our daughter? In addition, all the support for the RV-41 work would be withdrawn, leaving those poor people in even worse shape than they are. The hospital would be more shorthanded ... Many people would suffer because of our idealism. As a doctor, I find these possible consequences unacceptable.'

Ellie drove off the bicycle path into a small park about five hundred metres from the first buildings of Central City. 'Why are we stopping here?' Robert asked. 'They're expecting us at the hospital.'

'I want to take five minutes to see the trees, smell the flowers, and hug Nicole.'

After Ellie dismounted, Robert helped her disengage the baby carrier from her back. Ellie then sat on the grass with Nicole in her lap. Neither of the adults said anything while they watched Nicole study the three blades of grass that she had grabbed with her chubby hands.

At length Ellie spread out a blanket and laid her daughter gently upon it. She approached her husband and put her arms around his neck. 'I love you, Robert, very, very much,' she said. 'But I must say that sometimes I do not agree with you at all.'

9

The light from the solitary window in the cell made a pattern on the dirt wall opposite Nicole's bed. The bars on the window created a reflected square with a tic-tac-toe design, a near perfect three-by-three matrix. The light in her cell signaled to Nicole that it was time to rise. She crossed the room from the wooden bunk on which she had been sleeping and washed her face in the basin. She then took a deep breath and tried to summon her strength for another day.

Nicole was fairly certain that her latest prison, where she had been for about five months, was somewhere in the New Eden farming strip between Hakone and San Miguel. She had been blindfolded when they had moved her the last time. Nicole had quickly concluded, however, that she was in a rural location. Occasionally a strong smell of animals drifted into her cell through the forty-centimetre-square window just below the ceiling. In addition, Nicole could see no reflected light of any kind outside the window when it was night in New Eden.

These last months have been the worst, Nicole thought as she stood on tiptoe to push a few grams of flavoured rice through the window. *No conversation, no reading, no exercise. Two meals a day of rice and water*. The little red squirrel who visited her each morning appeared outside. Nicole could hear him. She backed across the cell so she could see him eating the rice.

'You are my only company, my handsome friend,' Nicole said out loud. The squirrel stopped eating and listened, always alert for any possible danger. 'And you have never understood a single word that I have said.'

The squirrel didn't stay long. When he had finished eating his ration of rice, he departed, leaving Nicole alone. For several minutes she stared out the window where the squirrel had been, wondering what was happening with her family.

Until six months earlier, when her trial for sedition had been 'indefinitely postponed' at the last minute, Nicole had been allowed one visitor each week for one hour. Even though the conversation had been chaperoned by a guard, and any discussion of politics or current events had been strictly prohibited, she had eagerly awaited those weekly sessions with Ellie or Patrick. Usually it had been Ellie who had come. From some very carefully worded statements by both her children, Nicole had deduced that Patrick was involved in some kind of government work and was only available at limited times.

Nicole had been first angry, and then depressed, when she had learned that Benjy had been institutionalised and would not be permitted to see her. Ellie had tried to assure her mother that Benjy was all right, considering the circumstances. There had been very little discussion of Katie. Neither Patrick nor Ellie had known how to explain to Nicole that their older sister had really shown no interest in visiting her mother.

Ellie's pregnancy was always a safe topic of conversation during those earlier visits. Nicole was thrilled to touch her daughter's stomach, or to talk about the special feelings of a mother-to-be. If Ellie would mention how active the baby was, Nicole would share and compare her own experiences ('When I was pregnant with Patrick,' Nicole said one time, 'I was never tired. You, on the other hand, were a mother's nightmare – always thrashing around in the middle of the night when I wanted to sleep'); if Ellie was not feeling well, Nicole would prescribe foods or physical activities that had helped her deal with the same conditions.

Elite's last visit had been two months before the due date for the baby. Nicole had been moved to her new cell the following week, and had not talked to a human being since then. The mute biots who attended Nicole never gave any indication that they even heard her questions. Once, in a pique of frustration, she had shouted at the Tiasso giving her the weekly bath. 'Don't you understand?' she had said. 'My daughter was supposed to have a baby, my grandchild, sometime last week. I need to know if they are all right.'

In her previous cells Nicole had always been allowed to read. New book-discs had been brought to her from the library whenever she had asked, so the days between visits had passed fairly quickly. She had reread almost all her father's historical novels, as well as some poetry, history, and a few of her more interesting medical books. Nicole had been especially fascinated by the parallels between her life and the lives of her two childhood heroines, Joan of Arc and Eleanor of Aquitaine. Nicole buttressed her own strength by noting that neither of the two other women allowed her basic attitudes to change despite long and difficult periods in prison.

Right after she was moved, when the Garcia who attended her in the new cell did not return her electronic reader with her personal effects, Nicole thought that a simple mistake had been made. However, after she asked for the reader several times and it still never appeared, she realised that she was now being denied the privilege of reading.

The time passed very slowly for Nicole in her new cell. For several hours each day she deliberately paced about, trying to keep her body and mind active. She attempted to organise these pacing sessions, steering them away from thoughts about her family, which inevitably caused her feelings of loneliness and depression to intensify, and toward more general philosophic concepts or ideas. Often at the conclusion of these sessions she would focus on some past event in her life and try to derive some new or meaningful insight from it.

During one such session Nicole remembered sharply a sequence of events that had taken place when she was fifteen years old. By that time she and her father were already comfortably ensconced at Beauvois and Nicole was performing brilliantly at school. She decided to enter the national competition to select three girls to play Joan of Arc in the set of pageants that would commemorate the 750th anniversary of the maid's martyrdom at Rouen. Nicole threw herself into the contest with a passion and single-mindedness that both thrilled and worried her father. After Nicole won the regional contest at Tours, Pierre even stopped working on his novels for six weeks to help his beloved daughter prepare for the national finals at Rouen.

Nicole placed first in both the athletic and intellectual components of the contest. She even scored very high in the acting evaluations. She and her father had been certain that she was going to be selected. But when the winners were announced, Nicole had been a second runner-up.

For years, Nicole thought as she walked around her cell in New Eden, *I thought that I had failed. What my father said about France not being ready for a copper-skinned Joan of Arc did not matter. In my mind I was a failure. I was devastated. My self-esteem did not really recover until the Olympics, and then it was only a few days before Henry knocked me down again.*

The price was terrible, Nicole continued. *I was completely self-absorbed for years because of my lack of self-esteem. It was much later before I was finally happy with myself. And only then was I able to give to others.* She paused for a moment in her thoughts. *Why is it that so many of us go through the same experience? Why is youth so selfish, and why must we first find ourselves to realise how much more there is to life?*

When the Garcia who always brought her meals included some fresh bread and a few raw carrots with her dinner, Nicole suspected that there was about to be a change in her regimen. Two days later the Tiasso came into her cell with a portable bathtub, a hairbrush, some makeup, a mirror, and even a small bottle of perfume. Nicole took a long, luxurious bath and freshened herself for the first time in months. As the biot picked up the wooden tub and prepared to leave, it handed her a note. 'You will have a visitor tomorrow morning,' the note said.

Nicole could not sleep. In the morning she chattered like a little girl to her friend the squirrel, discussing both her hopes and her anxieties about the coming rendezvous. She fussed with her face and hair several times before declaring both of them to be hopeless. The time went by very slowly.

At long last, just before lunch, she heard human footsteps coming down the corridor toward her cell. Nicole rushed forward expectantly. 'Katie,' she yelled when she saw her daughter walking around the final corridor.

'Hello, Mother,' Katie said, unlocking the door and entering the cell. The two women hugged for many seconds. Nicole did not try to restrain the tears that were pouring from her eyes.

They sat on Nicole's bed, the only furniture in the cell, and talked amiably for several minutes about the family. Katie informed Nicole that she had a new granddaughter ('Nicole des Jardins Turner,' she said. 'You should be very proud'), and then pulled out about twenty photographs. The pictures included recent snapshots of the baby with her parents, Ellie and Benjy together in a park somewhere, Patrick in a uniform, and even a couple of Katie in an evening dress. Nicole studied them, one by one, her eyes brimming repeatedly. 'Oh, Katie,' she exclaimed several times.

When she was finished, Nicole thanked her daughter profusely for having brought the photographs. 'You can have them, Mother,' Katie said, standing up and walking over to the window. She opened her purse and pulled out cigarettes and a lighter.

'Darling,' Nicole said hesitantly, 'would you please not smoke in here? The ventilation is terrible. I would smell it for weeks.'

Katie stared at her mother for a few seconds and then placed her cigarettes and lighter back in her purse. At that moment a pair of Garcias arrived outside the cell with a table and two chairs.

'What's this?' Nicole asked,

Katie smiled. 'We're going to have lunch together,' she said. 'I've had something special prepared for the occasion – chicken in a mushroom and wine sauce.'

The food, which smelled divine, was soon carried into the cell by a third Garcia and placed on the covered table beside the fine china and silver. There was even a bottle of wine and two crystal glasses.

It was difficult for Nicole to remember her manners. The chicken was so delicious, the mushrooms so tender, that she ate her meal without talking. Every so often, when she took a swallow of the wine, Nicole would murmur 'Umm' or 'This is fantastic,' but she basically said nothing until her plate was completely clean.

Katie, who had become a very light eater, nibbled at her food and watched her mother. When Nicole was finished, Katie called in a Garcia to take away the dishes and bring some coffee. Nicole had not had a good cup of coffee for almost two years.

'So, Katie,' Nicole said with a warm smile after thanking her for the meal, 'how about you? What are you doing with yourself?'

Katie laughed coarsely. 'Same old shit,' she said. 'I'm now director of entertainment for the whole Vegas resort ... I book all the acts into the clubs ... Business is great even though ...' Katie caught herself, remembering that her mother knew nothing of the war in the second habitat.

'Have you found a man who can appreciate all your attributes?' Nicole asked tactfully.

'Not one who will stay around.' Katie was self-conscious about her answer and suddenly became agitated. 'Look, Mother,' she said, leaning across the table. 'I didn't come here to discuss my love life ... I have a proposition for you – or rather, the family has a proposition for you that we all support.'

Nicole looked at her daughter with a puzzled frown.

She noticed for the first time that Katie had aged considerably in the two years since she had last seen her. 'I don't understand,' Nicole said. 'What kind of a proposition?'

'Well, as you may know, the government has been preparing its case against you for some time. They are now ready to go to trial. The charge of course is sedition, which carries a mandatory death penalty. The prosecutor has told us that the evidence against you is overwhelming, and that you are certain to be convicted. However, because of your past services to the colony, if you will plead guilty to the lesser charge of involuntary sedition, he will drop ...'

'But I am not guilty of anything,' Nicole said firmly.

'I know that, Mother,' Katie replied with a trace of impatience. 'But we – Ellie, Patrick, and I – all agree that there is a high likelihood that you will be convicted. The prosecutor has promised us that if you will simply plead guilty to the reduced charge, you will be moved immediately to nicer surroundings and allowed to visit with your family, including your new granddaughter ... He even hinted that he might intercede with the authorities to allow Benjy to live with Robert and Ellie ...'

Nicole was in turmoil. 'And all of you think that I should accept this plea bargain and acknowledge my guilt, even though I have steadfastly proclaimed my innocence since the moment I was arrested?'

Katie nodded. 'We don't want you to die,' she said. 'Especially for no reason.'

'For no *reason*.' Nicole's eyes suddenly flashed. 'You think I would be dying for no *reason*!' She pushed away from the table, stood up, and paced around the, cell. 'I would be dying for *justice*,' Nicole said, more to herself than to Katie, 'in my mind at least, even if there is not a single soul anywhere else in the universe who can understand it.'

'But Mother,' Katie now interjected, 'what purpose would it serve? Your children and granddaughter would be deprived forever of your company, Benjy would remain in that foul institution ...'

'So now here's the deal,' Nicole interrupted, her voice rising, 'a more insidious version of Faust's pact with the devil ... Abandon your principles, Nicole, and acknowledge your guilt, even though you have not transgressed at all. And do not sell your soul for mere personal Earthly reward. No, that would be too easy to reject ... You are asked to take the deal because your family will benefit. Can there be any possible appeal to a mother that is more likely to sway her?'

Nicole's eyes were on fire. Katie reached into her purse, pulled out a cigarette, and lit it with a trembling hand.

886

'And who is it that comes to me with such a proposition?' Nicole continued. She was now shouting. 'Who brings me delicious food and wine and pictures of my family to soften me up for the self-inflicted knife that will surely kill me with much more pain than any electric chair? Why, it is my own daughter, the beloved issue of my womb.'

Nicole suddenly moved forward and grabbed Katie. 'Do not play Judas for them, Katie,' Nicole said, shaking her frightened daughter. 'You are so much better than that. In time, if they convict and execute me on these specious charges, you will appreciate what I am doing.'

Katie freed herself from her mother's grasp and staggered backward. She took a drag from her cigarette. 'This is bullshit, Mother,' she said a moment later. 'Total bullshit. You're just being your usual self-righteous ... Look, I came here to help you, to offer you a chance to go on living. Why can't you listen to someone else just one time in your goddamn life?'

Nicole stared at Katie for several seconds. Her voice was softer when she spoke again. 'I have been listening to you, Katie, and I do not like what I have heard. I have also been watching you ... I don't think for a moment that you came here today to help *me*. That would be completely inconsistent with what I have seen of your character these last few years. There must be something in all this for you.

'Nor do I believe that you in any way represent Ellie and Patrick. If that were the case, they would have come with you. I must confess that for a while earlier I was confused and feeling that perhaps I was causing too much pain for all my children. But in these last few minutes I have seen what is going on here very clearly ... Katie, my dear Katie ...'

'Don't you touch me again,' Katie shouted as Nicole approached her, Katie's eyes were full of tears. 'And spare me your self-righteous pity.'

The cell was momentarily quiet. Katie finished her cigarette and tried to compose herself. 'Look,' she said at length, 'I don't give a shit what you feel about me – that's not important – but why, Mother, why can't you think about Patrick and Ellie and even little Nicole? Is being a saint so important to you that they should suffer because of it?'

'In time,' Nicole replied, 'they will understand.'

'In time,' Katie said angrily, 'you'll be dead. In a very short time ... Do you realise that the moment I walk out of here and tell Nakamura that there's no deal, the date for your trial will be set? And that you have no chance at all, absolutely no fucking chance?'

'You cannot scare me, Katie.'

'I cannot scare you, I cannot touch you, I cannot even appeal to your judgment. Like all good saints, you listen to your own voices.'

Katie took a deep breath. 'Then I guess this is it ... Goodbye, Mother.' Despite herself, fresh tears appeared in Katie's eyes.

Nicole wept openly. 'Goodbye, Katie,' she said. 'I love you.'

10

'The defence may now make its closing statement.'

Nicole rose from her chair and walked around the table. She was surprised that she was so tired. The two years in prison had definitely diminished her legendary stamina.

She slowly approached the jury of four men and two women. The woman in the front row, Karen Stolz, had been originally from Switzerland. Nicole had known the woman fairly well when Mrs Stolz and her husband had owned and operated the bakery around the corner from the Wakefield home in Beauvois.

'Hello again, Karen,' Nicole said quietly, stopping directly in front of the jurors. They were sitting in two rows of three seats each. 'How are John and Marie? They must be teenagers by now.'

Mrs Stolz squirmed in her seat. 'They're fine, Nicole,' she replied very softly.

Nicole smiled. 'And do you still make those wonderful cinnamon rolls every Sunday morning?'

The crack of the gavel resounded through the courtroom. 'Mrs Wakefield,' Judge Nakamura said, 'this is hardly the time for small talk. Your closing statement is limited to five minutes and the clock has already started.'

Nicole ignored the judge. She leaned across the barrier between her and the jury, her eyes focusing on a magnificent necklace around Karen Stolz's neck. 'The jewels are beautiful,' she said in a whisper. 'But they would have paid much, much more.'

Again the gavel cracked. Two guards quickly approached Nicole, but she had already backed away from Mrs Stolz. 'Ladies and gentlemen of the jury,' Nicole said, 'all this week you have listened as the prosecution has repeatedly insisted that I have incited resistance to the legitimate government of New Eden. For my putative actions I have been charged with sedition. You must now decide, on the basis of the evidence presented at this trial, if I am guilty. Please remember as you deliberate that sedition is a capital offence – a guilty verdict carries with it a mandatory death penalty.

'In my closing statement, I would like to examine carefully the structure of the prosecution's case. The testimony on the first day, all of which was totally irrelevant to the charges against me and, I believe, was permitted by Judge Nakamura in clear violation of the colony codicils covering testimony in capital offense trials ...'

'Mrs Wakefield,' Judge Nakamura angrily interrupted, 'as I have told you before this week, I cannot tolerate such disrespectful comments in my court-room. One more similar remark and I will not only cite you for contempt, I will also terminate your closing statement altogether.'

'That entire day, the prosecution attempted to show that my sexual moral-ity was questionable, and that therefore I was somehow a likely candidate to engage in political conspiracy,' Nicole continued, without so much as glanc-ing at the judge. 'Ladies and gentlemen, I would be happy to discuss privately with you the unusual circumstances associated with the conception of each of my six children. However, my sex life – past, present, or even future – has no bearing whatsoever on this trial. Except for its possible value as entertain-ment, that first day of testimony was absolutely meaningless.'

There were a few titters in the packed gallery, but the guards quickly quieted the crowd. 'The prosecution's next set of witnesses,' Nicole contin-ued, 'spent many hours implicating my husband for seditious activities. I freely admit that I am married to Richard Wakefield. But his guilt – or lack of it, for that matter – is not of any importance at this trial either. Only evidence that purports to show me guilty of sedition is germane to your verdict here.

'The prosecution has suggested that my seditious acts originated with my involvement in the video that eventually resulted in the establishment of this colony. I acknowledge that I did help prepare the video that was transmitted from Rama to the Earth, but I categorically deny that I either conspired from the beginning with the aliens or in any way schemed with the extraterres-trials who built this spaceship against my fellow humans.

'I participated in the making of that video, as I indicated yesterday when I allowed the prosecutor to cross-examine me, because I felt I had no choice. My family and I were at the mercy of an intelligence and power far beyond anything any of us had ever imagined. There was a significant concern that failure to accede to their request for help with the video would have resulted in reprisals against us.'

Nicole returned to the defence table briefly and drank some water. She then turned around to face the jury again. 'That leaves only two possible sources for any real evidence to convict me of sedition – my daughter Katie's testimony and that strange audio recording, a disjointed collection of com-ments that I made to other members of my family after I was imprisoned, that you heard yesterday morning.

'You are all well aware how easily recordings like that can be twisted and manipulated. The two, key audio technicians both admitted yesterday on the witness stand that they had listened to hundreds of hours of conversation between my children and me before coming up with that thirty minutes of "damaging evidence", no more than *eighteen seconds* of which were taken from any single conversation. To say that my comments on that recording were presented out of context would be an understatement.

'With respect to the testimony of my daughter Katie Wakefield, I can only say, with great sorrow, that she lied repeatedly in her original remarks. I have not ever had any knowledge of my husband Richard's supposedly illegal activities and I have certainly never supported him in them.

'You recall that under cross-examination by me, Katie became confused about the facts and ultimately repudiated her earlier testimony before collapsing on the witness stand. The judge has advised you that my daughter has recently been in fragile mental health, and that you should ignore the comments she made under emotional duress during my questioning. I beseech you to remember every word that Katie said, not only when the prosecutor was asking her questions, but also during the time that I was trying to obtain the specific dates and places for the seditious actions that she had ascribed to me.'

Nicole approached the jurors one final time, carefully making eye contact with each of them. 'Ultimately, you must judge where the truth lies in this case. I face you now with a heavy heart, disbelieving even as I stand here the events that have led to my being accused of these serious crimes. I have served both the colony and the human species well. I am not guilty of any of the charges against me. Whatever power or intelligence exists in this amazing universe will recognise that fact, regardless of the outcome of this trial.'

The outside light was fading quickly. A contemplative Nicole leaned against the wall in her cell, wondering if this would be the last night of her life. She shuddered involuntarily. Since the verdict had been announced, Nicole had gone to sleep each night expecting to die the next day.

The Garcia brought her dinner soon after it was dark. The food had been much better the last few days. As she slowly ate her grilled fish Nicole reflected on the five years since she and her family had met that first scouting party from the Pinta. *What went wrong here?* Nicole asked herself. *What were our fundamental mistakes?*

She could hear Richard's voice in her head. Always cynical and distrustful of human behaviour, he had suggested at the end of the first year that New Eden was too good for humanity. 'We'll eventually ruin it as we have the Earth,' he had said. 'Our genetic baggage – the whole bit, you know, territorialism and aggression and reptilian behaviour – is too strong for education and enlightenment to overcome. Look at O'Toole's heroes, both of them, Jesus and that young Italian, St Michael of Siena. They were destroyed because they suggested that humans should try to be more than clever chimpanzees.'

But here, in New Eden, Nicole thought, *there was so much opportunity for a better world. The basics of life were provided. We were surrounded by unambiguous evidence that there was intelligence in the universe far beyond ours. That should have produced an environment in which …*

She finished her fish and pulled the small chocolate pudding over in front of her. Nicole smiled to herself, remembering how much Richard had loved chocolate. *I have missed him very much, she thought. Especially his conversation and his insight.*

Nicole was startled to hear footsteps coming toward her cell. A deep chill of fear coursed through her body. Her visitors were two young men, each of them carrying lanterns. They were wearing the uniforms of Nakamura's special police.

The men came into the cell in a very businesslike manner. They did not introduce themselves. The older one, probably in his mid-thirties, quickly pulled out a document and began to read. 'Nicole des Jardins Wakefield,' he said, 'you have been convicted of the crime of sedition and will be executed at oh-eight hundred tomorrow morning. Your breakfast will be served at six thirty, ten minutes after first light, and we will come to take you to the execution chamber at seven thirty. You will be strapped into the electric chair at oh-seven fifty-eight and current will be applied exactly two minutes later ... Do you have any questions?'

Nicole's heart was beating so rapidly she could hardly breathe. She struggled to calm herself. 'Do you have any questions?' the policeman repeated.

'What is your name, young man?' Nicole asked, her voice breaking.

'Franz,' the man answered after a puzzled hesitation.

'Franz what?' Nicole said.

'Franz Bauer,' he replied.

'Well, Franz Bauer,' Nicole said, trying to force a smile. 'Can you please tell me how long it will take me to die? After you apply the current, of course.'

'I don't really know,' he said, somewhat flustered. 'You'll lose consciousness almost instantly, in just a couple of seconds. But I don't know how long ...'

'Thank you,' Nicole said, starting to feel faint. 'Could you go now, please? I would like to be alone.' The two men opened the door to the cell. 'Oh, by the way,' Nicole added, 'could you possibly leave the lantern? And maybe a pen and paper, or even an electronic notebook?'

Franz Bauer shook his head. 'I'm sorry,' he said. 'We cannot.'

Nicole waved him away and crossed to the far side of her cell. *Two letters,* she said to herself, breathing slowly to gather strength. *I only wanted to write two letters. One to Katie and one to Richard. I've made my final peace with everyone else.*

After the policemen had departed Nicole recalled the long hours that she had spent in the pit in Rama II many years before, when she had expected to die from starvation. She had passed what she had then thought were her last days reliving the happy moments of her life. *That's not necessary now,* she thought. *There is no event from my past that has not been thoroughly scrutinised already. That's the benefit of two years in prison.*

Nicole was surprised to discover that she was angry about not being able to write the final two letters, *I'll bring the subject up again in the morning. They'll let me write the letters if I make enough noise.* Despite herself, Nicole smiled. 'Do not go gently ...' she quoted out loud.

Suddenly she felt her pulse rate increase again. In her mind's eye Nicole saw an electric chair in a dark room. She was sitting in it; a strange helmet was wrapped around her head. The helmet began to glow and Nicole saw herself slump forward.

Dear God, she thought, wherever and whatever you are. Please give me some courage now. I am very frightened.

Nicole sat down on her bed in the darkness of her room. In a few minutes she felt better, almost calm. She found herself wondering what the instant of death would be like. *Is it just like going to sleep, and then there's nothing? Or does something special happen at that very last moment, something that no living person can ever know?*

There was a voice calling her from far away. Nicole stirred but did not wake up completely. 'Mrs Wakefield,' the voice called again.

Nicole sat up quickly in her bed, thinking it was morning. She felt a surge of fear as her mind told her that she had only two more hours to live. 'Mrs Wakefield,' the voice said, 'over here, outside your cell ... It's Amadou Diaba.'

Nicole rubbed her eyes and strained to see the figure in the dark by the door. 'Who?' she said, slowly walking across the room.

'Amadou Diaba. Two years ago you helped Dr Turner do my heart transplant.'

'What are you doing here, Amadou? And how did you get inside?' ,

'I came to bring you something. I bribed everybody necessary. I had to see you.'

Even though the man was only five metres away from her, Nicole could see only his vague outline in the darkness. Her tired eyes were playing tricks on her as well. Once, when she tried especially hard to focus, she momentarily thought her visitor was her great-grandfather Omeh. A sharp chill raced through her body.

'All right, Amadou,' Nicole said at length. 'What is it that you have brought me?'

'I must explain it first,' he said. 'And even then it may not make any sense ... I don't understand it fully myself. I just know that I had to bring it to you tonight.'

He paused a moment. When Nicole did not say anything, Amadou told his story very rapidly. 'The day after I was selected for Lowell Colony, while I was still in Lagos, I received this strange message from my Senoufo grandmother, telling me that it was very urgent that I come to see her. I went at my first opportunity, which was two weeks later, after I had received still another message from my grandmother insisting that my visit was a matter of "life and death".

'When I arrived at her village in the Ivory Coast, it was the middle of the night. My grandmother awakened and dressed immediately. Accompanied by our village medicine man, we took a long trek across the savanna that very night. I was exhausted by the time we reached our destination, a little village named Nidougou.'

'Nidougou?' Nicole interrupted.

'That's right,' Amadou replied. 'Anyway, there was a strange, wizened man there who must have been some kind of super Shaman. My grandmother and our medicine man stayed in Nidougou while this man and I made the strenuous climb up a nearby barren mountain to the side of a small lake. We arrived just before sunrise. "Look," the old man said when the first rays of the sun hit the lake. "Look into the Lake of Wisdom. What do you see?"

'I told him I saw thirty or forty melon-like objects resting on the bottom of one side of the lake. "Good," he said with a smile. "You are indeed the one."

'"I am the one what?" I asked.

'He never answered. We walked around the lake, nearer to where the melons had been submerged – we couldn't see them any longer as the sun rose higher in the sky – and the super shaman pulled out a small vial. He dipped it into the water, put a cap on it, and handed it to me. He also gave me a small stone, which looked and was shaped like the melon-like objects on the bottom of the lake.

'"These are the most important gifts you will ever receive," he said.

'"Why?" I said.

'A few seconds later his eyes became completely white and he fell into a trance, chanting in rhythmic Senoufo. He danced for several minutes and then suddenly jumped into the cold lake for a swim.

'"Wait a minute," I shouted. "What shall I do with your gifts?"

'"Take them with you everywhere," he said. "You will know the time to use them."'

Nicole thought that the beating of her heart was so loud that even Amadou could hear it. She extended her arm through the bars of her cell and touched his shoulder. 'And last night,' she said, 'a voice in a dream, or maybe it wasn't a dream after all, told you to bring the vial and the stone to me tonight.'

'Exactly!' Amadou said. He paused. 'How did you know?'

Nicole did not answer. She could not speak. Her entire body was trembling. Moments later, when Nicole felt the two objects in her hand, her knees were so weak that she thought she was going to fall. She thanked Amadou twice and urged him to leave before he was discovered.

She walked slowly across the cell to her bed. *Can it be? And how can it be? All this somehow known from the beginning? Manna melons on the Earth?* Nicole's system was overloaded. *I have lost control,* she thought, *and I have not even drunk from the vial yet.*

Just holding the vial and the stone reminded Nicole vividly of the incredible vision she had experienced at the bottom of the pit in Rama II. Nicole opened the vial. She took two deep breaths and swallowed its contents hurriedly.

At first she thought nothing was happening. The blackness all around her did not seem to change. Then suddenly a great orange ball formed in the middle of the cell. It exploded, spreading colour all across the darkness. A red ball followed, then a purple one. While Nicole was recoiling from the brilliance of the purple explosion, she heard a loud laugh outside her window. She glanced in that direction. The cell disappeared. Nicole was outside in a field.

It was dark, but she could still see outlines of objects. Off in the distance Nicole heard the laugh again. *Amadou*, she called in her mind. Nicole raced across the field at blinding speed. She was catching the man. As she drew closer, his face changed. It was not Amadou at all. It was Omeh.

He laughed again and Nicole stopped. *Ronata*, he called. His face was growing. Larger, ever larger, it was as big as a car, then as big as a house. His laughter was deafening. Omeh's face was a huge balloon, rising high, ever higher into the dark night. He laughed once more and his balloon face exploded, showering Nicole with water. She was drenched. She was submerged, swimming underneath the water. When Nicole surfaced she was in the oasis pond in the Ivory Coast, where as a seven-year-old girl she had confronted the lioness during the Poro. The same lioness was prowling the perimeter of the pond. Nicole was a little girl again. She was very frightened.

I want my mother, Nicole thought. *Lay thee down now and rest, may thy slumber be blessed*, she sang. Nicole started to walk out of the water. The lioness did not bother her. Nicole glanced at the animal once more and the face of the lioness had changed into the face of her mother. Nicole ran over to embrace her mother. Instead, Nicole became the lioness herself, prowling on the shore of the oasis pond in the middle of the African savanna.

There were now six swimmers altogether in the pond, all children. As lioness Nicole continued to sing the Brahms Lullaby, one by one the children emerged from the water. Genevieve was first, then Simone, Katie, Benjy, Patrick, and Ellie. Each of them walked past her, heading into the savanna. Nicole raced after them.

She was running on an infield in a packed stadium. Nicole was a human again, young and athletic. Her final jump was announced. As she headed for the top of the triple jump runway, a Japanese judge approached her. It was Toshio Nakamura. *You are going to foul*, he said with a scowl.

Nicole thought she was flying as she sped down the approach. She hit the board perfectly, soared into the air on her hop, executed a balanced skip, and powered far out into the pit with her jump. She knew it had been a good one. Nicole bounded over to where she had left her warm-ups. Her father and Henry both came over to give her a hug. *Well done*, they said in unison. *Very well done*.

Joan of Arc brought the gold medal to the victory stand and hung it around Nicole's neck. Eleanor of Aquitaine handed her a dozen roses. Kenji

Watanabe and Judge Mishkin stood beside her and offered their congratulations. The announcer said that her jump was a new world record. The crowd was giving her a standing ovation. Nicole looked out at the sea of faces and noticed that there weren't just humans in the crowd. The Eagle was there, in a special box, sitting beside an entire section of octo-spiders. Everyone was saluting her, even the avians and the spherical creatures with the gossamer tentacles and the dozen caped eels pressed against the window of a gigantic enclosed bowl. Nicole waved to them all.

Her arms changed to wings and she began to fly. Nicole was a hawk soaring high above the farming strip in New Eden. She looked down on the building where she had been imprisoned. Nicole turned west and found Max Puckett's farm. Even though it was the middle of the night, Max was outside, working on what appeared to be an addition to one of his barns.

Nicole continued to fly west, heading toward the bright lights of Vegas. She descended when she reached the complex, flying behind the big nightclubs, one by one. Katie was sitting outside on some back steps, all by herself. She had her face buried in her hands and her body was shaking. Nicole tried to comfort her but the only sound was a hawk's cry in the night. Katie looked up at the sky, puzzled.

She flew over to Positano, near the habitat exit, and waited for the outside door to open. Startling the guard, hawk Nicole departed from New Eden. She reached Avalon in less man a minute. Robert, Ellie, little Nicole, and even an orderly were all in the lounge with Benjy in the ward. Nicole had no idea why they were all awake in the middle of the night. She cried to them. Benjy came over to the window and gazed out into the darkness.

Nicole heard a voice calling her. It was faint, far to the south. She flew rapidly to the second habitat, entering through the gaping hole that the humans had cut into the exterior wall. After speeding through the annulus and finding a portal, she soared over the green region in the interior. She could no longer hear the voice. But Nicole could see her son Patrick camped with other soldiers near the base of the brown cylinder.

An avian with four cobalt rings met her in midair. *He's not here anymore*, it said. *Try New York*. Nicole exited quickly from the second habitat and returned to the Central Plain. She heard the voice again. Up, up she went. Hawk Nicole could barely breathe.

She flew south over the perimeter wall enclosing the Northern Hemicylinder. The Cylindrical Sea was below her. The voice was now more distinct. It was Richard. Her hawk heart was pounding furiously.

He was standing on the shore, in front of the skyscrapers, waving at her. *Come to me*, Nicole, his voice said. She could see his eyes even in the dark. Nicole flew down and landed on Richard's shoulder.

There was blackness around her. Nicole was back in her cell. Was that a bird she heard flying just outside her window? Her heart was still fluttering.

She walked across the small room. *Thank you, Amadou*, she said. *Or Omeh*. She smiled. *Or God*.

Nicole stretched out on her bed. A few seconds later she was asleep.

RAMA REVEALED

PROLOGUE

In one of the outlying spiral arms of the Milky Way Galaxy, an inconspicuous, solitary yellow star slowly orbits the galactic centre thirty thousand light-years away. This stable star, the Sun, takes 225 million years to complete one revolution in its galactic orbit. The last time the Sun was in its present position, giant reptiles of fearsome power had just begun to establish their dominion on the Earth, a small blue planet that is one of the satellites of the Sun.

Among the planets and other bodies in the family of the Sun, it is only on this Earth that any complex, enduring life has ever developed. Only on this special world did chemicals evolve into consciousness and then ask, as they began to understand the wonders and dimensions of the universe, if miracles similar to the ones that had produced them had indeed occurred elsewhere.

After all, these sentient Earthlings argued, there are a hundred billion stars in our galaxy alone. We are fairly certain that at least 20 per cent of these stars have orbiting planets, and that a small but significant number of these planets have had, at some time in their history, atmospheric and thermal conditions conducive to the formation of amino acids and other organic chemicals that are the *sine qua non* for any biology we can reasonably hypothesise. At least once in history, here on Earth, these amino acids discovered self-replication, and the evolutionary miracle that eventually produced human beings was set into motion. How can we presume that this sequence occurred only that single time in all history? The heavier atoms necessary to create us have been forged in the stellar cataclysms exploding across this universe for billions of years. Is it likely that only here, in this one place, these atoms have concatenated into special molecules and evolved into an intelligent being capable of asking the question, 'Are we alone?'

The humans on Earth began their search for cosmic companions first by building telescopes with which they could see their immediate planetary neighbours. Later, when their technology had developed to a higher level, sophisticated robotic spacecraft were sent to examine these other planets and to ascertain whether or not there were any signs of biology. These explorations proved that no intelligent life has ever existed on any other body in our solar system. If there is anyone out there, the human scientists concluded, any peer species with whom we might eventually communicate, they must be found beyond the void that separates our solar system from all the other stars.

At the end of the twentieth century in the human time system, the great antennae of the Earth began to search the sky for coherent signals, to determine if perhaps some other intelligence might be sending us a radio message. For over a hundred years the search continued, intensifying during the halcyon days of international science in the early twenty-first century, and then diminishing later, in the final decades of the century, after the fourth separate set of systematic listening techniques still failed to locate any alien signals.

By 2130, when the strange cylindrical object was first identified hurtling towards our solar system from the reaches of interstellar space, most thoughtful humans had decided that life must be scarce in the universe and that intelligence, if indeed it existed anywhere except on Earth, was exceedingly rare. How else, the scientists contended, can we possibly explain the lack of positive results from all our careful extraterrestrial search efforts of the last century?

The Earth was therefore stunned when, upon closer inspection, the object entering our solar system in 2130 was identified unambiguously as an artefact of alien origin. Here was undeniable proof that advanced intelligence existed, or at least *had* existed at some prior epoch, in another part of the universe. When an ongoing space mission was diverted to rendezvous with the drab cylindrical behemoth, which turned out to have dimensions greater than the largest cities on Earth, the investigating cosmonauts found mystery after mystery. But they were unable to answer the most fundamental questions about the enigmatic alien spacecraft. The intruder from the stars provided no definitive clues about its origin or purpose.

That first group of human explorers not only catalogueed the wonders of Rama (the name chosen for the gigantic cylindrical object before it was known to be an extraterrestrial artefact), but also explored and mapped its interior. After the exploration team left Rama and the alien spaceship dived around the Sun, departing from the solar system at hyperbolic velocity, scientists thoroughly analysed all the data that had been gathered during the mission. Everyone acknowledged that the human visitors to Rama had never encountered the actual creators of the mysterious spacecraft. However, the careful postflight analysis did reveal one inescapable principle of Raman redundancy engineering. Every critical system and subsystem in the vehicle had two back-ups. The Ramans designed everything in threes. The scientists considered it very likely that two more similar spacecraft would soon follow.

The years immediately after the visit from Rama I in 2130 were full of expectation on the Earth. Scholars and politicians alike proclaimed that a new era in human history had begun. The International Space Agency (ISA), working with the Council of Governments (COG), developed careful procedures for handling the next visit from the Ramans. All telescopes were trained on the heavens, competing with each other for the acclaim that would come to the individual or observatory who first located the next Rama spacecraft. But there were no additional sightings.

In the second half of the 2130s an economic boom, fueled partially during its last stages by worldwide reactions to Rama, came to an abrupt halt. The world was plunged into the deepest depression in its history, known as the Great Chaos, which was accompanied by widespread anarchy and destitution. Virtually all scientific research activity was abandoned during this sorrowful era, and after several decades in which they were forced to address more mundane problems, people on the Earth had nearly forgotten the unexplained visitor from the stars.

In 2200 a second cylindrical intruder arrived in the solar system. The citizens of Earth dusted off the old procedures that had been developed after the first Rama had departed, and prepared to rendezvous with Rama II. A crew of twelve was chosen for the mission. Soon after the rendezvous, the dozen reported that the second Rama spacecraft was nearly identical to its predecessor. The humans encountered new mysteries and wonders, including some alien beings, but were still unable to answer questions about the origin and purpose of Rama.

Three strange deaths among the crew created great concern back on the Earth, where all aspects of the historic mission were followed on television. When the giant cylinder underwent a midcourse manoeuvre that placed it on a trajectory that would impact the Earth, this concern changed to alarm and fear. The leaders of the world reluctantly concluded that, in the absence of any other information, they had no choice except to assume that Rama II was hostile. They could not allow the alien spacecraft to impact the Earth, or to come close enough that it might deploy any advanced weapons it might possess. A decision was made to destroy Rama II while it was still a safe distance away.

The exploration crew was ordered home, but three of its members, two men and a woman, were still on board Rama II when the alien spaceship avoided a nuclear phalanx launched from the Earth. Rama manoeuvred away from the hostile Earth and departed at high speed from the solar system, carrying both its intact secrets and the three human passengers.

It took thirteen years at relativistic velocities for Rama II to travel from the neighbourhood of Earth to its destination, a huge engineering complex called The Node that was located in a distant orbit around the star Sirius. The three humans on board the giant cylinder added five children and grew into a family. As they investigated the marvels of their home in space, the family again encountered the extraterrestrial species they had met earlier. However, by the time they reached The Node, the humans had already convinced themselves that these other aliens were, like them, only passengers in Rama.

The human family remained at The Node for slightly more than a year.

During this time the Rama spacecraft was refurbished and outfitted for its third and final journey to the solar system. The family learned from The Eagle, a non-biological creation of the Nodal Intelligence, that the purpose of the Rama series of spacecraft was to acquire and catalogue as much information as possible about spacefarers in the galaxy. The Eagle, who had the head, beak, and eyes of an eagle plus the body of a human, also informed them that the final Rama spacecraft, Rama III, would contain a carefully designed Earth habitat that could accommodate two thousand people.

A video was transmitted from The Node to the Earth announcing the imminent return of the third Rama spaceship. This video explained that an advanced extraterrestrial species wished to observe and study human activity over an lextended period of time and requested that two thousand representative humans be sent to rendezvous with Rama III in orbit around Mars.

Rama III made the voyage from Sirius back to the solar system at a velocity more than half the speed of light. Inside the spacecraft, sleeping in special berths, were most of the human family who had been at The Node. In Mars orbit this family greeted the other humans from Earth and the pristine habitat inside Rama was quickly settled. The resultant colony, which was called New Eden, was completely enclosed and separated from the rest of the alien spacecraft by thick walls.

Almost immediately Rama III accelerated again to relativistic velocities, blasting out of the solar system in the direction of the yellow star Tau Ceti. Three years passed without any outside interference in human affairs. The citizens of New Eden became so involved with their everyday lives that they paid scant attention to the universe outside their settlement.

When a set of crises stressed the fledgling democracy in the paradise that had been created for the humans by the Ramans, an opportunistic tycoon seized power in the colony and began to ruthlessly suppress all opposition. One of the original Rama II explorers fled from New Eden at this time, eventually making contact with a symbiotic pair of alien species living in the adjacent enclosed habitat. His wife remained in the human colony and tried unsuccessfully to be a conscience for the community. She was imprisoned after a few months, convicted of treason, and eventually scheduled for execution.

As the environmental and living conditions inside New Eden continued to deteriorate, human troops invaded the adjacent living area in the Northern Hemicylinder of Rama and engaged in a war of annihilation against the symbiotic pair of alien species. Meanwhile, the mysterious Ramans, known only through the genius of their engineering creations, continued their detailed observation from afar, aware that it was only a matter of time until the humans came into contact with the advanced species inhabiting the region to the south of the Cylindrical Sea ...

ESCAPE

1

'Nicole.'

At first the soft, mechanical voice seemed to be part of her dream. But when she heard her name repeated, slightly louder, Nicole awakened with a start.

A wave of intense fear swept through her. *They have come for me*, Nicole thought immediately. *It is morning. I am going to die in a few hours.*

She took a slow, deep breath and tried to quell her mounting panic. A few seconds later Nicole opened her eyes. It was completely dark in her cell. Puzzled, Nicole looked around for the person who had called her.

'We are here, on your cot, beside your right ear,' the voice said very softly. 'Richard sent us to help you escape ... but we must move quickly.'

For an instant Nicole thought that perhaps she was still dreaming. Then she heard a second voice, very similar to the first but nevertheless distinct. 'Roll over on your right side and we will illuminate ourselves.'

Nicole rolled over. Standing on the cot next to her head she saw two tiny figures, no more than eight or ten centimetres high, each in the shape of a woman. They were glowing momentarily from some internal light source. One had short hair and was dressed in the armor of a fifteenth century European knight. The second figure was wearing both a crown upon her head and the full, pleated dress of a medieval queen.

'I am Joan of Arc,' the first figure said.

'And I am Eleanor of Aquitaine.'

Nicole laughed nervously and stared in astonishment at the two figures. Several seconds later, when the robots' internal lights were extinguished, Nicole had finally composed herself enough to speak. 'So Richard sent you to help me escape?' she said in a whisper. 'Just how do you propose to do that?'

'We've already sabotaged the monitoring system,' tiny Joan said proudly. 'And reprogrammed a Garcia biot ... It should be here in a few minutes to let you out.'

'We have a nominal escape plan, along with several contingencies,' Eleanor added. 'Richard has been working on it for months – ever since he finished making us.'

Nicole laughed again. She was still absolutely stunned. 'Really?' she said.

'And may I ask just where my genius of a husband is at this moment?'

'Richard is in your old lair underneath New York,' Joan replied. 'He said to tell you that nothing has changed there. He is following our progress with a navigation beacon ... Incidentally, Richard sends his love. He hasn't forgotten ...'

'Be still for a moment, please,' Eleanor interrupted as Nicole automatically scratched at the tickling sensation behind her right ear. 'I'm deploying your personal beacon right now, and it's very heavy for me.'

Moments later Nicole touched the tiny instrument package next to her ear and shook her head. 'And can he *hear* us also?' she asked.

'Richard decided we couldn't risk voice transmissions,' Eleanor answered. 'They could be too easily intercepted by Nakamura ... However, he will be monitoring our physical location.'

'You may get up now,' Joan said, 'and put on your clothes. We want to be ready when the Garcia arrives.'

Will wonders never cease? Nicole thought while she was washing her face in the dark in the primitive basin. For a few brief seconds Nicole imagined that the two robots might be part of a clever New Eden government plot and that she was going to be killed trying to escape. *Impossible*, she told herself a few moments later. *Even if one of Nakamura's minions could create robots like these, only Richard would know enough about me to make a Joan of Arc and an Eleanor of Aquitaine ... anyway, what differrence does it make if I'm killed while trying to escape? My electrocution is scheduled for eight o'clock this morning.*

There was the sound of a biot approaching outside her cell. Nicole tensed, still not completely convinced that her two tiny friends were indeed telling her the truth. 'Sit back down on the cot,' she heard Joan say behind her, 'so Eleanor and I can climb into your pockets.' Nicole felt the two robots scrambling up the front of her shirt. She smiled. *You are amazing, Richard,* she thought. *And I'm ecstatic that you are still alive.*

The Garcia biot was carrying a flashlight. It strode into Nicole's cell with an air of authority. 'Come with me, Mrs Wakefield,' it said in a loud voice. 'I have orders to move you to the preparations room.'

Again Nicole was frightened. The biot certainly wasn't acting friendly. *What if ...* But she had very little time to think. The Garcia led Nicole through the corridor outside her cell at a rapid pace. Twenty metres later, they passed both the regular set of biot guards and a human commanding officer, a young man Nicole had never seen before. 'Wait,' the man yelled from behind them just as Nicole and the Garcia were about to climb the stairs. Nicole froze.

'You forgot to sign the transfer papers,' the man said, holding out a document to the Garcia. 'Certainly,' the biot replied, entering its identification number on the papers with a flourish. After less than a minute Nicole was outside the large house where she had been imprisoned for months. She took a deep breath of the fresh air and started to follow the Garcia down a path towards Central City.

'No,' Nicole heard Eleanor call from her pocket. 'We're not going with the biot. Go west. Toward that windmill with the light on top. And you must run. We must arrive at Max Puckett's before dawn.'

Her prison was almost five kilometres from Max's farm. Nicole jogged down the small road at a steady pace, urged on periodically by one of the two robots, who were keeping careful track of the time. It was not long until dawn. Unlike on the Earth, where the transition from night to day was gradual, in New Eden dawn was a sudden, discontinuous event. One moment it would be dark and then, in the next instant, the artificial sun would ignite and begin its mini-arc across the ceiling of the colony habitat.

'Twelve more minutes until light,' Joan said, as Nicole reached the bicycle path that led the final two hundred metres to the Puckett farmhouse. Nicole was nearly exhausted, but she kept running. Two separate times during her run across the farmland she had felt a dull ache in her chest. *I am definitely out of shape*, she thought, chastising herself for not having exercised regularly in her prison cell. *As well as approximately sixty years old.*

The farmhouse was dark. Nicole stopped on the porch, catching her breath, and the door opened a few seconds later. 'I have been waiting for you,' Max said, his earnest expression underscoring the seriousness of the situation. He gave Nicole a quick hug. 'Follow me,' he said, moving quickly off toward the barn.

'There have been no police cars yet on the road,' Max said when they were inside the barn. 'They probably have not yet discovered that you're gone. But it's only a matter of minutes now.'

The chickens were all kept on the far side of the barn. The hens had a separate enclosure, sealed off from the roosters and the rest of the building. When Max and Nicole entered the henhouse, there was a huge commotion. Animals scurried in all directions, clucking and squawking and beating their wings. The stench in the henhouse nearly overpowered Nicole.

Max smiled. 'I guess I forget how bad chicken shit smells to everyone else,' he said, 'I've grown so used to it myself.' He slapped Nicole lightly on the back. 'Anyway, it's another level of protection for you, and I don't think you'll be able to smell the shit from your hideout.'

Max walked over to a corner of the henhouse, chased several hens out of the way, and bent down on his knees. 'When those weird little robots of Richard's first appeared,' he said, pushing aside hay and chicken feed, 'I couldn't decide where I should build your hideout. Then I thought about this place.' Max pulled up a couple of boards to expose a rectangular hole in the floor of the barn. 'I sure as hell hope I was right.'

He motioned for Nicole to follow him and then crawled into the hole. They were both on their hands and knees in the dirt. The passageway, which ran parallel to the floor for a few metres and then turned downward at a steep angle, was extremely cramped. Nicole kept bumping up against Max in front of her and the dirt walls and ceiling all around her. The only light was the small flashlight that Max was carrying in his right hand. After fifteen metres the small tunnel opened into a dark room. Max stepped carefully down a rope ladder and then turned to help Nicole descend. A few seconds later they both walked into the centre of the room, where Max reached up and switched on a solitary electric light.

'It's not a palace,' he said as Nicole glanced around, 'but I suspect it's a damn sight better than that prison of yours.'

The room contained a bed, a chair, two shelves full of food, another shelf with electronic bookdiscs, a few clothes hanging in an open closet, basic toiletries, a large drum of water that must have barely fitted through the passageway, and a deep, square latrine in the far corner.

'Did you do all this yourself?' Nicole asked.

'Yep,' Max replied. 'At night ... during the last several weeks. I didn't dare ask anybody to help.'

Nicole was touched. 'How can I ever thank you?' she said.

'Don't get caught.' Max grinned. 'I don't want to die any more than you do ... Oh, by the way,' he added, handing Nicole an electronic reader into which she could place the bookdiscs, 'I hope the reading material is all right. Manuals on raising pigs and chickens are not the same as your father's novels, but I didn't want to attract too much attention by going to the bookstore.'

Nicole crossed the room and kissed him on the cheek. 'Max,' she said lightly, 'you are such a dear friend. I can't imagine how you ...'

'It's dawn outside now,' Joan of Arc interrupted from Nicole's pocket. 'According to our timeline, we are behind schedule. Mr Puckett, we must inspect our egress route before you leave us.'

'Shit,' said Max. 'Here I go again, taking orders from a robot no longer than a cigarette.' He lifted Joan and Eleanor out of Nicole's pockets and placed them on the top shelf behind a can of peas. 'Do you see that little door?' he said. 'There's a pipe on the other side. It comes out just beyond the pig trough ... Why don't you check it out?'

During the minute or two that the robots were gone, Max explained the situation to Nicole. 'The police will be searching everywhere for you,' he said. 'Particularly here, since they know that I am a friend of the family. So I'm going to seal the entrance to your hideout. You should have everything you need to last for at least several weeks.

'The robots can come and go freely, unless they are eaten by the pigs,' Max continued with a laugh. 'They will be your only contact with the outside world. They'll let you know when it's time to move to the second phase of our escape plan.'

'So I won't see you again?' Nicole asked.

'Not for at least a few weeks,' Max answered. 'It's too dangerous ... One more thing: if there are police on the premises, I will cut off your power. That will be your signal to stay especially quiet.'

Eleanor of Aquitaine had returned and was standing on the shelf next to the can of peas. 'Our egress route is excellent,' she announced. 'Joan has departed for a few days. She intends to leave the habitat and communicate with Richard.'

'Now I must leave also,' Max said to Nicole. He was silent for a few seconds. 'But not before I tell you one thing, my lady friend ... As you probably know, I have been a fucking cynic all my life. There are not very many people who impress me. But you have convinced me that maybe some of us are superior to chickens and pigs.' Max smiled. 'Not many of us,' he added quickly, 'but at least some.'

'Thank you, Max,' Nicole said.

Max walked over to the ladder. He turned around and waved before he began his climb.

Nicole sat down in the chair and took a deep breath. From the sounds in the direction of the tunnel, she surmised correctly that Max was sealing the entrance to her hideout by placing the big bags of chicken feed directly over the hole.

So what happens now? Nicole asked herself. She realised that she had thought about very little except her approaching death during the five days since the conclusion of her trial. Without the fear of her imminent execution to structure her thought patterns, Nicole was able to let her mind drift freely.

She thought first of Richard, her husband and partner, from whom she had been separated now for almost two years. Nicole recalled vividly their last evening together, a horrible Walpurgisnacht of murder and destruction that had begun on a hopeful note with her daughter Ellie's marriage to Dr Robert Turner. *Richard was certain that we were also marked for death*, she remembered. *And he was probably right ... because he escaped, they made him the enemy and left me alone for a while,*

I thought you were dead, Richard, Nicole thought. *I should have had more faith ... But how in the world did you end up in New York again?*

As she sat in the only chair in the underground room, her heart ached for the company of her husband. A montage of memories paraded through her mind. She first saw herself again in the avian lair in Rama II, years and years earlier, temporarily a captive of the strange birdlike creatures whose language was jabbers and shrieks. It had been Richard who had found her there. He had risked his own life to return to New York to determine if Nicole was still alive. If Richard had not come, Nicole would have been marooned on the island of New York for ever.

Richard and Nicole had become lovers during the time that they were struggling to figure out how to cross the Cylindrical Sea and return to their cosmonaut colleagues from the Newton spacecraft. Nicole was both surprised and amused by the strong stirrings inside her caused by her recollection of their early days of love. *We survived the nuclear missile attack together. We even survived my wrongheaded attempt to produce genetic variation in our offspring by sleeping with another man.*

Nicole winced at the memory of her own naïvety so many years before. *You forgave me, Richard, which could not have been easy for you. And then we grew even closer at The Node during our design sessions with The Eagle.*

What was The Eagle really? Nicole mused, shifting her train of thought. *And who or what created him?* In her mind was a vivid picture of the bizarre creature who had been their only contact while they had stayed at The Node during the refurbishing of the Rama spaceship. The alien being, who had had the face of an eagle and a body similar to a man's, had informed them that he was an advancement in artificial intelligence designed especially as a companion for humans. *His eyes were incredible, almost mystical,* Nicole remembered. *And they were as intense as Omeh's.*

Her great-grandfather Omeh had worn the green robe of the tribal shaman of the Senoufo when he had come to see Nicole in Rome two weeks before the launch of the Newton spacecraft. Nicole had met Omeh twice before, both times in her mother's native village in the Ivory Coast: once during the Poro ceremony when Nicole was seven, and then again three years later at her mother's funeral. During those brief encounters Omeh had started preparing Nicole for what the old shaman had assured her would be an extraordinary life. It had been Omeh who had insisted that Nicole was indeed the woman who the Senoufo chronicles had predicted would scatter their tribal seed 'even to the stars.'

Omeh, The Eagle, even Richard, Nicole thought. *Quite a group, to say the least.* The face of Henry, Prince of Wales, joined the other three men and Nicole remembered for a moment the powerful passion of their brief love affair in the days immediately after she had won her Olympic gold medal. She recalled sharply the pain of rejection. *But without Henry,* she reminded herself, *there would not have been a Genevieve.* While Nicole was remembering the love she had shared with her daughter on Earth, she glanced across the room at the shelf containing the electronic bookdiscs. Suddenly distracted, she crossed to the shelf and started reading titles. Sure enough, Max had left her some manuals on raising pigs and chickens. But that was not all. It looked as if he had given Nicole his entire private library.

Nicole smiled as she pulled out a book of fairy tales and inserted it into her reader. She flipped through the pages and stopped at the story of Sleeping Beauty. The phrase 'and they lived happily ever after' summoned another vivid memory, this one of herself as a small child, maybe six or seven, sitting on her father's lap in their house in the Parisian suburb of Chilly-Mazarin.

I longed as a little girl to be a princess and live happily ever after, she thought. *There was no way I could have known then that my life would make even the fairy tales seem ordinary.*

Nicole replaced the bookdisc on the shelf and returned to her chair. *And now,* she thought, idly surveying the room, *when I thought this incredible life was over, I seem to have been given at least a few more days.*

She thought again of Richard and her intense longing to see him returned. *We have shared much, my Richard. I hope I can again feel your touch, hear your laughter, and see your face. But if not, I will try not to complain. My life has already seen its share of miracles.*

2

Eleanor Wakefield Turner arrived at the large auditorium in Central City at seven-thirty in the morning. Although the execution was not scheduled to take place until eight o'clock, there were already about thirty people in the front seats, some talking, most just sitting quietly. A television crew wandered around the electric chair on the stage. The execution was being broadcast live, but the policemen in the auditorium were nevertheless expecting a full house, for the government had encouraged the citizens of New Eden to witness personally the death of their former governor.

Ellie had argued with her husband the night before. 'Spare yourself this pain, Ellie,' Robert had said, when she had told him that she intended to attend the execution. 'Seeing your mother one last time cannot be worth the horror of watching her die.'

But Ellie had known something that Robert did not know. As she took her seat in the auditorium, Ellie tried to control the powerful feelings inside her. *There can be nothing on my face,* she told herself, *and nothing in my body language. Not the slightest hint. Nobody must suspect that I know anything about the escape.* Several pairs of eyes suddenly turned around to look at her. Ellie felt her heart skip before she realised that someone had recognised her and that it was completely natural for the curious to stare at her.

Ellie had first encountered her father's little robots Joan of Arc and Eleanor of Aquitaine only six weeks before, when she was outside of the main habitat, over in the quarantine village of Avalon helping her physician husband Robert take care of the patients who were doomed by the RV-41 retrovirus inside their bodies. Ellie had just finished a pleasant and encouraging late-evening visit with her friend and former teacher Eponine. She had left Eponine's room and was walking along a dirt lane, expecting to see Robert at any moment. All of a sudden she had heard two strange voices calling her name. Ellie had searched the area around her before finally locating the pair of tiny figures on the roof of a nearby building.

After crossing the lane so that she could see and hear the robots better, the stunned Ellie had been informed by Joan and Eleanor that her father Richard was still alive. It had taken her a few moments to recover from the shock. Then Ellie had begun to question the robots. She had become quickly convinced that Joan and Eleanor were telling the truth; however, before Ellie had ascertained why her father had sent the robots to her, she had seen her husband approaching in the distance. The figures on the rooftop had then told her hurriedly that they would return soon. They had also cautioned Ellie not to tell anyone of their existence, not even Robert, at least not yet,

Ellie had been overjoyed that her father was still alive. It had been almost impossible for her to keep the news a secret, even though she was well aware of the political significance of her information. When, almost two weeks later, Ellie had been again confronted in Avalon by the little robots, she had been ready with a torrent of questions. However, on that occasion Joan and Eleanor had been programmed to discuss another subject – a possible forthcoming attempt to break Nicole out of prison. The robots told Ellie during this second meeting that Richard acknowledged such an escape would be a dangerous endeavor. 'We would never attempt it,' the robot Joan said, 'unless your mother's execution were absolutely certain. But if we are not prepared ahead of time, there can be no possibility of a last-minute escape.'

'What can I do to help?' Ellie had asked.

Joan and Eleanor had handed her a sheet of paper, on which there was a list of items including food, water, and clothing. Ellie had trembled when she recognised her father's handwriting.

'Cache these things at the following location,' the robot Eleanor had said, handing Ellie a map. 'No later than ten days from now.' A moment later another colonist had come into sight and the two robots had vanished.

Enclosed inside the map had been a short note from her father. 'Dearest Ellie,' it had said, 'I apologise for the brevity. I am safe and healthy, but deeply concerned about your mother. Please, please gather up these items and take them to the indicated spot in the Central Plain. If you cannot accomplish the task by yourself, please limit your support to a single person. And make certain that whoever you pick is as loyal and dedicated to Nicole as we are. I love you.'

Ellie had quickly determined that she would need help. But whom should she select as an accomplice? Her husband Robert was a bad choice for two reasons. First, he had already shown that his dedication to his patients and the New Eden hospital was a higher priority in his mind than taking a political stand. Second, anyone caught helping Nicole escape would certainly be executed. If Ellie were to involve Robert in the escape plan, then their daughter Nicole might be left without both her parents.

What about Nai Watanabe? There was no question about her loyalty, but Nai was a single parent with twin four-year-old sons. It was not fair to ask her to take the chance. That left Eponine as the only reasonable choice. Any worries that Ellie might have had about her afflicted friend had been quickly dispelled. 'Of course I'll help you,' Eponine had replied immediately. 'I have nothing to lose. According to your husband, this RV-41 is going to kill me in another year or two anyway.'

Eponine and Ellie had clandestinely gathered the required items, one at a time, over a period of a week. They had wrapped them securely in a small sheet that was hidden in the corner of Eponine's normally cluttered room in Avalon. On the appointed day, Ellie had signed out of New Eden and walked across to Avalon, ostensibly to 'monitor carefully' a full twelve hours of Eponine's biometry data. Actually, explaining to Robert why she wanted to spend the night with Eponine had been much more difficult than convincing the single human guard and the Garcia biot at the habitat exit of the legitimacy of her need for an overnight pass.

Just after midnight Ellie and Eponine had picked up their sheet and crept cautiously into the streets of Avalon. Being very careful to avoid the roving biots that Nakamura's police used to patrol the small outside village at night, the two women had sneaked through the outskirts of the town and into the Central Plain. They had then hiked for several kilometres and deposited the cache in the designated location. A Tiasso biot had confronted them outside Eponine's room upon their return and had asked what they were doing wandering around at such an absurd hour.

'This woman has RV-41,' Ellie had said quickly, sensing the panic in her friend. 'She is one of my husband's patients. She was in extreme pain and could not sleep, so we thought that an early morning walk might help ... Now, if you'll excuse us ...'

The Tiasso had let them pass. Ellie and Eponine had been so frightened that neither of them had spoken for ten minutes.

Ellie had not seen the robots again. She had no idea whether or not an actual escape had been attempted. As the time for her mother's execution now drew near and the auditorium seats around her began to fill, Ellie's heart was pounding furiously. *What if nothing has happened?* She thought. *What if Mother is really going to die in twenty more minutes?*

Ellie glanced up at the stage. A two-metre stack of electronics, metallic grey, stood next to the large chair. The only other object on the stage was a digital clock that currently read 0742. Ellie stared at the chair. Hanging from the top was a hood that would fit over the victim's head. Ellie shuddered and fought against nausea. *How barbaric,* she thought. *How could any species that considers itself advanced tolerate this kind of gruesome spectacle?*

Her mind had just cleared away the execution images when there was a tap on her shoulder. Ellie turned around. A large, frowning policeman was leaning across the aisle in her direction. 'Are you Eleanor Wakefield Turner?' he asked,

Ellie was so frightened she could barely respond. She nodded her head. 'Will you come with me, please?' he said. 'I need to ask you a couple of questions.'

Ellie's legs were shaking as she edged by three people in her row and entered the aisle. *Something's gone wrong,* she thought. *The escape has been foiled. They've found the cache and somehow know that I'm involved.*

The policeman took her to a small conference room on the side of the auditorium. 'I'm Captain Franz Bauer, Mrs Turner,' he said. 'It is my job to dispose of your mother's body after she has been executed. We have, of course, arranged for the customary cremation with the undertaker. However,' At this point Captain Bauer stopped, as if he were carefully selecting his words, 'in view of the past services that your mother has rendered for the colony, I thought perhaps that you, or some member of your family, might like to take care of the final procedures.'

'Yes, of course, Captain Bauer,' Ellie replied, weak with relief. 'Certainly. Thank you very much,' she added quickly.

'That will be all, Mrs Turner,' the policeman said. 'You may now return to the auditorium.'

Ellie stood up and discovered that she was still shaky.

She put one hand on the table in the middle of the room. 'Sir?' she said to Captain Bauer.

'Yes?' he replied.

'Would it be possible for me to see my mother alone, just for an instant, before ... ?'

The policeman studied Ellie at length. 'I don't think so,' he said, 'but I will ask on your behalf.'

'Thank you very ...'

Ellie was interrupted by the ring of the telephone. She delayed her departure from the conference room long enough to see the shocked expression on Captain Bauer's face. 'Are you absolutely certain?' she heard him say as she left the room.

The crowd was growing restive. The big digital clock on the stage read 0836. 'Come on, come on,' the man behind Ellie grumbled. 'Let's get on with it.'

Mother has escaped. I know it, Ellie said to herself joyfully. Ellie forced herself to stay calm. *That's why everything here is so confused.*

Captain Bauer had informed everyone at five minutes past eight that the 'activities' would be delayed 'a few minutes,' but in the last half-hour there had been no additional announcements. In the row in front of Ellie, a wild rumour was circulating that the extraterrestrials had rescued Nicole from her cell.

Some of the people had already started to leave when Governor Macmillan walked onto the stage. He looked harried and upset, but he broke quickly into his official open smile when he began addressing the crowd.

'Ladies and gentlemen,' he said, 'the execution of Nicole des Jardins Wakefield has been postponed. The government has discovered some small irregularities in the paperwork associated with her case – nothing really important, of course – but we felt these issues should be cleared up first, so that there can be no question of any impropriety. The execution will be rescheduled in the near future. All the citizens of New Eden will be informed of the details.'

Ellie sat in her seat until the auditorium was nearly empty. She half expected to be detained by the police when she tried to leave, but nobody stopped her. Once outside, it was difficult for her not to scream with joy. *Mother, Mother*, Ellie thought, tears finding their way into her eyes, *I am so happy for you.*

She suddenly noticed that several people were looking at her. *Uh-oh*, Ellie thought. *Am I giving myself away?* She met the other eyes with a polite smile. *Now, Ellie, comes your greatest challenge. You cannot under any circumstances behave as if you are not surprised.*

As usual, Robert, Ellie, and little Nicole stopped in Avalon to visit with Nai Watanabe and the twins after completing their weekly calls on the seventy-seven remaining RV-41 sufferers. It was just before dinner. Both Galileo and Kepler were playing in the dirt street in front of the ramshackle house. When the Turners arrived, the two little boys were involved in an argument.

'She is too,' the four-year-old Galileo said heatedly.

'Is not,' Kepler replied with much less passion.

Ellie bent down beside the twins. 'Boys, boys,' she said in a friendly voice. 'What are you fighting about?'

'Oh, hi, Mrs Turner,' Kepler answered with an embarrassed smile. 'It's really nothing. Galileo and I ...'

'I say that Governor Wakefield is already dead,' Galileo interrupted forcefully. 'One of the boys at the centre told me, and he should know. His daddy is a policeman.'

For a moment Ellie was taken aback. Then she realised that the twins had not made the connection between Nicole and her. 'Do you remember that Governor Wakefield is my mother, and little Nicole's grandmother?' Ellie said softly. 'You and Kepler met her several times before she went to prison.'

Galileo wrinkled his brow and then shook his head.

'I remember her ... I think,' Kepler said solemnly. 'Is she dead, Mrs Turner?' the ingenuous youngster then added after a brief pause.

'We don't know for certain, but we hope not,' Ellie replied. She had almost slipped. It would have been so easy to tell these children. But it would only take one mistake. There was probably a biot within earshot.

As Ellie picked up Kepler and gave him a hug, she remembered her chance encounter with Max Puckett at the electronic supermarket three days earlier, in the middle of their ordinary conversation, Max had suddenly said, 'Oh, by the way, Joan and Eleanor are fine and asked me to give you their regards.'

Ellie had become excited, and had asked a leading question about the two little robots. Max had ignored it completely. A few seconds later, just as Ellie was about to say something else, the Garcia biot who was in charge of the market had suddenly appeared beside them.

'Hello, Ellie. Hello, Robert,' Nai said now from the doorway of her house. She extended her arms and took Nicole from her father. 'And how are you, my little beauty? I haven't seen you since your birthday party last week.'

The adults went inside the house. After Nai checked to ensure that there were no spy biots in the area, she drew close to Robert and Ellie. 'The police interrogated me again last night,' she whispered to her friends. 'I'm starting to believe there may be some truth in the rumour.'

'*Which* rumour?' Ellie said. 'There are so many.'

'One of the women who works at our factory,' Nai said, 'has a brother in Nakamura's special service. He told her, one night after he had been drinking, that when the police showed up at Nicole's cell on the morning of the execution, the cell was empty. A Garcia biot had signed her out. They think it was the same Garcia that was reportedly destroyed in that explosion outside the munitions factory.'

Ellie smiled, but her eyes said nothing in response to the intense, inquiring gaze from her friend. *Of all the people*, she thought, *I cannot tell her*.

'The police have also questioned me,' Ellie said matter-of-factly. 'Several different times. According to them, the questions are all designed to clear up what they call the "irregularities" in Mother's case. Even Katie has had a visit from the police. She dropped by unexpectedly last week and remarked that the postponement of Mother's execution was certainly peculiar.'

'My friend's brother,' Nai said after a short silence, 'says that Nakamura suspects a conspiracy.'

'That's ridiculous,' Robert scoffed. 'There is no active opposition to the government anywhere in the colony.'

Nai drew even closer to Ellie. 'So what do you think is really happening?' she whispered. 'Do you think your mother has actually escaped? Or did Nakamura change his mind and execute her in private to stop her from becoming a public martyr?'

Ellie looked first at her husband and then at her friend. *Tell them, tell them*, a voice inside her said. But she resisted. 'I have no idea, Nai,' Ellie answered. 'I have, of course, considered all the possibilities you have mentioned. As well as a few others. But we have no way of knowing ... Even though I am certainly not what you would call a religious person, I have been praying in my own way that Mother is all right.'

3

Nicole finished her dried apricots and crossed the room to drop the package in the waste-basket. It was nearly full. She tried to compress the waste with her foot, but the level barely changed.

My time is running out, she thought, her eyes mechanically scanning the food remaining on the shelf. *I can last maybe five more days. Then I must have some new supplies.*

Both Joan and Eleanor had been gone for forty-eight hours. During the first two weeks of Nicole's stay in the room underneath Max Puckett's barn, one of the two robots had been with her all the time. Talking with them had been almost like talking with her husband, Richard, at least originally, before Nicole had exhausted all the topics the little robots had stored in their memories.

These two robots are his greatest creations, Nicole said to herself, sitting down in the chair. *He must have spent months on them.* She remembered Richard's Shakespearean robots from the Newton days. *Joan and Eleanor are far more sophisticated than Prince Hal and Falstaff. Richard must have learned a lot from the engineering of the human biots in New Eden.*

Joan and Eleanor had kept Nicole informed about the major events occurring in the habitat. It was an easy task for them. Part of their programmed instruction was to observe and to report by radio to Richard during their periodic sorties outside of New Eden, so they passed the same information on to Nicole. She knew, for example, that Nakamura's special police had searched every building in the settlement, ostensibly looking for anyone hoarding critical resources, in the first two weeks after her escape. They had also come to the Puckett farm, of course, and for four hours Nicole had sat perfectly still in total darkness in her hide-out. She had heard some noises above her, but whoever had conducted the search had not spent much time in the barn.

More recently, it had often been necessary for both Joan and Eleanor to be outside of the hide-out at the same time. They told her that they were busy coordinating the next phase of her escape. Once, Nicole had asked the robots how they managed to pass so easily through the check-point at the entrance to New Eden. 'It's really very simple,' Joan had said. 'Cargo trucks pass through the gate a dozen times a day, most carrying items to and from the troops and construction personnel over in the other habitat, some going out to Avalon. We're almost impossible to notice in any large load.'

Joan and Eleanor had also brought Nicole up to date on all the colony history since she had been imprisoned. Nicole now knew that the humans had invaded the avian/sessile habitat and essentially routed its occupants. Richard had not wasted robot memory space or his own time by supplying Joan and Eleanor with too many of the details about the avians and sessiles; however, Nicole did know that Richard had managed to escape to New York with two avian eggs, four manna melons containing embryos of the bizarre sessile species, and a critical slice of an actual adult sessile.

She also knew that the two avian hatchlings had been born a few months earlier and that Richard was being kept extremely busy tending to their needs.

It was difficult for Nicole to imagine her husband, Richard, playing both mother and father to a pair of aliens. She remembered that when their own children had been small, Richard had not shown much interest in their development, and he had often been insensitive to the children's emotional needs. Of course he had been marvellous at teaching them facts, especially abstract concepts from mathematics and science. But Nicole and Michael O'Toole had remarked to each other several times during their long voyage on Rama II that Richard did not seem to be capable of dealing with children on their own level.

His own childhood was so painful, Nicole thought, recalling her conversations with Richard about his abusive father. *He must have grown up with no capacity to love or trust other people ... All his friends were fantasies or robots he had created himself ...* She paused for a moment in her thinking. *But during our years in New Eden he definitely changed ... I never had a chance to tell him how proud I was of him. That was why I wanted to leave the special letter ...*

The solitary light in her room suddenly went out and Nicole was surrounded by darkness. She sat quite still in her chair and listened carefully for any sounds. Although Nicole knew that the police were again on the premises, she could hear nothing. As she became more frightened, Nicole realised how important Joan and Eleanor had become to her. During the first visit to the Puckett farm by the special police, both the little robots had been in the room to comfort her.

Time passed very slowly. Nicole could hear the beating of her heart. After what seemed like an eternity, she heard noises above her. It sounded as if there were many people in the barn. Nicole took a deep breath and tried to steady herself. Seconds later, she nearly jumped out of her skin when she heard a soft voice beside her reciting a poem.

> Invade me now, my ruthless friend,
> And make me cower in the dark.
> Remind me that I'm all alone

And draw upon my face your mark.
How is it that you capture me,
When all my thoughts deny your force?
Is it the reptile in my brain
That lets your terror run its course?

Baseless Fear undoes us all
Despite our quest for lofty goals.
We would-be Galahads don't die,
Fear just freezes all our souls.
It keeps us mute when feeling love,
Reminding us what we might lose.
And if by chance we meet success,
Fear tells us which safe route to choose.

Nicole recognised eventually that the voice belonged to the robot Joan, and that she was reciting Benita Garcia's famous pair of stanzas about fear, written after Benita had been thoroughly politicised by the poverty and destitution of the Great Chaos. The friendly voice of the robot and the familiar lines of the poem temporarily mitigated Nicole's panic. For a while she listened more calmly despite the fact that the noises above her were growing in amplitude.

When Nicole heard the sound of the movement of the large bags of chicken-feed stored above the entrance to her hide-out, however, her fright was suddenly renewed. *This is it*, Nicole said to herself. *I am going to be captured.*

Nicole wondered briefly if the special police would kill her as soon as they found her. Then she heard loud metallic pounding at the end of the passage to her room and was unable to remain seated. As she rose, Nicole felt two sharp pains in her chest and her breathing became laboured. *What's wrong with me?* she was thinking when Joan spoke up from beside her.

'After the first search,' the robot said, 'Max was afraid that he had not camouflaged your entrance well enough. One night while you were asleep he inserted into the top of the hole a full drainage system for the henhouse, with the discharge pipes running out above your hide-out. That pounding you heard was someone beating on the pipes.'

Nicole held her breath while a muffled conversation took place on the surface above her. After a minute, she again heard the movement of the bags of chicken-feed. *Good old Max*, Nicole thought, relaxing somewhat. The pain in her chest subsided. After several more minutes the noises above her ceased altogether. Nicole heaved a sigh and sat down in the chair. But she did not fall asleep until the lights were on again.

The robot Eleanor had returned by the time Nicole awakened. She explained to Nicole that Max was going to start ripping out the drainage system in the next few hours and that Nicole was finally going to leave her hide-out. Nicole was surprised when, after crawling through the tunnel, she encountered Eponine standing beside Max.

The two women embraced, 'Ça va bien? Je ne t'ai pas vue depuis si long-temps,' Eponine said to Nicole.

'Mais mon amie, pourquoi es-tu ici? J'ai pensé que ...'

'All right, you two,' Max interrupted. 'You'll have plenty of time later to become reacquainted. Right now we need to hurry. We're already behind schedule because I took too long to remove that damn drain ... Ep, take Nicole inside and dress her. You can explain the plan while you're putting on your clothes ... I need to shower and shave.'

As the two women walked in the dark from the barn to Max's house, Eponine informed Nicole that everything was in place for her escape from the habitat.

'During the last four days Max has hidden the diving gear, piece by piece around the shore of Lake Shakespeare. He also has another full set stored in a warehouse in Beauvois, in case someone has removed your mask or air tanks from their hiding-places. While you and I are at the party, Max will make sure that everything is all right.'

'What party?' a confused Nicole asked.

Eponine laughed as they entered the house. 'Of course,' she said. 'I forgot that you haven't been following the calendar. Tonight is Mardi Gras. There is a big party in Beauvois, and another over in Positano. Almost everyone will be out tonight. The government has been encouraging people to attend, probably to keep their minds off the other colony problems.'

Nicole looked very strangely at her friend, and Eponine laughed again. 'Don't you understand? Our biggest difficulty was figuring out how to get you all the way across the colony to Lake Shakespeare without being seen. Everyone in New Eden knows your face. Even Richard agreed that this was our only reasonable opportunity. You'll be in costume, and wearing a mask ...'

'Have you talked to Richard, then?' Nicole asked, starting to comprehend at least the outline of the plan.

'Not directly,' replied Eponine. 'But Max has communicated with him through the little robots. Richard was responsible for the drainage system idea that misled the police on their last visit to the farm. He was worried that you would be discovered ...'

Thank you again, Richard, Nicole thought as Eponine continued to talk. *I must owe you my life at least three times now.*

The women entered the bedroom, where a magnificent white dress was spread out upon the bed. 'You will attend the party as the queen of England,' Eponine said. 'I have been working on your dress non-stop all week. With this full mask and these long white gloves and leggings, none of your hair or skin will show. We shouldn't need to stay at the party for more than an hour or so, and you won't say much to anybody, but if anyone should ask, simply tell them that you're Ellie. She's staying home tonight with your granddaughter.'

'Does Ellie know I have escaped?' Nicole asked a few seconds later. She was experiencing a strong yearning to see both her daughter and little Nicole, whom she had never even met.

'Probably,' said Eponine. 'At least she knew that an attempt was likely ... It was Ellie who first involved *me* in your escape. Ellie and I cached your supplies out on the Central Plain.'

'So you haven't seen her since I've been out of prison?'

'Oh, yes. But we haven't said anything. Right now Ellie must be very careful. Nakamura is watching her like a hawk ...'

'Is anyone else involved?' Nicole asked, holding up the dress to see how it would fit.

'No,' answered Eponine. 'Just Max, Ellie, and I ... And of course Richard and the little robots.'

Nicole stood in front of the mirror for several seconds. *So here I am, finally the queen of England, at least for an hour or two.* She was certain that the idea for the specific costume had also come from Richard. *Nobody else could have made a choice so appropriate.* Nicole adjusted the crown upon her head. *With this white face,* she thought, *Henry might have even made me queen.*

Nicole was deep in a memory of many years earlier when Max and Eponine emerged from the bedroom. Nicole began to laugh immediately. Max was dressed in a scanty green outfit and was carrying a trident. He was Neptune, king of the sea, and Eponine was his sexy mermaid princess.

'You both look great!' Queen Nicole said, with a wink at Eponine. 'Wow, Max,' she added a second later in a teasing voice, 'I had no idea you had such an imposing body.'

'It's ridiculous,' Max grumbled. 'I have hair everywhere – all over my chest, down my back, in my ears, even ...'

'Except it's a little thin up here,' Eponine said, patting his head after removing his crown.

'Shit,' said Max. 'Now I know why I've never lived with a woman ... Come on, you two, let's get going. And by the way, the weather is wacky again tonight. You'll both need a shawl or a jacket during our ride in the buggy.'

'The buggy?' Nicole said, glancing at Eponine.

Her friend smiled. 'You'll see in a minute,' Eponine said.

When the New Eden government had requisitioned all the trains to convert the lightweight extraterrestrial alloys into war planes and other weaponry, the colony of New Eden had been left without a comprehensive transportation system. Luckily most of the citizens had purchased bicycles, and a full set of bicycle paths had been developed during the first three years after the initial settlement. Otherwise, it would have been very difficult for people to move about in the colony.

By the time of Nicole's escape, the old train tracks had all been removed and roads had been laid where the tracks had once been. These roads were used by the electric cars (restricted to government leaders and key military personnel), the transport trucks (which also ran on stored electricity), and the creative and varied other transportation devices constructed by individual citizens of New Eden. Max's buggy was such a device. In front it was a bicycle. The back half, however, was a large pair of soft seats, almost a couch, resting on two wheels and a strong axle, much like the horse-drawn buggies three centuries earlier on the Earth.

King Neptune struggled with the pedals as the costumed trio eased onto the road toward Central City. 'Shit,' Max said as he strained to accelerate, 'why did I ever agree to this absurd plan?'

Nicole and Eponine laughed in the seat behind him. 'Because you're a wonderful man,' Eponine said, 'and you wanted us both to be comfortable ... Besides, can you imagine a queen riding a bicycle for almost ten kilometres?'

The temperature was indeed on the cool side. Eponine spent a few minutes explaining to Nicole how the weather continued to grow more and more unstable. 'There was a recent report on television,' she said, 'that the government intends to settle many of the colonists in the second habitat. Its environment is still unspoiled ... Nobody has any confidence that we will ever fix the problems here in New Eden.'

As they neared Central City, Nicole worried that Max was becoming chilled. She offered him the shawl Eponine had loaned her, which he eventually accepted. 'You could have picked a warmer costume,' Nicole said teasingly.

'Having Max be King Neptune was also Richard's idea,' Eponine said. 'That way, if he needs to carry any of your diving equipment tonight, he will look perfectly natural.'

Nicole was surprisingly emotional as the buggy slowed in the growing traffic and wound its way through the colony's main buildings in Central City. She remembered a night, years before, when she had been the only human awake in New Eden. On that same night, after checking her family one last time, an apprehensive Nicole had climbed into her berth and prepared to sleep for the many-year trip back to the solar system.

An image of The Eagle, that strange manifestation of alien intelligence who had been their guide at The Node, appeared in her mind's eye. *Could you have predicted all this?* Nicole wondered, synthesising quickly the entire colony history since that first rendezvous with the passengers from Earth on board the Pinta. *And what do you think of us now?* Nicole grimly shook her head, acutely embarrassed by the behaviour of her fellow humans.

'They never replaced it,' Eponine was saying from the seat beside her. They had entered the main plaza.

'I'm sorry,' Nicole said. 'I'm afraid I was day-dreaming.'

'That wonderful monument your husband designed, the one that kept track of where Rama was in the galaxy ... Remember, it was destroyed the night the mob wanted to lynch Martinez ... Anyway, it was never replaced.'

Again Nicole was deep in her memory. *Maybe that's what being old is*, she thought. *Too many memories always crowding out the present*. She recalled the unruly mob and the red-haired boy who hollered, 'Kill the nigger bitch ...'

'What ever happened to Martinez?' Nicole asked softly, fearful of the answer.

'He was electrocuted soon after Nakamura and Macmillan took over the government. The trial dominated the news for several days.'

They had passed through Central City and were continuing south toward Beauvois, the village where Nicole and Richard and their family had lived before Nakamura's *coup. It could have been so different,* she thought, looking at Mount Olympus towering over them on her left. *We could have had paradise here. If only we had tried harder ...*

It was a train of thought that Nicole had followed a hundred times since that terrible night, the same night that Richard had hurriedly departed from New Eden. Always there was the same profound sorrow in her heart, the same burning tears in her eyes.

We humans, she remembered saying once to The Eagle at The Node, *are capable of such dichotomous behaviour. At times, when there is caring and compassion, we truly seem little lower than the angels. But more often, our greed and selfishness overwhelm our virtues and we become indistinguishable from the basest creatures from which we have evolved.*

4

Max had been gone from the party for almost two hours. Both Eponine and Nicole were becoming alarmed. As the two women tried to cross the crowded dance floor together, a pair of men dressed as Robin Hood and Friar Tuck stopped them.

'You are not Maid Marian,' Robin Hood said to Eponine, 'but Maid-Mer is nearly the same.' He laughed heartily at his own joke, extended his arms, and began to dance with Eponine.

'May a lowly priest enjoy a dance with Her Majesty?' the other man said. Nicole smiled to herself. *What harm can there be in a single dance?* she thought. She slipped into Friar Tuck's arms and they began moving slowly around the floor.

Friar Tuck was a talkative fellow. After every several bars of the music, he would pull away from Nicole and ask a question. As planned, Nicole would indicate her response with a head movement or a gesture. Toward the end of the song, the priest in costume began to laugh. 'Verily,' he said, 'I believe I am dancing with a mute. A graceful one, no doubt, but nevertheless a mute.'

'I have a bad cold,' Nicole said softly, trying to disguise her voice.

After she had spoken, Nicole detected a definite change in the friar's manner. Her concern increased when, after the dance was over, the man continued to hold her hands and to stare at her for several seconds.

'I've heard your voice somewhere before,' he said seriously. 'It's very distinctive ... I wonder if we've met. I'm Wallace Michaelson, the senator from the western section of Beauvois.'

Of course, Nicole thought in panic. *I remember you now. You were one of the first Americans in New Eden to support Nakamura and Macmillan.*

Nicole did not dare to say anything else. Fortunately, Eponine and Robin Hood returned to join Nicole and Friar Tuck before the silence had become dangerously long. Eponine sensed what had occurred and acted quickly. 'The queen and I,' she said, taking Nicole by the hand, 'were on our way to the powder room when you Sherwood Forest outlaws ambushed us. If you will now excuse us, with thanks for the dance, we will continue toward our original destination.'

As the women walked away, the two men dressed in green watched them carefully. Once inside the ladies' room, Eponine first opened all the stalls to ensure that she and Nicole were alone. 'Something's happened,' Eponine then whispered. 'Probably Max had to go to the warehouse to replace your equipment.'

'Friar Tuck is a senator from Beauvois,' Nicole said. 'He almost recognised my voice ... I don't think I'm safe here.'

'All right,' said Eponine nervously after a moment's hesitation. 'We will follow the alternate plan ... We'll go out front and wait underneath the big tree.'

Both women saw the small ceiling camera at the same time. It made just the slightest sound as it changed its orientation to follow them around the room. Nicole tried to remember every word that she and Eponine had said. *Was there anything that suggested who we were?* she wondered. Nicole was worried especially about Eponine, since her friend would continue to live in the colony after Nicole had either escaped or was captured.

When Nicole and Eponine returned to the ballroom, Robin Hood and his favourite priest gestured for the ladies to come toward them. In response Eponine motioned toward the front door, put her fingers to her lips to indicate that she was going outside to smoke, and then crossed the room with Nicole. Eponine glanced over her shoulder as she opened the outside door. 'The green men are following us,' she whispered to Nicole.

About twenty metres away from the entrance to the ballroom, which was in reality the gymnasium for Beauvois Middle School, there was a large elm tree that had been one of the few already-grown trees transported to Rama originally from the Earth. When Eponine and Queen Nicole reached the tree, Eponine reached into her purse, pulled out a cigarette, and lit it quickly. She blew the smoke away from Nicole. 'I'm sorry,' she whispered to her friend.

'I understand,' Nicole had just finished saying when Robin Hood and Friar Tuck walked up beside them.

'Well, well,' Robin Hood said, 'so our mermaid princess is a smoker. Don't you know that you're taking years off your life?'

Eponine started to give her standard reply, to tell the man that RV-41 would kill her long before smoking would, but she decided that any conversation might encourage the men to stay. She just smiled wanly, inhaled deeply on her cigarette, and blew smoke above her head into the branches of the tree.

'Both the friar here and I were hoping that you ladies would join us for a drink,' Robin Hood said, ignoring the fact that neither Eponine nor Nicole had responded to his earlier comment.

'Yes,' added Friar Tuck, 'we would like to know who you are ...' He stared at Nicole. 'I'm certain we've met before, your voice is so familiar.'

Nicole faked a cough and looked around. There were three policemen within a radius of fifty metres. *Not here,* she thought. *Not now. Not when I am so close.*

'The queen is not feeling well,' Eponine said. 'We may be leaving early. If not, we'll find you when we come back ...'

'I'm a doctor,' Robin Hood interrupted, moving closer to Nicole. 'Maybe I can help.'

Nicole could feel the tension in her heart. Again her breath was short and labored. She coughed again and turned away from the two men.

'That's a terrible cough, Your Majesty,' she heard a familiar voice say. 'We'd better take you home.'

Nicole glanced up at another man dressed in green. Max, a.k.a. King Neptune, was smiling broadly at her. Behind him Nicole could see the buggy parked no more than ten metres away. Nicole was joyful and relieved. She gave Max a huge hug and almost forgot the danger all around her. 'Max,' she said, before he put his finger to her lips.

'I know both you ladies are just delighted that King Neptune has finished his business for the evening,' he then said with a flourish, 'and can now squire you away to his castle, away from outlaws and other unsavoury elements.'

Max looked at the other two men, who were enjoying his performance even though he had foiled their plans for the evening. 'Thank you, Robin. Thank you, Friar Tuck,' Max said as he helped the ladies into the buggy seat. 'Your kind attention to my friends is most appreciated.'

Friar Tuck approached the buggy, obviously to ask one more question, but Max pedaled away. 'It is a night of costumes and mystery,' he said, waving at the man. 'But we cannot tarry, for the sea is calling us.'

'You were fantastic,' Eponine said, giving Max another kiss.

Nicole nodded her head. 'You may have missed your calling,' she said. 'Maybe you should have been an actor instead of a farmer.'

'I played Mark Antony in our high school play in Arkansas,' Max said, handing Nicole the diving mask for a final adjustment. 'The pigs loved my rehearsals ... "Friends, Romans, Countrymen ... lend me your ears ... I come to bury Caesar, not to praise him."'

The three of them laughed. They were standing in a small clearing about five metres from the shore of Lake Shakespeare. The trees and tall underbrush concealed them from the nearby road and bicycle path. Max lifted up the air tank and helped Nicole adjust it on her back.

'Is everything ready, then?' he asked.

Nicole nodded.

'The robots will meet you at the cache,' Max said. 'They told me to remind you not to descend too rapidly ... You have not done any diving in a long time.'

Nicole stood in silence for several seconds. 'I don't know how to thank you two,' she said awkwardly. 'Nothing I can think of to say seems adequate.'

Eponine walked over to Nicole and gave her a hug. 'Be safe, my friend,' she said. 'We love you very much.'

'Me too,' Max said a moment later, choking slightly as he embraced her. They both waved to Nicole as she backed into the lake.

Tears were running out of Nicole's eyes and collecting on the bottom of her mask. She waved one last time when the water was up to her waist.

The water was colder than Nicole had expected. She knew that the temperature variations in New Eden had been much greater since the colonists had taken over management of their own weather, but she had not considered that the changes in weather patterns would have altered the temperature of the lake.

Nicole changed the amount of air in her vest to slow her descent. *Do not hurry,* she counseled herself. *And stay relaxed. You have a long swim ahead of you.*

Joan and Eleanor had drilled Nicole repeatedly on the procedure she should follow to locate the long tunnel that ran under the habitat wall. She switched on her flashlight and studied the aquaculture farm off to her left. *Three hundred metres toward the centre of the lake, directly perpendicular to the back wall of the salmon-feeding area,* she remembered. *Stay at a depth of twenty metres until you see the concrete platform below you.*

Nicole swam easily, but she was tiring quickly nevertheless. She recalled a discussion with Richard from years before, when they had had been contemplating swimming together across the Cylindrical Sea to escape from New York. 'But I am not that good a swimmer,' Nicole had said. 'I may not be able to make it.'

Richard had assured her at the time that since she was such an exceptional athlete, she would have no problem with a long swim. *Now here I am, swimming for my life, following the same escape route Richard used two years ago,* Nicole thought. *Except that I am more or less sixty years old. And out of shape.*

Nicole found the concrete platform, descended another fifteen metres while carefully watching all her gauges, and eventually located one of the eight large pumping stations that were scattered on the bottom of the lake to keep the water continuously circulating. *Now the tunnel entrance is supposed to be hidden just under one of these big motors.* Nicole did not find it easily. She kept swimming past it because of all the new growth around the pumping complex.

The tunnel was a four-metre diameter circular pipe, completely full of water. It had been included as an emergency escape route in the original habitat design at the insistence of Richard, whose engineering background had taught him always to allow for unforeseen contingencies. From the entrance in Lake Shakespeare to the exit, out in the Central Plain beyond the walls of the habitat, was a swim of slightly over one kilometre. It had taken Nicole ten minutes longer than planned to find the entrance. She was already a very tired woman as she began her final swim.

During her two years in prison, Nicole's only exercise had been the walking, sit-ups, and push-ups that she had done at irregular intervals. Her aging muscles were no longer able to endure extreme fatigue without cramping. Three times during her swim through the tunnel, Nicole's leg muscles cramped. Each time she struggled, treading water, and forced herself to relax until the cramp completely dissipated. Her forward progress was very slow. Toward the end of her swim Nicole became frightened that she would run out of air before she reached the tunnel exit.

In the last hundred metres Nicole's body ached all over. Her arms did not want to push through the water and her legs had no strength left to kick. It was then that the ache began in her chest. The dull, disconcerting pain stayed with her even after her depth gauge indicated that the tunnel had turned slightly upward.

When she finally reached the end of the passage and stood up in a small underground room with only half a metre of water on the floor, Nicole almost collapsed. For several minutes she tried unsuccessfully to regain an equilibrium level in her breathing and pulse rate. Nicole did not even have enough strength left to lift off the metal exit cover above her head. Worried that she had pushed herself beyond safe physical limits, Nicole decided to remain in the tunnel and take a short nap.

She awakened two hours later when she heard a bizarre pitter-patter above her. Nicole stood directly under me cover and listened carefully. She could hear voices, but could not isolate what was being said. *What's going on?* she asked herself, her heart rate suddenly accelerating. *If I've been discovered by the police, why don't they just open the cover?*

Nicole moved quietly in the darkness over to her diving gear, which was sitting against the wall on the opposite side of the tunnel. Using her tiny flashlight, she examined her gauges to determine how much air remained in the tank. *I could submerge for a few minutes, but not many*, she thought.

Suddenly there was a sharp knock on the cover. 'Are you down there, Nicole?' the robot Joan asked. 'If so, identify yourself immediately. We have some warm clothes up here for you, but we are not strong enough to move the cover.'

'Yes, it's me,' Nicole cried with relief. 'I'll climb out as soon as I can.'

In her wet suit Nicole became quickly chilled in the bracing outside air of Rama, where the temperature was only a few degrees above freezing. Her teeth chattered during the eighty-metre walk in the dark to where her food and dry clothing were cached.

When the trio reached the supplies, Joan and Eleanor instructed Nicole to put on the army uniform that Ellie and Eponine had left for her. When Nicole asked why, the robots explained that to reach New York, it was necessary for them to pass through the second habitat. 'In case we are discovered,' Eleanor said when she was safely sitting in Nicole's shirt pocket, 'it will be easier to talk our way out of trouble if you are wearing a soldier's uniform.'

Nicole put on the long underwear and the uniform. When she was no longer cold, she realised that she was extremely hungry. While she was eating her feast, Nicole placed all the other items that had been wrapped in the sheet into the backpack she had been carrying under her diving-vest.

There was a problem entering the second habitat. Nicole and the two robots in her pocket had not encountered any humans at all in the Central Plain, but the entrance to what had once been the home of the avians and sessiles was guarded by a sentry. Eleanor had gone forward to scout and had reported the difficulty. The trio stopped three to four hundred metres away from the main traffic route between the two habitats.

'This must be a new security precaution, added since your escape,' Joan said to Nicole. 'We've never had any difficulties coming and going.'

'Are there no other routes that lead to the inside?' Nicole asked.

'No,' Eleanor answered. 'The original probe site was here. It has since been considerably widened, of course, and a bridge was built across the moat so that the troops can move quickly. But there are no other entrances.'

'And must we absolutely go through this habitat to reach Richard and New York?'

'Yes,' Joan replied. 'That huge grey barrier to the south, the one that forms the wall of the second habitat for many kilometres, prevents movement in and out of the Northern Hemicylinder of Rama. It's possible that we could fly over it, if we had an airplane that could reach an altitude of two kilometres, and a very clever pilot, but we don't ... Besides, Richard is expecting us to come through the habitat.'

They waited and waited in the dark and cold. Periodically one of the two robots would check the entrance, but there was always a sentry present. Nicole became tired and frustrated. 'Look,' she said at one point, 'we can't stay here forever. There must be some other plan.'

'We have no knowledge of any alternate or contingency plans in this situation,' Eleanor said, reminding Nicole for once that they were only robots.

During a brief nap the exhausted Nicole dreamed that she was lying, naked, on the top of a very large and very flat ice cube. Avians were striking at her from the sky, and hundreds of little robots like Joan and Eleanor had surrounded her on the surface of the ice. They were chanting something in unison.

When Nicole awakened, she felt somewhat refreshed. She talked with the two robots and they worked out a new plan. The three of them decided not to move until there was a break in the traffic through the entrance to the second habitat. At that time, the robots would decoy the sentry so that Nicole could proceed inside. Joan and Eleanor instructed Nicole then to walk cautiously to the other side of the bridge and turn right along the shore of the moat. 'Wait for us,' Eleanor said, 'in the small cove about three hundred metres from the bridge.'

Twenty minutes later, Joan and Eleanor made a terrible commotion along the far wall, about fifty metres from the entrance. Nicole walked unmolested into the interior of the habitat when the sentry left his post to investigate the noise. On the inside, a long stairway wound back and forth, dropping the several hundred metres from the entrance altitude to the level of the wide moat that circumscribed the entire habitat. There were lights on the stairway at periodic intervals, and Nicole could see more lights on the bridge in front of her, but the overall illumination was quite sparse. Nicole tensed when she saw a pair of construction workers coming up the stairs in her direction. But they climbed right past her with only minimal acknowledgment. Nicole was thankful she was wearing the uniform.

As she waited beside the moat, Nicole stared toward the centre of the alien habitat and tried to make out the fascinating features the little robots had described to her: the huge brown cylindrical structure, rising fifteen hundred metres straight up, that had once housed both the avian and sessile colonies; the great hooded ball that hung from the habitat ceiling and provided light; and the ring of mysterious white buildings, alongside a canal, that encircled the cylinder.

The hooded ball had not been illuminated for months, not since the first human incursion into the avian/sessile domain. The only lights that Nicole could see were small and widely scattered, obviously placed in the habitat by the human invaders. Thus all she could discern was a vague silhouette of the great cylinder, a shadow whose edges were very fuzzy. *It must have been glorious when Richard first entered,* Nicole thought, moved by the thought that she was in a location that had recently been the home of another sentient species. *So here also,* her mind continued, *we extend our hegemony, trampling underfoot all life-forms that are not as powerful as we.*

Eleanor and Joan took longer than expected to rejoin Nicole. The threesome then made slow progress along the side of the moat. One of the robots was always out front, scouting, making certain that contacts with other humans were avoided. Twice, in the part of the habitat that was very much like a jungle on Earth, Nicole waited quietly while a group of soldiers or workmen passed by on the road to their left. Both times she studied the new and interesting plants around her with fascination. Nicole even found a creature half-way between a leech and an earthworm trying to enter her right boot. She picked it up and put it in her pocket.

It had been almost thirty-two hours since she had backed into Lake Shakespeare when she and the two robots finally arrived at the spot for the rendezvous. They were on the far side of the second habitat, away from the entrance, where the normal density of human beings was at its lowest. A submarine surfaced within minutes after their arrival. The side of the submarine opened and Richard Wakefield, a gigantic smile upon his bearded face, rushed forward toward his beloved wife. Nicole's body shook with joy when she felt his arms around her.

5

Everything was so familiar. Except for Richard's clutter, accumulated during his months alone, and the conversion of the nursery into the bedroom of the two avian hatchlings, the lair underneath New Yoric was exactly the same as it had been when Richard, Nicole, Michael O'Toole, and their children had departed from Rama years before.

Richard had parked the submarine at a natural harbor on the south side of the island, in a place he had called The Port.

'Where did you get the sub?' Nicole had asked him while they were walking together toward the lair.

'It was a gift,' Richard had said. 'Or at least I think it was. After the super-chief of the avians showed me how to operate it, he or she disappeared, leaving the submarine here.'

Walking in New York had been an eerie experience for Nicole. Even in the dark the skyscrapers reminded her vividly of the years that she had lived on this mysterious island in the middle of the Cylindrical Sea.

How many years has it been since we left New York? Nicole had thought as Richard and she, holding hands, had stood beside the barn where Francesca Sabatini had left Nicole supposedly to perish in the bottom of a pit. But Nicole had known there was no way to give an accurate answer to her question. The intervening time could not have been measured in any normal way, since they had made two long interstellar voyages at relativistic velocities, the second one asleep in a special berth with extraterrestrial technology retarding their ageing process by careful manipulation of their enzymes and their metabolism.

'The only changes made in the Rama spacecraft on each visit to The Node,' Richard had said sometime later, while Nicole was still musing about the wonders of relativity, 'are those necessary to accommodate the next mission. So nothing has changed in here. The black screen is still there in the White Room, as well as our old keyboard. The procedures for making requests from the Ramans, or whatever our hosts should be called, are still intact also.'

'And what about the other lairs?' Nicole had asked during the descent down the ramp to their living-level. 'Have you visited them?'

'The avian lair is a tomb,' Richard had replied. 'I've been all through it several times. Once, I entered the octospider lair cautiously, but I went only as far as that cathedral room with the four tunnels leading away ...'

Nicole had interrupted him, laughing. 'The ones we called Eenie, Meenie, Mynie, and Moe ...'

'Yes,' Richard had continued. 'Anyway, I didn't feel comfortable there. I had the feeling, although I could not identify anything specific, that the lair was still inhabited. And that the octos, or whatever might be living there, were watching my every step.' This time it was his turn to laugh. 'Believe it or not, I was also worried about what would happen to Tammy and Timmy if I didn't return for any reason.'

Nicole's first introduction to Tammy and Timmy, the pair of avian hatchlings that Richard had raised from infancy, was priceless. Richard had built a half-door to the nursery and had closed it securely when he had left to meet Nicole inside the second habitat. Since the birdlike creatures couldn't yet fly, they had remained safely inside the nursery during Richard's absence. As soon as they heard his voice in the lair, however, the hatchlings began to shriek and jabber. They did not even stop squawking when Richard opened their door and cradled both of them in his arms.

'They're telling me,' Richard shouted to Nicole above the frightful noise, 'that I shouldn't have left them alone.'

Nicole was laughing so hard that tears were forming in her eyes. Both of the hatchlings had their long necks extended toward Richard's face. They interrupted their jabbers and shrieks only for short periods, during which time they rubbed the undersides of their beaks softly against Richard's bearded cheek. The avians were still small, about seventy centimetres tall when standing on their legs, but their necks were so long that they appeared to be much larger.

Nicole watched with admiration as her husband tended to his alien wards. He cleaned up their wastes, made certain that they had fresh food and water, and even checked the softness of their haylike beds in the corner of the nursery. *You have come a long, long way, Richard Wakefield*, Nicole thought, remembering his reluctance years earlier to deal with any of the more mundane duties associated with parenting. She was deeply touched by his obvious affection for the gangly hatchlings. *Is it possible*, Nicole found herself wondering, *that each of us has inside this kind of selfless love? And that we must somehow work through all the problems that both heredity and environment have created before we can find it?*

Richard had stored the four manna melons and the slice from the sessile in one corner of the White Room. He explained to Nicole that he hadn't noticed any changes in either the melons or the sessile material since he had arrived in New York. 'Maybe the melons can rest dormant for a long time, like seeds,' Nicole offered after listening to Richard's explanation of the complex life cycle of the sessile species.

'That's what I was thinking,' Richard said. 'Of course I have no idea at all under what conditions the melons might germinate ... The species is so strange and so complicated, I wouldn't be surprised if the process is controlled somehow by that small piece of the sessile.'

On their first evening together, Richard had difficulty getting the hatchlings to go to sleep. 'They're afraid I'm going to leave them again,' Richard explained when he returned to the White Room after the third time that Tammy's and Timmy's furious squawks had interrupted his dinner with Nicole. At length, Richard programmed Joan and Eleanor to amuse the avians. It was the only way he could keep his alien wards quiet so that he could have some time alone with Nicole.

They made love slowly and tenderly. Richard had admitted while he was undressing that he wasn't certain how well ... But Nicole had informed him that his performance, or lack thereof, was of absolutely no consequence. She insisted that it would be a delight just to hold his body next to hers and that any actual sexual stimulation would be a marvellous bonus. They were, of course, compatible, as they had been since the first time they had slept together. Richard and Nicole held hands, side by side, after intercourse. They said nothing. Several tears formed in Nicole's eyes and edged out slowly on to her face, eventually flowing sideways into her ears. She smiled in the dark. She was for the moment gloriously happy.

For the first time ever, there was no hurry in their lives. Every night they talked easily, sometimes even while they were making love. Richard told Nicole more about his childhood and adolescence than he ever had before. He included his most painful memories of his father's abuse, as well as the harrowing details of his disastrous first marriage to Sarah Tydings.

'I now realise that Sarah and Dad had something fundamental in common,' Richard said late one evening. 'They were both incapable of granting me the approval I so desperately sought – and somehow they both knew that I would continue to try to obtain that approval, even if it meant abandoning everything else in my life.'

Nicole shared with Richard for the first time all the drama of her fortyeight-hour affair with the Prince of Wales right after she had won her Olympic gold medal. She even admitted to Richard that she had yearned to marry Henry and that she had been completely devastated when she had realised that the prince had excluded Nicole as a candidate to be the queen of England primarily because of her skin colour. Richard was fascinated by the story that Nicole told. But never once did he seem even the least bit threatened or jealous.

He has become more mature, Nicole was thinking several nights later, while her husband was finishing his nightly task of tucking the hatchlings into bed. 'Darling,' Nicole said when Richard joined her in their bedroom in the lair, 'there's something that I want to tell you. I have been waiting for the right time ...'

'Uh-oh.' Richard feigned a frown. 'This sounds serious ... I hope it won't take long, for I had some plans of my own for us this evening.'

He crossed the room and started to kiss her ... 'Please, Richard, not now,' she said, pushing him away gently. 'This is very important to me.'

Richard backed up a couple of steps. 'When I thought I was going to be executed,' Nicole said slowly, 'I realised that all my personal affairs were in order, except for two. There were still things that I wanted to say, both to you and to Katie. I even asked the policeman who explained the execution procedure to me if he would give me pen and paper so that I could write two final letters.'

Nicole paused a moment, as if she were searching for exactly the right words. 'During those terrifying days, I couldn't remember, Richard,' she continued, 'if I had ever told you, explicitly, how glad I was that we had been husband and wife ... I also didn't want to die without ...'

She paused a second time, glanced briefly around the room, and then looked directly into Richard's eyes again. 'There was one more thing I wanted to accomplish with that last letter,' Nicole said. 'I believed at the time that it was necessary to make my life complete, so that I could depart from this world without any loose ends ... Richard, I wanted to apologise for my insensitivity back when you and Michael and I ... I made a mistake then by going to Michael's bed too soon when I feared ...'

Nicole took a deep breath. 'I should have had more faith,' she said. 'Not that I would for a minute remove either Patrick or Benjy from the world, but I realise now that I surrendered too quickly to my loneliness. I wish ...'

Richard touched his finger to her lips. 'No apology is necessary, Nicole,' he said softly. 'I know that you have loved me well.'

They settled into an easy rhythm in their simple existence. In the mornings they would walk around New York, usually arm in arm, exploring anew every corner of the island domain they had called home once before. Because it was always dark, the city looked different now. Only their flashlight beams illuminated the enigmatic skyscrapers whose details were indelibly imprinted in their memories.

Often they walked along the ramparts of the city, looking out at the waters of the Cylindrical Sea. One morning they spent several hours standing in one place, the very spot where they had entrusted their lives to the three avians years and years before. Together they recalled both their fear and their excitement at the moment when the great bird creatures had lifted them off the ground to carry them across the sea.

Every day after lunch Nicole, who had always needed more sleep than her husband, would take a short nap. Richard would use the keyboard to order more food or supplies from the Ramans, or take the hatchlings topside for some exercise, or work on one of his myriad projects scattered around the lair. In the evening, after a leisurely dinner, they would lie together, side by side, and talk for hours before making love or just falling asleep. They talked about everything: The Eagle, the Ramans, the existence of God, the politics in New Eden, books of all kinds, and most of all, their children.

Although they could converse enthusiastically about Ellie, Patrick, Benjy, or even Simone, whom they had not seen for many years, it was difficult for Richard to talk about Katie for any length of time. He regularly castigated himself for not having been stricter with his favourite daughter during her childhood, and blamed her irresponsible behaviour as an adult on his permissiveness. Nicole tried to console and reassure him, reminding Richard that their circumstances in Rama had been unusual and that, after all, nothing in his background had prepared him for the proper discipline required of a parent.

One afternoon when Nicole awakened from her nap, she could hear Richard mumbling to himself down the hall. Curious, she stood up quietly and walked down to the room that had once been Michael O'Toole's bedroom. Nicole stood at the door and watched Richard put the final touches on a large model that occupied most of the room.

'Voila,' he said, turning around to acknowledge that he had heard Nicole's footsteps. 'It won't win any aesthetic awards,' Richard said with a grin, motioning in the direction of the model, 'but it's a reasonable representation of our part of the universe, and it certainly has provided me with plenty of food for thought.'

A flat rectangular platform covered most of the floor. Thin vertical rods of varying heights had been inserted at twenty locations around the platform. At the top end of each rod was at least one coloured sphere, representing a star.

The vertical rod in the centre of the model, which had a yellow sphere attached to its top, rose about a metre and a half off the platform. 'This, of course,' Richard said to Nicole, 'is our Sun ... And here we are – or I should say Rama is – over in this quadrant, about one-fourth of the way between the Sun and our closest similar star, Tau Ceti ... Sirius, where we were when we stayed at The Node, is back over there ...'

Nicole walked around in the model depicting the stellar neighbourhood of the Sun. 'There are twenty star systems within twelve and a half light-years of our home,' Richard explained, 'including six binary systems and one triplet group, our nearest neighbours, the Centauris, over here. Note that the Centauris are the only stars inside the five-light-year sphere.'

Richard pointed at the three separate balls representing the Centauris. Each was a different size and colour. The trio, attached to each other with tiny wires, were resting on top of the same vertical rod, just inside an open wire sphere centreed at the Sun and marked with a large number 5.

'During my many days of solitude down here,' Richard continued, 'I often found myself wondering *why* Rama is going in this particular direction. Do we have a specific destination? It would seem so, since our path has not varied since our initial acceleration. And if we are going to Tau Ceti, what will we find there? Another complex like The Node? Or will the *same* Node perhaps have moved during the intervening time? ...'

Richard stopped. Nicole had walked over to the edge of the model and was stretching her arms up to a pair of red stars at the end of a three-metre rod. 'I assume you varied the length of these rods to demonstrate the full three-dimensional relationship of all these stars,' she said.

'Yes ... That particular binary group you are touching, incidentally, is called Struve 2398,' Richard replied in his human catalogue voice. 'They have a very high declination and are slightly over ten light-years away from the Sun.'

Seeing the slight grimace on Nicole's face, Richard laughed at himself and crossed the room to take her hand. 'Come over here with me,' he said, 'and I will show you something really interesting.'

They walked to the other side of the model and stood facing the Sun, half-way between the stars Sirius and Tau Ceti. 'Wouldn't it be fantastic if our Node really *has* moved,' Richard said excitedly, 'and we will see it again, over here, on the opposite side of our solar system?'

Nicole laughed. 'Of course,' she said, 'but we have absolutely no evidence ...'

'But we do have brains, and imaginations,' Richard interrupted. 'And The Eagle *did* tell us that the entire Node was capable of moving. It just seems to me ...' Richard stopped in mid-sentence and then changed the subject slightly. 'Haven't you ever asked yourself,' he said, 'where our Rama space-craft went, after we left The Node, during all those years that we were asleep? Suppose, for example, that the avians and the sessiles were picked up over here somewhere, around the Procyon binaries, perhaps, or maybe even over here, around Epsilon Eridani, which easily could have been on our trajectory. We know that there are planets around Eridani. At a significant fraction of the speed of light, Rama could have easily doubled back to the Sun ...'

'Hold it, Richard,' Nicole said. 'You're way ahead of me on this subject. Why don't we start at the beginning ...' She sat down on the platform in the interior of the model, next to a red ball elevated only a few centimetres by a very short rod, and crossed her legs. 'If I understand your hypothesis, our current voyage will end at Tau Ceti?'

Richard nodded. 'The trajectory is too perfect for it to be a coincidence. We will reach Tau Ceti in another fifteen years or so, and I believe our experiment will be concluded.'

Nicole groaned. 'I'm already old,' she said. 'By then, if I'm even still alive, Til be as withered as a prune ... Just out of curiosity, what do you think will happen to us after our "experiment is concluded", as you put it?'

'That's where we need our imaginations ... I suspect that we'll be unloaded from Rama, but what happens to us next is completely open ... I suppose our fate will be dependent in some way on what has been observed all this time ...'

'So you definitely agree with me that The Eagle and his buddies back at The Node have been watching us?'

'Absolutely. They have made such a huge investment in this project ... I'm certain they're monitoring everything that's going on here in Rama ... I must admit I'm surprised that they have left us completely to our own devices and have *never* interfered in our affairs, but that must be their method.'

Nicole was silent for a few seconds. She played absent-mindedly with the red ball beside her (Richard told her that it represented the star Epsilon Indi). 'The judge in me,' she said sombrely, 'fears what any reasonable extra-terrestrial would conclude about us, based on our behaviour in New Eden.'

Richard shrugged. 'We've been no worse in Rama than we have been for centuries on Earth ... Besides, I can't accept that any truly advanced aliens would be making such subjective judgments. If this process of observing spacefarers has been going on for tens of thousands of years, as The Eagle suggested, then the Ramans must have developed quantitative metrics for assessing all aspects of the civilizations they encounter ... They are almost certainly more interested in our exact natures, and what this means in some larger sense, than whether we are bad or good.'

'I suppose you're right,' Nicole said wistfully. 'But it's depressing that we, as a species, behave so barbarically, even when we are fairly certain we're being observed.' She paused and reflected. 'So in your opinion our long interaction with the Ramans, beginning with that first spaceship over a hundred years ago, is almost over?'

'I think so,' Richard replied. 'Somewhere in the future, possibly when we reach Tau Ceti, our part of this experiment will be concluded. My guess is that after all the data on the creatures currently inside Rama are entered in the Great Galactic Data Base, Rama will be emptied. Who knows, maybe soon thereafter this great cylindrical spacecraft will appear in another planetary system where a different spacefarer is living, and another cycle will begin.'

'And that brings us back to my earlier question, which you really did not answer ... What will happen to us then?'

'Maybe we, or our offspring, will be sent on a slow journey back to the Earth ... Or maybe we will be deemed expendable and terminated once all the data have been collected.'

'Neither of those outcomes is very appealing,' Nicole said. 'And I must say that although I agree with you that we are heading for Tau Ceti, all the rest of your hypothesis strikes me as pure conjecture.'

Richard grinned. 'I have learned a lot from you, Nicole ... Everything else in my hypothesis is intuitive. It *feels* right to me, based on everything I have learned about the Ramans.'

'But wouldn't it be more straightforward to imagine that the Ramans simply have way-stations scattered throughout the galaxy, and that the two nearest to us are at Sirius and Tau Ceti?'

'Yes,' Richard replied, 'but my gut feel is that it's unlikely. The Node was such an awesome engineering creation. If similar facilities exist every twenty or so light-years in the galaxy, there would be *billions* of them altogether ... And remember, The Eagle definitely said The Node could move.'

Nicole acknowledged to herself that it was unlikely that a facility as astonishing as The Node had been duplicated billions of times in some great cosmic assembly process. Richard's hypothesis did make some sense. *But how sad*, Nicole thought briefly, *that our entry in the galactic data base will contain so much negative information.*

'So where do the avians, sessiles, and our old friends the octospiders fit into your scenario?' Nicole asked a minute later. 'Are they just part of the same experiment, with us? ... And if so, are you suggesting that there is also a colony of octos onboard and that we just haven't met them yet?'

Richard nodded again. 'That conclusion is inescapable. If the final phase of each experiment is observing a representative sample of the spacefarers under controlled conditions, it makes sense that the octos are here also ...' He laughed nervously. 'There may even be some of our same friends from Rama II on the spacecraft with us at this very moment.'

'What a lovely set of ideas to think about before sleeping,' Nicole said with a smile. 'If you're right, you and I have fifteen more years to spend on a spacecraft that's inhabited not only by humans who want to capture and kill us, but also by huge, possibly intelligent arachnids whose nature we do not understand.'

'Remember,' Richard said with a grin, 'I could be wrong.'

Nicole stood up and walked toward the door.

'Where are you going?' Richard asked.

'To my bed,' Nicole replied with a laugh. 'I think I'm developing a headache. I can only contemplate the infinite for a finite period of time.'

6

The next morning, when Nicole opened her eyes, Richard was standing over her holding two full backpacks. 'We're going to explore and look for octospiders,' he said excitedly, 'behind the black screen ... I've left enough food and water to last Tammy and Timmy for two days and I've programmed Joan and Eleanor to find us if there is an emergency.'

Nicole watched her husband closely while she was eating her breakfast. His eyes were full of energy and life. *This is the Richard I remember the best*, Nicole said to herself. *Adventure has always been the most important component in his life.*

'I've been back here twice,' Richard said as soon as they had ducked under the raised screen. 'But I've never reached the end of this first passageway.'

The screen had closed behind them, leaving Richard and Nicole in the dark. 'There's no problem with being trapped here on this side, is there?' Nicole asked while they both checked their flashlights.

'Not at all,' Richard replied. 'The screen will not raise or lower more often than once every minute or so. But if anyone or anything is still in this general area a minute from now, the screen will automatically lift again.'

'Now, I should warn you before we start walking,' he continued a few seconds later, 'this is a *very* long passageway. I have followed it before, for at least a kilometre, and I have never found anything. Not even a turn-off. And there is absolutely no light. So the first part will be very boring – but it *must* eventually lead to something, for the biots bringing our supplies must be coming along this path.'

Nicole took his hand in hers. 'Just remember, Richard,' she said easily. 'We're not as young as we once were.'

Richard shone his flashlight first on Nicole's hair, which was now completely grey, and then on his own grey beard. 'We *are* a couple of old farts, aren't we?' he said gaily.

'Speak for yourself,' Nicole rejoined, squeezing his hand.

The passageway was much longer than a kilometre. As Richard and Nicole trudged along, they talked mostly about his astonishing experiences in the second habitat. 'I was absolutely terrified when the elevator door opened and I saw the myrmicats for the first time,' Richard said.

He had already finished describing to Nicole his stay with the avians and had just reached the point in his chronology where he had descended to the bottom of the cylinder. 'I was literally frozen with fear. They were only three or four metres away. Both of them were staring at me. The creamy fluid in their huge oval lower eyes was moving from side to side, and the pairs of eyes up on the stalks were bending around to see me from another point of view.' Richard shuddered. 'I will never forget that moment.'

'Now, let me make certain I have the biology straight,' Nicole said a few minutes later, as they approached what appeared to be a branching in the underground corridor. 'The myrmicats develop in the manna melons, live fairly short but highly active lives, and then die inside a sessile, where their entire life experiences, you theorise, are somehow added to the neural net's base of knowledge. The life cycle completes when new manna melons grow in the interior of the sessiles. These fledgling creatures are then harvested at the appropriate time by the active myrmicat population.'

Richard nodded. 'That may not be exactly right,' he said, 'but it must be close.'

'So what we're missing is only the necessary set of conditions for the manna melons to begin the germination process?'

'I was hoping you would help me with that puzzle,' Richard said. 'After all, Doctor, you are the only one of us with any formal biological training.'

The corridor became a Y, each of the two continuations making a forty-five-degree angle with the long, straight passageway from their lair. 'Which way, Cosmonaut des Jardins?' Richard asked with a smile, shining his flashlight in both directions. Neither of the two tunnels had a single distinguishing characteristic.

'Let's go to the left first,' Nicole said a few seconds later after Richard had created an outline map in his portable computer. The left pathway started to change after only a few hundred metres. The corridor widened into a descending ramp that wound around an extremely thick pole and dropped at least a hundred metres deeper into the shell of Rama. As they climbed down, Richard and Nicole could see lights below them. At the bottom, they encountered a long, wide canal with broad, flat banks. To their left, they saw a pair of crab biots scuttling away from them on the opposite side of the canal, as well as a bridge in the distance, beyond the biots. To their right, a barge was moving down the canal, carrying a full load of diverse but unknown objects, grey and black and white in colour, to some ultimate destination in the underground world.

Richard and Nicole surveyed the scene around them and then looked at each other. 'We're back in wonderland, Alice,' Richard said with a short laugh. 'Why don't we have a snack while I enter all this real estate in my trusty computer?'

While they were eating, a centipede biot approached on their side of the canal, stopped briefly as if to study them, and then passed on by. It climbed the ramp Richard and Nicole had just descended. 'Did you see any crab or centipede biots in the second habitat?' Nicole asked.

'No,' said Richard.

'And we purposely designed them out of the plans for New Eden, didn't we?'

Richard laughed. 'Indeed we did. You convinced both The Eagle and me that ordinary humans would not be able to deal easily with them.'

'So does their presence here imply the existence of a third habitat?' Nicole asked.

'Possibly. After all, we have no idea what's now in the Southern Hemicylinder. We have not seen it since Rama was refurbished. But there's another explanation as well. Suppose the crabs, centipedes, and other Raman biots just go with the territory, if you know what I mean. Maybe they are functioning in all parts of Rama, on all voyages, unless specifically proscribed by a given spacefarer.'

As Richard and Nicole finished lunch, another barge came into view on their left. Like its predecessor, it was loaded with stacks of white, black, and grey objects. 'These are different from the first ones,' Nicole remarked. 'These piles remind me of the spare centipede biot parts that were stored in my pit.'

'You could be right,' Richard said, standing up. 'Let's follow the canal and see where it leads us.' He glanced around, first at the arched ceiling ten metres above their heads and then back at the ramp behind them. 'Unless I have made an error in my computations, or the Cylindrical Sea is much deeper than I think, this canal runs from south to north under the sea itself.'

'So following the barge will take us back under the Northern Hemicylinder?' Nicole asked.

'I believe so,' Richard replied.

They followed the canal for more than two hours. Except for three spider biots, moving quickly as a team along the opposite bank, Richard and Nicole did not see anything else that was new. Two more barges passed them, carrying the same general kind of load downstream, and they intermittently encountered both centipede and crab biots without any interactions. They walked by one more bridge over the canal.

Richard and Nicole rested twice, drinking water or eating a snack while they talked. At the second rest stop Nicole suggested that perhaps they should turn back. Richard checked his watch. 'Let's give it another hour,' he said. 'If my sense of position is correct, we should be under the Northern Hemicylinder already. Sooner or later we must find where the barges are taking all that stuff.'

He was right. After another kilometre of hiking along the canal, Richard and Nicole saw a large pentagonal structure in the distance. As they drew closer, they could see that the canal flowed directly into the centre of the pentagon. The building itself, which straddled the canal, was six metres tall.

It had a flat roof, no windows, and a creamy white exterior. Each of its five sections or wings extended out twenty or thirty metres from the centre of the structure.

The walkway along the canal ended in some stairs that rose to a perimeter lane that ran around the entire pentagon. There was a similar configuration on the other side of the canal; a centipede biot was at that moment using the perimeter lane as a bridge to change from one side of the canal to the other.

'Where do you suppose it's going?' Nicole asked as the two of them stood aside to permit the biot to trundle by.

'Maybe to New York,' Richard answered. 'On my long walks before the avians hatched I sometimes saw one of them in the distance.'

They paused together outside the only door to the pentagon that was on the canal side of the building. 'I guess we're going in?' Nicole said.

Richard nodded and pushed open the small door. Nicole bent down and entered the building. Surrounding them was a large room, well lit, perhaps a thousand cubic metres altogether, with a ceiling five metres above the floor. Their walkway was elevated above the floor by two or three metres, so Richard and Nicole could watch most of the activities taking place below them. Biot robot workers they had never seen before, each designed for a specialised task, were unloading the two barges in the room and separating the cargo according to some predefined plan. Many of the individual pieces from the stacks were loaded onto truck biots, which disappeared through one of the back doors once they were full.

After a few minutes of observation, Richard and Nicole continued along the walkway to where it intersected another path just above the centre of the room. Richard stopped and made some notes in his computer. 'I presume this layout is as simple as it looks,' he said to Nicole. 'We can go either left or right – each way we go into another wing of the pentagon.'

Nicole chose the right walkway because the truck biots that she had thought were carrying parts for the centipede biot had gone in that direction. Her observations had been accurate. Soon after Richard and Nicole entered the second room, which was exactly the same size as the first, they realised that both a centipede and a crab biot were being manufactured on the floor below them. Richard and Nicole stopped to watch the process for several minutes.

'Absolutely fascinating,' Richard said, finishing his computer diagram of the biot factory. 'Are you ready to go?'

As Richard turned to face Nicole, she saw his eyes widen. 'Don't look now,' he said quietly a second later, 'but we have company.'

Nicole wheeled around and looked behind her. Across the room, forty metres behind them on the walkway, a pair of octospiders was slowly approaching them. Richard and Nicole had not heard their distinguishing sound, similar to dragging metallic brushes, because of the noise from the biot factory.

The octospiders stopped when they realised that the humans had noticed them. Nicole's heart was pumping furiously. She remembered clearly her last encounter with an octospider, when she had rescued Katie from the octo lair in Rama II. Then, as now, her overwhelming impulse had been to run.

She grabbed Richard's hand as they both stared at the aliens. 'Let's go,' Nicole said under her breath.

'I'm as frightened as you are,' he replied, 'but let's not leave just yet. They aren't moving. I want to see what they are going to do.'

Richard concentrated on the lead octospider and drew a careful picture in his mind. Its nearly spherical main body was charcoal grey, with a diameter of about a metre, and was featureless except for a vertical slit twenty or twenty-five centimetres wide that ran from the top to the bottom, where the body broke into the eight black and gold tentacles, each two metres long, that spread out across the floor. Inside the vertical slit were many unknown knobs and wrinkles (*Almost certainly sensors*, Richard thought) the largest of which was a big rectangular lens structure containing some kind of fluid.

As the two pairs of beings gazed at each other across the room, a broad band of bright purple colouring swept around the 'head' of the lead octospider. This band originated on one of the parallel edges of the vertical slit. It moved around the head, disappearing into the opposite edge of the slit almost 360 degrees later. It was followed in a few seconds by a complicated colour-band composed of red, green and a few colourless strips, which also made the same journey around the head of the octospider.

'That's exactly what happened when that octospider confronted Katie and me,' Nicole said nervously to Richard. 'She said it was talking to us.'

'But we have no way of knowing what it's saying,' Richard replied. 'Just because it can talk does not mean that it won't hurt us ...' As the lead octospider continued to talk in colour, Richard suddenly remembered an episode from years earlier, during his odyssey in Rama II. At the time he had been lying on a table, surrounded by five or six octos, all with coloured patterns on their heads. Richard recalled clearly the powerful terror that he had felt as he had watched some very small creatures, apparently under the control of the octospiders, crawl into his nose.

Richard's head began to throb with pain. 'They weren't all that nice to me before,' he said to Nicole. 'When they ...'

At that moment the far door to the room opened and four more octospiders entered. 'That's enough,' said Richard, feeling Nicole tense beside him. 'I think it's time for us to make an exit.'

Richard and Nicole walked quickly to the centre of the room, where the walkway, as in the previous room, joined with the path leading to the outside of the building. They turned toward the outside but stopped after taking a few steps. Four more octospiders were coming through this door as well.

They didn't need to confer. Richard and Nicole spun around, returned to the main interior walkway, and bolted in the direction of the third wing of the pentagon. This time they raced on, without turning to the outside, until they were inside the fourth wing. It was completely dark in this section. They slowed as Richard pulled out his flashlight to examine their surroundings. There was sophisticated-looking equipment on the floor below them, but no activity of any kind.

'Should we try the outside again?' Richard asked as he was putting his flashlight back in his shirt pocket. Seeing her nod, Richard took Nicole's hand and they ran together toward the intersection, where they turned right and headed out of the pentagon.

A few minutes later they were jogging down a dark corridor in completely unknown territory. Both of them were fatigued. Nicole was having difficulty breathing. 'Richard,' she said, 'I need to rest. I can't keep running like this.'

Richard and Nicole walked down the empty corridor for another fifty metres. They saw a door on their left. Richard cautiously opened the door, peered in, and scanned the room with his flashlight. 'It must be a storage-room of some kind,' he said. 'But it's currently empty.'

Richard walked into the room, glanced through its back door into another empty chamber, and then returned for Nicole. They sat down with their backs against the wall. 'When we return to our lair, darling,' Nicole said a few seconds later, 'I want you to help me check my heart. I have been having some strange pains lately.'

'Are you all right now?' Richard asked, concern reflected in his voice.

'Yes,' Nicole replied. She smiled in the dark and kissed her husband. 'As well as can be expected after narrowly escaping from a gaggle of octospiders.'

7

Nicole slept fitfully with her back against the wall and her head resting on Richard's shoulder. She had one nightmare after another, always waking with a start before dozing off again. In the last nightmare Nicole was on an island by the ocean with all her children. A huge tidal wave headed toward them on her dream screen. Nicole was frantic because her children were scattered all over the island. How could she possibly save all of them? She awakened with a shudder.

She nudged her husband in the dark. 'Richard,' Nicole said, 'wake up. Something's not right.'

At first Richard did not move. When Nicole touched him a second time, he slowly opened his eyes. 'What's the matter?' he said at length.

'I have the feeling we're not safe here,' she said. 'I think we should go.'

Richard switched on his flashlight and moved the beam slowly around the room. 'There's nobody here,' he said softly. 'And I don't hear anything either … Don't you think we should rest some more?'

Nicole's fears increased as they sat in silence. 'I'm still feeling a sense of danger, Richard,' she said finally. 'I know that you don't believe in anything you can't analyse, but I have learned to trust my premonitions.'

'All right,' Richard said unenthusiastically. He stood up and walked across the room, opening the back door, which led to a similar, adjacent area. He glanced inside. 'Nothing here either,' he said after several seconds. Richard next came back across the room and opened the door to the corridor they had used to escape from the pentagon. The moment the door was open, Nicole and he both heard the unmistakable sound of dragging brushes.

Nicole jumped to her feet. Richard closed the door without a sound and hurried over beside her. 'Come on,' he said in a whisper. 'We have to find another way out of here.'

They walked through the next room, then another and another. All were dark and empty. They lost their sense of direction as they raced through the unfamiliar territory. Eventually they came to a large double door at the far side of one of the many identical rooms. Richard told Nicole to stand back as he cautiously pushed open the door. 'Holy shit!' he exclaimed as soon as he looked into the room. 'What in the world is this?'

Nicole came up beside Richard and her eyes followed his flashlight beam as it fell on the bizarre contents of the adjoining chamber. The room was cluttered with large objects. The one closest to the door looked like a large amoeba on a skateboard, the next one like a gigantic ball of twine with two antennae sticking out of its centre. There was no sound in the room and nothing moved. Richard lifted his beam higher and let it move quickly around the rest of the crowded room.

'Go back,' Nicole said excitedly, catching a glimpse of something familiar. 'Over there. A few metres to the left of the other door.'

Seconds later the beam illuminated four humanlike figures, dressed in helmets and space suits, that were sitting against the far wall. 'It's the human biots,' Nicole said excitedly, 'the ones we saw just before we met Michael O'Toole at the bottom of the chairlift.'

'Norton and company?' Richard asked incredulously, a shiver of fear running down his spine.

'I bet it is,' Nicole responded.

They entered the room slowly and tiptoed around the many objects as they made their way toward the figures in question. Both Richard and Nicole knelt down beside the four apparent humans. 'This must be a biot dump,' Nicole said, after they had verified that the face behind the transparent helmet was indeed a copy of the Commander Norton who led the first Rama expedition.

Richard stood up and shook his head. 'Absolutely unbelievable,' he said. 'What are they doing here?' He let his flashlight beam wander around the room.

A second later Nicole screamed. No more than four metres away from her, an octospider was moving, or at least so it seemed in the peculiar light. Richard rushed to her side. The two of them quickly verified that what they were seeing was only an octospider biot, and then they both laughed for several minutes.

'Richard Wakefield,' Nicole said when she could finally contain her nervous laughter, 'may I go home now? I've had enough.'

'I guess so,' Richard said with a smile. 'As long as we can find the way.'

As they penetrated deeper and deeper into the maze of rooms and tunnels in the area around the pentagon, Nicole became convinced that they would never find their way out. Eventually Richard slowed the pace and started storing information in his portable computer. Afterward he was at least able to prevent their going in circles, but Richard never connected his growing map to any of the landmarks they had seen before they fled from the octospiders.

When both Richard and Nicole were starting to feel desperate, they chanced upon a small truck biot carrying an odd collection of small objects down a narrow corridor. Richard became more relaxed. 'Those things look as if they have been custom-made to someone's specifications,' he said to Nicole, 'like the objects delivered to us in the White Room. If we go back in the direction from which the biot came, then maybe we will locate where all our objects are manufactured. From there, it should be easy to find the path to our lair.'

It was a long hike. They were both completely exhausted several hours later when their corridor widened into a huge factory area with a very high ceiling. At the centre of the factory were twelve fat cylinders that looked like old-fashioned boilers on the Earth. Each was four or five metres high and a metre and a half wide. The boilers were arranged in four rows of three.

Conveyor belts, or at least the Rama equivalent, led into and out of each of the boilers, two of which were in operation at the moment. Richard was fascinated. 'Look over there,' he said, pointing at a vast warehouse floor covered with stacks of objects of all sizes and descriptions. 'That must be all the raw material. A request arrives at the central computer, which is probably in that hut behind the boilers, where it is processed and allocated to one of these machines. Biots go out, gather up the proper items, and place them on the conveyor belts. Inside the boilers these raw materials are altered significantly, for what comes out is the object ordered by whatever intelligent species is using the keyboard or its equivalent to communicate with the Ramans.'

Richard approached the closest active boiler. 'But the real question,' he said, overflowing with excitement, 'is what *kind* of process takes place inside these boilers? Is it chemical? Is it perhaps nuclear, involving element transmutations? Or have the Ramans some other technology for manufacturing completely beyond our ken?'

He knocked several times very hard on the outside of the active boiler. 'The walls are very thick,' he announced. Richard then bent down where the conveyor belt entered the boiler and started to stick his hand inside. 'Richard,' Nicole yelled, 'don't you think that's foolish?'

Richard glanced up at his wife and shrugged. As he bent down again to study the belt/boiler interface, a bizarre biot that looked like a camera box with legs scurried over from the back of the large room. It quickly wedged itself between Richard and the active conveyor belt and then expanded in size, forcing Richard away from the active process.

'Nice move,' Richard said appreciatively. He turned to Nicole. 'The system has excellent fault protection.'

'Richard,' Nicole now said, 'if you don't mind, can we please return to our major task? Or have you forgotten that we do not know the way back to our lair?'

'Just a little while longer,' Richard answered. 'I want to see what comes out of the active boiler closest to us. Maybe by seeing the output, after having already seen the input, I can infer the kind of intervening process.'

Nicole shook her head. 'I had forgotten what a knowledge junkie you are. You're the only human I have ever met who would stop to study a new plant or animal while he was completely lost in a forest.'

*

Nicole found another long passageway on the opposite side of the huge room. An hour later she finally convinced Richard to leave the fascinating alien factory. They had no way of knowing where this new passageway led, but it was their only hope. Again they walked and walked. Each time Nicole started to become tired or despondent, Richard would lift her spirits by extolling the wonder of everything they had seen since they had left their lair.

'This place is absolutely amazing, stupendous,' he said at one point, barely able to contain himself, 'I can't begin to assess what it all means ... Not only are humans not alone in this universe, we are not even near the top of the pyramid in terms of capability ...'

Richard's enthusiasm sustained them until finally, when they were both close to exhaustion, they saw ahead of them a branching in the corridor. Because of the angles, Richard felt certain that they had returned to the original Y no more than two kilometres from their lair. 'Yippee,' Richard yelled, picking up his pace. 'Look,' he shouted over at Nicole, his flashlight pointed in front of him, 'we're almost home.'

Something Nicole heard at that moment made her stop dead in her tracks. 'Richard,' she cried, 'turn off the light.'

He spun quickly around, nearly falling, and switched off his flashlight. In the next few seconds there was no doubt. The sound of dragging brushes was growing louder.

'Run for it,' yelled Nicole, bolting past her husband in a full sprint. Richard reached the intersection no more than fifteen seconds before the first of the octospiders. The aliens were coming up from the canal. As he was running away from them, Richard turned around and shone his flashlight behind him. In that brief instant he could see at least four coloured patterns moving in the darkness.

They brought all the furniture they could find into the White Room and created a barrier across the bottom of the black screen. For several hours Richard and Nicole watched and waited, expecting that at any moment the screen would lift up and their lair would be invaded by the octospiders. But nothing happened. At length they left Joan and Eleanor in the White Room as sentries and spent the night in the nursery with Tammy and Timmy.

'Why didn't the octospiders follow us?' Richard said to Nicole early the next morning. 'They almost certainly know the screen raises automatically. If they had come to the end of the corridor ...'

'Maybe they didn't want to frighten us again,' Nicole interrupted gently. Richard's brow furrowed and he gave Nicole a quizzical look. 'We still have no hard evidence that the octospiders are hostile,' Nicole continued, 'despite your feelings that you were mistreated as their prisoner during your odyssey years ago ... They did not harm Katie or me when they easily could have. And they did return you to us eventually.'

'By that time I was in a deep coma,' Richard replied. 'And no good to them anymore as a test subject ... Besides, how do you explain Takagishi? Or, for that matter, the attacks that were made on Prince Hal and Falstaff?'

'Each of those incidents has a plausible, nonhostile explanation. That's what is so confusing. Suppose Takagishi died of a heart attack. Suppose also that the octos preserved and stuffed his body to use as some sort of exhibit, for teaching other octospiders ... We might do the same thing ...'

Nicole paused before continuing. 'And the attack, as you call it, on Prince Hal and Falstaff, might have been just a misunderstanding ... What if your little robot had wandered into a very important place, maybe a nest, or the octospider equivalent of a church ... It would be natural for the octos to defend a key location.'

'I'm puzzled,' Richard said after a moment's hesitation. 'Here you are; defending the octospiders ... But you ran away from them yesterday even faster than I did.'

'Yes,' Nicole answered contemplatively. 'I admit that I was terrified. My animal instinct was to assume hostility and flee. Today I'm disappointed in myself. We humans are supposed to use our brains to overcome instinctive reactions ... Especially you and I. After everything we have seen in Rama and at The Node, we should be completely immune from xenophobia.'

Richard smiled and nodded. 'So are you suggesting now that maybe the octospiders were just trying to establish some kind of peaceful contact?'

'Perhaps,' Nicole answered. 'I don't know what they want. But I *do* know that I have never seen them do anything unambiguously hostile.'

Richard stared distractedly at the walls for a few seconds and then rubbed his forehead. 'I wish I could remember more of the details about my time with them. I still have these blinding headaches when I try to concentrate on that period of my life – only while I was inside the sessile were my memories of the octos not accompanied by pain.'

'Your odyssey was long ago,' Nicole said. 'Maybe the octospiders also are capable of learning and have adopted a different attitude toward us now.'

Richard stood up. 'All right,' he said. 'You have convinced me. The next time we see an octospider, we won't run away.' He laughed. 'At least not immediately.'

Another month passed. Richard and Nicole did not go behind the black screen again and they did not have any more encounters with the octospiders. They passed the days tending to the hatchlings (who were learning to fly) and enjoying each other. During much of their conversation they talked about their children and reminisced about the past.

'I guess we are now old,' Nicole said one morning as she and Richard were walking through one of the three central plazas of New York.

'How can you say that?' Richard replied with a mischievous grin. 'Just because we spend most of our time talking about what happened long ago, and our everyday bathroom functions occupy more of our attention and energy than sex, does that mean we're old?'

Nicole laughed. 'Is it as bad as that?' she said.

'Not quite,' Richard said in a kidding tone. 'I still love you like a schoolboy ... But every now and then that love is pushed aside by aches and pains that I never had before ... Which reminds me, wasn't I supposed to help you examine your heart?'

'Yes.' Nicole nodded. 'But there's really nothing you can do. The only instruments I brought with me in my medicine kit when I escaped were the stethoscope and the sphygmomanometer. I have used them both several times to examine myself ... I haven't been able to find anything unusual except an occasional leaky valve, and my shortness of breath has not recurred.' She smiled. 'It was probably all the excitement ... and age.'

'If our son-in-law the cardiologist were here,' Richard said, 'then he could give you a complete examination.'

They walked together in silence for several minutes. 'You miss the children a lot, don't you?' Richard said.

'Yes,' Nicole replied with a sigh. 'But I try not to think about them too much. I am happy to be alive and here with you – it's certainly much better than those last months in prison. And I have many wonderful memories of the children ...'

'God grant me the wisdom to accept the things I cannot change,' Richard quoted. 'It is one of your best qualities, Nicole ... I have always been envious of your equanimity.'

Nicole walked on slowly. *My what?* she said to herself, remembering clearly how obsessed she had been after Valeriy Borzov's death just after the Newton had docked with Rama. *I could not even sleep until I convinced myself that it was not my fault that he died.* She thought briefly about the intervening years. *Any equanimity, if it exists at all, has come fairly recently ... Motherhood and age both give you a different perspective on yourself and the world.*

A few moments later Richard stopped abruptly and turned to face Nicole. 'I love you very much,' he said, embracing her vigorously.

'What is this all about?' Nicole asked, puzzled by his sudden show of emotion.

Richard's eyes had a faraway look. 'During the last week,' he said excitedly, 'a wild and crazy plan has been developing in my brain. I have known from the outset that it was dangerous, and probably insane, but like all my projects it has taken hold of me ... Twice I have even gotten out of our bed in the middle of the night to work on the details ... I have wanted to tell you about it before now, but I needed to convince myself that it was indeed possible ...'

'I have no idea at all what you are talking about,' Nicole said impatiently.

'The children,' Richard said with a flourish. 'I have a plan for them to escape, to join us here in New York. I have even begun to reprogram Joan and Eleanor.'

Nicole stared at her husband, her emotions struggling with her reason. He started to explain his escape plan. 'Wait a minute, Richard,' Nicole interrupted after several seconds. 'There's an important question we must answer first ... What makes you think the children would even *want* to escape? They are not under indictment in New Eden, or in prison. Granted, Nakamura is a tyrant and life in the colony is difficult and depressing, but as far as I know, the children are as free as any of the other citizens. And if they were to try to join us and fail, their lives would be in danger ... Besides, our existence here, although fine for us, would hardly be considered a paradise for them.'

'I know ... I know ...' Richard replied, 'and perhaps I have been carried away by my desire to see them ... But what do we risk by sending Joan and Eleanor to talk to them? Patrick and Ellie are adults and can make up their own minds.'

'And what about Benjy and Katie?' Nicole asked.

A frown creased Richard's face. 'Obviously Benjy could not come by himself, so his participation depends on whether or not any of the others decide to help him. As for Katie, she is so unstable and unpredictable ... she might conceivably even decide to tell Nakamura ... I think we have no choice except to leave her out ...'

'A parent never gives up hope,' Nicole said softly, as much to herself as to Richard. 'By the way,' she added, 'does your scheme also include Max and Eponine? They are virtually members of the family.'

'Max is really the perfect choice to co-ordinate the escape from inside the colony,' Richard said, growing excited again. 'He did a fantastic job hiding you and then getting you to Lake Shakespeare without being detected. Patrick and Ellie will need someone mature and level-headed to guide them through all the details ... In my plan, Joan and Eleanor approach Max first. Not only is he already familiar with the robots, but also he will give his honest assessment as to whether or not the plan can work. If he tells us through the robots that the whole idea is preposterous, then we'll drop it.'

Nicole tried to imagine the joy she would feel at the moment of embracing any of her children again. It was impossible. 'All right, Richard,' she said, finally smiling. 'I admit that I'm interested ... Let's talk about it ... But we must promise ourselves that we won't do anything unless we are certain that we are not going to endanger the children.'

8

Max Puckett and Ellie Turner excused themselves from Eponine, Robert, and little Nicole shortly after dinner and walked outside at Max's farmhouse in New Eden. As soon as they were out of earshot, Max began telling Ellie about his recent visits from the little robots. Ellie could not believe what she was hearing. 'Surely you're mistaken,' she said in a loud voice to Max. 'They can't be suggesting that we just leave ...'

Max put a finger to his lips as they walked the final few metres to the barn. 'You can talk to them yourself,' he said in a whisper. 'But according to these little characters, there is plenty of room for all of us in that lair you lived in the first few years after you were born.'

It was dark inside the barn. Before Max switched on the light, Ellie had already glimpsed the tiny glowing robots beside her on one of the window-sills. 'Hello again, Ellie,' said little Joan, still dressed in her armour. 'Your mother and father are both fine and send their greetings.'

'We have come to see you tonight,' the robot Eleanor added, 'because Max thought it was necessary for you to hear for yourself what we have to say. Richard and Nicole are inviting you and your friends to join them in your old lair in New York, where your parents are living a Spartan but peaceful existence.'

'Everything about your lair,' Joan now said, 'is the same as it was when you were a small child. Food, clothing, and other objects are still supplied by the Ramans after requests are made by using the keyboard in the White Room. Unlimited supplies of fresh water are available at the cistern near the bottom of the entry staircase.'

Ellie listened, fascinated, while Joan reminded her of the living conditions under the island city on the southern side of the second habitat. Ellie tried to recall the lair from her memory, but the picture that came to her mind was surprisingly vague. What she could remember clearly from that period of her life were the last few days in Rama, including the spectacular rings of colour emanating from the Big Horn and drifting slowly toward the north of the giant cylinder. But her memory of the inside of the lair was foggy. *Why can't I remember at least the nursery more clearly?* she wondered. *Because too much has happened since? And made deeper impressions in my memory?*

A montage of images from her early childhood streamed through Ellie's mental vision. Some of the pictures were indeed from Rama, but far more of them were from the family apartment at The Node. The indelible features of The Eagle, a godlike figure to the child Ellie, seemed to preside over the montage.

Eleanor of Aquitaine had asked Ellie something, but, the young woman had not been paying attention. 'I'm sorry, Eleanor,' Ellie said, 'please repeat your question. I'm afraid I was temporarily lost in my childhood.'

'Your mother asked about Benjy. Is he still in the ward out in Avalon?'

'Yes,' Ellie replied. 'And doing as well as can be expected. His best friend in the whole world is now Nai Watanabe. When the war ended, she volunteered to work with those who had been assigned, for one reason or another, to the Avalon Ward. She spends time with Benjy almost every day and has helped him immensely. Her twins Kepler and Galileo love to play with him – Benjy is essentially just a big child himself – although Galileo is sometimes unkind and causes Nai considerable heartache.'

'As I told you,' Max said, turning the conversation back to their primary business, 'Nicole and Richard have left it up to our discretion to decide who should be involved if we do attempt a mass exodus. Will Benjy follow directions?'

'I think so,' Ellie said. 'As long as he trusts the person giving them. But there is no way we could tell him about the escape ahead of time. We couldn't possibly expect him not to say something about it. Secrecy and guile are not part of Benjy's personality. He will be overjoyed, but ...'

'Mr Puckett,' Joan of Arc interrupted, 'what should I tell Richard and Nicole?'

'Shit, Joanie,' Max replied, 'have a little patience ... Better still, come back again in a week, after Ellie, Eponine, and I have had more time to talk this thing through, and I'll give you a tentative answer ... And tell Richard I find the whole damn thing intriguing, even if it is certifiably insane.'

Max placed the two robots on the floor of the barn and they scampered away. When Max and Ellie were back outside in the fresh air, Max pulled a cigarette out of his pocket. 'I assume that it doesn't offend you *too* much if I smoke out here?' he said with a grin.

Ellie smiled, 'You don't want to tell Robert, do you, Max?' she then said quietly a moment later, as Max blew smoke-rings into the night air.

Max shook his head. 'Not yet,' he replied. 'Maybe not until the last moment.' He put his arm around Ellie, 'Young lady, I like your doctor husband, I really do, but sometimes I think his attitudes and priorities are a little strange. I can't say for certain that he wouldn't tell someone ...'

'Do you think, Max,' Ellie said, 'that maybe Robert has made a private vow of some kind never to act against authority again? And that he is afraid ...'

'Shit, Ellie, I'm no psychologist. I don't think either of us can possibly understand what killing two people in cold blood did to him. But I can say that there is a finite chance that he would not keep our secret – to avoid a painful personal decision, if nothing else.' Max inhaled deeply on his cigarette and stared at his young friend.

'You don't think he'll come, do you, Max? Not even if I want him to.'

Again Max shook his head. 'I don't know, Ellie. It will depend on how much he needs you and little Nicole. Robert has made room for the two of you in his life, but he still hides his feelings behind continuous work.'

'What about you, Max?' Ellie now asked. 'What do you *really* think of this whole scheme?'

'Eponine and I are both ready to go, to have ourselves a little *ad-ven-toor*,' Max said with a grin. 'It's just a matter of time before I get into serious trouble with Nakamura anyway.'

'And Patrick?'

'He'll love the idea. But I'm worried that he might say something to Katie. They have a special relationship ...'

Max stopped in mid-sentence when he saw that Robert, who was carrying his tired daughter, had come out onto the front porch.

'Oh, there you are, Ellie,' Robert said. 'I thought that maybe you and Max were lost in the barn ... Nicole is tired and I have a very early morning at the hospital ...'

'Of course, darling,' Ellie replied. 'Max and I were just sharing memories of my mother and father ...'

It must look like a perfectly normal day, Ellie thought as she showed her identification card to the Garcia biot in the atrium of the Beauvois supermarket. *I must do everything exactly as if this were an ordinary Thursday.*

'Mrs Turner,' the Garcia said a few seconds later, handing her a list printed out of the computer against the wall behind the biot, 'here is your ration allocation for the week. We are out of broccoli and tomatoes again, so we have included two extra measures of rice ... You may now proceed to the line to pick up your groceries.'

Little Nicole walked beside her as Ellie entered the main part of the supermarket. On the other side of a mesh screen, where in the early days of the colony the citizens of New Eden had done their own shopping, five or six Tiasso and Lincoln biots, all from the 300 series completely reprogrammed by the Nakamura government, were moving up and down the aisles filling the orders. Most of the shelves were empty. Even though the war had been over for some time, the unstable weather in New Eden, as well as the dislike of most of the farmers for Nakamura's heavy-handed ways, had kept food production at a minimum level. The government had found it necessary, therefore, to supervise the allocation of food. Only the governmental favourites had more than the bare essentials to eat.

There were half a dozen people in the queue in front of Ellie and her almost-two-year-old daughter. Ellie shopped with the same people every

Thursday afternoon. Most of them turned around when Ellie and Nicole entered the line.

'There's that darling little girl,' a pleasant woman with grey hair said. 'How are you today, Nicole?' she asked.

Nicole didn't answer. She just backed up a couple of steps and fastened herself tightly to one of her mother's legs. 'Nicole's still in her shy stage,' Ellie said. 'She only talks to people she knows.'

A Lincoln biot brought out two small boxes of food and handed them to the father and adolescent son at the head of the supermarket line. 'We won't be using a cart today,' the father said to the Lincoln. 'Please make a note of that on our record ... Two weeks ago, when we also hand-carried our groceries, nobody noted that we didn't take a cart and we were awakened in the middle of the night by a Garcia demanding that we return our cart to the store.'

There must be no trivial mistakes, Ellie said to herself. *No carts not returned, nothing that anyone could suspect before morning.* As she waited in the line, Ellie reviewed again the details of the escape plan that she and Patrick had discussed with Max and Eponine the previous day. A Thursday had been chosen because that was the day that Robert made his regular visits to the RV-41 sufferers in Avalon. Max and Eponine had applied for, and received, a pass to visit Nai Watanabe for dinner. They would look after Kepler and Galileo while Nai went to the ward for Benjy. Everything was in order. There was only one major uncertainty left.

Ellie had rehearsed her speech to Robert a hundred times. *His initial reaction will be negative*, she thought. *He will say it's too dangerous, that I am jeopardizing Nicole's security. And he'll be angry because I didn't tell him earlier.*

In her mind she had already answered all his objections and had carefully described the life they would have in New York in a positive light. But Ellie was still extremely nervous. She had not been able to convince herself that Robert would agree to come. And she had no idea what he would do if she declared that she and little Nicole were prepared to leave without him.

As her groceries were placed in the small shopping cart that she would return to the supermarket after unpacking everything at her home, Ellie squeezed her daughter's hand. *It is almost time*, she thought. *I must have courage. I must have faith.*

'How in the world do you *expect* me to react?' Robert Turner said. 'I come home from an exceptionally busy day at the hospital, my mind on the hundred things that I must do tomorrow, and you tell me over dinner that you want us to leave New Eden forever? And to go *tonight*? ... Ellie, dear Ellie, this whole thing is absurd. Even if it could work, I would need time to sort out everything ... I have projects ...'

'I know it's sudden, Robert,' Ellie said, growing fearful that she had underestimated the difficulty of her task, 'but I couldn't have told you any earlier. It would have been too dangerous. What if you had slipped and said something to Ed Stafford or another member of your staff, and one of the biots had overheard? ...'

'But I can't just leave without saying anything to anybody ...' Robert shook his head vigorously. 'Do you have any idea how many *years* of work would be wasted?'

'Couldn't you write down what needs to be done on each project?' Ellie suggested. 'And maybe summarise what's already been accomplished ...'

'Not in one night,' Robert replied emphatically. 'No, Ellie, it's really out of the question. We can't go. The long-term health of the colony may depend on the results of my research ... Besides, even if I accept that your parents are living comfortably in that bizarre place you described, wherever it is, it certainly does not sound like a good place to raise a child ... And you haven't even mentioned the possible danger to all of us. Our leaving will be viewed as treason. We could both be executed if we were caught. What would happen to Nicole then? ...'

Ellie listened to Robert's objections for another minute and then realised that the time had come for her declaration. Summoning all her courage, she walked around the table and took both her husband's hands. 'I have been thinking about this for almost three weeks, Robert ... You must understand how difficult this decision is for me ... I love you with all my heart, but if we must, Nicole and I will go without you ... I know that there is a lot of uncertainty in leaving, but life here in New Eden is definitely not healthy for any of us ...'

'No, no, *no*,' Robert said immediately, freeing himself from Ellie and starting to pace wildly around the room. 'I don't believe *any* of this. It's all a bad dream ...' He paused and looked across the room at Ellie. 'You cannot take Nicole with you,' he said with passion. 'Do you hear me? I forbid you to take our daughter ...'

'*Robert*,' Ellie interrupted him with a shout. Tears were now streaming down her cheeks. 'Look at me ... I am your wife, the mother of your daughter ... I love you. I beg you to *listen* to what I am saying.'

Nicole had come running into the room and was now crying beside her mother. Ellie composed herself before continuing. 'I don't believe that you are the only one in this family who is allowed to make decisions. I have that right as well. I can respect your desire not to go, but I am Nicole's mother. If you and I are to be separated, then I believe that it would be better for Nicole to come with me ...'

Ellie stopped. Robert's face was contorted in anger. He took a step toward her and, for the first time in her life, Ellie feared that Robert was going to hit her.

'What would be better for *me*,' Robert shouted, with his right hand raised in a fist, 'would be for you to forget this foolishness.'

Ellie backed up slightly. Nicole continued to cry. Robert struggled to control himself. 'I swore,' he said, his voice quavering with emotion, 'that nobody and nothing would ever cause me to hurt like that again ...'

Tears burst from his eyes. '*Goddamnit*,' he said, smashing his fist down on a nearby table. Without saying anything else, Robert sat down in the chair and buried his face in his hands.

Ellie consoled Nicole and said nothing for several seconds. 'I know how painful it was for you to lose your first family,' she said at length. 'But Robert, this is an entirely different situation. Nobody is going to harm Nicole and me.'

She walked over and put her arms around him. 'I'm not saying this is an easy decision, Robert,' Ellie said. 'But I'm convinced it's the right thing for Nicole and me.'

Robert returned Ellie's hug, but without much enthusiasm. 'I will not keep you and Nicole from going,' he said resignedly several seconds later. 'But I don't know what I am going to do. I would like to think about all this over the next several hours, while we're out in Avalon.'

'All right, dear,' Ellie replied, 'but please don't forget that Nicole and I need you even more than your patients do. You are our only husband and father.'

9

Nicole could not contain her excitement. As she put the finishing touches on the decorations in the nursery, she imagined what the room would be like when the human children were sharing it with the two avians. Timmy, who was now almost as tall as Nicole, clambered over beside her to inspect her handiwork. He uttered a few jabbers of appreciation.

'Just think, Timmy,' Nicole said, knowing that the avian could not understand her exact words but could interpret the timbre of her voice, 'when Richard and I return, we will be bringing you three new room-mates.'

'Are you ready, Nicole?' she heard Richard yell at that moment. 'It's almost time for us to leave.'

'Yes, darling,' she answered. 'I'm here in the nursery. Why don't you come and take a look?'

Richard stuck his head in the door and gave the new decorations a perfunctory inspection. 'Great, just great,' he said. 'Now we need to move. This operation requires precise timing.'

As they walked together to The Port, Richard informed Nicole that there had been no more reports from the Northern Hemicylinder. The lack of news could indicate that Joan and Eleanor were too involved with the escape, he said, or too close to a possible enemy, or even that the implementation of the escape plan was in trouble. Nicole could not remember seeing Richard so nervous before. She tried to calm him.

'We still don't know if Robert is coming?' Nicole asked a few minutes later as they approached the submarine.

'No. Nor anything at all about how he reacted when Ellie told him the plan. They did show up together in Avalon, as scheduled, but they were busy with his patients. Joan and Eleanor did not have a chance to talk to Ellie after they helped Nai pick up Benjy at the ward.'

Richard had checked out the submarine at least twice the day before. Nevertheless, he issued a sigh of relief when the operating system engaged and the craft slid into the water. When they were submerged in the waters of the Cylindrical Sea, both Richard and Nicole were quiet. Each of them was anticipating the emotional reunion that would take place in less than an hour.

Can there be a greater joy, Nicole was thinking, *than to be reunited with your children after expecting never to see them again?* Images of all six of her children filed slowly into Nicole's mind. Nicole saw Genevieve, her first child, born on the Earth after her union with Prince Henry. Next in line was serene Simone, whom Nicole had left at The Node with a husband almost sixty years her senior. The two oldest girls were followed in the mental procession by the four children still living in Rama, her wayward daughter Katie, her precious Ellie, and her two sons by Michael O'Toole, Patrick and the mentally handicapped Benjy. *They are all so different,* Nicole thought. *Each a miracle in his or her own way.*

I do not believe in universal truths, Nicole mused as the submarine drew closer to the tunnel under the wall of what was once the avian/sessile habitat, *but there cannot be many humans who have lived through the singular experience of parenting without being irrevocably changed by the process. We all wonder, as our children grow into adults, what we have done, or not done, that has contributed to, or detracted from, the happiness of these special beings we have brought into existence.*

The excitement inside Nicole was overwhelming. As Richard checked his watch and began to manoeuvre the submarine into position for the rendez-vous, her most recent recollections of Ellie, Patrick and Benjy danced among the tears in Nicole's eyes. She reached out and squeezed Richard's free hand as their ship broke through the surface of the water.

Through the window they could see eight figures standing on the shore at the appointed location. When the water stopped running down the window, Nicole recognised Ellie, her husband Robert, Eponine, Nai holding Benjy's hand, and the three small children, including her granddaughter and name-sake, whom Nicole had never seen before. She pounded on the window, knowing that it was senseless, and that none of the people on the shore could possibly hear or see her.

Richard and Nicole heard the gunshots as soon as they opened the door. A worried Robert Turner glanced behind him and then lifted little Nicole quickly off the ground. Ellie and Eponine each picked up one of the Watanabe twins. Galileo struggled against Eponine and received a reprimand from his mother Nai, who was trying to guide Benjy into the submarine.

Another round of gunfire, much closer, occurred just as the boarding party was crossing into the ship. There was no time for embraces. 'Max said to leave as soon as we were all on board,' Ellie said hurriedly to her parents. 'He and Patrick are holding off the platoon that was sent to capture us.'

Richard was preparing to close the door when two armed figures, one clutching at his side, burst from the nearby bushes. 'Get ready to go,' Patrick yelled, shouldering and firing his rifle twice. 'They are right behind us.'

Max stumbled, but Patrick half carried his wounded friend the final fifty metres to the submarine. Three of the colony soldiers fired upon the ship as it submerged in the moat. For a brief moment, none of the people on board the submarine said anything. Then the tiny compartment exploded in a cacophony of sound. Everyone was shouting and weeping. Both Nicole and Robert bent down over Max, who was sitting with his back against a wall.

'Are you seriously hurt?' Nicole asked.

'Hell, no,' Max replied with passion. 'There's just a solitary bullet in my gut somewhere. It takes much more firepower than that to kill a son-of-a-bitch like me.'

When Nicole stood up and turned around, Benjy was right behind her. 'Ma-ma,' he said, his arms outstretched and his big body trembling with joy. Nicole and Benjy exchanged a long and powerful embrace in the centre of the compartment. Benjy's sobs of happiness reflected the sentiment of every person on the ship.

While they were on board the submarine, the newcomers essentially suspended between two alien worlds, most of the conversation was personal. Nicole spent some private moments with each of her children and held her granddaughter for the first time. Little Nicole did not know what to make of this woman with the grey hair who wanted to hug and kiss her. 'This is your grandmother,' Ellie said, trying to persuade the child to return Nicole's affection. 'She is my mother, Nikki, and she has the same name that you have.'

Nicole knew enough about children to understand that it would take some time for the girl to accept her. At first there was some confusion about their common name, and every time someone said 'Nicole,' both the grandmother and the little girl would turn around. But after Ellie and Robert both started using 'Nikki' for the child, the rest of the group quickly followed suit.

Before the submarine even reached New York, Benjy was showing his mother that his reading had significantly improved. Nai had been an excellent teacher. Benjy had brought two books in his backpack, one a collection of the tales of Hans Christian Andersen written three centuries earlier. Benjy's favourite story was 'The Ugly Duckling,' which he read in its entirety as both his delighted mother and his teacher sat beside him. There was a wonderful, ingenuous excitement in his voice when the spurned duckling turned into a beautiful swan.

'I am very proud of you, darling,' Nicole said when Benjy was finished reading. 'And I thank you, Nai,' she said to her friend, 'from the bottom of my heart.'

'It's been a lot of fun working with Benjy,' the Thai woman replied. 'I had forgotten what a thrill it was to teach an interested and appreciative pupil.'

Robert Turner cleaned Max Puckett's wound and removed the bullet. His procedure was closely monitored by the five-year-old Watanabe twins, both of whom were fascinated by the inside of Max's body. The aggressive Galileo was always pushing for the better view; Nai had to adjudicate two brotherly disputes in favour of Kepler.

Dr Turner confirmed Max's statement that the wound was not serious and prescribed a short period of convalescence. 'I guess I'll just have to take it easy,' Max said, winking at Eponine. 'Which is what I was planning to do anyway. I don't think there will be too many pigs or chickens in this alien city of skyscrapers. And I don't know a goddamn thing about *bi-ots.*'

Nicole had a brief conversation with Eponine, just before the submarine arrived at The Port, in which she thanked Ellie's erstwhile teacher profusely for everything she and Max had done for the family. Eponine accepted the thanks graciously and told Nicole that Patrick had been 'absolutely fantastic' in helping them with all aspects of the escape. 'He has grown into a superb young man,' Eponine said.

'How is your health, then?' Nicole asked Eponine delicately a few moments later.

The Frenchwoman shrugged. 'The good doctor says the RV-41 virus is still there, poised and waiting for an opportunity to overwhelm my immune system. Whenever that happens, I should have between six months and a year more to live.'

Patrick informed Richard that Joan and Eleanor had tried to decoy the Nakamura platoon by making a lot of noise, as they had been programmed to do, and had almost certainly been captured and destroyed.

'I'm sorry about Joan and Eleanor,' Nicole said to Richard during a rare private moment on board the submarine. 'I know how much your little robots mean to you.'

'They served their purpose,' Richard replied. He forced a smile. 'After all, wasn't it you who told me once they're not the same as people?'

Nicole reached up and kissed her husband.

None of the new escapees had ever been in New York as an adult. Nicole's three children had all been born on the island and had lived there in their early childhood, but a child has a much different sense of place than an adult. Even Ellie, Patrick, and Benjy were awestruck when they first stepped on the shore and saw the tall, thin silhouettes reaching toward the Rama sky in the near-darkness.

Max Puckett was uncharacteristically speechless. He stood beside Eponine, holding her hand, and gawked at the thin, towering spires rising over two hundred metres above the island. 'This is too damn much for an Arkansas farm-boy,' he said at length, shaking his head. Max and Eponine walked at the end of the procession that was winding its way toward the lair which Richard and Nicole had converted into a multi-family apartment for all of them to share.

'Who built all this?' Robert Turner asked Richard as the troupe paused briefly in front of a giant polyhedron. Robert was growing increasingly apprehensive. He had been reluctant to come with Ellie and Nikki in the first place, and he was now rapidly becoming convinced that he had indeed made a big mistake.

'Probably the engineers at The Node,' Richard answered. 'Although we can't know for certain. We humans have added new construction in our habitat. It's possible that whoever, or whatever, lived here long ago might have built a few or even all of these amazing buildings.'

'Where are they now?' Robert asked next, more than a little frightened at the prospect of encountering beings with the technological expertise necessary to create such impressive edifices.

'We have no way of knowing. According to The Eagle, this Rama spacecraft has been making voyages to discover spacefaring species for thousands of years. Somewhere in our part of the galaxy is another spacefarer who would have been comfortable in an environment like this. What that creature was, or is, and why it wanted to live in and among these incredible skyscrapers is a riddle we will probably never answer.'

'What about the avians and the octospiders, Uncle Richard?' Patrick asked. 'Are they still living here in New York?'

'I have not seen any avians on the island since I arrived, except of course for the hatchlings that we are raising. But there are still octospiders around. Your mother and I encountered some of them when we were exploring behind the black screen.'

At that moment a centipede biot approached the procession from a side alley. Richard shone his flashlight in its direction. Robert Turner momentarily froze with fear, but he followed Richard's instructions and moved out of the way as the biot trundled by.

'Skyscrapers built by ghosts, octospiders, centipede biots,' Robert grumbled. 'What a lovely place!'

'In my opinion it's a hell of a lot better than living under that tyrant Nakamura,' Richard said. 'At least here we're free and can make our own decisions.'

'Wakefield,' Max Puckett shouted from the back of the line. 'What would happen if we didn't move out of the way of one of those centipede biots?'

'I don't know for sure, Max,' Richard replied. 'But it would probably go over or around you just as if you were an inanimate object.'

It was Nicole's turn to be the tour guide when they arrived at the lair. She personally showed each person his or her quarters. There was one room for Max and Eponine, another for Ellie and Robert, a room divided by a partition for Patrick and Nai, the large subdivided nursery for the three children, Benjy, and the two avians, and one final, small room that Richard and she had decided would be perfect as a common dining-area.

While the adults unpacked the meagre belongings they had loaded into backpacks, the children had their first experience with Tammy and Timmy. The avians did not know what to make of the little humans, especially Galileo, who insisted on pulling or tweaking anything he could touch. After about an hour of such treatment, Timmy scratched Galileo lightly with one of his talons as a warning, and the boy raised an incredible din.

'I just don't understand it,' Richard said to Nai in apology. 'The avians are really very gentle creatures.'

'I *do* understand,' Nai replied. 'Galileo was almost certainly up to some mischief.' She sighed. 'It's amazing, you know. You raise two children exactly the same way, and they turn out so differently. Kepler is so good he's almost an angel – I can hardly teach him to defend himself. And Galileo pays almost no attention to anything I tell him.'

When everyone had finished unpacking, Nicole completed the tour, including the two bathrooms, the corridors, the suspension tanks where the family had stayed during the period of high acceleration between the Earth and The Node, and finally the White Room, with the black screen and keyboard, which was also Richard and Nicole's bedroom. Richard demonstrated how the black screen worked by requesting, and receiving about an hour later, some new and simple toys for the children. He also gave Robert and Max each a copy of a short command dictionary that would allow them to use the keyboard.

The children were all asleep soon after dinner. The adults gathered in the White Room. Max asked questions about the octospiders. In the course of describing their adventures behind the black screen, Nicole mentioned her heart irregularities. Robert immediately showed concern and soon thereafter the doctor examined Nicole in her bedroom.

Ellie helped Robert with the examination. Robert had brought as much practical medical equipment as he could fit in his backpack, including all the miniaturised instruments and monitors necessary to do a full electrocardiogram (ECG). The results were not good, but not as bad as Nicole had privately feared. Before bedtime Robert informed the rest of the family that the years had definitely taken their toll on Nicole's heart, but that he didn't think she would require surgery in the immediate future. Robert advised Nicole to take it easy, even though he knew that his mother-in-law would probably ignore his prescription.

When everyone was asleep, Richard and Nicole moved the furniture to make room for their mats. They lay side by side, holding hands. 'Are you happy?' Richard asked.

'Yes,' Nicole answered, 'very. It's really wonderful to have all the children here.' She leaned over and gave Richard a kiss. 'I am also exhausted, husband of mine, but I'm not about to go to sleep without first thanking you for arranging all of this.'

'They're my children too, you know,' he said.

'Yes, darling,' Nicole said, lying down on her back again. 'But I know that you would never have done all this if it weren't for me. You would have been content to stay here with the hatchlings, all your gadgets, and the extra-terrestrial mysteries.'

'Maybe,' Richard said. 'But I also am delighted to have everyone in our lair … By the way, did you have a chance to talk to Patrick about Katie?'

'Only briefly,' Nicole replied. She sighed. 'I could tell from his eyes that he is still very worried about her.'

'Aren't we all?' Richard said softly. They lay in silence for a couple of minutes before Richard propped himself up on an elbow. 'I want you to know,' he said, 'that I think our granddaughter is absolutely precious.'

'So do I,' Nicole replied with a laugh, 'but there's not a chance that we could be considered unbiased on the subject.'

'Hey, does having Nikki with us mean that I can no longer call *you* Nikki, not even at special moments?'

Nicole turned her head to look at Richard. He was grinning. She had seen that particular expression on his face many times before. 'Go to sleep,' Nicole said with another short laugh. 'I'm too emotionally exhausted for anything else tonight.'

In the beginning time passed very quickly. There was so much to do, so much fascinating territory to explore. Even though it was perpetually dark in the mysterious city above them, the family made regular excursions into New York. Virtually every place on the island had a special story that Richard or Nicole could tell. 'It was here,' Nicole said one afternoon, shining her flashlight at the huge lattice that hung suspended between two skyscrapers like a spider web, 'that I rescued the trapped avian, who subsequently invited me into its lair.'

'Down there,' she said on another occasion, when they were in the large barn with its peculiar pits and spheres, 'I was trapped for many days and thought I was going to die.'

The extended family developed a set of rules to keep the children from getting into trouble. The rules were not needed for little Nikki, who hardly ever wandered far from her mother and doting grandfather, but the boys Kepler and Galileo were difficult to constrain. The Watanabe twins seemed to possess infinite energy. Once they were found bouncing on the hammocks in the suspension tanks, as if the hammocks were trampolines. Another time Galileo and Kepler 'borrowed' the family flashlights and went topside, without adult supervision, to explore New York. It was ten nervous hours before the boys were located in the maze of alleys and streets on the far side of the island.

The avians practised flying almost every day. The children delighted in accompanying their birdlike friends to the plazas, where there was more room for Tammy and Timmy to display their developing skills. Richard always took Nikki to watch the avians fly. In fact, he took his granddaughter with him everywhere he went. From time to time Nikki would walk, but mostly Richard carried her in a comfortable papoose-like contraption that he affixed to his back. The unlikely pair were inseparable. Richard became Nikki's main teacher as well. Very early he announced to everyone that his granddaughter was a mathematical genius.

At night he would regale Nicole with Nikki's latest exploits. 'Do you know what she did today?' he would say, usually when he and Nicole were alone in bed.

'No, dear,' was Nicole's standard reply; she knew very well that neither she nor Richard would sleep until he told her.

'I asked her how many black balls she would have if she already had three and I gave her two more.' (Dramatic pause.) 'And do you know what she answered?' (Another dramatic pause.) '*Five!* She said five. And this little girl just had her second birthday last week ...'

Nicole was thrilled by Richard's interest in Nikki. For both the little girl and the aging man, it was a perfect match. As a parent, Richard had never been able to overcome both his own repressed emotional problems and his acute sense of responsibility, so this was the first time in his life that he had experienced the joy of truly innocent love. Nikki's father, Robert, on the other hand, was a great doctor, but he was not a very warm person and he did not fully appreciate the purposeless time periods that parents must spend with their children.

Patrick and Nicole had several long talks about Katie, all of which left Nicole feeling extremely depressed. Patrick did not hide from his mother the fact that Katie was deeply involved in all of Nakamura's machinations, that she drank often and too much, and that she had been sexually promiscuous. He did not tell Nicole that Katie was managing Nakamura's prostitution business, or that he suspected his sister had become a drug addict.

10

Their near-perfect existence in New York continued until early one morning, when Richard and Nikki were topside together along the northern ramparts of the island. Actually it was the little girl who first saw the silhouettes of the ships in the dim Raman light. She pointed out across the dark water. 'Look, Boobah,' she said, 'Nikki sees something.'

Richard's weakened eyes could not detect anything in the darkness, and his flashlight beam did not travel far enough to reach whatever it was that Nikki was seeing. Richard pulled out the powerful binoculars that he always carried with him and confirmed that there were indeed two vessels in the middle of the Cylindrical Sea. Richard placed Nikki in the carrier on his back and hurried home to the lair.

The rest of the family was just waking up and had difficulty initially understanding why Richard was so alarmed. 'But who else could it be in a boat?' he said. 'Especially on the northern side. It has to be an exploration party sent by Nakamura.'

A family council was held over breakfast. Everyone agreed that they were facing a serious crisis. When Patrick confessed that he had seen Katie on the day of the escape, primarily because he had wanted to tell his sister goodbye, and that he had made a few unusual comments which had caused Katie to start asking questions, Nicole and the others became silent.

'I didn't say anything specific,' Patrick said apologetically, 'but it was still a dumb thing to do ... Katie is very smart. After we all disappeared, she must have put all the pieces together.'

'But what do we do now?' Robert Turner voiced everyone's apprehension. 'Katie knows New York very well – she was almost a teenager when she left here – and she can lead Nakamura's men directly to this lair. We'll be sitting ducks for them down here.'

'Is there any other place we can go?' Max asked.

'Not really,' Richard replied. 'The old avian lair is empty, but I don't know how we would feed ourselves down there. The octospider lair was also vacant when I visited it several months ago, but I haven't been inside their domain again since Nicole arrived in New York. We must assume, of course, based on what happened when Nicole and I went exploring, that our friends with the black and gold tentacles are still around. Even if they aren't living in their old lair anymore, we would still have the same problem of obtaining food if we were to move over there.'

'What about the area behind the screen, Uncle Richard?' Patrick asked. 'You said that's where our food is manufactured. Maybe we could find a couple of rooms there ...'

'I'm not very optimistic,' Richard said after a short pause, 'but your suggestion is probably our only reasonable option at this point.'

The family decided that Richard, Max, and Patrick would reconnoitre the region behind the black screen, both to find out exactly where the human food was being produced and to determine if another suitable living area existed. Robert, Benjy, the women, and the children would stay in the lair. Their assignment was to start developing the procedures for a rapid evacuation of their living-quarters, in case such action ever became necessary.

Before going, Richard finished testing a new radio system that he had designed in his spare time. It was strong enough that the explorers and the rest of the family would be able to remain in radio contact during the entire time that they were separated. The existence of the radio link made it easier for Richard and Nicole to convince Max Puckett to leave his rifle in the lair.

The three men had no difficulty following the map in Richard's computer and reaching the boiler room that Richard and Nicole had visited on their previous exploration. Max and Patrick both stared in wonder at the twelve huge boilers, the vast area of neatly arranged raw materials, and the many varieties of biots scurrying about. The factory was active. In fact, every single one of the boilers was involved in some kind of manufacturing process.

'All right,' Richard said into his radio to Nicole back in the lair. 'We're here and we're ready. Place the dinner order and we'll see what happens.'

Less than a minute later one of the boilers closest to the three men terminated whatever it was doing. Meanwhile, not far from the hut behind the boilers, three biots that looked like boxcars with hands moved out into the arrays of raw material, quickly picking up small quantities of many different items. These three biots next converged on the inactive boiler system near Richard, Max, and Patrick, where they emptied their containers onto the conveyor belt entering the boiler. Immediately the men heard the boiler surge into active operation. A long, skinny biot, resembling three crickets tied together in a row, each with a bowl-shaped carapace, crawled up on the conveyor belt system when the short manufacturing process was almost finished. Moments later, the boiler stopped again and the processed material came out on the conveyor belt. The segmented cricket biot deployed a scoop from its rear end, placed all the human food upon its backs, and scampered quickly away.

'Well, I'll be goddamned,' Max said, watching the cricket biot disappear down the corridor behind the hut. Before any of the men could say anything else, another set of boxcars with hands loaded the conveyor belts with thick, long rods, and in less than a minute the boiler that had made their food was operating for another purpose.

'What a fantastic system,' Richard exclaimed. 'It must have a complex interrupt process, with food orders at the top of the priority queue. I can't believe ...'

'Hold on just a damn minute,' Max interrupted, 'and repeat what you just said in normal English.'

'We have automatic translation subroutines back at the lair – I designed them originally when we were here years ago,' Richard said excitedly. 'When Nicole entered chicken, potatoes, and spinach into her own computer, a listing of keyboard commands which represent the complex chemicals in those particular foods was printed on her output buffer. After I signalled that we were ready, she typed that string of commands on the keyboard. They were immediately received here and what we saw was the response. At the time, all the processing systems were active; however, the Raman equivalent of a computer here in this factory recognised that the incoming request was for food, and made it the highest priority.'

'Are you saying, Uncle Richard,' Patrick said, 'that the controlling computer here shut down that operating boiler so that it could make our food?'

'Yes, indeed,' said Richard.

Max had moved some distance away and was staring at the other boilers in the huge factory. Richard and Patrick walked over beside him.

'When I was a little boy, about eight or nine,' Max said, 'my father and I went on our first overnight camping trip, up in the Ozarks several hours from our farm. It was a magnificent night and the sky was full of stars. I remember lying on my back on my sleeping bag and staring at all those tiny twinkling lights in the sky ... That night I had a big, big thought for an Arkansas farm-boy. I wondered how many alien children, out there somewhere in the universe, were looking up at the stars at exactly that moment and realizing, for the first time, how very small their tiny domain was in the overall scheme of the cosmos.'

Max turned around and smiled at his two friends. 'That's one of the reasons I remained a farmer,' he said with a laugh. 'With my chickens and pigs, I was always important. I brought them their food. It was a major event when ole Max showed up at their pen ...'

He paused for a moment. Neither Richard nor Patrick said anything. 'I think that deep down I always wanted to be an astronomer,' Max continued, 'to see if I could understand the mysteries of the universe. But every time I thought about billions of years and trillions of kilometres, I became depressed. I couldn't stand the feeling of complete and total insignificance that came over me. It was as if a voice inside my head was saying, over and over, "Puckett, you aren't shit. You are absolutely zero."'

969

'But *knowing* that insignificance, especially being able to *measure* it, makes us humans very special,' Richard said quietly.

'Now we're talking philosophy,' Max replied, 'and I'm completely out of my element. I'm comfortable with farm animals, tequila, and even wild midwestern thunderstorms. All this,' Max said, waving his arms at the boilers and the factory, 'scares the shit out of me. If I had known, when I signed up for that Martian colony, that I would meet machines that are smarter than people ...'

'Richard, Richard,' they all heard Nicole's anxious voice on the radio. 'We have an emergency. Ellie has just returned from the northern shore. Four large boats are about to land ... Ellie says she's positive she spotted a police uniform on one of the men ... Also, she has reported some kind of large rainbow in the south ... Can you get back here in a few minutes?'

'No we can't,' Richard answered. 'We're still tlown in the room with the boilers. We must be at least three and a half kilometres away ... Did Ellie say how many people might be on each boat?'

'I would guess about ten or twelve, Dad,' Ellie replied. 'I didn't stay around to count them ... But the boats were not the only unusual thing I saw while I was topside. During my run back to the lair, the southern sky lit up with wild bursts of colour that eventually became a giant rainbow ... It's near where you told us the Big Horn should be.'

Ten seconds later Richard shouted into the radio. 'Listen to me, Nicole, Ellie, all of you. Evacuate our lair immediately. Take the children, the hatch-lings, the melons, the sessile material, the two rifles, all the food, and as many personal belongings as you can comfortably carry. Leave *our* stuff alone – we have enough on our backs to survive in an emergency. Go directly to the octospider lair and wait for us in that large room that was a photo gallery years ago ... Nakamura's troops will come to our lair first. When they don't find us, if Katie's with them, they may go to the octospider lair as well, but I don't believe they will go into the tunnels there ...'

'What about you and Max and Patrick?' Nicole asked.

'We'll come back as fast as we can. If there is nobody ... by the way, Nicole, leave a transmitter, with the volume on high, in the White Room, and another in the nursery. That way we'll know if anybody is in our lair ... Anyway, as I was saying, if our home has not been invaded, we'll join you right away. If Nakamura's men are occupying our living-quarters, we'll try to find another entrance to the octospider lair from down here. There must be one ...'

'All right,' Nicole interrupted. 'We must get started with the packing ... I'll leave the receiver on in case you need us.'

'So you think we'll be safest in the octospider lair?' Max said after Richard had switched off his transmitter.

'It's a choice,' Richard said with a wan smile. 'There are too many unknowns here behind the screen. And we know for certain we won't be safe if Nakamura's police and troops find us ... The octospiders may not even be living in their lair anymore. Besides, as Nicole has said many times, we have no unambiguous evidence that the octos are hostile.'

The men moved as quickly as they could. At one point they halted briefly while Patrick transferred some of the weight off Richard's pack into his own. Both Richard and Max were sweating profusely by the time they reached the Y in the corridor.

'We must stop for a minute,' Max said to Patrick, who was out in front of his two older companions. 'Your Uncle Richard needs a rest.'

Patrick pulled a water-bottle from his pack and passed it around. Richard drank eagerly from the bottle, wiped his brow with a handkerchief, and after a minute's rest began jogging again towards the lair.

About five hundred metres away from the small platform behind the black screen, Richard's receiver began picking up indistinct noises from the inside of the lair. 'Maybe someone in the family forgot something important,' Richard said, slowing down to listen, 'and came back to retrieve it.'

A short time later the three men heard a voice they could not identify. They stopped and waited. 'It looks as if some kind of animal has been living back here,' the voice said. 'Why don't you come take a look?'

'Damn,' said a second voice. 'They have definitely been here recently ... I wonder how long ago they left.'

'Captain Bauer,' someone shouted. 'What do you want me to do with all this electronic gear?'

'Leave it for now,' the second voice answered. 'The rest of the troops should be down in a few minutes. We'll decide what to do then.'

Richard, Max, and Patrick sat quietly in the dark tunnel. For about a minute they didn't hear anything on the receiver. Apparently none of the members of the search party was in the White Room or the nursery during that time. Then the three men heard Franz Bauer's voice again.

'What's that, Morgan?' Bauer said. 'I can barely hear you ... There's some kind of racket ... What? Fireworks? colours? ... What in the world are you talking about? All right. All right. We'll come up immediately.'

For another fifteen seconds the receiver was quiet. 'Ah, here you are, Pfeiffer,' they then heard Captain Bauer say plainly. 'Round up the other men and let's go back upstairs. Morgan says there's an amazing fireworks demonstration in the southern sky. Most of the troops were already spooked by the skyscrapers and the dark. I'm going up to calm everyone's nerves.'

'This is our chance,' Richard whispered, rising to his feet. 'They will certainly be out of the lair for a few minutes.' He started to run and then stopped himself. 'We may need to separate ... Do both of you remember how to find the octospider lair?'

Max shook his head. 'I've never been over ...'

'Here,' Richard said, handing Max his portable computer. 'Enter an M and a P for an overview of New York. The octospider lair is marked with a red circle ... If you touch L, followed by another L, a map of the inside of their lair will be displayed ... Now let's go, while we still have some time.'

Richard, Max, and Patrick encountered no troops inside their lair. A pair of guards were stationed, however, a few metres away from the exit to New York. Fortunately, the guards were so transfixed by the fireworks in the Rama sky above their heads that they didn't hear the three men slipping up the stairs behind them. For safety, the threesome split up, each taking a different route to the octospider lair.

Richard and Patrick arrived at their destination within a minute of each other, but Max was delayed. As luck would have it, the route he had chosen led through one of the plazas where five or six of the colony troops had gathered for a better view of the fireworks. Max raced down an alley and huddled against one of the buildings. He pulled out the computer and studied the map on the monitor, trying to figure out an alternate path to the octospider lair.

Meanwhile, the spectacular fireworks show continued overhead. Max glanced up and was dazzled as a great blue ball exploded, throwing hundreds of rays of blue light in all directions. For almost a minute, Max watched the hypnotic display. It was grander than anything he had ever seen on Earth.

When Max finally reached the octospider lair, he descended the ramp quickly and entered the cathedral room from which the four tunnels led into the other parts of the lair. Max entered two Ls on the computer and the map of the octospider domain appeared on the tiny monitor. Max was so engrossed in the map that at first he did not hear the sound of dragging mechanical brushes accompanied by a soft, high-pitched whine.

He did not look up until the sound became quite loud. When Max finally raised his head, the large octospider was standing no more than five metres away from him. The sight of the creature sent powerful shivers down Max's spine. He stood quite still and fought against his desire to flee. The creamy liquid in the octospider's single lens moved from side to side, but the alien did not advance any closer to Max.

Out of one of the parallel indentations on both sides of the lens came a burst of purple colour, which circumnavigated the octospider's spherical head, followed by bands of other colours, all of which disappeared into the second of the two parallel slits. When the same colour-pattern repeated, Max, whose heart was pounding so fiercely he could feel it in his jaw, shook his head and said, 'I don't understand.' The octospider hesitated for a moment and then lifted two of its tentacles off the ground, clearly pointing in the direction of one of the four tunnels. As if to underscore its point, the octo shuffled in that general direction and then repeated the gesture.

Max stood up and walked slowly toward the indicated tunnel, being careful not to come too close to the octospider. When he reached the entrance, another series of colour splashes raced around the head of the alien. 'Thank

972

you very much,' Max said politely as he turned and walked into the passageway.

He didn't even stop to look at his map until he was three or four hundred metres into the tunnel. As Max walked along, the lights always came on automatically in front of him and were extinguished in the tunnel segments through which he had already passed. When he did finally examine the map carefully, Max discovered that he was not far from the designated room.

A few minutes later Max entered the chamber where the rest of the family was gathered. He had a big grin on his face. 'You'll never guess who I just met,' Max said only moments before Eponine greeted him with an embrace.

Soon after Max finished entertaining everyone with the story of his encounter with the octospider, Richard and Patrick cautiously backtracked to the cathedral room, stopping every hundred metres or so and listening carefully for the telltale sounds of the aliens. They heard nothing. Nor did they hear or see anything that indicated the forces dispatched from New Eden were in the vicinity. After about an hour, Richard and Patrick returned to the rest of the group and joined in the discussion of what they should do next.

The extended family had enough food for five days, maybe six if each portion was carefully rationed. Water was available at the cistern near the cathedral room. Everyone quickly agreed that the search party from New Eden, at least this first one, would probably not stay in New York too long. There was a short debate about whether or not Katie might have told Captain Bauer and his men the location of the octospider lair. On one critical point there was no argument – the next day or two was the most likely time period for them to be discovered by the other humans. As a result, except for physical necessities, none of the family left the large room in which they were staying for the next thirty-six hours.

At the end of that time the whole group, especially the hatchlings and the twins, had a bad case of cabin fever. Richard and Nai took Tammy, Timmy, Benjy, and the small children out into the passageway, trying unsuccessfully to keep them quiet, and led them away from the cathedral room, toward the vertical corridor with the protruding spikes that descended deeper into the octospider lair. Richard, who had Nikki on his back most of the time, warned Nai and the twins several times about the dangers of the area they were approaching. Even so, very soon after the tunnel widened and they arrived at the vertical corridor, the impetuous Galileo climbed into the barrel-shaped hole before his mother could stop him. He quickly became frozen with fright. Richard had to rescue the boy from his precarious perch on two spikes just a short distance below the level of the walkway that encircled the top of the huge abyss. The young avians, delighted to be able to fly again, soared freely around the area and twice dropped several metres into the dark chasm, but they never went deep enough to trigger the next lower bank of lights.

Before returning to the rest of the family, Richard took Benjy with him for a quick inspection of what Richard and Nicole had always called the octospider museum. This large room, located several hundred metres from the vertical corridor, was still completely empty. Several hours later, following Richard's suggestion, half of the extended family moved into the museum to give everyone more living-space.

On the third day of their stay in the octospider lair, Richard and Max decided that someone should try to discover if the colony troops were still in New York. Patrick was the logical choice to be the family scout. Richard's and Max's instructions to Patrick were straightforward – he was to proceed cautiously to the cathedral room and then up the ramp into New York. From there, using his flashlight and portable computer as little as possible, he should cross to the northern shore of the island and see if the boats were still there. Whatever the result of his investigation, he should return directly to the lair and give them a full report.

'There is one other thing to remember,' Richard said, 'that is extremely important. If at any time you hear either an octospider or a soldier, you are to turn around immediately and come back to us. But with this one added proviso: Under no circumstances should any human see you descend into this lair. You cannot do anything that will endanger the rest of us.'

Max insisted that Patrick should take one of the two rifles. Richard and Nicole did not argue. After receiving best wishes from everybody, Patrick set out on his scouting mission. He had only walked five hundred metres down the tunnel, however, when he heard a noise in front of him. He stopped to listen, but could not identify what he was hearing. After another hundred metres some of the sounds began to resolve themselves. Patrick definitely heard the sound of dragging brushes several times. There was some clanging as well, as if metal objects were hitting against each other, or against a wall. He listened for several minutes and then, remembering his instructions, he returned to his family and friends.

After a long discussion Patrick was sent out again. He was told this time to approach as close to the octospiders as he dared and to watch them quietly for as long as he could. Again he heard the dragging brush sound as he drew close to the cathedral room. But when Patrick actually reached the large chamber at the bottom of the ramp, there were no octospiders around. *Where had they gone?* he wondered. Patrick's first impulse was to turn around and go back in the direction from which he had come. However, since he had not encountered any actual octospiders yet, he decided that he might as well go up the ramp, out into New York, and carry out the remainder of his earlier assignment.

Patrick was shocked to discover, about a minute later, that the exit from the octospider lair had been sealed tight with a thick combination of metal rods and a cementlike material. He could barely see through the cover, and it was certainly sufficiently heavy that all the humans together would not be able to budge it. *The octospiders have done this,* he thought immediately, *but why have they trapped us here?*

Before returning to give his report, Patrick inspected the cathedral room and found that one of the four egress tunnels had also been sealed with what appeared to be a thick door or gate. *That must have been the tunnel that led to the canal,* he thought. Patrick remained in the area for another ten minutes, listening for the sounds of the octospiders, but heard nothing more.

11

'So the octospiders have never done anything hostile?' Max was saying angrily. 'Then what the hell do you call this? We're fucking trapped.' He shook his head vigorously. 'I thought it was stupid to come here in the first place.'

'Please, Max,' Eponine said. 'Let's not argue. Fighting among ourselves is not going to help.'

All the adults except Nai and Benjy had trekked the one kilometre down the passageway to the cathedral room to examine what the octospiders had done. The humans were indeed sealed inside the lair. Two of the three open tunnels leading out of the chamber went to the vertical corridor and the third, they quickly discovered, led to a large, empty storeroom from which there was no exit.

'Well, we'd better think of something fast,' Max said. 'We have only four days worth of food and absolutely no idea where to get any more.'

'I'm sorry, Max,' Nicole said, 'but I still think Richard's initial decision was correct. If we had stayed in our lair, we would have been captured and taken back to New Eden, where we almost certainly would have been executed ...'

'Maybe,' Max interrupted. 'And maybe not ... At least in that case the children would have been spared. And I don't think either Benjy or the doctor would have been killed ...'

'This is all academic,' Richard said, 'and doesn't deal with our main problem, which is, what do we do now?'

'All right, genius,' Max said with a sting in his voice. 'This has been your show so far. What do you suggest?'

Again Eponine interceded. 'You're being unfair, Max. It's not Richard's fault we're in this predicament ... And as I said before, it doesn't help ...'

'OK, OK,' Max said. He walked toward the passage that led to the store-room. 'I'm going in this tunnel to calm down and to smoke a cigarette.' He glanced back at Eponine. 'Do you want to share? We have exactly twenty-nine left after we smoke this one.'

Eponine smiled faintly at Nicole and Eflie. 'He's still pissed off at me for not taking all our cigarettes when we evacuated the lair,' she said quietly. 'Don't worry ... Max has a bad temper, but he gets over it fast ... We'll be back in a few minutes.'

'What *is* your plan, darling?' Nicole said to Richard a few seconds after Max and Eponine had left.

'We don't have much choice,' Richard said grimly. 'A bare minimum number of adults should stay with Benjy, the children, and the avians, while the rest of us explore this lair as quickly as possible. I have a hard time believing that the octospiders really intend for us to starve to death.'

'Excuse me, Richard,' Robert Turner now said, speaking for the first time since Patrick had reported that the exit to New York was sealed, 'but aren't you again assuming that the octospiders are friendly? Suppose they're not, or more likely in my opinion, suppose our survival is insignificant to them one way or the other, and that they simply sealed off this lair to protect themselves from all the humans who have recently appeared ...'

Robert stopped, apparently having lost his train of thought. 'What I was trying to say,' he continued a few seconds later, 'is that the children, including your granddaughter, are in considerable jeopardy, psychological as well as physical, I might add, in our current situation, and I would be against any plan that left them unprotected and vulnerable ...'

'You're right, Robert,' Richard interrupted. 'Several adults, including at least one man, must stay with Benjy and the children. In fact, Nai must have her hands full right this minute ... Why don't you, Patrick, and Ellie return to the children now? Nicole and I will wait for Max and Eponine and join you shortly.'

Richard and Nicole were alone after the others departed. 'Ellie says that Robert is angry most of the time now,' Nicole said quietly, 'but he doesn't know how to express his anger constructively ... He told her he thinks the whole enterprise has been a mistake from the beginning, and he spends hours brooding about it ... Ellie says she's even worried about his stability.'

Richard shook his head. 'Maybe it *was* a mistake,' he said. 'Maybe you and I should have lived the rest of our life here alone, I just thought ...'

At that moment Max and Eponine came back into the chamber. 'I want to apologise,' Max said, extending his hand, 'to both of you. I guess I let my fear and frustration get the best of me.'

'Thank you, Max,' Nicole answered. 'But an apology really isn't necessary. It would be ridiculous to assume that this many people could go through an experience like this without any disagreements.'

Everyone was together in the museum. 'Let's review the plan one more time,' Richard said. 'The five of us will climb down the spikes and explore the area around the subway platform. We will thoroughly investigate every tunnel we can find. Then, if we have not found any means of escape and the large subway is indeed there waiting, Max, Eponine, Nicole, and I will go on board. At that point Patrick will climb back up and rejoin you here in the museum.'

'Don't you think having all four of you on the subway is reckless?' Robert asked. 'Why not just two of you at first? ... What if the subway leaves and never comes back?'

'Time is our enemy, Robert,' Richard answered. 'If we weren't running so low on food, then we could follow a more conservative plan. In that case maybe only two of us would enter the subway. But what if the subway leads to more than one place? Since we have already decided that for safety we will explore only in pairs, it could take us a long time to find the escape route with just a single couple doing the searching.'

There was a protracted silence in the room until Timmy began to jabber at his sister. Nikki wandered over and began to stroke the avian's velvet underside. 'I don't pretend that I have all the answers,' Richard said. 'Nor do I underestimate the seriousness of our situation. But if there is a way out of here, and both Nicole and I believe that there must be, then the sooner we find it, the better.'

'Assuming that all four of you do take the subway,' Patrick now asked, 'how long do we wait for you here in the museum?'

'That's a difficult question,' Richard replied. 'You have enough food for four more days, and the plentiful water at the cistern should keep you alive for some period after that ... I don't know, Patrick. I guess you should stay here for at least two or three days ... After that, you have to make your own decision ... If it is at all possible, one or more of us will return.'

Benjy had been following the conversation with rapt attention. He obviously understood more or less what was happening, for he began to cry softly. Nicole went over to comfort him. 'Don't worry, son,' she said. 'Everything is going to be all right.'

The child-man looked up at his mother. 'I hope so, Mom-ma,' he said, 'but I'm scared.'

Galileo Watanabe suddenly jumped up and ran across the room to where the two rifles were leaning against the wall. 'If one of those octospider things comes in here,' he said, touching the closest rifle for a few seconds before Max lifted it free of the boy's grasp, 'then I'll shoot it. *Bang! Bang!*'

His shouts caused the avians to shriek and little Nikki to cry. After Ellie wiped away her daughter's tears, Max and Patrick shouldered the rifles and all five of the explorers said their goodbyes. Ellie walked out into the tunnel with them. 'I didn't want to say this in front of the children,' she said, 'but what *should* we do if we see an octospider while you're gone?'

'Try not to panic,' Richard answered.

'And don't do anything aggressive,' Nicole added.

'Grab Nikki and run like hell,' Max said with a wink.

Nothing unusual happened while they climbed down the spikes. Just as they had years earlier, the lights at the next lower level always turned on when anyone descending approached an unlit area. All five of the explorers were on the subway platform in less than an hour. 'Now we'll find out if those mysterious vehicles are still operating,' Richard said.

In the centre of the circular platform there was a smaller hole, also round and with metal spikes protruding from its sides, that descended deeper into the darkness. On opposite ends of the platform, ninety degrees away to the left and right from where the five of them were standing, two dark tunnels were cut into the rock and metal. One of the tunnels was large, five or six metres from top to bottom, while the opposite tunnel was almost exactly an order of magnitude smaller. When Richard approached to within twenty degrees of the large tunnel, it suddenly became illuminated and its interior could be clearly seen. The tunnel looked like a large sewer-pipe back on Earth.

The rest of the exploration party hurried over beside Richard as soon as the first whooshing sound was heard coming from the tunnel. Less than a minute later a subway sped around a distant corner and headed rapidly toward them, stopping with its front end a metre or so shy of where the spiked corridor continued to descend.

The inside of the subway was also illuminated. There were no seats, but there were vertical rods from the ceiling to the floor, scattered in the car in seemingly random fashion. The door slid open about fifteen seconds after the subway arrived. On the opposite side of the platform an identical vehicle, exactly one-tenth as large, pulled up and stopped no more than five seconds later.

Even though Max, Patrick, and Eponine had all heard stories about the two ghost subways many times, actually seeing the vehicles left all three of them full of apprehension. 'Are you really serious, my friend?' Max said to Richard after the two men quickly examined the outside of the larger subway. 'Do you really intend to *board* that damn thing if we find no other way out?'

Richard nodded.

'But it could go *any*where,' Max said. 'We don't have the foggiest fucking idea what it is, or who built it, or what the hell it's doing here. And once we're on board, we're completely helpless.'

'That's right,' Richard said. He smiled wanly. 'Max, you have an excellent grasp of our situation.'

Max shook his head. 'Well, we'd better find something down in this damn hole, because I don't know if Eponine and I ...'

'All right,' Patrick said, approaching the other two men. 'I guess it's time for the next phase of this operation ... Come on, Max, are you ready for some more spike climbing?'

Richard did not have any of his clever robots to place in the smaller subway. He did, however, have in his possession a miniature camera with a crude mobility system that he hoped would weigh enough to activate the smaller subway. 'Under any circumstances,' he told the others, 'the small tunnel does not provide a possible exit for us. I just want to determine for myself if anything significant has changed during these years. Besides, there does not seem to be any reason, at least not yet, for more than two of us to descend any farther.'

While Max and Patrick were climbing slowly down the additional spikes and Richard was absorbed with a final checkout of his mobile camera, Nicole and Eponine strolled around the platform. 'How's it going, farmer?' Eponine said to Max on the radio.

'Fine so far,' he replied. 'But we're only about ten metres below you. These spikes are not as close together as the ones above, so we're being more cautious.'

'Your relationship with Max must have really blossomed while I was in prison,' Nicole commented a few moments later.

'Yes, it did,' Eponine replied easily. 'Quite frankly, it surprised me. I didn't think a man was capable of having a serious affair with someone who ... you know ... but I underestimated Max. He is really an unusual person. Underneath that brusque, macho exterior ...'

Eponine stopped. Nicole was smiling broadly. 'I don't think Max really fools anybody – at least not those who know him. The tough, foul-mouthed Max is an act, developed for some reason, probably self-protection, back on that farm in Arkansas.'

The two women were silent for several seconds. 'But I don't think I have ever given him full credit either,' Nicole added. 'It is a tribute to him that he adores you so completely even though you two have never been able to really ...'

'Oh, Nicole,' Eponine said, suddenly emotional. 'Don't think I haven't wanted to, haven't dreamed about it. And Dr Turner has told us many times that the odds are very small that Max would contract RV-41 if we used protection ... But "very small" is not good enough for me. What if somehow, some way, I passed to Max this horrible scourge that is killing me? How could I ever forgive myself for condemning the man I love to death?'

Tears filled Eponine's eyes. 'We are intimate, of course,' she said. 'In our own safe way ... And Max has never once complained. But I can tell from his eyes that he misses ...'

'All right, now,' they heard Max say on the radio. 'We can see the bottom. It looks like a normal floor, maybe five more metres below us. There are two tunnels leading away, one the size of the smaller tunnel up at your level, and another that is really tiny. We're going on down for a closer inspection.'

The time had come for the explorers to enter the subway. Richard's mobile camera had not found anything substantively new and there was definitely no exit the humans could use on the only level below them in the lair. Richard and Patrick finished a private conversation in which they reviewed, in detail, what the young man was going to do when he returned to the others. Then they rejoined Max, Nicole, and Eponine, and the five of them walked slowly around the platform to the waiting subway.

Eponine had butterflies in her stomach. She remembered a similar feeling, when she was fourteen, just before her first one-woman art exhibit opened at her orphanage in Limoges. She took a deep breath.

'I don't mind saying it,' Eponine said. 'I'm scared.'

'Shit,' said Max, 'that's an understatement ... Say, Richard, how do we know this thing is not going to hurtle over that cliff you told us about, with us inside?'

Richard smiled but didn't reply. They reached the side of the subway. 'All right,' he said, 'since we don't know exactly how this thing is activated, we want to be very careful. We will all enter more or less simultaneously. That will preclude the possibility that the doors will close and the subway will take off when we are not all yet on board.'

Nobody said anything for almost a minute. They lined up four abreast, Max and Eponine on the side closest to the tunnel. 'Now I'm going to count,' Richard said. 'When I say three, we'll all step on together.'

'May I close my eyes?' Max asked with a grin. 'That made it easier for me on roller-coasters when I was a little boy.'

'If you like,' Nicole answered.

They stepped into the subway and each of them grabbed a vertical rod. Nothing happened. Patrick stood staring at them on the other side of the open door. 'Maybe it's waiting for Patrick,' Richard said quietly.

'I don't know,' Max mumbled, 'but if this fucking train doesn't move in a few seconds, I'm going to jump off.'

The door closed slowly only moments after Max's comment. There was time for two breaths each before the subway lurched into motion, accelerating rapidly into the illuminated tunnel.

Patrick waved and followed the subway with his eyes until it disappeared around the first corner. Then he put his rifle on his shoulder and began climbing up the spikes. *Please come back quickly*, he was thinking, *before the uncertainty becomes too much for all of us*.

He returned to their living-level in less than fifteen minutes. After taking a short drink from his water-bottle, he hurried down the tunnel to the museum. While he was walking, he was thinking about what he was going to say to everybody.

Patrick did not even notice that the room was dark when he crossed the threshold. When he entered, however, and the lights came on, he was momentarily disoriented. *I'm not in the right place*, he thought first. *I have taken the wrong tunnel. But no*, his jumbled mind now said, as he glanced quickly around the room, *this must be the room after all. I see a couple of feathers over there in the corner, and one of Nikki 's funny diapers ...*

With each passing second his heart beat faster. *Where are they?* Patrick said to himself, his eyes now darting frantically around the room for a second time. *What could have happened to them?* The longer he stared at the empty walls, carefully recalling all the conversation before he had departed, the more Patrick realised that his sister and friends could not possibly have left of their own volition. Unless there was a note! Patrick spent two minutes searching every nook in the room. There were no messages. *So someone, or something, must have forced them to leave*, he thought.

Patrick tried to think rationally, but it was impossible. His mind kept jumping back and forth between what he ought to do and terrible pictures of what might have happened to the others. At length he concluded that perhaps they had all moved back to the original room, the one his mother and Richard called the photo gallery, maybe because the lights in the museum were malfunctioning or for some other equally trivial reason. Buoyed by this thought, Patrick dashed out into the tunnel.

He reached the photo gallery three minutes later. It was also empty. Patrick sat down against the wall. There were only two directions his companions could have taken. Since Patrick had not seen anyone on his climb, the others must have gone toward the cathedral room and the sealed exit. As he walked down the long corridor, his hand tight around the rifle, Patrick convinced himself that the Nakamura troops had not left the island and that they had somehow broken into the lair and captured everybody else.

Just before he entered the cathedral room, Patrick heard Nikki crying. '*Mom-my, Mom-my*,' she screamed, folowed by a mournful wail. Patrick charged into the large room, not seeing anybody, and then turned up the ramp in the direction of his niece's cry.

On the landing beneath the still-sealed exit was a chaotic scene. In addition to Nikki's continued wailing, Robert Turner was walking around in a daze, his arms outstretched and his eyes upward, repeating over and over, 'No, God, no.' Benjy was quietly sobbing in a corner while Nai was trying, without much success, to comfort her twin sons.

When Nai saw Patrick, she jumped up and ran toward him. 'Oh, Patrick,' she said, tears running from her eyes, 'Ellie has been kidnapped by the octospiders.'

12

t was several hours before Patrick put together a coherent story about what had happened after his exploration party had left the museum room. Nai was still near shock from the experience, Robert could not talk for more than a minute without breaking into tears, and the children and Benjy frequently interrupted, often without making any sense. At first all Patrick knew for certain was that the octospiders had come and not only had kidnapped Ellie, but also had taken away the avians, the manna melons, and the sessile material. Eventually, however, after repeated questioning, Patrick thought he understood most of the details of what had occurred.

Apparently about an hour after the five explorers had departed, which would have been during the time that Richard, Patrick, and the others were down on the subway platform, the humans who had remained in the museum room heard the dragging-brush sound outside the door. When Ellie went out to investigate, she saw octospiders approaching from both directions. She returned to the room with her news and tried to calm Benjy and the children.

When the first octospider appeared in the doorway, all the humans moved as far away as they could, making space for the nine or ten octos who came inside. At first the creatures stood together in a group, their heads bright with the moving, coloured messages that they used to communicate. After a few minutes, one of the octospiders came slightly forward, pointed directly at Ellie by lifting one of its black and gold tentacles off the floor, and then went through a long sequence of colours that was quickly repeated. Ellie guessed (according to Nai – Robert, on the other hand, insisted that somehow Ellie *knew* what the octospider was saying) that the aliens were asking for the manna melons and the sessile material. She retrieved them from the corner and handed them to the lead octospider. It took the objects in three of its tentacles ('a sight to behold,' Robert exclaimed, 'the way they use those trunklike things and the cilia underneath') and passed them to its subordinates.

Ellie and the others thought that the octospiders would then leave, but they were sadly mistaken. The lead octo continued to face Ellie and flash his coloured messages. Another pair of octospiders started moving slowly in the direction of Tammy and Timmy. 'No,' Ellie said. 'No, you can't.'

But it was too late. The pair of octospiders wrapped many arms each around the hatchlings and then, oblivious of the jabbers and shrieks, carried the two avians away. Galileo Watanabe raced out and attacked the octospider that had three of its tentacles wrapped around Timmy. The octo simply used a fourth tentacle to lift the boy off the ground and hand him to one of its colleagues. Galileo was passed among them until he was put down, unhurt, in the far corner of the room. The intruders allowed Nai to rush over to comfort her son.

By this time three or four octospiders, the avians, the melons and the sessile material had all disappeared out into the hallway. There were still six of the aliens in the room. For about ten minutes they talked among themselves. All during this time, according to Robert ('I wasn't paying close attention,' Nai said. 'I was too frightened and too concerned about my children.'), Ellie was watching the coloured messages the octospiders were exchanging. At one point Ellie brought Nikki over to Robert and put their daughter in his arms. 'I think I understand a little of what they're saying,' Ellie said (the quotation is also according to Robert), her face absolutely white. 'They intend to take me as well.'

Again the lead octospider moved toward them and started speaking in colour, seemingly focusing on Ellie. Exactly what happened during the next ten minutes was a subject of considerable argument between Nai and Robert, with Benjy siding mostly with Nai. In Nai's version of the story, Ellie tried to protect everyone else in the room, to make some kind of bargain with the octospiders. With repeated hand gestures as well as speech, Ellie told the aliens that she would go with them, provided that the octospiders guaranteed that all the other humans in the room would be allowed to leave the lair safely.

'Ellie was explicit,' Nai insisted. 'She explained that we were trapped and did not have enough food. Unfortunately, they grabbed her before she was certain that they understood the bargain.'

'You're naïve, Nai,' Robert said, his eyes wild with confusion and pain. 'You don't understand how really sinister those creatures are. They hypnotised Ellie. Yes, they did. During the early part of their visit, when she was watching their colours so carefully. I'm telling you, she was not herself. All that malarkey about guaranteeing everyone safe passage was a subterfuge. She *wanted* to go with them. They altered her personality right there on the spot with those crazy coloured patterns. And nobody saw it but me.'

Patrick discounted Robert's account considerably because Ellie's husband was so distraught. Nai, however, agreed with Robert on two final points: Ellie did not struggle or protest after the first octospider enwrapped her, and before she disappeared from the room, she calmly recited to them a long list of minutiae dealing with the care of Nikki.

'How can anyone in her right mind,' Robert said, 'after having been seized by an alien, calmly rattle off what blankets her daughter hugs while she is sleeping, when Nikki last had a bowel movement, and other such things ... She was obviously hypnotised, or drugged, or something.'

The tale of how everyone happened to be on the landing beneath the sealed exit was relatively straightforward. After the octospiders left with Ellie, Benjy ran out into the corridor, screaming and yelling and vainly attacking the rearguard of the octos. Robert joined him and the two of them followed Ellie and the alien contingent all the way to the cathedral room. The gate was open to the fourth tunnel. One octospider held Benjy and Robert off with four long tentacles while the others departed. The final octospider then locked the gate behind itself.

The subway ride was exhilarating for Max. It reminded him of a trip he had made to a large amusement park outside of Little Rock when he was ten years old. The train was suspended above what looked like a metal tape and touched nothing as it sped through the tunnel. Richard conjectured that it was powered in some way by magnetism.

The subway stopped after about two minutes and the door quickly opened. The four explorers looked out at a plain platform, creamy white in colour, behind which was an archway about three metres high. 'I guess, according to Plan A,' Max said, 'Eponine and I should exit here.'

'Yes,' said Richard. 'Of course, if the subway doesn't move again, then Nicole and I will join you shortly.'

Max took Eponine's hand and stepped gingerly down on the platform. As soon as they were clear of the subway, the door closed. Several seconds later the train sped away.

'Well, isn't this romantic?' Max said after he and Eponine had waved goodbye to Richard and Nicole. 'Here we are, just the two of us, finally all alone.' He put his arms around Eponine and kissed her. 'I just want you to know, Frenchie, that I love you. I have no idea where in the fuck we are, but wherever it is, I'm glad to be here with you.'

Eponine laughed. 'I had a girl-friend at the orphanage whose fantasy was to be all alone on a desert island with a famous French actor named Marcel duBois, who had a mammoth chest and arms like tree trunks. I wonder how she would have felt in this place.' She looked around. 'I guess we're supposed to go under the archway.'

Max shrugged. 'Unless a white rabbit comes along that we can follow into some kind of a hole ...'

On the other side of the archway was a large rectangular room with blue walls. The room was absolutely empty and there was only one exit, through an open doorway into a narrow, illuminated corridor that ran parallel to the subway tunnel. All the walls in this corridor, which continued in both directions for as far as Max and Eponine could see, were the same blue colour as in the room behind the archway.

'Which way do we go?' Max asked.

'In this direction I can see what looks like two doors leading away from the subway,' Eponine said, pointing to her right.

'And there are two more this way as well,' Max said, looking left. 'Why don't we walk to the first doorway, look into it, and then decide on a strategy?'

Arm in arm they walked fifty metres down the blue corridor. What they saw when they came to the next doorway dismayed them. Another identical blue corridor, with occasional doorways along its length, stretched in front of them for many metres.

'Shit,' said Max. 'We are about to enter some kind of a maze ... We damn sure don't want to get lost.'

'So what do you think we should do?' Eponine asked.

'I think ...' Max said, hesitating, 'I think we should smoke a cigarette and talk this over.'

Eponine laughed. 'I couldn't agree with you more,' she said.

They proceeded very carefully. Each time they turned into another blue corridor, Max made marks with Eponine's lipstick on the wall, indicating the entire path back to the room behind the archway. He also insisted that Eponine, who was more adroit with a computer than he was, keep duplicate records on her portable. 'In case something comes along that removes my marks,' Max said.

In the beginning their adventure was fun, and the first two times they backtracked to the archway, just to prove they could do it, Max and Eponine felt a certain sense of accomplishment. But after an hour or so, when every turn kept producing another identical blue scene, their excitement began to wane. At length Max and Eponine stopped, sat down on the floor, and shared another cigarette.

'Now, why would any intelligent creature,' Max said, blowing smoke-rings into the air, 'create a place like this? ... Either we are unwittingly undergoing a test of some kind ...'

'Or there's something here that they don't want anybody to find easily,' Eponine finished. She took the cigarette from Max and inhaled deeply. 'Now, if that's the case,' she continued, 'then there must be some simple code that defines the location of the special place or thing, a code like one of those ancient combination-locks, second right, fourth left, and ...'

'Straight on until morning,' Max interrupted with a grin. He kissed Eponine briefly and then stood up. 'So what we should do is *assume* we're looking for something special and organise our search logically.'

When Eponine was on her feet, she looked at Max with a furrowed brow. 'Just exactly what did that last statement of yours mean?'

'I'm not certain,' Max replied with a laugh, 'but it sure as hell *sounded* intelligent.'

*

Max and Eponine had been walking up and down blue corridors for almost four hours when they decided it was time to eat. They had just started their lunch of Raman food when off to their left, at a full intersection of corridors, they saw something pass. Max jumped to his feet and ran to the intersection. He arrived not more than a few seconds before a tiny vehicle, maybe ten centimetres high, made a right turn into the next nearby hallway. Max scrambled forward and was barely able to see the vehicle disappear under a small archway, cut into the wall of another blue corridor, about twenty metres away.

'Come here,' he yelled at Eponine. 'I've found something.'

Eponine was quickly beside him. The top of the small archway in the wall was only about twenty-five centimetres above the floor, so both of them had to drop down on their knees, and then bend over some more, to see where the vehicle had gone. What they saw first was fifty or sixty tiny creatures, about the size of ants, climbing out of the buslike vehicle and then scattering in all directions.

'What the hell is this?' Max exclaimed.

'Look, Max,' Eponine said excitedly. 'Look carefully ... Those little creatures are octospiders ... You see ... They look just like the one you described to me ...'

'Well, I'll be damned,' Max said. 'You're right ... They must be baby octospiders.'

'I don't think so,' Eponine replied. 'The way they're going into those little hives, or houses, or whatever ... Look, there's a canal of some kind, and a boat ... '

'The camera,' Max shouted. 'Go back and get the camera ... There's an entire miniature city here.'

Max and Eponine had taken off their backpacks and other gear, including Eponine's camera, when they had sat down on the floor to eat. Eponine jumped up and raced back for the camera. Max continued to be fascinated by the complex miniature world he saw on the other side of the archway. A minute later he heard a faint scream and a cold shiver of fear coursed through him.

You stupid idiot, Max thought as he hurried back to where they had been eating. *Never, never leave your rifle.*

He made the last turn and hen stopped sharply. Between Max and where he had been eating with Eponine were five octospiders. One had enwrapped her with three of its tentacles, another had seized Max's rifle. A third octospider was holding Eponine's backpack, into which all her personal items had been neatly placed.

The look on her face was sheer terror. 'Help me, Max ... Please,' Eponine entreated.

Max stepped forward but was blocked by two of the octospiders. One of them sent a stream of coloured bands around its head. 'I don't understand what the fuck you're telling me,' Max shouted in frustration. 'But you must let her go.'

Like a football halfback, Max darted past the first two octospiders and had almost reached Eponine when he felt tentacles coiling around him, pinning his arms to his chest. Struggle was useless. The creature was unbelievably strong.

Three of the octospiders, including the one who had captured Eponine, began to move down the blue corridor away from him. 'Max ... Max,' the terrified Eponine cried. He could do nothing. After another minute Max could no longer hear Eponine's cries.

Max was enwrapped for about ten more minutes before he felt the powerful muscles that were holding him relax. 'So what happens now?' Max said when he was free. 'What are you bastards going to do next?'

One of the octos pointed toward his pack, which was still leaning against the wall where Max had left it. He slumped down beside it and pulled out some food and water. The octospiders talked to each other in colour while Max, who understood very well that he was being guarded, ate a few bites of his food.

These corridors are too narrow, he thought, thinking about trying to escape. *And those goddamn things are too big, especially with their long tentacles. I guess I'll just have to wait for whatever comes next.*

The two octospiders did not move from their post for hours. At length Max fell asleep on the floor between them.

When he woke up, Max was alone. He walked cautiously to the first corner and looked both ways down the blue corridor. He saw nothing. After spending a minute studying the lipstick marks on the wall and adding a few scribbles describing the location of the city of the tiny octospiders, Max returned to the room behind the subway platform.

He had no clear idea of what he should do next. Max spent several minutes wandering the blue corridors and yelling Eponine's name periodically, but his effort was wasted. He eventually decided to sit on the platform and wait for the subway. After more than an hour, Max was almost ready to return to the miniature octospider city when he heard the whoosh of the approaching subway. It was coming from the direction opposite the spiked vertical corridors.

As the subway drew near, he saw Richard and Nicole through the windows. 'Max!' they yelled simultaneously, even before the door opened.

Both Richard and Nicole were wildly excited. 'We have found it,' Richard exclaimed as he jumped down onto the platform. 'A large room, with a dome maybe forty metres high, in rainbow colours ... It's on the other side of the Cylindrical Sea – the subway goes right through the sea in a transparent tunnel ...' He paused as the subway whooshed away.

'It has bathrooms and beds and running water,' Nicole added rapidly.

'And fresh food, believe it or not ... some weird kinds of fruits and vegetables, but they're really great for all ...'

'Where's Eponine?' Nicole said suddenly, interrupting Richard in the
middle of his sentence.

'She's gone,' Max replied tersely.

'Gone?' said Richard. 'But how ... where?'

'Your non-hostile friends have kidnapped her,' Max said drily.

'Whaaat?' said Richard.

Max told the story slowly and accurately, without omitting anything
important. Both Richard and Nicole listened attentively until he was finished.
'They outsmarted us,' Richard commented at the end, shaking his head.

'Not *us*,' Max said in frustration. 'They outsmarted *me*. They lulled Ep and
me into believing we were solving some kind of puzzle in that maze of blue
corridors ... Shit. Just shit.'

'Don't be too hard on yourself,' Nicole said quietly, touching Max on the
shoulder. 'You had no way of knowing ...'

'But what colossal stupidity,' Max said, raising his voice. 'I bring along a
rifle for protection, and where is that rifle when our eight-legged monster
friends show up? Leaning against the fucking wall ...'

'We were initially in a similar place,' Richard said, 'except all our corridors
were red instead of blue. Nicole and I explored for about an hour and then
returned to the platform. The subway picked us up again in ten minutes and
then took us through the Cylindrical Sea.'

'Have you looked for Eponine at all?' Nicole asked.

Max nodded. 'Sort of. I wandered around and shouted her name a few
times.'

'Maybe we should give it another try,' Nicole suggested.

The three friends returned to the world of the blue corridors. When they
came to the first intersection, Max explained his lipstick marks on the wall
to Richard and Nicole. 'I guess we should split up,' Max said. 'That would
probably be a more efficient way to search for her ... Why don't we meet at
the room behind the archway in, say, half an hour?'

At the second corner Max, who was now by himself, found no lipstick
map. Puzzled, he tried to remember if he could possibly have failed to make
a map at every turn – or maybe he never even came this way ... While he
was deep in thought, he felt a hand on his shoulder and nearly jumped out
of his skin.

'Whoa,' said Richard, seeing his friend's face. 'It's only me ... Didn't you
hear me calling your name?'

'No,' said Max, shaking his head.

'I was only two corridors away ... There must be fantastic acoustic attenuation in this place ... Anyway, neither Nicole nor I found one of your maps
when we made our second turn. So we weren't certain ...'

'*Shit*,' said Max emphatically. 'Those clever bastards have cleaned the walls

... Don't you see? They have planned this entire affair from the beginning, and we have done exactly what they expected.'

'But Max,' Richard said, 'there's no way they could have accurately predicted *everything* we were going to do. Even *we* didn't even know our strategy completely. So how could they ...'

'I can't explain it,' Max said. 'But I feel it. Those creatures *deliberately* waited until Eponine and I were eating before they let us see that vehicle. They *knew* we would give chase and that they would have a chance to seize Eponine ... And somehow they were watching us all the time ...'

Even Max agreed that it was useless to search any longer for Eponine in the maze of blue corridors. 'She's almost certainly not here anymore,' he said dejectedly.

While the trio waited on the platform for the subway, Richard and Nicole told Max more details about the large room with the rainbow dome on the southern side of the Cylindrical Sea. 'OK,' said Max when they were finished, 'one connection is clear, even to this Arkansas farm-boy. The rainbow in the dome is obviously connected with the rainbow in the sky that distracted Nakamura's troops. So the rainbow people, whoever they are, don't want us to get captured. And they don't want us to starve to death ... They're probably the ones who built the subway, or at least that makes some sense to me. But what is the relationship between the rainbow people and the octospiders?'

'Before you told me about Eponine's kidnapping,' Richard replied, 'I was virtually certain they were one and the same. Now I don't know. It's difficult to interpret what you experienced as anything other than a hostile act.'

Max laughed. 'Richard, you have such a way with words. Why do you keep giving those ugly bastards the benefit of the doubt? I would have expected it from Nicole, but those octospiders once kept you prisoner for months, sent little creatures up your nose, and probably even tampered with your brain ...'

'We don't know that for sure,' Richard said quietly.

'All right,' said Max. 'But I think you're discounting a lot of evidence ...'

Max stopped when he heard the familiar whoosh. The subway arrived, heading in the direction of the octospider lair. 'Now why is it,' Max said with a trace of sarcasm just before they stepped into the train, 'that this subway always happens to be going in the right direction?'

Patrick had managed eventually to talk Robert and Nai into returning to the museum room. It had not been easy. Both the adults and the children had been severely traumatised by the octospider attack. Robert could not sleep at all, and the twins were plagued by dreams from which they would awaken screaming. By the time Richard, Nicole, and Max showed up, the remaining food was almost gone and Patrick had already started formulating contingency plans.

It was a subdued reunion. Both the kidnappings were discussed at length, leaving all the adults, even Nicole, acutely depressed. There was very little excitement about the rainbow dome in the south. But there was no question about what they should do. Richard summarised their situation succinctly. 'At least there's food under the dome,' he said.

They packed all their belongings in silence. Patrick and Max carried the children down the spiked vertical corridor. The subway appeared soon after everyone was on the platform. It did not stop at either of the two intermediate stations, just as Max had wryly predicted, but instead hurtled on into the transparent tunnel through the Cylindrical Sea. The strange and wonderful sea-creatures on the other sides of the tunnel wall, almost certainly all biots, fascinated the children and reminded Richard of his voyage to New York years earlier, when he had come to look for Nicole.

The vast chamber under the dome at the other end of the subway line was indeed staggering. Although Benjy and the children were more interested initially in the variety of fresh new food that was spread out along a long table on one side of the room, the adults all wandered around in amazement, not only staring at the brilliant colours of the rainbow far above their heads, but also examining all the alcoves off the back of the platform, where bathrooms and individual sleeping-suites were located.

Max marched off the dimensions of the main floor. It was roughly fifty metres wide, and forty metres from the subway platform to the alcove entrances. A few minutes later Patrick came over to talk to Max, who was now standing beside the slot cut into the platform for the subway. Everyone else was discussing the allocation of the sleeping-suites.

'I'm sorry about Eponine,' Patrick said, putting his hand on his friend's shoulder.

Max shrugged. 'In a way it's worse that Ellie is gone. I don't know if Robert or Nikki will ever recover completely.'

The two men stood side by side and stared at the long, dark, empty tunnel. 'You know, Patrick,' Max said grimly, 'I wish I could convince the farmer in me that our troubles are over and that the rainbow people are going to take care of us.'

Kepler came running up with a long vegetable that looked like a green carrot. 'Mr Puckett,' he said, 'you must try this. It's the best.'

Max accepted the little boy's gift and placed the vegetable in his mouth. He took a bite. 'This is good, Kepler,' he said, tousling the boy's hair. 'Thank you very much.'

Kepler raced back to the others. Max chewed the vegetable slowly. 'I always took excellent care of my pigs and chickens,' he said to Patrick. 'They had good food and great living conditions.' Max gestured with his right hand toward the dome and the table laden with food. 'But I also removed the animals, a few at a time, when I was ready to slaughter them or sell them at the market.'

THE RAINBOW CONNECTION

1

Nicole was lying on her back, awake again in the middle of the night. In the dim light of their bedroom she could see Richard sleeping soundlessly beside her. At length she rose quietly and crossed the room, exiting into the large main chamber of their temporary home.

The intelligence that controlled the illumination made it easy for the humans to sleep, always sharply reducing the light shining through the rainbow dome for roughly eight hours in each twenty-four-hour period. During these 'night' intervals, the main chamber underneath the dome was only softly lit, and the individual bedrooms cut into the walls, which had no lights of their own, were dark enough for restful sleep.

For several consecutive nights Nicole had slept fitfully, awakening often from disquieting dreams that she could not quite remember. This particular night, as she struggled unsuccessfully to recapture the images that had disturbed her rest, Nicole walked slowly around the perimeter of the large circular room in which her family and friends spent most of their time. On the far side of the chamber, near the empty subway platform, she stopped and stared into the dark tunnel that led through the Cylindrical Sea.

What is really going on here? Nicole wondered. *What power or intelligence is providing for us now?*

It had been four weeks since the small human contingent had first reached this magnificent cavern constructed underneath the Southern Hemicylinder of Rama. The new living-quarters had obviously been designed, at considerable effort, specifically for them. The bedrooms and the bathrooms in the alcoves were indistinguishable from those in New Eden. The first subway to return after they had arrived at the dome had brought more food and water, plus couches, chairs, and tables to furnish their living areas. The humans had even been supplied with dishes, glasses, and eating utensils. Who, or what, knew enough about everyday human activity to provide such detailed implements?

It is obviously someone who has observed us very carefully, Nicole was thinking. Her mind conjured up an image of The Eagle and she realised that she was engaging in wishful thinking. *But who else could it be? Only the Ramans and the Nodal Intelligence have enough information ...*

Her thoughts were broken by a sound behind her. Nicole turned and saw Max Puckett approaching from across the chamber. 'You can't sleep either?' he said as he drew near.

Nicole shook her head. 'These last few nights I've been having bad dreams.'

'I keep worrying about Eponine,' Max said. 'I can still see the terror in her eyes as she was dragged away.' He turned away in silence and faced the subway tunnel.

And what about you, Ellie? Nicole wondered, feeling a sharp pang of anxiety. *Are you safe with the octospiders? Or is Max correct about them? Are Richard and I deluding ourselves by believing the octos do not intend to harm us?*

'I can't just sit here any longer,' Max said quietly to Nicole. 'I must do something to help Eponine ... Or at least to convince myself I'm trying.'

'But what can you do, Max?' Nicole asked after a short pause.

'Our only contact with the outside world is that damn subway,' Max said. 'The next time it comes to bring us food and water, which should be either tonight or tomorrow, I intend to climb on board and stay there. When it leaves, I will ride until it stops. Then I will try to find an octospider and have myself captured.'

Nicole recognised the desperation in her friend's face. 'You're grasping at straws, Max,' she said softly. 'You will not find an octospider unless they are willing ... Besides, we need you.'

'Shit, Nicole, I'm not needed here.' Max had raised his voice. 'And there's absolutely nothing to *do*, except talk to each other and play with the children. At least in your lair there was always the option of taking a walk in the dark of New York ... Meanwhile, Eponine and Ellie may be dead, or wishing they were. It's time we *did* something ...'

As he was talking, they both saw lights flicker in the distant reaches of the subway tunnel. 'Here it comes again,' Max said. 'I'll help you unload after I finish packing my things.' He ran off in the direction of his bedroom.

Nicole stayed to watch the approaching subway. As always, lights came on in front of the train as it rushed through the tunnel. A few minutes later the subway pulled into its slot, an incision in the circular floor of the room, and stopped abruptly. After the doors opened, Nicole went over to examine the inside of the train.

In addition to four large jugs of water, the subway contained the usual collection of fresh produce that the humans had learned to eat and enjoy, plus a large squeeze-tube of a sticky substance that tasted not unlike a mixture of oranges and honey. *But where is all this food grown?* Nicole asked herself for the hundredth time as she began unloading the food. She recalled the many family discussions of the subject. The consensus conclusion was always that there must be large farms somewhere in the Southern Hemicylinder.

About *who* was feeding them there was less agreement. Richard was certain that they were being fed by the octospiders themselves, primarily because all their supplies passed through territory he considered to be octospider domain.

996

It was hard to argue with his logic. Max agreed that what they were eating was indeed being supplied by the octospiders. However, he attributed sinister motives to all octospider actions. If they were being fed by the octospiders, he asserted, then it was not for humanitarian purposes.

Why would the octospiders be our benefactors? Nicole wondered. *I agree with Max that feeding us is inconsistent with kidnapping Eponine and Ellie ... Isn't it just possible that some other species is involved? One that has chosen to intercede on our behalf?* Despite Richard's gentle ridicule in the privacy of their own bedroom, a part of Nicole clung stubbornly to the hope that there were indeed some 'rainbow people', higher in the development hierarchy than the octospiders, who were somehow interested in the preservation of the vulnerable humans and were ordering the octospiders to feed them.

The contents of the subway always included a surprise. At the back of the car this time were six balls of various sizes, each a different bright colour.

'Look, Max,' Nicole said. He had returned with his pack and was helping her unload. 'They have even sent balls for the children to play with.'

'Wonderful,' Max said sarcastically. 'Now we can all listen to the children argue about which ball belongs to whom.'

When they had finished emptying the subway, Max climbed into the car and sat down on the floor. 'How long will you wait?' Nicole asked.

'As long as it takes,' Max said grimly.

'Did you discuss what you're doing with anyone else?' Nicole inquired.

'Hell, no,' Max replied vehemently. 'Why should I? ... We're not operating a democracy here.' Max leaned forward in his sitting position. 'Sorry, Nicole, but I'm just generally pissed off right now. Eponine has been gone for a month, I've run out of cigarettes, and I'm easily annoyed.' He forced a smile. 'Clyde and Winona used to tell me, when I was acting like this, that I had a burr up my ass.'

'It's all right, Max,' Nicole said. She hugged him briefly before leaving. 'I just hope you'll be safe, wherever you go.'

The subway did not depart. Max stubbornly refused to leave the train, not even to go to the bathroom. His friends brought Max food, water, and the necessary materials for him to keep the train clean. By the end of the third day, the food supply was dwindling rapidly.

'Someone must talk to Max soon,' Robert said to the other adults after the children were asleep. 'It's clear that the subway is not going to move as long as he is on board.'

'I plan to discuss the situation with him in the morning,' Nicole said.

'But we're running out of food *now*,' Robert protested. 'And we don't know how long it takes ...'

'We can ration what we have left,' Richard interrupted, 'and make it last at least two more days ... Look, Robert, we're all tense and tired ... It will be better to talk to Max after a good night's sleep.'

'What do we do if Max does not willingly leave the subway?' Richard asked Nicole when they were alone.

'I don't know,' Nicole said. 'Patrick asked me the same question this afternoon ... He's afraid of what will happen if we try to force Max out of the train ... Patrick says that Max is very tired and very angry.'

Richard was sound asleep long before Nicole had stopped thinking about the best way to approach Max. *A confrontation should be avoided at all costs*, she thought. *That means I should talk to him alone, without any of the others even within earshot ... But what exactly should I say? And how do I respond if Max reacts neagatively?*

When Nicole finally fell asleep, she was exhausted. Again her dreams were troubled. In her first dream, the villa at Beauvois was on fire and she could not find Genevieve. Then the dream venue changed abruptly and Nicole was again seven years old in the Ivory Coast, participating in the Poro ceremony. She was swimming half-naked in the little pond in the centre of the oasis. On the banks of the pond the lioness was on the prowl, searching for the human girl who had disturbed her cub. Nicole submerged to avoid the sharp eyes of the lioness. When she came up for a breath, the lioness was gone, but three octospiders were now patrolling the pond.

'Mother, Mother,' Nicole heard Elite's voice say.

Treading water, Nicole's eyes raced around the perimeter of the pond. 'We're all right, Mother,' Ellie's voice distinctly said. 'Don't worry about us.'

But where was Ellie in the scene? Dreaming, Nicole saw a human silhouette in the woods behind the three octospiders and called out, 'Ellie, is that you, Ellie?'

The dark figure said 'Yes' in Ellie's voice and then walked out to where he could be seen in the moonlight. Nicole recognised the bright white teeth immediately.

'Omeh,' she shouted, a wave of terror running down her spine. 'Omeh ...'

Nicole was awakened by a persistent nudging. Richard was sitting beside her in the bed. 'Are you all right, darling?' he said. 'You were shouting Ellie's name ... and then Omeh.'

'I had another one of my vivid dreams,' Nicole said, rising and putting on her clothes. 'I was told that Eponine and Ellie are safe, wherever they are.'

Nicole finished dressing. 'Where are you going at this hour?' Richard asked.

'To talk to Max,' Nicole replied.

She hurried out of their bedroom and into the main chamber underneath the dome. For some reason, Nicole glanced up at the ceiling just when she entered the chamber. She saw something she had never noticed. There appeared to be a landing or platform cut several metres beneath the dome. *Why have I never seen that landing before?* Nicole wondered as she jogged towards the subway. *Because the shadows are so different during the day? Or because that landing has recently been constructed?*

Max was sleeping in a ball in the corner of the subway. Nicole entered very quietly. A few seconds before she touched him, Max murmured Eponine's name twice. Then his head jerked. 'Yes, dear,' he said quite distinctly.

'Max,' Nicole whispered in his ear. 'Wake up, Max.'

When Max awakened, he looked as if he had seen a ghost. 'I've had the most amazing dream, Max,' Nicole said. 'I now know that Ellie and Eponine are all right ... I've come to ask you to leave the subway, so it can bring us more food. I know how much you want to do something ...'

Nicole stopped. Max had risen to his feet and was preparing to descend from the subway. He still had a completely bewildered expression on his face. 'Let's go,' he said.

'Just like that?' Nicole said, astonished that she had encountered so little resistance.

'Yes,' said Max, stepping down from the train. Only a few moments after Nicole had also left the subway, the doors closed and the vehicle accelerated swiftly away from them.

'When you woke me up,' Max said as Nicole and he watched the subway disappear, 'I was in the middle of a dream. I was talking to Eponine. The instant before I heard your voice she told me you were going to bring me an important message.'

Max shuddered, then laughed and started walking toward the alcoves. 'Of course I don't believe in any of that ESP shit, but it certainly was a remarkable coincidence.'

The subway returned before it was dark again. This time there were two cars on the train. The front car was bright and open and full of food and water as it had always been before. The second car was totally dark. Its doors did not open and its windows were covered.

'Well, well,' Max said, walking to the edge of the subway slot and trying unsuccessfully to open the second car, 'what have we here?'

After the food and water had been unloaded from the front car, the subway did not depart as usual. The humans waited, but the mysterious second car refused to yield its secrets. At length Nicole and her friends decided to proceed with dinner. The conversation during the meal was subdued and full of wary speculation about their intruder.

When little Kepler innocently suggested that perhaps Eponine and Ellie might be inside the dark car, Nicole told the story again of finding Richard in a coma after his long sojourn with the octospiders. A sense of foreboding spread among the humans.

'We should keep a watch throughout the night,' Max suggested after dinner, 'so that there can be no possibility of any kind of devious trick while we're asleep. I'll take the first four-hour shift.'

Patrick and Richard also volunteered to help with the watch. Before going to bed, the whole family, including Benjy and the children, marched to the edge of the platform and stared at the subway. 'What could be inside, Ma-ma?' Benjy asked.

'I don't know, darling,' Nicole answered, hugging her son. 'I really have no idea at all.'

An hour before the lights in the dome brightened the next morning, Richard and Nicole were awakened by Patrick and Max. 'Come,' Max said to them excitedly, 'you've got to see this ...'

In the centre of the main chamber were four large black segmented creatures that were antlike in shape and structure. To each of their three body segments were attached both a pair of legs and another pair of prehensile appendages that were, as the humans watched, busily stacking material in piles. The creatures were a wonder to behold. Each of the long, snake like 'arms' had the versatility of an elephant's trunk, with one additional (and useful) capability. When any particular arm was not being used, either to lift something or to balance a weight being carried by its opposite member, that arm would withdraw into its 'case' in the side of the being, where it would remain tightly coiled until needed again. Thus, when the alien beings were not performing any task, their arms were out of sight and did not impede their movement.

The stunned humans continued to watch with rapt attention as the bizarre creatures, almost two metres long and a metre tall, quickly emptied the contents of the dark subway car, briefly surveyed their stacks, and then departed with the train. As soon as the aliens had disappeared, Max, Patrick, Richard, and Nicole walked over to examine the piles. There were objects of all shapes and sizes in the stacks, but the dominant single part was a long flat piece that resembled a conventional stair-step.

'If I had to guess,' Richard said, picking up a small item that was shaped like a fountain pen, 'I would say that this stuff is between cement and steel in bearing-strength.'

'But what is it for, Uncle Richard?' Patrick asked.

'They are going to build something, I would assume.'

'And who are they?' Max said.

Richard shrugged and shook his head. 'These creatures that just left struck me as advanced domestic animals, capable of complicated sequential tasks but not real thinking.'

'So they are not Mama's rainbow people?' Patrick said.

'Certainly not,' Nicole answered with a wan smile.

The rest of the humans, including the children, were thoroughly briefed about the new creatures during breakfast. All the adults agreed that if the aliens returned, as expected, there should be no interference with whatever task they were doing, unless it was determined that the creatures' activities constituted some kind of serious threat.

When the subway pulled into its slot three hours later, two of the new beings clambered out of the front car and hurried into the centre of the main chamber. Each was carrying a small pot, into which it dipped one of its arms frequently as it made bright red markings on the floor. Eventually these red lines circumscribed a region containing the subway platform, all the material that had been placed in stacks, and about half the area of the room.

Moments later, another dozen of the huge animals with the trunklike appendages poured forth from the two subway cars, several carrying on their backs large and heavy curvilinear structures. They were followed by two octospiders with unusually bright colours streaming around their spherical heads. The two octospiders sauntered into the centre of the chamber, where they inspected the piles of material and then ordered the antlike creatures to begin some kind of construction task.

'So the plot thickens,' Max said to Patrick as the two men watched together from a distance. 'It is indeed our octospider friends who are in control here, but just what in the world are they doing?'

'Who knows?' Patrick replied, mesmerised by what he was seeing.

'Look, Nicole,' Richard said a few minutes later, 'over by that large stack. That ant thing is definitely reading the octospider's colours.'

'So what do we do now?' Nicole said in a low voice.

'I guess we just watch and wait,' Richard answered.

All the construction activity took place inside the red lines that had been painted on the floor. Several hours later, after another subway load of the large curvilinear components was delivered and unloaded, the overall shape of what was being built became clear. On one side of the room a vertical cylinder, four metres in diameter, was being erected. Its top segment was eventually positioned even with the bottom of the dome. Inside the cylinder, the stair-steps were placed so that they wound up and around the centre of the structure.

The work continued unabated for thirty-six hours. The octospider architects supervised the giant ants with the versatile arms. The only significant break in the activity came when Kepler and Galileo, who tired of watching the alien construction after several hours, inadvertently allowed a ball to bounce across the red paint and into one of the antlike creatures. All work halted instantly and an octospider hurried over, both to retrieve the ball and seemingly to reassure the worker. With an adroit motion of two of its tentacles, the octospider threw the ball back to the children and the work resumed.

Everyone except Max and Nicole was asleep when the aliens finished their staircase, picked up their residual materials, and departed in the subway. Max walked over to the cylinder and stuck his head inside. 'Pretty impressive,' he said coyly, 'but what is it for?'

'Come on, Max,' Nicole replied, 'be serious. It's obvious that we are supposed to climb the stairs.'

'Shit, Nicole,' Max said. 'I know that. But *why? Why* do those octospiders want us to climb out of here? ... You know, they've manipulated us since the moment we entered their lair. They have kidnapped Eponine and Ellie, moved us into the Southern Hemicylinder, and refused to let me go back to New York ... What would happen if we decided not to go along with their plan?'

Nicole stared at her friend. 'Max, would it be all right with you if we postponed this conversation until we're all together in the morning? ... I'm very tired.'

'Certainly,' Max said. 'But tell that husband of yours I think we should do something completely unpredictable, like maybe even walking back through the tunnel to the octospider lair. I have an uneasy feeling about where all this is leading us.'

'We don't know all the answers, Max,' Nicole answered wearily, 'but I really don't see where we have much choice except to comply with their wishes as long as the octospiders control our food and water supply ... Maybe in this situation we must simply have some faith.'

'Faith?' said Max. 'That's just another word for not thinking.' He walked back over to the cylinder. 'And this amazing staircase could be taking us to hell as easily as heaven.'

2

In the morning the subway returned with new food and water. After it had departed and everyone had inspected the enclosed cylindrical structure, Max argued that the time had come for the humans to show that they were 'tired of being pushed around' by the octospiders. Max suggested that he, and anyone who wanted to go with him, should take the single remaining rifle and trek back through the tunnel under the Cylindrical Sea.

'But what exactly are you trying to accomplish?' Richard asked.

'I want them to capture me and take me to where they are holding Eponine and Ellie. Then I will know for certain they are all right. Nicole's dreams are really not sufficient ...'

'But Max,' Richard countered, 'your plan is not logical. Think about it. Even assuming that you are not run over by the subway while you're in the tunnel, how are you going to explain what you want to the octospiders?'

'I was hoping for some help from you, Richard,' Max said. 'I remember how you and Nicole communicated with the avians. Maybe you could use your computer skills to make a graphics picture of Eponine for me. Then I could show it to the octospiders, using my monitor ...'

Nicole sensed the entreaty in Max's voice. She touched Richard's hand. 'Why not?' she said. 'Someone could explore where the staircase leads while you create computer pictures of Eponine and Ellie for Max.'

'I would like to go with Max,' Robert Turner said suddenly. 'If there's any chance at all of finding Ellie, then I want to take it ... Nikki will be all right as long as she is here with her grandparents.'

Although Richard and Nicole were both concerned about what they were hearing, they chose not to express their anxieties in front of everyone else. Patrick was asked to climb the staircase and do some minimal exploring while Richard was performing his computer-graphics wizardry. Max and Robert went to their bedrooms to prepare for their trek. Meanwhile, Nicole and Nai were left alone with Benjy and the children in the main chamber.

'You think it's a mistake for Max and Robert to go back, don't you, Nicole?' Nai's question was asked, as always, in the gentle tone that characterised her personality.

'Yes,' said Nicole. 'But I'm not certain that my thoughts are relevant in this situation ... Both men feel bereft and frustrated. It is important to them that some action be taken that is aimed at reuniting them with their partners ... Even if the action doesn't make a lot of logical sense.'

'What do you think will happen to them?' Nai asked.

'I don't know,' Nicole replied. 'But I don't think Max and Robert will find Eponine and Ellie. In my opinion, each woman was kidnapped for a specific reason ... Although I have no idea *what* those reasons were, I believe the octospiders will not harm Eponine and Ellie and will eventually return them both to us.'

'You are very trusting,' Nai said.

'Not really,' said Nicole. 'My experiences with the octospiders lead me to believe that we are dealing with a species with a highly developed sense of morality ... I admit that the kidnappings do not *seem* to be in concert with that picture – and I don't fault either Max or Robert for coming to their own, very different conclusions about the octospiders – but I would bet that we will, in the long run, understand even the purpose of the kidnappings.'

'In the meantime,' Nai said, 'we face a difficult situation. If Max and Robert both leave and never return ...'

'I know,' said Nicole, 'but there's nothing we can really do about it. They have decided, Max especially, that they must make some kind of statement now. It's a little old-fashioned, macho even, but understandable. The rest of us must accommodate their needs, even if in our opinion their actions seem capricious.'

Patrick returned in less than an hour. He reported that the staircase ended on a landing that narrowed into a hallway behind the dome. That hallway eventually led to another, smaller staircase which climbed another ten metres and came out inside an igloo-shaped hut about fifty metres south of the cliff overlooking the Cylindrical Sea.

'And what was it like, outside in Rama?' Richard asked.

'The same as in the north,' Patrick answered. 'Cold, about five degrees Celsius I would estimate, and dark, with only traces of background light ... The igloo hut is warm and well lighted. There are beds and a single bathroom, certainly designed for us, but altogether not much living-space.'

'Are there no other corridors or passages?' Max asked.

'No,' said Patrick, shaking his head.

'Uncle Rich-ard has made great pic-tures of El-lie and Ep-o-nine,' Benjy said to his brother at this juncture. 'You should see them.'

Max pushed two buttons on his portable computer and an excellent rendition of Eponine's face appeared. 'Richard didn't have her eyes right the first time,' Max said, 'but I straightened him out ... Ellie was a much easier picture for him.'

'So are you all ready to go, then?' Patrick asked Max.

'Just about. We're going to wait until morning so that the light from this room will illuminate more of the tunnel.'

'How long do you think it will take to reach the other side?'

'An hour or so at a brisk pace,' Max said. 'I hope Robert can push himself that hard.'

'And what will you do if you hear a subway coming?' Patrick said.

'There's not much we can do,' Max replied with a shrug. 'We've already surveyed the tunnel and there's very little clearance. Your Uncle Richard says we must rely on the subway's "fault protection system".'

There was an argument at dinner about the rifle. Both Richard and Nicole were strongly opposed to Max's taking the rifle, not because they particularly wanted the weapon to stay with the rest of the family, but rather because they feared an 'incident' that might ultimately affect everyone. Richard was not very tactful with his remarks and angered Max.

'So, Mr Expert,' Max replied at one point, 'would you mind telling me just how you *know* that my rifle will be "useless" in finding Eponine.'

'Max,' Richard said stridently, 'the octospiders must ...'

'Let me, please, dear,' Nicole interceded. 'Max,' she said in a softer tone, 'I cannot imagine a scenario in which the rifle is a valuable asset for you on this trip. If you need it in any way to deal with the octospiders, then they must be hostile, and the fates of both Eponine and Ellie would have been decided long ago ... We just don't want ...'

'What if we encounter some other hostile creatures, non-octospiders,' Max said stubbornly, 'and we must protect ourselves? ... Or what if I need to use the rifle to signal Robert in some way? ... I can think of many situations ...'

The group was unable to resolve the issue. Richard was still frustrated when Nicole and he were undressing for bed. 'Can't Max understand,' Richard said, 'that the real reason he wants to have a gun is to give himself a feeling of security? And a false feeling at that? What if he does something hotheaded and the octospiders withdraw our food and water?'

'We can't worry about that now, Richard,' Nicole said. 'At this stage I don't think there's anything we can do except ask Max to be careful and remind him that he is our representative. No amount of talking is going to change his mind.'

'Then maybe we should call for a vote about whether or not he should take the rifle,' Richard said. 'And show Max that everyone is opposed to what he is doing.'

'My instinct tells me,' Nicole replied quickly, 'that any kind of vote would be absolutely the wrong way to handle Max. He already senses what everyone is feeling. A co-ordinated censure would alienate Max and could make an "incident" more likely to occur ... No, darling, in this case we must just hope that nothing untoward happens.'

Richard was quiet for almost a minute. 'I guess you're right,' he said finally. 'As usual ... Good night, Nicole.'

'Good night, Richard,' Nicole answered.

'We will wait here together for forty-eight hours,' Richard was saying to Max and Robert. 'After that time some of us may begin moving our things up to the igloo.'

'All right,' said Max, tightening the straps on his backpack. He grinned. 'And don't worry. I won't shoot one of your octospider friends unless it's absolutely necessary.' He turned to Robert. 'Well, mi amigo, are you ready for an adventure?'

Robert did not look comfortable wearing his backpack. He bent down awkwardly and picked up his daughter. 'Daddy will only be gone a short while, Nikki,' he said. 'Nonni and Boobah will both be staying here with you.'

Just before the two men departed, Galileo came running across the chamber with a small pack on his back. 'I'm going too,' he shouted. 'I want to fight the octospiders.'

Everyone laughed while Nai explained to Galileo why he couldn't go with Max and Robert. Patrick softened the little boy's disappointment by telling him that he could be the first one up the staircase when the family moved to the igloo.

The two men marched quickly into the tunnel. For the first few hundred metres they walked in silence, entertained by the fascinating sea-creatures on the other side of the transparent plastic or glass. Twice Max had to slow down to wait for Robert, who was in poor physical shape. The two men did not encounter any subways. After slightly more than an hour, their flashlight beams illuminated the first station on the other side of the Cylindrical Sea. When Max and Robert were within fifty metres of the station platform, all the lights switched on and they could see where they were going.

'Richard and Nicole visited this place,' Max said. 'Behind the archway there is a kind of atrium, and then a maze of red corridors.'

'What will we do here?' Robert asked. He was out of his element and completely content to follow Max's lead.

'I haven't decided exactly,' Max said. 'I guess we'll explore awhile and hope we find some octospiders.'

Much to Max's surprise, beyond the station platform, in the middle of the atrium floor, was a large blue painted circle, out of which ran a thick blue line that turned right at the beginning of the maze of red corridors. 'Richard and Nicole never mentioned a blue line,' Max said to Robert.

'It's obviously an idiot-proof set of directions,' Robert said. He laughed nervously. 'Following the thick blue line is as easy as following the yellow brick road.'

They walked into the first corridor. The blue line in the centre of the floor stretched a hundred metres in front of them and then turned left at a distant intersection.

'You think we should follow the line, don't you?' Max said to Robert.

'Why not?' Robert answered, taking a few steps along the corridor.

'It's *too* obvious,' said Max, as much to himself as to his companion. He clutched his rifle and followed Robert. 'Say,' he spoke again after they made their first left turn, 'you don't think this line was put here specifically for us, do you?'

'No,' Robert replied, stopping for a moment. 'How could anyone have known we were coming?'

'That's just what I asked myself,' Max mumbled.

Max and Robert walked on in silence, making three more turns following the blue line before coming to an archway that rose a metre and a half above the floor. They bent down and entered a large room with dark red ceilings and walls. The thick blue line ended in a large blue circle that was in the middle of the room.

Less than a second after they were both standing in the blue circle, the lights in the room went out. A crude, silent motion picture, whose image was about one metre square, immediately appeared on the wall directly in front of Max and Robert. In the centre of the image were Eponine and Eilie, both dressed in strange, smocklike yellow outfits. They were talking to each other and to some unknown person or thing who was off to the right, but of course Max and Robert could not hear anything they were saying. A few moments later, the two women moved a few metres to their right, past an octospider, and appeared beside a strange fat animal, vaguely resembling a cow, that had a flat white underbelly. Ellie held a snakelike pen against the white surface, squeezed it multiple times, and wrote the following message: *Don't worry. We're fine.* Both women smiled and the image abruptly terminated one second later.

As Max and Robert stood in the room thunderstruck, the ninety-second motion picture repeated twice in its entirety. By the time of the second repetition, the men had managed to collect themselves enough that they were able to pay careful attention to the details. Lights flooded the red room again when the movie was finished.

'Jesus Christ,' Max said, shaking his head.

Robert was joyful. 'She's alive!' he exclaimed. 'Ellie is still alive.'

'If we can believe what we've seen,' Max said.

'Come on, Max,' Robert said several seconds later. 'What possible reason could the octospiders have for making a film like that to deceive us? Wouldn't it be much easier for them to do nothing?'

'I don't know,' Max replied. 'But you answer a question for me. How did they know that the two of us, coming here together at this time, were worried about Ellie and Eponine? There are only two possible explanations. Either they have been watching everything we have been doing and saying since we entered their lair, *or* someone ...'

'... from our group has been providing information to the octospiders. Max, surely you don't think for an instant that either Richard or Nicole ...'

'No, of course not,' Max interrupted. 'But I'm having a damn hard time understanding how we could have been observed so carefully. We have not seen any suggestion of eavesdropping devices ... Unless some pretty sophisticated transmitters are planted *on* us, or *in* us, none of this makes any sense.'

'But how could they have done that without our knowledge?'

'Beats the shit out of me,' Max replied, bending down to walk through the archway. He stood up in the red corridor on the opposite side of the arch. 'Now, unless I miss my guess, that damn subway will be waiting for us when we arrive at the station and we'll be expected to return peacefully to the others. Everything is just too nice and neat.'

Max was correct. The subway was parked with its door open when Robert and he turned into the atrium from the maze of red corridors. Max stopped. He had a wild gleam in his eyes,

'I'm not going to board the damn train,' he said in a low voice.

'What are you going to do?' asked Robert, a little frightened.

'I'm going to go back into the maze,' Max said. He clutched his rifle, spun around, and raced back into the corridor. Max turned away from the blue line and ran about fifty metres before the first octospider appeared in front of him. It was quickly joined by several more octos, which spread across the corridor from one side to the other. They began to move toward Max.

Max stopped, looked at the advancing octospiders, and then glanced behind him. At the far end of the corridor another group of octospiders was moving in his direction.

'Wait just a damn minute,' Max shouted. 'I have something to say. You guys must understand at least part of our language or you could never have figured out that we were coming here ... I'm not satisfied. I want *proof* that Eponine is alive ...'

The octospiders, their heads rippling with colour, were almost upon him. A wave of fear swept through Max and he fired the rifle in the air as a warning. No more than two seconds later he felt a sharp sting in the back of his neck. Max collapsed immediately on the floor.

Robert, whose indecision had kept him standing in the station, raced across the platform at the sound of the gunfire. When he arrived in the red corridor, he saw two octospiders lifting Max off the floor. Robert stood aside as the extraterrestrials carried Max into the subway and gently deposited him in the corner of the car. The octospiders then gestured at the open subway door and Robert climbed inside. Less than ten minutes later the two men had returned to the chamber underneath the rainbow dome.

3

Max did not awaken for ten hours. During that time both Robert and Nicole examined him thoroughly and found no evidence of any wound or injury. Meanwhile, Robert repeatedly told the story of their adventure, except of course what happened during the critical minute when Max was by himself in the red corridor.

Most of the questions from the family were about what Robert and Max had seen in the motion picture. Were there any indications of stress in Ellie or Eponine, suggesting that perhaps they might have been coerced into making the film? Did they appear to have lost any weight? Did they look rested?

'I believe we now know much more about the nature of our hosts,' Richard said near the end of the family's second and more lengthy discussion of Robert's story. 'First and foremost, it is clear that the octospiders, or whatever species is in charge here, both observe us regularly and are able to understand our conversations. There is no other possible explanation for the fact that the film showed to Max and Robert featured Ellie and Eponine ...

'Second, their technological level, at least where motion pictures are concerned, is either several hundred years behind ours, or, if Robert is right when he insists that there could not have been a projecting device either in the room or behind the wall, they are so far advanced that their technology appears like magic to us. Thirdly ...'

'But Uncle Richard,' Patrick interrupted. 'Why didn't the motion picture have sound? Wouldn't it have been much easier for Eponine and Ellie just to *say* they were all right? Isn't it more likely that the octospiders are deaf than it is that their technology has not developed beyond silent movies?'

'What an interesting idea, Patrick,' Richard replied. 'That's something we have never even considered. And of course they don't need to hear to communicate ...'

'Creatures that have spent most of their evolutionary lives deep in the ocean are often deaf,' Nicole offered. 'Their primary sensory needs for survival are at other wavelengths, and with only a limited number of cells available for both the sensors and their processing, the ability to hear simply never develops.'

'I worked with the hearing impaired in Thailand,' Nai added, 'and I was fascinated by the fact that being unable to hear is not a significant drawback in an advanced culture. The sign language of the deaf has extraordinary range and is quite complex ... Humans on Earth no longer need to hear to hunt or to escape animals that might prey on them ... The octospider language of colours is more than adequate for communication ...'

'Hold on just a minute,' Robert said. 'Aren't we overlooking some pretty strong evidence that the octospiders *can* hear? How could they have known that Max and I were going out to find Ellie and Eponine if they didn't over-hear our conversation?'

There was silence for several seconds. 'They might have had the two women translate what was being said,' Richard suggested.

'But that would require two unlikely events,' Patrick said. 'First, if the octo-spiders are deaf, why would they have sophisticated miniaturised equipment available that would record sounds at all? Second, having Eponine and Ellie translate what we said for the octospiders implies a level of communication interaction that could hardly have developed in a month's time ... No, in my opinion, the octos probably determined the purpose of Max and Robert's trip on the basis of visual evidence – the portraits of the two women on the portable computer monitors.'

'Bravo,' shouted Richard. 'That's excellent thinking ...'

'Are you guys going to yak about this shit all night long?' Max said as he walked into the middle of the group.

Everyone jumped up. 'Are you all right?' Nicole asked.

'Sure,' said Max. 'I even feel well rested ...'

'Tell us what happened,' Robert interrupted. 'I heard your rifle fire, but by the time I came around the corner, a pair of octospiders was already carrying your body.'

'I don't know myself,' Max said. 'Just before I passed out I felt a stinging hot pain in the back of my neck ... That was it ... One of the octos behind me must have hit me with their equivalent of a tranquillising dart.'

Max rubbed the back of his neck. Nicole came over to inspect. 'I cannot even find a small hole now,' she said. 'They must use very thin darts.'

Max glanced at Robert. 'I don't suppose you retrieved the rifle.'

'I'm sorry, Max,' Robert said. 'I never even thought about it until after we were on the train.'

Max looked at his friends. 'Well, guys, I want you to know my rebellion is over. I'm convinced we cannot fight these creatures. So we might as well try to follow their plan.'

Nicole put a hand on her friend's shoulder. 'This is the new Max Puckett,' she said with a smile.

'I may be stubborn,' Max replied with a smile of his own, 'but I don't believe I'm stupid.'

'I don't think we're all supposed to move into Patrick's igloo,' Max said the next morning after another subway had come and replenished their food and water.

'Why do you say that?' Richard asked. 'Look at the evidence. The igloo was definitely designed for human habitation. Why else would they have built the staircase?'

'It just doesn't make sense,' Max replied. 'Especially for the children. There's not enough room to live for any period of time ... I think the igloo is some kind of way-station, a cabin in the woods, if you like.'

Nicole tried to imagine the ten of them living in the cramped quarters that Patrick had described. 'I can see your point, Max,' she said, 'but what do you suggest?'

'Why don't a few of us return to the igloo and look around carefully? Patrick's quick reconnoitre may have missed something ... Anyway, whatever we're supposed to do should be obvious. It wouldn't be like the octospiders, or whatever is guiding us, to leave us in uncertainty.'

Richard, Max, and Patrick were selected for the scouting mission. Their departure was delayed, however, so that Patrick could keep his promise to Galileo. Patrick followed the five-year-old up the long, winding staircase and down the hallway to the bottom of the second stairs. The boy was too exhausted to climb any more. In fact, when they were coming down from the dome, the little boy's legs gave out and Patrick had to carry Galileo the final twelve metres of the descent.

'Can you make it up a second time?' Richard asked Patrick.

'I believe so,' said Patrick, adjusting his pack.

'At least now he won't be waiting for us old farts all the time,' Max said with a grin.

The three men stopped to admire the view from the landing at the top of the cylindrical stairs. 'Sometimes,' Max said, as he took a long look at the magnificent colours of the rainbow strips in the dome only a few metres above him, 'I think that everything that has happened to me since I boarded the Pinta is a dream ... How do pigs, chickens, and even Arkansas fit into this picture? ... It's just too much.'

'It must be difficult,' Patrick said while they were walking along the hallway, 'to reconcile all this with your normal life on Earth. But consider my situation. I was born on an extraterrestrial spacecraft headed for an artificial world located near the star Sirius. I have spent more than half my life asleep. I have no idea what normal means ...'

'Shit, Patrick,' Max said, putting his arm around the young man, 'if I were you I would be as crazy as a bedbug.'

Later, when they were climbing the second stairs, Max stopped and turned to Richard below him. 'I hope you realise, Wakefield,' he said in a warm tone, 'that I'm just an ornery bastard and didn't mean anything personal during our arguments the last few days.'

Richard smiled. 'I understand, Max. I also know that I'm as arrogant as you are ornery ... I will accept your oblique apology if you will accept mine.'

Max feigned indignation. 'That wasn't a damn apology,' he said, walking up to the next step.

The igloo hut was just as Patrick had described it. The three men pulled on their jackets and prepared to go outside. Richard, who was the first one out the door, saw the other igloo before Max and Patrick had even taken their first breath of the bracing Rama air.

'That other igloo wasn't there, Uncle Richard,' Patrick insisted. 'I walked completely around the area.'

The second igloo, which was almost exactly one-tenth the size of the larger hut, was about thirty metres farther away from the cliff bordering the Cylindrical Sea. It was glowing in the Rama dark. As the men started walking toward it, the door of the smaller igloo opened and two tiny human figures came out. The figures were about twenty centimetres high and were illuminated from the inside.

'What the hell ...?' Max exclaimed.

'Look,' said Patrick excitedly, 'it's Mother and Uncle Richard!'

The two figures turned south in the darkness, away from the cliff and the sea. Richard, Max, and Patrick scrambled up beside them for a better view. The figures were dressed in exactly the same clothes that Richard and Nicole had worn the previous day. The attention to detail was extraordinary. The hair, faces, skin colouring – even the shape and colour of Richard's beard – were a perfect match for the Wakefields. The figures were also wearing backpacks.

Max stooped down to pick up the figure of Nicole but received an electrical jolt when he touched it. The figure turned in Max's direction and shook her head emphatically. The men followed the pair for another hundred metres and then stopped.

'There's not much doubt about what we're supposed to do next,' Richard said.

'Nope,' said Max. 'It looks as if you and Nicole are being summoned.'

The next afternoon Richard and Nicole packed several days' worth of food and water into their packs and said goodbye to their extended family. Nikki had slept between them the night before and was especially tearful when her grandparents departed.

It was quite a climb up the staircase. 'I should have taken the stairs more slowly,' Nicole said, breathing hard as she and Richard stood on the landing beneath the dome and waved one final time to everybody. Nicole could feel her heart beating arhythmically in her chest. She waited patiently for the palpitations to subside.

Richard was also out of breath. 'We're not as young as we were those many years ago in New York,' he said after a short silence. He smiled and put his arms around Nicole. 'Are you ready to continue our adventure?' he asked.

Nicole nodded. They walked slowly, hand in hand, down the long hallway. When they reached the second stairs, Nicole turned to Richard. 'Darling,' she said with sudden intensity, 'isn't it great to be alone again, just the two of us, even if it's only for a few hours? ... I love all the others, but it's a pain being so damn responsible all the time ...'

Richard laughed easily. 'It's a role you chose, Nicole,' he said, 'not one that was forced on you.'

He leaned down to kiss her on the cheek. Nicole turned her face toward him and kissed him strongly on the lips.

'Were you suggesting with that kiss,' Richard asked immediately with a wide grin, 'that we should spend tonight in the igloo and begin our journey tomorrow?'

'I think that you have been reading my mind, Mr Wakefield,' Nicole said with a coquettish smile. 'Actually, I was thinking how much fun it would be to imagine tonight that we were young lovers again ...' She laughed. 'At least our imaginations should still work all right.'

When they were three hundred metres south of the two igloos, Richard and Nicole could no longer see anything except whatever they illuminated with their flashlights. Although the floor beneath them, mostly dirt with an occasional collection of small rocks, was generally smooth, from time to time one or both of them would stumble when not paying careful attention.

'This may be a very long and tiring walk in the dark,' Nicole said when they stopped for some water.

'And cold too,' Richard said, taking a drink. 'Are you warm enough?'

'As long as we're moving,' Nicole said. She stretched out her arms and adjusted her backpack.

It was almost an hour before they saw a light in the sky to the south. The light was moving toward them and was growing larger.

'What do you think it is?' Nicole asked.

'Maybe the Blue Fairy?' Richard replied. 'When you wish upon a star, makes no difference who you are ...'

Nicole laughed. 'You're impossible,' she said.

'After last night,' Richard said as the light continued to move in their direction, 'I feel like a boy again.'

Nicole chuckled and shook her head. They held hands in silence while the ball of light continued to grow in size. A minute later it stopped twenty to thirty metres in front of them and about twenty metres above their heads. Richard and Nicole switched off their flashlights, for they could now see the terrain around them for a distance of more than a hundred metres.

Richard shaded his eyes and tried to determine the source of the illumination, but the light was too bright. He could not look directly at it. 'Whatever it is,' Nicole said after they were walking again, 'it appears to know where we're supposed to go.'

Two hours later, Richard and Nicole encountered a path heading to the southwest, with fields of growing plants on either side of the path. When they stopped for lunch, they wandered into the fields and discovered that one of their staple foods under the dome, a vegetable with a taste similar to a green bean but with the physical appearance of a yellow squash, was the principal crop being grown. These vegetables were interspersed with rows of a short, bright red plant that they had never seen before. Richard pulled one of the red plants out of the ground and dropped it immediately when the green, leathery sphere that had been beneath the surface began to writhe at the bottom of its red stalk. When it hit the ground, the creature scooted the few centimetres back to its original hole and buried its green sphere again in the same place.

Richard laughed. 'I guess I'll think twice before I do something like that again.'

'Look over there,' Nicole said a moment later. 'Isn't that one of the animals that built the staircase?'

They moved down the path and then back into the field itself for a better view. Coming towards them was indeed one of the large, antlike creatures with the six long arms. It was harvesting the vegetables with amazing efficiency, handling the three rows on either side of where its main body was located. Each arm, or trunk, was stripping the vegetables in a single row and stacking them in piles that were between the rows and about two metres apart. It was an astonishing sight, the six arms all operating simultaneously on different tasks, and at different distances from the main body.

When the creature reached the path, its arms quickly recoiled. It then moved six rows down the line and entered the field going in the opposite direction. The field was being harvested from south to north, so when Richard and Nicole started walking again, they passed through the part of the field that the giant ant thing had already finished. There they saw swift rodentlike creatures picking up the scattered piles and scampering away with them to the west.

Richard and Nicole came to several intersections while they were walking along the path among the fields, and each time the hovering light indicated which route they should take. The fields extended for many kilometres. They came upon several different crops, but Richard and Nicole, who were becoming hungry and weary, no longer stopped to examine each new vegetable.

At length they reached a flat open area covered with soft dirt. The light above them circled three times and then hovered over the centre of the area. 'I'm guessing that this is where we're supposed to spend the night,' Richard said.

'Gladly,' said Nicole, accepting Richard's help in removing her backpack. 'I don't think I'll have any trouble sleeping, even on this hard ground.'

They ate dinner and found a comfortable spot where they could sleep nestled together. When Richard and Nicole were both in the twilight zone between waking and sleeping, the light above them began to dim a little and then drop in altitude.

'Look,' Richard whispered, 'it's going to land.'

Nicole opened her eyes and watched as the light, continuing to dim, made a graceful arc and landed on the opposite side of the open area. It was still glowing slightly even after it was already on the ground. Although Richard and Nicole could not see the creature very well, they could tell that it was long and skinny and had wings more than twice as large as its body.

'It's a giant firefly,' Richard exclaimed when they could no longer see its outline.

'**B**iology for lights, biology for farm and construction equipment – do you have the impression that our octospider friends, or perhaps whatever is above them in some amazing symbiotic hierarchy, are the great biologists of the galaxy?'

'I don't know, Richard,' Nicole said as she finished her breakfast. 'But it certainly looks as if their technological evolution has followed a markedly different path from ours.'

They had both watched with wonder as the giant firefly, upon hearing their first movements after sleeping, had ignited itself and taken its accustomed hovering position above them. A few minutes later, a second, similar creature had approached them from the south. The two lights now combined to provide local illumination that was equivalent to daylight in New Eden.

Richard and Nicole had both slept well and were quite refreshed. Their two guides led them along paths through several more kilometres of fields, including one that was characterised by grasses over three metres tall. One hundred metres after making a sharp left turn in the tall grasses, Richard and Nicole found themselves at the edge of a vast array of shallow water-tanks that stretched in front of them as far as they could see.

They walked to the left for several minutes, until they came to what Richard properly identified as the north-east corner of the array. The system consisted of a series of long, narrow, rectangular tanks made out of a grey metallic alloy. Each of the individual tanks in the array was about twenty metres wide in the east–west direction and as much as several hundred metres long. The tanks were one metre high and were three-fourths filled with a liquid that appeared to be water. At the four corners of each narrow rectangle were bright, thick red cylinders, perhaps two metres tall, that were topped with white spheres.

Richard and Nicole walked the full hundred and sixty metres from east to west, examining each tank and all eight of the thick cylindrical poles marking where adjacent tanks shared common sides. They saw nothing in the tanks except the water. 'So is this some kind of purification plant?' Nicole asked.

'I doubt it,' Richard answered. They stopped at the western edge. 'Look at that mass of small, detailed parts affixed to the inside wall of this tank, just in front of the cylinder ... I would guess that those are complicated electronic components of some kind. There would be no need for all that in a simple water-purification system.'

Nicole looked askance at her husband. 'Come on, Richard, that's quite a leap of faith. How can you possibly claim to know the function of a bunch of three-dimensional squiggles on the inside of an alien water-tank?'

'I said I was guessing,' Richard responded with a laugh. 'I was only trying to make the point that it looks too complex to be a place to purify water.'

The guide lights above them were urging them to the south. The second bank of narrow tanks also contained nothing but water; however, when they reached the third set of rectangular tanks and cylindrical poles, Richard and Nicole discovered that the water was full of tiny fuzzy balls of many colours. Richard rolled up his sleeve and stuck his hand into the water, pulling out several hundred of the objects.

'Those are eggs,' Nicole said firmly. 'I know that fact with the same certainty that you knew those little gadgets on the insides of the tank wall were electronic components.'

Richard laughed again. 'Look,' he said, putting his mound of little objects in front of Nicole's eyes, 'there are really only five different kinds, if you study them closely.'

'Five different kinds of *what*?' Nicole asked.

The egglike things filled the entire length of the third set of tanks. By the time Richard and Nicole were approaching the fourth row of cylinders and another set of tanks, which were several more hundred metres to the south, both of them were growing tired. 'If we don't see anything new here,' she said, 'how about lunch?'

'You're on,' he answered.

But they could discern something new already when they were still fifty metres away from the fourth row of tanks. A square robot vehicle, perhaps thirty centimetres in length and width and another ten centimetres high, was moving swiftly back and forth between the cylindrical poles. 'I *knew* those were tracks for some kind of vehicle,' Nicole said, kidding Richard.

Richard was too fascinated to respond. In addition to the scurrying robot, which made a full cycle across the array from east to west every three minutes or so, there were several more wonders to observe. Each of the individual tanks here was further subdivided into two long pieces by a mesh fence parallel to the walls that was only slightly higher than the water level. On one side of the mesh was an absolute swarm of tiny swimming creatures in five different colours. On the other side, gleaming circles, resembling sand dollars, were scattered the complete length of the tank. The fence was positioned so that three-fourths of the tank volume was available to the gleaming circles, giving them far more room to manoeuvre than the densely packed swimmers.

Richard and Nicole bent over to study the activity. The sand dollars were moving in all directions. Because the water was teeming with so many creatures and so much activity, it took several minutes for Richard and Nicole to perceive the common pattern. At irregular intervals each of the sand dollars would propel itself over to the mesh fence using the whiplike cilia underneath its flat body and then, while anchored to the fence, would use another pair of cilia to capture a tiny swimmer and pull it through one of the holes in the mesh. While the sand dollar was against the fence, its light would dim. If it stayed long enough and caught several of the swimmers to eat, then its gleam would fade altogether.

'Watch what happens now when it leaves the fence,' Richard said to Nicole, pointing out one specific sand dollar just underneath them. 'As it swims along with its companions, its light will be slowly replenished.'

Richard hurried back to the nearest cylindrical pole and bent down on his knees on the ground. He dug into the soil with one of the tools from his pack. 'There's much more to this system underground,' he said excitedly. 'I bet this entire array is part of a gigantic power generator.'

He took three large, measured steps to the south, noted his position carefully, and leaned over the tank to count the sand dollars in the region between the cylindrical pole and him. It was a difficult count because of the constant motion of the gleaming circles.

'Roughly three hundred of them in three metres of tank length, making approximately twenty-five thousand per complete tank, or two hundred thousand in a complete row,' Richard said.

'Are you assuming, then,' Nicole asked, 'that these cylindrical poles are some sort of storage system? Like batteries?'

'Probably,' said Richard. 'What a fabulous idea! Find a living creature that generates electricity internally. Force it to give up its accumulated charge in order to eat. What could be better?'

'And that robot vehicle, moving back and forth between the poles, what is its purpose?'

'I would guess it's a monitor of some kind,' Richard replied.

Richard and Nicole ate their lunch and then finished their inspection of the putative power-plant. Altogether there were eight columns and eight rows in the array, for a total of sixty-four tanks. Only twenty were active at the time. 'Plenty of excess capacity,' Richard commented. 'Their engineers clearly understand the concepts of growth and margin.'

The giant fireflies now headed due east, along what appeared to be some kind of major highway. Twice Richard and Nicole encountered small herds of the large antlike creatures going in the opposite direction, but there were no interactions. 'Are those creatures intelligent enough to operate without supervision?' Nicole asked Richard. 'Or are we just not being allowed to see whatever beings give them instructions?'

'That's an interesting question,' Richard said. 'Remember how quickly the octospider came over to the ant thing when it was struck by the ball? Perhaps they have some limited intelligence, but cannot function well in new or unknown environments.'

'Like some people we have known,' Nicole said with a laugh.

Their long march to the east ended when their two guiding lights hovered over a large dirt field just off the road. The field was empty except for what looked at a distance like forty football goal-posts covered with ivy, arranged in five rows of eight posts each.

'Will you check the guidebook, please?' Richard said. 'It's easier to understand what we're seeing if we read about it first.'

Nicole smiled. 'We really are being given some kind of tour, aren't we? Why do you suppose our hosts want us to see all this?'

Richard was silent for a moment. 'I'm fairly certain that it's the octospiders who are the lords of all this territory,' he said finally, 'or at least they are the dominant species in a complicated hierarchy ... Whoever it was that picked us personally for this tour must believe that informing us about their capabilities will make future interactions easier.'

'But if it really is the octospiders,' Nicole said, 'why didn't they simply kidnap all of us as they did Ellie and Eponine?'

'I don't know,' Richard replied. 'Maybe their sense of morality is far more complicated than we have imagined.'

Both of the giant fireflies were dancing in the air over the collection of ivy-covered goal-posts. 'I think our tour guides are becoming impatient,' Nicole said.

If Richard and Nicole had not been so fatigued from their two days of arduous hiking, and if they had not already seen so many fabulous sights in this alien world that existed in the Southern Hemicylinder of Rama, they would have been both captivated and overwhelmed by the complex symbiosis they discovered in the next several hours.

What was all over the goal-posts was not ivy at all. What appeared to be individual leaves from a distance were in reality little cone-shaped nests, made of thousands of tiny creatures that resembled aphids. The creatures were glued together to form the nest by the sweet, sticky, honeylike substance the humans had enjoyed eating under the dome. The alien aphids manufactured large quantities of the substance as part of their normal diurnal activity.

During the time that Richard and Nicole were watching, convoys of snout-nosed beetles, who lived in mounds several metres high surrounding the entire enclave, burst from their homes every forty minutes or so and crawled all over the posts, harvesting the excess goo from the nests. The beetle creatures, which were about ten centimetres long when empty, swelled to three or four times their normal size before completing their harvest cycle and regurgitating the contents of their swollen bodies in sunken vats at the base of the posts.

Richard and Nicole did not talk much while they were watching the activity. The overall biological system displayed in front of them was both intricate and wonderful – another example of the astonishing advancements in symbiosis that had been made by their hosts. 'I bet,' said a weary Richard as he and Nicole prepared to sleep not far from one of the beetle mounds, 'that if we wait long enough, some beast of burden will show up to lift the vats of this honey, or whatever it is, out of the ground and then carry them to another site.'

As they were lying side by side on the dirt, they observed the two fireflies landing in the distance. Then it was suddenly dark. 'I don't believe all this just happened,' Nicole said. 'Not on another planet. Not anywhere. Natural evolution simply does not result in the kind of interspecies harmony we have witnessed the last two days.'

'What are you suggesting?' Richard asked. 'That all these creatures were somehow designed, like machines, to perform their functions?'

'It is the only explanation I can accept,' Nicole said, 'The octospiders, or somebody, must have reached the level of advancement where they can manipulate the genes to produce a plant or animal that does exactly what they want. *Why* do those beetle things deposit the honey substance in the vats? What is their biological pay-off for that action?'

'They must be compensated in some way that we have not yet discovered,' Richard said.

'Of course,' Nicole said. 'And behind that compensation is some incredible biological systems architect or engineer who is tuning all the interrelationships, not only so that each species is happy, however we choose to define that word, but also so that the architects themselves reap some profit – namely, food in the form of excess honey ... Now, do you believe that kind of optimization could possibly take place without some sophisticated genetic engineering involved?'

Richard was silent for almost a minute. 'Imagine,' he finally said slowly, 'a master biological engineer sitting at a keyboard, designing a living organism to meet certain system specifications ... It is a mind-boggling concept.'

Once more the beetles swarmed out of their mounds, barely missing the sleeping humans as they rushed for the goal-posts and their harvesting task. Nicole watched the beetles until they disappeared in the dark. Then she yawned and curled up on her side. *We humans have entered a new era*, she thought before she fell asleep. *In the future all history will be noted as* bc, *'before contact', and* ac, *'after contact'. For from that first moment when we knew unambiguously that simple chemicals had risen to consciousness and intelligence somewhere else in the vastness of our universe, the past history of our species became only an isolated paradigm, one small and relatively insignificant fragment in the infinite tapestry that depicts the astonishing variety of sentient life.*

*

After breakfast the next morning Richard and Nicole had a brief discussion about their dwindling food supply and then decided to take some of the honey substance from one of the vats. 'I guess if we're not supposed to do this,' Nicole said, glancing around while she was filling a small container, 'then some alien policeman will come along and stop us.'

Their guide lights moved directly south at first, leading Richard and Nicole toward a thick forest of very tall trees that extended as far as they could see in the east–west direction. The fireflies turned to the right and moved parallel to the edge of the trees. The forest on their left was dark and foreboding. From time to time Richard and Nicole heard strange, loud sounds coming from its interior.

Once Richard stopped and walked over to where the thick growth began. Between the trees were many smaller plants, with large leaves in green, red, and brown, as well as several different kinds of vine that laced together the middle and upper branches of the trees. Richard jumped back when he heard a sharp howl that sounded as if it were only a few metres away. His eyes searched the forest, but he could not find the source of the howl.

'There's something weird about this forest,' he said, turning back to Nicole. 'It feels out of place, as if it doesn't belong here.'

For over an hour the fireflies continued in a westerly direction. The bizarre sounds became more frequent as Richard and Nicole trudged slowly along in silence. *Richard is right*, Nicole thought wearily at one point. She was looking at the structure and order of the fields on her right and comparing them with the undisciplined growth on her left. *There is something different and disquieting about this forest.*

They took a brief rest in the middle of the morning. Richard calculated that they had already walked more than five kilometres since waking. Nicole asked for some of the fresh honey that was in Richard's backpack.

'My feet hurt,' she said, after eating and then taking a long drink of water. 'And my legs never stopped aching last night ... I hope we reach wherever we're going before too much longer.'

'I'm tired too,' Richard said. 'But we're not doing badly for a couple in their early sixties.'

'I feel older than that right now,' Nicole said. She stood up and stretched. 'You know, our hearts must be almost ninety. They may not have done much work all those years we were asleep, but they had to keep pumping nevertheless.'

As they were talking, a strange little spherical animal with a solitary eye, white fuzzy hair, and a dozen spindly legs darted out of the nearby forest and snatched the container of honey. The creature and the food were gone in an instant.

'What was that?' Nicole asked, startled.

'Something with a sweet tooth,' Richard said. He stared off into the forest, where the animal had disappeared. 'That is definitely another world over there.'

Half an hour later, the pair of fireflies moved off to the left and hovered over a path leading into the forest. The path was five metres wide and was lined on both sides by dense growth. Nicole's intuition told her not to follow the fireflies, but she said nothing. Her apprehension increased when, after Richard and she had taken a couple of steps into the forest, noises erupted from the trees all around them. They stopped, held hands, and listened.

'It sounds like birds, monkeys, and frogs,' Richard said.

'They must be signalling our presence,' Nicole said. She turned around and looked behind her. 'Are you sure we're doing the right thing?'

Richard pointed at the lights in front of them. 'We've been following those big bugs for two and a half days. It doesn't make much sense to lose faith in them now.'

They started walking down the path again. The caws, howls, and croaking sounds accompanied them. From time to time the kind of foliage on both sides of them would change a little, but it always remained dense and dark.

'There must be a group of alien gardeners,' Richard said at one point, 'who work the area around this path several times a week. Look how perfectly trimmed all the bushes and trees are ... They don't protrude one iota into the airspace above our heads.'

'Richard,' Nicole said a little later, 'if the sounds we are hearing are coming from alien animals, why don't we ever see one? Not a single creature has ever come out on the path.' She bent down and examined the dirt at her feet. 'And there is no visible evidence here of any life, not now and not ever ... Not even an ant ...'

'We must be walking on a magical path,' Richard said with a grin. 'Perhaps it leads to a gingerbread house and a wicked old witch ... Let us sing, Gretel, and perhaps we will feel better.'

The path, which had been absolutely straight for the first kilometre or so, began to meander. Because of its wandering, the sounds of the forest creatures surrounded Richard and Nicole. Richard sang popular songs from his adolescent years in England. Nicole joined him some of the time, when she knew the song, but mostly she spent her energy trying to contain her growing anxiety. She told herself not to think about what an easy target they would be for any large alien animal that might be lurking in the forest.

Richard suddenly stopped. He pulled two deep draughts of air through his nose into his lungs. 'Do you smell that?' he asked Nicole.

She sniffed the air. 'Yes,' she said, 'I do ... It's a little like gardenias.'

'Only much much better,' Richard said. 'It's positively divine.'

Ahead of them, the path turned abruptly to the right. At the turn there was a large bush beside the path that was covered with huge yellow flowers, the first flowers they had seen since they entered the forest. Each individual flower was the size of a basketball. As Richard and Nicole drew nearer to the bush, the enticing smell intensified.

Richard could not restrain himself. Before Nicole could say anything, he stepped the few metres off the path, stuck his face in one of the huge flowers, and inhaled deeply. The smell was magnificent. Meanwhile, one of the two fireflies flew back in their direction and began zigging and zagging in the sky over their heads.

'I don't think our guides approved of your sortie,' Nicole said.

'Probably not,' Richard replied, returning to the path. 'But it was worth it.'

More flowers, of all shapes, sizes, and colours, began to appear on both sides of the path. Neither of them had ever seen such a profusion of colour. At the same time, the sounds they had been hearing abated. A little later, when Richard and Nicole were in the middle of the flower region, the noises disappeared altogether.

The path narrowed to a couple of metres, barely wide enough for them to walk side by side and not brush the plants on which the flowers were growing. Richard left the trail several times to inspect and/or smell one of the amazing flowers. Each excursion caused the fireflies to swoop back in their direction. Despite Richard's enthusiasm for his trips into the forest, Nicole heeded the guides and remained on the path.

Richard was about eight metres off to the left, trying to obtain a closer look at a gigantic flower that looked like an Oriental carpet, when he disappeared suddenly from view. 'Ouch,' Nicole heard him yell as he fell to the ground.

'Are you all right?' she said immediately.

'Yes,' he said. 'I just tripped over some vines and fell into a bunch of thorns ... The bush surrounding me has red leaves as well as tiny, bizarre flowers that look like bullets ... They smell like cinnamon, incidentally.'

'Do you need any help?' Nicole asked.

'Nope ... I'll just climb out of here in a jiffy.'

Nicole glanced up and noticed that one of the two fireflies was racing off in the distance. *Now, what's that all about?* she was wondering when she heard Richard again.

'I may need some help after all,' he said. 'I seem to be stuck.'

Nicole took a cautious step off the path. The remaining firefly went crazy, zooming down almost into her face. Nicole was temporarily blinded.

'Don't come over here, Nicole,' Richard said abruptly a few seconds later. 'Unless I am losing my mind, I believe this plant is preparing to eat me.'

'*What?*' Nicole said, now frightened. 'Are you serious?' She waited impatiently for her eyes to recover from the overdose of light.

'Yes, I am,' Richard said. 'Get back on the path ... This bizarre bush has wrapped yellow tendrils around my arms and legs ... some crawling bugs are already drinking the blood caused by the thorns ... and there is an opening in the bush, toward which I am slowly being pulled, that looks like a distant cousin of some of the more unpleasant mouths I have seen in zoos ... I can even see some teeth.'

Nicole could hear the panic in Richard's voice. She took another step in his direction, but again the firefly blinded her.

'I can't see anything,' she yelled. 'Richard, are you still there?'

'Yes,' he answered. 'But I don't know for how much longer.'

They heard the sound of animals moving quickly through the forest, along with a high-pitched whine. Suddenly three octospiders appeared, brandishing peculiar long, skinny weapons. The octos fired a liquid spray at the carnivorous bush and within seconds the bush released Richard. The aggressive plant immediately hid its mouth again behind its many branches.

Richard stumbled over and hugged Nicole. They both yelled 'Thank you' as the trio of octospiders vanished into the forest as swiftly as they had appeared. Neither Richard nor Nicole noticed that the two fireflies were again hovering over their heads.

Nicole examined Richard carefully but found nothing except cuts and scratches. 'I think I'll stay on the path awhile,' he said, smiling wanly.

'That's probably not a bad idea,' Nicole replied.

They talked about what had happened as they continued to walk through the forest. Richard was still shaken. 'The branches close to my left shoulder pulled apart,' he said, 'and there was this hole, initially about the size of a baseball. But as the wave action of the tendrils carried me in that direction, the hole grew larger.' He shuddered. 'That's when I saw the little teeth, ringing the circumference. I had just started thinking about how it would feel to be eaten when our friends the octospiders arrived.'

'So what's going on here?' Nicole said a little later. They had left the flower region and were again surrounded by trees and jungle growth and intermittent animal noises.

'Damned if I know,' Richard replied.

The forest ended abruptly just as Richard and Nicole were becoming unbearably hungry. They stepped out upon an empty plain. In front of them, perhaps two kilometres away, a great green dome filled their view.

'Now what is ...'

'It's the Emerald City, darling,' Richard said. 'Certainly you recognise it from the old movie ... And inside is the Wizard of Oz, ready to grant all our wishes.'

Nicole smiled and kissed her husband. 'The wizard was a fake, you know,' she said. 'He didn't really have any power.'

'That's open to some question,' Richard said with a grin.

While they were talking, the two lights that had been guiding them sped away toward the green dome, leaving Richard and Nicole in near darkness. They pulled their flashlights out of their packs. 'Something tells me we're near the end of our hike,' Richard said, striding across the ground in the direction of the Emerald City.

They could see the gates through their binoculars from a distance of more than a kilometre. Both Richard and Nicole were becoming quite excited. 'Do you think that's the home city of the octospiders?' Nicole asked.

'Yes, indeed,' Richard said. 'It must be quite a place. The top of that green dome is at least three hundred metres above the ground. I would guess that the area underneath exceeds ten square kilometres ...'

'Richard,' Nicole asked when they were only about six hundred metres away, 'what is our plan? Are we just going to walk up and knock on the gate?'

'Why not?' Richard answered, his pace quickening.

When they were two hundred metres from the gate, it opened and three figures emerged. Richard and Nicole heard a yell as one of the figures began moving rapidly toward them. Richard stopped and used his binoculars again. 'It's Ellie,' he shouted. 'And Eponine ... They're with an octospider.'

Nicole had already dropped her pack and was jogging across the plain. She grabbed her beloved daughter in her arms and lifted her off the ground with the strength of her embrace, 'Oh, Ellie, Ellie,' she said, the tears cascading down her cheeks.

5

'This is our friend Archie ... He has been a big help to us while we have been staying here ... Archie, meet my mother and father.'

The octospider responded with a sequence that began with a brilliant crimson and was followed by a teal green, a lavender, two different yellows (one a saffron and the other a lemon, tending toward chartreuse), and a final purple. The band of colours ran completely around the octospider's spherical head and then disappeared back into the left side of the slit formed by the two long, parallel indentations in the middle of its face.

'Archie says it's a pleasure to meet you, especially after hearing so much about you,' Ellie said.

'You can read their colours?' Nicole asked, quite shocked.

'Ellie's great,' said Eponine. 'She's picked up their language very quickly.'

'But how do you speak to them?' Nicole asked.

'Their eyesight is incredibly keen,' Ellie replied, 'and they are remarkably intelligent ... Archie and a dozen others have already learned to read lips ... But we can talk about all that later, Mother. First tell me about Nikki and Robert. Are they all right?'

'Your daughter grows more adorable every day; and she misses you terribly ... But I'm afraid Robert has never completely recovered. He still blames himself for not having protected you better ...'

The octospider Archie politely followed the personal conversation for several minutes before tapping Ellie on the shoulder and then reminding her that her parents were probably tired and cold.

'Thanks, Archie,' Ellie said. 'Okay, here's the plan. The two of you are to come inside the city for at least tonight and tomorrow – a kind of hotel suite has been set up just inside the gate for the four of us – and the day after tomorrow, or whenever you are properly rested, we will all return to the others. Archie will go with us.'

'Why didn't the three of you simply come to where we were in the first place?' Richard said after a brief silence.

'I asked the same question, Dad ... and never did receive what I considered a satisfactory answer ...'

The bands of colour on Archie's head interrupted what Ellie was saying. 'All right,' she said to the octospider before turning back to her parents. 'Archie says the octos wanted you two especially to have a clear idea of what they are all about – anyway, we can discuss all this after we settle in our suite.'

The great gates of the Emerald City were thrown open when the four humans and their octospider companion were about ten metres away. Richard and Nicole were unprepared for the overwhelming variety of strange sights that greeted their eyes as they entered the city. Directly in front of them was a broad avenue, with continuous low structures on either side, leading to a tall, pink and blue, pyramid-shaped building several hundred metres in the distance.

Richard and Nicole were virtually in a trance when they took their initial steps into the octospider city. Neither of them would ever forget that incredible first moment. They were surrounded by a kaleidoscope of colour. Every element of the city, including the streets, the buildings, the unexplained decorations that lined the avenue, the plants in the garden (if that's indeed what they were), and the wide range of animal creatures that seemed to be scurrying in all directions, was emblazoned with bright colours. A group of four large worms, or snakes, resembling wriggling candy canes except much more profusely coloured, were coiled just inside the gate on the ground to Richard and Nicole's left. They had their heads lifted high, apparently straining to get a view of the alien visitors. Bright red and yellow animals with eight legs and lobsterlike claws were carrying thick green rods across an intersection fifty metres in front of Richard and Nicole.

Of course there were dozens, maybe hundreds of octo-spiders, all of whom had come to the gate area to catch a glimpse of the two newest humans to visit their city. They were sitting in groups in front of the buildings, standing beside the avenue, even walking on the rooftops. And they were all talking simultaneously in their bright bands of colour, accenting the static decorations of the street scene with dynamic bursts of various hues.

Nicole looked around, glancing only for a moment at each of the bizarre creatures staring at her. Then she leaned her head back and gazed at the green dome far above her head. Some kind of thin, flexible ribbing could be seen in isolated spots, but it was mostly covered over by a thick green canopy.

'The ceiling is all growing vines and other plants, along with the insectlike animals that harvest the useful fruits and flowers,' she heard Ellie say beside her. 'It is a complete living ecosystem that has the additional advantage of being an excellent covering for the city, sealing out the Raman cold and atmosphere. After the gates are closed, you'll see how comfortable the temperatures are normally inside the city.'

Scattered around under the dome were about twenty very bright sources of light, considerably larger than the individual fireflies that had guided Richard and Nicole through the octospider domain. Nicole tried to study one of the lights, but quickly gave up because it was too bright for her eyes. *Unless I miss my guess,* she thought, *all this illumination is provided by clusters of those fireflies that led us here.*

Was it fatigue or excitement or a combination of both that caused Nicole to lose her equilibrium? Whatever the reason, while she was gazing at the green dome above her, Nicole began to feel as if she were spinning around. She stumbled and reached out a hand for Richard. The burst of adrenaline that accompanied her dizziness and sudden fear caused her heart rate to surge.

'What is it, Mother?' Ellie said, alarmed at her mother's pallor.

'Nothing,' said Nicole, breathing slowly and deliberately. 'It's nothing ... I was just dizzy for a moment.'

Nicole glanced down at the ground to steady herself. The street was paved with brightly coloured squares that looked like ceramics. Sitting on the street no more than fifty centimetres in front of her were three of the strangest creatures that Nicole had ever seen. They were about the size of basketballs. Their hemispherical tops were royal blue undulating material that resembled, in some ways, both human brains and the part of a jellyfish that floats on top of the water. In the centre of this constantly moving mass was a dark, round hole, out of which were poking two long, thin antennae, perhaps twenty centimetres long, with ganglia or knots roughly two or three centimetres apart. When Nicole involuntarily recoiled, stepping back because she felt instinctively threatened by these bizarre animals, their antennae spun around and the trio scampered quickly to the side of the avenue.

Nicole glanced quickly around her. Bands of colour were streaming around the heads of all the octospiders she could see. Nicole knew that they were dissecting her latest reaction. She suddenly felt naked, lost, and completely overwhelmed. From somewhere deep inside her came an ancient and powerful signal of distress. Nicole was afraid that she was about to scream.

'Ellie,' she said quietly, 'I think I've had enough for today ... Can we go inside soon?'

Ellie took her mother by the arm and guided her toward a doorway in the second structure to the right of the avenue. 'The octos have been working day and night to convert these quarters. I hope they are satisfactory.'

Nicole continued to stare fixedly at the octospider street scene, but what she was seeing was no longer penetrating deep into her cognitive mind. *This is a dream,* she thought, as a group of thin green creatures that looked like bowling-balls on stilts walked through her field of view. *There cannot really be a place like this anywhere.*

'I too was feeling a little overwrought,' Richard was saying. 'We had that scare in the forest. And we have walked a long way in three days, especially for old folks ... It's not surprising that your mother became disorientated – that scene outside was weird.'

'Before he left,' Ellie said, 'Archie apologised in three different ways. He tried to explain that they had permitted free access to the gate area, thinking that you and Mother would be fascinated ... He hadn't thought about the fact that it might be a little too much ...'

Nicole sat up slowly in her bed. 'Don't worry, Ellie,' she said. 'I haven't really become that fragile ... I guess I just wasn't prepared, especially after so much exercise and emotion.'

'So would you like to rest some more, Mother, or would you prefer to have something to eat?'

'I'm fine, really,' Nicole reiterated. 'Let's go on with whatever you have planned ... By the way, Eponine,' she said, turning to the Frenchwoman, who had said very little since their initial greetings outside the city, 'I must apologise for our rudeness. Richard and I have been so busy talking with Ellie and seeing everything ... I forgot to tell you that Max sends his love. He made me promise that if I saw you, I would tell you that he misses you terribly.'

'Thanks, Nicole,' Eponine replied. 'I have thought of Max and the rest of you every day since the octospiders brought us here.'

'Have you been learning the octospider language too, like Ellie?' Nicole asked.

'No,' Eponine answered slowly, 'I've been doing something altogether different ...' She glanced around for Ellie, who had stepped out momentarily, presumably to arrange dinner. 'In fact,' Eponine continued, 'I had hardly seen Ellie for two weeks until we started making plans for your arrival.'

There was a strange silence for several seconds. 'Have you and Ellie been prisoners here?' Richard then asked in a low voice. 'And have you figured out why they kidnapped you?'

'No, not exactly,' Eponine replied. She stood up in the small room. 'Ellie,' she shouted, 'are you out there? Your father is asking questions ...'

'Just a minute,' they all heard Ellie yell. A few moments later she returned to the room with the octospider Archie behind her. Ellie read the look on her father's face. 'Archie is all right,' Ellie said. 'And we agreed that when we told you everything, he could be here ... To explain and clarify and maybe answer questions that we can't ...'

The octospider sat down among the humans and there was another temporary silence. 'Why do I have the feeling that this entire scene has been rehearsed?' Richard asked at length.

A worried Nicole leaned forward and took her daughter's hand. 'There's not any bad news, is there, Ellie? You did tell us that you would be coming back with us ...'

'No, Mother,' Ellie said. 'There are just a few things that Eponine and I want to tell you ... Ep, why don't you go first?'

Bands of colour were streaming around Archie's head as the octospider, who had obviously been following the conversation closely, changed his position to be more directly opposite Eponine. Ellie watched the bands carefully.

'What is he ... or *it* saying?' Nicole asked. She was still stunned by her daughter's proficiency with the alien language.

'"It" would be strictly proper, I guess,' Ellie said with a short laugh. 'At least that's what Archie told me when I explained pronouns ... But Ep and I have been using "he" and "him" when we refer to both Archie and Dr Blue ... Anyway, Archie wants us to inform you that both Eponine and I have been cared for very well, that we have not suffered in any way, and that we were only kidnapped by the octospiders because they had not been able to figure out how to establish a non-hostile and communicative interaction with us ...'

'Kidnapping is not exactly the proper way to begin,' Richard interrupted.

'I have explained all that to Archie and the others, Daddy,' Ellie continued, 'which is why he wants me to set the record straight now ... They *have* treated us magnificently, and I have seen no indication that their species is even capable of hostile acts ...'

'All right,' Richard said, 'your mother and I understand the gist of this preamble ...'

They were delayed momentarily by some comments in colour from Archie. After Ellie explained to the octospider the meanings of 'gist' and 'preamble,' she looked across at her parents. 'Their intelligence is really staggering,' Ellie said. 'Archie has never asked me the meaning of any word more than once.'

'When I arrived here,' Eponine began, 'Ellie was just beginning to understand the octospider language ... At first everything was terribly confusing ... But after a few days Ellie and I understood why the octospiders had kidnapped me.'

'We talked about it an entire evening,' Ellie interjected. 'We were both flabbergasted ... We couldn't figure out how they could possibly have known ...'

'Known *what*? Richard said. 'I'm sorry, ladies, but I'm having trouble following ...'

'They knew that I had RV-41,' Eponine said. 'And both Archie and Dr Blue, he's another octospider, a physician – we call him Dr Blue because when he's talking his cobalt blue band spills way outside the normal boundaries ...'

'Wait a minute,' Nicole said now, shaking her head vigorously. 'Let me get this straight. You're telling us the octospiders *knew* that Eponine had the RV-41 virus. How can that be possible?'

Archie went through a long colour sequence that Ellie asked him to repeat. 'He says that they have been monitoring all our activities very closely ever since we left New Eden. The octos deduced from our actions, he says, that Eponine had an incurable disease of some kind.'

Richard began to pace. 'That is one of the most amazing statements that I have ever heard,' he said with passion. He turned toward the wall, temporarily lost in his thoughts. Archie reminded Ellie that he could not understand anything unless Richard was facing him. At length Richard spun around. 'How could they *possibly* ... look, Ellie, aren't the octospiders deaf?'

When Ellie nodded affirmatively, Richard and Nicole learned their first little bit of the octospider language. Archie flashed a broad crimson band-(indicating the following sentence would be declarative – a broad purple band, Ellie explained, always precedes an interrogative sentence), followed by a magnificent aquamarine.

'Well, if they're deaf,' Richard exclaimed, 'how in the world could they have figured out that you had RV-41, unless they are masters of mind reading, or have a record of every ... no, even then it's not possible.'

He sat back down. There was another period of silence. 'Should I continue?' Eponine asked eventually. Richard nodded.

'As I was saying, Dr Blue and Archie explained to Ellie and me that they were really very advanced in biology and medicine ... and if we would try to co-operate with them, they would see if perhaps they had techniques that could cure me ... Assuming, of course, that I would be willing to submit to all the procedures ...'

'When we asked them *why* they wanted to cure Eponine,' Ellie said, 'Dr Blue told us that the octospiders were trying to make a grand gesture of friendship, something that would pave the way for harmonious interactions between our two species.'

Richard and Nicole were both absolutely astounded by what they were hearing. They looked at each other in disbelief as Ellie continued.

'Because I was still a beginner at the language,' Ellie said, 'it was very difficult to communicate what we knew about RV-41. Eventually, after many long, intense language sessions, we were able to tell the octospiders what we knew.'

'Both Ellie and I tried to remember everything Robert had ever said about the disease. All along, Dr Blue, Archie, and a couple of the other octospiders were around us. They never took a single note that we could see. But we never, ever told them the same information twice.'

'In fact,' Ellie added, 'whenever we inadvertently repeated ourselves, they reminded us that we had told them *that* before.'

'About three weeks ago,' Eponine continued, 'the octospiders informed us that their information-gathering process was over and that they were now ready to subject me to some tests. They explained that the tests might be painful at times and were extraordinary by human standards.'

'Most of the tests,' Ellie said, 'involved inserting living creatures, some microscopic and some that Eponine could actually see, into her body – either by injection ...'

'Or by allowing the creatures to enter through my, uh, I guess the best word would be orifices.'

Archie interrupted here and asked for the meanings of 'inadvertently' and 'orifices.' While Ellie was explaining, Nicole leaned over to Richard. 'Sound familiar?' she asked.

Richard nodded. 'But I never had any kind of interaction, at least not that I can remember ... I was isolated ...'

'I have experienced some weird feelings in my life,' Eponine was saying, 'but nothing quite like I felt the day five or six tiny worms, no bigger than a pin, crawled into the lower part of my body.' She shivered. 'I told myself that if I survived the days of having my insides invaded, I would never again complain about any physical discomfort.'

'Did you believe that the octospiders were going to be able to cure you?' Nicole asked.

'Not at first,' Eponine replied. 'But as the days passed, I began to think that it was possible. I certainly could see that they possessed medical capabilities altogether different from ours ... And I had the feeling they were making progress ...

'Then one day, after the testing was over, Ellie showed up in my room – throughout this time I was kept somewhere else in the city, probably in their equivalent of a hospital – and told me that the octospiders had isolated the RV-41 virus and understood how it operated on its host, namely, me. They had Ellie tell me then that they were going to insert a "biological agent" into my system which would seek out the RV-41 virus and destroy it completely. The agent would not be able to reduce the damage already done by the virus, which they assured me through Ellie was not that severe, but it would absolutely cleanse my system of RV-41.'

'I was told to explain to Eponine also,' Ellie said, 'that there could be some side effects from the agent. They didn't know exactly what to expect, for of course they had never used the agent in humans before, but their "models" predicted nausea and possibly headaches.'

'They were correct about the nausea,' Eponine said. 'I threw up every three or four hours for a couple of days. At the end of that time, Dr Blue, Archie, Ellie, and the other octospiders all gathered beside my bed to tell me that I was cured.'

'Whaaat?' said Richard, jumping to his feet again.

'Oh, Eponine,' Nicole said immediately, 'I'm so happy for you.' She stood up and hugged her friend.

'And you *believe* this?' Richard said to Nicole. 'You believe that the octospider doctors, who can't possibly yet understand very well how the human body works, could accomplish in several days what your brilliant son-in-law and his staff at the hospital could not do in four years?'

'Why not, Richard?' Nicole said. 'If it had been done by The Eagle at The Node, you would have accepted it immediately. Why can't the octospiders be much more advanced than we are in biology? Look at everything we saw ...'

'All right,' said Richard. He shook his head a few times and then turned to Eponine. 'I'm sorry,' he said, 'but it's just difficult for me to ... Congratulations. I too am delighted.' He embraced Eponine awkwardly.

While they had been talking, someone had noiselessly stacked fresh vegetables and water just outside their door. Nicole saw the materials for their feast when she went to use the bathroom.

'That must have been an astonishing experience,' she said to Eponine when she returned to where everyone else was sitting.

'That's an understatement,' Eponine said. She smiled. 'Even though I feel in my heart that I'm cured, I can't wait to have it confirmed by you and Dr Turner.'

Both Richard and Nicole were rxtremely tired after their large dinner. Ellie told her parents that there was more to talk about, but that she could wait until after Richard and Nicole had slept.

'I wish I could remember more about my period with the octospiders before we reached The Node,' Richard said, when he and Nicole were lying together on the large bed their hosts had provided. 'Then maybe I would understand better what I feel about the story that Ellie and Eponine told.'

'Do you still doubt that she's cured?' Nicole asked.

'I don't know,' Richard said. 'But I will admit that I am rather puzzled by the difference in behaviour between these octospiders and the ones who examined and tested me years before ... I cannot believe that the octos in Rama II would *ever* have rescued me from a voracious plant.'

'Maybe octospiders are capable of widely varying behaviour. That's certainly true for human beings. In fact, it's true for all higher-order mammals on Earth. Why should you expect all octospiders to be the same?'

'I know you're going to say that I'm being xenophobic,' Richard said, 'but it's difficult for me to accept these 'new' octospiders. They seem too good to be true. As a biologist, what do you think is their payoff, to use your word, for being "nice to us"?'

'It's a legitimate question, darling,' Nicole replied, 'and I don't know the answer. The idealist in me, however, wants to believe that we have encountered a species that behaves, most of the time, in a moral fashion because doing good is its own reward.'

Richard laughed. 'I should expected that answer. Especially after our discussion about Sisyphus back in New Eden.'

6

'Y ou would find their language fascinating, Daddy,' Ellie was saying when Nicole finally awakened after sleeping for eleven hours. Richard and Ellie were already eating breakfast. 'It's extremely mathematical. They use sixty-four colours altogether, but only fifty-one are what we would call alphabetical. The other thirteen are clarifiers – they are used to specify tenses, or as counters, or even to identify comparatives and superlatives. Their language is really quite elegant.'

'I can't imagine how a language can be elegant – your mother is the linguist in the family,' Richard said. 'I managed to learn to read German, but my speaking skills were atrocious.'

'Good morning, everybody,' Nicole said, stretching in her bed. 'What's for breakfast?'

'Some new and different vegetables ... or maybe they are fruits, for there's really no equivalence in our world ... Almost everything the octospiders eat is what we would probably call a plant, deriving its energy from light. Worms are about the only thing the octospiders eat regularly that does not get its primary energy from photons.'

'So all the plants in the fields that we passed are powered by a kind of photosynthesis?'

'Something similar,' Ellie replied, 'if I understood properly what Archie told me ... Very little is wasted in the octospider society ... Those creatures that you and Daddy call "giant fireflies" hover over each field for precisely scheduled periods of time each week or month ... And all the water is managed as carefully as the photons.'

'Where's Eponine?' Nicole asked while she surveyed the food laid out on the table in the middle of the room.

'She's off packing her things,' Ellie said. 'Besides, she thought that she really shouldn't participate in this morning's conversation.'

'Are we going to be shocked again, like last night?' Nicole asked lightly.

'Perhaps,' Ellie said slowly. 'I really don't know how you are going to react ... do you want to finish your breakfast before we start, or should I tell Archie we're ready?'

'You mean the octospider is going to be part of the conversation and Eponine is not?' Richard asked.

'It was her choice,' Ellie said. 'Besides, Archie, at least in his capacity as a representative of the octospiders, is far more involved in the subject-matter than Eponine.'

Richard and Nicole looked at each other. 'Do you have any idea at all what this is about?' Richard said.

Nicole shook her head. 'But we might as well begin,' she said.

After Archie took his seat among the Wakefields, Ellie informed her parents, and everyone laughed, that this time Archie would provide the 'preamble.' Ellie translated, at times hesitantly, as Archie began with an apology to Richard for the way Richard had been treated by Archie's 'cousins' years previously. Archie explained that *those* octospiders, the ones the humans had encountered in Rama II prior to arriving at The Node, were from a separate, splinter colony, only remotely related to the octospiders that were currently on board Rama. Archie emphasised that it was not until Rama III came into their sphere of influence for the third time that the octospiders, as a species, concluded that the great cylindrical spacecraft were important.

A few of the survivors of that *other* octospider colony, a 'vastly inferior group,' according to Archie (this was one of the places where Ellie asked him to repeat what he was saying), were still passengers on Rama III when the spacecraft was intercepted, early in its trajectory, by the current octospider colony that had been specifically selected to represent their species. The splinter-group survivors were removed from Rama, but all their records were preserved. Archie and the others in his colony learned the details of what had happened to Richard at that time and they now wished to make amends for that treatment.

'So all this preamble, in addition to being fascinating,' said Richard, 'is an elaborate apology to me?'

Ellie nodded and Archie flashed the broad crimson followed by the brilliant aquamarine.

'May I ask a question before we continue?' Nicole said. She turned toward the octospider. 'I assume, from what you told us, that you and your colony boarded Rama III during the period that we were all asleep. Did you know we were there?'

Archie answered that the octospiders had presumed the humans were living inside the far northern habitat in Rama, but had not known for certain until the external seal of the human habitat was first broken. By that time, according to Archie, the octospider colony had already been in place for twelve human years.

'Archie insisted that he make this apology himself,' Ellie said, glancing at her father and then waiting for him to respond.

'OK, I accept, I guess,' Richard replied. 'Although I have no idea what the proper protocol should be ...'

Archie asked Ellie to define 'protocol.' Nicole laughed. 'Richard,' she said, 'sometimes you are so stiff.'

'Anyway,' Ellie said again, 'in the interest of time, I will tell you everything else myself. According to Archie, the records from the splinter colony show that they conducted a number of experiments on you, most of which are outlawed in those octospider colonies Archie refers to as "highly developed". One experiment, Daddy, as you have often suggested, involved inserting into your brain a series of specialised microbes to void all your memory of the time period you stayed with the octospiders. I have reported to Archie and the others that the memory experiment was mostly but not completely successful ...

'The most complex experiment they conducted on your body was an attempt to alter your sperm. The splinter colony of octospiders knew no more about where Rama II was going than our family did. They thought that perhaps the humans and octospiders on board would be coexisting for centuries, maybe even eons, and the octospiders determined that it was absolutely essential for the two species to communicate.

'What they attempted to do was to change the chromosomes in your sperm so that your offspring would have both expanded language capability and greater visual resolution of colours. In short, they tried to engineer me genetically – for I was the only child born to you and Mother after your long odyssey – so that I would be able to communicate with them without undue difficulty. To accomplish this, they introduced a set of special creatures into your body ...'

Ellie stopped. Both Richard and Nicole were staring at her as if they were in shock.

'So you are some kind of hybrid?' Richard asked finally.

'Maybe a little,' said Ellie, laughing to defuse the tension. 'If I understand correctly, only a few thousand of the three billion kilobases that define my genome have been altered ... And speaking of that, Archie and the octospiders would like to invalidate, for their scientific research, that I am indeed the result of an altered sperm. They would like blood and other cell samples from both of you, so that they can conclude unequivocally that I could not have come from a "normal" union of the two of you. Then they would know for certain that my facility with their language was indeed "engineered" and not just incredible good luck.'

'What difference does it make at this point?' Richard asked. 'I would think that all that matters is that you can communicate ...'

'I'm surprised at you, Father – you who have always been such a knowledge junkie ... The octospider society places information at the top of the value scale. They are already virtually certain, as a result of the tests they have performed on me plus the records kept by the splinter group, that I am indeed the result of an altered sperm. Looking at both your genomes in detail, however, would allow them to confirm it.'

'All right,' said Nicole after only a brief hesitation. 'I'm willing.' She walked over and hugged Ellie. 'Whatever caused you to be, you are my daughter and I love you with all my heart.' Nicole glanced back at Richard. 'And I'm certain your father will agree as soon as he has had time to think about it.'

Nicole smiled at Archie. The octospider flashed the broad crimson, followed by a more narrow cobalt blue and a bright yellow. The sentence meant 'Thank you' in the octospider language.

The next morning Nicole wished that she had asked a few more questions before volunteering to help the octospiders with their scientific research. Just after breakfast, their constant alien companion Archie was joined by two other octospiders in the humans' small suite. One of the newcomers, introduced by Ellie as 'Dr Blue – a most distinguished medical scholar,' explained what was going to occur. Richard's procedure would be simple and straightforward. Essentially, the octos only wanted enough data on Richard to corroborate the historical record of his visit to the splinter colony years before.

As for Nicole, since the octospider data base contained no physiological information on her, and the octos had already learned from their detailed examination of Ellie that the way in which human genetic characteristics are expressed is dominated by the mother's contribution to the offspring, a much more elaborate procedure would be required. Dr Blue proposed to perform a complex series of tests on Nicole, the most important of which involved data gathering inside her body by a dozen tiny, coiled creatures that were about two centimetres long and the width of a pin. Nicole recoiled with horror when the octospider doctor held up an equivalent of a plastic bag and Nicole first saw the writhing, slimy creatures that were going to be inside her.

'But I thought all you needed was my genetic code,' Nicole said, 'and that's contained in each and every cell – It shouldn't be necessary ...'

Bright colours circled Dr Blue's head as the octospider interrupted before Nicole had a chance to finish her protest. 'Our techniques of extracting your genome information,' Dr Blue said through Ellie, 'are not yet very advanced. Our methods work best if we have many cells, chosen from several different organs and biological subsystems.'

The doctor then politely thanked Nicole again for her co-operation, finishing with the sequence of cobalt blue and bright yellow bands she had already learned to interpret. The blue part of the 'Thank you' spilled down the side of Dr Blue's head, producing a beautiful visual effect that momentarily distracted the linguist in Nicole. *So keeping those colour bands regular must be a learned behaviour,* she thought. *And our doctor has a kind of speech impediment.*

Nicole's attention was forcibly returned to the pending procedure a few moments later when Dr Blue explained that the coiled creatures would burrow through her skin into her body and then remain inside her for half an hour. *Yuch*, thought Nicole immediately, *they are like leeches.*

One was placed on her forearm. Nicole raised her arm up in front of her face and watched the tiny animal screw its way through her skin. Nicole felt nothing while the creature was invading her, but when it had disappeared she shuddered involuntarily.

Nicole was asked to lie down on her back. Dr Blue then showed her two small eight-legged creatures, one red and one blue, each the size of a fruit-fly. 'You may feel some discomfort soon,' Dr Blue said to Nicole through Ellie, 'as the coilers reach your internal organs. These little guys can be used for anesthesia if you would like some relief from the pain.'

Less than a minute later Nicole experienced a sharp stabbing sensation in her chest. Nicole's first thought was that something was cutting into one of the chambers of her heart. When Dr Blue saw Nicole's face wrenched in pain, he placed the two anesthetic bugs on Nicole's neck. In only seconds Nicole was suspended in a peculiar state between waking and dreaming. She could still hear Ellie's voice, continuing to explain what was happening, but she could not feel anything occurring inside her body.

Nicole found her gaze fixed on the front of the head of Dr Blue, who was supervising the entire procedure. Much to her astonishment, Nicole thought that she was beginning to recognise emotional expressions in the subtle surface wrinkles of the octospider's face. She remembered once as a child being certain that she had seen her pet dog smile. *There's so much to seeing,* her floating mind thought, *so much more than we ever use.*

She felt astonishingly peaceful. Nicole closed her eyes briefly and when she opened them again she was a ten-year-old girl, weeping beside her father as her mother's bier was consumed by flames in a burial ceremony befitting the Senoufo queen. The old man, her great-grandfather Omeh, dressed in a frightening mask to scare off any demons that might try to accompany Nicole's mother to the afterlife, came over beside her and took her hand. 'It is as the chronicles prophesied, Ronata,' he said, using Nicole's Senoufo name, 'our blood has been scattered to the stars.'

The variegated mask of the shaman disappeared into another set of colours, these in bands streaking around Dr Blue's head. Again Nicole heard Ellie's voice. *My daughter is a hybrid,* she thought to herself without emotion. *I have given birth to something that is more than human. A new kind of evolution has begun.*

Her mind drifted again and she was a great bird/plane flying high in the dark above the savannas of the Ivory Coast. Nicole had left the Earth, turned her back on the Sun, and blasted like a rocket toward the blackness and void beyond the solar system. In her mind's eye she could clearly see Omeh's face. 'Ronata,' he called into the night sky in the Ivory Coast, 'do not forget. You are the chosen one.'

And could he really have known, Nicole thought, still in the twilight zone between waking and sleeping, *all those years ago, in Africa, on Earth? And if so, how? Or is there still another dimension to seeing that we have only just begun to understand?*

*

Richard and Nicole were sitting together in the near-darkness. They were temporarily alone. Ellie and Eponine were out with Archie, making all the arrangements for the departure the next morning.

'You've been very quiet all day,' Richard said.

'Yes, I have,' Nicole answered. 'I have felt strange, almost drugged, ever since that last procedure this morning ... My memory is unusually active. I've been thinking about my parents. And Omeh. And visions I had years ago.'

'Were you surprised at the results of the tests?' Richard asked after a short silence.

'Not really. I guess so much has happened to us ... And you know, Richard, I can still remember when Ellie was conceived ... You were not really your-self again yet.'

'I talked to Ellie and Archie quite a bit this afternoon while you were napping. The changes the octospiders induced in Ellie are permanent, like mutations. Nikki probably has some of the same characteristics – it depends on the exact genetic mixture. Of course hers will be diluted by another genera-tion ...'

Richard didn't finish his thought. He yawned, and then reached over for Nicole's hand. They sat quietly together for several minutes before Nicole broke the silence.

'Richard, do you remember my telling you about the Senoufo chronicles? About the woman from the tribe, the daughter of a queen, who was proph-esied to carry the Senoufo blood "even unto the stars"?'

'Vaguely,' Richard answered. 'We haven't spoken about it for a long time.'

'Omeh was certain that I was the woman in the chronicles ... "the woman without companion", he called her ... Do you believe there is any possible way that we can have knowledge of the future?'

Richard laughed. 'Everything in nature follows certain laws. Those laws can be expressed as differential equations in time. If we know precisely the initial conditions of the system at any given epoch, and the exact equations representing the laws of nature, then theoretically we can predict all out-comes. We can't, of course, because our knowledge is always imperfect, and the rules of chaos limit the applicability of our estimation techniques ...'

'Suppose,' Nicole said, propping herself up on an elbow, 'there were indi-viduals or even groups who did not know mathematics, but could somehow *see* or *feel* both the laws and the initial conditions you mentioned. Couldn't they perhaps intuitively solve at least part of the equations and predict the future using insight that we cannot model or quantify?'

'It's possible,' said Richard. 'But remember, extraordinary claims require ...'

'... extraordinary evidence. I know,' said Nicole. She paused for a moment. 'I wonder what destiny is, then. Is it something we humans make up after the fact? Or is it real? And if destiny really exists as a concept, how can it be explained by the laws of physics?'

'I'm not following you, darling,' Richard said.

'It's confusing even to me,' Nicole said. 'Am I who I am because, as Omeh insisted when I was a little girl, it was always my destiny to travel in space? Or am I the person I am because of all the choices I have personally made and the skills I have consciously developed?'

Richard laughed again. 'Now you're very close to one of the fundamental philosophical conundrums, the debate between God's omniscience and man's free will.'

'I didn't mean to be,' said Nicole reflectively. 'I just can't shake the notion that nothing that has happened in my absolutely incredible life would have been a surprise to Omeh.'

7

Their departure breakfast was a feast. The octospiders provided more than a dozen different fruits and vegetables, as well as a hot, thick cereal made, according to Archie and Ellie, from the very tall grasses just north of the power plant. While they were eating, Richard asked the octospider what had happened to the avian hatchlings Tammy and Timmy, as well as the manna melons and the sessile material. He was not satisfied with the translated, somewhat vague response that all the other species were fine.

'Look, Archie,' Richard said in his characteristic brusque manner. He was now comfortable enough with his alien host that he no longer felt it necessary to be overly polite. 'I have far more than a casual interest in those creatures. I rescued them and raised them from birth by myself. I would like to see them, even if only briefly ... Under any circumstances, I think I deserve a more definitive answer to my question.'

Archie stood up, ambled out the door of the suite, and returned in a few minutes. 'We have arranged for you to see the avians for yourself later on today during our journey back to your friends,' he said. 'As for the other species, two of the eggs have just completed germination and are in the infant myrmicat stage. Their development is being closely monitored on the other side of our domain and it is not possible for you to visit them.'

Richard's face brightened. 'Two of them germinated! How did you accomplish that?'

'Eggs of the sessile species must be placed in a thermally controlled liquid for a month of your time before the embryonic development process will even begin,' Ellie interpreted Archie's colours very slowly. 'The temperature must be maintained within an extremely small range, less than a degree by your measures, at the same value that is optimal for the myrmicat manifestation of the species. Otherwise the growth and development process does not occur.'

Richard was on his feet. 'So that's the secret,' he said, nearly shouting. 'Dammit, I should have figured it out. I certainly had plenty of clues, both from the conditions inside their habitat and those murals they showed me ...' He began to pace around the room. 'But how did the octospiders know?' he said, with his back to Archie.

Archie replied quickly after Ellie's translation. 'We had information from the other octospider colony. Their records explained the entire metamorphosis of the sessiles.'

It seemed too simple to Richard. He suspected that maybe their alien colleague was not telling him the whole truth. Richard was ready to ask some more questions when Dr Blue came into the suite, followed by three other octospiders, two of whom were carrying a large hexagonal object wrapped in a paperlike material.

'What's this?' Richard asked.

'This is our official farewell party,' Ellie answered. 'Together with a present from the residents of the city.'

One of the new octos asked Ellie if all the humans could gather outside on the avenue for the departure ceremony. The humans picked up their belongings and walked through the hallway out into the brighter lights. Nicole was surprised by what she saw. Except for the octospiders who filed out of their suite behind them, the avenue was deserted. Even the colours of the gardens seemed more muted, as if they had somehow been temporarily brightened by all the surrounding activity two days earlier when Richard and Nicole had arrived.

'Where is everyone?' Nicole asked Ellie.

'It's very quiet on purpose,' her daughter replied. 'The octos didn't want to overwhelm you again.'

The five octospiders arranged themselves in a line in the middle of the avenue, with the pyramid-shaped building directly behind them. The two octos on the right side balanced the hexagonal package between them. It was larger than they were. The four humans were lined up opposite the octospiders, just in front of the gates to the city. The octospider in the centre, whom Ellie introduced as the 'Chief Optimiser' (after several failed attempts to find an exactly correct human word for Archie's description of the duties of the octospider leader), then stepped forward to speak.

The Chief Optimiser expressed its gratitude to Richard, Nicole, Ellie, and Eponine, including a personal note with each thank you, and said that it hoped this brief interaction would be the 'first of many' that would lead to more understanding between the two species. The octospider then indicated that Archie was going to return with the humans, not only so that the interaction could be continued and expanded, but also to demonstrate to the other humans that a mutual trust between the two species now existed.

During a brief pause Archie shuffled forward into the zone between the two lines and Ellie symbolically welcomed him to their traveling party. The two octos on the right then unveiled the present, which was a magnificent detailed painting of the sight that Richard and Nicole had seen at the moment of their entrance into the Emerald City. The painting was so lifelike that Nicole was momentarily stunned. A few moments later the humans all moved closer to the painting to study its details. All the weird creatures were in the picture, including the three royal blue undulators, whose two long, upright, knobby antennae thrust upward from a teeming body mass reminded Nicole how disoriented she had been the previous day.

As she examined the painting and wondered how it could have been created, Nicole recalled the near swoon that had accompanied her actual viewing of the scene. *Was I having a premonition of danger then?* she mused. *Or was it something else?* She glanced away from the painting and watched the octospiders talking among themselves. *Perhaps it was an epiphany, she thought, an instant burst of recognition of something way beyond my understanding.* Some force or power never before experienced by any human being. A chill ran down her back as the gates of the Emerald City began to open.

Richard was always concerned about naming things. After less than a minute of inspection of the creatures they were going to ride, he called them 'ostrichsaurs.'

'That's not very imaginative, darling,' Nicole chided him.

'Maybe not,' he said, 'but it is a perfect description. They are just like a giant ostrich with the face and neck of one of those herbivorous dinosaurs.'

The creature had four birdlike legs, a soft, feathery main body with an indented bowl in the middle where four humans could easily sit, and a long neck that could be extended three metres in any direction. Since the legs were about two metres long, the neck could reach the surrounding ground without difficulty.

The two ostrichsaurs were surprisingly swift. Archie, Ellie, and Eponine rode on one of the creatures, on whose side the large hexagonal painting had been tied with a kind of twine. Nicole and Richard were by themselves on the other ostrichsaur. There were no reins or other obvious means of controlling the creatures; however, before the group departed from the Emerald City, Archie spent almost ten minutes 'talking' to the ostrichsaurs.

'He's explaining the entire route,' Ellie said. 'And also outlining what to do in case of an accident.'

'What kind of an accident?' Richard asked, but Ellie simply shrugged in reply.

At first both Richard and Nicole hung on to the 'feathers' that surrounded the bowl in which they were sitting, but after a few minutes they relaxed. The ride was very smooth, with very little jostling up and down. 'Now, do you suppose,' Richard said after the Emerald City faded from view, 'these animals naturally evolved this way, with this near perfect bowl in the middle of their backs? Or did the octospider genetic engineers somehow breed them for transportation?'

'There's no doubt in my mind at all,' Nicole replied. 'I believe that most of the living things we have encountered, certainly including those dark, wriggling coiled things that crawled through my skin, have been designed for a specific function by the octospiders. How could it be otherwise?'

'But you can't believe these animals were designed from scratch,' Richard said. 'That would suggest an incredible technology, far beyond anything we can even imagine.'

'I don't know, darling,' Nicole said. 'Maybe the octospiders have travelled to many different planetary systems, in each place finding life-forms that could be slightly altered to fit into their grand symbiotic schemes. But I can't accept for a minute the idea that this harmonious biology just happened by natural evolution.'

The two ostrichsaurs and their five riders were guided by three of the giant fireflies. After a couple of hours, the group approached a vast lake stretching to the south and west. Both the ostrichsaurs squatted on the ground so that Archie and the four humans could descend.

'We're going to have lunch and a drink of water here,' Archie said to the others. He handed Ellie a container filled with food and then led the two ostrichsaurs over to the lake. Nicole and Eponine walked off in the direction of some blue plants growing at the edge of the water, leaving Richard and Ellie by themselves.

'Your proficiency in their language is very impressive, to say the least,' Richard said in between bites of food.

Ellie laughed. 'I'm afraid I'm not as good as you think. The octos purposely keep their sentences very simple for me. And they speak slowly, with broad bands. But I am improving ... You realise, don't you, that they are not using their true language when speaking to us? It's just a derivative form.'

'What do you mean?' Richard asked.

'I explained it to Mother back at the Emerald City. I guess she didn't have a chance to tell you.' Ellie swallowed before continuing. 'Their true language has sixty-four colour symbols, just as I mentioned, but eleven of them are not accessible to us. Eight lie in the infra-red part of the spectrum, and another three in the ultraviolet. So we can only distinguish clearly fifty-three of their symbols. This was quite a problem in the beginning. Luckily, five of the eleven outside symbols are clarifiers. Anyway, for our benefit they have developed what amounts to a new dialect of their language, using only the colour wavelengths that we can see. Archie says that this new dialect is already being taught in some of their advanced classes ...'

'Amazing,' Richard said. 'You mean they have adjusted their language to accommodate our physical limitations?'

'Not exactly, Father. They still use their true language when talking to each other. That's why I cannot always understand what they are saying. However, this new dialect has been developed, and is now being expanded, just to make communications with us as easy as possible.'

Richard finished his lunch. He was about to ask Ellie another question about the octospider language when he heard Nicole yell. 'Richard,' she shouted from fifty metres away, 'look over there, in the air, toward the forest.'

Richard craned his neck and shaded his eyes. In the distance he could see two birds flying toward them. For some reason his recognition was delayed until he heard the familiar shrieking sound. Then he jumped up and ran in the direction of the avians. Tammy and Timmy, now full-grown, swooped down out of the sky and landed beside him. Richard was overcome with joy as his wards jabbered incessantly and pressed their velvet underbellies against him for a rub.

They looked perfectly healthy. There was not a trace of sadness in their huge expressive eyes. A few minutes later Timmy suddenly stepped away, shrieked something in a very loud voice, and became airborne. Within a few minutes the avian returned with a companion, a female with an orange velvet covering unlike any Richard had ever seen. Richard was a little confused, but he did realise that Timmy was trying to introduce him to his mate.

The remainder of the reunion with the avians lasted only ten or fifteen minutes. Archie insisted, after he first explained that the vast lake system supplied almost half of the fresh water in the octospider domain, that the entourage needed to continue on its journey. Richard and Nicole were already in the bowl on the back of their ostrichsaur when the three avians departed. Tammy hovered over them for a goodbye jabber, obviously disturbing the creature on which they were riding. At length she followed her brother and his mate in their flight toward the forest.

Richard was strangely quiet as their mounts also headed north in the direction of the forest. 'They really mean a lot to you, don't they?' Nicole said.

'Absolutely,' her husband replied. 'I was all alone except for the hatchlings for a long time. Timmy and Tammy depended on me for their survival ... Committing myself to rescuing them was probably the first selfless act of my life. It opened up new dimensions of both anxiety and happiness for me.'

Nicole reached over and took Richard's hand. 'Your emotional life has had an odyssey of its own,' she said softly, 'every bit as diverse as the physical journey you have experienced.'

Richard kissed her. 'I still have a few demons that are not yet exorcised,' he said. 'Maybe, with your help, in another ten years I'll be a decent human being.'

'You don't give yourself enough credit,' Nicole said.

'To my *brain* I give plenty of credit,' Richard said with a grin, changing the tone of the conversation. 'And do you know what it is thinking right now? Where did that avian with the orange underbelly come from?'

Nicole looked puzzled. 'From the second habitat,' she replied. 'You yourself told us that there must have been a population of almost a thousand before Nakamura's troops invaded. The octospiders must have rescued a few also.'

'But I lived there for months,' Richard protested. 'And I never ever saw an avian with an orange underbelly. Not one. I would have remembered.'

'What are you suggesting?'

'Nothing. Your explanation is definitely consistent with Occam's Razor. But I'm starting to wonder if maybe our octospider buddies have some secrets they have not yet discussed with us.'

They reached the large igloo hut not far from the Cylindrical Sea after several more hours. The tiny glowing igloo that had been beside it was gone. Archie and the four humans dismounted. The octospider and Richard untied the hexagonal painting and stored it against the side of the igloo. Then Archie led the ostrichsaurs aside and gave them directions for their homeward trek.

'Can't they stay a little while?' Nicole asked. 'The children would be absolutely delighted with them.'

'Unfortunately, no,' Archie replied. 'We have only a few and they are very much in demand.'

Although Eponine, Ellie, Richard, and Nicole were all tired from their journey, they were still extremely excited about the forthcoming reunion. Before leaving the igloo hut, first Eponine and then Ellie used the mirror and freshened their faces. 'Please, all of you,' Eponine said, 'I ask one favour. Don't say anything about my cure to anybody until I have had a chance to tell Max in private. I want it to be my surprise.'

'I hope Nikki still recognises me,' Ellie said nervously as they descended the first staircase and entered the corridor that led to the landing. The whole group had a momentary panic, fearing the others might be asleep, until Richard did a computation with his master-schedule algorithm and assured everyone that it was the middle of the morning under the rainbow dome.

All five of them walked out onto the landing and gazed at the circular floor below them. The twins Kepler and Galileo were playing a game of tag, with little Nikki watching them and laughing. Nai and Max were unloading food from a subway that had apparently recently arrived. Eponine could not restrain herself. 'Max,' she shouted, 'Max!'

Max reacted as if he had been shot. He dropped the food he was carrying and turned toward the landing. He saw Eponine waving at him and broke like a thoroughbred for the cylindrical staircase. It could not have been more than two minutes before he emerged on to the landing and threw his arms around Eponine.

'Oh, Frenchie,' he said, lifting her half a metre off the ground and hugging her fiercely, 'how I have missed you!'

8

Archie could do all kinds of tricks with the coloured balls. The octospider could catch two balls at once and then throw them in distinctly different directions. Archie could even juggle all six of the balls simultaneously, using four tentacles, for he needed only the other four tentacles on the ground to maintain his balance. The children loved for him to swing all three of them at the same time. Archie never seemed to tire of playing with the smaller humans.

In the beginning, of course, the children had been afraid of the alien visitor. Little Nikki, despite Ellie's repeated assurances that Archie was friendly, was especially wary because of her memory of the terror of her mother's kidnapping. Benjy was the first to accept Archie as a playmate. The Watanabe twins were not coordinated enough to play complicated games, so Benjy was delighted to discover that Archie would gladly join him for an active game of catch or Benjy's version of dodge-ball.

Max and Robert were both disturbed by Archie's presence. Within an hour after the arrival of the four humans and the octospider, in fact, Max had confronted Richard and Nicole in their bedroom. 'Eponine tells me,' Max had said angrily, 'that the damn octospider is going to *live* with us here. Have you all lost your minds?'

'Think of Archie as an ambassador, Max,' Nicole had said. 'The octos want to establish regular communications with us.'

'But these same octospiders kidnapped your daughter and my girl-friend and held them against their will for over a month ... Are you telling me that we are to *ignore* their actions altogether?'

'There were extenuating reasons for the kidnappings,' Nicole had replied, exchanging a brief glance with Richard. 'And the women were treated very well ... Why don't you talk to Eponine about it?'

'Eponine has nothing but praise for the octospiders,' Max had said. 'It's almost as if she has been brainwashed ... I thought you two would be more reasonable.'

Even after Eponine had informed Max that the octospiders had cured her of RV-41, he was still skeptical. 'If it's true,' he had said, 'then it's the most wonderful news I've received since those little robots showed up at the farm and confirmed that Nicole had safely reached New York. But I am having a very hard time seeing those eight-legged monsters as our benefactors. I want Doc Turner to examine you very carefully. If he tells me you're cured, then I'll believe it.'

Robert Turner was overtly hostile to Archie from the beginning. Nothing Nicole or even Ellie could say could neutralise the anger that he still felt over Ellie's forcible kidnapping. His professional pride was also severely wounded by the apparent ease with which Eponine had been purportedly cured.

'You're expecting too much, Ellie, as always,' Robert said on the second night they were together. 'You come in here, all full of glowing reports about these aliens who snatched you away from Nikki and me, and you expect me to embrace them immediately. That's not fair. I need time to understand and to synthesise everything you're telling me ... Don't you realise that both Nikki and I were traumatised by your kidnapping? We have deep emotional scars caused by these same creatures you now want me to regard as friends ... I cannot change my opinion overnight.'

Robert was also troubled by Ellie's information about the genetic changes made in Richard's sperm, even though it did explain why his wife's genome had defied classification in the tests his colleague Ed Stafford had conducted back in New Eden.

'How can you be so calm about discovering that you're a hybrid?' he said to Ellie. 'Don't you understand what it means? When the octospiders altered your DNA to improve your visual resolution and to make learning their language easier, they tampered with a robust genetic code that has evolved naturally over millions of years. Who knows what disease susceptibilities, infirmities, or even negative changes in fertility may show up in you or subsequent generations? The octos may have unwittingly doomed all our grandchildren.'

Ellie was not able to mollify her husband. When Nicole began working with Robert to ascertain whether Eponine had indeed been cured of RV-41, she noticed that Robert bristled every time Nicole made a favourable statement about Archie or the octospiders.

'We must give Robert more time,' Nicole counselled her daughter a week after their return. 'He still feels that the octospiders violated him, not only by kidnapping you, but also by contaminating the genes of his daughter.'

'Mother, there is another problem as well. I almost feel that Robert is jealous in some peculiar way. He thinks that I spend too much time with Archie. He doesn't seem to accept the fact that Archie cannot communicate with anyone else unless I am there to interpret.'

'As I said, we must be patient. Eventually Robert will accept the situation.'

But in private Nicole had her doubts. Robert was determined to find some remnant of the RV-41 virus in Eponine and, when test after test with his relatively unsophisticated portable equipment showed no evidence of the pathogen in her system, he continued to request additional procedures. In Nicole's professional opinion, there was nothing to be gained from more testing. Although there existed a very small probability that the virus had eluded them and did still dwell somewhere in Eponine, Nicole felt that it was virtually certain that Eponine had been cured.

The two doctors clashed the day after Ellie had confided to her mother that Robert was jealous of Archie. When Nicole suggested that they terminate the tests on Eponine and pronounce her healthy, she was shocked to hear her son-in-law say that he proposed to open up Eponine's chest cavity and take a direct sample from the tissues around her heart.

'But Robert,' Nicole said, 'have you ever had a case where so many other tests have been virus-negative but the pathogen was still locally active in the cardiac region?'

'Only when death was imminent and the heart had already deteriorated,' he admitted. 'But that doesn't preclude that the same situation could occur earlier in the cycle of the disease.'

Nicole was staggered. She did not argue with Robert, for she could tell from the rigid set of his muscles that he had already decided on his next course of action. *But open heart surgery of any kind is risky, even in his skilled hands,* she thought. *In this environment any kind of accident could result in death. Please, Robert, come to your senses. If you do not, I will be forced to oppose you on Eponine's behalf.*

Max asked to talk to Nicole privately very soon after Robert recommended that the heart surgery be performed. 'Eponine is frightened,' Max confided, 'and I am too ... She came back from the Emerald City more full of life than I have ever seen her. Robert originally told me that the tests would be over in a couple of days. They have dragged on for almost two weeks and now he says he wants to take a tissue sample from her heart ...'

'I know,' said Nicole grimly. 'He told me last night he was going to recommend the open-heart procedure.'

'Help me, please,' Max said. 'I want to make certain that I understand the facts properly. You and Robert have examined her blood many times, as well as several other bodily tissues that sometimes show minute quantities of the virus, and all the specimens have been unambiguously negative?'

'That's correct,' Nicole said.

'Isn't it true also that every other time that Eponine has been examined, ever since she was first diagnosed as RV-41-positive years ago, her blood samples have indicated the presence of the virus?'

'Yes,' Nicole replied.

'Then why does Robert want to operate? Does he simply not want to believe that she is cured? Or is he just being extra-careful?'

'I cannot answer for him,' Nicole said.

She looked searchingly at her friend and knew both what his next question

1049

would be and how she would answer it. *There are difficult decisions that all of us must make in life,* she thought. *When I was younger I consciously tried to avoid placing myself in a position where I would be forced to make such decisions. Now I understand that by avoiding them I allow others to decide for me. And sometimes they are wrong.*

'If you were the doctor in charge, Nicole,' Max asked, 'would you operate on Eponine?'

'No, I would not,' Nicole replied carefully. 'I believe that it is almost certain that Eponine was indeed cured by the octospiders and that the risk of the operation cannot be justified.'

Max smiled and kissed his friend on the forehead. 'Thank you,' he said.

Robert was outraged. He reminded everyone that he had dedicated more than four years of his life to studying this particular disease, as well as trying to find a cure, and that he certainly knew more about RV-41 than all of them put together. How could they possibly trust an alien cure more than his surgical talent? How could his own mother-in-law, whose knowledge of RV-41 was limited to what he himself had taught her, have dared to offer an opinion different from his? He could not be placated by any of the group, not even by Ellie, whom he eventually banished from his presence after several unpleasant exchanges.

For two days Robert refused to come out of his room. He didn't even reply when his daughter Nikki wished him 'Sweet dreams, Daddy' before her naps and bedtime. His family and friends were deeply troubled by Robert's torment, but could not figure out how to ease his pain. The question of Robert's mental stability came up in several discussions. Everyone agreed that Robert had seemed out of place ever since the escape from New Eden and that his behaviour had become even more erratic and unpredictable after Ellie's kidnapping.

Ellie confided to her mother that Robert had been 'peculiar' with her since their recent reunion. 'He has not approached me even once, as a woman,' she said sorrowfully. 'It has been as if he felt I was contaminated by my experience ... He keeps saying weird things like, "Ellie, did you *want* to be kidnapped"?'

'I feel sorry for him,' Nicole replied. 'He is carrying such a heavy emotional burden, going all the way back to Texas. This has all been simply too much. We should have ...'

'But what can we do for him now?' Ellie interrupted.

'I don't know, darling,' Nicole said. 'I just don't know.'

Ellie tried to pass the difficult time helping Benjy with octospider language lessons. Her half brother was absolutely fascinated by everything about the aliens, including the hexagonal octospider painting that had been brought back from the Emerald City. Benjy stared at the picture several times a day and never missed an opportunity to ask questions about the amazing creatures depicted in the painting. Through Ellie, Archie always patiently answered whatever Benjy asked.

Benjy had decided, soon after he began playing regularly with Archie, that he wanted to learn to recognise at least a few phrases in the octospider lexicon. Benjy knew that Archie was able to read lips and he wanted to show the octospider that even a 'slow human', if properly motivated, could pick up enough understanding of the octospider language for a simple conversation.

Ellie and Archie started Benjy with the fundamentals. He learned the octospider colours for 'yes,' 'no,' 'please,' and 'thank you' without any difficulty. The numbers were fairly easy as well, because both the cardinals and the ordinals were essentially combination sequences of two basic colours, blood red and malachite green, that were used in a binary fashion and marked in the flow of the sentence by a salmon clarifier. What gave Benjy the most trouble was comprehending that the individual colours by themselves did not have any meaning. A burnt sienna band, for example, represented the verb 'to understand' if followed by a mauve and then a clarifier; however, if the burnt sienna/mauve combination was followed by a vermilion, the three-band symbol meant 'flowering plant'.

Nor were the individual colours members of an alphabet in the strictest sense. Sometimes the width of the colours, when compared with others in the longer sequence defining a single word, completely changed the meaning. The burnt sienna/mauve combination only meant 'to understand' if the two bands were of approximately equal width. The word defined by a narrow burnt sienna followed by a mauve of roughly double the width was 'capacity'.

Benjy struggled with the language, doing all the required repetitions, with an uncommon zeal. His ardour for learning warmed Ellie's heart at a time when she was deeply concerned about how the crisis with Robert would be resolved.

At the beginning of the third day of Robert's self-imposed exile in his room, the subway pulled into its slot, as expected, with their semi-weekly supply of food and water. Only this time there were two new octospiders on board. They disembarked and had a detailed conversation with Archie. The family gathered together, expecting some unusual news.

'Human troops are again in New York,' Archie reported, 'and they are in the process of breaking the seal to our lair. It's just a matter of time until they discover the subway tunnels.'

'So what should we do now?' Nicole asked.

'We would like you to come and live with us in the Emerald City,' Archie said. 'My colleagues anticipated this possibility and have already finished the design of a special section in the city just for you. It could be ready in a few more days.'

'And what if we don't want to go?' Max asked.

Archie conferred briefly with the other two octospiders. 'Then you can stay here and wait for the troops,' he said. 'We will provide as much food as we can, but we will begin dismantling the subway as soon as we have evacuated all our associates on the northern side of the Cylindrical Sea.'

Archie continued speaking, but Ellie stopped translating. She asked the octospider to repeat his next few sentences several times before turning, a little pale, to her friends and family.

'Unfortunately,' she translated, 'we octospiders must be concerned for our own welfare. Therefore, any of you who decide not to come with us will have your short-term memories blocked and will not be able to recall in detail any events from the last several weeks.'

Max whistled. 'So much for friendship and communication,' he said. 'When push comes to shove, all of the species use power.'

He walked over to Eponine and took her hand. She looked at him quizzically as Max pulled her over in front of Nicole. 'Will you marry us, please?' he said.

Nicole was flustered. 'Right now?' she asked.

'Right this very goddamn minute,' Max answered. 'I love this woman beside me and I want to have an orgy of a honeymoon with her up in that igloo hut before all hell breaks loose.'

'But I'm not qualified ...' Nicole protested.

'You're the best available,' Max interrupted. 'Come on, at least do a good approximation.' The speechless bride was beaming.

'Do you, Max Puckett, take this woman, Eponine,' Nicole said hesitantly, 'to be your wife?'

'I *do* and should have done months ago,' Max replied.

'And do you, Eponine, take this man, Max Puckett, to be your husband?'

'Oh, yes, Nicole, with pleasure.'

Max pulled Eponine toward him and kissed her passionately. 'Now, *Ar-chibald*,' he said as he and Eponine headed for the staircase, 'in case you're wondering, Frenchie and I intend to go with you to that Emerald City she talks so much about. But we'll be gone for the next twenty-four hours or so, maybe longer if Eponine's energy holds out, and we do not want to be disturbed.'

Max and Eponine walked briskly over to the cylindrical staircase and disappeared. Ellie had almost finished explaining to Archie what was going on with Max and Eponine when the newlyweds emerged on the landing and waved. Everyone laughed as Max pulled Eponine back toward the corridor.

Ellie sat by herself against the wall in the dim light. *It's now or never*, she thought. *I have to try one more time.*

She recalled the angry scene several hours earlier. 'Of course you want to go with your friend Archie the octospider,' Robert had said bitterly. 'And you expect to take Nikki with you.'

'Everyone else is going to accept the invitation,' Ellie had replied, not even attempting to hide her tears. 'Please come with us, Robert. They are a very gentle, very moral species.'

'They have brainwashed all of you,' Robert had said. 'Somehow they have seduced you into believing that they are even better than your own kind.' Robert had then looked at Ellie with disgust. 'Your own kind,' he had repeated. 'What a joke. Why, I guess you're as much an octospider as you are a human.'

'That's not true, darling,' Ellie had said. 'I've told you several times that only very small changes were made ... I'm as human as you are ...'

'Why, why, *why*?' Robert had suddenly shouted. 'Why did I let you talk me into coming to New York in the first place? I should have stayed behind, where I was surrounded by things I understood.'

Despite her pleas, Robert had been adamant He was not going to the Emerald City. He had even seemed strangely pleased that his short-term memory would be blocked by the octospiders. 'Perhaps,' he had said, laughing harshly, 'I will have no memory at all of your return. I will not recall that my wife and daughter are both hybrids and that my closest friends have no respect for my professional abilities. Yes,' he had continued, 'I will be able to forget this nightmare of the last few weeks and remember only that you were stolen away from me, as my first wife was, while I still loved you desperately.'

Robert had stalked around the room in anger. Ellie had tried to soothe and comfort him. 'No, no,' he had shouted, recoiling from her touch. 'It's too late. There is too much pain. I can't stand any more.'

In the early hours of the evening Ellie had sought counsel from her mother. Nicole had not been able to provide Ellie with any relief. Nicole had agreed that Ellie should not give up, but had cautioned her daughter that nothing in Robert's behaviour suggested that he might change his mind.

At Nicole's suggestion, Ellie approached Archie and asked a favour of the octospider. If Robert insisted on not going with them, Ellie entreated, would it be possible for Archie, or one of the other octospiders, to take Robert back to the lair, where he would be found quickly by the other humans? Archie had reluctantly agreed.

I love you, Robert, Ellie said to herself as she finally stood up. *And Nikki does too. We want you to come with us, for you are my husband and her father*. Ellie took a deep breath and entered her bedroom.

Even Richard had tears in his eyes as a mumbling Robert Turner, after exchanging a final hug with his wife and daughter, walked off haltingly behind Archie toward the subway only twenty metres away. Nikki was crying softly, but the girl couldn't have realised fully what was occurring. She was still too young.

Robert turned, waved slightly, and entered the train. In a few seconds it accelerated into the tunnel. Less than a minute later the sombre mood was broken by cries of joy from the landing above them.

'All right, down there,' Max shouted, 'you'd better be ready for a big party.'

Nicole looked up under the dome, and even at that distance, in the dim light, she could see the radiant smiles of the newlyweds. *And so it is*, she thought, her heart still heavy from her daughter's loss. *Sorrow and joy. Joy and sorrow. Wherever there are humans. On Earth. In new worlds beyond the stars. Now and forever.*

THE EMERALD CITY

1

The small driverless transport stopped at a circular plaza from which streets extended in five directions. A dark woman with grey hair and her octospider companion descended together from the car, leaving it empty. As the octospider and the human walked slowly away from the plaza, the transport departed with its interior lights now extinguished.

A solitary giant firefly preceded Nicole and Dr Blue as they continued their conversation in the near darkness. Nicole was careful to exaggerate each word so that her alien friend would have no difficulty reading her lips. Dr Blue replied in broad swaths of colour, using simple sentences that he knew Nicole understood.

When they reached the first of four cream-white, single-storey dwellings at the end of the cul-de-sac, the octospider lifted one of his tentacles from the street and shook hands with Nicole. 'Good night,' she replied with a wan smile. 'It was quite a day ... Thank you for everything.'

After Dr Blue went inside his house, Nicole walked over to the decorative fountain forming an island in the centre of the street and drank from one of the four spigots jetting forth a continuous stream of water at waist level. Some of the water that touched Nicole's face fell back into the basin, causing a flurry of activity in the shallow pool. Even in the dim light Nicole could see the swimming creatures darting to and fro. *The cleaners are everywhere*, she thought, *especially when we're around. The water that touched my face will be purified in seconds.*

She turned and approached the largest of the three remaining dwellings in the cul-de-sac. When Nicole crossed the threshold of her house, the outside firefly flew quickly down the street to the plaza. In the atrium, Nicole tapped the wall lightly one time, and in a few seconds a smaller firefly, barely glowing, appeared in the hallway in front of her. She stopped in one of the family's two bathrooms and then paused at the doorway of Benjy's room. He was snoring loudly. Nicole watched her son sleep for almost a full minute and then continued down the hallway to the master bedroom she shared with her husband.

Richard was also asleep. He did not respond to Nicole's soft greeting. She took off her shoes and left the bedroom. When she reached the study, Nicole tapped on the wall twice more and the illumination increased. The study was cluttered with Richard's electronic components, which he had had the octospiders gather for him over a period of several months. Nicole laughed to herself as she picked her way through the mess to her desk. *He always has a project*, she thought. *At least the translator will be very useful.*

Nicole sat in the chair at her desk and opened the middle drawer. She pulled out her portable computer, for which the octospiders had finally provided acceptable new power and storage subsystems. After calling up her journal from the menu, Nicole began typing on the keyboard, intermittently glancing at the small monitor to read what she was writing.

Day 221 –

I have arrived at home very late and, as I expected, everyone is asleep. I was tempted to take off my clothes and snuggle into bed beside Richard, but this day has been so extraordinary that I feel compelled to write while my thoughts and feelings are still fresh in my mind.

I had breakfast, as always, with our entire human clan here about one hour after dawn. Nai talked about what the children were going to do in school before their long nap, Eponine reported that both her heartburn and morning sickness had abated, and Richard complained that the 'biological wizards' (our octospider hosts, of course) were mediocre electrical engineers. I tried to participate in the conversation, but my growing anticipation and anxiety about this morning's meetings with the octospider doctors kept occupying my thoughts.

My stomach was full of butterflies when I arrived at the conference room in the pyramid just after breakfast. Dr Blue and his medical colleagues were prompt, and the octos launched immediately into a lengthy discussion of what they had learned from Benjy's tests. Medical jargon is hard enough to understand in one's own native language – it was nearly impossible for me at times to follow what they were saying with their colours. Often I had to ask them to repeat.

It did not take long for their answer to be apparent. Yes, the octospiders could definitely see, by comparison, where Benjy's genome was different from everyone else's. Yes, they agreed that the specific string of genes on chromosome 14 was almost certainly the source of Whittingham's syndrome. But no, they were sorry, they didn't see any way – not even using something I interpreted as a gene transplant – that they could cure his problem. It was too complex, the octospiders said, involving too many amino-acid chains, they had not had enough experience with human beings, there were too many chances that something might go terribly wrong ...

I cried when I understood what they were telling me. Had I expected otherwise? Had I thought that somehow the same miraculous medical capability that had freed Eponine from the curse of the RV-41 virus might be successful in curing Benjy's birth defect? I realised, in my despair, that I had indeed been hoping for a miracle, even though my brain recognised very clearly the significant difference between a congenital ailment and an acquired virus. Dr Blue tried his best to console me. I let my mother's tears flow there, in front of the octospiders, knowing that I would need my strength when I returned home to tell the others.

Nai and Eponine both knew the results as soon as they saw my face. Nai adores Benjy and never stops praising his determination to learn in spite of the obstacles. Benjy is amazing. He spends hours and hours in his room, working laboriously through all his lessons, struggling for days to grasp a concept in fractions or decimals that a gifted nine-year-old might learn in half an hour. Only last week Benjy beamed with pride when he showed me he could find the least common denominator to add the fractions ¼, ⅕, and ⅙.

Nai has been his main teacher. Eponine has been Benjy's pal. Ep probably felt worse than anybody this morning. She had been certain, because the octospiders had healed her so quickly, that Benjy's problem as well would succumb to their medical magic. It was not to be. Eponine sobbed so hard and so long this morning that I became concerned about the welfare of her baby. She patted her swollen belly and told me not to worry. Ep laughed and said, through her tears, that her reaction was probably mostly due to her overactive hormones.

All three of the men were clearly upset, but they didn't show much emotion. Patrick left the room quickly without saying anything. Max expressed his disappointment with an unusually colourful set of four-letter words. Richard just grimaced and shook his head.

We had all agreed, before the examination began, not to say anything to Benjy about the actual purpose of all the tests the octospiders were conducting. Could he have known? Might he have surmised what was going on? Perhaps. But this morning, when I told him that the octospiders had concluded that he was a healthy young man, I saw nothing in Benjy's eyes that even hinted he was aware of what had taken place. After I hugged him hard, fighting against another set of tears threatening to destroy my façade, I returned to my room and allowed the sorrow of my son's handicap to overcome me one more time.

I'm certain that Richard and Dr Blue conspired together to keep my mind busy the rest of the day. I had not been in my room for more than twenty minutes when there was a soft knock on the door. Richard explained that Dr Blue was in the atrium and that two other octospider scientists were waiting for me in the conference room. Had I forgotten that a detailed presentation on the octospider digestive system had been scheduled for me today?

The discussion with the octospiders turned out to be so fascinating that I was indeed able temporarily to forget that my son's handicap was beyond their medical magic. Dr Blue's colleagues showed me complex anatomical drawings of octospider insides, identifying all the major organs of their digestive sequence. The drawings were made on some kind of parchment or hide and were spread out across the large table. The octospiders explained to me, in their wonderful language of colours, absolutely everything that happens to food inside their body.

The most unusual feature of the octospider digestive process is the two large sacs, or buffers, at both ends of the system. Everything they eat goes directly into an intake buffer, where it can sit for as long as thirty days. The octospider's body itself, based on the activity level of the individual, automatically determines the rate at which the food in the bottom of the sac is accessed, broken down chemically, and distributed to the cells for energy.

At the other end is a waste buffer, into which is discharged all the material that cannot be converted into useful energy by the octospider's body. Every healthy octospider, I learned, has a small animal permanently living in this buffer. They showed me one of the tiny, centipedelike creatures that begins life as a minuscule egg deposited by its predecessor inside the host octospider. The 'waster' is essentially omnivorous. It consumes 99 per cent of the waste deposited in the buffer during the two human months that it takes to grow to maturity. When the waster reaches adulthood, it deposits a pair of new eggs, only one of which will germinate, and then leaves forever the octospider in which it has been living.

The intake buffer is located just behind and below the mouth. The octospiders eat very rarely; however, they absolutely gorge themselves when they do have meals. We had a long discussion about their eating habits. Two of the facts that Dr Blue told me were extremely surprising – first, that an empty octo intake buffer leads to *immediate* death, in less than a minute, and second, that a baby octospider must be *taught* to monitor the status of its food supply. Imagine! It does not know instinctively when it is hungry! When Dr Blue saw the astonishment on my face, he laughed (a jumbled-up sequence of short colour-bursts) and then hastened to assure me that unexpected starvation is not a leading cause of death among the octospiders.

After my three-hour nap (I still cannot make it through the long octospider day without some sleep – of our group only Richard is capable of forgoing the nap on a regular basis), Dr Blue informed me that, because of my keen interest in their digestive process, the octospiders had decided to show me a couple of other unusual characteristics of their biology.

I boarded a transport with the three octos, passed through one of the two gates out of our zone, and crossed the Emerald City. I suspect that this field trip was also planned to mitigate my disappointment about Benjy. Dr Blue reminded me while we were travelling (it was hard for me to pay close attention to what he was saying – once we were outside our zone, there were all kinds of fascinating creatures beside our car and along the street, including many of the same species that I saw briefly during my first few moments in the Emerald City) that the octospiders were a polymorphic genus and that there were six separate adult manifestations of the particular octo species that had colonised our Rama spacecraft. 'Remember,' he told me in colour, 'that one of the possible parameter variations is size.'

There is no way that I could have been prepared for what I saw about twenty minutes later. We descended from the transport outside a large warehouse. At each end of the windowless building were two mammoth, drooling octospiders, with heads at least ten metres in diameter, bodies that looked like small blimps, and long tentacles that were slate-grey instead of the usual black and gold. Dr Blue informed me that this particular morph had one, and only one, function: to serve as a food repository for the colony.

'Each "replete" (my translation of Dr Blue's colours) can store up to several hundred full buffers'-worth of food for an ordinary adult octospider,' Dr Blue said. 'Since our individual intake buffers hold thirty days'-worth of normal sustenance, forty-five on a reduced-energy diet, you can see what a vast storehouse a dozen of these repletes represent.'

As I watched, five octospiders approached one of their huge brothers and said something in colour. Within seconds the creature leaned forward, bent its head down almost to the ground, and ejected a thick slurry from the enlarged mouth just below its milky lens. The five normal-sized octos gathered around the mound of slurry and fed themselves with their tentacles.

'We practise this several times every day, with every replete,' Dr Blue said. 'These morphs must have practice, for they are not very smart. You might have noticed that none of them spoke in colour. They do not have any language-transmission capability, and their mobility is extremely limited. Their genomes have been designed so that they can efficiently store food, preserve it for long periods of time, and regurgitate it to feed the colony upon request.'

I was still thinking about the huge repletes when our transport arrived at what I was told was an octospider school. I commented, while we were crossing the grounds, that the large facility seemed deserted. One of the other doctors said something about the colony not having had a 'recent replenishment,' if I interpreted the colours correctly, but I never received a clear explanation of just what was meant by his remark.

At one end of the school facility, we entered a small building that had no furnishings. Inside were two adult octospiders and about twenty juveniles, maybe one-half the size of their larger companions. From the activity it was obvious that a repetitive drill of some kind was under way. I could not, however, follow the conversation between the juveniles and their teachers, both because the octospiders were using their full alphabet, including the ultraviolet and the infra-red, and because the juvenile 'talk' did not flow in the neat, regular bands that I have learned to read.

Dr Blue explained that we were witnessing part of a 'measuring class', where the juveniles were being trained to perform assessments of their own health, including estimating the magnitude of food contained in their intake buffers. After Dr Blue told me that 'measuring' was an integral part of the early learning curriculum for their juveniles, I inquired about the irregularity of the juvenile colours. Dr Blue informed me that these particular octos were very young, not much past 'first colour', and were barely able to communicate distinct ideas.

After we returned to the conference room, I was asked a set of questions about human digestive systems. The questions were extremely sophisticated (we went through the Krebs citric acid cycle step by step, for example, and discussed other elements of human biochemistry that I could barely remember), and I was struck again by how much more the octospiders know about us than we know about them. As always, it was never necessary for me to repeat an answer.

What a day! It began with the pain of discovering that the octospiders were not going to be able to help Benjy. Later on I was reminded of how resilient the human psyche is when I was actually lifted out of my despondency by the stimulation of learning more about the octospiders. I remain astonished by the range of emotions we humans possess – and how very quickly we can change and adapt.

Eponine and I were talking last night about our life here in the Emerald City and how our unusual living conditions will affect the attitudes of the child she is carrying. At one point Ep shook her head and smiled. 'You know what's so amazing?' she said. 'Here we are, an isolated human contingent living in an alien domain inside a gargantuan spacecraft hurtling toward an unknown destination ... Yet our days here are full of laughter, elation, sadness, and disappointment, just as they would be if we were still back on Earth.'

'This may look like a waffle,' Max said, 'and it may feel like a waffle when you first put it in your mouth, but it damn sure doesn't *taste* like a waffle.'

'Put more syrup on it,' Eponine said, laughing. 'And pass the plate over here.'

Max handed the waffles across the table to his wife. 'Shit, Frenchie,' he said, 'these last few weeks you've been eating everything in sight. If I didn't know better, I would think that you and that unborn child of ours both had one of those "intake buffers" Nicole was telling us about.'

'It would be handy, though,' Richard said distractedly. 'You could load up on food and not have to stop work just because your stomach was calling.'

'This cereal is the best yet,' little Kepler said from the other end of the table. 'I bet even Hercules would like it ...'

'Speaking of whom,' Max interrupted in a lower voice, glancing from one end of the table to the other, 'what is his, or its, purpose? That damn octospider shows up every morning two hours after dawn and just hangs around. If the children are having school with Nai, he sits in the back of the room ...'

'He plays with us, Uncle Max,' Galileo shouted. 'Hercules is really a lot of fun. He does everything we ask ... Yesterday he let me use the back of his head as a punching-bag.'

'According to Archie,' Nicole said between bites, 'Hercules is the official observer. The octospiders are curious about everything. They want to know all about us, even the most mundane details.'

'That's great,' Max replied, 'but we have a slight problem. When you and Ellie and Richard are gone, nobody here can understand what Hercules is saying. Oh, sure, Nai knows a few simple phrases, but nothing that's involved. Yesterday, for example, while everyone else was taking the long nap, that damned Hercules followed me into the crapper. Now, I don't know about you, but it's hard for me to do my business even with Eponine within earshot. With an alien staring at me from a few metres away, my sphincter was absolutely paralysed.'

'Why didn't you tell Hercules to go away?' Patrick said, laughing.

'I did,' Max answered. 'But he just stared at me with fluid running around in his lens and kept repeating the same colour-pattern that was totally unintelligible to me.'

'Can you remember the pattern?' Ellie said. 'Maybe I can tell you what Hercules was saying.'

'Hell, no, I can't remember it,' Max replied. 'Besides, it doesn't make any difference now ... I'm not sitting here trying to shit.'

The Watanabe twins broke into howls of laughter and Eponine frowned at her husband. Benjy, who had said very little during breakfast, asked to be excused.

'Are you all right, dear?' Nicole asked.

Benjy nodded and left the dining room in the direction of his bedroom.

'Does he know anything?' Nai said quietly.

Nicole shook her head quickly and turned to her granddaughter. 'Are you finished with your breakfast, Nikki?'

'Yes, Nonni,' the little girl replied. She excused herself and moments later was joined by Kepler and Galileo.

'I think that Benjy knows more than any of us give him credit for,' Max said as soon as the children were gone.

'You could be right,' Nicole said softly. 'But yesterday when I talked to him, I saw no indication that he ...' Nicole stopped in midsentence and turned to Eponine. 'By the way,' she said, 'how are *you* feeling this morning?'

'Great,' Eponine replied. 'The baby was very active before dawn. He kicked hard for almost an hour – I could even watch his feet moving around on my tummy. I tried to get Max to feel one of his kicks, but he was too squeamish.'

'Now, why do you call that baby "he", Frenchie, when you know damn well that I want a little girl who looks just like you ...'

'I don't believe you for a moment, Max Puckett,' Eponine interrupted. 'You only *say* you want a girl so that you won't be disappointed. Nothing would please you more than a boy you can raise to be your buddy ... besides, as you know, it's customary in English to use the pronoun "he" when the sex is not known or specified.'

'Which brings me to another question for our octospider *experts*,' Max said after taking a sip of quasi-coffee. He glanced first at Ellie and then at Nicole. 'Do either of you know what sex, if any, our octospider friends might be?' He laughed. 'I certainly haven't seen anything on their naked bodies that gives me a clue ...'

Ellie shook her head. 'I don't really know, Max. Archie did tell me that Jamie is not his child, and not Dr Blue's either, at least not in the strictest biological sense.'

'So Jamie must be adopted,' Max said. 'But is Archie the man and Dr Blue the woman? Or vice versa? Or are our next-door neighbours a gay couple raising a child?'

'Maybe the octospiders don't have what we call sex,' Patrick said.

'Then where do *new* octospiders come from?' Max asked. 'They certainly don't just materialise out of thin air.'

'The octospiders are so advanced biologically,' Richard said, 'they may have a reproduction process that would seem like magic to us.'

'I have asked Dr Blue about their reproduction several times,' Nicole said. 'He says it's a complicated subject, especially since the octospiders are poly-morphic, and that they'll explain it to me after I understand the other aspects of their biology.'

'Now, if I were an octospider,' Max said with a grin, 'I would want to be one of those fat slobs Nicole saw yesterday. Wouldn't it be great if your only function in life was to eat and eat, storing food for all your brethren ... What an existence! I knew a pig farmer's son back in Arkansas who was like a *re-plete*. Only he kept all the food for himself. Wouldn't even share it with the pigs ... I think he weighed almost three hundred kilograms when he died at the age of thirty.'

Eponine finished her waffle. 'Fat jokes in the presence of pregnant women show a lack of sensitivity,' she said, feigning indignation.

'Oh, shit, Ep,' Max replied, 'you know that none of that crap applies anymore. We're zoo animals here in the Emerald City, and we're stuck with each other. Humans only worry about what they look like if they're worried about being compared with someone else.'

Nai excused herself from the table. 'I have a few more preparations to com-plete for today's school lessons,' she said. 'Nikki will be starting on consonant sounds – she has already breezed through the alphabet drills.'

'Like mother, like daughter,' Max said. After Patrick left the dining-room, leaving only the two couples and Ellie at the table, Max leaned forward with a mischievous smile on his face. 'Are my eyes deceiving me,' he said, 'or is young Patrick spending a lot more time with Nai than he did when we first arrived?'

'I think you're right, Max,' Ellie said. 'I have noticed the same thing. He told me he feels useful helping Nai with Benjy and the children. After all, you and Eponine are engrossed with each other and the baby that is coming, my time is completely occupied between Nikki and the octospiders, Mother and Father are always busy ...'

'You're missing the point, young lady,' Max said. 'I'm wondering if we have another *cup-el* forming in our midst.'

'Patrick and Nai?' Richard asked, as if the idea had just occurred to him for the first time.

'Yes, dear,' Nicole said. She laughed. 'Richard belongs to that category of genius with very selective observational skills. No detail from one of his projects, no matter how small, goes unnoticed. Yet he misses obvious changes in people's behaviour. I remember once in New Eden when Katie started wearing low-cut dresses ...'

Nicole stopped herself. It was still difficult for her to talk about Katie without becoming emotional.

'Kepler and Galileo have both noticed that Patrick is around every day,' Eponine said. 'Nai says that Galileo has become quite jealous.'

'And what does Nai say about Patrick's attention?' Nicole asked. 'Is she happy with it?'

'You know Nai,' Eponine replied. 'Always gracious, always thinking of others. I think she's concerned about how any possible relationship between Patrick and her might affect the twins.'

All eyes turned toward the visitor who appeared in the doorway. 'Well, well. Good morning, Hercules,' Max said, standing up from his chair. 'What a pleasant surprise!... What can we do for you this morning?'

The octospider stepped into the dining-room as the colours streamed around his head. 'He says that he has come to help Richard with his automatic translator,' Ellie said. 'Especially the parts outside our visible spectrum.'

2

Nicole was dreaming. She was also dancing to an African rhythm around a campfire in an Ivory Coast grove. Omeh was leading the dance. He was dressed in the green robe he had been wearing when he had come to visit her in Rome a few days before the launch of the Newton. All of her human friends in the Emerald City, plus their four closest octospider acquaintances, were also dancing in the circle around the camp-fire. Kepler and Galileo were fighting. Ellie and Nikki were holding hands. Hercules the octospider was dressed in a bright purple African costume. Eponine was very pregnant and heavy on her feet. Nicole heard her name being called from outside the circle. Was it Katie? Her heart raced as she strained to recognise the voice.

'Nicole,' Eponine said beside her bed. 'I'm having contractions.'

Nicole sat up and shook the dream from her head. 'How often?' she asked automatically.

'They're irregular,' Eponine replied. 'I'll have a couple about five minutes apart, and then nothing for half an hour.'

Most likely they're Braxton-Hicks, Nicole was thinking. *She's still five weeks short of full term.*

'Come lie down on the couch,' Nicole said, putting on her robe. 'And tell me when the next contraction begins.'

Max was waiting in the living-room after Nicole finished washing her hands. 'Is she having the baby?' he asked.

'Probably not,' Nicole said. She began putting slight pressure on Eponine's mid-section, trying to locate the baby.

Meanwhile, Max paced fitfully around the room. 'I would absolutely kill for a cigarette right now,' he mumbled.

When Eponine had another contraction, Nicole noticed that there was some slight pressure on the undilated cervix. She was worried because she wasn't absolutely certain where the baby was. 'I'm sorry, Ep,' Nicole said after another contraction six minutes later. 'I *think* this is a false labour, a kind of practice exercise your body is going through, but I could be wrong ... I've never dealt with a pregnancy at this stage before without some kind of monitoring equipment to help me....'

'Some women *do* have babies this early, don't they?' Eponine asked.

'Yes. But it's rare. Only about one per cent of first-time mothers deliver more than four weeks before their due date. And it's almost always due to some kind of complication. Or heredity ... Do you know by any chance if you or any of your siblings were premature?'

Eponine shook her head. 'I never knew anything at all about my natural family,' she said.

Damnit, Nicole thought. *I'm almost positive that these are Braxton-Hicks contractions ... If only I could tell for certain ...*

Nicole told Eponine to dress and return to her home. 'Keep a record of your contractions. What is especially important is the interval between them. If they start occurring regularly, every four minutes or so without significant gaps, then come and get me again.'

'Might there be a problem?' Max whispered to Nicole while Eponine was dressing.

'Unlikely, Max, but there is always that possibility.'

'What do you think about asking our friends the biological wizards for some help?' Max asked. 'Please forgive me if I am offending you, it's just ...'

'I'm ahead of you, Max,' Nicole said. 'I had already decided to consult with Dr Blue in the morning.'

Max was nervous long before Dr Blue started to open what Max called the bug-jar. 'Hold on, Doc,' Max said, gently putting his hands on the tentacle holding the jar. 'Would you mind explaining to me just what you're doing before you let those creatures out?'

Eponine was lying down on the sofa in the Puckett living-room. She was naked, but mostly covered by a pair of sheets provided by the octospiders. Nicole had been holding Eponine's hand during most of the several minutes that the three octospiders had been setting up the portable laboratory. Now Nicole walked over beside Max so that she could translate what Dr Blue was saying.

'Dr Blue is not an expert in this field,' Nicole interpreted. 'He says that one of the other two octospiders will have to explain the details of the process.'

After a short conversation among the three octospiders, Dr Blue moved aside and another alien stood directly in front of Nicole and Max. Dr Blue then informed Nicole that this particular octo, whom he called the 'image engineer,' had only recently started learning the simpler octospider dialect used to communicate with humans. 'He might be a little difficult to understand,' Dr Blue told her.

'The tiny beings in the jar,' Nicole said several seconds later as the colours began streaming around the engineer's head, 'are called ... image quadroids, I guess would be a satisfactory translation ... Anyway, they are living miniature cameras that will crawl inside Eponine and take pictures of the baby. Each quadroid has the capability of ... several million photographic picture elements that can be allocated to as many as 512 images per octo-spider nillet. They can even create a moving picture if you choose.'

She hesitated and turned to Max. 'I'm simplifying all this, if that's all right. It's highly technical, and all in their octal mathematics. The engineer was explaining there at the end all the different ways in which the user can specify pictures – Richard would have absolutely loved it.'

'Remind me again how long a nillet is?' Max said.

'About twenty-eight seconds,' Nicole replied. 'Richard named all the time terms. The nillet is the shortest unit in octospider time: Eight nillets in a feng, eight fengs in a woden, eight wodens in a tert, and eight terts in an octospider day. Richard calculates their day at thirty-two hours, fourteen minutes, and a little more than six seconds.'

'I'm glad somebody understands all this,' Max said quietly.

Nicole faced the image engineer again and the conversation continued. 'Each image quadroid,' she translated slowly, 'enters the specified target area, takes its pictures, and then returns to the image processor – that's the grey box over against the wall – where it "dumps" its images, receives its reward, and returns to the queue.'

'What?' said Max. 'What kind of reward?'

'Later, Max,' Nicole said. She was struggling to understand a sentence that she had already asked the octospider to repeat. Nicole was silent for a few seconds before she shook her head and turned to Dr Blue. 'I'm sorry,' she said, 'but I still don't understand that last sentence.'

The two octospiders had a rapid exchange in their natural dialect and then the image engineer faced Nicole again. 'Okay,' she said at length, 'I think I've got it now ... Max, the grey box is some kind of a programmable data manager, both storing the data in living cells and preparing the outputs from the quadroids for projection on the wall, or wherever we want to see the image, according to the protocol selected ...'

'I have an idea,' Max interrupted. 'This is all way beyond me ... If you're satisfied that this contraption is not going to hurt Ep in any way, why don't we get on with it?'

Dr Blue understood what Max said. At a signal from Nicole, he and the other octospiders walked outside the Puckett home and retrieved what looked like a covered drawer from the parked transport. 'In this container,' Dr Blue said to Nicole, 'are a group of twenty or thirty of the smallest members of our species, morphs whose primary function is to communicate directly with the quadroids and the other tiny creatures that make this system work. The morphs will actually manage the procedure.'

'Well, I'll be goddamned,' said Max when the drawer opened and the tiny octospiders, only a couple of centimetres tall, scampered into the middle of the room. 'Those ...' Max stammered excitedly, 'are what Eponine and I saw back in the blue maze, in the lair on the other side of the Cylindrical Sea.'

'The midget morphs,' Dr Blue explained, 'take our directions and then organise the entire process. It is they who will actually program the grey box. Now all we need to start is a few specifications on what kind of images you want and where you want to see them.'

The large coloured picture on the wall in the Puckett living-room showed a perfectly formed, handsome boy foetus filling almost all of his mother's womb. Max and Eponine had been celebrating for an hour, ever since they had first been able to distinguish that their unborn child was indeed a boy. As the afternoon had progressed and Nicole had learned better how to specify what she wanted to see, the quality of the pictures had improved markedly. Now, the twice-life-size image on the wall was stunning for its clarity.

'Can I watch him kick one more time?' Eponine asked.

The image engineer said something to the lead midget morph and in less than a nillet there was a replay of young master Puckett kicking upward against his mother's tummy.

'Look at the strength of those legs,' Max exclaimed. He was more relaxed now. After he had recovered from the shock of the initial images, Max had become concerned about all the 'paraphernalia' surrounding his son in the womb. Nicole had calmed the first-time father by identifying the umbilical cord and the placenta and then assuring Max that everything was normal.

'So I'm not going to deliver my son any time soon?' Eponine asked when the replay of the movie was over.

'No,' Nicole answered. 'My guess is you have five or six more weeks. Often first babies are a little late. You may still have some of those intermittent contractions between now and the birth, but don't worry about them.'

Nicole thanked Dr Blue profusely, as did Max and Eponine. Then the octo-spiders gathered up all the components, both biological and non-biological, of their portable laboratory. When the octos had departed, Nicole crossed the room and took Eponine's hand. 'Es-tu heureuse?' she asked her friend.

'Absolument,' Eponine replied. 'And relieved as well. I thought that some-thing had gone wrong.'

'No,' Nicole said. 'It was just a simple false alarm.'

Max crossed the room and gave Eponine a hug. He was beaming. Nicole withdrew slightly and watched the tender scene between her friends. *There is no time a couple love each other as much*, she thought, *as just before the birth of their first baby.*

Nicole started to leave the house. 'Wait a minute,' said Max. 'Don't you want to know what we're going to name him?'

'Of course,' Nicole replied.

'Marius Clyde Puckett,' Max said proudly.

'Marius,' Eponine added, 'because he was the waif Eponine's dream lover in *Les Misérables* – I longed for a Marius during my long and lonely nights at the orphanage. And Clyde, after Max's brother back in Arkansas.'

'It's an excellent name,' Nicole said, smiling to herself as she turned to leave. 'An excellent name,' she repeated.

Richard could not contain his excitement when he came home later that afternoon. 'I have just spent two absolutely fascinating hours over in the conference room with Archie and the other octospiders,' he said to Nicole in his loudest voice. 'They showed me the entire apparatus they used with you and Eponine earlier today. Amazing. What incredible genius! No, wizardry is a better term – I've said it from the beginning, the damn octospiders are biological wizards.

'Just imagine ... They have living creatures that are cameras, another set of microscopic bugs that read the images and carefully store each individual pixel, a special genetic warping of themselves that controls the process, and a limited amount of electronics, where necessary, to perform the mundane data-management tasks ... How many thousands of years did it take for all this to occur? Who engineered it in the first place? It is absolutely mind-boggling!'

Nicole smiled at her husband. 'Did you see Marius? What did you think? ...'

'I saw all the pictures from this afternoon,' Richard continued to shout. 'Do you know how the midget morphs communicate with the image quadroids? They use a special wavelength range in the far ultraviolet part of the spectrum. That's right. Archie told me those little bugs and the midget octospiders actually have a common language. And that's not all. Some of the morphs know as many as eight different microspecies languages. Even Archie himself can communicate with forty other species, fifteen using their basic octospider colours and the rest in a range of languages that includes signs, chemicals, and other parts of the electromagnetic spectrum.'

Richard stood still for a moment in the middle of the room. 'This is incredible, Nicole, simply incredible.'

He was about to launch into another monologue when Nicole asked him how the regular octos and the midget morphs communicated. 'I never saw any colour patterns on the heads of the morphs today,' she said.

'All their conversation is in the ultraviolet,' Richard said, starting to pace again. Suddenly he turned and pointed at the centre of his forehead. 'Nicole,' he said, 'that lens thing in the middle of their slit is a veritable telescope, able to receive information at practically any wavelength. It's staggering. Somehow they have organised all these life-forms into a grand symbiotic system of complexity far beyond anything we could ever conceive of ...'

Richard sat down on the couch next to Nicole. 'Look,' he said, showing his arms to her, 'I *still* have goose bumps. I am in absolute awe of these creatures ... Jesus, it's a good thing they aren't hostile.'

Nicole looked at her husband with a furrowed brow. 'Why do you say that?'

'They could command an army of *billions*, maybe even *trillions*. I bet they even talk to their *plants*! You saw how quickly they scared off that thing in the forest ... Imagine what it would be like if your enemy could control all the bacteria, even the *viruses*, and make them do their bidding. What a frightening concept!'

Nicole laughed. 'Don't you think you're getting carried away? Just because they have genetically engineered a set of living cameras, it does not follow...'

'I know,' said Richard, jumping up from the couch. 'But I can't help thinking about the logical extension of what we have seen here today ... Nicole, Archie admitted to me that the *sole* purpose of the midget morphs is to be able to deal with the world of the tiny. The midgets can *see* things as small as a micrometre, that's one-*thousandth* of a millimetre ... Now extend that idea another several orders of magnitude. Imagine a species whose morphs span four or five relationships similar to the one between the normal octos and the midgets. Communication with bacteria might not be impossible after all.'

'Richard,' Nicole said at this juncture, 'don't you have anything at all to say about the fact that Max and Eponine are going to have a son? And that the boy looks perfectly healthy?'

Richard stood silent for a few seconds. 'It *is* wonderful,' he said a little sheepishly. 'I guess I should go next door and congratulate them.'

'You can probably wait until after dinner,' Nicole said, glancing at one of the special watches Richard had made for them. The watch kept human time in an octospider frame of reference.

'Patrick, Ellie, Nikki, and Benjy have been over at Max and Eponine's for the last hour,' Nicole continued, 'ever since Dr Blue stopped by with some parchment photographs of little Marius in the womb.' She smiled. 'As you would say, they should be home in about a feng.'

3

Nicole finished brushing her teeth and gazed at her reflection in the mirror. *Galileo was right,* she thought. *I am an old woman.*

She began rubbing her face with her fingers, methodically massaging the wrinkles that seemed to be everywhere. She heard Benjy and the twins playing outside and then both Nai and Patrick calling them to school. *I was not always old,* she said to herself. *There was a time when I too went to school.*

Nicole closed her eyes, attempting to remember what she had looked like as a young girl. She was unable to conjure up a clear picture of herself as a child. Too many other pictures from the intervening years blurred and distorted Nicole's image of herself as a schoolgirl.

At length she reopened her eyes and stared at the image in the mirror. In her mind she painted out all the bags and wrinkles on her face. She changed the colour of her hair and eyebrows from grey to a deep black. Finally she managed to see herself as a beautiful woman of twenty-one. Nicole felt a brief but intense yearning for those days of her youth. *For we were young, and we knew that we would never die,* she remembered.

Richard stuck his head around the corner. 'Ellie and I will be working with Hercules in the study,' he said. 'Why don't you join us?'

'In a few minutes,' Nicole answered. While she touched up her hair, Nicole reflected on the daily patterns of the human clan in the Emerald City. They usually all gathered for breakfast in the Wakefields' dining room. School ended before lunch. Then everyone except Richard napped, their accommodation to the eight-hour-longer day. Most afternoons Nicole and Ellie and Richard were with the octospiders, learning more about their hosts or sharing experiences from the planet Earth. The other four adults spent almost all their time with Benjy and the children in their enclave at the end of the cul-de-sac.

And where does all this take us? Nicole suddenly wondered. *For how many years will we be the guests of the octospiders? And what will happen if and when Rama reaches its destination?*

They were all questions for which Nicole had no answers. Even Richard had apparently stopped worrying about what was going on outside the Emerald City. He was completely absorbed by the octospiders and his translator project.

Now he only asked Archie for celestial navigation data every two months or so. Each time Richard would report to the others, without editorial comment, that Rama was still headed in the general direction of the star Tau Ceti.

Like little Marius, Nicole thought, *we are content here in our womb. As long as the outside world does not force itself upon us, we do not ask the overwhelming questions.*

Nicole left the bathroom and walked down the hall to the study. Richard was sitting on the floor between Hercules and Ellie. 'The easy part is tracking the colour pattern and having the sequence stored in the processor,' he was saying. 'The hardest part of the translation is automatically converting that pattern into a recognizable English sentence.'

Richard faced Hercules and spoke very slowly. 'Because your language is so mathematical, with every colour having an acceptable angstrom range defined a priori, all the sensor has to do is identify the stream of colours and the widths of the bands. The entire information content has then been captured. Because the rules are so precise, it's not even difficult to code a simple fault protection algorithm, for use with juveniles or careless speakers, in case any single colour errs to the left or the right in the spectrum.

'Changing what an octospider has said into our language, however, is a much more complex process. The dictionary for the translation is straightforward enough. Each word and the appropriate clarifiers can be readily identified. But it's damn near impossible to make the next step, into sentences, without some human intervention.'

'That's because the octospider language is fundamentally different from ours,' Ellie commented. 'Everything is specified and quantified, to minimise the possibility of misunderstanding. There is no subtlety or nuance. Look how they use the pronouns "we", "they", and "you". The pronouns are always marked with numerical clarifiers, including ranges when there are uncertainties. An octospider never says "a few wodens" or "several nillets" – always a number, or a numerical range, is used to specify the length of time more precisely.'

'From our point of view,' Hercules said in colour, 'there are two aspects to human language that are extremely difficult. One is the lack of precise specification, which leads to a massive vocabulary. The other is your use of indirectness to communicate ... I still have trouble understanding Max because often what he says is not literally what he means.'

'I don't know how to do this in your computer,' Nicole now said to Richard, 'but somehow all the quantitative information contained in each octospider statement must be reflected by the translation. Almost every verb or adjective they use has a connected numerical clarifier. How, for example, did Ellie just translate "extremely difficult" and "massive vocabulary"? What Hercules said, in octospider, was "difficult", with the number five used to clarify it, and "big vocabulary", with the number six as a clarifier for "big". All comparative clarifiers address the question of the strength of the adjective. Since their base number system is octal, the range for the comparatives is between one and seven. If Hercules had used a seven to clarify the word "difficult", Ellie would have translated the phrase as "impossibly difficult". If he had used a two as a clarifier in the same phrase, she might have said "slightly difficult".'

'Mistakes in the strengths of the adjectives, although important,' Richard said as he fiddled absentmindedly with a small processor, 'almost never lead to misunderstandings. Failure to interpret properly the verb clarifiers, however, is another issue altogether ... as I have learned recently from my preliminary tests. Take the simple octospider verb "to go", which means, as you know, to move unaided, without a transport. The maroon-purple-lemon yellow strip, each colour the same width, covers several dozen words in English, everything from "walk" to "stroll", "saunter", "run", and even "sprint".'

'That's the same point I was just making,' Ellie said. 'There is no translation without full interpretation of the clarifiers. For that particular verb, the octos use a double clarifier to address the issue of "how fast". In a sense, there are sixty-three different speeds at which they "go" ... To make matters even more complex, they may use a range clarifier as well, so their statement "Let's go" is subject to many, many possible translations.'

Richard grimaced and shook his head.

'What's the matter, Father?' Ellie asked.

'I'm just disappointed,' he answered. 'I had hoped to have a simplified version of the translator completed by now. But I made the assumption that the gist of what was being said could be determined without tracking *all* the clarifiers. To include all those short colour-strips will both increase the storage required and significantly slow down the translation. I may have trouble ever designing a translator that works in real time.'

'So what?' Hercules asked. 'Why are you so concerned about this translator? Ellie and Nicole already understand our language very well.'

'Not really,' Nicole said. 'Ellie is the only one of us who is *truly* fluent with your colours. I am still learning daily.'

'Although I originally began this project both as a challenge and as a means to force myself to become familiar with your language,' Richard replied to Hercules, 'Nicole and I were talking last week about how important the translator has become. She says, and I agree with her, that our human clan here in the Emerald City is dividing into two groups. Ellie, Nicole, and I have made our life more interesting because of our increasing interactions with your species. The rest of the humans, including the children, remain essentially isolated. Eventually, if the others don't have some way of communicating with you, they will become dissatisfied and/or unhappy. A good automatic translator is the key that will open up their lives here.'

The map was wrinkled and torn in a few places. Patrick helped Nai unroll it slowly and tack it to the wall of her dining room, which doubled as the schoolroom for the children.

'Nikki, do you remember what this is?' Nai asked.

'Of course, Mrs Watanabe,' the little girl replied. 'It's our map of the Earth.'

'Benjy, can you show us where your parents and grandparents were born?'

'Not again,' Galileo muttered audibly to Kepler. 'He'll never get it right. He's too dumb.'

'*Galileo Watanabe*,' came the swift response. 'Go to your room and sit on your bed for fifteen minutes.'

'That's all right, Nai,' Benjy said as he walked up to the map. 'I'm used to it by now.'

Galileo, almost seven years old by human accounting, stopped at the door to see if his sentence would be reprieved. 'What are you waiting for?' his mother scolded. 'I said for you to go to your room.'

Benjy stood quietly in front of the map for about twenty seconds. 'My mo-ther,' he said at length, 'was born here in France.' He backed away from the map briefly and located the United States on the opposite side of the Atlantic Ocean. 'My fa-ther,' Benjy said, 'was born here in Bos-ton, in A-mer-i-ca.'

Benjy started to sit down. 'What about your grandparents?' Nai prompted. 'Where were they born?'

'My mo-ther's mo-ther, my grand-mo-ther,' Benjy said slowly, 'was bom in Af-ri-ca.' He stared at the map for several seconds. 'But I do not re-member where that is.'

'I know, Mrs Watanabe,' said little Nikki immediately. 'May I show Benjy?'

Benjy turned and looked at the pretty girl with the jet-black hair. He smiled. 'You can tell me, Nik-ki.'

The girl rose from her chair and crossed the room. She placed her finger on the western section of Africa. 'Nonni's mother was born here,' she said proudly, 'in this green country ... It's called the Ivory Coast.'

'That's very good, Nikki,' Nai said.

'I'm sor-ry, Nai,' Benjy now said. 'I've been work-ing so hard on frac-tions I have-n't had an-y time for ge-og-ra-phy.' His eyes followed his three-year-old niece back to her seat. When he turned to face Nai again, Benjy's cheeks were, wet with tears. 'Nai,' he said, 'I don't feel like school to-day ... I think I'll go back to my own house.'

'OK, Benjy,' Nai said softly. Benjy moved toward the door. Patrick started to come over to his brother, but Nai waved him away.

The schoolroom was uncomfortably quiet for almost a minute. 'Is it my turn now?' Kepler finally asked.

Nai nodded and the boy walked up to the map. 'My mother was born here, in Thailand, in the town of Lamphun. That's where her father was also born. My grandmother on my mother's side was also born in Thailand, but in another city called Chiang Saen. Here it is, next to the Chinese border.' Kepler took one step to the east and pointed at Japan.

'My father, Kenji Watanabe, and both his parents were born in the Japanese city of Kyoto.'

The boy backed away from the map. He seemed to be struggling to say something. 'What is it, Kepler?' Nai asked.

'Mother,' the small boy said after an agonizing silence, 'was Daddy a bad man?'

'Whaat?' said Nai, completely stunned. She bent down to her son's level and looked him straight in the eyes. 'Your father was a wonderful human being ... He was intelligent, sensitive, loving, humorous – an absolute prince of a person. He ...'

Nai had to stop herself. She could feel her own emotions ready to erupt. She stood up, gazed at the ceiling for a brief moment, and regained her composure. 'Kepler,' she then said, 'why are you asking such a question? You adored your father. How could you have possibly ...'

'Uncle Max told us that Mr Nakamura came from Japan. We know that he is a bad man. Galileo says that since Daddy came from the same place ...'

'*Galileo*,' Nai's voice thundered, scaring all the children. 'Come here immediately.'

The boy scampered into the room and gave his mother a puzzled look.

'What have you been saying to your brother about your father?'

'What do you mean?' Galileo said, trying to look innocent.

'You told me that Daddy may have been a bad man, since he came from Japan like Mr Nakamura ...'

'Well, I don't remember Daddy very clearly. All I said was that maybe ...'

It took all of Nai's self-control to keep her from slapping Galileo. She grabbed the boy by both of his shoulders. 'Young man,' she said, 'if I *ever* hear you say one word against your father again ...'

Nai could not finish her sentence. She did not know what to threaten, or even what to say next. She suddenly felt completely overwhelmed by everything in her life.

'Sit down, please,' she said at length to her twin sons, 'and listen very carefully.' Nai took a deep breath. 'This map on the wall,' she said, pointing, 'shows all the countries on the planet Earth. In every nation there are all kinds of people, some good, some bad, most a complex mixture of good and bad. No country has only good people, or bad people. Your father grew up in Japan. So did Mr Nakamura. I agree with Uncle Max that Mr Nakamura is a very evil man. But the fact that he is bad has nothing to do with his being Japanese. Your father, Mr Kenji Watanabe, who was also Japanese, was as good a man as ever lived. I'm sorry that you cannot remember him and never really knew what he was like ...'

Nai paused for a moment. 'I will never forget your father,' she said in a softer voice, almost to herself. 'I can still see him returning to our home in New Eden in the late afternoon. The two of you always shouted together, "Hi Daddy, Hi Daddy", as he entered the house. He would kiss me, lift both of you in his arms, and take you out to the swing set in the backyard. Always, no matter how trying his day had been, he was patient and caring ...'

Her voice trailed off. Tears flooded Nai's eyes and she felt her body beginning to tremble. She turned her back and faced the map. 'Class dismissed for today,' she said.

Patrick stood beside Nai as the two of them watched the twins and Nikki playing with a big blue ball in the cul-de-sac. It was half an hour later. 'I'm sorry, Patrick,' Nai said. 'I didn't expect to become ...'

'You have nothing to be sorry for,' the young man replied.

'Yes, I do,' Nai said. 'Years ago I promised myself that I would never show such feelings in front of Kepler and Galileo. They can't possibly understand.'

'They've forgotten it already,' Patrick said after a brief silence. 'Look at them. They're totally engrossed in their game.'

At that moment the twins were having one of their typical arguments. As usual, Galileo was trying to gain an advantage for himself in a game that did not have rigorous rules. Nikki stood beside the boys, following every word of their dispute.

'Boys, boys,' Nai called out. 'Stop it. If you can't play without arguing, then you'll have to come inside.'

A few seconds later the blue ball was bouncing down the street toward the plaza and all three children were running gleefully after it. 'Would you like something to drink?' Nai asked Patrick.

'Yes, I would ... Do you have any more of that light green melon juice that Hercules brought last week? It was really tasty.'

'Yes,' answered Nai, bending down to the small cabinet in which they kept cool drinks. 'By the way, where is Hercules? I haven't seen him for several days.'

Patrick laughed. 'Uncle Richard has recruited him to work full-time on the translator. Ellie and Archie are even there with them every afternoon.' He thanked Nai for the glass of juice.

Nai took a sip of her own drink and walked back into the living-room. 'I know you wanted to comfort Benjy this morning,' she said. 'I only stopped you because I know your brother so well. He is very proud. He does not want anyone's pity.'

'I understood,' Patrick said.

'Benjy realised this morning, at some level, that even little Nikki – whom he still thinks of as a baby-will quickly surpass him in school. The discovery shocked him, and reminded him again of his own limitations.'

Nai was standing in front of the map of Earth, which was still affixed to the wall. 'Nothing on this map means anything significant to you, does it?' she said.

'Not really,' Patrick replied. 'I have seen many photographs and movies, of course, and when I was about the twins' age my father used to tell me about Boston, and the colour of the leaves in New England during the autumn, and the trip he took to Ireland with *his* father. But my memories are of other places. The lair in New York is quite vivid, as well as the astonishing year we spent at The Node.' He was silent for a moment. 'And The Eagle! What a creature! I remember him even more clearly than my father.'

'So do you consider yourself to be an Earthling?' Nai asked.

'That's an interesting question,' Patrick replied. He finished his drink. 'You know, I've never really thought about it ... Certainly I consider myself to be a human. But an Earthling? ... I guess not.'

Nai reached out and touched the map. 'My hometown of Lamphun, if it were larger, would have appeared here, just south of Chiang Mai. Sometimes it doesn't seem possible to me that I actually lived there as a child.'

Nai's fingers ran over the outline of Thailand as she stood quietly beside Patrick. 'The other night,' she said at length, 'Galileo threw a cup of water on my head while I was bathing the boys, and I suddenly had an incredibly vivid memory of the three days I spent in Chiang Mai with my cousins when I was fourteen years old ... It was the time of the Songkran Festival in April, and everyone in the city was celebrating the Thai New Year. There were parades and speeches – the usual stuff about how all the Chakri kings since the first Rama had prepared the Thai people for their important role in the world – but what I remember most clearly was riding around the city at night in the back of an electric pickup with my cousin Oni and her friends. Everywhere we went we threw a bucket of water on somebody – and they threw one on us. We laughed and laughed.'

'Why was everyone throwing water?' Patrick asked.

'I've forgotten now,' Nai said with a shrug. 'It had something to do with the ceremony. But the experience itself, the shared laughter, and even what it felt like to have my clothes absolutely soaked, and suddenly to be hit by another burst of water – all that I can recall in detail.'

They were again silent as Nai reached up to take the map off the wall. 'So I guess Kepler and Galileo will not consider themselves to be Earthlings either,' she mused. She rolled up the map very carefully. 'Maybe even studying the geography and history of the Earth is a waste of time.'

'I don't think so,' Patrick said. 'What else are the children going to study? And besides, all of us need to understand where we came from.'

Three young faces peered into the living-room from the atrium. 'Is it lunchtime yet?' asked Galileo.

'Almost,' Nai replied. 'Go wash up first ... *One at a time,*' she said, as the young feet pounded down the hallway.

Nai turned around abruptly and caught Patrick staring at her in an unusual way. She smiled. 'I have very much enjoyed your company this morning,' she said. 'You have made it easier for me to deal with everything.' Nai extended both her arms and took Patrick's hands in hers. 'You have been a big help to me with Benjy and the children these last two months,' she said, her eyes meeting his. 'And it would be foolish of me not to acknowledge that I have not felt nearly as lonely since you began coming over here every morning.'

Patrick made an awkward step toward Nai, but she held his hands firmly in place. 'Not yet,' she said gently. 'It's still too early.'

4

Less than a minute after the great firefly clusters in the Emerald City dome announced that another day had begun, little Nikki was in her grandparents' room. 'It's light, Nonni,' she said. 'They'll be coming for us soon.'

Nicole rolled over and gave her granddaughter a hug. 'We still have a couple of hours, Nikki,' she said to the excited girl. 'Boobah is still sleeping ... Why don't you go back to your room and play with your toys while we take a shower?'

When the disappointed girl finally left, Richard was sitting up, rubbing his eyes. 'Nikki has talked about nothing but this day for the last week,' Nicole said to him. 'She is always in Benjy's room, looking at the painting. Nikki and the twins have even given names to all those bizarre animals.'

Nicole reached unconsciously for the hairbrush beside the bed. 'Why is it that small children have such difficulty understanding the concept of time? Even though Ellie has made her a calendar and has been counting off the days one by one, Nikki has asked me every morning if "today's the day".'

'She's just excited. Everybody is,' Richard said, rising from the bed. 'I hope that we're not all disappointed.'

'How could we be?' Nicole replied. 'Dr Blue says that we will see sights even more amazing than those you and I saw when we entered the city for the first time.'

'I guess the whole menagerie will be out in force,' Richard said. 'By the way, do you understand what the octospiders are celebrating?'

'Sort of ... I guess the closest equivalent holiday I know about would be the American Thanksgiving. The octos call this "Bounty Day". They set aside a day to celebrate the quality of their life ... At least that's the way Dr Blue explained it to me.'

Richard started to go to the shower but stuck his head back in the room. 'Do you think they invited us to participate today because you told them about our family discussion at breakfast two weeks ago?'

'You mean when Patrick and Max said they wished they could return to New Eden?'

Richard nodded.

'Yes, I do,' Nicole answered. 'I think the octospiders had convinced themselves that we were all completely content here. Having us attend their celebration is part of their attempt to integrate us more into their society.'

'I wish I had all the damn translators finished,' Richard said. 'As it is, I only have two ... and they're not completely checked out. Should I give the second one to Max?'

'That would be a good idea,' Nicole said, crowding her husband in the doorway.

'What are you doing?' Richard said.

'I'm joining you in the shower,' Nicole answered with a laugh, 'unless, of course, you're too old to have company.'

Jamie came over from next door to tell them that the transport was ready. He was the youngest of their three octospider neighbours (Hercules lived by himself just on the other side of the plaza), and the humans had had the least contact with him. Jamie's 'guardians,' Archie and Dr Blue, explained that Jamie was very much involved with his studies and was approaching a major milestone in his life. Although at first glance Jamie looked almost exactly like the three adult octospiders the clan saw regularly, he was a little smaller than the older octos and the gold stripes in his tentacles were slightly brighter.

The humans had briefly been in a quandary about what to wear for the octospider celebration, but they had soon realised that their clothing was of absolutely no significance. None of the alien species in the Emerald City wore any coverings, a fact that the octospiders had often commented upon. When Richard had once suggested, only partly in jest, that perhaps the humans too should dispense with clothing while they were in the Emerald City – 'When in Rome ...' he had said – the group had quickly understood how fundamental clothing was to human psychological comfort. 'I could not be naked, even among you, my closest friends, without being extremely self-conscious,' Eponine had said, summarizing all their feelings.

The motley contingent of eleven humans and their four octospider colleagues traipsed down the street to the plaza. The very pregnant Eponine was at the back of the group, walking slowly and keeping one hand on her stomach. The women had all chosen to dress up a little – Nai was even wearing her colourful Thai silk dress with the blue and green flowers – but the men and children, except for Max (who had on the outrageous Hawaiian shirt he saved for special occasions), were in the T-shirts and jeans that had been their regular costume since the first day they had arrived at the Emerald City.

At least all their clothes were clean. In the beginning, finding a way to do the laundry had been an acute problem for the humans. However, once they had explained their difficulty to Archie, it was only a few days before he introduced them to the dromos, insect-sized beings that automatically cleaned their clothes.

The group boarded the transport at the plaza. Just before the gate marking the end of their zone, the transport stopped and two octospiders they had never seen before climbed into the car. Richard practised using his translator during the ensuing conversation between Dr Blue and the newcomers. Ellie read her father's monitor over his shoulder and congratulated him on the accuracy of the translation. The fidelity of the translation was fairly good, but the speed, at least at the normal octospider conversation rate, was much too slow. One sentence would be translated while three were 'spoken', causing Richard to reset the system regularly. He couldn't, of course, glean much from a conversation in which he missed two out of three sentences.

Once on the other side of the gate, the view from the transport was a mosaic of strange shapes and bright colours. Nikki's eyes stayed open at their widest levels as she, Benjy, and the twins, with much shouting, identified most of the animals from the octospider painting. The broad streets were full of traffic. There were not only many transports, which moved in both directions on rails like a city trolley, but also pedestrians of all species and sizes, creatures riding wheeled vehicles like unicycles and bicycles, and an occasional mixed group of beings on an ostrichsaur.

Max, who had never once been outside the human zone since his arrival, punctuated his observations with 'shits', 'damns', and some of the other words Eponine had requested that he remove from his vocabulary before the birth of their child. Max did not start to worry about Eponine's safety until, at the first transport stop after the gate, some strange new creatures crowded onto their car. Four of the newcomers headed immediately in Eponine's direction to examine the special seat the octospiders had installed in the transport because of her advanced pregnancy. Max stood protectively beside her, holding on to one of the vertical rails that were scattered throughout the ten-metre length of the car.

A pair of the new passengers were what the children called 'striped crabs,' eight-legged red-and-yellow creatures about Nikki's size, with round bodies covered with a hard shell and fearsome-looking claws. Both of them began immediately rubbing their antennae against one of Eponine's bare legs below her dress. They were only being curious, but the combination of the peculiar sensation and the bizarre appearance of the aliens caused Eponine to recoil from fright. Archie, who was standing on the other side of Eponine, reached down quickly with a tentacle and pushed the aliens gently away. One of the striped crabs then reared up on its back four legs, its claws snapping the air in front of Eponine's face, and apparently said something threatening with its rapidly vibrating antennae. An instant later Archie extended two tentacles, lifted the hostile striped crab off the floor of the transport, and deposited the creature on the street outside.

The scene dramatically altered the mood of all the humans. As Ellie translated Archie's explanation of what had occurred for Max and Eponine, the

Watanabe twins huddled up close to Nai, and Nikki stretched out her arms for her grandfather to pick her up.

'That species is not very intelligent,' Archie told his human friends, 'and we have had difficulty engineering out its aggressive tendencies. The particular creature that I threw off the bus has been a troublemaker before. The optimiser responsible for the species had already marked it – you may have noticed – with the two small green dots at the rear of the carapace. This latest transgression will certainly result in termination.'

When Ellie finished with the translation, the humans methodically inspected the other aliens on the transport, checking for any more green dots. Relieved that all the other creatures on board were safe, the adults relaxed somewhat.

'What did that "thing" say?' Richard asked Archie as the transport approached another stop.

'It was a standard threat response,' Archie replied, 'typical of animals with constrained intelligence capability. Its antenna patterns conveyed a crude message, with very little real information content.'

The transport continued down the avenue for eight or ten more nillets, stopping twice to receive additional passengers, including half a dozen octospiders and about twenty other creatures representing five different species. Four of the royal blue animals, the ones with the hemispherical tops that looked like they contained undulating brains, squatted right opposite Richard, who was still holding Nikki. Their collective assortment of eight knotted antennae extended upward toward Nikki's feet and became intertwined, as if they were communicating. When the human girl moved her feet slightly, the antennae were quickly retracted back into the strange mass that formed the bulk of the bodies of the alien creatures.

By this time it was very crowded in the transport. An animal the humans had never seen before, which Max later described accurately as a Polish sausage with a long nose and six short legs, raised itself up on one of the vertical bars and grabbed Nai's small purse with its two front paws. Jamie interceded before any damage was done to either the purse or Nai, but a few seconds later Galileo kicked the sausage hard, causing it to lose its grip on the bar. The boy explained that he had thought the sausage was preparing for another grab at the purse. The creature backed away into another section of the transport, its solitary eye fixed warily on Galileo.

'You'd better be careful,' Max said with a grin, tousling the boy's hair. 'Or the octos will place two green dots on your behind.'

The avenue was lined with one- and two-storey buildings, almost all painted with geometric patterns in brilliant colours. Garlands and wreaths of brightly coloured flowers and leaves festooned the doorways and the roofs. On one long wall, which Hercules told Nai was the back of the main hospital, a huge rectangular mural, four metres high and twenty metres long, depicted the octospider physicians ministering to their own injured, as well as helping many of the other creatures that lived in the Emerald City.

The transport slowed slightly and began to ascend a ramp. The vehicle crossed a bridge, several hundred metres long over a wide river or canal that contained boats, many frolicking octospiders, and several other unknown marine creatures. Archie explained that they were entering the heart of the Emerald City, where all the main ceremonies took place and the 'most important' optimisers lived and worked. 'Over there,' he said, pointing at an octagonal building about thirty metres tall, 'is our library and information centre.'

In response to Richard's question, Archie said that the canal, or moat, completely encircled the 'administrative centre'. 'Except on special occasions like today, or for some official purpose approved by the optimisers,' Archie said, 'only octospiders are allowed access to this area.'

The transport parked in a large, flat plain beside an oval structure that looked like a stadium, or perhaps an outdoor auditorium. Nai told Patrick, after they descended from the car, that she had felt more claustrophobic during the last part of the ride than at any time since she had been on the Kyoto subway at rush hour during her trip to meet Kenji's family.

'At least in Japan,' Patrick said with a brief shudder, 'you were surrounded by other human beings ... Here it was so weird. I felt as if I were being scrutinised by all of them. I had to close my eyes to maintain my sanity.'

As they disembarked and began moving toward the stadium, the humans walked in a group, surrounded by their four octospider friends and the other two octos who had boarded the transport before it had left the human zone. These six octospiders protected Nicole and the others from the teeming hordes of living creatures swarming in all directions. Eponine started feeling faint, as much from the combination of sights and smells as from the walking, so Archie stopped their procession about every fifty metres. Eventually they entered one of the gates and the octospiders led the humans to their assigned section.

There was only one seat in the section that had been reserved for the humans. In fact, Eponine may have had the only seat in the stadium. Looking around the upper deck of the arena with Richard's binoculars, Max and Patrick saw many beings leaning against, or holding on to, the sturdy vertical poles scattered throughout the terraces, but nowhere else could they find any seats.

Benjy was fascinated by the cloth bags that Archie and a few of the other octospiders were carrying. The bags, all of which were identical, were about the size of a woman's handbag and were off-white in colour. They hung at what might be called octospider hip level, attached over the head with a simple strap. Never before had any of the humans seen an octo with an accessory. Benjy had noticed the bags immediately and had asked Archie about them while they had been standing together at the plaza. Benjy had assumed that Archie had not understood his question at that time, and Benjy had in fact forgotten it himself until they reached the stadium and he saw the other similar bags.

Archie was uncharacteristically vague in his explanation of the purpose of the bag. Nicole had to ask the octospider to repeat his colours before she told Benjy what had been said. 'Archie says it's equipment he might need to protect us in an emergency.'

'What kind of e-quip-ment?' Benjy asked, but Archie had already moved several metres away and was talking with an octospider in an adjacent section.

The humans were separated from the other species both by two strips of taut metal rope around the tops and bottoms of the vertical poles on the outside of their enclave, and by their octospider protectors (or guards, as Max called them), who stationed themselves in the empty area between the different species. Beside the humans on the right was a group of several hundred of the aliens with the six flexible arms, the same creatures who had built the staircase under the rainbow dome. On the left and below the human clan, on the other side of a large empty area, were as many as a thousand brown, chunky, iguanalike animals with long, tapered tails and protruding teeth. The iguanas were the size of domestic cats.

What was immediately obvious was that the entire stadium was rigidly segregated. Each species was sitting with its own kind. What's more, except for the 'guards,' there were no octospiders on the upper deck. All fifteen thousand of the octos (Richard's estimate) who were present as spectators were sitting in the lower deck.

'There are several reasons for the segregation,' Archie explained, with Ellie translating for everyone else. 'First, what the Chief Optimiser says is going to be broadcast in thirty or forty languages simultaneously. If you look carefully, you'll see that each special section has an apparatus – here's yours, for example, what Richard calls a speaker – that presents what's being said in the language of that species. We have been working with the Chief Optimiser's text for days, preparing the proper translations. Since all the octos, including the various morphs, can understand our standard language of colour, they're all down on the lower deck, where there is no special translation equipment ...

'Let me show you what I'm talking about. Look over there (Archie extended a tentacle) do you see that group of striped crabs? See the two large vertical wires on that table at the front of their section? When the Chief Optimiser starts to speak, those wires will activate and present what is being said in their antenna language.'

Far below them, over the top of what would have been a sunken field in an Earth stadium, a vast cover with coloured stripes was suspended from stanchions attached to the bottom sections of the lower deck.

'Can you read what it says?' Ellie asked her father.

'What?' said Richard, still stunned by the magnitude of the spectacle.

'There's a message on the cover,' Ellie said, pointing downward. 'Read the colours.'

'So there is.' Richard read very slowly. 'Bounty means food, water, energy, information, balance, and ... What's the last word?'

'I would translate it as "diversity",' Ellie said.

'What does the message mean?' Eponine asked.

'I guess we're going to find out.'

A few minutes later, after Archie had told the humans that another reason for the species segregation was to confirm the octospiders' census statistics, the field cover was rolled up on two long, thick poles by two pairs of giant black animals. The pairs started on opposite sides of the middle of the arena and then moved toward the ends of the stadium, wrapping the cover around their poles to unveil the entire field.

Simultaneously, an additional cluster of fireflies descended from far above the stadium so that all the spectators could clearly see not only the abundance of fruits, vegetables, and grains stacked in hundreds of piles on both ends of the field, but also the two collections of diverse beings that were in separate regions on the floor of the arena, on either side of its middle. The first group of aliens was walking around in a large circle on a normal dirt surface. They were attached to each other by some kind of rope. Next to them was a large pool of water, in which another thirty or forty species, also connected to each other, were swimming in a second large circle.

In the absolute centre of the field was a raised platform, empty except for some scattered black boxes, with ramps descending in the direction of the two adjacent regions. As everyone watched, four octospiders broke from the circle in the swimming pool and climbed the ramp onto the platform. Another four octospiders left the group walking on the dirt surface and joined their colleagues. One of these eight octos then stood up on a box in the middle of the platform and began to speak in colour.

'We have gathered here today,' the voice from the speaker startled the humans. Little Nikki began to cry. At first it was extremely difficult for them to understand what they were hearing, for each syllable was stressed exactly the same and, although carefully pronounced, the sounds were not quite right, as if they were made by someone who had never heard a human speak. Richard was flabbergasted. He immediately abandoned his attempt to use his own real-time translator and bent down to study the octospider device.

Ellie borrowed Richard's binoculars so that she could follow the colours more readily. Even though she had to guess at some of the words because of the strip pieces outside her visible range, it was easier for her to watch than to concentrate fully on what was coming out of the octospider audio equipment.

Eventually the adults tuned their ears somewhat to the cadence and pronunciation of the alien voice and caught most of what was being said.

The octospider Chief Optimiser indicated that all was well in their bountiful realm and that the continued success of their complex and diverse society was reflected in the variety of foods found on the field. 'None of this bounty,' the speaker said, 'could have been produced without strong interspecies co-operation.'

Later in his brief message the Chief Optimiser handed out kudos for exceptional performance. Several specific species were singled out – for example, production of the honeylike substance had apparently been outstanding, for a dozen hovering fireflies spotlighted the snout-nosed beetle section for a few moments. About three fengs into the speech, the humans grew tired of the strain of listening to the strange voice and stopped following the speech altogether. The group was therefore surprised when the fireflies appeared over their heads and they were introduced to the alien multitudes. Thousands of strange eyes were aimed in their direction for half a nillet.

'What did he say about us?' Max asked Ellie, who had continued to translate the colours. Max had been talking to Eponine during the most recent part of the Chief Optimiser's speech.

'Just that we were new in the domain and that they were still learning about our capabilities. Then there were some numbers that must have been some way of describing us. I didn't understand that part.'

After another two species were briefly introduced, the Chief Optimiser started summarizing the main points of his speech. *'Mommy, Mommy,'* Nikki's terrified scream suddenly overpowered the alien voice. Somehow, while the adult humans were absorbed with the speech and the spectacle surrounding them, Nikki had climbed over the lower barrier around their section and entered the open space separating them from the iguana creatures. The octospider Hercules, who had been patrolling that area, had apparently not noticed her either, for he was unaware that one of the iguanas had stuck its head in the gap between the two metal ropes around its section and grabbed Nikki's dress with its sharp teeth.

The terror in the child's voice momentarily paralysed everyone but Benjy. He acted instantly, leaping over the barrier, rushing to Nikki's aid, and smashing the iguana creature in the head with all his strength. The startled alien let go of Nikki's dress. Pandemonium ensued. Nikki raced back to her mother's arms, but before Hercules and Archie could reach Benjy, the enraged alien had forced itself through the gap and jumped upon Benjy's back. He screamed from the intense pain of the iguana's teeth in his shoulder and began to flail about, trying to shake the creature off. A few seconds later the creature dropped to the ground, completely unconscious. Two green spots were clearly visible where the creature's tail joined the rest of its body.

The entire incident had occurred in less than a minute. The speech had not been interrupted. Except in the immediate surrounding sections, there had been no notice of the event. But Nikki was hopelessly frightened, Benjy was seriously injured, and Eponine had started having a contraction. Below them, the angry iguanas were straining against their metal ropes, disregarding the threats of the ten octospiders who had now moved into the space between the two species.

Archie told the humans that it was time for them to leave. There was no argument. Archie escorted them out of the stadium in a hurry, with Ellie carrying her sobbing daughter and Nicole frantically rubbing antiseptic taken from her medical bag into Benjy's wound.

Richard rose up on his elbows when Nicole came into the bedroom. 'Is he all right?' Richard asked.

'I believe so,' Nicole said with a heavy sigh. 'I'm still worried that there may be poisonous chemicals in that creature's saliva. Dr Blue has been very helpful. He has explained to me that the iguanas have no toxic venom, but he agrees we must watch out for some kind of allergic reaction in Benjy ... The next day or two will tell us whether or not we have a problem.'

'And the pain? Has it subsided?'

'Benjy refuses to complain. I think that he is actually quite proud of himself – as well he should be – and doesn't want to say anything that would detract from his moment as the hero of the family.'

'What about Eponine?' Richard said after a brief silence. 'Is she still having contractions?'

'No, they've stopped temporarily. But if she delivers in the next day or so, Marius will not be the first baby whose birth was induced by adrenaline.'

Nicole started to undress. 'Ellie's taking it the hardest ... She says that she is a terrible mother and that she will never forgive herself for not keeping a closer eye on Nikki ... A few minutes ago she even sounded like Max and Patrick. She was wondering aloud if maybe we should all go back to New Eden and take our chances with Nakamura. "For the children's sake," she said.'

Nicole finished undressing and climbed into bed. She kissed Richard lightly and put her hands behind her head. 'Richard,' she said, 'there is a very serious issue here ... Do you think the octospiders would even *permit* us to return to New Eden?'

'No,' he said after a pause. 'At least not all of us.'

'I'm afraid I agree with you,' Nicole said. 'But I don't want to say so to the others. Maybe I should bring the question up with Archie again.'

'He'll try to evade it, as he did the first time.'

They lay together holding hands for several minutes. 'What are you thinking about, darling?' Nicole asked when she noticed that Richard's eyes were still open.

'Today,' he said. 'Everything that happened today. I'm going back over it in my mind, scene by incredible scene. Now that I'm old and my memory isn't as good as it once was, I try to use refresh techniques ...'

Nicole laughed. 'You're impossible,' she said. 'But I love you anyway.'

5

Max was agitated. 'I, for one, do not want to stay in this place one minute longer than necessary. I no longer trust them. Look, Richard, you know damn well I'm right. Did you see how fast Archie took that tube thing out of his bag when the alien iguana jumped on Benjy's back? And he didn't hesitate a second to use it. Pffft was all I heard, and presto, that lizard was either dead or paralysed. He would have done the same thing to one of us if we had misbehaved.'

'Max, I think you're over-reacting,' Richard said.

'Am I? And is it another over-reaction that the entire scene yesterday reinforced in my mind just how powerless we are ...'

'Max,' Nicole interrupted, 'don't you think this is a discussion that we should have at another time, when we're not so emotional?'

'No,' Max replied emphatically. 'I do not ... I want to have it *now*, this morning. That's why I asked Nai to feed the children breakfast in her house.'

'But surely you're not suggesting that we should leave at this moment, when Eponine is due any minute,' Nicole said.

'Of course not,' Max said. 'But I think we should get our butts out of here as soon as she is able to travel. Jesus, Nicole, what kind of life can we have here anyway? Nikki and the twins are now scared shitless. I bet they won't be willing to leave our zone again for weeks, maybe not ever ... And that doesn't even address the bigger question of why the octospiders have brought us here in the first place. Did you see all those creatures in that stadium yesterday? Didn't you get the impression that *all* of them work for the octospiders in one way or another? Isn't it likely that we too will soon be occupying some niche in their system?'

Ellie spoke for the first time since the conversation started. 'I have always trusted the octospiders,' she said. 'I still do. I do not believe they have some kind of diabolical plot to integrate us into their overall scheme in a way that is unacceptable to us. But I did learn something yesterday, or I should say I relearned something. As a mother, it is my responsibility to provide for my daughter an environment in which she can flourish and have a chance to be happy ... I no longer think that's possible here in the Emerald City.'

Nicole looked at Ellie with surprise. 'So you would like to leave too?' she said.

'Yes, Mother.'

Nicole glanced around the table. She could tell from Eponine's and Patrick's expressions that they agreed with Max and Ellie. 'Does anyone know how Nai feels about this subject?' she inquired.

Patrick blushed slightly when Max and Eponine looked at him, as if he were expected to answer. 'We talked about it last night,' he said at length. 'Nai has been convinced, for some time, that the children have too narrow a life isolated here in our own zone. But she is also worried, especially after what happened yesterday, that there are significant dangers to the children if we try to live freely in the octospider society.'

'I guess that settles it,' Nicole said with a shrug. 'I will talk to Archie about our leaving at the first opportunity.'

Nai was a good storyteller. The children loved the school days when she would dispense with the planned activities and simply tell them stories instead. She had been telling the children both Greek and Chinese myths, in fact, the first day that Hercules had appeared to observe them. The children had given the octospider his name after he had helped Nai move the furniture in the room into a different configuration.

Most of the stories that Nai told had a hero. Since even Nikki still had some memory of the human biots in New Eden, the children were more interested in stories about Albert Einstein, Abraham Lincoln, and Benita Garcia than they were in historic or mythical characters with whom they had had no personal involvement.

On the morning after Bounty Day, Nai explained how, during the last phases of the Great Chaos, Benita Garcia used her considerable fame to help the millions of poor people in Mexico. Nikki, who had inherited the compassion of her mother and grandmother, was moved by the story of Benita's courageous defiance of the Mexican oligarchy and the American multinational corporations. The little girl proclaimed that Benita Garcia was her hero.

'Heroine,' the always precise Kepler corrected. 'And what about you, Mother?' the boy said a few seconds later. 'Did you have a hero or heroine when you were a little girl?'

Despite the fact that she was in an alien city on an extraterrestrial spacecraft at an unbelievable distance away from her hometown of Lamphun in Thailand, for an extraordinary fifteen or twenty seconds Nai's memory transported her back to her childhood, and she saw herself clearly, in a simple cotton dress, walking barefoot into the Buddhist temple to pay homage to Queen Chamatevi. Nai could also see the monks in their saffron robes, and she believed that for a moment she could even smell the joss in the viharn in front of the temple's principal Buddha.

'Yes,' she said, quite moved by the power of her flashback, 'I did have a heroine ... Queen Chamatevi of the Haripunchai.'

'Who was she, Mrs Watanabe?' Nikki said. 'Was she like Benita Garcia?'

'Not exactly,' Nai began. 'Chamatevi was a beautiful young woman who lived in the Mons kingdom in the south of Indochina over a thousand years ago. Her family was rich and closely connected to the king of the Mons. But Chamatevi, who was exceedingly well educated for a woman of that time, longed to do something different and unusual. Once upon a time, when Chamatevi was nineteen or twenty years old, a soothsayer visited ...'

'What's a soothsayer, Mother?' Kepler asked.

Nai smiled. 'Someone who predicts the future, or at least tries to,' she answered.

'Anyway, this soothsayer told the king that there was an ancient legend saying that a beautiful young Mons woman of noble birth would go north through the jungles to the valley of the Haripunchai and unite all the warring tribes of the region. This young woman, the soothsayer continued, would create a kingdom whose splendor would equal the Mons, and she would be known in many lands for her outstanding leadership. The soothsayer told this story during a feast at the court, and Chamatevi was listening. When the story was completed, the young woman came forward to the king of the Mons and told him that she must be the woman in the legend.

'Despite her father's opposition, Chamatevi accepted the king's offer of money and provisions and elephants, even though there was only enough food to last the five months of trekking through the jungle to the land of the Haripunchai. She knew that if the tribes of the north did not accept her as their queen, she would be forced to sell herself as a slave. But never for a moment was Chamatevi afraid.

'Of course the legend was fulfilled, the valley tribes embraced her as their queen, and she reigned for many years in what is known in Thai history as the Golden Age of the Haripunchai. When Chamatevi was very old, she carefully divided her kingdom into two equal parts, which she gave to her twin sons. She then retired to a Buddhist monastery to thank God for His love and protection. Chamatevi remained alert and healthy until she died at the age of ninety-nine.'

For reasons she did not completely understand, Nai felt herself becoming very emotional while she was telling the story. When she was finished, Nai could still see, in her mind's eye, the wall panels in the temple in Lamphun that illustrated Chamatevi's story. Nai had been so engrossed in her story that she had not even noticed that Patrick, Nicole, and Archie had all come into the schoolroom and were sitting on the floor behind the children.

'We have many similar stories,' Archie said a few minutes later, with Nicole translating, 'which we also tell to our juveniles. Most of them are very, very old. Are they true? It doesn't really matter to an octospider. The stories enter-tain, they instruct, and they inspire.'

'I'm sure the children would love to hear one of your stories,' Nai said to Archie. 'In fact, all of us would.'

Archie did not say anything for almost a nillet. His lens fluid was very active, moving back and forth, as if he were carefully studying the human beings staring at him. At length the coloured strips began to roll out of his slit and circumnavigate his grey head. 'A long, long time ago,' he began, 'on a faraway world blessed with bounteous resources and beauty beyond description, all the octospiders lived in a vast ocean. On the land there were many creatures, one of which, the ...'

'I'm sorry,' Nicole said both to Archie and the others, 'I don't know how to translate the next colour pattern.'

Archie used several new sentences to try to define the word in other terms. 'Those that have gone before ...' Nicole said to herself. 'Oh, well, it's probably not essential for the story that every word be exactly correct ... I'll simply call them the Precursors.

'On the land portions of this beautiful planet,' Nicole continued for Archie, 'were many creatures, of whom by far the most intelligent were the Pre-cursors. They had built vehicles that could fly into the air, they had explored all the neighbouring planets and stars, they had even learned how to create life from simple chemicals, where there had been no life before. They had changed the nature of the land and of the oceans with their incredible knowledge.

'It happened that the Precursors determined that the octospider species had enormous untapped potential, capabilities that had never been expressed during their many, many years of aquatic existence, and they began to show the octospiders how to develop and use their latent abilities. As the years passed, the octospider species, thanks to the Precursors, became the second most intelligent on the planet and evolved a very complicated and close relationship with the Precursors.

'During this time the Precursors helped the octospiders learn to live outside the water by taking oxygen directly from the air of the beautiful planet. Entire colonies of octos began to spend their whole lives on land. One day, after a major meeting between the chief optimisers of the Precursors and the octospiders, it was announced that all octospiders would become land creatures and give up their colonies in the oceans.

'Down at great depths in the sea was one small colony of octospiders, no more than a thousand altogether, that was managed by a local optimiser who did not think the chief optimisers of the two species had come to a correct decision. This local optimiser resisted the announcement and, although he and his colony were ostracised by the others and did not share in the bounty offered by the Precursors, he and many generations that followed him con-tinued to live their isolated, uncomplicated life on the bottom of the ocean.

'It happened that a great calamity struck the planet, and it became impossible to survive on the land. Many millions of creatures died and only those octospiders who could live comfortably in the water survived the thousands of years that the planet was laid waste.

'When eventually the planet recovered and a few of the ocean octospiders ventured out on land, they found none of their kindred – and none of the Precursors either. That local optimiser who had lived thousands of years before had been visionary. Without his action, every single octospider might have perished. And that's why, even today, smart octospiders retain their capability to live either on land or in water.'

Nicole had recognised, early in the story, that Archie was sharing with them something altogether different from anything he had ever told them before. Was it because of their conversation that morning, when she had told Archie that they wanted to return to New Eden soon after the Puckett child was born? She wasn't certain. But she did know that the legend Archie had related had told them things about the octospiders that the humans could never have figured out in any other way.

'That was truly marvellous,' Nicole said, touching Archie lightly. 'I don't know if the children enjoyed it ...'

'I thought it was neat,' Kepler said. 'I didn't know you guys could breathe water.'

'Just like an unborn baby,' Nai was saying, when an excited Max Puckett raced through the door.

'Come quickly, Nicole,' Max said. 'The contractions are only four minutes apart.'

As Nicole rose, she turned to Archie. 'Please tell Dr Blue to bring the image engineer and the quadroid system. And hurry!'

It was amazing to watch a birth from the outside and inside simultaneously. Nicole was giving directions to both Eponine and the octospider image engineer through Dr Blue. '*Breathe*, you must breathe through your contractions,' she would shout at Eponine. 'Move them closer, lower in the birth canal, with a little more light,' she would say to Dr Blue.

Richard was absolutely fascinated. He stood out of the way, over to one side of the bedroom, his eyes darting back and forth from the pictures on the wall to the two octospiders and their equipment. What was being shown in the images was delayed an entire contraction from what was happening on the bed. At the end of each contraction, Dr Blue would hand Nicole a small round patch, which Nicole would stick on the inside of Eponine's upper thigh. Within seconds the tiny quadroids that had been inside Eponine for the last contraction would race to the patch, and the new ones would then scramble up the birth canal. After a twenty- or thirty-second delay for data processing, another set of pictures would appear on the wall.

Max was driving everybody crazy. When he heard Eponine scream or moan, as she occasionally did near the peak of each contraction, he would rush over to her side and grab her hand. 'She's in terrible pain,' he would say to Nicole. 'You must do something to help her.'

Between contractions, when at Nicole's suggestion Eponine would stand up beside the bed to let the artificial gravity help with the birthing process, Max was even worse. The image of his unborn son wedged tightly in the birth canal, struggling with discomfort from the pressure of the previous contraction, would send him into a tirade. 'Oh, my God, look, look,' Max said after a particularly severe contraction. 'His head is *squashed*. Oh, fuck. There's not enough room. He's not going to make it.'

Nicole made a couple of major decisions a few minutes before Marius Clyde Puckett entered the universe. First, she concluded that the baby boy was not going to be born without some help. It would be necessary, she decided, for her to perform an episiotomy to mitigate the pain and tearing of the actual birth. Nicole also concluded that Max should be removed from the bedroom before he became hysterical and/or did something that might interfere with the birthing process.

Ellie sterilised the scalpel at Nicole's request. Max looked at the scalpel with wild eyes. 'What are you going to do with that?' he asked Nicole.

'Max,' Nicole said calmly as Eponine felt the advent of another contraction, 'I love you dearly, but I want you to leave the room. Please. What I am about to do will make it easier for Marius to be born, but it won't look pretty ...'

Max didn't move. Patrick, who was standing in the doorway, put a hand on his friend's shoulder as Eponine began to moan again. The baby's head was clearly pressing against the vaginal opening. Nicole began to cut. Eponine screamed in pain. 'No,' a frantic Max cried at the first sight of blood. '*No* ... Oh, shit ... oh, shit.'

'*Now* ... leave *now*,' Nicole yelled imperiously as she concluded the episiotomy. Ellie was swabbing up the blood as fast as she could. Patrick turned Max around, gave him a hug, and led him into the living-room.

Nicole checked the picture on the wall as soon as it was available. Little Marius was in perfect position. *What a fantastic technology*, she thought fleetingly. *It would change birthing altogether*.

She had no more time to reflect. Another contraction was beginning. Nicole reached up and took Eponine's hand. 'This could be it,' she said. 'I want you to push with all your might. All the way through the whole contraction.' Nicole told Dr Blue that no more images would be needed.

'Push,' Nicole and Ellie yelled together.

The baby crowned. They could see swatches of light brown hair.

'Again,' Nicole said. 'Push again.'

'I *can't*,' Eponine wailed.

'Yes, you can ... *push*.'

Eponine arched her back, took a deep breath, and moments later baby Marius squirted into Nicole's hands. Ellie was ready with the scissors to cut the umbilical cord. The boy cried naturally, without needing to be incited. Max rushed into the room.

'Your son has arrived,' Nicole said. She finished wiping off the excess fluid, tied off the umbilical, and handed the baby to the proud father.

'Oh my ... oh my ... What do I do now?' said the flustered but beaming Max, who was holding the child as if Marius were as fragile as glass and as precious as diamonds.

'You could kiss him,' Nicole said with a smile. 'That would be a good start.'

Max lowered his head and kissed Marius very gently. 'And you might bring him over to meet his mother,' Eponine said.

Tears of joy were streaming down the new mother's cheeks when she looked at her baby boy close up for the first time. Nicole helped Max lay the child across Eponine's chest. 'Oh, Frenchie,' Max then said, squeezing Eponine's hand, 'how I love you ... how very much I love you.'

Marius, who had been crying steadily since moments after his birth, quieted down in his new position on his mother's chest. Eponine reached down with the hand that Max was not holding and tenderly caressed her new son. Suddenly Max's eyes exploded with tears. 'Thank you, honey,' he said to Eponine. 'Thank you, Nicole. Thanks, Ellie.'

Max thanked everybody in the room multiple times, including the two octospiders. For the next five minutes Max was also a veritable hugging machine. Not even the octospiders escaped from his grateful embraces.

6

Nicole knocked lightly on the door and then stuck her head into the room. 'Excuse me,' she said. 'Is anybody awake?'

Eponine and Max both stirred, but no eyes opened to greet Nicole. Little Marius was nestled between his parents, sleeping contentedly. At length Max mumbled, 'What time is it?'

'Fifteen minutes *after* the scheduled time for our examination of Marius,' Nicole said. 'Dr Blue will be back in a little while.'

Max groaned and nudged Eponine. 'Come on in,' he said to Nicole. Max looked terrible. His eyes were red and puffy and both of them had double bags underneath. 'Why do babies not sleep for more than two hours at a time?' he asked with a yawn.

Nicole stood in the doorway. 'Some do, Max ... But every baby is different. Just after they're born, they usually follow the same routine they were comfortable with in the womb.'

'What are you complaining about anyway?' Eponine said, struggling to sit up. 'All you have to do is listen to some cries, change a diaper occasionally, and go back to sleep ... I have to stay awake while he nurses ... Have you ever tried to fall asleep while a little munchkin is sucking on your nipples?'

'What's this?' said Nicole, laughing. 'Have our new parents lost their neophyte aura in only four days?'

'Not really,' said Eponine, forcing a smile as she put on her clothes. 'But Jesus, I am so tired!'

'That's normal,' Nicole said. 'Your body has been through a trauma. You need rest. As I told you and Max the day after Marius was born when you insisted that we have a party, the only way you'll get enough sleep in the first two weeks is if you adapt *your* schedule to conform with *his*.'

'I believe you,' Max said. He stumbled out the door with his clothes and headed for the bathroom.

Eponine glanced at the light blue rectangular pad that Nicole had just taken out of her bag. 'Is that one of the new diapers?' she said.

'Yes,' Nicole answered. 'The octospider engineers have made some more improvements. By the way, their offer about the special waster is still open.

They don't have anything yet for Marius's urine, but they calculate that with the waster he would only poop ...'

'Max is completely against the idea,' 'Eponine interrupted. 'He says that his little boy is not going to be an experiment for the octospiders.'

'I wouldn't exactly call it an experiment,' Nicole said. 'The special waster species they have designed is only a slight modification from the ones that have been cleaning our toilets for six months now. And think of the trouble you would avoid ...'

'No,' Eponine said firmly. 'But thank the octospiders anyway.'

When Max returned, he was dressed for the day, although still unshaven. 'I wanted to tell you. Max,' Nicole said, 'before Dr Blue comes back, that I did finally have a long conversation with Archie about our leaving New Eden. When I explained to Archie that we all wanted to go, and tried to give him some of the reasons why, he told me it was not in his power to approve our leaving.'

'What does that mean?' Max asked.

'Archie said it was an issue for the Chief Optimiser.'

'Aha! So I must have been right all along,' Max said. 'We really *are* prisoners here, and not guests.'

'No, not if I understood correctly what Archie said. He told me that it "can be arranged, if necessary", but only the Chief Optimiser understands "all the factors" well enough to make an informed decision.'

'More goddamn octospider gobbledygook,' Max grumbled.

'I don't think so,' Nicole replied. 'I was actually encouraged ... But Archie said we will not be able to schedule a meeting with the Chief Optimiser until after the Matriculation is over ... That's the process that has been taking all of Jamie's time. Apparently it only happens every two years or so and involves the whole colony.'

'How long does this Matriculation thing last?' Max asked.

'Only another week. Richard, Ellie, and I have been invited to participate in some facet of the process tonight ... It sounds intriguing.'

'Marius and I won't be able to leave for several weeks anyway,' Eponine said to Max. 'So waiting a week is certainly no problem.'

At that moment Dr Blue knocked on the door. The octospider entered the bedroom with the specialised equipment that was going to be used in the examination of Marius. Max looked askance at a pair of plastic bags containing writhing creatures that looked like black pasta.

'What are those damn things?' Max asked with a scowl.

Nicole finished laying out her own instruments on the table beside the bed. 'Max,' she said with a smile, 'why don't you go next door for the next fifteen minutes or so?'

Max's brow furrowed. 'What are you going to do to my little boy? Boil him in oil?'

'No.' Nicole laughed. 'But from time to time it may sound as if that's what we're doing.'

Ellie picked up Nikki and gave her a hug. The little girl momentarily stopped crying. 'Mommy is going out with Nonni and Boobah and Archie and Dr Blue,' she said. 'We'll be back after your bedtime. You'll be fine here with Mrs Watanabe and Kepler ...'

'I don't *want* to stay here,' Nikki said in her most unpleasant voice. 'I want to go with Mommy.' She kissed Ellie on the cheek. The little girl's face was expectant.

When Ellie put the child back down on the floor a few seconds later, Nikki's beautiful face scrunched up and she began to wail. 'I don't *want* to ...' she screamed as her mother walked out the door.

Ellie shook her head as the five of them strolled toward the plaza. 'I wish I knew what to do for her,' Ellie said. 'Ever since that incident in the stadium, she has been clinging to me ...'

'It could be just a normal phase,' Nicole said. 'Children change very rapidly at her age. And Nikki's no longer the centre of attention, now that Marius is here.'

'I think the problem's deeper than that,' Ellie said several seconds later. She turned to Nicole. 'I'm sorry, Mother, but I believe Nikki's insecurity has more to do with Robert than with Marius.'

'But Robert has been gone for over a year,' Richard said.

'I don't think that matters,' Ellie replied. 'At some level Nikki must still remember what it was like to have two parents. To her it probably seems like first I abandoned her, then Robert. No wonder she is insecure.'

Nicole touched her daughter gently. 'But Ellie, if you're right, why is she just *now* reacting so strongly?'

'I can't say for certain,' Ellie said. 'Maybe the encounter with the iguana thing reminded her how vulnerable she was ... and how much she misses the protection of her father.'

They heard Nikki's loud wail behind them. 'Whatever is bothering her,' Ellie said with a sigh, 'I hope she outgrows it soon. When she cries like that, I feel as if a hot knife were cutting into my stomach.'

There was no transport at the plaza. Archie and Dr Blue kept on walking, heading for the pyramid, where the octospiders and the humans usually held their conferences. 'This is a very special evening,' Dr Blue explained, 'and there are many things that we must tell you before we leave your zone.'

'Where is Jamie?' Nicole asked as they were entering the building. 'I thought originally he was going with us. And while I'm at it, what ever happened to Hercules? We haven't seen him since Bounty Day.'

While they walked together up the ramp to the second floor of the pyramid, Dr Blue informed them that Jamie was with his fellow matriculating octospiders that evening and that Hercules had been 'reassigned'.

'Goodness,' said Richard jokingly, 'Hercules didn't even say goodbye.'

The octospiders, who still hadn't learned to recognise human humour very well, apologised for Hercules' lack of manners. They then mentioned that there would no longer be an octospider among the humans as a daily observer.

'Was Hercules fired for some reason?' Richard asked, still in a lighter vein. The two octospiders ignored the question altogether.

They entered the same conference room where Nicole had learned about the digestive process of the octospiders. Several large sheets of the parchment or hide on which the octos made their drawings and diagrams were over in the corner facing the wall. Dr Blue asked Richard, Nicole, and Ellie to sit down.

'What you are going to see later tonight,' Archie then said, 'has never been witnessed by a non-octospider since our colony was formed here in Rama. We are taking you with us in an attempt to increase the quality of communication between our two species. It is imperative that you understand, before we leave this room and head for the Alternate Domain, not only what you are going to see, but also how you are expected to behave.'

'Under no circumstances,' Dr Blue added, 'are you to disturb the proceedings or try to interact with anyone or anything along the way, either coming or going. You are to follow our instructions at all times. If you cannot or do not want to accept these conditions, then you must tell us now and we will not take you with us.'

The three humans looked at each other with alarm. 'You know us well,' Nicole said at length. 'I trust that we're not going to be asked to do something that is inconsistent with our values and principles. We could not ...'

'That's not our concern,' Archie interrupted. 'We are simply asking you to be passive observers, no matter what you see or experience. If you become confused or frightened and for some reason cannot locate one of us, sit down, wherever you are, with your hands at your sides, and wait for us to come.'

There was a brief pause. 'I cannot stress too much,' Archie continued, 'how important your behaviour is this evening. Most of the other optimisers objected when I requested that you be allowed to attend. Dr Blue and I have personally vouched for your ability not to do anything untoward.'

'Are our *lives* in danger?' Richard asked.

'Probably not,' Archie replied. 'But they *could* be. And if tonight were to turn into some kind of a fiasco because of something that one of you did, I'm not certain ...' In a very unusual action for an octospider, Archie did not finish his sentence.

'Are you telling us,' Nicole now said, 'that our request to return to New Eden is somehow tied up in all this?'

'Our mutual relationship,' Archie said, 'has reached a cusp. By sharing a critical portion of our Matriculation process with you, we are attempting to attain a new level of understanding. In that sense, the answer to your question is "Yes".'

*

They spent almost half a tert, two human hours, in the conference room. Archie began by explaining what the entire Matriculation activity was all about. Jamie and his companions, the octospider told them, had finished their adolescence and were about to make the transition to adulthood. As juveniles, their lives had been mostly controlled, and they had not been allowed to make any decisions of great significance. At the end of the Matriculation, Jamie and the other young octos would make a single monumental decision, one that would fundamentally alter the rest of their lives. It was the purpose of the Matriculation, and even much of the final year prior to the transition, to provide the adolescent octospiders with information that would help them make that important decision.

'Tonight,' Archie said, 'the juveniles will all be taken, as a group, over to the Alternate Domain to see a ...'

Neither Ellie nor Nicole could figure out at first how to translate into English what the young octospiders were going to see. Eventually, after some discussion between them and several sentences of clarification from Dr Blue and Archie, the women decided that the best interpretation for what Archie had said in colour was 'morality play'.

For the next several minutes the conversation digressed as Dr Blue and Archie explained, in response to questions from the humans, that the Alternate Domain was a specific section of the octospider realm that was not under the dome. 'South of the Emerald City,' Archie said, 'there is another settlement with a decidedly different life-style from ours. About two thousand octospiders live in the Alternate Domain at the present time, along with another three thousand or four thousand other creatures representing a dozen different species. Their lives are chaotic and unstructured. The alternate octospiders have no dome over their heads to protect them, no assigned tasks, no planned entertainment, no access to the information in the library, no roads or homes except those they collectively build for themselves, and a life expectancy about one-tenth that of the average octospider in the Emerald City.'

Ellie thought about how the Avalon area had been created by Nakamura to deal with the problems that the colonists in New Eden wanted to forget. She thought that perhaps the Alternate Domain was a similar settlement.

'Why,' she asked, 'have so many of your kindred – over ten per cent, if my math is accurate – been forced to live outside the dome?'

'No normal octospider has been forced to live in the Alternate Domain,' Dr Blue said. 'They are living there because of a personal choice.'

'But why?' all three humans said, almost in unison.

Dr Blue went over to the corner and retrieved a few of the charts. The two octospiders used the diagrams extensively during the long discussion that followed. First they explained that hundreds of generations earlier their biologists had correctly identified the connection between sexuality in their species and many other behavioural characteristics, including personal ambition, aggression, territoriality, and aging, to name the most important. This discovery had been made during a period of octospider history when the transition to Optimization was first occurring. But despite the supposedly universal acceptance of a theoretically better structure for octospider society, the transition was severely impeded by regular outbreaks of warfare, tribal dissension, and other mayhem. The octo biologists at the time speculated that only a sexless society, or one in which only a small fraction of the population was sexual, would be able to abide by the principles of Optimization, in which the desires of the individual were subordinated to the welfare of the colony as a whole.

A seemingly endless succession of conflicts convinced all of the forward-looking octospiders of the period that Optimization was only a foolish dream unless some method or technique could be found to combat the individualism that inevitably blocked acceptance of the new order. But what could be done? It was several more generations before a brilliant discovery was made. Research found that special chemicals in a sugar-cane-like product called barrican actually slowed down sexual maturation in the octospiders. Within several hundred years the octo genetic engineers had succeeded in designing and producing a variation of this barrican which, if ingested regularly, stopped the advent of sexual maturity altogether.

Test cases and test colonies succeeded beyond the wildest dreams of both the biologists and the progressive political scientists. Sexually immature octos were more responsive to the group concepts of Optimization. In addition, aging was also somehow retarded in those octos who ate barrican. Aging, the octospider scientists then learned very quickly, was tied to the same internal clock mechanism as puberty, and in fact the enzymes causing the cells not to replenish properly in older octospiders did not even activate until a specified time period *after* sexual maturity.

Octospider society underwent rapid changes, Archie and Dr Blue both asserted, after these colossal discoveries. Optimization took a firm hold everywhere. Octospider social scientists began to envision a society in which the individual octos would be nearly immortal, dying only from accidents or the sudden failure of a major and critical organ. Sexless octospiders populated all the colonies and, as the biologists had predicted, personal ambition and aggression became almost non-existent.

'All this history took place many generations ago,' Archie said, 'and is primarily background information to help you understand what the Matriculation is all about. Without going into the complex intervening history, Dr Blue will summarise where we are today in our particular colony.'

'Every octospider that you have encountered so far,' Dr Blue said, 'except for the midget morphs and the repletes, both of whom are permanently sexless, is a creature whose sexual maturity has been retarded by the barrican. Many years ago, before a rogue biologist showed how a different kind of sexuality could be genetically engineered into our species, only an octospider queen could produce offspring ...

'Among the normal adult octospider population there were two sexes, but the only significant differentiation between them was that one of the two had the ability, if mature, to fertilise a queen. Sexual adults copulated for pleasure, but because there was no issue from this contact, the distinctions between the sexes were blurred. In fact, long-term bonding in the colony was more frequent among members of the same sex, because of similar feelings and common points of view.

'Now the situation is vastly more complicated. In our octospider species, thanks to the genetic engineering genius of our predecessors, an adult female octo is capable of producing, as the result of a sexual union with a mature male octospider, a single, infertile juvenile of limited life expectancy and somewhat reduced capability. You have not yet seen one of these morphs because all of them live, by decree, in the Alternate Domain.'

Dr Blue paused and Archie continued. 'Right after Matriculation, each juvenile citisen of our colony decides whether he or she wishes to become sexually mature. If the answer is no, then the octo places his or her sexuality in trust with the optimisers and the colony as a whole. That's what Dr Blue, who is a female, and I each did long ago. Under octospider law, it is only immediately after Matriculation that an individual can make his or her own sexual choice without any consequences. The optimisers are not lenient toward those who decide to undergo a sexual metamorphosis, without explicit colony permission, after their careers have been carefully structured and planned.'

Again Dr Blue spoke. 'As we have presented it tonight, it might seem unlikely that a juvenile octospider would ever make the decision for early sexual maturity. However, in the interest of fairness we should point out that there are compelling reasons, at least in the minds of *some* young octospiders, for choosing to become alternates. First and foremost, a female octo knows that her chances of ever bearing offspring are significantly diminished if she chooses to remain nonsexual after Matriculation. Our history suggests that only in an emergency will a large number of these females ever be called upon to produce juvenile octospiders. In general, the reduced capability and infertility of this kind of offspring makes them less desirable, from the point of view of the colony as a whole, unless of course more octos are needed to support the infrastructure of the society.

'Some of the young octospiders don't like the regimentation and predictability of our life in the Emerald City and want an existence in which they can make all their own decisions. Others fear that the optimisers will place them in an improper career. All of those choosing early sexuality see the Alternate Domain as a free and exciting place, full of glamor and adventure. They discount what they are giving up ... and in their momentary exuberance, the quality of their life is more important than its likely duration ...'

Throughout the long conversation, Richard, Nicole, and Ellie asked many questions. As the evening progressed, all three of the humans started feeling overwhelmed. There was just too much information to digest in a single discussion.

'Wait a minute,' Richard said abruptly when Archie indicated it was past time for them to leave. 'I'm sorry ... there's something fundamental about this that I still don't understand. Why is this choice permitted at all? Why do the optimisers not simply decree that all the octospiders will always eat the barrican and remain sexless until the colony has a requirement for reproduction?'

'That's a very good question,' Archie replied, 'with a complex answer. Let me oversimplify, in the interests of time, by saying that our species believes in permitting some free choice. Also, as you will see tonight, there are some functions for which the alternates are uniquely suited and from which the whole colony derives benefits.'

fter leaving their zone, the transport followed a different route from
the one that had taken the humans to the stadium on Bounty Day.
This time it stayed on dimly lit streets on the periphery of the city. The
party encountered none of the busy, colourful scenes that they had seen in
their previous excursion. After several fengs the transport approached a large
closed gate very much like the one through which they had initially entered
the Emerald City.

Two octospiders came over and peered in the car. Archie said something to
them in colour, and one of the octospiders returned to what must have been
their equivalent of a guardhouse. In the distance Richard could see colours
flashing on a flat wall. 'She's checking with the authorities,' Dr Blue told the
humans. 'We're outside our expected arrival interval, so our exit code is no
longer valid.'

During a wait of several more nillets, the other octospider entered the
transport and inspected it thoroughly. None of the humans had ever experienced such stringent security precautions in the Emerald City, not even at
the stadium. Eliie's discomfort was heightened when the octospider security
officer, without saying anything to her, opened up her purse to see its contents. Eventually the inspector returned Ellie's purse and disembarked. The
gate swung open, the transport moved out from under the green dome, and
then it parked in the dark less than a minute later.

The transport was surrounded in the parking lot by thirty or forty other
vehicles. 'This area,' Dr Blue explained as they descended from the car and a
pair of fireflies joined them, 'is called the Arts District. It and the Zoo, which
is not too far from here, are the only two sections of the Alternate Domain
visited with any regularity by the octospiders who live in the Emerald City.
The optimisers do not approve many visitation requests to the alternate living
areas that are farther south – in fact, for most octospiders, the only comprehensive view of the Alternate Domain that they ever have is the tour during
the last week of Matriculation.'

The air was much colder than it had been in the Emerald City. Archie
and Dr Blue both started walking faster than the humans had ever seen an
octospider move before. 'We must hurry,' Archie turned and said, 'or we will

be late.' The human trio ran to keep up with the fast pace.

As they neared an illuminated area about three hundred metres from their transport, Archie and Dr Blue moved to either end of the line of humans so that they were walking five abreast. 'We're entering Artisan's Square,' Dr Blue said, 'which is where the alternates offer their artistic works for transfer.'

'What do you mean, "transfer"?' Nicole asked.

'The artists need credits for food and other essentials. They offer their works of art to an Emerald City resident who has credits to spare,' Dr Blue replied.

As much as Nicole might have wanted to pursue the conversation, she was immediately sidetracked by the dazzling array of unusual objects, make-shift stalls, octospiders, and other animals that greeted her eyes in Artisan's Squaje. The square, a large plaza seventy or eighty metres on a side, was directly across a broad avenue from the theatre that was their destination. Archie and Dr Blue, at the ends of their line, each extended a single tentacle along the collective backs of the humans so that the five of them moved as one across the bustling square.

The group was confronted by several octospiders holding out objects to transfer. Richard, Nicole, and Ellie quickly confirmed what Archie had told them during the long meeting, namely that the alternates did not conform to the official language specification used by the octospiders in the Emerald City. There were no neat colour bands sweeping around the heads of these octospiders, only sloppy sequences of coloured blotches of widely vari-able heights. One of the hawkers who accosted them was small, obviously a juvenile, and he or she, after being waved away by Archie, gave Ellie a sudden fright by wrapping a tentacle around Eliie's arm for a few fractions of a second. Archie seized the offender with three of his own tentacles and hurled him roughly out of the way, in the direction of one of the octospiders with a cloth bag over its shoulder. Dr Blue explained that the bag identified the octo as a policeman.

Nicole was walking so fast, and there was so much around her to see, that she found herself holding her breath. Although she had no idea what to make of many of the objects being offered for transfer in the square, she could recognise and appreciate the occasional painting, or piece of sculpture, or those tiny representations, in wood or some similar medium, of all the differ-ent animals who lived in the Emerald City. In one section of the square there were displays of coloured patterns pressed upon the parchment material – Dr Blue explained later, when they were inside the theatre, that the particular art form represented by the patterns was a combination, as she understood the human terms, of both poetry and calligraphy.

Just before they crossed the street, Nicole caught sight, on a wall twenty metres away on her left, of a large mural that was astonishingly beautiful. The colours were bold and eye-catching, the composition the work of an artist who understood both structure and optical appeal. The technical skill was also extremely impressive, but it was the emotions rendered in the bodies and faces of the octospiders and other creatures in the mural that fascinated Nicole.

'The Triumph of Optimization,' Nicole mumbled to herself as she craned her neck to read the title in colours across the upper portion of the mural. The painting had a spacecraft against a star background in one section, an ocean teeming with living things in another, and both a jungle and a desert in opposite corners. The central image, however, was a giant octospider, carrying a stave and standing on a pile of thirty or forty disparate animals, who were squirming in the dust underneath its tentacles. Nicole's heart nearly jumped out of her body when she saw that one of the trampled beings was a young human woman with brown skin, piercing eyes, and short curly hair.

'Look,' she yelled suddenly to the others, 'over there, at that mural.'

At that moment some kind of small animal was making itself a nuisance around their feet. It succeeded in distracting everyone's attention. The two octospiders dealt with the animal and pulled the line again toward the theatre. As she moved into the street, Nicole glanced back at the mural to make certain that she had not imagined the presence of a young woman in the picture. From the added distance the face of the woman and her features were vague, but Nicole was nevertheless convinced that she had definitely seen a human being in the artwork. *But how is that possible?* Nicole was asking herself as they entered the theatre.

Preoccupied with her discovery, Nicole listened with only half an ear to Richard's discussion with Archie about how he intended to use his translator during the play. She didn't even look when, after they took their standing positions in the fifth row above a theatre-in-the-round, Dr Blue pointed out with one of her tentacles the sector to the left of them containing Jamie and the other matriculating octospiders. *I must have made a mistake*, Nicole thought. She was seized by a powerful impulse to run back to the square and verify what she had seen. Then she remembered what Archie had told them about the importance of carefully following instructions on this particular evening. *I know I saw a woman in that painting*, Nicole told herself as three large fireflies flew down and hovered over the stage in the centre of the theatre. *But if I did, what does it mean?*

There were no intermissions in the play, which lasted slightly more than two wodens. The action was continuous, with one or more of the octospider actors occupying the lit stage at all times. No props were used and no costumes. At the beginning of the play the seven main 'characters' came forward and briefly introduced themselves – two matriculating octos, one of either sex, a pair of adoptive parents for each, and one alternate male whose bright and beautiful colours spread all the way to the end of his tentacles when he spoke.

The first several minutes of the actual play established that the two matriculating juveniles had been best friends for years and that, despite the good and sound advice of their assigned parents, they had selected early sexual maturity together. 'My desire,' the young female octospider said in her first monologue, 'is to produce a baby from a union with my cherished companion.' Or at least that's how Richard translated what she said. He was gleeful at the performance of his much-improved translator and, after remembering that the octospiders were deaf, he talked intermittently throughout the performance.

The four octo parents came together in the centre of the stage and expressed anxiety about what would happen when the 'powerful new emotions' that accompanied the sexual transformation were first encountered by their adopted children. They did, however, try to be fair, and all four of the adults admitted that their own choices not to become sexually mature after Matriculation meant that they could not give advice based on any actual experience.

In the middle of the play the two young octospiders were isolated at opposite corners of the stage, and the audience concluded from the pyrotechnics of the fireflies, plus a few brief statements from the octospider actors, that each of them had stopped eating the barrican and was alone in some kind of Transition Domain.

When later the two transformed octospiders walked across the stage and met in the centre, the colour patterns in their conversation had already altered. It was a powerful effect, however it was achieved by the actors, because not only were the individual colours brighter than they had been before the transition, but also the rigid, nearly perfect strips that had characterised the early conversations between the two juveniles were already marked with some different and interesting individual designs. Around them on the stage at this point were half a dozen other octospiders, all alternates, judging from their language-and a couple of Polish sausage animals chasing anything they could find. The pair were now clearly in the Alternate Domain.

Enter from the darkness off-stage the alternate male introduced at the beginning of the play. The octospider actor first made a brilliant display of horizontal and vertical patterns moving in both directions and then created advanced wave action, geometric structures, and even fireworks-like explosions of colour starting at random locations around his head. The newcomer's Technicolor display mesmerised the young female octo and won her away from the best friend of her childhood. Soon after, the interloper with the amazing colours, who had obviously parented the baby octo being carried in the frontal pouch of the female, left her 'weeping' (Richard's translation for sitting in the corner of the stage and sending out pulse after unstructured pulse of mixed colours) and alone.

At this point in the play the male octospider who had matriculated in the earlier scenes stormed into the light, saw his true love in despair with her baby, and jumped off into the darkness surrounding the stage. Moments later he returned with the alternate who had corrupted his girlfriend, and the two male octos engaged in a horrible but fascinating fight in the middle of the stage. Their heads a riot of expletive colour, they beat, twisted, choked, and battled each other for an entire feng. The younger male octo eventually won the fight, for the alternate lay motionless on the stage when the action was over. The sadness expressed in the closing remarks of the hero and the heroine made certain that the moral of the play was very clear. When the play was finished, Richard glanced at Nicole and Ellie and commented, with an irreverent grin, 'This is one of those downer plays, like *Othello*, where everyone dies in the end.'

Under the supervision of the octospider ushers, all with bags, the matriculating youngsters left the theatre first, followed next by Archie, Dr Blue, and their human companions. The orderly procession stopped just outside a few minutes later and formed a crowded ring around three other octospiders who were in the middle of the avenue. Richard, Nicole, and Ellie felt the presence of their friends' powerful tentacles across their backs as they moved into position to see what was taking place. Two of the octospiders in the centre of the street were holding staffs and wearing bags, while the third octo, who was crouching between them, was transmitting the colour message, in broad and unstructured bands, 'Please, help me.'

'This octospider,' one of the policemen said in crisp, measured strips, 'has consistently failed to earn her credits since coming to the Alternate Domain after her Matriculation four cycles ago. Last cycle she was warned that she had become an unacceptable drain upon our common resources, and recently, two days before Bounty Day, she was told to report for termination. Since that time she has been hiding among friends in the Alternate Domain ...'

The crouching octospider suddenly bolted and leaped into the audience near where the humans were standing. The crowd sagged back from the impact and Ellie, who was nearest the point where the escape attempt occurred, was knocked to the ground in the mêlée that ensued. In less than a nillet the police, with help from Archie and several of the matriculating juveniles, again had the fugitive under control.

'Failure to report for a scheduled termination is one of the worst crimes an octospider can commit,' the policeman then said. 'It is punishable by immediate termination upon apprehension.' One of the policemen pulled several wriggling, wormlike creatures from its shoulder-bag. The outlaw octo struggled hard the first time the two policemen tried to force the wormlike creatures into her mouth. However, after each of the policemen hit the renegade twice with a staff, the doomed octospider collapsed between her captors. Ellie, who had regained her footing by this time, was unable to suppress a scream of terror as the creatures entered the octo's mouth, and she began to regurgitate. Death came quickly.

None of the humans said a word as they walked arm in arm with Archie and Dr Blue across the square and into the parking area where their transport was waiting. Nicole was so stunned by what she had witnessed that she did not even remember to look for the painting that she thought had included a human face.

In the middle of the night Nicole, who had not been able to sleep, heard a noise in the living-room. She rose from her bed quietly and slipped into a robe. Ellie was sitting on the couch in the dark. Nicole sat down beside her daughter and took her hand.

'I couldn't sleep, Mother,' Ellie said. 'I have been going over everything in my mind and it doesn't make any sense. I feel as if I have been betrayed.'

'I know, Ellie,' Nicole said. 'I feel the same way.'

'I thought I knew the octospiders,' Ellie said. 'I trusted them. In many ways I thought they were superior to us, but after what I saw tonight ...'

'None of us is comfortable with killing,' Nicole said. 'Even Richard was horrified at first. But after we were in bed, he told me that he was certain the street scene was carefully staged for the benefit of the matriculators. He also said that we should be careful not to jump to too many conclusions or let ourselves react emotionally to one isolated incident ...'

'I have never before watched an intelligent being murdered before my very eyes. And what was her crime? Failure to report for termination?'

'We cannot judge them as we would judge human beings. The octospiders are an entirely different species, with a completely separate social organisation, one that may be even more complex than ours. We are only beginning to understand them ... Have you already forgotten that they cured Eponine of RV-41? And allowed us to use their technology when we were worried about Marius's birth?'

'No, I haven't,' Ellie replied. She was silent for several seconds. 'You know, Mother, I'm feeling as frustrated now as I did often in New Eden, when I kept wondering how human beings, who are capable of so much that is good, could possibly tolerate a tyrant like Nakamura. Now it looks as if the octospiders can be just as bad in their own way ... There is so much inconsistency everywhere ...'

Nicole tried to console her daughter with a hug. *There are no easy answers, my darling Ellie*, Nicole thought. In her mind's eye Nicole again saw a highlight montage of the night's incredible activities, including the fleeting glimpse in which she believed she had seen an unknown human woman in an octospider mural. *And what was that about, old woman?* she asked herself. *Was it really there, that face, or did your tired and imaginative brain create it to confuse you?*

8

Max finished shaving and washed the rest of the approximation of shaving cream off his face. Moments later he pulled the plug and the water disappeared from the stone basin. After wiping his face thoroughly with a small towel, Max turned to Eponine, who was sitting on the bed behind him nursing Marius.

'Well, Frenchie,' he said with a laugh, 'I must admit I'm damn nervous. I've never met a Chief Optimiser before.' He walked over beside her. 'Once, when I was in Little Rock for a farmers' convention, I sat next to the governor of Arkansas during a banquet ... I was a little nervous then too.'

Eponine smiled. 'It's hard for me to imagine you being nervous,' she said.

Max stood silently for several seconds, watching his wife and infant son. The baby made soft cooing sounds as he ate. 'You really enjoy this nursing business, don't you?'

Eponine nodded. 'It's a pleasure unlike any I have ever experienced. The sense of ... I don't know the exact word, maybe "communion" would be close ... is indescribable.'

Max shook his head. 'Ours is an amazing existence, isn't it? Last night, when I was changing Marius, I thought of how similar we probably were to millions of other human couples, doting on our first child ... yet just outside that door is an alien city run by a species ...' He did not finish his thought.

'Ellie has been different since last week,' Eponine said. 'She's lost her spark and talks about Robert more ...'

'She was horrified by the execution,' Max commented. 'I wonder if women are naturally more sensitive to violence. I remember after Clyde and Winona got married, when he brought her back to the farm, the first time she watched us slaughter a couple of pigs, her face became very white. She didn't say anything, but she never came to watch again.'

'Ellie won't talk much about that night,' Eponine said, switching Marius over to the other breast. 'And that's not like her at all.'

'Richard asked Archie about the incident yesterday, when he requested the components to build translators for the rest of us ... According to Richard, the damn octo was real foxy and did not give many straight answers. Archie

1110

would not even confirm what Dr Blue told Nicole about their basic termination policy.'

'It's pretty scary, isn't it?' she said. Eponine grimaced before continuing. 'Nicole insisted that she made Dr Blue repeat the policy to her several times, and she even tried several different versions in English, in Dr Blue's presence, to make certain that she had understood it correctly.'

'It's simple enough,' Max said with a forced grin, 'even for a farmer. "Any adult octospider whose total contribution to the colony over a defined period of time is not at least equal in worth to the resources necessary to sustain that individual will be entered onto the termination list. If the negative account is not corrected in a prescribed amount of time, the octospider will then be terminated".'

'According to Dr Blue,' Eponine said after a short silence, 'it's the optimisers who interpret the policies. They are the ones who decide what everything is worth ...'

'I know,' Max said, reaching down and caressing his baby son's back, 'and I think that's one of the reasons Nicole and Richard are anxious about today. Nobody has said anything explicit, but we have been using a lot of resources for a long time – and it's pretty damn hard to see what we've been contributing.'

'Are you ready, Max?' Nicole stuck her head in the door. 'Everyone else is out here by the fountain.'

Max bent down to kiss Eponine. 'Will you and Patrick be able to handle Benjy and the children?' he asked.

'Certainly,' Eponine replied. 'Benjy's no effort, and Patrick has been spending so much time with the children that he's become a child care specialist.'

'I love you, Frenchie,' Max said, waving goodbye.

There were five chairs for them outside the Chief Optimiser's operating area. Even when Nicole explained the word 'office' to Archie and Dr Blue a second time, their two octospider colleagues still insisted that 'operating area' was a better translation into English for the place where the Chief Optimiser worked.

'The Chief Optimiser is sometimes a little late,' Archie said apologetically. 'Unexpected events in the colony can force her to deviate from the planned schedule.'

'There must be something really unusual going on,' Richard said to Max. 'Punctuality is one of the hallmarks of the octospider species.'

The five humans waited silently for their meeting, each engrossed in his or her own thoughts. Nai's heart was pounding rapidly. She was both apprehensive and excited. She remembered having had a similar feeling as a schoolgirl when she was waiting for her audience with the king of Thailand's daughter, the Princess Suri, after Nai had won a top prize in a nationwide academic competition.

A few minutes later an octospider bade them enter the next room, where they were informed they would be joined in a moment by the Chief Optimiser and a few of her advisers. The new room had transparent windows. They could see activity all around them. Where they were sitting reminded Richard of a control area for a nuclear power-plant, or perhaps for a manned space flight. Octospider computers and visual monitors were everywhere, as were octospider technicians. Richard asked a question about something happening in a distant area, but before Archie could answer, three octospiders entered the room.

All five humans rose in a reflex action. Archie introduced the Chief Optimiser, the Deputy Chief Optimiser for the Emerald City, and the Optimiser Security Chief. The three octos each extended a tentacle to the humans and handshakes were exchanged. Archie motioned for the humans to sit down and the Chief Optimiser began speaking immediately.

'We are aware,' she said, 'that you have requested, through our representative, that you be allowed to return to New Eden to rejoin the other members of your species in Rama. We were not completely surprised by this request because our historical data indicate that most intelligent species with strong emotions, after a period of time living in an alien community, develop a sense of disconnection and yearn to return to a more familiar world. What we would like to do this morning is provide some additional information to you that could influence your request that we permit you to return to New Eden.'

Archie asked all the humans to follow the Chief Optimiser. The group passed through a room similar to the two in which they had been sitting and then entered a rectangular area with a dozen wall screens spread around the sides at octospider eye level.

'We have been monitoring closely the developments in your habitat,' the Chief Optimiser said when they were all together, 'ever since long before your escape. This morning we want to share with you some of the events that we have recently observed.'

An instant later all the wall screens switched on. Each contained a motion picture segment from the daily life among the humans remaining in New Eden. The quality of the videos was not perfect and no segment was continuous for longer than a few nillets, but there was no mistaking what was being presented on the screens.

For several seconds the humans were all speechless. They stood transfixed, glued to the images on the wall. On one of the screens Nakamura, dressed as a Japanese shogun, was making a speech to a large crowd in the square in Central City. He was holding up a large hand-drawn picture of an octospider. Although the videos were silent, it was apparent from his gestures and the pictures of the crowd that Nakamura was exhorting everyone to action against the octospiders.

'Well, I'll be goddamned,' Max said, his eyes moving from one screen to another.

'Look over here,' Nicole said. 'It's El Mercado in San Miguel.'

In the poorest of the four villages of New Eden, a dozen white and yellow toughs with karate bands around their heads were beating up four black and brown youths in full view of a pair of New Eden policemen and a sorrowful crowd of perhaps twenty villagers. Tiasso and Lincoln biots picked up the broken, bloodied bodies after the beatings and placed them in a large tricycle carriage.

On another screen a segment showed a well-dressed crowd, mostly white and Oriental, arriving for a party or a festival in Nakamura's Vegas. Bright lights beckoned them to the casino, over which a huge sign proclaimed 'Citizen Appreciation Day' and announced that every partygoer would receive a dozen free lottery tickets to celebrate the occasion. Two large posters of Nakamura, chest shots showing him smiling and wearing a white shirt and tie, flanked the sign.

A monitor on the wall behind the Chief Optimiser showed the interior of the Central City jail. A new felon, a female with a multicoloured hair-do, was being placed in a cell that already contained two other convicts. It appeared as if the newcomer were complaining about the crowded conditions, but the policeman just pushed her into the cell and laughed. When the policeman returned to his desk, the video revealed two photographs on the wall behind him, one of Richard and the other of Nicole, under both of which the word REWARD was written in large block letters.

The octospiders waited patiently as the humans' eyes moved from screen to screen. '*How* in the world?' Richard kept asking, shaking his head. Then the screens went suddenly blank.

'We have put together a total of forty-eight segments to show you today,' the Chief Optimiser said, 'all taken from observations made the last eight days in New Eden. The optimiser you call Archie will have a catalogue of the segments, which have been classified according to location, time, and event description. You may spend as much time here as you like, looking at the segments, talking among yourselves, and asking questions of the two octospiders who accompanied you here. I, unfortunately, have other tasks to perform ... If, at the end of your viewing, you wish to communicate with me again, I will make myself available.'

The Chief Optimiser then departed, followed by her two assistants. Nicole sat down in one of the chairs. She looked pale and weak. Ellie walked over beside her.

'Are you all right, Mother?' Ellie asked.

'I think so,' Nicole replied. 'Right after the videos began to play, I felt a sharp pain in my chest – probably from the surprise and excitement – but it has subsided now.'

'Do you want to go home and rest?' Richard asked.

'Are you kidding?' said Nicole with her characteristic smile. 'I wouldn't miss seeing this show even if there was a chance that I would drop dead in the middle.'

They watched the silent movies for almost three hours. It was clear from the videos both that there was no longer any individual freedom in New Eden and that most of the colonists were struggling to sustain even a meagre existence. Nakamura had consolidated his hold on the colony and crushed all the opposition. But the colony he ruled was peopled mostly by gloomy and unhappy citizens.

At first all the humans watched the same segment together, but after three or four had been played, Richard suggested that it was terribly inefficient for them to watch the segments one at a time. 'Spoken like a true optimiser,' said Max, who nevertheless agreed with Richard.

There was one segment in which Katie briefly appeared. It was a late-night scene from Vegas. The street prostitutes were plying their trade outside one of the clubs. Katie approached one of the women, had a brief conversation about some unknown subject, and then disappeared from view. Richard and Nicole couldn't help but notice that Katie looked terribly thin, even gaunt. They asked Archie to rerun the segment several times.

Another sequence was entirely devoted to the hospital in Central City. No words were needed for the viewers to understand that there were shortages of critical medicines, not enough staff members, and problems with equipment falling into disrepair. One particularly poignant scene showed a young woman of Mediterranean extraction, possibly Greek, dying after a painful breech childbirth. Her delivery room was lit with candles while the monitoring equipment that might have identified her difficulties and saved her life lay inexplicably unpowered beside the bed.

Robert Turner was everywhere in the hospital segment. The first time Ellie saw him walking through the halls, she burst into tears. She sobbed throughout the segment and then immediately requested a replay. Only when she was watching for a third time did she make any comment. 'He looks haggard,' she said, 'and overworked. He has never learned to take care of himself.'

When they were all emotionally exhausted and nobody requested the replay of another segment, Archie asked the humans if they wished to visit again with the Chief Optimiser. 'Not now,' Nicole said, reflecting everyone's opinion. 'We haven't had time to digest what we've seen.'

Nai asked if perhaps they could take some of the segments back to their homes in the Emerald City. 'I would like to see them again,' she said, 'at a more leisurely pace. And it would be great if we could show them to Patrick and Eponine.' Archie replied that he was sorry, but the segments could only be viewed in one of the octospider communication centres.

On the ride back to their zone, Richard was conversing with Archie and showing the octospider how well his real-time translator was working. Richard had just finished his final tests the day prior to the meeting with the Chief Optimiser. The translator could translate either the octospiders' natural dialect or the language specifically tailored to the visual spectrum of the humans. Archie acknowledged that he was impressed.

'By the way,' Richard added in a louder voice, so that all his compatriots could hear him, 'I guess there's not much chance that you'd tell us *how* you managed to obtain all those video segments from New Eden, is there?'

Archie did not hesitate to answer. 'Flying image quadroids,' he said. 'More advanced genus. Much smaller.'

Nicole translated for Max and Nai. 'Fuck me,' Max muttered under his breath. He rose and walked to the opposite end of the transport, shaking his head vigorously.

'I have never seen Max so solemn or so tense,' Richard said to Nicole.

'Nor have I,' she answered. They were taking an exercise walk an hour after having finished dinner with their family and friends. A lone firefly kept pace above Richard and Nicole as they repeated multiple times the walk from the end of their cul-de-sac to the plaza at the other end of the street.

'Do you think Max will change his mind about leaving?' Richard asked as they circled the fountain again.

'I don't know,' Nicole replied. 'I think he's still in shock, in a way. He detests the fact that the octospiders are able to watch everything we do. That's why he insists that he and his family will return to New Eden, even if everyone else stays here.'

'Have you had a chance to talk with Eponine alone?'

'The day before yesterday she brought Marius over just after naptime. While I was putting some medication on his diaper rash, she asked me if I had mentioned to Archie that they wanted to leave. She seemed frightened.'

They marched briskly into the plaza. Without stopping, Richard pulled out a small cloth and wiped the sweat from his brow. 'Everything has changed,' he said, as much to himself as to Nicole.

'I'm certain it's all part of the octospider plan,' Nicole replied. 'They didn't show us those videos only to demonstrate that all is not well in New Eden. They knew how we would react after we had had time to assess the real significance of what we had seen.'

The pair walked silently back in the direction of their temporary home. On the next swing around the fountain, Richard said, 'So do they observe everything we do, including even this conversation?'

'Of course,' Nicole replied. 'That was the primary message the octospiders transmitted to us by allowing us to see the videos ... We can have no secrets. Escape is out of the question. We are completely in their power ... I may be the only one, but I still do not believe that they intend to harm us ... And they might even allow us to return to New Eden ... Eventually.'

'It will never happen,' Richard said. 'Then they would have wasted a lot of resources for no measurable return, a decidedly nonoptimal situation. No,

I'm certain the octospiders are still trying to figure out our proper placement in their overall system.'

Richard and Nicole walked at top speed on their final lap. They finished at the fountain and both of them drank some water. 'How do you feel?' Richard asked.

'Fine,' Nicole answered. 'No pains, no shortness of breath. When Dr Blue examined me yesterday, she found no new pathology. My heart is just old and weak ... I should expect intermittent problems.'

'I wonder what niche we'll occupy in the octospider world,' Richard said a few moments later when they were washing their faces.

Nicole glanced at her husband. 'Aren't you the one,' she said, 'who laughed at me some months ago for making inferences about their motives? How can you be so certain now that you understand what the octospiders are trying to accomplish?'

'I'm not.' Richard grinned. 'But it's natural to assume that a superior species would at least be logical.'

Richard woke Nicole up in the middle of the night, 'I'm sorry to bother you, darling, but I have a problem.'

'What is it?' Nicole asked, sitting up in bed.

'It's embarrassing,' Richard said. 'That's why I haven't mentioned it earlier ... It started right after Bounty Day. I thought it would go away, but this last week the pain has become unbearable.'

'Come on, Richard,' Nicole said, a little irritated at having her sleep disturbed, 'get to the point. What pain are you talking about?'

'Every time I urinate, I have this burning sensation ...'

Nicole tried to stifle a yawn while she was thinking. 'And have you been urinating more frequently?' she asked.

'Yes ... how did you know?'

'Achilles should have been held by his prostate when he was dipped in the River Styx,' she said. 'It is certainly the weakest structure in the male anatomy. Roll over on your stomach and let me examine you.'

'Now?' said Richard.

'If you can wake me from a deep sleep because of your pain,' Nicole said with a laugh, 'then the least you can do is grit your teeth while I try to verify my instant diagnosis.'

Dr Blue and Nicole were sitting together in the octospider's house. On one of the walls four quadroid frames were projected. 'The image on the far left,' Dr Blue said, 'shows the growth as it looked that first morning, ten days ago, when you asked me to confirm your diagnosis. The second frame is a much magnified picture of a pair of cells taken from the tumour. The cell abnormalities – what you call cancer – are marked with the blue stain.'

Nicole smiled wanly. 'I'm having a little difficulty reorienting my thinking,' she said. 'You never use the colours for "disease" when you describe Richard's problem – only the word which in your language I define as "abnormality".'

'To us,' Dr Blue responded, 'a disease is a malfunction caused by an outside agent, such as a bacterium or a hostile virus. An irregularity in the cell chemistry leading to the manufacture of improper cells is a completely different kind of problem. In our medicine the treatment regimens are completely different for the two cases. This cancer in your husband is more closely related to aging, generically, than it is to a disease like your pneumonia or gastroenteritis.'

Dr Blue extended a tentacle toward the third picture. 'This image,' she said, 'shows the tumour three days ago, after the special chemicals carried by our microbiological agents had been carefully dispersed at the site of the abnormality. The growth has already begun to shrink because the production of the malignant cells has stopped. In the final image, taken this morning, Richard's prostate again looks normal. By this time all the original cancer cells have died, and no new ones have been produced.'

'So will he be all right now?' Nicole asked.

'Probably,' Dr Blue answered. 'We can't be absolutely certain because we still do not have as much data as we would like on the life cycle of your cells. There are a few unique characteristics about your cells – as there always are in species who have undergone an evolution distinct from any of our previously examined beings – that might permit a recurrence of the abnormality. However, based on our experience with many other living creatures, I would have to say that the development of another prostate tumour is unlikely.'

Nicole thanked her octospider colleague. 'This has been incredible,' she said. 'How wonderful it would be if your medical knowledge could somehow be transported back to Earth.'

The images vanished from the wall. 'There would be many social problems created as well,' Dr Blue said, 'assuming that I have properly understood our discussions of your home planet. If individual members of your species did not die from diseases or cell abnormalities, life expectancy would increase markedly. Our species went through a similar upheaval after our Golden Age of Biology, when octospider life spans doubled in just a few generations. It wasn't until optimization became firmly implanted as our governing structure that any kind of societal equilibrium was reached. We have plenty of evidence that without sound termination and replenishment policies, a colony of nearly immortal beings undergoes chaos in a relatively short period of time.'

Nicole's interest was piqued. 'I can appreciate what you're saying, at least intellectually,' she said. 'If everyone lives forever, or nearly so, and the resources are finite, the population will soon overwhelm the available food and living space. But I must admit, especially as an old person, that even the idea of a "termination policy" frightens me.'

'In our early history,' Dr Blue said, 'our society was structured much like yours, with almost all of the decision-making power resting with the older members of the species. It was easier to restrict replenishment, therefore, after life expectancy dramatically increased, than it was to deal with the difficult issue of planned terminations. After a comparatively brief period of time, however, the aging society began to stagnate. As Archie or any good optimiser would explain, the "ossification" coefficient of our colonies became so large that eventually all new ideas were rejected. These geriatric colonies collapsed, basically because they were not able to deal with the changing conditions of the universe around them.'

'So that's where Optimization comes in?'

'Yes,' said Dr Blue. 'If every individual embraces the precept that the welfare of the overall colony should be awarded the highest weight in the master objective function, then it quickly becomes clear that planned terminations are a critical element of the optimal solution. Archie would be able to show you quantitatively how disastrous it is, from the point of view of the colony as a whole, to spend huge amounts of collective resource on those citizens whose integrated remaining contribution is comparatively low. The colony benefits most by investing in those members who have a long, healthy lifetime still available and therefore a high probability of repaying the investment.'

Nicole repeated back to Dr Blue some of the octospider's key sentences, just to make certain that she had understood properly. Then she was silent for two or three nillets. 'I suppose,' Nicole said eventually, 'that even though your aging is delayed both by postponing sexual maturity and by your amazing medical capability, at some point preserving the life of an old octospider becomes prohibitively expensive, by some measure.'

'Exactly,' Dr Blue replied. 'We can extend the life of an individual almost forever. However, there are three major factors that make extra life extension decidedly nonoptimal for the colony. First, as you mentioned, the cost of the effort to extend life increases dramatically as each biological subsystem, or organ, begins to operate at less than peak efficiency. Second, as an individual octospider's time becomes more and more consumed with the process of simply staying alive, the amount of energy that he or she might have to contribute to the colony's welfare lessens considerably. Third, and the sociological optimisers proved this controversial point many years ago, although for some number of years after mental quickness and learning ability start to drop, accumulated wisdom more than compensates, in terms of value to the colony, for the diminished brainpower, there comes a time in the life of every octospider when the sheer weight of his or her past experience makes any additional learning extremely difficult. Even in a healthy octospider this phase of life, called the Onset of Limited Flexibility by our optimisers, signals a reduced ability to contribute to the colony.'

'So the Optimisers determine when it is termination time?'

'Yes,' said Dr Blue, 'but I don't know exactly how they do it. There is a probationary period first, during which time the individual octospider is entered on the termination list and given time to improve his or her net balance. This balance, if I have understood Archie's explanation, is calculated for each octospider by comparing its contributions made with the resources necessary to sustain that particular individual. If the balance does not improve, then termination is scheduled.'

'And how do those selected for termination react?' Nicole asked, involuntarily shuddering as she remembered facing her own execution.

'In different ways,' Dr Blue replied. 'Some, especially those who have been unhealthy, accept that they are not going to be able to redress the unsatisfactory balance and plan for their deaths in an organised fashion. Others ask for optimiser counseling and request new assignments that have a higher probability of allowing them to meet their contribution quotas ... That's what Hercules did just before your arrival.'

Nicole was momentarily speechless. A chill ran down her back. 'Are you going to tell me what happened to Hercules?' she said, finally summoning her courage.

'He was severely reprimanded for not providing proper protection for Nikki on Bounty Day,' Dr Blue said. 'Hercules was then reassigned and informed by the Termination Optimiser that there was virtually no way he could recover from the high negative assessment of his recent work. Hercules requested early and immediate termination.'

Nicole gasped. In her mind's eye she saw the friendly octospider standing in the cul-de-sac, juggling many balls to the delight of the children. *And now Hercules is dead*, she thought. *Because he didn't do his job. That's cruel and merciless.*

Nicole stood up and thanked Dr Blue again. She tried to tell herself that she should be rejoicing because Richard's prostate cancer had been cured, and should not be concerned about the death of a relatively meaningless octospider. But the image of Hercules continued to haunt her. *They are an altogether different species*, she told herself. *Do not judge them by human standards.*

As she was about to leave Dr Blue's house, Nicole suddenly had an overpowering desire to know more about Katie. She remembered that one recent night, after an especially vivid dream involving Katie, she had awakened and wondered if perhaps the octospider records might allow her to see more of Katie's life in New Eden.

'Dr Blue,' Nicole said as she was standing in the door, 'I would like to ask a favour. I don't know whether to ask you or Archie ... I don't even know if what I'm asking is possible.'

The octospider asked her what the favour was.

'As you know,' Nicole said, 'I have another daughter who is still living in New Eden. I saw her very briefly in one of the videos the Chief Optimiser showed us last month ... I would like very much to know what is happening in her life.'

9

During a conversation the next day, Archie told Nicole that her request to see videos of Katie could not be granted. Nevertheless, Nicole persisted, taking advantage of every opportunity when she was alone with Archie or Dr Blue to reiterate her request. Because neither of the octospiders ever indicated that images from Katie's life in New Eden did not exist in their files, Nicole was certain that the video data were available. Viewing these data became an obsession with her.

'Dr Blue and I talked today about Jamie,' Nicole said late one night after she and Richard were in bed. 'He has decided to enter optimiser training.'

'That's good,' said Richard sleepily.

'I told Dr Blue that she was lucky, as a parent, to be able to participate in the events in her child's life ... I then expressed again our concern about knowing so little about what's happened to Katie ... Richard,' Nicole said in a slightly louder voice, 'Dr Blue did not say today that I would be unable to see the videos of Katie. Do you think that signals a change in their attitude? Am I wearing down their resistance?'

Richard did not respond at first. After some prompting, he sat up in bed. 'Can't we go to sleep just this one night without another discussion of Katie and the damn octospider videos? Jesus, Nicole, you've talked about nothing else for over two weeks. You're losing your balance ...'

'I am *not*,' Nicole interrupted defensively. 'I'm simply concerned about what has happened to our daughter. I'm certain that the octospiders have many, many segments they could put together to show us. Don't *you* want to know ...'

'Of course I do,' Richard said, sighing heavily. 'But we've had this same conversation several times already. What is to be gained from having it again at this hour?'

'I *told* you,' Nicole said. 'I sensed a possible change in their attitude today. Dr Blue did not ...'

'I heard you,' Richard interrupted crossly, 'and I don't think it means anything. Dr Blue is probably as tired of discussing the subject as I am.' Richard shook his head. 'Look, Nicole, our little group is coming apart at the seams ... We desperately need some wisdom and sanity from you. Max grumbles every day about the octospiders' invasion of his privacy, Ellie is downright lugubrious except during the rare moments when Nikki causes her to smile, and now, in the middle of everything, Patrick has announced that he and Nai want to get married ... But you are so obsessed with Katie and the videos that you aren't even able to give advice to anybody else.'

Nicole gave Richard a harsh glance and lay down on her back. She didn't reply to his last comment.

'Please don't be sullen, Nicole,' Richard said about a minute later. 'I'm only asking you to be as objective about your own behaviour as you usually are about the actions of others.'

'I'm not being sullen,' Nicole replied, 'and I'm not ignoring everyone else. Anyway, why must I always be the one who is responsible for the happiness of our little family? Why can't somebody else play the role of group mother occasionally?'

'Because nobody else is you,' Richard said. 'You have always been everyone's best friend.'

'Well, now I'm tired,' Nicole said. 'And I have a problem of my own, an "obsession", according to you ... By the way, Richard, I'm disappointed in your apparent lack of interest. I always thought Katie was your favourite ...'

'That's unfair, Nicole,' Richard said quickly. 'Nothing would please me more than to know that Katie was all right ... But I do have other things on my mind ...'

Neither of them said anything for about a minute. 'Tell me something, dear,' Richard said then in a softer tone. 'Why has Katie become so important all of a sudden? What has changed? I don't remember your being so incredibly concerned about Katie before.'

'I have asked myself the same question,' Nicole said. 'And I don't have a straightforward answer. I do know that Katie has been in my dreams a lot lately, since even before we saw her in the video, and that I have been having an intense desire to talk with her ... Also, my first thought after Dr Blue told me about Hercules' death was that I *had* to see Katie again before I died ... I don't really know why, and I don't know either what I want to say to her, but the relationship still seems terribly incomplete to me ...'

Again there was a long silence in the bedroom. 'I'm sorry that I was a little insensitive just now,' Richard said.

It's all right, Richard, Nicole thought. *It wasn't the first time. Nor will it be the last. Even the best marriages have breakdowns in communication.*

Nicole reached over and caressed her husband. 'I accept your apology,' she said, kissing him on the cheek.

Nicole was surprised to see Archie so early in the morning. Patrick, Nai, Benjy, and the children had just left to go next door to the schoolroom. The rest of the adults had still not finished breakfast when the octospider appeared in the Wakefield dining-room.

Max was rude. 'Sorry, Archie,' he said, 'but we don't allow visitors – at least not those we can see – before our morning coffee, or whatever this shit is that we drink with breakfast each day.'

Nicole rose from the table as the octospider turned to leave. 'Don't pay any attention to Max,' she said. 'He is in a permanent bad mood.'

Max now jumped up from his chair, holding one of the mostly empty packages in which there was a little cereal remaining. He swooped the container through the air, first in one direction, then in another, before sealing it tight and handing the package to Archie. 'Have a few *quadroids*,' Max said in a loud voice. 'Or did they move too quickly for me?'

Archie did not reply. The rest of the humans felt awkward and embarrassed. Max returned to his place at the table beside Eponine and Marius. 'Shit, Archie,' he said, facing the octospider, 'I guess pretty soon you'll be marking me with a pair of those green dots. Or will you just terminate me instead?'

'*Max*,' Richard shouted. 'You're out of line ... At least think of your wife and son.'

'That's all I've been thinking about, friend,' he said, 'for almost a month now. And you know what, Richard? This Arkansas farm-boy cannot figure out *anything* he can do to change ...' His voice trailed off. Suddenly Max slammed his fist against one of the chairs. '*Goddamn it!*' he yelled. 'I feel so useless.'

Marius began to cry. Eponine scooted away from the table with the baby and Ellie went to help her. Nicole took Archie with her into the atrium, leaving Richard and Max alone. Richard leaned across the table. 'I think I know what you're feeling, Max,' he said gently, 'and I empathise with you ... But we don't improve our situation any by insulting the octospiders.'

'What difference does it make?' Max said, looking up at Richard. 'We are prisoners here, that's obvious. I have allowed my son to be born into a world where he will always be a prisoner. What kind of a father does that make me?'

While Richard was trying to soothe Max, Nicole was receiving from Archie the message that she had been seeking for weeks. 'We have obtained permission,' the octospider said, 'for you to use the data library today. We have compiled videos featuring your daughter Katie from our historical files.'

Nicole made Archie repeat his colours to make certain that she had not misunderstood.

Archie and Nicole did not converse as the transport carried them, without stopping, across the Emerald City to the tall building that housed the octospider library. Nor did Nicole pay much attention to the street scenes outside the transport. She was completely immersed in her own emotions and her thoughts of Katie. In her mind's eye she recalled, one after another, key moments from her life when Katie was a child. In the longest memory segment, Nicole relived both the terror and the joy of her descent into the octospider lair years earlier to find her missing four-year-old daughter. *You've always been missing, Katie,* Nicole thought. *In one way or another. I have never been able to keep you safe.*

Nicole could feel her heart pounding furiously when Archie finally led her into a room that was empty except for a chair, a large desk, and a wall screen. Archie indicated that Nicole should sit down in the chair. 'Before I show you how to use the equipment,' the octospider said, 'there are two things that I want to tell you. First, I want to respond officially, as the optimiser for your group, to the request by some of you to rejoin the others of your species in New Eden.'

Archie paused. Nicole collected herself. It was difficult for her to put Katie temporarily out of her mind, but she knew she had to concentrate completely on what Archie was about to tell her. The others in the group would expect a verbatim report.

'I'm afraid,' Archie continued a few moments later, 'that it is not possible for any of you to leave in the near future. I am not at liberty to tell you anything more than that the issue was considered by the Chief Optimiser herself, in a major staff meeting, and that your request was denied for security reasons.'

Nicole was stunned. She had not expected this news, certainly not at this time. She had told everyone that she thought they would be allowed ...

'So Max is right,' she said, fighting the tears that were threatening to flow. 'We are your prisoners.'

'You must interpret the decision for yourself,' Archie said. 'But I will tell you that insofar as I understand your language, I think the term "prisoner", which Max has often used lately, is not correct.'

'Then give me a *better* word, and some more explanation,' Nicole said angrily, rising from her chair. 'You know what the others will say ...'

'I cannot,' Archie replied. 'I have transmitted our entire message.'

Nicole paced around the room, her emotions swinging wildly from rage to depression. She knew how Max would react. Everyone would be angry. Even Richard and Patrick would remind her that she had been wrong. *But* why *won't they explain?* she thought. *It's not like them.* Nicole felt a slight pain in her heart and slumped into her chair.

'And what's the second thing you want to tell me?' Nicole said at length.

'I have personally worked with the data engineers,' Archie said, 'to prepare the video files you are about to access ... From what I know about human beings, and you specifically, I think that if you see this material, it will cause you extreme distress. I would like to ask you to consider not looking at the files at all.'

Archie had chosen carefully what he had said, doubtless because he understood how important the videos were to Nicole. His message was clear. *What I am about to see will cause me grief,* she thought. *But what choice do I have? Between nothing and grief,* she remembered, *I will choose grief.*

After Nicole thanked Archie for his concern and informed the octospider that she wanted to see the videos anyway, Archie pushed the chair in which she was sitting over in front of the desk and showed her how to control the data access. The time code had been translated by the octospiders into human numbers, in terms of days before the present, and there were four speeds at which the images could be shown, covering four octal orders of magnitude, from one-eighth real time to sixty-four times normal speed.

'The data on Katie are nearly complete,' Archie said, 'for about the last six months of your time. It is our normal data management process to filter and compress older data, based on its importance. The extended files on Katie show most of the key events for the past two years, but are fairly scarce before that.'

Nicole reached out for the controls. As she dialed up the most recent data entry and saw Katie's face appear on the screen, she felt Archie tapping on her shoulder. 'You may use this facility the rest of today,' the octospider said to her when she turned around, 'but that is all ... Since the amount of data available is enormous, I suggest you use the high speeds to locate events of interest.'

Nicole took a deep breath and turned back around to the screen.

She felt as if she could not cry anymore. Her eyes were nearly swollen shut from the constant stream of tears. Nicole had watched Katie inject herself with the drug kokomo at least half a dozen times already, but as she saw her daughter tie the rubber cord around her upper arm and plunge the needle into a bulging vein again, a new set of burning tears found their way into Nicole's eyes.

What she had seen in almost ten hours was so much worse than her most horrible imaginings that Nicole was utterly destroyed. Despite the fact that there was no sound with any of the pictures, it had been easy for Nicole to understand what Katie's life was all about. First, her daughter was a hopeless drug addict. At least four times a day, more if life was not going well for her, Katie retreated to her fancy apartment, either by herself or with friends, and used the elegant drug paraphernalia that she kept in a large locked box in her dressing-room.

Katie was charming immediately after the drug rush. She was friendly, funny, and full of both energy and apparent self-confidence. But if the drugs wore off while she was still partying, Katie was quickly transformed into a screaming, hostile bitch who ended many evenings alone with her needle in her apartment.

Katie's official job was the management of the Vegas prostitutes. In that position Katie was also responsible for recruiting new talent. At first Nicole's broken heart was unwilling to acknowledge what her eyes were telling her. But one long, sordid sequence, which began with Katie befriending a lovely but poor teenage Hispanic in San Miguel and ended with the girl, now magnificently dressed and bejeweled, becoming a temporary concubine for one of Nakamura's zaibatsu chiefs a few days later, forced Nicole to admit to herself that her daughter had absolutely no morals or scruples.

After Nicole had been watching the videos for many hours, Archie entered the room and offered her something to eat. Nicole declined. She knew that in her agitated state there was no way she could have retained any food in her stomach.

Why did Nicole keep watching for so long? Why didn't she just switch off the controls and leave the room? Later she would ask herself the same questions. Nicole concluded, when she thought about it later, that after the first few hours of watching she began, at least subconsciously, to search for the existence of some signs of hope in Katie's life. It was not in her nature to accept without argument that her daughter was fundamentally corrupt. Nicole longed desperately to see something in the videos that would suggest to her that Katie's future might be different.

Nicole eventually found two elements in Katie's unhappy life that Nicole somehow convinced herself were signs that her daughter might someday break out of her self-destructive pattern. During Katie's terrible bouts of depression, which occurred most often when her supply of drugs was low, Katie would often fly into a frenzy, smashing everything she could find in her apartment. Except for her framed photographs of Richard and Patrick. Toward the end of these frenetic tantrums, when her energy was exhausted, Katie would always take those two pictures off her dresser and lay them gently on her bed. She would then lie beside the photographs and sob for twenty to thirty minutes. To Nicole, this recurrent behaviour indicated that Katie still retained some love for her family.

The other hopeful element, in Nicole's mind, was Franz Bauer, the police captain who was Katie's regular consort. Nicole did not pretend to understand their bizarre relationship – one night the pair would have a terrible, obscene fight, and the next Franz would read Katie the poems of Rainer Maria Rilke as a prelude to several hours of endless, energetic sex – but she thought she could tell from the videos both that Franz loved Katie in his own strange way and that he did not approve of her drug addiction. During one of their fights, in fact, Franz picked up Katie's drug supply and threatened to flush it down the toilet. Katie went completely berserk and attacked Franz wildly with a hairbrush.

Hour after hour, Nicole continued to watch in an attempt to comprehend her daughter's tragic life. As the long day progressed and Nicole scanned through the earlier videos, some as early as the first days of Katie's drug addiction, Nicole discovered that Katie had even had a sordid affair with Nakamura himself and that the New Eden tyrant had regularly provided Katie with drugs during the time they were sexual partners.

By this time Nicole was numb. She was also so emotionally drained that she did not have the strength to move. When Nicole finally switched off the controls, she put her head down on the desk, cried for a few more minutes, and then fell asleep. Archie woke her four hours later and told her it was time to return home.

It was dark. The transport had been parked at the plaza for ten minutes, but Nicole had still not disembarked. Archie was standing beside her.

'There is no way that I can tell Richard about what I have seen today,' she said, glancing up at the octospider. 'He will be absolutely destroyed.'

'I understand,' Archie said sympathetically. 'Now you see why I suggested that you not watch the videos.'

'You were right,' Nicole said, slowly releasing her grasp on the vertical bar and resignedly extending one leg out of the car, 'but it's too late now. I can't erase the horrible pictures that are in my mind.'

'You told me earlier,' Archie said as soon as they were outside the transport, 'that it was obvious from the videos that Patrick had known something about the life Katie was leading before his escape. He elected not to tell you and Richard the worst details. Is it a violation of your personal principles to do something similar?'

'Thanks, Archie,' Nicole said, patting the octospider on the shoulder and almost smiling, 'for reading my mind ... You're beginning to know us too well.'

'We have a difficult time with truth in our society also,' Archie commented. 'One of our fundamental guidelines for new optimisers is to tell the truth at all times. It is acceptable to withhold information, the policy says, but not to pass falsehoods. The youngest optimisers are very zealous about telling the truth, without regard for the consequences ... Sometimes truth and compassion are not compatible.'

'I agree with you, my wise alien friend,' Nicole said with a heavy sigh. 'And now, after what I can definitely say was one of the worst days of my life, I face not one, but two very difficult tasks. I must tell Max that he will not be able to leave the Emerald City, and I must inform my husband, Richard, that his favourite daughter is a dope addict and a manager of whores. I hope that somewhere in this old and exhausted human is the strength necessary to handle those two duties properly.'

10

Richard was asleep when Nicole arrived at home. She was thankful that she did not need to explain anything right away. Nicole slipped into her nightgown and climbed gently into bed. But she could not fall asleep. Her mind kept jumping back and forth between the horrible images she had seen during the day and thoughts about what she was going to tell Richard and the others.

In her twilight state Nicole suddenly saw herself sitting on the terraces in Rouen beside her father, in the square where Joan of Arc had been burned to death eight hundred years earlier. Nicole was a teenager again, as she had been when her father had actually taken her to Rouen to see the conclusion of the Joan of Arc pageant. The oxcart carrying Joan was coming into the square and the people were shouting.

'Daddy,' the teenage Nicole said, yelling to be heard above the din, 'what can I do to help Katie?'

Her father had not heard the question. His attention was completely focused on the Maid of Orleans, or rather the French girl who was playing Joan. Nicole watched as the girl, who had the same clear and piercing eyes attributed to Joan, was tied to the stake. The girl began to pray softly as one of the bishops read her death sentence.

'What about Katie?' Nicole said again. There was no response. The audience around her on the terraces gasped as the piles of wood surrounding Joan were set on fire. Nicole stood up with the crowd as the flames spread quickly around the base of the huge wooden stake. She could clearly hear the prayers of St Joan, invoking the blessing of Jesus.

The flames moved closer to the girl. Nicole looked at the face of the teenager who had changed history and a cold shudder ran down her back. '*Katie*,' she screamed. '*No! No!*'

Nicole tried desperately to find some way out of the bleachers, but she was blocked on all sides. There was no way she could save her burning daughter. '*Katie! Katie!*' Nicole screamed again, flailing wildly at the people around her.

She felt arms around her chest. It took a few seconds for Nicole to realise that she had been dreaming. Richard was staring at her with alarm. Before Nicole could speak, Ellie walked into the bedroom in her robe.

'Are you all right. Mother?' she asked. 'I was up checking on Nikki and I heard you scream Katie's name ...'

Nicole glanced first at Robert, then at Ellie. She closed her eyes. She could still see Katie's anguished face, contorted in pain, just above the flames. Nicole opened her eyes again and looked at her husband and daughter. 'Katie is very unhappy,' she said, and then she burst into tears.

Nicole could not be consoled. Each time she would start to tell Richard and Ellie the details about what she had seen, she would start crying again. 'I feel so frustrated, so helpless,' Nicole said when she could finally control herself. 'Katie is in dire straits and there is absolutely nothing any of us can do to help her.'

Summarizing Katie's life without omitting anything except some of the more kinky sexual escapades, Nicole abandoned her tentative plan to soften her report. Both Richard and Ellie were stunned and saddened by the news.

'I don't know how you managed to sit there and watch for all those hours,' Richard said at one point. 'I would have been out of there in a few minutes.'

'Katie's so lost, so utterly lost,' said Ellie, shaking her head. A few minutes later little Nikki wandered into the bedroom looking for her mother. Ellie embraced Nicole and took Nikki back to their room.

'I'm sorry I was so distraught, Richard,' Nicole said a few minutes later, just before they went back to sleep.

'It's understandable,' Richard said. 'The day must have been absolutely horrible.'

Nicole wiped her eyes for the umpteenth time. 'I can only remember one other time in my life when I cried like this,' she said, managing a tiny smile. 'Back when I was fifteen. My father told me one day that he was thinking about proposing to this Englishwoman he was dating. I didn't like her – she was a cold and distant woman – but I didn't think it was proper for me to say anything negative to my father. Anyway, I was devastated. I picked up my pet mallard Dunois and raced down to our pond at Beauvois. I rowed out into the middle of the pond, brought the oars into the boat, and cried for several hours.'

They lay in silence for a few minutes. Then Nicole leaned over to kiss Richard. 'Thanks for listening to me,' she said, 'I needed the support.'

'It's not easy for me either,' Richard said. 'But at least I didn't actually *see* Katie, so somehow it seems ...'

'Oh, Jesus,' Nicole suddenly said, 'I almost forgot ... Archie also told me today that none of us would be permitted to return to New Eden. He said it was a security issue ... Max will be furious.'

'Don't worry about it now,' Richard said softly. 'Try to get some sleep. We'll talk about it in the morning.'

Nicole snuggled into Richard's arms and fell asleep.

*

'For *see-cur-i-tee reasons*,' Max yelled. 'Now, just what the fuck does that mean?'

Patrick and Nai both rose from the breakfast table. 'Just leave your food,' Nai said, motioning for the children to follow her. 'We can have some fruit and cereal in the schoolroom.'

Both Kepler and Galileo were reluctant to leave. They sensed that something important was going to be discussed. Only when Patrick came around the table toward them did they push back their chairs and rise.

Benjy was allowed to remain after he promised Nicole he would not repeat any of the conversation to the children. Eponine left the table to nurse the waking Marius in one of the corners of the room.

'I don't know what it means,' Nicole said to Max after the children had departed. 'Archie would not elaborate.'

'Well, this is just *god-damn* wonderful,' Max said. 'We can't leave, but those slimy friends of yours won't even tell us why. Why didn't you demand to see the Chief Optimiser right there on the spot? Don't you think they *owe* us some kind of explanation?'

'Yes, I do,' Nicole replied. 'And perhaps we should all ask for another audience with the Chief Optimiser. I'm sorry, Max, but I didn't handle the situation very well ... I was prepared to watch the videos of Katie and, quite frankly, Archie's pronouncement caught me off guard.'

'Shit, Nicole,' Max said, 'I don't blame you personally ... Anyway, since Ep, Marius, and I are the only ones who still want to return to New Eden, it's our job to appeal this decision ... I doubt if the Chief Optimiser has ever seen a two-month-old baby human in the flesh.'

The rest of the breakfast conversation was mostly about Katie and what Nicole had seen the day before in the videos. The family explained the gist of Katie's unhappy life without too many specifics.

When Patrick returned, he reported that the children were already busy with their lessons. 'Nai and I have been talking about a lot of things,' he said, addressing everyone at the table. 'First, Max, we would like to ask you to be a little more careful in front of the children with your negative comments about the octospiders ... They are now quite fearful when Archie or Dr Blue are around, and their reactions must be based on what they have overheard in our conversations.'

Max bridled and started to reply. 'Please, Max,' Patrick added quickly, 'you know that I'm your friend ... Let's not argue about it. Just think about what I've said and remember that we may all be staying here with the octospiders for a long time ...

'Secondly,' he continued, 'Nai and I both feel, especially in view of what we learned this morning, that the children should be learning the octospider language. We want them to start as soon as possible ... We think we need Ellie or Mother, plus an octospider or two ... not just to teach, but also to familiarise the children again with their alien hosts ... Hercules has been gone for a couple of months now ... Mother, will you talk to Archie about this, please?'

Nicole nodded and Patrick excused himself, saying that he needed to return to the classroom. 'Pat-rick has be-come a good teach-er,' Benjy volunteered. 'He is ve-ry pa-tient with me and the chil-dren.'

Nicole smiled to herself and looked across the breakfast table at her daughter. *Considering everything*, she thought, *our children have turned out fine. I should be thankful for Patrick, Ellie, and Benjy. And not worry myself sick about Katie.*

In one of the corners of her bedroom, Nai Watanabe finished her meditation and said the Buddhist morning prayers that had been part of her daily routine since she was a small child in Thailand. She crossed into the living-room, heading for the other bedroom to wake the twins, and found, much to her surprise, that Patrick was asleep on the couch. He was still dressed and her electronic reader was lying on his stomach.

She shook him gently. 'Wake up, Patrick,' she said. 'It's morning ... You've slept the whole night here.'

Patrick awakened quickly and apologised to Nai. As he was leaving, he told Nai that he had several issues to discuss with her, about Buddhism, of course, but he guessed that they could wait until a more convenient time. Nai smiled and kissed him lightly on the cheek before telling him that she and the boys would be over for breakfast in half an hour.

He is so young and earnest, Nai said to herself as she watched him walk away. *And I do enjoy his company ... But can anyone ever replace Kenji as my husband?*

Nai recalled the previous night. After the twins had fallen asleep, Patrick and she had had a long and serious talk. Patrick had pressed for an early marriage. She had replied that she would not be hurried, that she would agree to a specific date only when she felt entirely comfortable with the idea. Patrick had then awkwardly inquired about the possibility of what he called 'more sexual interaction' while they were waiting. Nai had reminded Patrick that she had told him from the beginning that there would be nothing but kisses until their wedding. To assuage his feelings, Nai had reassured Patrick that she found him very attractive physically and was definitely looking forward to lovemaking after they were married, but for all the reasons they had discussed a dozen times, Nai insisted that their 'sexual interaction' remain constrained for the time being.

Most of the rest of the evening the pair had talked about either the twins or Buddhism. Nai had expressed concern that their marriage might have a bad impact on Galileo, especially since the boy often cast himself in the role of his mother's protector. Patrick told Nai that he did not believe that his frequent clashes with Galileo had anything to do with jealousy. 'The boy just resents all authority,' Patrick had said, 'and resists discipline ... Kepler, on the other hand ...'

How many times in the past seven years, Nai thought, *has someone started a* comment with the phrase 'Kepler, on the other hand'? She remembered when Kenji was still alive and the boys were just starting to walk. Galileo was constantly falling down and running into things. Kepler, *on the other hand*, was careful and precise in his steps. He almost never fell.

The giant fireflies had still not brought dawn to the Emerald City. Nai continued to let her mind roam freely, as she often did after a peaceful meditation. She noted to herself that she had been making a lot of comparisons recently between Kenji and Patrick. *That's unfair of me*, she told herself. *I cannot marry Patrick until that process has completely stopped.*

Again she thought of the previous night. Nai smiled when she recalled their ardent discussion about the life of Buddha. *Patrick still has a child's naïvete, a pure idealism*, Nai said to herself. *It's one of the things about him I love the most.*

'I admire both Buddha's basic philosophy and his approach,' Patrick had said. 'I really do ... But I have a few problems ... How can you worship a man, for example, who leaves his wife and son and goes off to be a beggar ... What about his responsibility to his family?'

'You're taking Buddha's action out of its historical context,' Nai had replied. 'First, twenty-seven hundred years ago, in northern India, being a wandering mendicant was an acceptable way of life. There were some in every village, many in the towns. When a man wanted to seek "the truth", his normal first step was to disavow all material comforts ... Besides, you have forgotten that Buddha came from a very wealthy family. There was never any question about whether or not his wife and child would have food, shelter, clothing, or any other essential ...'

They had talked for two hours or so, and then kissed for a while before Nai had gone alone to her bedroom. Patrick had already returned to his reading about Buddhism by the time Nai had whispered good night from her doorway.

How difficult it is, Nai mused as the firefly dawn burst upon the octospider city, *to explain the relevance of Buddhism to someone who has never seen the Earth ... Yet even here, in this strange alien world among the stars, desire still causes suffering and human beings still search for spiritual peace. That's why*, she continued her thought, *some elements of Buddhism, and Christianity, and the other great religions of Earth, will last as long as there are still human beings anywhere.*

11

Richard bounced out of bed with more than his usual enthusiasm and began jabbering at Nicole. 'Wish me luck,' he said as he dressed. 'Archie said that we'll be gone all day.'

Nicole, who always woke up very slowly and intensely disliked frenetic activity of any kind in the early morning hours, rolled over and tried to enjoy the last few moments of her rest. She opened one eye slightly, saw that it was still dark, and closed it again.

'I haven't been this excited since I made those two final breakthroughs on the translator,' Richard said. 'I know that the octospiders are serious about putting me to work ... They're just trying to find the right task for me.'

Richard left the bedroom for several minutes. From the noises in the kitchen, the half-asleep Nicole could tell that Richard was preparing breakfast for himself. He returned eating one of the large pink fruits that had become his favourite. He stood beside the bed, chewing noisily.

Nicole opened her eyes slowly and looked at her husband. 'I assume,' she said with a sigh, 'that you are waiting for me to say something.'

'Yes,' he said. 'It would be nice if we could exchange a few pleasantries before I leave. After all, this could be the most important day for me since we arrived in the Emerald City.'

'You're certain,' Nicole said, 'that Archie intends to find a job for you?'

'Absolutely,' Richard replied. 'That's the whole purpose of today. He is going to show me some of their more complex engineering systems and try to ascertain where my talents can best be used ... At least that's what he told me yesterday afternoon.'

'But why are you leaving so early?' Nicole asked.

'Because there's so much to see, I guess ... Anyway, give me a kiss. He'll be here in a few minutes.'

Nicole kissed Richard dutifully and closed her eyes again.

The Embryo Bank was a large rectangular building located far to the south of the Emerald City, very close to where the Central Plain ended. Less than a kilometre from where the bank had been built, a set of three staircases, each with tens of thousands of individual steps, ascended the south polar bowl.

Above the Embryo Bank, in the near darkness of Rama, loomed the imposing, buttressed structures of the Big Horn and its six sharply pointed acolytes, each larger than any single engineering construction on the planet Earth.

Richard and Archie had mounted an ostrichsaur on the outskirts of the Emerald City. Together with an escort and a trio of fireflies, they had passed through the Alternate Domain in only a matter of minutes. Out in the southern reaches of the octospider realm there were very few buildings. Despite the occasional fields of grain, most of the territory through which they travelled on their southerly trek reminded Richard, even in the dim light, of the Northern Hemicylinder in Rama II, before the two habitats had been built.

Richard and his octospider friend entered the Embryo Bank through a pair of extra-thick doors that took them directly into a large conference room. There Richard was introduced to several other octospiders, who were obviously expecting his visit. Richard used his translator and the octos read his lips, although he had to speak slowly and distinctly because they were not nearly as skilled in the human language as Archie.

After some brief formalities, one of the octospiders led the pair to a series of control panels housing the equivalent of keyboards made from octo colour strips. 'We have almost ten million embryos stored here,' the lead octospider said in her introduction, 'representing over a hundred thousand distinct species and three times that many hybrids. Their natural life spans range in duration from half a tert to several million days, or about ten thousand of your human years. Their adult sizes range from a fraction of a nanometre to behemoths nearly as large as this building. Each embryo is stored in what are believed to be near-optimal conditions for its preservation. In fact, however, only about a thousand distinct environments, combinations of temperature, pressure, and ambient chemicals, are needed to span the range of required conditions.

'This building also houses an immense data-management and monitoring system. This system automatically tracks the conditions in each of the distinct environments and monitors the early development of the several thousand embryos that are always in active germination. The system has some automatic fault detection and correction, a dual-parameter warning structure, and also drives the displays which can exhibit status and/or catalogue information, both on the walls here or in any of the research areas on the upper floors.'

Richard's brain went into overdrive as he began to understand more clearly the purpose of the Embryo Bank. *What a fantastic concept*, he thought. *The octospiders store here all the seeds of other plant and animal species that might ever he needed for any purpose.*

'... Testing is continuous,' the lead octospider was saying, 'both to ensure the integrity of the storage and preservation systems and to provide specimens for the genetic engineering activities. At any given time approximately two hundred octospider biologists are actively engaged in genetic experiments here. The goal of these many experiments is to produce altered life-forms that will improve the efficiency of our society ...'

'Can you show me an example,' Richard interrupted, 'of such a genetic experiment?'

'Certainly,' the octospider replied. She shuffled over to the control panel and used three of her tentacles to press a sequence of coloured buttons. 'I believe you are familiar with one of our primary methods of power generation,' she said, as a video appeared on the wall. 'The basic principle is quite simple, as you know. The circular marine creatures generate and store electric charge in their bodies. We capture this charge along a wire mesh, against which the animals must press to reach their food supply. Although this system is quite satisfactory, our engineers have pointed out that it could be improved substantially if the behaviour of the creature could be altered somewhat.

'Look at this fast-motion close-up of half a dozen of the marine creatures that generate the power. Notice that during this brief motion picture each of the animals will go through three or four charge-discharge cycles. What feature of these cycles would be of primary interest to a system engineer?'

Richard watched the video carefully. *The sand dollars are dim after their discharge*, he thought, *but regain their full glow in a comparatively short period of time.*

'Assuming that the glow is a measure of the stored charge,' Richard said, suddenly wondering if he was undergoing some kind of a test, 'the system could be made more efficient by increasing the feeding frequency.'

'Exactly,' the lead octospider responded. Archie flashed a quick message to the host octo that was completed before Richard had even had a chance to aim the telescope on his translator. Meanwhile, a different picture appeared on the wall. 'Here are three genetic variants of the circular marine creature that are currently under test and evaluation. The leading replacement candidate is the one on the left. This prototype eats roughly twice as frequently as the component currently being used; however, the prototype has a metabolic imbalance that increases significantly its susceptibility to communicable diseases. All factors are being weighed in the current evaluation ...'

Richard was taken from one demonstration to another. Archie accompanied him at all times, but at each venue a different set of octospider specialists joined them for the prepared minilecture and the group discussion that always followed. One of the presentations was focused on the relationships between the Embryo Bank, the large zoo that occupied considerable territory in the Alternate Domain, and the barrier forest that formed a complete annulus around Rama, slightly less than a kilometre north of the Emerald City. 'All living species in our realm,' the presenter said, 'are either in active symbiosis, temporary observation in an isolated domain – in the zoo, the forest, or, in your specific case, in the Emerald City itself – or undergoing experimentation here at the Embryo Bank.'

After a long walk down many corridors, Richard and Archie attended a meeting of half a dozen octospiders evaluating a recommendation to replace an entire symbiotic chain of four different species. The chain was responsible for the production of a gelatin that cured a specific octospider lens malady. Richard listened with fascination as the test parameters of the proposed new symbiosis – resources consumed, reproduction rates, octospider interactions required, fault coefficients, and behaviour predictability – were compared with the existing system. The outcome of the meeting was that in one of the three manufacturing 'zones', the new symbiosis would be installed for several hundred operational days, after which time the decision would again be reviewed.

In the middle of the work day Archie and Richard were scheduled to be alone for half a tert. At Richard's request, they packed their lunches and drinks, remounted the ostrich-saur, commandeered a pair of fireflies, and wandered out into the cold and dark of the Central Plain. When he eventually dismounted, Richard walked around with his arms outstretched and gazed up into the vastness of Rama.

'Who among you,' Richard asked Archie, 'worries about, or even tries to figure out, the significance of all this?' He waved his arms in a circular motion.

The octospider replied that he didn't understand the question. 'Yes, you did, you sly thing,' Richard said, smiling. 'Except that this time-period was obviously set aside by your optimisers for a different kind of conversation between us ... What I want to discuss, Archie, is not in which specific engineering department in your Embryo Bank I would like to work so that I can make my "contribution" that will justify the "resources" necessary to sustain me ... what I want to talk to you about is what is *really* going on here. Why are we – humans, sessiles, avians, and you with all your menagerie – on this huge, mysterious spacecraft bound for the star we humans call Tau Ceti?'

Archie did not respond for almost thirty seconds. 'Members of our genus were told while they were at The Node, just as you were, that some higher intelligence is cataloguing life-forms in the galaxy, with a special emphasis on spacefarers. We assembled a typical colony, as requested, and established it inside this Rama vehicle so that the required detailed observations of our species could take place.'

'So you octospiders don't know anything more about *who* or *what* is behind this grand scheme than we humans do?'

'No,' Archie replied. 'In fact, we probably know less. None of the octospiders who spent time at The Node is still part of our colony. As I told you, that octospider contingent on Rama II was a different, inferior species. The only firsthand information about The Node that exists on board this spacecraft comes from you, your family, and whatever compressed data may reside inside that small volume of sessile material we are still keeping in our zoo.'

'And that's it?' Richard said. 'None of you asks any more questions?'

'We are trained as juveniles,' Archie answered, 'not to waste time on issues for which we are unable to obtain any significant data.'

Richard was momentarily silent. 'How do you know so much about the avians and the sessiles?' he then asked abruptly.

'I'm sorry, Richard,' Archie said after a brief pause, 'but I cannot talk with you about that subject now ... My assignment for this lunch period, as you surmised, is to ascertain whether or not you would be pleased to accept an engineering assignment in the Embryo Bank and, if so, which of the many areas you have seen today seems most interesting to you.'

'It's a hell of a commute,' Richard said, laughing. 'Yes, Archie,' he then added, 'everything is fascinating, especially what I call the encyclopedia department. I think I would like to work there – that way I could expand my meagre knowledge of biology ... But why are you asking me this question now? Aren't we going to have more "demonstrations" after lunch?'

'Yes,' Archie said. 'But this afternoon's schedule has been included primarily for completeness. Almost half of the Embryo Bank is devoted to microbiology. Management of that activity is more complex and involves communication with the midget morphs. It is difficult for us to imagine your working in any of those departments.'

Underneath the primary microbiological laboratory was a basement that could only be entered with special credentials. When Archie mentioned that large quantities of flying image quadroids were produced in that Embryo Bank basement, Richard virtually begged to observe the process. His official tour was halted and Richard stood idly around for several fengs while Archie obtained permission for them to visit the quadroid 'nursery'.

Two other octospiders guided them down a sequence of long ramps to the subterranean area. 'The nursery has been purposely built far below ground level,' Archie told Richard, 'for extra isolation and protection. We have three other similar facilities scattered around our domain.'

Holy shit, Richard said to himself when he and his three octospider companions walked out on a platform overlooking a large rectangular floor. His recognition was instant. Several metres below them, about a hundred midget morphs were scattered around the facility, performing unknown functions. Hanging down from the ceiling were eight rectangular lattices, each about five metres long and two metres wide, that were symmetrically placed around the room. Directly underneath each of the lattices was a large oval object with a hardened exterior. These eight objects resembled huge nuts and were surrounded by thick viny growths or webbing.

'I have seen a similar layout before, many years ago,' Richard said excitedly. 'Underneath New York. It was just before my first personal encounter with one of your cousins. Nicole and I were both scared out of our wits.'

'I think I read something about that incident,' Archie replied. 'Prior to our bringing Ellie and Eponine to the Emerald City, I studied all the old files on your species. Some of the data were compressed, so there were not many specifics ...'

'I remember that incident as if it were yesterday,' Richard interrupted. 'I had placed a couple of miniature robots on a small subway and they had disappeared into a tunnel. They came into an area like this one and, after climbing through some of that webbing, were chased and captured by one of your cousins ...'

'Doubtless the robots had stumbled into a quadroid nursery. Those octos acted to protect it. It's really very simple ...' Archie signaled their guide engineer that it was time for his explanation.

'The quadroid queens spend their gestation periods in special compartments that are just off the main floor,' the octo engineer said. 'Each queen lays thousands of eggs. When several million eggs have been laid, they are collected together and placed in one of those oval containers. The inside of the containers is maintained at a very high temperature, which markedly reduces the development time of the quadroids. The thick webbing around the containers absorbs the excess heat so that the working conditions are acceptable for the midget morphs who oversee the nursery ...'

Richard was partially listening, but his real focus was on a moment many years earlier. *Now it is all clear*, he said to himself. *And that tiny subway was for the midget morphs.*

'... Monitoring probes inside the containers identify exactly when the quadroids are ready to swarm. The lattices above are soaked with the proper chemical agents a few fengs prior to the automatic opening of the ovals. The new queens fly first, attracted to the lattice elements. The frenzied hordes of males follow, making visible black clouds despite their minuscule size. The quadroids are harvested from the lattice and go immediately into mass training ...'

'Very elegant,' Richard said. 'But I have a simple question. *Why* do the quadroids take all those pictures for you?'

'The short answer,' Archie replied, 'is that they have been genetically engineered over thousands of years to be receptive to our direction. We, or rather our midget morph specialists, speak the chemical language the quadroids use to communicate with each other. If they do what is asked of them, the quadroids are given food. If they perform satisfactorily over a long period of time, they are allowed the pleasures of sex.'

'Out of a given litter, or swarm, what percentage of the quadroids follow your directions?'

'The failure rate for first picture is about ten per cent,' the octospider engineer answered. 'Once the pattern has been established and the reward cycle reinforced, the failure rate drops dramatically.'

'Pretty damn impressive,' Richard said appreciatively. 'Maybe there's more to this biology stuff than I ever considered.'

*

On the ride back to the Emerald City, Richard and Archie discussed the comparative strengths and weaknesses of biological and non-biological engineering systems. It was mostly an esoteric, philosophical conversation with few definitive conclusions. They did agree, however, that the encyclopedia function, which was primarily the storage, manipulation, and presentation of vast amounts of information, was more optimally handled by non-biological systems.

As they drew near to the domed city, the green glow was suddenly extinguished. Night had come again to the centre of the octospider domain. Soon thereafter, an additional pair of fireflies appeared to give their ostrichsaur extra light.

It had been a long day and Richard was tired. When they entered the outskirts of the Alternate Domain, Richard thought he saw something flying in the darkness off to his right. 'What has happened to Tammy and Timmy?' he asked.

'They have both mated,' Archie replied, 'and have several offspring ... Their young hatchlings are cared for in the zoo.'

'Could I see them?' Richard said. 'You told me once, a few months ago, that someday it might be possible ...'

'I guess so,' Archie replied after a short silence. 'Even though the zoo is a restricted zone, the avian compound is very close to the entrance.'

When they reached the first large structure of the Alternate Domain, Archie dismounted and went inside the building. When he returned, the octospider said something to the ostrichsaur. 'We are only cleared for a brief visit,' Archie said as their mount turned off the main path and began to thread its way through the smaller lanes of the community.

Richard was introduced to the zookeeper, who drove them in a cart to a compound only about a hundred metres inside the zoo entrance. Both Tammy and Timmy were present. They recognised Richard immediately, and their jabbers and shrieks of pleasure filled the darkened skies. Tammy and Timmy introduced Richard to a new group of avian hatchlings in the compound. The juveniles were very shy around Richard, and would not let him touch them. However, Tammy and Timmy still loved to have their soft underbellies stroked by the man who had raised them from infancy. Richard felt powerful emotions as he recalled the days when he had been their sole protector in the lair underneath New York.

He said goodbye to his wards and boarded the cart with Archie and the zoo-keeper. Halfway back to the zoo entrance he heard a sound that jolted him into alertness and made his skin crawl with goose-bumps. He sat perfectly still and concentrated. The sound repeated just before the silent cart came to a stop.

'I could not possibly be mistaken,' Richard insisted to Nicole. 'I heard it twice. There is no other sound like the cry of a human child.'

'I'm not doubting you, Richard,' Nicole said. 'I'm just trying to exclude logically all other possible sources for the sound you heard. Juvenile avians do have a particular shriek that can sound a little like a baby crying ... and you were, after all, in a zoo. It could have been another animal.'

'No,' said Richard. 'I know what I heard. I have lived with enough children and heard enough cries in my life.'

Nicole smiled. 'Now the shoe is on the other foot, isn't it, darling? Do you remember your response when I told you I had seen a woman's face in that mural the night we went to see the octospider play? You scoffed at me and told me that I was "absurd", if I remember correctly.'

'So what's the explanation? Did the octospiders somehow kidnap some other humans from Avalon? And the incident was never reported? But how could they have ...'

'Did you say anything to Archie?' Nicole asked.

'No. I was too stunned. At first I was amazed that neither he nor the zoo-keeper made any comment, and then I remembered that the octospiders are deaf.'

They were both silent for several seconds. 'You weren't supposed to hear that cry, Richard,' Nicole then said. 'Our nearly perfect hosts have made a non-optimal slip-up.'

Richard laughed. 'Of course, they are recording this conversation. By tomorrow *they* will know that *we* know ...'

'Let's not say anything just yet to the others,' Nicole said. 'Maybe the octos will decide to share their secret with us ... By the way, when do you start to work?'

'Whenever I want,' Richard replied. 'I told Archie I had a few tasks of my own to finish first.'

'Sounds as if you had a fascinating day,' Nicole said. 'Everything was mostly quiet around here. Except for one thing. Patrick and Nai have set a date for their wedding ... Three weeks from tomorrow.'

'What?' Richard said. 'Why didn't you tell me earlier?'

Nicole laughed. 'I didn't have a chance ... You came in here talking non-stop about cries in the zoo, and avians, and quadroids, and the Embryo Bank ... I knew from experience that my news would have to wait until you wound down.'

'Well, mother of the groom,' Richard said a few seconds later, 'how do you feel?'

'Considering everything,' Nicole said, 'I'm very pleased ... You know how I feel about Nai ... It just strikes me as a strange time and place to start a marriage.'

12

They were sitting in the Wakefield living-room waiting for the appearance of the bride. Patrick was nervously wringing his hands. 'Be patient, young man,' Max said, crossing the room and putting his arm around Patrick. 'She'll be here ... A woman wants to look her finest on her wedding-day.'

'I didn't look my finest,' Eponine said. 'In fact, I don't even remember what I was wearing on my wedding day.'

'I remember it well, Frenchie,' Max said with a grin, 'especially up in the igloo. As I recall, most of the time you were wearing your birthday suit.'

Everyone laughed. Nicole entered the room. 'She'll be here in a few more minutes. Ellie is helping Nai with the final arrangement of her dress.' She glanced around. 'Where are Archie and Dr Blue?' she asked.

'They went to their house for a minute,' Ellie said. 'They have a special present for the bride.'

'I don't like having those octospiders around,' Galileo said in a nasty voice. 'They give me the creeps.'

'Starting next week, Galileo,' Ellie said gently, 'there will be an octospider with you in school nearly all the time ... She'll help you learn their language.'

'I don't want to learn their language,' the boy said defiantly.

Max walked over next to Richard. 'So how is the work going, amigo? We haven't seen much of you these last two weeks.'

'It's completely absorbing, Max,' Richard said enthusiastically. 'I'm working on an encyclopedia project, helping them design a new set of software to display all the critical information about the hundreds of thousands of species in the Embryo Bank ... The octospiders accumulate such an enormous wealth of data in their testing, yet they are surprisingly limited in their knowledge of how to manage it efficiently. Just yesterday, I began working with some recent test data on a set of microbiological agents that are classified, in the octospider taxonomy, by the range of plants and animals for which they are lethal ...'

Richard stopped as Archie and Dr Blue entered together carrying a box about a metre tall that was wrapped with their parchment. The octospiders set their present down in a corner and stood at the side of the room. Ellie arrived a moment later, humming Mendelssohn's Wedding March. Nai followed her.

Patrick's bride was wearing her Thai silk dress. It was adorned by the brilliant yellow and black flowers that the octospiders had given to Ellie. She had pinned them to the dress at strategic locations. Patrick rose to stand beside Nai in front of his mother. The couple held hands.

Nicole had been asked to perform the ceremony, and to keep it as simple as possible. As she prepared to begin her brief statement, Nicole's mind was suddenly flooded by memories of other wedding-days in her life. She saw Max and Eponine, Michael O'Toole and her daughter Simone, Robert and Ellie ... Nicole shuddered involuntarily as the memory of the sound of gunshots intruded into her mind. *Once again*, Nicole thought, forcing herself to return to the present, *we have gathered here together*.

She could barely speak. Nicole was overwhelmed by her feelings. *This is my last wedding*, she realised, almost thinking out loud. *There will not be another*.

A tear ran down her left cheek. 'Are you all right, Nicole?' the always sensitive bride asked quietly. Nicole nodded and smiled.

'Friends,' Nicole said, 'we have joined together today to witness and celebrate the wedding of Patrick Ryan OToole and Nai Buatong Watanabe. Let us form a circle around them, locking arms to show our love and support for their marriage.'

Nicole gestured to the two octospiders as the circle was forming and they too put their tentacles around the humans beside them.

'Do you, Patrick,' Nicole said, her voice cracking, 'take this woman, Nai, to love and cherish as your wife and partner in life?'

'I do,' said Patrick.

'And do you, Nai,' Nicole continued, 'take this man, Patrick, to love and cherish as your husband and partner in life?'

'I do,' said Nai.

'Then I announce that you are husband and wife.' Patrick and Nai embraced, and everyone shouted. The newlyweds shared their first married hug with Nicole.

'Did you ever talk to Patrick about sex?' Nicole asked Richard after the party was over and the crowd had dispersed.

'No,' said Richard. 'Max volunteered ... But it shouldn't be necessary. After all, Nai has been married before ... Goodness, you were certainly emotional tonight. What was that all about?'

Nicole smiled. 'I was thinking about other weddings, Richard. Simone and Michael's, Ellie and Robert's ...'

'That's one I would like to forget,' Richard said. 'For many reasons.'

'I thought, during the ceremony, that I was crying because this was probably the last wedding I would ever attend. But later, during the party, I thought of something else. Has it ever bothered you, Richard, that we have never had an official ceremony?'

'No,' Richard said, shaking his head. 'I had a ceremony with Sarah, and that was enough ...'

'But *you* have had a wedding, Richard. I never have. I have given birth to children from three different fathers, but I have never once been a bride.'

Richard was silent for several seconds. 'And you think that's why you were crying?'

'Maybe,' Nicole said. 'I don't know for certain.'

Nicole walked around while Richard was in deep thought. 'Wasn't that a magnificent statue of Buddha the octospiders gave to Nai?' she said. 'The artistry was superb ... I really thought both Archie and Dr Blue were enjoying themselves. I wonder why Jamie came to get them so early ...'

'Would you like to have a wedding ceremony?' Richard asked suddenly.

'At our age?' Nicole laughed. 'We're already grandparents.'

'Still, if it would make you happy ...'

'Are you proposing to me, Richard Wakefield?'

'I guess so,' he said. 'I wouldn't want you to be unhappy because you've never been a bride.'

Nicole crossed the room and kissed her husband. 'It might be fun,' she said. 'But let's not plan anything until Patrick and Nai are settled. I wouldn't want to steal their limelight.'

Richard and Nicole walked toward the bedroom with their arms around each other. They were startled to find their passage blocked by Archie and Dr Blue.

'You must come with us right away,' Archie said. 'This is an emergency.'

'*Now*?' Nicole replied. 'At this hour?'

'Yes,' said Dr Blue. 'Only the two of you. The Chief Optimiser is waiting ... She'll explain everything.'

Nicole felt her heart-rate surge as the adrenaline poured into her system. 'Do I need a coat?' she said. 'Will we be leaving the city?'

For some reason, Nicole's first thought had been that the summons was related to the child's cry that Richard had heard after his first visit to the Embryo Bank. Was the child sick? Perhaps dying? Then why weren't they going directly to the zoo, which was outside the dome, in the Alternate Domain?

The Chief Optimiser and her staff were indeed waiting. Two chairs were in the room. As soon as Richard and Nicole were seated, the octospider leader started speaking in colour.

'We have a major crisis under way,' she said, 'one that could unfortunately lead to war between our two species.' She waved a tentacle and video images began to appear on the wall. 'Early today, two helicopters began ferrying human troops from the island of New York to the northernmost section of our domain, right next to the Cylindrical Sea. Our quadroid data indicate not only that your species is preparing to launch an assault against us, but also that your leader Nakamura has convinced the human populace that we are your enemy. He has obtained the support of the senate for the war effort and, in a comparatively short period of time, has created an arsenal that could inflict substantial damage on our colony.'

The Chief Optimiser stopped while Richard and Nicole watched video snapshots showing bombs, bazookas, and machine-guns being manufactured in New Eden.

'Investigative forays have been carried out during the last four days by small groups of humans on the ground and the pair of helicopters in the air. These reconnaissance missions have penetrated as far south as the barrier forest and have covered the entire cylindrical range of our territory. Almost thirty per cent of our food, power, and water supply is contained in the region that the humans have reconnoitred.

'There has been no combat, for we have offered no resistance to the exploration activities. We have, however, placed signs in key places, using what we know of your language, informing the human troops that the entire Southern Hemicylinder is the realm of another advanced, but peaceful, species, and requesting that the humans return to their own region. Our signs have been ignored.

'Two days ago a troublesome incident occurred. While we were harvesting grain from one of our large fields, there was a helicopter overflight. The vehicle made a nearby landing and dispatched four soldiers. Without any provocation, these humans executed the three animals doing the harvesting – the same six-armed creatures the two of you saw on your initial tour of our domain – and set fire to the grain field. Since that incident, the content of our signs has changed, and we have made it clear that any other similar behaviour will be considered an act of war.

'Nevertheless, it is apparent from actions earlier today that our warnings have not been heeded and that your species is planning to start a conflict it cannot possibly win. I was today considering announcing a declaration of war, an extremely grave event in an octospider colony, with ramifications at every level of our society. Before I took the irreversible action, however, I consulted with those other optimisers whose opinions I most respected.

'The majority of my staff favoured the war declaration, seeing no way of convincing your fellow humans that a conflict with us would be a disaster for them. The octospider you call Archie, however, made a proposal to my staff that we think has some small probability of working. Even though our statistical analysts say war is still the most likely outcome, our principles demand that we do everything possible to avoid war ... Since Archie's proposal requires your involvement and co-operation, we have called you here tonight.'

The Chief Optimiser stopped speaking in colours and shuffled to the side of the room. Richard and Nicole glanced at each other. 'Did your translator follow all that?' she asked.

'Most of it,' Richard replied. 'I certainly understand the gist of the situation ... Do *you* have any questions? Or should we suggest they proceed with Archie's proposal?'

Nicole nodded in Archie's direction and their friend moved to the centre of the room. 'I have volunteered,' the octospider said, 'to negotiate personally with the human leaders in an attempt to stop this conflict before it escalates into full-scale war. To accomplish this, however, I must obviously have some help. If I suddenly appear in the camp of the human soldiers, they will kill me. Even if they do not, they will have no way of understanding what I am telling them. So some human who understands our language must accompany me to translate my colours or there's no way that a meaningful dialogue can be started ...'

After Richard and Nicole told the Chief Optimiser that they had no disagreement with the basic concept proposed by Archie, the two humans and their octospider colleague were left alone to discuss the details..Archie's idea was straightforward. Nicole and he would approach the camp near the Cylindrical Sea together and would request a meeting with Nakamura and the other human leaders. At that meeting Archie and Nicole would explain that the octospiders were a peace-loving species who had no territorial claims on the north side of the Cylindrical Sea. Archie would request that the humans withdraw from their camp and cease their overflights. If necessary, as a token of the goodwill of the octospiders, Archie would offer to supply quantities of food and water to help the humans through their current difficulties. A permanent relationship between the two species would be established and a treaty drafted to codify the agreement.

'Jesus,' Richard said after he finished translating Archie's comments. 'And I thought Nicole was an idealist!'

Archie did not understand Richard's remark. Nicole patiently explained to the octospider that the leaders of New Eden were not likely to be as reasonable as Archie was assuming. 'It is entirely possible,' Nicole said, to stress the danger of what Archie was proposing, 'that they will kill us *both* before we are ever allowed to say anything.'

Archie kept insisting that what he was proposing was bound to be accepted eventually because it was clearly in the best interests of the humans living in New Eden. 'Look, Archie,' Richard responded in frustration, 'what you said is just not correct. There are many human beings, including Nakamura, who do not give a shit what is good for the colony. In fact, the common welfare is not even a factor in the subconscious objective function, to use your terms, that governs their behaviour. All they care about is themselves. Every decision is weighed in terms of whether or not it will increase their own personal power or influence. In our history, leaders have often destroyed their own countries or colonies in attempts to retain their power.'

The octospider was stubborn. 'What you are describing just cannot be true in an advanced species,' Archie insisted. 'The fundamental laws of evolution clearly indicate that those species whose primary value is the welfare of the group will outlast those in which the individual is supreme. Are you suggesting that human beings are an aberration of some kind, a freak of nature violating a fundamental ...'

Nicole interrupted. 'This is all very interesting, you two,' she said, 'but we have some more pressing business. We must design a plan of action that has no pitfalls ... Richard, if you don't like Archie's plan, what do you suggest?'

Richard reflected for several seconds before speaking. 'I believe that Nakamura has committed New Eden to this action against the octospiders for many reasons, one of which is to preclude criticism of the domestic failures by his government. I do not think he will be dissuaded from his course unless the citizens are overwhelmingly against the war, and, I'm sorry to say, I don't think *that* will happen unless the colonists are convinced the war will be a disaster.'

'So you think threats are necessary?' Nicole said.

'As a minimum. What would be perfect would be a demonstration of military might by the octospiders,' Richard said.

'I'm afraid that's impossible,' Archie commented, 'at least under the current circumstances.'

'Why?' Richard asked. 'The Chief Optimiser spoke with confidence about winning any war that might occur. If you were to attack and utterly destroy that camp ...'

'Now it is *you* who do not understand *us*,' Archie said. 'Because war, or any conflict that can result in deliberate deaths, is such a non-optimal way of resolving disputes, our colony has very strict regulations governing concerted hostile actions. Controls are built into our society to make war absolutely the solution of the last resort. We have no standing army and no stockpile of weapons, for example ... And there are other restraints as well. All optimisers participating in a decision to declare war, as well as all octospiders engaging in an armed conflict, are immediately terminated after the war.'

'Whaaat?' said Richard, not believing his translator. 'That's not possible.'

'Yes, it is,' Archie said. 'As you can imagine, these factors significantly deter our participation in non-defensive hostilities. The Chief Optimiser knows that she signed her own death warrant two weeks ago when she authorised the beginning of war preparations. All eighty of the octospiders now living and working in the War Domain will be terminated when this war is either concluded or the threat of war has officially passed ... I myself, since I was part of the discussions today, will be placed on the termination lists if war is declared.'

Richard and Nicole were speechless. 'The only possible justification for war to an octospider,' Archie continued, 'is an unambiguous threat to the very survival of the colony. Once that threat is identified and acknowledged, our species undergoes a metamorphosis and prosecutes the war, without mercy, until either the threat is obliterated or our colony has been destroyed ... Generations ago, some very wise optimisers realised that those individual octospiders who were engaged in killing, and the design of killing, were so psychologically altered by their experiences that they became a significant detriment to the operation of a peaceful colony. That's why the termination codicils were enacted.'

Richard and Nicole were still silent even after Archie had finished talking. At length Richard started to ask Archie to leave the room so that he could speak privately to his wife, but he quickly remembered the ubiquitous quadroids. 'Nicole, darling,' he said finally, 'I don't think Archie's plan is quite right for several reasons. For one thing, I should be going with him instead of you ...'

When Nicole started to interrupt, Richard gestured with his hands for her to remain quiet, 'Now hear me out,' he said. 'Throughout our marriage, especially since we left The Node, you have always been the one out front, giving of your time and energy for the benefit of the family or the colony. Now it's my turn. In this particular instance, I believe that I am also better suited to the proposed task. I can more easily scare our fellow humans by conjuring up images of doomsday blows delivered by the octospiders ...'

'But you don't speak their language well,' Nicole protested. 'Without your translator ...'

'I've thought about that,' Richard said. 'And I think that Ellie and Nikki should go with Archie and me. First, with a child among us, the probability that we will be killed by the advance force is significantly reduced. Second, Ellie is completely fluent in the octospider language and can back me up if my translator is either not available or inadequate. Third, and this may be the most important reason, the only crime that Nakamura and his minions can possibly be attributing to the octospiders is Ellie's kidnapping. If she shows up, healthy and praising the alien enemy, then the war effort will be undermined.'

Nicole frowned. 'I don't like the idea of Nikki going along. It's much too dangerous. I would never forgive myself if something happened to that child ...'

'Nor would I,' Richard said. 'But I don't think Ellie will go without her ... Nicole, there are no *good* plans ... We will be forced to choose the least unsatisfactory option.'

During a brief pause in the conversation Archie spoke in colour. 'Richard's points are all excellent,' the octospider said to Nicole. 'And there is one additional reason why it might be better for you to remain here in the Emerald City – the rest of the humans who stay behind will need your leadership in the difficult days ahead.'

Nicole's mind was racing. She had not been prepared for Richard to volunteer to go. 'Are you telling me, Archie,' she said, 'that you *endorse* Richard's suggestions, including taking Ellie and Nikki with you?'

'Yes,' the octospider replied.

'But Richard,' Nicole then said, turning to her husband, 'you know how you hate what you call political crap. Are you certain you have thought this through?'

Richard nodded. Nicole shrugged. 'All right, then,' she said. 'We'll talk to Ellie. If she agrees, we have a plan.'

The Chief Optimiser thought that the amended proposal had some chance of success, but felt compelled to remind everyone that, based on the detailed octospider analysis of the likely outcome, there was still a high probability that both Archie and Richard would be killed, and a nonzero chance that Ellie and Nikki would not survive as well. Nicole's heart skipped a beat when she translated the octospider leader's reminder. The Chief Optimiser was not telling her anything that Nicole did not already know; however, Nicole had been so involved in the planning and discussions that she had not yet confronted any of the likely outcomes of their decisions.

Nicole said very little while the principals all agreed upon a baseline timetable. When she heard Richard say that Archie and he, with or without Ellie and Nikki, would leave the Emerald City one tert after dawn the next day, Nicole shuddered. *Tomorrow*, flashed quickly through her mind. *Tomorrow our lives will change again.*

She remained quiet on the transport ride back to their zone. While Richard and Archie talked about many different subjects, Nicole tried to wrestle with the growing fear inside her. An inner voice, one that she had not heard for years, was telling her that she would never see Richard again after tomorrow. *Is this perhaps some peculiar reaction on my part?* she asked herself critically. *Am I having trouble letting Richard be the hero?*

The strength of the premonition grew, despite Nioele's attempts to combat it. She remembered a terrible night many, many years earlier, when she had been in her bedroom in the little house in Chilly-Mazarin. Nicole had awakened screaming from a violent and vivid nightmare. 'Mommy is dead,' the ten-year-old girl had cried.

Her father had tried to console her and had explained that her mother was just away on a trip visiting her family in the Ivory Coast. The telegram announcing her mother's death had arrived at the house seven hours later.

'If you don't have any weapons stockpiled and no trained soldiers,' Richard was now saying, 'how in the world can you prepare for a war fast enough to defend yourself?'

'I cannot tell you that,' Archie replied. 'But believe me, I know for a fact that a conflict at this time between our two species could result in the total annihilation of the human civilization in Rama.'

Nicole could not calm her tormented soul. No matter how many times she told herself she was overreacting, the premonitory fear did not diminish. She reached over and took Richard's hand. He wrapped his fingers through hers and continued his conversation with Archie.

Nicole gazed intently at him. *I am proud of you, Richard*, she thought, *but I am also frightened.* She felt the tears creeping into her eyes. *And I am not yet ready to say goodbye.*

It was very late when Nicole went to bed. She had awakened Ellie gently, without disturbing Nikki and the Watanabe twins, who were sleeping in the Wakefield house so that Patrick and Nai could have their wedding-night alone. Ellie, of course, had had many questions. Richard and Nicole had explained the plan, including everything important they had learned from Archie and the Chief Optimiser earlier in the evening. Ellie had been fearful, but had finally agreed that Nikki and she would accompany Richard and Archie the next day.

Nicole could not fall into a deep sleep. After tossing and turning for an hour, she began a sequence of short, chaotic dreams. In her final dream Nicole was again seven years old back in the Ivory Coast, in the middle of her Poro ceremony. She was half-naked out in the water, with the lioness prowling around the perimeter of the pond. Little Nicole took a deep breath and dove under the water. When she surfaced, Richard was standing on the shore where the lioness had been. It was a young Richard smiling at her initially, but as Nicole watched, he aged rapidly and became the same Richard who was beside her that moment in the bed. She heard Omeh's voice in her ear. 'Look carefully, Ronata,' the voice said. 'And remember ...'

Nicole woke up. Richard was sleeping peacefully. She sat up in the bed and tapped on the wall one time. A solitary firefly appeared in the doorway, shining some light into the bedroom. Nicole stared at her husband. She looked at his hair and beard, grey from age, and remembered them when they had been black. She recalled fondly his ardour and humour during their courtship in New York. Nicole grimaced, took a deep breath, and kissed her index finger. She placed the finger on Richard's lips. He did not stir. Nicole sat quietly for several more minutes, studying every feature of her husband's face. Soft tears flowed down her cheeks and dropped from her chin onto the sheets. 'I love you, Richard,' she said.

WAR IN RAMA

1

REPORT Number 319
Time of Transmission: 156 307 872 574.2009
Time Since First Stage Alert: 111.9766
References: Node 23–419
Spacecraft 947
Spacefarers 47 249 (A & B)
32 806
2 666

During the last interval the structure and order in the spacefaring communities inside the spacecraft have continued to disintegrate. Despite the warnings of the octospiders (spacefarer # 2 666) and their laudable attempts to avoid a broad conflict with the humans (# 32 806), it is now even more likely that a disastrous war between the two species, which could leave only a few survivors, may take place in the next several intervals. The situation therefore meets all the prerequisite conditions for a stage two intercession.

Prior intercessionary activity has been declared a failure, primarily because the more aggressive of the two species, the humans, are fundamentally insensitive to the entire range of subtle intercessionary techniques. Only a few of the humans have responded to the many attempts to alter their hostile behaviour, and those who did react were unable to stop the genocide of the avians and sessiles (# 47 249, A & B) perpetrated by their rulers.

The humans are organised in the rigid, hierarchical manner often observed in pre-spacefaring species. They continue to be dominated by a leadership whose focus is the retention of personal power. The welfare of the human community and even its survival are subordinated in the implicit objective function of the current human leaders to the continuation of a political system which gives them absolute authority. There is consequently little likelihood that the threatened expanded conflict between the humans and the octospiders can be avoided by any logical appeals.

A small cadre of humans, including almost all of the family that lived at The Node for over a year, remains in residence in the main octospider city. Their interaction with their hosts has demonstrated that it is possible for the two species to live together in harmony. Recently a mixed delegation of those humans and one octospider have decided to make a concerted effort to prevent a full-scale interspecies war by contacting the leaders of the human colony directly. However, the probability that this delegation will be successful is very low.

Thus far the octospiders have taken no overt hostile action. Nevertheless, they have begun the process of preparing for a war against the humans. Although they will fight only if they determine that the survival of their community is in jeopardy, the advanced biological capabilities of the octospiders makes the outcome of such a war a foregone conclusion.

What is not certain is how the humans will react once the conflict escalates and they suffer heavy losses. It is possible that the war might terminate quickly and, in time, the two surviving communities might again reach a near equilibrium status. Based on the available observational data on the humans, however, there is a non-trivial probability that this species will continue the battle until most or all of them perish. Such an outcome would destroy all the vestiges of at least one of the two spacefaring societies remaining in the spacecraft. To preclude such a disadvantageous result for the project, consideration of a stage two intercession is recommended.

2

Nicole was awakened by the sound of the three children playing in the living-room. As she was slipping on her robe, Ellie came to the door of the bedroom and asked if she had seen Nikki's favourite doll. 'I think it's under her bed,' Nicole replied.

Ellie returned to her packing, Nicole could hear Richard in the bathroom. *It won't be long now*, she was thinking when her granddaughter suddenly appeared in the doorway. 'Mommy and I are leaving, Nonni,' the little girl said with a smile. 'We're going to see Daddy.'

Nicole opened her arms and the little girl ran over for a hug. 'I know, darling,' Nicole said. She held the girl tightly in her arms and then began to stroke her hair. 'I will miss you, Nikki,' she said.

A few seconds later the Watanabe twins both bounded into the room. 'I'm hungry, Mrs Wakefield,' Galileo said.

'Me too,' Kepler added.

Nicole reluctantly released her granddaughter and started walking across the bedroom. 'All right, boys,' she said. 'I'll have your breakfast in a few minutes.'

When the three children were almost finished eating, Max, Eponine, and Marius arrived at the door. 'Guess what, Uncle Max,' Nikki said before Nicole had even had a chance to greet the Pucketts. 'I'm going to see my daddy.'

The four hours flew by quickly. Richard and Nicole explained everything twice, first to Max and Eponine and then to the newlyweds, both of whom were still radiant from the pleasures of their wedding night. As the time neared for the departure of Richard, Ellie, and Nikki, the excitement and energy that had characterised the morning conversation began to wane. Butterflies started fluttering in Nicole's stomach. *Relax and smile*, she told herself. *You won't make it any easier by being sad*.

Max was the first to say goodbye. 'Come over here, Princess,' he said to Nikki, 'and give your Uncle Max a kiss.' The girl obediently followed directions. Max then stood up and crossed the room to where Ellie was talking with her mother. 'Take care of that little girl, Ellie,' he said, embracing her, 'and don't let the bastards get away with anything.' Max shook hands with Richard and then called the Watanabe twins to join him outside.

The mood in the room was swiftly altered. Despite her promise to herself that she would remain calm, Nicole felt a surge of panic as she suddenly realised that she had only a few minutes to complete her farewells. Patrick, Nai, Benjy, and Eponine had followed Max's cue and were hugging the departing trio.

Nicole tried to embrace Nikki again, but the little girl scurried away, running outside to play with the twins. Ellie finished saying goodbye to Eponine and turned to Nicole. 'I will miss you, Mother,' she said brightly. 'I love you very much.'

Nicole struggled to maintain her emotional equilibrium. 'I couldn't have asked for a better daughter,' she said. While the two women hugged, Nicole spoke softly in her daughter's ear. 'Be careful,' she said. 'There's a lot at stake ...'

Ellie pulled away and looked in her mother's eyes. She took a deep breath. 'I know, Mother,' she said somberly, 'and it frightens me, I hope I don't disappoint ...'

'You won't,' Nicole said lightly, patting her daughter's shoulders. 'Just remember what the cricket said in *Pinocchio*.'

Ellie smiled. '"And always let your conscience be your guide."'

'Archie's here!' Nicole heard Nikki shout. She looked around for her husband. *Where's Richard?* she thought in a fright. *I haven't said goodbye ...* Ellie was a blur as she headed for the door carrying two backpacks.

Nicole could hardly breathe. She heard Patrick say, 'Where's Uncle Richard?' and a voice from the study reply, 'I'm back here.'

She ran down the hall to the study. Richard was sitting on the floor amid electronic components and his own open backpack. Nicole stood in the doorway for a second, catching her breath.

Richard heard her behind him and turned around. 'Oh, hi, darling,' he said nonchalantly. 'I'm still trying to figure out how many back-up components I should take for my translators.'

'Archie's here,' Nicole said quietly.

Richard glanced at his watch. 'I guess it's time to go,' he said. He picked up a handful of electronic parts and stuffed them into his backpack. Then he stood up and walked towards Nicole.

'Uncle Richard,' Patrick yelled.

'I'm coming,' Richard shouted. 'Just a minute.'

Nicole began to tremble the moment Richard put his arms around her. 'Hey,' he said, 'it's all right ... We've been apart before.'

The fear inside Nicole had become so strong that she could not speak. She tried desperately to be brave, but it was impossible. She knew that this was the last time she would ever touch her husband.

She put one hand behind Richard's head and pulled away slightly so that she could kiss him. Nicole wanted to stop time, to make this one moment last an eternity. Her eyes took a photograph of Richard's face, and she kissed him gently on the lips.

'I love you, Nicole,' he said.

For an instant she didn't think she was going to be able to reply. 'I love you too,' she finally managed to say.

He hoisted his backpack and gave a little wave. Nicole stood in the doorway and watched him walk toward the door. Remember, she heard Omeh's voice say inside her head.

Nikki could hardly believe her good fortune. There in front of her, barely outside the gates of the Emerald City, an ostrichsaur was waiting for them, just as Archie had said. She moved about impatiently as her mother zipped her coat. 'Can I feed it, Mother?' she said. 'Can I? Can I?'

Even with the ostrichsaur sitting on the ground, Richard had to help Nikki mount the animal. 'Thank you, Boobah,' the girl said when she was comfortably nestled in the bowl.

'The timing has been worked out very carefully,' Archie told Richard and Ellie while they were moving along the path through the forest. 'We will arrive at the camp when all the troops are starting breakfast. That way everyone will see us.'

'How will we know precisely when to appear?' Richard asked.

'Some of the quadroids are being managed from the far northern fields. Soon after the first soldiers are awake and are moving around outside their tents, your avian friend Timmy, carrying a written announcement of our imminent arrival, will fly over their heads in the dark. Our message will indicate that we will be preceded by the fireflies and that we will be waving a white flag, as you suggested.'

Nikki noticed some strange eyes looking out at them from the dark of the forest. 'Isn't this fun?' she said to her mother. Ellie did not respond.

Archie stopped the ostrichsaur about a kilometre south of the human camp. The lanterns and other lights outside the distant tents in front of them looked like stars twinkling in the night. 'Timmy should be dropping our message just about now,' Archie said.

They had been moving cautiously in the dark for several hours, not wanting to use the fireflies because of the possibility that they might be noticed too early. Nikki was sleeping peacefully, her head in her mother's lap. Both Richard and Ellie were tense. 'What are we going to do,' Richard had inquired before they stopped, 'if the troops fire on us before we can say anything?'

'We'll turn around and retreat as fast as we can,' Archie had replied.

'And what happens if they come after us with the helicopters and the searchlights?' Ellie had asked.

'At full speed it will take the ostrichsaur almost four wodens to reach the forest,' Archie had said.

Timmy returned to the group and reported, in a brief jabber and colour conversation with Archie, that he had accomplished his mission. Richard and Timmy then said farewell to each other. The avian's large eyes expressed an emotion Richard had not seen before as Richard rubbed his underbelly. A few moments later, as Timmy flew away in the direction of the Emerald City, a pair of fireflies ignited beside the path and then headed in the direction of the human camp. Richard led the procession, clutching the white flag in his right hand. The ostrichsaur followed about fifty metres behind carrying Ellie, Archie, and the sleeping child.

Richard could see the soldiers with his binoculars when their party was about four hundred metres away. The troops were standing around, looking in their general direction. Richard counted twenty-six of them altogether, including three with rifles poised and another pair scanning the darkness with binoculars.

As planned, Ellie, Nikki, and Archie dismounted when they were about two hundred metres from the camp. The ostrichsaur was sent back while the four of them walked towards the human soldiers. Nikki, who had not been ready to awaken, complained at first but became quiet when she sensed the importance of her mother's request to remain silent.

Archie walked between the two adult humans. Nikki was holding her mother's hand and scampering to keep up with the pace. 'Hello, there,' Richard shouted when he thought he was within earshot. 'This is Richard Wakefield. We come in peace.' He waved the white flag vigorously. 'I am with my daughter Ellie, my granddaughter Nikki, and an octospider representative.'

They must have been an amazing sight for the soldiers, none of whom had ever seen an octospider before. With the fireflies hovering over the heads of the troops, Richard and his party emerged from the Raman dark.

One of the soldiers stepped forward. 'I am Captain Enrico Pioggi,' he said, 'the commanding officer of this camp ... I accept your surrender on behalf of the armed forces of New Eden.'

Because the announcement of their impending arrival had been delivered to the camp less than half an hour earlier, the New Eden chain of command had not had time to formulate a plan of what to do with the prisoners. As soon as he had confirmed that a party of a man, a woman, a child, and an alien octospider were indeed approaching his camp, Captain Pioggi had again radioed the front headquarters in New York and requested instructions on how to proceed.

The colonel in charge of the campaign told him to 'secure the prisoners' and 'stand by for further orders.'

Richard had anticipated that none of the officers would be willing to take any definitive action until Nakamura himself had been consulted. He had told Archie, during their long ride on the ostrichsaur, that it would be important to use whatever time they might have with the soldiers in the camp to start rebutting the propaganda that the New Eden government was spreading.

'This creature,' Richard said in a loud voice after the prisoners had been searched and the curious troops were milling around them, 'is what we call an octospider. All octospiders are very intelligent – in some ways more intelligent than we are – and about fifteen thousand of them live in the Southern Hemicylinder, which extends from here to the base of the south polar bowl. My family and I have been living in their realm for over a year, of our own choice, I might add, and we have found the octospiders to be moral and peace-loving. My daughter Ellie and I have come forward with this octospider representative, whom we call Archie, to try to find some way of stopping a military confrontation between our two species.'

'Aren't you Dr Robert Turner's wife?' said one of the troops to Ellie. 'The one who was kidnapped by the octospiders?'

'Yes, I am,' Ellie said in a clear voice. 'Except that I wasn't kidnapped in the truest sense of the word. The octospiders wanted to establish communications with us and had been unable to do so. I was taken because they believed that I had the capacity to learn their language.'

'That thing *talks*?' another soldier said with disbelief.

Until that moment Archie, as planned, had been silent. The troops all stared dumbfounded as colours began pouring out of the right side of his slit and circumnavigating his head. 'Archie says greetings,' Ellie translated. 'He asks each of you to understand that neither he nor any member of his species wishes you any harm. Archie also wants me to inform you that he can read lips and will be happy to answer any questions you might have ...'

'Is this for real?' a soldier said.

Meanwhile, a frustrated Captain Pioggi was standing off to the side, providing an eyewitness account by radio to the colonel in New York. 'Yes, sir,' he was saying, 'colours on its head ... all different colours, sir, red, blue, yellow ... like rectangles, moving rectangles, they go around its head, and then more of them follow ... What's that, sir? ... The woman, the doctor's wife, sir ... She apparently knows what the colours mean ... No, sir, there aren't any coloured letters, just the coloured strips ...

'Right now, sir, the alien is talking to the soldiers ... No, sir, they are not using colours ... According to the woman, sir, the octospider can read lips ... like a hearing-impaired person, sir ... same technique I guess ... Anyway, it then answers in colour and the doctor's wife translates ...

'No weapons of any kind, sir ... Plenty of toys, clothes, weird-looking objects prisoner Wakefield says are electronic components ... Toys, sir, I said toys ... the little girl had a lot of toys in her backpack ... No, we don't have a scanner up here ... Right, sir ... Do you have any idea how long we might be waiting, sir?'

By the time Captain Pioggi finally received orders to send the prisoners to New York in one of the helicopters, Archie had thoroughly impressed all the soldiers at the camp. The octospider had begun the demonstration of his prodigious mental abilities by multiplying five- and six-place numbers in his head.

'Now, how do we know that the octospider thing is really coming up with the right answer?' one of the younger soldiers had asked. 'All it does is show a string of colours.'

'My man,' Richard had replied with a laugh, 'didn't you just verify on the lieutenant's calculator that the number my daughter gave was correct? Do you think *she* computed the product in *her* head?'

'Oh, yeah,' the youth said. 'I see what you mean.'

What really overwhelmed the soldiers was Archie's phenomenal memory. At Richard's urging, one of the troops listed a sequence of several hundred numbers on a sheet of paper and then read the sequence to Archie, a single number at a time. The octospider repeated them back through Ellie, without any errors. Some of the soldiers thought that there had been a trick involved, that maybe Richard was flashing coded signals to Archie. However, when Archie duplicated his feat under carefully controlled conditions, all the doubters were convinced.

The atmosphere in the camp was relaxed and amiable by the time the orders were received to transport the prisoners to New York. The first part of their plan had succeeded beyond their wildest imaginings. Nevertheless, Richard was nervous as they climbed on board the helicopter to cross a portion of the Cylindrical Sea.

They only stayed in New York for about an hour. Armed guards met the prisoners at the helicopter pad in the western plaza, confiscated their backpacks over Richard's and Nikki's loud protests, and marched them to The Port. Richard carried Nikki in his arms. He barely had time to admire his favourite skyscrapers looming overhead in the dark.

The yacht that carried them across the northern half of the Cylindrical Sea was similar to the pleasure boats that Nakamura and his cronies used on Lake Shakespeare. At no time during the crossing did any of the guards speak to them. 'Boobah,' Nikki whispered to Richard after several of her questions had gone unheeded, 'don't these men know how to talk?' She giggled.

A rover was waiting for them on a dock that had been recently constructed to support the new activities in New York and the Southern Hemicylinder. At considerable effort and expense, the humans had cut an opening through the southern barrier wall in an area adjacent to the avian/sessile habitat and had built a large docking facility.

Richard wondered at first why he and his companions had not been flown directly back to New Eden in the helicopter. After a few quick mental calculations, however, he correctly concluded that because of the enormous height of the barrier wall, which extended well up into the region where the artificial gravity caused by the spinning Rama spacecraft began to drop substantially, as well as the probable lack of skilled pilots, there was an upper limit placed on the altitude at which the hastily built helicopters were allowed to fly. *That means*, Richard was thinking as he boarded the rover, *that the humans must move all their equipment and personnel either through this dock or by means of the moat and tunnel underneath the second habitat.*

Their rover was driven by a Garcia biot. In front and behind them were two other rovers, both with armed humans. They sped across the darkness to the Central Plain.

Richard sat in the front seat beside the driver, with Archie, Ellie, and Nikki in the back. Richard had turned around in his seat and was reminding Archie of the five kinds of biots in New Eden when the Garcia interrupted him. 'The prisoner Wakefield is to face forward and remain silent,' the biot said.

'Isn't that just a little bit ridiculous?' Richard said lightly.

The Garcia pulled its right arm off the steering wheel and struck Richard hard in the face with the back of its hand. 'Face forward and remain silent,' the biot repeated, as Richard recoiled from the force of the slap.

Nikki started crying after the sudden display of violence. Ellie tried both to quiet and to comfort her. 'I don't like the driver, Mommy,' the little girl said. 'I really don't.'

It was night inside New Eden after they were ushered through the checkpoint at the entrance to the habitat. Archie and the three humans were placed into an open electric car driven by another Garcia biot. Richard noticed immediately that it was almost as cold in New Eden as it had been in Rama. The car bounced down the road, which was in an acute state of disrepair, and turned north at what had once been the train station for the village of Positano. Fifteen or twenty people were huddled around camp-fires on the concrete areas surrounding the old station, and another three or four were stretched out and sleeping underneath cardboard boxes and old clothing.

'What are those people doing, Mommy?' Nikki asked. Ellie did not answer because the Garcia turned around quickly with a hostile stare.

The neon lights of Vegas could already be seen in front of them when the car took a sharp left turn onto a residential lane in a wooded section that had once been part of Sherwood Forest. The car came to an abrupt halt in front of a large, rambling ranch house. Two Oriental men, armed with both pistols and daggers, approached the car. They gestured for the passengers to climb out of the car and then dismissed the biot. 'Come with us,' said one of the men.

Archie and his human companions entered the house and were taken down a long flight of stairs into a basement with no windows. 'There is food and water on the table,' the second man said. He turned and started to climb the stairs.

'Wait a minute,' Richard said. 'Our backpacks ... we need to have our backpacks.'

'They will be returned,' the man said impatiently, 'as soon as all the contents have been carefully checked.'

'And when do we see Nakamura?' Richard inquired.

The man shrugged. His face was expressionless. He walked quickly up the stairs.

3

The days passed very slowly.

Richard, Ellie, and Nikki were without a time reference at first, but they soon learned that octospiders had a wonderfully precise inner clock that is calibrated and enhanced during their juvenile education. After they converted Archie to using human time measurements (Richard used his oft-quoted 'When in Rome ...' to convince Archie to abandon, at least temporarily, his terts, wodens, fengs, and nillets), they discovered, by sneaking glances at their guard's digital watch when he brought food and water, that Archie's internal timing accuracy was better than ten seconds out of every twenty-four hours.

Nikki amused herself by constantly asking Archie the time. As a result, after repeated observation, Richard and even Nikki learned how to read Archie's colours for time-references and small numbers. In fact, as the days passed, the regular conversation in the basement significantly improved Richard's overall comprehension of the octospider language. Although his skill in understanding the colour strips was still not as advanced as Ellie's, after a week Richard could comfortably converse with Archie without needing Ellie as an interpreter.

The humans slept on futons on the floor. Archie curled up behind them for the few hours each night that he slept. One or the other of the two Oriental men replenished their supplies once each day. Richard never failed to remind the guards that they were still waiting for their backpacks and for their audience with Nakamura.

After eight days the daily sponge baths in the washbasin adjoining the basement toilet were no longer satisfactory. Richard asked if they could have access to a shower and some soap. Several hours later a large laundry tub was carried down the stairs. Each of the humans bathed, although Nikki was at first surprisingly reluctant to be naked in front of Archie. Richard and Ellie felt sufficiently better after bathing that they managed to share some optimism. 'There's no way he can keep our existence a secret forever,' Richard said. 'Too many of the troops saw us ... and it would not be possible for them not to say anything, no matter what Nakamura ordered.'

'I'm certain they will come for us soon,' Ellie added brightly.

By the end of their second week of imprisonment, however, their temporary optimism had waned. Richard and Ellie were beginning to lose hope. It didn't help that Nikki had become a complete brat, announcing regularly that she was bored and complaining about not having anything to do. Archie began to tell Nikki stories to keep her occupied. His octospider 'legends' (he had a long discussion with Ellie about the exact meaning of the word before he finally accepted the term) delighted the little girl.

It helped that Ellie's translations rang with the resonant phrases the girl already associated with bedtime fairy tales. 'Once upon a time, back in the days of the Precursors ...' Archie would begin a story, and Nikki would squeal with anticipation.

'What did the Precursors look like, Archie?' the little girl asked after one such story.

'The legends never say,' Archie replied. 'So I guess you can create whatever picture of them you want in your imagination.'

'Is that story true?' Nikki asked Archie on another occasion. 'Would the octospiders *really* never have left their own planet if the Precursors had not taken them into space first?'

'So the legends indicate,' Archie replied. 'They say that almost everything we knew until about fifty thousand years ago was taught to us originally by the Precursors.'

One night, after Nikki was asleep, Richard and Ellie asked Archie about the origin of the legends. 'They have been around for tens of thousands of your years,' the octospider said. 'The earliest documented records from our genus contain many of the stories I have shared with you these last few days ... There are several different opinions about how factual the legends are ... Dr Blue believes that they are basically accurate and probably the work of some master storyteller, an alternate, of course, whose genius was not recognised in his or her lifetime.

'If the legends can be believed,' Archie said in answer to another of Richard's questions, 'many, many years ago we octospiders were simple seafaring creatures whose natural evolution had produced only minimal intelligence and awareness. It was the Precursors who discovered our potential by mapping our genetic structure, and they who altered us over many generations into what we had become when the Great Calamity occurred.'

'What exactly happened to the Precursors?' Ellie asked.

'There are many stories, some contradictory. Most or all of the Precursors living on the primary planet we shared with them were probably killed in the Calamity. Some of the legends suggest that their remote colonial outposts around nearby stars survived for several hundred years, but ultimately succumbed as well. One legend says that the Precursors continued to thrive in other, more favourable star systems and became the dominant form of intelligence in the galaxy. We do not know. All that is known for certain is that the land portion of our primary planet was uninhabitable for many,

many years and that when the octospider civilization again ventured out of the water, none of the Precursors were alive.'

The group of four in the basement developed their own diurnal rhythm as the days stretched into weeks. Each morning, before Nikki and Ellie awakened, Archie and Richard would talk about a wide range of topics of mutual interest. By this time, Archie's lip-reading was nearly flawless, and Richard's comprehension of the octospider colours was good enough that the octospider was only rarely asked to repeat what he had said.

Many of the conversations were about science. Archie was especially fascinated by the history of science in the human species. He wanted to know what discoveries were made when, what prompted the key investigations or experiments in the first place, and what inaccurate or competing models explaining the phenomena were discarded as a result of each new understanding.

'So it was actually war that accelerated the development of both aeronautics and nuclear physics in your species,' Archie said one morning. 'What an amazing concept! ... You cannot possibly appreciate,' the octospider added a few seconds later, 'how staggering it is for me to experience, even vicariously, your incremental process of learning about nature ... Our history is totally different. In the beginning our species was completely ignorant. Shortly thereafter a new kind of octospider was created, one that could not only think, but also observe the world and understand what it was seeing. Our mentors and creators, the Precursors, already had explanations for everything. Our task as a species was quite simple. We learned what we could from our teachers. Naturally, we did not have any concept of the trial and error that is involved in science. For that matter, we had no idea at all of how any component in a culture evolves. The brilliant engineering of the Precursors allowed us to skip hundreds of millions of years of evolution.

'Needless to say, we were woefully unprepared for taking care of ourselves after the Great Calamity occurred. According to the more historical of our legends, our primary intellectual activity for the next several hundred years was to accumulate and understand as much of the Precursor information as we could find and/or remember. In the meantime, with our benefactors no longer around to provide ethical guidelines, our sociological progress was negative. We entered a long, long period in which it was questionable whether or not the new, intelligent octospiders created by the Precursors would indeed survive ...'

Richard was overwhelmed by the idea of what he called a 'derivative technological species.' 'I had never imagined,' he told Archie one morning with his usual excitement of discovery, 'that there might exist a spacefaring species that had *never* worked out on its own the laws of gravity and had *never* derived, in a long sequence of experiments, the essentials of physics, such as the characteristics of the electromagnetic spectrum. It is a mind-boggling thought ... But now that I understand what you are telling me, it seems quite natural. If species A, who are advanced spacefarers, encounters species B, intelligent but somewhere lower on the technological ladder, it is perfectly logical to assume that, after contact, species B would skip the rungs between ...'

'Our case, of course,' Archie explained, 'was even more unusual. The paradigm that you are describing is indeed quite natural and has happened, according to both our history and the legends, with great frequency. More spacefarers are derivative, to use your word, than naturally evolved. Take the avians and the sessiles, for example. Their symbiosis, which developed without any outside interference, had already existed in a star system not far from our home planet for thousands of years when they were first visited on an exploratory mission by the Precursors. The avians and sessiles would almost certainly never have developed a spacefaring capability of their own. However, after meeting the Precursors and seeing their first spacecraft, they asked for and received the technology necessary to achieve space flight ...

'Our situation is generically different, and definitely much more derivative. If our legends are true, the Precursors were already spacefarers when we octospiders were still totally insentient. At that epoch we were not even capable of conceiving of the idea of a planet, much less of the space surrounding it. Our fate was decided by the advanced beings with whom we shared our world. The Precursors recognised the potential in our genetic structure. Using their engineering skills, they improved us, gave us minds, shared their information with us, and created an advanced culture where none would probably have ever existed ...'

A deep bonding developed between Richard and Archie as a result of the regular early morning conversations. Unencumbered by any distractions, the two were able to share their fundamental love for knowledge. Each expanded the understanding of the other, thereby enriching their mutual appreciation for the wonders of the universe.

Nikki almost always woke up before Ellie. Soon after the girl had finished her breakfast, the group entered the second segment of their daily schedule. Although Nikki occasionally played games with Archie, she spent most of what might be called her morning in informal classes. She had three teachers. With Ellie, Nikki read a little, and did elementary addition and subtraction. She talked to her grandfather about science and nature, and had lessons with Archie on morals and ethics. She also learned the octospider alphabet and a few simple phrases. Nikki was very quick with the language of colour, a fact that the others attributed both to her altered genes and to her natural intelligence.

'Our juveniles spend a significant amount of their schooling time discussing and interpreting case studies that raise critical moral problems,' Archie told Richard and Ellie one morning during a discussion of education. 'Real-life situations are chosen as examples – although the actual facts may be slightly altered to sharpen the issues – and the young octospiders are asked to assess the acceptability of various possible responses. They do this in open discussion.'

'Is this to expose the juveniles at an early age to the concept of optimisation?' Richard asked.

'Not really,' Archie replied. 'What we are trying to do is to prepare the young for the real task of living, which involves regular interaction with others, with many behavioural choices. Each juvenile is strongly encouraged to use the case studies to develop his or her own value system. Our species believes that knowledge does not exist in a vacuum. Only when knowledge is an integral part of a way of living does it achieve any real significance ...'

Archie's case studies presented Nikki with simple but elegant ethical problems. The basic issues of lying, fairness, prejudice, and selfishness were all covered in the first eight lessons. The girl's responses to the situations often drew upon examples from her own life.

'Galileo will always say or do whatever he thinks will allow him to have his own way,' Nikki remarked during one lesson. 'To him, what *he* wants is more important than anything else ... Kepler is different. He never makes me cry ...'

Nikki napped in the afternoon. While she was sleeping, Richard, Ellie, and Archie often exchanged comments and insights that highlighted the similarities and differences between the two species. 'If I have understood correctly,' Ellie said one day after a lively conversation about how intelligent, sensitive beings should handle members of their community who exhibit antisocial behaviour, 'your society is much less tolerant than ours ... There is clearly a "preferred way of living" that is advanced by your communities. Those octospiders who do not embrace that preferred model are not only ostracised early, but also denied participation in many of life's more rewarding activities and "terminated" after a shorter than normal life span ...'

'In our society,' Archie said in reply, 'what is acceptable is always clear – there is no confusion, as there is in yours. Thus our individuals make their choices with full knowledge of the consequences. Incidentally, the Alternate Domain is not like one of your prisons. It is a place where octospiders, and other species as well, can live without the regimentation and optimization necessary for the continued development and survival of the colony. Some of the alternates live to be very old and are quite happy ....

'Your society, at least what I have observed of it, seems not to understand the fundamental inconsistency between individual freedom and the common welfare. The two must be carefully balanced. No group can survive, let alone thrive, unless what is good for the overall community is more important than individual freedom ... Take, for example, resource allocation. How can anyone with any intelligence possibly justify, in terms of the overall community, the accumulation and hoarding of enormous material assets by a few individuals when others do not even have food, clothing, and other essentials?...'

In the basement Archie was not the reticent and/or evasive octospider he had sometimes been in the Emerald City. He spoke openly about all aspects of his civilization, as if the common mission he was undertaking with his human colleagues had somehow freed him from all constraints. Was Archie consciously sending a message to the other humans who were almost certainly monitoring the conversation? Perhaps. But how much of the conversation could Nakamura's men have understood, since they knew nothing of the language of colour? No, it was more likely that Archie, better than any of the humans, realised that his death was imminent and wanted his final days to be as meaningful and stimulating as possible.

One night before Richard and Ellie went to sleep, Archie said that he had something 'personal' to tell them. 'I do not want to alarm you,' the octospider said, 'but I have consumed almost all of the supply of barrican that is in my intake buffer. If we stay here much longer and my barrican runs out, as you know I will begin to undergo sexual maturity. According to our files, I will become more aggressive and possessive at that time. I hope that I will not ...'

'Don't worry about it,' Richard said with a laugh. 'I have dealt with teenagers before. Certainly I can handle an octospider who no longer has a perfect temperarnent.'

One morning the guard bringing their food and water told Ellie to prepare herself and the girl to leave. 'When?' Ellie said.

'Ten minutes,' the guard replied.

'Where are we going?' Ellie inquired.

The guard said nothing and disappeared up the stairway.

While Ellie was doing her best to freshen herself and Nikki (they had brought only three changes of clothes with them and had had difficulty cleaning them), she reviewed with Richard and Archie what she would say if she was able to meet with Nakamura or any of the other colony leaders.

'Don't forget,' her father stressed in a rapid whisper over in one corner of the room, 'although it is all right to say that the octospiders are a peace-loving species, we will not be able to stop any war unless we convince Nakamura that he cannot possibly win an armed conflict. The point must be made that their technology has advanced far beyond ours.'

'But what if they ask for specifics?'

'You wouldn't be expected to know any details. Tell them that I can supply all the specifics.'

Ellie and Nikki were taken by electric car to the colony hospital in Central City. They were whisked through the emergency entrance and into a small, sterile office with two chairs, a couch or bed used for examinations, and some complex electronic equipment. Ellie and Nikki sat alone for ten minutes before Dr Robert Turner walked into the room.

He looked very old. 'Hi, Nikki,' he said, smiling and squatting down with his arms outstretched. 'Come give your daddy a hug.'

The girl hesitated for a moment and then ran across the room to her father. Robert picked her up and swung her around in his arms. 'It's so good to see you, Nikki,' he said.

Ellie stood up and waited. After several seconds Robert put his daughter back down on the floor and looked at his wife. 'How are you, Ellie?' he asked.

'Fine,' Ellie replied, suddenly feeling awkward. 'How are *you*, Robert?'

'About the same,' he said.

They met in the middle of the room and embraced. Ellie tried to kiss him tenderly, but their lips merely brushed before Robert turned away. She could sense the tension in his body.

'What is it, Robert?' Ellie said softly. 'What's wrong?'

'I've just been working too hard, as usual,' he replied. He moved over beside the examination bed. 'Would you take off your clothes and lie down here, please, Ellie? I want to make certain you're all right.'

'Right this minute?' an incredulous Ellie asked. 'Before we even talk about what has happened to us during the months that we've been apart?'

'I'm sorry, Ellie,' Robert said with a trace of a smile. 'I'm very busy tonight. The hospital is terribly understaffed. I talked them into releasing you by promising ...'

Ellie had walked around the bed and was standing very close to her husband. She reached down and took his hand. 'Robert,' she said gently, 'I am your wife. I love you. We have not seen each other for over a year. Surely you can take a minute ...'

Tears formed in Robert's eyes. 'What is it, Robert? Tell me.' Ellie had a sudden fright. *He's married someone else*, she thought in panic.

'What has happened to *you*, Ellie?' he said suddenly in a loud voice. 'How could you possibly tell those soldiers that you were not kidnapped, and that the octospiders were not hostile? ... You have made me a laughing-stock. Every single citizen in New Eden has heard me on television describing that terrible moment that you were abducted ... My memories are so horribly clear ...'

Ellie backed up at first when Robert began his outburst. As she stood there listening, still holding his hand, his anguish was obvious. 'I made those comments, Robert, because I was, and am, trying to do whatever I can to stop any conflict between the octospiders and us ... I am sorry if my remarks caused you pain.'

'The octospiders have brainwashed you, Ellie,' Robert said bitterly. 'I knew it as soon as Nakamura's men showed me the reports. Somehow they have tampered with your mind so that you are no longer in touch with reality.'

Nikki had started whimpering when Robert had first raised his voice. She did not understand what the disagreement between her parents was about, but she could tell that everything was not all right. She began to cry and to cling to her mother's leg.

'It's all right, Nikki,' Ellie said soothingly. 'Your father and I are just talking.'

When Ellie glanced up, Robert had taken a transparent skullcap out of a drawer and was holding it in his hand. 'So you're going to give me an EEG,' she said nervously, 'to make certain that I haven't become one of them?'

'It's not funny, Ellie,' Robert replied. 'My EEGs have all been weird since I returned to New Eden. I can't explain it, nor can the neurologist on my staff. He says he has never seen such radical changes in an individual's brain activity, except in the case of severe injury.'

'Robert,' Ellie said, taking his hand again. 'The octospiders planted a micro-biological block in your memory when you departed. To protect themselves. That could be part of the explanation for your peculiar brain waves.'

Robert looked at Ellie for a long time without speaking. 'They kidnapped you,' he said. 'They tampered with my brain ... Who knows what they may have done to our daughter ... How can you possibly defend them?'

Ellie submitted to the EEG and the results showed neither irregularities nor major differences from the routine brain testing that she had undergone during the early days of the colony. Robert seemed genuinely relieved. He then told Ellie that Nakamura and the government were prepared to drop all charges against her and would let her return home with Nikki, under house arrest temporarily, of course, if she would provide information about the octospiders. Ellie thought about the request for a few minutes and then agreed.

Robert smiled and gave her a brisk hug. 'Good,' he said. 'You'll start tomor-row ... I'll tell them right away.'

Richard had warned Ellie during the ride on the ostrichsaur that Nakamura might try to use her in some way, most likely to justify his continued prosecu-tion of the war. Ellie knew that by agreeing ostensibly to help the New Eden government she was committing herself to a very dangerous course. *I must be careful,* she told herself as she soaked in a hot bath-tub, *never to say anything that would hurt Richard or Archie. Or that would give Nakamura's troops an unfair advantage in a possible war.*

Nikki had been unfamiliar with her old bedroom at first, but after an hour or so of playing with some of her toys, she seemed quite content. She came into the bathroom, where Ellie was taking a bath, and stood next to the tub. 'When will Daddy be home?' she asked her mother.

'He'll be late, darling,' Ellie replied. 'After you've gone to bed.'

'I like my room, Mommy,' Nikki said. 'It's much better than that old base-ment.'

'I'm glad,' Ellie replied. The little girl smiled and left the bathroom. Ellie took a deep breath. *It would have served no purpose,* she rationalised, *if I had refused and we had been returned to confinement.*

4

Katie had not finished with her make-up when she heard the buzzer sound. She took a drag on the cigarette burning in the ashtray beside her and pushed the 'Talk' button. 'Who is it?' she said.

'It's me,' came the reply.

'What are you doing here in the middle of the day?'

'I have some important news,' Captain Franz Bauer said. 'Buzz me up.'

Katie inhaled deeply on the cigarette and stubbed it out. She stood up and looked at herself in the full-length mirror. She adjusted her hair slightly just before the knock on her door.

'This had better be important, Franz,' Katie said, letting him into the room, 'or your ass is mud. You know I have a disciplinary meeting with two of the girls in a few minutes and I hate to be late.'

Franz grinned. 'You caught them skimming again?... Jesus, Katie, I'd hate for you to be my boss.'

Katie looked at Franz impatiently. 'Well?' she said. 'What was too important for the telephone?'

Franz had begun to walk around the living-room. The room was tastefully decorated, with a black and white sofa and loveseat, two matching chairs, and several interesting *objets d'art* on both the end tables and the coffee-table. 'There's not any chance that your apartment is bugged, is there?'

'You tell *me*, Mr Police Captain,' Katie said. 'Now, really, Franz,' she added, glancing at her watch, 'I don't have ...'

'There is a reliable report,' Franz said, 'that your father is in New Eden at this very moment.'

'*Whaat*?' said Katie. 'How is that possible?' She was stunned. She sat down on the couch and reached for another cigarette from the coffee-table.

'A lieutenant of mine is close friends with one of your father's guards. He was told that Richard and one of those octospider creatures are being held in the basement of a private residence not far from here.'

Katie crossed the room and picked up the telephone. 'Darla,' she said, 'tell Lauren and Atsuko that the meeting today is off ... Something has come up ... Reschedule for two o'clock tomorrow afternoon ... Oh, that's right, I forgot ... Damnit ... All right, make it eleven in the morning ... No, eleven-*thirty*. I don't want to get up any earlier than necessary.'

Katie returned to the couch and picked up her cigarette. She took a huge drag and blew smoke-rings into the air over her head. 'I want to know everything that you have heard about my father.'

Franz informed Katie that, according to his sources, her father, her sister Ellie, her niece, and an octospider had suddenly appeared, carrying a white flag, at the troop encampment on the southern edge of the Cylindrical Sea about two months ago. They had been quite relaxed and had even joked with the soldiers, Franz said. Her father and sister had told the troops that they had come forward with an octospider representative to see if an armed conflict between the two species could be avoided through negotiation. Nakamura had ordered that the entire affair be kept secret and had taken them ...

Katie was pacing around the room. 'My father is not only alive,' she said excitedly, 'he is *here*, in New Eden ... Have I ever told you, Franz,' she said, 'that my father is absolutely the smartest human being who ever lived?'

'About a dozen times,' Franz said. He laughed. 'I can't imagine how anyone could be smarter than you.'

Katie waved her hand. 'He makes me look like an absolute idiot. He was always such a dear. I could get away with *anything*.' She stopped her pacing and inhaled on her cigarette. Her eyes sparkled as she exhaled the smoke. 'Franz,' she said. 'I *must* see him ... I absolutely must.'

'That's impossible, Katie,' he said. 'Nobody is even supposed to know that he's here. I could be fired, or worse, if anyone ever found out that I told you...'

'I'm pleading with you, Franz,' Katie said, crossing the room and grabbing him by the shoulders. 'You know how I hate asking anyone for favours ... but this is very important to me.'

Franz was delighted that for once, Katie was requesting something from *him*. Nevertheless, he told her the truth. 'Katie,' he said, 'you still don't understand. There is an armed guard around the house at all times. The entire basement is bugged with audio and video monitors. There is just no way.'

'There's *always* a way,' Katie said emphatically, 'if something is important enough.' She reached inside his shirt and began tweaking his right nipple. 'You *do* love me, don't you, Franz?' She kissed him, a full open-mouthed kiss, with her tongue darting teasingly across his. Katie pulled away slightly, continuing to play with his nipple.

'Of course I love you, Katie,' Franz said, already very much aroused. 'But I'm not crazy.'

Katie marched off into her bedroom and returned less than a minute later with two stacks of notes. 'I am going to see my father, Franz,' she said, throwing the money on the coffee-table. 'And you are going to help me ... You can bribe anyone you want with this money.'

Franz was impressed. The money was more than adequate. 'And what are you going to do for me?' he said almost jokingly,

'What am I going to do for *you*? Katie said. 'What am I going to do for you?' Katie took him by the hand and led him to the bedroom. 'Now, Captain Bauer,' she said in an accented voice, 'you just take off all your clothes and lie here on your back. You'll see what I am going to do for you.'

Katie's apartment had a sitting/dressing-room adjacent to her bedroom. She walked into the smaller room and closed the door. With a key she unlocked a large decorated box on the top of the counter and pulled out one of the full syringes she had prepared earlier in the day. Katie lifted her dress and tied a tight tourniquet around her upper thigh with a piece of small black tubing. She waited momentarily until she could clearly identify a blood-vessel in the mass of bruises on her thigh, and then she deftly inserted the syringe. After pressing all the fluid into her bloodstream, Katie waited a few seconds for the fantastic rush and then removed the tourniquet.

'What am I supposed to do while I'm waiting?'

'Rilke is in my electronic reader, darling,' she said, 'both in German and English. I'll only be a few more minutes.'

Katie was flying. She started humming a dance-tune while she threw the syringe away and returned the tourniquet to the box. She took off all her clothes, stopping twice to admire her body in the mirror, and put them in a pile upon the vanity stool. Then she opened a large drawer in the vanity and pulled out a blindfold.

She paraded into the bedroom. Franz's eyes feasted admiringly upon her lithe body. 'Look carefully,' Katie said, ''cause this is all you're going to see this afternoon.'

Katie draped her naked body casually across his and kissed him intermittently while she attached the blindfold. She made certain that the blindfold was snug and then jumped down from the bed. 'What happens now?' Franz asked.

'You'll just have to wait and see,' Katie said teasingly as she rummaged through a large drawer at the bottom of her dresser. The drawer contained a smorgasbord of sexual paraphernalia, including electronic aids of all kinds, lotions, ropes and other bondage equipment, masks, and assorted models of genitalia. Katie selected a small bottle of lotion, a vial of white powder, and some beads strung along a piece of thin cord.

Still humming and laughing to herself, Katie rejoined Franz on the bed and began to run her fingers over his chest. She kissed him provocatively with her body pressed against his and then sat up. After pouring the lotion on her hands and rubbing them together vigorously, Katie spread his legs, crawled onto his stomach with her back toward Franz's face, and began to apply the lotion to his most sensitive parts.

'Ummm,' Franz murmured as the warm lotion began to take effect. 'That's wonderful.'

Katie dusted his genitalia with the white powder and then mounted him very slowly. Franz was in ecstasy. Katie rocked back and forth in an easy rhythm for a few minutes. When she could tell that Franz was nearing a climax, she halted her motion temporarily and reached under him to insert the beads. She rocked two or three more times and then halted again.

'Don't stop now,' Franz shouted.

'Repeat after me,' Katie said with a chuckle, moving slowly back and forth one more time. 'I promise ...'

'Anything,' Franz yelled, 'just don't stop again.'

'I promise,' she continued, 'that Katie Wakefield will see her father sometime in the next few days.'

Franz repeated the promise and Katie rewarded him. When she pulled the cord just after he started his climax, Franz screamed at the top of his lungs like an animal in the forest.

Ellie did not like her two interrogators. They were both dry, humourless individuals who treated her with complete disdain. 'This isn't going to work, gentlemen,' she said in an exasperated tone at one point during the first day of questioning, 'if you insist on asking the same questions over and over ... I understood that I was being asked to supply some information about the octospiders ... Thus far the questions, which you are now repeating, have all been about my mother and my father.'

'Mrs Turner,' the first man said, 'the government is trying to gather all possible information about this case. Your mother and father have both been fugitives for many ...'

'Look,' Ellie interrupted, 'I have already told you that I know nothing whatsoever about how, when, or even why either of my parents left New Eden. Nor do I have any knowledge of whether they were helped to escape, in any way, by the octospiders. Now, unless you are prepared to change the line of questioning ...'

'It is not you, young lady,' the second man said, his eyes flashing, 'who decides what are appropriate questions in this inquiry. Perhaps you do not understand the seriousness of your situation. You will be granted freedom from prosecution, on a very serious charge, I might add, *only* if you co-operate totally with us.'

'Just what is the charge against me?' Ellie asked. 'I'm curious ... I have never been a criminal before.'

'You can be charged with first-degree treason,' the first man said. 'Deliberately aiding and abetting the enemy during a period of declared hostilities.'

'That's absurd,' Ellie replied, frightened nevertheless. 'I have no idea what you're talking about.'

'Do you deny that during the period of time that you were staying with the aliens you freely gave them information about New Eden that could be useful during a war?'

'Of course I did,' Ellie said, laughing nervously. 'I told them as much as I could about our colony. And they reciprocated. The octospiders shared all the same information with us.'

Both men scribbled furiously on their pads. *How did they get like this?* Ellie wondered. *How can a laughing, curious child be transformed into such a grim and hostile adult? Is that environment, or heredity?*

'Look, gentlemen,' Ellie said when the next question was asked, 'this is not going well for me. I would like to declare a recess and organise my thoughts. Maybe I'll even make a few notes before we reconvene ... I had envisioned an altogether different process, something much more relaxed ...'

The two men agreed to the break. Ellie walked down the hallway to where a government sitter was staying with Nikki. 'You can go now, Mrs Adams,' Ellie said. 'We're taking time off for lunch.'

Nikki could read the worried look on Ellie's face. 'Are those men being mean to you, Mommy?' she asked.

At length Ellie smiled. 'You could say that, Nikki,' she said. 'You certainly could say that.'

Richard completed the last of his walking laps around the basement and headed for the washbasin in the corner of the room. He stopped first at the table for a quick drink of water. Archie remained motionless on the floor behind Richard's mattress. 'Good morning,' Richard said as he wiped his sweat with a washcloth. 'Are you ready for some breakfast?'

'I'm not hungry,' the octospider replied in colour.

'You have to eat *some*thing,' Richard said cheerfully. 'I agree with you that the food is terrible, but you can't survive on water alone.'

Archie did not move or say anything. For the last several days, ever since the supply of his stored barrican had been exhausted, the octospider had not been very good company. Richard had been unable to engage Archie in their usual stimulating conversation and had become concerned about the octospider's health. Richard put some grain in a bowl, sprinkled water on it, and carried it over to his friend. 'Here,' he said gently, 'try to eat a little.'

Archie lifted a pair of tentacles and took the bowl. As he began to eat, a bright orange burst came out of his slit and moved half-way down one of his other tentacles before fading away.

'What was that?' Richard asked.

'An emotional expression,' Archie answered, his response accompanied by more irregular colour-bursts.

Richard smiled. 'OK,' he said, 'but what kind of emotion?'

After a long pause, Archie's coloured strips were more regimented. 'I guess you would call it depression,' the octospider said.

'Is that what happens when the barrican is gone?' Richard asked.

Archie did not reply. At length Richard returned to the table and prepared himself a big bowl of grain. Then he came back and sat beside Archie on the floor. 'You might as well talk about it,' Richard said softly. 'We have nothing else to do.'

From the motion in Archie's lens Richard could tell that the octo was studying him carefully. Richard took several spoonfuls of his breakfast before Archie began to speak.

'In our society,' Archie said, 'the young males and females who are under-going sexual maturation are taken away from their everyday lives and placed in a highly appropriate environment with individuals who have been through the process before. They are encouraged to describe what they are feeling and are reassured that the new and complex emotions they are experiencing are completely normal. Now I understand why such a programme of intense attention is necessary.'

Archie paused for a moment and Richard smiled sympathetically. 'These last few days,' the octospider continued, 'for the first time since I was a very young juvenile, my emotions have not accepted the domination of my mind. During optimiser training we learned how important it was, whenever a decision was to be made, to sift carefully through all the available evidence and remove all prejudice that might be due to personal emotional responses. With the intensity of the feelings I am having presently, it would be quite impossible to relegate them to a low priority.'

Richard laughed. 'Please don't misunderstand me, Archie – I'm not laugh-ing at you – but you just described, in a typical octospider phrase, what most humans feel all the time. Very few of us ever achieve the control of our "personal emotional responses" that we would like. This may be the first time that you have ever been able to really understand us, if you know what I mean.'

'It's terrible,' Archie said. 'I am feeling both an acute sense of loss – I miss Dr Blue and Jamie – and powerful anger toward Nakamura for holding us prisoner ... I fear that my outrage will cause me to take some action that is non-optimal.'

'But the emotions you are describing are not usually connected, at least in humans, with sexuality,' Richard said. 'Does the barrican also act as some kind of tranquiliser, subduing all feelings?'

Archie finished his breakfast before responding. 'You and I are very differ-ent creatures and, as I have mentioned before, it is dangerous to project from one species to another ... I remember our initial discussions about humans at the optimisers' meeting just after you had breached the integrity of your habitat ... In the middle of the meeting, the Chief Optimiser stressed that we must not look at your species in *our* terms. We must observe carefully, she said, obtain data, and correlate it consistently, without colouring the data with our own experience ...

'I suppose this all amounts to a disclaimer, in some sense, of what I am about to tell you. Nevertheless, it is my personal opinion, based on my observations of humans, that sexual desire is the driving force behind *all* the strong emotions in your species ... We octospiders undergo a step discontinuity at sexual maturation. We change from being completely sexless to sexual in a very short period of time. In humans the process is much slower and more subtle. Sexual hormones are present in varying quantities from early in your foetal development. I contend, and have told the Chief Optimiser this, that it is possible that *all* your uncontrollable emotions can be traced to these sexual hormones. A human without any sexuality might be capable of the same optimised thought as an octospider.'

'What an interesting idea!' Richard said excitedly, standing up and beginning to pace. 'So are you suggesting that even such things as a child's unwillingness to share a toy, for example, might be linked in some way to our sexuality?...'

'Perhaps,' Archie replied. 'Maybe Galileo is practising the possessiveness of his adult sexuality when he refuses to share one of his toys with Kepler ... Certainly the human child's devotion to the parent of the opposite sex is a precursor of adult attitudes ...'

Archie stopped, for Richard had turned his back and had increased his pacing. 'I'm sorry,' he said, returning a few moments later and again sitting on the floor beside the octospider. 'Something occurred to me just now, something I thought about briefly earlier this morning when we were talking about controlling our emotions ... Do you remember an earlier conversation in which you dismissed the concept of a personal God as an "evolutionary aberration" necessary for all developing species as a temporary bridge during transition from the first awareness phase to the Information Era? Have the recent changes in you altered in any way your attitude about God?'

A broad burst of multicoloured strips, which Richard recognised as laughter, spilled over most of the octospider's upper body. 'You humans,' Archie said, 'are absolutely preoccupied with this notion of God. Even those like you, Richard, who profess not to believe, still spend an inordinate amount of time thinking about or discussing the subject ... As I explained to you months ago, we octospiders value information foremost, as we were taught by the Precursors ... There is no verifiable information available about any God, especially not one who is involved in any way with the daily affairs of the universe ...'

'You didn't exactly understand my question,' Richard interrupted, 'or maybe I didn't phrase it precisely enough ... What I want to know is, in your new, more emotional state, can you understand why other intelligent beings might create a personal God as a device to give them comfort and also to explain all those things that they cannot comprehend?'

Archie laughed again with bursts of colour. 'You're very clever, Richard,' the octospider said. 'You want me to confirm what you think, namely that God also is an emotional concept, born out of a yearning not unlike sexual desire. Therefore God too is derived from sexual hormones ... I cannot go that far. I do not have enough information. But I can say, based on the turmoil inside *me* these last few days, that I now understand this word "yearning" which was meaningless to me before ...'

Richard smiled. He was pleased. Their exchanges had been like this daily before Archie's buffer had become empty of barrican. 'It would be great, wouldn't it,' Richard said suddenly, 'if we could still talk with all our friends back in the Emerald City?'

Archie knew what Richard was suggesting. The two of them had been careful never to mention the quadroids or even to hint that the octospiders had an intelligence-gathering system. They did not want to alert Nakamura and their guards. Now, as Richard watched silently, bands of colour streamed around Archie's head. Although the octospider was no longer using the derivative language that had been developed for communication with the humans, Richard was able to understand the gist of the transmission.

After formally greeting the Chief Optimiser and apologizing for the lack of success of their mission, Archie sent two personal messages, a short one to Jamie and a longer one to Dr Blue. During the transmission to his life partner Dr Blue, variegated bursts of colour broke out of the measured pattern of Archie's message. Richard, who had grown to know his basement companion well in their two months together, was both fascinated and touched by this beautiful display of uninhibited emotion.

When Archie was finished, Richard came over and put a hand on the octospider's back. 'Do you feel better now?' he asked.

'In some ways,' Archie replied. 'But I also feel worse at the same time. I am more aware now than I was before that I may never see Dr Blue or Jamie again ...'

'Sometimes I imagine what I would say to Nicole,' Richard interrupted, 'if I could talk to her on the telephone.' He spoke his words very correctly, exaggerating the movements of his mouth. 'I miss you very much, Nicole,' he said, 'and I love you with all my heart.'

Richard did not have very vivid dreams. Therefore, external sounds were not likely to be incorporated into an ongoing dream. When he heard what he thought was a shuffling of feet above him in the middle of the night, he awakened quickly.

Archie was sleeping. Richard looked around and realised that the night light in the toilet area was extinguished. Alarmed, he awakened his octospider companion.

'What is it?' Archie asked in colour.

'I heard something unusual upstairs,' Richard whispered.

There was a sound of the door to the basement stairs opening slowly. Richard heard a soft footstep, then another, on the top of the stairs. He strained his eyes, but Richard could see nothing in the near darkness.

'It's a woman and a policeman,' Archie said, his lens picking up the infra-red heat of the intruders. 'They have stopped for the moment on the third step.'

We're going to be killed, Richard thought. A powerful fear swept through him and he drew closer to Archie. He heard the slow closing of the basement door and then the footsteps descending the stairs.

'Where are they now?' he whispered.

'At the bottom,' Archie said. 'They are coming ... I think the woman is ...'

'Dad.' Richard heard a voice from his past. 'Where are you, Dad?'

Holy shit! It's Katie! 'Over here, Katie,' Richard replied, too loud, trying to contain his excitement.

A very small flashlight beam wandered around the wall behind his mattress and eventually landed on his bearded face. A few seconds later Katie tripped over Archie and literally fell into her father's arms.

She kissed and hugged him, tears running down her cheeks. Richard was so startled by the entire event that he was at first unable to respond to any of Katie's questions. 'Yes ... yes, I'm fine,' he said eventually. 'I can't believe it's you ... Katie, oh, Katie ... Oh, yes, that grey mass over there, the one you kicked a moment ago, is my friend and fellow prisoner, Archie the octospider...'

Several seconds later Richard exchanged a firm handshake in the dark with a man Katie introduced only as 'my friend.' 'We don't have much time,' Katie said hurriedly after several minutes of conversation about the family. 'We've short-circuited the power systems in this entire residential area, and they should be repaired before too much longer.'

'Are we going to escape, then?' Richard asked.

'No,' Katie said. 'They would certainly catch and kill you ... I just wanted to see you ... When I heard the rumour that you were being held somewhere in New Eden ... Oh, Daddy, how I have missed you! I love you so very much...'

Richard put his arms around his daughter and held her as she wept. *She is so thin*, he thought, *virtually a wraith*. 'I love you too, Katie,' Richard said. 'Here,' he added, pulling away slightly, 'shine the light on your face ... Let me see your beautiful eyes.'

'No, Daddy,' Katie said, burying herself again in his embrace. 'I look old and used ... I want you to remember me as I was. I have lived a hard ...'

'It's unlikely that they will be keeping you here much longer, Mr Wakefield,' the male voice in the dark interrupted. 'Almost everyone in the colony has heard the story of your appearance at the soldiers' camp.'

'Are you all right, Daddy?' Katie said after a short silence. 'Are they feeding you properly?'

'I'm fine, Katie ... but we havn't talked any about you. What have you been doing? Are you happy?'

'I've had another promotion,' she said rapidly. 'And my new apartment is beautiful ... You should see it ... And I have a friend who cares about me ...'

'I'm so glad,' Richard said as Franz reminded Katie that they needed to be going. 'You were always the smartest of the children ... You deserve some happiness.'

Katie suddenly began sobbing and lowered her head against her father's chest. 'Daddy, oh, Daddy,' she said through her tears, 'please hold me.'

Richard put his arms around his daughter. 'What is it, Katie?' he said softly.

'I don't want to lie to you,' Katie said. 'I work for Nakamura, managing prostitutes. And I'm a drug addict ... a complete and total drug addict.'

Katie cried for a long time. Richard held her tightly and patted her on the back. 'But I *do* love *you*, Daddy,' Katie said when she finally raised her head. 'I always have, and I always will ... I'm terribly sorry that I have disappointed you.'

'Katie, we must be leaving now,' Franz said firmly. 'If the power is restored while we are still in the house, we'll be in deep shit.'

Katie kissed her father hurriedly on the lips and stroked his beard affectionately with her fingers one final time. 'Take care of yourself, Daddy,' she said. 'And don't give up hope.'

The flashlight beam was a thin finger of light preceding the visiting pair as they quickly crossed the room to the bottom of the stairs. 'Goodbye, Daddy,' Katie said.

'I love you too, Katie,' Richard said as he heard the sound of his daughter's feet running up the stairs.

5

The octospider on the table was unconscious. Nicole handed Dr Blue the small plastic container that the alien physician had requested and watched as the tiny creatures were dumped onto the greenish-black fluid that covered the open wound. In less than a minute the fluid was gone and her octospider colleague deftly sewed up the incision using the forward five centimetres of three of her tentacles.

'That's the last one for today,' Dr Blue said in colour. 'As always, Nicole, we thank you for your help.'

The two of them walked together out of the operating area into an adjacent room. Nicole had not yet accustomed herself to the cleaning process. She took a deep breath before removing her protective gown and placing her arms in a large bowl filled with dozens of silverfishlike animals. Nicole fought against her personal revulsion as the slimy things clambered all over her arms and hands.

'I know this part is not pleasant for you,' Dr Blue said, 'but we really have no choice now that the forward water supply has been contaminated by the bombing ... And we can't take a chance that anything here might be toxic for you.'

'Is everything destroyed north of the forest?' Nicole asked while Dr Blue finished cleaning herself up.

'Almost,' the octospider replied. 'And it looks as if the human engineers have now finished their modifications to the helicopters. The Chief Optimiser fears that they will make their first flights over the forest in another week or two.'

'And there have been no replies to the messages you have sent?'

'None at all. We know that Nakamura has read them ... but the humans captured and killed the last messenger near the power-plant ... Despite the fact that our octospider was carrying a white flag.'

Nicole sighed. She remembered something Max had said the night before when she had expressed bewilderment that Nakamura was ignoring all the messages. 'Of course he is,' Max had shouted angrily. 'That man understands nothing but force ... All those stupid messages say is that the octos want peace and will be forced to defend themselves if the humans don't desist ...

The threats that follow are meaningless. What is Nakamura to think when his troops and helicopters move around unimpeded, destroying everything in sight?... Hasn't the Chief Optimiser learned anything about humans? The octospiders must engage Nakamura's army in some kind of battle ...'

'That's not their way,' Nicole had replied. 'They do not involve themselves in skirmishes or limited wars. They only fight when their survival is threatened ... The messages have spelled this all out very carefully and have repeatedly urged Nakamura to talk to Richard and Archie ...'

In the hospital, Dr Blue was flashing colours at Nicole. She shook her head and returned to the present. 'Are you going to wait today for Benjy?' the octospider asked. 'Or will you go directly over to the administrative centre?'

Nicole checked her watch. 'I think I'll go now. It usually takes me a couple of hours to digest all the quadroid data from the day before ... So much is happening ... Please tell Benjy to tell the others that I'll be home for dinner.'

She walked out of the hospital a few minutes later and headed for the administrative centre. Even though it was daytime, the streets of the Emerald City were nearly deserted. Nicole passed three octospiders, all hurrying on the other side of the road, and a pair of crab biots, who looked strangely out of place. Dr Blue had told Nicole that the crab biots had been recruited for Emerald City garbage duty.

The city has changed so much since the decree, Nicole thought. Most of the older octos are now over in the war domain. And we never saw a single biot here until a month ago, after most of the support creatures had supposedly been moved to another location. Max thinks many of them might have been terminated because of the shortages. Max always thinks the worst of the octospiders.

Often after work Nicole would accompany Benjy to the transport stop. Her son was also helping the short-handed staff at the hospital. As Benjy had become more aware of what was occurring in the Emerald City, it had grown increasingly difficult for Nicole to hide the seriousness of their situation.

'Why are our peo-ple fight-ing against the oc-to-spi-ders?' Benjy had asked the previous week. 'The octos don't want to hurt ...'

'The colonists in New Eden don't understand the octospiders,' Nicole had replied. 'And they won't let Archie and Uncle Richard explain anything.'

'Then they're stu-pid-er than I am,' Benjy had said gruffly.

Dr Blue and the other members of the octospider hospital staff who had not been reassigned because of the war were all very impressed with Benjy. In the beginning, when he had volunteered to help, the octospiders had had reservations about what he could do with his limited capabilities. Once a simple task had been explained to him by Nicole, however, and he had repeated it back to her, Benjy never made a mistake. With his strong, youthful body, he was especially helpful performing heavy labour, a valuable attribute now that so many of the larger creatures were no longer around.

While Nicole was walking towards the administrative centre, her head full of pleasant thoughts about Benjy, an image of Katie popped into her mind and juxtaposed itself next to a smiling portrait of her retarded son. In her mind's eye Nicole glanced back and forth between the two images. *As parents, she sighed, we often spend too much time focusing on intellectual potential instead of more substantive qualities. What matters most is not how much intellect the child has, but rather what he or she decides to do with it. Benjy has succeeded beyond our wildest imaginings, primarily because of who he is inside. As for Katie, never, in my worst nightmares ...*

Nicole broke her train of thought as she entered the building. An octospider guard waved at her and she smiled. When she reached her usual viewing-room, Nicole was surprised to find the Chief Optimiser waiting for her. 'I wanted to take this opportunity,' the head octospider said, 'both to thank you for the contribution you are making in this difficult period and to reassure you that all your family and friends here in the Emerald City will be cared for as if they were members of our species, no matter what happens in the next few weeks.'

The Chief Optimiser started to leave the room. 'The situation is deteriorating, then?' Nicole asked.

'Yes,' the octospider replied. 'As soon as the humans fly over the forest, we will be forced to retaliate.'

When the Chief Optimiser was gone, Nicole sat down in front of her console to scan through the quadroid data from the day before. She was not allowed access to all the information from New Eden, but she was permitted to call up the images of the daily activities of all the members of her family. Nicole could see each day what was happening in the basement with Richard and Archie, how Ellie and Nikki were adjusting to being back in New Eden, and what was occurring in Katie's world.

As time passed, Nicole watched Katie less and less. It was simply too painful for her. Observing her granddaughter Nikki, by contrast, was pure delight. Nicole especially enjoyed watching Nikki on those afternoons when the little girl went to the Beauvois playground to play with the other children of the village. Although the images were soundless, Nicole could almost hear the squeals of mirthful delight as Nikki and the others tumbled over one another in pursuit of an elusive soccer-ball.

Nicole had become very concerned about Ellie. Despite her daughter's heroic efforts, Ellie was not having any luck resuscitating her marriage. Robert had remained withdrawn in his workaholic pattern, using the demands of the hospital to keep him from facing all emotions, including his own. He was a dutiful but restrained parent with Nikki, only rarely showing any true delight. He did not make love with Ellie and would not talk about it, except to say that he was 'not ready' when she tearfully brought up the subject three weeks after they had been reunited.

During the long solitary viewing-sessions Nicole often wondered whether it was possible, as a parent, to observe one's offspring in difficulty without asking what might have been done, by the parent, that would have made the child's life easier. *Parenting is an adventure with no guaranteed outcomes*, Nicole thought, wincing while flipping quickly through the images of Ellie crying quietly at night. *The only thing you know for certain is that you will never convince yourself you have done enough.*

She always saved Richard for last. Although Nicole never really shook the premonition that she would not touch her husband again, she did not let that feeling detract from the daily pleasure she experienced sharing his life in the basement in New Eden. She especially enjoyed his conversations with Archie, even though it was often difficult for her to read his lips. Their discussions reminded Nicole of earlier days, after her escape from prison and New Eden, when Richard and she would talk and talk about everything. Watching Richard always left Nicole feeling uplifted and much more able to deal with her own loneliness.

The reunion between Richard and Katie caught her by surprise. She had not been following Katie's life closely enough to know that her daughter and Franz had successfully designed a plan to secure a short visit with Richard. Because the quadroid images covered the infra-red portion of the spectrum as well as the visible, Nicole actually had a better view of the reunion than the participants. She was deeply moved by Katie's action, and even more by Katie's sudden admission (which Nicole watched over and over, in super slow motion, to make certain she was properly leading Katie's lips) that she was a drug addict. *The first step to overcoming a problem*, Nicole remembered from somewhere, *is to admit to someone you love that the problem exists.*

There were happy tears in Nicole's eyes as she rode the nearly empty transport back to the human enclave in the Emerald City. Despite the fact that the bizarre world around her was deteriorating into chaos, for once Nicole was optimistic about Katie.

Patrick and the twins were outside when Nicole stepped off the transport at the end of the street. As she drew closer, she could tell that Patrick was trying to adjudicate one of the boys' innumerable disputes.

'He *always* cheats,' Kepler was saying. 'I told him that I wasn't going to play with him anymore and he hit me.'

'That's a lie,' Galileo replied. 'I hit him because he made a face at me … Kepler's a sore loser. If he can't win, he thinks it's all right to quit.'

Patrick separated the two boys and sent them, as punishment, to sit against opposite corners of the house. He then greeted his mother with a kiss and a hug.

'I have some big news,' Nicole said, smiling at her son. 'Richard had a surprise visitor today – Katie!'

Of course Patrick wanted to know all the details of the visit between his sister and Richard. Nicole summarised what she had seen, admitting that she was encouraged by Katie's confession of her drug habit. 'Don't read too much into her action,' Patrick admonished. 'The Katie I knew would rather die than be without her precious kokomo.'

Patrick had turned around and was almost ready to tell the twins that they could resume playing, when a pair of rockets raced skyward, bursting into bright red balls of light just underneath the dome. Moments later the city was plunged into darkness. 'Come on, boys,' Patrick said. 'We must go inside.'

'That's the third time today,' Patrick commented to Nicole as they followed Kepler and Galileo into the house.

'Dr Blue said they extinguish the city lights the moment any helicopter rises to within twenty metres of the top of the forest canopy. Under no circumstances do the octospiders want to risk showing the location of the Emerald City.'

'Do you think Archie and Uncle Richard will ever have a chance to meet with Nakamura?' Patrick asked.

'I doubt it,' Nicole replied. 'If he were going to see them, it should have happened before now.'

Eponine and Nai greeted Nicole and embraced her. The three women talked briefly about the blackout. Eponine was holding little Marius on her hip. The boy was a fat, happy baby with a major drooling habit. She wiped off his face with a cloth so that Nicole could kiss him,

'Aha,' she heard Max say behind her, 'the Queen of Frowns is now kissing the Prince of Drools.'

Nicole turned around and gave Max a hug. 'What's this Queen of Frowns bit?' she said lightly.

Max handed her a glass containing some clear liquid. 'Here, Nicole, I want you to drink this. It's not tequila, but it's the best substitute the octospiders could make from my description ... We're all hoping that maybe you'll find your sense of humour before you finish the drink.'

'Come on, Max,' Eponine said. 'Don't make Nicole think that we're all somehow involved ... This was *your* idea, after all. The only thing that Patrick, Nai, and I did was agree with you that she has been very serious lately.'

'Now, my lady,' Max said to Nicole, raising his glass and clinking it against hers, 'I want to propose a toast ... To all of us, who have absolutely no control over our future. May we love each other and share laughter until the end, whenever and however it might come.'

Nicole had not seen Max drunk since before she went to prison. At his insistence she took a small drink. Her throat and oesophagus burned and her eyes watered. The drink contained a lot of alcohol.

'Before dinner tonight,' Max now said, opening his arms in a dramatic flourish, 'we are going to tell farm jokes ... This will provide us some much-needed comic relief. You, Nicole des Jardins Wakefield, as our leader by example if not by election, will have the floor first.'

Nicole managed a smile. 'But I don't know any farm jokes,' she protested.

Eponine was relieved to see that Nicole was not offended by Max's behaviour. 'That's all right, Nicole,' Eponine said, 'none of us do … Max knows enough farm jokes for all of us.'

'Once upon a time,' Max began a few moments later, 'there was a farmer from Oklahoma who had a fat wife named Whistle. She was called Whistle because, at the climax of her love-making, she would close her eyes, screw up her mouth, and make a long whistling sound.'

Max belched. The twins giggled. Nicole worried that maybe it was not appropriate for the children to hear Max's story, but Nai was sitting behind her boys, laughing with them. *Relax*, Nicole told herself. *You really have become the Queen of Frowns.*

'Now, one night,' Max continued, 'this farmer and Whistle had a big brouhaha – that's a fight, to you, boys – and she went to bed early and fuming. The farmer sat by himself at the table, drinking some fine tequila. As the evening progressed, he became sorry that he had been such an ornery son of a bitch and began to apologise in a loud voice.

'Meanwhile, ole Whistle, who was now angry all over again because the farmer had awakened her, knew that when he finished drinking, her husband was going to enter the bedroom and try to seal his apology with some wild lovemaking. While the farmer emptied the bottle of tequila, Whistle slipped out of the house, went over to the pig-pen, and carried the youngest and smallest of the sows back into their bedroom.

'When the drunken farmer staggered into the dark bedroom later that night, singing one of his favourite hymns, Whistle was watching from the corner and the sow was in the bed. The farmer took all his clothes off and jumped under the sheets. He grabbed the sow by the ears and kissed her on the lips. The sow squealed and the farmer pulled back. "Whistle, my love," he said, "did you forget to brush your teeth tonight?"

'His wife bolted from the corner and began beating the farmer on the head with a broom …'

Everyone was laughing. Max was so amused by his own joke that he could not sit upright. Nicole glanced around the room. *Max is right*, she thought. *We need this. We have been worrying too much.*

'… My brother Clyde,' Max said, 'knew more farm jokes than anyone I ever met. He courted Winona with them, or so he claimed. Clyde used to tell me that a "laughing woman already has one hand on her panties" … When we would go duck-hunting with the guys, we'd never shoot a single goddamn duck. Clyde would start telling stories, and we'd be laughing and drinking … After a while we'd forget why we got up at five ayem to go and sit in the cold …'

Max stopped talking and there was a momentary quiet in the room. 'Damn,' he said after the brief silence. 'For a while there I was imagining I was back in Arkansas.' He stood up. 'I don't even know now which way Arkansas is from here, or how many billions of kilometres away it is …' Max shook his head. 'Sometimes, when I'm dreaming and it's real lifelike, I think the dream is reality. I believe I'm back in Arkansas. Then when I wake up I am lost, and I think for a few seconds that this life we're living here in the Emerald City is the dream.'

'The same thing happens to me,' Nai said. 'Two nights ago I dreamed I was doing my morning meditation in the hawng pra in my family home in Lamphun. As I was reciting my mantra, Patrick awakened me. He told me that I was talking in my sleep. For a few seconds, however, I didn't know who he was … It was frightening.'

'All right,' Max said after a protracted silence. He turned to Nicole. 'I guess we're ready for the news of the day. What do you have to tell us?'

'The quadroid videos today were very peculiar,' a smiling Nicole replied. 'For the first few minutes, I was certain I had entered the wrong database … Image after image showed a pig, or a chicken, or a drunken Oklahoma farm-boy trying to court a sweet young thing … In the last series of pictures a farmer was trying to drink tequila, eat fried chicken, and make love with his sweetheart all at the same time … which reminds me, that chicken sure looked good. Is anyone else hungry?'

6

'I think they were somewhat reassured by what the Chief Optimiser told me,' Nicole said to Dr Blue. 'Max, of course, had his doubts ... He doesn't believe taking care of us will be a very high priority if the situation really becomes desperate.'

'That's very unlikely,' the octospider replied. 'Any further escalation of hostilities will be met by a massive retaliation ... Many octospiders have been working on our war plans for almost two months.'

'Have I understood correctly, then,' Nicole asked, 'that every individual member of your species who has been involved in the design and prosecution of this war will be terminated when it is over?'

'Yes,' Dr Blue replied, 'although they will not all die immediately ... They will be notified that they have been placed on the termination list ... The new Chief Optimiser will define the exact schedule for the terminations, depending on the needs of the colony and the pace of replenishment.'

Nicole and her octospider colleague were sharing lunch at the hospital. They had spent the morning trying unsuccessfully to save the lives of two of the six-armed utility creatures who had been blasted by human troops while they were working in one of the few remaining grain-fields on the north side of the forest.

During their lunch, a centipede biot trundled by in the hall beside them. Dr Blue noticed that Nicole followed the biot with her eyes for several seconds. 'When we first came inside Rama,' the octospider said, 'before we had developed our full cadre of support animals, we used the available biots for routine tasks, like maintenance ... Now we need their help again.'

'But how do you give them instructions?' Nicole asked. 'We were never able to communicate with them at all.'

'Their programming is done in firmware, at the time of their manufacture ... What we did in the early days, using a kind of keyboard analogous to the one you had in your lair, was ask the Ramans to alter the programming for our specific uses ... That's what all the biots are here for ... to be turned into useful servants by the passengers on board.'

Well, Richard, Nicole thought, *that's at least one concept we missed altogether. In fact, I don't think the idea ever even occurred to us ...*

'... We wanted our settlement here in Rama to be indistinguishable from any of our other colonies,' Dr Blue continued, 'so as soon as we no longer needed the biots, we requested that they be removed from our domain in Rama.'

'And since then you have had no direct contact at all with the Ramans?'

'Not much,' Dr Blue replied. 'But we have maintained the capability to communicate with the high-technology factories underneath the surface, primarily so that we can request the manufacture of certain raw materials that we do not have in our warehouses ...'

A door opened from the corridor and an octospider entered. It talked rapidly with Dr Blue in their language, using very narrow colour bands. Nicole recognised the words 'permission' and 'this afternoon,' but very little else.

After the visitor had departed, Dr Blue told Nicole that she had a surprise for her. 'Today one of our queens is going to have her egg rush. Her attendants are estimating it will take place in half a tert. The Chief Optimiser has approved my request for you to observe ... To my knowledge, you are the only alien, except for the Precursors, of course, who has ever had the privilege of witnessing an egg rush ... I think you will find it very interesting.'

During the transport ride to the Queen's Domain, which was in a part of the Emerald City that Nicole had never visited before, Dr Blue reminded Nicole of some of the more unusual aspects of octospider reproduction. 'In normal times, each of the three queens in our colony is fertilised once every three to five years, and only a small fraction of the fertilised eggs is permitted to grow to maturity. Because of the war preparations, however, the Chief Optimiser recently declared a Replenishment Event. All three of our queens are now producing a full set of eggs. They have been fertilised by the new warrior males, those octospiders selected for the war effort who have recently passed through sexual, transition. This activity is very important, for it ensures, at least symbolically, that each of these octospiders will have continued genetic involvement in the colony ... Remember, they know, as soon as they are designated as warriors, that their termination time is not too far away.'

Whenever I think that we have a lot in common with the octospiders, Nicole was thinking, *I see something so bizarre that I am reminded how very different we are. But, as Richard would say, how could it be otherwise? They are the product of a process totally alien to us.*

'... Don't be alarmed at the size of the queen ... and please, under no circumstances should you express anything but delight at what you see. When I first suggested that you attend the egg rush, one of the Chief Optimiser's staff members objected, saying that there was no way you could fully appreciate what you were seeing. Some of the other staff members were worried that you might display discomfort or even disgust and thereby detract from the experience for the other octospiders in attendance ...'

Nicole assured Dr Blue that she would do nothing untoward during the ceremony. She was indeed flattered that she had been included in the activity, and was feeling considerable excitement when the transport deposited them outside the thick walls of the Queen's Domain.

The building Nicole entered with Dr Blue was dome-shaped and built of blocks of white rock. It was about ten metres tall inside and covered a ground area of roughly thirty-five hundred square metres. There was a large map just inside the door in the atrium area, and a written message in colour identifying where the egg rush would take place. Nicole followed Dr Blue and several other octospiders up a pair of ramps and then down a long corridor. At the end of the hallway they turned right and entered a balcony area that overlooked a rectangular floor fifteen metres long and five or six metres wide.

Dr Blue took Nicole to the front row, where a railing a metre high protected the audience from falling onto the floor four metres below. Behind them the five elevated rows filled up quickly. Across the way, there was another, similar viewing area that would hold about sixty octospiders.

Looking down, Nicole could see a pool of water resembling a canal that ran the length of the floor and then disappeared under an arch on the right. There were narrow walkways on either side of the pool. On the opposite side, however, the walkway expanded into a broad platform three metres or so before it encountered the rock wall that formed the entire left side of the large room. This wall, painted with many different colours and designs, contained a hundred or so protruding silver rods or spikes, each standing out a metre from where it was embedded in the wall. Nicole noticed immediately the similarity between the wall and the vertical corridor, shaped like a barrel, that she and her friends had descended inside the octospider lair beneath New York.

Less than ten minutes after the two balcony areas were filled, the Chief Optimiser shuffled through a doorway on the lower level, stood on the walkway beside the pool, and made a short speech. Dr Blue helped Nicole translate as the Chief Optimiser reminded the onlookers that although the exact timing of an egg rush was never known, it was likely the queen would be ready to enter the room in several more fengs. After making a few comments about the critical importance of replenishment in the continuity of the colony, the Chief Optimiser made her exit.

The wait began. Nicole passed the time observing the octospiders in the balcony area across from her, and trying to eavesdrop on their conversations. She could understand a little of what was being said, but not everything. Nicole commented to herself that she still had a long way to go befor she would be fluent in their natural language.

Finally the great doors at the left end of the far walkway opened and the massive queen lumbered in. She was huge, at least six metres tall, with a gigantic swollen body above her eight long tentacles. She stopped on the platform and said something to the audience. Bright colours spilled in profusion all over her body, creating a vivid spectacle. Nicole could not understand what the queen was saying because she could not follow the exact sequence of colours pouring out of the slit.

The queen slowly turned toward the wall, extended her tentacles, and began the laborious process of pulling herself up onto the spikes. Throughout the climb, disordered bursts of colour decorated her body. Nicole assumed these were emotional expressions of some kind, perhaps pain and fatigue. Looking around her, Nicole noticed that the octospiders in the audience were all silent, their heads dark and devoid of colour.

When the queen had finally positioned herself in the centre of the wall, she wrapped all eight tentacles around the spikes and exposed her cream-coloured underbelly. While she had been working in the hospital, Nicole had become quite familiar with octospider anatomy, but she had never imagined that the soft tissue underneath their bellies could be distended so much. As Nicole watched, the queen began rocking slightly, moving forward and back-ward, gently bouncing off the rock wall with each motion. The emotional colour display continued. The colours reached their peak intensity when a geyser of greenish black fluid spewed forth from the queen's underside, followed immediately by an immense outpouring of white objects of different sizes contained in a thick, viscous fluid.

Nicole was stupefied. Below her, a dozen or so octospiders on either side of the pool were hurriedly brushing into the water the eggs and fluid that had landed on the walkways. Another eight octos were pouring the unknown contents of huge containers into the pool. The water was now teeming with octospider blood, eggs, and the high-viscosity fluid that was ejected along with the eggs. In less than a minute the entire slurry in the pool moved under the arch to the right.

The queen had not yet changed position. Once the pool below them was clear running water again, all lenses turned to watch the queen. Nicole was staggered by how much the octospider had already shrunk. She estimated that the queen must have lost half her body-weight in the fraction of a second it took the egg mass and accompanying fluids to pour forth from her body. The queen was bleeding still, and two normal-sized octospiders had climbed up the wall to minister to her. At this point Dr Blue tapped Nicole on the shoulder, indicating it was time to leave.

Sitting by herself in one of the small rooms in the octospider hospital, Nicole played the egg rush scene over and over in her mind. She had not expected that the event would affect her so emotionally. Nicole had only half watched while Dr Blue explained to her, after they had returned to the hospital, that the containers emptied into the slurry were full of tiny animals that would seek out and kill specific embryos. In that way the octospiders controlled, she said, the exact composition of the next generation, including the number of queens, repletes, midget morphs, and all the other variations.

The mother in Nicole was struggling to understand what it would feel like to be an octospider queen during an egg rush. In some undefinable way, Nicole felt deeply connected to that mammoth creature that had crawled up onto the spikes. During the instant of the egg rush, Nicole's loins had contracted, and she had recalled both the pain and the exhilaration of her own six births. *What is there about the birth process,* she wondered, *that unites all creatures who have ever experienced it?*

She remembered a long-past conversation in Rama II, after Simone and Katie had been born, when she tried to explain to Michael O'Toole what it felt like to give birth to a child. Nicole had reluctantly concluded, after hours of talking, that it was an experience that could never be adequately transferred from one person to another. *The world is divided into two groups,* she had said at the time. *Those that have experienced birth and those that have not.* Now, tens of years and billions of kilometres later, she wanted to add a corollary to her earlier observation. *Those who are mothers have more in common, fundamentally, with mothers of other species than they have with humans who have never given birth.*

As she continued to reflect on the scene that she had witnessed, Nicole was overwhelmed by a desire to communicate with the queen octospider, to know what that other intelligent mother had been thinking and feeling just prior to and during the egg rush. Had the queen, amid the pain and wonder of the moment, felt an epiphanic serenity, a vision of her own offspring and their offspring continuing into the unforeseen future, the miraculous cycle of life? Had there been a deep and ineffable peace in the seconds just after the rush, a peace unlike any the creature had ever known at any time other than immediately after birth?

Nicole knew that the imaginary conversation she was having with the queen could never take place. Again she closed her eyes, attempting to reconstruct the exact bursts of colour she had seen on the queen's body immediately before and after the event. Had those surges of colour told the other octospiders what the queen was feeling? Were they somehow able, Nicole wondered, with their rich language of colour, to communicate complex feelings like ecstasy better than humans, with their, limited language of words?

There were no answers. Nicole realised that there were tasks waiting for her outside the room, in the octospider hospital, but she was not ready for her solitude to end. She did not want the strong emotions she was feeling to be diminished by the demands of everyday life.

As the time passed, Nicole began also to experience a profound loneliness. She did not at first connect her loneliness directly to the egg rush. Nicole was, however, quite aware that she was having a strong desire to talk to a close friend, preferably Richard. She wanted to share with someone what she had seen and felt in the Queen's Domain. In her isolation Nicole suddenly remembered a few lines from a relevant poem by Benita Garcia. She opened her portable computer and, after a short search, found the entire poem.

In moments of deep doubt or intense pain,
When I am overpowered by my life,
I search around me everywhere I can.
For kindred souls who know what I know not,
For those who have the strength to mitigate
What makes me tremble, weep, and often brood.
They tell me that I cannot live *my* way
Where all my feelings rule my conscious mind.
I must control myself before the act,
Or else accept what I have long endured,
The brutal days of feeling lost and blind.

There have been times, not many but a few,
When someone has possessed the soothing balm,
Providing surcease for my angst or pain.
But age has taught me now one simple rule.
Inside myself I must the screams contain,
Whatever devils must be wrestled there.
The lessons learned will not be lost again.
We walk alone upon our final trip.
No hand can help us on that day of death,
It's best we learn, while time is still our friend,
To trust ourselves, and save our precious breath.

Nicole read the words several times. Immediately thereafter she realised that she was completely exhausted, she put her head down on the only table in the room and fell asleep.

Dr Blue tapped gently on Nicole's shoulder with one of her tentacles. Nicole stirred and opened her eyes. 'You've been asleep for almost two hours,' the octospider said. 'They have been expecting you over at the administrative centre.'

'What's going on?' Nicole asked, rubbing her eyes. 'Why is anyone waiting for me?'

'Nakamura has made a major speech in New Eden. The Chief Optimiser wants to discuss it with you.'

Nicole jumped up quickly and then reached out to touch the desk. In a few seconds her dizziness was gone. 'Thank you again, Dr Blue, for everything,' she said. 'I'll be on my way in another minute.'

7

'**I** really don't think Nikki should be allowed to watch the speech,' Robert said. 'It wili certainly scare her.'

'What Nakamura says will affect her life as much as it will ours,' Ellie replied. 'If she wants to watch, I think we should let her ... After all, Robert, she has lived with the octospiders ...'

'But she can't possibly understand what any of this really means,' Robert argued. 'She's not even four years old yet.'

The issue remained unresolved until a few minutes before the New Eden dictator was scheduled to appear on television. At that time Nikki approached her mother in the living-room. 'I'm not going to watch,' the little girl said with astonishing insight, 'because I don't want you and Daddy to fight.'

One of the rooms in Nakamura's palace had been converted into a television studio. It was from this studio that the tyrant usually addressed the citizens of New Eden. His last speech had been three months earlier, when he had announced that troops were going to be deployed in the Southern Hemicylinder to confront the 'alien menace.' Although the government-controlled newspapers and television had regularly been featuring news items from the front, many of them fabricating the 'intense resistance' being offered by the octospiders, this would be Nakamura's first public comment on the progress and direction of the war in the south.

For the address, Nakamura had ordered his tailors to make him a new shogun's outfit, complete with ornamented sword and dagger. He was appearing in Japanese martial dress, he told his aides, to stress his role as the 'lead warrior and protector' of the colonists. On the day of the broadcast Nakamura's attendants helped him put on a pair of heavy, constraining girdles so that he would project the 'powerful and menacing' look of the warrior.

Mr Nakamura spoke standing up, staring directly at the camera. His scowl never changed during his entire speech.

'We have all sacrificed in recent months,' he began, 'to support our valiant soldiers doing battle south of the Cylindrical Sea with a heinous and ruthless alien enemy. Our intelligence now informs us that these octospiders, who were described to you in detail by Dr Robert Turner after his brave escape, are planning a major attack against New Eden in the very near future. At this critical moment in our history, we must redouble our resolve and stand united against the alien aggressor.

'Our generals at the front have recommended that we penetrate beyond the barrier forest protecting most of the octospider domain and interdict their supplies and war materiel before they can launch their attack. Our engineers, working night and day for the survival of the colony, have made modifications to our helicopter fleet that will permit this interdiction to take place. We will strike in the near future. We will convince the aliens that they cannot attack us with impunity.

'Meanwhile, our warriors have finished securing the entire area of Rama between the Cylindrical Sea and the barrier forest. During the fierce battles, we have destroyed many hundreds of the enemy, as well as water and power facilities. Our casualties have been modest, primarily because of our superb battle plans and the heroism of our troops. But we must not become over-confident. On the contrary, we have every reason to believe that we have not yet even engaged the elite Death Corps that Dr Turner heard mentioned while he was being held captive. It is this Death Corps, we are certain, that will be in the alien vanguard if we do not move quickly to preclude an attack on New Eden. Remember, time is our enemy. We must strike now and totally demolish their war-making capability.

'There is one other brief item I would like to report tonight. Recently the traitor Richard Wakefield and an octospider companion surrendered to our troops in the south. They say that they are representing the alien military command and have come forward to talk about peace. I suspect a trick here, a Trojan horse of some kind, but it is my duty as your leader to conduct a hearing into this matter in the next few days. Rest assured that I will not negotiate away our security. I will report the outcome of this hearing very soon after it is completed.'

'But Robert,' Ellie said, 'you know that much of what he is saying is a *lie* ... There is no Death Corps, and the octospiders have not offered any resistance. How can you say nothing? How can you let him attribute statements to you that you never made?'

'It's all politics, Ellie,' Robert replied. 'Everybody knows that. Nobody really believes ...'

'But that's even worse. Don't you see what is happening?'

Robert started to leave the house. 'Where are you going now?' Ellie asked.

'Back to the hospital,' Robert replied. 'I have rounds to make.'

Ellie couldn't believe it. She stood there for a few seconds, staring at her husband. Then she erupted. '*That's* your response,' she shouted. 'Business as usual. A lunatic announces a plan that will most likely result in all of us being killed, and for you it's business as usual ... Robert, who are you? Don't you care about anything?'

Robert moved toward her angrily. 'Don't start again with that "holier than thou" attitude,' he said. 'You are not always right, Ellie, and you do not know for certain that we'll all be killed. Maybe Nakamura's plan will work.'

'You're kidding yourself, Robert. You turn the other way and tell yourself that as long as your little world is not affected, maybe it's OK ... You're wrong, Robert. Dead wrong. And if you won't do anything about it, then I *will*.'

'And what will you do?' Robert said, his voice rising. 'Tell the world that your husband is a *liar*? Try to convince everyone that those slimy octospiders are peaceful? No one will believe you, Ellie ... And I'll tell you one more thing: The minute you open your mouth, you'll be arrested and tried for treason. They'll kill you, Ellie, just like they're going to kill your father ... Is that what you want? Never to see your daughter again?'

Ellie recognised the mixture of pain and anger in Robert's eyes. *I don't know him,* flashed through her mind, followed by *How can this be the same man who has spent thousands of hours caring for dying patients? It doesn't make any sense.*

Ellie chose not to say anything more. 'I'm going now,' Robert said at length. 'I'll be home around midnight.'

She walked to the back of the house and opened Nikki's door. Luckily the girl had slept through the argument. Ellie was deeply depressed when she returned to the living-room. She wished more than ever that she had stayed in the Emerald City. But she hadn't, so what was she going to do now? *It would be so easy if I didn't have Nikki to think about,* Ellie said to herself. She shook her head slowly, back and forth, and finally allowed herself to shed the tears she had been restraining.

'So how do I look?' Katie said, pirouetting in front of Franz.

'Beautiful, ravishing,' he replied. 'Better than I have ever seen you look.'

She was wearing a simple black dress, custom-fitted to her thin body. The dress had a defining white stripe running down both sides. It was cut low in the front, highlighting her necklace of diamonds and gold, but was not so low that it would be considered improper.

Katie glanced at her watch. 'Good,' she said. 'For once I'm early.' She crossed the room to the table and lit a cigarette.

Franz's uniform was newly pressed and his shoes perfectly shined. 'Then I guess we have time,' he said, following Katie to the couch, 'for my surprise.' He handed her a small velvet box.

'What's this?' Katie asked.

'Open it,' Franz said.

Inside was a diamond ring, a solitaire. 'Katie,' Franz said awkwardly, 'will you marry me?'

Katie glanced at Franz and then looked away. She inhaled slowly on her cigarette and blew the smoke into the air above her. 'I'm flattered, Franz,' she said, standing up and kissing him on the cheek, 'I really am ... but it just wouldn't work.' She closed the box and handed him back the ring.

'Why not?' Franz asked. 'Don't you love me?'

'Yes, I do ... I guess ... if I'm capable of such an emotion ... But Franz, we've been through this before. I'm just not the kind of woman you should marry.'

'Why can't you let *me* decide that, Katie?' Franz said. 'How do you know what "kind of woman" I need?'

'Look, Franz,' Katie said, showing some agitation, 'I'd rather not talk about this now. As I said, I'm very flattered ... but I'm already nervous about this hearing for my father and you know I don't deal well with too much shit at once ...'

'You'll always have some reason for not wanting to talk about it,' Franz said angrily. 'If you love me, I think I deserve more of an explanation. And now ...'

Katie's eyes flashed. 'You want an explanation *now*, Captain Bauer ... All right, I'll give you one ... Follow me, if you please ...' Katie led him into her dressing-room. 'Now stand there, Franz, and watch very closely.'

Katie reached into her dresser. She pulled out a syringe and a piece of black tubing. She placed her right leg on the vanity stool and hiked her dress up above the bruises on her thigh. Franz instinctively turned his head away.

'No,' Katie said, reaching out with one hand and turning his head back to face her. 'You cannot look away, Franz ... You must see me as I am.'

She pulled down her panty hose and tied the tube in place. Katie glanced up to make certain Franz was still watching. There was pain in her eyes. 'Don't you see, Franz?' she said. 'I cannot marry you because I'm already married ... to this magic drug that never disappoints me ... Don't you understand? ... There's no way that you could ever compete with kokomo.'

Katie plunged the syringe into a vein and waited several seconds for the rush. 'You might be fine for a few weeks, or even months,' Katie said now, speaking more rapidly, 'but sooner or later you'd come up short ... And I would replace you in my heart with old reliable again.'

She wiped off the two drops of blood with a tissue and placed the syringe in the sink. Franz looked distraught. 'Cheer up,' Katie said, patting him lightly on the cheek. 'You haven't lost your bed partner ... I'll still be here for whatever kinky things we can dream up together ...'

Franz turned away and placed the velvet box back in one of the pockets of his uniform. Katie walked over to the table and took one final drag from the cigarette that had been left burning in the ashtray. 'Now, Captain Bauer,' Katie said, 'we have a hearing to attend.'

The hearing was held in the ballroom on the main floor of Nakamura's palace. About sixty chairs had been set up in four rows along the walls for 'special guests'. Nakamura himself, wearing the same Japanese costume in which he had appeared on television two days earlier, sat in a large, embroidered chair above a raised platform at one end of the room. Two bodyguards, also in samurai dress, were beside him. The ballroom was completely decorated in a sixteenth century Japanese motif, adding to the image Nakamura was trying to create of himself as the all-powerful shogun of New Eden.

Richard and Archie, who had only been told the hearing was going to occur four hours before they left the basement, were brought in by three policemen and instructed to sit on small pillows on the floor, twenty metres in front of Nakamura. Katie noticed that her father looked tired and very old. She resisted an impulse to run out and talk to him.

A functionary announced that the hearing was now under way and reminded all the spectators that they were to say nothing and interfere in no way with the proceedings. As soon as the announcement was completed, Nakamura stood up and swaggered down the two broad steps connecting his chair to the raised platform.

'This hearing has been convened by the New Eden government,' he said gruffly, walking back and forth, 'to determine if the alien enemy representative is prepared, on behalf of his species, to accept the unconditional surrender that we demand as a necessary prerequisite for ceasing the hostilities between us. If ex-citizen Wakefield, who is able to communicate with the alien, has been able to convince the alien of the wisdom of accepting our demands, including relinquishing all weapons of war and preparing for our occupation and administration of all alien lands, then we are prepared to be merciful. As a reward for his services in ending this terrible conflict, we would be willing to commute Mr Wakefield's death sentence to life imprisonment.

'If, however,' Nakamura now raised his voice, 'this convicted traitor and his alien accomplice surrendered to our victorious troops as part of some treacherous plot to undermine our collective will to punish the aliens for their aggressive attacks against us, then we will use these two as examples to send an unambiguous message to our enemy. We want the alien leaders to know that the citizens of New Eden stand steadfast against their expansionist aims.'

Up until this moment Nakamura had been addressing the entire audience. Now he turned to face the two prisoners isolated in the middle of the ballroom floor. 'Mr Wakefield,' he said, 'does the alien beside you have the authority to speak for his species?'

Richard stood up. 'To the best of my knowledge, yes,' he answered.

'And is the alien then prepared to ratify the document of unconditional surrender that you have been shown?'

'We only received the document a few hours ago and I have not yet had time to talk about all its contents. I have explained the most important parts to Archie, but I don't yet know ...'

'They are stalling,' Nakamura thundered, addressing the audience and waving a piece of paper in the air. 'This single sheet contains all the terms of the surrender.' He turned again to face Richard and Archie. 'The question requires only a simple answer,' Nakamura said. 'Is it yes or no?'

Colour bands rolled around Archie's head and there was a murmur in the audience. Richard watched Archie, whispered a question to his octospider colleague, and then interpreted Archie's response. He looked at Nakamura. 'The octospider wants to know,' Richard said, 'exactly what happens if the document is ratified. What are the events that take place then, and in what order – none of this is spelled out in the agreement.'

Nakamura paused briefly. 'First, all the alien soldiers must come forward with their weapons and surrender to our troops now in the south. Second, the alien government, or whatever is its equivalent, must turn over to us a complete inventory of everything that exists in their domain. Third, they must announce to all members of their species that we are going to occupy their colony and that all aliens are to co-operate in every way with our soldiers and citizens.'

Richard and Archie had another brief conversation. 'What will happen to all the octospiders and the other animals who support this society?' Richard asked.

'They will be permitted to resume their normal lives, with some constraints, of course. Our laws and our citizens will be put in place as the acting government of the occupied lands.'

'And will you, then,' Richard said, 'write an amendment or an appendix to this surrender document, guaranteeing the lives and safety of the octospiders, as well as the other animals, providing they do not violate any of the laws promulgated in the occupied territory?'

Nakamura's eyes narrowed. 'Except for those individual aliens who are found to have been responsible for the aggressive war that has been launched against us, I will personally guarantee the safety of those octospiders who obey the laws of occupation ... But these are details. They do not need to be written in the surrender document.'

This time Richard and Archie engaged in a long discussion. From the side of the room, Katie watched her father's face closely. She thought in the beginning that he was disagreeing with the octospider, but later in the conversation Richard seemed subdued, almost resigned. It looked as if her father were memorizing something ...

The long pause in the proceedings was irritating Nakamura. The special guests were starting to whisper among themselves. Finally Nakamura spoke again. 'All right,' he said. 'That's enough time. What is your answer?'

Colours were still streaking around Archie's head. At length, the patterns stopped and Richard took a step forward toward Nakamura. Richard hesitated a moment before speaking.

'The octospiders want peace,' he said slowly, 'and would like to find a way to end this conflict. If they were not a moral species, they might agree to ratify this surrender document just to buy some time. But the octospiders are not like that. My alien friend, whose name is Archie, would not make an agreement for his species unless he was certain both that the treaty was proper for his colony and that his fellow octospiders would honour it.'

Richard paused. 'We do not need a speech,' Nakamura said impatiently, 'just answer the question.'

'The octospiders,' Richard said in a louder voice, 'sent Archie and me to negotiate an honourable peace, *not* to surrender unconditionally. If New Eden is not willing to negotiate and to make an agreement that respects the integrity of the octospider domain, then they have no choice. Please,' Richard now shouted, looking back and forth at the guests on both sides of the room, 'understand that you cannot win if the octospiders really fight. So far they have put up no resistance at all. You must convince your leaders to enter into balanced discussions ...'

'*Seize the prisoners*,' Nakamura ordered.

'... or you will all perish. The octospiders are much more advanced than we are. Believe me. I know. I have been living with them for more than ...'

One of the policemen struck Richard on the back of the head and he fell to the floor, bleeding. Katie jumped up, but Franz restrained her with both arms. Richard was holding the side of his head as Archie and he were ushered out of the room.

Richard and Archie were in a small jail cell at the police station in Hakone, not far from Nakamura's palace. 'Is your head all right?' Archie asked in colour.

'I think so,' Richard answered, 'although it is still swelling.'

'They'll kill us now, won't they?' Archie asked.

'Probably,' Richard said grimly.

'Thanks for trying,' Archie said after a short silence.

Richard shrugged. 'I didn't do much good ... Anyway, it's you who should be thanked. If you hadn't volunteered, you would still be safe and sound in the Emerald City.'

Richard walked over to the washbasin in the corner to clean the cloth he was holding against his head wound. 'Didn't you tell me that most humans believe in life after death?' Archie asked after Richard had rejoined him in the front of the cell.

'Yes,' Richard replied. 'Some people believe we're reincarnated and return to live again, as another human or even as some other animal. Many others believe that if a good life has been lived, there is a reward, an eternal life in a beautiful, stressless place called heaven ...'

'And you, Richard,' Archie's colours interrupted. 'What do you personally believe?'

Richard smiled and thought for several seconds before answering. 'I've always believed that whatever there was in us that was unique and defined our special, individual personality disappeared at the moment of death. Oh, sure, our chemicals may be recycled into other living creatures, but there is no real continuity, not in terms of what some humans call the soul ...'

He laughed. 'Right now, however, when my logical mind says I could not possibly have much more time to live, a voice inside is begging me to embrace one of those fairy tales about the afterlife ... It would be easy, I admit ... But such a last-minute conversion would be inconsistent with the way I have lived all these years ...'

Richard walked slowly over to the front of their cell. He put his hands on the bars and stared down the corridor for several seconds without saying anything. 'And what do octospiders think happens after death?' he asked softly, turning around to face his cellmate.

'The Precursors taught us that each life is a finite interval, with a beginning and an end. Any individual creature, although a miracle, is not that important in the overall scheme of things. What matters, the Precursors said, is continuity and renewal. In their view each of us is immortal, not because anything related to a specific individual lives forever, but because each life becomes a critical link, either culturally or genetically or both, in the never-ending chain of life. When the Precursors engineered us out of ignorance, they taught us not to fear death, but to go willingly in support of the renewal that would follow.'

'So you experience no sorrow and no fear as your death approaches?'

'Ideally,' Archie replied. 'That is the accepted way in our society to face death. It is far easier, however, if an individual is surrounded, at the time of termination, by friends and others who represent the renewal that his death will enable.'

Richard walked over and put his arm around Archie. 'You and I have only each other, my friend,' he said. 'Plus the knowledge that we have tried, together, to stop a war that will probably end up killing thousands. There can't be many causes ...'

He stopped when he heard the door to the cell-block open. The local police captain, along with one of his men, stood to the side as four biots, two Garcias and two Lincolns, all wearing gloves, came down the hallway to their cell. None of the biots spoke. One of the Garcias opened the door and all four biots crowded into the cell with Richard and Archie. The captain closed the cell-block door. Moments later the lights went out, there was the sound of a scuffle for several seconds, Richard screamed, and a body fell against the bars of the cell. Then it was quiet.

'Now, Franz,' Katie said as they opened the door to the police station, 'don't be afraid to pull rank. He's just a local captain. He's not going to tell you that you can't see the prisoners.'

They walked inside only a second or two after the cell-block door closed behind the biots. 'Captain Miyazawa,' Franz said in his most official tone, 'I am Captain Franz Bauer from headquarters ... I have come to visit the prisoners.'

'I have strict orders from the highest authority, Captain Bauer,' the police-man replied, 'not to allow *anyone* into that cell-block.'

The room was suddenly plunged into darkness. 'What's going on?' Franz said.

'We must have blown a fuse,' Captain Miyazawa replied. 'Westermark, go outside and check the circuit breakers.'

Franz and Katie heard a scream. After what seemed to be an eternity, they heard the cell-block door open and the sound of footsteps. Three biots disappeared out the front door of the station as the lights flickered on again.

Katie ran to the door. 'Look, Franz,' she yelled. 'Blood, they have blood on their clothes.' She spun around, frantic. 'We must see my father.'

Katie outran the three police officers down the corridor. 'Oh, God,' she screamed as she neared the cell and saw her father lying on the floor against the bars. There was blood everywhere. 'He's dead, Franz,' Katie wailed. 'Daddy's dead!'

8

Nicole had watched the video twice before. Despite her swollen eyes and utter emotional exhaustion, she asked if she could see it one more time. Beside her Dr Blue handed her a cup of water. 'Are you certain?' the octospider asked.

She nodded. *One more time*, Nicole thought, *is not too much. I want every frame, no matter how horrible, preserved for ever in my mind.*

'Please start at the hearing,' Nicole requested. 'Normal speed until the biots enter the cell-block. Then slow it down to one-eighth.'

Richard never wanted to be a hero, Nicole was thinking as the video replayed the scene at the hearing. *That wasn't his style. He only went with Archie so that it wouldn't be necessary for me.* She winced when the guard struck Richard and he tumbled to the floor. *The plan was hopeless from the beginning*, she told herself as the New Eden policemen led Richard and Archie out of Nakamura's palace. *The octospiders all knew it. I knew it. Why didn't I speak up after my premonition?*

Nicole asked Dr Blue to fast-forward the video to the final minutes. *At least they had each other at the end*, she thought as Richard and Archie were sharing their final conversation. *And Archie tried to protect him* ... The four biots appeared on the screen and the video slowed. Nicole saw surprise change to fear in Richard's eyes as the biots entered the cell.

When the lights were extinguished, the picture quality changed. The infra-red images taken by the quadroids were more like photo negatives, highlighting the heat levels in each frame. The biots looked eerie. Their eyes bulged out of their heads in the infra-red pictures.

The instant the cell was dark, one of the Garcias grabbed Richard by the throat. The other three took off their gloves, exposing sharp, pointed fingers and knife-edged hands. Four of Archie's powerful tentacles enwrapped the Garcia trying to strangle Richard. As the Garcia's frame crumbled and the biot collapsed in a heap on the floor of the cell, the other three biots attacked Archie furiously. Richard tried to help in the battle. A Lincoln caught Archie's neck with a savage blow from its hand and nearly decapitated the octospider. Richard screamed as he was drenched by Archie's internal body fluid. With Archie out of the fight, the remaining biots devastated Richard, puncturing his body over and over with jabs from their fingers. He fell against the front of the cell and slipped down onto the floor. His blood and Archie's, which were different colours in the infra-red image, ran together and formed a pool on the floor of the cell.

The video continued, but Nicole was no longer seeing anything. Now, for the first time, she understood that her husband, Richard, the only really close friend she had ever had in her adult life, was actually dead. On the screen Franz led the sobbing Katie down the corridor and then the monitor went blank. Nicole did not move. She sat perfectly still, staring forward where the images had been just seconds before. There were no tears in her eyes, her body was not trembling, she seemed completely in control. Yet she could not move.

A low level of light came on in the viewing-room. Dr Blue was still sitting beside her. 'I don't think,' Nicole said slowly, surprised that her voice sounded so far away, 'that I realised the first two times ... I mean, I must have been in shock ... maybe I still am.' She couldn't continue. Nicole was having trouble breathing.

'You need a drink of water and some rest,' Dr Blue said.

Richard has been killed. Richard is dead. 'Yes, please,' Nicole said faintly. *I will never see him again. I will never talk to him again.* 'Cold water, if you have any.' *I saw him die. Once. Twice. Three times. Richard is dead.*

There was another octospider in the viewing-room. They were talking, but Nicole could not follow their colours. *Richard is gone forever. I am alone.* Dr Blue held the water up to Nicole's lips, but she could not drink. *Richard has been killed.* There was nothing but blackness.

Someone was holding her hand. It was a warm, pleasant hand, gently caressing hers. She opened her eyes.

'Hello, Mother,' Patrick said softly. 'Are you feeling any better?'

Nicole closed her eyes again. Where am I? she thought. Then she remembered. *Richard is dead. I must have fainted.*

'Ummm,' she said.

'Would you like some water?' Patrick asked.

'Yes, please,' she whispered. Her voice sounded strange.

Nicole tried to sit up and drink the water. She could not make it.

'Take it easy,' Patrick said. 'There's no hurry.'

Her mind began to work. *I must tell them,* she thought. *Richard and Archie are dead. The helicopters are coming. We must be very careful and protect the children.* 'Richard,' she managed to say.

'We know, Mother,' Patrick replied.

How do they know? Nicole thought. *I'm the only one left here who can read colours ...*

'The octospiders went to a lot of trouble to write everything down. It wasn't perfect English, but we certainly understood what they were telling us ... They told us about the war too ...'

Good, Nicole thought. *They know. I can sleep.* From somewhere in her head there was still an echo. *Richard is dead.*

'From time to time I can hear the bombs, but as far as I can tell none of them yet has hit the dome.' It was Max's voice. 'Maybe they haven't figured out where the city is.'

'It would be completely dark from the outside,' Patrick said. 'They have thickened the canopy and there are no lights on the streets.'

'The bombs must be hitting the Alternate Domain. There would be no way the octos could hide its existence,' Max said.

'What are the octospiders doing?' Patrick asked. 'Do we even know if they're counter-attacking?'

'Not for certain,' Max replied, 'but I can't believe they're still sitting around doing nothing.'

Nicole heard soft footsteps in the hallway. 'The boys are really developing a bad case of cabin fever,' Nai said. 'Do you think it would be all right if I let them play outside? ... The all-clear flares were half an hour ago.'

'I don't see why not,' Patrick said. 'But tell them to come in if they see a flare or hear any bombs.'

'I'll be out there with them,' Nai said.

'What's my wife doing?' Max asked.

'Reading with Benjy,' Nai replied. 'Marius is asleep.'

'Why don't you ask her to come over for a few minutes?'

Nicole rolled over on her other side. She thought about trying to sit up, but she felt so tired. She began daydreaming, remembering her childhood. *What does it take to be a princess?* little Nicole asked her father. *Either a king for a father, or a prince for a husband,* he answered. He smiled and kissed her. *Then I'm already a princess,* she told him. *For you're a king to me ...*

'How is Nicole?' Eponine asked.

'She stirred again this morning,' Patrick replied. 'Dr Blue's note said that she may be able to sit up tonight or tomorrow. It also said they have verified that the attack was not severe, that the heart was not permanently damaged, and that she is responding well to the treatment.'

'Can I see her now?' Benjy asked.

'No, Benjy, not yet,' said Eponine, 'she's still resting.'

'The octospiders have really been great, haven't they?' Patrick said. 'Even in the middle of this war, they have taken time to write us such complete messages ...'

'They've even made a believer out of me,' Max said. 'And I never thought that was possible.'

So I had a heart attack, Nicole thought. *I didn't just collapse because Richard ...* she could not complete the sentence at first ... *because he is gone.*

She drifted in the twilight zone between waking and sleeping until she heard a familiar voice calling her name. *Is that you, Richard?* Nicole said excitedly. *Yes, Nicole,* he answered. *Where are you? I want to see you,* she said, and his face appeared in a cloud in the middle of her dream-screen. *You look great,* she said, *are you all right? Yes,* Richard answered, *but I must talk to you.*

What is it, darling? Nicole asked. *You must go on without me,* he said. *You must set an example for the others.* His face began to alter as the shapes of the clouds changed. *Of course,* Nicole said, *but where are you going?* She could not see him any more. *Goodbye,* his voice said. *Goodbye, Richard,* Nicole answered.

When she woke up the next time, her mind was clear. Nicole sat up in bed and looked around her. It was dark, but she could tell she was in her own room in the house in the Emerald City.

Nicole could hear no sounds. She assumed it was night. She pushed off the covers and swung her legs over the edge of the bed. *So far, so good,* she thought. Nicole eased herself off the bed and stood up very slowly. Her legs were wobbly.

There was a glass of juice on the end table beside the bed. Nicole took two cautious steps, holding on to the bed with her right hand, and picked up the glass. The juice was delicious. Pleased with herself, Nicole started toward the closet to find some clothes. She became woozy after a few steps, however, and headed back toward the bed.

'Mother,' she heard Patrick say, 'is that you?' She could see his silhouette in the doorway.

'Yes, Patrick,' she answered.

'Here,' he said, 'why don't we have some light?' He knocked on the wall and a firefly flew into the middle of the room. 'Goodness,' he said, 'what are you doing up?'

'I can't stay in bed forever,' Nicole answered.

'But you should take it easy at first,' Patrick said, coming over beside her and helping her the rest of the way to bed.

She grabbed his arm. 'Listen to me, son,' Nicole said. 'I have no intention of being an invalid, nor do I want to be treated like one. I expect to be my old self in a few days, a week at the most.'

'Yes, Mother,' Patrick said with a concerned smile.

Dr Blue was delighted with her recovery. After four more days Nicole walked, albeit slowly, and, with a little help from Benjy, all the way to the transport stop and back to the house.

'Don't push yourself too hard,' Dr Blue told Nicole during an evening examination. 'You're doing great, but I worry ...'

When the octospider was finished and was preparing to leave the room. Max entered and announced that two more octospiders were waiting at the front door. Dr Blue hurried out, returning a few minutes later with the Chief Optimiser and one of the members of her staff.

The Chief Optimiser first apologised, both for coming unexpectedly and for not waiting until Nicole had completely recovered. 'However,' the octospider leader then said, 'we are now in an emergency situation and we felt that we needed to communicate with you immediately.'

Nicole felt her pulse-rate rise and tried to calm herself. 'What has happened?' she said.

'You have probably noticed that there have been no bombings for the last several days,' the Chief Optimiser said. 'The humans temporarily stopped the helicopter attacks while they were evaluating our ultimatum ... Five days ago we took the same written message to each of three troop encampments. The message said that we could no longer tolerate the bombings and that we would use our superior technology to launch a decisive attack if the hostilities were not ceased immediately ... As an illustration of our technological capabilities, we included in the message a nillet-by-nillet chronology of everything both Nakamura and Macmillan had done during two workdays last week.

'The human leaders were frantic. They suspected that we had somehow bribed some high official of the government and now knew all of their war plans as well. Macmillan recommended accepting our cease-fire and withdrawing from our territory. Nakamura was furious. He banished Macmillan from his presence and reorganised his command structure. Privately, he admitted to his security chief that any retreat would ruin his position in the colony.

'The day before yesterday someone suggested to Nakamura that perhaps your daughter Ellie might have some knowledge of how we had obtained our information. She was taken to the palace and interrogated by Nakamura himself. At first slightly cooperative, Ellie acknowledged that in certain fields we were more advanced than the humans. She also said that she believed it was entirely within our capabilities to obtain information about events in New Eden without using any spies or other conventional means of gathering intelligence.

'Because she was so forthright, Nakarnura became convinced that Ellie knew more than she was telling. He asked her questions for hours, about many subjects, including our military capabilities and the geography of our domain. Ellie astutely avoided giving away any critical information – she never mentioned the Emerald City, for example – and repeatedly answered that she had never seen any weapons or even any soldiers. Nakamura did not believe her. At length he had her thrown in prison and beaten. Since then Ellie has remained defiantly silent, despite additional rough treatment.'

The Chief Optimiser paused. Nicole had paled during his description of Ellie's mistreatment. The octospider leader turned to Dr Blue. 'Should I continue?' she said.

Max and Patrick were standing in the doorway. They could not, of course, understand what the Chief Optimiser was saying, but they could see the pallor on Nicole's face. Patrick walked into the room. 'My mother has been quite ill ...' he said.

'It's all right,' Nicole said, waving him away. She took a deep breath. 'Please go on,' she said to the Chief Optimiser.

'Nakamura,' the Chief Optimiser continued, 'has now convinced himself and his main lieutenants that our threat is a bluff. He believes that even though our technology is very advanced in some areas, we possess no military capabilities. In his last staff meeting, only a few terts ago, he agreed to a plan to bomb us into submission, using all available firepower. The first of the massive raids will come in the morning.

'We have therefore reluctantly concluded that we must now fight back. Failure to act could put the survival of our colony in jeopardy. Before coming to see you, I authorised the implementation of War Plan number 41, one of our intermediate-strength responses. This plan does not result in the total annihilation of all the colonists in New Eden, but should be devastating enough to bring the war to a quick end. Our analysts estimate that between twenty and thirty per cent of the humans will die ...'

The Chief Optimiser stopped when she saw the pained expression on Nicole's face. Nicole asked for something to drink. 'Are we allowed to know any more details about your attack?' Nicole said slowly after she finished drinking the glass of water.

'We have chosen a microbiological agent, chemically much like an enzyme, that interferes with cell reproduction in your species. Young, healthy humans below the age of forty or so have sufficiently strong natural defences that they will withstand the onslaught of the agent. Older or unhealthy humans will succumb quickly. Their cells will not be able to reproduce properly and their bodies will simply stop functioning ... We have used blood, skin, and other cells taken from all of you here in the Emerald City to verify our theoretical predictions. We are quite certain that the young will be unharmed.'

'Our species regards biological warfare as immoral,' Nicole said after a brief pause.

'We are aware,' the Chief Optimiser said, 'that within your system of values, some kinds of warfare are more acceptable than others. To us, all war is unacceptable. We fight only if we absolutely must. We can't imagine it makes any difference to the dead being if it has been killed by a gun, a bomb, a nuclear weapon, or a biological agent. Besides, we must fight back with whatever weapons we possess.'

There was a long silence. Nicole sighed and shook her head. 'I guess,' she said at length, 'I should be thankful that you have told us what is happening in this stupid war, even though the spectre of so many deaths is very frightening. I wish there could have been some other outcome ...'

The three octospiders prepared to leave the room. Max and Patrick were asking Nicole questions before the visitors had even departed from the house. 'Hold it,' Nicole said wearily. 'Call the others in here first. I only want to explain what the octospiders told me a single time.'

*

Nicole could not sleep. No matter how hard she tried, she could not stop thinking about the people who were going to die in New Eden. Faces, older faces, mostly, faces of people that Nicole had known and worked with during her active days in the colony, swam in and out of her mind.

And what about Katie and Ellie? Nicole thought. *What if the octospiders have made a mistake?* She pictured Ellie as she had last seen her, in her house with her husband and her daughter. Nicole recalled the arguments that she had witnessed between Ellie and Robert. His tired, worn visage remained fixed in her mental image. *And Robert,* she thought, *oh, my God. He's older, and doesn't take care of himself at all.*

Nicole squirmed in her bed, frustrated by her inability to do anything. Finally she decided to sit up in the darkness. *I wonder if it's too late,* Nicole asked herself. Again she thought of Robert. *I don't agree with him. I'm not even certain he's a good husband for Ellie. But he is still Nikki's father.*

A plan had begun to develop in her mind. Nicole gingerly slid out of bed and walked across to the closet. She put on some clothes. *I might not be able to help,* she was thinking, *but at least I'll know that I tried.*

Nicole was especially quiet in the hall. She did not want to wake Patrick or Nai, who had been sleeping in Ellie's room since her heart attack. *They would just make me go back to bed.*

Outside, in the Emerald City, it was almost as dark as it had been inside the house. Nicole stood at the doorway, hoping that her eyes would adjust enough that she could find the house next door. Eventually she could make out some shadows. She stepped off the porch, heading to the right.

Her progress was slow. She would take half a dozen steps and then stop to look around. It took her several minutes to reach the atrium of Dr Blue's house.

Now, with any luck, Nicole thought, remembering, *she should be sleeping in the second room on the left.* When she entered the octospider's sleeping-quarters, Nicole tapped lightly on the wall. A firefly dimly illuminated a pair of octospiders in a single heap. Dr Blue and Jamie were sleeping with their bodies pressed together and their tentacles tangled in a confusing pattern. Nicole walked over and touched Dr Blue on the top of the head. There was no response. She tapped a little harder the second time and Dr Blue's lens material began to move around.

'What are you doing here?' Dr Blue said in colour a few seconds later.

'I need your help,' Nicole answered. 'It's important.'

The octospider moved very slowly, trying to untangle her tentacles without disturbing Jamie. She was unsuccessful; the young octospider awakened anyway. Dr Blue told Jamie to go back to sleep and shuffled into the atrium with Nicole.

'You should be in bed,' Dr Blue said.

'I know,' Nicole replied. 'But this is an emergency. I need to talk to the Chief Optimiser, and I would like for you to go with me.'

'At this time of night?'

'I don't know how much time we have,' Nicole said. 'I must see the Chief Optimiser before those biological agents start killing people in New Eden ... I'm worried about Katie, and all of Ellie's family as well ...'

'Nikki and Ellie will not be harmed. Katie should be young enough too, if I understood ...'

'But Katie's system is screwed up by all the drugs,' Nicole interrupted the colours. 'Her body probably acts as if it's old ... and Robert is all worn-out from working all the time.'

'I'm not certain I understand what you are telling me,' said Dr Blue. 'Why is it that you want to see the Chief Optimiser?'

'To plead for special treatment for Katie and Robert, assuming of course that Ellie and Nikki are all right. There must be some way, with your biological magic, that they can be singled out and spared. That's why I want you to come with me ... to support my case.'

The octospider didn't say anything for several seconds. 'All right, Nicole,' she said finally, 'I will go with you. Even though I think you should be resting in bed ... And I doubt if there's anything that can be done.'

'Thank you very much,' Nicole said, forgetting herself for a moment and hugging Dr Blue around the neck.

'You must promise me one thing,' Dr Blue said as they walked together out the front door. 'You must not push yourself too hard tonight ... Tell me if you are feeling weak.'

'I'll even lean on you as we walk,' Nicole said with a smile.

They moved slowly into the street, the unlikely pair. Two of Dr Blue's tentacles were supporting Nicole at all times. Nevertheless, the day's activities and emotions had taken a toll on Nicole's meagre energy supply. She was feeling fatigue before they reached the transport stop.

She stopped to rest. The distant sounds she had been hearing, but not noticing, became more prominent. 'Bombs,' Nicole said to Dr Blue. 'A lot of them.'

'We were told to expect helicopter raids,' the octospider said. 'But I wonder why there were no flares ...'

Suddenly part of the domed canopy over their heads exploded in a great fireball. Moments later Nicole heard a deafening sound. She held tightly to Dr Blue and stared at the inferno above her. In the flames she thought she could see the remnants of a helicopter. Burning pieces of the dome were falling from the sky, some landing no more than a kilometre away.

Nicole could not catch her breath. Dr Blue could see the strain on her face. 'I'll never make it,' Nicole said. She clutched the octospider with all the strength she had remaining. 'You must go see the Chief Optimiser without me,' she said. 'As my friend. Ask her, no, *beg* her to do something for Katie and Robert ... Tell her it's a personal favour ... For me ...'

'I'll do what I can,' Dr Blue replied. 'But first we must take you back ...'

'*Mother*,' Nicole heard Patrick yell behind her. He was running down the street toward them. When he reached them, Dr Blue boarded the transport. Nicole looked up at the dome just as a helicopter blade, wrapped in burning foliage, fell out of the sky and crashed in the distance.

9

Katie dropped the syringe in the sink and looked at herself in the mirror. 'There,' she said out loud, 'that's much better ... I'm not trembling any more.' She was wearing the same dress she had worn to her father's hearing. Katie had made that decision also the week before, when she had told Franz what she was planning to do.

She turned around, watching her reflection critically. *What is that swelling on my forearm?* she wondered. Katie had not noticed it before. On her right arm, half-way between her elbow and her wrist, there was a lump the size of a golf ball. She rubbed it. The swelling felt tender when she pressed it, but it neither hurt nor itched unless she touched it directly.

Katie shrugged and walked into her living-room. The papers she had prepared were lying on the coffee-table. She smoked a cigarette while she organised the document. Then she placed the papers in a large envelope.

The phone call from Nakamura's office had come that morning. The sweet female voice had told Katie that Nakamura could see her at five o'clock in the afternoon. When she had put down the phone, Katie had hardly been able to contain herself. She had almost given up hope that she would be able to see him at all. Three days earlier, when she had called to make an appointment 'to talk about their mutual business,' Nakamura's receptionist had told her that he was extremely busy with the war effort and was not scheduling unrelated meetings.

Katie checked her watch again. It was fifteen minutes until five. To walk from her apartment to the palace would take ten minutes. She picked up the envelope and opened the door of her apartment.

The wait was destroying her self-confidence. It was already six o'clock and Katie had not even been admitted yet to the inner sanctum, the Japanese part of the palace where Nakamura worked and lived. Twice she had gone to the rest-room, both times inquiring on her way back to her seat if the wait would be much longer. The girl at the desk next to the door had twice responded with a vague, unknowing gesture.

Katie was struggling with herself. The kokomo was starting to wear off, and she was having doubts. While smoking a cigarette in the rest-room, she had tried to forget her anxieties by thinking about Franz. She had remembered the last time that they had made love. His eyes had been heavy with sadness when he had departed. *He does love me*, Katie thought, *in his own way ...*

The Japanese girl was standing at the door. 'You may go in now,' she said. Katie crossed back through the waiting-room and entered the main part of the palace. She took off her shoes, placed them on a shelf, and walked on the tatami in her stocking feet. An escort, a policewoman named Marge, greeted her and instructed Katie to follow her.

Clutching her envelope of papers in her hand, Katie walked behind the policewoman for ten or fifteen metres until a screen opened on their right. 'Please go in,' Marge said.

Another policewoman, Oriental but not Japanese, was waiting in the room. She was wearing a gun in a holster on her hip. 'Security around Nakamura-san is especially tight right now,' Marge explained. 'Please take off all your clothes and jewellery.'

'All my clothes?' Katie asked. 'Even my panties?'

'Everything,' the other woman said.

Her clothes were all folded neatly and placed in a basket marked with her name. The jewellery went into a special box. While Katie was naked, Marge checked her everywhere, including her private parts. She even inspected the inside of Katie's mouth, holding her tongue depressed for almost thirty seconds. Katie was then handed a blue and white yukata and a pair of Japanese slippers. 'You may now go with Bangorn to the last waiting-room,' Marge said.

Katie picked up her envelope and started to leave. The Oriental police-woman stopped her. '*Every*thing stays here,' she said.

'But this is a business meeting,' Katie protested. 'What I want to discuss with Mr Nakamura is in this envelope.'

The two women opened the envelope and took out the papers. They held each individual paper up to the light and then passed them, one at a time, through some kind of screening-machine. Finally they replaced the papers in the envelope and the woman named Bangorn motioned for Katie to follow her.

The final waiting-room was another fifteen metres down the hall. Again Katie had to sit and wait. She could feel herself starting to shake. *How could I have ever thought this might work?* she said to herself. *What a fool I am!*

As she sat, Katie began to yearn desperately for some kokomo. She could not recall ever wanting anything so much. Fearful that she was going to start crying, she asked Bangorn if she could go again to the rest-room. The police-woman accompanied her. At least Katie was able to wash her face.

When the two of them returned, Nakamura himself was standing in the waiting-room. Katie thought her heart was going to jump out of her chest. *This is it*, said her inner voice. Nakamura was wearing a yellow and black kimono covered with bright flowers. 'Hello, Katie,' he said with a leering smile. 'I have not seen you for a long time.'

'Hello, Toshio-san,' she replied with her voice breaking.

Katie followed him into his office and sat down, cross-legged, at a low table. Nakamura was opposite her. Bangorn stayed in the room, standing unobtrusively over in a corner. *Oh, no*, Katie said to herself when the police-woman did not leave. *What do I do now?*

'I thought,' Katie said to Nakamura a moment later, trying to sound normal, 'that a report on our business was long overdue.' She pulled the papers out of the envelope. 'Despite the poor economy, we have managed to increase our profits by ten per cent. In this summary sheet,' she said, handing a page to Nakamura, 'you can see that although the Vegas revenues are down, the local take, where the prices are cheaper, is up substantially. Even in San Miguel ...'

He glanced at the paper quickly and then put it down on the table. 'You don't need to show me any data,' Nakamura said. 'Everyone knows what a superb businesswoman you are.' He reached over to his left and retrieved a large black-lacquer box. 'Your performance has been outstanding,' he said. 'If times were not so tough, you would definitely merit a large rise ... As it is, I would like to offer you this gift as a token of my appreciation.'

Nakamura pushed the box across the table to Katie.

'Thank you,' she said, admiring the mountains and snow inlaid on its top. It was indeed beautiful.

'Open it,' he said, reaching for one of the wrapped candies in the bowl on the table.

Katie opened the box. It was full of kokomo. A genuine smile of delight crossed her face. 'Thank you, Toshio-san,' she said. 'You are most generous.'

'You may sample it,' he said, now grinning. 'You won't insult me.'

Katie put a small amount of the powder on her tongue. It was top-quality. Without hesitation, she pinched a chunk of powder out of the box and held it against her left nostril with her little finger. Closing off the right nostril, Katie inhaled deeply. She took slow, deep breaths while the rush took effect. Then she laughed. 'Whewee,' Katie said uninhibitedly. 'That's great stuff!'

'I thought you would like it,' Nakamura said. He idly tossed his candy-wrapper in the small wastebasket next to the table. *It will be in there some-where*, Katie remembered Franz telling her. *In some inconspicuous spot. Look in the wastebaskets. Look behind the curtains.*

The New Eden dictator was smiling at her from across the table. 'Was there anything else?' he asked.

Katie took a deep breath as she smiled. 'Only this,' she said. She stretched forward, put her elbows on the table, and kissed him on the lips. She felt the policewoman's rough hands on her shoulders moments later. 'That's a small token of my thanks for the kokomo.'

She had not misjudged him. The lust in his eyes was unmistakable.

Nakamura waved Bangorn away. 'You may leave us,' he said to the police-woman as he rose from his sitting position. 'Come over here, Katie. Give me a real kiss.'

Katie checked the small waste-basket as she danced around the table. There was nothing except candy-wrappers in it. *Of course*, she thought. *That would be too obvious. Now I must make this good.* She teased Nakamura first with one kiss, and then with another. Her tongue tickled his lips and tongue. Then she pulled away quickly, still laughing. Nakamura started to follow her.

'No,' she said, backing up toward the door. 'Not yet ... we're just getting started.'

Nakamura stood still and grinned. 'I had forgotten how talented you are,' he said. 'Those girls are lucky to have you as a mentor.'

'It takes an exceptional man to bring out the best in me,' Katie said, locking and bolting the door. Her eyes roamed quickly around the office and landed on another small waste-basket, over in the far corner. *That would be the perfect place*, she said to herself excitedly.

'Are you just going to stand there, Toshio,' Katie said now, 'or are you going to get me a drink?'

'Of course,' Nakamura said, moving toward the hand-carved liquor cabinet under the solitary window. 'Straight whiskey, wasn't it?'

'Your memory is phenomenal,' Katie said.

'I remember you very well,' Nakamura said as he prepared two drinks. 'How could I ever forget all those games – especially the princess and the slave, that was my favourite ... We had such fun there for a while.'

Until you insisted on bringing in others. And golden showers. And even more disgusting things, Katie thought. *You made it clear that I was not enough by myself.* 'Boy,' she barked suddenly in an imperious tone, 'I am thirsty ... Where is my drink?'

A quick frown crossed Nakamura's face before he broke into a wide smile. 'Yes, Your Highness,' he said, bringing her a drink with his head held low. He bowed. 'Is there anything else, Your Highness?' he said obsequiously.

'Yes,' Katie responded, taking the drink with her left hand and reaching aggressively under Nakamura's kimono with her right. She watched him close his eyes. Katie kissed him hard while continuing to arouse him.

She pulled away abruptly. While he was watching her, Katie slowly took off her yukata. Nakamura advanced. Katie stuck out her arms. 'Now, boy,' she ordered, 'turn down those lights and lie over there on the mat, on your back, next to the table.'

Nakamura dutifully complied. Katie walked over to where he was lying. 'Now,' she said in a gentler tone, 'you do remember what your princess needs, don't you? Slowly, very slowly, without any hurry.' She reached down and fondled him. 'I do believe that Musashi is almost ready ...'

Katie kissed Nakamura, caressing his face and neck with her fingers. 'Now close your eyes,' she whispered in his ear, 'and count to ten, very slowly.'

'Ichi, ni, san ...' he said breathlessly.

With astonishing celerity, Katie swept across the room to the other waste-basket. She pushed aside some papers and found the gun.

'... shi, go, ryoku ...'

Her heart pounding furiously, Katie picked up the gun, turned around, and headed back towards Nakamura.

'... shichi, hachi, kyu ...'

'This is for what you did to my father,' Katie said, sticking the barrel of the gun against his forehead. She pulled the trigger just as the astonished Nakamura opened his eyes.

'And this is for what you did to me,' she said, firing three bullets into his genitals in rapid succession.

The guards broke down the door in seconds. But she was too quick. 'And this, Katie Wakefield,' she said in a loud voice, sticking the gun in her mouth, 'is for what you did to yourself.'

Ellie awakened when she heard the keys rustling in the lock on her cell. She rubbed her eyes. 'Is that you, Robert?' she asked.

'Yes, Ellie,' he said. He came into the cell just as she stood up. Robert put his arms around Ellie and hugged her fiercely. 'I'm so glad to see you,' he said. 'I came as soon as Hans told me the guards had abandoned the station.'

Robert kissed his puzzled wife. 'I'm terribly sorry, Ellie,' he said. 'I was very, very wrong.'

It took Ellie a few seconds to gather her bearings. 'They *abandoned* the station?' she said. 'Why, Robert? What's going on?'

'Complete and total chaos,' he said heavily. He looked utterly defeated.

'What do you mean, Robert?' Ellie said, suddenly afraid. 'Nikki's all right, isn't she?'

'She's fine, Ellie ... But people are dying in droves ... And we don't know why ... Ed Stafford collapsed an hour ago and was dead before I could even examine him ... It's some kind of monstrous plague.'

The octospiders, Ellie thought immediately. *They have finally fought back.* She held her husband against her while he wept. After several seconds he pulled away and spoke. 'I'm sorry, Ellie ... There has been so much turmoil ... Are you all right?'

'I'm OK, Robert ... No one has questioned or tortured me for several days. But where's Nikki?'

'She's with Brian Walsh at our house. You remember Brian, Patrick's computer friend? He's been helping me take care of Nikki since you've been gone ... Poor guy, he found both his parents dead the day before yesterday when he woke up.'

Ellie walked out of the police station with Robert. He was talking continu-ously, rambling from subject to subject, but Ellie was able to comprehend a few things from his almost incoherent chatter. According to Robert, there had been over three hundred unexplained deaths in New Eden in just the last two days. And the end was nowhere in sight. 'It's strange,' he muttered. 'Only one child has died ... Most of the victims have been old.'

In front of the Beauvois police station, a desperate woman in her mid-thirties recognised and then grabbed Robert. 'You must come with me, Doctor, immediately,' the woman yelled in a shrill voice. 'My husband is unconscious ... He was sitting there with me eating lunch and he began to complain of a headache. When I came back from the kitchen, he was lying on the floor ... I'm afraid he's dead.'

'You see ...' Robert said, turning to Ellie.

'Go with her,' Ellie said, 'and then to the hospital if you must ... I'll go home and take care of Nikki. We'll be waiting for you.' She leaned over and kissed him. Ellie started to say something to Robert about the octospiders but decided against it.

'Mommy, Mommy,' Nikki yelled. She ran down the hall and jumped into Ellie's arms. 'I've missed you, Mommy.'

'And I have missed you, my angel,' Ellie said. 'What have you been doing?'

'I've been playing with Brian,' Nikki answered. 'He's a very nice man. He reads to me and teaches me all about numbers.'

Brian Walsh, who was in his early twenties, came around the corner holding a children's book. 'Hello, Mrs Turner,' he said. 'I don't know if you remember me ...'

'Of course I do, Brian. And I'm just Ellie ... I really do want to thank you for helping with Nikki ...'

'I'm glad to do it, Ellie. She's a great kid ... She's kept my mind off a lot of painful thoughts ...'

'Robert told me about your parents,' Ellie interrupted. 'I'm terribly sorry.'

Brian shook his head. 'It was so weird. They were both perfectly fine the night before, when they went to bed.' Tears came into his eyes. 'They looked so peaceful ...'

He turned away and pulled out a handkerchief to wipe his eyes. 'Several of my friends say this plague, or whatever it is, was caused by the octospiders. Do you think that maybe ...?'

'Possibly,' Ellie said. 'We may have pushed them too far.'

'Are we *all* going to die now?' Brian asked.

'I don't know,' Ellie answered. 'I really don't.'

They stood in awkward silence for several seconds. 'Well, at least your sister got rid of Nakamura,' Brian said suddenly.

Ellie was certain she had not heard the sentence correctly. 'What are you talking about, Brian?' she asked.

'You didn't hear about it? ... Four days ago Katie assassinated Nakamura ... and then killed herself.'

Ellie was stunned. She stared at Brian in utter disbelief. 'Daddy told me about Aunt Katie yesterday,' Nikki said to her mother. 'He said he wanted to be the one to tell me.'

Ellie could not say anything. Her head was spinning. She managed to say goodbye to Brian and to thank him again. Then she sat down on the couch. Nikki crawled up beside her mother and put her head on Ellie's lap. They sat together quietly for a long time.

'And how has your father been while I've been gone?' Ellie finally asked.

'Mostly fine,' the little girl replied. 'Except for the lump.'

'What lump?' Ellie said.

'On his shoulder,' Nikki said. 'As big as my fist. I saw it there when he was shaving, three days ago. He said it must be a spider bite or something.'

10

'Benjy and I are leaving for the hospital,' Nicole announced.

The others were still finishing their breakfast. 'Sit down, Nicole, please,' said Eponine. 'At least finish your coffee.'

'Thanks anyway,' she replied. 'But I promised Dr Blue we would come in early today. There were a lot of casualties in yesterday's raid.'

'But you've been working very hard, Mother,' Patrick said. 'And not sleeping nearly enough.'

'It helps to stay busy,' Nicole said. 'That way I don't have any time to think...'

'Let's go, Mama,' Benjy said, coming into the room and handing Nicole her coat. While he was standing beside his mother, Benjy smiled and waved at the twins, who had been uncharacteristically quiet. Galileo made a bizarre face and both Benjy and Kepler laughed.

'She hasn't yet allowed herself to grieve over Katie's death,' Nai said softly a minute later, as soon as Nicole had left. 'That worries me. Sooner or later...'

'She's afraid, Nai,' Eponine said. 'Maybe of another heart attack. Maybe even for her sanity ... Nicole is still in denial.'

'There you go, Frenchie, with that damn psychology again,' Max said. 'Don't worry about Nicole ... She's stronger than any of us. She'll weep for Katie when she's ready.'

'Mother hasn't been to the viewing-room since her heart attack. When Dr Blue told her about the assassination and Katie's suicide, I felt certain Mother would want to see some of the videos ... to see Katie one last time ... or at least to see how Ellie was doing ...'

'Best goddamn thing your sister ever did, Patrick,' Max commented, 'killing that bastard. Whatever else anybody could say about her, she had courage.'

'Katie had a lot of outstanding qualities,' Patrick said sadly. 'She was brilliant, she could be charming ... she just had that other side.'

There was a brief silence around the breakfast table. Eponine was about to say something when there was a glow of light at the front door. 'Uh-oh,' she said, standing up. 'I'm going to move Marius next door. The raids are starting again.'

Nai turned to Galileo and Kepler. 'Finish up quickly, boys ... We're going back into that special house Uncle Max made for us.'

Galileo screwed up his face. 'Not again,' he complained.

Nicole and Benjy had barely reached the hospital when the first bombs started falling through the tattered dome. The heavy raids had been occurring daily. More than half of the Emerald City ceiling was now gone. Bombs had fallen on almost every section of the city.

Dr Blue greeted them and immediately sent Benjy down to the receiving area. 'It's terrible,' the octospider physician said to Nicole. 'Over two hundred dead from yesterday alone.'

'What is happening in New Eden?' Nicole asked. 'I would have thought that by now ...'

'The micro-agents are working somewhat slower than predicted,' Dr Blue replied. 'But they are finally having an impact. The Chief Optimiser says the raids should cease in another day or two, at the most. She and her staff are drawing up plans for the next phase ...'

'Surely the colonists will not continue the war,' Nicole said, forcing herself not to think too much about what was occurring in New Eden, 'especially not with Nakamura dead.'

'We feel we must be prepared for any contingency,' Dr Blue said. 'But I certainly hope you're right.'

As they were moving down the corridor together, they were approached by another octospider doctor, the one that Benjy had named Penny because of the round mark, resembling a New Eden coin, just to the right of her slit. Penny described to Dr Blue the terrible scenes she had witnessed earlier that morning out in the Alternate Domain. Nicole was able to understand most of what Penny said, not only because the octospider repeated herself several times, but also because Penny used very simple sentences in their language of colour.

Penny informed Dr Blue that medical personnel and supplies were desperately needed immediately to help with the wounded in the Alternate Domain. Dr Blue tried to explain to Penny that there were not even enough staff members available to handle all the patients in the hospital.

'I could go with Penny for a few hours this morning,' Nicole suggested, 'if that would be any help.'

Dr Blue glanced at her human friend. 'Are you certain you feel up to it, Nicole?' the octospider asked. 'I understand it's pretty gruesome out there.'

'I have been getting stronger every day,' Nicole replied. 'And I want to be where I'm most needed.'

Dr Blue told Penny that Nicole would be able to assist her in the Alternate Domain for a maximum of a tert, as long as Penny accepted the responsibility for escorting Nicole back to the hospital. Penny agreed and thanked Nicole for volunteering to help.

Soon after they boarded the transport, Penny explained to Nicole what was happening in the Alternate Domain.

'The wounded are taken to any building that is still undamaged, where they are examined, treated with emergency medicines if necessary, and scheduled for transportation to the hospital ... The situation has been getting worse each day. Many of the alternates have already given up hope.'

The rest of the transport ride was equally depressing. In the light from the few scattered fireflies, Nicole could see destruction everywhere. To open the south gate, the guards had to push aside two dozen alternates, a few of them wounded, who were clamouring to enter the city. After the transport passed the gate, the devastation around them increased. The theatre where Nicole and her friends had attended the morality play was in shambles. More than half of the structures near the Arts District had been flattened. Nicole started feeling sick. *I had no idea it was this bad*, she was thinking. Suddenly a bomb exploded on top of the transport.

Nicole was thrown out of the car onto the street. Dazed, she struggled slowly to her feet. The transport had been severed into two twisted pieces. Penny and the other octospider doctor were buried in the debris. Nicole attempted for several minutes to reach Penny, but eventually realised it was hopeless. Another bomb exploded nearby. Nicole grabbed her small medical bag, which had been thrown into the street beside her, and staggered down a side-lane in search of a shelter.

A solitary octospider was lying motionless in the middle of the lane. Nicole bent down and pulled her flashlight from her bag. There was no activity in the octospider's lens. She rolled the octo over on its side and immediately saw the wound in the back of its head. A large mass of white corrugated material had oozed out of the wound onto the street. Nicole shuddered and almost gagged. She glanced around her quickly for something to cover the dead octospider. A bomb hit a building not more than two hundred metres away. Nicole stood up and walked on.

She found a small shed on the right side of the lane, but it was already occupied by five or six of the little Polish sausage animals. They chased her away, one of them snapping at her heels for twenty or twenty-five metres. At length the animal was gone and Nicole stopped to catch her breath. She spent a few minutes examining herself and discovered, much to her amazement, that she had no significant injuries, only a few isolated bruises.

There was a hiatus in the bombing. The Alternate Domain was eerily quiet. In front of Nicole, about a hundred metres down the street, a firefly was hovering over a building that appeared to be undamaged. Nicole saw a pair of octospiders, one of whom was obviously wounded, enter the building. *That must be one of the temporary hospitals*, she said to herself. She started to walk in that direction.

A few seconds later, Nicole heard a peculiar sound, barely above the threshold of her hearing. At first the sound did not register in her mind, but the second time she heard the cry, Nicole stopped abruptly in the street. A chill ran down her spine. *That was a baby's cry*, she thought, standing completely still. She heard nothing for several seconds. *Could I have imagined it?* Nicole asked herself.

Nicole strained her eyes and looked in the semi-darkness to her right, in what she imagined had been the direction of the cry. She could make out a wire fence, lying mostly on its side, about forty metres down an intersecting lane. She glanced again at the nearby building. *The octospiders need me in there*, Nicole thought. *But how can I not* ... The cry resounded in the night, clearer this time, rising and falling in amplitude like the typical wail of a desperate human baby.

She walked hurriedly over to the toppled fence. A broken sign in colour was lying on the ground in front of it. Nicole knelt down and picked up a piece of the sign. When she recognised the octospider colours for 'zoo', her heart rate surged. *Richard heard the cry when he was at the zoo*, she remembered.

There was an explosion about a kilometre away to her left, and then another, much closer. The helicopters had returned for another sortie. The baby's wail became continuous. Nicole tried to keep moving in the direction of the cry, but her progress was slow. It was difficult to isolate the wail amid the noise from the explosions.

A bomb burst in front of her less than a hundred metres away. In the silence that followed, Nicole heard nothing. *Oh, no*, her heart cried out, *not now. Not when I am this close*. There was another explosion in the distance, followed by another period of quiet. *It might be some other kind of animal*, she remembered telling Richard. *Somewhere in the universe there may be a creature that sounds like a human baby*.

All Nicole could hear was the sound of her own breathing. *What should I do now?* she asked herself. *Continue the search and hope somehow ... or turn and go back ...*

Her thoughts were interrupted by the return of the piercing wail. Nicole moved as fast as she dared. *No*, she kept saying to herself, her mother's heart torn apart by the desperate cry, *it's unmistakable. There cannot be any other sound like that*. A battered fence ran along the right side of the narrow lane. She crossed through it. In the shadows ahead of her Nicole saw some movement.

The crying baby was sitting on the ground next to the lifeless form of an adult human, presumably its mother. The woman was lying face down on the dirt. Blood covered the lower half of the adult's body. After quickly determining that the woman was indeed dead, Nicole reached down gingerly and picked up the dark-haired child. Astonished by the action, the baby fought against her and split the night with a powerful bawl. Nicole put the child against her shoulder and patted it lightly on the back. 'There, there,' she said as the baby continued to shriek, 'everything is going to be all right.'

In the dim light Nicole could see that the child's bizarre clothes, which were little more than two layers of heavy sacks with holes cut in appropriate places, were smeared with blood. Despite the baby's protests and thrashing, Nicole gave the child a quick examination. Except for a flesh wound in the leg and the filth that covered her entire body, the little girl appeared to be all right. Nicole estimated that she was about a year old.

Ever so gently, Nicole laid the girl down on a small fresh cloth taken from the medical bag. While Nicole was cleaning up the child, she felt the girl jerk and recoil each time a bomb exploded in the vicinity. Nicole tried to soothe her by singing Brahms's Lullaby. Once during the time that Nicole was dressing the leg-wound, the girl stopped crying temporarily and stared at Nicole with her huge, surprisingly blue eyes. She offered no protest even when Nicole took a damp cleansing-pad and began to wipe the dirt off her skin. A little later, however, when Nicole was cleaning underneath the girl's shirts of sackcloth and found, to her astonishment, a small rope necklace against the baby's tiny chest, the child started howling again.

Nicole gathered the crying baby in her arms and stood up. *She is undoubtedly hungry*, Nicole thought, looking around the area for some kind of hut or shelter. *There must be some food near by.* Under a deep overhanging rock about fifteen metres away, which had clearly been an enclosed area before the bombing raids began, Nicole found a large pan of water, some small objects of unknown purpose, a sleeping pad, and several more of the sacks out of which the clothing of both the woman and the child were made. But there was no food. Nicole tried unsuccessfully to get the girl to drink from the pan. Then she had another idea.

Returning to the body of the dead mother, Nicole determined that there was still some good milk left in her breasts. The woman had obviously died recently. Nicole lifted the mother's torso and slid in behind her on the ground. Supporting the mother's body against her own, Nicole held the baby girl against her mother's breasts and watched her eat.

The child ate hungrily. In the middle of the feeding, a bomb blast illuminated the dead woman's features. It was the same face Nicole had seen in the octospider painting in Artisan's Square. *So I did not imagine it*, Nicole thought.

The baby girl fell asleep when she was finished nursing. Nicole wrapped her in one of the extra sacks and placed her softly on the ground. Nicole now examined the dead mother thoroughly for the first time. Based on the gaping wounds in the woman's lower mid-section and right thigh, Nicole surmised that two large pieces of a single bomb had torn through her and that she had subsequently bled to death. While she was inspecting the thigh wound, Nicole felt a strange bulge in the woman's right buttock. Curious, she lifted the woman's body slightly off the ground and ran her fingers over and around the bulge. It felt as if some hard object had been implanted underneath the skin.

Nicole retrieved her medical bag and then, with her small scissors, made an incision just to one side of the bulge. She pulled out an object that appeared to be silver in the dim light. It was the size and shape of a small cigar, twelve to fifteen centimetres in length, and about two centimetres in diameter. A puzzled Nicole twirled the object around in her right hand and tried to imagine what it could be. It was incredibly smooth, with no discernible breaks anywhere. *Probably this is some kind of identifier for the zoo*, she was thinking when a bomb exploded nearby, waking the sleeping girl.

Over in the direction of the Emerald City, bombs were falling with increasing intensity. While Nicole comforted the child, she thought about what she should do next. A large fireball raced toward the sky as one of the falling bombs caused an even larger explosion on the ground. In the temporary light, Nicole could see that she and the child were on the top of a small hill, very close to the edge of the developed part of the Alternate Domain. The Central Plain began no more than a hundred metres to the west.

Nicole stood up with the girl on her shoulder. She was near exhaustion. 'We're going out there, away from the bombs,' she said out loud to the baby, motioning in the direction of the Central Plain. Nicole tossed the cylindrical object in her medical bag and grabbed a pair of the clean sacks. *These may be useful in the cold*, Nicole thought, throwing the heavy sacks over her shoulders.

It took an hour for her to trudge with the baby and the sacks to a spot in the Central Plain that Nicole thought was far enough away from the bombs. She lay down on her back, the child cradled on her chest, and wrapped the sacks around both of them. Nicole was asleep in seconds.

Nicole was awakened by the movement of the girl. She had been having a conversation with Katie in her dream, but Nicole could not recall what they had been saying to each other. She sat up and changed the baby, using a clean cloth from her medical bag. The child stared at Nicole curiously with her wide blue eyes. 'Good morning, little girl, whoever you are,' Nicole said brightly. The child smiled for the first time.

It was no longer completely dark. Firefly clusters illuminated the Emerald City in the distance, and the gaping holes in the dome allowed the light to shine on the surrounding area of Rama. *The war must have ended*, Nicole thought, *or at least the raids. Otherwise there would not be so much light in the city.*

'Well, my newest friend,' Nicole said, standing up and stretching after placing the baby carefully on one of the clean sacks, 'let's see what adventures are in store for us today.'

The girl quickly crawled off the sack into the dirt of the Central Plain. Nicole picked her up and replaced her in the middle of the sack. Again she crawled toward the dirt. 'Whoa, there, little one,' Nicole said with a laugh, picking the girl up a second time.

It was difficult for Nicole to gather up their belongings while she was holding the child in her arms. Eventually she succeeded and began walking slowly toward civilization. They were about three hundred metres from the closest buildings of the Alternate Domain. During her walk, Nicole decided that she would go first to the hospital to find Dr Blue. Assuming that she had correctly concluded that the war was over or at least had been temporarily halted, Nicole planned to spend the morning finding out everything she could about the child. *Who were her parents,* Nicole formed the questions in her mind, *and how long ago were they kidnapped from New Eden?* She was angry with the octospiders. *Why didn't you tell me there were other human beings in the Emerald City?* Nicole intended to ask the Chief Optimiser. *And how can you defend the way you treated this child and her mother?*

The girl, who was wide awake, would not sit still in Nicole's arms. Nicole became uncomfortable. She decided to stop for a rest. While the child was playing in the dirt, Nicole stared at the destruction in front of her, both in the Alternate Domain and, in the distance, in the part of the Emerald City that she could see. Nicole suddenly felt very sad. *What is it all for?* she asked herself. An image of Katie entered her mind, but Nicole pushed it aside, choosing instead to sit down in the dirt and entertain the child. Five minutes later they heard the whistle.

The sound was coming from the sky, from Rama itself. Nicole jumped to her feet, her pulse immediately skyrocketing. She felt a slight pain in her chest, but nothing could diminish her excitement. 'Look,' she shouted to the baby girl, 'look over there, in the south!'

In the distant southern bowl, streamers of coloured light were playing around the tip of the Big Horn, the massive spire that thrust upward along the spin axis of the cylindrical spacecraft. The streamers coalesced and formed a red ring near the tip of the spire. A few moments later this huge red ring sailed slowly north along the axis of Rama. Around the Big Horn, more colours danced until they formed into a second ring, orange in colour, which eventually followed the red ring, also in a northerly direction in the sky of Rama.

The whistle continued. It was not a harsh or shrill whistle. To Nicole it almost sounded musical. 'Something's going to happen,' Nicole said exultantly to the girl, 'something good!'

The little girl had no idea what was occurring, but she laughed heartily when the woman picked her up and tossed her skyward. And for her the rings were definitely eye-catching. Now a yellow and a green ring were both crossing the black sky of Rama, and the red one in the front of the procession had just reached the Cylindrical Sea.

Again Nicole tossed the child a foot or two in the air. This time the girl's necklace escaped from under her shirts and nearly flew off her head. Nicole caught the girl and gave her a hug. 'I had almost forgotten about your necklace,' Nicole said. 'Now that we have some decent light, may I take a look at it?'

The girl giggled as Nicole pulled the rope necklace over her head. At the bottom of the necklace, carved on a round piece of wood about four centimetres in diameter, was the outline of a man with arms upraised, surrounded on all sides by what appeared to be a fire. Nicole had seen a similar wood carving many years before, on Michael O'Toole's desk in his room inside the Newton. *Saint Michael of Siena*, Nicole said to herself, turning the carving over.

On the back the word 'Maria' was carefully printed in lower-case letters. 'That must be your name,' Nicole said to the girl. 'Maria ... Maria.' There was no indication of recognition. The child started to frown just before Nicole laughed and tossed her into the air one more time.

A few minutes later Nicole put the squirming child down again. Maria immediately crawled into the dirt. Nicole kept one eye on Maria and one eye on the coloured rings in the Rama sky. All eight rings could now be seen, the blue, brown, pink, and purple over the Southern Hemicylinder and the first four in the line in the sky above the north. As the red ring vanished in the northern bowl, another red ring formed at the tip of the Big Horn.

Just like all those years ago, Nicole thought. But her mind was not really focused on the rings yet. She was searching her memory, trying to remember every missing persons report that had ever been filed in New Eden. There had been a handful of boating accidents on Lake Shakespeare, she recalled, and every now and then one of the patients in the mental hospital at Avalon had disappeared ... *But how could a couple vanish like that? And where was Maria's father?* There were many questions that Nicole wanted to ask the octospiders.

The dazzling rings continued to float above her head. Nicole remembered that day long ago when Katie, as a girl of ten or eleven, had been so thrilled by the huge rings in the sky that she had screamed with joy. *She was always my most uninhibited child*, Nicole thought, unable to stop herself. *Her laugh was so complete, so genuine ... Katie had so much potential.*

Tears filled Nicole's eyes. She wiped them away and with great effort Nicole forced herself to concentrate on Maria. The child was sitting down, merrily eating the dirt from the Central Plain. 'No, Maria,' Nicole said, gently touching the child's hands. 'That's dirty.'

The girl screwed up her beautiful face and began to cry. *Like Katie*, Nicole thought immediately. *She couldn't stand me telling her 'No'.* Memories of Katie now flooded into her mind. Nicole saw her daughter first as a baby, then as a precocious early adolescent at The Node, and finally as a young woman in New Eden. The deep heartache that accompanied the images of her lost daughter completely overwhelmed Nicole. Tears ran down her cheeks and her body began to shake with sobs. 'Oh, Katie,' Nicole yelled out loud. '*Why? Why? Why?*'

She buried her face in her hands. Maria had stopped crying and was giving Nicole a strange look.

'It's all right, Nicole,' a voice behind her said. 'It will all be over soon.'

Nicole thought her mind was playing tricks. She turned around slowly. The Eagle was approaching with outstretched arms.

The third red ring had reached the northern bowl and there were no more coloured lights around the Big Horn. 'So will all the lights come on when the rings are finished?' Nicole asked The Eagle.

'What a good memory,' he said. 'You might be right.'

Nicole was again holding Maria in her arms. She kissed the child gently on the cheek and Maria smiled. 'Thank you for the girl,' Nicole said. 'She is wonderful ... and I understand what you're telling me.'

The Eagle faced Nicole. 'What are you talking about?' he said. 'We didn't have anything to do with the child.'

Nicole searched the alien's mystical blue eyes with her own. She had never seen a pair of eyes that had such a wide range of expression. But Nicole had had no recent practice reading what The Eagle was saying with his eyes. Was he teasing her about Maria? Or was he serious? Surely it wasn't just chance that she discovered the child so soon after Katie killed herself ...

You're being too rigid in your thinking, Nicole recalled Richard saying to her at The Node. *Just because The Eagle is not biological like you and me does not mean that he's not alive. He's a robot all right, but he's much smarter than we are ... and much more subtle ...*

'So have you been hiding in Rama all this time?' Nicole asked several seconds later.

'No,' The Eagle replied. He did not elaborate.

Nicole smiled. 'You've already told me that we haven't reached The Node or an equivalent place, and I'm certain that you didn't just drop by for a social visit ... Are you going to tell me why you *are* here?'

'This is a stage two intercession,' The Eagle said. 'We have decided to interrupt the observation process.'

'OK,' Nicole said, placing Maria back down on the ground, 'I understand the concept. But what exactly will happen now?'

'Everyone will go to sleep,' The Eagle said.

'And after they awaken? ... ' Nicole asked.

'All I can tell you is that everyone will go to sleep.'

Nicole stepped away in the direction of the Emerald City and raised her arms to the sky. Only three coloured rings remained now, and they were all far away, over above the Northern Hemicylinder. 'Just out of curiosity – I'm not complaining, you understand ...' Nicole said with a trace of sarcasm. She paused and turned around to face The Eagle. 'Why didn't you intercede a long time ago? *Before* all this' – she waved her arm towards the Emerald City – 'occurred? *Before* there were so many deaths ...'

The Eagle didn't answer immediately. 'You can't have it both ways, Nicole,' he said at length. 'You can't have both free will and a benevolent higher power who protects you from yourself.'

'Excuse me,' Nicole said with a puzzled look on her face. 'Did I mistakenly ask a religious question?'

'Not really,' The Eagle replied. 'What you must understand is that our objective is to develop a complete catalogue of all the spacefarers in this region of the Galaxy. We are not judgemental. We are scientists. We do not care if it is your natural predilection to destroy yourself. We *do* care, however, if the likely future return from *our* project no longer justifies the significant resources we have assigned.'

'Huh?' said Nicole. 'Are you telling me that you're not interceding to stop the bloodshed, but for some other reason?'

'Yes,' said The Eagle. 'However, I'm going to change the subject because our time is extremely limited. The lights will be coming on in two more minutes. You will be asleep a minute after that ... If you have anything you wish to communicate to the girl child ...'

'Are we going to *die*?' Nicole said, suddenly frightened.

'Not immediately,' said The Eagle. 'But I cannot guarantee that everyone will live through the sleeping-period.'

Nicole dropped down in the dirt beside the girl. Maria had another clod in her mouth and wet dirt lined her lips. Nicole wiped her face off very gently and offered the child a drink of water from a cup. To Nicole's surprise, Maria sipped at the water, spilling it down her chin.

Nicole smiled and Maria giggled. Nicole stuck her finger under the girl's chin and tickled her. Maria's giggles erupted into laughter, the pure, uninhibited, magical laughter of the small child. The sound was so beautiful, and touched Nicole so deeply, that her eyes filled up with tears. *If that's the last sound I ever hear*, she thought, *it's all right* ...

Suddenly all of Rama was filled with light. It was an awesome spectacle. The Big Horn and its six surrounding acolytes, attached by massive flying buttresses, dominated the sky above them. 'Forty-five seconds?' Nicole said to The Eagle.

The alien bird-man nodded. Nicole reached over and picked up the girl. 'I know that nothing that has happened to you recently makes any sense, Maria,' Nicole said, holding the child in her lap, 'but I want you to know that you have already been terribly important in my life and I love you very much.'

There was a look of astonishing wisdom in the little girl's eyes. She leaned forward and put her head on Nicole's shoulder. For a few seconds Nicole did not know what to do. Then she began patting Maria on the back. And singing softly. 'Lay thee down ... Now and rest ... May thy slumber be blessed ...'

RETURN TO THE NODE

1

The dreams came before the light. They were disconnected dreams, random images sometimes expanding into short, unified sets without apparent purpose or direction. colours and geometric patterns were the earliest dreams she remembered. Nicole could not recall when they had started. At some point she had thought for the first time, *I am Nicole. I must still be alive*, but that had been long ago. Since then she had seen, in her mind's eye, entire scenes, including the faces of other people. Some she had recognised. *That's Omeh*, she had said to herself. *That's my father*. She had felt sadness as she had awakened more each time. Richard had been in her last several dreams. And Katie. *They're both dead*, Nicole had remembered. *They died before I went to sleep.*

When she opened her eyes, she could still see nothing. The darkness was complete. Slowly Nicole became more aware of her surroundings. She dropped her hands beside her and felt the soft texture of the foam with her fingers. She turned over on her side with very little effort. *I must be weightless*, Nicole thought, her mind beginning to function after years of being dormant. *But where am I?* she asked herself before falling asleep again.

The next time she awakened, Nicole could see a solitary light source at the other end of the closed container in which she was lying. She wiggled her feet free of the white foam and held them up in front of the light. They were both covered with clear slippers. She stretched out to see if she could touch the light source with her toes, but it was too far away.

Nicole put her hands in front of her eyes. The light was so dim that she could not see any details, only a dark outline that silhouetted all the fingers. There was not enough room in the container for her to sit up, but she could manage to reach the top with one hand, if she propped herself up with the other. Nicole pressed her fingers against the soft foam. Behind the foam was a hard surface, wood or possibly even metal.

The slight activity wore her out. She was breathing rapidly and her heart rate had increased. Her mind became more alert. Nicole remembered clearly the last moments before she had gone to sleep in Rama. *The Eagle came*, she thought, *just after I found that baby girl in the Alternate Domain .... So where am I now? And how long have I slept?*

She heard a gentle knocking on the container and lay back down in the foam. *Someone has come. My questions will be answered soon.* The lid of the container was slowly raised. Nicole shielded her eyes from the light. She saw The Eagle's face and heard his voice.

The two of them were sitting together in a large room. Everything was white. The walls, the ceiling, the small round table in front of them, even the chairs, the cup, the bowl, and the spoon were white. Nicole took another sip of the warm soup. It tasted like chicken broth. Over to her left the white container in which she had been lying rested against the wall. There were no other objects in the room.

'... About sixteen years altogether, traveller's time, of course,' The Eagle was saying. *Traveller's time*, Nicole thought. *That's the same term that Richard used.* '... We did not retard your aging nearly as efficiently as before. Our preparations were somewhat hurried.'

Despite the weightlessness, it seemed to Nicole that every physical act was a monumental effort. Her muscles had been inactive for too long. The Eagle had helped her shuffle the few steps between the container and the table. Her hands had trembled a little while she had drunk the water and eaten the soup.

'So am I now about eighty?' she asked The Eagle in a halting voice, one that she barely recognised.

'More or less,' the alien replied. 'It would be impossible to give you a meaningful age.'

Nicole stared across the table at her companion. The Eagle looked just the same as always. The powder-blue eyes on either side of his protruding grey beak had lost none of their mystical intensity. The feathers on the top of his head were still pure white, contrasting sharply with the dark grey feathers of his face, neck, and back. The four fingers on each hand, creamy white and featherless, were as smooth as a child's.

Nicole studied her own hands for the first time. They were wrinkled and discoloured from age spots. She turned them over and from somewhere in her memory she heard a laugh. *Phthisic*, Richard was saying. *Isn't that a great word? It means more withered than 'withered.' ... I wonder if I'll ever have a chance to use it ...* The memory faded. *My hands are phthisic*, Nicole thought.

'Don't you ever age?' she asked The Eagle.

'No,' he replied. 'At least not in the sense that you use the word ... I am regularly maintained and subsystems that are exhibiting performance degradation are replaced.'

'So you never die either?'

He hesitated for a moment. 'That's not completely accurate,' The Eagle said. 'Like all members of my group, I was created for a specific purpose. If there is no longer a need for me to exist and I cannot be readily programmed to accomplish some new, necessary function, then I will be unpowered.'

Nicole started to laugh but caught herself. 'I'm sorry,' she said, 'I know it's not funny ... but your choice of words struck me as peculiar ... "Unpowered" is such a ...'

'It's also the correct word,' The Eagle said. 'Inside me are several tiny power sources, as well as a sophisticated power-distribution system. All the power elements are essentially modular and therefore transferable from one of us to another. If I am no longer needed, the elements can be removed and used in another being.'

'Like an organ transplant,' Nicole said, finishing her water.

'Somewhat,' The Eagle replied. 'Which brings me to another issue ... During your long sleep, your heart actually stopped beating twice, the second time just after we arrived here in the Tau Ceti system ... We have managed to keep you alive with drugs and mechanical stimulation, but your heart is now extremely weak ... If you want to have an active life for any appreciable additional period, you will need to consider replacing your heart.'

'Is that why you left me in there' (Nicole pointed at the container) 'for so long?' she asked.

'Partially,' said The Eagle. He had already explained to Nicole that most of the others from Rama had awakened much earlier, some as long as a year ago, and that they were living in crowded conditions in another venue not very far away. 'But we were also concerned about how comfortable you might be over in the converted starfish ... We refurbished that spacecraft in a hurry, so there are not many amenities ... We were also concerned because you are by far our oldest human survivor ...'

That's right, Nicole said to herself. *The octospider attack wiped out everyone over forty or so ... I am the only old person left.*

The Eagle had stopped talking for a moment. When Nicole looked at the alien again, his mesmerizing eyes seemed to be expressing an emotion. 'Besides, you are special to us. You have played a key role in this endeavour...'

Is it possible, Nicole thought suddenly, still staring at The Eagle's fascinating eyes, *that this electronic creature actually has feelings? Could Richard have been right when he insisted that there are no aspects of our humanity that could not be eventually duplicated by engineering?*

'... We waited as long as we could to wake you,' The Eagle continued, 'to minimise the length of time that you would have to spend in less than ideal conditions. Now, however, we are preparing to enter another phase of our operations ... As you can see, this room was emptied, except for you, long ago. In another eight to ten days we will begin dismantling the walls. By then you should have recuperated enough ...'

Nicole asked again about her family and friends. 'As I told you before,' The Eagle said, 'everyone survived the long sleep. However, the adjustment to living in what your friend Max calls the Grand Hotel has not been easy for anybody. All of those who were with you in the Emerald City, plus the girl Maria and Ellie's husband, Robert, were originally assigned to two large rooms, side by side, in one section of the starfish. Everyone was told that the living arrangements were only temporary, and that eventually they would be transferred to better quarters. Nevertheless, Robert and Galileo were not able to adapt successfully to the unusual conditions in the Grand Hotel.'

'What happened to them?' Nicole asked with alarm.

'They were both transferred, for sociological reasons, to another, more highly regulated area of the spacecraft. Robert was moved first. He went into a severe depression shortly after he awakened from the long sleep and was never able to break out of it. Unfortunately, he died about four months ago ... Galileo is all right physically, although his antisocial behaviour has continued ...'

Nicole felt a deep sorrow upon hearing the news of Robert's death. *Poor Nikki*, she thought immediately, *she never really had a chance to know her father ... and Ellie, your marriage didn't turn out as you had hoped ...*

She sat in silence, wandering through her collection of memories of Robert Turner. *You were a complicated man*, Nicole thought, *talented and dedicated to your work. Yet on a personal level you were surprisingly dysfunctional. Perhaps a critical part of you died long ago ... in that courtroom in Texas, on a planet called Earth.*

Nicole shook her head.

'I guess,' she commented to The Eagle, 'that the energy I expended to save Katie and Robert from the octospider agents was wasted effort.'

'Not really,' The Eagle replied simply. 'It was important to you at the time.'

Nicole smiled and looked at her alien colleague. *Well, my omniscient friend*, she thought, stifling a yawn. *I must admit I'm glad to be back in your company ... You may not be alive yourself but you are certainly wise about living beings.*

'Let me help you back to bed,' he said. 'You've been up long enough for the first time.'

Nicole was very pleased with herself. She had finally managed a full lap around the perimeter of the room without stopping.

'Bravo,' The Eagle said, coming up beside her. 'You are making fabulous progress. We never thought that you would walk so well in such a short period of time.'

'I definitely need some water now,' she said, smiling. 'This old body is sweating furiously.'

The Eagle retrieved a glass of water from the table. When she was finished drinking, Nicole turned to her alien friend. 'Now are you going to keep your part of the bargain?' she said. 'Do you have a mirror and a change of clothes in that suitcase over there?'

'Yes, I do,' The Eagle answered. 'And I even brought the cosmetics you requested ... But first I want to examine you to see how your heart responded to the exercise.' He held a small black device in front of her and watched some markings appear on the tiny screen. 'That's good,' he said. 'No, that's excellent ... No irregularities at all. Just an indication that your heart is working very hard, which would be expected in a human your age.'

'May I see that?' Nicole asked, pointing at the monitoring device. The Eagle handed it to her. 'I suppose,' she said, 'that this thing is receiving signals from inside my body ... but what exactly are all those squiggles and strange symbols on the screen?'

'You have over a thousand tiny probes inside your body, more than half in the cardiac region. They not only measure the critical performance of your heart and other organs, but also regulate such important parameters as blood flow and oxygen allocation. Some of the probes even supplement the normal biological functions. What you are seeing on the screen is summary data from the time interval when you were exercising. It has been compressed and telemetered by the processor inside you.'

Nicole frowned. 'Maybe I shouldn't have asked. Somehow the idea of all that electronic junk inside me is not very comforting.'

'The probes are not really electronic,' The Eagle said, 'at least not in the way you humans use the word. And they are entirely necessary at this point in your life. If they weren't there, you wouldn't survive even one day ...'

Nicole stared at The Eagle. 'Why didn't you just let me die?' she asked. 'Do you have some purpose for me yet that justifies all this effort? Some function I must still perform?'

'Perhaps,' The Eagle said. 'But perhaps we thought you might like to see your family and friends one more time.'

'I find it difficult to believe,' Nicole said, 'that my desires play any significant role in your hierarchy of values.'

The Eagle did not respond. He walked over to the suitcase, which was sitting on the floor beside the table, and returned with a mirror, a damp cloth, a simple blue dress, and a cosmetics bag. Nicole slipped out of the white nightgown she had been wearing, wiped herself all over with the cloth, and put on the dress. She took a deep breath as The Eagle handed her the mirror. 'I'm not certain I'm ready for this,' she said with a wan smile.

Nicole would not have recognised the face in the mirror if she had not mentally prepared herself first. Her face looked to her like a crazy quilt of bags and wrinkles. All her hair, including her eyebrows and eyelashes, was now either white or grey. Nicole's first impulse was to cry, but she gamely fought back the tears. *My God*, she thought, *I am so old ... can this really be me?*

She searched the features in the mirror, guided by her memory, for vestiges of the lovely young woman she had been. Here and there she could see the outlines of what was once considered to be a beautiful face, but the eye had to know where to look. Her heart ached as Nicole suddenly remembered a simple incident years earlier, when she was a teenager walking along a country road with her father near her home in Beauvois. An old woman using a cane had been coming toward them and Nicole had asked her father if they could cross over the road to avoid her.

'Why?' her father had asked.

'Because I don't want to see her up close,' Nicole had said. 'She is old and ugly ... She makes me shiver.'

'You too will be old someday,' her father had answered, refusing to cross the road.

I am old and ugly, Nicole thought. *I even make myself shiver*. She handed the mirror back to The Eagle. 'You warned me,' she said wistfully. 'Maybe I should have listened.'

'Of course you're shocked,' The Eagle said. 'You have not seen yourself for sixteen years. Most humans have a difficult time with the aging process even if they follow it day by day.' He extended the cosmetics bag in her direction.

'No, thank you,' Nicole said despondently, refusing the bag. 'It's a hopeless situation. Not even Michelangelo could do anything with this face.'

'Suit yourself,' The Eagle said. 'But I thought you might want to use the cosmetics before your visitor arrives.'

'A visitor!' Nicole said, with both alarm and excitement. 'I'm going to have a visitor ... Who is it?' She reached out for the mirror and the cosmetics.

'I think I'll leave it as a surprise,' The Eagle said. 'Your visitor will be here in a few minutes.'

Nicole put on lipstick and powder, brushed her grey hair, and straightened out and plucked her eyebrows. When she was finished, she cast a disapproving look in the mirror. 'That's about all I can do,' she said, as much to herself as to The Eagle.

A few minutes later The Eagle opened the door on the other side of the room and went outside. When he returned there was an octospider with him.

From across the room Nicole saw the royal blue colour spill out of its boundaries. 'Hello, Nicole. How are you feeling?' the octospider said.

'*Dr Blue*!' Nicole yelled excitedly.

Dr Blue held the monitoring device in front of Nicole. 'I will be staying here with you until you are ready to be transferred,' the octospider physician said. 'The Eagle has other duties at present.'

Bands of colour raced across the tiny screen. 'I don't understand,' Nicole said, looking at the device upside down. 'When The Eagle used that thing, the readout was all in squiggles and other funny symbols.'

'That's their special-purpose technological language,' Dr Blue said. 'It's incredibly efficient, much better than our colours ... But of course I can't read any of it ... This device actually is polylingual. There's even an English mode.'

'So what do you speak when you communicate with The Eagle and I'm not around?' Nicole asked.

'We both use colours,' Dr Blue responded. 'They run across his forehead from left to right.'

'You're kidding,' Nicole said, trying to picture The Eagle with colours on his forehead.

'Not at all,' the octospider answered. 'The Eagle is amazing. He jabbers and shrieks with the avians, squeals and whistles with the myrmicats ...'

Nicole had never seen the word 'myrmicat' in the language of colour before. When she asked about the word, Dr Blue explained that six of the strange creatures were now living in the Grand Hotel and that another four were about to burst forth from germinating manna melons.

'Although all the octospiders and humans slept during the long voyage,' Dr Blue said, 'the manna melons were allowed to develop into myrmicats and then sessile material. They are already into their next generation.'

Dr Blue replaced the device on the table. 'So what's the verdict for today, Doctor?' Nicole asked.

'You're gaining strength,' Dr Blue replied. 'But you're alive because of all the supplemental probes that have been inserted. At some time you should consider ...'

'... replacing my heart ... I know,' said Nicole. 'It may seem peculiar, but the idea does not appeal to me very much ... I don't know exactly why I'm against it ... Maybe I haven't yet seen what remains to live for ... I know that if Richard were still alive ...'

She stopped herself. For an instant Nicole imagined she was back in the viewing-room, watching the slow-motion frames of the last seconds of Richard's life. She had not thought about that moment since she awakened.

'Do you mind if I ask you something very personal?' Nicole said to Dr Blue.

'Not at all,' the octospider said.

'We watched the deaths of Richard and Archie together,' Nicole said, 'and I was so distraught that I could not function ... Archie was murdered at the same time, and he was your lifelong partner. Yet you sat beside me and gave me comfort ... Did you not feel any sense of loss or sadness at Archie's death?'

Dr Blue did not respond immediately. 'All octospiders are trained from birth to control what you humans call emotions. The alternates, of course, are quite susceptible to feelings. But those of us who ...'

'With all due respect,' Nicole interrupted softly, touching her octospider colleague, 'I wasn't asking you a clinical question, doctor to doctor. It was a question from one friend to another.'

A short burst of crimson, then another of blue, unrelated, slowly flowed around Dr Blue's head. 'Yes, I felt a sense of loss,' Dr Blue said. 'But I knew it was coming. Either then or later. When Archie joined the war effort, his termination became certain ... And besides, my duty at that moment was to help you.'

The door to the room opened and The Eagle entered. The alien was carrying a large box full of food, clothing, and miscellaneous equipment. He informed Nicole that he had brought her space suit and that she was going to venture out of her controlled environment in the very near future.

'Dr Blue says that you can speak in colour,' Nicole said playfully. 'I want you to show me.'

'What do you want me to say?' The Eagle replied in orderly narrow colour bands that started on the left side of his forehead and scrolled to the right.

'That's enough,' Nicole said with a laugh. 'You are truly amazing.'

Nicole stood on the floor of the gigantic factory and stared at the pyramid in front of her. Off to her right, less than a kilometre away, a group of special-purpose biots, including a pair of mammoth bulldozers, were building a tall mountain. 'Why are you doing all this?' Nicole said into the tiny microphone inside her helmet.

'It's part of the next cycle,' The Eagle replied. 'We have determined that these particular constructions enhance the likelihood of obtaining what we want from the experiment.'

'So you already know something about the new spacefarers?'

'I don't know the answer to that,' The Eagle said. 'I have no assignment associated with the future of Rama.'

'But you told us before,' Nicole said, not satisfied, 'that no changes were made unless they were necessary ...'

'I can't help you,' The Eagle said. 'Come, get in the rover. Dr Blue wants to have a closer look at the mountain.'

The octospider looked peculiar in her space suit. In fact, Nicole had laughed out loud when she had first seen Dr Blue with the glove-fitting white fabric covering her charcoal body and her eight tentacles. Dr Blue also had a transparent helmet around her head, through which it was easy to read her colours.

'I was astonished,' Nicole said to Dr Blue, who was sitting beside her as the open rover moved across the flat terrain towards the mountain, 'when we first came outside ... No, that's not a strong enough word ... You and The Eagle had both told me that we were in the factory and that Rama was being prepared for another voyage, but I never expected all this.'

'The pyramid was built around you,' The Eagle interjected from the driver's seat in front of them, 'while you sleeping. If we had not been able to build without disturbing your environment, it would have been necessary to awaken you much earlier.'

'Doesn't this entire business just amaze you?' Nicole continued to face Dr Blue. 'Don't you wonder what kind of beings conceived of this grand project in the first place? And also created artificial intelligence like The Eagle? It is almost impossible to imagine ...'

'It's not as difficult for us,' the octospider said. 'Remember, we have known about superior beings from the beginning. We only exist as intelligent creatures because the Precursors altered our genes. We have never had a period in our history when we thought we were at the apex of life.'

'Nor will we, ever again,' mused Nicole. 'Human history, whatever it turns out to be, has now been profoundly and irrevocably altered.'

'Maybe not,' The Eagle said from the front seat. 'Our data base indicates that some species are not significantly impacted by contact with us. Our experiments are designed to allow for that possibility. Our contact occurs during a finite interval, with only a small percentage of the population. There is no continuous interaction unless the species under study takes overt action to create it ... I doubt if life on Earth at this very moment is much different than it would have been if no Rama spacecraft had ever visited your solar system.'

Nicole leaned forward in her seat. 'Do you know that for a fact?' she said. 'Or are you just guessing?'

The Eagle's answer was vague. 'Certainly your history was changed by Rama's appearance,' he said. 'Many major events would not have occurred if there had not been any contact. But a hundred more years from now, or five hundred ... How different will Earth be then from what it would have been ...'

'But the human point of view *must* have changed,' Nicole argued. 'Surely the knowledge that there exists in the universe, or at least existed in some earlier epoch, an intelligence advanced enough to build an interstellar robotic spacecraft larger than our greatest city cannot be cast aside as insignificant information ... It creates a different perspective for the entire human experience. Religion, philosophy, even the fundamentals of biology must be revised in the presence ...'

'I am glad to see,' The Eagle interrupted, 'that at least some small measure of your optimism and idealism has survived all these years ... Recall, however, that in New Eden the humans knew that they were living inside a domain especially constructed for them by extraterrestrials. And they were told, by you and others, that they were being continually observed. Even so, when it became apparent that the aliens, whoever they were, did not intend to interfere in the daily activities of the humans, the existence of those advanced beings became irrelevant.'

The rover arrived at the base of the mountain. 'I wanted to come over here,' Dr Blue said, 'out of curiosity. We did not have any mountains, as you know, in our realm on Rama. And not many in my region of our home planet when I was a juvenile ... I thought it would be nice to stand on the top ...'

'I have commandeered one of the large bulldozers,' The Eagle said. 'Our journey to the summit will only take ten minutes ... You may be frightened in spots because of the steepness of the climb, but it is perfectly safe, as long as you wear your seat-belts.'

Nicole was not too old to enjoy the spectacular climb. The bulldozer, as large as an office building, did not have very comfortable seats for passengers and some of the bumps were quite violent, but the vistas that opened up as the trio ascended were definitely worth the trouble.

The mountain was over a kilometre high and about ten kilometres around its approximately round circumference. Nicole could clearly see the pyramid in which she had been staying when the bulldozer was only a quarter of the way up the mountain. Further away, in all directions, the horizon was dotted with isolated construction projects of unknown purpose.

So now it all begins again, Nicole thought. *This rebuilt Rama will soon enter another set of star systems. And what will it find? Who are the spacefarers who will next walk across this ground? Or climb this mountain?*

The bulldozer halted on a plateau very near the summit and the three passengers disembarked. The view was breathtaking. As Nicole surveyed the scene, she recalled her wonder on that very first trip into Rama, when she had been riding down the chair-lift and the vast alien world had stretched out in front of her. *Thank you,* she thought, addressing The Eagle in her mind, *for keeping me alive. You were right. This experience alone and the memories it triggers are more than enough reason to continue.*

Nicole turned around to face the rest of the mountain. She saw something small flying in and out of some bushy-looking growths, red in colour, that were no more than twenty metres away. She walked over and captured one of the flying objects in her hand. It was the size and shape of a butterfly. Its wings were decorated with a variegated pattern without symmetry or any other design principle that Nicole could discern. She let one go and then captured another. The pattern on the second Raman butterfly was altogether different, but still rich in both colour and decoration.

The Eagle and Dr Blue walked up beside her. Nicole showed them what she was holding in her hand. 'Flying biots,' The Eagle said without additional comment.

Nicole marveled again at the tiny creature. *Something astonishing happens every day,* she remembered Richard saying. *And we are then always reminded of what a joy it is to be alive.*

2

N icole had barely finished her bath when the two biots entered the room. One was a crab and the other looked like a small truck. The crab used a combination of its powerful pincers and its formidable array of ancillary gadgetry to cut Nicole's sleeping-container into manageable pieces. The pieces were then stacked in the bed of the truck. On its way out of the room less than a minute later, the crab grabbed the white bath-tub and all the remaining chairs and piled them on top of the stacks in the truck bed. It then put the table on its own back and disappeared from the empty room behind the truck biot.

Nicole straightened her dress. 'I'll never forget the first time I saw a crab biot,' she commented to her two companions. 'It was on the huge screen in the Newton control centre, years and years ago. We were all terrified.'

'So today's the day,' Dr Blue said in colour several seconds later. 'Are you ready to check into the Grand Hotel?'

'Probably not,' Nicole said with a smile. 'From what you and The Eagle have said, I guess I have enjoyed my last moment of solitude.'

'Your family and friends are very excited about seeing you,' The Eagle said. 'I visited them yesterday and told them you would be coming ... You'll stay with Max, Eponine, Ellie, Marius, and Nikki. Patrick, Nai, Benjy, Kepler, and Maria are next door ... As I explained to you last week, Patrick and Nai have been treating Maria as their own daughter since shortly after everyone awakened ... They know the whole story of how you rescued Maria during the bombing ...'

'I don't know if "rescued" is exactly the correct word,' Nicole said, remembering clearly her last hours in the old Rama spacecraft. 'I picked her up because there was no one to look after her. Anybody would have done the same thing.'

'You saved her life,' The Eagle said. 'Not more than an hour after you left the zoo with the girl, three large bombs devastated her compound and the two adjacent sections. Maria certainly would have been killed if you hadn't found her.'

'She is now a beautiful and intelligent young woman,' Dr Blue said. 'I met her once briefly several weeks ago. Ellie says Maria is incredibly energetic.

According to Ellie, the girl is the first one awake in the morning and the last one in bed at night.'

Like Katie, Nicole couldn't help thinking. *Who are you, Maria?* she wondered. *And why were you sent into my life at just that moment?*

'... Ellie also told me that Maria and Nikki are inseparable,' Dr Blue continued. 'They study together, eat together, and talk incessantly about everything ... Nikki has told Maria all about you.'

'How is that possible?' Nicole said with a smile. 'Nikki was not yet four years old the last time that I saw her. Human children don't retain memories from that early ...'

'They definitely do if they sleep through the next fifteen years,' The Eagle said. 'Kepler and Galileo also have very clear recollections of their early days ... But we can talk while we travel. It's time for us to leave now.'

The Eagle helped Nicole and Dr Blue put on their space suits. Then he picked up the suitcase of Nicole's belongings. 'I've put your medical bag in here with your clothes, as well as the cosmetics you've been using these last several days,' he said.

'My medical bag?' Nicole said. She laughed. 'Goodness, I had almost forgotten ... I had it with me, didn't I, when I found Maria? ... Thank you.'

The trio walked out of the room, which was on the bottom floor of the large pyramid. A few minutes later they moved through the great arched entrance to the building. Outside, in the bright light of the factory, the rover was waiting for them. 'It will take us about half an hour to reach the high-speed elevators,' The Eagle said. 'Our shuttle is parked at the Dock, on the uppermost level.'

As the rover moved away, Nicole turned around and looked behind her. Beyond the pyramid was the tall mountain they had climbed three days before. 'So you really have no idea why the butterfly biots are there?' Nicole said into the microphone in her space helmet.

'No,' said The Eagle. 'My assignment covers only your cycle.'

Nicole continued to stare behind her. The rover passed a set of tall poles, ten or twelve altogether, connected by wires at the top, middle, and bottom. *All this will be part of the new Rama*, Nicole thought. Suddenly it occurred to her that she was about to leave the world of Rama for the very last time. A powerful feeling of sadness swept over her. *This has been my home*, she said to herself, *and I am going away forever*.

'Would it be possible,' Nicole said to The Eagle without turning around, 'for me to see any of the other parts of Rama before we leave for good?'

'What for?' The Eagle asked.

'I'm not exactly certain ...' Nicole answered. 'Maybe just so I can linger for an extra hour in my memories.'

'The two bowls and the Southern Hemicylinder have already been completely remodelled. You would not recognise them. The Cylindrical Sea has been drained and removed. Even New York is in the process of being dismantled ...'

'But it's not completely destroyed yet, is it?' Nicole asked.

'No, not yet,' replied The Eagle.

'Then can we go there, please, just for a short while?'

Please indulge an old woman, Nicole thought. *Even though she does not understand why herself.*

'All right,' The Eagle said, 'but we'll be delayed. New York is in another part of the factory.'

They were standing on a parapet near the top of one of the tall skyscrapers. Most of New York was gone, the buildings bulldozed into heaps by the awesome power of the large biots. What was left was twenty or thirty buildings around one plaza.

'There were three lairs underneath the city,' Nicole was explaining to Dr Blue. 'One for us, one for the avians, and a third occupied by your cousins ... I was down inside the avian lair when Richard came to rescue me ...' She stopped. Nicole realised that she had told Dr Blue the story before and that octospiders never forgot anything. 'Do you mind?' she asked.

'Please continue,' the octospider said.

'During the whole time that we were here, none of us on this island knew that there were entrances to some of these buildings. Isn't that amazing? Oh, how I wish that Richard were still alive and I could have seen his face when The Eagle opened the door to the octahedron ... He would have been so shocked ...

'Anyway,' Nicole said, 'Richard came back inside Rama to find me ... And then we fell in love and figured out how to escape from the island using the avians ... It was such a glorious time, so many years ago ...'

Nicole stepped forward, grabbed the rail with both hands, and gazed around her. In her mind's eye she could see New York as it had been. *Over there were the ramparts. Out beyond was the Cylindrical Sea ... and somewhere in the middle of those ugly heaps of metal was the barn and the pit in which I nearly died.*

The tears came suddenly, surprising her. They poured out of Nicole's eyes and ran down her cheeks. She did not turn around. *Five of my six children were born over there*, Nicole thought, *underneath that ground. Just outside our lair we found Richard after he had been gone for two years. He was comatose.*

The memories came tumbling into her mind, one after another, each bringing a vague heartache and a new flow of tears. Nicole could not stop them. At one moment she was again descending into the octospider lair to save her daughter Katie, at another she was feeling the excitement and exhilaration of soaring over the Cylindrical Sea, attached by a harness to three avians. *We must eventually die*, Nicole thought, wiping her eyes with the back of her hand, *because there is not any room left in our brains for more memories.*

As Nicole gazed out across the broken landscape of New York, transforming it in her mind's eye into what it had been years before, she had a sharp recollection of an even earlier epoch in her life. She remembered a cold late-autumn evening at Beauvois during her last days on Earth, just before Genevieve and she had gone skiing at Davos. Nicole was sitting with her father and her daughter in front of the fireplace in their villa. Pierre had been very reflective that evening. He had shared with Nicole and Genevieve many special moments from his courtship with Nicole's mother.

Later, at bedtime, Genevieve had asked her mother a question. 'Why does Grampa talk so much about what happened long ago?' the teenager had said.

'Because that is what is important to him,' Nicole had answered.

Forgive me, Nicole thought, still staring out at the skyscrapers in front of her. *Forgive me, all you elderly people whose stories I ignored. I did not mean to be rude or condescending. I just did not understand what it meant to be old.*

Nicole sighed, took a deep breath, and turned around. 'Are you all right?' Dr Blue asked.

She nodded. 'Thank you for this,' Nicole said to The Eagle, her voice breaking. 'I'm ready to go now.'

She saw the lights as soon as their small shuttle cleared the hangar. Even though the lights were still over a hundred kilometres away, they were already a magnificent sight against the background of blackness and distant stars.

'This Node has an extra vertex,' The Eagle said, 'forming a perfect tetrahedron. The Node you visited near Sinus did not have a Knowledge Module.'

Nicole stared out the window of their shuttle, holding her breath. It looked unreal, like a figment of her imagination, this illuminated construction turning slowly in the distance. There were four large spheres at the vertices, connected to each other by six linear transportation corridors. Each of the spheres was exactly the same size. Each of the six long thin lines connecting them was exactly the same length. At this distance, the individual lights inside the transparent Node blurred together, so the entire facility appeared to be a great tetrahedral torch in the darkness of space.

'It's beautiful,' Nicole said, unable to find any other words to express the awe she was feeling.

'You should see it from the observation deck of our living-quarters,' Dr Blue said from beside her. 'It is dazzling. We are close enough that we can see the different lights inside the spheres and even follow the vehicles zooming back and forth along the transportation corridors. Many of the residents at the Grand Hotel stay on deck for hours at a time, amusing themselves by making guesses about the activities represented by the movement of the lights inside.'

Nicole felt goose bumps rising on her arm as she stared silently at The Node. She heard a faraway voice, Francesca Sabatini's voice, and a poem that Nicole had first memorised as a schoolgirl.

Tyger! Tyger! burning bright,
In the forests of the night,
What immortal hand or eye
Could frame thy fearful symmetry?

Did he who made the Lamb make thee? Nicole thought as the tetrahedron of light continued to turn. She remembered a late-night conversation with Michael O'Toole while they were staying at The Node near Sirius. 'We must unfetter God after this experience,' he had said. 'And remove our homocentric limitations on Him ... The God who created the architects of The Node must surely be amused by our pathetic attempts to define Him in terms we humans can readily understand.'

Nicole was fascinated by The Node. Even from this distance, as it turned slowly around, the different aspects presented by the tetrahedron were hypnotizing. As she watched, the facility moved into a position where one of the four equilateral triangles forming its empty faces was in a plane perpendicular to the flight-path of the shuttle. The Node looked entirely different, as if it had no depth. The fourth vertex, which was in reality some thirty kilometres beyond the plane on the other side from Nicole, appeared to be a nexus of light in the centre of the facing triangle.

When the shuttle abruptly changed direction, The Node was no longer visible. Instead, off in the distance, Nicole could see a solitary light yellow star. 'That's Tau Ceti,' The Eagle said to her, 'a star very much like your sun.'

'And why, if I may ask,' Nicole said, 'is this Node here, in the neighbourhood of Tau Ceti?'

'It is an optimum temporary placement,' The Eagle answered, 'to support our data-acquisition activities in this part of the galaxy.'

Nicole nudged Dr Blue. 'Do your engineers sometimes speak meaningless gobbledygook in colour?' she said with a smile. 'Our host just gave us a non-answer.'

'We are more humble as a species than you are,' the octospider replied. 'Again, it's probably because of our relationship with the Precursors. We don't pretend that we should be able to understand everything.'

'We have spoken very little about your species, during the time since I awakened,' Nicole said to Dr Blue, suddenly feeling self-centred and apologetic, 'although I do remember your telling me that your former Chief Optimiser, her staff, and all those who prosecuted the war had all been terminated in an orderly manner. Is the new leadership working out all right?'

'More or less,' Dr Blue answered, 'considering the difficulty of our living-situation. Jamie works at the lower echelon of the new staff, and he is busy almost every waking hour. We have not really been able to reach anything like an equilibrium in our colony because there is constant outside friction.'

'Most of which is caused by the humans on board,' The Eagle added. 'We haven't discussed this subject before, Nicole,' he continued, 'but now is probably a good time ... We have been surprised by the failure of your fellow beings to adapt to interspecies living. Only a very few of them are comfortable with the idea that other species may be as important and capable as they are.'

'I told you that soon after we met years ago,' Nicole said. 'I pointed out to you that for a variety of historical and sociological reasons, there is a vast range in the way that humans respond to new ideas and concepts.'

'I know you did,' The Eagle replied, 'but our experience with you and your family misled us. Until we woke up all the survivors, we had reached the tentative conclusion that what happened in New Eden, with the aggressive and territorial humans seizing control, was an anomaly, to be explained by the particular composition of the colonists. Now, after watching a year of interactions at the Grand Hotel, we have concluded that we did indeed have a typical collection of humans inside Rama.'

'It sounds as if I may be entering an unpleasant situation,' Nicole said. 'Are there other things that I need to know before we arrive?'

'Not really,' The Eagle said. 'We now have everything under control. I'm certain your colleagues will share with you the most important details from their experiences ... Besides, the current situation is only temporary, and this phase is almost over.'

'At first,' Dr Blue said, 'all the survivors from Rama were scattered throughout the starfish. In each ray there were some humans, some octospiders, and a few of our support animals that were permitted to survive because of their critical role in our social structure. That was all changed a few months later, primarily because of the continued aggressive hostility of the humans ... Now the living-quarters for each species are concentrated in a single region ...'

'Segregation,' Nicole said ruefully. 'It is one of the defining characteristics of my species.'

'Interspecies interaction occurs now only in the cafeteria and other common rooms in the centre of the starfish,' said The Eagle. 'More than half the humans, however, never leave their ray except to eat, and they studiously avoid interaction even then ... From our point of view, human beings are astonishingly xenophobic. There are not many examples in our data base of spacefarers who are as sociologically backward as your species.'

The shuttle turned in a new direction and again the magnificent tetrahedron filled their view. They were much closer now. Many individual light sources could be resolved, both inside the spheres and in the long, slender transportation lines that connected them. Nicole gazed at the beauty in front of her and sighed heavily. The conversation with Dr Blue and The Eagle had depressed her. *Maybe Richard was right,* Nicole thought to herself, *maybe humanity cannot be changed unless its entire memory is wiped clean and we begin anew, in a fresh environment, with an upgraded operating system.*

*

Nicole's stomach was churning as the shuttle approached the starfish. She told herself not to worry about silly things, but she nevertheless felt uncomfortable about her appearance. Nicole looked in the mirror as she touched up her make-up. She was not able to mitigate her anxiety. *I am old*, she thought. *The children will think I'm ugly.*

The starfish was not nearly as large as Rama had been. It was easy for Nicole to understand why it was so crowded inside. The Eagle had explained to her that the intercession had been a contingency plan and that Rama had arrived at The Node, as a result, several years earlier than originally scheduled. This particular starfish, an obsolete spacecraft that had somehow been spared the recycling process, had been remodeled into a temporary hotel to house the occupants of Rama until they could be moved elsewhere.

'We have given strict orders,' The Eagle said, 'that your entry should be as smooth as possible. We don't want your system taxed any more than necessary. Big Block and his army have cleared the halls and common areas leading from the shuttle station to your room.'

'So you will not be going with me?' Nicole asked The Eagle.

'No,' he replied. 'I have work to do over at The Node.'

'I will accompany you through the observation deck, as far as the entrance to the human ray,' Dr Blue said. 'Then you will be on your own. Luckily your quarters are not far from the ray entrance.'

The Eagle remained in the shuttle while Nicole and Dr Blue disembarked. The alien bird-man waved goodbye to them as they entered the air lock. When, a few minutes later, they moved into a large dressing room on the other side of the air lock, Nicole and Dr Blue were greeted by the robot known as Big Block.

'Welcome, Nicole des Jardins Wakefield,' the giant robot said. 'We are glad that you have finally arrived ... Please put your space suit on the bench to your right.'

Big Block, who was just under three metres tall, almost two metres wide, and constructed of rectangular blocks similar to those played with by human children, looked exactly like the robot that had supervised the engineering tests Nicole and her family had undergone at The Node near Sirius years earlier, before their return to the solar system. The robot hovered over Nicole and the smaller octospider.

'Although I am certain,' Big Block said in his mechanical voice, 'that you will not cause any problems, I want to remind you that all commands given by me or one of the similar, smaller robots are to be followed without hesitation. It is our purpose to keep order in this spaceship ... Now follow me, please.'

Big Block turned around, pivoting on the joints in its mid-section, and rolled forward on its single cylindrical foot. 'This large room is called the observation deck,' the robot said. 'Ordinarily it is the most popular of our common rooms. We have emptied it temporarily tonight to make it easier for you to reach your living-quarters.'

Dr Blue and Nicole stopped for a minute in front of the huge window facing The Node. The view was indeed spectacular, but Nicole could not focus her attention on the beauty and order of the superb extraterrestrial architecture. She was anxious to see her family and friends.

Big Block remained on the observation deck while Nicole and her octospider companion walked along the wide hallway that encircled the spacecraft. Dr Blue explained to Nicole how to locate and identify the places where the small trams stopped. The octospider also informed Nicole that the humans were in the third ray, moving in either direction from the shuttle station, with the octospiders in the two rays immediately clockwise from the station. 'The fourth and fifth rays,' Dr Blue said in colour, 'are designed differently. All the other creatures live there, as well as those humans and octospiders who have been placed under guard.'

'Is Galileo, then, in some kind of prison?' Nicole asked.

'Not exactly,' Dr Blue replied. 'There are just many more of the smaller block robots in that part of the starfish.'

They stepped off the tram together after traveling half-way around the starfish. When they reached the entrance to the human ray, Dr Blue held the monitoring device in front of Nicole and read the output colours on the screen. Based on the initial data that she saw, the octospider used the cilia underneath one of her tentacles to request more information.

'Is something wrong?' Nicole asked.

'Your heart has undergone a few palpitations in the last hour,' Dr Blue said. 'I just wanted to check the amplitude and frequency of the irregularities.'

'I'm very excited,' Nicole said. 'It's normal in humans for excitement to cause ...'

'I know,' Dr Blue said, 'but The Eagle instructed me to be very careful.' There were no colours on the octospider's head for several seconds while Dr Blue studied the data on her screen. 'I guess it's all right,' she said finally, 'but if you experience the slightest chest-pain or surprising shortness of breath, do not hesitate to push the emergency button in your room.'

Nicole gave Dr Blue a hug. 'Thank you very much,' she said. 'You have been wonderful.'

'It has been my pleasure,' Dr Blue said. 'I hope everything goes all right ... Your room is number forty-one, down that hallway, about the twentieth door on the left. The tram stops every five rooms.'

Nicole took a deep breath and turned around. The smaller tram was waiting for her. She shuffled toward it, sliding her feet on the floor, and boarded after a farewell wave to Dr Blue. A minute or two later Nicole was standing in front of an ordinary door with the number forty-one painted on it.

She knocked. The door opened immediately and five smiling faces greeted her. 'Welcome to the Grand Hotel,' said Max, with a wide grin and his arms open wide. 'Come in and give an Arkansas farm-boy a hug.'

Nicole felt a hand on hers as soon as she stepped into the room. 'Hello, Mother,' Ellie said. Nicole turned and looked at her youngest daughter. Ellie was greying at the temples, but her eyes were as clear and sparkling as ever.

'Hello, Ellie,' Nicole said, breaking into tears. They would not be the last tears she would shed during the several hours of the reunion.

Their room was a square, approximately seven metres on a side. Along the back wall was an enclosed bathroom, with a wash-basin, a shower, and a toilet. Next to the bathroom was a large open closet that contained all their clothes and other belongings. At bedtime the sleeping-mats, which were rolled up each day, were removed from the closet and placed upon the floor.

The first night Nicole slept between Ellie and Nikki, with Max, Eponine, and Marius on the other side of the room beside the table and six chairs that were the only furniture in their living-quarters. Nicole had been so exhausted that she had fallen asleep even before the lights had been switched off and everyone else had finished preparing for bed. After sleeping for about five hours, Nicole had awakened abruptly, temporarily uncertain where she was.

As she lay in the dark and the silence, Nicole thought about the events of the previous evening. During the reunion she had been so overwhelmed by her emotions that she had not really had time to sort out her reactions to what she was seeing and hearing. Immediately after Nicole had entered the room, Nikki had gone next door for the others. For the next two hours there had been eleven people in the crowded room, at least three or four of them talking all the time. Nicole had had brief conversations with each person individually during those two hours, but it had been impossible for her to discuss anything in depth.

The four young people, Kepler, Marius, Nikki, and Maria, had all been very shy. Maria, whose stunning blue eyes stood out in contrast to her copper skin and long black hair, had dutifully thanked Nicole for rescuing her. She had also politely acknowledged that she had no memories of any kind from the time period before she went to sleep. Nikki had been nervous and diffident in her brief tete-a-tete with her grandmother. Nicole thought she had detected some fear in Nikki's eyes; however, Ellie told Nicole later that what she had seen had probably been awe, that so many stories had been told about Nicole that Nikki felt she was meeting a legend.

The two young men had been polite, but not forthcoming. Once during the evening Nicole had seen Kepler staring at her from across the room with great intensity. Nicole reminded herself that she was the first really old human the boys had ever seen. *Young men in particular*, Nicole thought, *have difficulty with women who are old and phthisic. It shatters their fantasies about members of the opposite sex.*

Benjy had welcomed Nicole with an uninhibited embrace. He had lifted her off the floor with his strong arms and yelled with joy. 'Ma-ma, Ma-ma,' he had said, turning around in circles with Nicole's head above his. Benjy had seemed quite well. Nicole had been startled to discover that his hairline had receded and that he now looked decidedly avuncular. Later she had told herself that Benjy's appearance was really not that surprising, since he was roughly forty years old.

Her greetings from Patrick and Ellie had been very warm. Ellie had looked tired, but she had said it was because she had had a full day. Ellie had explained to Nicole that she had taken it upon herself to stimulate inter-species social activity at the Grand Hotel. 'It's the least I can do,' Ellie had said, 'since I speak the octospider language ... I'm hoping that you'll give me a hand as soon as you have your strength.'

Patrick had spoken quietly to Nicole about his concern for Nai. 'This Galileo situation is tearing her apart, Mother,' her son had said. 'She is furious because the blockheads, as we call them, removed Galileo from the normal living areas without much explanation and without anything that we would call "due process". She is also angry because she is not allowed to spend more than two hours a day with him ... I'm certain she is going to ask you for assistance.'

Nai had changed. The spark and softness were gone from her eyes and she was uncharacteristically negative, even in her first remarks. 'We are living in the worst kind of police state here, Nicole,' Nai had said. 'Far worse than under Nakamura. After you are settled, I have many things to tell you.'

Max Puckett and his adorable French wife, Eponine, had both aged, like everyone else, but it was clear that their love for each other and for their son, Marius, sustained them on a day-to-day basis. Eponine had shrugged when Nicole asked her if the crowded living conditions bothered her. 'Not really,' she had replied. 'Remember, I lived in the orphanage in Limoges as a child ... Besides, I'm just delighted to be alive and have Max and Marius. For years I never thought I would live long enough to have any grey hair.'

As for Max, he had remained his ornery, irrepressible self. His hair too was mostly grey, and he had lost a little of the bounce in his step. But Nicole could tell from his eyes that he was enjoying his life. 'There's this fellow I see regularly in the smoking-lounge,' Max had told Nicole during the evening, 'who is a big admirer of yours ... He somehow escaped the plague, although his wife didn't ... Anyway,' Max had then grinned, 'I thought I'd fix you two up as soon as you have some free time ... He's a little younger than you are, but I doubt if that will be a problem ...'

Nicole had asked Max about the problems between the humans and the octospiders. 'You know,' Max had said, 'the war may have taken place fifteen or sixteen years ago, but none of the humans has any intervening memories to soften his anger. Everyone here lost somebody, a friend or a relative or a neighbour, in that horrible plague. And they can't quickly forget that it was the octospiders who caused it.'

'In response to the aggression of the human armies,' Nicole had said.

'But most of the humans don't see it that way. Maybe they believe the propaganda Nakamura told them and not the "official" war history, presented by your friend The Eagle soon after we were moved here ... The truth is that most of the humans hate and fear the octospiders. Only about twenty per cent of the people have made any attempt to mix socially, despite Ellie's courageous efforts, or to learn anything about the octos. Most of the humans stay in our ray ... Unfortunately, the cramped living-quarters do not help to alleviate the problem.'

Nicole now rolled over on her side. Her daughter Ellie was sleeping facing her. Ellie's eyes were twitching. *She's dreaming*, Nicole thought. *I hope not about Robert* ... She thought again about her reunion with her family and friends. *I guess The Eagle knew what he was doing in keeping me alive. Even if he doesn't have anything specific for me to do ... As long as I don't become an invalid or a burden, I can be helpful here.*

'This will be your first major Grand Hotel experience,' Max said to Nicole. 'Every time I go to the cafeteria during open hours, I am reminded of Bounty Day in the Emerald City ... Those weird creatures that came along with the octospiders may be fascinating, but I'm a damn sight more comfortable when they're not around.'

'Can't we wait until it's our period, Dad?' Marius asked. 'The iguanas frighten Nikki. They gawk at us with their yellow eyes and make such repulsive clucking noises while they are eating.'

'Son,' Max said, 'you and Nikki can wait with the others until our segregated lunch-time, if you want. Nicole wants to eat with *all* the residents. It's a matter of principle to her ... Your mother and I are going to accompany her to ensure that she learns the cafeteria routine.'

'Don't worry about me,' Nicole said. 'I'm sure that Ellie or Patrick ...'

'Nonsense,' Max interrupted. 'Eponine and I are delighted to join you ... Besides, Patrick has gone with Nai to see Galileo, Ellie is over in the recreation room, and Benjy is reading with Kepler and Maria.'

'I appreciate your understanding, Max,' Nicole said. 'It is important for me to make the right kind of statement, especially at the beginning ... The Eagle and Dr Blue didn't tell me much about the details of the trouble ...'

'You don't need to explain,' Max replied. 'In fact, last night after you fell asleep, I told Frenchie I was certain that you would want to mix.' He laughed. 'Don't forget, we know you very well.'

After Eponine joined them, they walked out in the hallway. It was mostly empty. A few people were walking in the corridor on their left, away from the centre of the starfish, and a man and a woman were standing together at the entrance to the ray.

The trio waited two or three minutes for the tram to arrive. As they drew near to the final stop, Max leaned over to Nicole. 'Those two people standing at the ray entrance,' he said, 'are not just passing time ... They're both big activists on the Council ... Very opinionated and very pushy.'

Nicole took the arm that Max offered her as they disembarked. 'What do they want?' she whispered as the pair started walking toward them.

'I don't know,' Max mumbled quickly, 'but we'll find out soon enough.'

'Good day, Max ... Hello, Eponine,' the man said. He was a portly man in his early forties. He looked at Nicole and broke into a wide politician's smile. 'You must be Nicole Wakefield,' he said, reaching out to shake hands. 'We've all heard so very much about you ... Welcome ... Welcome. I'm Stephen Kowalski.'

'And I'm Renée du Pont,' the woman said, advancing and also extending her hand in Nicole's direction.

After exchanging a few pleasantries, Mr Kowalski asked Max what the three of them were doing. 'We're taking Mrs Wakefield to lunch,' Max replied simply.

'It's still common time,' the man said with another big smile. He checked his watch. 'Why don't you wait forty-five minutes more and Renee and I will join you ... We're on the Council, you know, and we would like very much to speak to Mrs Wakefield about our activities ... Certainly the Council will want to hear from her in the very near future.'

'Thanks for the offer, Stephen,' Max said. 'But we're all hungry. We want to eat now.'

Mr Kowalski's brow furrowed. 'I wouldn't do that if I were you, Max,' he said. 'There's a lot of tension at the moment ... After that incident yesterday in the swimming-pool, the Council voted unanimously to boycott all collective activities for the next two days ... Emily was especially incensed that Big Block put Garland on probation and took no disciplinary action of any kind against the offending octospider ... That's the fourth consecutive time that the blockheads have ruled against us.'

'Come on, Stephen,' Max said. 'I heard the story at dinner last night ... Garland was still in the pool fifteen minutes *after* our special time had expired ... He grabbed the octo first.'

'It was a deliberate provocation,' Renée du Pont said. 'There were only three octospiders in the pool ... There was no reason for one of them to be in the lane where Garland was swimming laps.'

'Besides,' Stephen said, 'as we discussed in the Council last night, the specifics of this particular incident are not our primary concern. It is essential that we send a message to both the blockheads and the octospiders, so that they know we are united as a species ... The Council is going to meet in special session again tonight to draw up a list of grievances ...'

Max was becoming angry. 'Thank you for keeping us informed, Stephen,' he said brusquely. 'Now if you'll just step aside, we would like to go to lunch.'

'You're making a mistake,' Mr Kowalski said. 'You will be the only humans in the cafeteria ... We will, of course, report this conversation at the meeting of the Council tonight.'

'Go ahead,' said Max.

Max, Eponine, and Nicole walked out into the main corridor that formed an annulus around the central core of the starfish. 'What's the Council?' Nicole asked.

'A group, self-appointed, I might add, that pretends to represent all the humans,' Max replied. 'At first they were just a nuisance, but in the last few months they have actually begun to wield some power ... They've even recruited poor Nai into their ranks by offering to help solve the Galileo problem.'

The big tram stopped about twenty metres to their right and a pair of the iguanas disembarked. Two of the block robots, who had been standing unobtrusively off to the side, walked out into the corridor between the humans and the strange animals with the fearsome teeth. As the iguanas passed around them back along the wall, Nicole recalled the attack on Nikki at the Bounty Day ceremony.

'Why are they here?' Nicole asked Max. 'I would have thought that they were too disruptive ...'

'Big Block and The Eagle have both explained to full human assemblies, on two separate occasions, that the iguanas are essential for the production of that barrican plant, without which the octo society would be all screwed up ... I didn't follow all the details of the biological explanation, but I do remember that fresh iguana eggs were a vital link in the process ... The Eagle stressed repeatedly that only the bare minimum number of iguanas were being maintained here in the Grand Hotel.'

The trio was near the entrance to the cafeteria. 'Have the iguanas caused much trouble?' Nicole asked.

'Not really,' Max said. 'They can be dangerous, as you know, but if you cut through all the crap put out by the Council, you conclude that there have only been a few incidents in which the iguanas launched an unprovoked attack ... Most of the altercations have been started by humans ... Our boy Galileo killed two of them one night in the cafeteria during one of his violent outbursts.'

Max noticed Nicole's strong reaction to his last comment. 'I don't want to be telling tales out of school,' he said, shaking his head, 'but this Galileo business has really torn our little family apart ... I promised Eponine I would let you talk to Nai about it first.'

The smaller block robots were constructed in the same general pattern as Big Block. A dozen of them were serving food in the cafeteria, and six or eight others were standing around the eating-area. When Nicole and her friends entered, four or five hundred octospiders, including two giant repletes and eighty or so midget morphs eating on the floor in the corner, were sitting in the cafeteria. Many of them turned to watch as Max, Eponine, and Nicole passed through the line. A dozen iguanas, seated not far from the serving line, stopped eating and eyed the humans warily.

Nicole was surprised at the large variety of things to eat. She chose some fish and potatoes, as well as some octospider fruit and their orange-tasting honey for her bread.

'Where does all this fresh food come from?' she asked Max as they sat at a long empty table.

Max pointed up. 'There's a second level to this starfish. All the food for everybody is raised up there ... We eat very well, although the Council has complained about the lack of meat.'

Nicole took a couple of bites of her food. 'I think I ought to tell you,' Max said quietly, leaning across the table, 'that a pair of octospiders is headed in your direction.'

She turned around. Two octospiders were indeed approaching. Out of the corner of her eye Nicole also gaw Big Block hurrying toward their table. 'Hello, Nicole,' the first octospider said in colour. 'I was one of Dr Blue's assistants in the Emerald City Hospital ... I just wanted to welcome you and thank you again for helping us out ...'

Nicole searched vainly for a distinguishing mark on the octospider. 'I'm sorry,' she said in a friendly tone, 'I can't place you exactly ...'

'You called me Milky,' the octospider said, 'because at the time I was recovering from a lens operation and I had excess white fluid ...'

'Ah, yes,' Nicole said with a smile. 'I remember you now, Milky ... Didn't we have a long discussion at lunch one day about old age? As I recall, you had a hard time believing that we humans remained alive, whether we were useful or not, until we died of natural causes.'

'That's right,' Milky answered. 'Well, I don't want to disturb your lunch, but my friend very much wanted to meet you.'

'And to thank you also,' said Milky's companion, 'for being so fair about everything ... Dr Blue says that you have been an example for all of us ...'

Other octospiders began to rise from where they were sitting in the cafeteria and to line up behind the first two octos. The colours for 'thank you' were visible on most of their heads. Nicole was deeply moved. At Max's suggestion, she stood up and spoke to the line of octospiders. 'Thank you all,' she said, 'for your warm welcome. I realiy do appreciate it ... I hope I have a chance to speak to each of you while we are living here together.'

Nicole's eyes drifted to the right of the line of octos and she saw her daughter Ellie with Nikki standing beside her. 'I came as soon as I could,' Ellie said, coming over and kissing her mother on the cheek. 'I should have known ...' she added with a slight smile. She gave Nicole a vigorous hug. 'I love you, Mother,' Ellie said. 'And I have missed you so very much.'

*

'I explained to the Council,' Nai said, 'that you had just arrived and did not fully understand the significance of the boycott. I believe they were satisfied.'

Nai opened the door and Nicole followed her into the laundry area. Using the washers and dryers they had seen in New Eden as a basis, the aliens who had outfitted the Grand Hotel in a hurry had built the free laundry room not far from the cafeteria. Two other women were in the large room. Nai purposely chose to use the machines at the far opposite side, so that she could have a private conversation with Nicole.

'I asked you to come with me today,' Nai said as she began to sort the clothing, 'because I wanted to talk to you about Galileo ...' She paused, struggling. 'Forgive me, Nicole, my feelings on this subject are so strong ... I'm not certain ...'

'It's all right, Nai,' Nicole said softly. 'I understand ... Remember, I'm a mother too.'

'I'm desperate, Nicole,' Nai continued. 'I need your help ... Nothing that has ever happened in my life, not even Kenji's murder, has affected me like this situation. I am consumed by anxiety for my son ... Even meditation does not give me any peace.'

Nai had divided the clothes into three piles. She put them into three washing-machines and returned to Nicole's side.

'Look,' she said, 'I'll be the first to admit that Galileo's behaviour has not been perfect ... After the long sleep, when we were moved over here, he was very slow to become involved with the others ... He would not participate in the classes Patrick, Ellie, Eponine, and I set up for the children, and when he did, he would not do any homework ... Galileo was surly, difficult, and unpleasant to everyone except Maria.

'He never would talk to me about what he was feeling ... The only thing he seemed to enjoy was going over to the recreation room for muscle-building exercises. He has, incidentally, become very proud of his physical strength.'

Nai paused for a moment. 'Galileo is not a *bad* person, Nicole,' she said apologetically. 'He is just confused ... He went to sleep as a six-year-old and woke up at the age of twenty-one, with the body and desires of a young man.'

She stopped. Tears had formed in her eyes. 'How could he have been *expected* to know how to act ...' Nai said with difficulty. Nicole reached out with her arms, but Nai did not accept her offer. 'I have tried, but I haven't been able to help him,' Nai continued. 'I don't know *what* to do ... And I'm afraid now it's too late.'

Nicole recalled her own sleepless nights in New Eden when she had often wept out of frustration about Katie. 'I understand, Nai,' she said softly. 'I really do.'

'One time, only one time,' Nai said after a pause, 'did I ever have a glimpse beneath that cold exterior Galileo wears so proudly ... It was in the middle of the night after the business with Maria, when he returned from his session with Big Block. We were out in the corridor together, only the two of us, and he was wailing and beating on the wall ... "I wasn't going to hurt her, Mom, you must believe me," he yelled. "I love Maria ... I just couldn't stop myself".'

'What happened with Galileo and Maria?' Nicole asked when Nai stopped again for a few seconds. 'I haven't heard the story.'

'Oh,' Nai said, surprised, 'I was certain that someone would have told you about it by now.' She hesitated for a moment. 'Max said at the time that Galileo had tried to rape Maria and that he might have succeeded if Benjy had not come back to the room and dragged him off the girl ... Later Max admitted to me that he might have over-reacted when he used the word "rape" but that Galileo had definitely been "out of line" ...

'My son told me that Maria had encouraged him, at least initially, and that they had dropped to the floor while kissing ... She was still enthusiastically participating, according to Galileo, until he started pulling down her pants ... That was when the struggle began ...'

Nai tried to calm herself. 'The rest of the story, no matter who tells it, is not very pleasant ... Galileo admits that he hit Maria several times after she started screaming and that he held her down and continued to pull off her pants ... He had locked the door. Benjy broke it down with his shoulder and threw himself at Galileo with all his force ... Because of the noise and the property damage, Big Block was there, as well as many onlookers ...'

There were more tears in Nai's eyes. 'It must have been horrible,' Nicole said.

'That night my life was shattered,' Nai said. 'Everyone condemned Galileo. When Big Block put him on probation and returned Galileo to the family unit, Max, Patrick, and even Kepler, his own brother, thought the punishment was too light. And if I ever hinted that maybe, just maybe, beautiful little Maria *might* have been partially responsible for what occurred, I was told by everybody that I was "unbalanced" and "blind to the facts" ...

'Maria played her part perfectly,' Nai continued, with undisguised acrimony in her voice. 'She admitted later that she had willingly kissed Galileo – they had kissed twice before, she said – but insisted that she had started saying "No" *before* he pulled her down on the floor. Maria wept for an hour immediately after the incident. She could barely talk. All the men tried to comfort her, including Patrick. They were all convinced before she even said anything that Maria was blameless.'

Soft bells sounded, indicating that the washing cycle was complete. Nai rose slowly, walked over to the machines, and put the clothes in a pair of dryers.

'We all agreed that Maria should move next door with Max, Eponine, and Ellie,' Nai began again. 'I thought that time would heal the wounds. I was wrong. Galileo was ostracised by everyone in the family, except for me.

Kepler would not even speak to his brother. Patrick was civil, but distant ... Galileo withdrew deeper into his shell, stopped attending classes altogether, and spent most of his waking hours by himself in the weight room.

'About five months ago I approached Maria and basically begged her to help Galileo ... It was humiliating, Nicole,' Nai said, tears entering her eyes again. 'There I was, an adult woman, pleading for favours from a teenage girl ... I had first asked Patrick, Eponine, and then Ellie, each in turn, if they would talk to Maria for me. Only Ellie had made an effort to intercede, and she informed me, after her attempt, that the appeal would have to come directly from me.

'Maria finally agreed to talk to Galileo,' Nai said bitterly, 'but only after forcing me to listen to a harangue about how she still felt "violated" by Galileo's attack. She also stipulated both that a sincere, written apology from Galileo should precede the meeting and that I should be personally present during their discussion to preclude any unpleasantness.'

Nai shook her head. 'Now, I ask you, Nicole,' she said, 'how in the world could a sixteen-year-old girl who has been awake for only two years in her entire life have *possibly* become so sophisticated? Somebody, and my guess is Max and Eponine, had been counselling her on how to behave. Maria *wanted* to humiliate me and to make Galileo suffer as much as possible. She certainly succeeded.'

'I know it seems unlikely,' Nicole spoke for the first time in many minutes, 'but I have met people with incredible natural gifts who know intuitively at a very early age how to deal with any possible situation. Maria may be one of them.'

Nai ignored her comment. 'The meeting went very well. Galileo co-operated. Maria accepted the apology that he wrote for her. For the next few weeks she seemed to go out of her way to include Galileo in whatever the young people were doing ... But he was still a stranger in their group, an outsider. I could see it. And I suspect that he could too.

'Then one day in the cafeteria, while the five of them were sitting together – the rest of us had eaten early and had already returned to our rooms – a pair of iguanas sat down at the other end of their table. According to Kepler, the iguanas were purposely repulsive. They lowered their heads into their bowls, noisily sucking up those wriggling worms they love so much, and then stared at the girls, especially Maria, with their beady yellow eyes. Nikki made some comment about not being hungry any more and Maria agreed with her.

'At that point Galileo rose from his seat, took a couple of steps toward the iguanas, and said "Shoo, go away," or something similar. When they didn't move, he took another step in their direction. One of the iguanas jumped at him. Galileo grabbed that first iguana by the neck and shook it ferociously. It died of a broken neck. The second iguana also attacked, seizing Galileo's forearm with its powerful teeth. Before the blockheads arrived to break up the fracas, Galileo had beaten the iguana to death against the top of the table.'

Nai seemed surprisingly calm as she finished the story. 'They took Galileo away. Three hours later Big Block came to our rooms and informed us that Galileo would be permanently detained in another part of the spacecraft. When I asked why, the super blockhead told me the same thing that he has told me every time since when I have asked the question: "We have determined that your son's behaviour is not acceptable."'

Another sequence of short bells announced that the drying cycle was complete. Nicole helped Nai fold the clothes on the long table. 'I'm allowed to see him only two hours each day,' Nai said. 'Although Galileo is too proud to complain, I can tell that he is suffering ... The Council has listed Galileo as one of the five human beings being "retained" without proper justification, but I do not know if their grievances are being seriously heard by the blockheads.'

Nai stopped folding clothes and put her hand on Nicole's forearm. 'That's why I'm asking you for help,' she said. 'In the alien hierarchy, The Eagle ranks even higher than Big Block. It's obvious that The Eagle pays careful attention to what you say ... Would you, please, for my sake, talk to him about Galileo?'

'It's the right thing,' Nicole said to Ellie, taking her belongings from the closet. 'I should have been in the other room from the beginning.'

'We talked about it before you came,' Ellie said. 'But both Nai and Maria said it was all right for the girl to move back next door so that you could be here with Nikki and me.'

'Nevertheless ...' Nicole said. She put her clothes on the table and looked at her daughter. 'You know, Ellie, I've only been here a few days, but it strikes me as terribly peculiar how absorbed everyone is in the day-to-day trivia of life ... And I'm not talking only about Nai and her concerns. The people with whom I have chatted in the cafeteria, or in the other common rooms, spend an astonishingly small percentage of their time discussing what's *really* going on here. Only two people have asked me questions about The Eagle. And up at the observation deck last night, while a dozen of us were staring out at that staggering tetrahedron, nobody wanted to discuss *who* might have built it, and for what purpose.'

Ellie laughed. 'Everyone else has been here for a year already, Mother. They asked all those questions long ago, for many weeks, but they did not receive any satisfactory answers. It's human nature, when we cannot answer an infinite question, to dismiss it until we have some new information.'

She picked up all her mother's things. 'Now, we have told everyone to leave you alone and let you take a nap today. Nobody should be coming in the room for the next two hours. *Please*, Mother, use this opportunity to rest ... When Dr Blue left last night, she told me that your heart was showing signs of fatigue, despite all the supplemental probes.'

'Mr Kowalski was certainly not happy,' Nicole commented, 'about having an octospider in our ray.'

'I explained it to him. So did Big Block. Don't worry about it.'

'Thank you, Ellie,' Nicole said. She kissed her daughter on the cheek.

4

'**A**re you ready, Mother?' Ellie asked, coming in the door.

'I guess so,' Nicole answered. 'Although I certainly feel foolish. Except for the game yesterday with you, Max, and Eponine, I haven't played bridge for years.'

Ellie smiled. 'It doesn't matter how well you play, Mother. We talked about that last night.'

Max and Eponine were waiting in the hallway at the tram stop. 'Today will be very interesting,' Max said after greeting Nicole. 'I wonder how many others will show up.'

The Council had voted the night before to extend the boycott again for three additional days. Although Big Block had responded to the list of grievances and even persuaded the octospiders, who outnumbered the humans eight to one, to yield more time in the common areas for the exclusive use of the humans, the Council had felt that many of the responses were still not adequate.

There had also been a discussion at the Council meeting about how to enforce the boycott. Some of the more vocal attendees at the meeting had wanted to establish punishments for those who ignored the boycott resolution. The meeting had concluded with an agreement that Council officers would 'actively engage' those humans who continued to disregard the Council's recommendations to avoid interactions with all other species.

The tram in the main corridor was nearly empty. A half-dozen octospiders were in the first car, and three or four more octos plus a pair of iguanas were sitting in the second. Nicole and her friends were the only humans on board.

'Three weeks ago, before this latest round of tension began,' Ellie said, 'we had twenty-three tables for our weekly bridge tournament. I thought we were making a lot of progress. We were averaging five or six new human attendees each week.'

'How in the world, Ellie,' Nicole asked as the tram stopped and another pair of octospiders boarded their car, 'did you ever think up the idea for these bridge tournaments? When you first mentioned playing cards with the octospiders to me, I thought you were out of your mind.'

Ellie laughed. 'In the beginning, soon after we had all settled here, I knew that it would take some kind of organised activity to encourage interaction. People were just not going to walk up to an octospider and begin a conversation, not even with a blockhead or me along as an interpreter ... Games seemed like a pretty good way to stimulate mixing. That worked for a little while, but it quickly became obvious that there was no game at which the most proficient human could match any of the octospiders. Even with handicaps ...'

'Late in the first month,' Max broke in, 'I played chess with your buddy Dr Blue ... She gave me a rook and two pawn advantage to start the game, and still cleaned my plough ... It was very demoralizing ...'

'The final blow was our first Scrabble tournament,' Ellie continued. 'All of the prizes went to the octospiders, even though all the words used were in English! That was when I realised that I had to come up with a game in which humans and octospiders did not play *against* each other ...

'Bridge turned out to be perfect. Each pair consists of one human and one octospider. It is not necessary for the partners to talk to each other. I have prepared convention cards in both languages, and even the dullest human can learn in one session the octo numbers from one to seven and their symbols for the four suits ... It has worked fabulously well.'

Nicole shook her head. 'I still think you are crazy,' she said with a smile. 'Although I will acknowledge a touch of brilliance as well.'

There were only fourteen other people in the card room of the recreation complex at the time the bridge tournament was scheduled to start. Ellie adapted well, deciding to have two separate games, one for the 'mixed pairs,' as she called them, and another contest solely for the octospiders.

Dr Blue was Nicole's partner. They agreed on a five-card major bidding approach, one of six codified by Ellie, and sat down at a table near the door. Because the seats for the octospiders were higher than those for the humans, Nicole and her partner were sitting eye to eye. Or, more appropriately, eye to lens.

Nicole had never been an exceptional bridge-player. She had learned to play originally as a student at the University of Tours, when her father, concerned that she did not have enough friends, had encouraged her to become involved in extracurricular activities. Nicole had also played some bridge in New Eden, where the game was the social rage during the first year after settlement. However, despite some natural flair for the game, Nicole had always thought that bridge consumed too much time and that there were too many other, more important things to do.

It was apparent to Nicole from the outset that Dr Blue, as well as the other octospiders who came to the table with their human partners to play in the duplicate tournament, was a superb card-player. On the second hand Dr Blue played a "three no trump" contract that was exceedingly difficult, using finesses and a terminal squeeze like a human bridge professional.

'Well done,' Nicole said to her octospider partner after Dr Blue made the contract plus one overtrick.

'It's very simple once you know where all the cards are,' Dr Blue answered in colour.

It was fascinating to watch the octospiders handle the mechanics of the game. They removed the cards from the traveling boards with the two last joints of a solitary tentacle, aided by the cilia, of course, and then held their hands in front of their lenses with three tentacles, one on either side and a third one in the middle. To place a card on the table, an octospider used whichever tentacle was closest to the card in question, balancing it among the cilia during iis descent.

Nicole and Dr Blue engaged in their usual lively conversation between hands. Dr Blue had just told Nicole that the new Chief Optimiser had been puzzled by the latest action from the Council, when the door to the card room opened and in walked three humans, followed by Big Block and one of the smaller blockheads.

The woman in the lead, whom Nicole recognised as Emily Bronson, the president of the Council, glanced around the room and then headed for Nicole's table. A move had just been called, and Nicole and Dr Blue had been joined by the octospider Milky and her partner, a pleasant-looking middle-aged woman named Margaret.

'Why, Margaret Young, I'm astonished to see you here,' Emily Bronson said. 'You must not have *heard* that the Council extended the boycott last night.'

The two men who had entered the room with Ms Bronson, one of whom was Garland of the swimming-pool incident, had followed her over to Nicole's table. All three of them were standing over Margaret.

'Emily ... I'm sorry,' Margaret replied with her eyes downcast. 'But you know how I love bridge ...'

'There's a lot more than games at stake here,' Ms Bronson said.

Ellie had risen from a nearby table and now made an appeal to Big Block to stop the disruption. But Emily Bronson was too quick. 'All of you,' she said in a loud voice, 'are showing your disloyalty by being here. If you leave now, the Council will not hold it against you ... If you stay, however, after having been warned ...'

Big Block now intervened and informed Ms Bronson that she and her friends were indeed disrupting the game. As the trio turned to leave, more than half of the humans rose from their chairs to follow.

'This is preposterous,' a voice with astonishing clarity and power said. Nicole was standing in her place, leaning on the table with one hand. 'Sit back down,' she said in the same tone. 'Do not allow yourself to be bullied by a hatemonger.'

All the bridge players returned to their seats. 'Shut up, old woman,' Emily Bronson said in anger from across the room. 'This is none of your concern.' Big Block escorted her and her companions out of the door.

*

'You don't have any idea, do you, Mrs Wakefield, what any of the objects are?'

'Your guess is as good as mine, Maria,' Nicole answered. 'They probably had special meaning, in some way, for your mother. I thought at the time that the silver cylinder implanted under your mother's skin was some kind of zoo identifier, but since none of the zookeeping staff survived the bombing and very few of the records remain, it's unlikely that we will ever be able to verify my hypothesis.'

'What's a "hypothesis"?' the girl asked.

'It's a tentative assumption or explanation for what's happened, when there's really not sufficient evidence to come to any definite answers,' Nicole said. 'By the way, I must say that your English is quite impressive.'

'Thank you, Mrs Wakefield.'

They were sitting together in the communal lounge just off the observation deck. Nicole and Maria were both drinking fruit juice. Although Nicole had been in the Grand Hotel for a week already, this was the first time she had had a private moment with the girl she had found amid the octospider zoo ruins sixteen years earlier.

'Was my mother really pretty?' Maria asked.

'She was striking, I remember that,' Nicole said, 'even though I couldn't see her very well in the dim light. She appeared to have your same colouring, maybe a little lighter, and was of medium build. I would have guessed she was thirty-five years old or maybe slightly less.'

'And there were no signs of my father?' Maria asked.

'None that I saw,' Nicole said. 'Of course, under the circumstances I did not make a very thorough search ... It's possible that he might have been wandering somewhere in the Alternate Domain looking for help. The fence that enclosed your compound had been flattened in the bombing. I worried, when we woke up the next morning, that your father might have been looking for you, but I later convinced myself, based on what I had seen in your shelter, that you and your mother lived alone.'

'So is it your hypothesis that my father had already died?' Maria said.

'Very good,' Nicole replied. 'No, not necessarily ... I wouldn't be that specific ... It just did not look as if anyone else had lived there in your enclosure for some time.'

Maria took a drink of her juice and there was a momentary silence at the table. 'You told me the other night, Mrs Wakefield,' the girl said, 'when we were talking with Max and Eponine, that you presumed my mother, or maybe both my parents, had been kidnapped much earlier by the octospiders, from a place called Avalon ... I didn't understand completely what you were saying ...'

Nicole smiled at Maria. 'I appreciate your politeness, Maria,' she said. 'But you're certainly part of the family ... you can call me Nicole.' Her mind drifted back to New Eden – it seemed so long ago – and then Nicole realised that the girl was waiting for an answer to her comment.

'Avalon was a settlement outside of New Eden,' Nicole said, 'in the dark and cold of the Central Plain. It was originally created by the government of the colony to quarantine those people who had a deadly virus called RV-41. After Avalon was built, the dictator of New Eden, a man named Nakamura, convinced the Senate that Avalon was also a perfect place for other "abnormal" humans, including those who protested against the government and those who were mentally ill or retarded ...'

'It doesn't sound like a very nice place,' Maria commented.

Benjy was there for over a year, Nicole was thinking. He never talks about it. She began feeling guilty about not having spent enough private time with Benjy since she had awakened. *But he has never once complained.*

Again Nicole had to force herself to pay attention to her conversation with Maria. *We old people have drifting thoughts*, she said to herself. *Because so many things we see and hear remind us of memories.*

'I have done some checking already,' Nicole said. 'Unfortunately, all the administrative personnel from Avalon died in the war ... I have described your mother to a few of the people who spent considerable time in Avalon, but none of them remember her.'

'Do you think she was a mental patient?' Maria asked.

'That's possible,' Nicole replied. 'We may never know for certain ... Your necklace, incidentally, is our best clue to your mother's identity. She was clearly a devotee of the order of the Catholic church started by Saint Michael of Siena ... There are some other Michaelites on board, Ellie says. I intend to talk with them when I have the time.'

Nicole stopped and turned toward the observation deck, where a commotion had started. A few humans and a large group of octospiders were pointing out the window and gesticulating wildly. A couple of people raced off toward the main corridor, presumably to bring back others to observe whatever it was they were seeing.

Nicole and Maria left their table, walked up the steps to the deck, and looked out the large window. In the distance, beyond the tetrahedron of lights, a huge, flat-topped spacecraft that resembled an aircraft-carrier was approaching The Node. Nicole and Maria watched for several minutes without speaking as the new spacecraft loomed larger and larger.

'What is it?' Maria asked.

'I have no idea,' Nicole answered.

The observation deck filled rapidly. The doors were constantly opening as more humans, octospiders, iguanas, and even a pair of avians came into the room. The crowd began to press against Nicole and Maria.

The flat-topped vehicle was extremely long, longer even than the transportation corridors connecting the spheres of The Node. Several dozen big transparent 'bubbles' were scattered around its surface. The carrier stopped near one of the spherical vertices of The Node and extended a long transparent tube that fit neatly into the side of the sphere.

The deck was in turmoil. All kinds of creatures were pushing, pressing to move closer to the window. A pair of iguanas leaped upward against the window in the weightlessness and were quickly joined by ten to twenty humans. Nicole began to feel claustrophobic and tried to move out of the way. There was no room through the mob. Nicole was pushed in all directions. She lost contact with Maria. A strong wave caught Nicole from the side and smacked her against the wall. Nicole felt a sharp pain in her left hip upon impact. In the ensuing melee, she might have been trampled and injured even more except that Big Block and the blockheads swept into the mob and restored order.

Nicole was badly shaken when Big Block reached her. The pain in her hip was unbearable. She could not walk.

'It's just part of being old,' The Eagle said. 'You must be more careful.' He and Nicole were alone in her apartment. The others were eating breakfast.

'I do not like being fragile,' Nicole said. 'Nor do I like not doing things because I'm afraid of injuring myself.'

'Your hip will heal,' The Eagle said. 'But it will take a while. You're lucky it's only badly bruised and not broken. At your age a broken hip can make a human a permanent invalid.'

'Thanks for the words of reassurance,' Nicole said. She took a small sip of her coffee. She was lying on her mat with her head lifted up slightly by several pillows. 'But enough about me. Let's move on to more important things ... What is that flat spacecraft all about?'

'The other humans have already started calling it the Carrier,' The Eagle said. 'That's a very appropriate name.'

There was a short silence. 'Come on, come on,' Nicole said in a cranky voice, 'don't play coy with me ... I'm lying here doped up and still in pain ... It shouldn't be necessary for me to drag the information out of you.'

'This phase of the operation will soon be over,' the alien said. 'Some of you will be transferred to the Carrier, and the rest of you will move over to The Node.'

'And what happens then?' Nicole asked. 'And how is it decided who goes where?'

'I can't tell you that yet,' The Eagle said. 'But I will tell you that you will be going to The Node ... Although if you tell anyone else what I have just shared with you, I will not in the future give you any more advance information ... We want the transition to be orderly ...'

'You always want things to be orderly ... Ouch,' Nicole said as she changed positions slightly. 'And I must say you have not given me very significant information.'

'You know more than anyone else.'

'Big deal,' Nicole grumped, taking another sip of coffee. 'By the way, do you have any fancy doctors over there in The Node who can wave a magic wand over this bruise and make it go away?'

'No,' said The Eagle, 'but we can give you a new hip if you like. Or a pseudo-hip, as I guess you would call it.'

Nicole shook her head. She winced as she jostled her hip while putting her coffee cup on the floor. 'Being old is shit,' she said.

'I'm sorry,' The Eagle said. He started to leave. 'I'll look in on you whenever I can ...'

'Before you go,' Nicole said, 'I have one other item of business ... Nai wanted me to ask you to intercede on Galileo's behalf ... She would like him returned to the family.'

'It's irrelevant now,' The Eagle said as he was leaving. 'You'll all be out of here in four or five days ... Goodbye, Nicole. Don't try to walk – use the wheelchair I brought you. Your hip won't heal unless you keep your weight off of it.'

5

I t was early in the morning, before most of the humans had awakened. Nicole had been out in the long hallway for half an hour experimenting with the controls on the arm of her wheelchair. She had been surprised that the chair could move so swiftly and quietly. As she raced past the series of conference rooms half-way down the kilometre-long corridor, Nicole wondered what kind of advanced technology was contained inside the sealed metal box beneath her chair. *Richard would have loved this wheelchair*, she thought. *He probably would have tried to take it apart.*

She passed a few humans out in the hallway, most shuffling along in an attempt at a morning-exercise walk. Nicole laughed to herself as a pair of shufflers moved quickly out of her way. *I must look very strange*, she thought, *a grey-haired old woman zooming down the hall in a wheelchair.*

She turned around just after she drove by the small tram, which was carrying a handful of passengers toward the common areas for an early breakfast. Nicole continued to press the acceleration button on her chair until she was going faster than the tram. The people in the tram stared at her with astonishment as she passed them. Nicole waved and grinned. A few moments later, however, when a door a hundred metres in front of her opened abruptly and two women walked out into the corridor, Nicole realised that it was not safe for her to be driving so fast. She slowed down, still chuckling to herself at the thrill the speed had given her.

As she drew near to her own apartment, Nicole saw The Eagle standing at the end of the ray where it merged with the annulus encircling the starfish. She drove over beside him.

'You look like you're having fun,' The Eagle said.

'I am,' Nicole said with a laugh. 'This chair is a fantastic toy. It has almost made me forget about the pain in my hip.'

'Did you sleep all right last night?' The Eagle asked.

'Much better, thank you,' Nicole replied. 'As you and I had discussed, I slept on my side with my injured hip elevated. Incidentally, whatever you gave last night really reduced the discomfort.'

The Eagle waved toward a lounge on the other side of the annulus. 'Let's go over there, please,' the alien said. 'I would like to talk to you in private.'

Nicole drove her chair across the main annulus until she reached the ramp leading to the lounge. The Eagle, who was walking behind her, motioned for her to continue. A dozen octospiders were sitting around the room. The Eagle and Nicole chose a spot off to the right, where they could be alone.

'The Carrier has almost finished its tasks over at The Node,' The Eagle said. 'Twelve hours from now it will make a short stop near this vehicle to pick up some more passengers ... I will announce after lunch who will be moving to the Carrier.'

The alien turned and looked directly at Nicole with his intense blue eyes. 'Some of the humans may not be pleased with my announcement ... After the decision was made to split your species into two separate groups, it was immediately apparent to me that it would be impossible to achieve a division that would not make some people unhappy ... I would like some help from you in making this process as smooth as possible.'

Nicole studied the remarkable face and eyes of her alien companion. She thought she remembered seeing, once before, a similar look from The Eagle. *Back at The Node*, she recalled, *when I was asked to do the video*.

'What is it that you want me to do?' Nicole asked.

'We have decided to allow a degree of flexibility in this process. Although all the individuals on the list for transfer to the Carrier *must* accept their assignments, we will permit some of those who are assigned to The Node to request reconsideration. Since there will be no interaction between the two vehicles, in the case of strong emotional attachments, for example, we would not want to force ...'

'Are you telling me,' Nicole interrupted, 'that this split may permanently break up families?'

'Yes, it may,' The Eagle replied. 'In a few instances, a husband or a wife has been assigned to the Carrier, while the spouse is on the list for The Node. Similarly, there are some cases where parents and their children will be separated ...'

'Jesus,' exclaimed Nicole. 'How in the world can you, or anyone, arbitrarily decide to separate a husband and a wife who have chosen to live together, and expect them to be happy? ... You'll be lucky if there is not a widespread revolt after you make your announcement.'

The Eagle hesitated for a few seconds. 'There was nothing arbitrary in our process,' the alien said at length. 'For months now we have been carefully studying voluminous data on every single creature currently living in the starfish. The records include complete information from all the years in Rama as well ... Those who have been assigned to the Carrier do not, in one way or another, meet our necessary criteria for transfer to The Node.'

'And what exactly are those criteria?' Nicole asked quickly.

'All I can tell you now is that The Node will feature an interspecies living-environment ... Those individuals who have limited adaptability have been assigned to the Carrier,' The Eagle replied.

'It sounds to me,' Nicole said after a few seconds, 'as if some subset of the humans in the Grand Hotel has been rejected, for some reason, and not found "acceptable" ...'

'If I understand your choice of words,' The Eagle now interrupted, 'you are inferring that this split divides the two groups on the basis of merit. That is not exactly the case. It is our belief that most of those in either group will, in the long run, be happier in the environment to which they have been assigned.'

'Even without their spouses or children?' Nicole said. She frowned. 'Sometimes I wonder if you have really observed what motivates the human species. "Emotional attachments", to use your words, are usually the most essential component in any human's happiness ...'

'We know that,' The Eagle said. 'We had a special review of every single case where families will be broken apart by the split, and we made some accommodations as a result. In our judgment, the remaining family divisions, which are not as numerous as this discussion might suggest, are all supported by the observational data.'

Nicole stared at The Eagle and shook her head vigorously. 'Why was this split never mentioned before?... Never once in all the discussions of the impending transfer did you ever even suggest that we were going to be divided into two groups ...'

'We hadn't decided ourselves until fairly recently. Recall that our intercession with the affairs on Rama took us into a contingency regime in our planning matrix ... Once it became clear that some kind of split would be necessary, we didn't want to upset the status quo ...'

'Bullshit,' Nicole said suddenly. 'I don't believe that for a moment. You *knew* what you were going to do long ago ... You just didn't want to listen to any objections ...'

Using the controls on the arm of her chair, Nicole turned around and faced away from her alien companion. 'No,' she said firmly, 'I will not be your accomplice in this matter ... And I am angry that you have compromised my integrity by not telling me the truth before now ...'

She pushed the acceleration button and started toward the main corridor.

'Is there nothing I can do to change your mind?' The Eagle said, following her.

Nicole stopped. 'I can only imagine one scenario in which I would help you ... Why don't you explain the differences between the two living-environments and let each individual from each species decide for him or herself?'

'I'm afraid we can't do that,' The Eagle said.

'Then count me out,' Nicole said, activating her wheelchair again.

Nicole was in a foul mood by the time she reached the door to her apartment. She leaned forward in her chair and entered the combination sequence on the panel in the middle of the door.

'Hello, Mrs Wakefield,' Kepler said as Nicole entered the room. 'Patrick and Mother are out looking for you. They were worried when they didn't find you in the hallway.'

Nicole drove past the young man and into the room. Benjy came out of the bathroom with only a towel wrapped around him. 'Hello, Ma-ma,' he said with a big smile. He noticed the look of displeasure on Nicole's face and hurried over beside her. 'What's wrong?' he asked. 'You have-n't hurt your-self a-gain? ...'

'No, Benjy,' Nicole said. 'I'm fine. I just had a disturbing conversation with The Eagle.'

'What a-bout?' Benjy said, taking her hand.

'I'll tell you later,' Nicole said after a brief hesitation. 'After you dry off and get dressed.'

Benjy smiled and kissed his mother on the forehead before returning to the bathroom. The sinking feeling in her stomach that Nicole had experienced during her conversation with The Eagle now returned. *Oh my God,* she thought suddenly. *Not Benjy. Surely The Eagle was not trying to tell me that we are going to be separated from Benjy.* She remembered The Eagle's comment about 'limited capabilities' and started to panic. *Not now. Please not now. Not after all this time.*

Nicole thought about a special moment from years earlier, when the family had been at The Node for the first time. She had been alone in her bedroom. Benjy had entered tentatively to find out if he was welcome to join the family on its trip back to the solar system. He had been immensely relieved to discover that he was not going to be separated from his mother. *He has suffered enough already,* Nicole said to herself, recalling Benjy's assignment to Avalon while she was in prison in New Eden. *The Eagle must know that, if he has really studied all the data.*

Despite her conscious attempts to remain calm, Nicole could not stifle the combination of fear and frustration that was rising inside her. *I would have preferred to die in my sleep,* she thought bitterly, fearing the worst. *I cannot say goodbye to Benjy now. It will break his heart. And mine too.*

A solitary tear slipped out of her left eye and rolled down Nicole's cheek. 'Are you all right, Mrs Wakefield?' a concerned Kepler asked.

'Yes, thank you, Kepler,' Nicole said, wiping her face with the back of her hand. She smiled. 'We old people are very emotional,' she said. 'It's nothing to worry about.'

There was a knock on the door. Kepler went to answer it. Patrick and Nai entered the room, followed by The Eagle. 'We found this friend of yours in the hallway, Mother,' Patrick said, greeting her with a kiss. 'He told us that the two of you had been having a conference ... Nai and I were worried ...'

The Eagle walked over beside Nicole. 'There was another subject I wanted to talk to you about as well,' The Eagle said. 'Could you please join me outside for another couple of minutes?'

'I guess I have no choice,' Nicole answered. 'But I am not going to change my mind ...'

A full tram passed The Eagle and Nicole just as they exited from the apartment. 'What is it?' Nicole asked impatiently.

'I wanted to inform you that all the different manifestations of the sessile species, as well as the remaining avians, will be in the group that is transferred to the Carrier this evening. If you still have any desire, as you indicated to me once during a conversation shortly after you first awakened here, to interact with the sessile and to experience what Richard described ...'

'Tell me something else first,' Nicole interrupted, grabbing The Eagle by the forearm with surprising strength.

'Will Benjy and I be separated by this split you're going to announce this afternoon?'

The Eagle hesitated for several seconds. 'No, you will not,' he said eventually. 'But I shouldn't be telling you any of the details ...'

Nicole heaved a sigh of relief. 'Thank you,' she said simply, managing a smile.

There was a protracted silence. 'The sessiles,' The Eagle started again, 'will not be available to you after ...'

'Yes, yes,' Nicole said. 'That's a great idea. Thank you very much. I would like to pay my respects to a sessile ... After I eat breakfast, of course ...'

The smaller block robots were very much in evidence in the ray that housed the avians and the sessiles. The ray was divided into several separate regions by walls that ran from the floor to the ceiling. The blockheads policed the entrances and exits from these regions and were also stationed at each of the tram-stops.

The avians and sessiles lived at the back of the ray, in the last of the separate compounds. Both a blockhead and an avian were guarding the entrance when The Eagle and Nicole arrived. The Eagle jabbered and shrieked in response to a series of questions from the avian. After they entered the compound, a myrmicat approached them. It began to communicate with The Eagle in bursts of high-frequency sound that originated from the small circular orifice below its dark brown, milky oval eyes. Nicole marveled at the fidelity of The Eagle's whistling response. She also watched in fascination as the second pair of myrmicat eyes, attached to stalks raised ten to twelve centimetres above its forehead, continued to pivot and survey the surroundings. When The Eagle had finished his conversation with the myrmicat, the six-legged creature, who resembled a giant ant when standing still, raced down the hall with the speed and grace of a cat.

'They know who you are,' The Eagle said. 'They are delighted that you have come for a visit.'

Nicole glanced up at her companion. '*How* do they know me?' she said. 'I have only occasionally seen a few of them in the common areas, and I have never actually interacted ...'

'Your husband is a god to this species ... None of them would be here if it were not for him. They know you from your images that were inside his memory ...'

'How is that possible?' Nicole asked. 'Richard died sixteen years ago ...'

'But the record of his stay with them is carefully preserved in their collective memory,' The Eagle said. 'Every myrmicat emerges from its manna melon with significant knowledge of the key components of its own culture and history ... The embryonic process that occurs inside the melon not only provides physical nourishment for the growing and developing being, but also passes critical information directly into the brain, or its equivalent, anyway, of the fledgling myrmicat.'

'Are you telling me,' Nicole said, 'that these creatures begin their education before they are *born*? And that there is stored knowledge inside those manna melons I used to eat that is somehow implanted in the minds of the unborn myrmicats?'

'Exactly,' The Eagle replied. 'I don't see why you should be so astounded. Physically, these creatures are nowhere near as complex as your species. The embryonic development process for a human is vastly more subtle and complicated than theirs. Your newborns arrive in the world with a staggering array of physical attributes and capabilities. Your infants, however, are still dependent on other members of the species for both their survival and their education. The myrmicats are born "smarter" and therefore more independent, but they have much less potential for total intellectual development.'

They both heard a shrill sound coming from a myrmicat fifty metres or so down the corridor. 'It is calling us,' The Eagle said.

Nicole moved her wheelchair slowly forward and settled at a speed consistent with The Eagle's walking pace. 'Richard never told me that these creatures preserve information from generation to generation.'

'He didn't know,' The Eagle said. 'He *did* figure out their metamorphic cycle, and that the myrmicats passed information to the neural net or web or whatever the final manifestation should be called ... But he didn't even suspect that the most important elements of that collective information were also stored in the manna melons and passed to the next generation ... Needless to say, it's a very strong survival mechanism.'

Nicole was fascinated by what The Eagle was telling her. *Imagine*, she was thinking, *if somehow human children could be born already knowing the essentials of our culture and history. Suppose something like the placenta contained, in compressed form, enough information ... It sounds impossible, but it must not be. If at least one creature can do it, then eventually ...*

'How much data are passed through the manna melons to the new-borns of the species?' Nicole asked as they drew near to the beckoning myrmicat.

'About one-thousandth of one per cent of the information present in a fully mature specimen like the one in which Richard resided. The primary function of the final manifestation of the species is to manipulate, process, and compress the data into a package for inclusion in the manna melons ... Just how this data-management process works is something we have been studying ...

'The neural net you will encounter in the next few minutes, incidentally,' The Eagle continued, 'was originally just a small sliver of material, containing critical data compressed using what must be a brilliant algorithm ... We have estimated that in that small cylinder Richard carried to New York years ago was an information content equivalent to the memory capacity of a hundred adult human brains.'

'Amazing,' Nicole said, shaking her head.

'That's only the beginning,' The Eagle said. 'Each of the four manna melons carried by Richard had its own special set of compressed data. They all germinated into myrmicats in the octospider zoo. The neural net now contains all those expences as well ... I expect that you're in for quite an adventure.'

Nicole stopped her wheelchair. 'Why didn't you tell me all this earlier? I might have spent more time ...'

'I doubt it,' The Eagle interrupted. 'Your first priority was to re-establish your connections to your own species ... I don't think you were ready for this until now.'

'You have been manipulating me by controlling what I see and experience,' Nicole said without rancour.

'Perhaps,' The Eagle answered.

Nicole was surprisingly fearful when she finally encountered the neural net up close. The Eagle and she were together in a room not unlike the apartment Nicole shared in the human ray. A pair of myrmicats was sitting behind them, against the wall. The sessile net or web occupied about 15 per cent of the room, back in the right corner. There was a gap in the centre of the dense, soft white material that was just large enough for Nicole and her wheelchair. Nicole complied with The Eagle's request to roll up her shirt-sleeves and lift her dress above her knees.

'I suppose,' she then said with some trepidation, 'that it expects me to drive into that space and that it will wrap its filaments around my body.'

'Yes,' said The Eagle. 'And it has been told by one of the myrmicats to release you at your request ... I will stay here the entire time, if that's any comfort to you.'

'Richard,' Nicole said, still delaying her entrance, 'told me that it took a long time for any real communication to develop ...'

'That will not be a problem now,' responded The Eagle. 'Certainly part of the information stored in the original sliver was data about methods that could be used to communicate efficiently with human beings.'

'All right, then,' Nicole said, passing her hand nervously through her hair, 'here I go. Wish me luck.'

She drove into the gap in the cottony network and turned off the power in her wheelchair. In less than a minute the creature had surrounded her and Nicole could not even see the outline of The Eagle across the room. Nicole tried to reassure herself. *This will not hurt me*, she said as she felt first hundreds and then thousands of tiny threads attaching themselves to her arms, legs, neck, and head. As she expected, the density of threads was highest around her head. She recalled Richard's description. *The individual filaments were incredibly thin, but they must have had very sharp parts underneath. I didn't even realise that they were inserted well inside the outer layers of my skin until I tried to pull one off.*

Nicole stared at a particular clump of threads about a metre away from her face. As this ganglion eased slowly toward her, the other elements in the delicate mesh shifted position. A shiver ran down her spine. Her mind accepted, finally, that the net surrounding her was a living creature. It was only moments later that the images began.

She realised immediately that the sessile was reading from her memory. Pictures from earlier in her life flashed through Nicole's mind at a fantastic rate, none lingering long enough even to provoke an emotion. There was no order to the images – a childhood memory from the woods behind her home in the Parisian suburb of Chilly-Mazarin would be followed by a picture of Maria laughing heartily at one of Max's stories.

This is the data-transfer stage, Nicole thought, remembering Richard's analysis of the time he had spent inside the neural net. *The creature is copying my memory into its own. At a very high rate.* She wondered briefly what in the world the sessile would do with all the images from her memory. Then suddenly in her mind's eye Nicole vividly saw Richard himself in a large chamber that had a vast, incomplete mural on its walls. The image became a full motion picture set in the chamber. The clarity of the individual frames was overwhelming. Nicole felt as if she were watching a colour television set located somewhere inside her brain. She could even see the details of the mural. As Nicole watched, a myrmicat directed Richard's attention to specific items in the wall paintings. Around the room a dozen other myrmicats were sketching or painting the unfinished sections of the mural.

The artwork was superb. It had all been created to give Richard information about what he could do to help the alien species survive. Part of the mural was a textbook about their biology, which explained in pictures the three manifestations of their species (manna melon, myrmicat, and sessile or neural net) and the relationships between them. The images Nicole saw were so sharp that she felt she had been transported to the room where Richard had been. She was therefore startled when the internal film she was watching suddenly underwent a jump-discontinuity and presented a picture of the last goodbye between Richard and his guide myrmicat.

Richard and the myrmicat were in a tunnel at the bottom of the brown cylinder. The motion picture lingered lovingly on every detail of this final farewell. The bearded Richard looked overburdened carrying the four heavy manna melons, two leathery avian eggs, and the cylinder of web material in the pack on his back. But even Nicole, seeing the determination in Richard's eyes as he departed from the doomed myrmicat habitat, could understand why he was such a hero to their species. *He risked his life*, she reminded herself, *to save them from extinction.*

More images flooded her mind, pictures from the octospider zoo recording events after the germination of the manna melons Richard had originally carried to New York. Despite their clarity, Nicole couldn't bring herself to concentrate on the images very closely. She was still thinking about Richard. *Not since I awakened have I allowed myself to miss your company, Nicole said to herself, because I thought such behaviour showed weakness. Now, seeing your face again so clearly and remembering how much we shared, I realise how ridiculous it is to force myself not to think about you. If we outlive those we have loved, why cannot it be a perfectly acceptable source of pleasure to relive the highlights of that love?*

A fleeting image of three human beings, a man, a woman, and a tiny baby, raced through Nicole's mind, catching her attention. *Wait*, Nicole almost screamed out loud. *Back up. There was something that I wanted to see.* The neural net did not read her message. It continued with the progression of pictures. Nicole suspended her thoughts about Richard and focused intently on the images appearing on the television inside her brain.

Less than a minute later she saw the trio again, walking with the octospider zoo-keeper past the front of the area housing the myrmicats. Maria was in her mother's arms. Her father, a dark and handsome man with grey at his temples, was dragging one of his legs as if it were broken. *I have never seen that man before*, Nicole thought. *I would have remembered him.*

There were no more images of Maria or her parents. The stream of pictures racing through Nicole's mind showed the transfer of the myrmicats to another venue, away from the zoo and the Emerald City, sometime before the bombing began. Nicole presumed that the last sequence of images she was shown took place during the time that all the humans and octospiders in Rama were asleep. *Not long thereafter*, Nicole thought, *if I understand their life cycle correctly, the four myrmicats resulting from Richard's melons became net material. With all these memories intact.*

The pictures in her mind became altogether different. Now Nicole was seeing some images of scenes that she believed were from the home planet of the sessiles, ones that Richard had once excitedly described to her during their time together after she had escaped from New Eden.

Nicole had purposely positioned her right hand next to the control panel of her wheelchair when she had entered the web. When she now pressed the power button and then reverse, the slight motion of the chair immediately registered with the sessile. The images stopped instantly, and the threads of the creature were subsequently withdrawn.

6

The next day, an hour before the beginning of the lunch period, a part of one wall in each starfish apartment transformed into a large television screen. The residents were then informed that an important announcement was forthcoming in thirty minutes.

'This is only the third time,' Max told Nicole as they waited, 'that we have had any kind of general transmission. The first was immediately after we arrived here and the second was when it was decided to segregate our living-quarters.'

'What's going to happen now?' Marius asked.

'I suspect we're going to find out the details of our move,' Max answered. 'At least that's the leading rumour.'

At the appointed time, The Eagle's face appeared on the monitor. 'Last year, when you were all awakened and moved from Rama,' The Eagle said, simultaneously giving the same message in coloured strips moving across his forehead, 'we told you that this vehicle would not be your permanent home. We are now ready to transfer you to other locations, where your living-conditions will be markedly better.'

The Eagle paused a few seconds before continuing. 'All of you will not be transferred to the same place. About one-third of the current starfish residents will move to the Carrier, that huge, flat spacecraft that has been stationed near The Node for most of the last week. During the next few hours, the Carrier will finish its business over at The Node and move in this direction. Those of you who are transferring to the Carrier will do so after dinner tonight.

'The rest of you will be moved to The Node in another three or four days. Nobody will be left here on the starfish ... I would like to stress again that the accommodations in both places will be excellent and far superior to those in this vehicle.'

The Eagle stopped for fifteen seconds, as if he were allowing time for his audience to react to what he had already said. 'When this meeting is over,' The Eagle then said, 'each of the apartment television screens will repeatedly cycle through the list of all creatures on board, ordered by apartment number, and display the transfer assignments. Reading the displays is very simple. If your name and/or identification code appears on the monitor in black letters against a white background, you will be transferred to the Carrier. If your name is written in white letters against a black background, you will remain here for the next few days and will eventually be moved over to The Node.

'For your information, on the Carrier each species will have its own self-contained living-area. There will be no interspecies mixing, except of course for the required symbiotic arrangements. By contrast ...'

'That ought to please the leaders of the Council,' Max commented quickly. 'They have been agitating for complete separation for months ...'

'... the living-situation at The Node will involve regular interspecies communication and activity ... We have attempted, in assigning individuals to the two locations, to place each of you in the environment best suited for his or her personality. Our selections were done carefully, based upon our observations both here at the starfish and during the years on Rama ...

'It is important that all of you realise that there will be *no* interaction between the two groups after the transfers take place. Let me say that in another way, to make certain there is no misunderstanding. Those moving to the Carrier tonight will *never* again see any of the residents who are going to be transferred to The Node.

'If you have been assigned to the Carrier,' The Eagle continued, 'you should begin packing immediately and should be completely ready to move before you come to dinner. If you are among those who have been designated to move to The Node and do not believe that your assignment is appropriate, you may request that your assignment be reconsidered. Tonight, after all residents currently assigned to the Carrier have completed their transfers, I will meet in the cafeteria with those who think they want to switch from The Node to the Carrier ...

'If any of you have questions, I will be at the big desk in the lounge for the next hour ...'

'What did The Eagle say to you?' Max asked Nicole.

'The same thing he said to the twenty other people in the lounge who were asking the same question,' Nicole replied. 'No changes are possible for those who have been assigned to the Carrier ... Reconsideration will only be given to those scheduled for transfer to The Node.'

'Was that when Nai ... uh, broke down?' Eponine asked.

'Yes,' Nicole said. 'Until then she had held herself together fairly well. When she initially came over to our apartment, after the lists had been shown for the first time, I thought she was remarkably calm ... She obviously must have convinced herself initially that Galileo's assignment was some kind of clerical mistake.'

'I can understand how she must feel,' Eponine said. 'I'll admit that my heart skipped a few beats until I saw that all the rest of us were together on the list to be transferred to The Node.'

'I bet that Nai is not the only one upset by the assignments,' Max said. He stood up and started to walk around the room. 'This is really a mess,' he said, shaking his head. 'What in the world would *we* have done if Marius had been assigned to the Carrier?'

'That's easy,' Eponine answered quickly. 'You and I would both have applied to go with our son.'

'Yep,' said Max after a momentary pause. 'I suspect you're right.'

'That's what Patrick and Nai are now discussing next door,' Nicole said. 'They asked the young people to leave so they could talk in private.'

'Do you think Nai can handle all this additional stress so soon after the ... incident?' Eponine asked.

'She really has no choice,' Max said. 'They only have a couple more hours to make a decision.'

'She seemed much better to me twenty minutes ago,' Nicole said. 'The light sedative had definitely taken effect ... Both Patrick and Kepler were being very gentle with her ... I think Nai frightened herself most of all with her outburst.'

'Did she actually attack The Eagle?' Eponine asked.

'No ... One of the blockheads restrained her immediately when she screamed,' Nicole said. 'But she was out of control ... she might have done anything.'

'Shit,' said Max, 'if you had told me while we were living in the Emerald City that Nai even had the capacity for violence, I would have told you ...'

'Nobody who has been a parent,' Nicole said, interrupting, 'can possibly understand the powerful feelings that a mother has where her children are concerned. Nai has been frustrated for months ... I can't condone her reaction, but I can certainly understand ...'

Nicole stopped. The knock on the door repeated. Patrick entered the room a few seconds later. His face betrayed his anxiety. 'Mother,' he said, 'I need to talk to you.'

'Eponine and I can go out in the hallway,' Max said. 'If that would help ...'

'Thanks, Max ... Yes, I would appreciate it,' Patrick said with difficulty. Nicole had never seen him so upset.

'I don't know what to do,' Patrick said as soon as he was alone with Nicole. 'Everything is happening so fast ... I don't think Nai is being rational, but I don't seem to be able ...' His voice trailed off. 'Mother, she wants us *all* to apply for reconsideration. Everyone. You, me, Kepler, Maria, Max ... All of us ... She says otherwise Galileo will feel abandoned.'

Nicole looked at her son. He was close to tears. *He hasn't had enough life to deal with a crisis like this,* she thought quickly. *He's only been awake for a little more than ten years.*

'What is Nai doing now?' Nicole said softly.

'She's meditating,' Patrick answered. 'She said it would calm and heal her spirit ... and give her strength ...'

'And are you supposed to convince the rest of us?'

'Yes, I guess ... But Mother, Nai has not even considered that anyone might not agree with what she is proposing. She believes that what we should all do is absolutely clear.'

Patrick's pain was obvious. Nicole wished that she could reach out, touch him, and make his agony go away. 'What do you think we should do?' Nicole asked after a period of silence.

'I don't know,' Patrick said, starting to pace around the room. 'Like everyone else, I noticed as soon as the list was posted that all the active Council members were being transferred to the Carrier, as well as most of the humans who had been removed from the normal living-quarters. The people we like and respect, as well as almost all the octospiders except some of the alternates, are going to The Node ... But I sympathise with Nai. She can't bear the thought that Galileo will be isolated, permanently cut off from the only support system he has ever known ...'

What would you do, a voice inside Nicole's head asked her, *if you were Nai? Didn't you panic earlier today when you were afraid that you might be separated from Benjy?*

'... Will you talk to her, Mother,' Patrick entreated, 'as soon as she has finished meditating? She will listen to you. Nai has always said how much she respects your wisdom.'

'And is there anything particular that you want me to say to her?' Nicole asked.

'Tell her ...' Patrick said, wringing his hands, 'tell her it's not her place to decide what would be best for everyone in our group. She should focus on her own decision.'

'That's good advice,' Nicole said. She gazed at her son. 'Tell me, Patrick,' she said several seconds later, 'have you decided what you are going to do if Nai switches to the Carrier and none of the rest of us does?'

'Yes, I have, Mother,' Patrick said quietly. 'I will go with Nai and Galileo.'

Nicole parked her wheelchair in a corner in front of the observation window. She was alone, as she had requested. The afternoon had been so emotional that she felt completely drained. Nicole had thought initially that her meeting with Nai had gone quite well. Nai had listened carefully to Nicole's advice, without much comment. Nicole had therefore been quite astonished an hour later when Nai, seething with anger, had confronted her along with Max, Eponine, and Ellie.

'Patrick tells me that *none* of you are going to come with us,' Nai had said. 'Now I see what rewards I have earned for my steadfast devotion all these years ... I dragged my twin boys away from their own home out of loyalty to you, my friends ... I deprived Galileo and Kepler of ever knowing a normal childhood because of my respect and admiration for you, Nicole, my role model ... And now, when for once I ask a favour ...'

'You're being unfair, Nai,' Ellie had said softly. 'We all love you and are deeply disturbed about this whole thing ... We would go with you and Galileo if we thought ...'

'Ellie, Ellie,' Nai had said, dropping on her knees beside her friend and bursting into tears. 'Have you forgotten all the hours I spent with Benjy out in Avalon? ... Yes, I admit that I did it of my own volition, but would I have given so much of myself to Benjy if he was not your brother and you were not my best friend? I *love* you, Ellie ... I need your support ... Please, please come with us. You and Nikki, at least ...'

Ellie had also wept. Before the confrontation was over, there was not a dry eye in the room. In the end Nai had apologised profusely to everyone.

Nicole took a deep breath and stared out the window. She knew that she needed a break from all the emotional turmoil. Twice during the afternoon she had felt twinges of pain in her chest. *Even all those magical probes*, she thought, *cannot protect me if I do not take care of myself.*

The huge Carrier was now stationed only several hundred metres away. It was an awesome engineering construction, far larger even than it had seemed when it was over by The Node. The spacecraft was parked sideways, so only a part of it could be seen from the window. The top of the Carrier was a long flat plane broken only by small, scattered equipment complexes and the transparent domes, or bubbles, as they had originally been called, that were located in an orderly pattern throughout the length and breadth of the plane. Some of the domes were quite large. One, directly in front of the window, rose over two hundred metres above the flat plane. Other domes were very small. Parts of eleven of the transparent bubbles were visible from the observation window. During the approach of the Carrier earlier in the afternoon, when the entire spacecraft could be seen, a total of seventy-eight domes had been counted.

The underbelly of the Carrier had an external surface of metallic grey. It extended below the plane about a kilometre, with gently sloping sides and a rounded bottom. From a distance the underbelly looked insignificant compared to the vast flat surface which was at least forty kilometres long and fifteen kilometres wide. However, up close it was clear that an enormous volume was contained inside that drab structure.

As Nicole watched in fascination, a small indentation in the side of the grey exterior, just below the surface, expanded and grew into a round tube moving outward from the Carrier. The tube drew near to the starfish and then, after some minor vernier corrections, was affixed to the main air lock.

Nicole smiled to herself. *Just another unbelievable day*, she thought, *in my amazing existence.* She changed position in her chair and felt some slight discomfort in her hip. *I wish there was something I could do for Nai*, she said to herself. *But making everybody sacrifice themselves for Galileo is not the right solution.*

She felt a touch on her arm and turned to the side. It was Dr Blue. 'How are you feeling?' the octospider said in colour.

'Better now,' Nicole replied. 'But I had some bad moments earlier this afternoon.'

Dr Blue scanned Nicole with the monitoring device. 'There were at least two major irregularities,' Nicole told her doctor. 'I remember both of them quite clearly.'

The octospider doctor studied the colours flashing on the small monitor. 'Why didn't you call me?' she said.

'I thought about it,' Nicole answered. 'But so much was going on ... And I figured you were busy with your own ...'

Dr Blue handed Nicole a small flask containing a light blue liquid. 'Drink this,' the octospider said. 'It will limit your cardiac response to emotional stress over the next twelve hours.'

'And will we still be together, you and I,' Nicole asked, 'after the Carrier departs? ... I didn't study your part of the list very carefully.'

'Yes,' Dr Blue answered. 'Eighty-five per cent of our species will be transferred to The Node. More than half the octospiders moving to the Carrier are alternates.'

'So, my friend,' Nicole said after drinking the liquid, 'what do you make of all this transfer business?'

'Our best guess,' Dr Blue said, 'is that this entire experiment has reached a significant branch point and that the two groups will be involved in radically different activities.'

Nicole laughed. 'That's not very specific,' she said.

'No, it's not,' the octospider calmly agreed.

There were eighty-two humans and nine octospiders present in the cafeteria when The Eagle convened the reconsideration meeting five minutes after the last starfish resident originally scheduled for transfer to the Carrier had departed through the air lock. Only those who had officially requested reconsideration were permitted to attend the meeting. Many other members of all species were still lingering on the observation deck and in the common areas, talking about the departure procession and/or waiting to learn the outcome of The Eagle's meeting.

Nicole had returned to her post at the observation window. She was sitting in her wheelchair, staring out at the Carrier and reflecting on the scenes she had witnessed during the last hour. Most of the departing humans had been in a festive mood, openly delighted that they would no longer be living among aliens. There had been some sad farewells at the door to the air lock, but actually surprisingly few.

Galileo had been allowed to spend ten minutes with his family and friends in the common area. Patrick and Nai had assured the young man, who had demonstrated very little emotion of any kind, that they and his brother, Kepler, who was still packing, would be joining him in the Carrier before the evening was over.

1281

Galileo had been one of the last humans to leave the starfish. He had been followed by the small contingent of avians and myrmicats. The neural-net material and, the remaining manna melons had been packed in large crates and had been carried by a contingent of the block robots. *I'll probably never see any of your kind again*, Nicole had thought as the trailing avian had turned and issued a shriek of goodbye to the onlookers.

'Each of you,' The Eagle said as he began the meeting in the cafeteria, 'has requested that your assignment be reconsidered and that you be allowed to switch your future home from The Node to the Carrier ... At this time I want to explain two additional differences between the living-environments in the Carrier and The Node. If, after weighing this new information, you still wish to have your assignment changed, then we will accommodate you ...

'As I told you this afternoon, there will be no inter-species mixing in the Carrier. Not only will each species be isolated in its own habitat, but also there will be *no* interference of any kind by *any other* intelligence, including the one I represent, in the affairs of each species. Not now, not ever. Each species in the Carrier will be on its own. By contrast, life in the interspecies world at The Node will be supervised. Not as heavily as it has been here on the starfish, but supervised nevertheless. We believe that oversight and monitoring are essential when different species are living together ...

'The second additional factor may be the most important of all. There will be no reproduction in the Carrier. All of the individuals who inhabit the Carrier, of *every* species, will be rendered forever sterile. Every element necessary for a long and happy life will be provided for those living in the Carrier, but nobody will be allowed to reproduce. By contrast, there will be no reproduction constraints imposed at The Node ...

'Please let me finish,' The Eagle said as several members of the audience tried to interrupt with questions. 'You each have two more hours to decide ... If you still want to transfer to the Carrier, simply bring the bags you have already packed and request Big Block to open the air lock ...'

Nicole was not surprised that Kepler no longer wanted to switch to the Carrier. The young man had clearly had a difficult time making up his mind in the first place and had only requested reconsideration out of loyalty to his mother. Since that time, he had spent most of the afternoon with Maria, whom he obviously adored.

Kepler enlisted everyone in the extended family in case there was an argument with his mother, but no dispute developed. Nai agreed that Kepler should not be deprived of the pleasure of being a father. Nai even magnanimously suggested that Patrick might want to reevaluate his own decision, but her husband was quick to point out that she was past her childbearing years and, besides, he had already been a father, in many ways, to Galileo and Kepler.

Nicole, Patrick, Nai, and Kepler were left alone in one of the apartments for the very final goodbyes. It had been a day of tears and raging emotions. All four of them were emotionally exhausted. Two mothers said goodbye, forever, to two sons. There was a touching symmetry in the final comments. Nai requested that Nicole guide Kepler with her wisdom; Nicole asked Nai to continue to give Patrick her unselfish, unconditional love.

Patrick then lifted both the heavy bags and threw them over his shoulders. As Nai and he walked out the door, Kepler stood beside Nicole's wheelchair, holding her phthisic hand. Only after the door closed did the river of tears run from Nicole's eyes. *Goodbye, Patrick*, she thought with a heartache. *Goodbye, Genevieve, Simone, and Katie. Goodbye, Richard.*

7

The dreams came one after another, sometimes without any break. Henry laughed at her for being black, then a supercilious colleague from medical school stopped her from making a bad mistake during a routine tonsillectomy. Later Nicote walked on a sandy beach with dark clouds hovering overhead. A silent caped figure beckoned in the distance. *That's death*, Nicole said to herself in the dream. But it was a cruel joke. When she reached the figure and touched its outstretched hand, Max Puckett removed his cape and laughed.

She was crawling on her bare knees in a dark underground cement pipe. Her knees had begun to bleed. *I'm over here*, Katie's voice said. *Where are you?* Nicole asked, frustrated. *I'm be-hind you, Ma-ma*, Benjy said. Water began to fill up the pipe. *I cannot find them. I cannot help them.*

Nicole was swimming, with difficulty. There was a strong current in the pipe. It swept her away, carried her outside, became a creek in a forest. Nicole's clothes caught on a bush that overhung the creek. She stood up and brushed herself off. She began walking on a path.

It was night. Nicole could hear a few birds and see the moon above her through the occasional breaks in the tall trees. The path wound back and forth. She came to a junction. *Which way should I go?* Nicole asked herself in the dream. *Come with me*, Genevieve said, emerging from the forest and taking her hand,

What are you doing here? Nicole said. Genevieve laughed. *I could ask you the same thing.*

A young Katie was coming toward them on the path. *Hello, Mother*, she said, reaching out for Nicole's other hand. *Do you mind if I walk with you? Not at all*, answered Nicole.

The forest thickened around them. Nicole heard footsteps behind her and turned around while she was still walking. Patrick and Simone returned her smiles. *We're almost there*, Simone said. *Where are we going?* Nicole asked. *You must know, Mrs Wakefield*, Maria answered. *You told us to come.* The girl was now walking beside Patrick and Simone.

Nicole and the five young people entered a small clearing. In the middle was a burning camp-fire. Omeh walked around from the other side of the fire and greeted them. After they formed a new circle around the fire, the shaman threw his head back and began to chant in Senoufo. As Nicole watched, Omeh's face began to peel away, revealing his frightening skull. Still the chant continued. *No, no*, said Nicole. *No. No.*

'Ma-ma,' Benjy said. 'Wake up, Mama ... You're having a bad dream.'

Nicole rubbed her eyes. She could see a light on the other side of the room. 'What time is it, Benjy?' she said.

'It's late, Ma-ma,' he answered with a smile. 'Kepler has gone to breakfast with the others ... We wan-ted to let you sleep.'

'Thank you, Benjy,' Nicole said, moving slightly on her mat. She felt the pain in her hip. She glanced around the room and remembered that Patrick and Nai were gone. *For ever*, Nicole thought briefly, fighting the return of her sorrow.

'Would you like to take a show-er?' Benjy asked. 'I could help you un-dress and car-ry you o-ver to the stall.'

Nicole looked up at her balding son. *I was wrong to worry about you*, she thought. *You would do fine without me.* 'Why, thank you, Benjy,' she said. 'That would be very nice.'

'I'll try to be gen-tle,' he said, unbuttoning his mother's gown. 'But please tell me if I hurt you.'

When Nicole was completely naked, Benjy picked her up in his arms and started to walk toward the shower. He stopped after he had taken two steps. 'What's wrong, Benjy?' Nicole asked.

Benjy grinned sheepishly. 'I didn't think the plan through ve-ry well, Ma-ma,' he said. 'I should have ad-just-ed the wa-ter first.'

He turned around, set Nicole back down on her mat, and crossed me room to the shower. Nicole heard the water running.

'You like it med-i-um hot, don't you?' he called out.

'That's right,' Nicole answered.

Benjy returned and picked her up a few seconds later. 'I put two tow-els down on the floor,' he said, 'so it would-n't be too hard or too cold for you.'

'Thank you, son,' Nicole said.

Benjy talked to her while Nicole sat on the towels on the floor of the shower and let the refreshing water pour over her body. He brought her soap and shampoo when she requested them. When she was finished, Benjy helped his mother dry off and dress. Then he carried her over to her wheelchair.

'Bend down here, please,' Nicole said as she settled into her chair. She kissed him on the cheek and squeezed his hand. 'Thank you for everything, Benjy,' she said, unable to stop the tears that were forming in her eyes. 'You have been a marvellous help.'

Benjy stood beside his mother, beaming. 'I love you, Ma-ma,' he said. 'It makes me hap-py to help you.'

'And I love you too, son,' Nicole said, squeezing his hand again. 'Now, are you going to join me for breakfast?'

'That was my plan,' said Benjy, still smiling.

Before they were finished eating, The Eagle walked up to Nicole and Benjy in the cafeteria. 'Dr Blue and I will be waiting for you in your room,' The Eagle said. 'We want to give you a thorough physical examination.'

Sophisticated medical equipment had already been set up in the apartment when Nicole and Benjy returned. Dr Blue injected additional microprobes directly into Nicole's chest and later sent another set of probes into her kidney region. The Eagle and Dr Blue conversed in the octospider's native colour language throughout the half-hour examination. Benjy assisted his mother when she was asked to stand or move around. He was completely fascinated by The Eagle's ability to speak in colour.

'How did you learn to do that?' Benjy asked The Eagle at one point in the examination.

'Technically speaking,' The Eagle replied, 'I didn't learn anything ... My designers added a pair of specialised subsystems to my structure, one that would allow me to interpret the octospider colours and the other to make the colour patterns on my forehead.'

'Did-n't you have to go to school or any-thing?' Benjy persisted.

'No,' The Eagle said simply.

'Could your de-sign-ers do that for *me*? Benjy asked several seconds later, when The Eagle and Dr Blue had resumed their discussion of Nicole's condition.

The Eagle turned around and looked at Benjy. 'I'm a ve-ry slow learn-er,' Benjy said. 'It would be won-der-ful if some-one could just put ev-ery-thing in-to my brain.'

'We don't quite know how to do that yet,' The Eagle said.

When the examination was over, The Eagle asked Benjy to pack all of Nicole's things. 'Where are we going?' Nicole asked.

'We're going for a ride in the shuttle,' The Eagle said. 'I want to discuss your physical condition with you in some detail and take you where any emergency could be quickly handled.'

'I thought the blue liquid and all those probes inside me were enough ...'

'We'll talk about it later,' the Eagle said, interrupting her. He took Nicole's bag from Benjy. 'Thank you for all your help,' the alien said.

'Let me make certain that I have understood this last half hour of discussion,' Nicole said into the microphone of her helmet as the shuttle neared the half-way point between the starfish and The Node. 'My heart will not last more than ten days at most, despite all your medical magic; my kidneys are currently undergoing terminal failure; and my liver is showing signs of severe degradation. Is that a fair summary?'

'It is indeed,' said The Eagle.

Nicole forced a smile. 'Is there any good news?'

'Your mind is still functioning admirably, and the bruise on your hip will eventually heal, provided the other ailments don't kill you first.'

'And what you are suggesting,' Nicole said, 'is that I should check into your equivalent of a hospital today over at The Node and have my heart, kidneys, and liver all replaced by advanced machines that can perform the same functions?'

'There may be some other organs that need to be replaced as well,' The Eagle said, 'as long as we are performing a major operation. Your pancreas has been malfunctioning intermittently, and your entire sexual system is out of spec ... A complete hysterectomy should be considered.'

Nicole was shaking her head. 'At what point does all of this become senseless? No matter what you do now, it's only a matter of time until some other organ fails. What would be next? My lungs? Or maybe my eyes? ... Would you even give me a brain transplant if I could no longer think?'

'We could,' The Eagle replied.

Nicole was quiet for almost a minute. 'It may not make much sense to you,' she said, 'because it certainly isn't what I would call logical ... but I am not very comfortable with the idea of becoming a hybrid being.'

'What do you mean?' The Eagle asked.

'At what point do I stop being Nicole des Jardins Wakefield?' she said. 'If my heart, brain, eyes, and ears are replaced by machines, am I still Nicole? Or am I someone, or something, else?'

'The question has no relevance,' The Eagle said. 'You're a doctor, Nicole. Consider the case of a schizophrenic who must take drugs regularly to alter the functions of the brain. Is that person still who he or she was? It's the same philosophical question, just a different degree of change.'

'I can see your point,' Nicole said after another brief silence. 'But it doesn't change my feelings ... I'm sorry. If I have a choice, and you have led me to believe that I do, then I will decline ... At least for today anyway.'

The Eagle stared at Nicole for several seconds. Then he entered a different set of parameters into the control system of the shuttle. The vehicle changed its heading.

'So are we going back to the starfish?' Nicole asked.

'Not immediately,' The Eagle said. 'I want to show you something else first.' The alien reached into the pouch around his waist and pulled out a small tube containing a blue liquid and an unknown device. 'Please give me your arm. I don't want you to die before this afternoon is over.'

As they approached the Habitation Module of The Node, Nicole complained to The Eagle about the 'less than forthright' way the dividing of the starfish residents into two groups had been handled. 'As usual,' Nicole said, 'you cannot be accused of telling a lie – just of withholding critical information.'

'Sometimes,' The Eagle said, 'there are no good ways for us to complete a task. In those cases we choose the least unsatisfactory course of action ...

What did you expect us to do? Tell the residents in the beginning that we couldn't take care of everyone forever, generation after generation? There would have been chaos ... Besides, I don't think you give us enough credit. We rescued thousands of beings from Rama, most of whom probably would have died in an interspecies conflict without our intervention ... Remember that everyone, including those assigned to the Carrier, will be allowed to complete his or her life.'

Nicole was silent. She was trying to imagine what life on the Carrier would be like without any reproduction. Her mind carried the scenario into its likely distant future, when there would be only a few individuals left. 'I wouldn't want to be the last human left alive in the Carrier,' she said.

'There was a species in this part of the galaxy about three million years ago,' The Eagle said, 'that flourished as a spacefarer for almost a million years. They were brilliant engineers and built some of the most amazing buildings ever seen. Their sphere of influence spread rapidly until they dominated a region covering more than twenty star systems. This species was learned, compassionate, and wise. But they made one fatal error ...'

'What was that?' Nicole asked on cue.

'Their equivalent to your genome contained an order of magnitude more information than yours. It had been the result of four billion years of natural evolution and was extremely complicated. Their initial experiments with genetic engineering, both on other species and on themselves, were an unqualified success. They *thought* they understood what they were doing. However, without their knowledge, slowly but surely the robustness of the genes that were being transferred from generation to generation was deteriorating ... When they finally understood what they had done to themselves, it was too late. They had preserved no pristine specimens from the early days, before they had begun to modify their own genes. They could not go back. There was nothing they could do.'

'Imagine,' The Eagle said, 'not just being the last member of your group on an isolated spaceship like the Carrier, but being one of the terminal survivors of a species rich in history, art, and knowledge ... Our encyclopedia contains many such stories, each containing at least one object-lesson.'

The shuttle moved through an open port in the side of the spherical module and came to a gentle stop against a wall. Automatic gantries on each side were deployed to keep the vehicle from drifting. There was a ramp from the passenger side of the shuttle to a walkway, which in turn led toward the hub of the transportation complex.

Nicole laughed. 'I was so engrossed in our conversation,' she said, 'that I didn't even look at this module from the outside.'

'You wouldn't have seen much that was new,' The Eagle said.

The alien then turned to Nicole and did something very unusual. He reached across the shuttle and took both of her gloved hands. 'In less than an hour,' he said, 'you are going to experience something that will astound you and also arouse your emotions. Originally, we had planned that this excursion would be a complete surprise. But with your weakened condition, we can't risk the possibility that your system might be overpowered by emotional input ... Therefore, we have decided to tell you first what we're about to do.'

Nicole felt her heart-rate increase. *What is he talking about?* she thought. *What could be so unusual ... ?*

'... We will board a small car that will travel several kilometres into this module. At the end of this short journey you will be reunited with your daughter Simone and Michael O'Toole.'

'*What?*' Nicole shouted, tearing her hands away from The Eagle and placing them on the side of her helmet. 'Did I hear you correctly? Did you say that I was going to see Simone and Michael?'

'Yes,' The Eagle replied. 'Nicole, please try to relax ...'

'My God!' Nicole exclaimed, ignoring his comment. 'I cannot believe it. I just cannot believe it ... I hope that this is not some kind of cruel trick ...'

'I assure you that it is not ...'

'But how can Michael still be alive?' Nicole asked. 'He must be at least a hundred and twenty years old ...'

'We have helped him with our medical magic, as you call it.'

'Oh, Simone, *Si-mone*!' Nicole cried. 'Can it be? Can it really be?'

The tears had been delayed because of Nicole's shock. Now they poured out of her eyes. Despite the pain in her hip and the unwieldy space-helmet, Nicole almost jumped across the seat to give The Eagle a hug. 'Thank you, oh, thank you,' she said. 'I cannot tell you how much this means to me.'

The Eagle steadied Nicole's wheelchair on the escalator as they descended into the centre of the main transportation complex. She looked around briefly. The station was identical to the one she remembered from The Node near Sirius. It was about twenty metres tall and laid out in a circle. Half a dozen moving sidewalks surrounded the central display, each running into a different arched tunnel leading away from the complex. Above the tunnels, to the right, were a pair of multi-level structures.

'Do the intermodule trains depart from up there?' Nicole asked, remembering a ride with Katie and Simone when the girls were both young.

The Eagle nodded. He pushed her wheelchair onto one of the moving sidewalks and they left the centre of the station. They travelled several hundred metrés in a tunnel before the moving sidewalk stopped. 'Our car should be just to the right, in the first corridor,' The Eagle said.

The small car, which opened from the top, had two seats. The Eagle lifted Nicole into the passenger seat and then folded the wheelchair into a compressed configuration no larger than a briefcase, which he stored in a pocket area inside the vehicle. Shortly thereafter, the car moved forward through the maze of light cream windowless passageways. Nicole was extraordinarily quiet. She was trying to convince herself that she was indeed about to see the daughter whom she had left in another star system years and years ago.

The ride through the Habitation Module seemed interminable. At one point they stopped and The Eagle told Nicole she could remove her helmet. 'Are we close?' she asked.

'Not yet,' he answered, 'but we are already in their atmospheric zone.'

Twice they encountered fascinating aliens in vehicles moving in the opposite direction, but Nicole was too excited to pay attention to anything except what was going on inside her head. She was barely even listening to The Eagle. *Calm down*, one of Nicole's inner voices said. *Don't be absurd*, another voice replied, *I'm about to see a daughter I haven't seen for forty years. There's no way I could remain calm.*

'... In its own way,' The Eagle was saying, 'their life has been as extraordinary as yours. Different, of course, altogether different. When we took Patrick over to see them very early this morning ...'

'What did you say?' Nicole asked abruptly. 'Did you say that Patrick saw them this morning? You took Patrick to see his father?'

'Yes,' said The Eagle. 'We had always planned for this reunion, as long as everything went according to schedule ... Ideally neither you nor Patrick would have seen Simone and Michael and their children ...'

'*Children!*' Nicole exclaimed. 'I have more grandchildren!'

'... until after you were settled at The Node, but when Patrick requested reconsideration ... Well, it would have been heartless to let him leave forever without ever seeing his natural father ...'

Nicole could no longer contain herself. She reached over and kissed The Eagle on his feathered cheek. 'And Max said you were nothing but a cold machine. How wrong he was! ... Thank you ... For Patrick's sake, I thank you ...'

She was trembling from excitement. A moment later Nicole could not breathe. The Eagle quickly stopped the small car.

'Where am I?' Nicole said, emerging from a deep fog.

'We are parked just inside the enclosed area where Michael, Simone, and their family live,' The Eagle said. 'We have been here for about four hours. You have been sleeping.'

'Did I have a heart attack?' Nicole asked.

'Not exactly ... Just a significant malfunction. I considered taking you immediately back to the hospital, but I decided to wait until you awakened. Besides, I have most of the same medications here with me ...'

The Eagle looked at her with his intense blue eyes. 'What do you want to do, Nicole?' he said. 'Visit with Simone and Michael as planned, or go back to the hospital? It's your choice, but understand ...'

'I know,' Nicole interrupted him with a sigh, 'I must be careful not to become too excited ...' She glanced at The Eagle. 'I want to see Simone, even if it's the last act of my life … Can you give me something that will calm me but will not make me goofy or put me to sleep?'

'A mild tranquiliser will only help,' The Eagle said, 'if you consciously work to contain your excitement.'

'All right,' Nicole said. 'I'll do my best.'

The Eagle eased the car onto a paved road lined with tall trees. As they drove, Nicole was reminded of the autumn in New England she spent with her father when she was a teenager. The leaves on the trees were red, gold, and brown.

'It's beautiful,' Nicole said.

The car rounded a curve and drove past a white fence enclosing a grassy area. There were four horses in the enclosure. A pair of human teenagers were walking among them. 'The children are real,' The Eagle said. 'The horses are simulations.'

At the top of a gentle hill was a large two-story white house with a sloped black roof. The Eagle pulled into the circular drive and stopped the car. The front door of the house opened an instant later and a tall, beautiful, jet-black woman with greying hair came outside.

'*Mother!*' Simone yelled as she raced for the car.

Nicole barely had time to open her door before Simone flung herself into her mother's arms. The two women hugged and kissed, weeping profusely. Neither of them could speak.

't was a bitter-sweet visit from Patrick,' Simone said, putting down her coffee-cup. 'He was here for over two hours, but it seemed like only a few minutes.'

The three of them were sitting at a table that looked out on the rolling farmland that surrounded the house. Nicole was temporarily staring out the window at the bucolic scene. 'It's mostly an illusion, of course,' Michael said. 'But a very good one ... Unless you knew better, you would think you were in Massachusetts or southern Vermont.'

'This whole dinner has seemed like a dream,' Nicole said. 'I have not yet accepted that any of this is really happening.'

'We felt that way last night,' Simone said, 'when we were told that we were going to see Patrick this morning ... Neither Michael nor I slept a wink.' She laughed. 'At one point during the night we had convinced ourselves that we were going to meet a "fake" Patrick, and we thought of questions we could ask that nobody except the real Patrick could answer.'

'Their technological skills are awesome,' Michael said. 'If they wanted to create a robot Patrick and pass him off as the genuine article, it would be very difficult for us to ascertain the truth.'

'But they didn't,' Simone said. 'I knew within minutes that it was really Patrick ...'

'How did he seem to you?' Nicole asked. 'In all the (confusion of the last day, I didn't have a chance to talk to him very much.'

'Resigned, mostly,' Simone said, 'but certain that he had made the correct decision. He said it would probably be weeks before he had sorted through all the emotions he had experienced in the last twenty-four hours.'

'That must be true for all of us,' Nicole said.

There was a brief silence at the table. 'Are you tired, Mother?' Simone asked. 'Patrick told us about your health problems, and when we received the message this afternoon that you had been delayed ...'

'Yes, I'm a little tired,' Nicole said. 'But I certainly couldn't sleep ... At least not immediately ...' She backed her wheelchair away from the table and lowered her seat. 'I would, however, like to use the powder-room.'

'Certainly,' Simone said, jumping up. 'I'll come with you.'

Simone accompanied her mother down a long hall with a simulated wooden floor. 'So you have six children living with you here,' Nicole said, 'including three that you carried?'

'That's right,' Simone said. 'Michael and I had two boys and two girls by the "natural method", as you called it ... The first of the boys, Darren, died when he was seven ... It's a long story. If we have time, I'll tell it to you tomorrow ... All the rest of the children were developed from embryos in their laboratories ...'

They had reached the door to the powder-room. 'Do you know how many children The Eagle and his colleagues have "developed"?' Nicole asked.

'No,' Simone answered. 'But they did tell me that they took more than a thousand healthy eggs from my ovaries.'

On the way back to the dining-room, Simone explained that all the children who had been born by the 'natural method' had lived their whole lives with Michael and her. Their spouses, who were of course also the product of Michael's sperm and her eggs, had been selected as the result of a comprehensive genetic matching technique developed by the aliens.

'So these were arranged marriages?' Nicole asked.

'Not exactly,' Simone said. She laughed. 'Each natural child was introduced to several possible mates, all of whom had passed the genetic screening.'

'And you've had no problems with your grandchildren?'

'Nothing that is "statistically significant", to use Michael's term,' Simone replied.

When they reached the dining-room, the table was empty. Michael told them that he had moved the coffee-pot and cups into the study. Nicole activated her wheelchair controls and followed them into a large, masculine study with dark wood bookshelves, and a fire burning in the fireplace.

'Is the fire real?' Nicole asked.

'Indeed it is,' Michael said. He leaned forward in his soft chair. 'You have been asking about the children,' he said, 'and we certainly want you to meet them, but we didn't want to overwhelm you ...'

'I understand,' Nicole said, taking a sip from a fresh cup of coffee, 'and I agree with you ... We certainly could not have had such a leisurely, informative dinner if there had been six more people ...'

'And don't forget the fourteen grandchildren,' Simone said.

Nicole looked at Michael and smiled. 'I'm sorry, Michael,' she said, 'but *you* are the part of this evening that is the most unreal. Whenever I look at you, my mind balks. You must be forty years older than I am, but you look not a day over sixty, and definitely younger than when we left you at The Node. How is this possible?'

'Their technology is absolute magic,' he said. 'They have reworked virtually every part of me. My heart, lungs, liver, entire digestive and excretory systems, and most of my endocrine glands have all been replaced, some several times, by smaller, more efficient functional equivalents. My bones, muscles, nerves, and blood-vessels are all buttressed by millions of microscopic implants that not only ensure the critical functions are accomplished, but also, in many cases, biochemically rejuvenate the aged cells. My skin is a special material they only recently perfected, which has all the good properties of real human skin but never ages or develops warts or moles ... Once a year I go over to their hospital. I'm unconscious for two days, and when I emerge I am literally a new man.'

'Would you mind coming over here,' Nicole said, 'and letting me touch you?' She laughed. 'I don't need to put my fingers through the holes in your hands, or anything like that, but you can certainly understand that what you are telling me is difficult to believe.'

Michael O'Toole crossed the room and knelt beside the wheelchair. Nicole reached out and touched the skin on his face. It was smooth and supple, like a young man's. His eyes were fresh and clear. 'And your brain, Michael,' Nicole asked softly. 'What have they done to your brain?'

He smiled. Nicole noticed that there were no wrinkles in his forehead. 'Many things,' he said. 'When my memory started to slip, they reconditioned my hippocampus. They even supplemented it with a small structure of their own, to give me more capacity, they said ... About twenty years ago they also installed what they described as a "better operating system", to sharpen my thinking processes ...'

Michael was less than a metre away from her. The light from the fire reflected off his face. Nicole was suddenly swept away by a flood of memories. She recalled what close friends they had been in Rama, as well as their moments of intimacy when Richard had been gone and presumed lost. She touched his face again.

'And are you still Michael O'Toole?' she asked. 'Or have you become something else, part-human and part-alien?'

He stood up without saying anything and walked back to his chair. He moved like an athlete, not like a man who was more than one hundred and twenty years old. 'I don't know how to answer your question,' he said. 'I can remember clearly all the details of my childhood in Boston, and every other important phase of my life. As far as I know, I am still more or less the same ...'

'Michael is still extremely interested in religion and creation as well,' Simone spoke for the first time in a long while. 'But he has changed a little – all of us are altered by our experiences in life ...'

'I have remained a devout Roman Catholic,' Michael said, 'and I still say my daily prayers ... But naturally my view of God, and of humanity too, has been drastically changed by what Simone and I have seen ... If anything, my faith has strengthened ... primarily because of my enlightening conversations with ...'

He stopped and glanced across the room at Simone. 'In the early years, Mother,' she said, 'when Michael and I were alone at The Node, near Sirius, there were many difficulties ... We had only each other to talk with ... I was still just a girl, and Michael was a mature man ... I could not discuss physics or religion or many of his other favourite topics ...'

'There were no major problems, you understand,' Michael said. 'Still, we were both lonely, in a peculiar sort of way ... What we had together was remarkable and enriching ... But we both needed something else, something additional ...'

'The Nodal Intelligence, or whatever we should call the power that was taking care of us, sensed our difficulty. It also recognised that The Eagle could not fulfill our individual needs. So a companion, like The Eagle, in a sense, was created for each of us.'

'It was a stroke of genius,' Simone said, 'that removed the emotional tension that was threatening our perfect marriage. When Saint Michael ...'

'Let me tell it, please,' Michael interrupted. 'One night, almost two years after you and the others had left, Simone was in the bedroom of the apartment nursing Katya when there was a knock on our door ... I assumed that it was The Eagle ... When I opened the door, however, a young man with dark, curly hair and blue eyes, a perfect reconstruction of Saint Michael of Siena, was standing there. He informed me that The Eagle would no longer be interacting with us and that he would be my new intermediary with the intelligence governing The Node ...'

'Saint Michael,' Simone said, 'came equipped with a vast set of knowledge of Earth history, and Catholicism, and physics, and all the other subjects about which I was totally ignorant ...'

'*Plus*,' Michael said, rising from his chair, 'he was willing to answer questions about what was going on around us at The Node ... Not that The Eagle wasn't, but Saint Michael was much warmer, more personal. It was as if he had been sent by them, or by God, to be a companion for my mind.'

Nicole glanced back and forth from Michael to Simone. Michael's face was positively radiant. *His religious fervour has not waned*, she thought. *It has only been redirected.*

'And is this Saint Michael character still around?' Nicole asked, swallowing the last sip of her coffee.

'Absolutely,' Michael said. 'We did not introduce Patrick to him – the time was too short, as Simone said – but we definitely want you to meet him.' Michael walked across the room, suddenly bubbling with energy. 'Do you remember all those infinite questions Richard used to ask, about who built The Node and Rama, and what was the purpose of this and that? Saint Michael knows all the answers. And he explains everything so eloquently!'

'Goodness,' said Nicole, with just a slight trace of sarcasm in her voice, 'he sounds fantastic ... Much too good to be true ... When will I have the privilege of meeting Saint Michael?'

'Right now, if you would like,' Michael O'Toole said expectantly.

'All right,' Nicole said, stifling a yawn. 'But remember I'm a tired, ailing, crotchety old woman ... I can't stay up for ever.'

Michael walked briskly to the far door of the study. 'Saint Michael,' he called, 'would you come in please and meet Simone's mother, Nicole?'

A few seconds later what looked like a young human priest in his early twenties, dressed in a dark blue robe, entered the room and crossed to Nicole's wheelchair. 'I am delighted,' Saint Michael said, with a beatific smile. 'I have heard about you for years.'

Nicole extended her hand and studied the alien intently. There was absolutely nothing she could see that would identify this individual as anything other than a human being. *My God*, Nicole thought quickly, *not only is their technology fantastic, but also their rate of learning is staggering.*

'Now let's get one thing straight at the outset,' she said to Saint Michael with a wry smile, 'there are too many Michaels here. I do *not* intend to address you regularly as Saint Michael. It's not my style. Do I just call you Saint, or Mike, or even Mikey – what do you prefer?'

'When they're both around I call my husband Big Michael,' Simone said. 'That seems to work fine.'

'All right,' Nicole said. 'As Richard always said, "When in Rome" ... Sit down, Michael, here close to my wheelchair ... Big Michael has praised you so highly I don't want my bad hearing to cause me to miss any of your pearls of wisdom.'

'Thank you, Nicole,' Saint Michael said with a smile of his own. 'Michael and Simone have extolled your virtues as well, but they clearly understated the cleverness of your wit.'

He has a personality too, Nicole thought. *Will wonders never cease?*

An hour later, after Simone had helped her to bed in the guest-room at the end of the hall, Nicole was lying on her side staring toward the windows. Although she was very tired, she could not sleep. Her mind was too active, going over and over the events of the day.

Maybe I should ring for something to help me sleep, Nicole thought, her hand automatically feeling for the button on the table beside her bed. *Simone said Saint Michael would come if I called. And that he could do anything The Eagle could.* Having assured herself that she could indeed summon help if her insomnia persisted, Nicole turned back to her most comfortable sleeping position and allowed her mind to float freely.

Her thoughts focused on what she had seen or heard since she had arrived at this isolated enclave in which Michael, Simone, and their family lived. Saint Michael had explained that this pseudo-New England was a small section inside the Habitation Module of The Node and that there were several hundred other species who were semi-permanent residents in the near vicinity. Why, Nicole had asked, had Big Michael and Simone chosen an everyday existence separate from all the others?

'For years,' Nicole remembered Michael O'Toole responding, 'we lived in a multi-species environment. In fact, both during and after our four natural children were born, we were whisked, or so it seemed, from place to place, testing both our adaptability and compatibility with a wide range of other plant and animal species. Saint Michael confirmed at the time what we suspected, namely that our hosts were purposely exposing us to a variety of environments to garner more information about us ... Each new venue was another challenge ...'

Big Michael paused for a moment, as if he were struggling emotionally. 'The psychological hardships were immense in those early days. As soon as we adapted to a given set of living-conditions, they were abruptly changed ... I still believe that Darren's death would not have occurred if everything hadn't been so strange in that underground world ... And we nearly lost Katya when she was only two or so and her curiosity was mistaken by a squidlike sea-creature as an act of aggression ...'

'After we were put to sleep the second time,' Simone said, 'and transported to this Node, both Michael and I were exhausted from the years of tests. The children were grown by then and starting to have families of their own. We requested, and were granted, some privacy ...'

'We still go out into the other world,' Michael added, 'but we interact with the exotic beings from distant star systems because we want to, not because it is a necessity ... Saint Michael briefs us regularly on the comings and goings of the basketball creatures, the sky-hoppers, and the flying turtles. He is our information window to the rest of The Node.'

Saint Michael is extraordinary, Nicole thought, *and much more advanced even than The Eagle. He answers all questions with such certitude. But there's something about him that makes me wonder. Are all those crisp answers about God and the origin and destiny of the universe really correct? Or has Saint Michael somehow been programmed, based on Michael's love of catechismal processes, to be his perfect alien companion?*

Nicole rolled over in bed and considered her own relationship with The Eagle. *Maybe I'm just jealous*, she thought, *because Michael seems to have learned so much ... and The Eagle has been unwilling or unable to answer my questions ... But who is better off, the child with a mentor who knows and tells everything or the one whose teacher helps the child find her own answers? ... I don't know ... I don't know ... But that was one hell of an impressive performance by Saint Michael at the easel.*

'Don't you see, Nicole?' Big Michael had jumped up from his chair for the umpteenth time. 'We're all participating in God's great experiment. This *entire* universe, not just our own galaxy, but all the galaxies that stretch to the end of the heavens, will provide one single data-point for God ... He, She, or It is searching for perfection, for that small range of initial parameters which, once the universe is set into motion by the transformation of energy into matter, will evolve, over billions of years, into one perfect harmony, a testimony to the Creator's consummate skill ...'

Nicole had had some difficulty following the higher mathematics, but she had certainly understood the gist of the diagrams that Saint Michael had drawn on the easel in the study. 'So at this moment,' Nicole had said to the alien with the curly hair and the blue eyes, 'there are countless other universes evolving, each having been started by God with different initial conditions, and God has somehow slipped you, The Eagle, The Node, and Rama *inside* this particular evolution process to acquire information? And the purpose of all this is so that God can define some mathematical construct associated with creation that will always produce a harmonious result?'

'Exactly,' Saint Michael had responded. Again he had pointed at the diagram on the easel. 'Imagine that this co-ordinate system I have drawn is a symbolic, two-dimensional representation of the available hypersurface of parameters defining the creation instant, the moment that energy is first transformed into matter. Any arrangement or vector representing a specific set of initial conditions for the universe may be depicted as a single point in my diagram. What God is, and has been, searching for is a very special closed dense set located on this mathematical hypersurface. This special set He is seeking has the property that *any* of its elements, that is, any arrangement of conditions for the instant of creation chosen from *within* this set, will produce a universe that will eventually end in harmony.'

'It's a nearly impossible problem,' Big Michael said, 'to create a universe that will end up with all living beings proclaiming the glory of God. If there is not enough matter, the explosion and inflation of the creation instant results in a universe that expands forever, without sufficient interaction of the individual components during evolution to produce and sustain life. If there is too much matter, then there is insufficient time for life and intelligence to develop fully before gravity causes the Great Crunch that ends the universe.'

'Chaos confounds God as well,' Saint Michael explained. 'Chaos is an outgrowth of all the physical laws governing the evolution of any created universe. It prevents the accurate prediction of the outcomes of large-scale processes, so God cannot, a priori, simply calculate what is going to happen in the future and therefore, by analytical techniques, isolate the zones of harmony ... Experimentation is the only possible way for Him to discover what He is seeking ...'

'The structure opposing God's design is overwhelming,' Big Michael added. 'In order for God to succeed, not only must life and intelligence evolve from raw subatomic particles made into atoms by stellar cataclysms, but also this life must reach such a level of both spiritual self-awareness and technological capability that it can actively transform everything around it ...'

So God, Nicole thought in her room, remembering the discussion, *is the ultimate designer, the ultimate engineer. He or She or It shapes the moment of creation in such a way that, billions of years later, living beings attest to the wonder of creation ...*

'There's a part of this I still don't understand,' Nicole had said to the two

Michaels and Simone near the end of the evening. 'Why must God create so many universes to conduct this experiment? Once the existence of a harmonious outcome has been verified, doesn't the task become easy? Can't the initial conditions for that universe simply be replicated?'

'That's not a difficult enough problem for God,' Saint Michael had responded. 'God wants to know the extent of the zone of harmony in the hypersurface of creation parameters, plus all the mathematical characteristics of the zone ... Besides, I don't think you yet appreciate the scope of God's problem. Only a minuscule fraction of all possible universes can end up harmonious. The natural outcome of the transformation of energy into matter is a universe with no life at all, or, at best, aggressive, temporary living creatures who are more destructive than constructive. Even a small region of harmony inside an evolving universe is a miracle ... That's why the whole enterprise.is such a challenge for God.'

Big Michael had then jumped up again. 'What God is looking for is a universe which, before it dies in the Big Crunch, has achieved *total* harmony. That's not just every living species from every world working together for the mutual good, but every subatomic particle of His creation actively participating in that harmony ... For a while, I myself couldn't comprehend the full grandeur of this concept. Then Saint Michael told me about a species that makes living beings out of rock and dirt, as our biblical God did, by transmuting and rearranging the elements. *Total* harmony requires that advanced species like us use our technological tools to transform inanimate and non-living things into creatures that contribute to the harmony ...'

Nicole remembered that she had announced, at about this point in the conversation, that her mind was overloaded and she wanted to go to bed. Saint Michael had asked her to wait just a few more minutes so that he could summarise what he felt had been a slightly disorganised discussion. Nicole had agreed.

'Going back to your original question,' Saint Michael had said, 'each of The Nodes is part of a hierarchical intelligence gathering information throughout this particular galaxy. Most galaxies, including the Milky Way, have a single superstation, which we call the Prime Monitor, located somewhere near their centres. The set of Prime Monitors was created by God at the same moment the universe began and then was deployed to learn as much as possible about the evolutionary process. The Nodes, the Carriers, and all the other engineering constructs you have seen were in turn designed by the Prime Monitor. The entire activity, including what has been going on since the first Rama spacecraft entered your solar system years ago, has as its objective the development of quantitative criteria, for use by the Creator, that will enable subsequent universes to conclude in glorious harmony, despite the chaotic tendencies of the natural laws.'

Nicole had whistled. 'This conversation has been absolutely mind-boggling,' she had finally said, activating her wheelchair. 'And now I am exhausted.'

But not so exhausted that I can sleep, she thought. *How could anybody sleep after having had the purpose of the universe explained?* Nicole laughed to herself in bed. *I can't imagine what Richard would have said after that discussion ... A good theory, perhaps, but how does it explain the African dominance in the World Cup between 2140 and 2160? ... Or is the meaning of life no longer 42?* She laughed again. *Richard would have appreciated Saint Michael, no doubt, but he would have had hundreds of questions ... We would have made love as soon as we returned to the room and then talked all night ...*

She yawned and turned over on her side. As she drifted off to sleep, visions of universes exploding into being danced in her mind's eye.

9

Nicole woke up refreshed and with a surprising amount of energy. She started to push the button beside her bed, but decided against it. Instead she struggled into her wheelchair. She rolled over to the windows and pulled the curtains.

It was a beautiful morning outside. There was a little creek off to her left, and three children, probably between eight and ten years of age, were skipping stones across a small pool in the creek. As Nicole gazed out the windows at the perfectly simulated fields and trees and rolling hills, she felt temporarily young and full of life.

Maybe I should let them repair me after all, Nicole thought. *Replace all my damaged and worn-out parts ... I could live here, with Simone and Michael. Maybe I could even teach my great-grandchildren a thing or two ...*

The three children left the creek and raced across a green field to where the horses were enclosed. The boy ran the fastest, but he barely beat the smaller of the two girls.

The trio laughed together and called the horses over to the fence.

'The boy is Zachary,' Big Michael said from behind her. 'The two girls are Colleen and Simone ... Zachary and Colleen are Katya's children, Simone is Timothy's oldest.'

Nicole had not heard him enter the room. She turned around in her wheelchair. 'Good morning, Michael,' she said. Nicole glanced back at the window. 'The children are all gorgeous.'

'Thank you,' Michael said, walking over to the window. 'I am a very lucky man,' he said. 'God has granted me a fascinating life with unbelievable riches.'

They watched in silence as the children played. Zachary mounted a white horse and began to show off. 'I was sorry to hear about Richard's death,' Michael said. 'Patrick told us the story yesterday ... It must have been horrible for you.'

'It was,' Nicole replied. 'Richard and I had developed such a wonderful friendship ...' They faced each other. 'You would have been so proud of him, Michael ... He was a different man in his last years ...'

'I suspected as much,' Michael said. 'The Richard I knew would never have volunteered to place himself in jeopardy, especially to save the lives of others ...'

'You should have seen him with his granddaughter Nikki, Ellie's little girl. They were inseparable. He was her "Boobah" ... He found tenderness so late in life ...'

Nicole could not continue. A sudden heartache overwhelmed her. She drove over to the bedside table and took a drink from the bottle of blue liquid.

She returned to the window. Outside, the girls were now on horseback also and some kind of game was under way.

'Patrick told us that Benjy had grown into a fine adult,' Michael said, 'limited in some ways, of course, but quite remarkable considering his basic ability and the long periods of sleep ... He said that Benjy was a living tribute to your talents, all of them, and that you had worked with him tirelessly, never letting him use his handicap as an excuse ...'

It was Michael's turn to choke up. He turned to Nicole with tears easing out of both of his eyes and placed his hands in hers. 'There's no way I can ever thank you enough for raising those two boys with such care. Especially Benjy.'

Nicole looked up at him from her wheelchair. 'They are our sons, Michael,' she said. 'I love them very much.'

Michael wiped his nose and eyes with a pocket handkerchief. 'Simone and I want you to meet our children and grandchildren, of course,' he said, 'but we both agreed that there was something we should tell you first ... We didn't know exactly how you would respond ... However, it would not be fair not to tell you, because otherwise you might not understand why the children are reacting ...'

'What is it, Michael?' Nicole interrupted. She smiled. 'You're certainly having a hard time coming to the point.'

'I am indeed,' he said, crossing the room and pushing the button beside Nicole's bed twice in rapid succession. 'Nicole, what I am about to say is a bit delicate ... Remember last night, when we told you that both Simone and I had alien companions ...'

'Yes, Michael,' Nicole said.

She was still gazing out of the window. Michael joined her and took her hand. She stared out the window. Outside, a woman in her late forties, athletic, with dark copper skin, had left the house and was walking quickly toward the horse compound. Both the woman's figure and her gait seemed familiar to Nicole. The children saw the woman, waved, and came toward her on their horses.

Nicole watched Zachary yell the woman's name and suddenly she understood. Nicole was thunderstruck. The woman turned around briefly and Nicole saw herself, exactly as she had been when she had left The Node forty years earlier. It was difficult for her to keep her emotions under control.

'It was you that Simone missed the most,' Michael said, acknowledging the look of astonished recognition on Nicole's face. 'So it was only natural that the aliens fashioned a companion for her from your image ... She is a remarkable simulation. Not just her physical appearance, which you can see for yourself, but also her personality. Simone and I were amazed, especially in the beginning, at what a perfect duplication job they had done. The alien talked like you, walked like you, even thought like you ... Within a week Simone was calling her "Mother" and I was calling her "Nicole". She has been with us ever since.'

Nicole gazed at the simulation of herself without saying a word. *The facial expressions and even the gestures are correct*, she thought. She continued to stare fixedly as the woman approached the house with the three children.

'Simone thought you might be a little upset, or maybe feel displaced, when you discovered that this simulation of you had been living with the family for all these years. But I assured her that you would be fine, that it would simply take a little while for you to adjust to the idea ... After all, as far as I know, no human being has ever been replaced by a robot copy of herself before.'

The alien Nicole picked up one of the girls and twirled her around in the air. Then all four of them bounded up the steps and across the threshold of the house.

They call her Granny, Nicole thought. *She can run, and ride horses, and toss them in the air ... She is not phthisic and confined to a wheelchair.* An emotion that Nicole did not like, self-pity, began to grow inside her. *Maybe Simone has not even missed me that much*, she said to herself. *Her 'mother' has been here all these years, at her beck and call, never aging, never asking for anything ...*

Nicole sensed that she was going to cry. She pulled herself together. 'Michael,' she said, forcing a smile, 'why don't you give me a minute to prepare myself for breakfast?'

'Are you sure you don't need any help?' he asked.

'No, no ... I'll be fine ... I just want to wash my face and put on a little make-up.'

The tears came a few seconds after the door closed. *There is no place for me here either*, Nicole said to herself. *There is already a granny, a better one than I could ever be, even if she is only a machine ...*

Nicole said almost nothing on the ride back to the transportation centre. She was still quiet as the shuttle left the Habitation Module and pulled out into space.

'You don't want to talk about it, do you?' The Eagle said.

'Not really,' Nicole said into the microphone in her helmet.

'Are you glad you went?' The Eagle inquired several seconds later.

'Oh, yes ... absolutely,' she replied. 'It was one of the most outstanding experiences of my life ... Thank you very much.'

The Eagle adjusted the flight of the shuttle so that they were moving slowly backward. The huge illuminated tetrahedron dominated the view out their window.

'The replacement procedure could be performed this afternoon,' The Eagle said. 'By early next week you would look younger than Big Michael.'

'No, thanks,' said Nicole.

There was another long period of silence. 'You don't seem very happy,' The Eagle then said.

Nicole turned to look at her alien companion. 'I am,' she said. 'And I am especially happy for Simone and Michael ... It's wonderful that their life has been so fulfilling ...' Nicole took a deep breath. 'Maybe I'm just tired,' she said. 'So much has occurred in such a short period of time.'

'That's probably it,' The Eagle said.

Nicole was deep in thought, methodically reviewing everything that had happened to her since she had awakened. The faces of Simone and Michael's six children and fourteen grandchildren swept through her mind. *A handsome lot,* she said to herself, *but without much variation.*

It was another face, one she remembered clearly from her own mirror, that returned to her mind's eye most often. She had agreed with Simone and Michael that the other Nicole was an unbelievable likeness, an absolute triumph of advanced technology. What Nicole had not even been able to discuss with them was how strange it was meeting and carrying on a conversation with herself as a younger person. Or how peculiar she felt knowing that a machine had replaced her in the hearts and minds of her own family.

Nicole had watched silently while the other Nicole and Simone had laughed about an argument that Simone had had with her little sister Katie years before at The Node. As the alien had recalled the details of the story, Nicole's memory too had been refreshed. *Even her memory is better than mine ... What a perfect solution to the whole problem of aging and dying ... capture a person in the prime of her life, with all her powers intact, and preserve her forever as a legend, at least in the eyes of her loved ones.*

'How do I know for certain that the Michael and Simone that I talked with yesterday and this morning are the real humans and not just an even higher-fidelity simulation than the other Nicole?' Nicole asked The Eagle.

'Saint Michael said you asked several pointed questions about Big Michael's early life,' The Eagle said. 'Weren't you satisfied with the answers?'

'But I realised while we were in the car an hour ago that some of that information may have been in Michael's biographical file from the Newton, and I know that you had access to that data ...'

'For what purpose would we possibly have gone to such lengths to mislead you?' The Eagle said. 'And have we ever behaved in a similar fashion before?'

'How many more of Simone and Michael's children are still alive?' Nicole asked a few minutes later, changing the subject.

'Thirty-two more are here at this Node,' The Eagle answered. 'And more than a hundred in other places.'

Nicole shook her head. She remembered the Senoufo chronicles. *'And her progeny shall be spread among the stars'* ... *Omeh would be pleased*, she thought

'Have you perfected, then, your ex-utero development of humans from fertilised eggs?' Nicole said.

'More or less,' The Eagle replied.

Again they flew in silence for a long time. 'Why didn't you ever tell me about the Prime Monitors?' Nicole asked next.

'It wasn't permitted, at least not until you awakened ... And since then the subject hasn't come up.'

'And is everything Saint Michael said true? About God and chaos and the many universes?'

'As far as we know,' The Eagle said. 'At least that's what is programmed in our systems ... None of us here has ever actually seen a Prime Monitor.'

'And is it possible,' Nicole asked, 'that the whole story is a myth of some kind, created by an intelligence above you in the hierarchy, as the official explanation to give out to human beings?'

The Eagle hesitated. 'That possibility exists ... I would have no way of knowing.'

'Would you know if something different, some other explanation, had ever been programmed in your systems before?'

'Not necessarily,' The Eagle said. 'I am solely responsible for what is retained in my memory.'

Nicole's behaviour remained unusual. She interrupted her protracted periods of silence with bursts of apparently unrelated questions. At one point she asked why some Nodes had four modules and others three. The Eagle explained that the Knowledge Module created a tetrahedron out of the Nodal triangle in about every tenth or twelfth Node. Nicole wanted to know what was so special about the Knowledge Module. The Eagle told her that it was the repository of all the acquired information about this part of the galaxy.

'It's part-library and part-museum, containing a colossal amount of information in a variety of forms,' he said.

'Have you ever been inside this Knowledge Module?' Nicole asked.

'No,' The Eagle answered, 'but my current systems contain a complete description of it ...'

'Can I go there?' Nicole said.

'A living being must have special permission to enter the Knowledge Module,' The Eagle said.

When Nicole spoke again, she asked about what was going to happen to the humans who would be transferred to The Node in another day or two. The Eagle explained patiently, in response to one short question after another, that the people would live in the Habitation Module in a test environment with several other species, that they would be closely monitored, and that Simone, Michael, and their family might or might not be integrated with the humans who were moving to The Node.

Nicole made her decision several minutes before they reached the starfish. 'I want to stay here only for tonight,' she said slowly. 'So that I can say goodbye to everybody.'

The Eagle looked at her with a curious expression. 'Then tomorrow,' Nicole continued, 'if you can obtain permission, I want you to take me to the Knowledge Module ... Once I leave the starfish, I want all medication suspended ... And I want no heroic efforts if my heart goes into distress.'

Nicole looked straight ahead, through the front of her space-helmet and out the window of the shuttle. *It is definitely the right time*, she said to herself. *If only I have the courage not to waver.*

'Yes, Mother,' Ellie said, wiping her tears again. 'I *do* understand, I really do ... But I'm your daughter. I love you. No matter how much logical sense it might make to you, there's just no way I can be happy about never seeing you again.'

'So what am I supposed to do?' Nicole said. 'Let them change me into some kind of bionic woman so I can hang around for ever? And be the *grande dame* of the community, sententious and puffed up with self-importance? That is certainly not very appealing to me.'

'But everyone admires you, Mother,' Ellie said. 'Your family here loves you, and you could spend years getting to know all of Simone and Michael's family. You would never be a problem to any of us ...'

'That's not really the issue,' Nicole said. She turned her wheelchair around and faced one of the bare walls. 'The universe is in constant renewal,' she said, as much to herself as to Ellie. 'Everything – individuals, planets, stars, even galaxies – has a life cycle, a death as well as a birth. Nothing lasts forever. Not even the universe itself ... Change and renewal are an essential part of the overall process. The octospiders know this well. That's why planned terminations are an integral part of their overall replenishment concept.'

'But Mother,' Ellie said from behind her, 'unless there is a war, the octospiders only put individuals on the termination list who are no longer making enough of a contribution to their society to justify the resources being expended ... There is no cost to us for keeping you alive ... And your wisdom and experience are still valuable.'

Nicole turned around and smiled. 'You are a very bright woman, Ellie,' she said. 'And I will acknowledge that there is truth in what you are saying. But you are conveniently ignoring the two key elements in my decision, both of which I have already explained at great length ... For reasons neither you nor anybody else may be able to understand, it is important to me that I be able to choose my own time of death. I want to make that decision *before* I am either a burden or out of the mainstream of activity, and while I still have the respect of my family and friends. Second, it is my feeling that I do not have any defined niche in the post-transfer world. Therefore I cannot justify, in my own mind, the massive physiological intervention that will be necessary before I can function without being a problem for others ... From so many different points of view, now seems to be an excellent time for me to make my exit.'

'As I told you at the very beginning,' Ellie said, 'your cold, rational analysis, whether correct or not, should not be the only consideration. What about the feeling of loss that Benjy, Nikki, I, and the others will experience? And our sorrow will be increased by the knowledge that your death at this time could have been avoided ...'

'Ellie,' Nicole said, 'one of the reasons I came back to say goodbye to you and the others was to try to assuage any feeling of loss that you might have after my death ... Again, look at the octospiders. They do not grieve ...'

'Mother,' Ellie interrupted, fighting the return of the tears, 'we are *not* octospiders, we are human beings ... We *grieve* ... We feel desolate when someone we love dies. We know, in our minds, that death is inevitable and that it is all part of the universal scheme, but nevertheless we weep and feel an acute sense of loss ...'

Ellie paused for a moment. 'Have you forgotten how you felt when Richard and Katie died? ... You were devastated.'

Nicole swallowed slowly and looked at her daughter. *I knew this would not be easy*, she thought. *Maybe I shouldn't have come back ... Maybe it really would have been better if I had asked The Eagle to tell everyone I had died of a heart attack.*

'I know you were upset,' Ellie said softly, 'to find out that an alien robot had replaced you in Michael and Simone's family ... But you shouldn't over-react. Sooner or later all of their children and grandchildren will learn that there can be no substitute for the real Nicole des Jardins Wakefield.'

Nicole sighed. She felt she was losing the battle. 'I did acknowledge to you, Ellie, that I felt there was no place for me in Michael and Simone's family. But it is unfair for you to imply that my reaction to the other Nicole is the sole, or even the main reason for my decision.'

Nicole was becoming exhausted. She had planned to talk first to Ellie, then to Benjy, and finally to the rest of the group before she went to sleep. Ellie had been much more difficult than she had expected. *But were you being realistic?* Nicole asked herself. *Did you really think Ellie would say, great, Mother, it makes sense. I'm sorry to see you go, but I understand completely.*

There was a knock on the door of the apartment. The Eagle looked at the two women after the door was opened. 'Am I intruding?' the alien asked.

Nicole smiled. 'I think we are ready for a short break,' she said.

Ellie excused herself to go to the bathroom and The Eagle walked over to Nicole. 'How's it going?' he said, bending down to the level of the wheelchair.

'Not so well,' Nicole answered.

'I thought I'd drop by,' The Eagle said, 'to tell you that your request to visit the Knowledge Module has been approved. Assuming the basic situation you described to me in the shuttle is still valid ...'

1307

Nicole brightened. 'Good, ' she said. 'Now if I can just summon the courage to finish what I have started.'

The Eagle patted her on the back. 'You can do it,' he said. 'You are the most extraordinary human we have ever encountered.'

Benjy's head was resting on her chest. Nicole was on her back with her arm wrapped around her son. *So this may be the last night of my life*, she thought as she drifted toward sleep. A small tremor of fear rushed through her and she forced it aside. *I am not afraid of death*, Nicole said to herself, *not after what I have already experienced*.

The visit from The Eagle had refortified her. When her conversation with Ellie had resumed, Nicole admitted that there was merit in all of Ellie's points and that she didn't mean to cause distress for her friends and family, but that she was determined to proceed with her decision. Nicole had then pointed out to Ellie that Benjy and she, and to some extent the others, would have an opportunity for additional individual growth in her absence, because there would no longer be an authority figure around to whom they could appeal.

Ellie had told Nicole that she was a 'stubborn old woman,' but that, because of her love and respect, Ellie would try to be supportive in the few remaining hours. Ellie had also asked Nicole if she intended to do anything specific to hasten her death. Nicole had laughed and told her daughter that no unusual steps would be necessary, for The Eagle had assured her that without supplementary medication her heart would fail in a matter of hours.

The conversation with Benjy had not been that difficult. Ellie had volunteered to help explain everything and Nicole had accepted her offer. Benjy knew that his mother was suffering and in poor health, and he had no knowledge that the aliens possessed the medical ability to fix her problems. Ellie had assured Benjy that Max, Eponine, Nikki, Kepler, Marius, and Maria would all still be part of his everyday world.

Of the larger group, only Eponine had had tearful eyes when Nicole had informed them of her decision. Max had said that he wasn't completely surprised. Maria had expressed sadness that she hadn't spent more time with the woman who had 'saved her life'. Kepler, Marius, and even Nikki had all been unsure of themselves and hadn't known what to say.

While she was preparing for bed, Nicole had promised herself that she would locate Dr Blue first thing in the morning and say a proper goodbye to her octospider friend. Just before she had switched out the lights, Benjy had approached his mother and asked, since this would be their last night together, if he could cuddle with her 'like I did when I was a lit-tle boy.' Nicole had agreed, and after Benjy had snuggled up against her, tears had run across her face, moistening her ears and the sleeping mat below.

10

Nicole awakened early. Benjy was already up and dressed, but Kepler was still asleep on the far side of the room. Benjy patiently helped Nicole shower and dress, as he had before.

Max came into the apartment a few minutes later. After waking up Kepler, he walked over to Nicole's wheelchair and took her hand. 'I didn't say much last night, my friend,' Max said, 'because I couldn't find the right words ... Even now, they seem so inadequate ...'

Max turned his head away. 'Shit, Nicole,' he said in a breaking voice, without facing her. 'You know how I feel about you ... you are a beautiful, beautiful person.'

He stopped. The only sound in the room was the water running for Kepler's shower. Nicole squeezed his hand. 'Thank you, Max,' she said softly, 'it means a lot to me.'

'When I was eighteen,' Max said hesitantly, turning back to look at Nicole, 'my father died of a rare kind of cancer ... We all knew it was coming. Clyde and Mom and I had watched him wither away for several months ... But I still didn't believe it, even after he was lying in the coffin ... We had a small service at the cemetery, just our friends from the neighbouring farms plus an auto mechanic from De Queen, a man named Willie Townsend who got drunk with Dad every other Saturday night ...'

Max smiled and relaxed. He loved telling stories. 'Willie was a good ole son of a bitch, a bachelor, hard as nails on the outside, and soft as putty underneath ... He was jilted by the De Queen High School Homecoming Queen when he was a young man and never again had a girl-friend ... Anyway, Mom asked me if I would say a few words "over my dad" at the graveside service, and I agreed ... I wrote them myself, memorised them carefully, and even practised once out loud in front of Clyde ...

'Come the service, I was ready with my speech ... "My father, Henry Allan Puckett, was a fine man," I began. I then paused, as I had planned, and looked around. Willie was already sniffling and was looking down at the ground ... Suddenly I couldn't remember what I was supposed to say next. We all stood there in the hot Arkansas sun for what seemed like for ever but was probably only thirty seconds or so ... I never did remember the rest of my speech. Finally, out of both desperation and embarrassment, I said "Aw, fuck"' and Willie chimed in immediately with a loud "Amen" …'

Nicole was laughing. 'Max Puckett,' she said, 'there cannot be anyone like you anywhere in this universe.'

Max grinned. 'Last night, when Frenchie and I were in bed, we were talking about that other Nicole the aliens had created for Simone and Michael, and Ep wondered if they could make a robot Max Puckett for her. She liked the idea of having a perfect husband who always did exactly what she asked … Even at night … We laughed until our sides hurt trying to imagine, well, you know, what the robot might or might not be able to do in bed …'

'Shame on you, Max,' Nicole said.

'Actually it was Frenchie who really got imaginative … Anyway,' Max said, 'I was sent over here with a specific purpose, to inform you that we are having a catered breakfast next door, courtesy of the blockheads, as part of our attempt to say goodbye, or wish you *"bon voyage"*, or whatever is appropriate. And that it will start in exactly eight more minutes.'

Nicole was delighted to discover that the mood at breakfast was light and pleasant. She had stressed several times the night before that her departure should not be a time for sorrow, that it should be celebrated as the end of a wonderful life. Apparently her family and friends had taken her remarks to heart, for she saw only an occasional sombre face.

Ellie and Benjy sat on either side of Nicole at the long table set up by the block robots. Next to Ellie was Nikki, then Maria, and Dr Blue. On the other side Max and Eponine were beside Benjy, then Marius, Kepler, and The Eagle. During the meal Nicole noticed with surprise that Maria was actually conversing with Dr Blue. 'I didn't know you could read colours, Maria,' Nicole said, a clearly complimentary tone in her voice.

'Only a little,' the girl said, slightly embarrassed by the attention. 'Ellie has been teaching me.'

'That's great,' Nicole commented.

'Of course the real linguist in this group,' Max said, 'is that strange bird-man at the end of the table … We even saw him yesterday talking to the iguanas in bizarre clicks and screeches.'

'Yuch,' said Nikki, 'I wouldn't want to talk to one of those nasty creatures…'

'They have an altogether different way of looking at the world,' The Eagle said. 'Very simple, very primitive.'

'What I want to know,' Eponine said, leaning forward and directly addressing The Eagle, 'is what I have to do to get an alien robot companion of my own. I'll take one that looks like Max here, except is not ornery and has certain other improved attributes …'

Everyone laughed. Nicole smiled to herself as she looked around the table. *This is perfect*, she thought. *I couldn't have asked for a better farewell.*

*

Dr Blue and The Eagle gave her one last dose of the blue liquid while Nicole was arranging her bag. She was glad to have a private moment to tell Dr Blue goodbye. 'Thank you for everything,' Nicole said simply, hugging her octospider colleague.

'We will all miss you,' Dr Blue said in colour. 'The new Chief Optimiser wanted to organise a grand send-off, but I told her I did not think it would be appropriate ... She asked me to tell you goodbye on behalf of our entire species.'

They all accompanied her to the airlock. There was one final round of smiling hugs, at wheelchair level, and then The Eagle and Nicole passed through the airlock.

Nicole sighed as The Eagle lifted her into her seat in the shuttle and folded the wheelchair.

'They were great, weren't they?' Nicole said.

'They love and respect you very much,' The Eagle replied.

Once they left the starfish, the great tetrahedron of light was again turning slowly in their view. 'How do you feel?' The Eagle asked.

'Relieved,' Nicole said, 'and a little frightened.'

'That's to be expected,' The Eagle said.

'How long do you think I have?' Nicole asked several seconds later. 'Before my heart gives out?'

'That's hard to say exactly.'

'I know, I know,' Nicole said impatiently. 'But you guys are scientists ... You must have done some computations ...'

'Between six and ten hours,' The Eagle said.

In six to ten hours I will be dead, Nicole thought. The fear was more palpable now. She could not push it completely aside.

'What's it like to be dead?' Nicole asked.

'We thought you'd ask that question,' The Eagle answered. 'We are told that it's similar to being unpowered.'

'Nothingness, forever?' Nicole said.

'I guess so.'

'And the act of dying itself?' she said. 'Is there anything special about that?'

'We don't know,' The Eagle said. 'We were hoping that you would share with us as much as you can.'

They flew in silence for quite a while. Ahead of them, The Node grew quickly in size. At one point the spacecraft changed its orientation slightly and the Knowledge Module moved to the centre of their window. During the final approach, the other three vertices of The Node were below them.

'Do you mind if I ask a question?' The Eagle said.

'Not at all,' Nicole answered. She turned and smiled at the alien through her space-helmet. 'I hope you're not becoming timid at this late date.'

'I didn't want to disturb your thoughts.'

1311

'Actually at the moment I'm not thinking about anything specific,' Nicole said. 'My mind is just drifting.'

'Why do you want to spend your final moments in the Knowledge Module?' The Eagle asked.

Nicole laughed. 'Now, that's a preprogrammed question if ever I heard one,' she said. 'I can already see my answer stored in some almost endless file, under "Death: Human Beings", and other related categories.'

The Eagle did not say anything.

'When Richard and I were marooned in New York years ago,' Nicole said, 'and did not think we had much of a chance to escape, we talked about what we would like to be doing during the last moments before our deaths. We agreed that our first choice would be making love together. Our second choice was to be learning something new, to be experiencing the thrill of discovery one last time ...'

'That's a very advanced concept,' The Eagle said.

'And a practical one too,' Nicole said. 'Unless I miss my guess, this Knowledge Module of yours will be so intriguing that I will not even be aware that the last seconds of my life are ticking away ... As committed as I am to this action, I think fear would overpower me if I weren't actively engaged during my final hours.'

The Knowledge Module now filled their entire window. 'Before we enter,' The Eagle said, 'I want to give you some information about this place ... The spherical module is actually three separate concentric domains, each with a specific purpose. The outermost and smallest region is focused on knowledge associated with the present, or near present. The next inner region is where all the historical information about this part of the galaxy has been stored. The large inner sphere contains all the models for predicting the future, as well as stochastic scenarios for the next aeons ...'

'I thought you had never been inside,' Nicole said.

'I haven't,' The Eagle replied. 'But my Knowledge Module data base was updated and expanded last night ...'

A door in the outer surface of the sphere opened and the shuttle started to enter. 'Just a minute,' Nicole said. 'Do I understand that I will almost certainly never leave this module alive?'

'Yes,' said The Eagle.

'Then will you please turn this vehicle around slowly and let me take one last look at the outside world?'

The shuttle executed a slow yaw manoeuvre and Nicole, sitting forward in her seat, gazed fixedly out the window. She saw the other spherical modules of The Node, the transportation corridors, and, in the distance, the starfish, where her family and friends were packing their bags for their transfer. In one orientation the yellow star Tau Ceti, so much like the Sun, was the only large object in the window, and despite its radiance and the scattered light from The Node, Nicole could still discern a few other stars against the blackness of space.

Nothing in this scene will be changed by my death, Nicole thought. *There will just be one less pair of eyes to observe its splendour. And one less collection of chemicals risen to consciousness to wonder what it all means.*

'Thank you,' Nicole said after the full turn was completed. 'We may now proceed.'

11

Vehicles entering the Knowledge Module from space, as well as the tubes arriving from the other three modules, all ended up at a long slender station located on one side of the mid-level annulus that completely encircled the huge sphere.

'There are only two entrances, a hundred and eighty degrees apart, into each of the three concentric domains of the Knowledge Module,' The Eagle said as Nicole and he were carried swiftly along the annulus by a moving sidewalk. To their right was the transparent outer surface of the module. On their left was a cream-coloured, windowless wall.

'Will I be able to take off my suit and helmet soon?' Nicole asked from her wheelchair.

'Yes, after we enter the exhibits,' The Eagle said. 'I had to specify some kind of tour – they couldn't change the atmosphere of the entire module overnight – and in those places you will not need your space suit.'

'So you have already selected what we are going to see?'

'It was unavoidable,' The Eagle said. 'This place is immense, much larger than one of the hemicylinders of Rama, and absolutely crammed full of information ... I tried to design our tour based on my knowledge of your interests and our allocated time ... If it turns out that there are other things ...'

'No, no,' Nicole said. 'I wouldn't have any idea what to request. I'm certain that what you did was fine ...'

They were approaching a place where the moving sidewalk stopped and a broad corridor went off to the left. 'By the way,' The Eagle said, 'I didn't explain to you that our tour is restricted to the outer two regions ... The Predictions Domain is off limits for us.'

'Why is that?' Nicole asked, activating her wheelchair and moving along the corridor beside The Eagle.

'I don't know for certain,' he said. 'But it doesn't really matter, if I understand your purpose here. There will be more than enough to occupy you in the two available domains.'

In front of them was a high blank wall. As The Eagle and Nicole approached, a wide door in the wall opened inward, revealing a tall circular room with a ten-metre-diameter sphere in its centre. The wall and ceiling of the room were both cluttered with small fixtures or equipment and many strange markings. The Eagle told Nicole that he had no idea what any of it meant.

'What I *have* been told,' the alien said, 'is that the orientation for your visit to this domain is supposed to take place inside that sphere in front of us.'

The gleaming sphere divided in half at the midsection. The upper half of the hollow ball lifted up just enough that The Eagle and Nicole could pass underneath into the interior of the sphere. Once they were inside, the top half of the sphere returned to its original position and they were completely enclosed.

It was only dark for a second or two. Then small scattered lights illuminated some of the side of the sphere that was facing them. 'It's decorated with a lot of detail,' Nicole commented.

'What we're looking at,' The Eagle said, 'is a model of this entire domain. Our point of view is from the inside, as if we were at the very centre of the Knowledge Module and neither of the two inner domains existed ... You'll notice that the way the objects are placed along and against the surface, not only in front of and behind us, but also above and below us, nothing intrudes into the empty central space more than a fixed distance. The outer wall of the next concentric domain is located at that spot in the *real* module ... Now the lights will show you, on the model, where we will be going in the next few hours.'

A large sector of the inner sphere surface facing them, about 30 per cent of the area altogether, was suddenly visible in a soft light.

'Everything in the lit region,' The Eagle said, making a circular gesture with his hand, 'is associated with spacefaring. We will confine our tour to this portion of the domain ... The blinking red light on the surface in front of us is where we are presently ...'

As Nicole watched, a red line of lights moved quickly up the surface, stopping at a point above her head where there was a picture of the Milky Way Galaxy. 'We will go first to the geography section,' The Eagle said, pointing at the place where the line of lights had stopped, 'then to engineering, and finally to biology ... After a short break, we will continue into the second domain ... Any more questions before we start?'

They drove up what appeared to be an ascending ramp in a small car similar to the one they had used in the Habitation Module during Nicole's visit with Michael and Simone. Although the path in front and behind them was illuminated, whatever was beside the car was always in the dark.

'What's around us?' Nicole asked after they had been driving for almost ten minutes.

'Data storage mostly, plus a few exhibits,' The Eagle said. 'It is dark so that you are not unnecessarily distracted.'

Eventually they stopped beside another tall door. 'The room you are about to enter,' The Eagle said, setting up Nicole's wheelchair, 'is the largest single room in this domain. It is half a kilometre across at its widest point. Inside currently is a model of the Milky Way Galaxy. Once we enter, we will be standing on a mobile platform that we can command to take us to any point in the room ... It will be mostly dark inside, and there will be displays and structures both above us and below us. You might feel as if you are going to fall, but remember that you are weightless ...'

The view from the platform was spectacular. Even before they began to move toward the centre of the vast room, Nicole was overwhelmed. Lights representing stars were everywhere in the blackness that surrounded them. Single stars, binaries, combination triples. Small, stable yellow stars, red giants, white dwarfs – they even passed directly over an exploding super-nova. In every location, in every direction, there was something different and fascinating to see.

After a few minutes The Eagle stopped the platform. 'I thought we'd start here, where you are familiar with the territory,' he said.

Using a pointer with multiple light beams, he indicated a nearby yellow star. 'Do you recognise this place?'

Nicole was still staring at the endless lights in all directions. 'Are all hundred billion stars in the galaxy actually modeled in this room?' she asked.

'No,' The Eagle replied. 'What you are seeing here is only a large section of the galaxy ... I'll explain more to you in a few minutes when we go to the top of the room and can look down on the central galactic plane ... I brought you to this particular spot for another purpose.'

Nicole recognised the Sun, and the Centauri triple, its closest neighbour, and even Barnard's star and Sirius. She could not remember the names of most of the other stars in the local neighbourhood of the Sun. She did, however, manage to locate another solitary yellow star not too far away.

'Is that Tau Ceti?' she asked.

'Yes, indeed,' said The Eagle.

Tau Ceti seems so close to the Sun, Nicole thought, *but in reality it is so very far away. That means the galaxy is larger than any of us could possibly comprehend.*

'The distance from the Sun to Tau Ceti,' The Eagle said, as if he were reading her mind, 'is one ten-thousandth of the distance across the galaxy.'

Nicole shook her head as the platform began to move away from the Sun and Tau Ceti. *There is so much more than I had ever imagined*, she thought. *Even my journeys have taken place in an insignificantly small region of space.*

Off the moving platform to Nicole's right, The Eagle projected a three-dimensional line-drawing in the shape of a rectangular solid. By manipulating the black device that he was holding in his hand, he made the volume of the solid alternately larger and smaller.

'We have many different ways to control what is projected in this room,' The Eagle said. 'With this device we can change the scale and zoom in on any particular region of the galaxy ... Let me show you. Suppose I put the red light here, in the middle of the Orion Nebula. That marks the desired initial position of the platform. Then let me expand this geometrical shape to enclose about a thousand stars ... Now, presto ...'

It was pitch-black in the room for about a second. Then suddenly Nicole was again dazzled, but this time by a different set of lights. The clusters and individual stars were much more clearly defined. The Eagle explained that the entire room was now contained inside the Orion Nebula and that the longest room dimension was now the equivalent of a few hundred light-years, instead of sixty thousand light-years as before.

'This particular area is a stellar nursery,' The Eagle said, 'where stars and planets are just being born.' He moved the platform toward the right. 'Over here, for example, is an infant star system, in the early stages of formation, with many of the characteristics that your solar system had four and a half billion years ago.'

He inscribed a small solid figure around one of the stars, and a few seconds later the room was filled with the light of a young sun. Nicole watched a gigantic solar storm move across the moiling surface. A coronal burst arced high above her head, shooting a finger of orange and red into the blackness of space.

The Eagle steered the platform toward a much smaller, distant body, one of about a dozen accumulations of mass that could be identified in the region closely surrounding the young star. This particular planet had a slightly reddish molten surface. As they watched, a large projectile crashed into the hot fluid, ejecting material from the surface and setting up vigorous wave motion in all directions.

'According to our statistical data,' The Eagle said, 'this planet has a non-trivial probability of producing life after a few billion years of evolution, once this period of bombardment and formation is concluded. It will have a solitary, stable host star, an atmosphere with sufficient climatic variation, plus all the chemical ingredients ... Here, see for yourself. Keep your eyes on that planet. I am going to activate a special routine that scans quickly through the bottom half of the periodic chart and displays quantitative data about the comparative number of atoms of each kind that exist in that boiling stew ...'

A magnificent visual display appeared in the blackness above the infant planet. Each separate atom contained in the planet's mass was indicated both by a specific colour and by its number of neutrons and protons. The size of the atom showed its comparative frequency in the mix ... 'Note that there are significant densities of carbon, nitrogen, the halogens, and iron,' The Eagle said. 'These are the critical atoms. They were all created by nearby supernova in the not-too-distant past and have enriched the organizational possibilities of this forming body ... Without complex chemistry, there cannot be efficient life ... If iron were not available to be the central atom of haemoglobin, for example, on your planet, the oxygen distribution system of the many advanced life-forms would be much more inefficient ...'

So the process continues, Nicole thought, *aeon after aeon. Stars and planets form out of the cosmic dust. A few of the planets contain the right chemical stuff that might eventually lead to life and intelligence. But what organises this process? What unseen hand causes these chemicals to become more and more complex and structured in time, until they reach even the state of self-awareness? Is there some yet-to-be-formulated natural law about matter organising itself according to specified rules?*

The Eagle was now explaining how unlikely it was that life would evolve in star systems that contained only simple atoms like hydrogen and helium, and none of the more complex, higher-order atoms forged by dying stars in supernova explosions. Nicole began to feel an overpowering insignificance. She longed for something on a human scale.

'How small can you shrink this room?' Nicole said suddenly. She laughed at her own awkward phraseology. 'To be more precise,' she continued, 'what is the ultimate resolution of this system?'

'The finest level of detail possible,' The Eagle said, 'is at a scale of 4096 to 1. At the other extreme, we can display an intergalactic scene with a greatest dimension of fifty million light years ... Remember, our interest in activities outside the galaxy is limited ...'

Nicole was doing some mental calculations of her own. 'Since the longest dimension of this room is half a kilometre, at the highest level of detail this room would be filled by a piece of real estate roughly two thousand kilometres long?'

'That's right,' The Eagle said. 'But why are you asking?'

Nicole was becoming more excited. 'Could we zoom in on the Earth?' she asked. 'And let me fly over France?'

'Yes, I guess so,' The Eagle answered after a short hesitation. 'Although that is not what I had planned.'

'It would mean a lot to me.'

'All right,' The Eagle said. 'It will take a couple of seconds to set up, but we can do it ...'

The flight began over the English Channel. The Eagle and Nicole had been sitting on the platform at the top of the dark room for approximately three seconds when there was an explosion of light beneath them. After Nicole's eyes finally adjusted, she recognised the blue water underneath them and the shape of the Normandy coastline. Off in the distance the Seine emptied into the Channel.

She asked The Eagle to station the platform over the mouth of the Seine and then to move slowly toward Paris. The sight of the familiar geography evoked a strong emotional response in Nicole. She remembered clearly the days of her youth, when she had wandered carefree throughout this region with her beloved father.

The model below them was superb. It was even three-dimensional when the sizes of the geographical features and buildings below them were above the limits of resolution of the alien system. In Rouen, the famous church where Joan of Arc had temporarily recanted was half a centimetre tall and two centimetres long. Off in the direction of Paris, Nicole could see the familiar shape of the Arc de Triomphe rising from the surface of the model.

When they reached Paris, the platform hovered for a few seconds over the sixteenth *arrondissement*. Nicole's eyes fell briefly upon a particular building below her. The sight of that building, a modern convention centre, brought back an especially poignant moment from her adolescence. *To my precious daughter, Nicole, and all the young people of the world, I offer one simple insight,* she heard her father's voice say again. He was near the end of his speech accepting the Mary Renault Prize. *In my life I have found two things of priceless worth – learning and loving. Nothing else – not fame, not power, not achievement for its own sake – can possibly have the same lasting value.*

An image of her father filled Nicole's mind. *Thank you, Papa,* she thought. Thank you for taking such good care of me after Mother died. *Thank you for everything you taught me ...*

A powerful, painful yearning brought a rush of tears to Nicole's eyes. For an instant she was again a child, and she wanted desperately to talk to her father about her coming death. Slowly, deliberately, Nicole fought against the emotions that were threatening to overwhelm her. *This is not what I wanted to feel right now,* she said to herself with difficulty. *I wanted to leave all this behind ...*

She turned her face away from the model of France below her.

'What is it?' The Eagle asked.

Nicole forced a smile. 'I want to see something else,' she said. 'Something spectacular ... and new. How about an octospider city?'

'Are you certain?' The Eagle said.

Nicole nodded.

The room became dark immediately. Two seconds later, when Nicole turned around to face the light, the platform was flying over a vast ocean of deep green.

'Where are we?' she asked. 'And where are we going?'

'We're presently about thirty light-years away from your Sun,' The Eagle replied, 'on the first oceanic planet colonised by the octospiders after the disappearance of the Precursors ... We're over the sea, obviously, about two hundred kilometres away from the most famous of the octospider cities.'

Nicole felt a surge of excitement as the platform zoomed across the sea. In the distance she could already see the vague outline of some buildings. For a moment she imagined that she was an adventurous space traveller arriving at this planet for the first time, eager to see the wonders of the fabulous cities that other interstellar travellers had described.

This is wonderful, Nicole thought. She momentarily turned her attention to the ocean below her. 'Why is this water so green?' she asked The Eagle.

'The top metre of this part of the ocean is a rich ecosystem of its own, dominated by a special genus of photosynthesising plant whose varied species, all green in colour, provide housing and food for as many as ten million separate creatures ... Some of the individual plants cover more than a square kilometre of territory ... The Precursors created this domain originally ... The octospiders found it and improved upon it ...'

When Nicole glanced up, the speeding platform had nearly reached the city. Hundreds of buildings of various shapes and sizes were spread out below them. Most of the octospider city's buildings were built on the land, but some appeared to be floating on the water. The densest collection of these structures was along a narrow peninsula that extended slightly into the sea. At the end of that peninsula stood three huge green domes, very close together, that dominated the city skyline.

At the periphery of the city was a wide outer circle of eight smaller domes, each of which was connected by linear transportation features to the central domes. Each of these outer domes was a distinct and different colour. Almost all of the buildings in the section of the city surrounding an outer dome had been painted with the same colour. Out in the ocean, for example, the brilliant red dome had eight long, slender red spokes, representing other buildings, extending outward from it in a balanced geometrical pattern.

All the buildings of the city lay inside the circle defined by the eight coloured domes. Nicole's immediate favourite was a strange brown-coloured structure floating on the water. It appeared to be almost as large as the huge central domes. From above, the rectangular building looked like twenty layers of a densely packed lattice, with material from birds nests filling the open areas inside each of the hundreds of cells.

'What is that?' Nicole asked, pointing from the platform.

'These particular octospiders are very advanced in microbiology,' The Eagle replied. 'That structure, which extends incidentally another ten metres deep into the ocean, contains over a thousand different habitats for species in the micrometre size-range ... What you're looking at is essentially a supply-station, containing the excess population for each of these tiny beings. Octospiders needing any of these creatures come to this building to requisition them.'

Nicole's eyes feasted on the unusual architecture below her. In her mind's eye she could see herself walking on the streets, looking around in amazement at a variety of creatures far greater even than the menagerie she had encountered in the Emerald City. *I want to go there*, she said to herself. *I want to see ...*

She asked The Eagle to move the platform directly over one of the large green domes. 'Is the inside of this dome,' Nicole asked, 'similar to what was in the Emerald City?'

'Not really,' The Eagle replied. 'The scale is altogether different ... The octospider realm in Rama was a compressed microcosm. Functions which are normally separated on their planets by hundreds of kilometres of distance were forced, because of space limitations, to be located in more or less the same area ... In the advanced colonies of the octospider genus, for example, the alternates do not have a community just outside the city gates – they live on an entirely different planet.'

Nicole smiled. *A planet full of alternates*, she thought. *Now, that would be quite a sight.*

'... This particular city is the home for more than eighteen million octospiders, if we count all the different morpho logical variations,' The Eagle said. 'It is also the administrative capital for this planet. Within the gates of the city live close to ten billion individual creatures, representing fifty thousand species ... The extent of the city is roughly equivalent to Los Angeles or any of the great urban areas on your Earth ...'

The Eagle continued to tell her facts and statistics about the octospider city beneath their platform. Nicole, however, was thinking about something else. 'Did Archie live here?' she said, interrupting her alien companion's encyclopedic monologue. 'Or Dr Blue, or any of the octospiders that we met?'

'No,' The Eagle replied. 'In fact, they did not even come from this planet or star system ... The octospiders in Rama came from what is known as a "frontier colony", one especially designed genetically for interaction with other intelligent life-forms ...'

Nicole shook her head and smiled. *Of course*, she said to herself, *I should have suspected that they were special ...*

She was growing tired. After another few minutes Nicole thanked The Eagle and said that she had seen enough of the octospider city. In an instant the domes, the brown lattice structure, and the deep-green sea vanished. The Eagle returned the platform to the top of the large chamber.

Below Nicole the Milky Way was confined to a small space in the centre of the room. 'The universe is an ever-expanding sequence of neighbourhoods and voids,' The Eagle was saying. 'Look how empty it is around the Milky Way. Except for the two Magellanic Clouds, which really don't qualify as galaxies, Andromeda is our nearest galactic neighbour. But it is very far away. The distance across the greatest dimension of the Milky Way is only one-twentieth of the distance to Andromeda.'

Nicole was not thinking about Andromeda. She was absorbed in delightful philosophical musings about life on different worlds, about cities, and about the likely range of creatures made from simple atoms who had evolved, with or without help from superior beings, into consciousness. She savoured the moment, knowing that very soon there would be no more of the flights of imagination that had enriched her life so much.

12

'We spent so much time in that exhibit,' The Eagle said after he finished the scan, 'that I think maybe we should revise our tour.'

They were sitting side by side in the car. 'Is that your diplomatic way of telling me that my heart is failing more rapidly than you expected?' Nicole asked, forcing a smile.

'No, not really,' The Eagle said. 'We really *did* spend almost twice as much time as I had planned ... I hadn't even considered the overflight of France, for example, or the visit to the octospider city ...'

'That part was wonderful,' Nicole said. 'I wish I could go there again, with Dr Blue as my guide, and find out more about the way they live ...'

'So you liked the octospider city better than the spectacular views of the stars?'

'I wouldn't say that,' Nicole replied. 'It was all fantastic ... What I have seen already has reconfirmed that I chose the right place to ...' She did not finish the sentence. 'I realised while I was on the platform that death is not just the end of thinking and being aware,' she said, 'it is also the end of feeling ... I don't know why that wasn't obvious to me before.'

There was a short silence. 'So, my friend,' Nicole said brightly, 'where do we go from here?'

'I thought we'd go next to engineering, where you can see models of Nodes, Carriers, and other spacecraft, after which, if we still have enough time, I plan to take you to the biology section. Some of your ex-utero grandchildren are living in that region, in one of our better Earthlike habitats. Nearby is another compound housing a community of those intriguing aquatic eels or snakes that we encountered once together at The Node. And there is a taxonomic display that compares and contrasts, physically, all the spacefarers that have been studied in this region ...'

'It all sounds great,' Nicole said. She laughed suddenly. 'The human brain is amazing ... Guess what just popped into my mind ... The first lines of Andrew Marvell's poem "To His Coy Mistress" ... "Had we but world enough, and time, This coyness, lady, were no crime," ... Anyway, I was going to say that since we do not have forever, let's go first to the Carrier display. I would like to see the spacecraft in which Patrick, Nai, Galileo, and the others will be living ... After that, we'll see how much time is left.'

The car began to move. Nicole noted to herself that The Eagle had not said anything about the results of his scan. The fear came back, stronger now. '*The grave's a fine and private place*,' she recalled. '*But none, I think, do there embrace.*'

They were together on the flat surface of the Carrier model. 'This is a one sixty-fourth scale model,' The Eagle said, 'so you have some sense of how large the Carrier really is.'

Nicole stared off into the distance from her wheelchair. 'Goodness,' she said, 'this plane must be almost one kilometre long.'

'That's a decent guess,' The Eagle said. 'The top of the actual Carrier is roughly forty kilometres long and fifteen kilometres wide.'

'And each of these bubbles encloses a different environment?'

'Yes,' The Eagle said. 'The atmosphere and other conditions are controlled by the equipment that is here on the surface, as well as the additional engineering systems down below in the main volume of the spacecraft ... Each of the habitats has its own spin rate to create the proper gravity ... Partitions are available to separate species, if necessary, inside one of the bubbles. The residents from the starfish have been placed in the same domain because they are comfortable in more or less the same ambient conditions. However, they do not have any access to each other.'

They were moving down a path among the equipment emplacements and the bubbles. 'Some of these habitats,' Nicole said, examining a small oval protrusion rising above the plane no more than five metres, 'seem too small and confining to hold more than just a few individuals ...'

'There are some very small spacefarers,' The Eagle said. 'One species, from a star system not too far from yours, is only about a millimetre in length. Their largest spacecraft are not even as big as this car.'

Nicole tried to imagine an intelligent group of ants, or aphids, working together to build a spacecraft. She smiled at her mental picture.

'And all these Carriers just travel from Node to Node?' she asked, changing the subject;

'Primarily,' The Eagle said. 'When there are no longer any living creatures in a particular bubble, that habitat is reconditioned at one of The Nodes.'

'Like Rama,' Nicole said.

'In a way,' The Eagle said, 'but with many significant differences. We are always intently studying whatever species are inside a Rama-class spacecraft. We try to place them in as realistic an environment as possible, so that we can observe them under "natural conditions". By contrast, we do not *need* any more data about the creatures assigned to the Carrier fleet. That's why we don't intercede in their affairs.'

'Except to preclude reproduction ... By the way, in the structure of your ethics, is preventing reproduction somehow more humane, or whatever your equivalent word is, than terminating the creatures directly?'

'We think so,' The Eagle replied.

They had reached a location on the top of the Carrier model where a pathway branched off to the left back to the ramps and hallways of the Knowledge Module. 'I think I've accomplished what I wanted here,' Nicole said. She hesitated for a moment. 'But I do have a couple of other questions.'

'Go ahead,' The Eagle said.

'Assuming Saint Michael's description of the purpose of Rama and The Node and everything else is correct, aren't you yourself disturbing and changing the very process you're observing? It seems to me that just by being here and interacting ...'

'You're right, of course,' The Eagle said. 'Our presence here *does* slightly impact the course of evolution. It's a situation analogous to the Heisenberg Uncertainty Principle from physics ... We cannot observe without influencing ... Nevertheless, our interactions can be considered by the Prime Monitor and taken into account in the overall modeling of the process. And we do have rules that minimise the ways in which we perturb the natural evolution...'

'I wish that Richard could have been with me to hear Saint Michael's explanation of everything,' Nicole said. 'He would have been fascinated, and, I am sure, would have had some excellent questions.'

The Eagle did not reply. Nicole sighed. 'So what's next, Monsieur le Tour Director?' she said.

'Lunch,' said The Eagle. 'There are a couple of sandwiches, some water, and a delicious piece of your favourite octospider fruit in the car.'

Nicole laughed and turned her wheelchair on to the pathway. 'You think of everything,' she said.

'Richard didn't believe in heaven,' Nicole said as The Eagle completed another scan. 'But if he could have constructed his own perfect afterlife, it would definitely have included a place like this.'

The Eagle was studying the weird squiggles on the monitor in his hand. 'I think it would be a good idea,' he said, looking up at Nicole, 'to skip some of the tour ... And go directly to the most important exhibits in the next domain.'

'That bad, huh?' Nicole said. She was not surprised. The occasional pain she had been feeling in her chest before the visits to France and the octospider city had now become continuous.

The fear was constant now as well. In between every word, every thought, she was acutely aware that her death was not very far away. *So what are you afraid of?* Nicole asked herself. *How can nothingness be that bad?* Still the fear persisted.

The Eagle explained that there was not enough time for an orientation to the second domain. They passed through the gates into the second of the concentric spheres and drove for about ten minutes. 'The emphasis in this domain,' The Eagle said while driving, 'is on the way everything changes in time. There is a separate section for every conceivable element in the galaxy that is affected by, or affects, the galaxy's overall evolution ... I thought you'd be especially interested in this first exhibit.'

The room was similar to the one where The Eagle and Nicole had first seen the Milky Way, except that it was considerably smaller. Again they boarded a moving platform that allowed them to move around in the dark room.

'What you are going to watch,' The Eagle said, 'requires some explanation. It is essentially a time-lapse summary of the evolution of spacefaring civilisations in a galactic region containing your Sun and about ten million other star systems. This is approximately one ten-thousandth of the entire galaxy, but what you will see is representative of the galaxy as a whole ...

'You will not see any stars or planets or other physical structures in this display, although their locations are assumed in developing the model. What you will see, once we begin, are lights, each representing a star system in which a biological species has become a spacefarer by at least putting a space-craft in orbit around its own planet ... As long as the star system remains a living centre for active spacefarers, the light in that particular location will stay illuminated ...

'I am going to start the display about ten billion years ago, soon after what has evolved into the current Milky Way Galaxy was initially formed. Since there was so much instability and rapid change at the beginning, no space-farers emerged for a long time. Therefore, for the first five billion years or so, up until the formation of your solar system, I will run the display rapidly, at a rate of twenty million years per second ... For reference purposes, the Earth will begin to accrete roughly four minutes into this process. I will stop the display at that time.'

They were together on the platform in the large chamber. The Eagle was standing and Nicole was sitting beside him in her wheelchair. The only light was a small one on the platform that allowed the two of them to see each other. After staring around her at the total darkness for more than thirty seconds, Nicole broke the silence. 'Did you start the process?' she asked. 'Nothing's happening.'

'Exactly,' The Eagle replied. 'What we have observed, from watching other galaxies, some much older than the Milky Way, is that no life emerges until the galaxy settles down and develops stable zones. Life requires both a few steady stars in a relatively benign environment and stellar evolution, result-ing in the creation of the critical elements on the periodic chart that are so important in all biochemical processes. If all the matter is subatomic particles and the simplest atoms, the likelihood of the origin of life of any kind, much less spacefaring life, is very very small. Not until large stars go through their complete life cycles and manufacture the more complex elements like nitrogen, carbon, iron, and magnesium do the probabilities for the emergence of life become reasonable.'

Below them an occasional light flickered, but in the entire first four minutes, no more than a few hundred scattered lights appeared, and only one endured for longer than three seconds. 'Now we have reached the time of the formation of the Earth and the solar system,' The Eagle said, preparing to activate the display again.

'Wait a moment, please,' Nicole said. 'I want to make certain I understand ... Did you just show me that for the first half of galactic history, when there was no Earth and no Sun, comparatively few spacefarers evolved in the region around where the Sun would eventually form? ... And that of those spacefarers, almost all of them had a species life span of less than twenty million years, and only one managed to survive for as long as sixty million years?'

'Very good,' The Eagle said. 'Now I am going to add another parameter to the display ... If a spacefarer has succeeded in traveling outside his own star system and has established a permanent presence in another – which you humans have of course not yet done – then the display acknowledges that expansion by illuminating the other star system as well, with the same colour light. Therefore we can follow the spread of a specific spacefaring species ... I am also now going to change the rate of the display by a factor of two, to ten million years per second ...'

Only half a minute into the next period, a red light came on over in one corner of the room. Six to eight seconds later, it was surrounded by hundreds of other red lights. Together they shone with such intensity that the rest of the room, with its occasional solitary or pair of lights, seemed dark and uninteresting by comparison. The field of red lights then abruptly vanished in a fraction of a second. First the inner core of the red pattern went dark, leaving small groups of lights scattered at the edges of what had once been a gigantic region. A blink of the eye later and all the red lights were gone.

Nicole's mind was operating at peak speed as she watched the lights flashing around her. *That must be an interesting story,* she thought, reflecting on the red lights. *Imagine a civilization spread out over a region containing hundreds of stars. Then suddenly, pfft, that species is gone ... The lesson is inescapable ... For everything there is a beginning and an end ... Immortality exists only as a concept, not as a reality.*

She glanced around the room. A general recurring pattern was developing as more and more regions hosted an occasional passing light, indicating the emergence of more spacefaring civilizations. Still most of the spacefarers endured but a brief moment on average, much less than a full second, and even those that spread out and colonised adjoining star systems only rarely came into close proximity with a light signalling another spacefaring species.

There has been intelligence, and spacefaring, in our part of the galaxy since before there was an Earth, Nicole thought ... *But very few of these advanced creatures have ever had the thrill of sustained contact with their peers ...So loneliness too, is one of the underlying principles of the universe ... At least of this universe ...*

Eight minutes later The Eagle again froze the display. 'We have now reached a point in time ten million years before the present,' he said. 'On the Earth, the dinosaurs have long since disappeared, destroyed by their inability to adapt to the climate changes caused by the impact of a great asteroid ... Their disappearance, however, has allowed the mammals to flourish, and one of those mammalian evolutionary lines is starting to show the rudiments of intelligence ...'.

The Eagle stopped. Nicole was looking up at him with an intense, almost pained expression on her face. 'What's the matter?' the alien asked.

'Will *our* particular universe end in harmony?' Nicole asked. 'Or will we be one of those data-points that helps God define the region He is seeking by being *outside* the desired set?'

'What prompts you to ask that question right now?' The Eagle said.

'This whole display,' Nicole answered, waving with her hand, 'is an amazing catalyst. My mind has dozens of questions.' She smiled. 'But since I don't have time to ask them all, I thought I would ask the most important one first ...

'Just look at what has happened here,' she continued, 'even now, after ten billion years of evolution, the lights are widely scattered. And none of the groupings that exist have become permanent or widespread, even in this relatively small portion of the galaxy. Surely if our universe is going to end in harmony, sooner or later lights indicating spacefarers and intelligence should be illuminated at almost every star system in every galaxy ... Or have I misinterpreted what Saint Michael meant by harmony?'

'I don't think so,' The Eagle said.

'Where is our solar system in this current display?' Nicole now asked.

'Right there,' The Eagle said, using his light beam pointer.

Nicole glanced first at the area around the Earth and then quickly surveyed the rest of the room. 'So ten million years ago, there were about sixty space-faring species living among our closest ten thousand stellar neighbourhoods ... And one of these species, if I understand that cluster of dark green lights, originated not too far from us and had spread to include twenty or thirty star systems altogether ...'

'That's correct,' said The Eagle. 'Should I run the display forward again, at a slower rate?'

'In a little while,' Nicole said. 'I want to appreciate this particular configuration first ... Up until now everything has been happening in this display faster than I could possibly absorb it ...'

She stared at the group of green lights. Its outer edge was no more than fifteen light-years from where The Eagle had marked the solar system. Nicole motioned for The Eagle to start the display again and he told her the rate would now be only two hundred thousand years a second.

The green lights moved closer and closer to the Earth and then they suddenly disappeared. 'Stop,' yelled Nicole.

The Eagle halted the display. He looked at Nicole with a quizzical expression.

'What happened to those guys?' Nicole said.

'I told you about them a couple of days ago,' The Eagle said. 'They genetically engineered themselves out of existence.'

They almost reached the Earth, Nicole thought. *And how different all history would have been if they had ... They would have recognised immediately the intellectual potential of the protohumans in Africa and would doubtless have done to them what the Precursors did to the octospiders. Then we ...*

In her mind's eye, Nicole suddenly had an image of Saint Michael, calmly explaining the purpose of the universe in front of the fireplace in Michael and Simone's study.

'Could I see the beginning?' Nicole asked The Eagle.

'The beginning of what?' he replied.

'The beginning of everything,' Nicole said eagerly. 'The instant when this universe began and the entire process of evolution was set in motion.' She waved her hand toward the model below them.

'We can do that,' The Eagle said after a brief pause.

'We have no knowledge about anything *before* this universe was created,' The Eagle said a moment later as Nicole and he stood together on the platform in total darkness. 'We do assume, however, that some kind of energy existed before the instant of creation, for we have been told that the matter of this universe resulted from a transformation of energy.'

Nicole looked around her. 'Darkness everywhere,' she said, almost to herself. 'And somewhere in that darkness – if the word "somewhere" even has any meaning – there was energy. And a Creator ... Or might the energy have been *part* of the Creator?'

'We don't know,' The Eagle said after another short pause. 'What we *do* know is that the fate of every single element in the universe was determined in that initial instant. The way in which that energy was transformed into matter defined eighty billion years of history ...'

As The Eagle spoke, a blinding light filled the room. Nicole turned away from the source and covered her eyes. 'Here,' said The Eagle, reaching into his pouch. He handed Nicole a special pair of glasses.

'Why did you make the simulation so bright?' Nicole asked after adjusting her glasses.

'To indicate, at least in some measure, what those initial moments were like ... Look,' he said, pointing below them, 'I have stopped the model at 10^{-40} seconds after the creation instant. The universe has existed for only an infinitesimal length of time, yet already it is rich in physical structure. This incredible amount of light is all coming from that tiny chunk of cosmic broth below us ... All that "stuff" forming the early universe is completely alien to anything we could recognise or understand. There are no atoms, no molecules. The density of the quarks, leptons, and their friends is so great that a pinch of the "stuff" no larger than a hydrogen atom would weigh more than a large cluster of galaxies in our era ...'

'Just out of curiosity,' Nicole said, 'where are you and I at this moment?'

The Eagle hesitated. 'Nowhere would be the best answer,' he said eventually. 'For illustrative purposes we are outside the model of the universe. But we could be in another dimension. The mathematics of the early universe do not work unless there were initially more than four dimensions. Of course everything in space-time that will later become our universe is contained in that small volume producing the awesome light. The temperature over there, incidentally, if the model were a true representation, would be ten trillion times hotter than the hottest star that will eventually evolve.

'Our model here has also distorted the concepts of size and distance,' The Eagle continued after a brief pause. 'In a moment I will start the simulation of the early universe again, and we will be overpowered as that compact blob of radiation explodes outward at an astonishing rate ... While the simulation of what the cosmologists call the Inflation Era is occurring, the assumed size of this room will also be increasing rapidly. If we did not change the scale, you would be unable now to see the structure of the universe at 10^{-40} seconds without a fantastic microscope.'

Nicole stared below her at the source of light. 'So that minuscule warped globule of hot, heavy stuff was the seed of everything? From that tiny stew of subatomic particles came the great galaxies you showed me in the other domain? It doesn't seem possible ...'

'Not just those galaxies,' The Eagle said. 'The potential for *everything* in the cosmos is stored in that peculiar superheated soup ...'

The small globule suddenly began to expand at an enormous rate. Nicole had the feeling that the outside of the globule was going to touch her face at any moment. Millions of bizarre structures formed and disappeared in front of her eyes. Nicole watched in fascination as the material seemed to change its nature several times, moving through transitional states as peculiar and foreign as the earlier superheated globule.

'I have run time forwards in the model,' The Eagle said several seconds later. 'What you see out there now, approximately one million years after creation, would be recognizable to any dedicated student of physics. Some simple atoms have formed – three kinds of hydrogen, two of helium, for example. Lithium is the heaviest known atom that is plentiful ... The density of the universe is now roughly equivalent to the air on Earth, and the temperature has fallen to a comparatively comfortable one hundred million degrees, or twenty orders of magnitude *less* than it was at the time of the hot globule.'

He activated the platform and guided it among the lights and clumps and filaments. 'If we were really smart,' The Eagle said, 'we would be able to look at all this early matter and predict which "lumps" would eventually become galactic clusters ... It was at about this time that the first Prime Monitor appeared, the only intruder into this otherwise natural evolution process ... No monitoring could have been done earlier, because the process is so sensitive ... Any kind of observation during the first second of creation, for example, would have completely distorted the resultant evolution.'

The Eagle pointed at a tiny metallic sphere in the centre of several huge agglomerations of matter. 'That first Prime Monitor,' he said, 'was sent by the Creator, from another dimension of the early universe, into our evolving space-time system. Its purpose was to observe what was occurring and to create, as necessary, with its own intelligence, the other observing systems that would together gather all the pertinent information on the overall process.'

'So the Sun, the Earth, and every human being,' Nicole said slowly, 'resulted from the unpredictable natural evolution of this cosmos. The Node, Rama, and even you and Saint Michael were produced from a directed development designed originally by that first Prime Monitor ...'

She paused, glancing around her, and then turned to The Eagle. '*You* could have been predicted shortly after the moment of creation ... *I*, and even the existence of humanity, came from a process so mathematically perverse that we could not even have been predicted a hundred million years ago, which is only *one* per cent of the time since the beginning of the universe ...'

Nicole shook her head and then waved her hand. 'All right,' she said, 'that's enough ... I'm overloaded with the infinite.'

The great room became dark again except for the small lights on the floor of the platform. 'What is it?' The Eagle said, seeing a look of distress on Nicole's face.

'I'm not certain,' she said. 'I feel a kind of sadness, as if I had experienced a deep personal loss. If I have understood all this, then humans are far more special than you, or even Rama. The odds are very much against any creatures even nearly like us ever arising again, either in this universe or any other ... We are one of the fluke products of chaos. You, or at least something like you, probably existed in all those other universes the Creator is supposedly observing ...'

There was a momentary silence. 'I guess I had imagined,' Nicole continued, 'after listening to Saint Michael, that there would be human voices in that harmony God was seeking ... Now I realise that it is only on the planet Earth, in this particular universe, that our songs ...'

Nicole felt a sharp burst of pain in her chest. It remained intense. She struggled to breathe, convinced for several moments that the end was coming immediately.

The Eagle said nothing, but watched her carefully. When Nicole finally caught her breath, she spoke in short, broken clauses. 'You told me ... at lunch ... a personal place ... where I could see family and friends ...'

*

They talked briefly in the car while the pain was momentarily bearable. Both the Eagle and Nicole knew, widiout either of them saying anything, that the next attack would be the last.

They entered another of the exhibit areas in the Knowledge Module. This room was a perfect circle, with a space in a small floor section in the middle where The Eagle could stand next to Nicole's wheelchair. They crossed to their central location and watched as humanlike figures began to replay events from Nicole's adult life in each of the six separate theatre settings that closely surrounded them.

The verisimilitude of the replays was astonishing. Not only did all Nicole's family and friends look exactly as they had at the time that the events had taken place, but all the sets were perfect reconstructions as well. In one of the scenes Katie was water-skiing boldly near the shore of Lake Shakespeare, laughing and waving with the reckless abandon that was her trademark. In another Nicole watched a re-creation of the party the little troupe on Rama II had held to celebrate the one thousandth anniversary of the death of Eleanor of Aquitaine. Seeing Simone at age four and Katie at two, and both Richard and herself when they were still young and vigorous, brought tears to Nicole's eyes.

It has been an astonishing life, Nicole thought. She rolled her wheelchair into the scene from Rama II and the action stopped. Nicole leaned over and picked up the robot TB that Richard had created to amuse the little girls. It felt properly weighted in her hands.

'How in the world did you do this?'. Nicole asked.

'Advanced technology,' The Eagle replied. 'I couldn't explain it to you.'

'And if I went over there, where Katie is skiing, would the water feel wet to my touch?'

'Absolutely.'

Nicole rolled out of the scene holding the pseudo-robot in her hands. When she was gone, another TB materialised and the scene continued. *I had forgotten, Richard*, Nicole said to herself, *all your brilliant little creations*.

Her heart granted her a few more minutes to enjoy the vignettes taken from her life. Nicole thrilled again to the moment of Simone's birth, relived her first night of love with Richard not long after he found her in New York, and experienced for a second time the fantastic array of sights and creatures that had greeted Richard and her when the gates of the Emerald City had first opened to them.

'Can you replay any event from my life that I might want?' Nicole asked, feeling a sudden constriction in her chest.

'As long as it happened after you arrived at Rama and I can find it in the archives,' The Eagle replied.

Nicole gasped. The final heart attack was under way. 'Please,' she said, 'may I see my last conversation with Richard before he left ...'

It won't be long, a voice inside Nicole said. She clenched her teeth and tried to concentrate on the scene that had suddenly appeared in front of her. Richard was explaining to pseudo-Nicole why he was the one who should accompany Archie back to New Eden.

'I understand,' pseudo-Nicole said in the scene.

I understand, the real Nicole said to herself. *That is the most important statement anyone can ever make ... the whole key to life is understanding ... And now I understand that I am a mortal creature whose time of death has come.*

Another surge of intense pain was accompanied by a fleeting memory of a Latin line from an old poem. *'Timor Mortis conturbat me'* ... *but I will not be afraid because I understand.*

The Eagle was watching her closely. 'I would like to see Richard and Archie,' she said, labouring, 'their final moments ... in the cell ... just before the biots came.'

I will not be afraid because I understand.

'And my children, if they can somehow be here ... And Dr Blue.'

The room became dark. Seconds ticked by. The pain was terrible. *I will not be afraid ...*

The lights came on again. Richard and Archie were in their cell immediately in front of Nicole's wheelchair. She heard the biots open the cell-block door down the hall ...

'Freeze it there, please,' Nicole said with difficulty. Just to the left of the scene with Richard and Archie, her children and Dr Blue were lined up in a tableau. Nicole struggled to her feet and walked the few metres to be among them. Tears poured from her eyes as she touched the faces that she loved one final time.

The walls of her heart began to collapse. Nicole stumbled into the scene in Richard's cell and embraced the representation of her husband. 'I understand, Richard,' she said.

Nicole dropped to her knees slowly. She turned to face The Eagle. 'I understand,' she said with a smile.

And understanding is happiness, she thought.

ACKNOWLEDGEMENTS

RAMA II

Many different people contributed to this novel during numerous conversations over a two-year period. Those whose comments or insights were especially valuable include Bebe Barden, Paul Chodas, Clayton Frohman, Michael Classman, Bruce Jakosky, Roland Joffe, Gerry Snyder, and Ian Stewart.

Lou Aronica, Malcolm Edwards, and Russ Galen each made significant contributions to the book. Their editing insights were essential in shaping the final structure of the novel.

Special thanks are extended to Father Martin Slaught, whose religious acumen was indispensable in creating General O'Toole, and Peter Guber, who enabled the authors to meet for the first time over three years ago.

Finally, no acknowledgement would be complete without bouquets for Mr Lee's family. His wife, Stacey, and five young sons, Cooper, Austin, Robert, Patrick, and Michael, generously allowed him to make the necessary trips halfway around the world to Sri Lanka and granted him the private time that was required for the integration of this novel.

ACKNOWLEDGEMENTS

THE GARDEN OF RAMA

Many people made valuable contributions to this novel. First among them, in terms of overall impact, was our editor, Lou Aronica. His early comments shaped the structure of the whole novel and his insightful final editing significantly strengthened the flow of the book.

Our good friend and polymath Gerry Snyder was again extremely helpful, generously tackling any technical problem, whether large or small. If the medical passages in the story are accurate and have verisimilitude, then credit should go to Dr Jim Willerson. Any errors in the same passages are strictly the responsibility of the authors.

During the early writing, Jihei Akita went out of his way to help us find the proper locations for the Japanese scenes. He also was more than willing to discuss at length both the customs and history of his nation. In Thailand, Ms Watcharee Monviboon was an excellent guide to the marvels of that country.

The novel deals in considerable detail with women, especially the way they feel and think. Both Bebe Barden and Stacey Lee were always available for conversations about the nature of the female. Ms Barden was also especially helpful with the ideas for the life and poetry of Benita Garcia.

Stacey Kiddoo Lee made many direct contributions to *The Garden of Rama*, but it was her unselfish support of the entire effort that was absolutely critical. During the writing of the novel Stacey also gave birth to her fourth son, Travis Clarke Lee. For everything, Stacey, thank you very much.

ACKNOWLEDGEMENTS

RAMA REVEALED

We would like to thank Neal and Shelagh Ausman, as well as Gerry and Michelle Snyder, for representing the readers in making suggestions about topics that should be addressed in *Rama Revealed*. Gerry was also extremely helpful in discussions about the details of the octospider language.

Our Bantam editor Jennifer Hershey has been a source of strength and support throughout the development and writing of this novel, providing both unflagging encouragement and valuable recommendations about all aspects of the book. Thank you, Jennifer. We are also indebted to Richard Evans at Gollancz for several specific editorial remarks, including the suggestion of adding a prologue.

Lou Aronica and Russ Galen, our publisher and our agent, have helped us in countless ways during the five years since the Rama trilogy sequel was originally conceived. Their many contributions have allowed us to focus our energies on the actual writing of the novels.

Our final thanks go to our families, for their love and understanding throughout this time period. To Stacey Kiddoo Lee especially, we extend our heartfelt appreciation, not only for her willingness to manage a family of five small boys in the presence of difficult (and changing) constraints, but also for her insightful comments about Nicole and the other leading female characters of the trilogy.